The Big Book

of

SHERLOCK HOLMES

Stories

THE BIG BOOK

of

SHERLOCK HOLMES

Stories

Edited and with an Introduction by

OTTO PENZLER

PANTHEON BOOKS, NEW YORK

Introduction and compilation copyright © 2015 by Otto Penzler

All rights reserved. Published simultaneously in the United States in hardcover by Pantheon Books and in trade paperback by Vintage Books, divisions of Penguin Random House LLC, New York, and distributed in Canada by Random House of Canada, a division of Penguin Random House Canada Ltd., Toronto.

Pantheon Books and colophon are registered trademarks of Penguin Random House LLC.

Owing to limitations of space, permissions to reprint previously published material appear on pages 785–89.

Library in Congress Cataloging-in-Publication Data
The big book of Sherlock Holmes stories /
edited and with an introduction by Otto Penzler.
pages cm
ISBN 978-1-101-87089-1 (hardcover). ISBN 978-1-101-87261-1 (trade pbk.).
ISBN 978-1-101-87262-8 (eBook).
1. Holmes, Sherlock—Fiction.   2. Private investigators—England—Fiction.
3. Detective and mystery stories, English.   4. Detective and mystery stories, American.
5. Watson, John H. (Fictitious character)—Fiction.   I. Penzler, Otto, editor.
PR1309.D4B54 2015   823'.0108351—dc23   2014047958

www.pantheonbooks.com

Jacket painting © Thomas Gianni
Jacket design by Joe Montgomery

Printed in the United States of America

First Edition
2 4 6 8 9 7 5 3 1

CONTENTS

To provide a little guidance through this massive tome, I've divided the stories into several categories but admit, immediately, that the effort is of questionable validity, as many of the stories fall into more than one subdivision. (A. A. Milne and P. G. Wodehouse, for example, will be found in the "Literary Writers" section, but since they wrote parodies, they could be found there just as easily.) It's not unlike making lists of foods that are delicious and foods that are fattening: there will be overlap. The two most reasonable choices are to ignore the categorizations altogether or to suggest that you don't take them very much to heart and just enjoy the stories.

The Master

It seems that no author could resist writing parodies of Holmes and Watson—not even their creator.

Familiar as the Rose in Spring

These are the most popular and frequently reprinted Sherlock Holmes stories of all time.

The Literature of Crime

Compelled by either whim or serious affection, many literary lions have tried their hand at writing a Holmes adventure. Sometimes they produce a pure pastiche, echoing the tone of Conan Doyle, and sometimes the notion of a parody is irresistible.

In the Beginning

Holmes became such a towering literary presence within a few years of his first appearance that parodies were being published in newspapers and magazines at an alarming rate. Most of them were truly dreadful, no more than burlesques based on a single joke that often wasn't very funny. Some of the earliest (all are from the nineteenth century), and best, are included here, in chronological order—as good a way as any to be presented.

Holmesless

Even when he's not physically present, the personality and aura of Holmes cannot be ignored, filling the room with his spirit.

Not of This Place

We associate Holmes with a certain place and time, mainly London "where it is always 1895," as Vincent Starrett wrote so simply yet eloquently. However, Holmes appears in various guises, places, eras, and even spiritual levels in a wide range of stories. Also, while the essence of Holmes's genius lies in his observations and deductions, all based on razor-sharp logic, there are things that may not be rationally explained.

Keeping the Memory Green

The list of eminent men and women who have demonstrated great affection for "the best and wisest man whom [they] have ever known" (to quote Dr. Watson) is without limit. Although they enjoyed successful careers in other fields, they often kept Holmes by their sides, and those with sufficient talent provided evidence of that kinship by putting pen to paper.

You Think That's Funny?

Writing a pastiche of a well-known detective, true in tone and with a puzzling mystery, is extremely difficult. Writing a parody is a good deal easier—as the focus can be on a single element of that figure rather than on a range of characteristics—but writing a genuinely funny one may be the most difficult literary feat of all. Sadly, as you will see, not every writer in this section was up to the challenge, but they are included here because several have historical significance. Thankfully, the worst of the parodies are mercifully short.

Contemporary Victorians

Many of today's most successful mystery writers, most of whom have their own series detectives, have on occasion broken away from the work for which they have had their greatest success to write a new Sherlock Holmes adventure. The good news is that they achieved their goal with greater than expected excellence.

The Footsteps of a Gigantic Author

It is not only today's mystery writers who have turned their creativity to producing Sherlock Holmes stories. Many of the classic writers of an earlier time have also taken the challenge of adding an adventure to the list of the great detective's cases.

INTRODUCTION

OTTO PENZLER

ABOUT A HUNDRED years ago, Sherlock Holmes was described as one of the three most famous people who ever lived, the other two being Jesus Christ and Houdini. There are some who claim that he is a fictional character, but this notion is, of course, absurd. Every schoolchild knows what he looks like, what he does for a living, and most know many of his peculiar characteristics.

The tall, slender, hawk-nosed figure, with his deerstalker hat and Inverness cape, is instantly recognizable in every corner of the world. In addition to the superb stories describing his adventures written by his friend, roommate, and chronicler, Dr. John H. Watson (with the assistance of his literary agent, Sir Arthur Conan Doyle), Holmes has been impersonated on the stage, television, radio, and in countless motion pictures. More than twenty-five thousand books, stories, and articles have been written about him by famous authors, amateur writers, and scholars.

This collection of Sherlock Holmes parodies and pastiches is the largest ever assembled. It contains serious pastiches by distinguished literary figures, equally good stories by less exalted Sherlockians, and some truly dreadful parodies

included here for historical interest more than reading pleasure. They are, mercifully, brief.

Inevitably, I have drawn on the work of others. The first and greatest anthology of its kind is *The Misadventures of Sherlock Holmes* (1944), edited by Ellery Queen, a brilliant, pioneering anthologist whose best collections—*101 Years' Entertainment: The Great Detective Stories 1841–1941* (1941); its sequel, *To the Queen's Taste* (1946); *The Female of the Species* (1943); and others—are true cornerstones of detective fiction.

Other scholars and aficionados who have unearthed material and whose books have provided access to rare and obscure material are Robert Adey, Richard Lancelyn Green, Charles Press, Marvin Kaye, and Mike Ashley.

My deep affection for Holmes, now exceeding fifty years of reading, has resulted in the addition of stories to this massive tome that never before have been collected in a book devoted to the great detective. While I may not fully concur with Watson's assessment that Holmes is "the best and wisest man whom I have ever known," an accolade reserved for a very few dear friends, he has been a trusted and worthy companion for the greatest percentage of my life.

Sherlock (he was nearly named Sherrinford) was born on January 6, 1854, on the farmstead of Mycroft (the name of his older brother) in the North Riding of Yorkshire. He solved his first case (eventually titled "The Gloria Scott") while a twenty-year-old student at Oxford. Following graduation, he became the world's first consulting detective—a vocation he followed for twenty-three years.

In January 1881 he was looking for someone to share his new quarters at 221B Baker Street when a friend introduced him to Dr. John H. Watson. Before agreeing to share the apartment, the two men aired their respective shortcomings. Holmes confesses, "I get in the dumps at times, and don't open my mouth for days on end." He also smokes a vile shag tobacco and conducts experiments with loathsome-smelling chemicals. He fails, however, to mention an affection for cocaine. Although he ruefully notes his fondness for scratching away at the violin while in contemplation, he proves to be a virtuoso who can calm his roommate's raw nerves with a melodious air. Watson's admitted faults include the keeping of a bull pup, a strong objection to arguments because his nerves cannot stand them, a penchant for arising from bed "at all sorts of ungodly hours," and an immense capacity for laziness. "I have another set of vices when I'm well," he says, "but those are the principal ones at present." They become friends, and Watson chronicles the deeds of his illustrious roommate, often to the displeasure of Holmes, who resents the melodramatic and sensational tales. He believes that the affairs, if told at all, should be put to the public as straightforward exercises in cold logic and deductive reasoning.

Holmes possesses not only excellent deductive powers but also a giant intellect. Anatomy, chemistry, mathematics, British law, and sensational literature are but a few areas of his vast sphere of knowledge, although he is admittedly not well versed in such subjects as astronomy, philosophy, and politics. He has published several distinguished works on erudite subjects: *Upon the Distinction between the Ashes of the Various Tobaccos*; *A Study of the Influence of a Trade upon the Form of the Hand*; *Upon the Polyphonic Motets of Lassus*; *A Study of the Chaldean Roots in the Ancient Cornish Language*; and his magnum opus, *Practical Handbook of Bee Culture, with Some Observations upon the Segregation of the Queen*. His four-volume *The Whole Art of Detection* has not yet been published. When he needs information that his brain does not retain, he refers to a small, carefully selected library of reference works and a series of commonplace books. Since Holmes cares only about facts that aid his work, he ignores whatever he considers superfluous. He explains his theory of education thus:

I consider that a man's brain originally is like an empty attic, and you have to stock it with such furniture as you choose. A fool takes in all the lumber of every sort that he comes across, so that the knowledge which might be useful to him gets crowded out, or at best is jumbled up with a lot of other things, so that he has a difficulty in laying his hands upon it. . . . It is a mistake to think that that little room has elastic walls and can distend to any extent. Depend upon it there comes a time for every addition of knowledge you forget something you knew before.

An athletic body complements Holmes's outstanding intelligence. He seems even taller than his six feet because he is extremely thin. His narrow, hooked nose and sharp, piercing eyes give him a hawklike appearance. He often astonishes Watson with displays of strength and agility; he is a superb boxer, fencer, and singlestick player. He needs all his strength when he meets his nemesis, the ultimate archcriminal Professor James Moriarty, in a struggle at the edge of the Reichenbach Falls in Switzerland. The evenly matched adversaries, locked in battle, fall over the cliff; both were reported to be dead. All England mourned the passing of its great keeper of the law, but in 1894, after being missing for three years, Holmes returned. He had not been killed in the fall, after all, but had seen a good opportunity to fool his many enemies in the underworld. He had taken over the identity of a Danish explorer, Sigerson, and traveled to many parts of the world, including New Jersey, where he is believed to have had an affair with Irene Adler (who will always be *the* woman to Holmes), and to Tibet, where he learned the secret of long life from the Dalai Lama.

When Miss Adler (the famous and beautiful opera singer Holmes first meets in "A Scandal in Bohemia") died in 1903, Holmes retired to keep bees on the southern slopes of the Sussex Downs with his old housekeeper, Mrs. Martha Hudson. He came out of retirement briefly before World War I, but his life since then has been quiet.

Holmes has outlived the people who have participated at various times in his adventures. In addition to Mycroft, Watson, Moriarty, Irene Adler, and Mrs. Hudson, the best-known auxiliary personalities in the stories include Billy the Page Boy, who occasionally announces visitors to 221B; Mary Morstan, who becomes Mrs. Watson; The Baker Street Irregulars, street urchins led by Wiggins, who scramble after information for Holmes's coins; Lestrade, an inept Scotland Yard inspector; Stanley Hopkins, a Scotland Yard man of greater ability; Gregson, the "smartest of the Scotland Yarders," according to Holmes; and Colonel Sebastian Moran, "the second most dangerous man in London."

The first story written about Sherlock Holmes, *A Study in Scarlet*, originally appeared in *Beeton's Christmas Annual* for 1887 and subsequently was published in book form in London by Ward, Lock & Company in 1888; the first American edition was published by J. B. Lippincott & Company in 1890. Holmes is called to assist Scotland Yard on what Inspector Tobias Gregson calls "a bad business at 3, Lauriston Gardens." An American, Enoch J. Drebber, has been murdered, and Yard men can point to only a single clue, the word "Rache" scrawled upon the wall in blood. They believe it to be the first letters of a woman's name, Rachel, but Holmes suggests that it is the German word for "revenge." Soon, the dead man's private secretary, Stangerson, is also found murdered; the same word is written in blood nearby. A long middle section of this novel, dealing with Mormons, is an unusual flashback.

The Sign of Four first appeared simultaneously in the English and American editions of *Lippincott's Magazine* for February 1890. Spencer Blackett published the first English book edition in the same year; P. F. Collier published the first American book edition in 1891. Calling at 221B Baker Street for help is Mary Morstan, a fetching young lady by whom Watson is totally charmed; ultimately, he marries her. She is the daughter of a captain in the Indian Army who had mysteriously disappeared ten years earlier and had never been heard from again. Four years after the disappearance, Miss Morstan received an anonymous gift, a huge, lustrous pearl, and has received another like it each year thereafter. Holmes and Watson accompany her to a tryst with the eccentric Thaddeus Sholto, twin brother of Bartholomew Sholto and the son of a major who had been Captain Morstan's only friend in London. Holmes sets out to find a fabulous treasure and is soon involved with the strange Jonathan Small and Tonga.

"A Scandal in Bohemia" first appeared in *The Strand Magazine* in July 1891; its first book appearance was in *The Adventures of Sherlock Holmes* (1892). The first published short story in which Holmes appears features the detective in an uncharacteristic battle of wits with a lady and with no real crime to be solved. The king of Bohemia has had a rather indiscreet affair with the beautiful Irene Adler, who threatens to create an international scandal when he attempts to discard her and marry a noblewoman. Holmes is hired to obtain possession of a certain unfortunate photograph before it can be sent to the would-be bride's royal family. Holmes is outwitted, and he never stops loving Irene for fooling him.

In *The Hound of the Baskervilles* (1902), Sir Charles Baskerville, of Baskerville Hall, Dartmoor, Devon, has been found dead. There are no signs of violence at the scene, but his face is incredibly distorted with terror. Dr. James Mortimer enlists the aid of Holmes to protect the young heir to the estate, Sir Henry Baskerville. Watson goes to the grim moor to keep an eye on Sir Henry but is warned to return to London by a neighbor, Beryl Stapleton, the beautiful sister of a local naturalist, who hears a blood-chilling moan at the edge of the great Grimpen Mire and identifies it as the legendary Hound of the Baskervilles, calling for its prey.

The original stories about Holmes total sixty; more than a hundred times that number have been written by other authors. Even Conan Doyle wrote a parody of the characters, contained in this collection.

Today, of course, Holmes continues to be a multimedia superstar, appearing in two internationally successful movies starring Robert Downey, Jr., as Holmes; the *Sherlock* BBC television series starring Benedict Cumberbatch; and *Elementary*, the wildly popular CBS series starring Jonny Lee Miller as Holmes and Lucy Liu as Dr. Watson.

Although universally beloved, there were a few who were not enamored of the great detective, and his detractors were led by none other than Conan Doyle himself. Having had enough of Holmes and believing that he had far superior works to write, Conan Doyle famously threw him off the cliff at the edge of Switzerland's Reichenbach Falls, along with the insidious Professor Moriarty.

Here is Conan Doyle's own account of the death of Holmes, with an introductory note by the editor of the magazine in which it first appeared. It was originally published as "Conan Doyle Tells the True Story of Sherlock Holmes" in the December 15, 1900, issue of *Tit-Bits*; it has been reprinted as "A Gaudy Death" and as "Conan Doyle Tells the True Story of Sherlock Holmes's End." Fortunately, as is well known, Conan Doyle eventually bowed to public pressure and resurrected Holmes to write two more novels and thirty-six additional short stories.

CONAN DOYLE TELLS THE TRUE STORY OF SHERLOCK HOLMES'S END

To interview Dr. Conan Doyle, the creator of Sherlock Holmes, is not an easy matter. Dr. Doyle has a strong objection to the interview, even though he has no personal antipathy to the interviewer. Considerations, however, of his long and friendly relationship with the firm of George Newnes Ltd, in the pages of whose popular and universally read *Strand Magazine* Sherlock Holmes lived, and moved, and had his being, overcame Dr. Doyle's reluctance to be interviewed, and he consented to give the following particulars, which will be read with interest by his admirers all over the world.

Tit-Bits, 15 December 1900

BEFORE I TELL you of Sherlock Holmes's death and how it came about, it will probably be interesting to recall the circumstances of his birth. He originally made his appearance, you will remember, in a book which I wrote called *A Study in Scarlet*. The idea of the detective was suggested by a professor under whom I had worked at Edinburgh, and in part by Edgar Allen Poe's detective, which, after all, ran on the lines of all other detectives who have appeared in literature.

In work which consists in the drawing of detectives there are only one or two qualities which one can use, and an author is forced to hark back upon them constantly, so that every detective must really resemble every other detective to a greater or less extent. There is no great originality required in devising or constructing such a man, and the only possible originality which one can get into a story about a detective is in giving him original plots and problems to solve, as

in his equipment there must be of necessity an alert acuteness of mind to grasp facts and the relation which each of them bears to the other.

At the time I first thought of a detective—it was about 1886—I had been reading some detective stories, and it struck me what nonsense they were, to put it mildly, because for getting the solution of the mystery the authors always depended on some coincidence. This struck me as not a fair way of playing the game, because the detective ought really to depend for his success on something in his own mind and not on merely adventitious circumstances, which do not, by any means, always occur in real life. I was seedy at the time, and, not working much, had leisure to read, so I read half-a-dozen or so detective stories, both in French and English, and they one and all filled me with dissatisfaction and a sort of feeling how much more interesting they might be made if one could show that the man deserved his victory over the criminal or the mystery he was called upon to solve.

Then I began to think, suppose my old professor at Edinburgh were in the place of one of these lucky detectives, he would have worked out the process of effect from cause just as logically as he would have diagnosed a disease, instead of having something given to him by mere luck, which, as I said just now, does not happen in real life.

For fun, therefore, I started constructing a story and giving my detective a scientific system, so as to make him reason everything out. Intellectually that had been done before by Edgar Allan Poe with M. Dupin, but where Holmes differed from Dupin was that he had an immense fund of exact knowledge to draw upon in consequence of his previous scientific education. I mean by this, that by looking at a man's hand he knew what the man's trade was, as by looking at his trousers leg he could deduce the character of the man. He was practical and he was systematic, and his success in the detection of crime was to be the fruit, not of luck, but of his qualities.

With this idea I wrote a small book on the lines I have indicated, and produced *A Study in Scarlet*, which was made *Beeton's Christmas Annual* in 1887. That was the first appearance of Sherlock; but he did not arrest much attention, and nobody recognized him as being anything in particular. About three years later, however, I was asked to do a small shilling book for *Lippincott's Magazine*, which publishes, as you know, a special story in each number. I didn't know what to write about, and the thought occurred to me, "Why not try to rig up the same chap again?" I did it, and the result was *The Sign of Four*. Although the criticisms were favorable, I don't think even then Sherlock attracted much attention to his individuality.

About this time I began thinking about short stories for magazines. It occurred to me that a serial story in a magazine was a mistake, for those who had not begun the story at the beginning would naturally be debarred from buying a periodical in which a large number of pages were, of necessity, taken up with a story in which they had no particular interest.

It occurred to me, then, that if one could write a serial without appearing to do so—a serial, I mean, in which each instalment was capable of being read as a single story, while each retained a connecting link with the one before and the one that was to come by means of its leading characters—one would get a cumulative interest which the serial pure and simple could not obtain. In this respect I was a revolutionist, and I think I may fairly lay claim to the credit of being the inaugurator of a system which has since been worked by others with no little success.

It was about this time that *The Strand Magazine* was started, and I asked myself, "Why not put my idea in execution and write a series of stories with Sherlock Holmes?" whose mental processes were familiar to me. I was then in practice in Wimpole Street as a specialist, and, while waiting for my patients to come, I began writing to fill up my waiting hours. In this way I wrote three stories, which were afterwards published as part of *The Adventures of Sherlock Holmes*. I sent them to *The Strand Magazine*. The editor liked them, seemed keen on them, and asked for more. The more he asked for the more I turned out, until I had done a dozen. That dozen constituted the volume which was afterwards published as *The Adventures of Sherlock Holmes*.

That dozen stories being finished, I determined they should be the end of all Sherlock's doings. I was, however, approached to do some more. My instincts were against this, as I believe it is always better to give the public less than it wants rather than more, and I do not believe in boring it with this sort of stuff. Besides, I had other subjects in my mind. The popularity of Sherlock Holmes, however, and the success of the new stories with the common thread running through them brought a good deal of pressure on me, and at last, under that pressure, I consented to continue with Sherlock, and did twelve more stories, which I called *The Memoirs of Sherlock Holmes*.

By the time I had finished those I was absolutely determined it would be bad policy to do any more Holmes stores. I was still a young man and a young novelist, and I have always noticed that the ruin of every novelist who has come up has been effected by driving him into a groove. The public gets what it likes, and, insisting on getting it, makes him go on until he loses his freshness. Then the public turns round and says: "He has only one idea, and can only write one sort of story." The result is that the man is ruined; for, by that time, he has probably himself lost the power of adapting himself in fresh conditions of work. Now, why should a man be driven into a groove and not write about what interests him? When I was interested in Holmes I wrote about Holmes, and it amused me making him get involved in new conundrums; but when I had written twenty-six stories, each involving the making of a fresh plot, I felt that it was becoming irksome this searching for plots—and if it were getting irksome to me, most certainly, I argued, it must be losing its freshness for others.

I knew I had done better work in other fields of literature, and in my opinion *The White Company*, for example, was worth a hundred Sherlock Holmes stories. Yet, just because the Sherlock Holmes stories were, for the moment, more popular, I was becoming more and more known as the author of Sherlock Holmes instead of as the author of *The White Company*. My lower work was obscuring my higher.

I therefore determined to stop my Holmes stories, and as my mind was fully made up I couldn't see any better way than by bringing Holmes to an end as well as the stories.

I was in Switzerland for the purpose of giving a lecture at the time when I was thinking out the details of the final story. I was taking a walking tour through the country, and I came to a waterfall. I thought if a man wanted to meet a gaudy kind of death that was a fine romantic place for the purpose. That started the train of ideas by which Holmes just reached that spot and met his death there.

That is really how I came to kill Holmes. But when I did it I was surprised at the amount of interest people took in his fate. I never thought they would take it so to heart. I got letters from all over the world reproaching me on the subject. One, I remember, from a lady whom I did not know, began "you beast."

From that day to this I have never for an instant regretted the course I took in killing Sherlock. That does not say, however, that because he is dead I should not write about him again if I wanted to, for there is no limit to the number of papers he left behind or the reminiscences in the brain of his biographer.

My objection to detective stories is that they only call for the use of a certain portion of one's imaginative faculty, the invention of a plot, without giving any scope for character drawing.

The best literary work is that which leaves the reader better for having read it. Now, nobody can possibly be the better—in the high sense in which I mean it—for reading Sherlock Holmes, although he may have passed a pleasant hour in doing so. It was not to my mind high work, and no detective work ever can be, apart from the fact that all work dealing with criminal matters is a cheap way of rousing the interest of the reader.

For this reason, at the outset of my career it would have been bad to devote too much attention to Sherlock Holmes. If I had continued with him I should by this time have worn him out, and also the patience of the public, and I should not have written "Rodney Stone," "Brigadier Gerard," "The Stark Monro Letters," "The Refugees," and all the other books which treat of life from many different standpoints, some of which represent my own views, which Sherlock Holmes never did.

There is one fact in connection with Holmes which will probably interest those who have followed his career from the beginning, and to which, so far as I am aware, attention has never been drawn. In dealing with criminal subjects one's natural endeavour is to keep the crime in the background. In nearly half the number of the Sherlock Holmes stories, however, in a strictly legal sense no crime was actually committed at all. One heard a good deal about crime and the criminal, but the reader was completely bluffed. Of course, I could not bluff him always, so sometimes I had to give him a crime, and occasionally I had to make it a downright bad one.

My own view of Sherlock Holmes—I mean the man as I saw him in my imagination—was quite different from that which Mr. Paget pictured in *The Strand Magazine*. I, however, am eminently pleased with his work, and quite understand the aspect which he gave to the character, and am even prepared to accept him now as Mr. Paget drew him. In my own mind, however, he was a more beaky-nosed, hawk-faced man, approaching more to the Red Indian type, than the artist represented him, but, as I have said, Mr. Paget's pictures please me very much.

THE MASTER

The Field Bazaar

ARTHUR CONAN DOYLE

THE UNIVERSITY OF Edinburgh hosted a fund-raiser on November 19, 20, and 21, 1896, in order to build a sports pavilion. The Field Bazaar, which featured exhibitions, concerts, military bands, and theatrical performances, raised about three thousand pounds from its students and the general public, a substantial portion of which resulted from a special edition of *The Student*, the university's publication. The Bazaar Number featured work by an extraordinary array of many of Great Britain's most popular authors of the day, including Robert Barr, James M. Barrie, Walter Besant, Israel Zangwill, and Arthur Conan Doyle.

Conan Doyle was asked for a Sherlock Holmes story. He had already killed his detective, throwing him over the Reichenbach Falls in Switzerland, along with his nemesis, Professor Moriarty, so there was fervent interest to see whether he would bring him back for his contribution. He failed to do so but provided this pleasant self-parody instead. The special issue of *The Student* was in such demand, largely owing to the appearance of Holmes after an absence of three years, that it went into a second printing almost immediately.

"The Field Bazaar" was first published in the November 20, 1896, issue of *The Student*. The first separate edition was published in an edition of one hundred copies, privately printed for A. G. Macdonell (London, Athaeneum Press, 1934), for distribution to the Baker Street Irregulars in New York for the group's first dinner.

THE FIELD BAZAAR

Arthur Conan Doyle

"I SHOULD CERTAINLY do it," said Sherlock Holmes.

I started at the interruption, for my companion had been eating his breakfast with his attention entirely centred upon the paper which was propped up by the coffee pot. Now I looked across at him to find his eyes fastened upon me with the half-amused, half-questioning expression which he usually assumed when he felt that he had made an intellectual point.

"Do what?" I asked.

He smiled as he took his slipper from the mantelpiece and drew from it enough shag tobacco to fill the old clay pipe with which he invariably rounded off his breakfast.

"A most characteristic question of yours, Watson," said he. "You will not, I am sure, be offended if I say that any reputation for sharpness which I may possess has been entirely gained by the admirable foil which you have made for me. Have I not heard of debutantes who have insisted upon plainness in their chaperones? There is a certain analogy."

Our long companionship in the Baker Street rooms had left us on those easy terms of intimacy when much may be said without offence. And yet I acknowledge that I was nettled at his remark.

"I may be very obtuse," said I, "but I confess that I am unable to see how you have managed to know that I was . . . I was . . ."

"Asked to help in the Edinburgh University Bazaar."

"Precisely. The letter has only just come to hand, and I have not spoken to you since."

"In spite of that," said Holmes, leaning back in his chair and putting his finger tips together, "I would even venture to suggest that the object of the bazaar is to enlarge the University cricket field."

I looked at him in such bewilderment that he vibrated with silent laughter.

"The fact is, my dear Watson, that you are an excellent subject," said he. "You are never *blasé*. You respond instantly to any external stimulus. Your mental processes may be slow but they are never obscure, and I found during breakfast that you were easier reading than the leader in the *Times* in front of me."

"I should be glad to know how you arrived at your conclusions," said I.

"I fear that my good nature in giving explanations has seriously compromised my reputation," said Holmes. "But in this case the train of reasoning is based upon such obvious facts that no credit can be claimed for it. You entered the room with a thoughtful expression, the expression of a man who is debating some point in his mind. In your hand you held a solitary letter. Now last night you retired in the best of spirits, so it was clear that it was this letter in your hand which had caused the change in you."

"This is obvious."

"It is all obvious when it is explained to you. I naturally asked myself what the letter could contain which might have this effect upon you. As you walked you held the flap side of the envelope towards me, and I saw upon it the same shield-shaped device which I have observed upon your

4

old college cricket cap. It was clear, then, that the request came from Edinburgh University—or from some club connected with the University. When you reached the table you laid down the letter beside your plate with the address uppermost, and you walked over to look at the framed photograph upon the left of the mantelpiece."

It amazed me to see the accuracy with which he had observed my movements. "What next?" I asked.

"I began by glancing at the address, and I could tell, even at the distance of six feet, that it was an unofficial communication. This I gathered from the use of the word 'Doctor' upon the address, to which, as a Bachelor of Medicine, you have no legal claim. I knew that University officials are pedantic in their correct use of titles, and I was thus enabled to say with certainty that your letter was unofficial. When on your return to the table you turned over your letter and allowed me to perceive that the enclosure was a printed one, the idea of a bazaar first occurred to me. I had already weighed the possibility of its being a political communication, but this seemed improbable in the present stagnant conditions of politics.

"When you returned to the table your face still retained its expression and it was evident that your examination of the photograph had not changed the current of your thoughts. In that case it must itself bear upon the subject in question. I turned my attention to the photograph, therefore, and saw at once that it consisted of yourself as a member of the Edinburgh University Eleven, with the pavilion and cricket-field in the background. My small experience of cricket clubs has taught me that next to churches and cavalry ensigns they are the most debt-laden things upon earth. When upon your return to the table I saw you take out your pencil and draw lines upon the envelope, I was convinced that you were endeavouring to realize some projected improvement which was to be brought about by a bazaar. Your face still showed some indecision, so that I was able to break in upon you with my advice that you should assist in so good an object."

I could not help smiling at the extreme simplicity of his explanation.

"Of course, it was as easy as possible," said I.

My remark appeared to nettle him.

"I may add," said he, "that the particular help which you have been asked to give was that you should write in their album, and that you have already made up your mind that the present incident will be the subject of your article."

"But how—!" I cried.

"It is as easy as possible," said he, "and I leave its solution to your own ingenuity. In the meantime," he added, raising his paper, "you will excuse me if I return to this very interesting article upon the trees of Cremona, and the exact reasons for their pre-eminence in the manufacture of violins. It is one of those small outlying problems to which I am sometimes tempted to direct my attention."

How Watson Learned the Trick

ARTHUR CONAN DOYLE

ONE OF THE most remarkable English artifacts of the early part of the twentieth century was a dolls' house designed and built for Queen Mary, the wife of George V. Created as a gift to Queen Mary from the people, it was produced to serve as a historical document on how a royal family might have lived during that period in England.

In addition to furniture and other household items built on a scale of 1:12 (one inch to one foot), resulting in a structure more than three feet tall, it contains curious items that actually work, such as a shotgun that can be cocked, loaded, and fired; toilets that flush; and electric lights that illuminate with the flick of a switch. The garage holds six automobiles, including a Daimler and a Rolls-Royce. Perhaps most impressively, it has seven hundred and fifty original works of art.

Remarkably, it has a substantial library of tiny books, each written specifically for the dolls' house. Among the authors who contributed to the project were Rudyard Kipling (who wrote seven poems and illustrated the book himself), James M. Barrie, Aldous Huxley, John Buchan, M. R. James (who wrote a ghost story, "The Haunted Dolls' House"), Thomas Hardy, W. Somerset Maugham, and Arthur Conan Doyle, who produced this charming parody of Holmes and Watson.

The house is on display at Windsor Castle.

"How Watson Learned the Trick" was originally published in *The Book of the Queen's Dolls' House*, two volumes edited by A. C. Benson, Sir Lawrence Weaver, and E. V. Lucas (London, Methuen, 1924); it was limited to fifteen hundred copies.

HOW WATSON LEARNED THE TRICK

Arthur Conan Doyle

WATSON HAD BEEN watching his companion intently ever since he had sat down to the breakfast table. Holmes happened to look up and catch his eye.

"Well, Watson, what are you thinking about?" he asked.

"About you."

"Me?"

"Yes, Holmes. I was thinking how superficial are these tricks of yours, and how wonderful it is that the public should continue to show interest in them."

"I quite agree," said Holmes. "In fact, I have a recollection that I have myself made a similar remark."

"Your methods," said Watson severely, "are really easily acquired."

"No doubt," Holmes answered with a smile. "Perhaps you will yourself give an example of this method of reasoning."

"With pleasure," said Watson. "I am able to say that you were greatly preoccupied when you got up this morning."

"Excellent!" said Holmes. "How could you possibly know that?"

"Because you are usually a very tidy man and yet you have forgotten to shave."

"Dear me! How very clever!" said Holmes. "I had no idea, Watson, that you were so apt a pupil. Has your eagle eye detected anything more?"

"Yes, Holmes. You have a client named Barlow, and you have not been successful with his case."

"Dear me, how could you know that?"

"I saw the name outside his envelope. When you opened it you gave a groan and thrust it into your pocket with a frown on your face."

"Admirable! You are indeed observant. Any other points?"

"I fear, Holmes, that you have taken to financial speculation."

"How *could* you tell that, Watson?"

"You opened the paper, turned to the financial page, and gave a loud exclamation of interest."

"Well, that is very clever of you, Watson. Any more?"

"Yes, Holmes, you have put on your black coat, instead of your dressing gown, which proves that you are expecting some important visitor at once."

"Anything more?"

"I have no doubt that I could find other points, Holmes, but I only give you these few, in order to show you that there are other people in the world who can be as clever as you."

"And some not so clever," said Holmes. "I admit that they are few, but I am afraid, my dear Watson, that I must count you among them."

"What do you mean, Holmes?"

"Well, my dear fellow, I fear your deductions have not been so happy as I should have wished."

"You mean that I was mistaken."

"Just a little that way, I fear. Let us take the points in their order: I did not shave because I have sent my razor to be sharpened. I put on my coat because I have, worse luck, an early meeting with my dentist. His name is Barlow, and the letter was to confirm the appointment. The cricket page is beside the financial one, and I turned to it to find if Surrey was holding its own against Kent. But go on, Watson, go on! It's a very superficial trick, and no doubt you will soon acquire it."

FAMILIAR AS THE ROSE IN SPRING

The Unique "Hamlet"

Being an Unrecorded Adventure of Mr. Sherlock Holmes

VINCENT STARRETT

IT SEEMS TO me that Charles Vincent Emerson Starrett (1886–1974) succeeded in being one of America's greatest bookmen, and his young daughter offered the best tombstone inscription—"The Last Bookman"—for anyone who is a Dofob, Eugene Field's useful word for a "damned old fool over books," as Starrett admitted to being. Once, when a friend called at his home, Starrett's daughter answered the door and told the visitor that her father was "upstairs, playing with his books."

Starrett produced innumerable essays, biographical works, critical studies, and bibliographical pieces on a wide range of authors, all while managing the "Books Alive" column for the *Chicago Tribune* for many years. His autobiography, *Born in a Bookshop* (1965), should be required reading for bibliophiles of all ages.

He wrote numerous mystery short stories and several detective novels, including *Murder on "B" Deck* (1929), *Dead Man Inside* (1931), and *The End of Mr. Garment* (1932). His 1934 short story, "Recipe for Murder," was expanded to the full-length novel, *The Great Hotel Murder* (1935), which was the basis for the film of the same title and released the same year; it starred Edmund Lowe and Victor McLaglen.

Few would argue that Starrett's most outstanding achievements were his writings about Sherlock Holmes, most notably *The Private Life of Sherlock Holmes* (1933) and "The Unique 'Hamlet,'" described by Sherlockians for decades as the best pastiche ever written. It was privately printed in 1920 by Starrett's friend Walter M. Hill in a hardcover limited edition of unknown quantity. It is likely that ten copies were issued for the author with his name on the title page. The number of copies published with Hill's name on the title page has been variously reported as thirty-three, one hundred, one hundred ten, and two hundred. It was selected for *Queen's Quorum* (1951), Ellery Queen's selection of the one hundred six most important volumes of detective fiction ever written.

THE UNIQUE "HAMLET"

Being an Unrecorded Adventure of Mr. Sherlock Holmes

Vincent Starrett

1

"HOLMES," SAID I one morning, as I stood in our bay window, looking idly into the street, "surely here comes a madman. Someone has incautiously left the door open and the poor fellow has slipped out. What a pity!"

It was a glorious morning in the spring, with a fresh breeze and inviting sunlight, but as it was early few persons were as yet astir. Birds twittered under the neighboring eaves, and from the far end of the thoroughfare came faintly the droning cry of an umbrella repairman; a lean cat slunk across the cobbles and disappeared into a courtway; but for the most part the street was deserted, save for the eccentric individual who had called forth my exclamation.

Sherlock Holmes rose lazily from the chair in which he had been lounging and came to my side, standing with long legs spread and hands in the pockets of his dressing gown. He smiled as he saw the singular personage coming along; and a personage the man seemed to be, despite his curious actions, for he was tall and portly, with elderly whiskers of the variety called muttonchop, and eminently respectable. He was loping curiously, like a tired hound, lifting his knees high as he ran, and a heavy double watch chain bounced against and rebounded from the plump line of his figured waistcoat. With one hand he clutched despairingly at his tall silk hat, while with the other he made strange gestures in the air, in a state of emotion bordering on distraction. We could almost see the spasmodic workings of his countenance.

"What in the world can ail him?" I cried. "See how he glances at the houses as he passes."

"He is looking at the numbers," responded Sherlock Holmes with dancing eyes, "and I fancy it is ours that will give him the greatest happiness. His profession, of course, is obvious."

"A banker, I should imagine, or at least a person of affluence," I ventured, wondering what curious detail had betrayed the man's vocation to my remarkable companion in a single glance.

"Affluent, yes," said Holmes with a mischievous twinkle, "but not exactly a banker, Watson. Notice the sagging pockets, despite the excellence of his clothing, and the rather exaggerated madness of his eye. He is a collector, or I am very much mistaken."

"My dear fellow!" I exclaimed. "At his age and in his station! And why should he be seeking us? When we settled that last bill—."

"Of books," said my friend severely. "He is a book collector. His line is Caxtons, Elzevirs, and Gutenberg Bibles, not the sordid reminders of unpaid grocery accounts. See, he is turning in, as I expected, and in a moment he will stand upon our hearthrug and tell the harrowing tale of a unique volume and its extraordinary disappearance."

His eyes gleamed and he rubbed his hands together in satisfaction. I could not but hope that his conjecture was correct, for he had had little recently to occupy his mind, and I lived in constant fear that he would seek that stimulation his active brain required in the long-tabooed cocaine bottle.

As Holmes finished speaking, the doorbell echoed through the house; then hurried feet were sounding on the stairs, while the wailing voice of Mrs. Hudson, raised in protest, could only have been occasioned by frustration of her coveted privilege of bearing up our caller's card. Then the door burst violently inward and the object of our analysis staggered to the center of the room and pitched headforemost upon our center rug. There he lay, a magnificent ruin, with his head on the fringed border and his feet in the coal scuttle; and sealed within his motionless lips was the amazing story he had come to tell—for that it was amazing we could not doubt in the light of our client's extraordinary behavior.

Sherlock Holmes ran quickly for the brandy, while I knelt beside the stricken man and loosened his wilted neckband. He was not dead, and when we had forced the flask beneath his teeth he sat up in groggy fashion, passing a dazed hand across his eyes. Then he scrambled to his feet with an embarrassed apology for his weakness, and fell into the chair which Holmes invitingly held toward him.

"That is right, Mr. Harrington Edwards," said my companion soothingly. "Be quite calm, my dear sir, and when you have recovered your composure you will find us ready to listen."

"You know me then?" cried our visitor. There was pride in his voice and he lifted his eyebrows in surprise.

"I had never heard of you until this moment; but if you wish to conceal your identity it would be well," said Sherlock Holmes, "for you to leave your bookplates at home." As Holmes spoke he returned a little package of folded paper slips, which he had picked from the floor. "They fell from your hat when you had the misfortune to collapse," he added whimsically.

"Yes, yes," cried the collector, a deep blush spreading across his features. "I remember now; my hat was a little large and I folded a number of them and placed them beneath the sweatband. I had forgotten."

"Rather shabby usage for a handsome etched plate," smiled my companion; "but that is your affair. And now, sir, if you are quite at ease, let us hear what it is that has brought you, a collector of books, from Poke Stogis Manor—the name is on the plate—to the office of Sherlock Holmes, consulting expert in crime. Surely nothing but the theft of Mahomet's own copy of the Koran can have affected you so strongly."

Mr. Harrington Edwards smiled feebly at the jest, then sighed. "Alas," he murmured, "if that were all! But I shall begin at the beginning.

"You must know, then, that I am the greatest Shakespearean commentator in the world. My collection of *ana* is unrivaled and much of the world's collection (and consequently its knowledge of the veritable Shakespeare) has emanated from my pen. One book I did not possess: it was unique, in the correct sense of that abused word, the greatest Shakespeare rarity in the world. Few knew that it existed, for its existence was kept a profound secret among a chosen few. Had it become known that this book was in England—anywhere, indeed—its owner would have been hounded to his grave by wealthy Americans.

"It was in the possession of my friend—I tell you this in strictest confidence—of my friend, Sir Nathaniel Brooke-Bannerman, whose place at Walton-on-Walton is next to my own. A scant two hundred yards separate our dwellings; so intimate has been our friendship that a few years ago the fence between our estates was removed, and each of us roamed or loitered at will in the other's preserves.

"For some years, now, I have been at work upon my greatest book—my magnum opus. It was to be my last book also embodying the results of a lifetime of study and research. Sir, I know Elizabethan London better than any man alive; better than any man who ever lived, I think——." He burst suddenly into tears.

"There, there," said Sherlock Holmes gently. "Do not be distressed. Pray continue with your interesting narrative. What was this book—which, I take it, in some manner has disappeared? You borrowed it from your friend?"

"That is what I am coming to," said Mr. Harrington Edwards, drying his tears, "but as for help, Mr. Holmes, I fear that is beyond even you. As you surmise, I needed this book. Knowing its value, which could not be fixed, for the book is priceless, and knowing Sir Nathaniel's idolatry of it, I hesitated before asking for the loan of it. But I had to have it, for without it my work could not have been completed, and at length I made my request. I suggested that I visit him and go through the volume under his eyes, he sitting at my side throughout my entire examination, and servants stationed at every door and window, with fowling pieces in their hands.

"You can imagine my astonishment when Sir Nathaniel laughed at my precautions. 'My dear Edwards,' he said, 'that would be all very well were you Arthur Rambidge or Sir Homer Nantes (mentioning the two great men of the British Museum), or were you Mr. Henry Hutterson, the American railway magnate; but you are my friend Harrington Edwards, and you shall take the book home with you for as long as you like.' I protested vigorously, I can assure you; but he would have it so, and as I was touched by this mark of his esteem, at length I permitted him to have his way. My God! If I had remained adamant! If I had only——."

He broke off and for a moment stared blindly into space. His eyes were directed at the Persian slipper on the wall, in the toe of which Holmes kept his tobacco, but we could see that his thoughts were far away.

"Come, Mr. Edwards," said Holmes firmly. "You are agitating yourself unduly. And you are unreasonably prolonging our curiosity. You have not yet told us what this book is."

Mr. Harrington Edwards gripped the arm of the chair in which he sat. Then he spoke, and his voice was low and thrilling.

"The book was a *Hamlet* quarto, dated 1602, presented by Shakespeare to his friend Drayton, with an inscription four lines in length, written and signed by the Master, himself!"

"My dear sir!" I exclaimed. Holmes blew a long, slow whistle of astonishment.

"It is true," cried the collector. "That is the book I borrowed, and that is the book I lost! The long-sought quarto of 1602, actually inscribed in Shakespeare's own hand! His greatest drama, in an edition dated a year earlier than any that is known; a perfect copy, and with four lines in his own handwriting! Unique! Extraordinary! Amazing! Astounding! Colossal! Incredible! Un——."

He seemed wound up to continue indefinitely; but Holmes, who had sat quite still at first, shocked by the importance of the loss, interrupted the flow of adjectives.

"I appreciate your emotion, Mr. Edwards," he said, "and the book is indeed all that you say it is. Indeed, it is so important that we must at once attack the problem of rediscovering it. The book, I take it, is readily indentifiable?"

"Mr. Holmes," said our client, earnestly, "it would be impossible to hide it. It is so important a volume that, upon coming into its possession, Sir Nathaniel Brooke-Bannerman called a consultation of the great binders of the Empire, at which were present Mr. Riviere, Messrs. Sangorski and Sutcliffe, Mr. Zaehnsdorf, and certain others. They and myself, with two others, alone know of the book's existence. When I tell you that it is bound in brown levant morocco, with leather joints and brown levant doublures and flyleaves, the whole elaborately gold-tooled, inlaid with seven hundred and fifty separate pieces of various colored leathers, and enriched by the insertion of eighty-seven precious stones, I need not add that it is a design that never will be duplicated, and I mention only a few of its glories. The binding was personally done by Messrs. Riviere, Sangorski, Sutcliffe, and Zaehnsdorf, working alternately, and is a work of such enchantment that any man might gladly die a thousand deaths for the privilege of owning it for twenty minutes."

"Dear me," quoth Sherlock Holmes, "it must indeed be a handsome volume, and from your description, together with a realization of its importance by reason of its association, I gather that it is something beyond what might be termed a valuable book."

"Priceless!" cried Mr. Harrington Edwards. "The combined wealth of India, Mexico, and Wall Street would be all too little for its purchase."

"You are anxious to recover this book?" asked Sherlock Holmes, looking at him keenly.

"My God!" shrieked the collector, rolling up his eyes and clawing at the air with his hands. "Do you suppose——?"

"Tut, tut!" Holmes interrupted. "I was only teasing you. It is a book that might move even you, Mr. Harrington Edwards, to theft—but we may put aside that notion. Your emotion is too sincere, and besides you know too well the difficulties of hiding such a volume as you describe. Indeed, only a very daring man would purloin it and keep it long in his possession. Pray tell us how you came to lose it."

Mr. Harrington Edwards seized the brandy flask, which stood at his elbow, and drained it at a gulp. With the renewed strength thus obtained, he continued his story:

"As I have said, Sir Nathaniel forced me to accept the loan of the book, much against my wishes. On the evening that I called for it, he told me that two of his servants, heavily armed, would accompany me across the grounds to my home. 'There is no danger,' he said, 'but you will feel better'; and I heartily agreed with him. How shall I tell you what happened? Mr. Holmes, it was those very servants who assailed me and robbed me of my priceless borrowing!"

Sherlock Holmes rubbed his lean hands with satisfaction. "Splendid!" he murmured. "This is a case after my own heart. Watson, these are deep waters in which we are adventuring. But you are rather lengthy about this, Mr. Edwards. Perhaps it will help matters if I ask you a few questions. By what road did you go to your home?"

"By the main road, a good highway which lies in front of our estates. I preferred it to the shadows of the wood."

"And there were some two hundred yards between your doors. At what point did the assault occur?"

"Almost midway between the two entrance drives, I should say."

"There was no light?"

"That of the moon only."

"Did you know these servants who accompanied you?"

"One I knew slightly; the other I had not seen before."

"Describe them to me, please."

"The man who is known to me is called Miles. He is clean-shaven, short and powerful, although somewhat elderly. He was known, I believe, as Sir Nathaniel's most trusted servant; he had been with Sir Nathaniel for years. I cannot describe him minutely for, of course, I never paid much attention to him. The other was tall and thickset, and wore a heavy beard. He was a silent fellow; I do not believe that he spoke a word during the journey."

"Miles was more communicative?"

"Oh yes—even garrulous, perhaps. He talked about the weather and the moon, and I forget what else."

"Never about books?"

"There was no mention of books between any of us."

"Just how did the attack occur?"

"It was very sudden. We had reached, as I say, about the halfway point, when the big man seized me by the throat—to prevent outcry, I suppose—and on the instant, Miles snatched the volume from my grasp and was off. In a moment his companion followed him. I had been half throttled and could not immediately cry out; but when I could articulate, I made the countryside ring with my cries. I ran after them, but failed even to catch another sight of them. They had disappeared completely."

"Did you all leave the house together?"

"Miles and I left together; the second man joined us at the porter's lodge. He had been attending to some of his duties."

"And Sir Nathaniel—where was he?"

"He said good-night on the threshold."

"What has he had to say about all this?"

"I have not told him."

"You have not told him?" echoed Sherlock Holmes, in astonishment.

"I have not dared," confessed our client miserably. "It will kill him. That book was the breath of his life."

"When did all this occur?" I put in, with a glance at Holmes.

"Excellent, Watson," said my friend, answering my glance. "I was just about to ask the same question."

"Just last night," was Mr. Harrington Edwards' reply. "I was crazy most of the night, and didn't sleep a wink. I came to you the first thing this morning. Indeed, I tried to raise you on the telephone, last night, but could not establish a connection."

"Yes," said Holmes, reminiscently, "we were attending Mme. Trentini's first night. We dined later at Albani's."

"Oh, Mr. Holmes, do you think you can help me?" cried the abject collector.

"I trust so," answered my friend, cheerfully. "Indeed, I am certain I can. Such a book, as you remark, is not easily hidden. What say you, Watson, to a run down to Walton-on-Walton?"

"There is a train in half an hour," said Mr. Harrington Edwards, looking at his watch. "Will you return with me?"

"No, no," laughed Holmes, "that would never do. We must not be seen together just yet, Mr. Edwards. Go back yourself on the first train, by all means, unless you have further business in London. My friend and I will go together. There is another train this morning?"

"An hour later."

"Excellent. Until we meet, then!"

2

We took the train from Paddington Station an hour later, as we had promised, and began our journey to Walton-on-Walton, a pleasant, aristocratic little village and the scene of the curious accident to our friend of Poke Stogis Manor. Sherlock Holmes, lying back in his seat, blew earnest smoke rings at the ceiling of our compartment, which fortunately was empty, while I devoted myself to the morning paper. After a bit I tired of this occupation and turned to Holmes to find him looking out of the window, wreathed in smiles, and quoting Horace softly under his breath.

"You have a theory?" I asked, in surprise.

"It is a capital mistake to theorize in advance of the evidence," he replied. "Still, I have given some thought to the interesting problem of our friend, Mr. Harrington Edwards, and there are several indications which can point to only one conclusion."

"And whom do you believe to be the thief?"

"My dear fellow," said Sherlock Holmes, "you forget we already know the thief. Edwards has testified quite clearly that it was Miles who snatched the volume."

"True," I admitted, abashed. "I had forgotten. All we must do then, is to find Miles."

"And a motive," added my friend, chuckling. "What would you say, Watson, was the motive in this case?"

"Jealousy," I replied.

"You surprise me!"

"Miles had been bribed by a rival collector, who in some manner had learned about this remarkable volume. You remember Edwards told us this second man joined them at the lodge. That would give an excellent opportunity for the substitution of a man other than the servant intended by Sir Nathaniel. Is not that good reasoning?"

"You surpass yourself, my dear Watson," murmured Holmes. "It is excellently reasoned, and as you justly observe, the opportunity for a substitution was perfect."

"Do you not agree with me?"

"Hardly, Watson. A rival collector, in order to accomplish this remarkable coup, first would have to have known of the volume, as you suggest, but also he must have known upon what night Mr. Harrington Edwards would go to Sir Nathaniel's to get it, which would point to collaboration on the part of our client. As a matter of fact, however, Mr. Edwards's decision to accept the loan was, I believe, sudden and without previous determination."

"I do not recall his saying so."

"He did not say so, but it is a simple deduction. A book collector is mad enough to begin with, Watson; but tempt him with some such bait as this Shakespeare quarto and he is bereft of all sanity. Mr. Edwards would not have been able to wait. It was just the night before that Sir Nathaniel promised him the book, and it was just last night that he flew to accept the offer— flying, incidentally, to disaster also. The miracle is that he was able to wait an entire day."

"Wonderful!" I cried.

"Elementary," said Holmes. "If you are interested, you will do well to read Harley Graham on *Transcendental Emotion*; while I have myself been guilty of a small brochure in which I catalogue some twelve hundred professions and the emotional effect upon their members of unusual tidings, good and bad."

We were the only passengers to alight at Walton-on-Walton, but rapid inquiry developed that Mr. Harrington Edwards had returned on the previous train. Holmes, who had disguised himself before leaving the coach, did all the talking. He wore his cap peak backward, carried a pencil behind his ear, and had turned up the bottoms of his trousers; while from one pocket dangled the end of a linen tape measure. He was a municipal surveyor to the life, and I could not but think that, meeting him suddenly in the highway I should not myself have known him. At his suggestion, I dented the crown of my hat and turned my jacket inside out. Then he gave me an end of the tape measure, while he, carrying the other, went on ahead. In this fashion, stopping from time to time to kneel in the dust and ostensibly to measure sections of the roadway, we proceeded toward Poke Stogis Manor. The occasional villagers whom we encountered on their way to the station paid us no more attention than if we had been rabbits.

Shortly we came in sight of our friend's dwelling, a picturesque and rambling abode, sitting far back in its own grounds and bordered by a square of sentinel oaks. A gravel pathway led from the roadway to the house entrance and, as we passed, the sunlight struck fire from an antique brass knocker on the door. The whole picture, with its background of gleaming countryside, was one of rural calm and comfort; we could with difficulty believe it the scene of the curious problem we had come to investigate.

"We shall not enter yet," said Sherlock Holmes, passing the gate leading into our client's acreage; "but we shall endeavor to be back in time for luncheon."

From this point the road progressed downward in a gentle decline and the vegetation grew more thickly on either side of the road. Sherlock Holmes kept his eyes stolidly on the path before us, and when we had covered about a hundred yards he stopped. "Here," he said, pointing, "the assault occurred."

I looked closely at the earth, but could see no sign of struggle.

"You recall it was midway between the two houses that it happened," he continued. "No, there are few signs; there was no violent tussle. Fortunately, however, we had our proverbial fall of rain last evening and the earth has retained impressions nicely." He indicated the faint imprint of a foot, then another, and still another. Kneeling down, I was able to see that, indeed, many feet had passed along the road.

Holmes flung himself at full length in the dirt and wriggled swiftly about, his nose to the earth, muttering rapidly in French. Then he whipped out a glass, the better to examine something that had caught his eye; but in a moment he shook his head in disappointment and continued with his exploration. I was irresistibly reminded of a noble hound, at fault, sniffing in circles in an effort to re-establish a lost scent. In a moment, however, he had it, for with a little cry of pleasure he rose to his feet, zigzagged curiously across the road and paused before a bridge, a lean finger pointing accusingly at a break in the thicket.

"No wonder they disappeared," he smiled as I came up. "Edwards thought they continued up the road, but here is where they broke through." Then stepping back a little distance, he ran forward lightly and cleared the hedge at a bound.

"Follow me carefully," he warned, "for we must not allow our own footprints to confuse us." I fell more heavily than my companion, but in a moment he had me up and helped me to steady myself. "See," he cried, examining the earth; and deep in the mud and grass I saw the prints of two pairs of feet.

"The small man broke through," said Sherlock Holmes, exultantly, "but the larger rascal leaped over the hedge. See how deeply his prints are marked; he landed heavily here in the soft ooze. It is significant, Watson, that they came this way. Does it suggest nothing to you?"

"That they were men who knew Edwards's grounds as well as the Brooke-Bannerman estate," I answered; and thrilled with pleasure at my friend's nod of approbation.

He flung himself upon the ground without further conversation, and for some moments we both crawled painfully across the grass. Then a shocking thought occurred to me.

"Holmes," I whispered in dismay, "do you see where these footprints tend? They are directed toward the home of our client, Mr. Harrington Edwards!"

He nodded his head slowly, and his lips were tight and thin. The double line of impressions ended abruptly at the back door of Poke Stogis Manor!

Sherlock Holmes rose to his feet and looked at his watch.

"We are just in time for luncheon," he announced, and brushed off his garments. Then, deliberately, he knocked upon the door. In a few moments we were in the presence of our client.

"We have been roaming about in the neighborhood," apologized the detective, "and took the liberty of coming to your rear door."

"You have a clue?" asked Mr. Harrington Edwards eagerly.

A queer smile of triumph sat upon Holmes's lips.

"Indeed," he said quietly, "I believe I have solved your little problem, Mr. Harrington Edwards."

"My dear Holmes!" I cried, and "My dear sir!" cried our client.

"I have yet to establish a motive," confessed my friend; "but as to the main facts there can be no question."

Mr. Harrington Edwards fell into a chair; he was white and shaking.

"The book," he croaked. "Tell me."

"Patience, my good sir," counseled Holmes kindly. "We have had nothing to eat since sunup, and we are famished. All in good time. Let us first have luncheon and then all shall be made clear. Meanwhile, I should like to telephone to Sir Nathaniel Brooke-Bannerman, for I wish him also to hear what I have to say."

Our client's pleas were in vain. Holmes would have his little joke and his luncheon. In the end, Mr. Harrington Edwards staggered away to the kitchen to order a repast, and Sherlock Holmes talked rapidly and unintelligibly into the telephone and came back with a smile on his face. But I asked no questions; in good time this extraordinary man would tell his story in his own way. I had heard all that he had heard, and had seen all that he had seen; yet I was completely at sea. Still, our host's ghastly smile hung heavily in my mind, and come what would I felt sorry for him. In a little time we were seated at table. Our client, haggard and nervous, ate slowly and with apparent discomfort; his eyes were never long absent from Holmes's inscrutable face. I was little better off, but Sherlock Holmes ate with gusto, relating meanwhile a number of his earlier adventures—which I may some day give to the world, if I am able to read my illegible notes made on the occasion.

When the dreary meal had been concluded we went into the library, where Sherlock Holmes took possession of the easiest chair with an air of proprietorship that would have been amusing in other circumstances. He screwed together his long pipe and lighted it with almost malicious lack of haste, while Mr. Harrington Edwards perspired against the mantel in an agony of apprehension.

"Why must you keep us waiting, Mr.

Holmes?" he whispered. "Tell us, at once, please, who——who——." His voice trailed off into a moan.

"The criminal," said Sherlock Holmes smoothly, "is——."

"Sir Nathaniel Brooke-Bannerman!" said a maid, suddenly putting her head in at the door; and on the heels of her announcement stalked the handsome baronet, whose priceless volume had caused all this commotion and unhappiness.

Sir Nathaniel was white, and he appeared ill. He burst at once into talk.

"I have been much upset by your call," he said, looking meanwhile at our client. "You say you have something to tell me about the quarto. Don't say——that——anything—— has happened——to it!" He clutched nervously at the wall to steady himself, and I felt deep pity for the unhappy man.

Mr. Harrington Edwards looked at Sherlock Holmes. "Oh, Mr. Holmes," he cried pathetically, "why did you send for him?"

"Because," said my friend, "I wish him to hear the truth about the Shakespeare quarto. Sir Nathaniel, I believe you have not been told as yet that Mr. Edwards was robbed, last night, of your precious volume—robbed by the trusted servants whom you sent with him to protect it."

"What!" screamed the titled collector. He staggered and fumbled madly at his heart, then collapsed into a chair. "My God!" he muttered, and then again: "My God!"

"I should have thought you would have been suspicious of evil when your servants did not return," pursued the detective.

"I have not seen them," whispered Sir Nathaniel. "I do not mingle with my servants. I did not know they had failed to return. Tell me—— tell me all!"

"Mr. Edwards," said Sherlock Holmes, turning to our client, "will you repeat your story, please?"

Mr. Harrington Edwards, thus adjured, told the unhappy tale again, ending with a heart-broken cry of "Oh, Nathaniel, can you ever forgive me?"

"I do not know that it was entirely your fault," observed Holmes cheerfully. "Sir Nathaniel's own servants are the guilty ones, and surely he sent them with you."

"But you said you had solved the case, Mr. Holmes," cried our client, in a frenzy of despair.

"Yes," agreed Holmes, "it is solved. You have had the clue in your own hands ever since the occurrence, but you did not know how to use it. It all turns upon the curious actions of the taller servant, prior to the assault."

"The actions of——?" stammered Mr. Harrington Edwards. "Why, he did nothing—— said nothing!"

"That is the curious circumstance," said Sherlock Holmes. Sir Nathaniel got to his feet with difficulty.

"Mr. Holmes," he said, "this has upset me more than I can tell you. Spare no pains to recover the book and to bring to justice the scoundrels who stole it. But I must go away and think——think——."

"Stay," said my friend. "I have already caught one of them."

"What! Where?" cried the two collectors together.

"Here," said Sherlock Holmes, and stepping forward he laid a hand on the baronet's shoulder. "You, Sir Nathaniel, were the taller servant, you were one of the thieves who throttled Mr. Harrington Edwards and took from him your own book. And now, sir, will you tell us why you did it?"

Sir Nathaniel Brooke-Bannerman staggered and would have fallen had not I rushed forward and supported him. I placed him in a chair. As we looked at him we saw confession in his eyes; guilt was written in his haggard face.

"Come, come," said Holmes impatiently. "Or will it make it easier for you if I tell the story as it occurred? Let it be so, then. You parted with Mr. Harrington Edwards on your doorsill, Sir Nathaniel, bidding your best friend good-night with a smile on your lips and evil in your heart. And as soon as you had crossed the door, you slipped into an enveloping raincoat, turned up your collar, and hastened by a shorter road to the porter's lodge, where you joined Mr. Edwards and Miles as one of your own servants. You spoke no word at any time, because you feared to speak. You were afraid Mr. Edwards would recognize your voice, while your beard, hastily assumed, protected your face and in the darkness your figure passed unnoticed.

"Having strangled and robbed your best friend, then, of your own book, you and your scoundrelly assistant fled across Mr. Edwards's fields to his own back door, thinking that, if investigation followed, I would be called in, and would trace those footprints and fix the crime upon Mr. Harrington Edwards—as part of a criminal plan, prearranged with your rascally servants, who would be supposed to be in the pay of Mr. Edwards and the ringleaders in a counterfeit assault upon his person. Your mistake, sir, was in ending your trail abruptly at Mr. Edwards's back door. Had you left another trail, then, leading back to your own domicile, I should unhesitatingly have arrested Mr. Harrington Edwards for the theft.

"Surely you must know that in criminal cases handled by me, it is never the obvious solution that is the correct one. The mere fact that the finger of suspicion is made to point at a certain individual is sufficient to absolve that individual from guilt. Had you read the little works of my friend and colleague, Dr. Watson, you would not have made such a mistake. Yet you claim to be a bookman!"

A low moan from the unhappy baronet was his only answer.

"To continue, however; there at Mr. Edwards's own back door you ended your trail, entering his house—his own house—and spending the night under his roof, while his cries and ravings over his loss filled the night and brought joy to your unspeakable soul. And in the morning, when he had gone forth to consult me, you quietly left—you and Miles—and returned to your own place by the beaten highway."

"Mercy!" cried the defeated wretch, cowering in his chair. "If it is made public, I am ruined. I was driven to it. I could not let Mr. Edwards examine the book, for that way exposure would follow; yet I could not refuse him—my best friend—when he asked its loan."

"Your words tell me all that I did not know," said Sherlock Holmes sternly. "The motive now is only too plain. The work, sir, was a forgery, and knowing that your erudite friend would discover it, you chose to blacken his name to save your own. Was the book insured?"

"Insured for £100,000, he told me," interrupted Mr. Harrington Edwards excitedly.

"So that he planned at once to dispose of this dangerous and dubious item, and to reap a golden reward," commented Holmes. "Come, sir, tell us about it. How much of it was forgery? Merely the inscription?"

"I will tell you," said the baronet suddenly, "and throw myself upon the mercy of my friend, Mr. Edwards. The whole book, in effect, was a forgery. It was originally made up of two imperfect copies of the 1604 quarto. Out of the pair I made one perfect volume, and a skillful workman, now dead, changed the date for me so cleverly that only an expert of the first water could have detected it. Such an expert, however, is Mr. Harrington Edwards—the one man in the world who could have unmasked me."

"Thank you, Nathaniel," said Mr. Harrington Edwards gratefully.

"The inscription, of course, also was forged," continued the baronet. "You may as well know everything."

"And the book?" asked Holmes. "Where did you destroy it?"

A grim smile settled on Sir Nathaniel's features. "It is even now burning in Mr. Edwards's own furnace," he said.

"Then it cannot yet be consumed," cried Holmes, and dashed into the cellar, to emerge some moments later, in high spirits, carrying a charred leaf of paper in his hand.

"It is a pity," he cried, "a pity! In spite of its questionable authenticity, it was a noble specimen. It is only half consumed; but let it burn away. I have preserved one leaf as a souvenir of the occasion." He folded it carefully and placed it in his wallet. "Mr. Harrington Edwards, I fancy the decision in this matter is for you to announce. Sir Nathaniel, of course, must make no effort to collect the insurance."

"Let us forget it, then," said Mr. Harrington Edwards, with a sigh. "Let it be a sealed chapter in the history of bibliomania." He looked at Sir Nathaniel Brooke-Bannerman for a long moment, then held out his hand. "I forgive you, Nathaniel," he said simply.

Their hands met; tears stood in the baronet's eyes. Powerfully moved, Holmes and I turned from the affecting scene and crept to the door unnoticed. In a moment the free air was blowing on our temples, and we were coughing the dust of the library from our lungs.

3

"They are a strange people, these book collectors," mused Sherlock Holmes as we rattled back to town.

"My only regret is that I shall be unable to publish my notes on this interesting case," I responded.

"Wait a bit, my dear Doctor," counseled Holmes, "and it will be possible. In time both of them will come to look upon it as a hugely diverting episode, and will tell it upon themselves. Then your notes shall be brought forth and the history of another of Mr. Sherlock Holmes's little problems shall be given to the world."

"It will always be a reflection upon Sir Nathaniel," I demurred.

"He will glory in it," prophesied Sherlock Holmes. "He will go down in bookish circles with Chatterton, and Ireland, and Payne Collier. Mark my words, he is not blind even now to the chance this gives him for a sinister immortality. He will be the first to tell it."

"But why did you preserve the leaf from *Hamlet*?" I inquired. "Why not a jewel from the binding?"

Sherlock Holmes laughed heartily. Then he slowly unfolded the leaf in question, and directed a humorous finger to a spot upon the page.

"A fancy," he responded, "to preserve so accurate a characterization of either of our friends. The line is a real jewel. See, the good Polonius says: 'That he is mad, 'tis true; 'tis true 'tis pittie; and pittie 'tis 'tis true.' There is as much sense in Master Will as in Hafiz or Confucius, and a greater felicity of expression. . . . Here is London, and now, my dear Watson, if we hasten we shall be just in time for Zabriski's matinee!"

The Stolen Cigar-Case

BRET HARTE

SEVERAL EXPERT READERS, including Ellery Queen, have described this oft-reprinted story as the best Sherlock Holmes parody (though I confess to a weakness for several of those by Robert L. Fish). There are, however, greater connections between the two hugely popular authors of the Victorian era than that they have both written about Holmes.

Bret Harte (1836–1902) established a reputation as one of the first and greatest chroniclers of life in the American West, specifically the gold rush years of California, in such stories as "The Outcasts of Poker Flat" (1869), which has been the basis for several films as well as multiple operas, and "The Luck of Roaring Camp" (1868), which brought him nationwide fame and wealth. His success did not last long, however, and though he continued to be published on a regular basis, his stories found little favor in America, often dismissed as derivative and sentimental. He moved to England in 1885, where his work enjoyed a large and enthusiastic following. Harte lived there for the rest of his life—an oddity, as he was then known as "the quintessential American writer."

In his autobiography, Arthur Conan Doyle admitted that several of his early short stories, such as "The Mystery of Sasassa Valley" (1879) and "The American's Tale" (1880), were "feeble echoes of Bret Harte." Furthermore, the plot of Conan Doyle's "The Adventure of the Noble Bachelor" (1892) appears to bear a striking resemblance to Harte's narrative poem, "Her Letter."

"The Stolen Cigar-Case" was first published in the December 1900 issue of *Pearson's Magazine*; it was first published in book form in *Condensed Novels: New Burlesques* (Boston and New York, Houghton Mifflin, 1902).

THE STOLEN CIGAR-CASE

Bret Harte

I FOUND HEMLOCK Jones in the old Brook Street lodgings, musing before the fire. With the freedom of an old friend I at once threw myself in my old familiar attitude at his feet, and gently caressed his boot. I was induced to do this for two reasons; one that it enabled me to get a good look at his bent, concentrated face, and the other that it seemed to indicate my reverence for his superhuman insight. So absorbed was he, even then, in tracking some mysterious clue, that he did not seem to notice me. But therein I was wrong—as I always was in my attempt to understand that powerful intellect.

"It is raining," he said, without lifting his head.

"You have been out then?" I said quickly.

"No. But I see that your umbrella is wet, and that your overcoat, which you threw off on entering, has drops of water on it."

I sat aghast at his penetration. After a pause he said carelessly, as if dismissing the subject: "Besides, I hear the rain on the window. Listen."

I listened. I could scarcely credit my ears, but there was the soft pattering of drops on the pane. It was evident, there was no deceiving this man!

"Have you been busy lately?" I asked, changing the subject. "What new problem—given up by Scotland Yard as inscrutable—has occupied that gigantic intellect?"

He drew back his foot slightly, and seemed to hesitate ere he returned it to its original position. Then he answered wearily: "Mere trifles—nothing to speak of. The Prince Kapoli has been here to get my advice regarding the disappearance of certain rubies from the Kremlin; the Rajah of Pootibad, after vainly beheading his entire bodyguard, has been obliged to seek my assistance to recover a jewelled sword. The Grand Duchess of Pretzel-Brauntswig is desirous of discovering where her husband was on the night of the 14th of February, and last night"—he lowered his voice slightly—"a lodger in this very house, meeting me on the stairs, wanted to know 'Why they don't answer his bell.'"

I could not help smiling—until I saw a frown gathering on his inscrutable forehead.

"Pray to remember," he said coldly, "that it was through such an apparently trivial question that I found out, 'Why Paul Ferroll killed his Wife,' and 'What happened to Jones!'"

I became dumb at once. He paused for a moment, and then suddenly changing back to his usual pitiless, analytical style, he said: "When I say these are trifles—they are so in comparison to an affair that is now before me. A crime has been committed, and, singularly enough, against myself. You start," he said; "you wonder who would have dared attempt it! So did I; nevertheless, it has been done. *I* have been *robbed*!"

"*You* robbed—you, Hemlock Jones, the Terror of Peculators!" I gasped in amazement, rising and gripping the table as I faced him.

"Yes; listen. I would confess it to no other. But *you* who have followed my career, who know my methods; yea, for whom I have partly lifted the veil that conceals my plans from ordinary humanity; you, who have for years rapturously accepted my confidences, passionately admired my inductions and inferences, placed yourself at my beck and call, become my slave, grovelled at my feet, given up your practice except those few unremunerative and rapidly decreasing patients to whom, in moments of abstraction over *my* problems, you have administered strychnine for quinine and arsenic for Epsom salts; you, who have sacrificed everything and everybody to me—*you* I make my confidant!"

I rose and embraced him warmly, yet he was already so engrossed in thought that at the same moment he mechanically placed his hand upon his watch chain as if to consult the time. "Sit down," he said; "have a cigar?"

"I have given up cigar smoking," I said.

"Why?" he asked.

I hesitated, and perhaps coloured. I had really given it up because, with my diminished practice, it was too expensive. I could only afford a pipe. "I prefer a pipe," I said laughingly. "But tell me of this robbery. What have you lost?"

He rose, and planting himself before the fire with his hands under his coat tails, looked down upon me reflectively for a moment. "Do you remember the cigar-case presented to me by the Turkish Ambassador for discovering the missing favourite of the Grand Vizier in the fifth chorus girl at the Hilarity Theatre? It was that one. It was incrusted with diamonds. I mean the cigar-case."

"And the largest one had been supplanted by paste," I said.

"Ah," he said with a reflective smile, "you know that?"

"You told me yourself. I remember considering it a proof of your extraordinary perception. But, by Jove, you don't mean to say you have lost it?"

He was silent for a moment. "No; it has been stolen, it is true, but I shall still find it. And by myself alone! In your profession, my dear fellow, when a member is severely ill he does not prescribe for himself, but call in a brother doctor. Therein we differ. I shall take this matter in my own hands."

"And where could you find better?" I said enthusiastically. "I should say the cigar-case is as good as recovered already."

"I shall remind you of that again," he said lightly. "And now, to show you my confidence in your judgment, in spite of my determination to pursue this alone, I am willing to listen to any suggestions from you."

He drew a memorandum book from his pocket, and, with a grave smile, took up his pencil.

I could scarcely believe my reason. He, the great Hemlock Jones! accepting suggestions from a humble individual like myself! I kissed his hand reverently, and began in a joyous tone:

"First I should advertise, offering a reward. I should give the same information in handbills, distributed at the 'pubs' and the pastry-cooks. I should next visit the different pawnbrokers; I should give notice at the police station. I should examine the servants. I should thoroughly search the house and my own pockets. I speak relatively," I added with a laugh, "of course I mean *your* own."

He gravely made an entry of these details.

"Perhaps," I added, "you have already done this?"

"Perhaps," he returned enigmatically. "Now, my dear friend," he continued, putting the notebook in his pocket, and rising—"would you excuse me for a few moments? Make yourself perfectly at home until I return; there may be some things," he added with a sweep of his hand towards his heterogeneously filled shelves, "that may interest you, and while away the time. There are pipes and tobacco in that corner and whiskey on the table." And nodding to me with the same inscrutable face, he left the room. I was too well accustomed to his methods to think much of his unceremonious withdrawal, and made no doubt he was off to investigate some clue which had suddenly occurred to his active intelligence.

Left to myself, I cast a cursory glance over his shelves. There were a number of small glass jars, containing earthy substances labeled "Pavement and road sweepings," from the principal thoroughfares and suburbs of London, with the subdirections "For identifying foot tracks." There were several other jars labeled "Fluff from omnibus and road-car seats," "Cocoanut fibre and rope strands from mattings in public places," "Cigarette stumps and match ends from floor of Palace Theatre, Row A, 1 to 50." Everywhere were evidences of this wonderful man's system and perspicacity.

I was thus engaged when I heard the slight creaking of a door, and I looked up as a stranger entered. He was a rough-looking man, with a shabby overcoat, a still more disreputable muffler round his throat, and a cap on his head. Considerably annoyed at his intrusion I turned upon him rather sharply, when, with a mumbled, growling apology for mistaking the room, he shuffled out again and closed the door. I followed him quickly to the landing and saw that he disappeared down the stairs.

With my mind full of the robbery, the incident made a singular impression on me. I knew my friend's habits of hasty absences from his room in his moments of deep inspiration; it was only too probable that with his powerful intellect and magnificent perceptive genius concentrated on one subject, he should be careless of his own belongings, and, no doubt, even forget to take the ordinary precaution of locking up his drawers. I tried one or two and found I was right—although for some reason I was unable to open one to its fullest extent. The handles were sticky, as if someone had opened them with dirty fingers. Knowing Hemlock's fastidious cleanliness, I resolved to inform him of this circumstance, but I forgot it, alas! until—but I am anticipating my story.

His absence was strangely prolonged. I at last seated myself by the fire, and lulled by warmth and the patter of the rain on the window, I fell asleep. I may have dreamt, for during my sleep I had a vague semi-consciousness as of hands being softly pressed on my pockets—no doubt induced by the story of the robbery. When I came fully to my senses, I found Hemlock Jones sitting on the other side of the hearth, his deeply concentrated gaze fixed on the fire.

"I found you so comfortably asleep that I could not bear to waken you," he said with a smile.

I rubbed my eyes. "And what news?" I asked. "How have you succeeded?"

"Better than I expected," he said, "and I think," he added, tapping his note-book—"I owe much to *you*."

Deeply gratified, I awaited more. But in vain. I ought to have remembered that in his moods Hemlock Jones was reticence itself. I told him simply of the strange intrusion, but he only laughed.

Later, when I rose to go, he looked at me playfully. "If you were a married man," he said, "I would advise you not to go home until you had brushed your sleeve. There are a few short, brown sealskin hairs on the inner side of the fore-arm—just where they would have adhered if your arm had encircled a sealskin sacque with some pressure!"

"For once you are at fault," I said triumphantly, "the hair is my own as you will perceive; I had just had it cut at the hair-dressers, and no doubt this arm projected beyond the apron."

He frowned slightly, yet nevertheless, on my turning to go he embraced me warmly—a rare exhibition in that man of ice. He even helped me on with my overcoat and pulled out and smoothed down the flaps of my pockets. He was particular, too, in fitting my arm in my overcoat sleeve, shaking the sleeve down from the arm-hole to the cuff with his deft fingers. "Come again soon!" he said, clapping me on the back.

"At any and all times," I said enthusiastically. "I only ask ten minutes twice a day to eat a crust at my office and four hours sleep at night, and the rest of my time is devoted to you always—as you know."

"It is, indeed," he said, with his impenetrable smile.

Nevertheless I did not find him at home when I next called. One afternoon, when nearing my own home I met him in one of his favourite disguises—a long, blue, swallow-tailed coat, striped cotton trousers, large turn-over collar, blacked face, and white hat, carrying a tambourine. Of course to others the disguise was perfect, although it was known to myself, and I passed him—according to an old understanding between us—without the slightest recognition, trusting to a later explanation. At another time, as I was making a professional visit to the wife of a publican at the East End, I saw him in the disguise of a broken down artisan looking into the window of an adjacent pawnshop. I was delighted to see that he was evidently following my suggestions, and in my joy I ventured to tip him a wink; it was abstractedly returned.

Two days later I received a note appointing a meeting at his lodgings that night. That meeting, alas! was the one memorable occurrence of my life, and the last meeting I ever had with Hemlock Jones! I will try to set it down calmly, though my pulses still throb with the recollection of it.

I found him standing before the fire with that look upon his face which I had seen only once or twice in our acquaintance—a look which I may call an absolute concatenation of inductive and deductive ratiocination—from which all that was human, tender, or sympathetic, was absolutely discharged. He was simply an icy algebraic symbol! Indeed his whole being was concentrated to that extent that his clothes fitted loosely, and his head was absolutely so much reduced in size by his mental compression that his hat tipped back from his forehead and literally hung on his massive ears.

After I had entered, he locked the doors, fastened the windows, and even placed a chair before the chimney. As I watched those significant precautions with absorbing interest, he suddenly drew a revolver and presenting it to my temple, said in low, icy tones:

"Hand over that cigar-case!"

Even in my bewilderment, my reply was truthful, spontaneous, and involuntary. "I haven't got it," I said.

He smiled bitterly, and threw down his revolver. "I expected that reply! Then let me now confront you with something more awful, more deadly, more relentless and convincing than that mere lethal weapon—the damning inductive and deductive proofs of your guilt!" He drew from his pocket a roll of paper and a note-book.

"But surely," I gasped, "you are joking! You could not for a moment believe—"

"Silence!" he roared. "Sit down!"

I obeyed.

"You have condemned yourself," he went on pitilessly. "Condemned yourself on my processes— processes familiar to you, applauded by you, accepted by you for years! We will go back to the time when you first saw the cigar-case. Your expressions," he said in cold, deliberate tones, consulting his paper, "were: 'How beautiful! I wish it were mine.' This was your first step in crime—and my first indication. From 'I *wish* it were mine' to 'I *will* have it mine,' and the mere detail, 'How *can* I make it mine,' the advance was obvious. Silence! But as in my methods, it was necessary that there should be an overwhelming inducement to the crime, that unholy admiration of yours for the mere trinket itself was not enough. You are a smoker of cigars."

"But," I burst out passionately, "I told you I had given up smoking cigars."

"Fool!" he said coldly. "That is the *second* time you have committed yourself. Of course, you *told* me! What more natural than for you to blazon forth that prepared and unsolicited statement to *prevent* accusation. Yet, as I said before, even that wretched attempt to cover up your tracks was not enough. I still had to find that overwhelming, impelling motive necessary to affect a man like you. That motive I found in *passion*, the strongest of all impulses—love, I suppose you would call it," he added bitterly; "that night you called! You had brought the damning proofs of it in your sleeves."

"But," I almost screamed.

"Silence," he thundered, "I know what you would say. You would say that even if you had embraced some young person in a sealskin sacque what had that to do with the robbery. Let me tell you then, that that sealskin sacque represented the quality and character of your fatal entanglement! If you are at all conversant with light sporting literature you would know that a sealskin sacque indicates a love induced by sordid mercenary interests. You bartered your honour for it—that stolen cigar-case was the purchaser of the sealskin sacque! Without money, with a decreasing practice, it was the only way you could insure your passion being returned by that young person, whom, for your sake, I have not even pursued. Silence! Having thoroughly established your motive, I now proceed to the commission of the crime itself. Ordinary people would have begun with that—with an attempt to discover the whereabouts of the missing object. These are not my methods."

So overpowering was his penetration, that although I knew myself innocent, I licked my lips with avidity to hear the further details of this lucid exposition of my crime.

"You committed that theft the night I showed you the cigar-case and after I had carelessly thrown it in that drawer. You were sitting in that chair, and I had risen to take something from that shelf. In that instant you secured your booty without rising. Silence! Do you remember when I helped you on with your overcoat the other night? I was particular about fitting your arm in. While doing so I measured your arm with a spring tape measure from the shoulder to the cuff. A later visit to your tailor confirmed that measurement. It proved to be *the exact distance between your chair and that drawer!*"

I sat stunned.

"The rest are mere corroborative details! You were again tampering with the drawer when I discovered you doing so. Do not start! The stranger that blundered into the room with the muffler on—was myself. More, I had placed a little soap on the drawer handles when I purposely left you alone. The soap was on your hand when I shook it at parting. I softly felt your pockets when you were asleep for further developments. I embraced you when you left—that I might feel if you had the cigar-case, or any other articles, hidden on your body. This confirmed me in the belief that you had already disposed of it in the manner and for the purpose I have

shown you. As I still believed you capable of remorse and confession, I allowed you to see I was on your track twice, once in the garb of an itinerant negro minstrel, and the second time as a workman looking in the window of the pawnshop where you pledged your booty."

"But," I burst out, "if you had asked the pawnbroker you would have seen how unjust—"

"Fool!" he hissed; "that was one of *your* suggestions to search the pawnshops. Do you suppose I followed any of your suggestions—the suggestions of the thief? On the contrary, they told me what to avoid."

"And I suppose," I said bitterly, "you have not even searched your drawer."

"No," he said calmly.

I was for the first time really vexed. I went to the nearest drawer and pulled it out sharply. It stuck as it had before, leaving a part of the drawer unopened. By working it, however, I discovered that it was impeded by some obstacle that had slipped to the upper part of the drawer, and held it firmly fast. Inserting my hand, I pulled out the impeding object. It was the missing cigar-case. I turned to him with a cry of joy.

But I was appalled at his expression. A look of contempt was now added to his acute, penetrating gaze. "I have been mistaken," he said slowly. "I had not allowed for your weakness and cowardice. I thought too highly of you even in your guilt; but I see now why you tampered with that drawer the other night. By some incredible means—possibly another theft—you took the cigar-case out of pawn, and like a whipped hound restored it to me in this feeble, clumsy fashion. You thought to deceive me, Hemlock Jones: more, you thought to destroy my infallibility. Go! I give you your liberty. I shall not summon the three policemen who wait in the adjoining room—but out of my sight forever."

As I stood once more dazed and petrified, he took me firmly by the ear and led me into the hall, closing the door behind him. This reopened presently wide enough to permit him to thrust out my hat, overcoat, umbrella and over-shoes, and then closed against me forever!

I never saw him again. I am bound to say, however, that thereafter my business increased—I recovered much of my old practice—and a few of my patients recovered also. I became rich. I had a brougham and a house in the West End. But I often wondered, pondering on that wonderful man's penetration and insight, if, in some lapse of consciousness, I had not really stolen his cigar-case!

The Case of the Man Who Was Wanted

ARTHUR WHITAKER

LITTLE APPEARS TO be known of the elusive Arthur Whitaker (1882–?) other than that he was an architect and was writing between the years 1892 and 1910, with a brief reappearance in 1949. Whitaker's only connection to the Sherlockian world is the pastiche "The Case of the Man Who Was Wanted," which was shrouded in mystery itself when it was first published in 1948 in *Cosmopolitan Magazine*.

In 1942, the Associated Press released the news of a previously unpublished, long-lost Sherlock Holmes story, which it believed was written in Arthur Conan Doyle's hand. It was rumored that his son Adrian Conan Doyle had discovered the manuscript in a chest of family documents. However, it was later revealed that the manuscript was not handwritten, but typewritten, unlike any of Conan Doyle's Sherlockian manuscripts.

For several years, Adrian refused to release the story for publication, as Conan Doyle's daughter Jean claimed she knew it was not written by her father. The Baker Street Irregulars launched an appeal for its release, which was published in the *Saturday Review of Literature*, and in August 1948 *Cosmopolitan Magazine* obtained the manuscript and published it under Arthur Conan Doyle's name with great fanfare about the great detective's final adventure being published now for the first time. It was also published in London's *Sunday Dispatch* in January 1949.

Soon afterward, Conan Doyle's biographer, Hesketh Pearson, received a letter from Whitaker, explaining that he was the true author of "The Case of the Man Who Was Wanted" and he had sent the manuscript to Conan Doyle in 1911 with the hope that it be published as a collaboration between himself and the famous author. Adrian, obviously, refused his suggestion, but did send Whitaker a check for ten guineas. To prove the authenticity of his claim, Whitaker produced a carbon copy of the manuscript and, after a brief threat of legal action, the Conan Doyle family finally accepted that Whitaker was the true author of the pastiche.

THE CASE OF THE MAN
WHO WAS WANTED

Arthur Whitaker

DURING THE LATE autumn of 'ninety-five a fortunate chance enabled me to take some part in another of my friend Sherlock Holmes's fascinating cases.

My wife not having been well for some time, I had at last persuaded her to take a holiday in Switzerland in the company of her old school friend Kate Whitney, whose name may be remembered in connection with the strange case I have already chronicled under the title of "The Man with the Twisted Lip." My practice had grown much, and I had been working very hard for many months and never felt in more need myself of a rest and a holiday. Unfortunately I dared not absent myself for a long enough period to warrant a visit to the Alps. I promised my wife, however, that I would get a week or ten days' holiday in somehow, and it was only on this understanding that she consented to the Swiss tour I was so anxious for her to take. One of my best patients was in a very critical state at the time, and it was not until August was gone that he passed the crisis and began to recover. Feeling then that I could leave my practice with a good conscience in the hands of a *locum tenens*, I began to wonder where and how I should best find the rest and change I needed.

Almost at once the idea came to my mind that I would hunt up my old friend Sherlock Holmes, of whom I had seen nothing for several months. If he had no important inquiry in hand, I would do my uttermost to persuade him to join me.

Within half an hour of coming to this resolution I was standing in the doorway of the familiar old room in Baker Street.

Holmes was stretched upon the couch with his back towards me, the familiar dressing gown and old brier pipe as much in evidence as of yore.

"Come in, Watson," he cried, without glancing round. "Come in and tell me what good wind blows you here?"

"What an ear you have, Holmes," I said. "I don't think that I could have recognized your tread so easily."

"Nor I yours," said he, "if you hadn't come up my badly lighted staircase taking the steps two at a time with all the familiarity of an old fellow lodger; even then I might not have been sure who it was, but when you stumbled over the new mat outside the door which has been there for nearly three months, you needed no further announcement."

Holmes pulled out two or three of the cushions from the pile he was lying on and threw them across into the armchair. "Sit down, Watson, and make yourself comfortable; you'll find cigarettes in a box behind the clock."

As I proceeded to comply, Holmes glanced whimsically across at me. "I'm afraid I shall have to disappoint you, my boy," he said. "I had a wire only half an hour ago which will prevent me from joining in any little trip you may have been about to propose."

"Really, Holmes," I said, "don't you think this is going a little *too* far? I begin to fear you are a fraud and pretend to discover things by observation, when all the time you really do it by pure out-and-out clairvoyance!"

Holmes chuckled. "Knowing you as I do it's absurdly simple," said he. "Your surgery hours are from five to seven, yet at six o'clock you walk smiling into my rooms. Therefore you must have a *locum* in. You are looking well, though tired, so the obvious reason is that you are having, or about to have, a holiday. The clinical thermometer, peeping out of your pocket, proclaims that you have been on your rounds today, hence it's pretty evident that your real holiday begins tomorrow. When, under these circumstances, you come hurrying into my rooms—which, by the way, Watson, you haven't visited for nearly three months—with a new Bradshaw and a timetable of excursion bookings bulging out of your coat pocket, then it's more than probable you have come with the idea of suggesting some joint expedition."

"It's all perfectly true," I said, and explained to him, in a few words, my plans. "And I'm more disappointed than I can tell you," I concluded, "that you are not able to fall in with my little scheme."

Holmes picked up a telegram from the table and looked at it thoughtfully. "If only the inquiry this refers to promised to be of anything like the interest of some we have gone into together, nothing would have delighted me more than to have persuaded you to throw your lot in with mine for a time; but really I'm afraid to do so, for it sounds a particularly commonplace affair," and he crumpled the paper into a ball and tossed it over to me.

I smoothed it out and read: "To Holmes, 221B Baker Street, London, S.W. Please come to Sheffield at once to inquire into case of forgery. Jervis, Manager British Consolidated Bank."

"I've wired back to say I shall go up to Sheffield by the one-thirty a.m. express from St. Pancras," said Holmes. "I can't go sooner as I have an interesting little appointment to fulfil tonight down in the East End, which should give me the last information I need to trace home a daring robbery from the British Museum to its

instigator—who possesses one of the oldest titles and finest houses in the country, along with a most insatiable greed, almost mania, for collecting ancient documents. Before discussing the Sheffield affair any further, however, we had perhaps better see what the evening paper has to say about it," continued Holmes, as his boy entered with the *Evening News*, *Standard*, *Globe*, and *Star*. "Ah, this must be it," he said, pointing to a paragraph headed "Daring Forger's Remarkable Exploits in Sheffield."

Whilst going to press we have been informed that a series of most cleverly forged cheques have been successfully used to swindle the Sheffield banks out of a sum which cannot be less than six thousand pounds. The full extent of the fraud has not yet been ascertained, and the managers of the different banks concerned, who have been interviewed by our Sheffield correspondent, are very reticent.

It appears that a gentleman named Mr. Jabez Booth, who resides at Broomhill, Sheffield, and has been an employee since January, 1881, at the British Consolidated Bank in Sheffield, yesterday succeeded in cashing quite a number of cleverly forged cheques at twelve of the principal banks in the city and absconding with the proceeds.

The crime appears to have been a strikingly deliberate and well thought-out one. Mr. Booth had, of course, in his position in one of the principal banks in Sheffield, excellent opportunities of studying the various signatures which he forged, and he greatly facilitated his chances of easily and successfully obtaining cash for the cheques by opening banking accounts last year at each of the twelve banks at which he presented the forged cheques, and by this means becoming personally known at each.

He still further disarmed suspicion by crossing each of the forged cheques and paying them into his account, while, at the same time, he drew and cashed a cheque of his own for about half the amount of the forged cheque paid in.

It was not until early this morning, Thursday, that the fraud was discovered, which means that the rascal has had some twenty hours in which to make good his escape. In spite of this we have little doubt but that he will soon be laid by the heels, for we are informed that the finest detectives from Scotland Yard are already upon his track, and it is also whispered that Mr. Sherlock Holmes, the well-known and almost world-famed criminal expert of Baker Street, has been asked to assist in hunting down this daring forger.

"Then there follows a lengthy description of the fellow, which I needn't read but will keep for future use," said Holmes, folding the paper and looking across at me. "It seems to have been a pretty smart affair. This Booth may not be easily caught, for though he hasn't had a long time in which to make his escape we mustn't lose sight of the fact that he's had twelve months in which to plan how he would do the vanishing trick when the time came. Well! What do you say, Watson? Some of the little problems we have gone into in the past should at least have taught us that the most interesting cases do not always present the most bizarre features at the outset."

" 'So far from it, on the contrary, quite the reverse,' to quote Sam Weller," I replied. "Personally nothing would be more to my taste than to join you."

"Then we'll consider it settled," said my friend. "And now I must go and attend to that other little matter of business I spoke to you about. Remember," he said, as we parted, "one-thirty at St. Pancras."

I was on the platform in good time, but it was not until the hands of the great station clock indicated the very moment due for our departure, and the porters were beginning to slam the carriage doors noisily, that I caught the familiar sight of Holmes's tall figure.

"Ah! here you are Watson," he cried cheerily. "I fear you must have thought I was going to be too late. I've had a very busy evening and no time to waste; however, I've succeeded in putting into practice Phileas Fogg's theory that 'a well-used minimum suffices for everything,' and here I am."

"About the last thing I should expect of you," I said as we settled down into two opposite corners of an otherwise empty first-class carriage, "would be that you should do such an unmethodical thing as to miss a train. The only thing which would surprise me more, in fact, would be to see you at the station ten minutes before time."

"I should consider that the greatest evil of the two," said Holmes sententiously. "But now we must sleep; we have every prospect of a heavy day."

It was one of Holmes's characteristics that he could command sleep at will; unfortunately he could resist it at will also, and often have I had to remonstrate with him on the harm he must be doing himself, when, deeply engrossed in one of his strange or baffling problems, he would go for several consecutive days and nights without one wink of sleep.

He put the shades over the lamps, leaned back in his corner, and in less than two minutes his regular breathing told me he was fast asleep. Not being blessed with the same gift myself, I lay back in my corner for some time, nodding to the rhythmical throb of the express as it hurled itself forward through the darkness. Now and again as we shot through some brilliantly illuminated station or past a line of flaming furnaces, I caught for an instant a glimpse of Holmes's figure coiled up snugly in the far corner with his head sunk upon his breast.

It was not until after we had passed Nottingham that I really fell asleep and, when a more than usually violent lurch of the train over some points woke me again, it was broad daylight, and Holmes was sitting up, busy with a Bradshaw and boat timetable. As I moved, he glanced across at me.

"If I'm not mistaken, Watson, that was the Dore and Totley tunnel through which we have just come, and if so we shall be in Sheffield in a few minutes. As you see I've not been wasting my time altogether, but studying my Bradshaw, which, by the way, Watson, is the most useful book published, without exception, to anyone of my calling."

"How can it possibly help you now?" I asked in some surprise.

"Well it may or it may not," said Holmes thoughtfully. "But in any case it's well to have at one's fingertips all knowledge which may be of use. It's quite probable that this Jabez Booth may have decided to leave the country and, if this supposition is correct, he would undoubtedly time his little escapade in conformity with information contained in this useful volume. Now I learn from this *Sheffield Telegraph* which I obtained at Leicester, by the way, when you were fast asleep, that Mr. Booth cashed the last of his forged cheques at the North British Bank in Saville Street at precisely two fifteen p.m. on Wednesday last. He made the round of the various banks he visited in a hansom, and it would take him about three minutes only to get from this bank to the G.C. station. From what I gather of the order in which the different banks were visited, he made a circuit, finishing at the nearest point to the G.C. station, at which he could arrive at about two eighteen. Now I find that at two twenty-two a boat express would leave Sheffield G.C., due in Liverpool at four-twenty, and in connection with it the White Star liner *Empress Queen* should have sailed from Liverpool docks at six thirty for New York. Or again, at two forty-five a boat train would leave Sheffield for Hull, at which town it was due at four thirty in time to make a connection with the Holland steam packet, Comet, sailing at six thirty for Amsterdam.

"Here we are provided with two not unlikely means of escape, the former being the most probable; but both worth bearing in mind."

Holmes had scarcely finished speaking when the train drew up.

"Nearly five past four," I remarked.

"Yes," said Holmes, "we are exactly one and a half minutes behind time. And now I propose a good breakfast and a cup of strong coffee, for we have at least a couple of hours to spare."

After breakfast we visited first the police station where we learned that no further developments had taken place in the matter we had come to investigate. Mr. Lestrade of Scotland Yard had arrived the previous evening and had taken the case in hand officially.

We obtained the address of Mr. Jervis, the manager of the bank at which Booth had been an employee, and also that of his landlady at Broomhill.

A hansom landed us at Mr. Jervis's house at Fulwood at seven thirty. Holmes insisted upon my accompanying him, and we were both shown into a spacious drawing room and asked to wait until the banker could see us.

Mr. Jervis, a stout, florid gentleman of about fifty, came puffing into the room in a very short time. An atmosphere of prosperity seemed to envelop, if not actually to emanate from him.

"Pardon me for keeping you waiting, gentlemen," he said, "but the hour is an early one."

"Indeed, Mr. Jervis," said Holmes, "no apology is needed unless it be on our part. It is, however, necessary that I should ask you a few questions concerning this affair of Mr. Booth, before I can proceed in the matter, and that must be our excuse for paying you such an untimely visit."

"I shall be most happy to answer your questions as far as it lies in my power to do so," said the banker, his fat fingers playing with a bunch of seals at the end of his massive gold watch chain.

"When did Mr. Booth first enter your bank?" said Holmes.

"In January, 1881."

"Do you know where he lived when he first came to Sheffield?"

"He took lodgings at Ashgate Road, and has, I believe, lived there ever since."

"Do you know anything of his history or life before he came to you?"

"Very little I fear; beyond that his parents were both dead, and that he came to us with the best testimonials from one of the Leeds branches of our bank, I know nothing."

"Did you find him quick and reliable?"

"He was one of the best and smartest men I have ever had in my employ."

"Do you know whether he was conversant with any other language besides English?"

"I feel pretty sure he wasn't. We have one clerk who attends to any foreign correspondence we may have, and I know that Booth has repeatedly passed letters and papers on to him."

"With your experience of banking matters, Mr. Jervis, how long a time do you think he might reasonably have calculated would elapse between the presentation of the forged cheques and their detection?"

"Well, that would depend very largely upon circumstances," said Mr. Jervis. "In the case of a single cheque it might be a week or two, unless the amounts were so large as to call for special inquiry, in which case it would probably never be cashed at all until such inquiry had been made. In the present case, when there were a dozen forged cheques, it was most unlikely that some one of them should not be detected within twenty-four hours and so lead to the discovery of the fraud. No sane person would dare to presume upon the crime remaining undetected for a longer period than that."

"Thanks," said Holmes, rising. "Those were the chief points I wished to speak to you about. I will communicate to you any news of importance I may have."

"I am deeply obliged to you, Mr. Holmes. The case is naturally causing us great anxiety. We leave it entirely to your discretion to take whatever steps you may consider best. Oh, by the way, I sent instructions to Booth's landlady to disturb nothing in his rooms until you had had an opportunity of examining them."

"That was a very wise thing to do," said Holmes, "and may be the means of helping us materially."

"I am also instructed by my company," said the banker, as he bowed us politely out, "to ask you to make a note of any expenses incurred, which they will of course immediately defray."

A few moments later we were ringing the bell of the house in Ashgate Road, Broomhill, at which Mr. Booth had been a lodger for over seven years. It was answered by a maid who informed us that Mrs. Purnell was engaged with a gentleman upstairs. When we explained our errand she showed us at once up to Mr. Booth's rooms, on the first floor, where we found Mrs. Purnell, a plump, voluble, little lady of about forty, in conversation with Mr. Lestrade, who appeared to be just concluding his examination of the rooms.

"Good morning, Holmes," said the detective, with a very self-satisfied air. "You arrive on the scene a little too late; I fancy I have already got all the information needed to catch our man!"

"I'm delighted to hear it," said Holmes dryly, "and must indeed congratulate you, if this is actually the case. Perhaps after I've made a little tour of inspection we can compare notes."

"Just as you please," said Lestrade, with the air of one who can afford to be gracious. "Candidly I think you will be wasting time, and so would you if you knew what I've discovered."

"Still I must ask you to humor my little whim," said Holmes, leaning against the mantelpiece and whistling softly as he looked round the room.

After a moment he turned to Mrs. Purnell. "The furniture of this room belongs, of course, to you?"

Mrs. Purnell assented.

"The picture that was taken down from the mantelpiece last Wednesday morning," continued Holmes, "that belonged to Mr. Booth, I presume?"

I followed Holmes's glance across to where an unfaded patch on the wallpaper clearly indicated that a picture had recently been hanging. Well as I knew my friend's methods of reasoning, however, I did not realize for a moment that the little bits of spiderweb which had been behind the picture, and were still clinging to the wall, had told him that the picture could only have been taken down immediately before Mrs. Purnell had received orders to disturb nothing in the room; otherwise her brush, evidently busy enough elsewhere, would not have spared them.

The good lady stared at Sherlock Holmes in open-mouthed astonishment. "Mr. Booth took it down himself on Wednesday morning," she said. "It was a picture he had painted himself, and he thought no end of it. He wrapped it up and took it out with him, remarking that he was going to give it to a friend. I was very much surprised at the time, for I knew he valued it very much; in fact he once told me that he wouldn't part with it for anything. Of course, it's easy to see now why he got rid of it."

"Yes," said Holmes. "It wasn't a large picture, I see. Was it a water color?"

"Yes, a painting of a stretch of moorland, with three or four large rocks arranged like a big table on a bare hilltop. Druidicals, Mr. Booth called them, or something like that."

"Did Mr. Booth do much painting, then?" enquired Holmes.

"None, whilst he's been here, sir. He has told me he used to do a good deal as a lad, but he had given it up."

Holmes's eyes were glancing round the room again, and an exclamation of surprise escaped him as they encountered a photo standing on the piano.

"Surely that's a photograph of Mr. Booth," he said. "It exactly resembles the description I have of him?"

"Yes," said Mrs. Purnell, "and a very good one it is too."

"How long has it been taken?" said Holmes, picking it up.

"Oh, only a few weeks, sir. I was here when the boy from the photographer's brought them up. Mr. Booth opened the packet whilst I was in the room. There were only two photos, that one and another which he gave to me."

"You interest me exceedingly," said Holmes. "This striped lounge suit he is wearing. Is it the same that he had on when he left Wednesday morning?"

"Yes, he was dressed just like that, as far as I can remember."

"Do you recollect anything of importance that Mr. Booth said to you last Wednesday before he went out?"

"Not very much, I'm afraid, sir. When I took his cup of chocolate up to his bedroom, he said—"

"One moment," interrupted Holmes. "Did Mr. Booth usually have a cup of chocolate in the morning?"

"Oh, yes, sir, summer and winter alike. He was very particular about it and would ring for it as soon as he waked. I believe he'd rather have gone without his breakfast almost than have missed his cup of chocolate. Well, as I was saying, sir, I took it up to him myself on Wednesday morning, and he made some remark about the weather and then, just as I was leaving the room, he said, 'Oh, by the way, Mrs. Purnell, I shall be going away tonight for a couple of weeks. I've packed my bag and will call for it this afternoon.' "

"No doubt you were very much surprised at this sudden announcement?" queried Holmes.

"Not very much, sir. Ever since he's had this auditing work to do for the branch banks there's been no knowing when he would be away. Of course, he'd never been off for two weeks at a stretch, except at holiday times, but he had so often been away for a few days at a time that I had got used to his popping off with hardly a moment's notice."

"Let me see, how long has he had this extra work at the bank—several months, hasn't he?"

"More. It was about last Christmas, I believe, when they gave it to him."

"Oh, yes, of course," said Holmes carelessly, "and this work naturally took him from home a good deal?"

"Yes, indeed, and it seemed to quite tire him, so much evening and night work too, you see, sir. It was enough to knock him out, for he was always such a very quiet, retiring gentleman and hardly ever used to go out in the evenings before."

"Has Mr. Booth left many of his possessions behind him?" asked Holmes.

"Very few, indeed, and what he has are mostly old useless things. But he's a most honest thief, sir," said Mrs. Purnell paradoxically, "and paid me his rent, before he went out on Wednesday morning, right up to next Saturday, because he wouldn't be back by then."

"That was good of him," said Holmes, smiling thoughtfully. "By the way, do you happen to know if he gave away any other treasures, before he left?"

"Well not *just* before, but during the last few months he's taken away most of his books and sold them I think, a few at a time. He had rather a fancy for old books and has told me that some editions he had were worth quite a lot."

During this conversation, Lestrade had been sitting drumming his fingers impatiently on the table. Now he got up. "Really, I fear I shall have to leave you to this gossip," he said. "I must go and wire instructions for the arrest of Mr. Booth. If only you would have looked before at this old blotter, which I found in the wastebasket, you would have saved yourself a good deal of unnecessary trouble, Mr. Holmes," and he triumphantly slapped down a sheet of well-used blotting paper on the table.

Holmes picked it up and held it in front of a mirror over the sideboard. Looking over his shoulder I could plainly read the reflected impression of a note written in Mr. Booth's handwriting, of which Holmes had procured samples.

It was to a booking agency in Liverpool, giving instructions to them to book a first-class private cabin and passage on board the *Empress Queen* from Liverpool to New York. Parts of the note were slightly obliterated by other impressions, but it went on to say that a check was enclosed to pay for tickets, etc., and it was signed J. Booth.

Holmes stood silently scrutinizing the paper for several minutes.

It was a well-used sheet, but fortunately the impression of the note was well in the center, and hardly obliterated at all by the other marks and blots, which were all round the outer circumference of the paper. In one corner the address of the Liverpool booking agency was plainly decipherable, the paper evidently having been used to blot the envelope with also.

"My dear Lestrade, you have indeed been more fortunate than I had imagined," said Holmes at length, handing the paper back to him. "May I ask what steps you propose to take next?"

"I shall cable at once to the New York police to arrest the fellow as soon as he arrives," said Lestrade, "but first I must make quite certain the boat doesn't touch at Queenstown or anywhere and give him a chance of slipping through our fingers."

"It doesn't," said Holmes quietly. "I had already looked to see as I thought it not unlikely, at first, that Mr. Booth might have intended to sail by the *Empress Queen*."

Lestrade gave me a wink for which I would dearly have liked to have knocked him down, for I could see that he disbelieved my friend. I felt a keen pang of disappointment that Holmes's foresight should have been eclipsed in this way by what, after all, was mere good luck on Lestrade's part.

Holmes had turned to Mrs. Purnell and was thanking her.

"Don't mention it, sir," she said. "Mr. Booth deserves to be caught, though I must say he's always been a gentleman to me. I only wish I could have given you some more useful information."

"On the contrary," said Holmes, "I can assure you that what you have told us has been of the utmost importance and will very materially help us. It's just occurred to me, by the way, to wonder if you could possibly put up my friend Dr. Watson and myself for a few days, until we have had time to look into this little matter?"

"Certainly, sir, I shall be most happy."

"Good," said Holmes. "Then you may expect us back to dinner about seven."

When we got outside, Lestrade at once announced his intention of going to the police office and arranging for the necessary orders for Booth's detention and arrest to be cabled to the head of the New York police; Holmes retained an enigmatical silence as to what he purposed to do but expressed his determination to remain at Broomhill and make a few further inquiries. He insisted, however, upon going alone.

"Remember, Watson, you are here for a rest and holiday and I can assure you that if you did remain with me you would only find my program a dull one. Therefore, I insist upon your finding some more entertaining way of spending the remainder of the day."

Past experience told me that it was quite useless to remonstrate or argue with Holmes when once his mind was made up, so I consented with the best grace I could, and leaving Holmes, drove off in the hansom, which he assured me he would not require further.

I passed a few hours in the art gallery and museum and then, after lunch, had a brisk walk out on the Manchester Road and enjoyed the fresh air and moorland scenery, returning to Ashgate Road at seven with better appetite than I had been blessed with for months.

Holmes had not returned, and it was nearly half past seven before he came in. I could see at once that he was in one of his most reticent moods, and all my inquiries failed to elicit any particulars of how he had passed his time or what he thought about the case.

The whole evening he remained coiled up in an easy chair puffing at his pipe and hardly a word could I get from him.

His inscrutable countenance and persistent silence gave me no clue whatever as to his thought on the inquiry he had in hand, although I could see his whole mind was concentrated upon it.

Next morning, just as we had finished breakfast, the maid entered with a note. "From Mr. Jervis, sir; there's no answer," she said.

Holmes tore open the envelope and scanned the note hurriedly and, as he did so, I noticed a flush of annoyance spread over his usually pale face.

"Confound his impudence," he muttered. "Read that, Watson. I don't ever remember to have been treated so badly in a case before."

The note was a brief one:

The Cedars, Fulwood.

September sixth

Mr. Jervis, on behalf of the directors of the British Consolidated Bank, begs to thank Mr. Sherlock Holmes for his prompt attention and valued services in the matter concerning the fraud and disappearance of their ex-employee, Mr. Jabez Booth.

Mr. Lestrade, of Scotland Yard, informs us that he has succeeded in tracking the individual in question who will be arrested shortly. Under these circumstances they feel it unnecessary to take up any more of Mr. Holmes's valuable time.

"Rather cool, eh, Watson? I'm much mistaken if they don't have cause to regret their action when it's too late. After this I shall certainly refuse to act for them any further in the case, even if they ask me to do so. In a way I'm sorry because the matter presented some distinctly interesting features and is by no means the simple affair our friend Lestrade thinks."

"Why, don't you think he is on the right scent?" I exclaimed.

"Wait and see, Watson," said Holmes mysteriously. "Mr. Booth hasn't been caught yet, remember." And that was all that I could get out of him.

One result of the summary way in which the banker had dispensed with my friend's services was that Holmes and I spent a most restful and enjoyable week in the small village of Hathersage, on the edge of the Derbyshire moors, and returned to London feeling better for our long moorland rambles.

Holmes having very little work in hand at the

time, and my wife not yet having returned from her Swiss holiday, I prevailed upon him, though not without considerable difficulty, to pass the next few weeks with me instead of returning to his rooms at Baker Street.

Of course, we watched the development of the Sheffield forgery case with the keenest interest. Somehow the particulars of Lestrade's discoveries got into the papers, and the day after we left Sheffield they were full of the exciting chase of Mr. Booth, the man wanted for the Sheffield Bank frauds.

They spoke of "the guilty man restlessly pacing the deck of the *Empress Queen*, as she ploughed her way majestically across the solitary wastes of the Atlantic, all unconscious that the inexorable hand of justice could stretch over the ocean and was already waiting to seize him on his arrival in the New World." And Holmes after reading these sensational paragraphs would always lay down the paper with one of his enigmatical smiles.

At last the day on which the *Empress Queen* was due at New York arrived, and I could not help but notice that even Holmes's usually inscrutable face wore a look of suppressed excitement as he unfolded the evening paper. But our surprise was doomed to be prolonged still further. There was a brief paragraph to say that the *Empress Queen* had arrived off Long Island at six a.m. after a good passage. There was, however, a case of cholera on board, and the New York authorities had consequently been compelled to put the boat in quarantine, and none of the passengers or crew would be allowed to leave her for a period of twelve days.

Two days later there was a full column in the papers stating that it had been definitely ascertained that Mr. Booth was really on board the *Empress Queen*. He had been identified and spoken to by one of the sanitary inspectors who had had to visit the boat. He was being kept under close observation, and there was no possible chance of his escaping. Mr. Lestrade of Scotland Yard, by whom Booth had been so cleverly tracked down and his escape forestalled, had

taken passage on the *Oceania*, due in New York on the tenth, and would personally arrest Mr. Booth when he was allowed to land.

Never before or since have I seen my friend Holmes so astonished as when he had finished reading this announcement. I could see that he was thoroughly mystified, though why he should be so was quite a puzzle to me. All day he sat coiled up in an easy chair, with his brows drawn down into two hard lines and his eyes half closed as he puffed away at his oldest brier in silence.

"Watson," he said once, glancing across at me. "It's perhaps a good thing that I was asked to drop that Sheffield case. As things are turning out I fancy I should only have made a fool of myself."

"Why?" I asked.

"Because I began by assuming that somebody else wasn't one—and now it looks as though I had been mistaken."

For the next few days Holmes seemed quite depressed, for nothing annoyed him more than to feel that he had made any mistake in his deductions or got onto a false line of reasoning.

At last the fatal tenth of September, the day on which Booth was to be arrested, arrived. Eagerly but in vain we scanned the evening papers. The morning of the eleventh came and still brought no news of the arrest, but in the evening papers of that day there was a short paragraph hinting that the criminal had escaped again.

For several days the papers were full of the most conflicting rumors and conjectures as to what had actually taken place, but all were agreed in affirming that Mr. Lestrade was on his way home alone and would be back in Liverpool on the seventeenth or eighteenth.

On the evening of the last named day Holmes and I sat smoking in his Baker Street rooms, when his boy came in to announce that Mr. Lestrade of Scotland Yard was below and would like the favor of a few minutes' conversation.

"Show him up, show him up," said Holmes,

rubbing his hands together with an excitement quite unusual to him.

Lestrade entered the room and sat down in the seat to which Holmes waved him, with a most dejected air.

"It's not often I'm at fault, Mr. Holmes," he began, "but in this Sheffield business I've been beaten hollow."

"Dear me," said Holmes pleasantly, "you surely don't mean to tell me that you haven't got your man yet."

"I do," said Lestrade. "What's more, I don't think he ever will be caught!"

"Don't despair so soon," said Holmes encouragingly. "After you have told us all that's already happened, it's just within the bounds of possibility that I may be able to help you with some little suggestions."

Thus encouraged Lestrade began his strange story to which we both listened with breathless interest.

"It's quite unnecessary for me to dwell upon incidents which are already familiar," he said. "You know of the discovery I made in Sheffield which, of course, convinced me that the man I wanted had sailed for New York on the *Empress Queen*. I was in a fever of impatience for his arrest, and when I heard that the boat he had taken passage on had been placed in quarantine, I set off at once in order that I might actually lay hands upon him myself. Never have five days seemed so long.

"We reached New York on the evening of the ninth, and I rushed off at once to the head of the New York police and from him learned that there was no doubt whatever that Mr. Jabez Booth was indeed on board the *Empress Queen*. One of the sanitary inspectors who had had to visit the boat had not only seen but actually spoken to him. The man exactly answered the description of Booth which had appeared in the papers. One of the New York detectives had been sent on board to make a few inquiries and to inform the captain privately of the pending arrest. He found that Mr. Jabez Booth had actually had the audacity to book his passage and travel under his

real name without even attempting to disguise himself in any way. He had a private first-class cabin, and the purser declared that he had been suspicious of the man from the first. He had kept himself shut up in his cabin nearly all the time, posing as an eccentric semi-invalid person who must not be disturbed on any account. Most of his meals had been sent down to his cabin, and he had been seen on deck but seldom and hardly ever dined with the rest of the passengers. It was quite evident that he had been trying to keep out of sight, and to attract as little attention as possible. The stewards and some of the passengers who were approached on the subject later were all agreed that this was the case.

"It was decided that during the time the boat was in quarantine nothing should be said to Booth to arouse his suspicions but that the pursers, steward and captain, who were the only persons in the secret, should between them keep him under observation until the tenth, the day on which passengers would be allowed to leave the boat. On that day he should be arrested."

Here we were interrupted by Holmes's boy who came in with a telegram. Holmes glanced at it with a faint smile.

"No answer," he said, slipping it in his waistcoat pocket. "Pray continue your very interesting story, Lestrade."

"Well, on the afternoon of the tenth, accompanied by the New York chief inspector of police and detective Forsyth," resumed Lestrade, "I went on board the *Empress Queen* half an hour before she was due to come up to the landing stage to allow passengers to disembark.

"The purser informed us that Mr. Booth had been on deck and that he had been in conversation with him about fifteen minutes before our arrival. He had then gone down to his cabin and the purser, making some excuse to go down also, had actually seen him enter it. He had been standing near the top of the companionway since then and was sure Booth had not come up on deck again since.

"'At last,' I muttered to myself, as we all went down below, led by the purser who took us straight to Booth's cabin. We knocked but, getting no answer, tried the door and found it locked. The purser assured us, however, that this was nothing unusual. Mr. Booth had had his cabin door locked a good deal and, often, even his meals had been left on a tray outside. We held a hurried consultation and, as time was short, decided to force the door. Two good blows with a heavy hammer broke it from the hinges, and we all rushed in. You can picture our astonishment when we found the cabin empty. We searched it thoroughly, and Booth was certainly not there."

"One moment," interrupted Holmes. "The key of the door—was it on the inside of the lock or not?"

"It was nowhere to be seen," said Lestrade. "I was getting frantic, for by this time I could feel the vibration of the engines and hear the first churning sound of the screw as the great boat began to slide slowly down towards the landing stage.

"We were at our wits' end; Mr. Booth must be hiding somewhere on board, but there was now no time to make a proper search for him, and in a very few minutes passengers would be leaving the boat. At last the captain promised us that, under the circumstances, only one landing gangway should be run out and, in company with the purser and stewards, I should stand by it with a complete list of passengers ticking off each one as he or she left. By this means it would be quite impossible for Booth to escape us even if he attempted some disguise, for no person whatever would be allowed to cross the gangway until identified by the purser or one of the stewards.

"I was delighted with the arrangement, for there was now no way by which Booth could give me the slip.

"One by one the passengers crossed the gangway and joined the jostling crowd on the landing stage and each one was identified and his or her name crossed off my list. There were one hundred and ninety-three first-class passengers on board the *Empress Queen*, including Booth, and, when one hundred and ninety-two had disembarked, his was the only name which remained!

"You can scarcely realize what a fever of impatience we were in," said Lestrade, mopping his brow at the very recollection, "nor how interminable the time seemed as we slowly but carefully ticked off one by one the whole of the three hundred and twenty-four second-class passengers and the three hundred and ten steerage from my list. Every passenger except Mr. Booth crossed that gangway, but he certainly did not do so. There was no possible room for doubt on that point.

"He must therefore be still on the boat, we agreed, but I was getting panic-stricken and wondered if there were any possibility of his getting smuggled off in some of the luggage which the great cranes were now beginning to swing up onto the pier.

"I hinted my fear to detective Forsyth, and he at once arranged that every trunk or box in which there was any chance for a man to hide should be opened and examined by the customs officers.

"It was a tedious business, but they didn't shirk it, and at the end of two hours were able to assure us that by no possibility could Booth have been smuggled off the boat in this way.

"This left only one possible solution to the mystery. He *must* be still in hiding somewhere on board. We had had the boat kept under the closest observation ever since she came up to the landing stage, and now the superintendent of police lent us a staff of twenty men and, with the consent of the captain and the assistance of the pursers and stewards etc., the *Empress Queen* was searched and re-searched from stem to stern. We didn't leave unexamined a place in which a cat could have hidden, but the missing man wasn't there. Of that I'm certain—and there you have the whole mystery in a nutshell, Mr. Holmes. Mr. Booth certainly *was* on board the *Empress Queen* up to, and at, eleven o'clock on the morning of the tenth, and although he could not by any possibility have left it, we are nevertheless face to face with the fact that he wasn't there at five o'clock in the afternoon."

Lestrade's face as he concluded his curious and mysterious narrative bore a look of the most hopeless bewilderment I ever saw, and I fancy my own must have pretty well matched it, but Holmes threw himself back in his easy chair, with his long thin legs stuck straight out in front of him, his whole frame literally shaking with silent laughter. "What conclusion have you come to?" he gasped at length. "What steps do you propose to take next?"

"I've no idea. Who could know what to do? The whole thing is impossible, perfectly impossible; it's an insoluble mystery. I came to you to see if you could, by any chance, suggest some entirely fresh line of inquiry upon which I might begin to work."

"Well," said Holmes, cocking his eye mischievously at the bewildered Lestrade, "I can give you Booth's present address, if it will be of any use to you?"

"His what!" cried Lestrade.

"His present address," repeated Holmes quietly. "But before I do so, my dear Lestrade, I must make one stipulation. Mr. Jervis has treated me very shabbily in the matter, and I don't desire that my name shall be associated with it any further. Whatever you do you must not hint the source from which any information I may give you has come. You promise?"

"Yes," murmured Lestrade, who was in a state of bewildered excitement.

Holmes tore a leaf from his pocket book and scribbled on it: Mr. A. Winter, c/o Mrs. Thackary, Glossop Road, Broomhill, Sheffield.

"You will find there the present name and address of the man you are in search of," he said, handing the paper across to Lestrade. "I should strongly advise you to lose no time in getting hold of him, for though the wire I received a short time ago—which unfortunately interrupted your most interesting narrative—was to tell me that Mr. Winter had arrived back home again after a temporary absence, still it's more than probable that he will leave there, for good,

at an early date. I can't say how soon—not for a few days I should think."

Lestrade rose. "Mr. Holmes, you're a brick," he said, with more real feeling than I have ever seen him show before. "You've saved my reputation in this job just when I was beginning to look like a perfect fool, and now you're forcing me to take all the credit, when I don't deserve one atom. As to how you have found this out, it's as great a mystery to me as Booth's disappearance was."

"Well, as to that," said Holmes airily, "I can't be sure of all the facts myself, for of course I've never looked properly into the case. But they are pretty easy to conjecture, and I shall be most happy to give you my idea of Booth's trip to New York on some future occasion when you have more time to spare."

"By the way," called out Holmes, as Lestrade was leaving the room, "I shouldn't be surprised if you find Mr. Jabez Booth, alias Mr. Archibald Winter, a slight acquaintance of yours, for he would undoubtedly be a fellow passenger of yours, on your homeward journey from America. He reached Sheffield a few hours before you arrived in London and, as he has certainly just returned from New York, like yourself, it's evident you must have crossed on the same boat. He would be wearing smoked glasses and have a heavy dark mustache."

"Ah!" said Lestrade, "there *was* a man called Winter on board who answered to that description. I believe it must have been he, and I'll lose no more time," and Lestrade hurried off.

"Well, Watson, my boy, you look nearly as bewildered as our friend Lestrade," said Holmes, leaning back in his chair and looking roguishly across at me, as he lighted his old brier pipe.

"I must confess that none of the problems you have had to solve in the past seemed more inexplicable to me than Lestrade's account of Booth's disappearance from the *Empress Queen*."

"Yes, that part of the story is decidedly neat," chuckled Holmes, "but I'll tell you how I got at the solution of the mystery. I see you are ready to listen.

"The first thing to do in any case is to gauge the intelligence and cunning of the criminal. Now, Mr. Booth was undoubtedly a clever man. Mr. Jervis himself, you remember, assured us as much. The fact that he opened banking accounts in preparation for the crime twelve months before he committed it proves it to have been a long-premeditated one. I began the case, therefore, with the knowledge that I had a clever man to catch, who had had twelve months in which to plan his escape.

"My first real clues came from Mrs. Purnell," said Holmes. "Most important were her remarks about Booth's auditing work which kept him from home so many days and nights, often consecutively. I felt certain at once, and inquiry confirmed, that Mr. Booth had had no such extra work at all. Why then had he invented lies to explain these absences to his landlady? Probably because they were in some way connected, either with the crime or with his plans for escaping after he had committed it. It was inconceivable that so much mysterious outdoor occupation could be directly connected with the forgery, and I at once deduced that this time had been spent by Booth in paving the way for his escape.

"Almost at once the idea that he had been living a double life occurred to me, his intention doubtless being to quietly drop one individuality after committing the crime and permanently take up the other—a far safer and less clumsy expedient than the usual one of assuming a new disguise just at the very moment when everybody is expecting and looking for you to do so.

"Then there were the interesting facts relating to Booth's picture and books. I tried to put myself in his place. He valued these possessions highly; they were light and portable, and there was really no reason whatever why he should part with them. Doubtless, then, he had taken them away by degrees and put them someplace where he could lay hands on them again. If I could find out where this place was, I felt sure

there would be every chance I could catch him when he attempted to recover them.

"The picture couldn't have gone far for he had taken it out with him on the very day of the crime . . . I needn't bore you with details . . . I was two hours making inquiries before I found the house at which he had called and left it—which was none other than Mrs. Thackary's in Glossop Road.

"I made a pretext for calling there and found Mrs. T. one of the most easy mortals in the world to pump. In less than half an hour I knew that she had a boarder named Winter, that he professed to be a commercial traveler and was from home most of the time. His description resembled Booth's save that he had a mustache, wore glasses.

"As I've often tried to impress upon you before, Watson, details are the most important things of all, and it gave me a real thrill of pleasure to learn that Mr. Winter had a cup of chocolate brought up to his bedroom every morning. A gentleman called on the Wednesday morning and left a parcel, saying it was a picture he had promised for Mr. Winter, and asking Mrs. Thackary to give it to Winter when he returned. Mr. Winter had taken the rooms the previous December. He had a good many books which he had brought in from time to time. All these facts taken in conjunction made me certain that I was on the right scent. Winter and Booth were one and the same person, and as soon as Booth had put all his pursuers off the track he would return, as Winter, and repossess his treasures.

"The newly taken photo and the old blotter with its tell-tale note were too obviously intentional means of drawing the police onto Booth's track. The blotter, I could see almost at once, was a fraud, for not only would it be almost impossible to use one in the ordinary way so much without the central part becoming undecipherable, but I could see where it had been touched up.

"I concluded therefore that Booth, alias Winter, never actually intended to sail on the *Empress Queen*, but in that I underestimated his ingenuity. Evidently he booked *two* berths on the boat, one in his real, and one in his assumed name, and managed very cleverly to successfully keep up the two characters throughout the voyage, appearing first as one individual and then as the other. Most of the time he posed as Winter, and for this purpose Booth became the eccentric semi-invalid passenger who remained locked up in his cabin for such a large part of his time. This, of course, would answer his purpose well; his eccentricity would only draw attention to his presence on board and so make him one of the best-known passengers on the boat, although he showed so little of himself.

"I had left instructions with Mrs. Thackary to send me a wire as soon as Winter returned. When Booth had led his pursuers to New York, and there thrown them off the scent, he had nothing more to do but to take the first boat back. Very naturally it chanced to be the same as that on which our friend Lestrade returned, and that was how Mrs. Thackary's wire arrived at the opportune moment it did."

The *Cosmopolitan* editor's note: We are aware that there are several inconsistencies in this story. We have not tried to correct them. The story is published exactly as it was found except for minor changes in spelling and punctuation.

The Adventure of the Two Collaborators

JAMES M. BARRIE

WHILE THE SCOTTISH author James Matthew Barrie (1860–1937) remains universally loved for having created Peter Pan, he had many other extraordinary literary achievements in drama, novels, and short stories. Beginning his literary life as a journalist, first for the *Nottingham Journal*, then as a contributor to such popular magazines as *The Pall Mall Gazette*, in 1888 he published his first novel, *Better Dead*, a mystery that had minimal success. The publication of *Auld Licht Idylls* (1888), charming sketches of Scottish life, brought him recognition and critical praise, but it was three years later with the release of his sentimental novel *The Little Minister* (1891) that Barrie enjoyed enormous success. When he dramatized it, the ensuing popularity made him a devotee of the theater, and he began to write plays, many of which drew large and enduring audiences. Among those still produced are *The Admirable Crichton* (1902), about a butler who saves the family for whom he works when they are all stranded on an island after a shipwreck, and *Quality Street* (1901), about two sisters who start a school for upper-class children.

His adult novel *The Little White Bird* (1902) introduced Peter Pan, the character that inspired him to write the play *Peter Pan*, which debuted in London in 1904; the section of the novel about the boy who escaped being human at the age of seven to become a fairy was published separately as *Peter Pan in Kensington Garden* (1906). Barrie then wrote a full-length book using the same character titled *Peter and Wendy* (1911). The play has been produced countless times and made into several films, most notably the much-loved animated feature produced by Walt Disney in 1953.

Barrie and Arthur Conan Doyle collaborated on the book for an operetta, *Jane Annie* (1893), which by all accounts was a miserable failure. After it quickly closed, Barrie inscribed a copy of his book, *A Window in Thrums* (1889), to Conan Doyle, with this little parody written on the flyleaves. Conan Doyle claimed that it was the best parody of Holmes ever written (a generous assessment) and included it in his autobiography.

"The Adventures of the Two Collaborators" was first published in *Memories and Adventures* by Arthur Conan Doyle (London, Hodder & Stoughton, 1924).

THE ADVENTURE OF THE TWO COLLABORATORS

James M. Barrie

IN BRINGING TO a close the adventures of my friend Sherlock Holmes I am perforce reminded that he never, save on the occasion which, as you will now hear, brought his singular career to an end, consented to act in any mystery which was concerned with persons who made a livelihood by their pen. "I am not particular about the people I mix among for business purposes," he would say, "but at literary characters I draw the line."

We were in our rooms in Baker Street one evening. I was (I remember) by the centre table writing out "The Adventure of the Man Without a Cork Leg" (which had so puzzled the Royal Society and all the other scientific bodies of Europe), and Holmes was amusing himself with a little revolver practice.

It was his custom of a summer evening to fire round my head, just shaving my face, until he had made a photograph of me on the opposite wall, and it is a slight proof of his skill that many of these portraits in pistol shots are considered admirable likenesses.

I happened to look out of the window, and, perceiving two gentlemen advancing rapidly along Baker Street, asked him who they were. He immediately lit his pipe, and, twisting himself on a chair into a figure 8, replied:

"They are two collaborators in comic opera, and their play has not been a triumph."

I sprang from my chair to the ceiling in amazement, and he then explained:

"My dear Watson, they are obviously men who follow some low calling. That much even you should be able to read in their faces. Those little pieces of blue paper which they fling angrily from them are Durrant's Press Notices. Of these they have obviously hundreds about their person (see how their pockets bulge). They would not dance on them if they were pleasant reading."

I again sprang to the ceiling (which is much dented) and shouted: "Amazing! But they may be mere authors."

"No," said Holmes, "for mere authors only get one press notice a week. Only criminals, dramatists, and actors get them by the hundred."

"Then they may be actors."

"No, actors would come in a carriage."

"Can you tell me anything else about them?"

"A great deal. From the mud on the boots of the tall one I perceive that he comes from South Norwood. The other is obviously a Scotch author."

"How can you tell that?"

"He is carrying in his pocket a book called (I clearly see) 'Auld Licht Something.' Would anyone but the author be likely to carry about a book with such a title?"

I had to confess that this was improbable.

It was now evident that the two men (if such they can be called) were seeking our lodgings. I have said (often) that Holmes seldom gave way to emotion of any kind, but he now turned livid with passion. Presently this gave place to a strange look of triumph.

"Watson," he said, "that big fellow has for years taken the credit for my most remarkable doings, but at last I have him—at last!"

Up I went to the ceiling, and when I returned the strangers were in the room.

"I perceive, gentlemen," said Mr. Sherlock Holmes, "that you are at present afflicted by an extraordinary novelty."

The handsomer of our visitors asked in amazement how he knew this, but the big one only scowled.

"You forget that you wear a ring on your fourth finger," replied Mr. Holmes calmly.

I was about to jump to the ceiling when the big brute interposed.

"That tommyrot is all very well for the public, Holmes," said he, "but you can drop it before me. And, Watson, if you go up to the ceiling again I shall make you stay there."

Here I observed a curious phenomenon. My friend Sherlock Holmes *shrank*. He became small before my eyes. I looked longingly at the ceiling, but dared not.

"Let us cut out the first four pages," said the big man, "and proceed to business. I want to know why—"

"Allow me," said Mr. Holmes, with some of his old courage. "You want to know why the public does not go to your opera."

"Exactly," said the other ironically, "as you perceive by my shirt stud." He added more gravely: "And as you can only find out in one way I must insist on your witnessing an entire performance of the piece."

It was an anxious moment for me. I shuddered, for I knew that if Holmes went I should have to go with him. But my friend had a heart of gold. "Never!" he cried fiercely. "I will do anything for you save that."

"Your continued existence depends on it," said the big man menacingly.

"I would rather melt into air," replied Holmes proudly, taking another chair. "But I can tell you why the public don't go to your piece without sitting the thing out myself."

"Why?"

"Because," replied Holmes calmly, "they prefer to stay away."

A dead silence followed that extraordinary remark. For a moment the two intruders gazed with awe upon the man who had unravelled their mystery so wonderfully. Then, drawing their knives—

Holmes grew less and less, until nothing was left save a ring of smoke which slowly circled to the ceiling.

The last words of great men are often noteworthy. These were the last words of Sherlock Holmes: "Fool, fool! I have kept you in luxury for years. By my help you have ridden extensively in cabs where no author was ever seen before. *Henceforth you will ride in buses!*"

The brute sank into a chair aghast. The other author did not turn a hair.

The Sleuths

O. HENRY

IT IS UNLIKELY that a more beloved short story writer ever lived in America than William Sydney Porter (1862–1910), more commonly known as O. Henry. He never wrote a novel, but his miniature masterpieces encapsulated whole lives of ordinary people—his favorite subjects.

After being convicted of embezzlement, he spent time in prison, reputedly taking for his pseudonym the name of a kindly guard, and he wrote numerous stories about various crimes: robbery, kidnapping ("The Ransom of Red Chief" in 1910), extortion, safecracking ("A Retrieved Reformation" in 1903, commonly remembered as "Alias Jimmy Valentine" after the successful Broadway play and several film versions), and more. His book *The Gentle Grafter* (1908) was regarded so highly that Ellery Queen selected it for *Queen's Quorum*, the list of the one hundred six greatest mystery short story collections of all time.

He wrote three stories in which Shamrock Jolnes appeared. The first, "The Adventures of Shamrock Jolnes," was published on February 7, 1904; it featured observations and deductions by Jolnes but no crime. The last, "The Detective Detector," was published on March 26, 1905; Jolnes appears, but center stage is dominated by the Master Criminal.

"The Sleuths" was first published in the October 23, 1904, issue of the *New York Sunday World*; it was first collected in *Sixes and Sevens* by O. Henry (New York, Doubleday, Page, 1911).

THE SLEUTHS

O. Henry

IN THE BIG CITY a man will disappear with the suddenness and completeness of the flame of a candle that is blown out. All the agencies of inquisition—the hounds of the trail, the sleuths of the city's labyrinths, the closet detectives of theory and induction—will be invoked to the search. Most often the man's face will be seen no more. Sometimes he will reappear in Sheboygan or in the wilds of Terre Haute, calling himself one of the synonyms of "Smith," and without memory of events up to a certain time, including his grocer's bill. Sometimes it will be found, after dragging the rivers, and polling the restaurants to see if he may be waiting for a well-done sirloin, that he has moved next door.

This snuffing out of a human being like the erasure of a chalk man from a blackboard is one of the most impressive themes in dramaturgy.

The case of Mary Snyder, in point, should not be without interest.

A man of middle age, of the name of Meeks, came from the West to New York to find his sister, Mrs. Mary Snyder, a widow, aged fifty-two, who had been living for a year in a tenement house in a crowded neighbourhood.

At her address he was told that Mary Snyder had moved away longer than a month before. No one could tell him her new address.

On coming out Mr. Meeks addressed a policeman who was standing on the corner, and explained his dilemma.

"My sister is very poor," he said, "and I am anxious to find her. I have recently made quite a lot of money in a lead mine, and I want her to share my prosperity. There is no use in advertising her, because she cannot read."

The policeman pulled his moustache and looked so thoughtful and mighty that Meeks could almost feel the joyful tears of his sister Mary dropping upon his bright blue tie.

"You go down in the Canal Street neighbourhood," said the policeman, "and get a job drivin' the biggest dray you can find. There's old women always getting knocked over by drays down there. You might see 'er among 'em. If you don't want to do that you better go 'round to headquarters and get 'em to put a fly cop onto the dame."

At police headquarters, Meeks received ready assistance. A general alarm was sent out, and copies of a photograph of Mary Snyder that her brother had were distributed among the stations. In Mulberry Street the chief assigned Detective Mullins to the case.

The detective took Meeks aside and said:

"This is not a very difficult case to unravel. Shave off your whiskers, fill your pockets with good cigars, and meet me in the cafe of the Waldorf at three o'clock this afternoon."

Meeks obeyed. He found Mullins there. They had a bottle of wine, while the detective asked questions concerning the missing woman.

"Now," said Mullins, "New York is a big city, but we've got the detective business systematized. There are two ways we can go about finding your sister. We will try one of 'em first. You say she's fifty-two?"

"A little past," said Meeks.

The detective conducted the Westerner to

a branch advertising office of one of the largest dailies. There he wrote the following "ad" and submitted it to Meeks:

"Wanted, at once—one hundred attractive chorus girls for a new musical comedy. Apply all day at No. —— Broadway."

Meeks was indignant.

"My sister," said he, "is a poor, hard-working, elderly woman. I do not see what aid an advertisement of this kind would be toward finding her."

"All right," said the detective. "I guess you don't know New York. But if you've got a grouch against this scheme we'll try the other one. It's a sure thing. But it'll cost you more."

"Never mind the expense," said Meeks; "we'll try it."

The sleuth led him back to the Waldorf. "Engage a couple of bedrooms and a parlour," he advised, "and let's go up."

This was done, and the two were shown to a superb suite on the fourth floor. Meeks looked puzzled. The detective sank into a velvet armchair, and pulled out his cigar case.

"I forgot to suggest, old man," he said, "that you should have taken the rooms by the month. They wouldn't have stuck you so much for 'em."

"By the month!" exclaimed Meeks. "What do you mean?"

"Oh, it'll take time to work the game this way. I told you it would cost you more. We'll have to wait till spring. There'll be a new city directory out then. Very likely your sister's name and address will be in it."

Meeks rid himself of the city detective at once. On the next day some one advised him to consult Shamrock Jolnes, New York's famous private detective, who demanded fabulous fees, but performed miracles in the way of solving mysteries and crimes.

After waiting for two hours in the anteroom of the great detective's apartment, Meeks was shown into his presence. Jolnes sat in a purple dressing-gown at an inlaid ivory chess table, with a magazine before him, trying to solve the mystery of "They." The famous sleuth's thin, intellectual face, piercing eyes, and rate per word are too well known to need description.

Meeks set forth his errand. "My fee, if successful, will be $500," said Shamrock Jolnes.

Meeks bowed his agreement to the price.

"I will undertake your case, Mr. Meeks," said Jolnes, finally. "The disappearance of people in this city has always been an interesting problem to me. I remember a case that I brought to a successful outcome a year ago. A family bearing the name of Clark disappeared suddenly from a small flat in which they were living. I watched the flat building for two months for a clue. One day it struck me that a certain milkman and a grocer's boy always walked backward when they carried their wares upstairs. Following out by induction the idea that this observation gave me, I at once located the missing family. They had moved into the flat across the hall and changed their name to Kralc."

Shamrock Jolnes and his client went to the tenement house where Mary Snyder had lived, and the detective demanded to be shown the room in which she had lived. It had been occupied by no tenant since her disappearance.

The room was small, dingy, and poorly furnished. Meeks seated himself dejectedly on a broken chair, while the great detective searched the walls and floor and the few sticks of old, rickety furniture for a clue.

At the end of half an hour Jolnes had collected a few seemingly unintelligible articles—a cheap black hat pin, a piece torn off a theatre programme, and the end of a small torn card on which was the word "left" and the characters "C 12."

Shamrock Jolnes leaned against the mantel for ten minutes, with his head resting upon his hand, and an absorbed look upon his intellectual face. At the end of that time he exclaimed, with animation:

"Come, Mr. Meeks; the problem is solved. I can take you directly to the house where your sister is living. And you may have no fears concerning her welfare, for she is amply provided with funds—for the present at least."

Meeks felt joy and wonder in equal proportions.

"How did you manage it?" he asked, with admiration in his tones.

Perhaps Jolnes's only weakness was a professional pride in his wonderful achievements in induction. He was ever ready to astound and charm his listeners by describing his methods.

"By elimination," said Jolnes, spreading his clues upon a little table, "I got rid of certain parts of the city to which Mrs. Snyder might have removed. You see this hat pin? That eliminates Brooklyn. No woman attempts to board a car at the Brooklyn Bridge without being sure that she carries a hat pin with which to fight her way into a seat. And now I will demonstrate to you that she could not have gone to Harlem. Behind this door are two hooks in the wall. Upon one of these Mrs. Snyder has hung her bonnet, and upon the other her shawl. You will observe that the bottom of the hanging shawl has gradually made a soiled streak against the plastered wall. The mark is clean-cut, proving that there is no fringe on the shawl. Now, was there ever a case where a middle-aged woman, wearing a shawl, boarded a Harlem train without there being a fringe on the shawl to catch in the gate and delay the passengers behind her? So we eliminate Harlem.

"Therefore I conclude that Mrs. Snyder has not moved very far away. On this torn piece of card you see the word 'left,' the letter 'C,' and the number '12.' Now, I happen to know that No. 12 Avenue C is a first-class boarding house, far beyond your sister's means—as we suppose. But then I find this piece of a theatre programme, crumpled into an odd shape. What meaning does it convey. None to you, very likely, Mr. Meeks; but it is eloquent to one whose habits and training take cognizance of the smallest things.

"You have told me that your sister was a scrub woman. She scrubbed the floors of offices and hallways. Let us assume that she procured such work to perform in a theatre. Where is valuable jewellery lost the oftenest, Mr. Meeks? In the theatres, of course. Look at that piece of programme, Mr. Meeks. Observe the round impression in it. It has been wrapped around a ring—perhaps a ring of great value. Mrs. Snyder found the ring while at work in the theatre. She hastily tore off a piece of a programme, wrapped the ring carefully, and thrust it into her bosom. The next day she disposed of it, and, with her increased means, looked about her for a more comfortable place in which to live. When I reach thus far in the chain I see nothing impossible about No. 12 Avenue C. It is there we will find your sister, Mr. Meeks."

Shamrock Jolnes concluded his convincing speech with the smile of a successful artist. Meeks's admiration was too great for words. Together they went to No. 12 Avenue C. It was an old-fashioned brownstone house in a prosperous and respectable neighbourhood.

They rang the bell, and on inquiring were told that no Mrs. Snyder was known there, and that not within six months had a new occupant come to the house.

When they reached the sidewalk again, Meeks examined the clues which he had brought away from his sister's old room.

"I am no detective," he remarked to Jolnes as he raised the piece of theatre programme to his nose, "but it seems to me that instead of a ring having been wrapped in this paper it was one of those round peppermint drops. And this piece with the address on it looks to me like the end of a seat coupon—No. 12, row C, left aisle."

Shamrock Jolnes had a far-away look in his eyes.

"I think you would do well to consult Juggins," said he.

"Who is Juggins?" asked Meeks.

"He is the leader," said Jolnes, "of a new modern school of detectives. Their methods are different from ours, but it is said that Juggins has solved some extremely puzzling cases. I will take you to him."

They found the greater Juggins in his office. He was a small man with light hair, deeply absorbed in reading one of the bourgeois works of Nathaniel Hawthorne.

The two great detectives of different schools shook hands with ceremony, and Meeks was introduced.

"State the facts," said Juggins, going on with his reading.

When Meeks ceased, the greater one closed his book and said:

"Do I understand that your sister is fifty-two years of age, with a large mole on the side of her nose, and that she is a very poor widow, making a scanty living by scrubbing, and with a very homely face and figure?"

"That describes her exactly," admitted Meeks. Juggins rose and put on his hat.

"In fifteen minutes," he said, "I will return, bringing you her present address."

Shamrock Jolnes turned pale, but forced a smile.

Within the specified time Juggins returned and consulted a little slip of paper held in his hand.

"Your sister, Mary Snyder," he announced calmly, "will be found at No. 162 Chilton street. She is living in the back hall bedroom, five flights up. The house is only four blocks from here," he continued, addressing Meeks. "Suppose you go and verify the statement and then return here. Mr. Jolnes will await you, I dare say."

Meeks hurried away. In twenty minutes he was back again, with a beaming face.

"She is there and well!" he cried. "Name your fee!"

"Two dollars," said Juggins.

When Meeks had settled his bill and departed, Shamrock Jolnes stood with his hat in his hand before Juggins.

"If it would not be asking too much," he stammered—"if you would favour me so far— would you object to——"

"Certainly not," said Juggins pleasantly. "I will tell you how I did it. You remember the description of Mrs. Snyder? Did you ever know a woman like that who wasn't paying weekly instalments on an enlarged crayon portrait of herself? The biggest factory of that kind in the country is just around the corner. I went there and got her address off the books. That's all."

Holmes and the Dasher

A. B. COX

O N E O F T H E most ingenious and influential authors of the golden age of detective fiction (the two decades between the world wars), Anthony Berkeley Cox (1893–1971) has been sadly neglected, unknown to all but serious aficionados of the mystery genre. He founded London's prestigious Detection Club, reserved for only the best of the best authors of mystery fiction.

His professional writing life began with humorous stories, articles, and books using A. B. Cox as the byline, producing sketches for *Punch*, many later collected as *Jugged Journalism* (1925), and such trifling novels as *Brenda Entertains* (1925) and *The Professor on Paws* (1926). His first detective novel, *The Layton Court Mystery* (1925), published anonymously, introduced Roger Sheringham, one of the more original, and more fallible, amateur detectives of the era.

In *The Second Shot* (1930), Sheringham provides irrefutable logic to identify the killer, only to have the real murderer explain why he committed the crime. A similar scenario plays out in Cox's most famous book, *The Poisoned Chocolates Case* (1929). His primary achievement in these clever tours de force was to establish the importance of psychological evaluation—of the criminal, the detective, and even of the victim.

This was a major step toward the modern detective story, which is more concerned with the *why* of a crime than the *who* or the *how*. This was brought to its greatest heights in the first two books that Cox wrote under the Francis Iles pseudonym. *Malice Aforethought* (1931) is based on the real-life Armstrong case in which a cowardly doctor kills his detestable wife. The murderer is known from the start, much like an episode of the *Columbo* television series, but the reader's interest is held by how the crime is planned and whether it will go unpunished. Julian Symons wrote, "If there is one book more than another that may be regarded as the begetter of the postwar realistic crime novel, it is this one."

Even more significant is *Before the Fact* (1932), a psychological study of a potential murderer as seen through the eyes of his intended victim. The novel served as the basis for the great Alfred Hitchcock film *Suspicion* (1941), though the ending was changed to protect Cary Grant's image of movie innocence.

"Holmes and the Dasher" was originally published in *Jugged Journalism* (London, Herbert Jenkins, 1925).

HOLMES AND THE DASHER

A. B. Cox

I T W A S A pretty rotten sort of day in March, I remember, that dear old Holmes and I were sitting in the ancestral halls in Baker Street, putting in a quiet bit of meditation. At least Holmes was exercising the good old gray matter over a letter that had just come, while I was relaxing gently in an armchair.

"What-ho, Watson, old fruit," he said at last, tossing the letter over to me. "What does that mass of alluvial deposit you call a brain make of this, what, what?"

The letter went something like this, as far as I can remember; at least, I may not have got all the words quite right, but this was the sort of gist of it, if you take me:

Jolly old Mr. Holmes,—I shall be rolling round at about three o'clock to discuss a pretty ripe little problem with you. It's like this. Freddie Devereux asked me to marry him last night, as I can prove with witnesses; but this morning he says he must have been a bit over the edge (a trifle sozzled, if you get me), and that a proposal doesn't count in the eyes of the rotten old Law if made under the influence of friend Demon Rum, as it were. Well, what I mean is—what about it? In other words, it's up to you to see that Freddie and I get tethered up together in front of an altar in the pretty near future. Get me?

Yours to a stick of lip salve,
Cissie Crossgarters

"Well, Watson?" Holmes asked, splashing a little soda into his glass of cocaine. "As the jolly old poet says—what, what, what?"

"It seems to me," I said, playing for safety, "that this is a letter from a girl called Cissie Crossgarters, who wants to put the stranglehold on a chappie called Devereux, while he's trying to counter with an uppercut from the jolly old Law. At least, that is, if you take my meaning."

"It's astounding how you get at the heart of things, Watson," said Holmes, in that dashed sneering way of his. "But it is already three o'clock, and there goes the bell. If I'm not barking up the wrong tree, this will be our client. Cissie Crossgarters!" he added ruminatively. "Mark my words, Watson, old laddie, she'll be a bit of a dasher. That is, a topnotcher, as it were."

In spite of his faults I'm bound to say that Holmes certainly is the lad with the outsize brain; the fellow simply exudes intuition. The girl *was* a topnotcher. The way she sailed into our little sitting room reminded me of a ray of sunshine lighting up the good old Gorgonzola cheese. I mean, poetry and bright effects and whatnot.

"Miss Crossgarters?" asked Holmes, doing the polite.

"Call me Cissie," she said, spraying him with smiles. Oh, she was a dasher all right.

"Allow me to present my friend, colleague and whatnot, Bertie Watson," said Holmes, and she switched the smile onto me. I can tell you, I felt the old heart thumping like a motorbike as I squeezed the tiny little hand she held out to me. I mean, it was so dashed small. In fact, tiny, if you get me. I mean to say, it was such a dashed *tiny* little hand.

"Well?" said Holmes, when we were all seated, looking his most hatchet-faced and sleuthiest. "And what about everything, as it were? That is, what, what?"

"You got my letter?" cooed the girl, looking at Holmes as if he were the only man in the world. I mean, you know the sort of way they look at you when they want something out of you.

"You bet I did," said Holmes, leaning back and clashing his finger tips together, as was his habit when on the jolly old trail.

"And what do you think of it?"

"Ah!" said Holmes, fairly bursting with mystery. "That's what we've got to consider. But I may say that the situation appears to me dashed thick and not a little rotten. In fact, dashed rotten and pretty thick as well, if you take me. I mean to say," he added carefully, "well, if you follow what I'm driving at, altogether pretty well dashed thick and rotten, what?"

"You do put things well," said the girl admiringly. "That's just what I felt about it myself. And what had I better do, do you think?"

"Ah!" said Holmes again, clashing away like mad. "It's just that particular little fruity point that we've got to think over, isn't it? I mean, before we get down to action, we've got to put in a bit of pretty useful meditation and whatnot. At least, that's how the thing strikes me."

"How clever you are, Mr. Holmes!" sighed the girl.

Holmes heaved himself out of his chair. "And let me tell you that the best way of agitating the old bean into a proper performance of its duties is first of all to restore the good old tissues with a little delicate sustenance. In other words, what about something rather rare in tea somewhere first?"

"Oh, yes!" cried the girl. "How lovely!"

"Top-hole!" I said enthusiastically. I mean, the idea tickled me, what?

Holmes looked at me with a dashed cold eye. "You're not on the stage for this bit of dialogue, dear old laddie," he remarked in the way that writer chappies call incisively.

They trickled out together.

It was past midnight before Holmes returned.

"What ho!" I said doubtfully, still feeling a bit sore, if you understand me.

"What ho!" said Holmes, unleashing his ulster.

"What ho! What ho!"

"What ho! What ho! What?"

"I mean, what about Freddie Devereux?" I asked, to change the conversation.

"That moon-faced lump of mediocrity? What about him?"

"Well, what about him? About him and Miss Crossgarters, as it were. I mean to say, what about them, what?"

"Oh, you mean what about them? Well, I don't think he'll trouble her much more. You see, Cissie and I have got engaged to be married, what? I mean, what, what, what?"

An Irreducible Detective Story

STEPHEN LEACOCK

CANADA'S GREATEST HUMORIST, Stephen Butler Leacock (1869–1944) was born in England. When his family moved to Canada seven years later, "I decided to go with them," as he later wrote. In the early part of the twentieth century, he was the most famous humorist in the English-speaking world, according to *The Canadian Encyclopedia* (though this may come as a surprise to the many aficionados of Mark Twain). It seems precisely the correct credential for the position he subsequently held: professor of political economy and longtime chair of the Department of Economics and Political Science at McGill University.

Leacock was a prolific writer of nonfiction, mainly histories of Canada and England, and biographies, including of Mark Twain and Charles Dickens, but they are forgotten today, and if he is remembered at all, it is for his humorous stories and verse. He was a great champion of the *New Yorker*'s Robert Benchley and was a favorite humorist of comedians Groucho Marx and Jack Benny.

As a parodist, Leacock more than once turned to Sherlock Holmes (leaving him unnamed, called only The Great Detective). Other stories were "Maddened by Mystery, or The Defective Detective" (1911), "The Great Detective" (1928), and "What Happened Next?" (1937).

"An Irreducible Detective Story" was first published in *Further Foolishness: Sketches and Satires of the Follies of the Day* (New York and London, John Lane; Toronto, Gundy, 1916).

AN IRREDUCIBLE DETECTIVE STORY

Stephen Leacock

THE MYSTERY HAD now reached its climax. First, the man had been undoubtedly murdered. Second, it was absolutely certain that no conceivable person had done it.

It was therefore time to call in the great detective.

He gave one searching glance at the corpse. In a moment he whipped out a microscope.

"Ha! Ha!" he said, as he picked a hair off the lapel of the dead man's coat. "The mystery is now solved."

He held up the hair.

"Listen," he said, "we have only to find the man who lost this hair and the criminal is in our hands."

The inexorable chain of logic was complete.

The detective set himself to the search.

For four days and nights he moved, unobserved, through the streets of New York scanning closely every face he passed, looking for a man who had lost a hair.

On the fifth day he discovered a man, disguised as a tourist, his head enveloped in a steamer cap that reached below his ears.

The man was about to go on board the *Gloritania*.

The detective followed him on board.

"Arrest him!" he said, and then drawing himself to his full height, he brandished aloft the hair.

"This is his," said the great detective. "It proves his guilt."

"Remove his hat," said the ship's captain sternly.

They did so.

The man was entirely bald.

"Ha!" said the great detective, without a moment of hesitation. "He has committed not *one* murder but about a million."

The Doctor's Case

STEPHEN KING

FEW WRITERS IN the history of American literature have maintained as long-standing a position of popularity, as well as critical recognition, as Stephen Edwin King (1947–). Born in Portland, Maine, he graduated from the University of Maine with a BA in English. He sold stories to various publications, including *Playboy*. Heavily influenced by H. P. Lovecraft and the macabre stories published by EC Comics, he specializes in writing horror and supernatural fiction but has also published books in other genres, including mystery, western, and science fiction.

The first three pages of the manuscript of his first book, *Carrie* (1973), about a girl with psychic powers, were thrown into a wastebasket and famously rescued by his wife, Tabitha, who encouraged him to finish it. It was published in a modest hardcover edition but then had great success as a paperback, launching a career of such spectacular magnitude that King is a celebrity as recognizable as a movie star or athlete—not commonplace for authors.

In addition to numerous novels and short stories, King has written screenplays and nonfiction, proving himself an expert in macabre fiction and film. More than one hundred films and television programs have been made from his work, most notably *Carrie* (1976), *The Shining* (1980), *Stand by Me* (1986, based on the novella "The Body"), *The Shawshank Redemption* (1994, based on the short story "Rita Hayworth and the Shawshank Redemption"), and *The Green Mile* (1999). *Under the Dome* (2009), one of his longest novels, served as the basis for a popular television series of the same name that premiered in June 2013.

"The Doctor's Case" was originally published in *The New Adventures of Sherlock Holmes*, edited by Martin H. Greenberg and Carol-Lynn Rössel Waugh (New York, Carroll & Graf, 1987).

THE DOCTOR'S CASE

Stephen King

IT WAS A WET, dreary afternoon and the clock had just rung half past one. Holmes sat by the window, holding his violin but not playing it, looking silently out into the rain. There were times, especially after his cocaine days were behind him, when Holmes could grow moody to the point of surliness when the skies remained stubbornly gray for a week or more, and he had been doubly disappointed on this day, for the glass had been rising since late the night before and he had confidently predicted clearing skies by ten this morning at the latest. Instead, the mist which had been hanging in the air when I arose had thickened into a steady rain. And if there was anything which rendered Holmes moodier than long periods of rain, it was being wrong.

Suddenly he straightened up, tweaking a violin string with a fingernail, and smiled sardonically. "Watson! Here's a sight! The wettest bloodhound you ever saw!"

It was Lestrade, of course, seated in the back of an open waggon with water running into his close-set, fiercely inquisitive eyes. The waggon had no more than stopped before he was out, tossing the driver a coin, and striding toward 221B Baker Street. He moved so quickly that I thought he should run into our door.

I heard Mrs. Hudson remonstrating with him about his decidedly damp condition and the effect it might have on the rugs both downstairs and up, and then Holmes, who could make Lestrade look like a tortoise when the urge struck him, leaped across to the door and called

down, "Let him up, Mrs. H.—I'll put a newspaper under his boots if he stays long, but I somehow think—"

Then Lestrade was bounding up the stairs, leaving Mrs. Hudson to expostulate below. His colour was high, his eyes burned, and his teeth—decidedly yellowed by tobacco—were bared in a wolfish grin.

"Inspector Lestrade!" Holmes cried jovially. "What brings you out on such a—"

No further did he get. Still panting from his climb, Lestrade said, "I've heard gypsies say the devil grants wishes. Now I believe it. Come at once if you'd have a try, Holmes; the corpse is still fresh and the suspects all in a row."

"What is it?"

"Why, what you in your pride have wished for a hundred times or more in my own hearing, my dear fellow. The perfect locked-room mystery?"

Now Holmes's eyes blazed. "You mean it? Are you serious?"

"Would I have risked wet lung riding here in an open waggon if I was not?" Lestrade countered.

Then, for the only time in my hearing (despite the countless times the phrase has been attributed to him), Holmes turned to me and cried: "Quick, Watson! The game's afoot!"

On our way to the home of Lord Hull, Lestrade commented sourly that Holmes also had the *luck* of the devil; although Lestrade had commanded the waggon-driver to wait, we had no more than emerged from our lodgings when that exquisite rarity clip-clopped down the street: an empty hansom cab in what had become a driving rain. We climbed in and were off in a trice. As always, Holmes sat on the left-hand side, his eyes darting restlessly about, cataloguing everything, although there was precious little to see on *that* day . . . or so it seemed, at least, to the likes of me. I've no doubt every empty street-corner and rain-washed shop window spoke volumes to Holmes.

Lestrade directed the driver to what sounded like an expensive address in Saville Row, and then asked Holmes if he knew Lord Hull.

"I know *of* him," Holmes said, "but have never had the good fortune of meeting him. Now it seems I never shall. Shipping, wasn't it?"

"Shipping it was," Lestrade returned, "but the good fortune was all yours. Lord Hull was, by all accounts (including those of his nearest and—ahem!—dearest), a thoroughly nasty fellow, and as dotty as a puzzle-picture in a child's novelty book. He's finished practicing both nastiness and dottiness for good, however; around eleven o'clock this morning, just"—he pulled his turnip of a pocket-watch and looked at it— "two hours and forty minutes ago, someone put a knife in his back as he sat in his study with his will on the blotter before him."

"So," Holmes said thoughtfully, lighting his pipe, "you believe the study of this unpleasant Lord Hull is the perfect locked room I've been looking for all my life, do you?" His eyes gleamed skeptically through a rising rafter of blue smoke.

"I believe," Lestrade said quietly, "that it is."

"Watson and I have dug such holes before and never struck water yet," Holmes said, and he glanced at me before returning to his ceaseless catalogue of the streets through which we passed. "Do you recall the 'Speckled Band,' Watson?"

I hardly needed to answer him. There had been a locked room in that business, true enough, but there had also been a ventilator, a snake full of poison, and a killer evil enough to allow the one into the other. It had been devilish, but Holmes had seen to the bottom of the matter in almost no time at all.

"What are the facts, Inspector?" Holmes asked.

Lestrade began to lay them before us in the clipped tones of a trained policeman. Lord Albert Hull had been a tyrant in business and a despot at home. His wife was a mousy, terrified thing. The fact that she had borne him three sons seemed to have in no way sweetened his feelings toward her. She had been reluctant to speak of their social relations, but her sons had no such reservations; their papa, they said, had missed no opportunity to dig at her, to criticize her, or to jest at her expense . . . all of this when they were in company. When they were alone, he virtually ignored her. And, Lestrade, added, he sometimes beated her.

"William, the eldest, told me she always gave out the same story when she came to the breakfast table with a swollen eye or a mark on her cheek; that she had forgotten to put on her glasses and had run into a door. 'She ran into doors once and twice a week,' William said. 'I didn't know we had that many doors in the house.' "

"Hmmm!" Holmes said. "A cheery fellow! The sons never put a stop to it?"

"She wouldn't allow it," Lestrade said.

"Insanity," I returned. A man who would beat his wife is an abomination; a woman who would allow it an abomination and a perplexity.

"There was method in her madness, though," Lestrade said. "Although you'd not know it to look at her, she was twenty years younger than Hull. He had always been a heavy drinker and a champion diner. At age sixty, five years ago, he developed gout and angina."

"Wait for the storm to end and then enjoy the sunshine," Holmes remarked.

"Yes," Lestrade said. "He made sure they knew both his worth and the provisions of his will. They were little better than slaves—"

"—and the will was the document of indenture," Holmes murmured.

"Exactly so. At the time of his death, his worth was three hundred thousand pounds. He never asked them to take his word for this; he had his chief accountant to the house quarterly to detail the balance sheets of Hull Shipping . . . although he kept the purse-strings firmly in his own hands and tightly closed."

"Devilish!" I exclaimed, thinking of the cruel boys one sometimes sees in Eastcheap or Piccadilly, boys who will hold out a sweet to a starving dog to see it dance . . . and then gobble it themselves. Within moments I discovered this comparison was even more apt than I thought.

"On his death, Lady Rebecca Hull was to receive one hundred and fifty thousand pounds; William, the eldest, was to receive fifty thousand; Jory, the middler, forty; and Stephen, the youngest, thirty."

"And the other thirty thousand?" I asked.

"Seven thousand, five hundred each to his brother in Wales and an aunt in Brittany (not a cent for *her* relatives), five thousand in assorted bequests to the servants at the town-house and the place in the country, and—you'll like this, Holmes—ten thousand pounds to Mrs. Hemphill's Home for Abandoned Pussies."

"You're *joking*!" I cried, although if Lestrade expected a similar reaction from Holmes, he was disappointed. Holmes merely re-lighted his pipe and nodded as if he had expected this, or something like it. "With babies dying of starvation in the East End and homeless orphans still losing all the teeth out of their jaws by the age of ten in the sulphur factories, this fellow left ten thousand pounds to a . . . a boarding-hotel for *cats*?"

"I mean exactly that," Lestrade said pleasantly. "Furthermore, he should have left *twenty-seven times* that amount to Mrs. Hemphill's Abandoned Pussies if not for whatever happened this morning—and whoever who did the business."

I could only gape at this, and try to multiply in my head. While I was coming to the conclusion that Lord Hull had intended to disinherit both wife and children in favor of an orphanage for felines, Holmes was looking sourly at Lestrade and saying something which sounded to me like a total *non sequitur*. "I am going to sneeze, am I not?"

Lestrade smiled. It was a smile of transcendent sweetness. "Oh yes, my dear Holmes. I fear you will sneeze often and profoundly."

Holmes removed his pipe, which he had just gotten drawing to his satisfaction (I could tell by the way he settled back slightly in his seat), looked at it for a moment, and then held it out into the rain. I watched him knock out the damp and smouldering tobacco, more dumbfounded than ever. If you had told me then that I was to be the one to solve this case I believe I should have been impolite enough to laugh in your face. At that point I didn't even know what the case was *about*, other than that someone (who more and more sounded the sort of person who deserved to stand in the courtyard of Buckingham Palace for a medal rather than in the Old Bailey for sentencing) had killed this wretched Lord Hull before he could leave his family's rightful due to a gaggle of street cats.

"How many?" Holmes asked.

"Ten," Lestrade said.

"I suspected it was more than this famous locked room of yours that brought you out in the back of an open waggon on such a wet day," Holmes said sourly.

"Suspect as you like," Lestrade said gaily. "I'm afraid I must go on, but if you'd like, I could let you and the good doctor out here."

"Never mind," Holmes said. "When did he become sure that he was going to die?"

"Die?" I said. "How can you know he—"

"It's obvious, Watson," Holmes said. "It amused him to keep them in bondage by the means of his will." He looked at Lestrade. "No trust arrangements, I take it?"

Lestrade shook his head.

"Nor entailments of any sort?"

"None."

"Extraordinary!" I said.

"He wanted them to understand all would be theirs when he did them the courtesy of dying, Watson," Holmes said, "but he never actually intended for them to have it. He realized he was dying. He waited . . . and then he called them together this morning . . . this morning, Inspector, yes?"

Lestrade nodded.

"Yes. He called them together this morning and told them that he had made a new will which disinherited them one and all . . . except for the servants and the distant relatives, I suppose."

I opened my mouth to speak, only to discover I was too outraged to say anything. The image which kept returning to my mind was that of those cruel boys, making the starving East End curs jump with a bit of pork or a crumb of crust from a meat pie. I must add it never occurred to me to ask if such a will could not be disputed before the bar. Today a man would have a deuce of a time slighting his closest relatives in favor of a hotel for pussies, but in 1899, a man's will was a man's will, and unless many examples of insanity—not eccentricity but outright *insanity*—could be proved, a man's will, like God's, was done.

"This new will was properly witnessed?" Holmes asked, immediately putting his finger on the one possible loophole in such a wretched scheme.

"Indeed it was," Lestrade replied. "Yesterday Lord Hull's solicitor and one of his assistants appeared at the house and were shown into his study. There they remained for about fifteen minutes. Stephen Hull says the solicitor once raised his voice in protest about something—he could not tell what—and was silenced by Hull. Jory, the third son, was upstairs, painting, and Lady Hull was calling on a friend. But both Stephen and William saw them enter and leave. William said that when the solicitor and his assistant left, they did so with their heads down, and although William spoke, asking Mr. Barnes—the solicitor—if he was well, and making some social remark about the persistence of the rain, Barnes did not reply and the assistant seemed to actually cringe. It was as if they were ashamed, William said."

Well, there it was: witnesses. So much for *that* loophole, I thought.

"Since we are on the subject, tell me about the boys," Holmes said, putting his slender fingers together.

"As you like. It goes pretty much without saying that their hatred for the pater was exceeded only by the pater's boundless contempt for them . . . although how he could hold Stephen in contempt is . . . well, never mind, I'll keep things in their proper order."

"How good of you, Inspector Lestrade," Holmes said dryly.

"William is thirty-six. If his father had given him any sort of allowance, I suppose he would be a bounder. As he had little or none, he took long walks during the days, went out to the coffee-houses at night, or, if he happened to have a bit more money in his pockets, to a card-house, where he would lose it quickly enough. Not a pleasant man, Holmes. A man who has no purpose, no skill, no hobby, and no ambition (save to outlive his father), could hardly be a pleasant man. I had the queerest idea while I was talking to him—that I was interrogating an empty vase on which the face of the Lord Hull had been lightly stamped."

"A vase waiting for the pater's money to fill him up," Holmes commented.

"Jory is another matter. Hull saved most of his contempt for Jory, calling him from his earliest childhood by such endearing pet-names as 'fish-face' and 'keg-legs' and 'stoat-belly.' It's not hard to understand such names, unfortunately; Jory Hull stands no more than five feet tall, if that, is bow-legged, slump-shouldered, and of a remarkably ugly countenance. He looks a bit like that poet fellow, the pouf."

"Oscar Wilde?" asked I.

Holmes turned a brief, amused glance upon me. "I believe Lestrade means Algernon Swinburne," he said. "Who, I believe, is no more a pouf than you are, Watson."

"Jory Hull was born dead," Lestrade said. "After he remained blue and still for an entire minute, the doctor pronounced him so and put a napkin over his misshapen body. Lady Hull, in her one moment of heroism, sat up, removed the napkin, and dipped the baby's legs into the hot water which had been brought to attend the birth. The baby began to squirm and squall."

Lestrade grinned and lit a cigarillo with a match undoubtedly dipped by one of the urchins of whom I had just been thinking.

"Hull himself, always munificent, blamed this immersion for his bow legs."

Holmes's only comment on this extraordinary (and to my physician's mind rather suspect) story was to suggest that Lestrade had gotten a large body of information from his suspects in a short period of time.

"One of the aspects of the case which I thought would appeal to you, my dear Holmes," Lestrade said as we swept into Rotten Row in a splash and a swirl. "They need no coercion to speak; coercion's what it would take to shut 'em up. They've had to remain silent all too long. And then there's the fact that the new will is gone. Relief loosens tongues beyond measure, I find."

"Gone!" I exclaimed, but Holmes took no notice. He asked Lestrade about this misshapen middle child.

"Ugly as he is, I believe his father continually heaped vituperation on his head because—"

"Because Jory was the only son who had no need to depend upon his father's money to make his way in the world," Holmes said complacently.

Lestrade started. "The devil! How did you know that?"

"Rating a man with faults which all can see is the act of a man who is afraid as well as vindictive," Holmes said. "What was his key to the cell door?"

"As I told you, he paints," Lestrade said.

"Ah!"

Jory Hull was, as the canvases in the lower halls of Hull House later proved, a very good painter indeed. Not great; I do not mean to suggest he was. But his renderings of his mother and brothers were faithful enough so that, years later, when I saw color photographs for the first time, my mind flashed back to that rainy November afternoon in 1899. And the one of his fa-

ther, which he showed us later . . . perhaps it *was* Algernon Swinburne that Jory resembled, but his father's likeness—at least as seen through Jory's hand and eye—remainded me of an Oscar Wilde character: that nearly immortal *roué*, Dorian Gray.

His canvases were long, slow processes, but he was able to quick-sketch with such nimble rapidity that he might come home from Hyde Park on a Saturday afternoon with as much as twenty pounds in his pockets.

"I wager his father enjoyed *that*," Holmes said. He reached automatically for his pipe and then put it back. "The son a Peer of the Realm quick-sketching well-off American tourists and their sweethearts like a French Bohemian."

"He raged over it," Lestrade said, "but Jory wouldn't give over his selling stall in Hyde Park . . . not, at least, until his father agreed to an allowance of thirty-five pounds a week. He called it low blackmail."

"My heart bleeds," I said.

"As does mine, Watson," Holmes said. "The third son, Lestrade—we've almost reached the house, I believe."

As Lestrade had said, surely Stephen Hull had the greatest cause to hate his father. As his gout grew worse and his head more befuddled, Lord Hull surrendered more and more of the company affairs to Stephen, who was only twenty-eight at the time of his father's death. The responsibilities devolved upon Stephen, and the blame devolved upon him if his least decision proved amiss . . . and yet no financial gain devolved upon him should he decide well.

As the only of his three children with an interest in the business he had founded, Lord Hull should have looked upon his son with approval. As a son who not only kept his father's shipping business prosperous when it might have foundered due to Lord Hull's own increasing physical and mental problems (and all of this as a young man) he should have been looked upon with love and gratitude as well. Instead, Stephen had been rewarded with suspicion, jealousy and his father's belief—spoken more and more often—that his son "would steal the pennies from a dead man's eyes."

"The b——d!" I cried, unable to contain myself.

"He saved the business and the fortune," Holmes said, steepling his fingers again, "and yet his reward was still to be the youngest son's share of the spoil. What, by the way, was to be the disposition of the company by the new will?"

"It was to be handed over to the Board of Directors, Hull Shipping, Ltd., with no provision for the son," Lestrade said, and pitched his cigarillo as the hackney swept up the curving drive of a house which looked extraordinarily ugly to me just then, as it stood amid its dead lawns in the rain. "Yet with the father dead and the new will nowhere to be found, Stephen Hull comes into thirty thousand. The lad will have no trouble. He has what the Americans call 'leverage.' The company will have him as managing director. They should have done anyway, but now it will be on Stephen Hull's terms."

"Yes," Holmes said. "Leverage. A good word." He leaned out into the rain. "Stop short, driver!" he cried. "We've not quite done!"

"As you say, guv'nor," the driver returned, "but it's devilish wet out here."

"And you'll go with enough in your pocket to make your innards as wet and devilish as your out'ards," Holmes said, which seemed to satisfy the driver, who stopped thirty yards from the door. I listened to the rain tip-tapping on the roof while Holmes cogitated and then said: "The old will—the one he teased them with— *that* document isn't missing, is it?"

"Absolutely not. It was on his desk, near his body."

"Four excellent suspects! Servants need not be considered . . . or so it seems now. Finish quickly, Lestrade—the final circumstances, and the locked room."

Lestrade complied in less than ten minutes, consulting his notes from time to time. A month previous, Lord Hull had observed a small black spot on his right leg, directly behind the knee. The family doctor was called. His diagnosis was gangrene, an unusual but far from rare result of gout and poor circulation. The doctor told him the leg would have to come off, and well above the site of the infection.

Lord Hull laughed at this until tears streamed down his cheeks. The doctor, who had expected any other reaction than this, was struck speechless. "When they stick me in my coffin, sawbones," Hull said, "it will be with both legs still attached, thank you."

The doctor told him that he sympathized with Lord Hull's wish to keep his leg, but that without amputation he would be dead in six months . . . and he would spend the last two in exquisite pain. Lord Hull asked the doctor what his chances of survival should be if he were to undergo the operation. He was still laughing, Lestrade said, as though it were the best joke he had ever heard. After some hemming and hawing, the doctor said the odds were even.

"Bunk," said I.

"Exactly what Lord Hull said," Lestrade replied. "Except he used a term a bit more vulgar."

Hull told the doctor that he himself reckoned his chances at no better than one in five. "As to the pain, I don't think it will come to that," he went on, "as long as there's laudanum and a spoon to stir it within stumping distance."

The next day, Hull finally sprang his nasty surprise—that he was thinking of changing his will. Just how he did not say.

"Oh?" Holmes said, looking at Lestrade from those cool gray eyes that saw so much. "And who, pray, was surprised?"

"None of them, I should think. But you know human nature, Holmes; how people hope against hope."

"And how some plan against disaster," Holmes said dreamily.

This very morning Lord Hull had called his family into the parlor, and when all were settled, he performed an act few testators are granted, one which is usually performed by the wagging tongues of their solicitors after their own have been silenced forever. In short, he read them his new will, leaving the balance of his estate to Mrs. Hemphill's wayward pussies. In the silence which followed he rose, not without difficulty, and favored them all with a death's-head grin. And leaning over his cane, he made the following declaration, which I find as astoundingly vile now as I did when Lestrade recounted it to us in that hackney cab: "So! All is fine, is it not? Yes, very fine! You have served me quite faithfully, woman and boys, for some forty years. Now I intend, with the clearest and most serene conscience imaginable, to cast you hence. But take heart! Things could be worse! If there was time, the pharaohs had their favorite pets—cats, for the most part—killed before they died, so the pets might be there to welcome them into the after-life, to be kicked or petted there, at their masters' whims, forever . . . and forever . . . and forever." Then he began to laugh at them. He leaned over his cane and laughed from his doughy livid dying face, the new will—signed and witnessed, as all of them had seen—clutched in one claw of a hand.

William rose and said, "Sir, you may be my father and the author of my existence, but you are also the lowest creature to crawl upon the face of the earth since the serpent tempted Eve in the Garden."

"Not at all!" the old monster returned, still laughing. "I know four lower. Now, if you will pardon me, I have some important papers to put away in my safe . . . and some worthless ones to burn in the stove."

"He still had the old will when he confronted them?" Holmes asked. He seemed more interested than startled.

"Yes."

"He could have burned it as soon as the new one was signed and witnessed," Holmes mused. "He had all the previous afternoon and evening to do so. But that wasn't enough, was it? What do you suppose, Lestrade?"

"That he was teasing them. Teasing them with a chance he believed all would refuse."

"There is another possibility," Holmes said. "He spoke of suicide. Isn't it possible that such a man might hold out such a temptation, knowing that if one of them—Stephen seems most

likely from what you say—would do it for him, be caught . . . and swing for it?"

I stared at Holmes in silent horror.

"Never mind," Holmes said. "Go on."

The four of them had sat in paralyzed silence as the old man made his long slow way up the corridor to his study. There were no sounds but the thud of his cane, the laboured rattle of his breathing, the plaintive *miaow* of a cat in the kitchen, and the steady beat of the pendulum in the parlour clock. Then they heard the squeal of hinges as Hull opened his study door and stepped inside.

"Wait!" Holmes said sharply, sitting forward. "No one actually saw him go in, did they?"

"I'm afraid that's not so, old chap," Lestrade returned. "Mr. Oliver Stanley, Lord Hull's valet, had heard Lord Hull's progress down the hall. He came from Hull's dressing chamber, went to the gallery railing, and called down to ask if Hull was all right. Hull looked up—Stanley saw him as plainly as I see you right now, old fellow—and said he was feeling absolutely tip-top. Then he rubbed the back of his head, went in, and locked the study door behind him. By the time he reached the door (the corridor is quite long and it may have taken him as long as two minutes to make his way up it without help) Stephen had shaken off his stupor and had gone to the parlour door. He saw the exchange between his father and his father's man. Of course his father was back-to, but he heard his father's voice and described the same gesture: Hull rubbing the back of his head."

"Could Stephen Hull and this Stanley fellow have spoken before the police arrived?" I asked—shrewdly, I thought.

"Of course they could, and probably did," Lestrade said wearily. "But there was no collusion."

"You feel sure of that?" Holmes asked, but he sounded uninterested.

"Yes. Stephen Hull would lie very well, I think, but Stanley would do so badly. Accept my professional opinion or not just as you like, Holmes."

"I accept it."

So Lord Hull passed into his study, the famous locked room, and all heard the click of the lock as he turned the key—the only key there was to that *sanctum sanctorum*. This was followed by a more unusual sound: the bolt being drawn across.

Then, silence.

The four of them—Lady Hull and her sons, so shortly to be blue-blooded paupers—looked at each other in silence. The cat *miaowed* again from the kitchen and Lady Hull said in a distracted voice that if the housekeeper wouldn't give that cat a bowl of milk, she supposed she must. She said the sound of it would drive her mad if she had to listen to it much longer. She left the parlour. Moments later, without a word among them, the three sons also left. William went to his room upstairs, Stephen wandered into the music room. And Jory went to sit upon a bench beneath the stairs where, he had told Lestrade, he had gone since earliest childhood when he was sad or had matters of deep difficulty to think over.

Less than five minutes later a terrible shriek arose from the study. Stephen bolted out of the music room, where he had been plinking out isolated notes on the piano. Jory met him at the door. William was already halfway downstairs and saw them breaking in when Stanley, the valet, came out of Lord Hull's dressing room and went to the gallery railing for the second time. He saw Stephen Hull burst the study door in; he saw William reach the foot of the stairs and almost fall on the marble; he saw Lady Hull come from the dining room doorway with a pitcher of milk still in one hand. Moments later the rest of the servants had gathered. Lord Hull was slumped over his writing desk with the three brothers standing by. His eyes were open. There was a snarl on his lips, a look of ineffable surprise in his eyes. Clutched in his hand was his will . . . the old one. Of the new one there was no sign. And there was a dagger in his back."

With this Lestrade rapped for the driver to go on.

We entered between two constables as stone-faced as Buckingham Palace sentinels. Here was a very long hall, floored in black-and-white marble tiles like a chessboard. They led to an open door at the end, where two more constables were posted. The infamous study. To the left were the stairs, to the right two doors: the parlour and the music room, I guessed.

"The family is gathered in the parlour," Lestrade said.

"Good," Holmes said pleasantly. "But perhaps Watson and I might first have a look at this locked room."

"Shall I accompany you?"

"Perhaps not," Holmes said. "Has the body been removed?"

"It had not been when I left for your lodgings, but by now it should be gone."

"Very good."

Holmes started away. I followed. Lestrade called, "Holmes!"

Holmes turned, eyebrows upraised.

"No secret panels, no secret doors. Take my word or not, as you like."

"I believe I'll wait until . . ." Holmes began, and then his breath began to hitch. He scrambled in his pocket, found a napkin probably carried absently away from the eating-house where we had dined the previous evening, and sneezed mightily into it. I looked down and saw a large scarred tomcat, as out of place here in this grand hall as would have been one of those sulphur-factory urchins, twining about Holmes's legs. One of its ears was laid back against its scarred skull. The other was gone, lost in some long-ago alley battle, I supposed.

Holmes sneezed repeatedly and kicked out at the cat. It went with a reproachful backward look rather than with the angry hiss one would have expected from such an old campaigner. Holmes looked at Lestrade over the napkin with reproachful, watery eyes. Lestrade, not in the least put out of countenance, grinned. "Ten, Holmes," he said. "*Ten*. House is full of felines. Hull loved 'em." With that Lestrade walked off.

"How long, old fellow?" I asked.

"Since forever," he said, and sneezed again. I still believe, I am bound to add, that the solution to the locked room problem would have been as readily apparent to Holmes as it was to me if not for this unfortunate affliction. The word *allergy* was hardly known all those years ago, but that, of course, was his problem.

"Do you want to leave?" I was a bit alarmed. I had once seen a case of near asphyxiation as the result of such an aversion to sheep.

"He'd like that," Holmes said. I did not need him to tell me who he meant. Holmes sneezed once more (a large red welt was appearing on his normally pale forehead) and then we passed between the constables at the study door. Holmes closed it behind him.

The room was long and relatively narrow. It was at the end of something like a wing, the main house spreading to either side from an area roughly three-quarters of the way down the hall. Thus there were windows on both sides and the room was well-lit in spite of the gray, rainy day. There were framed shipping charts on most of the walls, but on one was a really handsome set of weather instruments in a brass-bound case: an anemometer (Hull had the little whirling cups mounted on one of the roof-peaks, I supposed), two thermometers (one registering the outdoor temperature and the other that of the study), and a barometer much like the one that had fooled Holmes into believing the bad weather would finally break. I noticed the glass was still rising, then looked outside. The rain was falling harder than ever, rising glass or no rising glass. We believe we know a great lot, with our instruments and things, but we don't know half as much as we think we do.

Holmes and I both turned to look at the door. The bolt was torn free, but leaning inward, as it should have been. The key was still in the lock, and still turned.

Holmes's eyes, watering as they were, were everywhere at once, noting, cataloging, storing.

"You are a little better," I said.

"Yes," he said, lowering the napkin and stuffing it indifferently back into his coat pocket. "He may have loved 'em, but he apparently didn't allow 'em in here. Not on a regular basis, anyway. What do you make of it, Watson?"

Although my eyes were slower than his, I was also looking around. The double windows were all locked with thumb-turns and small brass side-bolts. None of the panes had been broken. The framed charts and weather instruments were between these windows. The other two walls, before and behind the desk which dominated the room, were filled with books. There was a small coal-stove at the south end of the room but no fireplace . . . the murderer hadn't come down the chimney like St. Nicholas, not unless he was narrow enough to fit through a stove-pipe and clad in an asbestos suit, for the stove was still very warm. The north end of this room was a little library, with two high-backed upholstered chairs and a coffee-table between them. On this table was a random stack of books. The ceiling was plastered. The floor was covered with a large Turkish rug. If the murderer had come up through a trap-door, I hadn't the slightest idea how he could have gotten back under that rug without disarranging it, and it was not disarranged in the slightest: it was smooth, and the shadows of the coffee-table legs lay across it without a ripple.

"Did you believe it, Watson?" Holmes asked, snapping me out of something like a hypnotic trance. Something . . . something about that coffee-table . . .

"Believe what, Holmes?"

"That all four of them simply walked out of that parlour, in four different directions, four minutes before the murder?"

"I don't know," I said faintly.

"*I* don't believe it; not for a mo—" He broke off. "Watson! Are you all right?"

"No," I said in a voice I could hardly hear myself. I collapsed into one of the library chairs. My heart was beating too fast. I couldn't seem to catch my breath. My head was pounding; my eyes seemed to have suddenly grown too large for their sockets. I could not take them from the shadows of the coffee-table legs upon the rug. "I am most . . . most definitely not . . . not all right."

At that moment Lestrade appeared in the

study doorway. "If you've looked your fill, H—" He broke off. "What the devil's the matter with Watson?"

"I believe," said Holmes in a calm, measured voice, "that Watson has solved the case. Have you, Watson?"

I nodded my head. Not all of it, perhaps, but most. I knew who; I knew how.

"Is it this way with you, Holmes?" I asked. "When you . . . see?"

"Yes," he said.

"*Watson's* solved the case?" Lestrade said impatiently. "Bah! Watson's offered a thousand solutions to a hundred cases before this, Holmes, as you very well know—all of them wrong. Why, I remember just this late summer—"

"I know more about Watson than you shall ever know," Holmes said, "and this time he has hit upon it. I know the look." He began to sneeze again; the cat with the missing ear had wandered into the room through the door, which Lestrade had left open. It headed directly for Holmes with an expression of what seemed to be affection on its ugly face.

"If this is how it is for you," I said, "I'll never envy you again, Holmes. My heart should burst."

"One becomes enured even to insight," Holmes said, with not the slightest trace of conceit in his voice. "Out with it, then . . . or shall we bring in the suspects, as in the last chapter of a detective novel?"

"No!" I cried in horror. I had seen none of them; I had no urge to. "Only I think I must *show* you how it was done. If you and Inspector Lestrade will only step out into the hall for a moment—"

The cat reached Holmes and jumped into his lap, purring like the most satisfied creature on earth.

Holmes exploded into a perfect fusillade of sneezes. The red patches on his face, which had begun to fade, burst out afresh. He pushed the cat away and stood up.

"Be quick, Watson, so we can be away from this damned place," he said in a muffled voice,

and left his perfect locked room with his shoulders in an uncharacteristic hunch, his head down, and with not a single look back. Believe me when I say that a little of my heart went with him.

Lestrade stood leaning against the door, his wet coat steaming slightly, his lips parted in a detestable grin. "Shall I take Holmes's new admirer, Watson?"

"Leave it," I said, "but close the door."

"I'd lay a fiver you're wasting our time, old man," Lestrade said, but I saw something different in his eyes: if I'd offered to take him up on the wager, he would have found a way out of it.

"Close the door," I repeated. "I shan't be long."

He closed the door. I was alone in Hull's study . . . except for the cat, of course, which was now sitting in the middle of the rug, tail curled neatly about its paws, green eyes watching me.

I felt in my pockets and found my own souvenir from last night's dinner—bachelors are rather untidy people, I fear, but there was a reason for the bread other than general slovenliness. I almost always kept a crust in one pocket or the other, for it amused me to feed the pigeons that landed outside the very window where Holmes had been sitting when Lestrade drove up.

"Pussy," said I, and put the bread beneath the coffee-table—the coffee-table to which Lord Hull would have presented his back when he sat down with his two wills—the wretched old one and the even more wretched new one. "Pussy-pussy-pussy."

The cat rose and walked languidly beneath the table to investigate.

I went to the door and opened it. "Holmes! Lestrade! Quickly!"

They came in.

"Step over here." I walked to the coffee-table. Lestrade looked about and began to frown, seeing nothing; Holmes, of course, began to sneeze again. "Can't we have that wretched thing out of here?" he managed from behind the table-napkin, which was now quite soggy.

"Of course," said I. *"But where is it, Holmes?"*

A startled expression filled his eyes above the napkin. Lestrade whirled, walked toward Hull's writing desk, and behind it. Holmes knew his reaction should not have been so violent if the cat had been on the far side of the room. He bent and looked beneath the coffee-table, saw nothing but empty space and the bottom row of the two book-cases on the north wall of the room, and straightened up again. If his eyes had not been spouting like fountains, he should have seen the illusion then; he was right on top of it. But all the same, it was devilishly good. The empty space under that coffee-table had been Jory Hull's masterpiece.

"I don't—" Holmes began, and then the cat, who found Holmes much more to its liking than the bread, strolled out from beneath the table and began once more to twine ecstatically about his ankles. Lestrade had returned, and his eyes grew so wide I thought they might actually fall out. Even having seen through it, I myself was amazed. The scarred tomcat seemed to be materializing out of thin air; head, body, white-tipped tail last.

It rubbed against Holmes's leg, purring as Holmes sneezed.

"That's enough," I said. "You've done your job and may leave."

I picked it up, took it to the door (getting a good scratch for my pains), and tossed it unceremoniously into the hall. I shut the door behind it.

Holmes was sitting down. "My God," he said in a nasal, clogged voice. Lestrade was incapable of any speech at all. His eyes never left the table and the faded red Turkish rug beneath its legs: and empty space that had somehow given birth to a cat.

"I should have seen," Holmes was muttering. "Yes . . . but you . . . how did you understand so *quickly?*" I detected the faintest hurt and pique in that voice . . . and forgave it.

"It was *those,*" I said, and pointed at the shadows thrown by the table-legs.

"Of course!" Holmes nearly groaned. He slapped his welted forehead. "Idiot! I'm a perfect *idiot!*"

"Nonsense," I said tartly. "With ten cats in the house and one who has apparently picked you out for a special friend, I suspect you were seeing ten of everything."

Lestrade finally found his voice. "What about the shadows?"

"Show him, Watson," Holmes said wearily, lowering the napkin into his lap.

So I bent and picked one of the shadows off the floor.

Lestrade sat down in the other chair, hard, like a man who has been unexpectedly punched.

"I kept looking at them, you see," I said, speaking in a tone which could not help being apologetic. This seemed all wrong. It was Holmes's job to explain the whos and hows. Yet while I saw that he now understood everything, I knew he would refuse to speak in this case. And I suppose a part of me—the part that knew I would probably never have another chance to do something like this—*wanted* to be the one to explain. And the cat was rather a nice touch, I must say. A magician could have done no better with a rabbit and a top-hat.

"I knew something was wrong, but it took a moment for it to sink in. This room is extremely well lighted, but today it's pouring down rain. Look around and you'll see that not a single object in this room casts a shadow . . . *except for these table-legs.*"

Lestrade uttered an oath.

"It's rained for nearly a week," I said, "but both Holmes's barometer and the late Lord Hull's"—I pointed to it—"said that we could expect sun today. In fact, it seemed a sure thing. So he added the shadows as a final touch."

"Who did?"

"Jory Hull," Holmes said in that same weary tone. "Who else?"

I bent down and reached my hand beneath the right end of the coffee-table. It disappeared into thin air, just as the cat had appeared. Lestrade uttered another startled oath. I tapped the back of the canvas stretched tightly between the forward legs of the coffee-table. The books and the rug bulged and rippled, and the illusion, nearly perfect as it had been, was dispelled.

Jory Hull had painted the nothing under his father's coffee-table; had crouched behind the nothing as his father entered the room, locked the door, and sat at his desk with his two wills, the new and the old. And when he began to rise again from his seat, he rushed out from behind the nothing, dagger in hand.

"He was the only one who could execute such a piece of realism," I said, this time running my hand down the face of the canvas. We could all hear the low rasping sound it made, like the purr of a very old cat. "The only one who could execute it, and the only one who could hide behind it: Jory Hull, who was no more than five feet tall, bow-legged, slump-shouldered.

"As Holmes said, the surprise of the new will was no surprise. Even if the old man had been secretive about the possibility of cutting the relatives out of the will, which he wasn't, only simpletons could have mistaken the import of the visit from the solicitor and, more important, the assistant. It takes two witnesses to make a will a valid document at Chancery. What Holmes said about some people preparing for disaster was very true. A canvas as perfect as this was not made overnight, or in a month. You may find he had it ready—should it need to be used—for as long as a year—"

"Or five," Holmes interpolated.

"I suppose. At any rate, when Hull announced that he wanted to see his family in the parlour this morning, I suppose Jory knew the time had come. After his father had gone to bed last night, he would have come down here and mounted his canvas. I suppose he may have put down the false shadows at the same time, but if I had been him I should have tip-toed in here for another peek at the glass this morning, before the parlour gathering, just to make sure it was still rising. If the door was locked, I suppose he filched the key from his father's pocket and returned it later."

"Wasn't locked," Lestrade said shortly. "As a rule he kept it closed to keep the cats out, but rarely locked it."

"As for the shadows, they are just strips of felt, as you now see. His eye was good; they are about where they would have been at eleven this morning . . . if the glass had been right."

"If he expected the sun to be shining, why did he put down shadows at all?" Lestrade grumped.

"Sun puts 'em down as a matter of course, just in case you've never noticed your own, Watson."

Here I was at a loss. I looked at Holmes, who seemed grateful to have *any* part in the answer.

"Don't you see? That is the greatest irony of all! If the sun had shone as the glass suggested it would, the canvas would have *blocked* the shadows. Painted shadow-legs don't cast them, you know. He was caught by shadows on a day when there were none because he was afraid he would be caught by none on a day when his father's barometer said they would almost certainly be everywhere else in the room."

"I still don't understand how Jory got in here without Hull seeing him," Lestrade said.

"That puzzled me as well," Holmes said— dear old Holmes! I doubt if it puzzled him a bit, but that was what he said. "Watson?"

"The parlor where the four of them sat has a door which communicates with the music room, does it not?"

"Yes," Lestrade said, "and the music room has a door which communicates with Lady Hull's morning room, which is next in line as one goes toward the back of the house. But from the morning room one can only go back into the hall, Doctor Watson. If there had been *two* doors into Hull's study, I should hardly have come after Holmes on the run as I did."

He said this last in tones of faint self-justification.

"Oh, he went back into the hall, all right," I said, "but his father didn't see him."

"Rot!"

"I'll demonstrate," I said, and went to the writing-desk, where the dead man's cane still leaned. I picked it up and turned toward them. "The very instant Lord Hull left the parlour, Jory was up and on the run."

Lestrade shot a startled glance at Holmes; Holmes gave the Inspector a cool, ironic look in return. And I must say I did not understand the wider implications of the picture I was drawing for yet a while. I was too wrapped up in my own recreation, I suppose.

"He nipped through the first connecting door, ran across the music room, and entered Lady Hull's morning-room. He went to the hall door then and peeked out. If Lord Hull's gout had gotten so bad as to have brought on gangrene, he would have progressed no more than a quarter of the way down the hall, and that is optimistic. Now mark me, Inspector Lestrade, and I will show you how a man has spent a lifetime eating rich foods and imbibing the heavy waters ends up paying for it. If you doubt it, I shall bring you a dozen gout sufferers who will show you exactly what I'm going to show you now."

With that I began to stump slowly across the room toward them, both hands clamped tightly on the ball of the cane. I would raise one foot quite high, bring it down, pause, and then draw the other leg along. Never did my eyes look up. Instead, they alternated between the cane and that forward foot.

"Yes," Holmes said quietly. "The good Doctor is exactly right, Inspector Lestrade. The gout comes first; then, (if the sufferer lives long enough, that is), there comes the characteristic stoop brought on by always looking down."

"He knew it, too," I said. "Lord Hull was afflicted with worsening gout for five years. Jory would have marked the way he had come to walk, always looking down at the cane and his own feet. Jory peeped out of the morning room, saw he was safe, and simply nipped into the study. Three seconds and no more, if he was nimble." I paused. "That hall floor is marble, isn't it? He must have kicked off his shoes."

"He was wearing slippers," Lestrade said curtly.

"Ah. I see. Jory gained the study and slipped behind his stage-flat. Then he withdrew the dagger and waited. His father reached the end of the hall. He heard Stanley call down to his father. That must have been a bad moment for him. Then his father called back that he was fine, came into the room and closed the door."

They were both looking at me intently, and I understood some of the godlike power Holmes must have felt at moments like that, telling others what only you could know. And yet, I must repeat that it is a feeling I shouldn't have wanted to have too often. I believe the urge for such a feeling would have corrupted most men—men with less iron in their souls than was possessed by my friend Sherlock Holmes is what I mean.

"Jory—old Keg-Legs, old Stoat-Belly— would have made himself as small as possible before the locking-up went on, knowing that his father would have one good look round before turning the key and shooting the bolt. He may have been gouty and going a bit soft about the edges, but that doesn't mean he was going blind."

"His valet says his eyes were quite good," Lestrade said. "One of the first things I asked."

"Bravo, Inspector," Holmes said softly, and Inspector Lestrade favored him with a jaundiced glance.

"So he looked round," I said, and suddenly I could *see* it, and I supposed this was also the way with Holmes; this reconstruction which, while based only upon facts and deduction, seemed to be half a vision, "and he saw nothing but the study as it always was, empty save for himself. It is a remarkably open room, I see no closet door, and with the windows on both sides, there are no dark nooks even on such a day as this.

"Satisfied, he closed the door, turned his key, and shot the bolt. Jory would have heard him stump his way across to the desk. He would have heard the heavy thump and wheeze of the chair-cushion as his father sat down—a man in whom gout is well-advanced does not sit so much as position himself over a soft spot and then drop into it, seat-first—and then Jory would at last have risked a look out."

I glanced at Holmes. "Go on, old man," he said warmly. "You are doing splendidly. Absolutely first rate." I saw he meant it. Thousands would have called him cold, and they would not have been wrong, precisely, but he also had a large heart. Holmes simply protected it better than some men do.

"Thank you. Jory would have seen his father put his cane aside, and place the papers—the two packets of papers—on the blotter. He did not kill his father immediately, although he could have done; that's what's so gruesomely pathetic about this business, and that's why I wouldn't go into that parlour where they are for a thousand pounds. I wouldn't go in unless you and your men dragged me."

"How do you know he didn't do it immediately?" Lestrade asked.

"The scream came at least two minutes after the key was turned and the bolt drawn; I assume you have enough testimony on that to believe it. Yet it can only be seven paces from door to desk. Even for a gouty man like Lord Hull, it would have taken half a minute, forty seconds at the outside, to cross to the chair and sit down. Add fifteen seconds for him to prop his cane where you found it, and put his wills on the blotter.

"What happened then? What happened during that last minute or two, which must have seemed—to Jory Hull, at least—all but endless? I believe Lord Hull simply sat there, looking from one will to the other. Jory would have been able to tell the difference between the two easily enough; the parchment of the older would have been darker.

"He knew his father intended to throw one of them into the stove.

"I believe he waited to see which one it would be.

"There was, after all, a chance that his father was only having a cruel practical joke at his family's expense. Perhaps he would burn the new will, and put the old one back in the safe. Then he could have left the room and told his family the new will was safely put away. Do you know where it is, Lestrade? The safe?"

"Five of the books in that case swing out," Lestrade said briefly, pointing to a shelf in the library area.

"Both family and old man would have been satisfied then; the family would have known their earned inheritances were safe, and the old man would have gone to his grave believing he had perpetrated one of the cruellest practical jokes of all time . . . but he would have gone as God's victim or his own, and not Jory Hull's."

Again, that look I did not understand passed between Holmes and Lestrade.

"Myself, I rather think the old man was only savoring the moment, as a man may savor the prospect of an after-dinner drink in the middle of the afternoon or a sweet after a long period of abstinence. At any rate, the minute passed, and Lord Hull began to rise . . . but with the darker parchment in his hand, and facing the stove rather than the safe. Whatever his hopes may have been, there was no hesitation on Jory's part when the moment came. He burst from hiding, crossed the distance between the coffee-table and the desk in an instant, and plunged the knife into his father's back before he was fully up.

"I suspect the autopsy will show the thrust clipped through the heart's upper ventricle and into the lung—that would explain the quantity of blood expelled from the mouth. It also explains why Lord Hull was able to scream before he died, and that's what did for Mr. Jory Hull."

"Explain," Lestrade said.

"A locked room mystery is a bad business unless you intend to pass murder off as a case of suicide," I said, looking at Holmes. He smiled and nodded at this maxim of his. "The last thing Jory would have wanted was for things to look as they did . . . the locked room, the locked windows, the man with a knife in him where the man himself never could have put it. I think he had never forseen his father dying with such a squall. His plan was to stab him, burn the new will, riffle the desk, unlock one of the windows, and escape that way. He would have entered the house by another door, resumed his seat under the stairs, and then, when the body was finally discovered, it would have looked like robbery."

"Not to Hull's solicitor," Lestrade said.

"He might well have kept his silence," Holmes said, and then added brightly, "I'll bet Jory intended to open one of the windows and add a few tracks, too. I think we all agree it would have seemed a suspiciously convenient murder, under the circumstances, but even if the solicitor spoke up, nothing could have been *proved*."

"By screaming, Lord Hull spoiled everything," I said, "as he had been spoiling things all his life. The house was roused. Jory, probably in a panic, probably only stood there like a nit.

"It was Stephen Hull who saved the day, of course—or at least Jory's alibi, the one which had him sitting on the bench under the stairs when his father was murdered. He rushed down the hall from the music room, smashed the door open, and must have hissed for Jory to get over to the desk with him, at once, so it would look as if they had broken in toget—"

I broke off, thunderstruck. At last I understood the glances between Holmes and Lestrade. I understood what they must have seen from the moment I showed them the trick hiding place: it could not have been done alone. The killing, yes, but the rest . . .

"Stephen testified that he and Jory met at the study door," I said slowly. "That he, Stephen, burst it in and they entered together, discovered the body together. He lied. He might have done it to protect his brother, but to lie so well when one doesn't know what has happened seems . . . seems . . ."

"Impossible," Holmes said, "is the word for which you are searching, Watson."

"Then Jory and Stephen were in on it together," I said. "They planned it together . . . and in the eyes of the law, both are guilty of their father's murder! My God!"

"Not both of them, my dear Watson," Holmes said in a tone of curious gentleness. "*All* of them."

I could only gape.

He nodded. "You have shown remarkable insight this morning, Watson. For once in your life you have burned with a deductive heat I'll wager you'll never generate again. My cap is off to you, dear fellow, as it is to any man who is able to transcend his normal nature, no matter how briefly. But in one way you have remained the same dear chap as you've always been: while you understand how good people can be, you have no understanding of how black they *may* be."

I looked at him silently, almost humbly.

"Not that there was much blackness here, if half of what we've heard of Lord Hull was true," Holmes said. He rose and began to pace irritably about the study. "Who testifies that Jory was with Stephen when the door was smashed in? Jory, naturally. Stephen, naturally. But there were two others. One was William—the third brother. Am I right, Lestrade?"

"Yes. He said he was halfway down the stairs when he saw the two of them go in together, Jory a little ahead."

"How interesting!" Holmes said, eyes gleaming. "Stephen breaks in the door—as the younger and stronger of course he must—and so one would expect simple forward motion would have carried him into the room first. Yet William, halfway down the stairs, saw *Jory* enter first. Why was that, Watson?"

I could only shake my head numbly.

"Ask youself whose testimony, *and whose testimony alone*, we can trust here. The answer is the fourth witness, Lord Hull's man, Oliver Stanley. He approached the gallery railing in time to see Stephen enter the room, and that is perfectly correct, since *Stephen* was alone when he broke it in. It was *William*, with a better angle from his place on the stairs, who said he saw Jory precede Stephen into the study. William said so because he had seen Stanley and knew what he must say. It boils down to this, Watson: we know Jory was inside this room. Since both of his brothers testify he was *outside*, there was, at the very least, collusion. But as you say, the lack of confusion, the way they all pulled together so neatly, suggests something more."

"Conspiracy," I said dully.

"Yes. But, unfortunately for the Hulls, that's not all. Do you recall me asking you, Watson, if you believe that all four of them simply walked wordlessly out of that parlour in four different directions at the very moment they heard the study door locked?"

"Yes. Now I do."

"The *four* of them." He looked at Lestrade. "All four testified they were four, yes?"

"Yes."

"That includes Lady Hull. And yet we know Jory had to have been up and off the moment his father left the room; we know he was in the study when the door was locked, *yet all four—including Lady Hull*—claimed all four of them were still in the parlour when they heard the door locked. There might as well have been four hands on that dagger, Watson. The murder of Lord Hull was very much a family affair."

I was too staggered to say anything. I looked at Lestrade and saw a look on his face I had never seen before or ever did again; a kind of tired sickened gravity.

"What may they expect?" Holmes said, almost genially.

"Jory will certainly swing," Lestrade said. "Stephen will go to gaol for life. William Hull may get life, but will more likely get twenty years in Broadmoor, and there such a weakling as he will almost certainly be tortured to death by his fellows. The only difference between what awaits Jory and what awaits William is that Jory's end will be quicker and more merciful."

Holmes bent and stroked the canvas stretched between the legs of the coffee-table. It made that odd hoarse purring noise.

"Lady Hull," Lestrade went on, "would go to Beechwood Manor—more commonly known to the female inmates as Cut-Purse Palace—for five years . . . but, having met the lady, I rather suspect she will find another way out. Her husband's laudanum would be my guess."

"All because Jory Hull missed a clean strike," Holmes remarked, and sighed. "If the old man had had the common decency to die silently, all would have been well. He would, as Watson says, have left by the window. Taking his canvas with him, of course . . . not to mention his trumpery shadows. Instead, he raised the house. All the servants were in, exclaiming over the dead master. The family was in confusion. How shabby their luck was, Lestrade! How close was the constable when Stanley summoned him? Less than fifty yards, I should guess."

"He was actually on the walk," Lestrade said. "Their luck *was* shabby. He was passing, heard the scream, and turned in."

"Holmes," I said, feeling much more comfortable in my old role, "how did you know a constable was so nearby?"

"Simplicity itself, Watson. If not, the family would have shooed the servants out long enough to hide the canvas and 'shadows.' "

"Also to unlatch at least one window, I should think," Lestrade added in a voice uncustomarily quiet.

"They *could* have taken the canvas and the shadows," I said suddenly.

Holmes turned toward me. "Yes."

Lestrade raised his eyebrows.

"It came down to a choice," I said to him. "There was time enough to burn the new will or get rid of the hugger-mugger . . . this would have been just Stephen and Jory, of course, in the moments after Stephen burst in the door. They—or, if you've got the temperature of the characters right, and I suppose you do, *Stephen*—decided to burn the will and hope for the best. I suppose there was just time enough to chuck it into the stove."

Lestrade turned, looked at it, then looked back. "Only a man as black as Hull would have found strength enough to scream at the end," he said.

"Only a man as black as Hull would have required a son to kill him," Holmes returned.

He and Lestrade looked at each other, and again something passed between them, something perfectly communicated which I myself did not understand.

"Have you ever done it?" Holmes asked, as if picking up on an old conversation.

Lestrade shook his head. "Once came damned close," he said. "There was a girl involved, not her fault, not really. I came close. Yet . . . that was one."

"And these are four," Holmes returned. "Four people ill used by a foul man who should have died within six months anyway."

Now I understood.

Holmes turned his gray eyes on me. "What say you, Lestrade? Watson has solved this one, although he did not see all the ramifications. Shall we let Watson decide?"

"All right," Lestrade said gruffly. "Just be quick. I want to get out of this damned room."

Instead of answering, I bent down, picked up the felt shadows, rolled them into a ball, and put them in my coat pocket. I felt quite odd doing it: much as I had felt when in the grip of the fever which almost took my life in India.

"Capital fellow, Watson!" Holmes said. "You've solved your first case and became an accessory to murder all in the same day, and before tea-time! And here's a souvenir for myself—an original Jory Hull. I doubt it's signed, but one must be grateful for whatever the gods send us on rainy days." He used his pen-knife to loosen the glue holding the canvas to the legs of the coffee-table. He made quick work of it; less than a minute later he was slipping a narrow canvas tube into the inner pocket of his voluminous greatcoat.

"This is a dirty piece of work," Lestrade said, but he crossed to one of the windows and, after a moment's hesitation, released the locks which held it and raised it half an inch or so.

"Some is dirtier done than undone," Holmes observed. "Shall we?"

We crossed to the door. Lestrade opened it. One of the constables asked Lestrade if there was any progress.

On another occasion Lestrade might show the man the rough side of his tongue. This time he said shortly, "Looks like attempted robbery gone to something worse. I saw it at once, of course; Holmes a moment later."

"Too bad!" the other constable ventured.

"Yes, too bad," Lestrade said. "But the old man's scream sent the thief packing before he could steal anything. Carry on."

We left. The parlour door was open, but I kept my head as we passed it. Holmes looked, of course; there was no way he could not have done. It was just the way he was made. As for me, I never saw any of the family. I never wanted to.

Holmes was sneezing again. His friend was twining around his legs and miaowing blissfully. "Let me out of here," he said, and bolted.

An hour later we were back at 221B Baker Street, in much the same positions we occupied when Lestrade came driving up: Holmes in the window-seat, myself on the sofa.

"Well, Watson," Holmes said presently, "how do you think you'll sleep tonight?"

"Like a top," I said. "And you?"

"Likewise," he said. "I'm glad to be away from those damned cats, I can tell you that."

"How will Lestrade sleep, d'you think?"

Holmes looked at me and smiled. "Poorly tonight. Poorly for a week, perhaps. But then he'll be all right. Among his other talents, Lestrade has a great one for creative forgetting."

That made me laugh, and laugh hard.

"Look, Watson!" Holmes said. "Here's a sight!" I got up and went to the window, sure I would see Lestrade riding up in the waggon once more. Instead I saw the sun breaking through the clouds, bathing London in a glorious late afternoon light.

"It came out after all," Holmes said. "Tophole!" He picked up his violin and began to play, the sun strong on his face. I looked at his barometer and saw it was falling. That made me laugh so hard I had to sit down. When Holmes looked at me and asked what it was, I could only shake my head. Strange man, Holmes: I doubt if he would have understood, anyway.

THE LITERATURE
OF CRIME

The Brown Recluse

DAVIS GRUBB

THE NIGHT OF THE HUNTER (1953), the remarkable first novel by Davis Grubb (1919–1980), served as the basis for one of the great noir suspense films of all time. Invited to write the screenplay, Grubb instead wrote in-depth character sketches of the principal roles, allowing interpretation by the director, Charles Laughton, and the starring actor, Robert Mitchum. James Agee is listed as the writer of the screenplay but it was Laughton, with Grubb's profiles in hand, who deserves credit.

The novel, about a thief who finds widows in "lonely hearts" ads in newspapers, seduces them, and murders them and their children, was based on a true-life serial killer in Grubb's hometown of Moundsville, West Virginia, where the murderer was a member of one of the town's most prominent families. *The Night of the Hunter* was a finalist for the National Book Award.

Prior to the publication of his first novel, Grubb had been a painter but, afflicted with color blindness, he turned to writing for radio while producing numerous short stories for major magazines. Many of these stories later were adapted for television by Alfred Hitchcock for *Alfred Hitchcock Hour* and by Rod Sterling for *Night Gallery*.

Grubb wrote nine additional novels, none of which approached the success of *The Night of the Hunter*, but his crime drama, *Fools' Parade* (1969), was also filmed, starring James Stewart, George Kennedy, Kurt Russell, and Strother Martin.

"The Brown Recluse" was originally published in *Shadows 3*, edited by Charles L. Grant (New York, Doubleday, 1980).

THE BROWN RECLUSE

Davis Grubb

I POSSESS, AS you can see, the narrowest, smallest, most beautiful foot in the whole town of Glory.

I wear a size five and a half quadruple A, and since no Glory shoe store—and few anywhere in West Virginia, for that matter—carries my size, I have my shoes—my shoe, that is—especially crafted for me in Waltham, Massachusetts.

You see, my left leg below the knee is missing and has been from birth. And now that I have that blunt and admittedly unpleasant detail out in the open I feel well enough to continue my tale of Justice, of fog—and of murder.

Naturally, I adore this perfect right extremity of mine. And yet, having to make my way about on that one foot, with the aid of a particularly heavy orthopedic crutch made necessary by a slight curvature of the spine, this—one would suppose—might tend to make my foot heavy and calloused and broad. O, no, my dear, far from it! My five narrow little toes wink up at me every night as I draw from them my expensive French silk stocking. At night I soak my foot for hours in warm olive oil. I massage the soles and arch and ankle with Lanolin and vitamin E cream then. The result is a foot of perfection—one without callus or blemish. Each tiny nail has been lacquered with a special shade of polish blended for me exclusively by a Pittsburgh cosmetologist— the subtle flaming hue of the nasturtiums that grow in my small, old-fashioned garden. Is the association too farfetched?—the identification of myself with a flower? Yet what is a flower but beauty standing on its one leg and being swayed

and bent by the chance wind of Destiny? Should I be compared perhaps to a stork? No; with my beautiful foot, I think of myself as a blossom.

But men are cruel.

Everyone does not see me in this light.

Towns like Glory are cruel.

And so I live alone in this perfectly charming old frame house on Water Street—amid a yard overgrown with weeds and wildflowers; with tan bark walks and a spice bush and azalea and crab apple trees for jelly and Impatiens growing all around the crumbling, rococo porches.

My father willed me the property. I was an only child. My mother, Ellen, for whom I am named, died at my birth, which was difficult and which, obviously, injured me as well as her. My father was inconsolable after her death and within a year had resigned his job as Professor of Logic and Oriental Philosophy at the local Glory college.

He lived until I was nine.

I did not grieve for him, or my mother particularly, as I grew up under the austere stewardship of my father's two gaunt sisters who came to the big waterfront house to take over my care and rearing. They did little to help me through a particularly distressing adolescence; and then one of the sisters, the younger, ran away with a carnival medicine man from Chillicothe, Ohio, and the other, within a year, fell asleep after two pints of elderberry wine and drowned in my father's great Grecian bathtub.

I was nineteen, alone, and really quite well off, thanks to several oil wells which suddenly resumed production on land my father had owned downriver in Pleasant County.

And that was thirty years ago.

Forgive me while I shed my shoe. It is a hot August midday and such humidity—added to the strain of getting about—causes my foot to perspire. I must let nothing strain that exquisite member.

Look at me closely now, if you please, and tell me what you find. A rather pretty spinster nearing fifty, with striking titian hair, slender (if slightly bowed) figure, with one leg missing and at the end of the other, a foot without peer in all of Glory—perhaps in all of West Virginia.

Is that all you see?

Of course it is, since how—unless you were a mystic—could you see behind my large and rather wistful eyes a mind of absolute clarity and of extraordinary powers of ratiocination. Everyone says I inherited such brilliant powers of deduction from my father. I should somehow prefer to think they came from my mother's side of the family, though, I must confess, it is from my father that I derive my intense fascination for mystery stories in general, and for the tales of Sherlock Holmes in particular.

I seldom read mysteries anymore, even though the local Glory library has a quite good and up-to-date selection. They are so predictable. If the author plays fair and gives me the clues as he should, I can generally spot the killer by the end of page one hundred. And I sigh and go back to my father's deep, cool library bookshelves and pull down the bound *Strand* instalments of the Master's exploits. I know these tales by heart, of course, and yet I find more real mystery and suspense in them than in any of these jejune, modern exercises in deduction.

Somehow, I believe the fogs we have here in Glory, especially down here on Water Street, account for my fascination with this segment of nineteenth-century London tradition.

Slowly the river fogs creep in from our great Ohio River. The crickets and frogs down in the rushes and cattails persist for a while, after the world has grown pale and flocculent and pecu-

liarly hushed. But after a time, Mystery wins, and even they grow still.

They seem waiting, listening, watching.

For what?

One stares out the deep parlor windows and the pale lemon-damask curtains hanging there seem part of the piled mists beyond the wrinkled window panes.

Mystery is afoot.

And what *is* the world out there?

Is it truly the majestic Ohio out yonder—running deep and silent over its submerged secrets in the cunning and clandestine night? Or is it not, magically, incontrovertibly, suddenly the ancient Thames? And has not our Water Street and the end of Twelfth Street and the bricked, deserted wharf not suddenly become a fragment of London, east of Mansion House, beyond Limehouse and sinister, sleeping Soho—and those bricks gleaming with mists like black blood out there at the place where the wharf descends to the lapping shore—is not this perhaps actually a piece of London's waterfront with some satanic malevolence implicit within every shifting shadow and mist-drenched bough and glistening cobbled gutter?

Sometimes I stand in those mists, father's old blue-and-green Alpaca shawl hugged round my shoulders, and stare down the curling white phantoms in the moonlit street toward the looming black-brick dwelling, ugly beyond description, which stands at the end of Water Street at the place where the land, defoliated by the foul-breathing zinc smelter, provides its endless treasure of arrowheads and other Meso-American artifacts for summertime boys. This ugly edifice is the home of Charlie Gribble, the town banker, pillar of the community, bachelor, eccentric, sixtyish, irascible, unbending, with no single warm human virtue.

I call him the Brown Recluse. Naturally.

As you doubtless know, the Brown Recluse shares the distinction of being—along with the Black Widow—the most venomous spider in our land. It is sneaking and furtive and bites unexpectedly and is extremely lethal.

My appropriation of the name of this loathsome creature and giving it to Charlie Gribble is, as you shall see, quite natural.

Look at him pass along the misted, glistening, brick sidewalk beyond my honeysuckle and red raspberry bushes, homeward bound, his goldheaded walking stick ferrule ringing resoundingly on the stones as he hunches past in some still hour of the night after long hours at his cluttered, roll-top desk in the frosted-glass office at the bank, hours of piece-mealing painfully through reams of bank loans, mortgages, proposed foreclosures, imminent bankruptcies, corporation claims to mineral rights—the process of squeezing every last penny out of paper until the paper moans in pain.

Just see him hunker past through the mists which seem, like white spectral fingers, to clasp, cling, and then tear free of the shape of him—a veritable mortal incarnation of the Brown Recluse Spider in that particularly hideous and indescribably ugly brown Manx tweed cape he wears in every kind of weather. See how he seems to scuttle on eight legs rather than stride, like a man, on two. See how the furry, brown, venomous hulk of his shoulders in their repulsive vestiture resembles the shape of the insidious and lethal namesake. A moment later and he has scuttled off under the fog, like a Thing hiding under a stone. O, how one longs to overturn that sandstone shelter and drive the creature out into the open, into the light, where it can be seen. And crushed.

Next to money—and I am not even sure of this—the creature I have named the Brown Recluse has one obsession. And I am not sure whether or not I should not put this passion of his first. I mean, of course, his obsession with Sherlock Holmes.

I know it is difficult to imagine this miser, this money-grubber of unmitigated meanness, as the fanatic fan of the most romantic figure in perhaps all of English fiction. I used to ponder it over my solitary suppers in the pantry, when the lovely light of sundown came in golden lacy lights through the leaves beyond the kitchen window onto my mother's white linen tablecloth. Why, naturally, the Brown Recluse worshipped Sherlock Holmes. Sherlock Holmes, wiser even than Inspector Lestrade, was the absolute paradigm of proper law and order. And banking would rot without law and order. Moreover, there was in the Master's patient unraveling of the tangled skeins of proof and guilt, something close to Gribble's own patient, nitpicking perusal of a mortgage, a deed, a contract for coal or oil rights. O, how well I have named him the Brown Recluse. How patiently he would sit in the center of his mercantile web, throwing out sticky, fresh strands when necessary to entrap some poor man and then pounce, kill and suck out the last drops of some pitiful little legacy or the picayune and pathetic residue of some insurance check after hospital and funeral deductions were made. O, like Sherlock he was a patient, painstaking—and logical—man.

He was also my first and only lover.

I shan't distress you with the details of that short liaison—I don't like to dwell on it. Suffice it to say that it happened over a period of three months in the summer and early autumn of my twenty-ninth year and by Christmas—perhaps the saddest since my childhood—I had miscarried a child and almost hemorrhaged to death in the Glendale Hospital.

O, my diabolical, furry, brown darling—how well I have named you!

And you will think me perhaps strange when I tell you that the loss of my good name in Glory, the loss of my maidenhead, even the loss of my baby—these were not the facts that pinched most painfully in the end. What hurt me— what really maddened me—was the knowledge that the Brown Recluse's passion for Sherlock, the Master, had begun in this very room—over there, in the cool, dark shelves where my father's morocco-bound volumes of the *Strand* glow dully in the amber light of sundown from the stirring curtains above my ferns.

I must confess that in the last few weeks of our little interlude the Brown Recluse spent less time in my bedroom and more in that secluded, shrinelike corner of my father's library. It seemed to me at the time disquieting. I mean, I really do think of Father's books as a kind of chapel, a sort of dedicated retreat which somehow seemed more inviolable than my own body. He had no right to be down there! It seemed more of a rape than his taking of myself.

The night we parted he swinishly called me a cripple and when he left, by the side porch, scuttling off into the fog, he stole from my father's desk a silver-framed inscribed sepia photo portrait of Sir Arthur Conan Doyle himself.

In the eyes of the law it would have seemed a small thing, if even provable, and besides I was too sick that autumn to fight.

I wonder if I ever would have summoned gumption enough to fight—ever—if the Brown Recluse had not then done what he did.

The following April he—and six other Glory professional men—formed the first West Virginia chapter of the Baker Street Irregulars. Almost overnight he—this Brown Recluse—had become the county's expert, proprietor, and final arbiter of a subject so very dear to my heart—Sherlock Holmes, dear Dr. John Watson, Mrs. Hudson, Moriarity, Mycroft, and all that enchanted world of vanished, foggy, London nights. How dare he! If it hadn't been for his knowing me—if it had not been for that world I foolishly shared with him in that cool, sacred retreat of my father's bookshelves—he would not—. But wait! I have not told you the most outrageous part of all. This obscene person—this Brown Recluse—had formed a social club of other addicts to Holmesiana—and he had persuaded them *not* to admit me as a member!

How's that for cheek? Can you blame me for what followed?

Yet I won that round with the Brown Recluse, at least. Little, five-foot Harry Hornbrook and Ory Gallagher, Glory real estate partners along with Gene Voitle, the county sheriff— they had all three been students of my father at the Glory college. They had loved him. They had respected him. It was in those sunny campus autumns that Father had initiated them to

the inner sanctum of the neat little flat at 221B Baker Street. They had not forgotten.

And so they haggled, bullied, and cajoled the Brown Recluse until he had agreed to my membership.

Ory called me that night and told me the news. I was invited to the spring meeting. I was to be accepted into the organization with full rights and membership.

And pleased and victorious as I felt—how could I know that my troubles had only begun?

The fourth member of the Irregulars was Jake Bardall, who made his living as a carpenter and—in the winters—teaching manual training at Glory High School. The Irregulars had secured rooms on the third floor of the Snyder Hotel, and Jake promptly proposed that, with him and his sons doing all the work, they transform the quarters, and in particular the large front room, into an exact historical replica of the digs at 221B. It took Jake and the boys all that summer. The result was surprisingly good. Wives and sisters provided Victorian oil lamps and curtains and overstuffed turn-of-the-century chairs and a davenport from dusty attics. Abner Snyder, the hotel proprietor, raised some fuss over the bullet-hole pattern of the patriotic VR over the fireplace, but in the end, myth was master, and Ory, with an old banker's special .32, fired the initials into the golden oak mantelpiece. Gribble and the others went to work on the fine details—the hypodermic syringe and the coal scuttle and the files of cases.

And the Persian Slipper. For Sherlock Holmes's tobacco.

I don't know where the Persian Slipper came from. I never did know. I know it caught my eye at our first meeting during which we read aloud, examined, and took apart a fine Vincent Starrett—or was it Christopher Morley?—story in the style of the Canon.

It was the oddest, queerest, most beautiful slipper I had ever seen. It was made of some faded, jade-green stuff, like felt, obviously and authentically oriental. It was curled at the tip like some curious pastry, and from one end to the other it was crusted with tinted sequins and bright paste gems. O, it was so lovely! And something about the size of it caused my heart to stir—gently at first and then with a furious and almost unappeasable longing for possession. It was only a few millimeters greater in length than my foot. O, I knew I had to have the thing the moment I laid eyes on it!

My admission to the Irregulars occurred in the third year of their existence. I was not yet onto all the special rights and duties of the group—one of them, at least, downright eccentric.

I remember that night. Over on Roberts' Ridge men were working in the hay harvest, in the moonlight, and the sweet smell of slaughtered clover drifted down upon the misted river hush. It was a scent like the great cake of Creation rising in God's ovens! O, I stared across the table at which everyone was speculating on the date of the buried coins in the Musgrave Ritual (as if they were discernible!)—I stared across the glimmering lampshine at the mantelpiece. At the Persian Slipper.

Is it full of perique? I asked with a small smile. Or perhaps a nice latakia and shag cut English Burleigh?

Is what full of perique? asked the Brown Recluse in an unappeasably patronizing manner. Is what full of latakia or shag cut English Burleigh?

Why, the slipper, I said. The Persian Slipper. Isn't that where the Master keeps his pipe tobacco?

Jake Bardall intervened kindly.

Ordinarily, yes, Ms. Lathrop. Tonight being Persian Slipper Night we dumped it out. It's in that twist of paper you see beside it on the manteltop.

Slowly, irresistibly, I arose and left the doilied table and the circle of lampshine and went to the mantelpiece. O, it was so beautiful! I had never seen so lovely a slipper! Old? Of course. A little moth-eaten? Naturally. Eaten first by moths, I would guess, drawn to the halo of Aladdin's lamp in some ancient Arab midnight. Was there a sequin or a paste gem missing here or there? Of course—ripped off in some desper-

ate last moment escape by Sinbad the Sailor. O, I knew this was no stage prop, some scuffed and dusty Atlantic City souvenir donated by one of the Irregular wives or sisters. This was *the* Persian Slipper. It was the one, the only, the original Persian Slipper from the Master's mysterious and marvelous abode. Here was proof (as though any were needed!) that Sherlock Holmes had been real, actual, flesh and blood—and always would be. This had been *his* slipper.

The men were watching me curiously as I stood at this place to which, on my giant crutch, I had hobbled. They seemed to grasp the fact—yes, even the Brown Recluse seemed to know—that they were in the presence of deep human emotion. The room was still, save for the grassy whisper of the clock. Through the open window came faintly the sweetness of the slashed clover up somewhere above the fog which set its wisping, spectral fingers across the weathered sill.

Slowly I reached up and took the Persian Slipper in my fingers. My hand trembled with excitement. O, you dear, lovely, old thing. I must somehow—someday possess you.

Everyone there must have surely heard my murmur. Yes, even the Brown Recluse.

Yet no one moved, no one spoke—not even as I tucked the slipper firmly in the space between head and shoulder and hopped and scraped across the oriental carpet to the deep Morris chair where the Master might once have sat deep in a cocaine revery of Irene Adler or the abominable Dartmoor dog. I lowered myself slowly into the leather and rested my thick crutch on the carved arm. Then I reached down and slipped off my costly, but rather practical looking, five and a half quadruple A shoe. I lay it beside my stockinged foot. I wriggled my pretty painted toes in happy anticipation. Dare I do it?

I knew every eye was upon me in that moment. I did not look up.

I took the Persian Slipper out from the hollow between cheek and shoulder where I had held it and lowered it to my beautiful foot. I slipped it on. I did not stand up—O, no, this was not for walking. It was for feeling, for dreaming, for being in another time, another place. I did not look at the men. I did not look into the bilious, yellow eyes of the Brown Recluse who, even there, in the comfort of that little room, hunkered above us all in his hideous brown-tweed cape. I looked at the window—the pretty lace curtains blowing gently on either side of a potted begonia—and beyond the sill, the fog. And I knew—I mean I was quite logically convinced—that so long as the Persian Slipper so clasped my foot that I was in England—in the London of a misted metropolitan night—with street lamps glowing in the fleecy murk like Van Gogh sunflowers amid some drenching dark. And somewhere up the street, in Buckingham or Windsor, Victoria was sleeping more soundly thanks to me and Sherlock Holmes!

I tore my eyes from Fancy then and faced the five silent pairs of eyes.

It feels—O, it feels as though—as though it has always been there. On my foot. O, and did you each see my foot? Yes, you, Mister Gribble, yes, I know *you* have seen it! Did any of you ever see a lovelier foot?

I kicked my leg like a dancer, there in the lampshine. Now, there were fireflies out in the fog, but they were not really fireflies at all—they were the wink of carriage lamps on fleeing hansom cabs or glimmers of dusky, hangdog flames leaked out of dark lanterns carried by bodysnatchers and Resurrectionists from up in the Mews.

Can't you see? I said, that the Persian Slipper is really mine?

And so it may well be, said Harry Hornbrook with a kindly nod into the smoke of his Marsh Wheeling stogie. Next year.

Next year?

Why, yes, said Gene Voitle. If you win it.

Win it? I murmured. How vulgar. I don't believe I understand.

The Brown Recluse rose. He appeared more menacing, more virulent as his huge, brown-caped figure soared up out of his chair. He glowered meanly down at me.

This year, he said. It seems that I am the winner.

Winner? Will one of you be so kind as to explain?

I shall not tax you with the details of the answer which followed—nor the truly obscene ritual that ensued—save to say that in the initial year of its organization, the local chapter had voted to have an annual award—purely honorary—to the Irregular who solved a crime to have been committed by someone other than the person charged by the authorities in Glory or in the boundaries of the Ohio Valley.

As this was being explained to me (as I sat listening in disgust), the Brown Recluse came scuttling across the room, lifted the adorable slipper from my reluctant hands and replaced it on the mantelpiece after a moment of proprietary weighing of it in his own fingers.

It is not often, said Ory with a courteous nod to the sheriff, that law-enforcement officials in these times arrest the wrong person. But it does happen.

He lighted his cold bulldog brier. His friendly eyes twinkled as he regarded the sheriff.

No offense of course, Gene.

Voitle nodded and rubbed the tip of his bulbous, shiny nose.

No offense, of course, he said. But at least once a year during the last three years the law has been wrong. The Ashworth burglary three years ago, we arrested the wrong persons. The Moorhead holdup—that was another mistake. And this year we nabbed and charged those three Trentor kids for a car theft in Benwood, and again we were wrong.

He glanced appreciatively in the direction of the Brown Recluse.

But thanks to you, Charlie Gribble, Justice finally triumphed.

I don't understand, I said, though I think I was beginning to.

Simply this, Miss Lathrop, said the Brown Recluse suddenly, in that nasal voice of his which seems to penetrate and spoil every cranny of peace in a room. Every year for the past three years—since, indeed, I founded this chapter of the Baker Street Irregulars—I have proven the true author of a crime instead of the one wrongly accused.

How? I managed to gasp. You?

By the simple application of those rules of logic which your late father expounded and taught, he said. And with the methods of the Master—the great Sherlock Holmes—whom I have adored (and studied) since childhood.

I think not, I said icily. I think much more recently than that, Charlie.

Well, you are mistaken. My father had a large library of great books. He had many original Doyle manuscripts—he had the complete file of the *Strand* Holmes—he had every first edition. He even had—.

Yes, I think I know, I said, getting laboriously to my leg. He had an inscribed photograph of Doyle.

The spidery hulk wavered. A snicker of wet apology was heard.

Why, no, he said. He was never so fortunate as that. But to get on with it—I have won the Persian Slipper for two years and if my fellow members are to be believed—I am to win it again tonight.

A murmur of assent went round the group. The fog piled white as Dickens' dreams against the lacy panes and I was in the midst of a vanished England.

For a year, I said, nervously. You possess it for a year.

A year is the limit, said Ory. Unless—well, we've never been faced with *this* one.

What is that? I asked, my curiosity insatiable now.

The solving of one kind of case, said Harry Hornbrook. By one of the Irregulars—would mean that he could keep the Persian Slipper in perpetuity.

And what sort of case might that be?

Something, luckily, we haven't had to deal with in this fine little community, observed Sheriff Voitle.

I ask what it is—this special crime—to bring so special a reward for solving.

Murder.

Did you say murder?

Yes, murder. Any member who solves a murder is, at the next meeting, awarded the Persian Slipper.

To—to keep?

In perpetuity, said Harry then.

I don't mean to discourage you, ma'am, said Ory, but we got a pretty clever sheriff here. And we have Charlie Gribble.

Yes, I said, in a voice I struggled to steady. I know you have him. The Brown—

It came out despite myself.

—the Brown Recluse.

What did you say, my dear? asked Harry Hornbrook.

I said you must excuse me, I stammered, and scraped and hobbled to the door. I shan't stay for the award. I shall pass this meeting entirely by, I think, gentlemen. I have the most unremitting headache in years.

And I was gone from them—into the fogs of that London night, along the sacred Thames, along my lovely old Ohio.

The next three years passed by in dreary progression. A horse theft the first year and the true thief unveiled got the Brown Recluse the treasured Slipper award. The second year vandals broke into the Bowser Feed Company and stole six hundred pounds of chicken mash. Again the Brown Recluse got the honor. And the slipper. The third year he won it for locating another stolen car.

Stolen cars, horse thieves, chicken feed!

What a farce it was!

And the lovely Persian Slipper showing a little more wear, a little more age, a sequin missing here or there as the relentless years unfolded.

I determined one chilly September night in that last year that this should end. Abruptly. I had worked hard on all the cases in question. To tell the truth, all of the members were as eager to help me win the award as I was—I think they knew it meant something special to me. They seemed to relinquish all personal ambitions to possess it. But each year—though I did my homework faithfully (and, as nearly as possible, following the Master's methods)—the Persian Slipper went to the Brown Recluse.

Damn him!

I knew that cold September night that this spider must be crushed.

Forever.

I resolved that the Brown Recluse should be dead before morning.

I am not one of your modern cynics writing now in the mode so prevalent that dwells with obsessive and feverish particulars on acts of violence. So I shall be terse.

There is a venerable and gigantic elm at the corner, beyond the single street lamp, at Water Street and Twelfth. The tree is thought to be some six or seven hundred years old, and its great roots have thrust tough fingers under the brick sidewalk, giving it a lovely tilt and bulge and ripple. In the fog, with the feathered luminescence of the street lamp behind it, it looks like some enormous Druid priest—presiding over some mossy, sacred ritual.

It was behind this tree that I waited that biting September night. From where I leaned, I could scarcely make out the shape of my house, though I could distinguish the guttering candle flame in the window of the little fruit and vegetable storage room off the pantry.

I was frightened, but I was determined.

It was perhaps ten-thirty. I kept my eyes fixed, piercing as best they could the scarcely penetrable fog which lay on the land toward the center of town. Every light was a golden spider sending out myriad, shimmering strands to form, in each pocket of dark, a golden web. But the spider for which I waited was not golden. I had taken my crutch from the pit of my arm and braced myself securely against the great, ancient tree. Somewhere out on the river voices drifted from boys in skiffs, out gigging frogs. A dog barked, muffled, secret, beyond the mist. I faced up Twelfth Street, the direction from which he would come from the Bank. At the very moment when the town clock struck eleven in the tower of the courthouse somewhere up in the submerged village, I heard those footsteps. Foot-

steps and the unmistakable chink of the steel ferrule of the golden-headed walking stick as he struck it ahead of him along the rippled brick sidewalk. But, heavens—he was coming *from* the house, not *toward* it. He had gotten home early, it would seem, and now was returning to the bank for some late work—those dreary mercantile schemes which seem to occupy his professional life, at least.

If you ponder a moment, you will realize that I was on the wrong side of the tree for him not to glimpse me before I struck. He was far, far stronger than I—stronger than some men, I should wager—and I knew if he saw me with my heavy crutch raised he would fend away my blow easily and successfully ward it off. I could not permit that to happen.

With an effort so great that it tore at my very breath I scrambled around the half circumference of the huge tree trunk and stationed myself on the other side—and not a moment too soon.

He was almost opposite me now. I must wait until that split moment when he is past, yet not too far past, out of eyeshot, at least, but within striking distance. The moment arrived and I harvested it well.

I have not yet mentioned the strength in my right shoulder and arm with which almost forty-nine years of crutching myself about have endowed me. On that side I am quite powerful.

I shall never forget that moment. The street lamp like a blinding, baleful moon above us both. He—in that split instant with his back to me—that hated back, the dirty glow of the bilious brown-tweed cape below the scraggled hair and not very clean collar and raddled, fat neck. It was at this target that now, with all my mortal power, I aimed and swung the crutch.

The Circle of Willis, the poets call it. And the doctors. That area of cranial excellence and all living movement—the base of the skull above the nape. I felt the metal of the crutch standard strike and I felt something crunch and I heard an almost mindless gasp—a sound that seemed to have been an afterthought to dying. Without another noise the hideous victim slumped heavily to the glistening brick pavement.

And fitting the armpiece of the crutch back under my arm I hobbled slowly, remorselessly, and feeling wholly at peace with myself, toward the light in the pantry window.

I had a slender stemmed glass of Muscadet Bordeaux from a bottle my father had left in his small liquor cabinet in the library. I sat a long while in the dark of the parlor. My thoughts were as slow and grave as the procession of numerals on a clock face. My mind was entirely in order. Except for one thought—a fancy, at first, and then presently an obsession.

I thought I should now never possess the Persian Slipper. I thought the ghost of the Brown Recluse—the avenging shade named Charlie Gribble—would come back from the dead and announce (after much showy pretense of deduction) his own murderer. And in perpetuity—even if in Death—possess the adorable award. The more I thought of it the more I trembled. Even at this moment, it seemed, the ghost of the man I had murdered was pacing the sterile linoleum of his bedroom, pondering the solution to this latest and most intriguing of crimes—and then pointing his phosphorescent finger of accusations—quite accurately—at me!

Damn him!

I hobbled to the phone and sank onto the Ottoman beside it. I laid down my crutch (quite unstained by its recent fatal contact) and picked up the phone and dialed his number. O, yes I knew it. I would never forget it—a memory of the nights when—full of his child—I had frantically called and called to a phone which was off the hook or not answered at all.

I listened to the distant drone of the ring—somehow seeming a little fainter because of the fog against the windows.

Again it rang.

And again.

And seven times more. And I sat thinking myself quite mad and quite a silly fool to be sending those rings echoing through a house in which there was no one to answer. The eighth ring.

What kind of little play are you acting out inside yourself, dear Ellen Lathrop? I heard a voice murmur—not unkindly—inside my head.

And then the distant receiver was picked up.

O, I could hear the aching silence of that fog-bound bedroom in the receiver at my ear.

I could hear a breathing in the phone, too. But whose? In God's name whose? Tell me quickly before I am struck mad forever!

When the voice spoke I fell back in the chair in a half faint.

It was he. Yes, it was his voice. Charlie Gribble. The Brown Recluse.

And, to my even greater horror and dismay, he seemed, for the first time in years, quite affable and even talkative.

Ellen, he said. How nice it is to hear you. How are you. For some curious reason I was thinking about you a quarter hour or so ago. I meant to call you.

Are you—are you all right?

Not really, he said then, in fateful, unmistakable words of doom, though unawares of that. I'm concerned. Jim Smitherman, a colleague of mine from Wheeling, has been here for supper and we've been working since then on those old Bow Chemical mineral right suits you may have read about in the Glory *Argus*. Well, it was warm this afternoon when we came home from the bank (Why had I not seen them!) and Jim left his coat in my office. Around ten I asked for a file of documents Jim had brought down with him. It wasn't here. Obviously, Jim had left it at the bank. Jim knew exactly where the file was and offered to go back for it. By then this plagued river weather had changed and the fog was up and it was chilly. Damned chilly. I loaned Jim something to wear and he took it and left, and it's been an hour and he's not back yet.

I began to laugh then. O, I caught it in time, but I am sure he distinctly heard my laugh. And then I said some things I can't quite remember and hung up. Somehow I made it to bed and took some Veronal and slept—astonishingly untormented by the dream of having killed the wrong person.

At daybreak the chain reaction of certain incredible and astonishing events began. I settled down in father's cool library—like a forest cover of ancient oaks—with a bottle of Yardley's Smelling Salts and a box of Kleenex for my tears until sunrise.

Soon the fog would burn off—roll away and wisp away like the departing ghosts of some long white night. Morning sun would filter through the high canopy of maples and sycamores and elms and spin gold coins on the glowing green lawn. Sun motes and dandelions would intermingle there. I stared out through the front window, beyond the tiny statue of Michelangelo's "David" which father always kept there on the deep, white sill. Every morning I sat and stared there at a certain inevitable, unvarying matutinal event that would take place. It would happen almost simultaneously with the striking of father's old Dutch clock. I watched. I waited. Yes, here he came—weaving and stumbling along the uneven brick path: even on this fatal, fateful morning here he came—Ort Holliday, the town drunk, making his way home at sunrise with a skinful of cheap corncob wine or some foul, resinous bootleg distillation.

He was rounding Twelfth Street now and making his way unsteadily to the left and up Water Street toward my house, toward—yes, toward the gigantic old elm beneath which lay, on the wet, glittering bricks—

I watched, enthralled, rapt in suspense as he came closer. He stumbled once where the sidewalk tilted up suddenly and then steadied himself against Mart Brown's big willow and came on, past the street lamp now competing dismally with the misty, yet powerful sun. On and on. Stumbled, staggered, and leaned. And on.

I thought foolishly for a moment he was going to stumble on the body or that he would somehow stagger around it, seeing it but fancying it was merely a sample of the delirium that was waiting for him in his little shack down below the zinc smelter where Water Street dwindles out and is lost amid mesamerican memories. Surely, he had seen it by now! Good God, he

has passed it. No. No, he hasn't. He has seen it. He rubs his eyes, his swollen, sweating face. He stares again. He stoops unsteadily to have a better look. A cunning look replaces the fear on his face. He smiles tipsily, looks around to see if anyone may be watching at this strange prebreakfast hour when only coal miners and drunks are up and about. He pauses, his right hand poised unsteadily like the bill of a robin about to pounce on a worm. Now he makes his move. Swiftly the dirty hand darts down and under the dirty tweed cape, the inner jacket pocket, the inside pocket. The purse is in his hands now as he greedily snaps it open, plucks out a rather thick wad of bills, and without counting them stuffs them into his own coat pocket from which peeps the stained corner of a dirty bandanna. He rises, smiling, his raddled, smeary face working in slow emotion as he tries to persuade himself that his fortune is real. He seems curious as to how his obliging victim died. He leans again—almost as if suddenly sober, almost as though arranging things not as they are but as they should be.

Yes, yes, he nods to himself. Yes, yes.

His gray lips working wetly.

He stoops then and picks up a loose, mossy brick at the edge of the stacked, ornamental pavement. He sees blood on it—blood which has coiled oily across the walk from the wound somewhere up under the huddled, staring head.

He is standing there, the victim's purse already in his pocket, a brick smeared with gouts of the victim's own blood in his right hand, a memoryless vacant smile on his dissipated face—yes, standing there so when Sheriff Voitle and his deputy, on a last tour before shift change, came round the corner of Twelfth and Water Street in their Plymouth cruiser.

He was, of course, arrested, advised of his rights, arraigned and locked up in the Apple County jail.

I did something that morning and afternoon I have never done in my life. I went to father's little wine cabinet with its little brass key which chirps like a golden bird in the lock when you turn it. I saw that only one bottle of father's wine was left—the Bordeaux. So I selected one I had purchased and put there five years before—a perfectly delectable 1971 Château Calon-Ségur, Saint-Estèphe.

I drank all that morning. I drank past lunch while all around me Glory buzzed and whispered over the murder within its sacrosanct city limits. I drank until—at four that afternoon—I suddenly realized that the phone was ringing and had been ringing for, perhaps, two or three minutes. I did not stagger. I think, perhaps, that it is, moreover, quite impossible to stagger on one leg. I made my way quite steadily to the phone and picked it up.

It was he—the unspeakable—the dark, the dreary, the intended dead—the Brown Recluse.

I suppose you've heard, he said.

About the murder? Yes.

I was pleased and delighted at how carefully and distinctly my voice sounded. I was really quite drunk, you see, and I somehow believe that the adrenaline already in me from the excitement of the night had counteracted the wine. I had never spoken more distinctly.

I don't suppose you saw anything, Ellen, he said then. You're generally up and about at the time the murder took place. Sitting in the ladder-back chair in your father's library. At the window.

How well, I said, you remember all my night habits, Charlie.

Don't be unpleasant, Ellen, he said. Besides I didn't call you about that.

What then?

There's to be a special meeting of the Irregulars tonight at sundown. I think you might like to attend.

I was silent a moment.

What is the occasion? No meeting was scheduled until the fall meeting in October.

The occasion, he said, is the awarding of the Persian Slipper. This time in perpetuity.

To whom? Gene Voitle, I suppose. He solved the crime, I am told.

That's the plan, he said.

Well, what a windfall for Gene, I said. I mean he didn't really have to do any real detection.

Not in the manner of the Master. He just happened round the corner and his two eyes saw Ort Holliday standing there, the brick in his hand, the purse in his pocket.

That is why he is not going to be awarded the Persian Slipper.

Oh?

Well, wait, Ellen. Be at the meeting tonight. I don't want to spoil my denouement to this strange series of events. Be at the meeting. At sundown.

I shall be at the hotel at six at the latest, I said.

O, no, said the Brown Recluse. Not at the hotel.

What do you mean?

I mean this session of the Baker Street Irregulars isn't going to be held at 221B.

Where then?

Why, in front of your house, Ellen, as a matter of fact. At the scene of the murder.

Why there? I whispered.

Because it is there, said the Brown Recluse, that I am going to demonstrate that Ort Holliday did not—and could not possibly—have murdered Jim Smitherman.

Oh? How? Who then—?

You always were impatient, Ellen. A probing, curious mind, you have.

You *know* then?

Of course, I know.

I mean, you know who really murdered your friend?

I do, he said. And I shall prove it. At the big elm which grows in front of your house, Ellen. At tonight's emergency meeting of our dedicated little group.

My mouth opened but the words wouldn't work. I suddenly felt a severe headache. From the wine. From the pressure which seemed to be tightening, like a silver band, around my perspiring brow. From I knew not what.

Are you there, Ellen?

Yes. Yes. Yes, I'll be there. At six, I cried out and slammed down the receiver.

So he knew. How could he know? Had he anticipated such a crime and followed Smitherman's progress through the thick white night?

Nonsense. Had he set the whole thing up to trap me?—knowing I would mistake the brown cloaked figure and—O, I must pull myself together. These are chimeras, unbelievable and impossible conjectures.

I drank coffee. Mother's old blue-speckled coffee pot steamed and puffed all the remainder of that afternoon. As I drank the coffee and smoked cigarette after cigarette (I seldom smoke) a curious and aery self-assurance seemed to overcome me.

By five-thirty I was ready for whatever came. I think I was even quite sensibly resigned to this ultimate victory of the Brown Recluse—his winning of the coveted Persian Slipper in perpetuity. O, it stung. It hurt. I shall not deny that. But I tell you I felt in absolute possession of myself as the sun sank lower over the river, over the stained Ohio Hills, and six o'clock approached. Even the realization that my crime would be exposed and that he and not I would come into eternal possession of that yearned for possession—well, my mind seemed to stop at the threshold of that realization and to refuse to accept it. Somehow, this detestable Brown Recluse should not be so smiled on by Goddess Fortune.

The sun was low on the mine tipple across the great river when we began to gather. There was a chill in the air, as there had been the night before. I had bathed and massaged my foot in its special emollient cream for half an hour. I wore my black silk dress, black stocking, black shoe. I wore my grandmother's black onyx pendant on its tiny platinum chain. I wore my mother's good quarter-length beaver jacket—as soft and fresh as the day she put it in the cedar chest the afternoon of her death. I put a dab of mother's favorite perfume (and mine—Christmas Night by Houbigant) behind each ear and on the instep of my pretty, pretty foot. I gave my shoe a little shine. Then I came out—rather regally, I think—and made my way down the tanbark path toward the brick sidewalk, under the enormous and venerable tree, where the rest of the Irregulars were awaiting me.

Gene Voitle, his big gun clinging to his hip, looked vainglorious and a little defiant. He looked as determined as the Brown Recluse to win that precious award. I smiled. I knew that my expression betrayed nothing. And I was thankful for that, because the Brown Recluse never once took his beady, spidery eyes off my face, as the meeting began.

I don't know what this is all about, grumbled the sheriff. I don't know how there could be any more incriminating evidence than to find a man at the scene of a cold-blooded murder with the fatal weapon in his hand.

But the brick did not kill Jim Smitherman, said the Brown Recluse. Ort Holliday merely discovered the body and being the cut of man that he is and being, moreover, blind drunk, stole the dead man's wallet. Corpse robbing is, of course, a felony. But it is not the felony of first-degree murder, gentlemen.

And Ms. Lathrop. May I remind you I am here. And that I am not a gentleman, Charlie.

Forgive me, Ellen, he said with ungracious politeness. I had not forgotten your presence here. Oh, far from it.

The wind stirred the long, lovely willow fronds down by the landing where the river lapped on the old stones of the now deserted wharf. For a moment I dreamed one of the old steamboats—lovely as a white-clad bride—was feeling her way in for a landing. Sun motes danced like spinning gold pieces in the high grass and clinging, thick green moss on the brick pavement. The wind blew—that cold September wind. Soon the fog would be up— soon it would claim all, everything, the town, the world, in its white embrace—like a lover taking all from a lover, owning the clasped white earth. Soon it would be London out here where we stood and footpads and cut-purses would dart amid the moonstruck and radiant woolly world. Down yonder where the dark water lapped would not be the Glory wharf—it would be Shadwell Stair and the stair named Wapping Old. And the white queen sleeps more soundly in her Windsor bed because of the Master. And because of me.

Now, said the Brown Recluse. Let us stop this child's play, gentlemen. And—and dear Ellen.

Let us show who really murdered James Arthur Smitherman quite early this morning.

I spoke recklessly then.

Charlie Gribble, I said, in a level voice devoid of all the bitterness I might well have been justified in showing. Charlie, I guess this is the happiest moment of your life.

He pondered this.

Oddly enough, he said, it is one of the most uncomfortable. Even though I shall gladly accept and treasure forever the result of it. No, Ellen, it is quite a sad occasion, really.

In what way, sir?

Because it involves my proving that the real murderer was not Ort Holliday as Gene proposes, he said, but that it was someone much closer to us.

Closer? How?

One of us, he said, almost in a whisper, his little glass eyes fixed on mine, a faint smile whispering round his thin, gray lips. One of the Baker Street Irregulars is the murderer.

Oh, really, now, blurted two or three of the group at once. Come on now, Charlie. That's a little thick to cut. Who? Which one?

I'll get to that, said the Brown Recluse, strutting back and forth across the blood-stained bricks like some barnyard tyrant, crowing as he went. First though we must establish motive.

Well, the motive was plain enough, said the sheriff then. Robbery. The defendant already had the victim's wallet in his pocket when he was apprehended. With the murder weapon in his hand.

Again I say that was not the murder weapon, said the Brown Recluse.

I stared at him. He was not wearing the bilious brown tweed cape. That, I supposed, had gone to Empire Cleaners, with an admonition to return it to him in pristine, unstained state. Now he shivered in a shabby little Aquascutum trench coat, quite a few sizes too small. He strutted some more, picked his gold tooth, and inspected a particle of food on the end of it. He flicked it into the gold-dappled grass beside the bricks.

The blood on that brick was dry, he said. Already several hours old. For reasons known only to Holliday he picked the brick up—already clotted with the considerable flow from the deceased's wounds a few feet away. The blood was dry, I say. Clearly Holliday arrived at the scene of the crime a full two hours after it took place. Now are you asking us to suppose that he committed the crime say around four in the morning and then stood there till six with the bloody brick in his hand and the victim's purse in his coat—waiting until Gene yonder could chance upon him? I say that is sheer nonsense, gentlemen—Ellen.

O, he was so patronizing when he said my name. And yet I felt that wine of assurance warm in my veins. Somehow I should win. You see the key to the murder—to any murder—is the establishment of the strongest motive.

What was the motive, Charlie? asked Ory then. If it wasn't greed.

Oh, it was greed all right, said the Brown Recluse. But it wasn't the greed of a simple-minded drunkard for a purse containing forty—maybe fifty dollars and a few coins. It was a much greater greed.

Everyone waited. No one spoke.

The evidence of how great that greed is, he went on, is provided by the absence here this evening of one of our charter members.

I cocked my brow. What was happening here? My mind ransacked all possibilities. What was the repulsive creature getting at? O, I was more determined than ever that he should not possess my treasure. Yes, it had always been mine, I thought in that instant.

And everyone was looking around to see who was missing. Gene Voitle was there. I was there. Gribble was there. Jake Bardall, the carpenter, was there. Ory looked uncomfortable.

He cleared his throat.

Harry Hornbrook, he said. I know he'd be sorry to miss this meeting. I mean, a special meeting like this.

Where is Harry? Where is your real estate partner, Ory?

He went to Wheeling early this morning, Ory said. Took a plane to Pittsburgh. Planed out of there for Washington.

Tell us, Ory, said the Brown Recluse, strutting all the more, his pale, hairy wrists jutting out of the undersized trenchcoat like naked chicken bones. Tell us, he said, like some pop-injay of a small-town prosecuting attorney, why Harry said he was going to Washington.

Why to fight Bow Chemical's mineral rights contract—they bought up hundreds of them last year—to take over his coal lands.

Tell me, Sheriff Voitle, said the Brown Recluse then, would you have any idea where the original deeds for those mineral rights might be?

No, Charlie, I don't.

Perhaps I can inform you, said the Brown Recluse, like some shyster in a thirties movie, that until the murder in the early hours in this September morning, those original contracts—the sole arbitrating fulcrum for any claims in this case—these were in Jim Smitherman's briefcase.

Charlie, that's not so. I gave those contracts to Harry to take to Washington. You must know that.

You did not, said the Brown Recluse, and I knew when he was lying. (When a man lies to a woman in love she can forever spot a lie in that person's mouth.) He was rigging this, the fiend. He was setting up Harry Hornbrook—just so he could claim the Persian Slipper.

You know Harry has those mineral right deeds, said Ory, red-faced and perplexed before this array of unreason. He had to have them to show to the government boys. To make his claim.

I remember sending Jim back to the bank for them, said the Brown Recluse. He was return-ing with them—through the foggy town—when Harry struck. Struck and took the deeds. And flew the coop.

Ory picked his nose and then flickered his fingers nervously.

By God, Charlie, he said, you'd do anything to win that damned old Arabian nights shoe. Even betray a friend.

Respect for law and order, said the Brown Recluse, goes deeper than friendship. The Mas-ter would agree, I think.

Nobody said anything. Nobody argued.

But I knew, I think we all knew that Charlie Gribble was not through.

Relentlessly, he went on, building his vicious and preposterous case against the poor real es-tate partner. I had earlier noticed the bulge in the tawdry, tight little trench coat. Now his spidery fingers dove into this pocket and took out something round and perhaps four inches in diameter wrapped in a white, though blood-stained, handkerchief.

This, he announced pretentiously, is the murder weapon. I found it a few moments ago under those leaves and moss by the tree.

What is it, Charlie? asked the sheriff drawing near and scratching the back of his neck.

It is a glass paperweight, said the Brown Recluse. Affixed to the bottom of it so that it can be read easily is a printed advertisement for a Glory firm. It is a promotional give-away.

Which one, Charlie? the sheriff asked. Which company?

A real estate firm, it so happens, drawled the dreadful little spiderman. One quite prominent locally.

He cleared his throat in the manner of a bad actor.

The firm of Hornbrook and Gallagher, he said then.

Again all was still save for the wind and the rustle of the dear old tree. I was fascinated, as though watching the filming of something pre-recorded and all stacked up by whatever Fates there be. I felt a little giddy.

This paperweight was the weapon that killed Jim, said the Brown Recluse then. There is blood on it. And even a few hairs. And—

Oh, how dare you perpetrate this unbeliev-able folly! I blurted. You with your widely known shares in every chemical plant between Weirton and Nitro. You—a millionaire in chemical plants. Bow, I am sure, among them. You want that land for Bow, damn you, you—you Brown Recluse!

Ellen, control yourself, he stammered in a faint, scared voice. You shan't snatch this mo-ment of glory from me now.

I shall—damn you. And I shall snatch with the fingers of Truth!

But Harry Hornbrook's fingerprints are on this paperweight, dear lady. Can that be contro-verted?

Ory Gallagher was standing tensed, half crouching.

Every one of those paperweights has Harry's prints on them, for God's sake, Charlie. He distributed them. Mailed them out personally.

But the blood. The blood, my dear fellow, snapped the Brown Recluse, and I swear his voice had assumed a kind of fake Englishness. As the Master would say in this case, Elementary, my dear Gallagher.

Oh, this was unspeakable. Absolutely detestable.

He had trumped the whole thing up, this greed-head, in the hopes of causing Harry to lose his deed claim with the powerful chemical combine. And to win, as a kind of lagniappe, the lovely Persian Slipper.

I think, I said, that it is time that the woman's voice be heard, gentlemen.

I hobbled forward and stood swaying amid lovely beams of a sun which burned all the more fiercely as it declined behind a stripped-out hill. The wind blew and stirred my curls across my cheek.

My soul made choices in that instant.

In the manner of the Master, I announced with a modest lilt to my voice, I shall now demonstrate the true manner in which this crime was perpetrated.

I stared across the grass where the Brown Recluse stood, and I stared into the space six inches above his head, putting him forever beneath my regard.

In the first place, I said, we all know that he yonder wants those mineral rights for Bow Chemical. He is therefore prejudiced. He is also stupid—for the blood and hair on the paperweight will probably, under examination, prove to be the blood of one of his own Rhode Island red stewing hens. Establishing that, I shall continue.

Harry Hornbrook is a small man, I said. The deceased was a large man. I do not believe that Harry Hornbrook could have reached high enough to get a proper swing to deliver the fatal blow.

I hobbled around the dear old tree and stared at the empty case of a locust. Blessed creature, you have escaped and flown away into the moon.

I plucked it loose and watched it fall to the moss at the base of the tree. I smiled.

How could you, Charlie Gribble—how could you, Sheriff Voitle—be so blind as to have missed *this*?

They all gathered round.

This footprint, I said. In the sweet, thick moss which grows here. It is so clear. It is unmistakable.

The sheriff stooped and stared. Presently he nodded.

It is like the print of a child, he whispered. A child—maybe ten, eleven. Such a tiny shoe.

Oh, yes, I breathed. Do observe how small. In fact—I smiled over their heads. The sun still clung—a bright, striving crumb of fire upon the mine tipple across the already fog-wisping river—I think if you measure the print, sheriff, you will find it was made by a size five and a half quadruple A.

That's amazingly narrow, amazingly small, said Jake Bardall, who sold shoes on a commission mail-order business.

Oh, thank you—thank you, I said.

The thought seemed to strike everyone at once for at least three of them asked it.

Where is the other print? they chorused.

The wind blew so sweetly. O, I felt as if I could dance—dance—if only something soft and green, jade green, with sequins and paste gems were only clasping my dear little foot.

There was none, I said. The murder was committed by a one-legged person—quite strong in the shoulder and arm of the good side, as most such lame people are—and this one-legged person, to judge from the impression of the shoe in the moss, was probably a woman. Surely, no man would wear so small—so delicate—so petite a shoe.

Drawn by the sundown scents of frying steak in river-front pantries, a small brown dog came trotting past along the bricks and disappeared across Twelfth.

The murder weapon was metal, of considerable more weight than the piece of glass that the Brown—that Charlie Gribble has offered as exhibit A. No, this weapon—I leaned against the great, comforting tree and waved my crutch at them—this weapon, I said, was metal and tubular and of great weight. In fact, I went on, I believe this crutch of mine will, upon examination, prove to exactly fit the wound.

The dog barked at the screen door. Steaks and homefries and wilted-lettuce and gravy haunted the river wind.

No one spoke. I broke the silence.

Gentlemen, I said, I have given you your murderer. I have not confessed—I have irrefutably demonstrated. In the method of the canon—the technique of the Master.

I paused like a happy child about to leap a crying, country brook.

May I have the Persian Slipper? I whispered almost coquettishly. In perpetuity now.

The screen door slammed. But the supper sweetness dreamed sweetly on the wind and I could smell my azalea, too.

Yes, snapped the Brown Recluse. It's up in the hotel. At what used to be 221B. On the mantel.

Will you get it for me?

No, damn you. Get it for yourself.

My progress from the big elm and up the town that sundown evening is legend now. A dozen feet behind me purred Ory's Plymouth cruiser. Lord, did they think I'd make a run for it? It took me one hour and fifteen minutes. Word spread fast. Kids and old people, too, came out on porches and stared over iced-tea glasses at a middle-aged cripple slowly hobbling up brick sidewalks toward her freedom. Oh, the poor fools. Didn't they know I had won—won, at last?

The hardest part was making it up three flights of those hotel steps. And the long hallway with a door open and a poor young colored maid making up a room. I got there at last. I took the Persian Slipper down from its resting place on the mantel, under the patriotic VR. I sank into the Morris chair and, after a long spell, while all of them stood in the hall watching and craning their necks to see, I slipped my expensive hand-lasted shoe off my lovely foot. I wriggled my toes in the almost dark. I put on the Persian Slipper.

A strange thing has happened in the year since that night. I am sitting alone in my little room in a khaki, state uniform. The walls of the room are brown. Everything visible is some shade of brown. There is even a brownish cast to the beams of sunlight that manage to poke through my small window. Perhaps I am brown now, too—I have no mirror here. Only one spot of color blazes like a jewel in that dustbin of a place. Jade-green felt that curls into a cornucopia at the end, like a sweet, subtle pastry; bright sequins of lavender and mauve and cosmos blue, a glitter as of rubies and amethysts from the little gems of paste.

And I am free! No longer am I a flower pinned to earth on one leg—a stork incapable of delivering real babies. I am free. And that's because the Persian Slipper is touched with enchantment and makes it be London out there when the fog comes up. When the fog comes up and makes it be Soho and Limehouse in all that fleecy Dickens world of night. Because you see with my marvelous Persian Slipper I can browse and wander through that strip of Thames just east of Mansion House. And every night—when the fog is up—you'll find me there. If you look.

O, do come looking—do find me in that fog some night!

We can sit till morning and tell each other tales of Sherlock Holmes so wondrous that even he will not believe!

Or, if you prefer, we'll go to haunt a spider.

Poor Charlie Gribble. No one believes him when he tells them he's shrinking.

The Darkwater Hall Mystery

KINGSLEY AMIS

OF THE MANY elements of a full life for which Sir Kingsley William Amis (1922–1995) is famous, drinking may well head the list, though womanizing doesn't trail by very much. The fact that he may be the leading British humorist of the second half of the twentieth century should not be forgotten, however, nor his rank (by the London *Times*) as the ninth greatest British writer since World War II.

He was a bestselling novelist with more than two dozen books to his credit, including the first, *Lucky Jim* (1954), which made a great impact both critically and with more than respectable international sales. While regarded as one of the Grand Old Men of British letters late in life, famous as one of the great satiric writers of the twentieth century, he also was a great aficionado of popular fiction, especially mystery fiction and even more especially James Bond. He wrote *Colonel Sun* (1968), a Bond novel, under the pseudonym Robert Markham, and two nonfiction books about 007: *The James Bond Dossier* (1965) and *The Book of Bond, or Every Man His Own 007* (1965) under the pseudonym Lt.-Col. William ("Bill") Tanner. Other mystery novels written under his own name are *The Anti-Death League* (1966), *The Riverside Villas Murder* (1973), *Russian Hide-and-Seek* (1980), and *The Crime of the Century* (1987).

"The Darkwater Hall Mystery" was first published in the May 1978 issue of *Playboy*; it was first published in book form in a chapbook, *The Darkwater Hall Mystery* (Edinburgh, Tragara Press, 1978). Its first commercial book publication was in *Collected Short Stories* (London, Hutchinson, 1980).

THE DARKWATER HALL MYSTERY

Kingsley Amis

ON CONSULTING MY notes, their paper grown yellow and their ink brown with the passage of almost forty years, I find it to have been in the closing days of July, 1885, that my friend Sherlock Holmes fell victim, more completely perhaps than at any other time, to the innate melancholy of his temperament. The circumstances were not propitious. London was stiflingly hot, without a drop of rain to lay the dust which, at intervals, a damp wind swept up Baker Street. The exertions caused Holmes by the affair of the Wallace-Bardwell portfolio, and the subsequent entrapment of the elusive Count Varga, had taken their toll of him. His grey eyes, always sharp and piercing, acquired a positively hectic brightness, and the thinness of his hawk-like nose seemed accentuated. He smoked incessantly, getting through an ounce or more of heavy shag tobacco in a single day.

As his depression became blacker, he would sit in his purple dressing-gown with his fiddle across his knee and draw from it strange harmonies, sometimes sonorous, sometimes puzzling, more often harsh and disagreeable. Strange too, and quite as disagreeable, were the odours given off by his chemical experiments; I did not inquire their purpose. When he brought out his hair-trigger pistol and proceeded to add elaborate serifs to the patriotic V.R. done in bullet-pocks in the wall opposite his arm-chair, my impatience and my concern together dictated action. Nothing short of a complete rest, in conditions of comfort and ease such as I could not possibly provide, would restore my friend

to health. I moved swiftly; telegrams were exchanged; within little more than twelve hours Sherlock Holmes was on his way to Hurlstone in Sussex, the seat of that Reginald Musgrave whose family treasures he had so brilliantly rediscovered some five years earlier. Thus it was that events conspired to embroil me in what I must describe as a truly singular adventure.

It came about in the following fashion. That same afternoon, I had just returned from visiting a patient when the housekeeper announced the arrival of a Lady Fairfax. The name at once stirred something in my memory, but I had had no time to apprehend it before my visitor had crossed the threshold of the sitting-room. There entered a blonde young woman of the most unusual beauty and distinction of feature. I was at once aware in her of a discomposure obviously not at all derived from the sweltering weather, to which indeed her bearing proclaimed utter indifference. I encouraged this lovely but troubled creature to be seated and to divulge her purpose.

"It was Mr. Sherlock Holmes whom I came to see, but I understand he has gone away and is not expected back for a fortnight," she began.

"That is so."

"Can he not be recalled?"

I shook my head. "Quite out of the question."

"But I come on a matter of the utmost urgency. A life is in danger."

"Lady Fairfax," said I, "Holmes has been overworking and must have rest and a change of air. I speak not only as his friend but as his physician. I fear I cannot be influenced by any other consideration."

The lady sighed and lowered her gaze into her lap. "May I at least acquaint you with the main facts of the matter?"

"Do so by all means, if you feel it will be of service to you."

"Very well. My husband is Sir Harry Fairfax, the sixth baronet, of Darkwater Hall in Wiltshire. In his capacity as a magistrate, he had brought before him last year a man known locally as Black Ralph. The charge was poaching. There was no doubt of his guilt; he had erred before in this way and in others, and my husband's sentence of twelve months in gaol was lenient to a degree. Now, Black Ralph is at liberty again, and word has reached our servants that he means to revenge himself on my husband—to kill him."

"Kill him?" I ejaculated.

"Nothing less, Dr. Watson," said Lady Fairfax, clasping and unclasping her white-gloved hands as she spoke. "My husband scouts these threats, calling Black Ralph a harmless rascal with a taste for rhetoric. But the fellow is no mere drunken reprobate such as one finds in every village; I have seen him and studied him, and I tell you he is malignant, and in all likelihood mentally deranged as well."

I was at a loss. My visitor was by now extremely agitated, her vivid lips atremble and her fine blue eyes flashing fire. "He sounds most menacing," said I, "and I understand your desire for assistance. I chance to know a certain Inspector Lestrade at Scotland Yard who would be happy to lend you all the aid he could."

"Thank you, but my husband refuses to go to the police and has forbidden me to do so."

"I see."

"There must, however, be other consulting detectives in London whom I might approach. Perhaps you know of some of them?"

"Well," said I after a short space, "it's true that in the last year or so a number of—what shall I call them?—rivals of Sherlock Holmes have sprung up. But they're very slight and un-

satisfactory fellows. I could not in honesty recommend a single one."

There was a silence. The lady sighed once more and at last turned to me. "Dr. Watson, will *you* help me?"

I had half expected this preposterous suggestion, but was none the better armed against it when it came. "I? I am quite unfit. I'm a simple medical man, Lady Fairfax, not a detective."

"But you have worked with Mr. Holmes on his previous cases. You are his close friend and associate. You must have learned a great deal from him."

"I think I can say I know his methods, but there are aspects of his activities of which I am altogether ignorant."

"That would not prevent you from talking to my husband, from making him see the peril he faces. Nor from approaching Black Ralph, warning him, offering him money. Dr. Watson, I know you think me overwrought, fanciful, perhaps even deluded. Is it not the case, that you think so?"

This was uncommonly and uncomfortably shrewd, not only as an observation, but also as a turn of tactics. I made some motion intended to be evasive.

"Thank you for being so honest," was the smiling response. "Now I may be all you suppose, but I lay no obligation upon you, and would two or three comfortable days out of London in this weather be so great a burden?"

Sherlock Holmes once observed that the fair sex was my department. I never fully took his meaning, but if it was to the effect that I enjoyed any ascendancy in that sphere, he misreckoned. Otherwise I should scarcely have found myself, the evening after the interview just described, alighting at a remote railway halt some miles from Westbury.

At once a tall, broad-shouldered man in black accosted me, mentioning my name in a foreign accent. He was an obvious Spaniard—by name Carlos, as I was later to learn—with the dignified deportment of that race and an address that contrived to be at once courteous and proud. Courtesy was to the fore while he introduced himself as butler to Sir Harry Fairfax and installed me and my luggage in the smart wagonette that waited in the station yard; and yet his sombre looks bespoke a temperament to which the keeping of pledges and the avenging of slights were of deadly concern. Not that I took much note at the time; I was pleasantly struck by the baronet's civility in sending an upper servant to meet me, and soothed by the unhurried drive through the leafy lanes, where, as the shadows lengthened, a cooling breeze blew. I looked forward, too, to renewing my acquaintance with the charming Lady Fairfax, and, with a lively quickening of curiosity, to uncovering whatever might be the nature of the threat to her husband.

The carriage mounted a crest in the road and these agreeable feelings were soon dissipated. We had come to the edge of the chalky upland that forms most of the county and entered a region of clay and rock. Some half a mile off stood a tall house of grey stone mantled with ivy and of a design that even at this distance seemed ill-contrived. To one side of it lay a plantation of trees with foliage of a deep, almost bluish hue uncommon in England; on the other there wound a stream or small river. I knew at once that the house was our destination, and as soon as a curve in the stream brought the murky, weed-clogged flood close to the road, saw the force of its name. A moment later I was almost spilled from my seat by the wild shying of the pair of cobs that drew the wagonette. The cause was not far to seek—a human figure of indescribable menace lurking in the hedgerow. I caught a glimpse of a hairy fist shaken, of rotten teeth bared in a snarl, no more, but I would have been sure that it was Black Ralph I had seen even if the Spaniard's dark eye had not fixed me with a sufficiently eloquent look.

Darkwater Hall was no more prepossessing at close quarters. Weathering showed it to be not of recent erection, but its bulging windows and squat chimneys belonged to no period or style I had ever encountered. The interior was comparatively conventional. Carlos took me to a more

than adequate bedroom and quickly fetched me ample hot water, so I was able to make a very tolerable change and go to greet my hosts in renewed spirits.

With his fresh complexion, steady eye and open, unassuming manner, Sir Harry Fairfax was one of the finest types of English country gentlemen. I judged him to be about thirty years old. His brother Miles resembled him in age and nothing else, a sallow, sneering young man probably addicted to cigarettes and strong waters. From neither brother did I obtain what I had hoped the meeting would furnish, some clue or indication, something that would force out of the subconsciousness of my mind whatever it was that had stirred there when I heard the name of Fairfax; reference books had proved useless. For the moment, the memory stayed buried.

As before, I had no time to ponder the point, for my hostess, in a gown of azure velvet that showed off the brilliance of her eyes, steered me towards the fifth member of the party. Him I identified as an Army man (from the set of his shoulders) who had served some years in the tropics (from his deep tan), but whose career had not prospered (from his disappointed air), and was somewhat tickled to hear him introduced as Captain Bradshaw of the Assam Light Horse. No one who had failed to gain his majority by the age of forty-five, which I estimated Bradshaw to have reached, could be called a successful soldier. I hid a smile at the thought of the "Excellent, Watson!" which a well-known voice might have breathed into my ear, had its owner been present, and took to conversation.

"I was a sort of soldier myself when I was a youngster," said I.

"Oh yes? Where did you serve?"

"Afghanistan."

"You saw some action there, I take it."

"Not the sort that a fighting soldier sees, but enough. I was wounded and at last invalided out."

"What infernal luck."

"You're on leave, no doubt."

"Awaiting retirement," said Bradshaw in a tone as dejected as his bearing.

Miles Fairfax now cocked his unkempt head at me. "Welcome to Darkwater Hall, Dr. Watson. Life here may strike you as a trifle dull and rustic after the bustle and polish of London, but believe me, it has its points of interest."

"Indeed."

"I presume you're a medical doctor, not one who professes law or divinity?"

"Medicine's my trade, yes."

"Then the following fact, omitted by my brother when he introduced us, might amuse you. Although unlike in every possible way, he and I are twins."

"That's not so surprising," said I. "Many pairs of twins are no more alike than ordinary brothers and sisters, and we know how they can differ."

"Assuredly," said he at his most sarcastic. "Is it true, Doctor, that twins can be born several or even many hours apart?"

"It is."

"Not so in our case—eh, Harry? Twenty minutes was all that separated our respective arrivals in this world. But it was enough."

His sister-in-law put a gently restraining hand on his arm, but the fellow shook it off with a roughness that, had it been my place to do so, I should have considered correcting. I was now morally certain he was intoxicated.

"Yes," he went on with a growl, "twenty minutes settled the disposal of the baronetcy, the house, the estate, the money. God's will, what?"

"At least, Mr. Fairfax," said I, "it's evident you're a good loser."

That shot went home, and it silenced him for a while, but I was relieved when Carlos announced dinner, thus effecting a change of scene and mood. It proved to be a change not wholly for the better, in that the spacious room in which I now found myself was dominated by a most outlandish carving or relief occupying the section of wall above the fireplace. It was of some dark wood and I could not be sure what it portrayed, except that in one corner a human figure, half naked, was being bound to a post by others wearing hooded robes, while further off

I thought I saw a scaffold. All in all, it made an unequivocally distasteful impression upon me. The fare, however, was palatable enough, and the service most adroit and pleasant, provided by Carlos and a young woman I learned was his wife, named Dolores. With her raven hair, creamy skin and deep brown eyes she was in striking contrast to her mistress, but female beauty takes many forms.

I was in the midst of recounting, at the baronet's invitation, the full facts of the strange affair at Stoke Moran, when Lady Fairfax gave an abrupt gasp and raised her hands to her throat. I followed her horrified gaze and spied, through a gap in the curtains, a face I had seen for a moment earlier that day, a face once more contorted with malice.

"Black Ralph! At the window!" I cried, and jumped up from my chair. Bradshaw was already on his feet, standing between the lady and the point where the intruder had appeared. Sir Harry and I had left the house within seconds, but, though we searched thoroughly the nearer part of the grounds, we returned empty-handed, much to Miles's scoffing amusement. Some time later, my host contrived to disengage me from the rest of the company, having imputed to me a desire to be shown the contents of his gun-room. He enjoyed some friendly amusement at my expense when I cautioned him to stay away from the windows there until I had drawn the curtains over them.

"Do you imagine that Black Ralph has come back with a Gatling gun?" he asked with a smile.

"I imagine nothing, Sir Harry. I go by what I see and hear," and I told him of my earlier sighting of that villainous creature.

He was quite unmoved, attributing these visitations to the idle curiosity of a simpleton. "I am at no risk, Doctor," he ended firmly.

"Lady Fairfax thinks differently."

"That's her way. She watches over me with a care that would sometimes befit a mother more than a wife. Such matters will be resolved with the arrival of our first child."

"Is that happy event in positive prospect?"

"Not as yet."

Rather abruptly, he thrust into my hands a pair of antique duelling-pistols that had resided in a glass case, and inquired my opinion of them. I made what reply I could, as also when he passed me an early revolver from the time of Waterloo. After a moment he began to speak of his brother.

"Visitors are always apt to bring out the worst in him. I fancy he sees himself through their eyes and dislikes the sight. A man with no occupation, no interest in country pursuits—except shooting, at which he excels—and yet too indolent to make a move. Poor, poor Miles, the prisoner of his own nature, as we all are! And poor Bradshaw too."

"How so?"

"Well, frankly, Watson—and in the circumstances there seems little point in not being frank with you—Jack has been living here largely on my charity. I offer it gladly as he served under my father, but it galls him. And beneath that quiet exterior, you know, there's a cauldron of feelings. Not a stable character, Jack's. It told against him in the regiment, so the dad said."

In the pause that followed, I ran my eye over a weapon I recognised, one of the single-action Rossi-Charles rifles with the old aperture sight. Though inaccurate at anything of a range, they had been much prized at one time for never jamming and for their lightness and cheapness. I mentioned having come across them in Afghanistan and Sir Harry told me his father had picked this one up after Jellalabad. Forty years ago and more, I remember thinking to myself, and am still at a loss to say why I did—forty years ago, before I was born.

The rest of the evening passed pleasantly if inconclusively enough, and in due course the party dispersed. My bedroom was on the second floor, above which lay what I had taken to be a number of unoccupied or unused garrets and the like; I was slightly surprised, then, to hear, as I made ready to retire, the distinct sound of a door shutting somewhere above my head, and proceeded to listen with half an ear to a conversation of which I could at first make out nothing but that, of a small number of speakers, one or more was male and one or more female. My attention mounted as the voices grew in volume and feeling until, when it was plain that upstairs a tenacious woman faced an importunate man, I hung on every word, but no words were distinguishable, none save one, the interjection "No!" thrice pronounced in feminine accents, and accompanied by what was beyond all doubt the defiant stamp of a feminine foot. This evidently settled the matter; the colloquy at once died down and soon ceased, the door opened and shut again, and in a few moments all was still.

The whole incident had not lasted a minute, and its meaning and importance were far from certain. Nevertheless, I found some difficulty in composing my mind for sleep. The man's voice I had been unable to identify; the woman's was quite positively that of Lady Fairfax. What, I asked myself, could have taken her at such an hour to a part of the house so remote from where her own quarters must be situated?

When sleep came it was deep and dreamless. Next morning, thoroughly refreshed, I had barely finished breakfast when the household exploded into sudden clamour. It appeared that the gun-room had been broken into by a window and the Rossi-Charles rifle and half a dozen rounds of its ammunition removed. Nothing else was missing, according to Carlos, who, I gathered, was in virtual charge of his master's modest armoury. Mindful of Sherlock Holmes's dictum, that there is no branch of detective science so important as the art of tracing footsteps, I fetched the large magnifying-glass I had had the forethought to bring with me and set to work on the approaches to the window. But circumstance was against me in the very particular in which it so often favoured my friend; the ground, baked hard by the hot summer, yielded no trace of what I sought. I returned to the gun-room to find an altercation in progress.

"It is indeed suspicious—" Sir Harry was saying.

"Suspicious!" his wife flashed at him. "Might

a bullet in your heart come near to furnishing a certainty?"

"In law it is no more than suspicious, and even a magistrate cannot have a man confined on such grounds. I have no charge to bring."

Bradshaw, at the lady's other side, seemed disposed to agree, pointing out that there had been no witnesses to the burglary.

"Then," came the ready rejoinder, "Harry must be placed under guard, protected night and day."

"I refuse to be made a prisoner in my own house, and out of doors the plan would be quite impracticable, eh, Jack?"

"I shouldn't care to undertake it myself with anything less than a full platoon," declared the soldier.

"Then you must leave the Hall, go somewhere safe and secret until—"

"What, and give a rascal like Black Ralph the satisfaction of making me bolt like a rabbit? I'd sooner die."

His sincerity was unmistakable, and made an impression on all his hearers, even his brother, who for the moment forgot to sneer, though he remembered soon enough when I took a hand in the conversation.

First explaining the absence of footsteps outside, I added, "But I did find some fragments of glass on the soil, as we did on this side of the window."

"Is that so surprising?" was the baronet's question.

I answered it with another. "Is this door normally kept locked?"

"Why, yes, of course."

"How many keys are there?"

"Two. I have one, Carlos the other."

"Does he carry it with him at all times?"

"No, for the most part it's kept on a ring hanging up in his pantry."

"And is that generally known in the household?"

"It might well be, yes."

The younger twin said with a curl of his lip, "Your reasoning is pellucidly clear, Dr. Watson.

Any of us, and Carlos besides, could have let himself in here, broken the window from *inside* in order to suggest an intruder from *outside*, and made off with the rifle. How exquisitely ingenious!"

"Mr. Fairfax," said I, summoning up as much reasonableness as I could, "all I seek to do is to explore possibilities, however remote they may appear to be, and however absurd they may turn out in retrospect to have been."

"As the great Sherlock Holmes would be seeking to do, were he here."

"I am not too proud to learn from my betters," I observed a little tartly as I drew Sir Harry aside.

Before I could speak, he said with some warmth, "You don't seriously suppose, do you, Watson, that Carlos, or Jack Bradshaw, or my own brother would have stolen that weapon? For what conceivable motive?"

"Of course I don't suppose any such thing," said I. "This Black Ralph miscreant is obviously the culprit. No, I was merely—"

"Displaying your powers of observation?" he asked, his good humour at once restored.

"Very likely. Now you must tell me where to find the fellow. There's no time to be lost."

"I beg you to be careful, Watson."

"*You* are to be careful, Sir Harry. Keep to the house as far as you can. Take Bradshaw with you if you must venture out. Warn the servants."

He promised to do as I said, and his directions conducted me straight to the noisome hovel which was Black Ralph's abode, but my journey was vain. The slattern who answered my knock informed me that the man had left the previous day to visit his sister near Warminster and was not expected back for a week. I did not stay to puncture such an obvious tissue of falsehood. When an inquiry at the local tavern fell out equally fruitless, I returned to Darkwater Hall and addressed myself to questioning the servants, the source of the disquieting rumours that had reached Lady Fairfax in the first place.

My most puzzling informant was the girl Dolores, who fortunately spoke English well, though with a stronger accent than her husband. At first she had little to say, answering in curt monosyllables or merely shrugging her graceful shoulders by way of reply. But then, led by luck or instinct, I ventured to ask what were her personal views of her employer. At once her dark eyes blazed and I caught a glimpse of splendid white teeth.

"He is cold!" she cried. "He is a good man, this Sir Harry Fairfax, a fine English gentleman, but he is cold! His blood is like the blood of a fish!"

Making no move to restrain her, for we were out of hearing of the household at the time, I did no more than encourage her to explain herself.

"I cannot! How can I, to another Englishman?"

"Has he treated you unkindly?"

"Unkindly, never; I tell you he is a good man. But coldly, coldly!"

"In what way coldly?"

Again the girl did no more than shrug her shoulders. I sensed I would get no further along this path and took a new approach by asking whether Carlos also held the opinion that Sir Harry was a good man.

"Yes, yes," was the reply, accompanied by a toss of the head. "I think so. Or perhaps I should better say that I hope so, I greatly hope so."

"Why is that?"

But here once more I found there was no more progress to be made. I revolved in my mind this interview, together with other matters, through an agreeable luncheon and the earlier part of a confoundedly sultry afternoon. Half-past four found me in the drawing-room taking tea with my hostess.

"We won't wait for Harry," said she. "He often misses tea altogether."

"Where is Sir Harry at this moment?"

"At the stables. He should be safe enough there."

"I see there is a fourth cup."

"In case Miles should decide to join us."

"But you make no provision for Captain Bradshaw."

"Ah, he never takes tea. Nothing must be allowed to interfere with his afternoon walk. Jack Bradshaw is a very serious man."

"He is certainly very serious about you, Lady Fairfax."

"What do you mean?"

"He's in love with you, as you know. I learned it last night, at dinner. You showed signs of strong fear; Bradshaw had not seen what it was that had frightened you, but he could tell its direction from your gaze, and at once—before I was on my feet, and I moved quickly—interposed himself between you and the source of danger. Such speed comes from instinct founded on deep emotion, not from the conscious part of the mind."

The lady was not indignant, nor did she affect disbelief or surprise. I was sufficiently emboldened by this further evidence of her sagacity to inquire if I might go further in plain speaking.

"We shall make no progress if we allow ourselves to be circumscribed by false notions of delicacy," she replied.

"Very well. Remember that I am discussing remote contingencies, nothing more. Now—if I wanted to procure Sir Harry's demise, when should I best make my attempt?"

"When his life had recently been threatened by a convicted felon."

"Just so. What of my motive?"

"We know of one possibility, that your victim stands between you and the object of your passion. No doubt there are others."

"Certainly. Perhaps I'm the prey of a special kind of envy, or a sense that Fortune has been unjust to me."

"I follow you."

"Or again I may feel that my honour has been slighted so grievously that only death can redress the wrong."

"Do you call that plain speaking, Dr. Watson?" was a question never answered, for at that moment the tea-cup in that graceful hand shattered into fragments and the crack of a rifle was heard from the nearer distance. Bidding Lady Fairfax lie down, I hastened out through the open French windows and searched the adjacent shrubbery, but with no result. On my return to the house, I found the baronet with his arms about his wife, who was decidedly less shocked than many young women would have been after such an experience. After satisfying myself that she needed none of my professional care, I searched for the bullet that had passed between us and eventually retrieved it from the corner where it had ricochetted after hitting the back wall. This contact had somewhat deformed it, but I was soon satisfied that it had come from the Rossi-Charles rifle.

By now, Miles Fairfax had arrived from his sitting-room on the first floor, unaware, on his account, of anything amiss until summoned by a servant. Had he not heard the shot? He had indeed heard *a* shot, but had taken it for one more of the hundreds fired in the vicinity every year for peaceful purposes. Bradshaw appeared a little later, back, he declared, from his walk, and evidently much agitated at the narrowness of Lady Fairfax's escape.

He clutched his forehead wildly. "In Heaven's name, what lunatic would seek to harm so innocent a creature?" he cried.

"Oh, I think it must have been to me that harm was intended, Jack," said Sir Harry. "Consider where Watson was sitting. From any distance, it would have been perfectly possible to mistake him for me."

"Harry," said his wife in tones of resolve, "there must be no shoot tomorrow. I forbid it."

"What shoot is this?" I asked.

"A very modest affair, Doctor," returned Sir Harry. "We intend to do no more than clear some of the pigeons from the east wood. A few people from round about will be joining us."

"And is your intention known in the district?"

"Well, it is our yearly custom. I suppose it must be known."

"Don't go, dearest," implored the lady. "Let the others do as they please, but you remain behind."

I took it upon myself to intervene. "My dear Lady Fairfax," said I, "Sir Harry must be there.

It's our best chance. We must bring Black Ralph into the open and end this menace. I will be responsible for your husband's safety."

And, with the support of Bradshaw and, unexpectedly, that of Miles Fairfax, I carried the day. Later I made some preparations with which I will not weary the reader, and, in common with the rest of the household, retired early. I was drifting off to sleep when, just as on the previous night, I heard the door above me shut. In an instant I was fully awake. The voices began again, but with the immediate difference that the man was unmistakably Sir Harry Fairfax, speaking with a measured harshness that chilled the blood. I caught a phrase here and there— "castigation of sin" and "suffer condign punishment." They were enough to recall to me what hitherto the name of Fairfax and the sight of the fiendish representation in the dining-room had failed to do. It had been an eighteenth-century occupant of that baronetcy, one Sir Thomas Fairfax, who had conducted nameless rites in this very house, subjecting his own wife to indignities which I cannot set down here. At that moment I heard from upstairs the voice of the present Lady Fairfax raised in piteous entreaty and then what could have been nothing but the savage crack of a whip. A stifled scream followed.

I could hesitate no longer. Lighting a candle, I took my revolver from its hiding-place at the bottom of my travelling-bag, threw on a dressing-gown and made for the upper storey. Within seconds I had found the room I sought and paused outside it before committing myself.

After a moment, Sir Harry's voice, its unnatural harshness intensified, spoke from beyond the closed door. "Now, I say, you shall make an act of contrition!" There was another pause, and then the voice came again. "Ah. So you remain, devil. You are incorporate with the body you inhabit. You and she are one flesh. Then as one flesh shall you suffer chastisement!"

With the whiplash ringing in my ears I burst in and confronted two figures garbed after the fashion of a hundred years before. Emily Fairfax wore a gown of black bombazine; he who must be her husband was unrecognisable by reason of the red velvet mask that, apart from eye-holes, covered all his face above the mouth. That mouth was now open in consternation.

"Enough, Fairfax, enough!" I cried. "What is this hideous mummery? These, I suppose, were the practices of your accursed ancestor."

There was a moment of complete silence before the man removed his mask. When he had done so, his face wore an expression of what might have been taken for friendly concern. "I'm truly sorry, Doctor," he said in his normal tones. "We have troubled your rest. I can't think how I came to forget that your room was beneath this one."

"Thank Heaven you did forget," said I. "What is to be done with you, you vile creature? I am utterly staggered."

At this, Lady Fairfax broke into sudden laughter. "That is altogether understandable," said she. "My dear Dr. Watson, you have been scandalously put upon. How am I to explain? Perhaps I may show you this."

She handed me a tattered volume on whose cover I made out the legend, "Plays of Terror and the Macabre." I turned over its pages with a dawning comprehension which became complete when I reached, set out in cold print, the very words I had just heard Sir Harry pronounce. "You are acting," was the best I could find to say.

"Correct, my dear fellow," smiled the dreadful inquisitor of a minute before, cracking his whip against a battered escritoire—I saw now that the room was half full of such items of discarded furniture. "I think I told you how my poor wife misses the theatre, and this sort of tomfoolery was the best we could devise by way of a substitute."

"Last night," I said feebly—"last night I heard Lady Fairfax protesting in a strain I could have sworn held nothing simulated."

"Quite true," said the lady pleasantly; "last night I was tired after my travels, too tired for this sport."

"I will interrupt you no longer," I declared, and brushing aside the apologies of both, took myself out of that room as fast as I could. Doubtless I had made a fool of myself, but I was saved from the self-regarding shame that that thought usually brings by commiseration towards Lady Fairfax. Nobody could have failed to see that her object that night had been, not entertainment, but distraction from thought of what the next day might hold in store.

It was a day that began auspiciously enough, with a blue sky faintly veiled in mist, so often the prelude to a blazing noon. By eleven o'clock the shooting-party was on its way towards the wood. Besides myself, it included the Fairfax brothers and half a dozen neighbours, but not Captain Bradshaw, whom I had just heard explaining to a bewhiskered farmer that the recurrence of a bowel complaint, the effect of a germ picked up in India, forbade him to attend. Happening to catch my eye as he said this, he had hastily looked away, and with reason; I have never met a worse liar. The only servant present was a ruddy-cheeked youth carrying a rattle to put up the birds.

The sun was hot and high as we moved into the shadows of the wood, where there were many small noises. Almost at once Miles Fairfax stumbled at some irregularity of the ground, and but for my outthrust arm might have fallen.

"Are you all right?" I asked.

He hobbled a pace or two. "My damned ankle. I seem to have twisted it."

"Best let me have a look."

This natural suggestion seemed to fill him with wrath. "I haven't broken my leg, curse it!" he cried. "I don't need surgery! I'll be all right directly and will catch you up. Go on, all of you. Go on!"

It seemed we had no choice but to do as we were told. Presently the rattle sounded, flocks of pigeons took to the air and the guns blazed merrily away. I held my fire, maintaining a keen look-out and staying as close to Sir Harry as I could without forming one target with him. The party trod steadily on, deeper into the wood. I caught various movements among foliage, but none were of human agency. I had begun to fear, not what might happen, but that nothing would, when we reached a clearing some seventy yards across. At once there came the smart crack of a rifle-shot and Sir Harry cried out and fell. I was thunderstruck, but after a glance at the baronet's prostrate form I shouted to the party that they should lie flat and keep their heads down. They obeyed with alacrity. Another shot sounded, but the bullet went wild. I faced in the direction from which it had come and walked slowly forward.

"Aim here," I called, indicating my chest. "Here."

A third report followed; I heard the round buzzing through the air ten feet above my head. The fourth and fifth attempts were no better. When I had gone some twenty yards there was a receding flurry in the bushes. I followed at a run, but still had seen nothing when two shots rang out almost together and a howl of pain followed. Within a minute I had found what I sought—Bradshaw and Carlos each covering with a rifle the prostrate form of Black Ralph.

"Well done, lads," said I, grasping each by the arm, then turned my attention to the would-be assassin. My first good look at the scoundrel showed him to be of simous and ape-like appearance, and there was something animal in the way he whimpered over his injury. This was nothing much; a bullet had creased his knee-cap, temporarily incapacitating him but not, which would have been the case had it struck nearer, crippling him for life. All in all he was infernally lucky.

"Whose shot was it?" I asked.

"I'm not certain," said Bradshaw.

"I am certain," said the Spaniard with a gallant bow. "It was yours, Captain. Most brilliant, with a moving target at that range. And now you may leave it to me to deliver to the authorities this piece of filth."

Sir Harry's wound was lighter—a gash in the upper arm which had not bled excessively. When I reached him, he was being tenderly comforted by his brother Miles, whose whole nature seemed transformed, and who gave me such a

look, compounded of remorse for past conduct and a firm resolve for the future, as I shall never forget. On our return to Darkwater Hall, the wife's joy at her husband's safe homecoming affected us all, notably Bradshaw. I received so much praise for my supposed courage in exposing myself to Black Ralph's fire that I was forced at last to explain that it was undeserved.

"The rifle is the key," said I, the recovered weapon in my hand. "Like all its fellows, it's inaccurate. So when it was stolen I knew the culprit was someone ignorant of firearms. Then, when your tea-cup flew to pieces yesterday, Lady Fairfax, I knew more. To get a bullet out of this thingumbob between you and me at something like eighty yards the firer must be either a brilliant shot with many hours of practice behind him—impossible—or a very bad shot with the luck of the devil, one who had the luck of the devil again an hour ago; that staggered me, I must say. So you see, while Black Ralph was aiming at my chest I was safe. If he had just let fly at random he might conceivably have hit me."

Bradshaw seemed dissatisfied. "But even the most inaccurate weapon in the world is dangerous at short range," he observed.

"Indeed it is. That was why I kept my distance till there were no more shots in the locker. But of course I knew who was the villain of the piece within minutes of arriving in the house, despite all the questions I asked."

"By deduction?" asked Miles Fairfax with a friendly smile.

"Certainly not. I knew Black Ralph was a criminal, one glimpse of him was enough to show me he was a dangerous one, and everybody else I saw was simply incapable of such a monstrous deed as the one he tried to perpetrate today. It was obvious. And I thank God for that fact. In a case of the least difficulty I should have been the sorriest of substitutes for Sherlock Holmes."

Accompanied by Bradshaw, who told me he felt he had vegetated too long, I caught the evening train for London, where we supped pleasantly at the Savoy.

If I were recording here one of Holmes's adventures I should lay down my pen at this point, but since I mean to ensure that nobody shall see this account until fifty years after my death, I will take leave to say a little more.

I have been less than frank with the reader. By this I do not merely mean to confess that, in this narrative as in others, I have done what Holmes himself once accused me of doing and concealed "links in the chain"—the scheme I devised with Bradshaw and Carlos for apprehending Black Ralph is the most glaring example—in order to make a better story, though I hope the finale thus produced is not "meretricious." Nor do I mean to discuss the view, put forward by a Viennese colleague to whom I recently recounted the outline of this story, that Sir Harry Fairfax's amateur theatricals might have been something other than what I had taken them to be, and in some abstruse way—which I could not wholly follow—connected with his failure to produce an heir. But it is all too certain that he was still childless when, some ten years after the Black Ralph affair, he met his death in a riding accident, leaving his brother to inherit with sorrow the baronetcy and estates he had once so ardently coveted.

Enough of that. What I have to reveal is of another order altogether. The interview with Dolores, as set out above, is a lie. She did indeed impute to Carlos a groundless jealousy of Sir Harry. But the manner of this, and its circumstances, were wholly different from what I have implied. The two of us were in my bed. Even in these easy-going days of the third decade of the twentieth century I would not care to publish such a confession. I dare hope that the reader of the 1970s will find it unexceptionable; a vigorous bachelor of three-and-thirty, such as I then was, a beautiful and passionate girl, and an opportunity—is there anything there to outrage delicacy?

Dolores, what was it in you, or in me, or in both of us that brought it about that in your arms I experienced a joy more intense and more exquisite than any before or since? Was it that we were so different from each other or that we shared a strange communion of spirit? Was it the season? Was it—contrary to appearance—the place? To me, that is the real Darkwater Hall mystery, as impenetrable and as wonderful now as it was then, forty years ago.

John H. Watson, M.D.
Bournemouth
April, 1925

The Case of the Gifted Amateur

J. C. MASTERMAN

OF HIS MANY accomplishments, a career as a mystery writer was not the peak achievement of John Cecil Masterman (1891–1977). He was a distinguished academic, teaching modern history at Christ Church College, Oxford, resigning in the mid-1920s to devote his full time to sports, becoming an internationally acclaimed multisport star. He was an outstanding tennis player, field hockey champion, golfer, squash player, and a cricket player of such skill that he toured with the prestigious Marylebone Cricket Club. He was recognized as a gamesman worthy of inclusion in Stephen Potter's classic, *The Theory and Practice of Gamesmanship or The Art of Winning Games Without Actually Cheating* (1947). Masterman returned to Oxford after World War II to become Provost of Worcester College (1946–1961) and Vice-Chancellor of Oxford University (1957–1958). He was knighted in 1959.

Masterman's greatest achievement was undoubtedly his chairmanship of the Twenty Committee when World War II broke out. It was a secret group of British intelligence officials and gifted amateurs whose Double Cross System was designed to turn German spies into double agents working for the British, providing misinformation to be transmitted to German intelligence agencies. Although Masterman ran the Committee, he credited MI5 with originating the idea. It has been frequently reported that Ian Fleming, also involved in WWII intelligence, adapted Masterman's name for the Jill Masterson character in his James Bond novel *Goldfinger* (1959).

The two detective novels Masterman wrote are academic mysteries that feature Francis Wheatley Winn, an Oxford don who served as Watson to the novel's Sherlock Holmes, an amateur sleuth named Ernst Brendel, a likable Viennese lawyer. The success of *An Oxford Tragedy* (1933) did not inspire a sequel until 1957's *The Case of the Four Friends*.

"The Case of the Gifted Amateur" was first published in the December 1952 issue of *MacKill's Mystery Magazine*; it was first published in England in the January 18, 1954, issue of *The Evening Standard*. The first book appearance was in *Bits and Pieces* by J. C. Masterman (London, Hodder & Stoughton, 1961).

THE CASE OF THE GIFTED AMATEUR

J. C. Masterman

AMONGST ALL THE talented officers of Scotland Yard Chief Detective Inspector Lestrade was both the most astute and the most successful—so at least he often gave me to understand. Long after he had retired I used to visit him in the Nursing Home in Surrey in which he passed the last years of his life, and with the minimum of encouragement he would relate again the triumphs of himself, of Gregson, of Athelney Jones, of "young" Stanley Hopkins and the rest of those heroes who had flourished in what he considered the palmy days of the Yard.

Yet curiously enough he seldom mentioned the name of Sherlock Holmes, with whom his name had been linked in my own early memories. This I found difficult to understand, and I even, at one time, harboured the unworthy suspicion that he was in some way jealous of the reputation of the Baker Street detective. When I contrived to mention the latter's name he would make a faintly depreciatory comment and pass on to another part of the saga of his own career. Rarely, very rarely, he was more communicative about a man—or men, for a certain Dr. Watson had worked with Holmes in those bygone days—about whose doings I had an insatiable curiosity. Once only he related a story of the two to me.

"Mr. Sherlock Holmes was a clever man in his way, but not nearly so clever as he thought himself, and as for that Watson . . . ! My old chief at the Yard, I remember, used to call Mr. Sherlock Holmes 'the Gifted Amateur,' though why, I couldn't quite make out. You see, properly speaking, he wasn't an amateur at all, and as for being gifted—well—there were some of us at the Yard that could have given him half a stone and a beating any day."

Lestrade gave a wheezy chuckle of satisfaction.

"But he had some bright ideas, hadn't he? I suppose he was helpful to you now and then?"

"If you ask me," retorted Lestrade, "the boot was on the other leg. I can remember one case when I helped Holmes—and Watson too, for that matter—out of a pretty tight jam—not that they were as grateful to me as they might have been. I'll tell you about it."

It was in the year 1889, so far as I can remember, and it's in my mind that Mr. Sherlock Holmes had been having rather a lean time—why, even that Watson could hardly find any cases to write about at that time (you know the Doctor used to write up his friend's cases for what they call publicity purposes nowadays). When, therefore, the case of the Dark Diamond was handed over to me and I noticed that Dr. Watson was connected with it in his professional capacity it seemed to me that it was the only kind thing to do to let Holmes have a finger in the pie. I was a bit sorry for him, as you might say, besides I wasn't too sure that I could solve the mystery just as quickly and easily as I wanted to. So I walked round to Baker Street somewhere about teatime and found them both smoking in their room.

"Ah, Lestrade," said Holmes in his high-and-mighty manner, "you are often the harbinger of good tidings—what have you for me now?"

"I suppose Dr. Watson has told you about this case of Rheinhart Wimpfheimer's diamond?" I asked. Holmes smiled.

"Watson's account is a trifle confused. I should be glad if you would run over the case so that I may have the salient facts before me; possibly I may be able to help you."

The reports which I made in those days didn't miss much so I read out the notes which I had already made.

Mr. Rheinhart Wimpfheimer is well known as a man who has amassed a prodigious fortune in trade with the Orient; he is even better known as the greatest of all collectors of famous and curious jewels. In this field only one other person can compare with him, and that is his younger brother Mr. Solomon Wimpfheimer, a wealthy bachelor residing in Albany. Between the two brothers a keen but friendly rivalry has always existed, but the elder's collection is believed to be incomparably the finer. Mr. Rheinhart Wimpfheimer is himself a widower, living in some luxury at his residence, 123 Great Cumberland Place. Apart from the servants his household consists of himself, his unmarried daughter, aged about twenty-five, and his private secretary who assists him both in his business dealings and in his collecting. Many of his possessions have already been given or loaned to museums but some of the more precious are always kept in the house. Amongst them all, the famous Dark Diamond of Dungbura holds pride of place. So much is he attached to this wonderful stone that he carries it with him daily in a small chamois leather bag suspended from his neck. At night it is placed resting on the chamois leather bag on the table by his bedside.

"A moment, Lestrade," Holmes interrupted me. "Watson, pray pass me the third of those bulky volumes by your side. Ah—yes—I thought that there would be a note. The Dark Diamond of Dungbura, one of the most famous stones in the world owing to its size, its peculiar colour and its history. How or when it appeared in Dungbura, which is on the confines of Thibet, and how it passed from there to Europe are unknown, but it has since found a place in several of the greatest collections. Whereas most precious stones have a sinister reputation this one is reputed invariably to bring happiness and good fortune to its possessor. But I interrupt your orderly narrative, Lestrade. Proceed, if you will."

Early on Wednesday morning Mr. Rheinhart Wimpfheimer was suddenly taken ill. His usual medical attendant was on holiday and our friend Dr. Watson here was acting as his locum tenens. Dr. Watson was urgently summoned to the house at about nine and diagnosed the case as one of brain fever—correct me if I am wrong, Doctor.

"That is quite correct; I prescribed the usual remedies and promised to call again in the evening."

Dr. Watson called again in the evening and on his arrival found Mr. Wimpfheimer still unconscious. During the course of the visit, however, the patient had a short period of mental clarity and—I regret to say—vehemently expressed his desire to have the assistance of some physician more highly qualified than Dr. Watson.

"Ah, well," said Holmes, "after all he is a cultured man of unlimited wealth, and the services of a General Practitioner of limited experience and mediocre ability . . ."

"Holmes, this is unworthy of you," protested Watson. "You yourself have failed to obtain immediate success on some occasions."

"The dates?" replied Holmes acidly.

I hurried on with my report lest a quarrel should develop between the two friends. The patient relapsed into delirium and Dr. Watson gave instructions to the nurse and wrote down the names and addresses of some of his eminent fellow practitioners. He then left the house.

"The time, Watson?" inquired Holmes.

"It was 7 p.m.," replied Watson a little sulkily. "Mr. Wimpfheimer is a collector of furniture and *objets d'art* of all kinds. I passed at least four grandfather clocks on the staircase and, as all of them struck, the time was somehow impressed on my memory."

"Excellent, Watson. I am gratified that you are developing the power of observation. What happened next?"

A call was sent to Scotland Yard at ten o'clock this morning and I myself hurried round to 123 Great Cumberland Place where I found the house in a state of great commotion. When Sir Euston Pancras, the brain fever specialist, called that morning to examine the patient it was observed by the valet that the Dark Diamond of Dungbura which had lain on the table by the bedside the night before had vanished.

"It was there at the time of your visit, Watson?" inquired Holmes.

"It was—I observed it lying on the chamois leather bag on the table."

Between that time and the specialist's visit five persons entered the sickroom—the nurse who was on duty during the night, the nurse who relieved her this morning, the patient's confidential valet, his private secretary, and his daughter.

"What steps have you taken?" inquired Holmes. "Have you examined all these persons?"

No stone has been left unturned but the mystery seems insoluble. Of the five persons concerned none left the house except Miss Wimpfheimer who drove in a hansom to visit her uncle in Albany and tell him of his brother's progress. She left the house at about 9 p.m. and returned some three-quarters of an hour later. These persons are, moreover, all above suspicion. The valet and the secretary have been with Mr. Wimpfheimer for more than ten years, the first nurse retired to sleep almost immediately after she left the sickroom, and the second nurse did not leave the sickroom after she came on duty. The whole house has been searched from attic to cellar and the Diamond is not in it. I am forced to the conclusion that some burglar must have entered the room and abstracted the stone—but here again there are difficulties.

There are double windows in all the rooms and an elaborate system of burglar alarms; moreover Mr. Wimpfheimer has a dachshund to which he is devotedly attached; this animal never leaves him and sleeps in his bedroom. It is inconceivable that it should not have barked if a burglar had entered the room in the night-time. Still a burglar must have entered the room. The question is, how and when did he enter and how did he escape? You know my methods, Mr. Holmes—apply them (I often gave Mr. Sherlock Holmes pieces of advice of that kind and I think they were useful to him). Perhaps you may have some suggestion to make as to how the crime was accomplished.

Mr. Sherlock Holmes honoured me with one of his supercilious smiles.

"The case, my good Lestrade, though essentially a simple one, presents some features which are not without interest. I shall be glad to look into it for you."

"And when will you be prepared to restore the Diamond?" I asked with just the proper touch of sarcasm.

"Perhaps if you will honour Dr. Watson and myself with your company at breakfast tomorrow—let us say at 9:30—I may have some information for you."

I can see that room in Baker Street as clearly as though it was yesterday. When I returned the next morning Holmes, in his dressing-gown, was sitting in his chair at one side in a cloud of smoke and Dr. Watson was opposite him looking ill and worried. Perhaps, I thought, that Jezail bullet of which he was always talking was giving him a twinge of pain. His stethoscope, an old-fashioned instrument, was lying beside him, as though he was just about to start on a round of visits. Holmes waved me to a seat.

"Let me briefly elucidate the case," he began. "Last night I called at Great Cumberland Place. Disguised as a veterinary surgeon I explained that Mr. Wimpfheimer had given me an appointment some days before to examine the dachshund, and I was immediately admitted to the sickroom. The windows give no appearance of having been opened for some weeks at least; the physical formation of the dachshund enabled me, furthermore, to make an examination of the carpet."

"What was peculiarly noticeable about the carpet?" I asked.

"Nothing was noticeable about the carpet—that was peculiar. Your theory that a burglar must have entered the room is wholly untenable."

He paused and placed the tips of his long fingers together.

"We have therefore certain incontrovertible facts. The Diamond lay on the table when Watson paid his visit at 7 p.m.; it had disappeared when Sir Euston called at 10 in the morning—no burglar can have entered the room during that period; five persons, and five persons alone, entered the room during the night, all of them people of unimpeachable character; no one of them had any motive, so far as is known, for the theft. It is an old maxim of mine, however, that when the impossible has been excluded whatever remains, however improbable, must be the truth. Therefore one of those five persons stole the Diamond."

"Amazing, Holmes," exclaimed Watson. Holmes's pale face flushed a little at this compliment, but he continued his exposition.

"If we confine ourselves to the established facts we can carry the analysis further. The Diamond has been stolen from the bedroom, and stolen by one of the five persons who entered the bedroom. It is not in the house and therefore it has been removed from the house. It is a fair deduction that the thief who took it from the bedroom also removed it from the house. Moreover other considerations lead me to the same conclusion. No ordinary thief would choose the night when a trained and wakeful nurse sat at Mr. Wimpfheimer's bedside to make a burglarious entry, and indeed no professional thief would even contemplate stealing the Dungbura Diamond, for its peculiarities

would make it impossible for the thief to dispose of it. I therefore come to the conclusion that this was no ordinary theft. One solution and one only remains. Lestrade, the stone was abstracted not for vulgar gain but in order that it might be transferred to some other collection! There are no lengths to which collectors will not go—the pride of possession overcomes all scruples—and remember that the Dungbura Diamond brings happiness and good fortune to its possessor."

He paused dramatically.

"Mr. Solomon Wimpfheimer is a collector, Miss Wimpfheimer visited him in the evening to tell him of his brother's illness. We do not know what impelled this unhappy woman to transfer the Diamond from her father to her uncle but we do know that it was her hand which removed it from Great Cumberland Place. The case is completed. Breakfast can wait. Put on your hat, Watson, and we will stroll with Lestrade to Albany. There, unless I am much mistaken, we shall find the Diamond."

"But, but . . ." interrupted Watson. Holmes frowned at his friend. "I have demonstrated that the Diamond can have left Great Cumberland Place in no other way," he remarked severely.

"But—my stethoscope . . ." stammered Watson. We both turned towards him as the Doctor, clutching his side, appeared to faint and fell back in his chair.

For the first time in my experience Holmes seemed to be overcome by a human emotion. He rushed to his friend, tore open his shirt and applied the stethoscope to his chest.

"Alas, poor fellow," he cried, "he is dead. I can hear nothing."

"That," muttered Watson, "is what you must expect to hear when you use *my* stethoscope."

For my part I seized a bottle of seltzogene from the table and dashed it over the doctor's face. He gradually recovered, though he still clutched his side as though in great pain. It was then that I had one of those flashes of intuition which helped me so much in my career.

"Mr. Holmes," I said, "I believe that Dr.

Watson has something which he wishes to say to us." The Doctor nodded assent.

"Holmes," he said, "I cannot keep silence any longer. I have been in the Army and it is impossible for me to allow a breath of suspicion to rest on a pure and lovely woman. At all costs I must clear her reputation. When Mr. Wimpfheimer dismissed me in such cavalier fashion I felt a not unnatural resentment. At that moment, as he relapsed again into delirium, my eye caught the glint of the Diamond lying on its chamois leather bag on the table. The nurse left us to bring in some cooling drink which I had prescribed. In a flash my mind was made up—indeed my brain seemed to function with abnormal speed and certainty. A complete plan presented itself to me. I would seize the Diamond and convey it to Baker Street; you would find it in our room. I had no doubt that your keen analytical brain would connect the presence of the Diamond in Baker Street with my visit to Great Cumberland Place. I felt assured that the staunchness of your friendship would shield me from any undesirable consequences; I felt certain that you would find means, when a baffled Scotland Yard consulted you, to restore the stone to its owner, and to prove that it could in fact never have left Great Cumberland Place; you would then, I knew, generously allow Lestrade to take all the credit for the recovery. With me, to think is to act. To seize the Diamond was the matter of a moment; I rolled it into its bag and thrust them both into the mouth of my stethoscope. Thus burdened, I hurried from the house and hailed the first passing hansom. Inside I felt for the first time a spasm of nervousness, and I doubted the security of the hiding-place which I had chosen. I therefore removed the Diamond from the bag, pushed the bag back into the stethoscope and placed the Diamond in my mouth—a trick of concealment which I learned on the Afghan frontier. Then another doubt assailed me. It was essential for the success of my plan that you should not fail to find the Diamond. Should I place it in the tobacco in your Persian slipper (but you might

not smoke enough to reach it in time) or should I secrete it in your violin (but would you notice it there)? In this mental dilemma I allowed the muscles of my jaw to relax, the hansom gave a sudden lurch and, alas! I swallowed the Dark Diamond of Dungbura!"

"Impossible," exclaimed Holmes. "It is too large."

"I have swallowed much in my time," retorted Watson with quiet dignity. A new access of pain swept over him and his face contorted with agony.

"How he suffers," cried Holmes; "it is a tortured brain."

"No, no. Alimentary, my dear Holmes, alimentary," gasped Watson. "Take me to a hospital and I will stake my medical reputation that the Dark Diamond can speedily be recovered." Holmes drew me aside.

"Watson," he said, "has bungled shamefully, as I fear he often does—nevertheless we might still use some part of his strange plan. I could well restore the Diamond to Great Cumberland Place."

It was then that I took command of the situation.

"No, Mr. Holmes," said I, "that is out of the question. When the Yard undertakes a case of this kind it does not rest until success is achieved. Within twenty-four hours of taking over the case I have laid my hands on the criminal, who now writhes in your chair, and I have—within very narrow limits—located the stolen Diamond. With some assistance from the hospital I shall recover it and I shall restore it to its owner." But I noted a look of chagrin on Holmes's face, so I tapped him on the shoulder and tried to console him. "The Yard," I said, "cares little to whom the credit goes if only its task is achieved. After all, the confession which I extracted from Dr. Watson has saved me some hours of patient investigation; if, therefore, Mr. Wimpfheimer recovers I shall inform him that the Gifted Amateur, Mr. Sherlock Holmes, lent his assistance to us in the recovery of the Diamond."

.   .   .

A happy smile passed over the great Lestrade's wrinkled face.

"I am not denying," he said, "that my speed and efficiency in the handling of the case of the Dark Diamond was a big step upward in my professional career. Nor did I forget my promise to the Gifted Amateur. Mr. Rheinhart Wimpfheimer recovered and when, some three or four months later, I met Mr. Sherlock Holmes, he was wearing a handsome diamond tiepin which I do not remember to have seen in his possession before."

The Late Sherlock Holmes

JAMES M. BARRIE

(Published Anonymously)

JAMES MATTHEW BARRIE (1860–1937), the beloved Scottish playwright who created one of literature's iconic characters, Peter Pan, formed an unlikely friendship with Arthur Conan Doyle that survived many years and vast differences between two of the most popular writers of their time.

Conan Doyle was a sportsman. Fond of skiing, he has been credited with introducing that vigorous activity to Switzerland. An aficionado of pugilism, he was praised for his skill as a boxer and wrote two books with boxing themes: *Rodney Stone* (1896), which focused on bare-knuckle fighting during the Regency era, and *The Croxley Master: A Great Tale of the Prize Ring* (1907), about a boxing medical student. Famously, Conan Doyle was asked to referee the racially charged Jack Johnson–Jim Jeffries heavyweight championship fight in 1910. Johnson, the new champion, was an arrogant black man, so Jeffries, the old former champion, was called out of retirement in the interest of white supremacy. Conan Doyle declined the offer, stating that it was more likely to foster bigotry than combat it.

Barrie, on the other hand, stopped growing when he was still quite small (5'3½" according to his passport), was extremely introverted, and though he was married, his relationship was apparently unconsummated. "Boys can't love," he explained to his wife.

Nonetheless, Barrie and his friends, Jerome K. Jerome, Conan Doyle, P. G. Wodehouse, and others, founded a cricket club, called Allahakbarries. Conan Doyle was the only member who could actually play cricket. Barrie's friendship with Conan Doyle undoubtedly inspired him to write three Sherlock Holmes parodies, all of which are included in this collection.

"The Late Sherlock Holmes" was first published anonymously in the December 29, 1893, issue of *The St. James's Gazette*; it was first published in book form in the anthology *My Evening with Sherlock Holmes*, edited by John Gibson and Richard Lancelyn Green (London, Ferret Fantasy, 1981).

THE LATE SHERLOCK HOLMES

James M. Barrie

THE LATE SHERLOCK HOLMES, SENSATIONAL ARREST.

WATSON ACCUSED OF THE CRIME.

(By Our Own Extra-Special Reporters.)

12:30 p.m.—Early this morning Mr. W. W. Watson, M.D. (Edin.), was arrested at his residence, 12a, Tennison-road, St. John's-wood, on a charge of being implicated in the death of Mr. Sherlock Holmes, late of Baker-street. The arrest was quickly effected. The prisoner, we understand, was found by the police at breakfast with his wife. Being informed of the cause of their visit he expressed no surprise, and only asked to see the warrant. This having been shown him, he quietly put himself at the disposal of the police. The latter, it appears, had instructions to tell him that before accompanying them to Bow-street he was at liberty to make arrangements for the carrying on during his absence of his medical practice. Prisoner smiled at this, and said that no such arrangements were necessary, as his patient had left the country. Being warned that whatever he said would be used as evidence against him, he declined to make any further statement. He was then expeditiously removed to Bow-street. Prisoner's wife witnessed his removal with much fortitude.

THE SHERLOCK HOLMES MYSTERY.

The disappearance of Mr. Holmes was an event of such recent occurrence and gave rise to so much talk that a very brief *resume* of the affair is all that is needed here. Mr. Holmes was a man of middle age and resided in Baker-street, where he carried on the business of a private detective. He was extremely successful in his vocation, and some of his more notable triumphs must still be fresh in the minds of the public—particularly that known as "The Adventure of the Three Crowned Heads," and the still more curious "Adventure of the Man without a Wooden Leg," which had puzzled all the scientific bodies of Europe. Dr. Watson, as will be proved out of his own mouth, was a great friend of Mr. Holmes (itself a suspicious circumstance) and was in the habit of accompanying him in his professional peregrinations. It will be alleged by the prosecution, we understand, that he did so to serve certain ends of his own, which were of a monetary character. About a fortnight ago news reached London of the sudden death of the unfortunate Holmes, in circumstances that strongly pointed to foul play. Mr. Holmes and a friend had gone for a short trip to Switzerland, and it was telegraphed that Holmes had been lost in the terrible Falls of Reichenbach. He had fallen over or been precipitated. The Falls are nearly a thousand feet high; but Mr. Holmes in the course of his career had survived so many dangers, and the public had such faith in his turning-up as alert as ever next month, that no one believed him dead. The general confidence was strengthened when it became known that his companion in this expedition was his friend Watson.

WATSON'S STATEMENT.

Unfortunately for himself (though possibly under the compulsion of the police of

Switzerland), Watson felt called upon to make a statement. It amounted in brief to this: that the real cause of the Swiss tour was a criminal of the name of Moriarty, from whom Holmes was flying. The deceased gentleman, according to Watson, had ruined the criminal business of Moriarty, who had sworn revenge. This shattered the nerves of Holmes, who fled to the Continent, taking Watson with him. All went well until the two travellers reached the Falls of Reichenbach. Hither they were followed by a Swiss boy with a letter to Watson. It purported to come from the innkeeper of Meiringen, a neighbouring village, and implored the Doctor to hasten to the inn and give his professional attendance to a lady who had fallen ill there. Leaving Holmes at the Fall, Watson hurried to the inn, only to discover that the landlord had sent him no such letter. Remembering Moriarty, Watson ran back to the Falls, but arrived too late. All he found there was signs of a desperate struggle and a slip of writing from Holmes explaining that he and Moriarty had murdered each other and then flung themselves over the Falls.

POPULAR TALK.

The arrest of Watson this morning will surprise no one. It was the general opinion that some such step must follow in the interests of public justice. Special indignation was expressed at Watson's statement that Holmes was running away from Moriarty. It is notorious that Holmes was a man of immense courage, who revelled in facing danger. To represent him as anything else is acknowledged on all hands to be equivalent to saying that the People's Detective (as he was called) had

IMPOSED UPON THE PUBLIC.

We understand that printed matter by Watson himself will be produced at the trial in proof of the public contention. It may also be observed that Watson's story carries doubt on the face of it. The deadly struggle took place on a narrow path along which it is absolutely certain that the deceased must have seen Moriarty coming. Yet the two men only wrestled on the cliff. What the Crown will ask is,

WHERE WERE HOLMES'S PISTOLS?

Watson, again, is the authority for stating that the deceased never crossed his threshold without several loaded pistols in his pockets. If this were so in London, is it not quite incredible that Holmes should have been unarmed in the comparatively wild Swiss mountains, where, moreover, he is represented as living in deadly fear of Moriarty's arrival? And from Watson's sketch of the ground, nothing can be clearer than that Holmes had ample time to shoot Moriarty after the latter hove in sight. But even allowing that Holmes was unarmed, why did not Moriarty shoot him? Had he no pistols either? This is the acme of absurdity.

WHAT WATSON SAW.

Watson says that as he was leaving the neighbourhood of the Falls he saw in the distance the figure of a tall man. He suggests that this was Moriarty, who (he holds) also sent the bogus letter. In support of this theory it must be allowed that Peter Steiler, the innkeeper, admits that some such stranger did stop at the inn for a few minutes and write a letter. This clue is being actively followed up, and doubtless with the identification of this mysterious person, which is understood to be a matter of a few hours' time, we shall be nearer the unravelling of the knot. It may be added, from information supplied us from a safe source, that the police do not expect to find that this stranger was Moriarty, but rather

AN ACCOMPLICE OF WATSON'S,

who has for long collaborated with him in his writings, and has been a good deal mentioned in connection with the deceased. In short, the most sensational arrest of the century is on the *tapis*.

The murdered man's

ROOMS IN BAKER-STREET

are in possession of the police. Our representative called there in the course of the morning and spent some time in examining the room with which the public has become so familiar through Watson's descriptions. The room is precisely as when deceased inhabited it. Here, for instance, is his favourite chair in which he used to twist himself into knots when thinking out a difficult problem. A tin canister of tobacco stands on the mantelpiece (shag), and above it hangs the long-lost Gainsborough "Duchess," which Holmes discovered some time ago, without, it seems, being able to find the legal owner. It will be remembered that Watson, when Holmes said surprising things, was in the habit of "leaping to the ceiling" in astonishment. Our representative examined the ceiling and found it

MUCH DENTED.

The public cannot, too, have forgotten that Holmes used to amuse himself in this room with pistol practice. He was such a scientific shot that one evening while Watson was writing he fired all round the latter's head, shaving him by an infinitesimal part of an inch. The result is a portrait on the wall, in pistol-shots, of Watson, which is considered an excellent likeness. It is understood that, following the example set in the Ardlamont case, this picture will be produced in court. It is also in contemplation to bring over the Falls of Reichenbach for the same purpose.

THE MOTIVE.

The evidence in the case being circumstantial, it is obvious that motive must have a prominent part in the case for the Crown. Wild rumours are abroad on this subject, and at this stage of the case they must be received with caution. According to one, Watson and Holmes had had a difference about money matters, the latter holding that the former was making a goldmine out of him and sharing nothing. Others allege that the difference between the two men was owing to Watson's change of manner; Holmes, it is stated, having complained bitterly that Watson did not jump to the ceiling in

amazement so frequently as in the early days of their intimacy. The blame in this case, however, seems to attach less to Watson than to the lodgers on the second floor, who complained to the landlady. We understand that the legal fraternity look to

THE DARK HORSE

in the case for the motive which led to the murder of Mr. Holmes. This dark horse, of course, is the mysterious figure already referred to as having been seen in the vicinity of the Falls of Reichenbach on the fatal day. He, they say, had strong reasons for doing away with Mr. Holmes. For a long time they were on excellent terms. Holmes would admit frankly in the early part of his career that he owed everything to this gentleman; who, again, allowed that Holmes was a large source of income to him. Latterly, however, they have not been on friendly terms, Holmes having complained frequently that whatever he did the other took the credit for. On the other hand, the suspected accomplice has been heard to say "that Holmes has been getting too uppish for anything," that he "could do very well without Holmes now," that he "has had quite enough of Holmes," that he "is sick of the braggart's name," and even that "if the public kept shouting for more Holmes he would kill him in self-defence." Witnesses will be brought to prove these statements, and it is believed that the mysterious man of the Falls and this gentleman will be found to be one and the same person. Watson himself allows that he owes his very existence to this dark horse, which supplies the important evidence that the stranger of the Falls is also a doctor. The theory of the Crown, of course, is that these two medical men were accomplices. It is known that he whom we have called the dark horse is still in the neighbourhood of the Falls.

DR. CONAN DOYLE.

Dr. Conan Doyle is at present in Switzerland.

AN EXTRAORDINARY RUMOUR

reaches us as we go to press, to the effect that Mr. Sherlock Holmes, at the entreaty of the whole British public, has returned to Baker-street, and is at present (in the form of the figure 8) solving the problem of The Adventure of the Novelist and His Old Man of the Sea.

Sherlock Holmes and the Drood Mystery

EDMUND PEARSON

EDMUND LESTER PEARSON (1880–1937) is best known as a career librarian, humorist, expert on real-life crimes, reviewer of books, and the author of a weekly column of essays and stories titled "The Librarian" that was published in the *Boston Evening Transcript* from 1906 to 1920. Born in 1880 in Newburyport, Massachusetts, Pearson graduated from Harvard College in 1902 and went on to obtain a BLS from the New York State Library School in Albany in 1904. While at Harvard, he published his first writings in the school periodical, the *Harvard Advocate*. After graduating, Pearson held the position of Librarian in the Washington, D.C., Public Library, worked in the Library of Congress in the Copyright Division, and worked in the Military Information Division of the War Department. In 1914, he became the Editor of Publications at the New York Public Library.

Pearson's most famous work is a collection of essays on true crimes, *Studies in Murder* (1924), in which he details the Lizzie Borden murders, among other crimes. Other publications include *Murder at Smutty Nose and Other Murders* (1926) and *Five Murders* (1928), several autobiographical books focused on his childhood, and three books about books: *Books in Black or Red* (1923), *Queer Books* (1928), and *Dime Novels* (1929). In addition to "Sherlock Holmes and the Drood Mystery," Pearson's other works in the Sherlockian world are "Ave atque Vale, Sherlock!" in the July 20, 1927, issue of *The Outlook*, and "Sherlock Holmes Among the Illustrators" in the August 1932 issue of *The Bookman*.

"Sherlock Holmes and the Drood Mystery" originally appeared in the April 2, 1913, issue of the *Boston Evening Transcript*; it was first collected in *The Secret Book* (New York, Macmillan, 1914). It was later published as a separate pamphlet (Boulder, Colorado, Aspen Press, 1973).

SHERLOCK HOLMES AND
THE DROOD MYSTERY

Edmund Pearson

"WATSON," SAID SHERLOCK Holmes, beaming at me across the breakfast table, "can you decipher character from handwriting?"

He held an envelope toward me as he spoke. I took the envelope and glanced at the superscription. It was addressed to Holmes at our lodging in Baker Street. I tried to remember something of an article I had read on the subject of handwriting.

"The writer of this," I said, "was a modest self-effacing person, and one of wide knowledge, and considerable ability. He—"

"Excellent, Watson, excellent! Really, you outdo yourself. Your reading is quite Watsonian, in fact. I fear, however, you are a bit astray as to his modesty, knowledge, and so on. As a matter of fact, this letter is from Mr. Thomas Sapsea."

"The famous Mayor of Cloisterham?"

"Quite so. And for pomposity, egregious conceit coupled with downright ignorance, he has not his peer in England. So you did not score a bull's-eye there, my dear fellow."

"But what does he want of you?" I asked, willing to change the subject. "He isn't going to engage you to solve the mystery of Edwin Drood?"

"That is precisely what he is doing. He is all at sea in the matter. Come, what do you say to a run down to Cloisterham? We can look into this matter to oblige the mayor, and take a ramble through the cathedral. I'm told they have some very fine gargoyles."

An hour later, we were seated in a train for Cloisterham. Holmes had been looking through the morning papers. Now he threw them aside, and turned to me.

"Have you followed this Drood case?" he asked.

I replied that I had read many of the accounts and some of the speculations on the subject.

"I have not followed it as attentively as I should have liked," he returned, "the recent little affair of Colonel Raspopoff and the czarina's rubies has occupied me thoroughly of late. Suppose you go over the chief facts—it will help clear my mind."

"The facts are these," I said. "Edwin Drood, a young engineer about to leave for Egypt, had two attractions in Cloisterham. One was his affianced wife—a young school-girl, named Miss Rosa Bud. The other was his devoted uncle and guardian, Mr. John Jasper. The latter is choirmaster of the cathedral. There were, it seems, two clouds over his happiness. One of these was the fact that his betrothal to Miss Bud—an arrangement made by their respective parents while Edwin and Rosa were small children—was not wholly to the liking of either of the principals. They had, indeed, come to an agreement, only a few days before Edwin Drood's disappearance, to terminate the engagement. They parted, it is believed, on friendly, if not affectionate terms.

"The other difficulty lay in the presence, in Cloisterham, of one Neville Landless—a young student from Ceylon. Landless has, it seems, a strain of Oriental blood in his nature—he is of dark complexion and fiery temper. Actual quarrels had occurred between the two, with some violence on Landless's part. To restore them to friendship, however, Mr. Jasper, the uncle of Edwin, arranged for a dinner in his rooms on Christmas Eve, at which they were to be the only guests. The dinner took place, everything passed off amicably, and the two left, together, late in the evening, to walk to the river, and view the great storm which was raging. After that they parted—according to Landless—and Drood has never been seen again. His uncle raised the alarm next morning, Landless was detained, and questioned, while a thorough search was made for the body of Drood. Beyond the discovery of his watch and pin in the weir, nothing has been found. Landless had to be released for lack of evidence, but the feeling in Cloisterham was so strong against him that he had to leave. He is thought to be in London."

"H'm," remarked Holmes, "who found the watch and pin?"

"A Mr. Crisparkle, minor canon of the cathedral. Landless was living in his house, and reading with him. I may add that Landless has a sister—Miss Helena—who has also come to London."

"H'm," said Holmes. "Well, here we are at Cloisterham. We can now pursue our investigations on the spot. We will go to see Mr. Sapsea, the mayor."

Mr. Sapsea proved to be exactly the pompous Tory jackass that Holmes had described. He had never been out of Cloisterham, and his firm conviction of the hopeless inferiority of all the world outside England was so thoroughly provincial that I suspected him of some connection with "The Saturday Review." He was strong in his belief that young Neville Landless had murdered Drood and thrown his body in the river. And his strongest reason for this belief lay in the complexion of Landless.

"It is un-English, Mr. Holmes," said he, "it's un-English and when I see a face that is un-English, I know what to suspect of that face."

"Quite so," said Holmes; "I suppose that everything was done to find the body?"

"Everything, Mr. Holmes, everything that my—er—knowledge of the world could possibly suggest. Mr. Jasper was unwearied in his efforts. In fact he was worn out by his exertions."

"No doubt his grief at the disappearance of his nephew had something to do with that, as well."

"No doubt of it at all."

"Landless, I hear, is in London?"

"So I understand, sir, so I understand. But Mr. Crisparkle, his former tutor, has given me—in my capacity as magistrate—assurances that he can be produced at any moment. At present he can be found by applying to Mr. Grewgious, at Staple Inn. Mr. Grewgious is a guardian of the young lady to whom Edwin Drood was betrothed."

Holmes made a note of Mr. Grewgious's name and address on his shirt-cuff. We then rose to depart.

"I see," said the mayor, "that you are thinking of paying a call on this un-English person in London. That is where you will find a solution of the mystery, I can assure you."

"It is probable that I shall have occasion to run up to London this evening," said Holmes, "though I believe that Dr. Watson and I will stroll about Cloisterham a bit, first. I want to inspect your gargoyles."

When we were outside, Holmes's earliest remark was, "But I think we had better have a little chat with Mr. John Jasper."

We were directed to Mr. Jasper's rooms, in the gatehouse, by a singularly obnoxious boy, whom we found in the street, flinging stones at the passers-by.

"That's Jarsper's," said he, pointing for an instant toward the arch, and then proceeding with his malevolent pastime.

"Thanks," said Holmes, shortly, giving the imp sixpence, "here's something for you. And here," he continued, reversing the boy over his knee, and giving him a sound spanking, "here is something else for you."

On inquiry it appeared that Mr. Jasper was at home. He would see us, said the landlady, but she added that "the poor gentleman was not well."

"Indeed?" said Holmes. "What's the matter?"

"He do be in a sort of daze, I think."

"Well, well, this gentleman is a doctor—perhaps he can prescribe."

And with that we went up to Mr. Jasper's room. That gentleman had recovered, apparently, from his daze, for we heard him chanting choir music, as we stood outside the door. Holmes, whose love for music is very keen, was enraptured, and insisted on standing for several moments, while the low and sweet tones of the choir-master's voice, accompanied by the notes of a piano, floated out to us. At last we knocked and the singer admitted us.

Mr. Jasper was a dark-whiskered gentleman who dwelt in a gloomy sort of room. He had, himself, a gloomy and reserved manner. Holmes introduced us both, and informed Mr. Jasper that he was in Cloisterham at the request of the mayor, Mr. Sapsea, to look up some points in connection with the disappearance of Edwin Drood.

"Meaning his murder?" inquired Mr. Jasper.

"The word I used," said Holmes, "was disappearance."

"The word I used," returned the other, "was murder. But I must beg to be excused from all discussion of the death of my dear boy. I have taken a vow to discuss it with no one, until the assassin is brought to justice."

"I hope," said Holmes, "that if there is an assassin, I may have the good fortune—"

"I hope so, too. Meanwhile—" and Mr. Jasper moved toward the door, as if to usher us out. Holmes tried to question him about the events of Christmas Eve, prior to the young man's disappearance, but Mr. Jasper said that he had made his statement before the mayor, and had nothing to add.

"Surely," said Holmes, "I have seen you before, Mr. Jasper?"

Mr. Jasper thought not.

"I feel almost positive," said my friend; "in London, now—you come to London at times, I take it?"

Perhaps. But he had never had the pleasure of meeting Mr. Holmes. He was quite sure. Quite.

We departed, and as we strolled down the High Street, Holmes asked me if I would object to spending the night in Cloisterham.

"I shall rejoin you tomorrow," he added.

"But you are going away?"

"Yes, to London. I am going to follow Mr. Sapsea's advice," he added with a smile.

"I thought you wanted to see the gargoyles," I objected.

"So I did. And do you know, my dear fellow, I believe I have seen one of the most interesting of them all."

Holmes's remark was entirely enigmatic to me, and while I was still puzzling over it, he waved his hand and entered the omnibus for the station. Left thus alone in Cloisterham, I went to the Crozier, where I secured a room for the night. In passing the gatehouse I noticed a curious looking man with his hat in his hand, looking attentively at Mr. Jasper's window. He had, I observed, white hair, which streamed in the wind. Later in the afternoon, having dropped in at the cathedral to hear the vesper service, I saw the same man. He was watching the choir-master, Mr. Jasper, with profound scrutiny. This made me uneasy. How did I know but what another plot, like that which had been hatched against the nephew, was on foot against the uncle? Seated in the bar at the Crozier, after dinner, I found him again. He willingly entered into conversation with me, and announced himself as one Mr. Datchery—"an idle buffer, living on his means." He was interested in the Drood case and very willing to talk about it. I drew him out as much as I could, and then retired to my rooms to think it over.

That he wore a disguise seemed clear to me. His hair looked like a wig. If he was in disguise, who could he be? I thought over all the persons in any way connected with the case, when suddenly the name of Miss Helena Landless occurred to me. Instantly I was convinced that it must be she. The very improbability of the idea fascinated me. What more unlikely than that a young Ceylonese girl should pass herself off for an elderly English man, sitting in bars and drinking elderly English drinks? The improbable is usually true, I remembered. Then I recalled that I had heard that Miss Landless, as a child, used to dress up as a boy. I was now positive about the matter.

I was on hand to meet Holmes when he returned the next day. He had two men with him and he introduced them as Mr. Tartar and Mr. Neville Landless. I looked with interest at the suspected man, and then tried to have speech with Holmes. But he drew me apart.

"These gentlemen," said he, "are going at once to Mr. Crisparkle's. They will remain there until tonight, when I expect to have need of them. You and I will return to your hotel."

On the way I told him about Mr. Datchery, and my suspicions about that person. He listened eagerly, and said that he must have speech with Datchery without delay. When I told him of my belief that Datchery was the sister of Landless, in disguise, Holmes clapped me on the back, and exclaimed:

"Excellent, Watson, excellent! Quite in your old vein!"

I flushed with pride at this high praise from the great detective. He left me at the Crozier, while he went forth to find Datchery, and also, he said, to have a word with Mr. Jasper. I supposed that he was about to warn the choir-master that he was watched.

Holmes returned in capital spirits.

"We shall have our work cut out for us tonight, Watson," said he, "and perhaps we will have another look at the gargoyles."

During dinner he would talk of nothing except bee-keeping. He conversed on this topic, indeed, until long after we had finished our meal, and while we sat smoking in the bar. About eleven, an ancient man, called Durdles, came in, looking for Mister Holmes.

"Mr. Jarsper he's a-comin' down the stair, sir," said he.

"Good!" exclaimed Holmes, "come, Watson, we must make haste. This may be a serious business. Now, Durdles!"

The man called Durdles led us rapidly, and by back ways, to the churchyard. Here he showed us where we could stand, hidden behind a wall, and overlooking the tombs and gravestones. I could not imagine the object of this nocturnal visit. Holmes gave our guide some money, and he made off. While I stood there, looking fearfully about, I thought I saw the figures of two men behind a tomb, at some little distance. I whispered to Holmes, but he motioned for silence.

"Hush!" he whispered, "Look there!"

I looked where he indicated, and saw another figure enter the churchyard. He carried some object, which I soon guessed to be a lantern, swathed in a dark wrapping. He unfolded a part of this wrapping, and I recognized by the light the dark features of Mr. Jasper. What could he be doing here at this hour? He commenced to fumble in his pockets, and presently produced a key with which he approached the door of the tomb. Soon it swung open, and Mr. Jasper seemed about to step inside. But he paused for an instant, and then fell back, with a fearful scream of terror. Once, twice, did that awful cry ring through the silent churchyard. At its second repetition a man stepped from the tomb. Then Jasper turned, and ran frantically toward the cathedral.

The two men whom I had previously noticed sprang from behind a monument and pursued him.

"Quick!" said Holmes, "after him!"

We both ran in the same direction as fast as we could. Hindered by the darkness and by our unfamiliarity with the ground, however, we made poor progress. The fleeing choir-master and his two strange pursuers had already vanished into the gloom of the cathedral. When at last we entered the building the sound of hurrying footsteps far above us was all we could hear. Then, as we paused, for an instant at fault, there came another dreadful cry, and then silence.

Men with lights burst into the cathedral and led us up the staircase toward the tower. The twisting ascent was a long business, and I knew from Holmes's face that he dreaded what we might find at the top. When we reached the top there lay the choir-master, Jasper, overpowered and bound by Mr. Tartar. The latter, then, had been one of the men I had seen behind the monument.

"Where is Neville?" said Holmes quickly.

Tartar shook his head and pointed below.

"This man," said he, indicating Jasper, "fought with him, and now I fear he really has a murder to answer for."

One of the men in the group which had followed us to the top stepped forward and looked down toward Jasper. It was the man whom we had seen step out of the tomb. I started when I saw that except for the wig and a few changes in his costume it was the same man who had called himself "Datchery."

Jasper gazed up at him and his face was distorted with fear.

"Ned! Ned!" he cried, and hid his face on the stone floor.

"Yes, yer may hide yer face," said old Durdles, trembling with rage, "yer thought yer had murdered him,—murdered Mr. Edwin Drood, yer own nephew. Yer hocussed him with liquor fixed with pizen, same's yer tried to hocus Durdles, an' tried to burn him up with quicklime in the tomb. But Durdles found him, Durdles did."

He advanced and would have ground the head of the prostrate choir-master under his heel, if some men had not held him back.

"Of course," said Holmes to me on the train back to London next morning, "no one in Cloisterham thought of suspecting the eminently respectable Mr. Jasper. They started with the presumption of his innocence. He was a possible object of suspicion to me from the first. This was because he was one of the two men who last saw Edwin Drood. When we had our interview

with him—Jasper, I mean—I recognized him as the frequenter of a disreputable opium den near the docks. You may remember that I have had occasion to look into such places in one other little problem we studied together. He was, then, leading a double life. That was as far as I had gone when I returned to London last night. But while there I had a talk with Mr. Grewgious, as well as with poor young Landless and his sister. From them I learned that Jasper was in love with his nephew's betrothed, and had, indeed, been persecuting her with his attentions, both before and after Edwin's disappearance. From Mr. Grewgious's manner I became convinced that he, at any rate, viewed Jasper with profound suspicion. But he was a lawyer, and very cautious; he evidently had no certain proof. Other hints which were dropped led me to suspect that he was not mourning the death of young Drood.

"This was a curious thing—the whole crux to the mystery lay in it. I sat up all night, Watson, and consumed about four ounces of tobacco. It needed some thinking. Why, if Jasper had plotted murder, had he failed to carry it out? The opium, the opium, Watson—you know, yourself, that a confirmed opium-smoker is apt to fail, is almost sure to fail, in any great enterprise. He tries to nerve himself before the deed, and ten to one he merely stupefies himself, and the plot miscarries. This morning I saw Mr. Grewgious again, and charged him in so many words with keeping secret the fact that Drood was alive. He admitted it, and told me that Drood was in Cloisterham masquerading as Datchery."

"But why should he do that?" I asked, "why did he let Neville rest under suspicion of murder?"

"Because he had no certain proof of Jasper's guilt," said Holmes, "and he was trying to collect evidence against him. He was himself drugged when the attempt was made upon his life, he was rescued on that occasion by Durdles, and his disappearance was connived at by Mr. Grewgious. The lawyer further told me of the ring which Edwin Drood carried with him, and which the would-be murderer overlooked when he took the watch and pin. Then, it was only necessary for me to drop a hint to Jasper about the ring. That sent him back to the tomb, into which he supposed he had flung Drood's body to be consumed by quicklime. There he found the living, and not the dead Edwin Drood, as you saw. But the opium was really the clew to the whole thing—I went to see the old hag who keeps the den he frequented, and learned from her that he babbled endlessly about the murder in his dreams. He had arrived at a point where he could not distinguish between the real attempt at murder and a vision. He acted as in a vision when he tried to commit the deed, and so it failed.

"As for your theory about Miss Landless being Datchery—well, my dear fellow, I am glad for the sake of that proper, clerical gentleman, Mr. Crisparkle, that his intended wife has not been masquerading in trousers at the Cloisterham inns. Poor Landless—I shall never forgive myself for his death. His murderer will meet the fate he richly deserves, without a doubt.

"And now, Watson, we were discussing bees. Have you ever heard of planting buckwheat near the hives? I am told they do wonderfully on buckwheat."

The Rape of the Sherlock

Being the Only True Version of Holmes's Adventures

A. A. MILNE

FEW CHARACTERS IN the world of children's literature are as beloved as Christopher Robin and Winnie-the-Pooh, created by Alan Alexander Milne (1882–1956) with four iconic books written for his son. Born in London, Milne went to Cambridge and became a journalist, eventually taking the position of assistant editor of *Punch*.

Although not a prolific writer of mystery fiction, he did produce one of the most influential detective novels of all time when he produced *The Red House Mystery* (1922) near the beginning of the golden age of detective fiction. In this popular book, described by Alexander Woollcott as "one of the three best mystery stories of all time," Milne introduces the jolly, "oh, what fun!" approach to crime in the person of Antony Gillingham, a slightly zany amateur detective whose nickname is "Madman." Milne's play *The Fourth Wall* (1928; U.S. title: *The Perfect Alibi*) was a success; the audience saw the murder committed and then witnessed every logical step taken to uncover and apprehend the criminal.

"The Rape of the Sherlock" was Milne's first published piece of fiction, as he recounts in his book *It's Too Late Now: the Autobiography of a Writer* (1939). He submitted it to *Punch*, which rejected it, but it was accepted by London's *Vanity Fair*. To describe it as trivial overpraises it. It is included here as a curiosity—nothing more.

"The Rape of the Sherlock: Being the Only True Version of Holmes's Adventures" was first published in the October 15, 1903, issue of London's *Vanity Fair*.

THE RAPE OF THE SHERLOCK

Being the Only True Version of Holmes's Adventures

A. A. Milne

IT WAS IN the summer of last June that I returned unexpectedly to our old rooms in Baker Street. I had that afternoon had the unusual experience of calling on a patient, and in my nervousness and excitement had lost my clinical thermometer down his throat. To recover my nerve I had strolled over to the old place, and was sitting in my arm-chair thinking of my ancient wound, when all at once the door opened, and Holmes glided wistfully under the table. I sprang to my feet, fell over the Persian slipper containing the tobacco, and fainted. Holmes got into his dressing-gown and brought me to.

"Holmes," I cried, "I thought you were dead."

A spasm of pain shot across his mobile brow.

"Couldn't you trust me better than that?" he asked, sadly. "I will explain. Can you spare me a moment?"

"Certainly," I answered. "I have an obliging friend who would take my practice for that time."

He looked keenly at me for answer. "My dear, dear Watson," he said, "you have lost your clinical thermometer."

"My dear Holmes—" I began, in astonishment.

He pointed to a fairly obvious bulge in his throat.

"I was your patient," he said.

"Is it going still?" I asked, anxiously.

"Going fast," he said, in a voice choked with emotion.

A twinge of agony dashed across his mobile brow. (Holmes's mobility is a byword in military Clubs.) In a little while the bulge was gone.

"But why, my dear Holmes—"

He held up his hand to stop me, and drew out an old cheque-book.

"What would you draw from that?" he asked.

"The balance," I suggested, hopefully.

"What conclusion I meant?" he snapped.

I examined the cheque-book carefully. It was one on Lloyd's Bank, half-empty, and very, very old. I tried to think what Holmes would have deduced, but with no success. At last, determined to have a dash for my money, I said:

"The owner is a Welshman."

Holmes smiled, picked up the book, and made the following rapid diagnosis of the case:

"He is a tall man, right-handed, and a good boxer; a genius on the violin, with an unrivalled knowledge of criminal London, extraordinary powers of perception, a perfectly enormous brain; and, finally, he has been hiding for some considerable time."

"Where?" I asked, too interested to wonder how he had deduced so much from so little.

"In Portland."

He sat down, snuffed the ash of my cigar, and remarked:

"Ah! Flor—de—Dindigul—I—see,—do—you—follow—me—Watson?" Then, as he pulled down his "Encyclopaedia Britannica" from its crate, he added:

"It is my own cheque-book."

"But Moriarty?" I gasped.

"There is no such man," he said. "It is merely the name of a soup."

From a Detective's Notebook

P. G. WODEHOUSE

O N E O F T H E most popular and beloved humorists of the twentieth century, Sir Pelham "Plum" Grenville Wodehouse (1881–1975) had a long, illustrious, and prolific literary career that began with works in several genres, including straightforward detective stories. "From a Detective's Notebook" is similar to some of his later ventures into the literature of mystery or crime, which are generally nonsensical, such as *Hot Water* (1932), *Pigs Have Wings* (1952), and *Do Butlers Burgle Banks?* (1968).

As a young man he became a banker, but by the time he was twenty-two, he was earning more as a writer than as a banker and resigned to devote his full time to producing short stories, novels, and occasional pieces, which he did with enormous success for the next seven decades. His first novel was *The Pothunters* (1902), but his greatest creations, the Hon. Bertie Wooster and his friend and valet, Jeeves, did not make their appearance until *The Saturday Evening Post* published "Extricating Young Gussie" in 1915. Wooster is the good-hearted but intellectually challenged young man who ceaselessly finds himself in difficulties with his aunt, a girl, or the law, relying on Jeeves to get him out of trouble.

For much of his life, Wodehouse spent half his time in America and half in England; he became a U.S. citizen in 1955. He wrote scores of screenplays and teleplays beginning in 1930, and provided the book and lyrics for numerous musicals, including *Anything Goes* (1934), for which he wrote the book with Guy Bolton; Cole Porter wrote the music and lyrics.

Shortly before his death, he was given a knighthood as Commander of the Order of the British Empire by Queen Elizabeth II.

"From a Detective's Notebook" was first published in the May 1959 issue of *Punch*; it was first collected in *The World of Mr. Mulliner* (London, Barrie & Jenkins, 1972).

FROM A DETECTIVE'S NOTEBOOK

P. G. Wodehouse

WE WERE SITTING round the club fire, old General Malpus, Driscoll the QC, young Freddie ffinch-ffinch and myself, when Adrian Mulliner, the private investigator, gave a soft chuckle. This was, of course, in the smoking-room, where soft chuckling is permitted.

"I wonder," he said, "if it would interest you chaps to hear the story of what I always look upon as the greatest triumph of my career?"

We said No, it wouldn't, and he began.

"Looking back over my years as a detective, I recall many problems the solution of which made me modestly proud, but though all of them undoubtedly presented certain features of interest and tested my powers to the utmost, I can think of none of my feats of ratiocination which gave me more pleasure than the unmasking of the man Sherlock Holmes, now better known as the Fiend of Baker Street."

Here General Malpus looked at his watch, said "Bless my soul," and hurried out, no doubt to keep some appointment which had temporarily slipped his mind.

"I had at first so little to go on," Adrian Mulliner proceeded. "But just as a brief sniff at a handkerchief or shoe will start one of Mr. Thurber's bloodhounds giving quick service, so is the merest suggestion of anything that I might call fishy enough to set me off on the trail, and what first aroused my suspicions of this sinister character was his peculiar financial position.

"Here we had a man who evidently was obliged to watch the pennies closely, for when we are introduced to him he is, according to Doctor Watson's friend Stamford, 'bemoaning himself because he could not find someone to go halves with him in some nice rooms which he had found and which were too much for his purse.' Watson offers himself as a fellow lodger, and they settle down in—I quote—'a couple of comfortable bedrooms and a large sitting-room at 221B Baker Street.'

"Now I never lived in Baker Street at the turn of the century, but I knew old gentlemen who had done so, and they assured me that in those days you could get a bedroom and sitting-room and three meals a day for a pound a week. An extra bedroom no doubt made the thing come higher, but thirty shillings must have covered the rent, and there was never a question of a man as honest as Doctor Watson failing to come up with his fifteen each Saturday. It followed, then, that even allowing for expenditure in the way of Persian slippers, tobacco, disguises, revolver cartridges, cocaine, and spare fiddle-strings, Holmes would have been getting by on a couple of pounds or so weekly. And with this modest state of life he appeared to be perfectly content. In a position where you or I would have spared no effort to add to our resources he simply did not bother about the financial side of his profession. Let us take a few instances at random and see what he made as a 'consulting detective.' Where are you going, Driscoll?"

"Out," said the QC, suiting action to the word.

Adrian Mulliner resumed his tale.

"In the early days of their association Watson

speaks of being constantly bundled off into his bedroom because Holmes needed the sitting-room for interviewing callers. 'I have to use this room as a place of business,' he said, 'and these people are my clients.' And who were these clients? 'A grey-headed, seedy visitor, who was closely followed by a slipshod elderly woman,' and after these came 'a railway porter in his velveteen uniform.' Not much cash in that lot, and things did not noticeably improve later, for we find his services engaged by a stenographer, an average commonplace British tradesman, a commissionaire, a City clerk, a Greek interpreter, a landlady ('You arranged an affair for a lodger of mine last year') and a Cambridge undergraduate.

"So far from making money as a consulting detective, he must have been a good deal out of pocket most of the time. In *A Study in Scarlet* Inspector Gregson says there has been a bad business during the night at 3 Lauriston Gardens off the Brixton Road and he would esteem it a great kindness if Holmes would favour him with his opinions. Off goes Holmes in a hansom from Baker Street to Brixton, a fare of several shillings, dispatches a long telegram (another two or three bob to the bad), summons 'half a dozen of the dirtiest and most ragged street Arabs that ever I clapped eyes on,' and gives each of them a shilling, and finally, calling on Police Constable Bunce, the officer who discovered the body, takes half a sovereign from his pocket and after 'playing with it pensively' presents it to the constable. The whole affair must have cost him considerably more than a week's rent at Baker Street, and no hope of getting it back from Inspector Gregson, for Gregson, according to Holmes himself, was one of the smartest of the Scotland Yarders.

"Inspector Gregson! Inspector Lestrade! These clients! I found myself thinking a good deal about them, and it was not long before the truth dawned upon me that they were merely cheap actors, hired to deceive Doctor Watson. For what would the ordinary private investigator have said to himself when starting out in business? He would have said, 'Before I take on

work for a client I must be sure that that client has the stuff. The daily sweetener and the little something down in advance are of the essence,' and would have had those landladies and those Greek interpreters out of that sitting-room before you could say 'blood-stain.' Yet Holmes, who could not afford a pound a week for lodgings, never bothered. Significant?"

On what seemed to me the somewhat shallow pretext that he had to see a man about a dog, Freddie ffinch-ffinch now excused himself and left the room.

"Later," Adrian Mulliner went on, "the thing became absolutely farcical, for all pretence that he was engaged in a gainful occupation was dropped by himself and the clients. I quote Doctor Watson: 'He tossed a crumpled letter across to me. It was dated from Montague Place upon the preceding evening and run thus:

Dear Mr. Holmes,—I am very anxious to consult you as to whether or not I should accept a situation which has been offered me as a governess. I shall call at half past ten to-morrow if I do not inconvenience you.

Yours faithfully,
Violet Hunter

"Now, the fee an investigator could expect from a governess, even one in full employment, could scarcely be more than a few shillings, yet when two weeks later Miss Hunter wired 'please be at the Black Swan Hotel at Winchester at midday to-morrow,' Holmes dropped everything and sprang into the 9:30 train."

Adrian Mulliner paused and chuckled softly.

"You see where all this is heading?"

I said No, I didn't. I was the only one there, and had to say something.

"Tut, tut, man! You know my methods. Apply them. Why is a man casual about money?"

"Because he has a lot of it."

"Precisely."

"But you said Holmes hadn't."

"I said nothing of the sort. That was merely the illusion he was trying to create."

"Why?"

"Because he needed a front for his true activities. Sherlock Holmes had no need to worry about fees. He was pulling in the stuff in sackfulls from another source. Where is the big money? Where has it always been! In crime. Bags of it, and no income tax. If you want to salt away a few million for a rainy day you don't spring into 9:30 trains to go and see governesses, you become a master criminal, sitting like a spider in the centre of its web and egging your corps of assistants on to steal jewels and naval treaties."

"You mean . . ."

"Exactly. He was Professor Moriarty."

"What was that name again?"

"Professor Moriarty."

"The bird with the reptilian head?"

"That's right."

"But Holmes hadn't a reptilian head."

"Nor had Moriarty."

"Holmes said he had."

"And to whom? To Watson. So as to get the description given publicity. Watson never saw Moriarty. All he knew about him was what Holmes told him. Well, that's the story, old man."

"The whole story?"

"Yes."

"There isn't any more?"

"No."

I chuckled softly.

The Ruby of Khitmandu

HUGH KINGSMILL

(Writing as Arth_r C_n_n D_yle and E. W. H_rn_ng)

THE ENGLISH AUTHOR, journalist, parodist, biographer, anthologist, and literary critic Hugh Kingsmill Lunn (1889–1949) dropped his last name as a partial pseudonym for what he described as professional reasons, perhaps in order not to be confused with his brothers, Arnold Lunn and Brian Lunn.

Although Kingsmill is described in numerous reference books as a mystery writer, among his other literary accomplishments, he did not, in fact, write a single crime novel, though he wrote some short stories in the genre, several of which were collected in a book of parodies, *The Table of Truth* (1933), which he has identified as one of his favorite books. Several of his biographies are notable, especially *The Return of William Shakespeare* (1929), *Frank Harris* (1932), *Samuel Johnson* (1933), and *D. H. Lawrence* (1938).

The dual byline on this story reflects the fame of the now somewhat-forgotten E. W. Hornung, the creator of Raffles, the notorious gentleman jewel thief. Although he appeared in only four books between 1899 and 1909, Raffles short stories vied with Sherlock Holmes in popularity in the late nineteenth and early twentieth century, and it was not uncommon for parodists to match the nearly infallible detective against the equally successful safecracker.

"The Ruby of Khitmandu" was first published in the April 1932 issue of *The Bookman*; it was first collected in book form in the author's *The Table of Truth* (London, Jarrolds, 1933).

THE RUBY OF KHITMANDU

Hugh Kingsmill

(Synopsis—The Maharajah of Khitmandu, who is staying at Claridge's, is robbed of the famous Ruby of Khitmandu. Sherlock Holmes traces the theft to Raffles, who agrees to hand over the ruby to Holmes, on condition that he and his confederate Bunny are not proceeded against. Raffles has just explained the situation to Bunny. They are in the rooms of Raffles in the Albany.)

Chapter XV
(*Bunny's Narrative*)

MY HEART FROZE at the incredible words which told me that Raffles, of all men, was throwing up the sponge without a struggle, was tamely handing over the most splendid of all the splendid trophies of his skill and daring to this imitation detective, after outwitting all the finest brains of the finest crime-investigating organization in the world. Suddenly the ice turned to fire, and I was on my feet, speaking as I had never spoken to living man before. What I said I cannot remember. If I could, I would not record it. I believe I wept. I know I went down on my knees. And Raffles sat there with never a word! I see him still, leaning back in a luxurious armchair, watching me with steady eyes sheathed by drooping lids. There was a faint smile on the handsome dare-devil face, and the hands were raised as if in deprecation; nor can I give my readers a more complete idea of the frenzy which had me in its grip than by recording the plain fact that I was utterly oblivious to the strangeness of the spectacle before me. Raffles apologetic, Raffles condescending to conciliate me—at any other time such a reversal of our natural rôles had filled me with unworthy exultation for myself, and bitter shame for him. But I was past caring now.

And then, still holding his palms towards me, he crossed them. I have said that during the telling of his monstrous decision he had the ruby between the thumb and forefinger of his right hand. Now the left hand was where the right had been, and the ruby was in it. I suppose I should have guessed at once, I suppose I should have read in his smile what it needed my own eyes to tell me, that there was a ruby in his right hand too! So that was the meaning of the upraised hands! I swear that my first sensation was a pang of pure relief that Raffles had not stooped to conciliate me, my second a hot shame that I had been idiot enough even for one moment to believe him capable of doing so. Then the full significance of the two rubies flashed across me.

"An imitation?" I gasped, falling back into my chair.

"An exact replica."

"For Holmes?"

He nodded.

"But supposing he—"

"That's a risk I have to take."

"Then I go with you."

A savage gleam lit up the steel-blue eyes.

"I don't want you."

"Holmes may spot it. I must share the risk."

"You fool, you'd double it!"

"Raffles!" The cry of pain was wrung from me before I could check it, but if there was weakness in my self-betrayal, I could not regret it when I saw the softening in his wonderful eyes.

"I didn't mean it, Bunny," he said.

"Then you'll take me!" I cried, and held my breath through an endless half-minute, until a consenting nod brought me to my feet again. The hand that shot out to grasp his was met half-way, and a twinkling eye belied the doleful resignation in his "What an obstinate rabbit it is!"

Our appointment with Holmes was for the following evening at nine. The clocks of London were striking the half-hour after eight when I entered the Albany. My dear villain, in evening dress, worn as only he could wear it, was standing by the table; but there was that in his attitude which struck the greeting dumb upon my lips. My eyes followed the direction of his, and I saw the two rubies side by side in their open cases.

"What is it, Raffles?" I cried. "Has anything happened?"

"It's no good, Bunny," he said, looking up. "I can't risk it. With anyone else I'd chance it, and be damned to the consequences, too. But Holmes—no, Bunny! I was a fool ever to play with the idea."

I could not speak. The bitterness of my disappointment, the depth of my disillusion, took me by the throat and choked me. That Raffles should be knocked out I could have borne, that he should let the fight go by default—there was the shame to which I could fit no words.

"He'd spot it, Bunny. He'd spot it." Raffles picked up one of the cases. "See this nick?" he asked lightly, for all the world as if blazing eyes and a scarlet face were an invitation to confidences. "I've marked this case because it holds the one and only Ruby of Khitmandu, and on my life I don't believe I could tell which ruby was which, if I once got the cases mixed."

"And yet," I croaked from a dry throat, "you think Holmes can do what you can't!"

"My dear rabbit, precious stones are one of his hobbies. The fellow's written a monograph on them, as I discovered only to-day. I'm not saying he'd spot my imitation, but I am most certainly not going to give him the chance," and he turned on his heel and strode into his bedroom for his overcoat.

The patient readers of these unworthy chronicles do not need to be reminded that I am not normally distinguished for rapidity of either thought or action. But for once brain and hand worked as surely and swiftly as though they had been Raffles's own, and the rubies had changed places a full half-minute before Raffles returned to find me on my feet, my hat clapped to my head, and a look in my eyes which opened his own in enquiry.

"I'm coming with you," I cried.

Raffles stopped dead, with an ugly glare.

"Haven't you grasped, my good fool, that I'm handing Holmes the real stone?"

"He may play you false."

"I refuse to take you."

"Then I follow you."

Raffles picked up the marked case, snapped it to, and slipped it into his overcoat pocket. I was outwitting him for his own good, yet a pang shot through me at the sight, with another to follow when the safe closed on the real ruby in the dummy's case. And the eyes that strove to meet his fell most shamefully as he asked if I still proposed to thrust my company upon him. Through teeth which I could hardly keep from chattering I muttered that it was a trap, that Holmes would take the stone and then call in the police, that I must share the danger as I would have shared the profits. A contemptuous shrug of the splendid shoulders, and a quick spin on his heel, were all the answer he vouchsafed me, and not a word broke the silence between us as we strode northwards through the night.

There was no tremor in the lean strong hand which raised the knocker on a door in Baker Street. He might have been going to a triumph instead of to the bitterest of humiliations. And it might be a triumph, after all! And he would owe it to me! But there was little enough of exultation in the heart which pounded savagely as I followed him upstairs, my fingers gripped tightly round the life-preserver in my pocket.

"Two gentlemen to see you, sir," wheezed the woman who had admitted us. "And one of them," drawled an insufferably affected voice, as we walked in, "is very considerately advertising the presence of a medium-sized life-preserver in his right overcoat pocket. My dear Watson, if you must wave a loaded revolver about, might I suggest that you do so in the passage? Thank you. It is certainly safer in your pocket. Well, Mr. Raffles, have you brought it?"

Without a word, Raffles took the case out, and handed it across to Holmes. As Holmes opened it, the fellow whom he had addressed as Watson leaned forward, breathing noisily. Criminals though we were, I could not repress a thrill of pride as I contrasted the keen bronze face of my companion with the yellow cadaverous countenance of Holmes, and reflected that my own alas indisputably undistinguished appearance could challenge a more than merely favourable comparison with the mottled complexion, bleared eyes, and ragged moustache of the detective's jackal.

"A beautiful stone, eh, Watson?" Holmes remarked, in the same maddening drawl, as he held the ruby to the light. "Well, Mr. Raffles, you have saved me a good deal of unnecessary trouble. The promptitude with which you have bowed to the inevitable does credit to your quite exceptional intelligence. I presume that you will have no objection to my submitting this stone to a brief examination?"

"I should not consider that you were fulfilling your duty to your client if you neglected such an elementary precaution."

It was perfectly said, but then was it not Raffles who said it? And said it from the middle of the shabby bear-skin rug, his legs apart and his back to the fire. Now, as always, the center of the stage was his at will, and I could have laughed at the discomfited snarl with which Holmes rose, and picking his way through an abominable litter of papers disappeared into the adjoining room. Three minutes, which seemed to me like twice as many hours, had passed by the clock on the mantelpiece, when the door opened again. Teeth set, and nerves strung ready, I was yet, even in this supreme moment, conscious of a tension in Raffles which puzzled me, for what had he, who believed the stone to be the original ruby, to fear? The menacing face of the detective brought my life-preserver half out of my pocket, and the revolver of the man Watson wholly out of his. Then, to my unutterable relief, Holmes said, "I need not detain you any longer, Mr. Raffles. But one word in parting. Let this be your last visit to these rooms."

There was a threat in the slow-dropping syllables which I did not understand, and would have resented, had I had room in my heart for any other emotion than an overwhelming exultation. Through a mist I saw Raffles incline his head with a faintly contemptuous smile. And I remember nothing more, till we were in the open street, and the last sound I expected startled me back into my senses. For Raffles was chuckling.

"I'm disappointed in the man, Bunny," he murmured with a laugh. "I was convinced he would spot it. But I was ready for him."

"Spot it?" I gasped, fighting an impossible suspicion.

"Yes, spot the dummy which my innocent rabbit was so insultingly sure was the one and only Ruby of Khitmandu."

"What!" My voice rose to a shriek. "Do you mean it was the dummy which was in the marked case?"

He spun round with a savage "Of course!"

"But you said it was the real one."

"And again, of course!"

Suddenly I saw it all. It was the old, old wretched story. He would trust no one but himself. He alone could bluff Holmes with a dummy stone. So he had tried to shake me off with the lie about restoring the real stone. And my unwitting hand had turned the lie to truth! As I reeled, he caught my arm.

"You fool! You infernal, you unutterable fool!" He swung me round to face his blazing eyes. "What have you done?"

"I swapped them over. And be damned to you!"

"You swapped them over?" The words came slowly through clenched teeth.

"When you were in your bedroom. So it *was* the one and only ruby you gave him after all," and the hand that was raised to strike me closed on my mouth as I struggled to release the wild laughter which was choking in my throat.

Chapter XVI
(*Dr. Watson's Narrative*)

I must confess that as the door closed on Raffles and his pitiful confederate I felt myself completely at a loss to account for the unexpected turn which events had taken. There was no mistaking the meaning of the stern expression on the face of Holmes when he rejoined us after examining the stone. I saw at once that his surmise had proved correct, and that Raffles had substituted an imitation ruby for the original. The almost laughable agitation with which the lesser villain pulled out his life-preserver at my friend's entrance confirmed me in this supposition. It was clear to me that he was as bewildered as myself when Holmes dismissed Raffles instead of denouncing him. Indeed, his gasp of relief as he preceded Raffles out of the room was so marked as to bring me to my feet with an ill-defined impulse to rectify the extraordinary error into which, as it seemed to me, Holmes had been betrayed.

"Sit down!" Holmes snapped, with more than his usual asperity.

"But Holmes!" I cried. "Is it possible you do not realize—"

"I realize that, as usual, you realize nothing. Take this stone. Guard it as you would guard the apple of your eye. And bring it to me here at eight to-morrow morning."

"But Holmes, I don't understand—"

"I have no time to discuss the limitations of your intelligence."

I have always been willing to make allowances for my friend's natural impatience with a less active intelligence than his own. Nevertheless, I could not repress a feeling of mortification as he thrust the case into my hand, and propelled me into the passage. But the night air, and the brisk pace at which I set out down Baker Street, soon served to restore my equanimity. A long experience of my friend's extraordinary powers had taught me that he often saw clearly when all was darkness to myself. I reflected that he had no doubt some excellent reason for letting the villains go. No man could strike more swiftly and with more deadly effect than Holmes, but equally no man knew better how to bide his time, or could wait more patiently to enmesh his catch beyond the possibility of escape. While these thoughts were passing through my mind, I had been vaguely conscious of two men walking ahead of me, at a distance of about a hundred yards. Suddenly one of them reeled, and would have fallen had not his companion caught his arm. My first impression was that I was witnessing the spectacle, alas only too common a one in all great cities, of two drunken men assisting each other homewards. But as I observed the couple in pity mingled with repulsion, the one who had caught the other's arm raised his hand as if to deliver a blow. I felt for my revolver, and was about to utter a warning shout, when I perceived that they were the very men who had just been occupying my thoughts. The need for caution instantly asserted itself. Halting, I drew out my pipe, filled it, and applied a match. This simple stratagem enabled me to collect my thoughts. It was plain that these rascals had quarrelled. I recalled the familiar adage that when thieves fall out honest men come by their own, and I summoned all my powers to imagine what Holmes would do in my place. To follow the rogues at a safe distance, and act as the development of the situation required, seemed to me the course of action which he would pursue. But I could not conceal from myself that his view of what the situation might require would probably differ materially from my own. For an instant I was tempted to hasten back to him with the news of this fresh development. But a moment's reflection convinced me that to do so would be to risk the almost certain loss of my quarry. I had another, and I fear a less excusable, motive for not returning. The brusquerie of my dismissal still rankled a little. It would be gratifying if I could, this once, show my imperious friend that I was capable of making an independent contribution to the unravelling of a problem. I therefore quickened my steps, and soon diminished the distance between myself and my quarry to about fifty yards. It was obvious that the dispute was still in progress. Raffles himself maintained a sullen silence, but the excitable voice and gestures of his accomplice testified that the quarrel, whatever its nature, was raging with unabated vehemence.

They had entered Piccadilly, and I was still at their heels, when they turned abruptly into Albany Courtyard. By a fortunate coincidence I had for some weeks been visiting the Albany in my professional capacity, having been called in by my old friend General Macdonagh, who was now at death's door. I was therefore known to the commissionaire, who touched his hat as I hastened past him. With the realization that this was where Raffles lived, the course of action I should adopt became clear to me. He had the latchkey in his door, as I came up.

"By Heavens!" his companion cried. "It's Watson!"

"*Dr.* Watson, if you please, Bunny." The scoundrel turned to me with a leer. "This is indeed a charming surprise, Doctor."

Ignoring the covert insolence of the man, I demanded sternly if he would accord me a brief audience in his rooms.

"But of course, my dear Doctor. Any friend of Mr. Holmes is our friend, too. You will excuse me if I lead the way."

My hand went to my revolver, and as the door of his rooms closed behind us, I whipped it out, at the same time producing the case which contained the imitation ruby.

"Here is your imitation stone," I cried, tossing the case on to the table. "Hand over the real one, or I shall shoot you like a dog."

Accomplished villain though he was, he could not repress a start of dismay, while his miserable confederate collapsed on a sofa with a cry of horror.

"This is very abrupt, Doctor," Raffles said, picking the case up and opening it. "May I ask if you are acting on the instructions of Mr. Holmes? It is, after all, with Mr. Holmes that I am dealing."

"You are dealing with me now. That is the only fact you need to grasp."

"But Mr. Holmes was entirely satisfied with the stone I handed him."

"I am not here to argue. Will you comply with my request?"

"It is disgraceful of Holmes to send you to tackle the pair of us single-handed."

"*Mr.* Holmes, you blackguard! And he knows nothing of what I am doing."

"Really? Then I can only say he does not deserve such a lieutenant. Well, Bunny, our triumph was, I fear, a little premature."

A minute later, I was in the passage, the case containing the genuine stone in my breast pocket. Through the closed door there rang what I took to be the bitter, baffled laugh of an outwitted scoundrel. In general, I am of a somewhat sedate temper, but it was, I confess, in a mood which almost bordered on exultation that I drove back to Baker Street, and burst in on Holmes.

"I've got it! I've got it!" I cried, waving the case.

"Delirium tremens?" Holmes enquired coldly, from his arm-chair. I noticed that he was holding a revolver.

"The original ruby, Holmes!"

With a bound as of a panther Holmes leaped from his chair and snatched the case from my hand. "You idiot!" he snarled. "What have you done?"

Vexed and bewildered, I told my story, while Holmes stared at me with heaving chest and flaming eyes. My readers will have guessed the truth, which Holmes flung at me in a few disconnected sentences, interspersed with personal observations of an extremely disparaging nature. It was indeed the original ruby which Raffles had brought with him, and which Holmes, suspecting that Raffles would attempt to retrieve it while he slept, had entrusted to my keeping. The warning which Holmes had given Raffles not to visit him again was now explained, as was also the vigil with a loaded revolver on which my friend had embarked when I burst in on him.

The arrest a fortnight later of Raffles and the man Bunny, and the restoration of the famous ruby to its lawful owner, will be familiar to all readers of the daily papers. During this period the extremely critical condition of General Macdonagh engaged my whole attention. His decease was almost immediately followed by the unexpected deaths of two other patients, and in the general pressure of these sad events I was unable to visit Holmes in order to learn from his own lips the inner story of the final stages in this remarkable case.

The Adventure of the Remarkable Worm

AUGUST DERLETH

AUGUST WILLIAM DERLETH (1909–1971) was born in Sauk City, in Wisconsin, where he remained his entire life, most of which appears to have been spent at the typewriter, as he wrote more than three thousand stories and articles, and published more than a hundred books, including detective stories (featuring Judge Peck and the Sherlock Holmes–like character Solar Pons), supernatural stories, and what he regarded as his serious fiction: a very lengthy series of books, stories, poems, journals, etc., about life in his small town, which he renamed Sac Prairie.

When Derleth learned that Arthur Conan Doyle had no plans to write more Holmes stories, he wrote to ask permission to continue the series; Conan Doyle graciously declined. Nonetheless, Derleth proceeded, inventing a name that was syllabically reminiscent of Sherlock Holmes, and wrote his first pastiches about Solar Pons, ultimately producing more stories about Pons than Conan Doyle did about Holmes.

Pons is all but a clone of Holmes. Both have prodigious powers of observation and deduction, able to tell minute details about those they have just met, deduced in seconds of observation. They also are physically similar, both being tall and slender. Holmes stories are narrated by Dr. John H. Watson, Pons stories by Dr. Lyndon Parker, with whom he shares rooms at 7B Praed Street; their landlady is Mrs. Johnson. Holmes's elder brother, Mycroft, has even greater gifts than Sherlock, and Solar Pons's brother, Bancroft, is also superior.

Among the few differences between Holmes and Pons are their time frames. The most memorable Holmes adventures took place in the 1880s and 1890s, whereas Pons flourished in the 1920s and 1930s. Pons is also a more cheerful figure than Holmes, less given to depression and bouts of drug use.

Several of the Pontine tales have titles taken from the famous unrecorded cases to which Watson often alluded, including "Ricoletti of the Club Foot (and his Abominable Wife)," "The Aluminum Crutch," "The Politician, the Lighthouse, and the Trained Cormorant," and the present story.

"The Adventure of the Remarkable Worm" was first published in *Three Problems for Solar Pons* (Sauk City, Wisconsin, Mycroft & Moran, 1952).

THE ADVENTURE OF THE REMARKABLE WORM

August Derleth

"AH, PARKER!" EXCLAIMED Solar Pons, as I walked into our quarters at 7B Praed Street late one mid-summer afternoon in the early years of the century's third decade, "you may be just in time for another of those little forays into the criminological life of London in which you take such incomprehensible delight."

"You have taken a case," I said.

"Say, rather, I have consented to an appeal."

As he spoke, Pons laid aside the pistol with which he had been practising, an abominable exercise which understandably disturbed our long-suffering landlady, Mrs. Johnson. He reached among the papers on the table and flipped a card so that it fell before me on the table's edge, the message up.

"Dear Mr. Pons,

"Mr. Humphreys always said you were better than the police, so if it is all right I will come there late this afternoon when Julia comes and tell you about it. The doctor says it is all right with Mr. P., but I wonder.

"Yours resp., Mrs. Flora White."

Pons regarded me with a glint in his eye as I read it.

"A cryptogram?" I ventured.

Pons chuckled. "Oh, come, Parker, it is not as difficult as all that. She is only agitated and perhaps indignant."

"I confess this is anything but clear to me."

"I do not doubt it," said Pons dryly. "But it is really quite simple on reflection. She makes reference to a Mr. Humphreys; I submit it is that fellow Athos Humphreys for whom we did a bit of investigation in connection with that little matter of the Penny Magenta. She wishes to consult us about a matter in which a doctor has already been consulted. The doctor has not succeeded in reassuring her or allaying her alarm. She cannot come at once because she cannot leave her patient alone. The patient, therefore, is at least not dead. She must wait until Julia comes, which will be late this afternoon; it is not amiss, therefore, to venture that Julia is her daughter or at least a schoolgirl, who must wait upon dismissal of classes before she can take Mrs. White's place and thus free our prospective client to see us.

"Since it is now high time for her to make an appearance, she has probably arrived in that cab which has just come to a stop outside."

I stepped to the window and looked down. A cab was indeed standing before our lodgings, and a heavy woman of middle age was ascending the steps of Number 7. She was dressed in very plain house-wear, which suggested that she had come directly away from her work. Her only covering, apart from an absurdly small feathered hat, was a thin shawl, for the day was cool for August.

In a few moments Mrs. Johnson had shown her in, and she stood looking from one to the other of us, her florid face showing but a moment's indecision before she smiled uncertainly at my companion.

"You're Mr. Pons, ain't yer?"

"At your service, Mrs. White," replied Pons with unaccustomed graciousness, as his alert eyes took in every detail of her appearance. "Pray sit down and tell us about the little problem which vexes you."

She sat down with growing confidence, drew her shawl a little away from her neck, and began to recount the circumstances which had brought her to our quarters. She spoke in an animated voice, in a dialect which suggested not so much Cockney as transplanted provincial.

She explained how she "says to Mr. 'Umphreys," and he "says to me to ask his friend, Solar Pons; so I done like he said," as soon as her niece came from school. Pons sat patiently through her introduction until his patience was rewarded. He did not interrupt her story, once she began it.

She was employed as a cleaning woman at several houses. This was her day at the home of Idomeno Persano, a solitary resident of Hampstead Heath, an ex-patriate American of Spanish parentage. He had bought a house on the edge of the heath eleven years before, and since that time had led a most sedentary life. He was known to frequent the heath in the pursuit of certain entomological interests. As a collector of insects and information pertinent thereto, he was attentive to the children of the neighborhood; they knew him as a benign old fellow, who was ever ready to give them sixpence or a shilling for some insect to add to his collection.

Persano's life appeared to be in all respects retiring. Judging by what Mrs. White told in her rambling manner, he corresponded with fellow entomologists and was in the habit of sending and receiving specimens. He had always seemed to be a very easy-going man, but one day a month ago, he had received a post-card from America which had upset him very much. It had no writing on it but his name and address, and it was nothing but a comic picture card. Yet he had been very agitated at receipt of it, and since that time he had not ventured out of the house.

Mrs. White had been delayed in coming to

her employer's home on this day; so it was not until afternoon that she reached the house. She was horrified to find her employer seated at his desk in an amazing condition. She thought he had gone stark mad. She had striven to arouse him, but all she could draw from him was a muttered few words which sounded like "the worm—unknown to science." And something about "the dog"—but there had never been a dog in the house, and there was not now. Nothing more. He was staring at a specimen he had apparently just received in the post. It was a worm in a common matchbox.

"Och, an 'orrible worm, Mr. Pons. Fair give me the creeps, it did!" she said firmly.

She had summoned a physician at once. He was a young *locum tenens*, and confessed himself completely at sea when confronted with the ailing Persano. He had never encountered an illness of quite such a nature before, but he discovered a certain paralysis of the muscles and came to the conclusion that Persano had had a severe heart attack. From Mrs. White's description, the diagnosis suggested coronary trouble. He had administered a sedative and had recommended that the patient be not moved.

Mrs. White, however, was not satisfied. As soon as the doctor had gone, she had consulted "Mr. 'Umphreys," with the result that she had sent the note I had seen by messenger. Now she was here. Would Mr. Pons come around and look at her employer?

I could not refrain from asking, "Why did you think the doctor was wrong, Mrs. White?"

"I feels it," she answered earnestly. "It's intuition, that's what, sir. A woman's intuition."

"Quite right, Mrs. White," said Pons in a tolerant voice which nettled me the more. "My good friend Parker is of that opinion so commonly held by medical men, that his fellow practitioners are somehow above criticism or question by lay persons. I will look at Mr. Persano, though my knowledge of medicine is sadly limited."

"And 'ere," said our client, "is the card 'e got."

So saying, she handed Pons a colored postcard of a type very common in America, a type evidently designed for people on holiday wishing to torment their friends who are unable to take vacations. It depicted in cartoon form a very fat man running from a little dog which had broken his leash. The drawing was bad, and the lettered legend was typical: "Having a fast time at Fox Lake. Wish you were here." The obverse bore nothing but Persano's address and a Chicago postmark.

"That is surely as innocuous a communication as I have ever seen," I said.

"Is it not, indeed?" said Pons, one eyebrow lifted.

"I could well imagine that it would irritate Persano."

"'Upset' was the word, I believe, Mrs. White?"

"That he was, Mr. Pons. Fearful upset. I seen 'im, seein' as how 't was me 'anded it to 'im. I says to 'im, 'Yer friends is havin' a time on their 'oliday,' I says. When 'e seen it, 'e went all white, and was took with a coughin' spell. 'E threw it from him without a word. I picked it up and kept it; so 'ere 'tis."

Pons caressed the lobe of his right ear while he contemplated our client. "Mr. Persano is a fat man, Mrs. White?"

Her simple face lit up with pleasure. "That 'e is, Mr. Pons, though 'ow yer could know it, I don't see. Mr. 'Umphreys was right. A marvel 'e said yer was."

"And how old would you say he is?"

"Oh, in 'is sixties."

"When you speak of your employer as having been 'upset,' do you suggest that he was frightened?"

Our client furrowed her brows. "'E was upset," she repeated doggedly.

"Not angry?"

"No, sir. Upset. Troubled, like. 'Is face changed color; 'e said something under 'is breath I didn't 'ear; 'e threw the card away, like as if 'e didn't want ter see it again. I picked it up and kep' it."

Pons sat for a moment with his eyes closed.

Then he took out his watch and consulted it. "It is now almost six o'clock. The matter would seem to me of some urgency. You've kept your cab waiting?"

Mrs. White nodded. "Julia will be that anxious."

"Good!" cried Pons, springing to his feet. "We will go straight back with you. There is not a moment to be lost. We may already be too late."

He doffed his worn purple dressing-gown, flung it carelessly aside, and took up his Inverness and deerstalker.

Throughout the ride to the scene of our client's experience, Pons maintained a meditative silence, his head sunk on his chest, his lean fingers tented where his hands rested below his chin.

The house on the edge of Hampstead Heath was well isolated from its neighbors. A substantial hedge, alternating with a stone wall, ran all around the building, which was of one storey, and not large. Our client bustled from the cab, Pons at her heels, leaving me to pay the fare. She led the way into the house, where we were met by a pale-faced girl who was obviously relieved to see someone.

"Been any change, Julia?" asked Mrs. White.

"No, 'm. He's sleeping."

"Anybody call?"

"No 'm. No one."

"That's good. Yer can go 'ome now, that's a good girl." Turning to us, our client pointed to a door to her left. "In there, Mr. Pons."

The light of two old-fashioned lamps revealed the scene in all its starkness. Mrs. White's employer sat in an old Chippendale wing chair before a broad table, no less old-style than the lamps which shed an eerie illumination in the room. He was a corpulent man, but it was evident at a glance that he was not sleeping, for his eyes were open and staring toward the curious object which lay before him—an opened match-box with its contents, which looked to my untutored eye very much like a rather fatter-than-usual caterpillar. A horrible smile—the *risus sardonicus*—twisted Persano's lips.

"I fancy Mr. Persano is in your department, Parker," said Pons quietly.

It took but a moment to assure me of what Pons suspected. "Pons, this man is dead!" I cried.

"It was only an off-chance that we might find him alive," observed Pons. He turned to our client and added, "I'm afraid you must now notify the police, Mrs. White. Ask for Inspector Taylor at Scotland Yard. Say to him that I am here."

Mrs. White, who had given forth but one wail of distress at learning of her employer's death, rallied sufficiently to say that there was no telephone in the house. She would have to go to a neighbor's.

The moment our client had gone, Pons threw himself into a fever of activity. He took up one of the lamps and began to examine the room, dropping to his knees now and then, scrutinizing the walls, the book-shelves, the secretary against one wall, and finally the dead man himself, examining Persano's hands and face with what I thought to be absurd care.

"Is there not a peculiar color to the skin, Parker?" he asked at last.

I admitted that there was.

"Is it consistent with coronary thrombosis?"

"It isn't usual."

"You saw that faint discoloration of one finger," continued Pons. "There is some swelling, is there not?"

"And a slight flesh wound. Yes, I saw it."

"There is some swelling and discoloration of exposed portions of the body surely," he went on.

"Let me anticipate you, Pons," I put in. "If the man has been poisoned, I can think of no ordinary poison which would be consistent with the symptoms. Arsenic, antimony, strychnine, prussic acid, cyanide, atropine—all are ruled out. I am not prepared to say that this man died of unnatural causes."

"Spoken with commendable caution," observed Pons dryly. "I submit, however, that the evident symptoms are inconsistent with coronary thrombosis."

"They would seem so."

With this Pons appeared to be satisfied. He gave his attention next to the table before which Persano's body sat. The surface of the table was covered with various objects which suggested that Persano had been in the process of trying to identify the remarkable worm when he was stricken. Books on entomology and guides to insect-life lay open in a semi-circle around the opened match-box with its strange occupant; beyond, in the shadow away from the pool of light from the lamp on the table, lay a case of mounted insects in various stages of their evolution from the larval through the pupal. This, too, suggested that Persano was searching for some points of similarity between them and the specimen unknown to science.

I reached out to take up the match-box, but Pons caught my arm.

"No, Parker. Let us not disturb the scene. Pray observe the discarded cover of the box. Are there not pin-pricks in it?"

"The creature would need air."

Pons chuckled. "Thank heaven for the little rays of humor which your good nature affords us!" he exclaimed. "The worm is dead; I doubt that it ever was alive. Besides, the parcel was wrapped. Let us just turn the cover over."

He suited his actions to his words. It was at once evident that the pin-pricks spelled out a sentence. Together with Pons, I leaned over to decipher it.

"Little dog catches big cat."

I flashed a glance at Pons. "If that's a message, certainly it is in code."

"Surely a limited message, if so," demurred Pons.

"But it's nothing more than child's play," I protested. "It can have no meaning."

"Little, indeed," agreed Pons. "Yet I fancy it may help to establish the identity of the gentleman who brought about Idomeno Persano's death."

"Oh, come, Pons, you are having me!"

"No, no, the matter is almost disappointingly elementary," retorted Pons. "You know my methods, Parker; you have all the facts. You need only apply them."

With this he came to his knees at the wastebasket, where he sought diligently until he found a box six inches square, together with cord and wrapping paper.

"This would appear to be the container in which the worm arrived," he said, examining the box. "Well filled with packing, so that the specimen should not be jolted, I see. Does that convey nothing to you, Parker?"

"It is the customary way of sending such specimens."

"Indeed." He looked to the wrapping. "The return address is plainly given. 'Fowler. 29 Upper Brook Street.' Yet is was posted in Wapping, a little detail I daresay Persano overlooked. Some care for details is indicated. Fowler will doubtless turn out to be a known correspondent in matters entomological, but most definitely not the source of this remarkable worm."

At this moment Mrs. White returned, somewhat out of breath. At her heels followed the young *locum tenens* she had evidently gone to fetch after telephoning Scotland Yard; and, bringing up the rear, came Inspector Walter Taylor, a feral-faced young man in his thirties who had more than once shown an unusual aptitude for the solution of crime within his jurisdiction.

With his arrival, the Inspector immediately took charge, and soon Pons and I were on our way back to 7B Praed Street, Pons bearing with almost gingerly care, with Inspector Taylor's permission, a little parcel containing the extraordinary worm which had sent Idomeno Persano to madness and death.

In our quarters once more, Pons carefully uncovered the remarkable worm and placed it, still in its match-box, under the light on his desk. Thus seen, it was truly an imposing sight. It was furred, like a caterpillar, but also horned, like some pupal stages, with not one horn, but four, one pair rising from the back close to its head,

the other facing the first pair, but rising from the other end of the worm. Its head was bare of fur and was featured by a long proboscis, from which uncoiled a slender, thread-like tongue. It appeared to have no less than four rows of feet, double rows extending all the way along its length, as multitudinous as those of a centipede, and very similar in construction. Double antennae rose from back of its head, reaching to the height of the horns, while its tail was thick and blunt. It was perhaps four inches in length, and at least two inches in diameter.

"Have you ever seen its like before?" asked Pons delightedly, his eyes twinkling.

"Never. How could I, if even science does not know it?"

"Ah, Parker, do not be so ready to take someone's word for such a judgment. There is no such thing, technically, as a worm unknown to science. Any worm discovered by a scientist can be readily enough classified, even if not immediately identified with precision."

"On the contrary," I retorted with some spirit. "It lies before us."

"Let me put it this way, Parker—if the worm is unknown to science, there is no such worm."

"I'm afraid we are reversing roles, Pons," I said with asperity. "Is it not you who scores me constantly for my didacticism?"

"I am guilty of the charge," he admitted. "But in this case, I must give you no quarter. This worm is unknown to science for precisely the reason I have stated—there is no such worm."

"But it lies here, refuting you!"

"Pray look again, my dear fellow. I submit that the head of this interesting creature is nothing less than the head of a sphinx moth—commonly known also as a hawk moth or humming-bird moth—quite possibly the common striped sphinx, *Deilephila Lineata*. The elaborate legs are nothing more than complete centipedes cunningly fitted in—six of them, I should say; these appear to be a centipede commonly found in the northern part of North America, *Scutigera forceps*. The antennae apparently derive from two sources—the furred pair suggest the *Actias Luna*, or common Luna moth; the long, thin green pair are surely those of *Pterophylla camellifolia*, the true katydid. The fur is as equally a fabrication, and the horns—ah, Parker, the horns are little masterpieces of deception! This is a remarkable worm indeed. How closely did you examine the wound in Persano's finger?"

"I examined it with my customary care," I answered somewhat stiffly.

"What would you say had caused it?"

"It appeared to be a gash, as if he had run his finger into a nail or a splinter, though the gash was clean."

"So that you could, if pressed, suggest that Persano had come to his death by venom administered through a snake's fang?"

"Since my imagination is somewhat more restricted, of scientific necessity, than yours, Pons . . . ," I began, but he interrupted me.

"Like this," said Pons.

He seized hold of a tweezers and caught the remarkable worm of Idomeno Persano between them. Instantly the four horns on the creature's thick body shot forth fangs; from two of them a thin brown fluid still trickled.

"Only one of these found its mark," said Pons dryly. "It seems to have been enough." He gazed at me with twinkling eyes and added, "I believe you had the commendable foresight not to include snake venom in that list of poisons you were confident had not brought about Persano's death."

For a moment I was too nonplussed to reply. "But this is the merest guesswork," I protested finally.

"You yourself eliminated virtually all other possibilities," countered Pons. "You have left me scarcely any other choice."

"But what of the dog?" I cried.

"What dog?" asked Pons with amazement he did not conceal.

"If I recall rightly, Mrs. White said that Persano spoke of a dog. A dog's tooth might well have made that gash."

"Ah, Parker, you are straying afield," said Pons with that air of patient tolerance I always found so trying. "There was no such dog. Mrs. White herself said so."

"You suggest, then, that Mrs. White misunderstood her employer's dying words?"

"Not at all. I daresay she understood him correctly."

"I see. Persano spoke of a dog, but there was no dog," I said with a bitterness which did not escape Pons.

"Come, come, Parker!" replied Pons, smiling. "One would not expect you to be a master of my profession any more than one could look to me as a master of yours. Let us just see how skillfully this is made."

As he spoke, he proceeded with the utmost care to cut away the fur and the material beneath. He was cautious not to release the spring again, and presently revealed a most intricate and wonderfully wrought mechanism, which sprang the trap and forced the venom from small rubber sacks attached to the fangs by tubes.

"Are those not unusually small fangs?" I asked.

"If I were to venture a guess, I should say they belonged to the coral or harlequin snake, *Micrurus fulvius*, common to the southern United States and the Mississippi Valley. Its poison is a neurotoxin; it may have been utilized, but certainly not in its pure state. It was most probably adulterated with some form of alkaloid poison to prolong Persano's death and complicate any medication Persano may have sought. The snake belongs to the Proteroglyphs, or front-fanged type of which cobras and mambas are most common in their latitudes. The 'worm' was designed to spring the fangs when touched; it was accordingly well packed so that its venom would not be discharged by rough handling in transit." He cocked an eye at me. "Does this deduction meet with your approval, Parker?"

"It is very largely hypothetical."

"Let us grant that it is improbable, if no more so than the worm itself. Is it within the bounds of possibility?"

"I would not say it was not."

"Capital! We make progress."

"But I should regard it as a highly dubious method of committing murder."

"Beyond doubt. Had it failed, its author would have tried again. He meant to kill Persano. He succeeded. If he tried previously to do so, we have no record of it. Persano was a secretive man, but he had anticipated that an attempt would be made. He had had what was certainly a warning."

"The post-card?"

Pons nodded. "Let us compare the writing on the card with that on the wrapping of the package."

It required little more than a glance to reveal that the script on the wrapping of the package which had contained the lethal worm was entirely different from that on the post-card. But if Pons was disappointed, he did not show it; his eyes were fairly dancing with delight, and the hint of a smile touched his thin lips.

"We shall just leave this for Inspector Taylor to see. Meanwhile, the hour is not yet nine; I shall be able to reach certain sources of information without delay. If Taylor should precede my return, pray detain him until I come."

With an annoyingly enigmatic smile, Pons took his leave.

It was close to midnight when my companion returned to our quarters. A fog pressed whitely against the windows of 7B, and the familiar sounds from outside—the chimes of the clock a few streets away, the rattle of passing traffic, the occasional clip-clop of a hansom cab—had all but died away.

Inspector Taylor had been waiting for an hour. I had already shown him the remarkably ingenious instrument of death designed by the murderer of Idomeno Persano, and he had scrutinized the post-card, only to confess himself as baffled as I by any meaning it might have. Yet he had an unshakable faith in my companion's striking faculties of deduction

and logical synthesis and made no complaint at Pons's delay.

Pons slipped so silently into the room as to startle us.

"Ah, Taylor, I trust you have not been kept waiting long," he said.

"Only an hour," answered the Inspector.

"Pray forgive me. I thought, insofar as I had succeeded in identifying the murderer of Idomeno Persano, I might trouble also to look him up for you."

"Mr. Pons, you're joking!"

"On the contrary. You will find him at the 'Sailor's Rest' in Wapping. He is a short, dark-skinned man of Italian or Spanish parentage. His hair is dark and curly, but showing grey at the temples. He carries a bad scar on his temple above and a little retracted from his right eye. There is a lesser scar on his throat. His name in Angelo Perro. His motive was vengeance. Persano had appeared against him in the United States a dozen years ago. Lose no time in taking him; once he learns Persano is dead, he will leave London at the earliest moment. Come around tomorrow, and you shall have all the facts."

Inspector Taylor was off with scarcely more than a mutter of thanks. It did not occur to him to question Pons's dictum.

"Surely this is somewhat extraordinary even for you, Pons," I said, before the echo of Taylor's footsteps had died down the stairs.

"You exaggerate my poor powers, Parker," answered Pons. "The matter was most elementary, I assure you."

"I'm afraid it's quite beyond me. Consider—you knew nothing of this man, Persano. You made no enquiries. . . ."

"On the contrary, I knew a good deal about him," interrupted Pons. "He was an expatriate American of independent means. He dabbled in entomology. He lived alone. He had no telephone. He was manifestly content to live in seclusion. Why?—if not because he feared someone? If he feared someone, I submit it is logical to assume that the source of his fear lay in the United States."

"But what manner of thing did he fear that he could be upset by this card?" I asked.

Pons tossed the card over to me "Though it may tell you nothing, Parker, manifestly it conveyed something to Persano."

"It could surely not have been in the address. It must be in the picture."

"Capital! Capital!" cried Pons, rubbing his hands together. "You show marked improvement, Parker. Pray proceed."

"Well, then," I went on, emboldened by his enthusiasm, "the picture can hardly convey more than that a big fat man is running away from a little dog who has broken his leash."

"My dear fellow, I congratulate you!"

I gazed at him, I fear, in utter astonishment. "But, Pons, what other meaning has it?"

"None but that. Coupled with the suggestion of the holiday which appears in the commercial lettering, the card could readily be interpreted to say: 'Your holiday is over. The dog is loose.' A fat man running to escape a dog. Persano was corpulent."

"Indeed he was!"

"Very well, then. The post-card is the first incidence of a 'dog' in the little drama which is drawing to a close at Inspector Taylor's capable hands in Wapping. Mrs. White, you recalled to my attention only a few hours ago, told us that her late employer muttered 'the dog' several times before he lapsed into silence. That was the second occurrence. And then, finally, this match-box cover announces 'Little dog catches big cat.' My dear fellow, could anything be plainer?"

"I hardly know what to say. I have still ringing in my ears your emphatic pronouncement that there was no dog in the matter," I said coldly.

"I believe my words were 'no such dog.' Your reference was clearly to a quadruped, a member of the Canis group of Carnivora. There is no such dog."

"You speak increasingly in riddles."

"Perhaps one of these clippings may help."

As he spoke, Pons took from his pocket a trio of clippings cut from *The Chicago Tribune* of seven weeks before. He selected one and handed it to me.

"That should elucidate the matter for you, Parker."

The clipping was a short news-article. I read it with care.

"Chicago, June 29: Prisoners paroled from Ft. Leavenworth yesterday included four Chicagoans. They were Mao Hsuieh-Chang, Angelo Perro, Robert Salliker, and Franz Witkenstein. They were convicted in 1914 on a charge of transporting and distributing narcotics. They had served eleven years. Evidence against them was furnished by a fifth member of the gang known as 'Big Id' Persano, who was given a suspended sentence for his part in their conviction. 'Big Id' dropped out of sight immediately after the trial. The four ex-convicts plan to return to Chicago."

Two of the convicts were pictured in the article; one of them was Perro. Pons must have made the rounds of hotels and inns in Wapping, showing Perro's photograph, in order to find him at the "Sailor's Rest."

"I take it 'Big Id' was our client's employer," I said, handing the clipping back to him.

"Precisely."

"But pray tell me, how did you arrive at Perro as the murderer?"

"Dear me, Parker, surely that is plain as a pikestaff?"

I shook my head. "I should have looked to the Chinaman. The device of the worm is Oriental in concept."

"An admirable deduction. Quite probably they were all in it together and the worm was the work of the Chinaman. But the murderer was Perro. I fear your education in the Humanities has been sadly neglected.

"The card, which was postmarked but two days after this item appeared in the papers, was an announcement from a friend of Persano's to tell him that the 'little dog' was free. The 'little dog' undoubtedly had information about Persano's whereabouts, and knew how to find him, even if Persano perhaps did not realize how much of his life in London was known in America. Persano understood the card at once.

"Had Perro not wished Persano to know who meant to kill him, I might have had a far more difficult time of it. 'Little dog catches big cat.'

Perro is a little man. Persano was big. Perro is the Spanish for 'dog.' It should not be necessary to add that Persano is the Spanish for 'Persian.' And a Persian is a variety of cat.

"An ingenious little puzzle, Parker, however elementary in final analysis."

The Enchanted Garden

H. F. HEARD

THE ENGLISH SOCIAL historian and author of science and mystery fiction Henry FitzGerald Heard (1889–1971) was born in London, studied at Cambridge University, then turned to writing essays and books on historical, scientific, religious, mystical, cultural, and social subjects, signing them Gerald Heard, the name under which all his nonfiction appeared. He moved to the United States in 1937 to head a commune in California, and later appeared as a character in several Aldous Huxley novels, notably as William Propter, a mystic, in *After Many a Summer Dies the Swan* (1939).

A Taste for Honey (1941) introduced Mr. Mycroft, a tall, slender gentleman who has retired to Sussex to keep bees. The story is told by Sydney Silchester, a reclusive man who loves honey, which he obtains from Mr. and Mrs. Heregrove, the village beekeepers, until he discovers the lady's body, black and swollen from bee stings. After the coroner's inquest, Silchester turns to Mr. Mycroft for a fresh supply of honey and receives a warning about Heregrove's killer bees.

Anthony Marriott, along with Robert Bloch, the author of *Psycho* (1959) and many other novels and stories, adapted the novel for a truly awful contemporary screenplay titled *The Deadly Bees* (1966). For an episode of television's *The Elgin Hour*, Alvin Sapinsley wrote the script for "Sting of Death," which starred Boris Karloff as Mr. Mycroft; it aired on February 22, 1955.

Mr. Mycroft appeared in two additional novels by Heard: *Reply Paid* (1942) and *The Notched Hairpin* (1949). Among Heard's other science fiction and mystery novels, perhaps his best-known work is the short story "The President of the U.S.A., Detective," which won the first prize in *Ellery Queen's Mystery Magazine*'s contest in 1947.

"The Enchanted Garden" originally was published in the March 1949 issue of *Ellery Queen's Mystery Magazine*.

THE ENCHANTED GARDEN

H. F. Heard

" 'NATURE'S A queer one,' said Mr. Squeers," I remarked.

"I know what moves you to misquote Dickens," was Mr. Mycroft's reply.

Here was a double provocation: first, there was the injury of being told that the subject on which one was going to inform someone was already known to him, and secondly, there was the insult that the happy literary quotation with which the information was to be introduced was dismissed as inaccurate. Still it's no use getting irritated with Mr. Mycroft. The only hope was to lure his pride onto the brink of ignorance.

"Then tell me," I remarked demurely, "what I have just been reading?"

"The sad, and it is to be feared, fatal accident that befell Miss Hetty Hess who is said to be extremely rich, and a 'colorful personality' and 'young for her years'—the evidence for these last two statements being a color photograph in the photogravure section of the paper which establishes that her frock made up for its brevity only by the intense virility of its green color."

I am seldom untruthful deliberately, even when considerably nonplussed; besides it was no use: Mr. Mycroft was as usual one move ahead. He filled in the silence with: "I should have countered that naturalists are the queer ones."

I had had a moment to recover, and felt that I could retrieve at least a portion of my lost initiative. "But there's no reason to link the accident with the death. The notice only mentions that she had had a fall a few weeks previously. The cause of death was 'intestinal stasis.' "

"Cause!" said Mr. Mycroft. He looked and sounded so like an old raven as he put his head on one side and uttered "caws," that I couldn't help laughing.

"Murder's no laughing matter!" he remonstrated.

"But surely, *cher maître*, you sometimes are unwilling to allow that death can ever be through natural causes!"

"Cause? There's sufficient cause here."

"*Post hoc, propter hoc*." I was glad to get off one of my few classic tags. "Because a lady of uncertain years dies considerably *after* a fall from which her doctor vouched there were no immediate ill effects, you would surely not maintain that it was *on account* of the fall that the rhythm of her secondary nervous system struck and stopped for good? And even if it was, who's to blame?"

"Cause." At this third quothing of the Raven I let my only comment be a rather longer laugh—and waited for my lecture. Mr. Mycroft did not fail me. He went on: "I'll own I know nothing about causality in the outer world, for I believe no one does really. But I have spent my life, not unprofitably, in tracing human causality. As you're fond of Dickens, I'll illustrate from Copperfield's Mr. Dick. The *causes* of King Charles's head coming off may have been due to four inches of iron going through his neck. I feel on safer ground when I say it was due to his failing to get on with his parliament. You say Miss Hess died naturally—that is to say (1) her death, (2) her accident a fortnight before, and

(3) the place where that accident took place, all have only a chance connection. Maybe your case would stand were I not watching *another* line of causality."

"You mean a motive?"

"Naturally."

"But motives aren't proof! Or every natural death would be followed by a number of unnatural ones—to wit, executions of executors and legatees!"

"I don't know whether I agree with your rather severe view of human nature. What I do know is that when a death proves to be far too happy an accident for someone who survives, then we old sleuths start with a trail which often ends with our holding proofs that not even a jury can fail to see."

"Still," I said, "suspicion can't always be right!"

What had been no more than an after-lunch sparring-match suddenly loomed up as active service with Mr. Mycroft's, "Well, the police agree with you in thinking that there's no proof, and with me in suspecting it *is* murder. That's why I'm going this afternoon to view the scene of the accident, unaccompanied—unless, of course, you would care to accompany me?"

I may sometimes seem vain but I know my uses. So often I get a ringside seat because, as Mr. Mycroft has often remarked, my appearance disarms suspicion.

"We are headed," Mr. Mycroft resumed as we bowled along in our taxi, "for what I am creditably informed is in both senses of the word a gem of a sanctuary—gem, because it is both small and jewelled."

We had been swaying and sweeping up one of those narrow rather desolate canyons in southern California through which the famous "Thirteen suburbs in search of a city" have thrust corkscrew concrete highways. The lots became more stately and secluded, the houses more embowered and enwalled, until the ride, the road, and the canyon itself all ended in a portico of such Hispano-Moorish impressiveness that it might have been the entrance to a

veritable Arabian Nights Entertainments. There was no one else about, but remarking, "This is Visitors' Day," Mr. Mycroft alit, told our driver to wait, and strolled up to the heavily grilled gate. One of the large gilt nails which bossed the gate's carved timbers had etched round it in elongated English so as to pretend to be Kufic or at least ordinary Arabic the word PRESS. And certainly it was as good as its word. For not only did the stud sink into the gate, the gate followed suit and sank into the arch, and we strolled over the threshold into as charming an enclosure as I have ever seen. The gate closed softly behind us. Indeed, there was nothing to suggest that we weren't in an enchanted garden. The ground must have risen steeply on either hand. But you didn't see any ground—all manner of hanging vines and flowering shrubs rose in festoons, hanging in garlands, swinging in delicate sprays. The crowds of blossom against the vivid blue sky, shot through by the sun, made the place intensely vivid. And in this web of color, like quick bobbins, the shuttling flight of hummingbirds was everywhere. The place was, in fact, alive with birds. But not a single human being could I see.

Birds are really stupid creatures and their noises, in spite of all the poetry that has been written about them, always seem to me tiring. Their strong point is, of course, plumage. I turned to Mr. Mycroft and remarked that I wished the Polynesian art of making cloaks of birds' feathers had not died out. He said he preferred them alive but that he believed copies of the famous plumage-mantles could now be purchased for those who liked to appear in borrowed plumes.

"This, I understand," continued Mr. Mycroft, "is supposed to be the smallest and choicest of all the world's bird sanctuaries. It is largely reserved for species of that mysterious living automaton, the hummingbird," and as was the way with the old bird himself, in a moment he seemed to forget why we were there. First, he scanned the whole place. The steep slopes came down till only a curb-path of marble divided the banks of flowers from a floor of water. At the farther end of this was a beautiful little statue holding high a lance, all of a lovely, almost peacock-green hue. And from this lance rose a spray of water, a miniature fountain. This little piece of art seemed to absorb him and as he couldn't walk on the water and examine it, he took binoculars from his pocket and scanned it with loving care. Then his mind shifted and slipping the glasses back in his pocket, he gave the same interest to the birds. His whole attention now seemed to be involved with these odd little bird-pellets. Hummingbirds are certainly odd. To insist on flying all the time you are drinking nectar from the deep flask of a flower always seems to me a kind of *tour de force* of pointless energy. In fact, it really fatigues me a little even to watch them. But the general plan of the place was beautiful and restful: there was just this narrow path of marble framing the sheet of water and this wall of flowers and foliage. The path curved round making an oval and at the upper end, balancing the fine Moorish arch through which we had entered, there rose a similar horseshoe arch, charmingly reflected in the water above which it rose. It made a bridge over which one could pass to reach the marble curb on the other side of the water.

"A bower," remarked Mr. Mycroft. He loitered along, cricking back his neck farther and farther to watch the birds perched on sprays right against the sky. He had now taken a pen from his pocket and was jotting down some ornithological observation. Poor old dear, he never could enjoy but must always be making some blot of comment on the bright mirror of—well, what I mean is that I was really taking it in and he was already busy manufacturing it into some sort of dreary information. And poor Miss Hess, she too must wait till he came back to her actual problem, if indeed there was one.

I watched him as he stepped back to the very edge of the marble curb so that he might better view a spray of deep purple bougainvillea at which a hummingbird was flashing its gorget. Yes, it would have been a pretty enough bit of color contrast, had one had a color camera to snap it, but: I had seen a sign on the gate outside asking visitors not to take photographs. So I watched my master. And having my wits about me I suddenly broke the silence. "Take care," I shouted. But too late. Mr. Mycroft had in his effort to see what was too high above him stepped back too far. The actual edge of the marble curb must have been slippery from the lapping of the ripples. His foot skidded. He made a remarkable effort to recover. I am not hard-hearted but I could not help tittering as I saw him—more raven-like than ever—flap his arms to regain his balance. And the comic maneuver served perfectly—I mean it still gave me my joke and yet saved him from anything more serious than a loss of gravity. His arms whirled. Pen and paper scrap flew from his hands to join some hummingbirds but the Mycroft frame, under whose over-arching shadow so many great criminals had cowered, collapsed not gracefully but quite safely just short of the water.

I always carry a cane. It gives poise. The piece of paper and even the pen—which was one of those new "light-as-a-feather" plastic things—were bobbing about on the surface. Of course, Mr. Mycroft, who was a little crestfallen at such an absent-minded slip, wouldn't let me help him up. In fact he was up before I could have offered. My only chance of collecting a "Thank-you" was to salvage the flotsam that he had so spontaneously "cast upon the waters." I fished in both the sopped sheet and the pen, and noticed that Mr. Mycroft had evidently not had time to record the precious natural-history fact that he had gleaned before his lack of hindsight attention parted the great mind and the small sheet. Nor when I handed him back his salvaged apparatus did he do so; instead he actually put both pen and sopped sheet into his pocket. "Shaken," I said to myself; "there's one more disadvantage of being so high up in the clouds of speculation."

As we continued on our way along the curb and were approaching the horseshoe Moorish arch-bridge, Mr. Mycroft began to limp. My real fondness for him made me ask, "Have you strained anything?"

Mr. Mycroft most uncharacteristically answered, "I think I will rest for a moment."

We had reached the place where the level marble curb, sweeping round the end of the pond, rose into the first steps of the flight of stairs that ran up the back of the arch. These stairs had a low, fretted rail. It seemed to me that it might have been higher for safety's sake, but I suppose that would have spoiled the beauty of the arch, making it look too heavy and thick. It certainly was a beautiful piece of work and finished off the garden with charming effectiveness. The steps served Mr. Mycroft's immediate need well enough, just because they were so steep. He bent down and holding the balustrade with his left hand, lowered himself until he was seated. So he was in a kind of stone chair, his back comfortably against the edge of the step above that one on which he sat. And as soon as he was settled down, the dizziness seemed to pass, and his spirits obviously returned to their old bent. He started once more to peek about him. The irrelevant vitality of being interested in anything mounted once again to its usual unusual intensity.

After he had for a few moments been swinging his head about in the way that led to his fall—the way a new-born baby will loll, roll, and goggle at the sky—he actually condescended to draw me into the rather pointless appreciations he was enjoying. "You see, Mr. Silchester, one of their breeding boxes." He pointed up into the foliage, which here rose so high that it reared a number of feet above the highest pitch of the arch.

"Surely," I asked, for certainly it is always safer with Mr. Mycroft to offer information armored in question form, "surely breeding boxes are no new invention?"

Mr. Mycroft's reply was simply, "No, of course not," and then he became vague.

I thought: Now he'll start making notes again. But no, poor old pride-in-perception was evidently more shaken by his fall than I'd thought. I felt a real sympathy for him, as I stood at a little distance keeping him under observation but pretending to glance at the scene which, though undoubtedly pretty, soon began to pall for really it had no more sense or story about it than a kaleidoscope. Poor old thing, I repeated to myself, as out of the corner of my eye, I saw him let that big cranium hang idly. But the restless, nervous energy still fretted him. Though his eyes were brooding out of focus, those long fingers remained symptomatic of his need always to be fiddling and raveling with something. How important it is, I reflected, to learn young how to idle well. Now, poor old dear, he just can't rest. Yes, Britain can still teach America something: a mellow culture knows how to meander; streams nearer their source burst and rush and tumble.

The Mycroft fingers were running to and fro along the curb of the step against which he was resting his back. I thought I ought to rouse him. He must be getting his fingernails into a horrid condition as they aimlessly scraped along under that ledge and the very thought even of someone rasping and soiling his nails sets my teeth on edge.

My diagnosis that the dear old fellow was badly shaken was confirmed when I suggested, "Shall we be getting on?" and he answered, "Certainly." And I must say that I was trebly pleased when, first, Mr. Mycroft took my extended hand to pull him to his feet, then accepted my arm as we went up the bridge and down its other side, and once we were outside the gate let me hold the door of the cab open for him. At that moment from an alcove in the gate-arch popped a small man with a book. Would we care to purchase any of the colored photographs he had for sale, and would we sign the visitors' book? I bought a couple and said to Mr. Mycroft, "May I sign Mr. Silchester and friend?"— for this was a ready way for him to preserve his anonymity, when he remarked, "I will sign," and in that large stately hand the most famous signature was placed on the page.

As we swirled down the canyon, Mr. Mycroft gave his attention to our new surroundings. Suddenly he exclaimed, "Stop!" The cab bumped to a standstill. The spot he had chosen was certainly a contrast to our last stop. Of course, once outside the houses of the rich, this countryside *is* pretty untidy. We had just swished round one of those hairpin curves all these canyon roads make as they wiggle down the central cleft. The cleft itself was in slow process of being filled by the cans and crocks that fall from the rich man's kitchen. Something, disconcerting to a sane eye even at this distance, had caught Mr. Mycroft's vulture gaze. Even before the cab was quite still, he was out and went straight for the garbage heap. I need not say that not only did I stay where I was, I turned away. For that kind of autopsy always makes me feel a little nauseated. Mr. Mycroft knows my reasonable limits. He had not asked me to go with him and when he came back he spared me by not displaying his trophy, whatever it might be. I caught sight of him stuffing a piece of some gaudy colored wrapping-paper into his pocket as he climbed into the seat beside me, but I was certainly more anxious not to notice than he to conceal.

Nor, when we reached home, did Mr. Mycroft become any more communicative. Indeed, he went straight to his study and there, no doubt, unloaded his quarry. He did not, as a matter of fact, put in an appearance till dinner. Nor did the dinner rouse him. I can hardly blame him for that. For I, too, was a little abstracted and so have to confess that I had ordered a very conventional repast, the kind of meal that you can't remember five minutes after you have ordered it or five minutes after it has been cleared away—a dinner so lacking in art that it can arouse neither expectation nor recollection.

Truth to tell, I was not a little disconcerted at the tameness of our "adventure." Mr. M. had as good as told me that he would disclose a plot and a pretty ugly one, but all we had seen was a charming enough stage, set for comedy rather than tragedy. And not a soul in view, far less a body.

The only incident, and surely that was tamely comic and I had to enjoy even that by myself, was Mr. Mycroft's skid. Indeed, as we sat on in silence I was beginning to think I might say

something—perhaps a little pointed—about pointless suspicion. But on looking across at Mr. M. who was sitting dead still at the other side of the table, I thought the old fellow looked more than a little tired. So I contented myself with the feeling that his fall had shaken him considerably more than he chose to allow.

But as I rose to retire, after reading my half-chapter of Jane Austen—for me an unfailing sedative—the old fellow roused himself.

"Thank you for your company, Mr. Silchester. Quite a fruitful day." Perhaps he saw I was already "registering surprise." For he added, "I believe we sowed and not only reaped this afternoon but if you will again give me your company, we will go tomorrow to gather the harvest."

"But I thought today was Visitors' Day?"

"Oh," he carelessly remarked, "I expect the proprietor will be glad of callers even the day after. The place was quite deserted, wasn't it? Maybe he's thinking of closing it. And that would be a pity before we had seen all that it may have to offer."

Well, I had enjoyed the little place and was not averse to having one more stroll round it. So, as it was certain we should go anyhow, I agreed with the proviso, "I must tell you that though I agree the place is worth a second visit for its beauty, nevertheless I am still convinced that to throw a cloud of suspicion over its innocent brightness might almost be called professional obsessionalism."

I was rather pleased at that heavy technical-sounding ending and even hoped it might rouse the old man to spar back. But he only replied, "Excellent, excellent. That's what I hoped you'd think and say. For that, of course, is the reaction I trust would be awakened in any untrained—I mean, normal mind."

The next afternoon found us again in the garden, I enjoying what was there and Mr. M. really liking it as much as I did but having to spin all over its brightness the gossamer threads of his suspicions and speculations. The water was flashing in the sun, the small spray-fountain playing, birds dancing—yes, the place was the nicest *mis-en-scène* for a meditation on murder that anyone could ask. Again we had the place to ourselves. Indeed, I had just remarked on the fact to Mr. M. and he had been gracious enough to protrude from his mystery mist and reply that perhaps people felt there might still be a shadow over the place, when a single other visitor did enter. He entered from the other end. I hadn't thought there was a way in from that direction but evidently behind the bridge and the thicket there must have been. He strolled down the same side of the small lake as we were advancing up. But I didn't have much chance to study him for he kept on turning round and looking at the bridge and the fountain. I do remember thinking what a dull and ugly patch his dreary store suit made against the vivid living tapestries all around us. The one attempt he made to be in tune was rather futile: he had stuck a bright red hibiscus flower in his button-hole. And then that thought was put out of my mind by an even juster judgment. Mr. M. was loitering behind— sometimes I think that I really do take things in rather more quickly than he—at least, when what is to be seen is what is meant to be seen. He pores and reflects too much even on the obvious. So it was I who saw what was going forward and being of a simple forthright nature took the necessary steps at once. After all, I did not feel that I had any right to be suspicious of our host who was certainly generous and as certainly had been put in a very unpleasant limelight by police and press. My duty was to see that what he offered so freely to us should not be abused or trespassed on. As the man ahead turned round again to study the fountain and the arch I saw what he was doing. He had a small color camera pressed against him and was going to take a photo of the fountain and the bridge. Now, as we knew, visitors were asked expressly not to do this. So I stepped forward and tapped him on the shoulder, remarking that as guests of a public generosity we should observe the simple rule requested of us. He swung round at my tap. My feelings had not been cordial at first sight, his action had alienated them further, and now a close-up

clinched the matter. His hat was now pushed back and showed a head of billiard-baldness; his eyes were weak and narrowed-up at me through glasses, rimless glasses that like some colorless fly perched on his nose—that hideous sight-aid called rightly a *pince-nez*.

Suddenly his face relaxed. It actually smiled, and he said, "That is really very kind of you. It is a pity when the rule is not kept for it does deprive the pension house for pets of a little income—almost all that one can spare for that excellent work. I am grateful, grateful." I was taken aback, even more so with the explanation. "I have the responsibility for this place. Owing to a very ungenerous press campaign we are not getting the visitors we used to. So I thought I would take a few more photos for the sales-rack at the gate. Yes, I am the owner of this little place, or as I prefer to say, the trustee of it in the joint interests of the public and philanthropy. May I introduce myself?—I am Hiram Hess, Jr."

After my *faux pas* I stumbled out some kind of apology.

"Please don't make any excuse. I only wish all my guests felt the same way in our common responsibility," he replied. "Indeed, now that you have done me one kindness, you embolden me to ask for another. I believe that the public has been scared away and this seems a heaven-sent opportunity."

All this left me somewhat in the dark. I am not averse to being treated as an honored guest and murmured something about being willing to oblige. Then I remembered Mr. M. and that I was actually taking the leading part in a scene and with the "mystery character" to whom he had in fact introduced me. I turned round and found Mr. M. at my heels. I think I made the introduction well and certainly the two of them showed no signs of not wishing to play the parts in which I was now the master of ceremonies. Mr. Hess spoke first: "I was just about to ask your friend . . ."—"Mr. Silchester," I prompted—"whether he would add another kindness. I was told only yesterday by a friend that natural history photos sell better if they can be combined with human interest of some sort. Of course when I was told that, I saw at once he was right. It must be, mustn't it?" Mr. M. made a "Lord Burleigh nod." "I am glad you agree. So I suggested that I might ask a movie star to pose. But my friend said No, I should get a handsome young man whose face has not been made wearisome to the public and that would give a kind of mystery element to the photo. People would ask, 'In what movie did that face appear?'" I own that at this personal reference—I am a Britisher, you know—I felt a little inclined to blush. "And," hurried on Mr. Hess, "now, the very day after I am told what to do, I am offered the means to do it!"

Frankness has always been my forte. Like many distinguished and good-looking people, I like being photographed and these new colored ones are really most interesting. "I would be most happy to oblige," I said, and turned to see how Mr. M. would react to my taking the play out of his hands. Of course this odd little man couldn't be a murderer. I'm not a profound student of men but that was now perfectly clear to me. Mr. M. merely treated us to another of his "Lord Burleigh nods" and then, "While you are posing Mr. Silchester, may I walk about?"

"Please look upon the place as your own" left Mr. M. free to stroll away and he seemed quite content to use his fieldglasses looking at the birds and blooms.

"Now," said Mr. Hess, all vivacity and I must confess, getting more likable every moment, "my idea is that we put the human interest, if I may so describe my collaborator, right in the middle of the scene. You will be the focus round which the garden is, as it were, draped." Then he paused and exclaimed, "Why, of course, that's the very word—why didn't I think of it before? I wonder whether you would be kind enough to agree—it would make the picture really wonderful."

Again I was a little at a loss, but the small man's enthusiasm was quite infectious. "How can I help further?" I asked.

"Well, it was the word *drape* that shot the idea into my head, darting like one of these sweet birdkins. Don't you think, Mr. Silchester, that men's clothes rather spoil the effect here?"

He looked down on his own little store suit and smiled. It was true enough but a sudden qualm shook my mind. The thought of stripping and posing, with Mr. Mycroft in the offing—well, I felt that awkward blush again flowing all over me. Whether my little host guessed my confusion or not, his next words put me at ease. "Do you think that you'd consent to wear just for the photo a robe I have?"

My relief that I was not to be asked to disrobe but to robe made me say, "Of course, of course," and without giving me any further chance to qualify my consent, off hurried little Hess. He was not gone more than a couple of minutes—not enough time for me to go back to where Mr. Mycroft was loitering near the gate at the other end of the pool—before once again he appeared, but nearly hidden even when he faced me. For what he was holding in his arms and over his shoulder was one of those Polynesian feather cloaks of which I had remarked to Mr. Mycroft that I thought they were one of the finest of all dresses ever made by man.

"Of course," Hess said, "this isn't one of the pieces that go to museums. I always hoped that somehow I would make a picture of this place in which this cloak would play the leading part."

All the while he said this he was holding out the lovely wrap for me to examine and as he finished he lightly flung the robe over my shoulder. "Oh, that's it, that's it!" he said, standing back with his head on one side like a bird. And looking down, I could not help thinking that I too was now like a bird and, to be truthful, a very handsome one.

So, without even casting a look behind me to see if Mr. Mycroft was watching and perhaps smiling, I followed Mr. Hess as he led the way, saying over his shoulder, heaped with the Polynesian robe, "I said right in the centre and I mean to keep my word." It was clear what he meant, for already he was mounted on the steps of the horseshoe-arch bridge and was going up them. Yes, I was to be the *clou* of the whole composition. When we reached the very apex of the arch, he held out the cloak to me, remarking, "You will find it hangs better if you'll just slip off your coat." I agreed and obeyed. I had already laid aside my cane. He was evidently quite an artist and was determined to pose me to best possible effect. He tried a number of poses and none seemed to him good enough. "I have it!" he finally clicked out. "Oh, the thing gets better and better! Why you aren't in the movies . . . But of course after this . . . photogenic—why, it's a mild word! I'm not asking for anything theatrical—only an accent, as it were—just the natural inevitable drama, one might say. The cloak itself sets the gesture. You see, the sun is high above and you are the centre of this pool of flowers and birds. And so we would get perfect action, perfect face lighting, and perfect hang of drapery if you would just stretch up your arms to the sun and let the light pour on your face. You stand here, with your back to the garden— its high-priest offering all its life to the sun."

While the little man had been saying this, he had been arranging the robe to make it hang well, tucking it in at my feet. "The shoes mustn't show, you know," he said, as he stooped like a little bootblack and arranged my train; then he shifted my stance until he had me close to the balustrade, for only there could he get the light falling full on my upturned face. One couldn't help falling in with his fancy—it was infectious. I rolled up my sleeves so that now, as I stood looking into the sun, I confess I could not help feeling the part. I forgot all about my old spider, Mr. Mycroft. I was one with nature, transformed by the robe which covered every sign of the civilized man on me, and by my setting. Mr. Hess darted back to the other side of the arch, up which we had come, and began—I could see out of the corner of my upturned eye—to focus his camera.

And then he seemed to spoil it all. After some delay he became uncertain. Finally, he came back up to me. "It's magnificent. I've never had the chance to take such a photo. But that's what so often happens with really great opportunities and insights into art and high beauty, isn't it?"

I was more than a little dashed. "Do you mean that you have decided not to take the photo?" I asked. Perhaps there was a touch of resentment in my voice. After all, I had been to a great deal of inconvenience; I had lent myself to a very unusual amount of free model work and laid myself open to Mr. Mycroft's wry humor which would be all the more pointed if the photo was never taken.

"No—Oh, of course not!" But the tone had so much reservation in it that I was not in the slightest reassured, and even less so when he showed his hand, for then I was certain he had just thought up a none-too-unclever way of getting out of the whole business. "But as I've said, and as I know you know, whenever one glimpses a true summit of beauty one catches sight of something even more remarkable beyond."

I snapped out, "Am I to presume that on reconsideration you would prefer not a high light but a foil, not myself but my old sober friend down by the gate?"

I had been growing quite resentful. But my resentment changed to outrage at the absurdity of his answer. It was a simple "Yes." Then seeing me flush, he hurriedly added, "I do believe that majestic old figure would make a perfect foil to yours."

Of course, this was an amend of sorts, but of a very silly sort. For could the man be such a fool as to think that while I might be generous and accommodating to a fault my old friend would fall in with this charade?

"I think," I said with considerable dignity, beginning to draw the robe away from my shoulders, "that when you want models, Mr. Hess, you had better pay for them."

But my arm got no further than halfway down the coat-sleeve. For my eyes were held. Looking up at the sun makes you a little dizzy and your sight blotchy, but there was no doubt what I was seeing. That silly little Hess had run along the curb and as I watched was buttonholing Mr. Mycroft. I didn't wait to struggle into my jacket but running down the steps went to where they stood together by the exit. I couldn't hear what was being said but was sure I guessed. Yet, in a moment, I was again at a loss. For instead of Mr. Mycroft turning down the grotesque offer, beckoning to me, and going out of the gate, Mr. M. was coming toward me, and he and Hess were talking quite amicably. Of course, I could only conclude that Hess had been spinning some new kind of yarn but all I could do was to go right up to them and say, "Perhaps you will be good enough to tell me what you have arranged!"

I was still further bewildered when it was Mr. M. who answered, "I think Mr. Hess's idea is excellent. If the picture is to be the success which he hopes, it should have contrast and, if I may put it in that way, significance—a picture with a story. Wasn't that your telling phrase, Mr. Hess?"

Hess beamed: "Precisely, precisely! Mr. Mycroft is so instantly intuitive." And the little fellow looked Mr. M. up and down with a mixture of surprise and complacency that I found very comic and sedative to my rightly ruffled feelings. Still I was quite in the dark as to what had happened to make the three of us so suddenly and so unexpectedly a happy family with—of all people—Mr. M. as the matchmaker. Hess, however, was bubbling over to tell me:

"Do forgive me, rushing off like that. So impulsive. But that's the way I am—'stung with the sudden splendor of a thought.' You see, that was the way I was with you, wasn't I? And I know you're an artist too and so you must know that when one idea comes, generally an even brighter one comes rushing on its heels," he tittered. "I was also a bit frightened, I must confess," he ran on. "What if Mr. Mycroft had refused? I knew if I asked you, you'd say he would; and of course you'd have been right. So I just rushed on to my fate, risked losing the whole picture—the best so often risks the good, doesn't it?"

While the little fellow had been pouring out this excited rigmarole, he had been leading us back to the bridge and as Mr. M. followed without any kind of unwillingness, I fell in too. After all, it looked as though we were going to get the photo. As we reached the steps it was Mr. M.

who forestalled Hess just as Hess was about to give us some directions. "You would like us, wouldn't you, to pose on the other side of the bridge-top?"

"Yes, that's it—just where I had Mr. Silchester."

I took up my position, picking up the robe, putting down my jacket. Hess arranged the fall of the robe as before. I must admit he was neat at that sort of thing. He moved me to exactly the spot I had held, asked me once more to raise my bared arms to the sun and throw back my head—"Just like a priest of Apollo," was his phrase, a phrase which I didn't quite like Mr. M. hearing. And even when Hess remarked to Mr. Mycroft, "with Mr. Silchester it's an inevitable piece of casting, isn't it?"—Mr. M. replied only, "Yes, quite a pretty piece of casting." I could only imagine that now Mr. Mycroft saw that the little fellow was obviously as harmless as a hummingbird—and about as brainless.

But Hess couldn't stay content with one triumph; he must try to crown it with another. "And you, Mr. Mycroft, you too are going to be perfectly cast," and he chuckled.

"I am ready to fall in with any of your plans for philanthropy," was Mr. Mycroft's answer. The pomposity might have been expected but the agreeability was certainly one more shock of surprise.

"Now," and the little man had put down his camera and was fussing like a modiste round a marchioness client whom she was fitting for a ball dress, "now, Mr. Silchester is set and ready. You, Mr. Mycroft, would you please just sit here, just behind him, on the balustrade. You see, my idea has about it something of what great artists call inevitability! The group casts itself—it's a great piece of moving sculpture. Here is Mr. Silchester gazing with stretched-out arms at the glorious orb of day, his face flooded with its splendor, the very symbol of youth accepting life—life direct, warm, pulsing, torrential . . ." As he ran on like this I began to have a slight crick in my neck, and with one's head thrown back my head began to throb a little and my eyes got quite dizzy with the sunlight. "Now, please, Mr. Silchester," said the voice at my feet, "hold the pose for just a moment more while I place Mr. Mycroft," and I heard our little artist in *tableau vivant* cooing to Mr. Mycroft. "And you, you see, are the wisdom of age, grey, wise, reflective, a perfect contrast, looking down into the deep waters of contemplation."

Evidently Mr. Mycroft fell in with all this, even to having himself shifted until he was right behind me. I remember I was a little amused at the thought of Mr. Mycroft being actually put at my feet and, more, that there I stood with the leading role and with my back to him—he who was so used to being looked up to. Perhaps it was this thought that gave one more stretch to the tiring elastic of my patience. And in a moment more evidently Mr. Mycroft's cooperation had been so full that Hess was content. The little fellow ran back down the steps of the other side of the bridge and I could just see from the corner of my rather swimming eyes that he had picked up his camera and was going to shoot us. But again he was taken with a fussy doubt. He ran back to us. We were still too far apart. He pushed us closer till my calves were actually against Mr. Mycroft's shoulder blades.

"The composition is perfect in line and mass," murmured Hess, "it is a spot of highlighting color that's wanted and right near the central interest, the upturned, sun-flooded face. Mr. Silchester, please don't move an inch. I have the very thing here."

I squinted down and saw the little fellow flick out from his button-hole the hibiscus blossom which he was wearing. I saw what was coming. The beautiful Samoans did always at their feasts wear a scarlet hibiscus set behind the ear so that the blossom glowed alongside their eye. In silence I submitted as Hess fitted the flower behind my left ear and arranged the long trumpet of the blossom so that it rested on my cheek bone. Then at last he was content, skipped back to his camera, raised it on high, focussed. . . . There was a click—I am sure I heard that. And I'm equally sure there was a buss, or twang. And

then involuntarily I clapped my hands to my face and staggered back to avoid something that was dashing at my eye. I stumbled heavily backwards against Mr. Mycroft, felt my balance go completely, the cloak swept over my head and I plunged backwards and downwards into the dark.

My next sensation was that I was being held. I hadn't hit anything. But I was in as much pain as though I had. For one of my legs was caught in some kind of grip and by this I was hanging upside down. For suddenly the bell-like extinguisher in which I was pending dropped away—as when they unveil statues—and I was exposed. Indeed I could now see myself in the water below like a grotesque narcissus, a painfully ludicrous pendant.

How had I managed to make such a grotesque stumble? I could only suppose that the long gazing at the sun had made me dizzy and then some dragon-fly or other buzzing insect had darted at me—probably at that idiotic flower—which in spite of my fall still stuck behind my ear. That had made me start and I had overturned. For though the flower held its place, the cloak was gone and now lay mantling the surface of the pond some six feet below me.

These observations, however, were checked by another dose of even more severe pain. I was being hauled up to the balustrade above me by my leg and the grip that paid me in foot by foot was Mr. Mycroft's sinewy hands. When my face came up far enough for me to see his, his was quite without expression. He did have the kindness to say, "Sun dizziness, of course," and then over his shoulder where I next caught sight of the anxious face of little Hess, "Don't be alarmed. I caught him just in time. I fear, however, that your valuable cloak will not be the better for a wetting."

The little fellow was full of apologies. While this went on Mr. Mycroft had helped me into my jacket, given me my cane and led me, still shaken, to the gate, accompanied all the way by a very apologetic Hess. When we were there Mr. Mycroft closed the incident quietly. "Don't apologize, Mr. Hess. It was a brilliant idea, if the execution fell a little below expectation," and then putting his hand up to my ear, "I am sure you would like this flower as a souvenir of an eventful day. I hope the picture-with-a-meaning will develop."

As we swirled away in a taxi, every sway of the car made me nearly sick. When we were home Mr. Mycroft broke the silence: "I have a call to make and one or two small things to arrange."

Mr. Mycroft didn't come back till dinner was actually being put on the table and he too looked as fresh as snow, after a hot shower and a clean change of linen, I felt. He was kind, too, about the meal. The avocado-and-chive paste served on hot crackers he praised by the little joke that the paste showed symbolically how well my suavity and his pungency really blended. The Pacific lobster is a creature of parts but it needs skill to make it behave really *à la Thermidor*, and I was pleased that the chef and I had made my old master confess that he would not know that it was not a Parisian *langouste*. The chicken *à la King* he smilingly said had something quite regal about it while the *bananes flambées* he particularly complimented because I had made them out of a locally grown banana which, because it is more succulent than the standard varieties, lends itself to better blending with alcohol. Indeed, he was so pleased that while the coffee was before us he asked whether I'd like to hear the end of the story in which I had played so important a part. Of course I admitted that nothing would give me more pleasure. But I was more than usually piqued when he said quietly, "Let me begin at the end. As we parted I said I was going to make a call. It has been answered as I wished. Do not fear that we shall have to visit the bird sanctuary again. It is closed—permanently. Now for my story. It seemed for both of us to be marked by a series of silly little misadventures. First, it was my turn to fall and you kindly helped me. Then, on our second call, it was your turn to endure the humiliation of an upset. But each served its purpose."

"But what did you gain from skidding on our first visit?" I asked.

"This," said Mr. Mycroft, rising and taking from the mantelshelf, where I had seen him place his fountain pen when he sat down to dinner, the little tube.

"That was only a recovery, not a gain," I said.

"No," he replied, "it garnered something when it fell. To misquote—as both of us like doing—'Cast your pen upon the waters and in a few moments it may pick up more copy than if you'd written for a week with it!'"

My "What do you mean?" was checked as he carefully unscrewed the top.

"See those little holes," he said, pointing to small openings just under the shoulder of the nib; then he drew out the small inner tube. It wasn't of rubber—it was of glass and was full of fairly clear water.

"This is water—water from the pond in the bird sanctuary. It looks like ordinary pond-water. As a matter of fact, it contains an unusually interesting form of life in it."

I began to feel a faint uneasiness.

"Oh, don't be alarmed. It is safely under screw and stopper now and is only being kept as Exhibit A—or, if you like it better, a stage-property in a forthcoming dramatic performance which will be Act Three of the mystery play in which you starred in Act Two, Scene Two."

"But I don't quite see . . ." was met by Mr. Mycroft more graciously than usual with, "There's really no reason why you should. I couldn't quite see myself, at the beginning. Yes, I do indeed admire such richness of double-dyed thoroughness when I come across it. It is rare for murderers to give one such entertainment, so elaborate and meticulous. They usually shoot off their arrows almost as soon as it enters their heads that they can bring down their bird and without a thought of how it may strike a more meditative mind afterwards. But this man provided himself with a second string of rather better weave than his first."

Well, when Mr. Mycroft gets into that kind

of strain it is no use saying anything. So I swallowed the I.D.S. formula that was again rising in my throat and waited.

"You remember, when you helped me to my feet and the pen had been salvaged, that with your aid we completed the round of the little lake. But when we had gone no farther than the beginning of the high-backed bridge, I felt I must rest. Do you recall what I did then?"

Could I recall! Naturally, for that was the very incident that had confirmed my suspicion that Mr. Mycroft was really shaken. I answered brightly:

"You sat, I can see it now, and for a moment you appeared to be dazed. And while you rested, as the beautiful old song, *The Lost Chord*, expresses it, your 'fingers idly wandered.' But I noticed that they must be getting dirty, because, whether you knew it or not, they were feeling along under the jutting edge of the slab that made the step against which your back was resting."

"Admirable. And the quotation is happy, for my fingers were idly wandering (to go on with the old song) over the 'keys'!"

Mr. Mycroft cocked his old head at me and went on gaily, "And may I add that I am not less pleased that you thought the old man was so shaken that he really didn't know what he was doing! For that is precisely the impression that I had to give to another pair of eyes watching us from nearby cover. Well, after that little rest and glance about at those sentimental birdy-homes, the breeding boxes, I told you we could go home. And now may I ask you three questions?" I drew myself up and tried to sharpen my wits. "First," said my examiner, "did you observe anything about the garden generally?"

"Well," I replied, "I remember you called my attention to the little Nereid who held a spear from which the jet of the small fountain sprang?"

"Yes, that's true and indeed in every sense of the word, to the point. But did you notice something about—I will give you a clue—the flowers?"

"There were a lot of them!"

"Well, I won't hold you to that longer. I couldn't make out myself whether it had any significance. Then in the end I saw the light—yes, the light of the danger signal! Does that help you?"

"No," I said, "I remain as blind as a bat to your clue."

"Then, secondly, if the flowers failed to awake your curiosity, what about the birds?"

"Again, a lot of them and I did like that minah bird with its charmingly anaemic hostess voice."

"No, that was off the trail. I'll give you another clue—what about the breeding boxes?"

"Well, they're common enough little things, aren't they?"

"All right," he replied with cheerful patience, "now for my last question. When we were coming back do you remember any special incident?"

Then I did perk up. "Yes, of course—the contrast stuck in my mind. After being bathed in all that beauty we passed a dump corner and you got out and hunted for curios in the garbage."

"And brought back quite a trophy," said the old hunter as he pulled something out of his pocket, remarking "Exhibit B."

And then, do you know, my mind suddenly gave a dart—I do things like that every now and then. The thing he had pulled out and placed on the table was only a piece of cellophane or celluloid. It was also of a very crude and common red. It was the color that made my mind take its hop, a hop backwards. "I don't know what that dirty piece of road-side flotsam means but I now recall something about the garden—there wasn't a single red flower in it!"

Mr. Mycroft positively beamed. His uttered compliment was of course the "left-handed" sort he generally dealt me. "Mr. Silchester, I have always known it. It is laziness, just simple laziness, that keeps you from being a first-rate observer. You can't deny that puzzles interest you, but you can't be bothered to put out your hand and pluck the fruit of insight crossed with foresight."

I waved the tribute aside by asking what the red transparency might signify.

"Well," he said, "it put an idea into your head by what we may call a negative proof. Now, go one better and tell me something about it, itself, from its shape."

"Well, it's sickle-shaped, rather like a crescent moon. No," I paused, "no, you know I never can do anything if I strain. I have to wait for these flashes."

"All right," he said, "we will humor your delicate genius. But I will just say that it is a beautiful link. The color and the shape—yes, the moment I saw it lying there like a petal cast aside, my mind suddenly took wings like yours." He stopped and then remarked, "Well, the time has come for straight narrative. We have all the pieces of the board, yourself being actually the queen. It only remains to show you how the game was played. First, a tribute to Mr. Hess not as a man but as a murderer—an artist, without any doubt. Here are the steps by which he moved to his first check and how after the first queen had been taken—I refer to his aunt and her death—he was himself checkmated.

"You have noted that the garden has no red flowers and I have also suggested that the breeding box by the bridge interested me. About the water from the pond I have been frank and will shortly be franker. So we come to our second visit. It was then that our antagonist played boldly. How often have I had occasion to remind you that murderers love living over again the deaths they dealt, repeating a kill. That was Mr. Hess's wish. Of course, it wasn't pure love of art—he certainly knew something about me." Mr. Mycroft sighed, "I know you don't believe it, but I don't think you can imagine how often and how strongly a detective wishes to be unknown. To recognize you must remain unrecognized." He smiled again.

"Now note: You go up to him and ask him not to take photos. He shows first a startled resentment at your impudence, then a generous courtesy as proprietor for your interference on his behalf. Next, a sudden happy thought—how well you would look as part of the picture he was planning. He dresses you up, taking care to place you in a position in which you'll trip and fall. Now he has the middle link in his chain. But you were merely a link. You see, his real plan is to get me down too. He could, you will admit, hardly have hoped to lure me to act as model for a sun worshipper. But put you in that role and then he might persuade me to get into the picture also. Then, when you went over backwards, you would pull me into the pond as well."

"But," I said, "we should have had no more than a bad wetting."

"I see you are going to call for all my proofs before you will yield to the fact that we were really in the hands of a man as sane as all careful murderers are. You remember that charming little statuette which so took my fancy when we first visited the garden? It was of bronze. Not one of those cheap cement objects that people buy at the road-side and put in their gardens. It is a work of art, a museum-piece."

"It had patinated very nicely," I remarked, just to show I could talk *objet d'art* gossip as well as the master.

"I'm glad you observed that," he replied. "Yes, bronze is a remarkable material and worthy of having a whole Age named after it. More remarkable, indeed, than iron, for though iron has a better edge, it won't keep if constantly watered."

"What are you driving at?" For now I was getting completely lost in the old spider's spinning.

"That pretty little sham spear from which the water sprayed wasn't sham at all. It was a real spear, or shall we say, a giant hollow-needle. Because it was bronze it would keep its point unrusted. The only effect the water would have—and that would add to its lethal efficacy—would be to give it a patina. Further, I feel sure from the long close look I was able to give when we were being posed for our plunge, the blade of the spear had been touched up with a little acetic acid. That would no doubt corrode the fine edge a little but would make it highly poisonous—though not to the life in the pool."

"Why are you so interested in the pond-life?" I asked.

Mr. Mycroft picked up the small tube which he had removed from the fountain pen and which was now standing on a small side-table. "You'll remember, I said this pippet contains an interesting form of life—a very powerful form, if not itself poisoned. So powerful that, like most power-types, it tends to destroy others, yes, far higher types. This is really a remarkably fecund culture of a particularly virulent strain of typhoid bacillus."

I drew back. I don't like things like that near where I eat.

"Oh, it is safe enough so long as you don't drink it." I gasped. "So, you see, that was his plan. But, thoughtful man that he was, it was only his second string. He was a very thorough worker and had two concealed tools. If you fall over a bridge headlong and just underneath you is a Nereid holding a charming little wand, there is a good chance that you will fall, like the heroic Roman suicides, on your spear and so end yourself; and if the spear has round its socket some poison, the wound is very likely to give you blood-poisoning. But of course you may miss the point. People falling through the air are apt to writhe which may alter quite considerably the point at which they make their landing, or in this case, their watering. Well, thoughtful Mr. Hess realized how much human nature will struggle against gravitational fate—so he provided himself with a wider net. For when people fall headlong over a bridge, the natural reaction of panic is to open the mouth. So when they strike the water, they inevitably swallow a mouthful. And a little of this brew goes a long way."

"Now, now," I broke in, "I don't think any jury will send the nephew to join the aunt on that evidence."

"Why not?" was Mr. Mycroft's unexpectedly quiet rejoinder.

"First," I said, picking off the points on my fingers just as Mr. Mycroft sometimes does when closing a case, "granted this tube does contain typhoid germs, they may have been in this water from natural pollution. Proof that Hess poisoned the water cannot be sustained.

Secondly, let me call the attention of judge and jury to the fact that when Miss Hess died a fortnight after her slight ducking, she did not die of typhoid. The cause of death was 'intestinal stasis.' Typhoid kills by a form of dysentery. Emphatically, that condition is polar to stasis."

"You are quite right," rejoined Mr. Mycroft, "the old-fashioned typhoid used to kill as you have described. But, would you believe it, the typhus germ has had the cunning to reverse his tactics completely. I remember a friend of mine telling me some years ago of this, and he had it from the late Sir Walter Fletcher, an eminent student of Medical Research in Britain. It stuck in my mind: the typhoid victim can now die with such entirely different symptoms that the ordinary doctor, unless he has quite other reasons to detect the presence of the disease, does not even suspect that his patient has died of typhoid, and with the best faith in the world fills in the death certificate never suggesting the true cause. Yes," he went on meditatively, "I have more than once noticed that when a piece of information of that sort sticks in my mind, it may be prophetic. Certainly in this case it was."

I felt I might have to own defeat on that odd point when Mr. Mycroft remarked, "Well, let's leave Miss Hess and the medical side alone for a moment. Let's go back to the garden. I referred to you as the middle link. I have to be personal and even perhaps put myself forward. Mr. Hess was not averse to murdering you—if that was the only way of murdering me. We see how he maneuvered you to pose and then having got you in place, he set out to get me. You would stagger back, knock me off my perch, and both of us would plunge into the poisonous water, and one might be caught on the poisonous point. It was beautifully simple, really."

"You have got to explain how he would know that I would suddenly get dizzy, that a dragonfly or something would buzz right into my eyes and make me stagger."

"Quite easy—I was just coming to that. That was the first link in the chain. Now we can bring everything together and be finished with that really grim garden. Please recall the thing you noticed."

"No red flowers," I said dutifully and he bowed his acknowledgment.

"Next, the two things which you couldn't be expected to puzzle over. The breeding box which you did see but did not understand, and the undercurb of the step which even I didn't see but felt with my hand. That breeding box had the usual little doorway or round opening for the nesting bird to enter by, but to my surprise the doorway had a door and the door was closed. Now, that's going too far in pet-love sentimentality and although very cruel people are often very kind to animals, that kind of soapy gesture to birdmother comfort seemed to me strange—until I noticed, on the under-side of the next box, a small wheel. When I felt under the jamb of the step, I found two more such wheels—flanged wheels, and running along from one to the other, a black thread. Then when I knew what to look for, I could see the same black thread running up to the wheel fixed in the bird-box. I couldn't doubt my deduction any longer. That little door could be opened if someone raised his foot slightly and trod on the black thread that ran under the step curb.

"Now, one doesn't have to be a bird fancier to know that birds don't want to breed in boxes where you shut them up with a trap-door. What then could this box be for? You do, however, have to be something of a bird specialist to know about hawking and hummingbirds. The main technique of the former is the hood. When the bird is hooded it will stay quietly for long times on its perch. Cut off light and it seems to have its nervous reactions all arrested. Could that box be a hood not merely for the head of a bird but for *an entire bird*? Now we must switch back, as swoopingly as a hummingbird, to Miss Hess. You remember the description?"

It was my turn to be ready. I reached round to the paper rack and picked out the sheet that had started the whole adventure. I read out, "The late Miss Hess, whose huge fortune has gone to a very quiet recluse nephew whose one interest is birds,

was herself a most colorful person and wonderfully young for her years." I added, "There's a colored photo of the colorful lady. She's wearing a vivid green dress. Perhaps that's to show she thought herself still in her salad days?"

"A good suggestion," replied Mr. Mycroft generously; "but I think we can drive our deductions even nearer home. Of course, I needed first-hand information for that. But I had my suspicions before I called."

"Called where?"

"On the doctor of the late lady. He was willing to see me when I could persuade him that his suspicions were right and that his patroness had really been removed by foul means. Then he told me quite a lot about the very odd person she was. She was shrewd in her way. She kept her own doctor and she paid him handsomely and took the complementary precaution of not remembering him in her will. Yes, he had every reason for keeping her going and being angry at her being gone. She was keen on staying here and not only that but on keeping young. But her colorfulness in dress was something more, he told me, than simply 'mutton dressing itself up to look like lamb.' She was color-blind and like that sort—the red-green colorblindness—she was very loath to admit it. That bright green dress of the photo pretty certainly seemed to her bright red."

I was still at a loss and let the old man see it.

"Now comes Hess's third neat piece of work. Note these facts: the aunt is persuaded to come to the garden—just to show that the nephew has turned over a new page and is being the busy little bird lover—sure way to keep in the maiden lady's good graces. He takes her round." Suddenly Mr. Mycroft stopped and picked up the celluloid red crescent. "Many color-blind persons have eyes that do not like a glare. The thoughtful nephew, having led auntie round the garden, takes her up the bridge to view the dear little birdie's home. She has to gaze up at it and he has thoughtfully provided her with an eye-shade—green to her, red to him; and red to something else. "Certain species of hummingbirds are particularly sensitive to red—all animals, of course, prefer red to any other color. When young these particular hummingbirds have been known to dash straight at any object that is red and thrust their long bill toward it, thinking no doubt it is a flower. They will dart at a tomato held in your hand. Well, the aunt is gazing up to see the birdie's home; she's at the top of the bridge, just where you stood. Nephew has gone on, sure that aunt is going to follow. He is, in fact, now down by that lower step. He just treads on the concealed black thread. The door flies open, the little feathered bullet which had been brooding in the dark sees a flash of light and in it a blob of red. The reflex acts also like a flash. It dashes out right at Miss Hess's face. Again a reflex. This time it is the human one. She staggers back, hands to face—not knowing what has swooped at her—the flight of some of these small birds is too quick for the human eye.

Of course she falls, takes her sup of the water, goes home shaken, no doubt not feeling pleased with nephew but not suspicious. After a fortnight we have a condition of stasis. The sound, but naturally not very progressive doctor, sees no connection. The police and public are also content. Nevertheless, she dies."

"And then?" I said, for I was on tiptoe of interest now.

"Well, Hess couldn't put a red eye-hood over your eyes, hoping you'd think it green and so make you a mark for his bird-bullet. So he put an hibiscus behind your ear. Each fish must be caught with its own bait, though the hook is the same. His effort with us was even more elaborate than with his aunt. What a pity that artists can't be content with a good performance but must always be trying to better it! Well, the bird sanctuary is closed and with it the sanctuary of a most resourceful murderer."

A Study in Handwriting

RING W. LARDNER

SPORTSWRITING HAS PRODUCED more than its share of outstanding literary figures. While such distinguished practitioners of "literature under pressure" as Ernest Hemingway and Jack London gained the majority of their fame after turning to other forms of prose, a few, including Ringgold Willmer Lardner (1885–1933) never strayed far from it.

He got his first job as a sports columnist while still a teenager and moved from newspaper to newspaper for many years before settling in at the *Chicago Tribune* in 1913, which became the home paper for his syndicated column, "In the Wake of the News." While his columns purported to be journalism, they frequently lapsed into satire and often were entirely fiction. Lardner became one of the country's greatest humorists and many of his short stories, mainly about baseball, have become classics. His first successful book, *You Know Me Al* (1916), was written in the form of letters by "Jack Keefe," a minor league baseball player, to a friend using a unique and hilarious vernacular.

Lardner became disillusioned with his beloved game of baseball when he learned of the infamous "Black Sox" scandal; he had been close to players on the Chicago White Sox team and felt betrayed when they conspired to throw the 1919 World Series to the Cincinnati Reds.

"A Study in Handwriting" was first published in the March 16, 1915, "In the Wake of the News" column for the *Chicago Tribune*, and syndicated in more than one hundred newspapers.

A STUDY IN HANDWRITING

Ring W. Lardner

"I CANNOT REJOICE over the ever-increasing popularity of the typewriter," said Sherlock Holmes, as he lounged in the most comfortable chair provided by our landlady, and refilled, for the sixth time within an hour, a particularly malodorous pipe. "It is spoiling one of the most absorbing ways of studying the human race.

"One can judge from a typewritten letter very little concerning its author; merely whether or not he is an expert with the machine. But a man's handwriting will tell a careful student a writer's likes and dislikes as plainly as he could state them himself, to say nothing of his occupation, his characteristics, his immense thoughts, his—"

"Do you mean to state," I interrupted, "that you can accurately describe a man's vocation, his traits, his opinions, by a study of his handwriting?"

"Just so," returned my companion with a smile, "and if you would look into it, I am sure you would find it as interesting a study as your medicine and surgery."

"I am sure I would find it all bosh," I returned shortly.

"Try it and see," said Holmes, and thrusting his long tapering fingers into the inside pocket of his lounging coat, he drew forth a letter. "Glance at this," handing it to me, "and tell me what you learn of the writer."

I spread the missive on my knee and looked at it for perhaps five minutes. It was written on hotel stationery in a graceful, legible hand, and read:

Editor: Chicago Tribune:

Of all the silly tommy rot and cheap Barrel House seen or heard, that contained under the heading "In the Wake of the News" has them all beat to a frazzle.

It appears to me that R. W. L——would make a good wit at a real wake and were he the corpse, I'd say thank God.

I've decided to switch to another paper, and talking the matter over with other fellow drummers the general opinion appears to be the same. Namely L——is a dead one.

Yours very truly,
XXXXX

"Well," said Holmes at length, "what do you make of him?"

"Nothing," I said, "except that he writes clearly and legibly."

"O, Watson, Watson!" exclaimed my companion, and threw up his hands in mock horror. "Where are your brains?"

"In my head, I hope," I said with some asperity. "But I did not make any ridiculous assertion as to my clairvoyant powers. It was you, I believe, who started the discussion. And it is surely your duty to make good your claim or admit that you were talking nonsense, as I believe to be the case."

Holmes smiled quietly and reaching over, took back the letter he had given me. He pondered it in silence for some moments before he spoke.

"Watson," he said, "it is as far from nonsense as anything could be. This power or knack, or whatever you choose to call it has served me in good stead in some of my most important cases. But I see you are still a skeptic and it is therefore my part to convert you. I have already made my study of this particular letter and will state my conclusions to you as briefly as I can.

"To begin with, I see the writer has recently been in Sheboygan, Wisconsin. He has a bit of spare time on his hands, either while stopping at the Grand hotel, which is centrally located and homelike, owned by R. J. Warner and protected by the electric fire alarm system, or right afterwards. He is not a personal friend of the editor of *The Tribune*. He uses slang. He has no patience with a certain department of *The Tribune* called 'In the Wake of the News.' He is hard-hearted. He is religious. He makes his decisions only after careful thought and dis-

cussion. He is democratic. He is interested in the opinion of his fellows and not above talking with them. He is a salesman who travels. He is inconsiderate. I think that is about all. Do you follow me?"

"Holmes, you are wonderful," I exclaimed. "But surely you will tell me how you reached some of your conclusions. For instance, how do you deduce that the writer is inconsiderate?"

"From his handwriting, of course," returned my companion. "Study the formation of the letters in this sentence: 'I've decided to switch to another paper.' If he were considerate of the feelings of others, would he be so blunt with the person addressed? Wouldn't he rather allow the editor to find out gradually that he was no longer a subscriber?"

"It is clear as day," I admitted. "And how long did it take you to master this trick?"

"Trick!" said Holmes, disgustedly scratching the bridge of his aquiline nose with a gold-handled toothpick.

The Case of Death and Honey

NEIL GAIMAN

DESCRIBED AS ONE of the world's ten most important postmodern writers, Neil Richard MacKinnon Gaiman (1960–) is also one of its most popular and beloved. His literary output has included journalism, poetry, short stories, novels, books for children and young adults, and the comic books and graphic novels that brought him his first, and perhaps greatest, fame.

While writing for DC Comics, he was asked to revive a moribund character, The Sandman, and he did, turning it into one of the most successful series of all time. *The Sandman* gives the account of Dream, known by many names, including Morpheus. In January 1989, the series began; it concluded in March 1996. His first novel, *Good Omens* (1990), was coauthored with Terry Pratchett; his first solo novel was a novelization of a four-part BBC television series, *Neverwhere* (1996). Among his many other works are the horror/fantasy novel for young readers, *Coraline* (2002), which was released in 2009; *Anansi Boys* (2005), which debuted at number one on the *New York Times* bestseller list; *American Gods* (2001); and *The Ocean at the End of the Lane* (2013).

It would take a mighty effort to count the number of awards Gaiman has won in various genres, including horror, fantasy, comics, and children's books.

"The Case of Death and Honey" was first published in *A Study in Sherlock*, edited by Laurie R. King and Leslie S. Klinger (New York, Bantam Books, 2011).

THE CASE OF DEATH AND HONEY

Neil Gaiman

I T W A S A mystery in those parts for years what had happened to the old white ghost man, the barbarian with his huge shoulder bag. There were some who supposed him to have been murdered, and, later, they dug up the floor of Old Gao's little shack high on the hillside, looking for treasure, but they found nothing but ash and fire-blackened tin trays.

This was after Old Gao himself had vanished, you understand, and before his son came back from Lijiang to take over the beehives on the hill.

This is the problem, *wrote Holmes in 1899*: ennui. And lack of interest. Or rather, it all becomes too easy. When the joy of solving crimes is the challenge, the possibility that you cannot, why then the crimes have something to hold your attention. But when each crime is soluble, and so easily soluble at that, why then there is no point in solving them.

Look: this man has been murdered. Well then, someone murdered him. He was murdered for one or more of a tiny handful of reasons: he inconvenienced someone, or he had something that someone wanted, or he had angered someone. Where is the challenge in that?

I would read in the dailies an account of a crime that had the police baffled, and I would find that I had solved it, in broad strokes if not in detail, before I had finished the article. Crime is too soluble. It dissolves. Why call the police and tell them the answers to their mysteries? I leave it, over and over again, as a challenge for them, as it is no challenge for me.

I am only alive when I perceive a challenge.

The bees of the misty hills, hills so high that they were sometimes called a mountain, were humming in the pale summer sun as they moved from spring flower to spring flower on the slope. Old Gao listened to them without pleasure. His cousin, in the village across the valley, had many dozens of hives, all of them already filling with honey, even this early in the year; also, the honey was as white as snow-jade. Old Gao did not believe that the white honey tasted any better than the yellow or light brown honey that his own bees produced, although his bees produced it in meagre quantities, but his cousin could sell his white honey for twice what Old Gao could get for the best honey he had.

On his cousin's side of the hill, the bees were earnest, hardworking, golden brown workers, who brought pollen and nectar back to the hives in enormous quantities. Old Gao's bees were ill-tempered and black, shiny as bullets, who produced as much honey as they needed to get through the winter and only a little more: enough for Old Gao to sell from door to door, to his fellow villagers, one small lump of honeycomb at a time. He would charge more for the brood-comb, filled with bee larvae, sweet-tasting morsels of protein, when he had brood-comb to sell, which was rarely, for the bees were angry and sullen and everything they did, they did as little as possible, including make more bees, and Old Gao was always aware that each piece of brood-comb he sold meant bees he would not have to make honey for him to sell later in the year.

Old Gao was as sullen and as sharp as his bees. He had had a wife once, but she had died in childbirth. The son who had killed her lived for a week, then died himself. There would be nobody to say the funeral rites for Old Gao, no-one to clean his grave for festivals or to put offerings upon it. He would die unremembered, as unremarkable and as unremarked as his bees.

The old white stranger came over the mountains in late spring of that year, as soon as the roads were passable, with a huge brown bag strapped to his shoulders. Old Gao heard about him before he met him.

"There is a barbarian who is looking at bees," said his cousin.

Old Gao said nothing. He had gone to his cousin to buy a pailful of second-rate comb, damaged or uncapped and liable soon to spoil. He bought it cheaply to feed to his own bees, and if he sold some of it in his own village, no-one was any the wiser. The two men were drinking tea in Gao's cousin's hut on the hillside. From late spring, when the first honey started to flow, until first frost, Gao's cousin left his house in the village and went to live in the hut on the hillside, to live and to sleep beside his beehives, for fear of thieves. His wife and his children would take the honeycomb and the bottles of snow-white honey down the hill to sell.

Old Gao was not afraid of thieves. The shiny black bees of Old Gao's hives would have no mercy on anyone who disturbed them. He slept in his village, unless it was time to collect the honey.

"I will send him to you," said Gao's cousin. "Answer his questions, show him your bees, and he will pay you."

"He speaks our tongue?"

"His dialect is atrocious. He said he learned to speak from sailors, and they were mostly Cantonese. But he learns fast, although he is old."

Old Gao grunted, uninterested in sailors. It was late in the morning, and there was still four hours walking across the valley to his village, in the heat of the day. He finished his tea. His cousin drank finer tea than Old Gao had ever been able to afford.

He reached his hives while it was still light, put the majority of the uncapped honey into his weakest hives. He had eleven hives. His cousin had over a hundred. Old Gao was stung twice doing this, on the back of the hand and the back of the neck. He had been stung over a thousand times in his life. He could not have told you how many times. He barely noticed the stings of other bees, but the stings of his own black bees always hurt, even if they no longer swelled or burned.

The next day a boy came to Old Gao's house in the village, to tell him that there was someone—and that the someone was a giant foreigner—who was asking for him. Old Gao simply grunted. He walked across the village with the boy at his steady pace, until the boy ran ahead, and soon was lost to sight.

Old Gao found the stranger sitting drinking tea on the porch of the Widow Zhang's house. Old Gao had known the Widow Zhang's mother, fifty years ago. She had been a friend of his wife. Now she was long dead. He did not believe anyone who had known his wife still lived. The Widow Zhang fetched Old Gao tea, introduced him to the elderly barbarian, who had removed his bag and sat beside the small table.

They sipped their tea. The barbarian said, "I wish to see your bees."

Mycroft's death was the end of Empire, and no-one knew it but the two of us. He lay in that pale room, his only covering a thin white sheet, as if he were already becoming a ghost from the popular imagination, and needed only eye-holes in the sheet to finish the impression.

I had imagined that his illness might have wasted him away, but he seemed huger than ever, his fingers swollen into white suet sausages.

I said, "Good evening, Mycroft. Dr. Hopkins tells me you have two weeks to live, and stated that I was under no circumstances to inform you of this."

"The man's a dunderhead," said Mycroft, his breath coming in huge wheezes between the words. "I will not make it to Friday."

"Saturday at least," I said.

"You always were an optimist. No, Thursday evening and then I shall be nothing more than an exercise in practical geometry for Hopkins and the funeral directors at Snigsby and Malterson, who will have the challenge, given the narrowness of the doors and corridors, of getting my carcass out of this room and out of the building."

"I had wondered," I said. "Particularly given the staircase. But they will take out the window frame and lower you to the street like a grand piano."

Mycroft snorted at that. Then, "I am fifty-four years old, Sherlock. In my head is the British Government. Not the ballot and hustings nonsense, but the business of the thing. There is no-one else knows what the troop movements in the hills of Afghanistan have to do with the desolate shores of North Wales, no-one else who sees the whole picture. Can you imagine the mess that this lot and their children will make of Indian Independence?"

I had not previously given any thought to the matter. "Will India become independent?"

"Inevitably. In thirty years, at the outside. I have written several recent memoranda on the topic. As I have on so many other subjects. There are memoranda on the Russian Revolution—that'll be along within the decade, I'll wager—and on the German problem and . . . oh, so many others. Not that I expect them to be read or understood." Another wheeze. My brother's lungs rattled like the windows in an empty house. "You know, if I were to live, the British Empire might last another thousand years, bringing peace and improvement to the world."

In the past, especially when I was a boy, whenever I heard Mycroft make a grandiose pronouncement like that I would say something to bait him. But not now, not on his death-bed. And also I was certain that he was not speaking of the Empire as it was, a flawed and fallible construct of flawed and fallible people, but of a British Empire that existed only in his head, a glorious force for civilisation and universal prosperity.

I do not, and did not, believe in empires. But I believed in Mycroft.

Mycroft Holmes. Four-and-fifty years of age. He had seen in the new century but the Queen would still outlive him by several months. She was almost thirty years older than he was, and in every way a tough old bird. I wondered to myself whether this unfortunate end might have been avoided.

Mycroft said, "You are right, of course, Sherlock. Had I forced myself to exercise. Had I lived on bird-seed and cabbages instead of porterhouse steak. Had I taken up country dancing along with a wife and a puppy and in all other ways behaved contrary to my nature, I might have bought myself another dozen or so years. But what is that in the scheme of things? Little enough. And sooner or later, I would enter my dotage. No. I am of the opinion that it would take two hundred years to train a functioning Civil Service, let alone a secret service . . ."

I had said nothing.

The pale room had no decorations on the wall of any kind. None of Mycroft's citations. No illustrations, photographs, or paintings. I compared his austere digs to my own cluttered rooms in Baker Street and I wondered, not for the first time, at

Mycroft's mind. He needed nothing on the outside, for it was all on the inside—everything he had seen, everything he had experienced, everything he had read. He could close his eyes and walk through the National Gallery, or browse the British Museum Reading Room—or, more likely, compare intelligence reports from the edge of the Empire with the price of wool in Wigan and the unemployment statistics in Hove, and then, from this and only this, order a man promoted or a traitor's quiet death.

Mycroft wheezed enormously, and then he said, "It is a crime, Sherlock."

"I beg your pardon?"

"A crime. It is a crime, my brother, as heinous and as monstrous as any of the penny-dreadful massacres you have investigated. A crime against the world, against nature, against order."

"I must confess, my dear fellow, that I do not entirely follow you. What is a crime?"

"My death," said Mycroft, "in the specific. And Death in general." He looked into my eyes. "I mean it," he said. "Now isn't that a crime worth investigating, Sherlock, old fellow? One that might keep your attention for longer than it will take you to establish that the poor fellow who used to conduct the brass band in Hyde Park was murdered by the third cornet using a preparation of strychnine."

"Arsenic," I corrected him, almost automatically.

"I think you will find," wheezed Mycroft, "that the arsenic, while present, had in fact fallen in flakes from the green-painted bandstand itself onto his supper. Symptoms of arsenical poison are a complete red-herring. No, it was strychnine that did for the poor fellow."

Mycroft said no more to me that day or ever. He breathed his last the following Thursday, late in the afternoon, and on the Friday the worthies of Snigsby and Malterson removed the casing from the window of the pale room and lowered my brother's remains into the street, like a grand piano.

His funeral service was attended by me, by my friend Watson, by our cousin Harriet and—in accordance with Mycroft's express wishes—by no-one else. The Civil Service, the Foreign Office, even the Diogenes Club—these institutions and their representatives were absent. Mycroft had been reclusive in life; he was to be equally as reclusive in death. So it was the three of us, and the parson, who had not known my brother, and had no conception that it was the more omniscient arm of the British Government itself that he was consigning to the grave.

Four burly men held fast to the ropes and lowered my brother's remains to their final resting place, and did, I daresay, their utmost not to curse at the weight of the thing. I tipped each of them half a crown.

Mycroft was dead at fifty-four, and, as they lowered him into his grave, in my imagination I could still hear his clipped, grey wheeze as he seemed to be saying, "Now *there* is a crime worth investigating."

The stranger's accent was not too bad, although his vocabulary seemed limited, but he seemed to be talking in the local dialect, or something near to it. He was a fast learner. Old Gao hawked and spat into the dust of the street. He said nothing. He did not wish to take the stranger up the hillside; he did not wish to disturb his bees. In Old Gao's experience, the less he bothered his bees, the better they did. And if they stung the barbarian, what then?

The stranger's hair was silver-white, and sparse; his nose, the first barbarian nose that Old Gao had seen, was huge and curved and put Old Gao in mind of the beak of an eagle; his skin was tanned the same colour as Old Gao's own, and was lined deeply. Old Gao was not certain that he could read a barbarian's face as he could read the face of a person, but he thought the man seemed most serious and, perhaps, unhappy.

"Why?"

"I study bees. Your brother tells me you have big black bees here. Unusual bees."

Old Gao shrugged. He did not correct the man on the relationship with his cousin.

The stranger asked Old Gao if he had eaten, and when Gao said that he had not the stranger asked the Widow Zhang to bring them soup and rice and whatever was good that she had in her kitchen, which turned out to be a stew of black tree-fungus and vegetables and tiny transparent river fish, little bigger than tadpoles. The two men ate in silence. When they had finished eating, the stranger said, "I would be honoured if you would show me your bees."

Old Gao said nothing, but the stranger paid the Widow Zhang well and he put his bag on his back. Then he waited, and, when Old Gao began to walk, the stranger followed him. He carried his bag as if it weighed nothing to him. He was strong for an old man, thought Old Gao, and wondered whether all such barbarians were so strong.

"Where are you from?"

"England," said the stranger.

Old Gao remembered his father telling him about a war with the English, over trade and over opium, but that was long ago.

They walked up the hillside that was, perhaps, a mountainside. It was steep, and the hillside was too rocky to be cut into fields. Old Gao tested the stranger's pace, walking faster than usual, and the stranger kept up with him, with his pack on his back.

The stranger stopped several times, however. He stopped to examine flowers—the small white flowers that bloomed in early spring elsewhere in the valley, but in late spring here on the side of the hill. There was a bee on one of the flowers, and the stranger knelt and observed it. Then he reached into his pocket, produced a large magnifying glass and examined the bee through it, and made notes in a small pocket notebook, in an incomprehensible writing.

Old Gao had never seen a magnifying glass before, and he leaned in to look at the bee, so black and so strong and so very different from the bees elsewhere in that valley.

"One of your bees?"

"Yes," said Old Gao. "Or one like it."

"Then we shall let her find her own way home," said the stranger, and he did not disturb the bee, and he put away the magnifying glass.

The Croft
East Dene, Sussex

August 11th, 1922

My dear Watson,

I have taken our discussion of this afternoon to heart, considered it carefully, and am prepared to modify my previous opinions.

I am amenable to your publishing your account of the incidents of 1903, specifically of the final case before my retirement, under the following conditions.

In addition to the usual changes that you would make to disguise actual people and places, I would suggest that you replace the entire scenario we encountered (I speak of Professor Presbury's garden. I shall not write of it further here) with monkey glands, or a similar extract from the testes of an ape or lemur, sent by some foreign mystery-man. Perhaps the monkey-extract could have the effect of making Professor Presbury move like an ape—he could be some kind of "creeping man," perhaps?—or possibly make him able to clamber up the sides of buildings and up trees. I would suggest that he could grow a tail, but this might be too fanciful even for you, Watson, although no more fanciful than many of the rococo additions you have made in your histories to otherwise humdrum events in my life and work.

In addition, I have written the following speech, to be delivered by myself, at the end of your narrative. Please make certain that something much like this is there, in which I inveigh against living too long, and the fool-ish urges that push foolish people to do foolish things to prolong their foolish lives:

There is a very real danger to humanity, if one could live forever, if youth were simply there for the taking, that the material, the sensual, the worldly would all prolong their worthless lives. The spiritual would not avoid the call to something higher. It would be the survival of the least fit. What sort of cesspool may not our poor world become?

Something along those lines, I fancy, would set my mind at rest.

Let me see the finished article, please, be-fore you submit it to be published.

*I remain, old friend,
your most obedient servant,
Sherlock Holmes*

They reached Old Gao's bees late in the after-noon. The beehives were grey wooden boxes piled behind a structure so simple it could barely be called a shack. Four posts, a roof, and hangings of oiled cloth that served to keep out the worst of the spring rains and the summer storms. A small charcoal brazier served for warmth, if you placed a blanket over it and yourself, and to cook upon; a wooden pallet in the center of the structure, with an ancient ceramic pillow, served as a bed on the occasions that Old Gao slept up on the mountainside with the bees, particularly in the autumn, when he harvested most of the honey. There was little enough of it compared to the output of his cousin's hives, but it was enough that he would sometimes spend two or three days waiting for the comb that he had crushed and stirred into a slurry to drain through the cloth into the buckets and pots that he had car-ried up the mountainside. Finally he would melt the remainder, the sticky wax and bits of pollen and dirt and bee slurry, in a pot, to extract the beeswax, and he would give the sweet water back

to the bees. Then he would carry the honey and the wax blocks down the hill to the village to sell.

He showed the barbarian stranger the eleven hives, watched impassively as the stranger put on a veil and opened a hive, examining first the bees, then the contents of a brood box, and fi-nally the queen, through his magnifying glass. He showed no fear, no discomfort: in everything he did the stranger's movements were gentle and slow, and he was not stung, nor did he crush or hurt a single bee. This impressed Old Gao. He had assumed that barbarians were inscrutable, unreadable, mysterious creatures, but this man seemed overjoyed to have encountered Gao's bees. His eyes were shining.

Old Gao fired up the brazier, to boil some water. Long before the charcoal was hot, how-ever, the stranger had removed from his bag a contraption of glass and metal. He had filled the upper half of it with water from the stream, lit a flame, and soon a kettleful of water was steam-ing and bubbling. Then the stranger took two tin mugs from his bag, and some green tea leaves wrapped in paper, and dropped the leaves into the mug, and poured on the water.

It was the finest tea that Old Gao had ever drunk: better by far than his cousin's tea. They drank it cross-legged on the floor.

"I would like to stay here for the summer, in this house," said the stranger.

"Here? This is not even a house," said Old Gao. "Stay down in the village. Widow Zhang has a room."

"I will stay here," said the stranger. "Also I would like to rent one of your beehives."

Old Gao had not laughed in years. There were those in the village who would have thought such a thing impossible. But still, he laughed then, a guffaw of surprise and amusement that seemed to have been jerked out of him.

"I am serious," said the stranger. He placed four silver coins on the ground between them. Old Gao had not seen where he got them from: three silver Mexican pesos, a coin that had be-come popular in China years before, and a large silver yuan. It was as much money as Old Gao might see in a year of selling honey. "For this money," said the stranger, "I would like some-one to bring me food: every three days should suffice."

Old Gao said nothing. He finished his tea and stood up. He pushed through the oiled cloth to the clearing high on the hillside. He walked over to the eleven hives: each consisted of two brood boxes with one, two, three, or, in one case, even four boxes above that. He took the stranger to the hive with four boxes above it, each box filled with frames of comb.

"This hive is yours," he said.

They were plant extracts. That was obvious. They worked, in their way, for a limited time, but they were also extremely poisonous. But watching poor Professor Presbury during those final days—his skin, his eyes, his gait—had convinced me that he had not been on entirely the wrong path.

I took his case of seeds, of pods, of roots, and of dried extracts and I thought. I pondered. I cogitated. I reflected. It was an intellectual problem, and could be solved, as my old maths tutor had always sought to demonstrate to me, by intellect.

They were plant extracts, and they were lethal.

Methods I used to render them non-lethal rendered them quite ineffective.

It was not a three pipe problem. I suspect it was something approaching a three hundred pipe problem before I hit upon an initial idea—a notion, perhaps—of a way of processing the plants that might allow them to be ingested by human beings.

It was not a line of investigation that could easily be followed in Baker Street. So it was, in the autumn of 1903, that I moved to Sussex, and spent the winter reading every book and pamphlet and monograph so far published, I fancy, upon the care and keeping of bees. And so it was that in early April of 1904, armed only with theoretical knowledge, I took delivery from a local farmer of my first package of bees.

I wonder, sometimes, that Watson did not suspect anything. Then again, Watson's glorious obtuseness has never ceased to surprise me, and sometimes, indeed, I had relied upon it. Still, he knew what I was like when I had no work to occupy my mind, no case to solve. He knew my lassitude, my black moods when I had no case to occupy me.

So how could he believe that I had truly retired? He knew my methods.

Indeed, Watson was there when I took receipt of my first bees. He watched, from a safe distance, as I poured the bees from the package into the empty, waiting hive, like slow, humming, gentle treacle.

He saw my excitement, and he saw nothing.

And the years passed, and we watched the Empire crumble, we watched the Government unable to govern, we watched those poor heroic boys sent to the trenches of Flanders to die, all these things confirmed me in my opinions. I was not doing the right thing. I was doing the only thing.

As my face grew unfamiliar, and my finger-joints swelled and ached (not so much as they might have done, though, which I attributed to the many bee-stings I had received in my first few years as an investigative apiarist) and as Watson, dear, brave, obtuse Watson, faded with time and paled and shrank, his skin becoming greyer, his mustache becoming the same shade of grey, my resolve to conclude my researches did not diminish. If anything, it increased.

So: my initial hypotheses were tested upon the South Downs, in an apiary of my own devising, each hive modelled upon Langstroth's. I do believe that I made every mistake that ever a novice beekeeper could or has ever made, and in addition, due to my investigations, an entire hiveful of mistakes that no beekeeper has ever made before, or shall, I trust, ever make again. "The Case of the Poisoned Beehive," Watson might have called many of them, although "The Mystery of the Transfixed Women's Institute" would have drawn more attention to my researches, had anyone been interested enough to investigate. (As it was, I chided Mrs. Telford for simply taking a jar of honey from the shelves here without consulting me, and I ensured that, in the future, she was given several jars for her cooking from the more regular hives, and that honey from the experimental hives was locked away once it had been collected. I do not believe that this ever drew comment.)

I experimented with Dutch bees, with German bees and with Italians, with Carniolans and Caucasians. I regretted the loss of our British bees to blight and, even where they had survived, to interbreeding, although I found and worked with a small hive I purchased and grew up from a frame of brood and a queen cell, from an old Abbey in St. Albans, which seemed to me to be original British breeding stock.

I experimented for the best part of two decades, before I concluded that the bees that I sought, if they existed, were not to be found in England, and would not survive the distances they would need to travel to reach me by international parcel post. I needed to examine bees in India. I needed to travel perhaps farther afield than that.

I have a smattering of languages.

I had my flower-seeds, and my extracts and tinctures in syrup. I needed nothing more.

I packed them up, arranged for the cottage on the Downs to be cleaned and aired once a week, and for Master Wilkins—to whom I am afraid I had developed the habit of referring, to his obvious distress, as "Young Villikins"—to inspect the beehives, and to harvest and sell surplus honey in Eastbourne market, and to prepare the hives for winter.

I told them I did not know when I should be back.

I am an old man. Perhaps they did not expect me to return.

And, if this was indeed the case, they would, strictly speaking, have been right.

Old Gao was impressed, despite himself. He had lived his life among bees. Still, watching the stranger shake the bees from the boxes, with a practised flick of his wrist, so cleanly and so sharply that the black bees seemed more surprised than angered, and simply flew or crawled back into their hives, was remarkable. The stranger then stacked the boxes filled with comb on top of one of the weaker hives, so Old Gao would still have the honey from the hive the stranger was renting.

So it was that Old Gao gained a lodger.

Old Gao gave the Widow Zhang's granddaughter a few coins to take the stranger food three times a week—mostly rice and vegetables, along with an earthenware pot filled, when she left at least, with boiling soup.

Every ten days Old Gao would walk up the hill himself. He went initially to check on the hives, but soon discovered that under the stranger's care all eleven hives were thriving as they had never thrived before. And indeed, there was now a twelfth hive, from a captured swarm of the black bees the stranger had encountered while on a walk along the hill.

Old Gao brought wood, the next time he came up to the shack, and he and the stranger spent several afternoons wordlessly working together, making extra boxes to go on the hives, building frames to fill the boxes.

One evening the stranger told Old Gao that the frames they were making had been invented by an American, only seventy years before. This seemed like nonsense to Old Gao, who made frames as his father had, and as they did across the valley, and as, he was certain, his grandfather and his grandfather's grandfather had, but he said nothing.

He enjoyed the stranger's company. They made hives together, and Old Gao wished that the stranger was a younger man. Then he would stay there for a long time, and Old Gao would have someone to leave his beehives to, when he died. But they were two old men, nailing boxes together, with thin frosty hair and old faces, and neither of them would see another dozen winters.

Old Gao noticed that the stranger had planted a small, neat garden beside the hive that he had claimed as his own, which he had moved away from the rest of the hives. He had covered it with a net. He had also created a "back door" to the hive, so that the only bees that could reach the plants came from the hive that he was renting. Old Gao also observed that, beneath the netting, there were several trays filled with what appeared to be sugar solution of some kind, one coloured bright red, one green, one a startling blue, one yellow. He pointed to them, but all the stranger did was nod and smile.

The bees were lapping up the syrups, though, clustering and crowding on the sides of the tin dishes with their tongues down, eating until they could eat no more, and then returning to the hive.

The stranger had made sketches of Old Gao's bees. He showed the sketches to Old Gao, tried to explain the ways that Old Gao's bees differed from other honeybees, talked of ancient bees preserved in stone for millions of years, but here the stranger's Chinese failed him, and, truthfully, Old Gao was not interested. They were his bees, until he died, and after that, they were the bees of the mountainside. He had brought other bees here, but they had sickened and died, or been killed in raids by the black bees, who took their honey and left them to starve.

The last of these visits was in late summer. Old Gao went down the mountainside. He did not see the stranger again.

It is done.

It works. Already I feel a strange combination of triumph and of disappointment, as if of defeat, or of distant storm-clouds teasing at my senses.

It is strange to look at my hands and to see, not my hands as I know them, but the hands I remember from my younger days:

knuckles unswollen, dark hairs, not snow-white, on the backs.

It was a quest that had defeated so many, a problem with no apparent solution. The first Emperor of China died and nearly destroyed his empire in pursuit of it, three thousand years ago, and all it took me was, what, twenty years?

I do not know if I did the right thing or not (although any "retirement" without such an occupation would have been, literally, maddening). I took the commission from Mycroft. I investigated the problem. I arrived, inevitably, at the solution.

Will I tell the world? I will not.

And yet, I have half a pot of dark brown honey remaining in my bag; a half a pot of honey that is worth more than nations. (I was tempted to write, *worth more than all the tea in China*, perhaps because of my current situation, but fear that even Watson would deride it as cliché.)

And speaking of Watson . . .

There is one thing left to do. My only remaining goal, and it is small enough. I shall make my way to Shanghai, and from there I shall take ship to Southampton, a half a world away.

And once I am there, I shall seek out Watson, if he still lives—and I fancy he does. It is irrational, I know, and yet I am certain that I would know, somehow, had Watson passed beyond the veil.

I shall buy theatrical makeup, disguise myself as an old man, so as not to startle him, and I shall invite my old friend over for tea.

There will be honey on buttered toast served for tea that afternoon, I fancy.

There were tales of a barbarian who passed through the village on his way east, but the people who told Old Gao this did not believe that it could have been the same man who had lived in Gao's shack. This one was young and proud, and his hair was dark. It was not the old man who had walked through those parts in the spring, although, one person told Gao, the bag was similar.

Old Gao walked up the mountainside to investigate, although he suspected what he would find before he got there.

The stranger was gone, and the stranger's bag.

There had been much burning, though. That was clear. Papers had been burnt—Old Gao recognised the edge of a drawing the stranger had made of one of his bees, but the rest of the papers were ash, or blackened beyond recognition, even had Old Gao been able to read barbarian writing. The papers were not the only things to have been burnt; parts of the hive that the stranger had rented were now only twisted ash; there were blackened, twisted strips of tin that might once have contained brightly coloured syrups.

The colour was added to the syrups, the stranger had told him once, so that he could tell them apart, although for what purpose Old Gao had never enquired.

He examined the shack like a detective, searching for a clue as to the stranger's nature or his whereabouts. On the ceramic pillow four silver coins had been left for him to find—two yuan and two pesos—and he put them away.

Behind the shack he found a heap of used slurry, with the last bees of the day still crawling upon it, tasting whatever sweetness was still on the surface of the still-sticky wax.

Old Gao thought long and hard before he gathered up the slurry, wrapped it loosely in cloth, and put it in a pot, which he filled with water. He heated the water on the brazier, but did not let it boil. Soon enough the wax floated to the surface, leaving the dead bees and the dirt and the pollen and the propolis inside the cloth.

He let it cool.

Then he walked outside, and he stared up at the moon. It was almost full.

He wondered how many villagers knew that his son had died as a baby. He remembered his wife, but her face was distant, and he had no portraits or photographs of her. He thought that there was nothing he was so suited for on the face of the earth as to keep the black, bulletlike bees on the side of this high, high hill. There was no other man who knew their temperament as he did.

The water had cooled. He lifted the now solid block of beeswax out of the water, placed it on the boards of the bed to finish cooling. He took the cloth filled with dirt and impurities out of the pot. And then, because he too was, in his way, a detective, and once you have eliminated the impossible whatever remains, however unlikely, must be the truth, he drank the sweet water in the pot. There is a lot of honey in slurry, after all, even after the majority of it has dripped through a cloth and been purified. The water tasted of honey, but not a honey that Gao had ever tasted before. It tasted of smoke, and metal, and strange flowers, and odd perfumes. It tasted, Gao thought, a little like sex.

He drank it all down, and then he slept, with his head on the ceramic pillow.

When he woke, he thought, he would decide how to deal with his cousin, who would expect to inherit the twelve hives on the hill when Old Gao went missing.

He would be an illegitimate son, perhaps, the young man who would return in the days to come. Or perhaps a son. Young Gao. Who would remember, now? It did not matter.

He would go to the city and then he would return, and he would keep the black bees on the side of the mountain for as long as days and circumstances would allow.

Murder to Music

ANTHONY BURGESS

ONE OF THE greatest writers of the second half of the twentieth century, John Anthony Burgess Wilson (1917–1993) produced thirty-three novels, many of which enjoyed great success, but his most famous work is *A Clockwork Orange* (1962), the dystopian novel that served as the basis for the controversial, violent, and disturbing 1971 film written and directed by Stanley Kubrick.

His writing included short stories, literary criticism, screenplays, poetry, librettos, essays, parodies, travel writing, and translations. In spite of his acclaim as a bestselling and sophisticated literary novelist, Burgess preferred to be regarded as a composer first and foremost, having produced more than two hundred fifty musical works, including three symphonies.

"Murder to Music" is not Burgess's only contribution to the literature of Sherlock Holmes. On the 1979–80 television series *Sherlock Holmes and Doctor Watson*, Burgess is given credit as a writer and consultant on some episodes, suggesting a level of Sherlockian interest and scholarship not often recognized among aficionados of the great detective. In the series, which lasted for twenty-four episodes, Holmes is played by Geoffrey Whitehead and Watson by Donald Pickering. Several episodes were remakes of the 1954–55 *Sherlock Holmes* television series that stars Ronald Howard as Holmes and Howard Marion-Crawford as Watson.

"Murder to Music" was first published in *The Devil's Mode* by Anthony Burgess (London, Hutchinson, 1989).

MURDER TO MUSIC

Anthony Burgess

SIR EDWIN ETHERIDGE, the eminent specialist in tropical diseases, had had the kindness to invite me to share with him the examination of a patient of his in the Marylebone area. It seemed to Sir Edwin that this patient, a young man who had never set foot outside England, was suffering from an ailment known as *latah*—common enough in the Malay archipelago but hitherto unknown, so far as the clinical records, admittedly not very reliable, could advise, in the temperate clime of northern Europe. I was able to confirm Sir Edwin's tentative diagnosis: the young man was morbidly suggestible, imitating any action he either saw or heard described, and was, on my entrance into his bedroom, exhausting himself with the conviction that he had been metamorphosed into a bicycle. The disease is incurable but intermittent: it is of physical rather than nervous provenance, and can best be eased by repose, solitude, opiates, and tepid malt drinks. As I strolled down Marylebone Road after the consultation, it seemed to me the most natural thing in the world to turn into Baker Street to visit my old friend, lately returned, so the *Times* informed me, from some nameless assignment in Marrakesh. This, it later transpired, was the astonishing case of the Moroccan poisonous palmyra, of which the world is not yet ready to hear.

I found Holmes rather warmly clad for a London July day, in dressing gown, winter comforter and a jewelled turban which, he was to inform me, was the gift of the mufti of Fez—donated in gratitude for some service my friend was not willing to specify. He was bronzed and clearly inured to a greater heat than our own, but not, except for the turban, noticeably exoticised by his sojourn in the land of the Mohammedan. He had been trying to breathe smoke through a hubble-bubble but had given up the endeavour. "The flavour of rose water is damnably sickly, Watson," he remarked, "and the tobacco itself of a mildness further debilitated by its long transit through these ingenious but ridiculous conduits." With evident relief he drew some of his regular cut from the Turkish slipper by the fireless hearth, filled his curved pipe, lighted it with a vesta and then looked at me amiably. "You have been with Sir Edwin Etheridge," he said, "in, I should think, St. John's Wood Road."

"This is astonishing, Holmes," I gasped. "How can you possibly know?"

"Easy enough," puffed my friend. "St. John's Wood Road is the only London thoroughfare where deciduous redwood has been planted, and a leaf of that tree, prematurely fallen, adheres to the sole of your left boot. As for the other matter, Sir Edwin Etheridge is in the habit of sucking Baltimore mint lozenges as a kind of token prophylactic. You have been sucking one yourself. They are not on the London market, and I know of no other man who has them specially imported."

"You are quite remarkable, Holmes," I said.

"Nothing, my dear Watson. I have been perusing the *Times*, as you may have observed from its crumpled state on the floor—a womanish habit, I suppose, God bless the sex—with a view to informing myself on events of national import, in which, naturally enough, the enclosed world of Morocco takes little interest."

"Are there not French newspapers there?"

"Indeed, but they contain no news of events in the rival empire. I see we are to have a state visit from the young king of Spain."

"That would be his infant majesty Alfonso the Thirteenth," I somewhat gratuitously amplified. "I take it that his mother the regent, the fascinating Maria Christina, will be accompanying him."

"There is much sympathy for the young monarch," Holmes said, "especially here. But he has his republican and anarchist enemies. Spain is in a state of great political turbulence. It is reflected even in contemporary Spanish music." He regarded his violin, which lay waiting for its master in its open case, and resined the bow lovingly. "The petulant little fiddle tunes I heard in Morocco day and night, Watson, need to be excised from my head by something more complex and civilized. One string only, and usually one note on one string. Nothing like the excellent Sarasate." He began to play an air which he assured me was Spanish, though I heard in it something of Spain's Moorish inheritance, wailing, desolate and remote. Then with a start Holmes looked at his turnip watch, a gift from the Duke of Northumberland. "Good heavens, we'll be late. Sarasate is playing this very afternoon at St. James's Hall." And he doffed his turban and robe and strode to his dressing room to habit himself more suitably for a London occasion. I kept my own counsel, as always, concerning my feelings on the subject of Sarasate and, indeed, on music in general. I lacked Holmes's artistic flair. As for Sarasate, I could not deny that he played wonderfully well for a foreign fiddler, but there was a smugness in the man's countenance as he played that I found singularly unattractive. Holmes knew nothing of my feelings and, striding in in his blue velvet jacket with trousers of a light-clothed Mediterranean cut, a white shirt of heavy silk and a black Bohemian tie carelessly knotted, he assumed in me

his own anticipatory pleasure. "Come, Watson," he cried. "I have been trying in my own damnably amateurish way to make sense of Sarasate's own latest composition. Now the master himself will hand me the key. The key of D major," he added.

"Shall I leave my medical bag here?"

"No, Watson. I don't doubt that you have some gentle anaesthetic there to ease you through the more tedious phases of the recital." He smiled as he said this, but I felt abashed at his all too accurate appraisal of my attitude to the sonic art.

The hot afternoon seemed, to my fancy, to have succumbed to the drowsiness of the Middle Sea, as through Holmes's own inexplicable influence. It was difficult to find a cab and, when we arrived at St. James's Hall, the recital had already begun. When we had been granted the exceptional privilege of taking our seats at the back of the hall while the performance of an item was already in progress, I was quick enough myself to prepare for a Mediterranean siesta. The great Sarasate, then at the height of his powers, was fiddling away at some abstruse mathematics of Bach, to the accompaniment on the pianoforte of a pleasant-looking young man whose complexion proclaimed him to be as Iberian as the master. He seemed nervous, though not of his capabilities on the instrument. He glanced swiftly behind him towards the curtain which shut off the platform from the wings and passages of the administrative arcana of the hall but then, as if reassured, returned wholeheartedly to his music. Meanwhile Holmes, eyes half-shut, gently tapped on his right knee the rhythm of the intolerably lengthy equation which was engaging the intellects of the musically devout, among whom I remarked the pale red-bearded young Irishman who was making his name as a critic and a polemicist. I slept.

I slept, indeed, very soundly. I was awakened not by the music but by the applause, to which Sarasate was bowing with Latin extravagance. I glanced covertly at my watch to find that a great deal of music had passed over my sleeping brain;

there must have been earlier applause to which my drowsy grey cells had proved impervious. Holmes apparently had not noted my somnolence or, perhaps noting it, had been too discreet to arouse me or, now, to comment on my boorish indifference to that art he adored. "The work in question, Watson," he said, "is about to begin." And it began. It was a wild piece in which never fewer than three strings of the four were simultaneously in action, full of the rhythm of what I knew, from a brief visit to Granada, to be the *zapateado*. It ended with furious chords and a high single note that only a bat could have found euphonious. "Bravo," cried Holmes with the rest, vigorously clapping. And then the noise of what to me seemed excessive approbation was pierced by the crack of a single gunshot. There was smoke and the tang of a frying breakfast, and the young accompanist cried out. His head collapsed onto the keys of his instrument, producing a hideous jangle, and then the head, with its unseeing eyes and an open mouth from which blood relentlessly pumped in a galloping tide, raised itself and seemed to accuse the entire audience of a ghastly crime against nature. Then, astonishingly, the fingers of the right hand of the dying man picked at one note of the keyboard many times, following this with a seemingly delirious phrase of a few different notes which he repeated and would have continued to repeat if the rattle of death had not overtaken him. He slumped to the floor of the platform. The women in the audience screamed. Meanwhile the master Sarasate clutched his valuable violin to his bosom—a Stradivarius, Holmes later was to inform me—as though that had been the target of the gunshot.

Holmes was, as ever, quick to act. "Clear the hall!" he shouted. The manager appeared, trembling and deathly pale, to add a feebler shout to the same effect. Attendants somewhat roughly assisted the horrified audience to leave. The red-bearded young Irishman nodded at Holmes as he left, saying something to the effect that it was as well that the delicate fingers of the amateur should anticipate the coarse questing paws of the Metropolitan professionals, adding that

it was a bad business: that young Spanish pianist had promised well. "Come, Watson," said Holmes, striding towards the platform. "He has lost much blood but he may not be quite dead." But I saw swiftly enough that he was past any help that the contents of my medical bag could possibly provide. The rear of the skull was totally shattered.

Holmes addressed Sarasate in what I took to be impeccable Castilian, dealing every courtesy and much deference. Sarasate seemed to say that the young man, whose name was Gonzáles, had served as his accompanist both in Spain and on foreign tours for a little over six months, that he knew nothing of his background though something of his ambitions as a solo artist and a composer, and that, to the master's knowledge, he had no personal enemies. Stay, though: there had been some rather unsavoury stories circulating in Barcelona about the adulterous activities of the young Gonzáles, but it was doubtful if the enraged husband, or conceivably husbands, would have pursued him to London to effect so dire and spectacular a revenge. Holmes nodded distractedly, meanwhile loosening the collar of the dead man.

"A somewhat pointless procedure," I commented. Holmes said nothing. He merely peered at the lowest segment of the nape of the corpse's neck, frowned, then wiped one hand against the other while rising from a crouch back to his feet. He asked the sweating manager if the act of assassination had by any chance been observed, either by himself or by one of his underlings, or, failing that, if any strange visitant had, to the knowledge of the management, insinuated himself into the rear area of the hall, reserved exclusively for artists and staff and protected from the rear door by a former sergeant of marines, now a member of the corps of commissionaires. A horrid thought struck the manager at once, and followed by Holmes and myself, he rushed down a corridor that led to a door which gave on to a side alley.

That door was unguarded for a very simple reason. An old man in the uniform trousers of the corps, though not, evidently because of the heat, the jacket, lay dead, the back of his grey head pierced with devilish neatness by a bullet. The assassin had then presumably effected an unimpeded transit to the curtains which separated the platform from the area of offices and dressing rooms.

"It is very much to be regretted," said the distraught manager, "that no other of the staff was present at the rear, though if one takes an excusably selfish view of the matter, it is perhaps not to be regretted. Evidently we had here a cold-blooded murderer who would stop at nothing." Holmes nodded and said:

"Poor Simpson. I knew him, Watson. He spent a life successfully avoiding death from the guns and spears of Her Imperial Majesty's enemies, only to meet it in a well-earned retirement while peacefully perusing his copy of *Sporting Life*. Perhaps," he now said to the manager, "you would be good enough to explain why the assassin had only poor Simpson to contend with. In a word, where were the other members of the staff?"

"The whole affair is very curious, Mr. Holmes," said the manager, wiping the back of his neck with a handkerchief. "I received a message just after the start of the recital, indeed shortly after your good self and your friend here had taken your seats. The message informed me that the Prince of Wales and certain friends of his were coming to the concert, though belatedly. It is, of course, well known that His Royal Highness is an admirer of Sarasate. There is a small upper box at the back of the hall normally reserved for distinguished visitors, as I think you know."

"Indeed," said Holmes. "The Maharajah of Johore was once kind enough to honour me as his guest in that exclusive retreat. But do please go on."

"Naturally, myself and my staff," the manager continued, "assembled at the entrance and remained on duty throughout the recital, assuming that the distinguished visitor might arrive only for the final items." He went on to say that, though considerably puzzled, they had remained in the vestibule until the final applause,

hazarding the guess that His Royal Highness might, in the imperious but bonhomous manner that was his wont, command the Spanish fiddler to favour him with an encore in a hall filled only with the anticipatory majesty of our future King Emperor. Thus all was explained save for the essential problem of the crime itself.

"The message," Holmes demanded of the manager. "I take it that it was a written message. Might I see it?"

The manager drew from an inner pocket a sheet of notepaper headed with the princely insignia and signed with a name known to be that of His Royal Highness's private secretary. The message was clear and courteous. The date was the seventh of July. Holmes nodded indifferently at it and, when the police arrived, tucked the sheet unobtrusively into a side pocket. Inspector Stanley Hopkins had responded promptly to the summons delivered, with admirable efficiency, by one of the manager's underlings in a fast cab.

"A deplorable business, inspector," Holmes said. "Two murders, the motive for the first explained by the second, but the second as yet disclosing no motive at all. I wish you luck with your investigations."

"You will not be assisting us with the case, Mr. Holmes?" asked the intelligent young inspector. Holmes shook his head.

"I am," he said to me in the cab that took us back to Baker Street, "exhibiting my usual duplicity, Watson. This case interests me a great deal." Then he said somewhat dreamily: "Stanley Hopkins, Stanley Hopkins. The name recalls that of an old teacher of mine, Watson. It always takes me back to my youthful days at Stoneyhurst College, where I was taught Greek by a young priest of exquisite delicacy of mind. Gerard Manley Hopkins was his name." He chuckled a moment. "I was given taps from a tolly by him when I was a callow atramontarius. He was the best of the younger crows, however, always ready to pin a shouting cake with us in the haggory. Never creeping up on us in the silent oilers worn by the crabbier jebbies."

"Your vocabulary, Holmes," I said. "It is a foreign language to me."

"The happiest days of our lives, Watson," he then said somewhat gloomily.

Over an early dinner of cold lobster and a chicken salad, helped down by an admirable white burgundy well chilled, Holmes disclosed himself as vitally concerned with pursuing this matter of the murder of a foreign national on British soil, or at least in a London concert room. He handed me the presumed royal message and asked what was my opinion of it. I examined the note with some care. "It seems perfectly in order to me," I said. "The protocol is regular, the formula, or so I take it, is the usual one. But, since the manager and his staff were duped, some irregularity in obtaining the royal notepaper must be assumed."

"Admirable, Watson. Now kindly examine the date."

"It is today's date."

"True, but the formation of the figure seven is not what one might expect."

"Ah," I said, "I see your meaning. We British do not place a bar across the number. This seven is a continental one."

"Exactly. The message has been written by a Frenchman or an Italian or, as seems much more probable, a Spaniard with access to the notepaper of His Royal Highness. The English and, as you say, the formula are impeccable. But the signatory is not British. He made a slight slip there. As for the notepaper, it would be available only to a person distinguished enough to possess access to His Royal Highness's premises and to a person unscrupulous enough to rob him of a sheet of notepaper. Something in the configuration of the letter *e* in this message persuades me that the signatory was Spanish. I may, naturally, be totally mistaken. But I have very little doubt that the assassin was Spanish."

"A Spanish husband, with the impetuousness of his race, exacting a very summary revenge," I said.

"I think the motive of the murder was not at all domestic. You observed my loosening the collar of the dead man and you commented with professional brusqueness on the futility of my act. You were unaware of the reason for it." Holmes, who now had his pipe alight, took a pencil and scrawled a curious symbol on the tablecloth. "Have you ever seen anything like this before, Watson?" he puffed. I frowned at the scrawl. It seemed to be a crude representation of a bird with spread wings seated on a number of upright strokes which could be taken as a nest. I shook my head. "That, Watson, is a phoenix rising from the ashes of the flames that consumed it. It is the symbol of the Catalonian separatists. They are republicans and anarchists and they detest the centralizing control of the Castilian monarchy. This symbol was tattooed on the back of the neck of the murdered man. He must have been an active member of a conspiratorial group."

"What made you think of looking for it?" I asked.

"I met, quite by chance, a Spaniard in Tangiers who inveighed in strong terms against the monarchy which had exiled him and, wiping the upper part of his body for the heat, disclosed quite frankly that he had an identical tattoo on his chest."

"You mean," I said incredulously, "that he was in undress, or, as the French put it, *en deshabille*!"

"It was an opium den in the Kasbah, Watson," Holmes said calmly. "Little attention is paid in such places to the refinements of dress. He mentioned to me that the nape of the neck was the more usual site of the declaration of faith in the Catalonian republic, but he preferred the chest, where, as he put it, he could keep an eye on the symbol and be reminded of what it signified. I had been wondering ever since the announcement of the visit to London of the young Spanish king whether there might be Catalonian assassins around. It seemed reasonable to me to look on the body of the murdered man for some indication of a political adherence."

"So," said I, "it is conceivable that this young Spaniard, dedicated to art as he seemed to be, proposed killing the harmless and innocent Alfonso the Thirteenth. The intelligence services of the Spanish monarchy have, I take it, acted promptly though illegally. All the forces of European stability should be grateful that the would-be assassin has been himself assassinated."

"And the poor old soldier who guarded the door?" Holmes riposted, his sharp eyes peering at me through the fog of his tobacco smoke. "Come, Watson, murder is always a crime." And then he began to hum, not distractedly, a snatch of tune which seemed vaguely familiar. His endless repetition of it was interrupted by the announcement that Inspector Stanley Hopkins had arrived. "I expected him, Watson," Holmes said, and when the young police officer had entered the room, he bafflingly recited:

"And I have asked to be / Where no storms come, / Where the green swell is in the havens dumb, / And out of the swing of the sea."

Stanley Hopkins gaped in some astonishment, as I might have myself had I not been long inured to Holmes's eccentricities of behaviour. Before Hopkins could stutter a word of bewilderment, Holmes said: "Well, inspector, I trust you have come in triumph." But there was no triumph in Hopkins's demeanour. He handed over to Holmes a sheet of paper on which there was handwriting in purple ink.

"This, Mr. Holmes, was found on the dead man's person. It is in Spanish, I think, a language with which neither I nor my colleagues are at all acquainted. I gather you know it well. I should be glad if you would assist our investigation by translating it."

Holmes read both sides of the paper keenly. "Ah, Watson," he said at length, "this either complicates or simplifies the issue, I am not as yet sure which. This seems to be a letter from the young man's father, in which he implores the son to cease meddling with republican and anarchistic affairs and concentrate on the practice of his art. He also, in the well-worn phrase, wags a will at him. No son of his disloyal to the concept of a unified Spain with a secure monarchy need expect to inherit a *patrimonio*. The father appears to be mortally sick and threatens to deliver a dying curse on his intransigent offspring. Very Spanish, I suppose. Highly dramatic. Some passages have the lilt of operatic arias. We need the Frenchman Bizet to set them to music."

"So," I said, "it is possible that the young man had announced his defection from the cause, possessed information which he proposed to make public or at least refer to a quarter which had a special interest in it, and then was brutally murdered before he could make the divulgation."

"Quite brilliant, Watson," said Holmes, and I flushed discreetly with pleasure. It was rarely that he gave voice to praise untempered by sarcasm. "And a man who has killed so remorselessly twice is all too likely to do so again. What arrangements, inspector," he asked young Hopkins, "have the authorities made for the security of our royal Spanish visitors?"

"They arrive this evening, as you doubtless know, on the last of the packets from Boulogne. At Folkestone they will be transferred immediately to a special train. They will be accommodated at the Spanish embassy. Tomorrow they travel to Windsor. The following day there will be luncheon with the prime minister. There will be a special performance of Messrs. Gilbert and Sullivan's *Gondoliers*—"

"In which the Spanish nobility is mocked," said Holmes, "but no matter. You have given me the itinerary and the programme. You have not yet told me of the security arrangements."

"I was coming to that. The entire Metropolitan force will be in evidence on all occasions, and armed men out of uniform will be distributed at all points of vantage. I do not think there is anything to fear."

"I hope you are right, inspector."

"The royal party will leave the country on the fourth day by the Dover-Calais packet at one twenty-five. Again, there will be ample forces of security both on the dockside and on the boat itself. The home secretary realizes the extreme importance of the protection of a visiting monarch—especially since that regrettable incident when the Czar was viciously tripped over in the Crystal Palace."

"My own belief," Holmes said, relighting his pipe, "is that the Czar of all the Russias was intoxicated. But again, no matter." A policeman in uniform was admitted. He saluted Holmes first and then his superior. "This is open house for the Metropolitan force," Holmes remarked with good-humoured sarcasm. "Come one, come all. You are heartily welcome, sergeant. I take it you have news."

"Beg pardon, sir," the sergeant said, and to Hopkins, "We got the blighter, sir, in a manner of speaking."

"Explain yourself, sergeant. Come on, man," snapped Hopkins.

"Well, sir, there's this kind of Spanish hotel, meaning a hotel where Spaniards go when they want to be with their own sort, in the Elephant and Castle it is."

"Appropriate," Holmes interjected rapidly. "It used to be the Infanta of Castile. Goat and Compasses. God encompasses us. I apologize. Pray continue, sergeant."

"We got there and he must have known what was coming, for he got on the roof by way of the skylight, three storeys up it is, and whether he slipped or hurled himself off, his—neck was broke, sir." The printing conventions of our realm impose the employment of a dash to indicate the demotic epithet the sergeant employed. "Begging your pardon, sir."

"You're sure it's the assassin, sergeant?" asked Holmes.

"Well, sir, there was Spanish money on him and there was a knife, what they call a stiletto, and there was a revolver with two chambers let off, sir."

"A matter, inspector, of checking the bullets extracted from the two bodies with those still in the gun. I think that was your man, sergeant. My congratulations. It seems that the state visit of his infant majesty can proceed without too much foreboding on the part of the Metropolitan force. And now, inspector, I expect you have some writing to do." This was a courteous way of dismissing his two visitors. "You must be tired, Watson," he then said. "Perhaps the sergeant would be good enough to whistle a cab for you. In the street, that is. We shall meet, I trust, at the Savoy Theatre on the tenth. Immediately before curtain time. Mr. D'Oyly Carte always has two complimentary tickets

waiting for me in the box office. It will be interesting to see how our Iberian visitors react to a British musical farce." He said this without levity, with a certain gloom rather. So I too was dismissed.

Holmes and I, in our evening clothes with medals on display, assisted as planned at the performance of *The Gondoliers*. My medals were orthodox enough, those of an old campaigner, but Holmes had some very strange decorations, among the least recondite of which I recognized the triple star of Siam and the crooked cross of Bolivia. We had been given excellent seats in the orchestral stalls. Sir Arthur Sullivan conducted his own work. The infant king appeared to be more interested in the electric light installations than in the action or song proceeding on stage, but his mother responded with suitable appreciation to the jokes when they had been explained to her by the Spanish ambassador. This was a musical experience more after my heart than a recital by Sarasate. I laughed heartily, nudged Holmes in the ribs at the saltier sallies and hummed the airs and choruses perhaps too boisterously, since Lady Esther Roscommon, one of my patients, as it happened, poked me from the row behind and courteously complained that I was not only loud but also out of tune. But, as I told her in the intermission, I had never laid claim to any particular musical skill. As for Holmes, his eyes were on the audience, and with opera glasses too, more than on the stage proceedings.

During the intermission, the royal party very democratically showed itself in the general bar, the young king graciously accepting a glass of British lemonade, over which, in the manner of a child unblessed by the blood, he smacked his lips. I was surprised to see that the great Sarasate, in immaculate evening garb with the orders of various foreign states, was taking a glass of champagne with none other than Sir Arthur Sullivan. I commented on the fact to Holmes, who bowed rather distantly to both, and expressed wonder that a man so eminent in the sphere of the more rarefied music should be hobnobbing with a mere entertainer, albeit one honoured by the Queen. "Music is music," Holmes explained, lighting what I took to be a Tangerine panatella. "It has many mansions. Sir Arthur has sunk, Watson, to the level he finds most profitable, and not only in terms of monetary reward, but he is known also for works of dreary piety. They are speaking Italian together." Holmes's ears were sharper than mine. "How much more impressive their reminiscences of aristocratic favour sound than in our own blunt tongue. But the second bell has sounded. What a waste of an exceptionally fine leaf." He referred to his panatella, which he doused with regret in one of the brass receptacles in the lobby. In the second half of the entertainment Holmes slept soundly. I felt I needed no more to experience the shame of an uncultivated boor when I succumbed to slumber at a more elevated musical event. As Holmes had said, somewhat blasphemously, music has many mansions.

The following morning, a hasty message from Sir Edwin Etheridge, delivered while I was at breakfast, summoned me to another consultation in the bedroom of his patient on St. John's Wood Road. The young man was no longer exhibiting the symptoms of *latah;* he seemed now to be suffering from the rare Chinese disease, which I had encountered in Singapore and Hong Kong, known as *shook jong.* This is a distressing ailment, and embarrassing to describe outside of a medical journal, since its cardinal feature is the patient's fear that the capacity of generation is being removed from him by malevolent forces conjured by an overheated imagination. To combat these forces, which he believes responsible for a progressive diminution of his tangible generative asset, he attempts to obviate its shrinkage by transfixation, usually with the sharpest knife he can find. The only possible treatment was profound sedation and, in the intervals of consciousness, a light diet.

I very naturally turned onto Baker Street after the consultation, the fine weather continuing with a positively Hispanic effulgence. The great world of London seemed wholly at peace. Holmes, in dressing gown and Moorish turban,

was rubbing resin onto his bow as I entered his sitting room. He was cheerful while I was not. I had been somewhat unnerved by the sight of an ailment I had thought to be confined to the Chinese, as I had been disconcerted earlier in the week by the less harmful *latah*, a property of hysterical Malays, both diseases now manifesting themselves in a young person of undoubtedly Anglo-Saxon blood. Having unburdened myself of my disquiet to Holmes, I said, perhaps wisely, "These are probably the sins visited by subject races on our imperialistic ambitions."

"They are the occluded side of progress," Holmes said, somewhat vaguely, and then, less so, "Well, Watson, the royal visit seems to have passed without mishap. The forces of Iberian dissidence have not further raised their bloody hands on our soil. And yet I am not altogether easy in my mind. Perhaps I must attribute the condition to the irrational power of music. I cannot get out of my head the spectacle of that unfortunate young man struck lifeless at the instrument he had played with so fine a touch, and then, in his death agony, striking a brief rhapsody of farewell which had little melodic sense in it." He moved his bow across the strings of his violin. "Those were the notes, Watson. I wrote them down. To write a thing down is to control it and sometimes to exorcise it." He had been playing from a scrap of paper which rested on his right knee. A sudden summer gust, a brief hot breath of July, entered by the open window and blew the scrap to the carpet. I picked it up and examined it. Holmes's bold hand was discernible in the five lines and the notes, which meant nothing to me. I was thinking more of the *shook jong.* I saw again the desperate pain of an old Chinese who had been struck down with it in Hong Kong. I had cured him by countersuggestion and he had given me in gratitude all he had to give—a bamboo flute and a little sheaf of Chinese songs.

"A little sheaf of Chinese songs I once had," I said musingly to Holmes. "They were simple but charming. I found their notation endearingly simple. Instead of the clusters of black blobs which, I confess, make less sense to me than the shop signs in Kowloon, they use merely a system of numbers. The first note of a scale is one, the second two, and so on, up to, I think, eight."

What had been intended as an inconsequent observation had an astonishing effect on Holmes. "We must hurry," he cried, rising and throwing off turban and dressing gown. "We may already be too late." And he fumbled among the reference books which stood on a shelf behind his armchair. He leafed through a Bradshaw and said: "As I remembered, at eleven fifteen. A royal coach is being added to the regular boat train to Dover. Quick, Watson—into the street while I dress. Signal a cab as if your life depended on it. The lives of others may well do so."

The great clock of the railway terminus already showed ten minutes after eleven as our cab clattered to a stop. The driver was clumsy in telling out change for my sovereign. "Keep it, keep it," I cried, following Holmes, who had not yet explained his purpose. The concourse was thronged. We were lucky enough to meet Inspector Stanley Hopkins, on duty and happy to be near the end of it, standing alertly at the barrier of Platform 12, whence the boat train was due to depart on time. The engine had already got up its head of steam. The royal party had boarded. Holmes cried with the maximum of urgency:

"They must be made to leave their carriage at once. I will explain later."

"Impossible," Hopkins said in some confusion. "I cannot give such an order."

"Then I will give it myself. Watson, wait here with the inspector. Allow no one to get through." And he hurled himself onto the platform, crying in fluent and urgent Spanish to the embassy officials and the ambassador himself the desperate necessity of the young king's leaving his compartment with all speed, along with his mother and all their entourage. It was the young Alfonso XIII, with a child's impetuousness, who responded most eagerly to the only exciting thing that had happened on his visit, jumping from the carriage gleefully, anticipat-

ing adventure but no great danger. It was only when the entire royal party had distanced itself, on Holmes's peremptory orders, sufficiently from the royal carriage that the nature of the danger in which they had stood or sat was made manifest. There was a considerable explosion, a shower of splintered wood and shattered glass, then only smoke and the echo of the noise in the confines of the great terminus. Holmes rushed to me, who stood obediently with Hopkins at the barrier.

"You let no one through, Watson, inspector?"

"None came through, Mr. Holmes," Hopkins replied, "except—"

"Except"—and I completed the phrase for him—"your revered maestro, I mean the great Sarasate."

"Sarasate?" Holmes gaped in astonishment and then direly nodded. "Sarasate. I see."

"He was with the Spanish ambassador's party," Hopkins explained. "He went in with them but left rather quickly because, as he explained to me, he had a rehearsal."

"You fool, Watson! You should have apprehended him." This was properly meant for Hopkins, to whom he now said: "He came out carrying a violin case?"

"No."

I said with heat: "Holmes, I will not be called a fool. Not, at any rate, in the presence of others."

"You fool, Watson, I say again and again, you fool! But, inspector, I take it he was carrying his violin case when he entered here with the leave-taking party?"

"Yes, now you come to mention it, he was."

"He came with it and left without it?"

"Exactly."

"You fool, Watson! In that violin case was a bomb fitted with a timing device which he placed in the royal compartment, probably under the seat. And you let him get away."

"Your idol, Holmes, your fiddling god. Now transformed suddenly into an assassin. And I will not be called a fool."

"Where did he go?" Holmes asked Hopkins, ignoring my expostulation.

"Indeed, sir," the inspector said, "where *did* he go? I do not think it much matters. Sarasate should not be difficult to find."

"For you he will be," Holmes said. "He had no rehearsal. He has no further recitals in this country. For my money he has taken a train for Harwich or Liverpool or some other port of egress to a land where your writ does not run. You can of course telegraph all the local police forces in the port areas, but from your expression I see that you have little intention of doing that."

"Exactly, Mr. Holmes. It will prove difficult to attach a charge of attempted massacre to him. A matter of supposition only."

"I suppose you are right, inspector," said Holmes after a long pause in which he looked balefully at a poster advertising Pear's Soap. "Come, Watson. I am sorry I called you a fool."

Back in Baker Street, Holmes attempted to mollify me further by opening a bottle of very old brandy, a farewell gift from another royal figure, though, as he was a Mohammedan, it may be conjectured that it was strictly against the tenets of his faith to have such a treasure in his possession, and it may be wondered why he was able to gain for his cellar a part of the Napoleonic trove claimed, on their prisoner's death, by the British authorities on St. Helena.

For this remarkable cognac was certainly, as the ciphers on the label made clear, out of a bin that must have given some comfort to the imperial captive. "I must confess, Watson," said Holmes, an appreciative eye on the golden fluid in his balloon glass, one of a set presented to him by a grateful khedive, "that I was making too many assumptions, assuming, for instance, that you shared my suspicions. You knew nothing of them and yet it was yourself, all unaware, who granted me the key to the solution of the mystery. I refer to the mystery of the fingered swan song of the poor murdered man. It was a message from a man who was choking in his own blood, Watson, and hence could not speak as others do. He spoke as a musician and as a musician, moreover, who had some knowledge of an exotic system of notation. The father who wagged his will, alas, as it proved, fruitlessly, had

been in diplomatic service in Hong Kong. In the letter, as I recall, something was said about an education that had given the boy some knowledge of the sempiternality of monarchical systems, from China, Russia, and their own beloved Spain."

"And what did the poor boy say?" After three glasses of the superb ichor, I was already sufficiently mollified.

"First, Watson, he hammered out the note D. I have not the gift of absolute pitch, and so was able to know it for what it was only because the piece with which Sarasate concluded his recital was in the key of D major. The final chord was in my ears when the young man made his dying attack on the keyboard. Now, Watson, what we call D, and also incidentally the Germans, is called by the French, Italians and Spaniards *re*. In Italian this is the word for 'king,' close enough to the Castilian *rey*, which has the same meaning. Fool as I was, I should have seen that we were being warned about some eventuality concerning the visiting monarch. The notes that followed contained a succinct message. I puzzled about their possible meaning, but your remark this morning about the Chinese system of note-naming, note-numbering, rather, gave me the answer—only just in time, I may add. In whatever key they were played, the notes would yield the numerical figuration one-one-one-five—C-C-C-G, or D-D-D-A: the pitch is of no importance. The total message was one-one-one-five-one-one-seven. It forms a melody of no great intrinsic interest—a kind of deformed bugle call—but the meaning is clear now that we know the code: the king is in danger at eleven fifteen on the morning of the eleventh day of July. It was I who was the fool, Watson, for not perceiving the import of what could have been dying delirium but in truth was a vital communication to whoever had the wit to decipher it."

"What made you suspect Sarasate?" I asked, pouring another fingerful of the delicious liquor into my glass.

"Well, Watson, consider Sarasate's origins. His full name is Pablo Martín Melitón de Sarasate y Navascuéz and he is a son of Barcelona. A

Catalonian, then, and a member of a proud family with an anti-monarchist record. I ascertained so much from judicious enquiries at the Spanish embassy. At the same time I discovered the Chinese background of the youthful Gonzáles, which, at the time, meant nothing. The republicanism of the Sarasate family should have been sufficient to cast a shadow of suspicion over him, but one always considers a great artist as somehow above the sordid intrigues of the political. There was, as I see now, something atrociously cold-blooded in the arrangement whereby the murder of his accompanist was effected only at the conclusion of his recital. Kill the man when he has fulfilled his artistic purpose—this must have been the frigid order delivered by Sarasate to the assassin. I do not doubt that the young Gonzáles had confided in Sarasate, whom, as a fellow musician and a great master, he had every apparent reason to trust. He informed him of his intention to betray the plans of the organization. We cannot be sure of the nature of his motivation—a sudden humane qualm, a shaken state of mind consequent on the receipt of his father's letter. The assassin obeyed Sarasate's order with beat-counting exactitude. My head spins to think of the master's approbation of such a murderous afterpiece to what was, you must admit, a recital of exceptional brilliance."

"The brilliance was, for me, confirmed more by the applause of others than by any judgment of my own. I take it that Sarasate was responsible for another performance less brilliant—the note from His Royal Highness's secretary and the exotic number seven."

"Evidently, Watson. At the Savoy Theatre you saw him chatting amiably with Sir Arthur Sullivan, a crony of the Prince. *Grazie a Dio*, he said among other things, that his long cycle of recitals had finished with his London performance and he could now take a well-earned rest. Any man unscrupulous enough to collaborate with that noted sneerer at the conventions Mr. William Schwenck Gilbert would be quite ready to pick up a sheet or so of the Prince's private notepaper and pass it on without enquiring into the purpose for which it was required."

"Well, Holmes," I now said, "you do not, I take it, propose to pursue Sarasate to condign punishment, to cut off his fiddle-playing career and have him apprehended as the criminal he undoubtedly is?"

"Where is my proof, Watson? As that intelligent young inspector trenchantly remarked, it is all supposition."

"And if it were not?"

Holmes sighed and picked up his violin and bow. "He is a supreme artist whom the world could ill afford to lose. Do not quote my words, Watson, to any of your church-going friends, but I am forced to the belief that art is above morality. If Sarasate, before my eyes and in this very room, strangled you to death, Watson, for your musical insensitivity, while an accomplice of his obstructed my interference with a loaded pistol, and then wrote a detailed statement of the crime, signed with the name of Pablo Martín Melitón de Sarasate y Navascuéz, I should be constrained to close my eyes to the act, destroy the statement, deposit your body in the gutter of Baker Street and remain silent while the police pursued their investigations. So much is the great artist above the moral principles that oppress lesser men. And now, Watson, pour yourself more of that noble brandy and listen to my own rendering of that piece by Sarasate. I warrant you will find it less than masterly but surely the excellence of the intention will gleam through." And so he stood, arranged his music stand, tucked his fiddle beneath his chin and began reverently to saw.

IN THE BEGINNING

An Evening with Sherlock Holmes

JAMES M. BARRIE

(Published Anonymously)

COINCIDENTALLY, JAMES MATTHEW BARRIE and Arthur Conan Doyle, two of the most popular and successful writers of the Victorian and Edwardian eras, attended Edinburgh University at the same time. The university had a greater influence on Conan Doyle, as that is where he encountered Dr. Joseph Bell, the professor whose skill at observation and rational deduction served as the model for Sherlock Holmes.

In later years, Barrie and Conan Doyle formed a friendship, albeit one that was slightly tempered late in their lives when Barrie forbade any talk of spiritualism, the subject that had consumed most of Conan Doyle's thoughts and energy in the last twenty years of his life.

Barrie and Conan Doyle had both published books with moderate success and both found fame and imminent fortune in the same year, 1891, Barrie with the publication of *The Little Minister*, Conan Doyle with *The Strand Magazine*'s publication of the first Sherlock Holmes short stories (after the first two Holmes novels, *A Study in Scarlet*, 1887, and *The Sign of Four*, 1890). The staggering public adulation of Holmes, Watson, and Conan Doyle that followed the publication of the Holmes stories (the first, "A Scandal in Bohemia," appeared in July 1891, followed by additional stories every month) made the detective a household name, thus ripe for parody. The first author to seize the opportunity was Barrie, who anonymously wrote "An Evening with Sherlock Holmes" a mere four months after the first Holmes story, for the November 28, 1891, issue of *The Speaker: A Review of Politics, Letters, Science, and the Arts*, a short-lived London journal that published work by Oscar Wilde and other British literary lights. The story bears the distinction of being the earliest parody of Holmes.

AN EVENING WITH SHERLOCK HOLMES

James M. Barrie

I AM THE sort of man whose amusement is to do everything better than any other body. Hence my evening with Sherlock Holmes.

Sherlock Holmes is the private detective whose adventures Mr. Conan Doyle is now editing in the *Strand* magazine. To my annoyance (for I hate to hear anyone praised except myself) Holmes's cleverness in, for instance, knowing by glancing at you what you had for dinner last Thursday, has delighted press and public, and so I felt it was time to take him down a peg. I therefore introduced myself to Mr. Conan Doyle and persuaded him to ask me to his house to meet Sherlock Holmes.

For poor Mr. Holmes it proved to be an eventful evening. I had determined to overthrow him with his own weapons, and accordingly when he began, with well-affected carefulness, "I perceive, Mr. Anon, from the condition of your cigar-cutter, that you are not fond of music," I replied blandly, "Yes, that is obvious."

Mr. Holmes, who had been in his favourite attitude in an easy chair (curled up in it), started violently and looked with indignation at our host, who was also much put out.

"How on earth can you tell from looking at his cigar-cutter that Mr. Anon is not fond of music?" asked Mr. Conan Doyle, with well-simulated astonishment.

"It is very simple," said Mr. Holmes, still eyeing me sharply.

"The easiest thing in the world," I agreed.

"Then I need not explain?" said Mr. Holmes haughtily.

"Quite unnecessary," said I.

I filled my pipe afresh to give the detective and his biographer an opportunity of exchanging glances unobserved, and then pointing to Mr. Holmes's silk hat (which stood on the table) I said blandly, "So you have been in the country recently, Mr. Holmes?"

He bit his cigar, so that the lighted end was jerked against his brow.

"You saw me there?" he replied almost fiercely.

"No," I said, "but a glance at your hat told me you had been out of town."

"Ha!" said he triumphantly, "then yours was but a guess, for as a matter of fact I—"

"Did not have that hat in the country with you," I interposed.

"Quite true," he said smiling.

"But how—" began Mr. Conan Doyle.

"Pooh," said I coolly, "this may seem remarkable to you two who are not accustomed to drawing deductions from circumstances trivial in themselves (Holmes winced), but it is nothing to one who keeps his eyes open. Now as soon as I saw that Mr. Holmes's hat was dented in the front, as if it had received a sharp blow, I knew he had been in the country lately."

"For a long or short time?" Holmes snarled. (His cool manner had quite deserted him.)

"For at least a week," I said.

"True," he said dejectedly.

"Your hat also tells me," I continued, "That you came to this house in a four-wheeler—no, in a hansom."

"—" said Sherlock Holmes. "Would you mind explaining?" asked our host.

"Not at all," I said. "When I saw the dent in Mr. Holmes's hat, I knew at once that it had come unexpectedly against some hard object. Probably the roof of a conveyance, which he struck against while stepping in. These accidents often happen at such a time to hats. Then though this conveyance might have been a four-wheeler, it was more probable that Mr. Holmes would travel in a hansom."

"How did you know I had been in the country?"

"I am coming to that. Your practice is, of course, to wear a silk hat always in London, but those who are in the habit of doing so acquire, without knowing it, a habit of guarding their hats. I, therefore, saw that you had recently been wearing a pot-hat and had forgotten to allow for the extra height of the silk hat. But you are not the sort of man who would wear a little hat in London. Obviously, then, you had been in the country, where pot-hats are the rule rather than the exception."

Mr. Holmes, who was evidently losing ground every moment with our host, tried to change the subject.

"I was lunching in an Italian restaurant to-day," he said, addressing Mr. Conan Doyle, "and the waiter's manner of adding up my bill convinced me that his father had once—"

"Speaking of that," I interposed, "do you remember that as you were leaving the restaurant you and another person nearly had a quarrel at the door?"

"Was it you?" he asked.

"If you think that possible," I said blandly, "you have a poor memory for faces."

He growled to himself.

"It is this way, Mr. Doyle," I said. "The door of this restaurant is in two halves, the one of which is marked 'Push' and the other 'Pull.' Now Mr. Holmes and the stranger were on different sides of the door, and both pulled. As a consequence the door would not open, until one of them gave way, then they glared at each other and parted."

"You must have been a spectator," said our host.

"No," I replied, "but I knew this as soon as I heard that Mr. Holmes had been lunching in one of those small restaurants. They all have double doors which are marked 'Push' and 'Pull' respectively. Now, nineteen times in twenty, mankind pushes when it ought to pull, and pulls when it should push. Again, when you are leaving a restaurant there is usually someone entering it. Hence the scene at the door. And, in conclusion, the very fact of having made such a silly mistake rouses ill-temper, which we vent on the other man, to imply that the fault was all his."

"Hum!" said Holmes savagely. "Mr. Doyle, the leaf on this cigar is unwinding."

"Try anoth—" our host was beginning, when I interposed with—

"I observe from your remark, Mr. Holmes, that you came straight here from the hairdresser's."

This time he gaped.

"You let him wax your mustache," I continued. (For of late Mr. Holmes has been growing a mustache.)

"He did and before I knew what he was about," Mr. Holmes replied.

"Exactly," I said, "and in your hansom you tried to undo his handiwork with your fingers."

"To which," our host said with sudden enlightenment, "some of the wax stuck, and is now tearing the leaf of the cigar!"

"Precisely," I said, "I knew he had come from a hairdresser's the moment I shook hands with him."

"Good-night," said Mr. Holmes, seizing his hat (he is not as tall as I thought him at first), "I have an appointment at ten with a banker, who—"

"So I have been observing," I said. "I knew it from the way you—"

But he was gone.

Detective Stories Gone Wrong:
The Adventures of Sherlaw Kombs

ROBERT BARR

(Writing as Luke Sharp)

THE BRITISH WRITER, journalist, and short story writer Robert Barr (1850–1912) is best known for *The Triumphs of Eugène Valmont* (1906), his superb collection of stories about the French detective. It contains one of the most famous and ingenious mystery stories of all time, "The Absent-Minded Coterie." As the first important volume of humorous detective stories in English literature, it was selected by Ellery Queen for his pioneering work, *Queen's Quorum*, which described the one hundred six most important collections of detective stories from 1845 to 1950.

Perhaps Barr's even greater contribution to Victorian and Edwardian fiction was the founding of *The Idler*, which was devoted to popular fiction and became one of the leading British magazines of the day. Barr brought along the famous humorist Jerome K. Jerome to be coeditor and the magazine soon published many of the leading illustrators and authors of the day, including Mark Twain, Rudyard Kipling, Arthur Conan Doyle, E. W. Hornung, H. G. Wells, and Barr himself; it was issued from 1892 until 1911.

An adept parodist, Barr targeted Sherlock Holmes twice and was one of the first to make sport of the detective, though this did not damage his friendship with Conan Doyle. In his autobiography, Conan Doyle described him as "a volcanic Anglo—or rather Scot-American, with a violent manner, a wealth of strong adjectives, and one of the kindest natures underneath it all."

"Detective Stories Gone Wrong: The Adventures of Sherlaw Kombs" was first published under the Luke Sharp pseudonym in the May 1892 issue of *The Idler*; it was first collected in book form under the title "The Great Pegram Mystery" in *The Face and the Mask* by Robert Barr (London, Hutchinson, 1894), acknowledging the true authorship.

DETECTIVE STORIES GONE WRONG:
THE ADVENTURES OF SHERLAW KOMBS

Robert Barr

I DROPPED IN on my friend, Sherlaw Kombs, to hear what he had to say about the Pegram mystery, as it had come to be called in the newspapers. I found him playing the violin with a look of sweet peace and serenity on his face, which I never noticed on the countenances of those within hearing distance. I knew this expression of seraphic calm indicated that Kombs had been deeply annoyed about something. Such, indeed, proved to be the case, for one of the morning papers had contained an article eulogizing the alertness and general competence of Scotland Yard. So great was Sherlaw Kombs's contempt for Scotland Yard that he never would visit Scotland during his vacations, nor would he ever admit that a Scotchman was fit for anything but export.

He generously put away his violin, for he had a sincere liking for me, and greeted me with his usual kindness.

"I have come," I began, plunging at once into the matter on my mind, "to hear what you think of the great Pegram mystery."

"I haven't heard of it," he said quietly, just as if all London were not talking of that very thing. Kombs was curiously ignorant on some subjects, and abnormally learned on others. I found, for instance, that political discussion with him was impossible, because he did not know who Salisbury and Gladstone were. This made his friendship a great boon.

"The Pegram mystery has baffled even Gregory, of Scotland Yard."

"I can well believe it," said my friend, calmly.

"Perpetual motion, or squaring the circle, would baffle Gregory. He's an infant, is Gregory."

This was one of the things I always liked about Kombs. There was no professional jealousy in him, such as characterizes so many other men.

He filled his pipe, threw himself into his deep-seated armchair, placed his feet on the mantel, and clasped his hands behind his head.

"Tell me about it," he said simply.

"Old Barrie Kipson," I began, "was a stockbroker in the City. He lived in Pegram, and it was his custom to—"

"Come in!" shouted Kombs, without changing his position, but with a suddenness that startled me. I had heard no knock.

"Excuse me," said my friend, laughing, "my invitation to enter was a trifle premature. I was really so interested in your recital that I spoke before I thought, which a detective should never do. The fact is, a man will be here in a moment who will tell me all about this crime, and so you will be spared further effort in that line."

"Ah, you have an appointment. In that case I will not intrude," I said, rising.

"Sit down; I have no appointment. I did not know until I spoke that he was coming."

I gazed at him in amazement. Accustomed as I was to his extraordinary talents, the man was a perpetual surprise to me. He continued to smoke quietly, but evidently enjoyed my consternation.

"I see you are surprised. It is really too simple to talk about, but, from my position opposite the mirror, I can see the reflection of objects in the street. A man stopped, looked at one of my cards, and then glanced across the street. I recognized my card, because, as you know, they are all in scarlet. If, as you say, London is talking of this mystery, it naturally follows that *he* will talk of it, and the chances are he wished to consult with me upon it. Anyone can see that, besides there is always—*Come* in!"

There was a rap at the door this time.

A stranger entered. Sherlaw Kombs did not change his lounging attitude.

"I wish to see Mr. Sherlaw Kombs, the detective," said the stranger, coming within the range of the smoker's vision.

"This is Mr. Kombs," I remarked at last, as my friend smoked quietly, and seemed half-asleep.

"Allow me to introduce myself," continued the stranger, fumbling for a card.

"There is no need. You are a journalist," said Kombs.

"Ah," said the stranger, somewhat taken aback, "you know me, then."

"Never saw or heard of you in my life before."

"Then how in the world—"

"Nothing simpler. You write for an evening paper. You have written an article condemning the book of a friend. He will feel bad about it, and you will condole with him. He will never know who stabbed him unless I tell him."

"The devil!" cried the journalist, sinking into a chair and mopping his brow, while his face became livid.

"Yes," drawled Kombs, "it is a devil of a shame that such things are done. But what would you, as we say in France."

When the journalist had recovered his second wind he pulled himself together somewhat. "Would you object to telling me how you know these particulars about a man you say you have never seen?"

"I rarely talk about these things," said Kombs with great composure. "But as the cultivation of the habit of observation may help you in your profession, and thus in a remote degree benefit me by making your paper less deadly dull, I will tell you. Your first and second fingers are smeared with ink, which shows that you write a great deal. This smeared class embraces two subclasses, clerks or accountants, and journalists. Clerks have to be neat in their work. The ink smear is slight in their case. Your fingers are badly and carelessly smeared; therefore, you are a journalist. You have an evening paper in your pocket. Anyone might have any evening paper, but yours is a Special Edition, which will not be on the streets for half an hour yet. You must have obtained it before you left the office, and to do this you must be on the staff. A book notice is marked with a blue pencil. A journalist always despises every article in his own paper not written by himself; therefore, you wrote the article you have marked, and doubtless are about to send it to the author of the book referred to. Your paper makes a specialty of abusing all books not written by some member of its own staff. That the author is a friend of yours, I merely surmised. It is all a trivial example of ordinary observation."

"Really, Mr. Kombs, you are the most wonderful man on earth. You are the equal of Gregory, by Jove, you are."

A frown marred the brow of my friend as he placed his pipe on the sideboard and drew his self-cocking six-shooter.

"Do you mean to insult me, sir?"

"I do not—I—I assure you. You are fit to take charge of Scotland Yard tomorrow—I am in earnest, indeed I am, sir."

"Then heaven help you," cried Kombs, slowly raising his right arm.

I sprang between them.

"Don't shoot!" I cried. "You will spoil the carpet. Besides, Sherlaw, don't you see the man means well? He actually thinks it is a compliment!"

"Perhaps you are right," remarked the detective, flinging his revolver carelessly beside his pipe, much to the relief of the third party. Then, turning to the journalist, he said, with his customary bland courtesy—

"You wanted to see me, I think you said. What can I do for you, Mr. Wilber Scribbings?"

The journalist started.

"How do you know my name?" he gasped.

Kombs waved his hand impatiently.

"Look inside your hat if you doubt your own name."

I then noticed for the first time that the name was plainly to be seen inside the top-hat Scribbings held upside down in his hands.

"You have heard, of course, of the Pegram mystery—"

"Tush," cried the detective; "do not, I beg of you, call it a mystery. There is no such thing. Life would become more tolerable if there ever *was* a mystery. Nothing is original. Everything has been done before. What about the Pegram affair?"

"The Pegram—ah—case has baffled everyone. The *Evening Blade* wishes you to investigate, so that it may publish the result. It will pay you well. Will you accept the commission?"

"Possibly. Tell me about the case."

"I thought everybody knew the particulars. Mr. Barrie Kipson lived at Pegram. He carried a first-class season ticket between the terminus and that station. It was his custom to leave for Pegram on the 5:30 train each evening. Some weeks ago, Mr. Kipson was brought down by the influenza. On his first visit to the City after his recovery, he drew something like three hundred pounds in notes, and left the office at his usual hour to catch the 5:30. He was never seen again alive, as far as the public have been able to learn. He was found at Brewster in a first-class compartment on the Scotch Express, which does not stop between London and Brewster. There was a bullet in his head, and his money was gone, pointing plainly to murder and robbery."

"And where is the mystery, might I ask?"

"There are several unexplainable things about the case. First, how came he on the Scotch Express, which leaves at six, and does not stop at Pegram? Second, the ticket examiners at the terminus would have turned him out if he showed his season ticket; and all the tickets sold for the Scotch Express on the 21st are accounted for. Third, how could the murderer have escaped? Fourth, the passengers in two compartments on each side of the one where the body was found heard no scuffle and no shot fired."

"Are you sure the Scotch Express on the 21st did not stop between London and Brewster?"

"Now that you mention the fact, it did. It was stopped by signal just outside of Pegram. There was a few moments' pause, when the line was reported clear, and it went on again. This frequently happens, as there is a branch line beyond Pegram."

Mr. Sherlaw Kombs pondered for a few moments, smoking his pipe silently.

"I presume you wish the solution in time for tomorrow's paper?"

"Bless my soul, no. The editor thought if you evolved a theory in a month you would do well."

"My dear sir, I do not deal with theories, but with facts. If you can make it convenient to call here tomorrow at 8 a.m. I will give you the full particulars early enough for the first edition. There is no sense in taking up much time over so simple an affair as the Pegram case. Good afternoon, sir."

Mr. Scribbings was too much astonished to return the greeting. He left in a speechless condition, and I saw him go up the street with his hat still in his hand.

Sherlaw Kombs relapsed into his old lounging attitude, with his hands clasped behind his head. The smoke came from his lips in quick puffs at first, then at longer intervals. I saw he was coming to a conclusion, so I said nothing.

Finally he spoke in his most dreamy manner. "I do not wish to seem to be rushing things at all, Whatson, but I am going out tonight on the Scotch Express. Would you care to accompany me?"

"Bless me!" I cried, glancing at the clock. "You haven't time, it is after five now."

"Ample time, Whatson—ample," he murmured, without changing his position. "I give myself a minute and a half to change slippers and dressing-gown for boots and coat, three seconds for hat, twenty-five seconds to the street, forty-two seconds waiting for a hansom, and then seven minutes at the terminus before the express starts. I shall be glad of your company."

I was only too happy to have the privilege of going with him. It was most interesting to watch the workings of so inscrutable a mind. As we drove under the lofty iron roof of the terminus I noticed a look of annoyance pass over his face.

"We are fifteen seconds ahead of our time," he remarked, looking at the big clock. "I dislike having a miscalculation of that sort occur."

The great Scotch express stood ready for its long journey. The detective tapped one of the guards on the shoulder.

"You have heard of the so-called Pegram mystery, I presume?"

"Certainly, sir. It happened on this very train, sir."

"Really? Is the same carriage still on the train?"

"Well, yes, sir, it is," replied the guard, lowering his voice, "but of course, sir, we have to keep very quiet about it. People wouldn't travel in it, else, sir."

"Doubtless. Do you happen to know if anybody occupies the compartment in which the body was found?"

"A lady and gentleman, sir; I put 'em in myself, sir."

"Would you further oblige me," said the detective, deftly slipping half a sovereign into the hand of the guard, "by going to the window and informing them in an offhand casual sort of way that the tragedy took place in that compartment?"

"Certainly, sir."

We followed the guard, and the moment he had imparted his news there was a suppressed scream in the carriage. Instantly a lady came out, followed by a florid-faced gentleman, who scowled at the guard. We entered the now empty compartment, and Kombs said:

"We would like to be alone here until we reach Brewster."

"I'll see to that, sir," answered the guard, locking the door.

When the official moved away, I asked my friend what he expected to find in the carriage that would cast any light on the case.

"Nothing," was his brief reply.

"Then why do you come?"

"Merely to corroborate the conclusions I have already arrived at."

"And might I ask what those conclusions are?"

"Certainly," replied the detective, with a touch of lassitude in his voice. "I beg to call your attention, first, to fact that this train stands between two platforms, and can be entered from either side. Any man familiar with the station for years would be aware of that fact. This shows how Mr. Kipson entered the train just before it started."

"But the door on this side is locked," I objected, trying it.

"Of course. But every season ticket holder carries a key. This accounts for the guard not seeing him, and for the absence of a ticket. Now let me give you some information about the influenza. The patient's temperature rises several degrees above normal, and he has a fever. When the malady has run its course, the temperature falls to three-quarters of a degree below normal. These facts are unknown to you, I imagine, because you are a doctor."

I admitted such was the case.

"Well, the consequence of this fall in temperature is that the convalescent's mind turns towards thoughts of suicide. Then is the time he should be watched by his friends. Then was the time Mr. Barrie Kipson's friends did *not* watch him. You remember the 21st, of course. No? It was a most depressing day. Fog all around and mud underfoot. Very good. He resolves on suicide. He wishes to be unidentified, if possible, but forgets his season ticket. My experience is that a man about to commit a crime always forgets something."

"But how do you account for the disappearance of the money?"

"The money has nothing to do with the matter. If he was a deep man, and knew the stupidness of Scotland Yard, he probably sent the notes to an enemy. If not, they may have been given to a friend. Nothing is more calculated to prepare the mind for self-destruction than the prospect of a night ride on the Scotch Express, and the view from the windows of the train as it passes through the northern part of London is particularly conducive to thoughts of annihilation."

"What became of the weapon?"

"That is just the point on which I wish to satisfy myself. Excuse me for a moment."

Mr. Sherlaw Kombs drew down the window on the right-hand side, and examined the top of the casing minutely with a magnifying glass. Presently he heaved a sigh of relief, and drew up the sash.

"Just as I expected," he remarked, speaking more to himself than to me. "There is a slight dent on the top of the window frame. It is of such a nature as to be made only by the trigger of a pistol falling from the nerveless hand of a suicide. He intended to throw the weapon far out of the window, but had not the strength. It might have fallen into the carriage. As a matter of fact, it bounced away from the line and lies among the grass about ten feet six inches from the outside rail. The only question that now remains is where the deed was committed, and the exact present position of the pistol reckoned in miles from London, but that, fortunately, is too simple even to need explanation."

"Great heavens, Sherlaw!" I cried. "How can you call that simple? It seems to me impossible to compute."

We were now flying over northern London, and the great detective leaned back with every sign of *ennui*, closing his eyes. At last he spoke wearily:

"It is really too elementary, Whatson, but I am always willing to oblige a friend. I shall be relieved, however, when you are able to work out the A B C of detection for yourself, although I shall never object to helping you with the words of more than three syllables. Having made up

his mind to commit suicide, Kipson naturally intended to do it before he reached Brewster, because tickets are again examined at that point. When the train began to stop at the signal near Pegram, he came to the false conclusion that it was stopping at Brewster. The fact that the shot was not heard is accounted for by the screech of the air-brake, added to the noise of the train. Probably the whistle was also sounding at the same moment. The train being a fast express would stop as near the signal as possible. The air-brake will stop a train in twice its own length. Call it three times in this case. Very well. At three times the length of this train from the signal-post towards London, deducting half the length of the train, as this carriage is in the middle, you will find the pistol."

"Wonderful!" I exclaimed.

"Commonplace," he murmured.

At this moment the whistle sounded shrilly, and we felt the grind of the air-brakes.

"The Pegram signal again," cried Kombs, with something almost like enthusiasm. "This is indeed luck. We will get out here, Whatson, and test the matter."

As the train stopped, we got out on the right-hand side of the line. The engine stood panting impatiently under the red light, which changed to green as I looked at it. As the train moved on with increasing speed, the detective counted the carriages, and noted down the number. It was now dark, with the thin crescent of the moon hanging in the western sky throwing a weird half-light on the shining metals. The rear lamps of the train disappeared around a curve, and the signal stood at baleful red again. The black magic of the lonesome night in that strange place impressed me, but the detective was a most practical man. He placed his back against the signal-post, and paced up the line with even strides, counting his steps. I walked along the permanent way beside him silently. At last he stopped, and took a tape-line from his pocket. He ran it out until the ten feet six inches were unrolled, scanning the figures in the wan light of the new moon. Giving me the end, he placed his knuckles on the metals, motioning me to proceed down the embankment. I stretched out the line, and then sank my hand in the damp grass to mark the spot.

"Good God!" I cried, aghast. "What is this?"

"It is the pistol," said Kombs quietly.

It was!

Journalistic London will not soon forget the sensation that was caused by the record of the investigations of Sherlaw Kombs, as printed at length in the next day's *Evening Blade*. Would that my story ended here. Alas! Kombs contemptuously turned over the pistol to Scotland Yard. The meddlesome officials, actuated, as I always hold, by jealousy, found the name of the seller upon it. They investigated. The seller testified that it had never been in the possession of Mr. Kipson, as far as he knew. It was sold to a man whose description tallied with that of a criminal long watched by the police. He was arrested, and turned Queen's evidence in the hope of hanging his pal. It seemed that Mr. Kipson, who was a gloomy, taciturn man, and usually came home in a compartment by himself, thus escaping observation, had been murdered in the lane leading to his house. After robbing him, the miscreants turned their thoughts towards the disposal of the body—a subject that always occupies a first-class criminal mind after the deed is done. They agreed to place it on the line, and have it mangled by the Scotch Express, then nearly due. Before they got the body halfway up the embankment the express came along and stopped. The guard got out and walked along the other side to speak with the engineer. The thought of putting the body into an empty first-class carriage instantly occurred to the murderers. They opened the door with the deceased's key. It is supposed that the pistol dropped when they were hoisting the body in the carriage.

The Queen's evidence dodge didn't work, and Scotland Yard ignobly insulted my friend Sherlaw Kombs by sending him a pass to see the villains hanged.

Sherlock Holmes vs. Conan Doyle

ANONYMOUS

THE SHERLOCK HOLMES stories published in *The Strand Magazine* in 1891 and 1892 were a national sensation, so it is not surprising that when the first twelve were collected and published as *The Adventures of Sherlock Holmes* the book became an instant bestseller. The first printing of ten thousand copies was published on October 14, 1892. Demand required a second printing, and then a third. It has never been out of print, either in Great Britain or the United States (where it was published one day after the English edition).

With astonishing speed, a parody written by an anonymous journalist was published on October 29, 1892, in *The National Observer*, a London magazine. The publication began as the *Scots Observer* until it was moved from Edinburgh, coincidentally Arthur Conan Doyle's birthplace, to London in 1889, after which it was renamed the *National Observer*. One of its editors was the famed poet William Ernest Henley. Among the writers it published were Rudyard Kipling, George Bernard Shaw, Thomas Hardy, James M. Barrie, H. G. Wells, and the unknown humorist who anonymously produced "Sherlock Holmes vs. Conan Doyle."

In this little episode, one of the very first recorded Sherlock Holmes parodies, the detective speaks his mind about the man who seems to get it all wrong when chronicling his adventures: Arthur Conan Doyle.

SHERLOCK HOLMES VS. CONAN DOYLE

Anonymous

IN VIEW OF the recent publication of Mr. Sherlock Holmes's more celebrated cases (writes our representative) I called upon the famous scientific detective for the purpose of elucidating if possible some of his more eventful and thrilling episodes in his adventures.

I found the celebrated sleuth-hound, whose fame is now European, seated before a comfortable fire in his cosily furnished rooms in Baker Street. His chin was sunk upon his chest, and his lynx eyes were fixed upon the ceiling with that hawk-like expression which his portraits have rendered so familiar to us.

"Good evening," he said, without turning his head or altering his gaze, as I entered. "You could not have come at a better time. I was just off to bed. You wish to interview me," he added, as his eyes literally pierced me through and through.

"You wear a high hat on Sundays, you are fond of cream tarts, Mr. William Watson is your favourite author, and seventeen years and six months ago you had a cousin who died."

"Really, Mr. Holmes," I stammered in amazement. "It is quite true, though how on earth you know—"

"It is very simple," he said, smiling. "Moreover, it saves me from *ennui*—it and cocaine. Life, my dear sir (your name, by the way, begins with a D, as I see from your handkerchief), is only interesting because it is mysterious. What is ordinary is merely that which is not remarkable, and if you could open all the windows and sail over this vast city, you would behold strange secrets. I do not seem to be able to persuade you of the importance of the improbable," he said reflectively.

"I have come, Mr. Holmes," I began hastily, knowing from Dr. Conan Doyle's account of his weakness for this vein of reflection, and fearing to be taken beyond my depths; "I have come to ask you about the book—"

"You mean," he interrupted, "my treatise on the 742 ways of saying the word 'damn!'"

"No, I refer to Dr. Doyle's collection of your adventures."

"I have heard of the man," said Mr. Holmes. "It is my business to know about all kinds of people. But I've never met him. If you will look in my Index, under the heading Plagiarists—"

"But," I objected, "Dr. Doyle is a novelist."

"True, but he is also a plagiarist—the very worst kind of plagiarist, seeing that he steals from life. Oddly enough, as there was no classical concert this evening, I was just dipping into the very book to which you refer."

He waved his hand towards the table, and leaned back in his chair with a little soft laugh. As he put his fingertips together and, closing his eyes, assumed a languid expression of weariness. I guessed what was coming, and so seized my opportunity and my note book.

"It is perhaps," Mr. Holmes resumed, "just as well, my good man, that people will not stick to the truth, otherwise my occupation—and it is a pleasant way of passing the time—would be gone. This man (who is a stranger to me), has compiled a book purporting to be my adventures. It is, in fact, a garbled version of some very inferior incidents in my professional career;

but where or how he got hold of them, I cannot say, although my mind is already made up.

"You see Watson could never keep his tongue quiet, and he was the densest of men I ever saw, as you may have perceived. If a man wore a muddy coat, he would wonder how I knew he had been splashed. And then Scotland Yard has always been jealous of me. They may have given me away.

"But in any case, it is of no consequence. Dr. Doyle, by the way, I am in a position to state, has written eight other books; and this one appeared originally in the columns of a magazine, where it ran for twelve months. Am I not right?"

"Certainly, but how—"

"It is merely the faculty of observation," he replied. "By examining the book, I find out all that. Obviously, too, he is a man of few scruples and no respect for the truth. He is an unfair man, striving, like all in his class, to make 'copy' where he can.

"I have been grossly misrepresented by him. Do you really think I made that blunder in 'A Scandal in Bohemia'? Do you imagine I had as little a finger in 'The Engineer's Thumb' or 'The Copper Beeches' as he makes out? And do you suppose I interfered as ineffectually in the 'Five Pips' as he represents?"

"What do you suppose was his object, Mr. Holmes?"

The famous detective looked me full in the face.

"Gain," said he simply.

I stared back in astonishment.

"Yes," he resumed; "it is all easy when you see the explanation. You see the book is large and expensively brought out; moreover it is issued by a publisher who caters to the millions. Hence it is clear a very large sale is anticipated. Why? Because the book is supposed to contain a popular element, and that popular element is myself.

"Now, it follows that Dr. Doyle must have heard of me, through Watson or the police; that he saw I should suit his game (which was money); having invented spurious stories about me that he hit upon a publisher similarly unscrupulous. With my name and a fairly accurate account of those interesting cases of mine, 'The Blue Carbuncle' and 'The Speckled Band,' he made a good start; and after that anything would sell, even stuff like 'The Engineer's Thumb' or 'The Noble Husband.' It is a case of moral degeneration."

"What else do you gather of Dr. Doyle?" I asked.

Mr. Holmes yawned.

"He is evidently a smoker; for your smoker always attributes the odious vice to his hero (I need hardly say I never touch tobacco). It is clear too he is not a teetotaler."

"One word more, and I have done: Should you say Dr. Doyle was young or old?"

Mr. Holmes got up and stretched himself. "I need only refer you to the colour of the book."

The Duke's Feather

R. C. LEHMANN

(Writing as Cunnin Toil)

THE FULL AND diverse life of Rudolph Chambers Lehmann (1856–1929) included several separate careers. He entered the Henley Royal Regatta for twelve straight years (1877–1888) and finished dead last in every heat in which he competed; nonetheless, he wrote *The Complete Oarsman* (1908), for many years the standard text on the subject, and was a coach at Oxford, Cambridge, Trinity (Dublin), and Harvard.

He was a member of the bar and the High Sheriff of Buckinghamshire, where the family had a house large enough to be given a name, Fieldhead, and was elected to serve in Parliament from 1906 to 1910 as a member of the Liberal Party. But it is as a literary figure that he is most remembered today. A founder of *Granta* while an undergraduate at Cambridge University in 1889, a magazine that continues to flourish today, he was also a frequent contributor to the British humor magazine *Punch* for thirty years, producing light verse, parodies, and sketches, soon being added to the editorial staff. The Picklock Holes stories, the first series of Sherlock Holmes parodies, were published from August to November 1894 and were collected in book form as *The Adventures of Picklock Holes* in 1901. Other works collected from his contributions to *Punch* are *A Spark Divine: A Book for Animal-Lovers* (1913) and *The Vagabond and Other Poems from* Punch (1918).

"The Duke's Feather" was first published in the August 19, 1893, issue of *Punch*; it was first published in book form under the author's real name in *The Adventures of Picklock Holes* (London, Bradbury, Agnew, 1901).

THE DUKE'S FEATHER

R. C. Lehmann

TWO MONTHS HAD passed without my hearing a word of Holes. I knew he had been summoned to Irkoutsk by the Czar of Russia in order to help in investigating the extraordinary theft of one of the Government silver mines, which had completely and mysteriously disappeared in one night. All the best intellects of the terrible secret police, the third section of the Government of the Russian Empire, had exhausted themselves in the vain endeavor to probe this mystery to the bottom. Their failure had produced a dangerous commotion in the Empire of the Czar; there were rumors of a vast Nihilist plot, which was to shake the Autocracy to its foundations; and, as a last resource, the Czar, who had been introduced to Holes by Olga Fiaskoffskaia, the well-known Russian secret agent at the Court of Lisbon, had appealed to the famous detective to lend his aid in discovering the authors of a crime which was beginning to turn the great white Czar into ridicule in all the bazaars of Central Asia. Holes, whose great mind had been lying fallow for some little time, had immediately consented; and the last I had seen of him was two months before the period at which this story opens, when I had said good-bye to him at Charing Cross Station.

As for myself, I was spending a week in a farmhouse situated close to the village of Blobley-in-the-Marsh. Three miles from the gates of the farmhouse lay Fourcastle Towers, the ancestral mansion of Rear-Admiral the Duke of Dumpshire, the largest and strangest landowner of the surrounding district. I had a nodding acquaintance with His Grace, whom I had once attended for scarlatina when he was a midshipman. Since that time, however, I had seen very little of him, and, to tell the truth, I had made no great effort to improve the acquaintance. The Duke, one of the haughtiest members of our blue-blooded aristocracy, had been called by his naval duties to all parts of the habitable globe; I had steadily pursued my medical studies, and, except for the biennial visit which etiquette demanded, I had seen little or nothing of the Duke. My stay at the farmhouse was for purposes of rest. I had been overworked, that old tulwar wound, the only memento of the Afghan Campaign, had been troubling me, and I was glad to be able to throw off my cares and my black coat and to revel for a week in the rustic and unconventional simplicity of Wurzelby Farm.

One evening, two days after my arrival, I was sitting in the kitchen close to the fire, which, like myself, was smoking. For greater comfort I had put on my old mess-jacket. The winter wind was whistling outside, but besides that only the ticking of the kitchen clock disturbed my meditations. I was just thinking how I should begin my article on modern medicine for the *Fortnightly Review*, when a slight cough at my elbow caused me to turn round. Beside me stood Picklock Holes, wrapped in a heavy, close-fitting fur *moujik*. He was the first to speak.

"You seem surprised to see me," he said.

"Well, perhaps that is natural; but really, my dear fellow, you might employ your time to better purpose than in trying to guess the number of words in the first leading article in the *Times* of the day before yesterday."

I was about to protest when he stopped me.

"I know perfectly well what you are going to say, but it is useless to urge that the country is dull, and that a man must employ his brain somehow. That kind of employment is the merest wool-gathering."

He plucked a small piece of Berlin worsted—I had been darning my socks—off my left trouser, and examined it curiously. My admiration for the man knew no bounds.

"Is that how you know?" I asked. "Do you mean to tell me that merely by seeing that small piece of fancy wool on my trousers you guessed I had been trying to calculate the number of words in the *Times* leader? Holes, Holes, will you never cease from astounding me?"

He did not answer me, but bared his muscular arm and injected into it a strong dose of morphia with a richly chased little gold instrument tipped with a ruby.

"A gift from the Czar," said Holes, in answer to my unspoken thoughts. "When I discovered the missing silver mine on board the yacht of the Grand Duke Ivanoff, his Imperial Majesty first offered me the Chancellorship of his dominion, but I begged him to excuse me, and asked for this pretty toy. Bah, the Russian police are bunglers."

As he made this remark the door opened and Sergeant Bluff of the Dumpshire constabulary entered hurriedly.

"I beg your pardon, sir," he said, addressing me, with evident perturbation, "but would you step outside with me for a moment. There's been some strange work down at—"

Holes interrupted him.

"Don't say any more," he broke in. "You've come to tell us about the dreadful poaching affray in Hagley Wood. I know all about it, and tired as I am I'll help you to find the criminals."

It was amusing to watch the sergeant's face.

He was ordinarily an unemotional man, but as Holes spoke to him he grew purple with astonishment.

"Beggin' your pardon, sir," he said, "I didn't know about no—"

"My name is Holes," said my friend calmly.

"What, Mr. Picklock Holes, the famous detective?"

"The same, at your service; but we are wasting time. Let us be off."

The night was cold, and a few drops of rain were falling. As we walked along the lane Holes drew from the sergeant all the information he wanted as to the number of pheasants on the Duke's estate, the extent of his cellars, his rent-roll, and the name of his London tailor. Bluff dropped behind after this cross-examination with a puzzled expression, and whispered to me:

"A wonderful man that Mister Holes. Now how did he know about this 'ere poaching business? *I* knew nothing about it. Why I come to you, sir, to talk about that retriever dog you lost."

"Hush," I said. "Say nothing. It would only annoy Holes and interfere with his inductions. He knows his own business best." Sergeant Bluff gave a grumbling assent, and in another moment we entered the great gate of Fourcastle Towers and were ushered into the hall, where the Duke was waiting to receive us.

"To what am I indebted for the honor of this visit?" said His Grace, with all the courtly politeness of one in whose veins ran the blood of the Crusaders. Then, changing his tone, he spoke in fierce sailor language: "Shiver my timbers! What makes you three stand there like that? Why, blank my eyes, you ought to—" What he was going to say will never be known, for Holes dashed forward.

"Silence, Duke," he said, sternly. "We come to tell you that there has been a desperate poaching affray. The leader of the gang lies insensible in Hagley Wood. Do you wish to know who he was?"

So saying, he held up to the now terrified eyes of the Duke the tail feather of a golden pheasant. "I found it in his waistcoat pocket," he said, simply.

"My son, my son!" shrieked the unfortunate Duke. "Oh Alured, Alured, that it should have come to this!" And he fell to the floor in convulsions.

"You will find Earl Mountravers at the cross-roads in Hagley Wood," said Holes to the sergeant. "He is insensible."

The Earl was convicted at the following Assizes and sentenced to a long term of penal servitude. His ducal father has never recovered from the disgrace. Holes, as usual, made light of the matter and of his own share in it.

"I met the Earl," he told me afterwards, "as I was walking to your farmhouse. When he ventured to doubt one of my stories, I felled him to the earth. The rest was easy enough. Poachers? Oh dear no, there were none. But it is precisely in these cases that ingenuity comes in."

"Holes," I said, "I admire you more and more every day."

The Sign of the "400"

Being a Continuation of the Adventures of Sherlock Holmes

ROY L. McCARDELL

ROY L. MCCARDELL (1870–1940), who referred to himself as "Old Doctor McCardell," began writing and selling his pieces at the age of twelve. He was a journalist, humorist, and writer of book reviews, songs, poetry, sketches, articles, the stage play *The Gay Life*, and more than a thousand movie scenarios. *Puck*, the first successful American humor magazine, published his adolescent works. After Arthur Brisbane recruited him to *The Evening Sun*, he went on to work at various magazine and newspapers, including the *New York World*. He joined the *Puck* staff in his adult life and served as the editor of multiple magazines and newspapers, including the *New York Morning Telegraph* and *Metropolitan Magazine*.

In the 1890s, he suggested to Ballard Smith at the *New York World* the idea of a weekly colored comic supplement on Sundays. This idea soon came into fruition when *The Yellow Kid*, created by Richard F. Outcault, came into being. *The Yellow Kid* is famous for its inspiration of what is known as yellow journalism— the kind that uses bold headlines to sell newspapers but doesn't necessarily report fact-supported news. *The Yellow Kid* helped increase the *World*'s circulation from 140,000 to 800,000 within six months.

McCardell is generally regarded as the first person to be put on salary by a motion picture studio. At the turn of the twentieth century, he was hired by the American Mutoscope and Biograph Company to produce stories and scenarios for films, and wrote more than a thousand scripts, including the Theda Bara vehicle *A Fool There Was* in 1915.

His prolific writing career rewarded him on several fronts, including with prize money as the winner of at least two major competitions—one thousand dollars for a scenario he submitted to the *Morning Telegraph* and ten thousand dollars for his serial scenario, *The Diamond from the Sky*, acquired by the American Film Manufacturing Company.

"The Sign of the '400': Being a Continuation of the Adventures of Sherlock Holmes" had been credited to R. K. Munkittrick for many years, but recent research unearthed its true authorship. It was first published in the October 24, 1894, issue of *Puck*. McCardell's only foray into the world of Holmes and Conan Doyle, it appears to be the first Holmes parody written by an American.

THE SIGN OF THE "400"

Being a Continuation of the Adventures of Sherlock Holmes

Roy L. McCardell

FOR THE NONCE, Holmes was slighting his cocaine and was joyously jabbing himself with morphine—his favorite 70 per cent solution—when a knock came at the door; it was our landlady with a telegram. Holmes opened it and read it carelessly.

"H'm!" he said. "What do you think of this, Watson?"

I picked it up. "COME AT ONCE. WE NEED YOU. SEVENTY-TWO CHINCHBUGGE PLACE, S. W.," I read.

"Why, it's from Athelney Jones," I remarked.

"Just so," said Holmes; "call a cab."

We were soon at the address given, 72 Chinchbugge Place being the town house of the Dowager Countess of Coldslaw. It was an old-fashioned mansion, somewhat weather-beaten. The old hat stuffed in the broken pane in the drawing room gave the place an air of unstudied artistic negligence, which we both remarked at the time.

Athelney Jones met us at the door. He wore a troubled expression. "Here's a pretty go, gentlemen!" was his greeting. "A forcible entrance has been made to Lady Coldslaw's boudoir, and the famous Coldslaw diamonds are stolen."

Without a word Holmes drew out his pocket lens and examined the atmosphere. "The whole thing wears an air of mystery," he said, quietly.

We then entered the house. Lady Coldslaw was completely prostrated and could not be seen. We went at once to the scene of the robbery. There was no sign of anything unusual in the boudoir, except that the windows and furniture had been smashed and the pictures had

been removed from the walls. An attempt had been made by the thief to steal the wallpaper, also. However, he had not succeeded. It had rained the night before and muddy footprints led up to the escritoire from which the jewels had been taken. A heavy smell of stale cigar smoke hung over the room. Aside from these hardly noticeable details, the despoiler had left no trace of his presence.

In an instant Sherlock Holmes was down on his knees examining the footprints with a stethoscope. "H'm!" he said; "so you can make nothing out of this, Jones?"

"No, sir," answered the detective; "but I hope to; there's a big reward."

"It's all very simple, my good fellow," said Holmes. "The robbery was committed at three o'clock this morning by a short, stout, middle-aged, hen-pecked man with a cast in his eye. His name is Smythe, and he lives at 239 Toff Terrace."

Jones fairly gasped. "What! Major Smythe, one of the highest thought-of and richest men in the city?" he said.

"The same."

In half an hour we were at Smythe's bedside. Despite his protestations, he was pinioned and driven to prison.

"For heaven's sake, Holmes," said I, when we returned to our rooms, "how did you solve that problem so quickly?"

"Oh, it was easy, dead easy!" said he. "As soon as we entered the room, I noticed the cigar smoke. It was cigar smoke from a cigar that had been given a husband by his wife. I could tell that, for I have made a study of cigar smoke. Any other but a hen-pecked man throws such cigars away. Then I could tell by the footprints that the man had had appendicitis. Now, no one but members of the '400' have that. Who then was hen-pecked in the '400,' and had had appendicitis recently? Why, Major Smythe, of course! He is middle-aged, stout, and has a cast in his eye."

I could not help but admire my companion's reasoning, and told him so. "Well," he said, "it is very simple if you know how."

Thus ended the Coldslaw robbery, so far as we were concerned.

It may be as well to add, however, that Jones's arrant jealousy caused him to resort to the lowest trickery to throw discredit upon the discovery of my gifted friend. He allowed Major Smythe to prove a most conclusive alibi, and then meanly arrested a notorious burglar as the thief, on the flimsiest proof, and convicted him. This burglar had been caught while trying to pawn some diamonds that *seemed* to be a portion of the plunder taken from 72 Chinchbugge Place.

Of course, Jones got all the credit. I showed the newspaper accounts to Holmes. He only laughed, and said: "You see how it is, Watson; Scotland Yard, as usual, gets the glory." As I perceived he was going to play "Sweet Marie" on his violin, I reached for the morphine, myself.

HOLMESLESS

Codeine (7 Per Cent)

CHRISTOPHER MORLEY

ONE OF THE greatest bookmen in the history of American letters, Christopher Morley (1890–1957) was a novelist, poet, short story writer, journalist, dramatist, and literary critic. Virtually all his work had a gentle kindness of spirit and deep-seated morality. More than any other subject, however, his work exulted in books and the joys they could impart. He was an editor of *Bartlett's Familiar Quotations* and a judge for the Book-of-the-Month Club for nearly three decades.

His first novel, *Parnassus on Wheels* (1917), is a tender romance about a bookseller and the horse-drawn bookshop with which he travels throughout New England. A near-sequel is *The Haunted Bookshop* (1919), which is a bit more sprightly and involves the same gently heroic bookseller and an assassination attempt on President Woodrow Wilson.

Aficionados of Sherlock Holmes will forever be in Morley's debt on several fronts. First, before there was a *Baker Street Journal*, the one literary home for Sherlockian essays, anecdotes, and other information (real and imagined) was in Morley's "The Bowling Green" column for the New York *Evening Post*, beginning in 1920, and then for *The Saturday Review of Literature* from 1924.

Doubleday hired Morley to write the introduction to the Memorial Edition of *The Complete Sherlock Holmes* in 1930, the year Arthur Conan Doyle died. "In Memoriam" remains arguably the single greatest essay ever written about Holmes and Watson. A few years later, in 1934, he was the prime force behind the formation of the Baker Street Irregulars, one of dozens of clubs he organized, the most famous for many years having been the Three Hours for Lunch Club.

"Codeine (7 Per Cent)" was first published in the November 1945 issue of *Ellery Queen's Mystery Magazine*; it was first published in book form in *To the Queen's Taste*, edited by Ellery Queen (Boston, Little, Brown, 1946).

CODEINE (7 PER CENT)

Christopher Morley

I HADN'T SEEN Dove Dulcet, former literary agent and amateur detective, for a long time—not since he went into Naval Intelligence in '39. But last winter the Baker Street Irregulars, that famous club of Sherlock Holmes devotees, invited him to be a guest at their annual dinner. Dulcet is shy and would have preferred not to speak, but of course he was called on and made a very agreeable little impromptu which I supposed the B & O from Washington had given him time to think out.

What Dulcet did was propose a toast to Sherlock Holmes's unknown sister. She was a good deal younger than either Mycroft or Sherlock, he suggested. The basis of his fancy was Sherlock's famous remark to Miss Hunter when she was offered that dubious position as governess at the Copper Beeches. "It is not the situation which I should like to see a sister of mine apply for," said Sherlock Holmes. Dulcet maintained that no man would say that unless he actually *did* have a sister; and offered ingenious suggestions why Watson had never mentioned her.

The Irregulars, who were getting a bit noisy by then (it was late in the evening), accused Dulcet of being "whimsical," and chaffed him a good deal. There's something in Dove's innocent demeanor, his broad bland face and selvage of saffron-colored hair under an ivory scalp, that encourages good-natured teasing. He was twitted about the supposed inefficiency of our Intelligence Services—how G2, for instance, was caught actually moving its offices on D-Day, with all its phones and devices cut off so they didn't even know what was happening. He replied that maybe that was exactly what G2 wanted people to think; perhaps they had Planned It That Way. He suggested gently (he speaks in a voice so soft that people really keep quiet in order to listen) that sometimes the Intelligence people work longer ahead than we suppose. I noticed that he paused then a moment, as though he had more to say and thought better of it. "And now, gentlemen," he concluded, "you'll pardon me if I excuse myself and retire. I've got one of those delicious fin de siècle rooms here at the old Murray Hill and I can't wait to get to it. You know the kind of thing, a big brass bedstead, and lace drapes, and a rose-colored secretary with wonderful scroll work." Of course this gave the stags a laugh, and I caught a small private wink from him as he sat down. So presently I followed him up to his room.

"That was an ingenious surmise of yours," I said, "about Holmes having a sister."

"No surmise at all," he said. "I knew her. Or rather, to be exact, I know her daughter. Violet Hargreave; she works for me."

"Good heavens!" I exclaimed. "*Hargreave?* The New York Police Department? As mentioned in *The Dancing Men?*"

"Of course. Violet's mother married Sherlock's friend, Wilson Hargreave. She was Sibyl Holmes, one of the Holmeses who stayed in this country. I didn't want to mention names at your dinner. In our kind of job you don't do it. When I went into Intelligence I took Violet with me. She's absolutely indispensable. Wonderful gift for languages; we use her mostly as an agent overseas."

If I had asked further questions Dove would have shut up; he always says that the first shot you take in Government work is a transfusion of clam-juice. But we are very old friends and he trusts me. He poured me a drink and then fetched his wallet from under his pillow.

"I had this in my pocket tonight," he said, taking out a letter. "I would have loved to mention it when one of your members was talking about cryptography, codes, ciphers, and so on. The best codes are the simplest, not methodical at all but based on some completely personal association. She's safe at home now, so I can show you how Violet used to get her stuff out of Berlin when it wasn't easy. Sometimes it was only a few words on a picture postcard; the Nazis never seemed to suspect anything so naïve as that. When she had more to say she used some stationery she swiped from the Museum of Natural History, to look professional, and then overprinted a new letterhead."

I examined the paper. At the top of the sheet was the legend AMERICAN MUSEUM OF NATURAL HISTORY, and under it:

Professor Challenger's Expedition
Oceanic Ornithology
c/o S.Y. *Matilda Briggs*

"She couldn't get much on a postcard, not with a handwriting like that," I said, glancing at the lines of large heavily-inked script. "Very different from the small neat hand of her uncle."

"She has several handwritings, as occasion requires. Go ahead and read the letter."

It went thus:

Dear Friend:

Everything very interesting, and German scientists most helpful. Hope to come back by way of Pacific, Hawaii and Alleutians, studying migrations of gulls and goonies. If can take Kodiak will have wonderful pic-

*tures. Goonies (*phalacrocorax carbo, *a kind of cormorant, dangerous to lighthouse keepers) have regular schedule, fly Midway or Wake in October, Alleutians in June. Hope to get mail at Honolulu before you take up Conk-Singleton papers.*

Yours always,
Violet H. Hargreave

"She really is an ornithologist, isn't she," I said.

"So the Berlin censor thought, as he let it come through. Does nothing else strike you?"

"Well, I haven't got my convex lens," I said. "Are there any secret watermarks in the paper? The only thing I notice is that surely a scientific investigator should spell geography correctly. Isn't there only one *l* in Aleutians?"

"Good man. Of course that would tickle the German censor; he'd just think another ignorant American. You can be quite sure any member of the Holmes family would know how to spell. That's our private signal. Whenever Violet spells something wrong I know there's a double meaning. So the gulls and goonies are Japs."

"Say, she's good! And the allusions to the Holmes cases—sure, I get it. Cormorant and lighthouse keeper—that suggests politician; the story of *The Veiled Lodger*; it means get this warning across to the government. But what about Conk-Singleton?"

"Don't you remember the end of *The Six Napoleons*? Holmes says, before you get out the Conk-Singleton papers *put the pearl in the safe.* Just what we didn't do with Pearl Harbor."

"But what's the date of this letter?" I exclaimed. "Why, it's spring of '41, six months before Pearl Harbor."

"I told you we have to work ahead of time," Dove said. "Violet had just been tipped off, in Berlin, about the secret terms of the German–Japanese alliance. Hitler told the Japs he'd be in Moscow by Christmas, they'd be perfectly safe to strike in December. And you can check those goony dates, which by the way are correct for the bird migrations. The Japs landed at Attu and Kiska in June, just as she said."

"I always wondered what they thought they could do up there on those godforsaken rocks."

"Maybe they were attracted by the name of that group. Ever notice it on the map? The Rat Islands."

I was beginning to get the inwardness of this Baker Street code. "Goodness, even the name of the yacht, *Matilda Briggs*—in the *Sussex Vampire*; why, yes, that was the story of the Giant Rat of Sumatra—"

"For which the world *is not prepared*," Dove finished for me.

"Golly, the State Department must have turned handsprings when you decoded this for them."

Dove was discreetly silent.

I looked over the letter once more. "Kodiak . . . they thought she meant Kodak. I suppose you couldn't make any mistake, it was sure to refer to the Japanese?"

"Well, there Violet was really cute. You spoke of the handwriting."

"Yes, she must have used a very broad pen, a stub."

"She picked up the idea from her Uncle Mycroft. Don't you remember his immortal remark, in *The Greek Interpreter*—about the letter written with a J-pen, that is a stub pen—by a middle-aged man with a weak constitution."

"I guess that's me," I said feebly. "Still I don't get it."

"J-pen, Japan."

We finished what Dove called our auld lang snort. I was thinking hard. "Whenever you get a letter with a wrong spelling," I said guiltily, "do you suspect a secret meaning?—Gosh, do you suppose when broadcasters mispronounce a word on the radio it's really a code?"

"Get out of here," said Dove. "I want my rest."

Mrs. Hudson's Case

LAURIE R. KING

AUTHORS OF SHERLOCK HOLMES parodies and pastiches have taken many liberties with the character but few were as controversial as the decision made by Laurie R. King (1952–) to marry him, a condition in which few readers of the canon expected to find him. Nonetheless, the series about Mary Russell and Holmes has gone on to be so admired and loved by readers that the books have become regulars on national bestseller lists.

When Mary was fifteen years old, she encountered an elderly gentleman who she soon came to know was Sherlock Holmes, retired and keeping bees in Sussex. He mentors her in her early years as a crime solver, and they develop a close friendship, resulting in a marriage arrangement seven years after that first meeting. Mary Russell was introduced in *The Beekeeper's Apprentice* (1994), the first of more than a dozen adventures.

With Leslie S. Klinger, King has coedited several Sherlock Holmes works of nonfiction (the two-volume *The Grand Game*, 2011–2012) and two anthologies of short stories inspired by the Holmes canon: *A Study in Sherlock* (2011) and *In the Company of Sherlock Holmes* (2014).

King has also produced a second successful series of detective novels featuring Kate Martinelli, a lesbian police officer in San Francisco, introduced in *A Grave Talent* (1993), which won the Edgar Award for best first novel of the year, as well as the (British) Crime Writers' Association John Creasey Dagger for best first novel. Among King's seven novels in neither series is *Califia's Daughters* (2004), a science fiction novel released under the pseudonym Leigh Richards.

"Mrs. Hudson's Case" was originally published in *Crime Through Time*, edited by Miriam Grace Monfredo and Sharan Newman (New York, Berkley, 1997).

MRS. HUDSON'S CASE

Laurie R. King

AS HAS BEEN noted by a previous biographer, Mrs. Hudson was the most long-suffering of landladies. In the years when Sherlock Holmes lived beneath her Baker Street roof, she faced with equanimity his irregular hours, his ill temper, his malodorous and occasionally dangerous chemical experiments, his (again) occasionally malodorous and even dangerous visitors, and all the other demands made on her dwelling and her person. And yet, far from rejoicing when Holmes quit London for the sea-blown expanses of the Sussex Downs, in less than three months she had turned her house over to an estate agent and followed him, to run his household as she had formerly run her own. When once I dared to ask her why, late on a celebratory evening when she had rather more drink taken than was her wont, she answered that the devil himself needed someone to look after him, and it made her fingers itch to know that Mr. Holmes was not getting the care to which he was accustomed. Besides, she added under her breath, the new tenants had not been in place for a week before she knew she would go mad with boredom.

Thus, thanks to the willingness of this good woman to continue suffering in the service of genius, Holmes's life went on much as before.

Not that he was grateful, or indeed even aware of her sacrifice. He went on, as I said, much as before, feeling vexed when her tidying had removed some vital item or when her regular market-day absence meant that he had to brew his own coffee. Deep in his misogynis-

tic soul, he was not really convinced that women had minds, rights, or lives of their own.

This may be unfair; he was certainly always more than ready to dismiss members of his own sex. However, there is no doubt that a woman, be she lady or governess, triggered in him an automatic response of polite disinterest coupled with vague impatience: it took a high degree of determination on the part of a prospective client who happened to be female to drag him into a case.

Mrs. Hudson, though, was nothing if not determined. On this day in October of 1918 she had pursued him through the house and up the stairs, finally bearding him in his laboratory, where she continued to press upon him the details of her odd experience. However, her bristling Scots implacability made little headway against the carapace of English phlegm that he was turning against her. I stood in the doorway, witness to the meeting of irresistible force and immovable object.

"No, Mrs. Hudson, absolutely not. I am busy." To prove it (although when I had arrived at his house twenty minutes earlier I had found him moping over the newspapers) he turned to his acid-stained workbench and reached for some beakers and a couple of long glass tubes.

"All I'm asking you to do is to rig a wee trap," she said, her accent growing with her perturbation.

Holmes snorted. "A bear trap in the kitchen, perhaps? Oh, a capital idea, Mrs. Hudson."

"You're not listening to me, Mister 'Olmes. I told you, I wanted you to fix up a simple cam-

220

era, so I can see who it is that's been coming in of rights and helping himself to my bits and pieces."

"Mice, Mrs. Hudson. The country is full of them." He dropped a pipette into a jar and transferred a quantity of liquid into a clean beaker.

"*Mice!*" She was shocked. "In *my* kitchen? Mr. Holmes, *really.*"

Holmes had gone too far, and knew it. "I do apologize, Mrs. Hudson. Perhaps it was the cat?"

"And what call would a cat have for a needle and thread?" she demanded, unplaced. "Even if the beastie could work the latch on my sewing case."

"Perhaps Russell . . . ?"

"You know full well that Mary's been away at University these four weeks."

"Oh, very well. Ask Will to change the locks on the doors." He turned his back with an optimistic attempt at finality.

"I don't want the locks changed, I want to know who it is. Things have gone missing from all the neighbours, little things mostly, but it's not nice."

I had been watching Holmes's movements at first idly, then more closely, and now I took a step into the room and caught at Mrs. Hudson's sleeve. "Mrs. Hudson, I'll help you with it. I'm sure I can figure out how to booby trap a camera with a flash. Come, let's go downstairs and decide where to put it."

"But I thought—"

"Come with me, Mrs. Hudson."

"Mary, are you certain?"

"*Now*, Mrs. Hudson." I tightened my grip on her substantial arm and hauled, just as Holmes removed his finger from the end of the pipette and allowed the substance it held to drop into the already seething mixture in the beaker. He had not been paying attention to his experiment; a cloud of noxious green gas began instantly to billow up from the mouth of the beaker. Mrs. Hudson and I went with all haste down the stairs, leaving Holmes to grope his way to

the shutters and fling them open, coughing and cursing furiously.

Once in her kitchen, Mrs. Hudson's inborn hospitality reasserted itself, and I had to wait until she had stirred up a batch of rock cakes, questioned me about my progress and my diet up at Oxford in this, my second year there. She then put on the kettle, washed up the bowls, and swept the floor before finally settling in a chair across the soft scrubbed wood table from me.

"You were saying," I began, "that you've had a series of break-ins and small thefts."

"Some food and a bit of milk from time to time. Usually stale things, a heel of bread and a knob of dry cheese. Some wool stockings from the darning basket, two old blankets I'd intended for the church. And as I said, a couple of needles and a spool of black thread from the sewing case." She nodded at the neat piece of wooden joinery with the padded top that sat in front of her chair by the fire, and I had to agree, no cat could have worked its latch.

"Alcohol?"

"Never. And never have I missed any of the household money I keep in the tea caddy or anything of value. Mrs. Prinnings down the road claims she lost a ring to the thief, but she's terribly absentminded, she is."

"How is he getting in?"

"I think he must have a key." Seeing my expression, she hastened to explain. "There's always one on the hook at the back door, and one day last week when Will needed it, I couldn't find it. I thought he maybe borrowed it earlier and forgot to return it, that's happened before, but it could have been the thief. And I admit I'm not always good at locking up all the windows at night. Which is probably how he got in in the first place."

"So change the locks."

"The thing is, Mary, I can't help but feel it's some poor soul who is in need, and although I certainly don't want him to waltz in and out, I do want to know who it is so that I know what to do. Do you follow me?"

I did, actually. There were a handful of ex-soldiers living around the fringes of Oxford, so badly shell-shocked as to be incapable of ordinary social intercourse, who slept rough and survived by what wits were left them. Tragic figures, and one would not wish to be responsible for their starvation.

"How many people in the area have been broken into?"

"Pretty near everyone when it first started, the end of September. Since then those who have locks use them. The others seem to think it's fairies or absentmindedness."

"Fairies?"

"The little people are a curious lot," she said. I looked closely to be sure that she was joking, but I couldn't tell.

Some invisible signal made her rise and go to the oven, and sure enough, the cakes were perfect and golden brown. We ate them with fresh butter and drank tea (Mrs. Hudson carried a tray upstairs, and returned without comment but with watering eyes) and then turned our combined intellects to the problem of photographing intruders.

I returned the next morning, Saturday, with a variety of equipment. Borrowing a hammer, nails, and scraps of wood from old Will, the handyman, and a length of fine fishing twine from his grandson, by trial and error Mrs. Hudson (interrupted regularly by delivery boys, shouts from upstairs, and telephone calls) and I succeeded in rigging a trip wire across the kitchen door.

During the final stages of this delicate operation, as I perched on the stepladder adjusting the camera, I was peripherally aware of Holmes's voice raised to shout down the telephone in the library. After a few minutes, silence fell, and shortly thereafter his head appeared at the level of my waist.

He didn't sneer at my efforts. He acted as if I were not there, as if he had found Mrs. Hudson rolling out a pie crust rather than holding out a selection of wedges for me to use in my adjustments.

"Mrs. Hudson, it appears that I shall be away for a few days. Would you sort me out some clean collars and the like?"

"*Now*, Mr. Holmes?"

"Any time in the next ten minutes will be fine," he said generously, then turned and left without so much as a glance at me. I bent down to call through the doorway at his retreating back.

"I go back to Oxford tomorrow, Holmes."

"It was good of you to come by, Russell," he said, and disappeared up the stairs.

"You can leave the wedges with me, Mrs. Hudson," I told her. "I'm nearly finished."

I could see her waver with the contemplation of rebellion, but we both knew full well that Holmes would leave in ten minutes, clean linen or no, and whereas I would have happily sent him on his way grubby, Mrs. Hudson's professional pride was at stake. She put the wedges on the top of the stepladder and hurried off.

She and Holmes arrived simultaneously in the central room of the old cottage just as I had alighted from the ladder to examine my handiwork. I turned my gaze to Holmes, and found him dressed for Town, pulling on a pair of black leather gloves.

"A case, Holmes?"

"Merely a consultation, at this point. Scotland Yard has been reflecting on our success with the Jessica Simpson kidnapping, and in their efforts to trawl the bottom of this latest kidnapping, have decided to have me review their efforts for possible gaps. Paperwork merely, Russell," he added. "Nothing to excite you."

"This is the Oberdorfer case?" I asked. It was nearly a month since the two children, twelve-year-old Sarah and her seven-year-old brother Louis, had vanished from Hyde Park under the expensive nose of their nurse. They were orphans, the children of a cloth manufacturer with factories in three countries and his independently wealthy French wife. His brother, who had taken refuge in London during the war, had anticipated a huge demand of ransom. He was still waiting.

"Is there news?"

"There is nothing. No ransom note, no sightings, nothing. Scotland Yard is settling to the opinion that it was an outburst of anti-German sentiment that went too far, along the lines of the smashing of German shopkeepers' windows that was so common in the opening months of the war. Lestrade believes the kidnapper was a rank amateur who panicked at his own audacity and killed them, and further thinks their bodies will be found any day, no doubt by some sportsman's dog." He grimaced, tucked in the ends of his scarf, buttoned his coat against the cool autumnal day, and took the portmanteau from Mrs. Hudson's hand.

"Well, good luck, Holmes," I said.

"Luck," he said austerely, "has nothing to do with it."

When he had left, Mrs. Hudson and I stood looking at each other for a long minute, sobered by this reminder of what was almost certainly foul murder, and also by the revealing lack of enthusiasm and optimism in the demeanour of the man who had just driven off. Whatever he might say, our success in the Simpson case two months earlier had been guided by luck, and I had no yearning to join forces in a second kidnap case, particularly one that was patently hopeless.

I sighed, and then we turned to my trap. I explained how the camera worked, told her where to take the film to be developed and printed, and then tidied away my tools and prepared to take my own departure.

"You'll let me know if anything turns up?" I asked. "I could try to make it back down next weekend, but—"

"No, no, Mary, you mustn't interfere with your studies. I shall write and let you know."

I stepped cautiously over the taut fishing wire and paused in the doorway. "And you'll tell me if Holmes seems to need any assistance in this Oberdorfer case?"

"That I will."

I left, ruefully contemplating the irony of a man who normally avoided children like the plague (aside from those miniature adults he had scraped off the streets to form his "Irregulars"

in the Baker Street days); these days he seemed to have his hands full of them.

I returned to Oxford, and my studies, and truth to tell the first I thought about Mrs. Hudson's problem was more than a week later, on a Wednesday, when I realized that for the second week in a row her inevitable Tuesday letter had not come. I had not expected the first one, though she often wrote even if I had seen her the day before, but not to write after eight days was unprecedented.

I telephoned the cottage that evening. Holmes was still away, Mrs. Hudson thought, interviewing the Oberdorfer uncle in Paris, and she herself sounded most peculiar. She seemed distracted, and said merely that she'd been too busy to write, apologized, and asked if there was anything in particular I was wanting?

Badly taken aback, I stammered out a question concerning our camera trap.

"Oh, yes," she said, "the camera. No, no, nothing much has come of that. Still, it was a good idea, Mary. Thank you. Well, I must be gone now, dear, take care."

The line went dead, and I slowly put up the earpiece. She hadn't even asked if I was eating well.

I was hit by a sudden absurd desire to leave immediately for Sussex. I succeeded in pushing it away, but on Saturday morning I was on the train south, and by Saturday afternoon my hand was on the kitchen door to Holmes's cottage.

A moment later my nose was nearly on the door as well, flattened against it, in fact, because the door did not open. It was locked.

This door was never locked, certainly not in the daytime when there was anyone at home, yet I could have sworn that I had heard a scurry of sound from within. When I tried to look in the window, my eyes were met by a gaily patterned teatowel, pinned up neatly to all the edges.

"Mrs. Hudson?" I called. There was no answer. Perhaps the movement had been the cat. I went around the house, tried the French doors and found them locked as well, and continued around to the front door, only to have it open as I stretched out my hand. Mrs. Hudson stood in the narrow opening, her sturdy shoe planted firmly against the door's lower edge.

"Mrs. Hudson, there you are! I was beginning to think you'd gone out."

"Hello there, Mary. I'm surprised to see you back down here so soon. Mr. Holmes isn't back from the Continent yet, I'm sorry."

"Actually, I came to see you."

"Ah, Mary, such a pity, but I really can't have you in. I'm taking advantage of Mr. Holmes's absence to turn out the house, and things are in a dreadful state. You should have checked with me first, dear."

A brief glance at her tidy, uncovered hair and her clean hand on the door made it obvious that heavy housecleaning was not her current preoccupation. Yet she did not appear afraid, as if she was being held hostage or something; she seemed merely determined. Still, I had to keep her at the door as long as I could while I searched for a clue to her odd behaviour.

Such was my intention; however, every question was met by a slight edging back into the house and an increment of closure of the door, until eventually it clicked shut before me. I heard the sound of the bolt being shot, and then Mrs. Hudson's firm footsteps, retreating towards the kitchen.

I stood, away from the house, frankly astonished. I couldn't even peer in, as the sitting-room windows overlooking the kitchen had had their curtains tightly shut. I considered, and discarded, a full frontal assault, and decided that the only thing for it was stealth.

Mrs. Hudson knew me well enough to expect it of me, of that I was fully aware, so I took care to stay away that evening, even ringing her from my own house several miles away to let her know that I was not outside the cottage, watching her curtains. She also knew that I had to take the Sunday night train in order to be at the Monday morning lectures, and would then begin to relax. Sunday night, therefore, was when I took up my position outside the kitchen window.

For a long time all I heard were busy kitchen sounds—a knife on a cutting board, a spoon scraping against the side of a pot, the clatter of a bowl going into the stone sink. Then without warning, at about nine o'clock Mrs. Hudson spoke.

"Hello there, dear. Have a good sleep?"

"I always feel I should say 'good morning,' but it's nighttime," said a voice in response, and I was so startled I nearly knocked over a pot of herbs. The voice was that of a child, sleep-clogged but high-pitched: a child with a very faint German accent.

Enough of this, I thought. I was tempted to heave the herb pot through the window and just clamber in, but I was not sure of the condition of Mrs. Hudson's heart. Instead I went silently around the house, found the door barred to my key, and ended up retrieving the long ladder from the side of the garden shed and propping it up against Holmes's window. Of course the man would have jimmy-proof latches. Finally in frustration I used a rock, and fast as Mrs. Hudson was in responding to the sound of breaking glass, I still met her at the foot of the stairs, and slipped past her by feinting to the left and ducking past her on the right.

The kitchen was bare.

However, the bolt was still shot, so the owner of the German voice was here somewhere. I ignored the furious Scots woman at my back and ran my eyes over the scene: the pots of food that she would not have cooked for herself alone, the table laid for three (one of the place settings with a diminutive fork and a china mug decorated with pigs wearing toppers and tails), and two new hairbrushes lying on a towel on the side of the sink.

"Tell them to come out," I said.

She sighed deeply. "You don't know what you're doing, Mary."

"Of course I don't. How can I know anything if you keep me in the dark?"

"Oh, very well. I should have known you'd keep on until you found out. I was going to move them, but—" She paused, and raised her voice. "Sarah, Louis, come out here."

They came, not, as I had expected, from the pantry, but crawling out of the tiny cupboard in the corner. When they were standing in the room, eyeing me warily, Mrs. Hudson made the introductions.

"Sarah and Louis Oberdorfer, Miss Mary Russell. Don't worry, she's a friend. A very nosy friend." She sniffed, and turned to take another place setting from the sideboard and lay it out—at the far end of the table from the three places already there.

"The Oberdorfers," I said. "How on earth did they get here? Did Holmes bring them? Don't you know that the police in two countries are looking for them?"

Twelve-year-old Sarah glowered at me. Her seven-year-old brother edged behind her fearfully. Mrs. Hudson set the kettle down forcefully on the hob.

"Of course I do. And no, Mr. Holmes is not aware that they are here."

"But he's actually working on the case. How could you—"

She cut me off. Chin raised, grey hair quivering, she turned on me with a porridge spoon in her hand. "Now don't you go accusing me of being a traitor, Mary Russell, not until you know what I know."

We faced off across the kitchen table, the stout, aging Scots housekeeper and the lanky Oxford undergraduate, until I realized simultaneously that whatever she was cooking smelled superb, and that perhaps I ought indeed to know what she knew. A truce was called, and we sat down at the table to break bread together.

It took a long time for the various threads of the story to trickle out, narrated by Mrs. Hudson (telling how, in Holmes's absence, she could nap in the afternoons so as to sit up night after night until the door had finally been opened by the thief) and by Sarah Oberdorfer (who coolly recited how she had schemed and prepared, with map and warm clothes and enough money to get them started, and only seemed troubled at the telling of how she had been forced to take to a life of crime), with the occasional contribution by young Louis (who thought the whole thing a great lark, from the adventure of hiding among the baggage in the train from London to the thrill of wandering the Downs, unsupervised, in the moonlight). It took longer still for the entire thing to become clear in my mind. Until midnight, in fact, when the two children, who had from the beginning been sleeping days and active at night to help prevent discovery, were stretched out on the carpet in front of the fire in the next room, colouring pictures.

"Just to make sure I have this all straight," I said to Mrs. Hudson, feeling rather tired, "let me go over it again. First, they say they were not kidnapped, they fled under their own power, from their uncle James Oberdorfer, because they believed he was trying to kill them in order to inherit his late brother's, their father's, property."

"You can see Sarah believes it."

I sighed. "Oh yes, I admit she does. Nobody would run away from a comfortable house, hide in a baggage car, and live in a cave for three weeks on stolen food if she didn't believe it. And yes, I admit that there seems to have been a very odd series of accidents." Mrs. Hudson's own investigative machinery, though not as smooth as that of her employer, was both robust and labyrinthine: she had found through the servant sister of another landlady who had a friend who—and so forth.

There was a great deal of money involved, with factories not only here and in France, but also in Germany, where the war seemed on the verge of coming to its bloody end. These were two very wealthy orphans, with no family left but one uncle. An uncle who, according to below-the-stairs rumour collected by Mrs. Hudson's network of informants, exhibited a smarmy, shallow affection to his charges. I put my head into my hands.

It all rested on Sarah. A different child I might have dismissed as being prone to imaginative stories, but those steady brown eyes of hers, daring me to disbelieve—I could see why Mrs. Hudson, by no means an easy mark for a sad story, had taken them under her wing.

"And you say the footman witnessed the near-drowning?" I said without looking up.

"If he hadn't happened upon them they'd have been lost, he said. And the maid who ate some of the special pudding their uncle brought them was indeed very ill."

"But there's no proof."

"No." She wasn't making this any easier for me. We both knew that Holmes, with his attitudes towards children, and particularly girl children, would hand these two back to their uncle. Oh, he would issue the man a stern warning that he, Holmes, would in the future take a close personal interest in the safety of the Oberdorfer heirs, but after all, accidents were unpredictable things, particularly if Oberdorfer chose to return to the chaos of war-ravaged Germany. If he decided the inheritance was worth the risk, and took care that no proof was available . . .

No proof here either, one way or the other, and this was one case I could *not* discuss with Holmes.

"And you were planning on sending them to your cousin in Wiltshire?"

"It's a nice healthy farm near a good school, and who would question two more children orphaned by zeppelin bombs?"

"But only until Sarah is sixteen?"

"Three years and a bit. She'd be a young lady then—not legally of course, but lawyers would listen to her."

I was only eighteen myself, and could well believe that authorities who would dismiss a twelve-year-old's wild accusations would prick their ears at a self-contained sixteen-year-old. Why, even Holmes . . .

"All right, Mrs. Hudson, you win. I'll help you get them to Wiltshire."

I was not there when Holmes returned a week later, drained and irritable at his failure to enlighten Scotland Yard. Mrs. Hudson said nothing, just served him his dinner and his newspapers and went about her business. She said nothing then, and she said nothing later that evening when Holmes, who had carried his collection of papers to the basket chair in front of the fire and prepared to settle in, leapt wildly to his feet, bent over to dig among the cushions for a moment, then turned in accusation to his housekeeper with the gnawed stub of a coloured pencil in his outstretched palm.

She never did say anything, not even three years later when the young heir and his older sister (her hair piled carefully on top of her head, wearing a grown woman's hat and a dress a bit too old for her slim young frame) miraculously materialized in a solicitor's office in London, creating a stir in three countries. However, several times over the years, whenever Holmes was making some particularly irksome demand on her patience, I saw this most long-suffering of landladies take a deep breath, focus on something far away, and nod briefly, before going on her placid way with a tiny, satisfied smile on her face.

The Final Problem

BLISS AUSTIN

IN HIS LIFETIME a standout chemist and metals engineer, Dr. James Bliss Austin (1904–1988) today is celebrated for his two exceptional hobbies: preserving historic Japanese block prints and being one of the most prominent Sherlockians of his generation. Austin was in the first group of fifteen ever to receive an investiture in the Baker Street Irregulars (1944). Like several other early members of the BSI, he became a noted collector of Conan Doyle's signed first editions and foreign translations.

Today, Austin's own byline is eagerly sought by modern-day students of Sherlock Holmes. For more than forty years he was a frequent contributor to anthologies, magazines, and limited-edition pamphlets about the great detective. Among the gems he produced were "What Son Was Watson?" (1944), "Thumbing His Way to Fame" (1946), "The Atomic Holmeses" (1947), "On the Writing of Some of the Most Remarkable Books Ever Penned" (1978), and "William Gillette on the Air" (1982). Though he preferred literary criticism and writing about manuscripts as cultural objects, Austin also wrote Sherlockian poetry and historical retrospectives. Only on rare occasions did he venture into the world of short fiction.

Austin prepared the present story for an *Ellery Queen's Mystery Magazine* detective genre contest. More than eight hundred entries were received, with the top fifteen stories published in book form as *The Queen's Awards*. By way of a prank, Austin's protagonists were also the contest's judges and his Sherlockian cronies: Christopher Morley, Howard Haycraft, as well as Frederic Dannay and Manfred B. Lee, who jointly were Ellery Queen. The quartet enjoyed the joke so much that they awarded Austin a surprise honorable mention and placed "The Final Problem" at the caboose-end of the anthology as a "dividend and bloodhound bonus" for their readers.

"The Final Problem" was first published in *The Queen's Awards* (Boston, Little, Brown, 1946).

THE FINAL PROBLEM

Bliss Austin

CHRISTOPHER MORLEY FLUNG his arm out wide in a sweeping gesture and with a low bow pushed Howard Haycraft ahead of him into Ellery Queen's study. It was a large room about fifteen feet square, completely lined from floor to ceiling with shelves which were ram-jam-full of books, so full in fact that there was no shelf-space for the hundreds of other volumes which cluttered the room. Piles of books leaning Pisa-like were stacked on the floor, on table tops, even on chairs, so that Queen was having some difficulty in finding a place to seat his guests. At last he succeeded in excavating two comfortable armchairs to which he escorted the visitors. He then settled himself in a red-leather easy chair, flanked on one side by a heterogeneous collection of copies of the *Strand*, *Black Cat*, and *Golden Book*, and on the other by a commodious smoking stand which served as a private cemetery for innumerable corpses of cigars, cigarettes, and pipe dottle. The whole effect seemed staged to give the appearance of a throne, so that Haycraft could not refrain from quoting:

"The King was in the counting house—"

"No, no," laughed Morley. "The Queen was in the parlor."

To their surprise Ellery did not join their laughter. Instead, his face clouded, he rose from his chair and crossed over to his desk, from a drawer of which he took a playing card.

"Speaking of Kings and Queens," he said, "what do you make of this?"

"Obviously," replied Haycraft, "it's a King of Spades. What about it?"

"Only this," said Ellery, "it came to me in the morning mail in a plain envelope with a typed address and bearing a New York postmark. Frankly, I'm quite puzzled over it because I can't figure out who sent it—or why."

"Probably some friend of yours is indulging a misplaced sense of humor," suggested Morley. "I notice it's a Bicycle card. Perhaps someone whose manuscript you rejected is threatening to take you for a ride."

"Or," added Haycraft, "someone is trying to take the Queen with a King."

"Which would be quite a trick," replied Queen, falling in with the bantering mood of the others.

He replaced the card in his desk drawer and was returning to his chair when he caught sight of the heap of tobacco ashes on the smoking stand.

"Pardon me, gentlemen," he said, "I forget my duty as a host." And pushing aside a row of old magazines he revealed an array of boxes and jars containing cigars, cigarettes, and pipe tobacco.

"What are you smoking, Ellery?" asked Haycraft, helping himself to a cigarette.

"This," replied Queen, drawing from his pocket a fat and aromatic cigar.

"A Merlinda!" gasped Morley, recognizing the cigar band. "How long has *EQMM* supported you in this style?"

"Since the notices about the Short Story Contest, to be exact," said Ellery, as he lit the cigar. "I'm sorry that I don't have one for each of you but you will find those Cabañas in the humidor quite good. There's a story that goes with my cigar. I may as well tell it to you since it concerns one of the manuscripts submitted in the contest.

"Several days ago, I received a story from a young fellow named Hugh Ashton, a graduate student at Hale. So far as I can discover he has never written anything before, and for a first effort it's amazing. I don't want to influence your judgment, but I don't mind telling you that it's a honey—as we say in Hollywood, it's colossal!

"Unfortunately, the manuscript needs a bit of editing. Ashton seems to realize that himself because shortly after the story arrived he phoned me to say that a friend of his on the faculty had offered to polish it for him. This Professor was to be in New York yesterday—so he asked, as a special favor, that I meet him at the Hale Club and return the manuscript to him along with any suggestions I might care to make. I agreed to meet the Professor—for two reasons. First, because Ashton's story is so clever that I don't want to lose it, and second, because I was piqued by the Professor's name. What do you suppose it was?"

"Elementary, my dear Queen," said Morley. "It was Moriarty, James Moriarty, I should guess."

"Right," said Queen. "So yesterday morning I went to the Hale Club and as I approached the door, a man stepped up and said: 'Mr. Queen? Professor Moriarty.'"

"What did he look like?" asked Haycraft.

"I'll bet I know," put in Morley, and shutting his eyes as if to aid his memory he recited: "He is extremely tall and thin, his forehead domes out in a wide curve, and his two eyes are deeply sunken in his head. He is clean-shaven, pale and ascetic-looking, retaining something of the professor in his features. His shoulders are rounded from much study and his face protrudes forward and is forever slowly oscillating from side to side in a curiously reptilian fashion. He peers at you with great curiosity in his puckered eyes."

"*Bravo!*" laughed Ellery. "That's not quite

right but it will do. To go on, I was studying him carefully when he jolted me by saying—"

"Don't tell me," broke in Morley again, "that he actually told you that you had less frontal development than he expected?"

"Exactly," replied Queen. "I told him it was evident that he was a keen student of Sherlock Holmes, at which he smiled and said that the Moriartys always have been. He then invited me into the Club where we had oyster cocktails without cocktail sauce, blast it! In the end I traded the manuscript of the story for this cigar."

Here Queen paused and looked at the cigar a trifle apprehensively, as if he were not sure that the swap had been an advantageous one.

"The Professor promised to do the rewriting at once, so you will have a chance to read the story for yourselves very soon, I hope. And now let's get on to selecting the prize-winning stories in *EQMM*'s first short story contest. There are, as you know, fifteen finalists so far."

He rose and started toward his desk on which stood a pile of fifteen manuscripts, but before he got there he began to sway and stumble. He opened his mouth as if to say something but seemed to have difficulty in drawing his breath. Suddenly he pitched forward to the floor, knocking over several piles of books and magazines, so that he lay almost buried under them. Haycraft and Morley, stupefied, remained frozen in their chairs, but finally roused themselves and rushed to Ellery's side. By the time they got to him and swept away the books, it was too late.

Ellery Queen was dead.

Sometime later, Ellery's physician, Dr. Dundy, entered the study accompanied by two men whom Morley and Haycraft, standing in glum silence, recognized as Ellery's father, Inspector Richard Queen, and Sergeant Thomas Velie.

"Inspector," said Morley, "I never dreamed I would meet you under such distressing circumstances. This is simply dreadful."

The Inspector, overcome, sank into a chair

and mumbled some reply which no one heard. His eyes, usually so bright and alert, were glazed over with a dull film. For the first time in his life, he showed his age. He sat motionless, like a man in deep shock.

Morley averted his head, then turned briskly to the physician.

"Well, what's the verdict?" he asked.

"We aren't quite certain," the doctor replied. "That's why we should like to have your help. Could you tell us exactly what happened?"

"There isn't much to tell. Ellery, Haycraft, and I are the judges in the Short Story Contest which Ellery's *Mystery Magazine* is sponsoring. Ellery invited us here this morning to discuss the final selections for the prize winners. We had been here only a few minutes—in fact, Ellery was just going to his desk when he fell to the floor—"

"I would particularly like to get his symptoms straight," said the doctor with a glance at the Inspector. "As I understand it, he tried to say something but couldn't; his face became livid and convulsed and his teeth clenched. Right?"

"Right," replied Morley.

Here the Inspector roused himself and spoke clearly for the first time.

"Did Ellery seem in good spirits?"

"Quite," said Haycraft. "Except that he was puzzled by the fact that someone had sent him a King of Spades in this morning's mail."

"Who did that?" asked Sergeant Velie.

"He didn't know," said Morley. "But it's over there in his desk drawer if you want to see it."

Velie went quickly to the desk, found the card, and handed it to the Inspector, who examined it absent-mindedly.

Dr. Dundy resumed his questioning. "Was there anything else unusual?"

"Not much," replied Morley. "He told us about an extraordinarily good story submitted by a graduate student at Hale—Ashton, I think the name was—but it was rather poorly written and needed editing. The other day Ashton called Ellery on the phone to say that a friend of his on the Hale faculty had offered to rewrite it for

him. So he asked Ellery to meet his friend at the Hale Club yesterday. Ellery did, and that's about all there is."

"Did he offer you anything to drink?" asked Velie. "Any of that Harvey's Bristol Cream sherry that he liked so much?"

"No—only cigarettes and cigars," said Morley.

"What did Ellery smoke?" asked the doctor.

"A cigar the Professor from Hale had given him," said Haycraft. "He was about half through it when—"

The Inspector rose suddenly from his chair, sharp and bird-like at the hint of a clue.

"A half-smoked cigar? Where's the butt?"

"Come to think of it, I haven't seen it," said Morley. "It must be on the floor somewhere."

Sergeant Velie started rummaging through the fallen books and magazines. The others joined him when there came a somewhat muffled shout from the doctor who emerged from the kneehole of the desk with a cigar butt in his hand.

"Is this it?" he asked.

Morley took a look at the band and nodded.

Without another word, the doctor handed the butt to the Inspector who examined it carefully and finally sniffed it. He handed it back to the doctor who likewise sniffed it and laid it carefully on the desk.

"I had hoped I was wrong," he said to the Inspector, "but I guess it's a case for you after all."

The Inspector gave a little shudder, his eyes filming over again. Then the film passed as quickly as it had appeared. He set his narrow shoulders and turned to Morley and Haycraft.

"Gentlemen," he said, "the significance of the King of Spades is now all too clear. Someone was threatening Ellery's life. Dr. Dundy was suspicious as soon as he heard the symptoms. Now there is no doubt about it. That cigar reeks of cyanide. Ellery was murdered."

"Good God—*no!*" Morley shouted.

The Inspector continued, his voice thin and hard: "I'm in it now two ways, and by heaven I'll find the man who did it if it's the last thing I do!

Velie, call headquarters and get the boys started while I ask these gentlemen a few questions."

As Velie disappeared, he continued: "First thing I want to know is the name of the Professor who gave Ellery the cigar?"

"James Moriarty," replied Haycraft hesitantly.

"Please," said the Inspector. "This is no time for any of your damned Baker Street Irregular shenanigans."

"So help me, Inspector," put in Morley, "that's exactly what Ellery told us."

"All right, all right, skip it," said the Inspector. "What else do you know about him? Where does he live? What does he teach?"

"All we know is that Ashton said he was on the faculty at Hale," replied Haycraft.

"Didn't he tell you anything about his looks?" snapped the Inspector, making no effort to conceal his growing impatience.

"Only roughly," said Morley. "When I heard the name I quoted the description of the real Moriarty as given by Dr. Watson in *The Final Problem*. Ellery said it wasn't exact but it would do."

He went to a shelf, took down a book, thumbed through it, then offered the open volume to the Inspector.

"Read it for yourself."

At this point Sergeant Velie returned. The Inspector ignored the book in Morley's hand. "There's nothing further to be gained here," said the Inspector, "but I should like to know where I can reach both of you at any time."

"If you don't mind," said Morley, "Haycraft and I would like to take these manuscripts up to my place and look them over. Here's my address and phone number."

"Make a note of it, Velie," said the Inspector, already leaving the room.

While Morley spoke to Velie, Haycraft gathered up the manuscripts on the desk.

"Who would have thought," said Morley, after Velie's departure, "that the Short Story Contest would turn out to be the Ellery Queen Memorial Competition?"

. . .

Late that evening Morley and Haycraft were sitting in Morley's smoke-filled study. The *EQMM* manuscripts lay on Morley's desk untouched; neither had had any heart for looking at them. They had discussed Ellery's murder for hours and were now gloomily silent. Suddenly the phone rang. Morley dashed for the instrument, upsetting his chair in his haste.

"Hello," he said. "Yes . . . Yes . . . I'm sure I can. I'll ask Howard. . . . It's Velie," he said to Haycraft. "The Inspector wants to know if we'll meet him in Grand Central at nine in the morning and go up to Old Haven for a day or two."

"Try and stop me," said Haycraft.

Morley talked again to Velie. Then came a long pause during which Morley listened intently. Finally, with a mere "Goodbye," he hung up.

"Velie says there isn't any Professor Moriarty on the Hale Faculty, nor is there anyone who answers the description we have."

"I can't say I'm surprised," said Haycraft.

"Nor I," replied Morley. "What does surprise me is that this morning a crushed body was found at the foot of a big cliff near Old Haven called North Rock. It was the body of Hugh Ashton."

Next morning, on the train to Old Haven, Morley and Haycraft opened up with a barrage of questions, but the Inspector briskly silenced them.

"I still don't know much more than you do," he said, "except that I have vaguely confirmed the description of the Professor. We have just been over at the Hale Club and questioned the doorman who was on duty at the time Ellery and the Professor came in. He recognized Ellery from a picture published recently in connection with some affair of the Baker Street Irregulars. The other chap he didn't know and didn't even notice much except that he recalls him as being tall and dark, which certainly isn't much help.

As neither of them was a member of the Club he started to speak to them when the tall fellow explained that they had an appointment to meet Professor Gill of the Chemistry Department and asked if he had come in yet. The doorman turned away to look at the board which indicates which members are in the building; when he turned back he saw them disappearing upstairs in the direction of the lounge. Sometime later they came downstairs and went to the door where Ellery said goodbye and left. The tall fellow went back upstairs again and wasn't seen by anyone afterward. Professor Gill, of course, never showed up. I just had him on the phone and he says he never had any such appointment, knows no Moriarty, and can't think of anyone who fits that description. Gill does—did—know Hugh Ashton, who took a number of his courses."

"But what about Ashton?" asked Morley.

"He was a graduate student in chemistry, living with a few other students in a small dormitory on the top floor of the chemistry laboratory. He seems to have been fairly smart, not too well-off, and well liked by both students and faculty. Night before last he went out early in the evening, telling a friend that he was going for a walk. He never came back and yesterday morning his body was found at the foot of North Rock. Presumably he had fallen off the cliff. Our main problem, though, is to find this Professor Moriarty."

"We certainly don't know much about him even now," said Haycraft.

"Except," replied the Inspector, "that he is tall, dark, gaunt, and has a high forehead."

"I wouldn't be too sure of any of that," said Morley. "Besides, you haven't mentioned the really significant items."

"Such as?" asked the Inspector.

"First," replied Morley, "he is undoubtedly a keen student of Sherlock Holmes. Second, he has an exaggerated sense of humor, a talent for the dramatic, and a taste for the bizarre. Third, he knew Hugh Ashton. Fourth, he is a man of considerable resourcefulness and has the instincts of a born killer—a most dangerous combination."

The Inspector did not take kindly to this little lecture.

"Sometimes," he growled, "I wish you grown men would forget all this Baker Street Irregular nonsense."

As they got off at the Old Haven station, a tall, well-knit, blond, young man stepped up to them and addressed the Inspector.

"Inspector Queen, I believe? My name is Moran. The Chief asked me to take care of you during your visit here. I am happy to meet you and to be of service, though I could wish that it was under less tragic circumstances. You can count on us to do all we can to help find Ellery's murderer."

"Thank you," replied the Inspector. "I am glad to meet you, Colonel—I've heard a lot about you."

Morley almost jumped. "Colonel! Good God, what next?"

"I don't know what your plans are, Inspector," said Moran, "but the Chief thought you would probably like to talk to the President of the University and to Professor Gill, so he has made an appointment with them for eleven. As you still have twenty minutes, I suggest you go to the hotel and check in. I have my car here and will be glad to take you."

"Tell me, Colonel," said the Inspector, as they drove slowly through the crooked streets of the town, "how did you recognize me so easily?"

Moran laughed. "You know my methods, Watson. It was Morley who gave the show away. I knew that the four of you were coming and I had seen pictures of both Morley and Haycraft in the ads of your son's *Mystery Magazine*. I must say I wouldn't have spotted Haycraft from his picture but Morley's beard is unmistakable. Once I had the crowd spotted, the rest was easy. Sergeant Velie was so obviously himself that I knew you must be Inspector Queen."

Detecting a Sherlockian flavor to this explanation, the Inspector promptly changed the subject.

"Anything new on Ashton?"

"Nothing yet," replied Moran, "but the Medical Examiner's report is due sometime this morning. By the way, I knew Ashton while we were both undergraduates. We were in some chemistry classes together and were fellow stooges in some of the Dramat productions. On graduation, he decided to do post-graduate work and I joined the Army Air Corps."

Then glancing at Morley, he went on:

"I was a Lieutenant-Colonel before I finally got shot up and was discharged. That's where the Colonel comes from. When I came back, I joined the Old Haven police, with whom I had some slight acquaintance during my practical-joking student days. Well, here's the hotel."

It did not take long to get their rooms and a few moments later they were at the President's office, where the President and Professor Gill were waiting for them. Both were greatly disturbed over the double tragedy and both were most anxious to do what they could. But after two hours of questioning and discussion, they were no further advanced than before. The group was about to go out to lunch when a phone call came through for Moran.

"It's the medical report," he said as he hung up. "I'm afraid it doesn't help much either. Except that Ashton was not killed by the fall from North Rock. He was poisoned with cyanide first, then thrown over."

Lunch, in which the visitors from New York were joined by Moran and Professor Gill, was a depressing affair. When it was over, the Inspector asked to see Ashton's room.

"Certainly," replied Professor Gill, to which Moran added that he would drive them out to the chemistry laboratory.

This proved to be a large squat pile of red brick and stone, surmounted by turrets and battlements, the latter decorated with a number of small shields each carrying the likeness of some piece of chemical apparatus. To the great disgust of Professor Gill, Moran insisted on taking them off to one end of the building to show them a shield on which the architects had placed a foaming mug of beer. He then led them through a large gothic arch and up a small winding staircase which brought them to the top floor, into a short corridor with a row of oak doors along one side. He went straight to the third which he opened with a tagged key taken from his pocket; the room was small, barely large enough for the bed, dresser, and desk which it contained. Its walls of rough plaster were decorated with an assortment of pin-ups of the type usually seen in a student's room. Along one wall was a small bookcase packed with chemistry texts and detective stories.

"We have been over it pretty thoroughly," Colonel Moran said, "but we haven't found anything worthwhile. Nothing has been taken away, so you are welcome to see what you can turn up."

The Inspector and Velie did a quick but thorough job of searching the room but could find nothing which shed any light on the case.

"So far as I can see," said the Inspector, "this doesn't tell us much except that Ashton was industrious, methodical, and a detective-story fan."

"And yet," said Morley, "there's one thing that puzzles me. Where is the manuscript that Ashton wrote?"

"I suppose Moriarty, whoever he is, has it," said Moran.

"But an author usually keeps a copy," replied Morley. "Surely there must have been some notes or a first draft. Moran, did you say nothing had been removed?"

"Nothing."

"Then I'm going to have another look," replied Morley.

After a few minutes of searching Morley began riffling through some sheets of carbon paper. Suddenly he examined one sheet intently, then another.

"Here's something!" he exclaimed. "Some of

these carbons have been used to write the out-line of a story!"

The Inspector snatched the carbons and looked at them through the light.

"I'll take these," he said. "They may be the break we're looking for."

"Wouldn't you like," suggested Moran, "to go to North Rock to see where Ashton's body was found?"

"That's next," agreed the Inspector.

A little later they were standing at the base of the tall and broken cliff of red traprock, gazing at the spot where the crumpled remains of Hugh Ashton had been discovered early the morning before. There was little to be seen except a few blood-spattered rocks. They were about to leave when they heard a sudden noise above them. Looking up they were horrified to see a large rock rolling down toward them. It was almost upon them when suddenly it veered and with a great clatter bounded past them a few feet away.

Morley shook his fist at the sky. "This is too much—much too much!"

The Inspector started up the path which as-cended the cliff from the rear, the others follow-ing excitedly. Reaching the summit, they saw no sign of anyone. Morley dropped to his knees and searched through the grass.

"What are you up to, Chris?" asked Haycraft, still panting.

Morley stood up. "Look at this," he said, holding out the band of a Merlinda cigar.

"What about it?" said Moran.

"Don't you realize its significance?" asked Morley.

"I suppose you mean it proves that Moriarty was here," Inspector Queen said thoughtfully.

They returned to the hotel for dinner. The Inspector was still in a thoughtful mood. When their after-dinner smoke was over, he excused himself and retired to his room where he took out the sheets of carbon paper and studied them. Later he brightened noticeably and began to make some notes. Still later, with a bitter smile, he clipped the sheets neatly together, undressed, and went to bed.

At about the same time, in a room not far away, Morley knocked the dottle from his pipe and muttered: "It must be so!" Then he too went to bed.

It seemed to Inspector Queen that he had hardly got to sleep when he woke with a feeling that someone was in his room. Looking round, he thought the darkness seemed deeper by his desk. He sat up but as he did so the deeper dark-ness moved. Suddenly something exploded on his chin and he was knocked flat on his back. Re-covering, he rolled out of bed just in time to see a dark figure passing through his door into the corridor. The door closed with a slam but he had it open again in a few seconds and immediately collided with a burly form. Both fell to the floor locked in each other's arms. Suddenly his oppo-nent relaxed.

"Take it easy, Inspector," said the voice of Sergeant Velie, "it's only me. What's up?"

"That's exactly what I'd like to know!" re-plied the bewildered Inspector.

With the assistance of the Sergeant and much rubbing of his chin, he returned to his bed.

"Now," he said, glaring at Velie, "what were you doing in my room?"

"Me?" asked Velie. "I was sound asleep next door when I hear you yell, so I come tearing over only to have you slug me. What's the angle?"

"I woke up and realized someone was in the room over by my desk. Before I could do any-thing something hit me on the chin and knocked me flat. Then whoever it was beat it out the door."

"Did he take anything?"

"Blast it if I know," said the Inspector. "Let's take a look."

He scrambled out of bed and ran to the desk.

"Now I begin to see," he said. The carbon paper and his notes were gone.

Next morning Morley and Haycraft were in Moran's office early, waiting for the Inspector. Moran reported the night's events, as phoned to him by Velie. In spite of all efforts by the police, efforts which Moran himself had directed, there was no clue to the identity of the midnight intruder nor any trace of the missing papers.

"Well," said Haycraft, "it doesn't do us much good now that they are gone but at least this proves that those carbon papers are important."

"I wouldn't be too sure," replied Morley. "In fact, I'm inclined to believe they may be just a red herring. You see, they don't quite fit into the pattern."

"A Sherlockian deduction, no doubt," came a voice from the door where a haggard-looking Inspector stood. "Just let me tell you, Mr. Morley, that those carbon papers broke the case. The thief, whoever he is, didn't get there quite soon enough. I'd got what I wanted from them earlier in the evening and what I got will lead us to the murderer of Ellery and Ashton. Not only that but it clears up a long-unsolved case in New York."

Morley looked troubled. He combed his beard with his fingers, then said slowly: "I wonder if I could speak to you alone, Inspector."

"Not now," replied the Inspector. "I want to make some phone calls to New York. I don't want to go off half-cocked, like some people I know."

After what seemed like hours of phoning, the Inspector returned.

"I haven't all the answers yet," he said, "but I've got enough to know I'm on the right track. Moran, have you a pack of cards?"

"No," said Moran, "but I can get one."

He went out, returning in a few minutes with a new pack.

"And now," said the Inspector, "could I have an envelope, please?"

While Moran was getting one, the Inspector selected the Ace of Spades from the deck.

"I'm sorry I can't explain all this to you yet," he said, "but I think I've found out who sent Ellery the King of Spades, and I thought it would be a nice touch to let him know that the Ace takes the King."

He slipped the Ace into a stamped envelope, scribbled an address on it, and went out to post it himself. When he returned Morley asked again if he could speak to him alone.

The two retired to the next room but were back in a few minutes, Morley flushed and the Inspector furious.

"I'll hear no more of this foolishness about Sherlock Holmes," he shouted.

"Some day," muttered Morley, as he and Haycraft left, "you won't consider it so foolish."

It was midafternoon before Morley and Haycraft decided to risk another visit to Moran's office. They found the Inspector, Velie, and Moran in the midst of a heated argument. Shortly before, the Inspector had received a mysterious phone call from someone in Old Haven, a call which had been traced to a corner drugstore. He had been asked to meet this person at midnight at the back door of the chemistry laboratory, which led out into a large vacant lot, partly a park, dotted with clumps of trees and bushes, and crisscrossed with several paths. The voice had warned that the Inspector was to come alone, that any attempt to bring along a companion would only result in disaster. The Inspector agreed to come by himself and was about to ask a few questions when the mysterious caller hung up.

Velie and Moran were now objecting to his promise to go alone. They said it was too dangerous. But the Inspector was deaf to all arguments. He insisted he could take care of himself. Morley and Haycraft somewhat timidly added their pleas but the Inspector remained adamant. Finally, Morley and Haycraft, seeing that nothing was to be accomplished, left with the announcement that they were going back to their hotel and would join the rest at dinner. But they didn't go to the hotel directly. At Morley's insistence they made a short call on Professor Gill first.

About 10:30 that evening, three figures arrived at the back door of the laboratory. One of the figures opened the door and they all entered cautiously, then crossed the darkened room to a large bay window in the opposite wall.

"From here," said Professor Gill to Morley and Haycraft, "we can have a good view of the door leading to the square without being seen ourselves."

They looked out and saw the outline of a similar bay window on the other side of the door. The three men settled down to wait for the arrival of the Inspector. Time dragged. All three were nervous and the smell of the place began to oppress both Morley and Haycraft. Once they thought they heard sounds down the corridor, as if someone might be moving in the room beyond the door, but these faint noises soon ceased and after that there was only the silence of an empty building.

About a quarter to twelve, they heard someone moving along one of the paths leading to the door and presently they saw the gleam of a flashlight. It was Professor Gill who recognized the visitor.

"Why, it's the laboratory watchman," he said. "What on earth is he doing out there?"

The man made a hurried search of the nearby shrubbery. Finally, he came to the door of the laboratory, opened it, and passed inside.

Gill made a movement to intercept the watchman but Morley objected. "It would be fatal if anyone saw us."

"Then we'd better hide," said Gill, "because he'll be looking in here in a minute."

They hardly had time to conceal themselves—Morley behind a bank of cylinders, Haycraft behind a large tank filled with water, and Professor Gill in a fume hood—before the door opened and the watchman flicked on the lights. Not seeing anything out of the ordinary, he quickly turned the lights off and went on down the corridor. Creeping out from their hiding places, the three men saw lights gleaming in the bay window beyond the door. These likewise were quickly turned out and they heard the watchman's footsteps grow fainter as he walked farther down the corridor.

This little incident heightened the tension; they grew more impatient by the minute. Haycraft, who had a luminous dial watch, slowly checked off the time. At two minutes to twelve, Morley, with eyes glued to the window, gave a low warning—someone was moving up the path toward the door. They soon recognized the In-

spector who advanced cautiously, peering into the several clumps of bushes as he came toward the door. Then he began to pace nervously up and down the walk while the three men inside the laboratory strained to watch for the appearance of the mysterious stranger. The minutes dragged unbearably. Suddenly there was a sound, but not from the square. Muffled footsteps came down from the second-floor corridor of the laboratory. Could it be the watchman returning? The footsteps grew louder. Then the door swung open and a tall, dark figure emerged. At the sound of the door opening, the Inspector had retreated into the shadow of a large clump of bushes but the shadowy figure spotted him. "You evidently don't know me," it said. "Permit me to introduce myself—Professor James Moriarty."

The Inspector moved forward out of the deep shadow. The voice, obviously imitating that of Professor Moriarty on a well-known radio program, went on:

"I daresay you weren't expecting me."

"Frankly, I wasn't," replied the Inspector. "But since you are here, I'll make the most of it. You and I have much to settle between us."

"Indeed, we have," said the Professor. "For example, I find myself placed in such a position through your continual persecution that I am in positive danger of losing my liberty. The situation is becoming an impossible one."

Hearing this quotation from *The Final Problem*, Morley controlled himself only with the utmost difficulty.

Moriarty went on: "I am quite sure that a man of your intelligence will see that there can be but one outcome to this affair. It is necessary that you withdraw."

"I'll see you in the chair first," replied the Inspector.

"I feared as much," continued the Professor. "It seems a pity but I have done what I could. Now you have worked things in such a fashion that I have but one resource left."

Suddenly there was a flash of light jetting out from the Professor's right hand. The Inspector staggered back, dropped to his knees. Three quick flashes spurted out of the bay window beyond the door. This time it was the Professor who staggered and fell. Morley and Haycraft, squeezing through the casements in their bay window, stared in amazement as Sergeant Velie emerged in similar fashion from the window beyond the door.

They ran to the Inspector's side. It was too late. Fiercely they turned to the other figure.

"Look," exclaimed Haycraft, "he's wearing a wig!"

They stripped off the wig and focused a light on the murderer's face.

It was the face of Colonel Moran.

Several days later, a sorrowful group was gathered in Morley's study.

"This affair illustrates again," Morley was saying as he poured drinks, "what folly it is to disregard the teachings of Holmes. I was struck from the very beginning by the way in which the whole case was dressed up in the Holmesian tradition. The use of the name of James Moriarty and the obvious impersonation of the Professor as described in the canon were quite transparent. When I found a Colonel Moran also involved, it seemed too pat—especially after I came to realize that Moran possessed all of the qualifications of the Professor. Haycraft will recall that I told Inspector Queen that Moriarty was a keen student of Holmes, had an exaggerated sense of humor, a talent for the dramatic, a taste for the bizarre, and the instincts of a killer. Moran had all of these. One of his first remarks to us when we arrived was: 'You know my methods, Watson!' Also, he told us that as an undergraduate he was a practical joker and insisted on showing us the shield with the mug of beer on it. Again, he himself told us that he and Ashton had been in Dramat productions which indicated not only a talent for the dramatic but some experience in make-up. Finally, it was not unreasonable that a young man who had distinguished himself in the war by the sav-

agery of his tactics should be fundamentally a born killer. Well, I gave him the benefit of the doubt because I couldn't see any possible motive. But when that rock was pushed down on us it was too much. That was obviously patterned after Holmes's account of what happened at the Reichenbach Falls and indicated conclusively that a Moran was involved. Before he died Moran admitted that he had arranged it but refused to divulge the name of his accomplice. The more I thought about it the more convinced I became that Moran was implicated, and that night I resolved to put the case before the Inspector. But he stubbornly refused to listen, though it is only fair to say that he had good reason, since he too was on the right trail.

"The rest of the story I got from Moran on his deathbed at the hospital. It seems, for reasons we shall probably never know, that he shared the secret of a notorious murder which completely baffled the police in New York several years ago. The killer, I suspect, was someone dear to him.

"One night in a drunken brawl at which Ashton was present, he let slip a few things that Ashton, who was much interested in crimes and detective fiction, recognized as significant. Ashton began to blackmail Moran in a small way. Finally, Moran balked and tried to bluff. About that time Ellery announced the Short Story Contest, so Ashton wrote the case up in a way that the New York police would see through and sent the manuscript to Ellery. He then told Moran what he had done and said he would get the manuscript back only if Moran paid over a large sum of money to Ashton.

"Moran could not raise so much money; also he was afraid that Ellery might already have seen the clue which the story provided, so he resolved to do away with both Ellery and Ashton. We know how he murdered Ellery with cyanide taken from Ashton's laboratory. He killed Ashton much the same way—offered him a drink loaded with poison, then carted the body out and tossed it over the cliff. As a police official he gambled on being one of the first into Ashton's room, so that he could destroy all traces of the manuscript. Unfortunately for him he forgot the carbon paper, which he then had to steal from the Inspector's room. But the Inspector had already arrived at the truth—as Moran knew from the address to which the Inspector mailed the Ace of Spades. So he phoned the Inspector and arranged the fatal rendezvous.

"It was a clever touch of Moran's to get the night watchman to search the bushes and laboratory rooms to see that the coast was clear, but the watchman, thank Heaven, didn't do a good job. Meanwhile, Moran put on his make-up and appeared again as James Moriarty."

There was silence when Morley finished. Then Haycraft raised his glass.

"In memoriam—the Queens," he said.

"In memoriam—the Queens," the others echoed.

"And yet," said Morley, putting his glass down, "Sherlock Holmes returned from his encounter with Moriarty, and I shouldn't be at all surprised if the Queens, *père et fils*, manage to do the same."

NOT OF THIS PLACE

The Adventure of the Bogle-Wolf

ANTHONY BOUCHER

IT IS UNCOMMON for an author to achieve great success in any genre, but William Anthony Parker White (1911–1968), pseudonym Anthony Boucher, enjoyed distinguished careers as a writer of both mystery and science fiction, as well as an established reputation as a first-rate critic, translator, editor, and anthologist. Born in Oakland, California, he received a BA from the University of Southern California and an MA in German from the University of California, Berkeley. He later became sufficiently proficient in French, Spanish, and Portuguese to translate mystery stories into English, becoming the first to translate Jorge Luis Borges into English. Under the Boucher pseudonym, he wrote well-regarded fair-play detective novels, beginning with *The Case of the Seven of Calvary* (1937), followed by *Nine Times Nine* (1940), which was voted the ninth-best locked-room mystery of all time in a poll of fellow writers and critics; it was written under the pseudonym H. H. Holmes, an infamous nineteenth-century serial killer. He wrote prolifically in the 1940s, producing at least three scripts a week for such popular radio programs as *Sherlock Holmes*, *The Adventures of Ellery Queen*, and *The Casebook of Gregory Hood*. He also wrote numerous science fiction and fantasy stories, reviewed books in those genres as H. H. Holmes for the *San Francisco Chronicle* and *Chicago Sun-Times*, and produced notable anthologies in the science fiction, fantasy, and mystery genres. He served as the longtime mystery reviewer of *The New York Times* (1951–1968) and *Ellery Queen's Mystery Magazine* (1957–1968). He was one of the founders of the Mystery Writers of America in 1946. The annual World Mystery Convention is familiarly known as the Bouchercon in his honor, and the Anthony Awards are also named for him.

"The Adventure of the Bogle-Wolf" was originally published in *The Illustrious Clients Second Case-Book*, edited by J. N. Williamson (Indianapolis, Indiana, privately printed for the Illustrious Clients, 1949).

THE ADVENTURE OF THE BOGLE-WOLF

Anthony Boucher

IT WAS ON a chill January afternoon in 1889 that I sat before the fire in my Paddington home, thoroughly exhausted from some hours of such strenuous activity as I had not known since our pursuit of the Andaman Islander on the Thames. I did not stir when I heard the bell, not recalling until its fifth clang that among the other vexations of this day was the fact that it was the maid's afternoon out. Charging my pipe load of Arcadia mixture to revive my flagging spirits, I reluctantly answered the summons.

It was with a mixture of joy and apprehension that I beheld upon the step the familiar figure of my friend Sherlock Holmes. Pleased though I was to see him, I nevertheless feared that he might find me, in my present condition, regrettably slow in responding to the challenge of whatever game might be afoot. But Holmes seemed as inactively disposed as I, inclined to do nothing, after our exchange of greetings, but follow me back to the fire, sink into the chair on the opposite side, and companionably stoke up his villainous black clay.

"London has grown dull," Holmes complained as I performed the expected rites with the tantalus and gasogene which had been his wedding present to us. "And dullness, my dear Watson, is the only insufferable malady. It is over two months since my pretended illness, which so deeply concerned you, enabled Inspector Morton to arrest that devil, Mr. Culverton Smith; and in all that time not a single problem of interest has come my way. Oh, the newspapers devoted some space, of course, to that wretched affair of the Taliaferro opals; but a four-year old child could have seen that the thief must be an albino Lascar." He broke off and regarded me with some concern. "My dear fellow, you aren't ill, are you?"

"The January chill," I hastened to explain. "Here; this will take the edge off it for both of us."

"*Ennui* . . . " Holmes murmured. "The French, Watson, have certain invaluable words. Consider, too, their use of our own word, *spleen* . . . One needs my grandmother's language to describe my state at the moment. The concretely expressed gratitude of the reigning family of Holland would in itself be sufficient to maintain my modest needs for years to come; but my mind needs a case. I must sharpen my teeth, Watson, on whatever bone I can find.

"This afternoon," he continued after a pause and a sip, "I called by at the Diogenes Club, but Mycroft was engaged on a mission of such secrecy that its nature might not be hinted even to me. I needed a mere five minutes to determine, from the ash beside Mycroft's habitual chair and the smudge of violet ink on the clerk's left forefinger, that his errand concerned a certain highly placed young gallant whose activities it would be wiser for me to ignore. Then I came to you, my old friend, in the hope that your practice—ever growing, I trust?—might have produced some little problem of a teasing, if petty, sort."

"No problem," I said wearily, and added, "from my practice."

"If I cannot find stimulating distraction somewhere . . ." His normally incisive voice trailed off, and the thumb of his right hand made the significant gesture of depressing a hypodermic syringe.

"In God's name, Holmes!" I cried. "You would not return to that?"

He sat in silence for a moment, smoking and smiling. Then he asked casually, "Polar or grizzly?"

"Polar," I responded automatically, and then leapt to my feet. "Holmes," I exclaimed, "this is too much! That you should want some stimulating distraction, as you call it, I can understand; but that you should invade the privacy of your friends, spying on them in their domestic moments like the pettiest enquiry agent—"

His welcome laugh and a gesture of his long thin hand interrupted my indignation. "Watson, Watson," he lamented, shaking his head. "Will you never learn that I practice neither black magic nor sneaking skulduggery? When I find a healthy young man in a state of complete exhaustion, dust on his hands and on the knees of his trousers, his rug awry and the furniture misplaced, and when moreover he winces at my causual allusion to a four-year old child, it is obvious that he has been spending the afternoon entertaining an infant, and at least in part by imitating animals on all fours. To one who knows your character as I do, Watson, it is equally obvious that the child would find you most acceptable in the role of a bear. It remained only to ask, 'Polar or grizzly?'—though in view of your predilection for tales of arctic adventure, that answer, too, should have been obvious. I regret that I seem to be losing my touch."

"Now—" I began.

"I know," he interrupted me with some acerbity. "Now it is all perfectly simple—once I have explained it. To see the answer it is explained— that, I might point out, is the desideratum. However, I might go on to deduce that the child belongs to a friend of your wife's (since I recall no couples with children in your own acquaintance), and that your wife and the child's mother have gone out together. Probably, in view of the day and the hour, to a matinee. Quite possibly, in view of the season, to a pantomime—which might perhaps indicate an older child in the family, taken to the theatre while this one, too young for public appearance, is left with the friend's obliging husband."

"Holmes," I exclaimed, "King James the First should have known you before he wrote his studies on witchcraft."

"Tush, Watson," my friend protested. "That was the merest guesswork. But there is no guesswork in concluding from the faint cries which I detect from the upper story that the young man in question has awakened from his nap and demands attention."

"This," I announced to Holmes when I had done my clumsy best to freshen the child after his nap, "is Master Elias Whitney."

"Ah? A namesake, no doubt, of the late Principal of the Theological College of St. George's?"

"His nephew," I replied, marveling as always at this man who had at his fingertips every fact of English life. "His mother, Kate, is a dear friend of Mary's. His father . . ." But professional reticence caused me to say no more of his poor father, little dreaming how the perverse proclivity which at that time caused me so much concern as a medical man was later to lead me into the adventure which I have chronicled elsewhere as the Man with the Twisted Lip.

"Ah there, young feller," Holmes said genially.

Young Elias gravely contemplated the piercing eyes, the hawklike features, the firmly sensitive lips of my friend, and delivered his verdict. "Funny man," he said.

I could not repress a smile, nor a lively sense of anticipation as I watched to see what species of animal Holmes would be obliged to portray for the young gentleman's entertainment. But I was disappointed in my expectations as young Elias disregarded the temptations of the rug which had been the Arctic Circle, settled himself on the hassock by the fire, and demanded, "Tell story."

Holmes's eyes twinkled. "He's found your

weak spot, Watson, my lad—a confirmed story teller, in and out of school. Well, if he must have animals, tell him of our experiences at Baskerville Hall."

I was about to protest as to the suitability for young ears of that gruesome narrative when the boy himself said, "No. Tell story about boglebear."

"He's come to the right shop," Holmes observed. "Your Scottish ancestry, my dear fellow, must team with stories of bogles."

"He means," I explained patiently, "a polar bear, such as I had the honor of portraying. No, Elias, I'm sorry, but I don't know any stories about polar bears. But I can recall that in my own childhood I was always partial to stories about wolves. Would one of those interest you?"

"Bogle-wolf?" Elias suggested.

"I am not positive on the subject, but I strongly doubt that there is such a beast as a polar wolf. This wolf is simply an ordinary wolf, such as one may encounter, at least in fairy tales, upon any corner. It lived in a deep dark forest—"

"Corners in forest?" Elias asked with interest.

Holmes had refilled his glass from the tantalus and settled back in the chair. "Pray continue, Watson," he urged. "I find fairy tales particularly suitable for you, in view of the romantic touches in your narratives of my own adventures. I am eager to see you at work."

"No," I answered Elias. "There were no corners in the forest, only a long winding pathway which led from one cottage to another. Now in the first cottage there lived a little girl called Red Riding Hood—"

"Know bout Riding Good," Elias said.

I felt somewhat rebuffed. "Would you prefer another story, then?"

"No. Like Riding Good. Tell bout Riding Good."

"The public," Holmes observed, "always prefers a story which it already knows."

I told about "Riding Good." Since the story may perhaps be familiar to the reader from his own nursery days, I shall here omit the details of the narrative, which I told in full as it was often related to us by our old Nannie in those happy sunlit days when Harry and I were children. I told of the first meeting with the wolf, of the wolf's nefarious practices upon grandmother, of Red Riding Hood's horrible interview with the disguised wolf, of her gradual realization of her great peril, and of the final intrusion of the gallant woodcutter (whom I described, I confess, with certain of the more outstanding physical traits of my friend) and his destruction of the wolf and restoration of grandmother—a detail, I am given to understand, frequently omitted from modern versions.

I was flattered by the rapt attention of young Elias, and I was not only flattered but puzzled by the equally rapt attention of Sherlock Holmes. As I progressed with my narrative, his eyes lit up, he followed my every word, and soon, after an automatic reach for the absent Persian slipper, extracted his pouch, loaded the clay, and surrounded himself with those poisonous clouds which I had come to associate with the final stages of a problem.

When I had concluded, he sprang to his feet and took several eager paces about the room. "That's done it, Watson!" he exclaimed, and there was the old life in his voice. "Elias!" He pointed a long forefinger at the child, who visibly quailed before it. "Do you want to know the *truth* about Red Riding Hood?"

"Know troof bout Riding Good?" the child repeated numbly.

"What dolts men can be!" Holmes ejaculated to himself. "To repeat that story for generations and never to perceive its meaning! And yet in the very words of this child there was a hint of the truth. *Bogle-wolf* . . . Surely you must see it, Watson?"

"See what?" I stammered.

"There are two essential points. Fix your mind on them, Watson. First, Red Riding Hood noticed the wolfishness of 'grandmother' only gradually—almost feature by feature. Second, after the wolf was killed, there was grandmother."

"But my dear Holmes—"

"You still do not understand? Then listen." His eyes sparkled. "It was, indeed, a bogle-wolf: it was a *werewolf*, a wolf which is only the lupine shape of a malevolent and anthropophagous human being. And that human being was . . . *Grandmother*!

"It is perfectly clear. Red Riding Hood did not look up at once and see that the form in bed was a wolf. No; little by little, she noticed the appearance of wolfish characteristics. It is obvious that she was watching the werewolf change from human being to wolf.

"And when the wolf was killed, there was grandmother. Not springing alive from the stomach—that is palpably a later rationalization, impossible even by the standards of the fairy tale. But there was grandmother, lying on the floor, stretched out by the blow of the woodman's axe—for the werewolf, when slain, always resumes its human form."

"Holmes," I gasped, "you are right. That must be the truth. So simple and yet so startling. And after all these centuries, you alone—"

With a lightning motion of his lithe body, Holmes whirled on young Elias. "Now, young feller, you know. Tell your mother that while she was attending the pantomime, you, my lad, have been the first boy in the world to learn the truth about Red Riding Hood!"

The boy sat silent for a moment, gazing at the man before him. Then his mouth parted and his eyes screwed up. He was still silent for what seemed like minutes, but at last an anguished wail came from that horribly distorted countenance. In all the adventures which I have shared with my friend Sherlock Holmes, I have never heard a scream of such pure and undiluted rage, agony and frustration.

So loud was the scream that we did not hear the key in the front door. Our first warning of the ladies' return was the whirlwind entrance of Kate Whitney, who dashed to the hassock, seized her agonized offspring in her arms, and vainly tried to still his screams.

My wife, entering with the still panto-rapt young Isa, turned on me furiously. "James!" she cried, loudly enough to be heard even over those wails. "What *have* you been doing to that child?"

"James," Sherlock Holmes observed. "A pet name, no doubt? And to think that I should have known you for so long, my dear fellow, without troubling to discover that your middle initial must stand for Hamish."

Mary turned to face him. "Mr. Holmes," she said, with ominous politeness. Her eyes took in the disordered rug, the rearranged furniture, the lowered level of the tantalus.

Kate Whitney's voice kept repeating, "What did the mans do to ums?" At last Master Elias controlled his hysteria sufficiently to point a damning finger at Sherlock Holmes.

"Bad man!" he said accusingly. "Bad man spoil Riding Good. Spoil it all up!" And he resumed his vociferous vocalizations.

I spoke as loudly and as calmly as I could. I said, "About that little matter of the Vatican Vaccination Scandal, old man. Don't you think we could talk it over in the consulting room?"

The glare in Mary's eyes softened a little. Close to my ear she whispered, "Another commission?" and I mumbled, "The usual percentage." She relaxed, and even let me take the tantalus with us.

"There," said Sherlock Holmes later, "you have the typical instance for the public's reaction to truth. You must never expect the scientific attitude from the popular mind, which always prefers the accepted falsehood to the unfamiliar truth. I have been contemplating a small monograph upon such delusory traditions; I am sure, for example, that since your friend Doyle wrote his legend about what he terms the *Marie Celeste*, the correct name *Mary Celeste* will fall into complete disuse. And yet we must try where we may to restore truth, and scorn the public hostility. *Populus me sibilat . . .*"

". . . *at numni*," I paraphrased glumly, recalling my unfortunate half-promise to Mary, "*desunt in arca . . .*"

The Martian Crown Jewels

POUL ANDERSON

AN IMMENSELY POPULAR, successful, and critically acclaimed writer of science fiction, Nordic mythology, and magic realism, Poul William Anderson (1926–2001) was noted for his meticulous research, calling his writing "fantasy with rivets"; if he referenced a particular type of armor, he would carefully detail its production.

He wrote more than a hundred books, mostly with a theme of individual liberty and free will, derived from his admiration for the founding fathers and the Constitution. While his philosophical position drew the enmity of his more left-wing colleagues, he remained a popular figure in his literary community, being chosen as president of the Science Fiction and Fantasy Writers of America, which named him a Grand Master and later inducted him into the Science Fiction Fantasy Hall of Fame. He won numerous writing awards during his lifetime, including seven Hugos and three Nebulas.

Anderson had a long-lived interest in Sherlock Holmes, observing that "there is considerable overlap between followers of science fiction and of the great detective." There can be no doubt that his affection for Sherlockian matters owes its inception to Karen Kruse, who founded a Sherlock Holmes society while still in high school. He met her at a world science fiction convention in Chicago in 1952. They married in 1953 and remained together until his death.

Anderson's other Sherlockian stories were "The Adventure of the Misplaced Hound," written with Gordon R. Dickson (1953), "Eve Times Four" (1960), and the much-praised "The Queen of Air and Darkness" (1971).

"The Martian Crown Jewels" was first published in the February 1958 issue of *Ellery Queen's Mystery Magazine*; it was first collected in book form in *A Treasury of Great Science Fiction*, edited by Anthony Boucher (Garden City, New York, Doubleday, 1959).

THE MARTIAN CROWN JEWELS

Poul Anderson

THE SIGNAL WAS picked up when the ship was still a quarter million miles away, and recorded voices summoned the technicians. There was no haste, for the ZX28749, otherwise called the *Jane Brackney*, was right on schedule; but landing an unmanned spaceship is always a delicate operation. Men and machines prepared to receive her as she came down, but the control crew had the first order of business.

Yamagata, Steinmann, and Ramanowitz were in the GCA tower, with Hollyday standing by for an emergency. If the circuits *should* fail—they never had, but a thousand tons of cargo and nuclear-powered vessel, crashing into the port, could empty Phobos of human life. So Hollyday watched over a set of spare assemblies, ready to plug in whatever might be required.

Yamagata's thin fingers danced over the radar dials. His eyes were intent on the screen. "Got her," he said. Steinmann made a distance reading and Ramanowitz took the velocity off the Dopplerscope. A brief session with a computer showed the figures to be almost as predicted.

"Might as well relax," said Yamagata, taking out a cigarette. "She won't be in control range for a while yet."

His eyes roved over the crowded room and out its window. From the tower he had a view of the spaceport: unimpressive, most of its shops and sheds and living quarters being underground. The smooth concrete field was chopped off by the curvature of the tiny satellite. It always faced Mars, and the station was on the far side, but he could remember how the planet hung enor-mous over the opposite hemisphere, soft ruddy disc blurred with thin air, hazy greenish-brown mottlings of health and farmland. Though Phobos was clothed in vacuum, you couldn't see the hard stars of space: the sun and the floodlamps were too bright.

There was a knock on the door. Hollyday went over, almost drifting in the ghostly gravity, and opened it. "Nobody allowed in here during a landing," he said. Hollyday was a stocky blond man with a pleasant, open countenance, and his tone was less peremptory than his words.

"Police." The newcomer, muscular, round-faced, and earnest, was in plain clothes, tunic and pajama pants, which was expected; everyone in the tiny settlement knew Inspector Gregg. But he was packing a gun, which was not usual.

Yamagata peered out again and saw the port's four constables down on the field in official spacesuits, watching the ground crew. They carried weapons. "What's the matter?" he asked.

"Nothing . . . I hope." Gregg came in and tried to smile. "But the *Jane* has a very unusual cargo."

"Hm?" Ramanowitz's eyes lit up in his broad plump visage. "Why weren't we told?"

"That was deliberate. Secrecy. The Martian crown jewels are aboard." Gregg fumbled a cigarette from his tunic.

Hollyday and Steinmann nodded at each other. Yamagata whistled. "On a robot ship?" he asked.

"Uh-huh. A robot ship is the one form of transportation from which they could not be stolen. There were three attempts made when they went to Earth on a regular liner, and I hate to think how many while they were at the British Museum. One guard lost his life. Now my boys are going to remove them before anyone else touches that ship and scoot 'em right down to Sabaeus."

"How much are they worth?" wondered Ramanowitz.

"Oh . . . they could be fenced on Earth for maybe half a billion UN dollars," said Gregg. "But the thief would do better to make the Martians pay to get them back . . . no, Earth would have to, I suppose, since it's our responsibility." He blew nervous clouds. "The jewels were secretly put on the *Jane*, last thing before she left on her regular run. I wasn't even told till a special messenger on this week's liner gave me the word. Not a chance for any thief to know they're here, till they're safely back on Mars. And that'll be *safe!*"

"Some people did know, all along," said Yamagata thoughtfully. "I mean the loading crew back at Earth."

"Uh-huh, there is that." Gregg smiled. "Several of them have quit since then, the messenger said, but of course, there's always a big turnover among spacejacks—they're a restless bunch." His gaze drifted across Steinmann and Hollyday, both of whom had last worked at Earth Station and come to Mars a few ships back. The liners went on a hyperbolic path and arrived in a couple of weeks; the robot ships followed the more leisurely and economical Hohmann A orbit and needed 258 days. A man who knew what ship was carrying the jewels could leave Earth, get to Mars well ahead of the cargo, and snap up a job there—Phobos was always shorthanded.

"Don't look at me!" said Steinmann, laughing. "Chuck and I knew about this—of course—but we were under security restrictions. Haven't told a soul."

"Yeah. I'd have known it if you had," nodded Gregg. "Gossip travels fast here. Don't resent this, please, but I'm here to see that none of you

boys leaves this tower till the jewels are aboard our own boat."

"Oh, well. It'll mean overtime."

"If I want to get rich fast, I'll stick to prospecting," added Hollyday.

"When are you going to quit running around with that Geiger in your free time?" asked Yamagata. "Phobos is nothing but iron and granite."

"I have my own ideas about that," said Hollyday stoutly.

"Hell, everybody needs a hobby on this Godforsaken clod," declared Ramanowitz. "I might try for those sparklers myself, just for the excitement—" He stopped abruptly, aware of Gregg's eyes.

"All right," snapped Yamagata. "Here we go. Inspector, please stand back out of the way, and for your life's sake don't interrupt."

The *Jane* was drifting in, her velocity on the carefully precalculated orbit almost identical with that of Phobos. Almost, but not quite—there had been the inevitable small disturbing factors, which the remote-controlled jets had to compensate, and then there was the business of landing her. The team got a fix and were frantically busy.

In free fall, the *Jane* approached within a thousand miles of Phobos—a spheroid five hundred feet in radius, big and massive, but lost against the incredible bulk of the satellite. And yet Phobos is an insignificant airless pill, negligible even beside its seventh-rate planet. Astronomical magnitudes are simply and literally incomprehensible.

When the ship was close enough, the radio directed her gyros to rotate her, very, very gently, until her pickup antenna was pointing directly at the field. Then her jets were cut in, a mere whisper of thrust. She was nearly above the spaceport, her path tangential to the moon's curvature. After a moment Yamagata slapped the keys hard, and the rockets blasted furiously, a visible red streak up in the sky. He cut them again, checked his data, and gave a milder blast.

"Okay," he grunted. "Let's bring her in."

Her velocity relative to Phobos's orbit and rotation was now zero, and she was falling. Yamagata slewed her around till the jets were pointing vertically down. Then he sat back and mopped his face while Ramanowitz took over; the job was too nerve-stretching for one man to perform in its entirety. Ramanowitz sweated the awkward mass to within a few yards of the cradle. Steinmann finished the task, easing her into the berth like an egg into a cup. He cut the jets and there was silence.

"Whew! Chuck, how about a drink?" Yamagata held out unsteady fingers.

Hollyday smiled and fetched a bottle. It went happily around. Gregg declined. His eyes were locked to the field, where a technician was checking for radioactivity. The verdict was clean, and he saw his constables come soaring over the concrete, to surround the great ship with guns. One of them went up, opened the manhatch, and slipped inside.

It seemed a very long while before he emerged. Then he came running. Gregg cursed and thumbed the tower's radio board. "Hey, there! Ybarra! What's the matter?"

The helmet set shuddered a reply: "Senor . . . Senor Inspector . . . the crown jewels are gone."

Sabaeus is, of course, a purely human name for the old city nestled in the Martian tropics, at the juncture of the "canals" Phison and Euphrates. Terrestrial mouths simply cannot form the syllables of High Chlannach, though rough approximations are possible. Nor did humans ever build a town exclusively of towers broader at the top than the base, or inhabit one for twenty thousand years. If they had, though, they would have encouraged an eager tourist influx; but Martians prefer more dignified ways of making a dollar, even if their parsimonious fame has long replaced that of Scotchmen. The result is that though interplanetary trade is brisk and Phobos a treaty port, a human is still a rare sight in Sabaeus.

Hurrying down the avenues between the stone mushrooms, Gregg felt conspicuous. He was glad the airsuit muffled him. Not that the grave Martians stared; they varkled, which is worse.

The Street of Those Who Prepare Nourishment in Ovens is a quiet one, given over to handicrafters, philosophers, and residential apartments. You won't see a courtship dance or a parade of the Lesser Halberdiers on it: nothing more exciting than a continuous four-day argument on the relativistic nature of the null class or an occasional gunfight. The latter are due to the planet's most renowned private detective, who nests here.

Gregg always found it eerie to be on Mars, under the cold deep-blue sky and the shrunken sun, among noises muffled by the thin oxygen-deficient air. But for Syaloch he had a good deal of affection, and when he had gone up the ladder and shaken the rattle outside the second-floor apartment and had been admitted, it was like escaping from nightmare.

"Ah, Krech!" The investigator laid down the stringed instrument on which he had been playing and towered gauntly over his visitor. "An unexpected bleassure to see hyou. Come in, my tear chab, to come in." He was proud of his English—but simple misspellings will not convey the whistling, clicking Martian accent.

The Inspector felt a cautious way into the high, narrow room. The glowsnakes which illuminated it after dark were coiled asleep on the stone floor, in a litter of papers, specimens, and weapons; rusty sand covered the sills of the Gothic windows. Syaloch was not neat except in his own person. In one corner was a small chemical laboratory. The rest of the walls were taken up with shelves, the criminological literature of three planets—Martian books, Terrestrial micros, Venusian talking stones. At one place, patriotically, the glyphs representing the reigning Nestmother had been punched out with bullets. An Earthling could not sit on the trapezelike native furniture, but Syaloch had courteously provided chairs and tubs as well: his clientele was also triplanetary.

"I take it you are here on official but confidential business," Syaloch got out a big-bowled pipe. Martians have happily adopted tobacco, though in their atmosphere it must include potassium permanganate.

Gregg started. "How the hell do you know that?"

"Elementary, my dear fellow. Your manner is most agitated, and I know nothing but a crisis in your profession would cause that."

Gregg laughed wryly.

Syaloch was a seven-foot biped of vaguely storklike appearance. But the lean, crested, red-beaked head at the end of the sinuous neck was too large, the yellow eyes too deep: the white feathers were more like a penguin's than a flying bird's, save at the blue-plumed tail: instead of wings there were skinny red arms ending in four-fingered hands. And the overall posture was too erect for a bird.

Gregg jerked back to awareness. God in Heaven! The city lay gray and quiet: the sun was slipping westward over the farmlands of Sinus Sabaeus and the desert of the Aeria: he could just make out the rumble of a treadmill cart passing beneath the windows—and he sat here with a story which could blow the Solar System apart!

His hands, gloved against the chill, twisted together. "Yes, it's confidential, all right. If you can solve this case, you can just about name your own fee." The gleam in Syaloch's eyes made him regret that, but he stumbled on: "One thing, though. Just how do you feel about us Earthlings?"

"I have no prejudices. It is the brain that counts, not whether it is covered by feathers or hair or bony plates."

"No, I realize that. But some Martians resent us. We do disrupt an old way of life—we can't help it, if we're to trade with you—"

"K'teh. The trade is on the whole beneficial. Your fuel and machinery—and tobacco, yesss—for our kantz and snull. Also, we were getting too . . . stale. And of course space travel has added a whole new dimension to criminology. Yes, I favor Earth."

"Then you'll help us? And keep quiet about something which could provoke your planetary federation into kicking us off Phobos?"

The third eyelids closed, making the long-beaked face a mask. "I give no promises yet, Gregg."

"Well . . . damn it, all right, I'll have to take the chance." The policeman swallowed hard. "You know about your crown jewels."

"They were lent to Earth for exhibit and scientific study."

"After years of negotiation. There's no more priceless relic on all Mars—and you were an old civilization when we were hunting mammoths. All right. They've been stolen."

Syaloch opened his eyes, but his only other movement was to nod.

"They were put on a robot ship at Earth Station. They were gone when that ship reached Phobos. We've damn near ripped the boat apart trying to find them—we did take the other cargo to pieces, bit by bit—and they aren't there!"

Syaloch rekindled his pipe, an elaborate flint-and-steel process on a world where matches won't burn. Only when it was drawing well did he suggest: "It is possible the ship was boarded en route?"

"No. It isn't possible. Every spacecraft in the System is registered, and its whereabouts are known at any time. Furthermore, imagine trying to find a speck in hundreds of millions of cubic miles, and match velocities with it . . . no vessel ever built could carry that much fuel. And mind you, it was never announced that the jewels were going back this way. Only the UN police and the Earth Station crew *could* know till the ship had actually left—by which time it'd be too late."

"Most interesting."

"If word of this gets out," said Gregg miserably, "you can guess the results. I suppose, we'd still have a few friends left in your Parliament—"

"In the House of Actives, yesss . . . a few. Not in the House of Philosophers, which is of course the upper chamber."

"It could mean a twenty-year hiatus in Earth-

Mars traffic—maybe a permanent breaking off of relations. Damn it, Syaloch, you've *got* to help me find those stones!"

"Hm-m-m. I pray your pardon. This requires thought." The Martian picked up his crooked instrument and plucked a few tentative chords. Gregg sighed.

The colorless sunset was past, night had fallen with the unnerving Martian swiftness, and the glowsnakes were emitting blue radiance when Syaloch put down the demifiddle.

"I fear I shall have to visit Phobos in person," he said. "There are too many unknowns for analysis, and it is never well to theorize before all the data have been gathered." A bony hand clapped Gregg's shoulder. "Come, come, old chap. I am really most grateful to you. Life was becoming infernally dull. Now, as my famous Terrestrial predecessor would say, the game's afoot . . . and a very big game indeed!"

A Martian in an Earthlike atmosphere is not much hampered, needing only an hour in a compression chamber and a filter on his beak to eliminate excess oxygen and moisture. Syaloch walked freely about the port clad in filter, pipe, and *tirstokr* cap, grumbling to himself at the heat and humidity.

He donned a spacesuit and went out to inspect the *Jane Brackney*. The vessel had been shunted aside to make room for later arrivals, and stood by a raw crag at the edge of the field, glimmering in the hard spatial sunlight. Gregg and Yamagata were with him.

"I say, you *have* been thorough," remarked the detective. "The outer skin is quite stripped off."

The spheroid resembled an egg which had tangled with a waffle iron: an intersecting grid of girders and braces above a thin aluminum hide. The jets, hatches, and radio mast were the only breaks in the checkerboard pattern, whose depth was about a foot and whose squares were a yard across at the "equator."

Yamagata laughed in a strained fashion.

"No. The cops fluoroscoped every inch of her, but that's the way these cargo ships always look. They never land on Earth, you know, or any place where there's air, so streamlining would be unnecessary. And since nobody is aboard in transit, we don't have to worry about insulation or air-tightness. Perishables are stowed in sealed compartments."

"I see. Now where were the crown jewels kept?"

"They were supposed to be in a cupboard near the gyros," said Gregg. "They were in a locked box, about six inches high, six inches wide, and a foot long." He shook his head, finding it hard to believe that so small a box could contain so much potential death.

"Ah . . . but *were* they placed there?"

"I radioed Earth and got a full account," said Gregg. "The ship was loaded as usual at the satellite station, then shoved a quarter mile away till it was time for her to leave—to get her out of the way, you understand. She was still in the same free-fall orbit, attached by a light cable—perfectly standard practice. At the last minute, without anyone being told beforehand, the crown jewels were brought up from Earth and stashed aboard."

"By a special policeman?"

"No. Only licensed technicians are allowed to board a ship in orbit, unless there's a life-and-death emergency. One of the regular station crew—fellow named Carter—was told where to put them. He was watched by the cops as he pulled himself along the cable and in through the manhatch." Gregg pointed to a small door near the radio mast. "He came out, closed it, and returned on the cable. The police immediately searched him and his spacesuit, just in case, and he positively did not have the jewels. There was no reason to suspect him of anything—good steady worker—though I'll admit he's disappeared since then. The *Jane* blasted a few minutes later and her jets were watched till they cut off and she went into free fall. And that's the last anyone saw of her till she got here—without the jewels."

"And right on orbit," added Yamagata. "If by some freak she had been boarded, it would have thrown her off enough for us to notice as she came in. Transference of momentum between her and the other ship."

"I see." Behind his faceplate, Syaloch's beak cut a sharp black curve across heaven. "Now then, Gregg, were the jewels actually in the box when it was delivered?"

"At Earth Station, you mean? Oh, yes. There are four UN Chief Inspectors involved, and HQ says they're absolutely above suspicion. When I sent back word of the theft, they insisted on having their own quarters and so on searched, and went under scop voluntarily."

"And your own constables on Phobos?"

"Same thing," said the policeman grimly. "I've slapped on an embargo—nobody but me has left this settlement since the loss was discovered. I've had every room and tunnel and warehouse searched." He tried to scratch his head, a frustrating attempt when one is in a spacesuit. "I can't maintain those restrictions much longer. Ships are coming in and the consignees want their freight."

"*Hnachla*. That puts us under a time limit, then." Syaloch nodded to himself. "Do you know, this is a fascinating variation of the old locked room problem. A robot ship in transit is a locked room in the most classic sense." He drifted off.

Gregg stared bleakly across the savage horizon, naked rock tumbling away under his feet, and then back over the field. Odd how tricky your vision became in airlessness, even when you had bright lights. That fellow crossing the field there, under the full glare of sun and floodlamps, was merely a stipple of shadow and luminance . . . what the devil was he doing, tying a shoe of all things? No, he was walking quite normally—

"I'd like to put everyone on Phobos under scop," said Gregg with a violent note, "but the law won't allow it unless the suspect volunteers—and only my own men have volunteered."

"Quite rightly, my dear fellow," said Syaloch.

"One should at least have the privilege of privacy in his own skull. And it would make the investigation unbearably crude."

"I don't give a fertilizing damn how crude it is," snapped Gregg. "I just want that box with the Martian crown jewels safe inside."

"Tut-tut! Impatience has been the ruin of many a promising young police officer, as I seem to recall my spiritual ancestor of Earth pointing out to a Scotland Yard man who—hm—may even have been a physical ancestor of yours, Gregg. It seems we must try another approach. Are there any people on Phobos who might have known the jewels were aboard this ship?"

"Yes. Two men only. I've pretty well established that they never broke security and told anyone else till the secret was out."

"And who are they?"

"Technicians, Hollyday and Steinmann. They were working at Earth Station when the *Jane* was loaded. They quit soon after—not at the same time—and came here by liner and got jobs. You can bet that *their* quarters have been searched!"

"Perhaps," murmured Syaloch, "it would be worthwhile to interview the gentlemen in question."

Steinmann, a thin redhead, wore truculence like a mantle; Hollyday merely looked worried. It was no evidence of guilt—everyone had been rubbed raw of late. They sat in the police office, with Gregg behind the desk and Syaloch leaning against the wall, smoking and regarding them with unreadable yellow eyes.

"Damn it, I've told this over and over till I'm sick of it!" Steinmann knotted his fists and gave the Martian a bloodshot stare. "I never touched the things and I don't know who did. Hasn't any man a right to change jobs?"

"Please," said the detective mildly. "The better you help the sooner we can finish this work. I take it you were acquainted with the man who actually put the box aboard the ship?"

"Sure. Everybody knew John Carter. Everybody knows everybody else on a satellite station." The Earthman stuck out his jaw. "That's why none of us'll take scop. We won't blab out all our thoughts to guys we see fifty times a day. We'd go nuts!"

"I never made such a request," said Syaloch.

"Carter was quite a good friend of mine," volunteered Hollyday.

"Uh-huh," grunted Gregg. "And he quit too, about the same time you fellows did, and went Earthside and hasn't been seen since. HQ told me you and he were thick. What'd you talk about?"

"The usual." Hollyday shrugged. "Wine, women, and song. I haven't heard from him since I left Earth."

"Who says Carter stole the box?" demanded Steinmann. "He just got tired of living in space and quit his job. He couldn't have stolen the jewels—he was searched."

"Could he have hidden it somewhere for a friend to get at this end?" inquired Syaloch.

"Hidden it? Where? Those ships don't have secret compartments." Steinmann spoke wearily. "And he was only aboard the *Jane* a few minutes, just long enough to put the box where he was supposed to." His eyes smoldered at Gregg. "Let's face it: the only people anywhere along the line who ever had a chance to lift it were our own dear cops."

The Inspector reddened and half rose from his seat. "Look here, you—"

"We've got *your* word that you're innocent," growled Steinmann. "Why should it be any better than mine?"

Syaloch waved both men back. "If you please. Brawls are unphilosophic." His beak opened and clattered, the Martian equivalent of a smile. "Has either of you, perhaps, a theory? I am open to all ideas."

There was a stillness. Then Hollyday mumbled: "Yes. I have one."

Syaloch hooded his eyes and puffed quietly, waiting.

Hollyday's grin was shaky. "Only if I'm right, you'll never see those jewels again."

Gregg sputtered.

"I've been around the Solar System a lot," said Hollyday. "It gets lonesome out in space. You never know how big and lonesome it is till you've been there, all by yourself. And I've done just that—I'm an amateur uranium prospector, not a lucky one so far. I can't believe we know everything about the universe, or that there's only vacuum between the planets."

"Are you talking about the cobblies?" snorted Gregg.

"Go ahead and call it superstition. But if you're in space long enough . . . well, somehow, you *know*. There are beings out there—gas beings, radiation beings, whatever you want to imagine, there's something living in space."

"And what use would a box of jewels be to a cobbly?"

Hollyday spread his hands. "How can I tell? Maybe we bother them, scooting through their own dark kingdom with our little rockets. Stealing the crown jewels would be a good way to disrupt the Mars trade, wouldn't it?"

Only Syaloch's pipe broke the inward-pressing silence. But its burbling seemed quite irreverent.

"Well—" Gregg fumbled helplessly with a meteoric paperweight. "Well, Mr. Syaloch, do you want to ask any more questions?"

"Only one." The third lids rolled back, and coldness looked out at Steinmann. "If you please, my good man, what is your hobby?"

"Huh? Chess. I play chess. What's it to you?" Steinmann lowered his head and glared sullenly.

"Nothing else?"

"What else is there?"

Syaloch glanced at the Inspector, who nodded confirmation.

"I see. Thank you. Perhaps we can have a game sometime. I have some small skill of my own. That is all for now, gentlemen."

They left, moving like things in the haze of a dream through the low gravity.

"Well?" Gregg's eyes pleaded with Syaloch. "What's next?"

"Very little. I think . . . yesss, while I am here I should like to watch the technicians at work. In my profession, one needs a broad knowledge of all occupations."

Gregg sighed.

Ramanowitz showed the guest around. The *Kim Brackney* was in and being unloaded. They threaded through a hive of spacesuited men.

"The cops are going to have to raise that embargo soon," said Ramanowitz. "Either that or admit why they've clamped it on. Our warehouses are busting."

"It would be politic to do so," nodded Syaloch. "Ah, tell me . . . is this equipment standard for all stations?"

"Oh, you mean what the boys are wearing and carrying around? Sure. Same issue everywhere."

"May I inspect it more closely?"

"Hm?" *Lord, deliver me from visiting firemen!* thought Ramanowitz. He waved a mechanic over to him. "Mr. Syaloch would like you to explain your outfit," he said with ponderous sarcasm.

"Sure. Regular spacesuit here, reinforced at the seams." The gauntleted hands moved about, pointing. "Heating coils powered from this capacitance battery. Ten-hour air supply in the tanks. These buckles, you snap your tools into them, so they won't drift around in free fall. This little can at my belt holds paint that I spray out through this nozzle."

"Why must spaceships be painted?" asked Syaloch. "There is nothing to corrode the metal."

"Well, sir, we just call it paint. It's really gunk, to seal any leaks in the hull till we can install a new plate, or to mark any other kind of damage. Meteor punctures and so on." The mechanic pressed a trigger and a thin, almost invisible stream jetted out, solidifying as it hit the ground.

"But it cannot readily be seen, can it?" objected the Martian. "I, at least, find it difficult to see clearly in airlessness."

"That's right. Light doesn't diffuse, so . . .

well, anyhow, the stuff is radioactive—not enough to be dangerous, just enough so that the repair crew can spot the place with a Geiger counter."

"I understand. What is the half-life?"

"Oh, I'm not sure. Six months, maybe? It's supposed to remain detectable for a year."

"Thank you." Syaloch stalked off. Ramanowitz had to jump to keep up with those long legs.

"Do you think Carter may have hid the box in his paint can?" suggested the human.

"No, hardly. The can is too small, and I assume he was searched thoroughly." Syaloch stopped and bowed. "You have been very kind and patient, Mr. Ramanowitz. I am finished now, and can find the Inspector myself."

"What for?"

"To tell him he can lift the embargo, of course." Syaloch made a harsh sibilance. "And then I must get the next boat to Mars. If I hurry, I can attend the concert in Sabaeus tonight." His voice grew dreamy. "They will be premiering Hanyech's *Variations on a Theme by Mendelssohn*, transcribed to the Royal Chlannach scale. It should be most unusual."

It was three days afterward that the letter came. Syaloch excused himself and kept an illustrious client squatting while he read it. Then he nodded to the other Martian. "You will be interested to know, sir, that the Estimable Diadems have arrived at Phobos and are being returned at this moment."

The client, a Cabinet Minister from the House of Actives, blinked. "Pardon, Freehatched Syaloch, but what have you to do with that?"

"Oh . . . I am a friend of the Featherless police chief. He thought I might like to know."

"*Hraa.* Were you not on Phobos recently?"

"A minor case." The detective folded the letter carefully, sprinkled it with salt, and ate it. Martians are fond of paper, especially official Earth stationery with high rag content. "Now, sir, you were saying—?"

The parliamentarian responded absently. He would not dream of violating privacy—no, never—but if he had X-ray vision he would have read:

"Dear Syaloch,

"You were absolutely right. Your locked room problem is solved. We've got the jewels back, everything is in fine shape, and the same boat which brings you this letter will deliver them to the vaults. It's too bad the public can never know the facts—two planets ought to be grateful to you—but I'll supply that much thanks all by myself, and insist that any bill you care to send be paid in full. Even if the Assembly had to make a special appropriation, which I'm afraid it will.

"I admit your idea of lifting the embargo at once looked pretty wild to me, but it worked. I had our boys out, of course, scouring Phobos with Geigers, but Hollyday found the box before we did. Which saved us a lot of trouble, to be sure. I arrested him as he came back into the settlement, and he had the box among his ore samples. He has confessed, and you were right all along the line.

"What was that thing you quoted at me, the saying of that Earthman you admire so much? 'When you have eliminated the impossible, whatever remains, however improbable, must be true.' Something like that. It certainly applies to this case.

"As you decided, the box must have been taken to the ship at Earth Station and left there—no other possibility existed. Carter figured it out in half a minute when he was ordered to take the thing out and put it aboard the Jane. *He went inside, all right, but still had the box when he emerged. In that uncertain light nobody saw him put it 'down' between four girders right next to the hatch. Or as you remarked, if the jewels are not in the ship, and yet not away from the ship, they must be on the ship. Gravitation would hold them in place. When the* Jane *blasted off, ac-*

celeration pressure slid the box back, but of course the waffle-iron pattern kept it from being lost; it fetched up against the after rib and stayed there. All the way to Mars! But the ship's gravity held it securely enough even in free fall, since both were on the same orbit.

"Hollyday says that Carter told him all about it. Carter couldn't go to Mars himself without being suspected and watched every minute once the jewels were discovered missing. He needed a confederate. Hollyday went to Phobos and took up prospecting as a cover for the search he'd later be making for the jewels.

"As you showed me, when the ship was within a thousand miles of this dock, Phobos gravity would be stronger than her own. Every spacejack knows that the robot ships don't start decelerating till they're quite close; that they are then almost straight above the surface; and that the side with the radio mast and manhatch—the side on which Carter had placed the box—is rotated around to face the station. The centrifugal force of rotation threw the box away from the ship, and was in a direction toward Phobos rather than away from it. Carter knew that this rotation is slow and easy, so the force wasn't enough to accelerate the box to escape velocity and lose it in space. It would have to fall down toward the satellite. Phobos Station being on the side opposite Mars, there was no danger that the loot would keep going till it hit the planet.

"So the crown jewels tumbled onto Phobos, just as you deduced. Of course Carter had given the box a quick radioactive spray as he laid it in place, and Hollyday used that to track it down among all those rocks and crevices. In point of fact, its path curved clear around this moon, so it landed about five miles from the station.

"Steinmann has been after me to know why you quizzed him about his hobby. You forgot to tell me that, but I figured it out for myself and told him. He or Hollyday had to

be involved, since nobody else knew about the cargo, and the guilty person had to have some excuse to go out and look for the box. Chess playing doesn't furnish that kind of alibi. Am I right? At least, my deduction proves I've been studying the same canon you go by. Incidentally, Steinmann asks if you'd care to take him on the next time he has planet leave.

"Hollyday knows where Carter is hiding, and we've radioed the information back to Earth. Trouble is, we can't prosecute either of them without admitting the facts. Oh, well, there are such things as blacklists.

"Will have to close this now to make the boat. I'll be seeing you soon—not professionally, I hope!

Admiring regards,
Inspector Gregg"

But as it happened, the Cabinet minister did not possess X-ray eyes. He dismissed unprofitable speculation and outlined his problem. Somebody, somewhere in Sabaeus, was farniking the krats, and there was an alarming zaksnautry among the hyukus. It sounded to Syaloch like an interesting case.

Sherlock Among the Spirits

ANONYMOUS

EVIDENCE STRONGLY SUGGESTS that Gilbert Keith Chesterton (1874–1936) was a great fan of Sherlock Holmes and Arthur Conan Doyle. In addition to being a popular and successful author, notably for his five volumes of stories about Father Brown, Chesterton was an illustrator whose caricatures were published in many magazines and books, and he frequently made Holmes the subject of his colored inks.

Early in his life he turned from most artistic pursuits to write in many genres, including poetry, journalism, detective fiction, religion, biography, and art and literary criticism, becoming a profoundly influential voice in both religious thought and literature, founding the important and eponymous magazine, *G. K.'s Weekly* (1925–1936) after editing its predecessor, *The New Witness*, for seven years.

In its pages were theological and political articles by such significant authors as H. G. Wells and George Bernard Shaw, but also pieces about spiritualism, the great late-life preoccupation of Conan Doyle. Chesterton had been involved in this area of study himself, and he published this anonymous parody of Holmes and his encounter with a medium. It has been speculated that Chesterton himself wrote it, but there is no evidence to definitively state that this is true.

"Sherlock Among the Spirits" was first published in the August 15, 1925, issue of *G. K.'s Weekly*.

SHERLOCK AMONG THE SPIRITS

Anonymous

THE SPIRITUALIST SÉANCE, which my friend Conan Doyle had induced me to hold in my old rooms in Baker Street, was just over. It had been a tremendous revelation. The medium, Dr. Magog, whom I assumed from the first to be a charlatan (for my training had been strictly scientific and rational), because of his long white hair and beard and his Lithuanian name, astounded me with the accuracy of his suggestions. He even converted Sir Arthur's other friend Dr. Challenger, whom readers of the *Strand Magazine* may remember as having discovered a world of prehistoric animals, whose manners and demeanour he seemed to share. He had begun by having grave doubts, which he expressed by hurling the table to the end of the room and dancing on several of the enquirers after truth; but half way through the proceedings he burst into sobs that shook the building.

I could understand his feelings. The medium mentioned things that could only be known in the innermost domestic circle; such as a knock given to a girl when she was a child, now recalled by the spirit of her brother killed in the war. Sometimes this intimacy was even distressing; as in the picture called up before us of a girl sobbing in a remote chateau in France, and the gloomy admission by a young man present that the memory moved him to remorse. Perhaps the most remarkable case was that of the spirit of a daughter who told her father not to neglect his appearance from grief at her death, seeing that the Shining Ones liked to see him in a single eyeglass and spats. Now the man in question was indescribably shaggy and shabby, but he ad-

mitted that he had indeed been thus adorned in happier days.

I was brooding on these things after the others had left, when I heard a step on the stair that told of one of them returning. Dr. Magog himself hurriedly re-entered the room, saying: "I had forgotten my hat. Interesting occasion, wasn't it?"

"You absolutely amazed me," I answered.

"You have often told me so, my dear Watson," he replied.

I sprang to my feet and stood stiffened with incredulous stupefaction, for I had caught a note of something more marvelous than any psychical marvels.

He seated himself languidly and removed the white wig, showing the unmistakable frontal development of the greatest detective in the world. "If you had used my methods, Watson," he said, "you would have known that a man never forgets his hat except when he is wearing a wig. It was a deplorable lapse. Well, you see, I converted Challenger."

"A wonderful achievement," I said. "The discoverer of the prehistoric world."

"A very appropriate occupation, Watson," he said. "I should say Dr. Challenger's powers of scientific observation were just about equal to noticing one of the larger Plesiosauri a few yards off. With a little more attention to minutiae he might even see a mammoth on the mat."

"But how on earth did you manage it?" I asked. "How did you know of that nursery incident, for instance?"

"The girl was good looking and healthy and

she had false teeth. More probably she had them knocked out; and who should knock them out if not her brother?"

"And what about the eyeglass and spats," I demanded.

"I have myself written a little monograph on 'The Monacle of Crime,' and we saw something of its devastating effect when we looked into that little problem of the Haunted Hat Peg. The man had different markings in the two eye sockets, in a way only produced by the single eyeglass. Did you ever know a shabby, unshaven man to wear a single eyeglass? His beard bristled like that of all men who were once clean shaven. I guessed the spats; but I was careful only to say that the higher intelligences would like to see them. There is no accounting for taste."

"And how did you know," I asked, lowering my voice, "that the young man had broken the heart of a lady in a chateau?"

"He hadn't," replied Sherlock Holmes, "but I could see by his face he would be the last man to deny it. Rather too obvious, Watson. Will you pass me my violin?"

The Case of the Missing Patriarchs

LOGAN CLENDENING

ALTHOUGH AN OUTSTANDING scholar and collector of Sherlock Holmes, Logan Clendening (1884–1945) is now forgotten except for his single short-short story, which Ellery Queen described as "one of the shortest and cleverest pastiches of Sherlock Holmes ever conceived," and Edgar W. Smith, the head of the Baker Street Irregulars, called a classic piece, even suggesting "The Navel Treatise" as a possible alternative title.

Born in Kansas City, Missouri, Clendening became one of the city's greatest doctors and most beloved citizens, as famous for his wit and charm as he was for his literary scholarship and medical expertise. His column, "Diet and Health," was syndicated in nearly four hundred newspapers, and his most important book, *The Human Body* (1927), was a bestseller that remained in print through successive editions for many years. Its success encouraged him to give up private practice for writing and journalism. His sense of humor came to the front when he was asked why he had quit private practice. He replied, "My boy, about this country are several headstones marking my progress in the operating field. I desisted, I may say, almost by universal acclaim."

When the great Sherlockian scholar and collector Vincent Starrett was forced by financial difficulties to sell his Holmes collection, Clendening wrote to him. "I hear that you have just parted with your own collection, and I think you ought to start another. Why not start with mine? It is small but goodish—it contains a number of the better pieces that you might have difficulty duplicating—and I am boxing it up this afternoon and getting it off to you tomorrow morning. You will really take a load off my mind if you will accept it."

"The box," Starrett wrote in his autobiography, *Born in a Bookshop* (1965), "contained some twenty of the most desirable items in the field, including the desperately rare first printing of *A Study in Scarlet*. It was the nucleus of a new collection. . . . I suppose no finer thing ever was done for one collector by another."

"The Case of the Missing Patriarchs" was privately printed in an edition of thirty copies for friends of Edwin B. Hill (Ysleta, Texas, 1934).

THE CASE OF THE MISSING PATRIARCHS

Logan Clendening

SHERLOCK HOLMES IS dead. At the age of eighty he passed away quietly in his sleep. And at once ascended to Heaven.

The arrival of few recent immigrants to the celestial streets has caused so much excitement. Only Napoleon's appearance in Hell is said to have equaled the great detective's reception. In spite of the heavy fog which rolled in from the Jordan, Holmes was immediately bowled in a hansom to audience with the Divine Presence. After the customary exchange of amenities, Jehovah said:

"Mr. Holmes, we too have our problems. Adam and Eve are missing. Have been, 's a matter of fact, for nearly two aeons. They used to be quite an attraction to visitors and we would like to commission you to discover them."

Holmes looked thoughtful for a moment.

"We fear that their appearance when last seen would furnish no clue," continued Jehovah. "A man is bound to change in two aeons."

Holmes held up his long, thin hand. "Could you make a general announcement that a contest between an immovable body and an irresistible force will be staged in that large field at the end of the street—Lord's, I presume it is?"

The announcement was made and soon the streets were filled with a slowly moving crowd. Holmes stood idly in the divine portico watching them.

Suddenly he darted into the crowd and seized a patriarch and his whimpering old mate; he brought them to the Divine Presence.

"It is," asserted Deity. "Adam, you have been giving us a great deal of anxiety. But, Mr. Holmes, tell me how you found them."

"Elementary, my dear God," said Sherlock Holmes, "they have no navels."

The Devil and Sherlock Holmes

LOREN D. ESTLEMAN

A DEEP-SEATED AFFECTION for Sherlock Holmes resulted in Loren D. Estleman's (1952–) first two published books, *Sherlock Holmes vs. Dracula, or The Adventure of the Sanguinary Count* (1978) and *Dr. Jekyll and Mr. Holmes* (1979), as well as the recent short story collection, *The Perils of Sherlock Holmes* (2012).

Nevertheless, among his seventy published books, it is Estleman's twenty-three novels about Detroit private investigator Amos Walker for which he is best known. Beginning with *Motor City Blue* (1980), this hard-boiled series has been praised by fans as diverse as Harlan Coben, Steve Forbes, John D. MacDonald, John Lescroart, and the Amazing Kreskin. As one of the most honored writers in America, Estleman was given the Eye, the lifetime achievement award of the Private Eye Writers of America, from which he has also received four Shamus Awards.

He has been nominated for a National Book Award and an Edgar Award, winning twenty additional national writing awards, notably the Owen Wister Award for Lifetime Contributions to Western Literature, the highest honor given by the Western Writers of America.

"The Devil and Sherlock Holmes" was first published in *Ghosts in Baker Street*, edited by Martin H. Greenberg, Jon Lellenberg, and Daniel Stashower (New York, Carroll & Graf, 2006).

THE DEVIL AND SHERLOCK HOLMES

Loren D. Estleman

THE YEAR 1899 stands out of particular note in my memory; not because it was the last but one of the old century (the numerologists are clear upon this point, but popular opinion differs), but because it was the only time during my long and stimulating association with Sherlock Holmes that I came to call upon his unique services as a client.

It was the last day of April, and because I had not yet made up my mind whether to invest in South African securities, I was refreshing my recollection by way of recent numbers of the *Times* and *Telegraph* about developments in the souring relationship between the Boers and the British in Johannesburg. The day was Sunday, and my professional consulting-room was empty. This situation presented the happy prospect of uninterrupted study outside the melancholy surroundings of my lonely quarters in my wife's temporary absence, as well as a haven from personal troubles of more recent vintage.

I was, therefore, somewhat disgruntled to be forced to disinter myself from the pile of discarded sections to answer the bell.

"Ah, Watson," greeted Sherlock Holmes. "When I find you squandering your day of rest in conference with your cheque-book, I wonder that I should have come in chains, to haunt you out of your miser's destiny."

I was always pleased to encounter my oldest of friends, and wrung his hand before I realised that he had once again trespassed upon my private reflections. It was not until I had relieved him of his hat, ulster, and stick, and we were comfortable in my worn chairs with glasses of brandy in hand to ward off the spring chill, that I asked him by what sorcery he'd divined my late activity.

"The printers' ink upon your hands, on a day when no newspapers are delivered, is evidence; the rest is surmise, based upon familiarity with the company and the one story that has claimed the interest of every journal in the country this past week. Having experienced war at firsthand, you are scarcely an enthusiast of sword-rattling rhetoric; but you are a chronic investor, who prides himself upon his determination to wrest every scrap of intelligence from a venture before he takes the plunge. The rest is simple arithmetic."

"You haven't lost your touch," said I, shaking my head.

"And yet I fear I shall, should I remain in this calm another week. There isn't a criminal with imagination left on our island. They have all emigrated to America to run for public office."

His voice was jocular, but he appeared drawn. I recognised with alarum the look of desperation which had driven him to unhealthy practices in the past. Instead, he had come to me, and I was heartily glad to serve as substitute.

"Well, I don't propose to ask you to investigate the *Uitlanders* in South Africa," I remarked.

He threw his cigarette, which he had just lit, into the grate, a gesture of irritation.

"The fare would be a waste. Anyone with eyes

in his head can see there will be war, and that it will be no holiday for Her Majesty's troops. Heed my advice and restrict your gambling to the turf."

Holmes was prickly company when he was agitated. Fortunately, I did not have to cast far to strike a subject that might distract him from his boredom, which in his case could be fatal. The situation had been nearly as much on my mind of late as the squabbling on the Ivory Coast. However, a cautious approach was required, as the circumstances were anathema to his icy faculties of reason.

"As a matter of fact," I teased, "I have been in the way of a matter that may present some features of interest. However, I hesitate to bring it up."

"Old fellow, this is no time in life to acquire discretion. It suits you little." He lifted his head, as a hound does when the wind shifts from the direction of a wood where game is in residence.

"My dear Holmes, let's pretend I said nothing. The thing is beneath you."

"You are an open book, unequal to the skills of a confidence-man dangling bait. Get on with you, and leave the techniques of obverse alienism to the likes of Dr. Freud." In spite of the irony in his speech, he was well and truly on the scent.

"It is just that I know your opinions on the subject."

"What subject is that?" he demanded.

"The supernatural."

"Bah! Spare me your bogey tales."

He pretended disappointment, but I knew him better than to accept appearances. He could disguise his person from me with wigs and rubber noses, but not his smouldering curiosity.

"You are aware, perhaps, that I am a consulting physician to the staff of St. Porphyry's Hospital in Battersea?"

"I know St. Poor's," he said. "My testimony at the Assizes sent a murderer there, bypassing the scaffold, and there are at least two bank robbers jittering in front of gullible medical experts who ought to be rotting in Reading Gaol."

I could not determine whether he was wishing incarceration upon the robbers or the doctors. Either way, I was annoyed.

"St. Porphyry's is a leader in the modern treatment of lunacy. It's not a bolt-hole for charlatans."

"I did not mean to suggest it was. Pray continue. This penchant for withholding the most important feature until the end may please the readers of your tales, but it exhausts my store of patience."

"To be brief," said I, "there is a patient there at present who's convinced himself he's the Devil."

He nodded thoughtfully. "That's on its way towards balancing the account. Bedlam has two Christs and a Moses."

"Have they succeeded in convincing anyone besides themselves?"

He saw my direction, and lit another cigarette with an air of exaggerated insouciance. Thus did I know he was sniffing at the pit I had dug and covered with leaves.

"It's no revelation that he's found some tormented souls in residence who agree with him. There's more sport in bear-baiting."

"It isn't just some of the patients, Holmes," I said, springing the trap. "There are at least two nurses on the staff, and one doctor, who are absolutely unshakeable in the conviction that this fellow is Satan Incarnate."

Within the hour, we were aboard a coach bound for Battersea, the telegraph poles clicking past, quite in time with the working of Holmes's brain. He hammered me with questions, seeking to string the morsels of information I'd already provided into a chronological narrative. It was an old trick of his, not unlike the process of mesmerisation; he worried me for every detail, mundane though it may have been, and in so doing caused me to recall incidents that had been related to me, and which I had seen for myself, but had since forgotten.

My regular practice having stagnated, I had succumbed at last to persistent entreaties from my friend and colleague, Dr. James Menitor, chief alienist at St. Porphyry's, to observe the behaviour of his more challenging patients twice a week and offer my opinion upon their treatment. In this I suspect he thought my close exposure to Holmes's detective techniques would prove useful, and I had been rather too flattered by his determination, and intrigued by the diversion, to put him off any longer.

Dr. Menitor was particularly eager to consult with me in the case of a patient known only as John Smith; at which point in my narration I was interrupted by a derisive snort from Holmes.

"A *nom de romance*," said he, "lacking even the virtue of originality. If I cannot have imagination in my criminals, let me at least have it in my lunatics."

"It was the staff who christened him thus, in lieu of any other identification. Dr. Menitor insists upon treating patients as individuals, not as mere case numbers. Smith was apprehended verbally accosting strollers along the Thames, and committed by Scotland Yard for observation. It seems he told the constable that he was engaged on his annual expedition to snare souls."

"I hadn't realised there was a season. When was this?"

"Three days ago. It was fortuitous you dropped in upon me when you did, for Mr. Smith has indicated he will be returning to the netherworld this very night."

"*Walpurgisnacht*," said Holmes.

"Bless you," said I; for I thought he had sneezed.

"Thank you, but I am quite uncongested. *Walpurgisnacht* is a Teutonic superstition; not worthy of discussion in our scientific age, but possibly of interest to the deluded mind. Has your John Smith a foreign accent?"

"No. As a matter of fact, his speech is British upper class. I wonder that no one has reported him missing."

"I know a number of families in the West End with good reason not to in that situation." He shrugged. "It appears I am guilty, then, of a non sequitur. The date may not be significant. What has he done to support his claim, apart from wandering the hospital corridors, snatching at gnats?"

"Would that were the case. He has already nearly caused the death of one patient and jeopardised the career of a nurse whose professional behaviour was impeccable before he arrived."

Holmes's eyes grew alight in the reflection of the match he had set to his pipe. Violence and disgrace were details dear to his detective's heart.

I continued my report. On his first day in residence, Smith was observed in close whispered conversation with a young man named Tom Turner, who suffered from the conviction that he was Socrates, the ancient Greek sage. Dr. Menitor had been pleased with Turner's progress since he'd been admitted six months previously, wearing a bedsheet wrapped about him in the manner of a toga, bent over and speaking in a voice cracked with age, when in fact he was barely four-and-twenty; he had of his own volition recently resumed contemporary dress, and had even commenced to score off his delusion with self-deprecating wit, an encouraging sign that sanity was returning.

All that changed after his encounter with John Smith.

Minutes after the pair separated, young Turner had opened a supply closet and was prevented from ingesting the contents of a bottle of chlorine bleach only by strenuous intervention by a male orderly who'd happened to be passing. Placed in restraints in the infirmary, the young man raved in his cracked old voice that he must have his hemlock, else how could Socrates fulfill his destiny?

"A madman who reads Plutarch. Perhaps not such an oddity after all."

"Holmes, please!" I deplored his callousness.

"*Mea culpa*, my friend. Pray continue, and I shall endeavour not to be impertinent."

Mollified, I went on.

Confronted by Dr. Menitor after the episode, John Smith smiled blandly.

"Good physician," he said, "when he was Socrates, his acquaintance was worthy of pursuing, but as a plain pudding of the middle class, he was a bore. I am overstocked with Tom Turners, but my inventory of great philosophers is dangerously low."

"Holmes," said I, "neither Menitor nor myself can explain just what Smith said to Turner that overturned the work of months. He will not be drawn out upon the subject."

"And what of the disgraced nurse?"

"Martha Brant has worked at St. Porphyry's for twenty years without so much as a spot on her record. It was her key to the supply closet Turner had in his possession when he was apprehended."

"Stolen?"

"Given, by her own account."

"Hum."

"When questioned, she confessed to removing the key from its ring and surrendering it to Turner. She insisted that she was commanded to do so by Smith. She became hysterical during the interrogation. Dr. Menitor was forced to sedate her with morphine and confine her to a private room, where she remains, attended by another nurse on the staff. Before she lost consciousness, Miss Brant insisted that Smith is the Prince of Lies, precisely as he claims."

"What has been done with Smith in the meantime?"

"At present, he is locked up in the criminal ward. However, that has not stopped him from exercising an unhealthy influence upon all of St. Porphyry's. Since his incarceration, a previously dependable orderly has been sacked for stealing food from the kitchen pantry and selling it to the owner of a public-house in the neighbourhood, and restlessness among the patients has increased to the point where Menitor refuses to step outside his own consulting-room without first placing a loaded revolver in his pocket. The orderlies have all been put on their guard, for an uprising is feared.

"It's for my friend I'm concerned," I continued. "He has been forced to replace the nurse in charge of Miss Brant and assign her to less demanding duties elsewhere in the hospital;

the poor girl has come to agree with her that Smith is the Devil. It's true that she's a devout Catholic, belonging to an order that believes in demonic obsession and the cleansing effects of exorcism. However, Miss Brant herself is a down-to-earth sort who was never before heard to express any opinion that was not well-founded in medical science. And when I was there yesterday, I found Menitor in a highly agitated state, and disinclined to rule out the Black Arts as a cause for his present miseries. I fear the situation has unhinged him.

"I hope you will consider me your client in this affair," I concluded.

"Hum," said Holmes again, and pulled at his pipe. "Under ordinary circumstances, I would dismiss this fellow Smith as nothing more than a talented student of the principles taught by the late Franz Mesmer. However, I doubt even that estimable practitioner was capable of entrancing the entire population of a London hospital."

"It is more than that. I've met the fellow, and I can state with absolute certainty that I've never encountered anyone who impressed me so thoroughly that he is the living embodiment of evil. This was before the Turner incident, and we exchanged nothing more than casual greetings; yet his mere presence filled me with dread."

"Insanity is a contagion, Watson. I've seen it before, and no amount of persuasion will force me to concede that prolonged exposure to it is less dangerous than an outbreak of smallpox. Do you limit your visits to St. Poor's, lest you contract it as well. I have never been stimulated by your intellect, but I have come to rely upon your granite pragmatism. Sense is not common, and wisdom is anything but conventional. You must guard them as if they were the crown jewels."

"Is it then your theory that this situation may be explained away as mass hysteria?"

"I refuse to theorise until I have made the acquaintance of Mr. John Smith."

St. Porphyry's Hospital was Georgian, but only in so far as it had been rebuilt from the ruins of the Reformation. Parts of it dated back to William the Conqueror, and I once knew an antiquarian who insisted it was constructed on the site of a Roman temple. It had been by turns a redoubt, a prison, and an abbey, but the addition of some modern architectural features had softened somewhat the medieval gloom I felt whenever I entered its grounds; but not today. The air itself crawled with the horrors of human sacrifice.

The dread sensation increased when we crossed the threshold. An agitated orderly conducted us down the narrow corridor that led past the common room—the heavy door to which was locked up tight—to Dr. Menitor's consulting-room at the back. A stout rubber truncheon hung from a strap round his wrist, and he gripped it with knuckles white. The ancient walls seemed to murmur an unintelligible warning as we passed; it was the sound of the patients, muttering to themselves behind locked doors. This general confinement was by no means a common practice in that establishment. It had been added since my last visit.

We found my friend Menitor in an advanced state of nervous excitement, worse than the one I had left him in not twenty-four hours before. He appeared to have lost weight, and his fallen face was as white as his hair, which I had sworn still bore traces of its original dark colour at our parting. He shook our hands listlessly, dismissed the orderly with an air of distraction, and addressed my companion in a bleating tone I scarcely credited as his.

"I am honoured, Mr. Holmes," said he, "but I fear even your skills are no match for the fate that has befallen this institution to which I have dedicated my entire professional life. St. Porphyry's is damned."

"Has something happened since I left?" I asked, alarmed by his resignation.

"Two of my best orderlies have quit, and I've taken to arming the rest, much good has it done them. None will go near Room Six, even to push a plate of bread through the portal in the door. 'You cannot starve the Devil,' said one, when I attempted to upbraid him for this insubordina-tion. And who am I to lay blame? I'd sooner face a pack of Rider Haggard's lions than approach that colony of Hell."

"Come, come." Holmes was impatient. "Consider: If Smith's assertion is genuine, no door fashioned by the hand of Man can hold him. His continued presence there is proof enough he's either mad or a charlatan."

"You don't know him, Mr. Holmes. We're just his playthings. It pleases him at present to remain where he is and turn brave men into cowards and good women into familiars. When he tires of that, he'll slither out through the bars and bid the maws of the underworld to open and swallow us all."

His voice rose to a shrill cackle—cut off suddenly, as by the sheer will of whatever reason he retained within him.

I went into action without waiting for Holmes's signal. I forced him into a chair with my hand upon his shoulder, strode to the cabinet where he kept a flask of brandy, poured a generous draught into a glass, and commanded him to drink.

He drank off half the elixir in one motion. It seemed to fortify him. He took another sip and set the glass on the corner of his desk. Colour climbed his sallow cheeks.

"Thank you, John. I apologise, Mr. Holmes. I don't mind telling you I've questioned my own rationality throughout this affair. It's more comforting to believe myself mad than to accept the only other explanation that suggests itself."

Holmes's own cold tones were as bracing as the spirits.

"Only the sane question their sanity, Doctor. Until this business is concluded, however, I suggest you let Haggard be and turn your attention towards the Messrs. Gilbert and Sullivan. Their shoguns and pirates are healthier fare in trying times. Later, perhaps, you will agree to collaborate with me on a monograph about the unstable nature of the criminal mind in general. Certainly only an irrational individual would consider committing a felony as long as Sherlock Holmes is in practice."

"Bless you, sir, for the attempt; but I fear I've passed the point where an outrageous remark will lift the bleakness from my soul. Smith has taken the hindmost, and that unfortunate is I."

At that moment, the clock upon his mantel struck seven. Menitor started.

"Five hours left!" he moaned. "He's pledged to quit this world at midnight, and we shall all accompany him."

"I, for one, never embark upon a long voyage without first taking the measure of the captain," Holmes said. "Where is the key to Room Six?"

A great deal of persuasion, and another injection of brandy, were necessary before Dr. Menitor would part with the key to the room in which John Smith had been shut. He wore it, like the poetic albatross, on a cord round his neck. Holmes took it from his hand and instructed me to stay behind with Menitor.

I shook my head. "I'm going with you. We've faced every other devil together. Why not the Dark Lord himself?"

"Your other friend needs you more."

"He will sleep. I slipped a mild solution of morphine into his second drink." In fact, Menitor was already insensate in his chair, with a more peaceful expression upon his face than he had worn in days.

Holmes nodded curtly. "Then by all means, let us deal with the devil we don't know."

The criminal ward occupied most of the ancient keep, with Room Six at the top. Sturdy bars in the windows separated the occupant from a hundred-foot drop to the flags below. I had brought my old service revolver, and Holmes instructed me to stand back with it cocked and in hand as he turned the key in the lock.

This precaution proved unnecessary, as we found the patient seated peacefully upon the cot that represented the room's only furnishing. He was dressed neatly but simply in the patched clothing that had been donated to the hospital by the city's charitable institutions, and the shoes he'd worn when he was brought there, shiny black patent-leathers to match his formal dress, from which all the tailor's labels had been removed.

In appearance, there was little about John Smith to support his demonic claim. He was fair, with a windblown mop of blonde curls, moustaches in need of trimming, and a sprinkling of golden whiskers to attest to his three days without a razor. He was a dozen or so pounds overweight. I should have judged his age to be about thirty, and yet there was a quality in his eyes—large, and of the palest blue imaginable—that suggested the bleakness of an uninhabited room, as if they had witnessed more than one lifetime and remained unchanged.

There was, too, an attitude of mockery in his smile, outwardly polite and welcoming, that seemed to reduce everything and everyone he turned it upon to insignificance. I do not know if it was these features or the man himself who filled me with such dread and loathing. I closed the door and stationed myself with my back to it, the revolver in my pocket now, but still cocked in my hand.

"Mr. Sherlock Holmes," he greeted in his soft, modulated voice, gentled further by a West End accent. "The engravings in the public journals do you little justice. You have the brow of a philosopher."

"Indeed? A late gentleman of my acquaintance once remarked that there was less frontal development than he'd expected."

"Dear Professor Moriarty. Thank you for that unexpected gift. I did not have him down for another decade when you pitched him over those falls."

Holmes was unimpressed by this intelligence; the story of his last meeting with that blackguardly academic was well known to readers of the account I had published in *The Strand* magazine.

"Shall I address you familiarly as Lucifer, or Your Dark Majesty?" Holmes asked evenly. "I'm ignorant as to the protocol."

"Smith will do. I find it difficult to keep track of all my titles myself. How did you make out on that Milverton affair, by the way? The Dreyfuss business had me distracted."

At this Holmes hesitated, and I was hard put to disguise my astonishment. The case of the late blackmailer Charles Augustus Milverton had only recently been concluded, in a most shocking fashion, and its circumstances enjoined me from reporting it publicly for an indefinite period. Holmes's involvement was unknown even to Scotland Yard.

He changed the subject, dissembling his own thoughts on Smith's sources.

"I have come to ask you what was your motive in attempting to destroy Tom Turner," said he. "I shan't accept that fable you told Dr. Menitor."

Smith replied, "I must have my amusements. Arranging wars and corrupting governments requires close concentration over long periods. You have your quaint chemical experiments to divert you from your labours upon your clients' behalf; I have my pursuit of unprepossessing souls. Exquisite miniatures, I call them. One day I hope to show you my display."

"It's a pity Turner escaped your net."

"Fortunately, St. Porphyry's offers a variety of other possibilities." The patient appeared unmoved by Holmes's thrust.

"So I am told. A career ruined, another besmirched, and a third severely straitened. Will you add violent insurrection to your exhibit?"

"Alas, there may not be time. I depart at midnight."

"Do you miss home so much?"

"I am not going home just yet. If Menitor gave you that impression, he misunderstood me. This has been a pleasant holiday, but there is work for me in Whitehall and upon the continent. Your Foreign Secretary shows indications of being entirely too reasonable at Bloemfontein, and the Kaiser is far too comfortable with his country's borders. Also, the Americans have grown complacent with the indestructibility of their presidents. A trip abroad may be warranted. It isn't as if the situation at home will go to Hell in my absence." He chuckled.

"Blighter!" I could no longer restrain myself.

He turned that infernal smile upon me, and with it those vacant, soulless eyes.

"I congratulate you, Doctor. In matters of detective science you remain Holmes's trained baboon, but as a master of classic British understatement you have no peer."

"Your own grasp of the obvious comes close," Holmes observed. "How pedestrian that you should choose this of all nights to plan your escape."

"It's hardly an escape. It's pleased me to have stayed this long in residence. *Walpurgisnacht*, that brief excursion when dead walk and witches convene, has a paralysing effect upon those who still credit it. However, it requires renewal from time to time. Perhaps after tonight, you will believe as well."

Holmes made a little bow. "I accept the challenge, Mr. Smith. We shall return at midnight."

"Shall I offer you kingdoms then?"

The detective paused with his hand on the door. "I beg your pardon?"

"I should admire to have you sit at my right hand throughout eternity, as your mind is nearly as clever and devious as my own. Upon second thought, however, kingdoms would offer you scarce temptation, as any comic-opera monarch who has tried to purchase your loyalty with promises of great wealth can attest. Cocaine, perhaps. Or morphine: bushels and barrels of it without end. My poppy fields are vast beyond measure. You need never suffer the horrors of static reality again."

Outside the room, Holmes locked the door, his hand trembling ever so faintly as he twisted the key. He led me down the first flight of stairs, a finger to his lips. On the landing he stopped.

"We are out of earshot now, Watson. What is your opinion?"

"He is cruel enough to be whom he says he is. I should have smote him with my pistol for that despicable last remark."

"I meant about his timetable. Midnight is but four and one-half hours distant, and he has pledged to quit these premises today."

"I don't trust him, Holmes. Whatever devilry he has planned won't wait."

"I disagree. In his way he considers himself

an honourable fellow. Tricksters never cheat. It robs them of their triumph."

"However did he know about the Milverton case?"

"That was a bit of a knockup, was it not? Milverton may have had a partner after all—either Smith, or one he's been in communication with. Smuggled intelligence is a parlour trick. Mind-readers and spiritualists have been using it for years. We shall ask him after the stroke of twelve. How long will Menitor sleep?"

"Until early morning, I should say."

"While he is incommoded, you are St. Poor's ranking medical authority. I advise you to place a guard upon Smith's door and another outside, at the base of the tower. I suspect our friend is too enamoured of his confidence skills to attempt anything so vulgar as an escape by force or an assault upon the bars of his window, to say nothing of the precipitous drop that awaits; still, one cannot be too careful. While we are waiting, I suggest we avail ourselves of the comforts of that public-house you mentioned earlier."

Holmes's expression was eager. It carried no hint of the irritable *ennui* he had worn to my consulting-room. Although I was loath to own to it, I had the Devil to thank for that, at least.

"You must think of it as if you'd borrowed from our century, and must repay the full amount," Holmes explained. "You would not return ninety-nine guineas and imagine that you had discharged your debt of one hundred. Therefore, you cannot consider that the twentieth century has begun until 1900 has come and gone."

We had enjoyed a meal of bangers-and-mash at our corner table, and were now relaxing over whiskies-and-soda; taking our time over the latter lest their depressant qualities rob us of reflexes we might need later that evening. Holmes had refused to discuss Smith since we had entered the public-house.

"I understand it now that you have explained it," said I, "but I doubt your example will prevent all London from attending the pyrotech-

nics display over the Thames come the first of January."

"Appearances are clever liars; much like friend Smith."

I saw then that he was ready to return to the subject of our visit to Battersea.

"Is it your theory, then, that he is posing as a madman?"

"I have not made up my mind. Madmen lie better than most, for they manage to convince themselves as well as their listeners. If he is posing, we shall know once midnight has passed and he is still a guest of St. Poor's. A lunatic, once confronted with the evidence of his delusion, either becomes agitated or substitutes another for the one that has betrayed him. A liar attempts to explain it away. Conventional liars are invariably rational."

"But what could be his motive?"

"That remains to be seen. He may be acting in concert with an accomplice, distracting me from some other crime committed somewhere far away from this place to which we've been decoyed: Your position on the staff, and your reputation as my companion, may have given them the idea.

"Yes," he continued; "I think that scenario more likely than Smith enjoying making mischief and laying the guilt at Satan's door. Or such is my hope. In these times of temptation, any unscrupulous or lecherous man of the cloth is capable of the latter. I am no connoisseur of the ordinary."

"What do you think he meant when he spoke of Africa and Germany and America?"

"If I were Beelzebub, or pretending to be, I couldn't think of better places for calamity."

The publican announced that the establishment would be closing shortly. He was a narrow, rat-faced fellow, quite the opposite of the merry rubicund alesman of quaint English legend, and just the sort who would purchase provisions from a hospital orderly with no questions asked.

"What need for watches, when we have merchants?" Holmes enquired. "Shall we watch the patient in Room Six unfold his leathery wings and fly to the sound of mortals in torment?"

There was a different orderly at the door, built along the lines of a prizefighter, who held his truncheon as if it were an extension of his right arm. His predecessor had told him of our expected return. He reported that all was quiet. After a brief visit to Dr. Menitor's consulting-room to confirm that he continued to sleep soundly beneath the blanket I had spread over him, I rejoined Holmes, who had retained the key to John Smith's cell. I gripped my revolver as he unlocked the door.

Smith looked as if he had not moved in our absence. He sat with his hands resting on his thighs and his mocking smile firmly in place.

"How was the service?" he asked.

Holmes was unshaken by this assumption of our recent whereabouts.

"You're inconsistent. If you indeed saw into our minds, you would know the answer to that question."

"You confuse me with my former Master. I am not omniscient."

"In that case, the service was indifferent, but the fare above the average—surprising, in view of the proprietor's *laissez-faire* attitude regarding the source of his stock. We would have brought you a sample, but it might slow your flight."

Smith chuckled once more, in that way that chilled me to the bone.

"I shall miss you, Holmes. I am sorry my holiday can't be extended. I should have admired to snare your soul. I could build a new display with it in the centre."

"And to think only a few hours ago you offered me a seat at the head table."

"That offer has expired."

"Still, you exalt me. Dr. Watson is the better catch. He has the fairest soul in all of England, and the noblest heart."

Smith stroked his chin thoughtfully, as if he expected to find a spade-shaped beard there out of a children's illustrated guide to Holy Writ.

"I shall not be gone forever. If I return in a year, will you wager your friend's fair soul that I cannot vanquish you in a game of wits?"

"Twaddle!" I exclaimed; and looked to Holmes for support. But his reaction surprised and unnerved me. When he was amused, his own cold chuckle was nearly a match for Smith's. Instead, he appeared to grow a shade more pale, and raised a stubborn chin.

"You will forgive me if I decline the invitation," said he simply.

Smith shrugged. "It is one minute to midnight."

"You have no watch," I said.

"I told the time before there were clocks and watches."

I groped for the timepiece in my pocket, eager to prove him wrong, if only by seconds. Holmes stopped me with a nearly infinitesimal shake of his head. His eyes remained upon Smith. I clutched the revolver in my pocket, tightly enough to make my hand ache.

The first throb of Big Ben's iron bell penetrated the keep's thick wall.

"One minute, precisely," Smith said. "I don't pretend to think you will accept my word on that."

The bell bonged a second time; a third, fourth. We three remained absolutely motionless.

Upon the seventh stroke, the play of a cloud against the moon cast Smith's face in precise halves of light and dark, making of it a Harlequin mask. Still none of us stirred.

Eight.

Nine. The shadow passed; his visage was fully illuminated once again.

Ten.

Eleven. Another cloud, larger and denser than its predecessor, blotted out the light. The man seated on the cot was a figure drenched in black. I nearly squeezed the trigger in my confusion as to what he might be up to in the shadows. Only my old military training, and my long exposure to Holmes's own iron nerve, allowed me to hold my fire.

Came the final knell. It seemed to reverberate long after it had passed. Silence followed, as complete as the grave.

"Right." Holmes stirred. "Wake up, Smith. St. Walpurgis has fled, and you are still with us."

The moon now fell full upon the seated man. He raised his head. Relief swept through me. I relaxed my grip. Circulation returned tingling to my hand.

John Smith blinked, looked round.

"What is this place?" His gaze fell upon Holmes. "Who the devil are you?"

To this day, I cannot encompass the change that took place in the man in Room Six after Big Ben had finished his ageless report. He was still the same figure, fair and blue-eyed and inclining towards stout, but the mocking smile had vanished and his eyes had become expressive, as if whoever had decamped from them days before had returned. Most unsettling of all, his upper-class British accent was gone, replaced by the somewhat nasal tones of an American of English stock.

"Stop staring at me, you clods, and tell me where you've taken me. By God, you'll answer to Lord Penderbroke before this day is out. He's expecting me for dinner."

The young man's story would not be shaken, even when Holmes admitted failure and sent for Inspector Lestrade, whose brutish technique for obtaining confessions made up to a great extent for his shortcomings as a practical investigator. It was eventually corroborated when Lord Penderbroke himself was summoned and confirmed the young man's identity as Jeffrey Vestle, son of the Boston industrialist Cornelius Vestle, who had dispatched him to London to request the hand of his lordship's daughter in marriage and merge their American fortune with noble blood. Young Vestle had failed to keep a dinner appointment three days before, and the police had been combing the regular hospitals and mortuaries to determine whether he'd come to misfortune; private hospitals and lunatic asylums were at the bottom of the list.

Lestrade, in conference with Holmes and me in Dr. Menitor's consulting-room, was shame-faced.

"I daresay you have the advantage of me this one time, Mr. Holmes. The constables who brought the fellow here didn't recognise him from the description."

Holmes was grave.

"You won't hear it from me, Inspector. When the first stone is cast, you will hardly be the one it strikes."

Lestrade thanked him, although it was clear he knew not what to make of the remark, or of the grim humour in which it was delivered.

The mystery of the Devil of St. Porphyry's Hospital is a first in the matter that I was the client of record; but it is a first also in that I have chosen to place it before the public without a solution.

Dr. Menitor was satisfied, for with the departure of "John Smith," exited also the curse that seemed to have befallen his institution. He erased the mark from Nurse Brant's record and reinstated the temporarily larcenous orderly, assigning their lapses to strain connected with overwork, as he had dismissed his own emotional crisis, and thanked Holmes and me profusely for our intervention.

Holmes himself never refers to the case, except to hold it up as an example of *amnesia dysplacia*, a temporary loss of identity upon young Vestle's part, complicated by dementia, and brought on by stress, possibly related to his forthcoming nuptials.

"I might, in his place, have been stricken similarly," he says. "I met Penderbroke's daughter." But the humour rings hollow.

He considers his role in the affair that of a passive observer, and therefore not one of his successes. In this I am inclined to agree, but for a different reason.

I do not know that "John Smith" was the Devil, having left Jeffrey Vestle's body for a brief holiday from his busy schedule; I cannot say that Holmes's scientific explanation for the phenomenon—in which, I am bound to say, Dr.

Menitor concurred—is not the correct one. I fervently hope it is. However, it does not explain how Smith/Vestle knew of the Milverton business, cloaked in secrecy as it was by the only two people who could give evidence (and never would, as to do so would lay us open to a charge of complicity in murder). At the time of that incident, the young Bostonian was three thousand miles away in Massachusetts, and in no position to connect himself with either Milverton or his fate. I am at a loss to supply such a connection, and too sensitive of Holmes's avoidance of the issue to bring it up.

Lack of evidence is not evidence, and such evidence as I possess is at best circumstantial.

Within months of Smith's leaving Vestle's body, the Bloemfontein Conference in South Africa came to grief over the British Foreign Secretary's refusal to back away from his political position and an ultimatum from Paul Krueger, the Boer leader, precipitating our nation into a long and tragic armed conflict with the Boers.

Less than two years later, on September 6, 1901, William McKinley, the American President, was fatally shot by a lone assassin in Buffalo, New York.

All the world knows what happened in August 1914, when Kaiser Wilhelm II invaded France, violating Belgium's neutrality and bringing Germany to war with England, and eventually the world. That prediction of Smith's took longer to become reality, but its effects will be with us for another century at least.

Regardless of whether Sherlock Holmes sparred with the Devil, or of whether the Devil exists, I know there is evil in our world. I know, too, that there is a great good, and I found myself in the presence of both in Room Six at St. Poor's.

For one fleeting moment, my friend put aside his pragmatic convictions and refused, even in jest, to gamble with Satan over my soul. I say again that he was the best and the wisest man I have ever known; and I challenge you, the reader, to suggest one better and wiser.

KEEPING THE
MEMORY GREEN

The Strange Case of the Megatherium Thefts

S. C. ROBERTS

IN THE WORLD of Sherlock Holmes, Sir Sydney Castle Roberts (1887–1966) was the well-known author of such classic Holmesian volumes as *Doctor Watson: Prolegomena to the Study of a Biographical Problem* (1931), a chapbook that was the first study devoted entirely to Watson; *Christmas Eve* (1936), a one-act play parodying Holmes that Roberts had privately printed as a gift for his friends and acquaintances in the Sherlockian community; and *Holmes and Watson: A Miscellany* (1953), a collection of scholarly essays about the great detective and his amanuensis. His affection for Holmes and his devotion to studying and writing about him earned him the presidency of the Sherlock Holmes Society of London.

Roberts's accomplishments, however, went far beyond Holmes. He was recognized as a major figure in British publishing and education, serving as Secretary of Cambridge University Press from 1922 to 1948, Master of Pembroke College, Cambridge, from 1948 to 1958, Vice-Chancellor of the University of Cambridge from 1949 to 1951, and Chairman of the British Film Institute from 1952 to 1956. He was given a knighthood in 1958. Three portraits of Roberts hang in the National Portrait Gallery, London.

Among his many works are books about Cambridge, publishing, and such biographies as *The Story of Doctor Johnson: Being an Introduction to Boswell's Life* (1919), *Doctor Johnson in Cambridge: Essays in Boswellian Imitation* (1922), *Lord Macaulay: The Pre-eminent Victorian* (1927), and *Adventures with Authors* (1966).

"The Strange Case of the Megatherium Thefts" was first published as a privately printed chapbook in an edition of one hundred twenty-five copies (Cambridge, University Press, 1945); it was first commercially published in *Holmes and Watson: A Miscellany* (London, Oxford University Press, 1953).

THE STRANGE CASE OF THE MEGATHERIUM THEFTS

S. C. Roberts

I HAVE ALREADY had occasion, in the course of these reminiscences of my friend Sherlock Holmes, to refer to his liking for the Diogenes Club, the club which contained the most unsociable men in London and forbade talking save in the Strangers' Room. So far as I am aware, this was the only club to which Holmes was attracted, and it struck me as not a little curious that he should have been called upon to solve the extraordinary mystery of the Megatherium Thefts.

It was a dull afternoon in November and Holmes, turning wearily from the cross-indexing of some old newspaper-cuttings, drew his chair near to mine and took out his watch.

"How slow life has become, my dear Watson," he said, "since the successful conclusion of that little episode in a lonely west-country village. Here we are back amongst London's millions and nobody wants us."

He crossed to the window, opened it a little, and peered through the November gloom into Baker Street.

"No, Watson, I'm wrong. I believe we are to have a visitor."

"Is there someone at the door?"

"Not yet. But a hansom has stopped opposite to it. The passenger has alighted and there is a heated discussion in progress concerning the fare. I cannot hear the argument in detail, but it is a lively one."

A few minutes later the visitor was shown into the sitting-room—a tall, stooping figure with a straggling white beard, shabbily dressed and generally unkempt. He spoke with a slight stutter.

"M-Mr. Sherlock Holmes?" he inquired.

"That is my name," replied Holmes, "and this is my friend, Dr. Watson."

The visitor bowed jerkily and Holmes continued: "And whom have I the honour of addressing?"

"My n-name is Wiskerton—Professor Wiskerton—and I have ventured to call upon you in connexion with a most remarkable and puzzling affair."

"We are familiar with puzzles in this room, Professor."

"Ah, but not with any like this one. You see, apart from my p-professorial standing, I am one of the oldest members of——"

"The Megatherium?"

"My dear sir, how did you know?"

"Oh, there was no puzzle about that. I happened to hear some reference in your talk with the cabman to your journey having begun at Waterloo Place. Clearly you had travelled from one of two clubs and somehow I should not associate you with the United Services."

"You're p-perfectly right, of course. The driver of that cab was a rapacious scoundrel. It's s-scandalous that——"

"But you have not come to consult me about an extortionate cab-driver?"

"No, no. Of course not. It's about——"

"The Megatherium?"

"Exactly. You see, I am one of the oldest m-members and have been on the Committee

278

for some years. I need hardly tell you the kind of standing which the Megatherium has in the world of learning, Mr. Holmes."

"Dr. Watson, I have no doubt, regards the institution with veneration. For myself, I prefer the soothing atmosphere of the Diogenes."

"The w-what?"

"The Diogenes Club."

"N-never heard of it."

"Precisely. It is a club of which people are not meant to hear—but I beg your pardon for this digression. You were going to say?"

"I was g-going to say that the most distressing thing has happened. I should explain in the first place that in addition to the n-noble collection of books in the Megatherium library, a collection which is one of our most valuable assets, we have available at any one time a number of books from one of the circulating libraries and——"

"And you are losing them?"

"Well—yes, in fact we are. But how did you know?"

"I didn't know—I merely made a deduction. When a client begins to describe his possessions to me, it is generally because some misfortune has occurred in connexion with them."

"But this is m-more than a m-misfortune, Mr. Holmes. It is a disgrace, an outrage, a——"

"But what, in fact, has happened?"

"Ah, I was c-coming to that. But perhaps it would be simpler if I showed you this document and let it speak for itself. P-personally, I think it was a mistake to circulate it, but the Committee over-ruled me and now the story will be all over London and we shall still be no nearer a solution."

Professor Wiskerton fumbled in his pocket and produced a printed document marked *Private and Confidential* in bold red type.

"What do you m-make of it, Mr. Holmes? Isn't it extraordinary? Here is a club whose members are selected from among the most distinguished representatives of the arts and sciences and this is the way they treat the c-club property."

Holmes paid no attention to the Professor's

rambling commentary and continued his reading of the document.

"You have brought me quite an interesting case, Professor," he said, at length.

"But it is more than interesting, Mr. Holmes. It is astonishing. It is inexplicable."

"If it were capable of easy explanation, it would cease to be interesting and, furthermore, you would not have spent the money on a cab-fare to visit me."

"That, I suppose, is true. But what do you advise, Mr. Holmes?"

"You must give me a little time, Professor. Perhaps you will be good enough to answer one or two questions first?"

"Willingly."

"This document states that your Committee is satisfied that no member of the staff is implicated. You are satisfied yourself on that point?"

"I am not s-satisfied about anything, Mr. Holmes. As one who has s-spent a great part of his life amongst books and libraries, the whole subject of the maltreatment of books is repugnant to me. Books are my life-blood, Mr. Holmes. But perhaps I have not your s-sympathy?"

"On the contrary, Professor, I have a genuine interest in such matters. For myself, however, I travel in those byways of bibliophily which are associated with my own profession."

Holmes moved across to a shelf and took out a volume with which I had long been familiar.

"Here, Professor," he continued, "if I may rid myself of false modesty for the moment, is a little monograph of mine *Upon the Distinction Between the Ashes of the Various Tobaccos*."

"Ah, most interesting, Mr. Holmes. Not being a smoker myself, I cannot pretend to appraise your work from the point of view of scholarship, but as a bibliophile and especially as a c-collector of out-of-the-way monographs, may I ask whether the work is still available?"

"That is a spare copy, Professor; you are welcome to it."

The Professor's eyes gleamed with voracious pleasure.

"But, Mr. Holmes, this is m-most generous of you. May I b-beg that you will inscribe it? I derive a special delight from what are called 'association copies.'"

"Certainly," said Holmes, with a smile, as he moved to the writing-table.

"Thank you, thank you," murmured the Professor, "but I fear I have distracted you from the main issue."

"Not at all."

"But what is your p-plan, Mr. Holmes? Perhaps you would like to have a look round the Megatherium? Would you care, for instance, to have luncheon to-morrow—but no, I fear I am engaged at that time. What about a c-cup of tea at 4 o'clock?"

"With pleasure. I trust I may bring Dr. Watson, whose co-operation in such cases has frequently been of great value?"

"Oh-er-yes, certainly."

But it did not seem to me that there was much cordiality in his assent.

"Very well, then," said Holmes. "The document which you have left with me gives the facts and I will study them with great care."

"Thank you, thank you. To-morrow, then, at 4 o'clock," said the Professor, as he shook hands, "and I shall t-treasure this volume, Mr. Holmes."

He slipped the monograph into a pocket and left us.

"Well, Watson," said Holmes, as he filled his pipe, "What do you make of this curious little case?"

"Very little, at present. I haven't had a chance to examine the data."

"Quite right, Watson. I will reveal them to you." Holmes took up the sheet which the Professor had left.

"This is a confidential letter circulated to members of the Megatherium and dated November 1889. I'll read you a few extracts:

"'In a recent report the Committee drew attention to the serious loss and inconvenience caused by the removal from the Club of books from the circulating library. The practice has continued.... At the end of June, the Club paid for no less than 22 missing volumes. By the end of September 15 more were missing.... The Committee were disposed to ascribe these malpractices to some undetected individual member, but they have regretfully come to the conclusion that more members than one are involved. They are fully satisfied that no member of the staff is in any way implicated.... If the offenders can be identified, the Committee will not hesitate to apply the Rule which empowers expulsion.'

"There, Watson, what do you think of that?"

"Most extraordinary, Holmes—at the Megatherium, of all clubs."

"*Corruptio optimi pessima*, my dear Watson."

"D'you think the Committee is right about the servants?"

"I'm not interested in the Committee's opinions, Watson, even though they be the opinions of Bishops and Judges and Fellows of the Royal Society. I am concerned only with the facts."

"But the facts are simple, Holmes. Books are being stolen in considerable quantities from the club and the thief, or thieves, have not been traced."

"Admirably succinct, my dear Watson. And the motive?"

"The thief's usual motive, I suppose—the lure of illicit gain."

"But what gain, Watson? If you took half a dozen books, with the mark of a circulating library on them, to a secondhand bookseller, how much would you expect to get for them?"

"Very little, certainly, Holmes."

"Yes, and that is why the Committee is probably right in ruling out the servants—not that I believe in ruling out anybody or anything on *a priori* grounds. But the motive of gain won't do. You must try again, Watson."

"Well, of course, people are careless about books, especially when they belong to someone else. Isn't it possible that members take these books away from the club, intending to return them, and then leave them in the train or mislay them at home?"

"Not bad, my dear Watson, and a perfectly reasonable solution if we were dealing with a loss of three or four volumes. In that event our Professor would probably not have troubled to enlist my humble services. But look at the figures, Watson—twenty-two books missing in June, fifteen more in September. There's something more than casual forgetfulness in that."

"That's true, Holmes, and I suppose we can't discover much before we keep our appointment at the Megatherium tomorrow."

"On the contrary, my dear Watson, I hope to pursue a little independent investigation this evening."

"I should be delighted to accompany you, Holmes."

"I am sure you would, Watson, but if you will forgive me for saying so, the little inquiry I have to make is of a personal nature and I think it might be more fruitful if I were alone."

"Oh, very well," I replied, a little nettled at Holmes's superior manner, "I can employ myself very profitably in reading this new work on surgical technique which has just come to hand."

I saw little of Holmes on the following morning. He made no reference to the Megatherium case at breakfast and disappeared shortly afterwards. At luncheon he was in high spirits. There was a gleam in his eye which showed me that he was happily on the trail.

"Holmes," I said, "you have discovered something."

"My dear Watson," he replied, "your acuteness does you credit. I have discovered that after an active morning I am extremely hungry."

But I was not to be put off.

"Come, Holmes, I am too old a campaigner to be bluffed in that way. How far have you penetrated into the Megatherium mystery?"

"Far enough to make me look forward to our tea-party with a lively interest."

Being familiar with my friend's bantering manner, I recognized that it was no good pressing him with further questions for the moment.

Shortly after 4 o'clock Holmes and I presented ourselves at the portals of the Megatherium. The head porter received us very courteously and seemed, I thought, almost to recognize Sherlock Holmes. He conducted us to a seat in the entrance-hall and, as soon as our host appeared, we made our way up the noble staircase to the long drawing-room on the first floor.

"Now let me order some tea," said the Professor. "Do you like anything to eat with it, Mr. Holmes?"

"Just a biscuit for me, Professor, but my friend Watson has an enormous appetite."

"Really, Holmes——" I began.

"No, no. Just a little pleasantry of mine," said Holmes, quickly. I thought I observed an expression of relief on the Professor's face.

"Well, now, about our p-problem, Mr. Holmes. Is there any further information that I can give you?"

"I should like to have a list of the titles of the books which have most recently disappeared."

"Certainly, Mr. Holmes, I can get that for you at once."

The Professor left us for a few minutes and returned with a paper in his hand. I looked over Holmes's shoulder while he read and recognized several well-known books that had been recently published, such as *Robbery under Arms*, *Troy Town*, *The Economic Interpretation of History*, *The Wrong Box*, and *Three Men in a Boat*.

"Do you make any particular deductions from the titles, Mr. Holmes?" the Professor asked.

"I think not," Holmes replied; "there are, of course, certain very popular works of fiction, some other books of more general interest, and a few titles of minor importance. I do not think one could draw any conclusion about the culprit's special sphere of interest."

"You think not? Well, I agree, Mr. Holmes. It is all very b-baffling."

"Ah," said Holmes suddenly, "this title reminds me of something."

"What is that, Mr. Holmes?"

"I see that one of the missing books is *Plain*

Tales from the Hills. It happens that I saw an exceptionally interesting copy of that book not long ago. It was an advance copy, specially bound and inscribed for presentation to the author's godson who was sailing for India before the date of publication."

"Really, Mr. Holmes, really? That is of the greatest interest to me."

"Your own collection, Professor, is, I suspect, rich in items of such a kind?"

"Well, well, it is not for me to b-boast, Mr. Holmes, but I certainly have one or two volumes of unique association value on my shelves. I am a poor man and do not aspire to first folios, but the p-pride of my collection is that it could not have been assembled through the ordinary channels of trade. . . . But to return to our problem, is there anything else in the Club which you would like to investigate?"

"I think not," said Holmes, "but I must confess that the description of your collection has whetted my own bibliographical appetite."

The Professor flushed with pride.

"Well, Mr. Holmes, if you and your friend would really care to see my few t-treasures, I should be honoured. My rooms are not f-far from here."

"Then let us go," said Holmes, with decision.

I confess that I was somewhat puzzled by my friend's behaviour. He seemed to have forgotten the misfortunes of the Megatherium and to be taking a wholly disproportionate interest in the eccentricities of the Wiskerton collection.

When we reached the Professor's rooms I had a further surprise. I had expected not luxury, of course, but at least some measure of elegance and comfort. Instead, the chairs and tables, the carpets and curtains, everything, in fact, seemed to be of the cheapest quality; even the bookshelves were of plain deal and roughly put together. The books themselves were another matter. They were classified like no other library I had ever seen. In one section were presentation copies from authors; in another were proof-copies bound in what is known as "binder's cloth"; in another were review copies; in another

were pamphlets, monographs, and off-prints of all kinds.

"There you are, Mr. Holmes," said the Professor, with all the pride of ownership. "You may think it is a c-collection of oddities, but for me every one of those volumes has a p-personal and s-separate association—including the item which came into my hands yesterday afternoon."

"Quite so," said Holmes, thoughtfully, "and yet they all have a common characteristic."

"I don't understand you."

"No? But I am waiting to see the remainder of your collection, Professor. When I have seen the whole of your library, I shall perhaps be able to explain myself more clearly."

The Professor flushed with annoyance.

"Really, Mr. Holmes, I had been warned of some of your p-peculiarities of manner; but I am entirely at a loss to know what you are d-driving at."

"In that case, Professor, I will thank you for your hospitality and will beg leave to return to the Megatherium for consultation with the Secretary."

"To tell him that you can't f-find the missing books?"

Sherlock Holmes said nothing for a moment. Then he looked straight into the Professor's face and said, very slowly:

"On the contrary, Professor Wiskerton, I shall tell the Secretary that I can direct him to the precise address at which the books may be found."

There was silence. Then an extraordinary thing happened.

The Professor turned away and literally crumpled into a chair; then he looked up at Holmes with the expression of a terrified child:

"Don't do it, Mr. Holmes. Don't do it, I b-b-beseech you. I'll t-tell you everything."

"Where are the books?" asked Holmes, sternly.

"Come with me and I'll show you."

The Professor shuffled out and led us into a dismal bedroom. With a trembling hand he felt in his pocket for his keys and opened a cupboard alongside the wall. Several rows of books were revealed and I quickly recognized one or two titles that I had seen on the Megatherium list.

"Oh, what m-must you think of me, Mr. Holmes?" the Professor began, whimpering.

"My opinion is irrelevant," said Sherlock Holmes, sharply. "Have you any packing-cases?"

"No, but I d-daresay my landlord might be able to find some."

"Send for him."

In a few minutes the landlord appeared. Yes, he thought he could find a sufficient number of cases to take the books in the cupboard.

"Professor Wiskerton," said Holmes, "is anxious to have all these books packed at once and sent to the Megatherium, Pall Mall. The matter is urgent."

"Very good, sir. Any letter or message to go with them?"

"No," said Holmes, curtly, "but yes—stop a minute."

He took a pencil and a visiting-card from his pocket and wrote "With the compliments of" above the name.

"See that this card is firmly attached to the first of the packing-cases. Is that clear?"

"Quite correct, sir, if that's what the Professor wants."

"That is what the Professor most particularly wants. Is it not, Professor?" said Holmes, with great emphasis.

"Yes, yes, I suppose so. But c-come back with me into the other room and l-let me explain."

We returned to the sitting-room and the Professor began:

"Doubtless I seem to you either ridiculous or despicable or both. I have had two p-passions in my life—a passion for s-saving money and a passion for acquiring b-books. As a result of an unfortunate dispute with the Dean of my faculty at the University, I retired at a c-comparatively early age and on a very small p-pension. I was determined to amass a collection of books; I was equally determined not to s-spend my precious savings on them. The idea came to me that my library should be unique, in that all the books

in it should be acquired by some means other than p-purchase. I had friends amongst authors, printers, and publishers, and I did pretty well, but there were many recently published books that I wanted and saw no m-means of getting until—well, until I absent-mindedly brought home one of the circulating library books from the Megatherium. I meant to return it, of course. But I didn't. Instead, I b-brought home another one. . . ."

"*Facilis descensus . . .*," murmured Holmes.

"Exactly, Mr. Holmes, exactly. Then, when the Committee began to notice that books were disappearing, I was in a quandary. But I remembered hearing someone say in another connexion that the b-best defence was attack and I thought that if I were the first to go to you, I should be the last to be s-suspected."

"I see," said Holmes. "Thank you, Professor Wiskerton."

"And now what are you going to do?"

"First," replied Holmes, "I am going to make certain that your landlord has those cases ready for despatch. After that, Dr. Watson and I have an engagement at St. James's Hall."

"A trivial little case, Watson, but not wholly without interest," said Holmes, when we returned from the concert hall to Baker Street.

"A most contemptible case, in my opinion. Did you guess from the first that Wiskerton himself was the thief?"

"Not quite, Watson. I never guess. I endeavour to observe. And the first thing I observed about Professor Wiskerton was that he was a miser—the altercation with the cabman, the shabby clothes, the unwillingness to invite us to lunch. That he was an enthusiastic bibliophile was, of course, obvious. At first I was not quite certain how to fit these two characteristics properly together, but after yesterday's interview I remembered that the head porter of the Megatherium had been a useful ally of mine in his earlier days as a Commissionaire and I thought a private talk with him might be useful.

His brief characterization put me on the right track at once—'Always here reading,' he said, 'but never takes a square meal in the club.' After that, and after a little hasty research this morning into the Professor's academic career, I had little doubt."

"But don't you still think it extraordinary, in spite of what he said, that he should have taken the risk of coming to consult you?"

"Of course it's extraordinary, Watson. Wiskerton's an extraordinary man. If, as I hope, he has the decency to resign from the Megatherium, I shall suggest to Mycroft that he puts him up for the Diogenes."

The Adventure of the Noble Husband

PETER CANNON

ALTHOUGH BEST KNOWN for his scholarly writings about H. P. Lovecraft and fictional works based on the famed horror writer's Cthulhu Mythos, Peter Cannon (1951–), currently an editor at *Publishers Weekly* specializing in mystery fiction, has also produced several works involving Sherlock Holmes. His short novel *Pulptime: Being a Singular Adventure of Sherlock Holmes, H. P. Lovecraft, and the Kalem Club, as if Narrated by Frank Belknap Long, Jr.* (1984) combines two of his fields of interest.

Among Cannon's critical and appreciative studies of Lovecraft are his graduate theses: *A Case for Howard Phillips Lovecraft* (Honors thesis, Stanford, 1973) and *Lovecraft's New England* (MA thesis, Brown University, June 1974). Again combining his areas of expertise, he wrote "You Have Been in Providence, I Perceive" (*Nyctalops*, March 1978), which illustrates the influences of the Sherlock Holmes stories upon Lovecraft. This was followed by another analysis of Holmes's influence on Lovecraft, "Parallel Passages in 'The Adventure of the Copper Beeches' and 'The Picture in the House' "; it was published in *Lovecraft Studies* 1, No. 1 (Fall 1979).

Cannon's Lovecraftian fiction includes *Scream for Jeeves: A Parody* (1994), which narrates some of Lovecraft's stories in the voice of P. G. Wodehouse's Bertie Wooster; *The Lovecraft Chronicles* (2004), a novel based on Lovecraft's life; and several short stories in the Cthulhu Mythos genre, including "Azathoth in Arkham" and "The Revenge of Azathoth," both sequels to "The Thing on the Doorstep"; and "The Madness Out of Space," originally presented as a lost story by Lovecraft. A collection of his stories was published as *Forever Azathoth* (1999).

"The Adventure of the Noble Husband" was first published in *The Confidential Casebook of Sherlock Holmes*, edited by Marvin Kaye (New York, St. Martin's Press, 1998).

THE ADVENTURE OF
THE NOBLE HUSBAND

Peter Cannon

IN SURVEYING THE many cases of Mr. Sherlock Holmes in which I had the privilege to participate, I confess that I have often been torn whether or not to publish the results. More than once in my eagerness to set a stirring story before the public I have, to my shame, shown scant regard for the privacy of Holmes's more illustrious clients. Still, I am confident I know where to draw the veil. I doubt that I shall ever release the full facts regarding Ackerley, the bigamous banana king, who for years maintained a household in Richmond and a "secret orchard" in Castlenau, with neither family the wiser. Tawdry affairs such as this one are best left to moulder in their year-books on the shelves. And yet there are a few cases in this sensitive category which beg for disclosure, if only long after the eminent parties involved have passed on. Such was the adventure of the noble husband, a matter that threatened to destroy not only the good name of one of Britain's most revered authors but also my relationship with my literary agent.

One summer afternoon in the year 1900, finding myself in the vicinity of our old Baker Street lodgings after a professional call, I decided to drop by 221B. Mrs. Hudson informed me that a client had just arrived, but as Holmes customarily welcomed my presence at these interviews I did not hesitate to mount the stairs. In the sitting room I discovered Sherlock Holmes listening to a small, respectably dressed woman with a plain, pale face—an utterly unprepossessing type such as one might pass on the street with scarcely a glance.

"Ah, Watson. I would like you to meet Mrs. Hawkins," said my friend. "I trust you won't mind, Mrs. Hawkins, but Dr. Watson often does me the courtesy—"

"Oh, Mr. Holmes, I'm afraid I . . ." The stranger rose from her chair, her wan cheeks suddenly flushed. She pressed a handkerchief to her mouth to conceal a cough. Then it struck me; I knew this woman, though not under the name of Mrs. Hawkins. As soon as she recovered her composure, she spared us both further embarrassment by introducing, or rather I should say, reintroducing herself.

"It's Mrs. Doyle, Dr. Watson," she said, extending a tiny hand. "We met once years ago, through my husband, who I believe still acts as your literary agent."

"Oh, yes. Quite so," I answered. Her palm trembled in mine. "I regret, however, that it has been ages since he and I last met. How is Mr. Doyle, if I may ask?"

During the silence that ensued, only the sound of Holmes thrumming his fingers against his chair could be heard.

"I am very sorry, madam," the detective said at last, "but if you are indeed the wife of Arthur Conan Doyle, the historical novelist and, more to the point, my colleague Dr. Watson's literary agent, you present me with a potential conflict of interest. I cannot help you."

The woman gave a little gasp.

"I could refer you, if you wish. A Mr. Adrian Mulliner—"

"Oh no, Mr. Holmes, only you can help! Forgive me. Hawkins is my maiden name. I feared you would dismiss me without a hearing if I had revealed my identity immediately. You must understand. I've come all the way from Hindhead. For months I've been in agony over whether or not to seek you out. Please, Mr. Holmes, allow me at least to finish my story."

With these words the woman sank back in her chair and began to cry quietly into her handkerchief. Again she coughed, in a manner that suggested some serious lesion of the lungs. I hardly dared look Holmes in the eye. One would have to be a heartless fiend to ignore her distress.

"Very well, madam," Sherlock Holmes said gently. "As I had barely time to note that you are fond of animals and devoted to your children, a girl and a boy if I am not mistaken, before Watson here arrived, you might as well repeat for him what you have already confided to me."

"Thank you, Mr. Holmes," she answered, her tears now dried. "You are truly a gentleman. As I said before, we met fifteen years ago in Southsea, Portsmouth, on account of my brother Jack, one of Arthur's resident patients. Alas, poor Jack proved to have cerebral meningitis and succumbed within weeks. In my bereavement I naturally turned to Arthur for consolation, and he responded with a warmth that betrayed a deeper sympathy. We married that summer, and a kinder, more protective husband no woman could dare dream for, Mr. Holmes. If you have read my husband's book *The Stark Munro Letters*, you may have gained some notion of the sweet, affectionate home life that was ours in those early days."

Holmes's hooded eyes flickered in acknowledgment, though I was certain he had never opened *The Stark Munro Letters*, let alone any of the popular works penned by my literary agent. For my own part I was doing my best to stifle a smile, despite the gravity of the woman's narrative, as it was not every day that a client failed to express instant astonishment at one of my friend's personal deductions. Mrs. Doyle was either very simple—or very clever.

"This idyll, like all perfect things, could not last, I regret to say," our visitor continued. "First, in '93, I was diagnosed with consumption. My quiet life became enforced. In the autumn of '96 we moved from London to Surrey, for the sake of my health. That first spring in the country, Arthur started to behave oddly. At the time of our engagement he warned me that he tended to long silences and that I mustn't mind, but thoughtful contemplation soon all but gave way to mournful brooding. Of late, when not withdrawn in silence, Arthur has been full of restless energy. He has taken up the banjo, practicing for hours, despite an obvious lack of musical aptitude. As for golf and cricket, games at which he excels, he now plays them with an enthusiasm more befitting a youth half his age."

"Pardon me, madam," interrupted the detective, "but just how old is your husband?"

"Arthur turned forty-one in May."

"Pray go on."

"He has grown increasingly irritable, too. While patient and paternal as always with me and the children, he has allowed himself to get drawn into silly literary feuding."

"A pity, madam, but perhaps not so surprising for a man who has advanced in his career from provincial doctor to world-renowned author."

"You may be right, Mr. Holmes, but there's more." The woman coughed into her knotted handkerchief, then took a deep breath. "In March, just before he left for South Africa—"

"South Africa?" interjected Holmes.

"Yes, to join a field hospital as unofficial supervisor."

"Most admirable. Pray continue."

"As I was saying, this past March I observed Arthur unawares in the garden at Undershaw, our house in Hindhead. He picked a snowdrop and carried it into the library. After his departure I examined his shelves and found pressed between the leaves of a volume of romantic verses three snowdrop flowers—one fresh, the other two dried and withered."

My friend leaned forward, eyes glinting. This was the kind of curious detail he relished.

"Oh, Mr. Holmes, a man does not do such a sentimental thing unless he is in love—in love with another woman!" With this the woman broke into sobs.

"What do you propose I do, madam?" said Sherlock Holmes after a decent interval.

"Please determine whether or not my Arthur remains true."

"And if I confirm your worst fears?"

"Oh, I do not know, Mr. Holmes, I do not know. I am ill, sir, gravely ill. My time draws short in this world. You must believe that Arthur's happiness matters more to me than my own. That he has found room for another in that great heart of his I can accept. But, as long as I live, I shall not abide his being unfaithful!"

Our visitor resumed her sorry weeping. I was deeply moved, and despite the mask of the perfect reasoner he affected, I knew my friend could not be untouched by such pure and intense emotion.

"Where is your husband now, madam?"

"On his way back from South Africa. His ship, the *Briton*, is due to dock next week in Plymouth."

"Ah, then we have some time."

"Oh, my dear Mr. Holmes!"

"Please, Mrs. Doyle. Before I can give my assent, I must first consult Dr. Watson on the ethics of my taking you on as a client. If you wouldn't mind waiting downstairs, I dare say Mrs. Hudson should already have the water on the hob for tea."

After further expressions of gratitude, the woman put on her shawl, which was covered with cat hair, and gathered a shopping bag marked with the emblem of Hamley's toy emporium, containing, I saw as I held the door for her, a doll and a set of tin soldiers. "Thank you, Dr. Watson. Since I so rarely travel to London these days," she said, smiling at her purchases, "I feel obliged to bring home something for Mary and Kingsley to show my expedition has not been unfruitful."

We stood listening to her dainty tread fade down the steps. Then the detective collapsed into his chair, his features unfathomable. A minute passed before he spoke:

"Well, Watson, as I have said to you in the past, the fair sex is your department. What is your assessment?"

"To be blunt, Holmes, if we are to credit what Mrs. Doyle tells us, her husband is suffering from acute . . . frustration. The overindulgence in sport, the banjo playing, the literary feuding, for a healthy male in his prime—"

"Enough, Watson," said Holmes. "Like you, I have concluded that the man is in dire danger of violating his marital vows. The real issue for me, my dear fellow, is your role here. It has never been my policy to pry into your affairs, but just how well do you know your literary agent?"

"Not well, Holmes, though our relations have always been cordial and correct. As fellow medical men we have traded a tale or two of the dissecting room, and Doyle did present me with an inscribed copy of his story collection *Round the Red Lamp*, but there all confidences end. I am grateful that he continues in his capacity as my agent, despite his rising fame as an author, though again it has been some while since I have put any work his way."

After believing Holmes had fallen to his death in '91 in the grasp of his archfoe Professor Moriarty, I was too grief-stricken to publish any adventures beyond that of "The Final Problem." My friend's abrupt resurrection three years later provided an additional jolt which reinforced my silence.

"Tell me, Watson. I confess I am ignorant of literary practices," said Sherlock Holmes, "but why on earth have you not submitted your fanciful melodramas directly to *The Strand* magazine?"

"Well, Holmes, if you can keep a secret, this chap Doyle has done more than act as middleman. He has touched up my prose here and there, checked details, consistency of names and dates, that sort of thing. After all, he's a professional, I a mere amateur."

I was not about to admit that in many instances my agent had been a virtual co-author.

Indeed, to safeguard my posthumous reputation, the extent of Doyle's hand in my own writings must forever remain in mystery.

"Do you, then, have any objections to my assuming Mrs. Doyle's case?"

"None at all, Holmes."

"I am sure Mulliner could handle this affair ably enough in my stead."

"No, Holmes. A lady's honour is at stake. She trusts only you. If a scandal ensues from your investigation, I am prepared to risk the loss of her husband's services—of which I may have no real need in future anyway."

"Good old Watson! How fortunate for your wives to have a man of your loyalty."

"Thank you, Holmes."

For a few moments we sat in a silence that was almost comfortable.

"The old queen cannot live forever," my friend resumed. "Her son, the heir, has already set the moral tone for the new century that looms. With her will pass an age that for all its cant and hypocrisy still upholds the gentlemanly virtues. I suspect, dear fellow, that you and I shall find ourselves increasingly out of step with the laxer times ahead. In the meanwhile, let us put Mrs. Doyle out of her suspense, then join her in a cup of tea."

Later that month the newspapers heralded Arthur Conan Doyle's return from South Africa, on holiday from his exertions in the Boer War. He was badly in need of rest, so a clandestine message from his wife informed Holmes; though that would not prevent him from coming up to London to play for Surrey at Lord's. The detective determined that it might be interesting to learn who might be watching among the crowd. "For now I prefer to theorize in the background," he said before I set off alone for St. John's Wood. "Besides, Watson, you instinctively appreciate the nuances of a game, like the subtleties of women, which I with my logical mind find completely baffling."

In truth I was fond of cricket, if more as a ca-sual peruser of the box scores in the pink sheet than as a spectator on the grounds. In the event I welcomed the chance to visit Lord's, though by the time I entered the gate the teams had adjourned for lunch. I headed for the pavilion, where I nodded to more than a few former patients and consumed strawberries and cream. It was while I was so engaged that I heard a familiar voice at my side.

"Watson, old chap!"

I turned and there stood the tall, athletic figure of my literary agent, Arthur Conan Doyle, wearing whites. He looked a bit gaunt but otherwise exuded robust good cheer.

"My dear Doyle," I said, dropping my spoon. We clasped hands.

"I say, this is a stroke of luck," my companion began in that solid, precise way of his. "I've been meaning to get in touch with you since my return from South Africa—a frightful situation there, you know; it's all in my forthcoming book, *The Great Boer War*. At any rate, on board the ship home I met a journalist named Fletcher Robinson. Told me the most wonderful West Country legend about a spectral hound." Conan Doyle winked. "Back in the eighties, I understand, a crime connected with this hound brought a certain private consulting detective—"

"Sounds promising, Doyle," I interrupted hastily, "but I'd rather we—"

I disliked discussing business in so public a place, but fortunately the arrival of a third party put an end to this line of conversation.

"Ah, Jean," said the author, addressing a young woman dressed in a summer frock that showed to advantage her long, slender neck and beautifully sloped shoulders. "I'd like you to meet my client, Dr. John Watson. Watson, may I present Miss Jean Leckie."

"I'm delighted to meet you, Dr. Watson," said the woman in a Scots accent like a melody. "I used so much to enjoy the adventures of your friend Mr. Sherlock Holmes in *The Strand*. Pray, is there any hope of his return?"

Usually when confronted with this question, as I had been all too often since the appearance of "The Final Problem," my answer was curt. On this occasion, I have to admit, I was no proof against the charm of my lovely interlocutor's smile and went so far as to say that I had not ruled out the possibility.

We were shortly joined by a fourth individual, a balding young fellow in the colours of the opposing Middlesex team. As tall and strapping as Doyle himself, he was carrying a book.

"Good day, Mr. Doyle," said the youth, who despite his imposing build had a shy, quiet manner about him. "I hope I'm not intruding. My name is Wodehouse. You may recall you bowled me out for six this morning."

"Ah, yes, Wodehouse," replied Conan Doyle with a grin. "One of the stars of the Dulwich eleven your final term, I hear."

"My friend Fletcher Robinson tells me the two of you met aboard the *Briton*, Mr. Doyle."

"Indeed, a capital chap. Spoke highly of you as a cricketer—and as an aspiring journalist."

"I confess that for the moment I work in a bank, but literature is my great love. I'm a particular fan of yours, Mr. Doyle." A faint blush mantled the young man's cheek. "Would you be so good as to sign my copy of your latest book?" Here Wodehouse produced the volume he had under his arm, *The Green Flag and Other Stories of War and Sport*, by A. Conan Doyle. The author scribbled on the title page with a pen supplied by his admirer.

"Thank you very much, Mr. Doyle."

"Always glad to oblige a fellow cricketer, my lad. Oh, pardon me, my manners suffered somewhat on the veldt. Allow me to introduce Miss Leckie"—Wodehouse bowed—"and Dr. Watson."

"Pleased to meet you, Dr. Watson. Yet another literary man, are you not? Author of *The Adventures* and *The Memoirs of Sherlock Holmes*?"

I acknowledged the compliment, though mindful of the fact that if you failed to publish, after a while the public tended to forget you, no matter how keenly they may have received you at first.

Attention soon shifted back to Doyle and his recent writing, then to his musical efforts. "It was I who encouraged Arthur to take up the banjo, to accompany my singing," said Miss Leckie. "He hasn't told me yet whether he had the chance to practice in South Africa, though I gather his butler was threatening to resign until his timely departure from England." She laughed, and we all joined in, no one more heartily than the banjo-playing author himself.

"Maybe Mr. Doyle should consider trying the banjolele instead," suggested the young cricketer.

This sparked more laughter, leading to talk between Miss Leckie and Wodehouse of notable stringed-instrument performers that season on the London music-hall stage. Doyle drew me aside.

"Isn't she a peach, Watson?"

"Miss Leckie is most congenial."

"An excellent horsewoman, rides to hounds, trained as an opera singer in Dresden." The man gave a huge sigh. "I won't pretend with you, old boy. I've already confided in a number of my close friends, as well as my mother. To my immense relief 'the Ma'am,' as I call her, has given her blessing. I know how it must seem. But I can assure you—"

That my literary agent should be sharing such a confidence was more than a little disconcerting, even though of course he was confirming the very information I most vitally sought. Perhaps the strain of attending the wounded in South Africa, combined with his excitement at seeing Miss Leckie after so long an absence, explained his lack of reserve. Fortunately, at this juncture Wodehouse interrupted to say he needed to go grab a bite before returning to the pitch. Shortly after he left we were joined by a couple who greeted Doyle like a long-lost brother, which in a real sense he was.

"Ah, Connie, Willie, I'd like you to meet a friend of mine, Miss Jean Leckie. And this is my client, Dr. John Watson."

I had never met Ernest William Hornung, better known as E. W. Hornung, chronicler of

Raffles, the "amateur cracksman," and Conan Doyle's brother-in-law, but I certainly knew him by reputation. While his wife, Constance, caught up with her celebrity brother, I exchanged a few words with my fellow detective-story writer.

"Can we look forward to any new adventures of Mr. Sherlock Holmes, Dr. Watson?" asked the man in a facetious tone I found irritating.

"I think not, Mr. Hornung."

"Come, come, sir. Everyone knows Mr. Holmes has resumed his London practice. It's been years now. When are you going to reveal how he survived that plunge into the Reichenbach Falls?"

"Some things are best left in mystery, Mr. Hornung."

"Dear me, Dr. Watson, you are obstinate. If you refuse to honour us with further tales of your detective friend, then I suppose we lesser authors will just have to do our humble best to fill the gap."

While the exploits of Raffles were all very amusing in their way, they were thin stuff compared with my own. Listening to this man prate, I began to think that perhaps it was time, after all, to "resurrect" Holmes, not that I was about to give my rival the satisfaction of saying so. I made a mental note to talk to Doyle later about that spectral hound legend, assuming we were still on speaking terms after the resolution of the present case.

With relief I turned to the conversation between the ladies, while Doyle reviewed for Hornung some of the finer points of that morning's match. Mrs. Hornung queried Miss Leckie politely about her family, but it soon became clear that she was more interested in a topic closer to home.

"Where did you say you and my brother met, Miss Leckie?"

"At a party, Mrs. Hornung. My parents were entertaining at the Glebe House, in Blackheath."

"You say this was in March, Miss Leckie?"

"March three years ago, Mrs. Hornung."

"To be precise, March fifteenth," Doyle chipped in, giving Miss Leckie's hand a quick squeeze. For an instant both Hornungs frowned.

"I see," said his sister. "Well, we must all have lunch together sometime."

"Right now you must all excuse me," said Doyle, looking at his watch. "Play resumes promptly on the hour."

"Good-bye, then, Arthur. Shall we be seeing you at Undershaw?"

"On the morrow, Connie."

The Hornungs made their farewells to Miss Leckie. Their frozen smiles, if I am any judge, left behind a distinct air of disapproval. But Miss Leckie, with whom I found myself suddenly alone, seemed not to mind if she even noticed.

"Oh, Dr. Watson, isn't Arthur the best and wisest man you have ever known!"

That evening I returned to Baker Street and gave Holmes my report.

"I must congratulate you, Watson," said the detective, "for all your discovery has fallen to you like ripe fruit from a tree. Your literary agent proclaims his attachment to this Miss Leckie as nothing less than an open secret!"

"Yes, Holmes, but I am certain it is no liaison, at least not yet."

"Ah, there lies the nub of the matter. That Doyle has managed to resist temptation for more than three years shows the utmost chivalry. But for how many more years can he or any man in his position hold out? Especially if he must face censorious relatives who could provoke him into doing something rash."

"One has to sympathize with the poor fellow, Holmes."

"Sympathy is all very well, Watson, but one has also to act. The situation is in real danger of coming to a crisis. Tomorrow I shall catch the first train for Hindhead, where I think a little undercover work will be in order."

"Must you go alone, Holmes?"

"Yes, Watson. Were you to accompany me to Surrey and Doyle learned of your presence, he might view your popping up so soon again as rather more than coincidence."

Over the next few days, in between my rounds, I had ample opportunity to reflect on this complex business. Who was in the wrong and who in the right became less and less obvious the more I considered my literary agent's predicament, and I could not help wishing that his wife had spared Holmes and me her problem in the first place. I had no word from Holmes. Then, four days after his departure from London, the wire came urging me to meet him at Paddington in time for an early afternoon train to Gloucester.

I arrived on the platform just as the final whistle was sounding.

"Quick, Watson!" shouted Sherlock Holmes from a carriage window. Moments later I was sitting opposite my friend in an otherwise unoccupied compartment.

"Watson, I only pray that we are not too late."

"Too late for what?"

"Let me start at the beginning. Once settled at an hotel in Hindhead, I sought to gain the confidence of one of the staff at Undershaw. This proved difficult, as the Doyles employ no women susceptible to the charms of the rakish alias I had chosen to assume. Then yesterday, by great good fortune, I was out for a stroll on the road to Undershaw when I ran into a tall, husky chap with a widow's peak. In his hand he had a book, *The Green Flag*. I struck up a conversation and soon ascertained that he was indeed young Wodehouse, as you had described in such telling detail, down for the weekend at the invitation of his new friend and fellow cricket enthusiast.

"Sensing that here was a young man of character, I decided to take him into my confidence. At first he was hesitant, but in the end he agreed to act as my agent-in-place. Like you, he regards a woman's honour as paramount. He told me he was aware that Mrs. Hornung had scheduled and then, at the last minute, cancelled a luncheon in the town for herself, her husband, her brother, and an unknown fourth party. I in-

structed Wodehouse to keep his ears open and report anything of significance.

"Early today Wodehouse rang me at my hotel. Over the billiard table late the night before, Hornung confronted Doyle on the matter of Miss Leckie. His taunts apparently hit home, for Doyle lost his temper and stormed out of the room. Wodehouse, who witnessed the entire ugly exchange, feared for his host's sanity. He and I agreed to rendezvous within the hour at the same spot as our encounter the previous day.

"Wodehouse had more news by the time we met. Doyle was still in a temper and announced that he had to go away on unspecified business. His guests were welcome to stay at Undershaw. After his departure Wodehouse went into the garden, where he was accosted by Mason, the Doyles's butler, who also serves as his master's valet. Mason was extremely agitated and in a mood to talk to someone. Just as I had, Mason must have instinctively recognized Wodehouse as trustworthy. He informed Wodehouse of a phone conversation he overheard his master make shortly before he left—in which Doyle reserved a room at the Everson Arms in Gloucester, under the name of Mr. and Mrs. Arthur Parker. The man evidently wanted to discuss possible courses of action, but Wodehouse said not to worry and rushed out to meet me."

"I say, Holmes, where was Mrs. Doyle during all this?"

"Too weak to leave her room, conveniently enough for everyone, so Wodehouse gathered. He never saw her, nor did I attempt to communicate with her. I immediately headed for the train station, while Wodehouse returned to Undershaw, vowing that if he ever became an author of fiction he would be sure to leave physical passion out of it. As soon as I got back to London I wired you and went straight to Paddington; hence here we both are, en route in a possibly futile effort to save a gentleman's honour and a lady's virtue."

Any discussion of how we might thwart the designs of the two lovers we agreed to postpone until we got to Gloucester. Upon arrival we discovered the Everson Arms across the street from the terminal, the sort of down-at-heel establishment that catered to commercial travellers and less reputable patrons. In the shabby lobby we decided that Holmes would inquire at the desk, while I would survey the public room, through a side door by the entrance. There, so as to seem an ordinary customer, I ordered a pint of bitter at the bar. I barely touched the glass to my lips when I heard a hearty voice behind me.

"I say, Watson old chap, this is a coincidence!"

I turned my head and there, beaming over my shoulder, was my literary agent.

"Doyle! My goodness, what a surprise," I replied, trying to sound as if I meant it.

"What on earth are you doing in Gloucester?"

I took a long sip of my bitter.

"By Jove, I've got it. You must be helping your friend Mr. Sherlock Holmes on a case. Well, I know better not to ask any further. If you aren't too busy, old boy, might you join us for a little supper?"

Doyle gestured toward a corner table, where I could see two women sitting—one the fair Miss Leckie, the other an elderly woman in black.

"I'll have to ask Holmes first."

"It's quite all right, Watson," said Holmes, who had suddenly materialized on my other side. "We would be delighted to join Mr. Doyle and . . . company."

The two men regarded each other warily and respectfully, as I imagined two gunfighters might have done on first meeting in a Wild West saloon.

"I don't believe I've had the pleasure, Mr. Holmes."

"The pleasure is entirely mine, sir," answered the detective mildly. They gripped hands. Sherlock Holmes was evidently willing to give my literary agent the benefit of the doubt, at least for the moment.

Doyle led us to the table, where he made the appropriate introductions—to Miss Leckie and to Mrs. Charles Altamont Doyle, his mother.

"The Ma'am was good enough to join our party at the last minute," the author explained. "The more the merrier I always say," he added with a laugh, which may have been a bit forced.

While there was undeniably a certain strain in the air, I have to say that supper passed agreeably. Holmes for one appeared wholly at his ease, discussing prospects in the prize ring with Doyle and the careers of various well-known sopranos with Miss Leckie. The senior Mrs. Doyle said little, presiding over the scene with quiet strength and dignity. As the public area filled up with voluble diners, conversation became increasingly an effort and we all focused on polishing our plates.

Afterwards, as everyone rose and said their farewells, Doyle drew me aside. "I say, Watson," he whispered. "I almost did a foolish thing tonight. A very foolish thing. Fortunately, the Ma'am arrived when she did, though the devil knows how she found out to intercept us here. An amazingly omniscient woman, the Ma'am. After her lecture on fidelity and chastity, I assured her that Miss Leckie and I would never, as long as Touie . . . Well, I trust I can rely on your discretion—and that of Mr. Holmes."

"You can indeed, Doyle," I promised.

Since we had to maintain our pretence that we had come to Gloucester on other business, Holmes and I lingered at the Everson Arms public bar while the lovers and their chaperone proceeded to the railway terminal, to catch a late train to London. Over a final pint of bitter I recounted Conan Doyle's parting comments to me.

"A noble husband, Watson," said Sherlock Holmes. "After this recent test of his mettle, I have no doubt the man will keep his word. The question now becomes what, if anything, we tell that saintly soul, his wife." We finished our pints in silence.

"It has been a long day, old fellow," announced my friend at last. "I am weary and in no mood to hurry back to London. While Gloucester may boast many respectable inns, I am sure the Everson Arms offers as comfortable a bed as any. They should have at least one available room, following the unexpected departure of 'Mr. and Mrs. Parker.'"

The next day, after a short sightseeing excursion to the Forest of Dean, we rode the train back to Paddington. I accompanied Holmes to Baker Street, where two missives awaited him. The first, a wire dated the previous afternoon, was from Wodehouse, stating that Doyle's man Mason had cabled Doyle's mother to alert her to the impending assignation. Mason was confident Mrs. Doyle would do what was necessary. The second was a letter written in a feeble female hand. Holmes read it aloud:

My dear Mr. Holmes,

I hope you will not think too badly of me, but I no longer require your services. While I shall always wonder about the other woman, I now realize that it is quite the best and wisest course not to risk disrupting things as they are. Ignorance is bliss, as they say.

Since his return from South Africa, Arthur has been so kind and attentive to me, while I, confined to my room, have been no use to anyone. This past weekend I was too ill even to receive house guests.

Forgive me my foolishness! With apologies for any unnecessary trouble I may have caused you and Dr. Watson, I am

Sincerely yours,
Louise Hawkins Doyle

"I say, Holmes," I said, unable on this occasion to suppress a smile. "Like Lady Chiltern in *An Ideal Husband*, Mrs. Doyle seems now content to await the perfect partner in the next world."

"Indeed, Watson," my friend replied, with only a hint of testiness, "though let us not forget the tragic example of the author of *An Ideal Husband*, who unlike the worthy Mr. Doyle permitted passion to overrule his better judgement."

Epilogue

The following year I resumed publication of these memoirs of mine with *The Hound of the Baskervilles*, while P. G. Wodehouse made his first professional magazine sale. In 1902, for his efforts in presenting the British position in the Boer War, Arthur Conan Doyle received his knighthood, though he accepted only reluctantly, at the insistence of his mother. Sherlock Holmes refused a knighthood the same year. Louise Hawkins Doyle died of tuberculosis in 1907. The year after, Sir Arthur married Jean Leckie, who bore him three children. According to his son Adrian, a few months before his death, Conan Doyle left his sickbed unseen to go out into the garden. A few minutes later the butler found him, collapsed in a passage with a heart attack. In his hand he clutched a snowdrop. It had been his custom to observe the anniversary of his meeting Jean Leckie, on the fifteenth of March, 1897, by picking the first snowdrop of the season.

A Night with Sherlock Holmes

WILLIAM O. FULLER

ALTHOUGH VERY WELL known during his lifetime as a journalist, raconteur, and friend of such literary luminaries as Mark Twain and Henry Van Dyke, William Oliver Fuller (1856–1941) is little read today.

Born in Rockland, Maine, he lived there his entire life. He became the postmaster of Rockland (1902–1914) while also working as a newspaperman, having founded the *Rockland Courier* when he was only eighteen. It was merged with the *Rockland Gazette* to form *The Courier-Gazette* in 1882, of which he was the editor and manager for decades. He was presented with the Silver Plaque of the Maine Press Association in 1937 for being the oldest editor in point of service (sixty-three years).

Known for his charm and wit, he was a successful lecturer, after-dinner speaker, and author. Near the turn of the previous century, he contributed humorous sketches to the New York *World* with such subject matter as "Unknown Husbands of Well-Known Wives." He also wrote books: *What Happened to Wigglesworth* (1901), a comic novel in which the life of man-about-the-house Ellery Wigglesworth is a walking accident waiting to happen, and *An Old Town by the Sea* (1908), the story of the Thomas Bailey Aldrich Memorial House in Portsmouth, produced when the house was dedicated in 1908. His close friend, Aldrich once described Fuller as the nearest in style to Charles Lamb of any writer he had ever known.

"A Night with Sherlock Holmes" was a paper read by Fuller to the 12mo Club on January 1, 1929. He claimed that he had received the manuscript directly from Arthur Conan Doyle. It was originally published in a limited edition of two hundred copies (Cambridge, Massachusetts, The Riverside Press, 1929). It was first commercially published under the title "The Mary Queen of Scots Jewel" in *The Misadventures of Sherlock Holmes*, edited by Ellery Queen (Boston, Little, Brown, 1944).

A NIGHT WITH SHERLOCK HOLMES

William O. Fuller

IT WAS ONE of those misty, rainy mornings in early summer when the streets of London contrive to render themselves particularly disagreeable, the pavements greasy with mud and the very buildings presenting their gloomy façades wreathed in a double melancholy. Returning from a professional call and finding Baker Street in my way, I had dropped in on my friend Sherlock Holmes, whom I found amid the delightful disorder of his room, his chair drawn up to a fire of coals and himself stretched abroad in it, pulling at his favorite pipe.

"Glad to see you, Watson," he called heartily. "Sit down here, light a cigar and cheer me up. This infernal wet spell has got on my nerves. You're just the company I require."

I helped myself to a cigar, put a chair to one side of the grate and waited for Holmes to talk, for I understood that in this frame of mind he had first to relieve himself of its irritability before a naturally pleasant mood could assert itself.

"Do you know, Watson," he began, after some moments of silent smoking, "I don't at all like your treatment of my latest adventure. I told you at the time that the part played by that country detective threw my methods into a comparison with his such as tends to overrate my abilities."

Holmes's querulous allusion to the now famous Amber Necklace Case, to my mind one of his most brilliant exploits, I could afford to let pass in silence, and did so.

"Not," he added, with a suggestion of the apologetic in his voice, "not that, on the whole, you let your pen of a ready chronicler carry you too pliantly into the realm of romance—but you must be careful, Watson, not to ascribe to me the supernatural. You know yourself how ordinary my science is when the paths of its conclusions are traced after me. As, for instance, the fact that I am about to have a caller—how I know this may for a moment appear a mystery to you, but in the sequel most commonplace."

There came on the instant a rap at the street door, and to my surprised look of inquiry Holmes replied, with a laugh:

"My dear Watson, it is kindergarten. You failed to hear, as I did an instant ago—for you were listening to my morose maunderings—the faint tooting of the horn of a motorcar, which it was easy to perceive was about turning the upper corner of our street; nor did you observe, as I was able to do, that in the proper space of time the unmistakable silence caused by the stopping of a motor engine was apparent under my window. I am persuaded, Watson, that a look out of that window will plainly disclose a car standing by my curb-stone."

I followed him across the room and peered over his shoulder as he put back the curtains. Sure enough, a motorcar had drawn up to the curb. Under its canopy top we perceived two gentlemen seated in the tonneau. The chauffeur stood at the street door, evidently waiting. At this moment Holmes's housekeeper, after a warning rap, walked into the room, bearing two cards on a tray, which she passed to Holmes.

"MR. WILLIAM S. RICHARDSON—MR. WIL-

LIAM O. FULLER," he said, reading the cards aloud. "H'm. Evidently our friend the Conqueror has many admirers in America. You may ask the gentlemen to walk upstairs, Mrs. Hudson," he added.

"How do you know your callers are from America?" I was beginning, when following a knock at the door, and Holmes's brisk "Come in!" two gentlemen entered, stopped near the threshold and bowed. They were garbed in raincoats; one, of medium height, smooth-shaven, resembling in features the actor Irving; the other, of smaller stature, distinguished by a pair of Mr. Pickwick spectacles.

"Pray come in, gentlemen," said Sherlock Holmes, with the courtesy of manner that so well becomes him. "Throw off your raincoats, take a cigar, sit here in these chairs by the fire, and while you talk of the circumstances that have given me the honor of a visit so soon after your arrival in London, I will busy myself in mixing a cocktail, one of the excellent devices which your American people have introduced to an appreciative British public."

The visitors responded readily to these overtures of cordiality; from a tray on the table selected with unerring discrimination what I knew to be Holmes's choicest cigars, and in a brief time the four chairs were drawn in a half-moon before the glowing grate. Introductions had quickly been got through with.

"Dr. Watson, as my somewhat o'erpartial biographer," said Holmes as he lighted his pipe, "was on the point of wondering, when interrupted by your entrance, at my having in advance pronounced upon the nationality of my callers."

The taller of the gentlemen—it was the one bearing the name of Richardson—smiled.

"I was myself struck by that allusion," he responded, "no less than by your other somewhat astonishing reference to our being but newly come to the city. In point of fact we have been here a period of something less than twenty-four hours."

Sherlock Holmes laughed pleasantly. "It is the simplest of matters when explained," he said, "as I have often pointed out to Dr. Watson. In the line of research to which I occasionally turn my attention, as he has so abundantly set forth in his published narratives, acquaintance must be had, as you will know, with a great variety of subjects. The motorcar, for instance, that ubiquitous invader of the realm of locomotion, naturally falls within the periphery of these attentions; nor could I long study its various interesting phases without coming to recognize the cars of different makes and nationalities. There are, if my memory is not at fault, some one hundred and thirty varieties of patterns easily distinguishable to one adept in this direction. When Watson looked out of the window, at my shoulder a moment ago, his investigations, pursued in quite different channels, did not disclose to him what was evident to me at a glance, namely, an American machine frequently encountered in this country. It was easy to guess that its occupants were also from the States.

"As to the other matter—among the earliest things the American man or woman of taste does on reaching London is to give an order to the engraver for his name card in the latest London style. The card this season, as we know, is small, the type a shaded variety of Old English. The cards brought me by the hand of Mrs. Hudson were of medium size, engraved in last year's script. Plainly my American callers had at the longest but a short time come to the city. A trifle hazardous—yes—but in these matters one sometimes has to guess point-blank—or, to quote one of your American navigators, 'Stand boldly to the South'ard and trust to luck!' You find this holds together, Watson?"

I confessed with a laugh that I was quite satisfied. The American gentlemen exchanged glances of gratification. Evidently, this exhibition of my friend's characteristic method of deduction afforded them the highest satisfaction.

"Which brings us," remarked Holmes, whose pipe was now drawing bravely, "to the real object of this visit, which I may say at once I am glad to be honored with, having a high appreciation of your country, and finding myself always indebted to one of your truly great writers, whose French detective I am pleased to consider a monumental character in a most difficult field of endeavor. My friend Watson has made some bold essays in that direction," added Holmes, with a deprecatory shake of the head, "but it is a moot question if he ever has risen to the exalted level of *The Murders in the Rue Morgue*."

As Sherlock Holmes ceased speaking, the visitors, who had turned grave, looked at each other questioningly.

"It is your story," said the one in spectacles.

The gentleman by the name of Richardson acknowledged the suggestion.

"Perhaps," he said, "I would best begin at the beginning. If I am too long, or obscure in my details, do me the honor to interrupt me."

"Let us have the whole story," said Holmes. "I naturally assume that you solicit my assistance under some conditions of difficulty. In such matters no details, however seemingly obscure, can be regarded as inessential, and I beg you to omit none of them."

The American flicked the ash from his cigar and began his story.

"My friend and I landed at Liverpool ten days or more ago, for a summer's motoring in your country. We journeyed by easy stages up to London, stopping here only long enough to visit our bankers and to mail two or three letters of introduction that we had brought from home."

"To mail—" interrupted Holmes; then he added with a laugh: "Ah, yes, you posted your letters. Pardon me."

"Long enough to post our letters," repeated the American, adopting the humorously proffered correction. "Then we pushed on for our arranged tour of the South of England. At Canterbury a note overtook us from the Lord M——, acknowledging receipt of our letter of introduction to that nobleman, and praying us to be his guests at dinner on Wednesday of the present week—yesterday—as later he should be out of the city. It seemed best, on a review of the circumstances, for us to return to London,

as his Lordship was one whom we particularly desired to meet. So Wednesday found us again in the city, where we took rooms at the Langham, in Portland Place. It wanting several hours of dressing time, we strolled out in a casual way, bringing up in Wardour Street. I don't need to tell you that in its abounding curio shops, which have extraordinary fascination for all American travelers, we found the time pass quickly. In one of the little shops, where I was somewhat known to the proprietor by reason of former visits, we were turning over a tray of curious stones, with possible scarf pins in mind, when the dealer came forward with a package that he had taken from his safe, and removing its wrappings said: 'Perhaps, sir, you would be interested in this?'

"It was a curious bit of antique workmanship—a gold bar bearing the figure of a boy catching a mouse, the whole richly set about with diamonds and rubies, with a large and costly pearl as a pendant. Even in the dingy light of the shop it sparkled with a sense of value.

"'It is from the personal collection of the Countess of Warrington,' said the dealer. 'It belonged originally to the unfortunate Mary Queen of Scots, and there is an accompanying paper of authentication, showing its descent through various hands for the past three hundred and forty years. You will see engraved here, in the setting, the arms of Mary.'"

Holmes, a past master in the science of heraldry, his voice exhibiting a degree of interest with which I was quite familiar, here broke in:

"Or, a lion rampant within a double tressure flory and counter flory, gules. Mary, as Queen of Scotland and daughter of James I, would bear the arms of Scotland. I know the jewel you are describing—indeed, I saw it one time when visiting at the country seat of the Countess, following a daring attempt at burglary there. You know the particulars, Watson. I have heard that since the death of the Countess, the family being straitened financially, some of her jewels have been put into discreet hands for negotiation."

"So the dealer explained," the visitor continued, "and he added, that as the jewels were so well known in England, they could be sold only to go abroad, hence the value of a prospective American customer. I confess that the jewel interested me. I had a newly married niece in mind for whom I had not yet found just the wedding gift that suited me, and this appeared to fit into the situation.

"'What is the price?' I asked.

"'We think one thousand pounds very cheap for it, sir,' said the dealer, in the easy manner with which your shopkeepers price their wares to Americans.

"After some further talk, our time being run out, my friend and I returned to the Langham and dressed for dinner. It was while dressing that a knock came at my room door. Opening it, I found a messenger from the curio dealer's, who, handing me a small package, explained that it was the jewel, which the dealer desired me to retain for more convenient examination. In the embarrassment of the moment I neglected to do the proper thing and return the package to the messenger, who indeed had touched his cap and gone while I yet stood in the door.

"'Look at this, Fuller,' I called, and stepped into his room—it is our traveling custom to have rooms connecting. 'Isn't this quite like an English shopkeeper, entrusting his property to a comparative stranger? It's a dangerous thing to have credit with these confiding tradesmen.'

"My friend's reply very clearly framed the situation.

"'It's a more dangerous thing,' he said, 'to be chosen as the safe-deposit of priceless heirlooms. It is scarcely the sort of thing one would seek to be made the custodian of in a strange city.'

"This was true. The dinner hour was close on our heels, a taxi was in waiting, there was no time to arrange with the office, and I dropped the package into my inner pocket. After all, it seemed a secure enough place. I could feel its gentle pressure against my side, which would be a constant guarantee of safety.

"We were received by Lord and Lady M—— with the open-handed cordiality that they always accord to visitors from our country. The company at table was not so large but that the conversation could be for the most part general, running at the first to topics chiefly American, with that charming exhibition of English naïveté and ignorance—you will pardon me—in affairs across the water. From this point the talk trailed off to themes quite unrelated but always interesting—the Great War, in which his Lordship had played a conspicuous part; the delicious flavor of wall-grown peaches; the health of the King; of her ladyship's recipe for barleywater; the recent disposal of the library and personal effects of the notorious Lord Earlbank. This by natural steps led to a discussion of family heirlooms, which speedily brought out the jewel, whose insistent pressure I had felt all through the courses, and which was soon passing from hand to hand, accompanied by feminine expressions of delight.

"The interest in the jewel appeared to get into the air. Even the servants became affected by it. I noticed the under butler, while filling the glass of Captain Pole-Carew, who was holding the trinket up to catch the varying angles of light, in which it flashed amazingly, fasten his eyes upon it. For an instant he breathed heavily and almost leaned upon the captain's shoulder, forgetting the wine he was in the act of decanting, and which, overflowing the glass, ran down upon the cloth. The jewel continued its circuit of the table and returned to my inner pocket.

"'A not over-safe repository, if I may venture the opinion,' said the captain, with a smile. I had occasion later to recall the cynical remark.

"We returned to our hotel at a late hour, and fatigued with the long day went directly to bed. Our rooms, as I have said, adjoined, and it is a habit in our travels at the day's end to be back and forth, talking as we disrobe. I allude to this fact as it bears upon the case. I was first in bed, and remember hearing Mr. Fuller put up the window before his light went out. For myself, I dropped off at once and must have slept soundly. I was awakened by hearing my name called loudly. It was Fuller's voice and I rushed at once into his room, hastily switching on the electric light. Fuller sat on the edge of the bed, in his pajamas—and as this part of the story is his, perhaps he would best tell it."

The visitor in the Pickwickian spectacles, thus appealed to, took up the narrative.

"I also had gone instantly to sleep," he said, "but by-and-by came broad awake, startled, with no sense of time, but a stifled feeling of alarm. I dimly saw near the side of my bed a figure, which on my suddenly sitting up made a hurried movement. With no clear idea of what I was doing, I made a hasty clutch in the dark and fastened my hand on the breast of a man's coat. I think my grip was a frenzied one, for as the man snatched himself away, I felt the cloth tear. In a second of time the man had crossed the room and I heard the window rattle as he struck the sash in passing through it. It was then I cried out, and Mr. Richardson came running in."

"We made a hasty examination of the room," the first speaker resumed. "My evening coat lay on the floor, and I remembered that when taking it off I had hung it on the post of Fuller's bed. It is to prolong an already somewhat lengthy story not to say at once that the jewel was gone. We stared at each other with rueful faces.

"'The man has gone through that window with it!' cried Fuller. He pointed with a clenched hand. Then he brought his hand back, with a conscious air, and opened it. 'This is a souvenir of him,' he said, and he held out a button—this button."

Sherlock Holmes reached quickly for the little article that the speaker held out and carefully examined it through his lens.

"A dark horn button," he said, "of German manufacture and recent importation. A few strands of thread pulled out with it. This may be helpful." Then he turned to his callers. "And what else?"

"Well—that is about all we can tell you. We did the obvious thing—rang for the night clerk and watchman and made what examination was possible. The burglar had plainly come along a narrow iron balcony, opening from one of the hotel corridors and skirting the row of windows that gave upon an inner courtyard, escaping by the same channel. The night watchman could advance only a feeble conjecture as to how this might be done successfully. The burglar, he opined, could have made off through the servants' quarters, or possibly was himself a guest of the house, familiar with its passages and now snugly locked in his room and beyond apprehension."

"Did you speak of your loss?" asked Holmes.

"No; that did not appear to be necessary. We treated the incident at the moment as only an invasion."

"Exceedingly clever," approved Holmes. "You Americans can usually be trusted not to drive in too far."

"We breakfasted early, decided that you were our only resource and—in short," concluded the visitor, with an outward gesture of the hands, "that is the whole story. The loss is considerable and we wish to entrust the matter to the discreet hands of Mr. Sherlock Holmes."

My friend lay back in his chair, intently regarding the button poised between his forefingers.

"What became of that under butler?" he asked abruptly.

A little look of surprise slipped into the countenance of the visitor. "Why, now that you call attention to it," he returned, after a moment's reflection, "I remember seeing the head butler putting a spoonful of salt upon the red splotch the spilled wine had made, then turning his awkward assistant from the room. It was so quietly done as to attract no special notice. Afterward, over our cigars in the library, I recall his lordship making some joking allusion to Watkins—so he called the man—being something of a connoisseur in jewelry—a collector in a small way. His Lordship laughingly conjectured that the sight of so rare a jewel had unnerved him. Beyond regarding the allusion in the way of a quiet apology for a servitor's awkwardness, I gave it no particular thought."

Sherlock Holmes continued to direct his gaze upon the button.

"Your story is interesting," he said after some moments of silence. "It will please me to give it further thought. Perhaps you will let me look in on you later at your hotel. It is possible that in the course of the day I shall be able to give you some news."

The visitors hereupon courteously taking their leave, Holmes and I were left alone.

"Well, Watson," he began, "what do you make of it?"

"There is an under butler to be reckoned up," I replied.

"You also observed the under butler, did you?" said Holmes abstractedly. After a pause he added: "Do you happen to know the address of Lord M——'s tailor?"

I confessed that this lay outside the circle of my knowledge of the nobility. Holmes put on his cap and raincoat.

"I am going out on my own, Watson," he said, "for a stroll among the fashionable West End tailor shops. Perhaps you will do me the honor to lunch with me at the Club. I may want to discuss matters with you."

Sherlock Holmes went out and I returned home. It was a dull day for patients, for which I was glad, and the lunch hour found me promptly at the Athenaeum, waiting at our accustomed corner table—impatiently waiting, for it was long past the lunch hour when Holmes came in.

"A busy morning, Watson," was his brief remark as he took his chair.

"And successful?"

To this Holmes made no reply, taking his soup with profound abstraction and apparently oblivious of his guest across the table. While I was accustomed to this attitude of preoccupation, it piqued me to be left so entirely out of his consideration. A review of his morning investigations seemed, under the circumstances, to be quite my due.

"I am going to ask you," began Holmes, when the meal had gone on to its close in silence, "to get tickets for the Alhambra tonight—four tickets. In the middle of the house, with an aisle seat.

Then kindly drop around to the hotel and arrange with our friends to go with us. Or, rather, for us to go with them—in their motorcar, Watson. Request them to pick us up at Baker Street. You will undertake this? Very good, Watson. Then—till I see you at my rooms!" And tossing off his coffee in the manner of a toast, Sherlock Holmes abruptly arose and left me, waving his cap as he went through the door.

It was useless to demur at this cavalier treatment. I had to content myself with the reflection that, as my friend mounted into the atmosphere of criminal detection, the smaller obligations fell away from him. During what was left of the day I was busy in executing the commissions which he had entrusted to me, and night found me at Baker Street, where I discovered Holmes in evening clothes.

"I was just speculating, Watson," he began, in an airy manner, "upon the extraordinary range and variety of the seemingly insignificant and lowly article of commerce known as the button. It is a device common in one form or another to every country. Its origin we should need to seek back of the dimmest borders of recorded history. Its uses and application are beyond calculation. Do you happen to know, my dear Doctor, the figures representing the imports into England for a single year of this ornamental, and at times highly useful, little article? Of horn buttons, for example—it were curious to speculate upon the astonishing number of substances that masquerade under that distinguishing appellation. Indeed, the real horn button when found—if I may quote from our friend Captain Cuttle—is easily made a note of."

It was in this bantering vein that Holmes ran on, not suffering interruption, until the arrival of our callers of the morning, in their motorcar, which speedily conveyed us to the Alhambra, that gorgeous home of refined vaudeville. The theater was crowded as usual. A few moments after our arrival, one of the boxes filled with a fashionable party, among whom our American friends recognized some of their dinner acquaintances of the previous evening. Later

I perceived Captain Pole-Carew, as he looked over the house, bow to our companions. Then his glance ranged to Sherlock Holmes, where I may have imagined it rested a moment, passing thence to a distant part of the galleries. Why we had been brought to this public amusement hall it was impossible to conjecture. That in some manner it bore upon the commission Holmes had undertaken I was fain to believe, but beyond that conclusion it was idle to speculate. At one time during the evening Holmes, who had taken the aisle seat, suddenly got up and retired to the lobby, but was soon back again and apparently engrossed in what went on upon the stage.

At the end of the performance we made our way through the slowly moving audience, visibly helped along by Holmes. In the lobby we chanced to encounter Captain Pole-Carew, who had separated from the box party. He greeted the Americans with some reserve, but moved along with us to the exit, near which our motorcar already waited. The captain had distantly acknowledged the introduction to Holmes and myself, and knowing how my friend resented these cool conventionalities, I was unprepared for the warmth with which he seconded the suggestion that the captain make one of our party in the drive home.

"Sit here in the tonneau," he said cordially, "and let me take the seat with the chauffeur. It will be a pleasure, I assure you."

The captain's manifest reluctance to join our party was quite overcome by Holmes's polite insistence. His natural breeding asserted itself against whatever desire he may have entertained for other engagements, and in a short time the car had reached his door in Burleigh Street.

Sherlock Holmes quickly dismounted. "We have just time for a cigar and a cocktail with the captain," he proposed.

"Yes, to be sure," said Captain Pole-Carew, but with no excess of heartiness. "Do me the honor, gentlemen, of walking into my bachelor home. I—I shall be charmed."

It was Sherlock Holmes who carried the thing off; otherwise I think none of us would have felt that the invitation was other than the sort that is perfunctorily made and expected to be declined, with a proper show of politeness on both sides. But Holmes moved gayly to the street door, maintaining a brisk patter of small talk as Pole-Carew got out his latchkey. We were ushered into a dimly lighted hall and passed thence into a large apartment, handsomely furnished, the living room of a man of taste.

"Pray be seated, gentlemen," said our host. "I expected my valet here before me—he also was at the theater tonight—but your motorcar outstripped him. However, I daresay we can manage," and the captain busied himself setting forth inviting decanters and cigars.

We had but just engaged in the polite enjoyment of Captain Pole-Carew's hospitality when Sherlock Holmes suddenly clapped his handkerchief to his nose, with a slight exclamation of annoyance.

"It is nothing," he said, "a trifling nose-bleed to which I am often subject after the theater." He held his head forward, his face covered with the handkerchief.

"It is most annoying," he added apologetically. "Cold water—er—could I step into your dressing room, Captain?"

"Certainly—certainly," our host assented; "through that door, Mr. Holmes."

Holmes quickly vanished through the indicated door, whence presently came the sound of running water from a tap. We had scarcely resumed our interrupted train of conversation when he reappeared in the door, bearing in his hand a jacket.

"Thank you, Captain Pole-Carew," he said, coming forward, "my nose is quite better. It has led me, I find, to a singular discovery. May I ask, without being regarded as impolite, if this is your jacket?"

I saw that Captain Pole-Carew had gone pale as he answered haughtily: "It is my valet's jacket, Mr. Holmes. He must have forgotten it. Why do you ask?"

"I was noticing the buttons," returned Holmes; "they are exactly like this one in my

A NIGHT WITH SHERLOCK HOLMES

pocket," and he held the dark horn button up to view.

"What of that?" retorted our host quickly; "could there not be many such?"

"Yes," Holmes acknowledged, "but this button of mine was violently torn from its fastening—as it might have been from this jacket."

"Mr. Holmes," returned Captain Pole-Carew with a sneer, "your jest is neither timely nor a brilliant one. The jacket has no button missing."

"No, but it had," returned Holmes coolly; "here, you will see, it has been sewn on, not as a tailor sews it, with the thread concealed, but through and through the cloth, leaving the thread visible. As a man unskilled, or in some haste, might sew it on. You get my meaning, Captain?"

Sherlock Holmes as he spoke had crossed the room to where Captain Pole-Carew, his face dark with passion, was standing on the hearthrug. Holmes made an exaggerated gesture in holding up the jacket, stumbled upon the captain in doing so, and fell violently against the mantel. In an effort to recover himself his arm dislodged a handsome vase, which fell to the floor and shivered into fragments. There was a cry from Captain Pole-Carew, who flung himself amid the fractured pieces of glass. Swift as his action was, Sherlock Holmes was quicker, and snatched from the floor an object that glittered among the broken fragments.

"I think, Mr. Richardson," he said calmly, recovering himself, "that, as a judge of jewelry, this is something you will take particular interest in."

Before any one of us was over the surprise of the thing, Captain Pole-Carew had quite regained his poise, and stood lighting his cigar.

"A very pretty play, Mr. Sherlock Holmes," he said. "I am indebted to you and your itinerant friends for a charming evening. May I suggest, however, that the hour is now late, and Baker Street, even for a motorcar, something of a distance?"

.   .   .

"Naturally," said Sherlock Holmes, when we had reached his rooms and joined him in a good-night cigar, "you expect me to lay bare the processes and so rob my performance of its sole element of fascination. Watson has taught you in his memoirs to expect it. My button quest was certainly directed against his Lordship's under butler, but at the first inquiry it turned up, to my surprise, the entirely unexpected valet of quite another person. It was a curious fact, the tailor declared, that he should twice in one day have calls for that identical button, and he innocently alluded to the valet of Pole-Carew. This was sufficient clue to start upon.

"Investigation in proper quarters not only established the palpable innocuousness of the under butler, but afforded such insight into the existent relations between the captain and his valet as I doubt not will again bring them into the sphere of my attentions. It was plainly the brain of the master that conceived the robbery, but the hand of the valet executed it. I even paid a most enjoyable visit to our friends at the Langham, as I had promised."

The Americans looked at each other.

"That could hardly be," they said. "We were not out of our rooms, and our only caller was a clerk from the curio shop with a message from the dealer—an impertinent old fellow he was, too, who followed us about the rooms with many senile questions as to our tour."

"In this profession I have to adopt many disguises," Holmes smilingly explained. "Of course I could have called on you openly, yet it amused me to fool you a bit. But a disguise would not serve my purpose in getting into Captain Pole-Carew's apartments, which was the thing now most desired. Looking back upon the achievement, I flatter myself that it was rather ingeniously pulled off. You know, Watson, of my association with the theaters and how easily under such a connection one can learn who has reserved boxes.

"I confess that here things played into my hand. I perceived that Pole-Carew recognized me—that is your doing, Watson—and I was not surprised when I saw his glance single out a person in the gallery, with whom he presently got into conversation. I say conversation, for Pole-Carew I discovered to be an expert in the lip language, an accomplishment to which I myself once devoted some months of study and which I have found very helpful in my vocation. It was an easy matter to intercept the message that the captain from his box, with exaggerated labial motion, *lipped* above the heads of the audience.

"'*Hide the vase!*' was the message, several times repeated. '*Hide the vase!*'

"That was the moment when I left the theater for consultation with a friendly detective in the lobby. I strongly suspect," said Sherlock Holmes, with a chuckle, "that the reason the captain failed to find his valet at home could be traced to the prompt and intelligent action of that friendly detective. Our foisting ourselves upon the reluctant captain was merely a clever bit of card forcing, arranged quite in advance, but the rest of it was simplicity itself.

"Inasmuch as you declare that it is the property only, and not a criminal prosecution, that you desire, I do not think anything remains?"

"Except," said the gentleman warmly, taking the jewel from his pocket, "to pay you for this extraordinary recovery."

Sherlock Holmes laughed pleasantly.

"My dear American sir," he replied, "I am still very much in your debt. You should not lose sight of Edgar Allan Poe."

The Adventure of the Wooden Box

LESLIE S. KLINGER

ONE OF THE world's foremost experts on Sherlock Holmes, Leslie Stuart Klinger (1946–) has written extensively on the subject and, more significantly, has edited some of the most distinguished scholarly works about Holmes of recent years.

His magnum opus is *The New Annotated Sherlock Holmes*, published in three massive volumes (2004–2005), in which he provides background information for virtually all references, no matter how arcane, within the sixty Holmes adventures written by Arthur Conan Doyle, as well as numerous maps, photographs, and other illustrations. The first two volumes, released together, won the Edgar Award for the Best Biographical/Critical Work of the year; the third volume was issued the following year. This three-volume edition, aimed at the general public, followed his annotations for the ten-volume *Sherlock Holmes Reference Library* (2001–2009), produced for more scholarly Sherlockians, with even more esoteric information.

Other Sherlock Holmes–related books edited by Klinger include the two-volume tome *The Grand Game* (2011–2012), coedited with mystery writer Laurie R. King, with whom he also edited two anthologies of short stories inspired by the Holmes canon: *A Study in Sherlock* (2011) and *In the Company of Sherlock Holmes* (2014).

Klinger has also edited *The New Annotated Dracula* (2008), *The Annotated Sandman* in four volumes (2012–2015), and *The New Annotated H. P. Lovecraft* (2015).

"The Adventure of the Wooden Box" was originally published as a chapbook by the Mysterious Bookshop (New York, 1999).

THE ADVENTURE OF THE WOODEN BOX

Leslie S. Klinger

IT WAS IN October 1900, with the turn of the century nigh upon us, that I shared with Sherlock Holmes the most bizarre case of our years together. That morning, the fog swirled languidly against the bay window as Holmes passed over the newspaper. "There, on page three, Watson. I believe he was a school chum of yours." I glanced at the headline to which Holmes's long finger pointed: "SURGEON ROBBED, SLAIN AT DOCKS."

"Smithfield and I were at Netley together," I said, after I had scanned the article. "Poor old Smithfield, stabbed to death."

"Did you know him well?"

"Hardly. He was a queer fellow, always afraid that someone was getting the better of him. It appears that someone finally did."

"Hmmm . . ." mused Holmes. "The description of the knife wounds is most suggestive of . . ."

Holmes's reverie was interrupted by a knock at our door, which I recognized as Mrs. Hudson's signal.

"Mr. Holmes—Inspector Hopkins is wanting to see you!" she announced.

"Send him up, Mrs. Hudson," cried Holmes. He turned to me, revealing that rare luster that sparked his penetrating eyes at the beginning of a case. "So, Watson, we may soon know more of your friend's demise. Ah, come in, Inspector Hopkins!" Holmes sprang from his chair, taking the wet, troubled-looking Scotland Yard man by the arm. "Watson, some brandy for our chilled friend!"

"Mr. Holmes, I don't know what to make of it," said Hopkins, after he warmed himself. "It looks to be a simple case of robbery and murder, but it troubles me. Have you read the account in the papers?"

"I trust you mean the Smithfield case," said Holmes.

"Why, yes," stammered the young detective. "I'm sorry."

"I thought as much," said Holmes. "Your name was mentioned in the account, and I rather thought those knife wounds might send you 'round."

"Mr. Holmes, you constantly amaze me! How did you know what was bothering me?"

"Tut, Inspector, even Scotland Yard may find it hard to explain as armed robbery a murder case in which the victim was found lying in the open with knife wounds in his chest!"

"I don't follow, Holmes," I interrupted.

"In the chest, my dear Watson! If one were set upon in a dark alley, such wounds might be possible. But chest wounds imply a frontal attack, Watson. If one's attacker approached from the front unexpectedly, signs of flight would surely be expected. Were there such signs, Inspector? I thought not from the newspaper account. Therefore we must consider the possibility that Dr. Smithfield allowed his assailant to approach him. Hardly consistent with armed robbery!"

"Exactly, Mr. Holmes! I had not thought it through, but even though the doctor's money was taken, my report of armed robbery did not sit right with me. What troubles me most, Mr.

Holmes, is why the doctor was down at the docks at so strange an hour."

"Splendid, Hopkins! You have stolen my next suggestion from my lips! Let us consider under what circumstances a gentleman would be out strolling by the docks at midnight and yet allow a brigand armed with a knife to come within striking distance. What do you say, Watson?"

"A beggar, perhaps?" I ventured.

"Or rather that he knew the man, eh?" Holmes paused to relight his pipe. "Does not an assignation suggest itself? Well, enough supposition. If I am to assist you, Hopkins, I must have facts. Theorizing before knowing the facts is not only useless; it may narrow one's view to the point where one ignores facts."

"Very well, Mr. Holmes," the young inspector replied. "You know that I try to follow your methods, and I will reveal to you what I have learned. As to the body of the doctor, you may examine it if you wish. I have determined that the wounds were made by a right-handed man, about six feet in height, with a broad-bladed knife, while standing close to the victim."

"Very good, Hopkins! I presume that you determined his height and habits from the angle of the wounds."

"Exactly, Mr. Holmes. The body revealed nothing further of an unusual nature, except that the doctor's left arm was bandaged tightly to his body, although he had no apparent wound on it."

"Indeed!" interjected Holmes, his eyes twinkling. "Were the bandages fresh?"

"I did not note," said Hopkins. "I also examined the ground near the body as carefully as I could in this morning's rain. The footprints were quickly washing away, and it was not easy to tell, but I could see no signs of a struggle. Of course, the rains may have taken their toll already by the time I arrived at the scene.

"Later this morning I went 'round to the doctor's house and spoke to his assistant, Philip Buckram, who lives with him. He could add little. No caller had come for the doctor after supper, and he had no idea why the doctor should

be at the waterfront so late. Buckram did see the doctor go out last evening, bundled up in his greatcoat. He noticed that the doctor was carrying under his arm a long, narrow box, which he had not seen before. We could find no sign of the box this morning. When I questioned him about the doctor's recent behavior, he reported that Smithfield had been extremely agitated since his return from America a fortnight ago."

"From America, you say?" said Holmes. "On what ship?"

"The barque *White Star* from Virginia," Hopkins answered, looking pleased.

"Excellent, excellent, my boy! You shall be a fine detective yet!" Holmes cheered.

"Thank you, Mr. Holmes," murmured the young man. "Now, if you would like to inspect the body . . ."

"I would rather see where the body was found," said Holmes, leaping up and seizing his hat and cape. "Come, Watson, there is sunshine on even the foggiest day!"

A quarter hour later, we were alighting from a cab in a grimy street near the waterfront. A constable welcomed us to the gloomy wharf, where the shadows of soot-covered warehouses made it ever twilit.

"Good afternoon, Constable," said Hopkins. "Show Mr. Holmes here to the spot where the body was found." The constable led us to a corner of the wharf near the road, where a street lamp hung.

"You are right, Inspector," said Holmes. "The rain seems to have left us little." Holmes bent to the ground and walked in widening circles, like a hunting dog seeking a scent. "Halloa!" he cried. He dropped to his knees in the dirt under the eaves of the adjacent warehouse.

"Halloa! Watson, what do you make of this? Inspector, you have not cast your eye far enough afield!"

I looked where Holmes pointed. A wide, flattened channel with straight sides was clearly visible on the patch of dry earth. "A box, Watson! Someone has pushed a box through the dirt here!" He peered under the building, where a small but cavernously dark space had been left by the builders. Seizing my umbrella, he flung himself on the ground and stretching out his long arm, proceeded to angle in the blackness until we heard a solid thump. Holmes manipulated further and then slid out by the handle a long, narrow box.

"Holmes!" I cried. "It is a casket, a child's casket!" Holmes nodded and, whipping out his glass, bent to examine the exterior of the box.

"For God's sake, Mr. Holmes, let us open it!" cried Hopkins. Holmes reluctantly pocketed his glass. "Go ahead, Constable," he said. The stalwart policeman stepped forward, hesitated a moment, then lifted the cover. He staggered back, uttering a cry of surprise. Hopkins and I pressed forward and gasped. There, amidst velvet cushions, lay a raggedly severed human arm. Holmes's eyes shone.

Reminding myself of the numerous men I had treated in the field and the cadavers I had dissected in the laboratories, I bent to the box and examined the arm professionally. "It is a male arm," I stated, determined not to be outdone by Hopkins, "adult, probably about thirty years of age. It appears to have been severed by a ragged series of cuts."

"Cut off in an industrial accident?" asked Hopkins.

"No," I said, remembering my patient Victor Hatherley, whom Holmes had consented to help. "No, it appears to have been cut off with a surgical saw, but rather clumsily."

"Or quickly," suggested Holmes. He stooped to examine the hands and fingers. "How long has it—he—been dead, would you say, Watson?"

"Well, the saw marks appear fresh. But the decomposition of the flesh is too advanced for death to have been recent, Holmes."

"Would you agree that the arm was not cut off a living man, Watson?"

"I can't say for certain, Holmes, but why . . ."

"The lack of blood, man! This arm, and presumably the remainder of its owner, has been embalmed!" He turned to Hopkins. "Inspector, I suggest that you inquire after a carpenter, approximately thirty years of age, about five feet ten inches in height, who smoked heavily, was of Semitic descent, and who recently died of heart disease. I should like to speak to his physician."

"But, Mr. Holmes . . ." Hopkins blurted, gesturing feebly at the coffin.

"Come, Hopkins, I thought you were learning my methods. His height we may estimate from the length of the arm. His heavy smoking is evident from the tobacco stains on his fingers, and the calluses on the hand are characteristic of carpentry. I thought I had lent you my little monograph on that subject. Dr. Watson will confirm that the clubbing of the fingertips displayed there suggests recent heart disease, and the color and texture of the skin manifest his descent. Elementary, eh, Watson?"

I nodded.

"And his age, Mr. Holmes?" asked Hopkins.

"Ah, there we must make a stab! The calluses are not so heavy as to indicate long years of carpentry, yet the profession requires a significant apprenticeship. I should estimate that our friend had just begun to establish himself as a master carpenter."

"We'll get on it right away, Mr. Holmes," Hopkins demurred.

"There is nothing further to see here, Inspector. I think, however, that I should like to talk to the captain of the *White Star*. He may be able to cast some light on Dr. Smithfield's anxiety. Watson, can you join me, or is your wife due back from the country today?"

I resisted his chaff regarding my domesticity, and we left the inspector to conduct his search for Holmes's one-armed carpenter. Once we were on our way to Pall Mall in a cab, I queried Holmes on his theories. "Really, Holmes, did you expect to find that gruesome box?" I asked.

"I rather expected to find something, Watson," he replied, "although not even I could have foretold its grisly nature. One does not expect a surgeon to keep a midnight assignation with a man unless something is to pass between them. If it were information, a telegram or a letter would suffice. Therefore I searched for some clue as to that box with which he had left and which must have been intended to pass. I hardly expected to be so dramatically rewarded. We must now wait to see whether the find is as informative as it is ghastly." With that, Holmes drew out his pipe and leaned back into the seat.

A brief inquiry in Pall Mall brought us to the offices of Jos. Brunard and Sons, Shipping Merchants, where the manager shook his head in dismay. "I'd like to help you, Mr. Holmes," he said, glancing covetously at the guinea in Holmes's hand, "but the *White Star* and all her crew have sailed for Boston. We can't afford to leave our ships idle in the harbor, and she docked here over a fortnight ago."

"I am interested in her last voyage," said Holmes. "Had she any untoward incidents?"

"None reported, sir," said the shipper.

"Might I see the list of crew and passengers?" asked Holmes, pressing the guinea on him.

"Certainly!" he responded eagerly, passing over a bound notebook.

Holmes glanced down the page. "Odd," he murmured. "Smithfield's name is not on the list. Think, man," he said to the shipper, "is there no one who can tell us of this ship?"

"Well," said the manager after some thought, "there is Billy Morse. He was a mate on the voyage, but he's caught sick and couldn't ship out. He'll be at the Royal Hotel down the street."

The Royal Hotel little reflected its name. Holmes inquired briefly with the clerk, then led the way up decrepit steps to a thin, greasy door. He knocked with authority.

"Leave me alone, I'm sick," a voice rasped.

"I must talk to you," said Holmes.

The door inched open. "What d'ye want?" asked the sailor, peering cautiously through the crack.

"Dr. Smithfield," said Holmes. "Was he a passenger on the *White Star* from Virginia?"

The sailor laughed, then coughed gaspingly. "A passenger—you might say. But what's it to you?"

"The doctor is dead," said Holmes. "Murdered by a sailor."

"A sailor, eh?" snarled Morse. "Well, I ain't surprised, a sniveling one, that. But it weren't me, matey."

Holmes pushed open the door, and the sailor staggered back to his cot. "I know it wasn't you, Morse, but Scotland Yard might not believe me. I must know how Smithfield came to be on board the *White Star*. After you tell us, you can get some more medicine." Holmes looked meaningfully at the empty gin bottle on the bedtable.

The sailor sighed, coughed rackingly, and lay back in the bedclothes. "We was sailing down to Cuba for some trade on our way back from Virginia," he began. "We had but two passengers, two tobacco traders bound for Scotland on holiday and too cheap to sail on a finer ship. We was passing through the Providence Channel when we spotted wreckage floating off the port bow. It was pieces of a ship, we could see, and broken up small like it had been chewed up by the sea. She must have foundered on the rocks—there are hidden troubles there for an unwise skipper. Anyway, we made a search for survivors in the water, but there weren't none. Just before we was ready to weigh anchor again, the bo'sun spotted men dancing and waving from one of the far-off islands. We sent a skiff on over there—I was in command—and when we beached, we found four howling maniacs, so's I thought. They was the sole survivors of the *Virginia Dare*, out of Savannah. Their ship had been smashed in a storm, and the four of them had managed somehow to be washed up on the island. I don't know how they lived there for two months—that island had nothin' on it, just a few bushes and a little water. They must have had a queer time of it, those four. Anyway, we took 'em on board and brought 'em by way of Cuba to London with us."

"And Smithfield was one of them, was he?" asked Holmes.

"Aye," said the seaman, "and not the queerest of the lot!"

"What do you mean?" I asked.

"Them others," he said, "they all had only one arm!"

As we rode back to Baker Street, my thoughts whirled. Visions of one-armed men and that bloody arm we had discovered danced in my brain. "Holmes, why did you say Smithfield was murdered by a sailor?" I began. "And what did you make of Morse's tale?"

"One question at a time, Watson. It was obvious that Smithfield was murdered by a sailor the moment I saw the knife wounds. First, wounds of that width could only have been made by a broad-bladed knife, such as seamen carry. Second, the upward angle of the wounds also suggest that the assailant was a sailor, who tend to carry a knife underhanded, while an amateur wielding a knife holds it with his thumb away from the blade. Those points, along with the district itself in which the body was found, strongly indicated a sailor. I admit that it is not certain, but the assertion was not lost on Morse."

"Then you do suspect him."

"No, no, Watson, that would be the sheerest coincidence. I merely wished to speed his co-operation. Every sailor has an innate fear of the law, and I used it to our advantage. As to Morse's tale, it provides the pattern into which our pieces now fit, I believe."

"I don't see how, Holmes. Did the arm in the casket belong to one of the castaways?"

"It is not likely, Watson. It is a long voyage for an arm in a small casket, from Georgia to London. And there are no carpenters among the list of castaways Morse gave us. You recall them? Smithfield, John Bennett, Savannah planter, Alfred Winton, a London merchant, and Jack Tiptree, a member of the crew of the *Virginia Dare*. I believe we should pay a visit to Mr. Winton's establishment, Watson, early tomorrow."

Early Tuesday, following a scanty breakfast, I found myself accompanying Holmes into a substantial-looking shop. "Mr. Winton, please," Holmes pleasantly inquired of the clerk. "One moment," he said. He turned, and a young man, more a schoolboy than a shopkeeper, stepped forward. "If it's my father you're looking for, gentlemen," he blurted, "I'm afraid he can't see you."

"It is important," said Holmes. "My name is Sherlock Holmes . . ."

"*The* Sherlock Holmes?" he cried. "And you must be Dr. Watson! Oh, I read of you every month in the *Strand*! Oh," and he turned gloomy, "but my father cannot see anyone, not even you, Mr. Holmes. They've sent him away!"

"Where?" I cried.

"For a rest," he said, obviously holding back tears. "When he came back from America, he was . . . sick. The doctors said he must stay with them until he's better. He doesn't talk right, Mr. Holmes, just gibberish!"

"There, there, now, lad," I offered, patting his shoulder, "you seem like a capable fellow. I'm sure he'll be proud of the way you've run the store while he's away." He shook my hand gratefully and went in the back of the store.

"It is as I feared," said Holmes when we were outside. "I hope we are not too late to save Bennett." I pondered his words and the fate of Winton as we rode back to Baker Street in silence. When we arrived, however, Mrs. Hudson handed Holmes a telegram.

"Too late, Watson!" He handed me the telegram. It was brief:

BENNETT TOOK HIS OWN LIFE SATURDAY IN
HOTEL ROOM.

—HOPKINS

"Why, Holmes?" I cried. "What is it that drove Winton mad and Bennett to suicide? And what about this Tiptree?"

"Soon it will all be clear," Holmes said. "Allow me to reveal the truth to you in my own way. Meanwhile, I think a meal and a pipe are in order, Watson, while we wait for the seeds I have sown to germinate."

Several hours later, a light tapping at the door woke me from my reverie. Holmes leapt up, and I could see Wiggins, chief of those street urchins whom Holmes employs, standing in the doorway, his cap in hand.

"Well?" said Holmes. Wiggins whispered in his ear. "Excellent, Wiggins!" cried Holmes.

"Share this with your fellows!" He gave the boy two guineas.

"Once again my lads shine," he rejoiced, turning to me. "Come, Watson! The game is at an end!"

I hurriedly took up my hat and coat and raced down the stairs, following closely on Holmes's heels. He summoned a cab, and, yelling "Old Yew Place" to the driver, we whistled off.

"Holmes, where are we going?" I shouted as we bounced along at a rapid rate.

"To the land of oblivion, Watson, to oblivion!" was his cryptic reply.

The cab pulled up in a dimly lit corner of the city which I had never seen. The district looked unsavory, and when Holmes led me by the arm to an unmarked door in a dark alley, I was glad to feel the bulk of my service revolver in my coat pocket. Holmes knocked twice, then once, and the door swung slowly open. "Tiptree," he whispered to the shadowy figure inside, and as we stepped in, the door slammed behind us. Immediately my nose identified my surroundings—an opium den!

Holmes led me knowingly through the candlelit gloom of the parlor to a low divan in the back room. There on the pallet lay a young man, of rough appearance, but with a face now bathed in drug-induced peace. This angelic face looked like part of a broken statue, for the man's left sleeve was empty. Holmes shook the sailor, and he stirred.

"Tiptree!" Holmes called. "Tiptree!" The young man started awake and lunged for the floor, but Holmes held his remaining arm in a vise-like grip. "We're not here to harm you, Tiptree. We know all about the island and the doctor's death. We only want to talk to you. Are you awake?"

The sailor peered at us, visibly shaking off his stupor. "Are you the police?" he asked.

"No," said Holmes. "I am Sherlock Holmes. We are the—um, unofficial investigators. But do not let that deceive you," Holmes warned. "I want to hear your story, even though I believe I know it already, and if I am not satisfied that you

are telling the truth, it will go hard with you. An American like you has few friends here in London." Holmes gripped his arm again, and Tiptree shivered.

"I feel as if I have stumbled into the inferno itself," he began, "and you may guide me out of it. My last moment of peace was on board the *Virginia Dare*. I shipped on her from Savannah, where my pa owns a plantation. I shipped for adventure, to see England, to make my own way. I remember that last night, looking out over her bow, where the sea was calm and stars shone, when the storm came upon us in a fury. I was swept over the bow in an instant by a giant wave, and I thought my life had ended as I plunged down under the sea. But I am a strong swimmer, and I strove upwards, up, my lungs burning, until I split the surface. I looked 'round just in time to see the ship thrown against the rocks, like a child's toy, the crew, my mates, and the passengers wailing and jumping for their lives. I was lucky, I guess, for I missed being caught in the rigging or the spiky rocks like most of 'em. A piece of the ship's keel came floating by me, and I lit out for it, and when I reached it, I hung on for dear life. I could hear the moans and cries of the others as they were tossed about by the gale, and each scream burned my soul, for I knew that they were a'gone.

"I guess I slept some, thought I don't know how, and when morning came, my piece of the ship—my savior, I thought then—had floated me up near an island. I blessed the Lord for his good grace and struck out for the land, leaving my little raft behind. With my remaining strength, I pulled myself up on the shore, where I lay for a while.

"I thought, then, that I was dreaming, for I heard voices. I opened my eyes to find three passengers standing over me, Mr. Bennett, Mr. Winton, and Dr. Smithfield. They too had God's grace to come to land. The doctor looked me over and found me as fit as they, so we set out to explore our haven from the sea.

"It was a barren place, sir, and I am sorry to say that my praises of the Lord died on my lips.

The island was small, and, but for some pools of brackish water and juiceless-looking bushes, it was dead too. We must have walked the island twice 'round, searching for a way by which we would live. We saw none.

"We talked over our said fortune among ourselves, again and again. Mr. Winton held his faith steadfast then. Rescuers would find us soon, he said. The others were not so hopeful. That first night, as I lay shivering in the mist-laden air, I dreamed I was again in the sea, and fishes swam into my mouth for dinner. It had been only one day, then, since eating, and I was brave.

"The next day the sun baked us, and we grew mightily thirsty. Dr. Smithfield searched our clothing and found a piece of jerky I'd forgotten, in a pocket. He ate it quickly before we could protest. 'I'm the doctor,' he said when he'd finished, as if to explain. We decided to try our luck at the pools, although the doctor protested. We drank greedily that day, though the water stank of rotting stuff, and when we were sick that night, heaving our empty stomachs, the doctor scolded us for not listening to him.

"The days passed, sir, how, I do not wish to recall. We ate the roots of the scraggly brush. We drank the waters of the pools to keep alive, 'though we wished we were dead when the heat hit us after. Finally, we were done—at our ropes' ends. Even the bushes had been exhausted. God had plucked us from the sea to starve.

"Then the doctor told us his notion. I wish we'd died then, Mr. Holmes. But we listened. The doctor told us of tribes in Africa, in faraway lands and on deserted islands, that ate human flesh. He told us of its properties of vitality, of the precious fluids it contained. Then he proposed that we eat our own flesh.

"Mr. Winton laughed madly at his idea. Mr. Bennett cursed the doctor for a blasphemer. I—I listened, Mr. Holmes. My belly listened.

"The doctor proposed that one of us sacrifice an arm. Rationing it out, a little at a time, a man's arm, he said, big as we were (though not so meaty, then, I swear), would feed us for three days. Then, if we must, another, and then . . . Well, even I could listen no more. The doctor shut up.

"The next day was hotter than ever. The sweat ran down my brow in little trickles, and I lapped it up at the corners of my mouth. The doctor started in again. This time we all listened. The doctor proposed to remove a left arm of one of us (he being the surgeon having to do it, of course), and we should thereby live until rescue. We weakly debated it again. Finally, we all agreed, and we drew lots to decide who should first lose his limb. I lost. In the twilight that night, when it was cool enough to move about, the doctor cut off my left arm with my seaman's knife. I fainted from the pain, I must admit. The doctor had tied up the wound as best he could, but I bled like a stuck pig. In my delirium, I felt my life flowing from me, and I prayed for death.

"But I did not die, and the next morning I ate. I ate, sir, of my own flesh, with the help of Mr. Winton and Mr. Bennett. We all ate. The doctor took the bigger portion, so as to be able to save us all, he said. We did not begrudge him then, for he had saved us—so I thought then."

Tiptree paused, clutching his left shoulder. "It burns at night, Mr. Holmes, burns like the devil is stabbing it with a hot poker." He lay back on the divan, then continued. "We ate the meat slowly, parceling it out to put off the day we knew was coming. We sucked the juices from it, savoring each morsel. By God, I am ashamed to say that it tasted—good. But the day came, and it was gone. We agreed, then, to repeat the vital surgery. This time, however, I protested that the doctor draw straws with the rested, having seen him continually take more for himself than the others. He protested violently, and the others reluctantly agreed with him. But I would not be swerved. I made him take an oath that if we were rescued, he too would submit to removal of a limb, so that he might not profit from our misery. He swore, the blackguard, and then he cut!

"After each of us had lost an arm, we despaired that our bloody pain was just a beginning to further dismemberment. Then, hope against hope, we were rescued! When we sighted the ship on the horizon, we ran, in a burst of lunatic energy, down to the sea, to throw ourselves toward the ship. They set a boat for us, and it struck me, as the boat pulled across the waves, what we had done. I turned to the others and babbled my fear and shame. The doctor quickly took up my cause, and finally we all swore not to breathe a word of what had transpired on our island. I made the doctor repeat his oath, then, too.

"They picked us up and nursed us on their way to London then. They eyed us queerly, for we were a strange bearded bunch of madmen, but we said not a word of what had happened, save of the wreck itself. Our island meat diet must have done us well, for by the time we reached port, we were all well enough to be set free in London. Before we left the ship, I took the doctor aside. He liked it little, I could tell, for now I was mingling with my betters in front of the crew and passengers. But I gripped his neck and reminded him of his oath and arranged to meet him by the waterfront last Monday night, two weeks after we docked. He was to show up there and prove to me—I would act for us three—that he'd mutilated himself as well.

"I thought of little else, Mr. Holmes, for that fortnight, except our vengeance. Perhaps I should have fallen on my knees and praised God for sending us the doctor to save us there. Instead, I paced my room, cursing the doctor, waiting, waiting for our meeting. I took to detective work, then, searching out his offices. I followed him secretly, watching for the deed to be done."

"Finally the night came. I went to the appointed spot and paced again, waiting, waiting. He came, then, late. He was clad in a greatcoat, and his left sleeve hung limp. My poisoned brain began to rejoice. He carried under his right arm a long, narrow box. 'Here!' he said, placing it on the ground, then turned to go. 'Wait!' I cried. 'I must see it!' I flung back the lid of the casket and exclaimed with satisfaction as I saw the severed arm within. I looked at him, then, with exultation, and to my horror, I saw his greatcoat

swung carelessly open, and beneath it, his left arm strapped to his body. My brain reeled, and I leapt then, seizing him by the collar. In a moment, before he could cry out, I released him, plucked my knife from my boot, and stabbed him. My arm worked uncontrollably, stabbing again and again, and it was not until he crumpled against me that I realized my deed. I quickly wiped my knife in the dirt and pushed the box with the horrible false arm deep under a nearby building, for in my madness I feared the arm might link me to him. In a moment of clarity, I seized his wallet, thinking I could make it appear robbery. Then I ran with demons chasing me.

"I remember little else since then, Mr. Holmes. I wandered nearby, and some Samaritan, taking pity on a cripple perhaps, dropped a guinea in my pocket. For that, sir, I bought peace here until you came."

"We will not disturb your peace again," said Holmes, as he pulled me from my chair and turned to go. "Opium has become the religion of the masses, I fear, Watson," he said, "but for some, Heaven must wait too long."

In the cab, I could not be silent. "What a piteous wretch, Holmes! And so young!"

"Perhaps he will kill his pain and rejoin the living someday."

"However did you find him, Holmes?" I asked.

"Quite elementary, Watson, when one has the resources of my Baker Street Irregulars at one's disposal. I had Wiggins direct a search of every gin-mill and pipe den near the waterfront. I fully expected the man to be drowning himself in one sea or another."

"But why did you suspect him of Smithfield's murder, Holmes?"

"Come, Watson, the connection was certain clear. I must confess that when I first saw the contents of the mysterious box, I suspected deviltry—real deviltry, Watson, compared with Black Masses and the lot. But then Hopkins found my deceased carpenter for me—a patient of Smithfield's, as I suspected. His arm in a box similar to that with which the doctor was seen—well, the box had to be Smithfield's. But why would he bring it? Obviously, to give someone, but for what purpose? And why was his own arm bandaged?

"It was then that I knew we must trace the *White Star*. Smithfield's agitation commenced with his return, and he would not speak of the trip to his assistant. Why? Morse's story gave me the final link. Actually, though Tiptree believes he has sinned originally, his cannibalism tale is not new. I believe the King's Bench heard a similar case in '95. But the bargain element was unique, and until I surmised that, the connection was obscure."

Holmes puffed meditatively on his pipe. "The ways of nature are strange. She gives life, and she takes it. Sometimes we meddle too freely with her course, Watson, but we never bend her permanently from her appointed goal."

The Case of the Unseen Hand

DONALD THOMAS

BEST KNOWN FOR his first-rate pastiches of Sherlock Holmes, Donald Serrell Thomas (1935–) has also written a well-received series about the Victorian policeman Sergeant Verity under the Francis Selwyn pseudonym, among his long list of published works.

As an expert on Victorian times, especially its crime and criminals, Thomas has written various biographies, such as *Swinburne, the Poet in His World* (1979), *Robert Browning: A Life Within Life* (1982), and *Lewis Carroll: A Portrait with Background* (1996), and histories, notably *The Victorian Underworld*, with Henry Mayhew (1998), which was nominated for a Dagger by the (British) Crime Writers' Association.

His Victorian-era mystery novels under the Selwyn name began with *Sergeant Verity and the Cracksman* (1974; U.S. title: *Cracksman on Velvet*), followed by five additional adventures. Even more successful has been the series about Holmes, enhanced by the author's knowledgeable background of the time in which the stories are set, written under his own name.

The first of the ongoing Holmes series was *The Secret Cases of Sherlock Holmes* (1997), followed by *Sherlock Holmes and the Running Noose* (2001; U.S. title: *Sherlock Holmes and the Voice from the Crypt*), *The Execution of Sherlock Holmes* (2007), *Sherlock Holmes and the King's Evil* (2009), *Sherlock Holmes and the Ghosts of Bly* (2010), and *Death on a Pale Horse: Sherlock Holmes on Her Majesty's Secret Service* (2013).

"The Case of the Unseen Hand" was first published in *The Secret Cases of Sherlock Holmes* (London, Macmillan, 1997).

THE CASE OF THE UNSEEN HAND

Donald Thomas

I

IN THAT SERIES of events which I call "The Case of the Unseen Hand," everything appeared to turn against us from the outset. Yet, at its conclusion, Sherlock Holmes enjoyed a private success that was seldom matched in any of his other investigations.

Readers of "The Golden Pince-Nez," a narrative made public in *The Return of Sherlock Holmes*, may recall my reference to the earlier triumph of the great detective in tracking and arresting Huret, the so-called "Boulevard Assassin" of Paris, in 1894. Holmes was rewarded for his services with a handwritten letter from the President of France and by the Order of the Legion of Honour. The presidential letter was written in January 1895 by Félix Faure, who had just then succeeded to the leadership of his country at a most difficult moment, following the assassination of President Carnot and a few months of unhappy tenure by Casimir-Périer.

Holmes had a natural sympathy for Félix Faure, as a man who had risen from humble circumstances to the highest position in France. It was unfortunate for Monsieur Faure, however, that a month before he assumed office, Captain Alfred Dreyfus, a young probationary officer of the French General Staff, had been condemned by court martial to life imprisonment in the steaming and unbroken heat of Devil's Island for betraying his country's military secrets to Germany. In the aftermath of the trial there were rioting crowds in the streets of Paris, demanding

the execution of Dreyfus. The President himself was attacked in public and spat upon for his leniency. The mob threatened death to any man courageous enough to doubt the guilt of "the traitor." Dreyfus was first "degraded" on the parade ground of the École Militaire and then transported to that infamous penal colony off the French Guianan coast of South America. He was confined to a tiny stone hut, day and night, in the breathless heat of Cayenne Île du Diable. Though escape was impossible from such a place, his ankles were locked in double irons attached to a bar across the foot of his cot. His true punishment was not imprisonment for life but death by slow torture. A firing-squad would have been a more humane sentence.

The facts alleged against Alfred Dreyfus were that he had sold his country's secrets to Colonel Max von Schwartzkoppen, Military Attaché at the German Embassy in Paris. The court martial was held *in camera* but the details of the accusations were public knowledge. The paper, which his prosecutors insisted was in the hand of Dreyfus, conveyed to Colonel Schwartzkoppen specifications of the new and highly secret 120 mm gun, its performance and deployment; the reorganisation plan of the French Artillery, and the Field Artillery Firing Manual. Only an officer of the General Staff could have held such information.

Sherlock Holmes, like Émile Zola and a host of impartial men and women, never believed in the guilt of Captain Dreyfus. My friend's skill in graphology convinced him that the handwriting on the letter to Colonel Schwartzkoppen was not that of Alfred Dreyfus but, perhaps, a half-successful attempt at imitation. Like Monsieur Zola, Holmes also deplored the bigotry of the prosecution, the whole manner of the court martial and condemnation. Years later, our *Dreyfusards* were proved right. Colonel Hubert Henry of the Deuxième Bureau and Lemercier-Picard, who had both forged further "evidence" to deepen the guilt of Dreyfus after his condemnation, committed suicide.

In the years that followed our adventure, the innocence of Dreyfus and the guilt of a certain Major Count Ferdinand Walsin-Esterhazy were to be established. Restored to his command, as a gallant officer of the Great War, Captain Dreyfus was to join Sherlock Holmes as a Chevalier of the Legion of Honour. The manner in which justice was done at last forms the background to my account of our own case.

II

In January 1899, when the presidency of Félix Faure and the imprisonment of Captain Dreyfus had already lasted for four years, Holmes and I travelled to Paris on behalf of the British government. Our confidential mission, which had been warmly supported by our friend Lestrade at Scotland Yard, was to meet the great Bertillon. Alphonse Bertillon was a former professor of anthropology, now head of the Identification Bureau at the Préfecture de Police. The "Bertillon System" had enabled the French police to identify a man or woman uniquely by measuring certain bony structures of the body, notably those of the head. It was claimed in Paris that these measurements would render all criminal disguises and false identities futile. The objection at Scotland Yard was that such a system was far too complicated for general use. In England, Sherlock Holmes and Sir Francis Galton had been working upon the simpler method of identification by fingerprints, which Bertillon had also pioneered. They had been set upon the task

by Mr. Asquith, as Home Secretary in 1893. At first their opponents argued that no jury would be persuaded to convict a defendant upon such a whimsical theory. Twelve years later, however, the Stratton brothers were to be hanged for the Deptford Street murder on the evidence of a single thumbprint.

When we set off for Paris in January 1899, it was our mission to persuade Professor Bertillon to join his efforts with ours in championing this simpler method of criminal detection. One of Bertillon's original objections had been that a great many surfaces retain no visible fingerprint. Holmes had answered this when he devised in our Baker Street rooms a system for making these unseen or "latent" fingerprints visible, by the use of silver nitrate powder or iodine fumes. Bertillon then demanded of him how such evidence was to be displayed in court. In reply, Holmes had painstakingly adapted a small Kodak camera by adding an open box to the front, so that the lens always looked down on the fingerprint from a uniform distance and was therefore permanently in focus. By this means, any number of photographs of a fingerprint might be made for a criminal trial. He had brought his prototype of the camera to display to the great French criminologist. All the same, there was no sign as yet that such advances would persuade Professor Bertillon to change his mind.

On a chill but windless January day, we crossed from Folkestone to Boulogne by the *Lord Warden* steamer. Holmes stood at the ship's rail, his sharp profile framed by his ear-flapped travelling-cap. As soon as we cast off from Folkestone harbour pier, it seemed that his interest in his French adversary underwent a significant change. Fingerprints and skull measurements were discarded from our conversation. He unfolded a sheet of paper and handed it to me.

"The affair of Captain Dreyfus, Watson. Read this. It is a private note from my disgraced friend Colonel Picquart, late of the Information Branch of the Deuxième Bureau. Even in this matter it seems that we cannot escape the shade of Bertillon. Picquart tells me that the professor is immoveable, convinced that the incriminating letter of 1894 is in the hand of Captain Dreyfus. For a man of Bertillon's capability to believe such a thing is quite beyond my comprehension. Unfortunately, however, his reputation as a criminal expert will count for far more in a courtroom than all Monsieur Zola's denunciations of injustice."

He shook his head and gave a quiet sigh, staring across the Channel. The sea lay calm as wrinkled satin towards the sands of France, pale and chill on the horizon of that winter afternoon.

"Then what will you do?" I asked, handing back to him the sheet of paper.

"I shall pray, Watson. Not for a miracle—merely for an opportunity to demonstrate to Professor Bertillon the error of his methods in graphology and identification alike. There is a battle to be fought and won for Captain Dreyfus but it must be fought at the right time and in the right place."

During the next few weeks our Baker Street quarters were exchanged for two bedrooms and a sitting-room at the Hôtel Lutétia in the Boulevard Raspail. It was an area of business and bustle, having more in common with the nearby railway terminus of the Gare Montparnasse than with the bohemian society of poets and artists which the name of that district more often suggests. The Hôtel Lutétia rose like the hull of an ocean liner above a quayside in this commercial avenue of tall houses with their grey mansard roofs, their elegant windows and balconies set in pale tidewashed stone. In front of many a grander building, a handsome *porte-cochère* entrance remained. Yet the days of Second Empire quiet had gone. As afternoon drew on, the winter sun threw up a dusty light from the constant traffic.

I was not present at the private discussions between Holmes and Professor Bertillon, which were concluded in a day or two. In truth, there was little to discuss so long as the two men remained immoveable. The silver nitrate, the iodine fumes, the special camera, were mere toys in Bertillon's view. To make matters worse, a further hostility arose in general conversation

when the professor repeated his view that the incriminating message of 1894 to the German Military Attaché was written in the hand of Captain Dreyfus. The first day's meeting ended with ill temper on both sides. Next morning Bertillon returned to the debate over scientific detection, insisting that fingerprints might be disfigured or erased, or even prevented by the wearing of gloves. They were no substitute for the measurement of criminal heads, where counterfeiting was an impossibility. With that, he indicated that his exchange of views with his English visitor was at an end. Holmes returned from the Préfecture de Police in a filthy temper, his vanity bruised, and his appetite for battle with the French anthropologist all the keener. I could not help thinking—though I judged it best not to say so at the time—that the sooner we returned to Baker Street, the better.

I had begun to look forward to our return and was already picturing myself among the comforts of home, when I heard my companion in the lobby of the hotel, informing the manager that we should require our rooms for at least another fortnight.

"But why?" I demanded, as soon as we were alone.

"Because, Watson, an innocent man is condemned to suffer the nightmare of Devil's Island until he drops dead from exhaustion or the brutality of the regime. Bertillon, the one expert whose word might yet save him, refuses to say that word. As it happens, he also rejects, unexamined, the only infallible method of criminal identification upon which others have lavished years of toil. I do not greatly care for Alphonse Bertillon. I swear to you that these two issues may yet become a personal matter between us."

"For God's sake, Holmes! You cannot fight a duel with the head of a French police bureau!"

"In my own way, Watson, that is just what I propose to do."

After so much bluster, as I thought it, Holmes became inexplicably a pattern of idleness. So much for his threats against Professor Bertillon! Like a man who feels that the best of life is behind him, he began to describe our visit to Paris as a chance that "might not come again." Yet I could not believe that it was some premonition of mortality that determined him to spend two or three weeks longer in the city. More probably it was his usual mode of life, in which he alternated between intense periods of obsessional activity—when he would sleep little and eat less—and weeks when he seemed to do little more than stare from his armchair at the sky beyond the window, without a thought in his head.

The indolence that came upon him now was not quite of the usual sort. He tasted something of bohemian café society at the Closerie des Lilas with its trees and its statue of Marshal Ney. He spent an entire day reading the icy tombstones of Montparnasse cemetery, as he was to do next day at Père Lachaise. For the most part, we walked the cold streets and parks as we had never done in any other city.

A frosty morning was our time for the tree-lined vista of the Avenue de la Grande Armée, the lakes and woods of the Bois de Boulogne extending before us in a chill mist. Down the wide thoroughfare, the closed carriages of fashionable society rattled on frozen cobbles. The shrubbery gardens of the adjacent mansions lay silent and crisp beyond the snowcaps of tall wrought-iron railings.

"My dear Holmes," I said that evening, "it is surely better that we should go our separate ways for a little. There is no purpose in our remaining longer in Paris. At least, there is no purpose for me. Let me return to London and attend to business there. You may stay here and follow when you think the time is right. There can be no use in both of us remaining."

"Oh, yes, Watson," he said quietly, "there is the greatest use in the world. It will require us both, of that I am sure."

"May I know what the use is?"

"The question cannot be pressed," he said vaguely. "The purpose must mature in its own time."

It matured at a snail's pace, as it seemed to me, for almost a week. During those days our morning rambles now took us through the red revolutionary *arrondissements* of the north-east.

We crossed the little footbridges of the Canal Saint-Martin. Holmes studied the sidings and marshalling-yards of Aubervilliers with the rapt attention that other visitors might give to the *Mona Lisa* in the Louvre. A late sun of the winter morning rose like a red ball through the mist across the heroic distance of the Place de la République, where the statue of Marianne stands like a towering Amazon protecting the booths and shooting galleries. By evening we were in the wide lamplit spaces of the Place de la Concorde, the tall slate roofs of the Quai d'Orsay rising through a thin river mist on the far bank.

Five days passed in this manner, as if Holmes were mapping the city in his head, noting the alleys, culs-de-sac, escape routes, and short cuts. That evening, there were footsteps on the stairs. At the door of our rooms, there appeared briefly and dimly a visitor who brought an envelope of discreet and expensive design with the gold initials "RF" interwoven. Holmes read the contents but said nothing.

Next morning, he came from his room in a costume more bizarre than any of his disguises as a tramp or a Lascar seaman. He was wearing the black swallow-tailed coat and white tie of court dress. Before I could ask what the devil this meant, there was a discreet tap at the door and our visitor of the previous evening reappeared, now similarly attired in formal dress. I caught a murmured exchange and the newcomer twice used the form of "Monsieur le Président," when indicating that time pressed. Holmes accompanied him without a word. I turned to the window and saw them enter a closed carriage, its black coachwork immaculately polished but without a single crest or other emblem to indicate its origins. I could only suppose it was for this summons that Holmes had been waiting while we walked the streets of Paris.

III

In the hours that passed before I saw him again, I no longer doubted that the "purpose" of our visit was working itself out. Holmes had used his influence, the Order of the Legion of Honour, as well as the reputation of a man who had rid Paris of the Boulevard Assassin, to obtain an audience with President Faure. The intention could only be to convince Félix Faure that Captain Dreyfus was no traitor and that the letter sent to Colonel Schwartzkoppen, the Military Attaché, would be shown on scientific examination to be the work of another hand.

It was late in the afternoon when my companion returned. He knew as well as I that there was no need for an explanation of his absence. He stood in the sitting-room of the hotel suite, a familiar figure in the unfamiliarity of his formal costume.

"Your patience may be rewarded, Watson," he said with the quick movement of his mouth, which was sometimes a smile and sometimes a nervous quirk, "I have put our case to President Faure."

"Our case?"

He smiled more easily. "Very well, then, the case of Alfred Dreyfus. The matter of the handwriting. We have, I believe, a chance to vanquish Professor Bertillon on both fronts. Who knows? If we succeed in this, there may be a path to victory over him in other matters. I have struck a bargain with Félix Faure. The evidence against Dreyfus will be reviewed. Indeed, though he still thinks the man guilty, in all probability, he has not set his face against a retrial."

"Then you have succeeded?" I asked the question because, to anyone who had known him for a length of time, it was evident that Holmes was holding back some unwelcome detail.

"Not quite," he said, another nervous movement plucking at his mouth. "I fear, Watson, you will not like our side of the bargain. We are to remain in Paris for a few more months."

"Months! What the devil for?"

"That, my dear friend, will be explained to you within the hour by President Faure's confidential secretary. It is not too much to say that the fate of France and the peace of Europe may depend upon the safety of the treasure we are to guard."

"Treasure!" I exclaimed. "What treasure?"

But Holmes waved his hand aside, recommending patience. He turned and went to his room, exchanging formal clothes for familiar tweeds and Norfolk jacket. Short of pursuing him and standing over him while he changed, there was little I could do. I walked about the tall corniced sitting-room on the first floor of the Hôtel Lutétia, folding a paper here and tidying a table there, in anticipation of a visit from the confidential secretary of the President of the Republic. Then I paused and stared down into the Boulevard Raspail with its busy traffic from the suburbs and markets. Would Félix Faure's confidential secretary really make a habit of visiting confidants in what was almost a public room? I thought of Sir Henry Ponsonby and Sir Arthur Bigge as Her Majesty's private secretaries, conducting confidential negotiations in the hotels of Bayswater or Pimlico. The idea was plainly absurd.

This was one of the rare occasions when I suspected that Holmes, on unfamiliar territory, was out of his depth. He had just reappeared in his tweed suiting, when there was a knock at the door. It was a hotel page-boy who had brought our visitor from the lobby. The stranger entered the sitting-room. As the page closed the door again, Holmes bowed, took the hand of the President's confidential secretary, and kissed it with instinctive gallantry. This newcomer was not the type of Sir Henry Ponsonby nor Sir Arthur Bigge, but one of the most striking young women upon whom I had ever set eyes.

IV

She might have been eighteen, though the truth was that she was thirty and already had a daughter who was ten years old. Yet there was such a soft round beauty in her face, a depth to her wide eyes, and a lustre in the elegant coiffure of her dark hair that she reminded one irresistibly of a London *débutante* in her first season. To describe her figure as elegant, narrow-waisted, and instinctively graceful in every movement is to resort to the commonplaces of portraiture. Yet Marguerite Steinheil was possessed of all these attributes and was never commonplace.

Such was Félix Faure's confidential secretary. Though I was struck by her beauty, even her modesty of demeanour on this occasion, the thought that preoccupied me was that no English politician's reputation could have withstood such an association with a young woman of so remarkable a presence as hers.

"Watson!" Holmes turned to me with a look of triumph. "Let me introduce to you Madame Marguerite Steinheil, the emissary of President Faure. Madame, allow me to present my colleague, Dr. John Watson, before whom you may speak as freely as to myself."

Somehow, I scarcely recall how, I mumbled my way through the pleasantries of formal introduction in the next few minutes. If I had thought before this that Sherlock Holmes had plunged into the Dreyfus affair beyond his depth, I was now utterly convinced of it. Madame Steinheil took her place on the chaise-longue, Holmes and I facing her from two upright gilded chairs. She spoke almost perfect English with an accent so light that it added to the charm of her voice.

"I believe," she said, "that I may soon be able to bring you good news of Captain Dreyfus, of whose innocence I have never myself entertained the least doubt. However, I may only help him, or help you, if you will assist me in return."

"Then you must explain that, madame," Holmes said quietly. "I believe it is the President whom we are to serve, is it not?"

She smiled quickly at him and said, "It is the same thing, Mr. Holmes. More than four years ago, I became his friend because of his interest in art. My husband, Adolphe Steinheil, is a portrait painter. Our drawing-room has long been a meeting-place for men and women from literature, art, music, and public life. We have a house and a studio in the Impasse Ronsin, off the Rue de Vaugirard, near the Gare Montparnasse. Félix Faure was a guest at my *salons*, a friend before he became President. After his election, he bought one of Adolphe's paintings for the private rooms in the Élysée Palace. He is the President but he is also the greatest friend in the world to me. I must make this confidence to you. My own father is dead but Félix Faure has been, in his way, a father to me and I, perhaps, like a daughter to him."

The more I heard of this, the less I liked it. I saw that Holmes's mouth tightened a little.

"Forgive me, Madame Steinheil, but you are not—are you?—a daughter. You are a confidential secretary and you will betray your trust if you seek to be anything more."

She put her hands together and stared down at them. Then she looked up with the same smile, the same openness of her face and gaze, that would have softened any accusation in the world.

"Mr. Holmes," she said quietly, "I need not tell you that the Third Republic of France was born from war and revolutionary bloodshed almost thirty years ago. Since then, there has been scandal, riot, and assassination. In England, I think, you have not known such things. Were you to see the secret papers of the past thirty years in our own country, you would be more deeply troubled still and perhaps a good deal more shocked than you have been even by the affair of Captain Dreyfus. These papers of which I speak are known to very few people. Naturally, they have been seen by fewer people still."

"Of whom you are doubtless one, madame!"

The cold precision of his voice was a harsh contrast to the softer tones of Marguerite Steinheil. Yet she was a match for him.

"Of whom I am one," she said, inclining her head. "Since the President came to office, he has suffered abuse in the Chamber of Deputies, he has been physically attacked in public and spat at. Lesser men would have resigned the office, as his predecessor did, and France would go down in civil war. But he will not resign, Mr. Holmes. He will fight. In order to fight, he must have a weapon. The pen, as you say, will prove mightier than the sword."

"If it is used with discretion," Holmes said gently.

She smiled again and then dropped her voice a little, as if fearing that even now she might be overheard.

"For the past three years, Félix Faure has been engaged upon his secret history of France since the Franco-Prussian War of 1870. It is to be his testament, his justification of steps that he must take, before the end of his *septennat*—his period of office."

"And you, madame?" Holmes inquired coolly. "What are you to him in such a crisis?"

There was no smile as she looked at him now.

"What am I in all this? Félix Faure saw in me a friend who would offer an undivided loyalty, a loyalty that is not to be found among the ministers and officials surrounding him. You have not lived in France during the past ten years, Mr. Holmes. From your well-ordered life in London, it is hard to imagine the scandal and near-revolution that plagues this city."

"One may deduce a little, even in London."

"No," she said, and shook her head with a whisper of disagreement, "Félix Faure was called to office among the mortal injuries which France seemed determined to inflict on herself. The Boulangists would overthrow republicanism and restore the monarchy. The Anarchists would plunge us in blood. We had watched the *bourse*—the stock exchange—and the Quai d'Orsay brought to near-ruin by the Panama corruption scandals and the disappearance of two hundred and fifty million francs. We had seen governments created in hope, only to collapse in dishonour after a few months. Six months before my friend was called to the highest office, President Carnot himself was stabbed to death at Lyons by a terrorist. President Casimir-Périer was driven from office by libel and ridicule within a few weeks. During those weeks came the Dreyfus affair."

Holmes was about to say something but seemed to think better of it.

"I watched that man's epaulettes torn from his tunic," the young woman continued softly, "on the parade ground of the École Militaire, his sword broken over the adjutant's knee. Mobs shouted for his death in the riots that followed. France had degenerated into such chaos that government itself seemed impossible. In our relations with the world, we had drifted from our alliance with Russia and were close to war with England over Fashoda and the Sudan. Félix Faure tried without success to persuade his ministers that a *rapprochement* with England and Russia was our sole salvation abroad. He failed to move them. How could he succeed when, as the secret papers confirm, his closest adviser in foreign affairs was a man whose mistress had for years been in the pay of the German Embassy? Four months ago, in October, matters were so grave that Monsieur Faure considered carrying out a military *coup d'état* as President, taking absolute power to impose order on the country by martial law."

"And you, madame?" Holmes still pressed for an answer to the most important question of all. "What were you to Félix Faure?"

"I was his eyes and ears throughout all this, as well as his amanuensis. I went privately to sittings of the Chamber of Deputies and the Senate, to certain receptions and parties. He is surrounded by enemies in government and now he knows it, through me. I was better able to identify certain men who might have destroyed him, had they been appointed to office. They are, Mr. Holmes, without scruples or principles under their masks of public virtue. They are *arrivistes* ready to sell themselves to achieve their ambitions."

Sherlock Holmes held her gaze dispassionately.

"As a woman, however, you were surely in greater danger of being compromised in your role of adviser than a man would have been?"

If Marguerite Steinheil blushed a little at the innuendo, I saw no sign of it.

"My sex was my advantage. No man is inscrutable to a woman, Mr. Holmes, especially when that woman is devoted to one whom she has decided to help, and when she is supposed to care for nothing more essential than music, flowers, or dress."

"But you do not play quite the same part now, I take it?"

"No," she said softly. "The dangers and the threats became so numerous that there could only be one answer—'The Secret History of France under the Third Republic.' It is a weapon so powerful that our adversaries dare not provoke its use. Every afternoon, the President adds several pages to it, on foolscap paper which I buy for him myself. At first these pages were locked in an iron box at the Élysée Palace itself. Then, in the crisis of last October, Félix Faure asked me to take home the pages as he wrote them. Until this afternoon, three people in the world knew of this precaution: the President and I, of course, and Monsieur Hamard, Chief of the Sûreté, a man of honour to whom Félix Faure would entrust his very life. Dr. Watson and yourself must now be admitted to the secret."

"Then I trust, madame, you will use such a weapon as a shield, not as a sword."

The young woman smiled at this. "A shield is all we ask, Mr. Holmes. The President's enemies cannot be sure what revelations drawn from the secret papers these chapters may contain. Yet he has taken good care that those from whom he has most to fear are aware of the consequences. If such pages were to be made public, the reputations of those men would be blasted. It would be impossible for them to hold office and they would be fortunate indeed to escape prosecution as common criminals. Perhaps you think such a threat unchivalrous? No doubt it is. I assure you, however, that there is nothing in those pages except what is the proven truth."

She paused and Holmes said nothing for a moment. He took his pipe from the pocket of his Norfolk tweeds and then replaced it.

"It is on this account that you wish Dr. Watson and I to remain in Paris?"

"Only for a while," she said gently. "In a month—two months at the most—enough of the work will be done. A copy will be made and deposited elsewhere, to make the work safe for posterity. Meanwhile, new pages and documents will be taken back each night to a hiding-place in the Impasse Ronsin. In the past weeks, the President has been warned by Monsieur Hamard that visitors to the Élysée Palace are being watched by those who may be agents of foreign powers but more probably of our enemies within France. Some of our visitors are being followed. It would not do for a single page of the history or a single document to fall into the hands of those who would destroy us."

Holmes spoke courteously but the scepticism in his eyes, as he regarded her, was inescapable to anyone who knew him.

"You have begun well, madame, by ensuring that the manuscript is removed from the Élysée Palace. You must surely have more enemies in that building than in the rest of the world. In a crisis, that is the first place where those whom you fear would search for it. As for the opinion of Monsieur Hamard, he and I have been acquainted ever since the case of the Boulevard Assassin. I hold him in the highest regard. If he warns you of a danger, you would be well advised to take heed."

"Indeed," she said, "it is on Monsieur Hamard's suggestion that I am here this afternoon. Knowing that you were in Paris to confer with his colleague Professor Bertillon, he believed you might be prepared to assist. He advises that, for the future, any papers which I take with me to the Impasse Ronsin each evening should be a decoy, documents of no importance. The pages of the manuscript itself will be entrusted to you. At a distance, you and Dr. Watson will be my escort and courier. When you are satisfied that no one is watching or following, you may deliver the envelope through the letter-box of the Impasse Ronsin."

Holmes looked unaccountably gloomy.

"Yes," he said thoughtfully. "Well, Madame Steinheil, I have had this put to me in similar terms by the President. It is hard for a humble ratepayer of Baker Street to oppose the will of a head of state. However, I shall ask you a question that I might not ask the President. What purpose is served by Dr. Watson and myself remaining in Paris to do something that any well-trained policeman might do? Indeed, you might employ a different officer each evening, so that whoever attempted to shadow you would not recognise him. As for the papers, you scarcely need more than a porter to convey your luggage."

There, I thought, he had tripped her. Marguerite Steinheil looked her prettiest at him.

"A President is surely entitled to ask for the best?"

"No, no, madame!" said Holmes with a flash of irritation. "That really will not do for an answer!"

She flinched a little. "Very well, then. Among the papers from which the narrative is drawn—in the pages of the narrative itself—will be found evidence to prove the innocence of Colonel Dreyfus beyond all argument."

"Then let that evidence be published now," Holmes said abruptly.

Again she shook her head. "The man who might put the case beyond any further argument is in Berlin. He has been forbidden from speaking by the Chief of the German General Staff and by the Kaiser himself. If our plan succeeds, they will find in a month or two that they can command him no longer."

There was a moment's silence. In that comfortable hotel sitting-room on the Boulevard Raspail, we pictured Dreyfus the innocent, the man of honour, riveted in his irons in the jungle mist of Cayenne Île du Diable, condemned to rot until death released him.

"*Fiat justitia, ruat coelum,*" Holmes said at last, still with reluctance. "Let justice be done, though the heavens fall. Madame, you shall have your way. God knows, it is a small enough price that we pay for the poor fellow's liberty."

After she had taken her leave, he sat without speaking. Then, as he was apt to do when something of great weight was on his mind, he walked to the window and stared out into the street. It was dark by now and the scene was one that might have been painted by Pissarro or Manet. Each flickering gas-lamp threw out a misty halo,

its shivering image reflected in pools of rain. The traffic of cabs and horse-buses dwindled from the brightly lit shops of the Rue de Rennes to the quiet elegance of the Boulevard St. Germain. Men and women hurried homeward by the darkened skyline of the Luxembourg Gardens.

"So," he said, turning at last, "we are to remain here in order to guard a few sheets of paper every evening, to prevent them from being snatched away in the street! Can you believe a word of it, Watson? It reminds me of nothing so much as that other useless occupation, the Red-Headed League, whose history you were good enough to preserve in your memoirs! A man was paid handsomely for the aimless daily exercise of copying out the whole of the *Encyclopaedia Britannica* by hand. A pretty piece of villainy lay behind that!"

I was a little shocked by his tone.

"You do not call Madame Steinheil a villain?"

"Of course I do not!" he said impatiently. "Wayward, perhaps. She has, I believe, the reputation of what is delicately called, among the fashionables of Rotten Row, a 'Pretty Horse-Breaker.'"

The vulgar phrase sounded oddly in his fastidious speech.

"Then you believe she has not told us the truth?"

"Not the whole truth! Of course not!" He looked at me in dismay, unable to see how I had missed the fact. "It does not require the two of us to prevent an envelope being snatched from her hand or to see whether she is followed. She knows that as well as you or I!"

"What else is there to prevent?"

"After all that we have heard from her of *coups d'état* and treason, you still do not see why our services are preferred to those of the Sûreté or the Deuxième Bureau?"

"I do not see what else she hopes we may prevent," I said with the least feeling of exasperation. "What is it?"

Sherlock Holmes gave a fatalistic sigh.

"In all probability," he said softly, "the assassination of the President of France."

V

During the next few days, the prediction seemed so preposterous that I had not the heart to remind him of it, even as a joke. Every afternoon, we took the same cab to the same drab stretch of the Rue de Vaugirard with its hospitals and public buildings. In the Impasse Ronsin, the tall house with its studio windows rose beyond a high street-wall and garden trees. As if at a signal, a second cab turned out on to the main thoroughfare and preceded us by way of the Boulevard des Invalides, the elegant span of the Pont Alexandre III, across the River Seine, and past the glass domes of the exhibition pavilions.

Sometimes, when the winter afternoon was sunny, the young woman would dismiss the cab at the river bridge and walk across the wide spaces of evergreen gardens with their regimented trees and little chairs, at the lower end of the Champs-Élysées. This was done to give us a better opportunity of seeing whether she was shadowed. From time to time a man might look sidelong at the narrow-waisted beauty, the collar of her coat trimmed with fur that lay more sensuously against the bloom of her cheek, the coquettish hat with its net veil crowning her elegant coiffure. Many wistful and casual glances came in her direction yet no one followed her.

Quickly and unobtrusively, she was admitted by the little gate in the gold-tipped iron railings of the presidential palace, at the corner of the Champs-Élysées and the Avenue de Marigny. Not a soul took the least notice. Several times, on her return, she got down from the cab among the little streets of the Left Bank that run from the *grands quais* of the Seine, opposite the Louvre. In the early dusk, she paused at the shopfronts of the Rue des Saints Pères in dark green or terracotta or black with gold. Curios and jewellery shone in the lamplit windows. The shelves of the *bibliothèques* glowed with the rich leather bindings of rare editions. Holmes and I knew from long experience that in such territory the hunter easily becomes the prey. The shadow must dawdle or feign interest or linger

in his cab, while his quarry visits one shop after another. If there was such a man on these evenings, the trained eye of Sherlock Holmes failed to see him.

On several afternoons, Holmes and I were admitted by the same little gate to the grounds of the Élysée Palace, by the authority of the President's *chef de cabinet*, Monsieur Le Gall. The President's office was on the ground floor of the left wing of the palace, looking out upon a private garden. Beyond the presidential office and the private study, these quiet apartments ended in an elegant bedroom, used by Félix Faure on the frequent nights when he worked into the small hours, so that Madame Faure should not be disturbed by his late arrival.

On our occasional visits to Le Gall, neither Holmes nor I was admitted beyond an outer office, where the *chef de cabinet* guarded the entrance to the presidential suite. It was on 16 February that we were last there. Madame Steinheil was a little later than usual, arriving at about 5:30 p.m. to collect the papers that the President had been writing. We were received by Le Gall in his outer office a half-hour later. To that moment, there was no sign of anyone—man nor woman—shadowing the "confidential secretary" who had been put under our care.

At the time of our arrival, Madame de Steinheil was already in the office or study of the presidential apartment, no doubt copying pages for the use of her patron. The President himself had just finished a conversation with a visitor who came out of the apartments, escorted by a chamberlain, taking his leave almost as soon as we had begun speaking to Le Gall. Even had I not seen his face in the newspaper photographs of the past few days, I should have guessed by his purple cassock and biretta that he was Cardinal Richard, Archbishop of Paris.

The purpose of the Cardinal's visit to the President was never revealed. As soon as His Eminence had left, however, Le Gall ushered Holmes and me to a waiting-room at one side. The door swung to but failed to catch, leaving us with a narrow aperture into the *chef de cabinet*'s office. A tall saturnine man in evening dress with a purple sash and the star of a royal order walked slowly past. On the far side of Le Gall's office, another door opened and closed. There was a murmur of voices. Holmes stretched in his armchair, took a pencil from his pocket, and wrote something in his notebook.

"The Prince of Monaco," he said quietly. "This promises well, Watson. My information is that, for several months, His Serene Highness has been the go-between of the President and the Kaiser in the matter of Captain Dreyfus. Berlin is less threatened by the scandal than Paris but it would suit both parties to have the matter settled."

Shortly after this, Le Gall or one of his assistants must have noticed that the waiting-room door was a little ajar. It was closed from outside, by whose hand we did not see. Whether the Prince of Monaco had left or the interview with the President continued was hidden from us.

In recollecting what followed, I believe it was about three-quarters of an hour that we had been waiting for our summons to escort Madame Steinheil back to the Impasse Ronsin. I was immersed in a Tauchnitz pocket-book and Holmes was reading the evening paper. Not a word passed between us until, without warning, Holmes threw the newspaper down and sprang to his feet.

"What in God's name was that, Watson?"

His face was drawn into an expression that mingled horror and dismay, a fearful look more intense than any other I can remember in the course of our friendship. The look in his eyes and the angle of his head assured me that Holmes, who had the most acute hearing of any man known to me, had caught something beyond my range.

"Do you not hear it, man? You must hear it!"

In two strides he was at the waiting-room door, which he flung open without ceremony. As he did so, I caught the shrill escalating screams of terror which rang through the private apartments of the President of France. They were a woman's screams.

Of Le Gall, there was no sign, though the fine double doors of white and gold that led to the President's office stood open. After so much talk of traitors and assassination, you may imagine what my thoughts were. The screams stopped for an instant, only to be resumed with greater urgency. They were not cries of pain but shrieks of unbridled fear. Perhaps, then, we should be in time to prevent whatever was threatened.

Holmes strode through the presidential office with the red buttoned leather of its chairs and the walnut veneer of the desk. Beyond that, the single door to the private study swung lightly in the draught. The curtains were still open. Outside, in the private garden, thin snow drifted down through the lamplight on to the lawns and formal paths. There was no one in the study itself but the far door opened into a small book-lined lobby. This lobby framed a further pair of doors—again in white and gold—which guarded the boudoir of the presidential suite. Those doors were closed and Le Gall stood facing them, pushing with his arms out and hands spread wide, as if seeking some means to force his way through. The shrieks, which now redoubled, were coming from the bedroom itself. I thought I heard the word "Assassin!" with its French emphasis and pronunciation.

Holmes pushed the *chef de cabinet* aside, for had we left it to Le Gall he would never have broken open the locked doors. My friend's right foot rose and he crashed the heel of his boot into the ornamental lock. The double doors shuddered but held. Holmes took a pace back and again smashed the heel of his boot into the fastening. One of the two doors burst open and flew back against the inner wall with a crack. Holmes was first through the opening, Le Gall after him. I brought up the rear with Holmes already calling out, "Here, Watson! As quickly as ever you can!"

I stood in the doorway and saw before me such a sight as I hope never to see again.

VI

The tangled bodies in their nakedness were like nothing so much as a detail from some canvas depicting a massacre. Félix Faure was a well-built man of the heavily handsome type. Approaching sixty years of age, he had a head that was broad and tall, pale blue eyes, and a long moustache. He lay face down, naked as he was born, the gross bulk of him sprawling and slack in a manner that meant only one thing to me. Under him, trapped by his weight, without a shift or a stitch upon her, lay Marguerite Steinheil. There were spots of blood upon her face and shoulders which had come from his nose or mouth.

It was a horrible and yet, in its way, a commonplace tableau to a medical man. The tragedy of an old lover and a young mistress, cerebral congestion, apoplexy occurring in the excitement of some venereal spasm, is a textbook fact that needs no moral commentary here. I reached Félix Faure in time to detect a pulse that faded under my touch. In the moment of his seizure, the dying man had clenched his fingers in the young woman's hair, adding to her terror beyond measure. With some caution, I straightened the fingers one by one. Holmes and I turned the dead President on to his back. Le Gall snatched a dressing-gown from the closet and wrapped Madame Steinheil in it. She stood before us, still crying out hysterically, until there was a crack like a pistol as Holmes slapped her across the face.

Le Gall's hand was on the bell.

"No!" shouted Holmes. "Wait!" Thereupon he took command of the situation while the *chef de cabinet* did his bidding. "Get this young woman dressed!"

It was easier said than done. Without going to indelicate lengths of description, I can record that Madame Steinheil had been wearing a corset, which few women could put on again without the assistance of a ladies' maid. So it was that she was helped into her outer clothes, the rest being bundled into a valise.

"Touch nothing, Watson, until I get back! Nothing!"

With that, Holmes led the poor trembling courtesan out by a side entrance into the snow. I watched them cross the lawn to the little gate, with Le Gall following. On the *chef de cabinet*'s authority, the private gate at the Avenue de Marigny was opened and Madame Steinheil was put into the cab, which had been previously ordered to wait for her, with directions to the driver to proceed directly to the Impasse Ronsin.

In my friend's absence, I had found a nightshirt in the armoire. Between us, we managed to draw it over the head of the corpse and impart some decency to the mortal remains of the late Félix Faure.

"Monsieur!" Holmes spun round on Le Gall. "Have the goodness to find a priest. Any priest! The Madeleine will be your nearest church."

Le Gall was like a man in a stupor.

"No," he said. "There is no purpose. The President is dead and formalities must follow their course."

"Formalities!" Holmes snapped at him, like a man waking a dreamer. "Do you not see that there is enough scandal in all this to have a revolution on the streets of Paris before tomorrow night? That is where formalities will get you! Find the first priest that you can and tell him President Faure is dying!"

Badly shaken though he was, the *chef de cabinet* went out. In five minutes Holmes and I had drawn the sheets over the body and Félix Faure lay on his back, his head on the pillow and his eyes closed. Holmes paced the room, looking here and there, as if for some lost clue to explain the tragedy. But the explanation lay only in the medical textbooks.

"Here, I think!" he said presently, picking up a small ochre-coloured bottle from the dressing-table. "What, my friend, do you make of this?"

As he held it before me, I could read only another parable of human frailty and old men's folly. There was little doubt that Félix Faure had taken a philtre of some kind which he hoped would aid his failing powers where women were concerned and which surely was the precipitating cause of his death. I thought, but did not say so, that he might have taken one of the capsules before the visit of the Prince of Monaco interrupted his intentions and had then taken another following it. For a man in his condition, it had been a most dangerous dose. Holmes took a small bag from his pocket and carefully dropped the bottle into it.

"It will not do, Watson, to leave such a thing where it may be found. The poor fellow is dead; let that be enough."

Though little more than five minutes had passed, Le Gall was back with a young priest in a cassock, a prison chaplain who had been passing the main entrance of the palace on the Rue du Faubourg St. Honoré as the *chef de cabinet* hurried towards the Madeleine. A little overawed by the magnificence of the death-chamber, the young chaplain murmured the phrases of absolution over the President's remains.

"Now," said Holmes to Le Gall, "you will have the goodness to send for a doctor and for Madame Faure, as quickly as possible. My colleague and I will take our leave by the gate into the Avenue de Marigny."

Le Gall, in his confusion and grief, promised that no reward we might ask was too great for having averted a scandal that would surely have led to civil disturbance and bloodshed. Even as matters stood, the Paris newspapers were not long in circulating a rumour that the President had met his death through the murderous cunning of a Judith or a Delilah employed by the fanatics of Captain Dreyfus.

"I will take no fee and no reward," said Holmes, "unless it be a trivial souvenir of a great man."

"Whatever you wish is yours," Le Gall insisted.

With great delicacy, my friend lifted a little box of pale rose-coloured Sèvres *porcelaine tendre*, an exquisite thing no more than two inches square that might have been a snuff-box.

"Is that all?" the *chef de cabinet* asked, embarrassed by so slight a gift.

"Yes," said Holmes quietly. "That is all. And now I think it best that, so far as we are concerned, we should leave Paris and this matter should be at an end."

VII

So it seemed to be. There were riots by an unthinking mob, encouraged in the right-wing press, who accused the *Dreyfusards* of murdering their President, but there was no revolution. Félix Faure was mourned and buried by the better part of his compatriots with a dignity befitting his rank. Dreyfus himself was still condemned to remain worse than a slave for life in the tropical hell of Devil's Island. Marguerite Steinheil and the "Secret History of the Third Republic" were two subjects which Holmes swore he never wished to hear mentioned again.

We gave our notice to the Hôtel Lutétia next day. As Holmes said several times, we had been made fools of by Madame Steinheil and had wasted valuable words on Professor Bertillon. Worst of all, the death of Félix Faure in the arms of his young mistress had perhaps dashed all hope among those who sought justice for Dreyfus. As our last resort, Holmes swore that nothing would do but he must go to Berlin and confront Colonel Schwartzkoppen. He would have confronted Kaiser Wilhelm himself, in his present mood, had he been granted an audience.

Two days later, on a dull February morning, our train pulled out from the Gare de L'Est, among the departure boards for Vienna and Prague, Munich and Berlin, under the long span of the shabby Rue Lafayette with its workshops and warehouses. Holmes stared out at the open ironwork of bridges that carried the grey streets of La Chapelle and La Villette above the broad expanse of railway tracks. In the grey light of winter we entered a canyon below tall stone houses with peeling shutters and mansard roofs; the darkness of a tunnel enclosed us.

"And this," said Holmes at last, "is to be our reward. Let it take a place among our curios, Watson."

He held lightly between his finger and thumb the little box of Sèvres porcelain. In his other hand lay several capsules, the contents of that box.

"The evil potion," I said without thinking.

"Not the most evil, however," Holmes remarked. "Not evil enough, perhaps, to kill a man. Think how easy even that would be to someone who knew the weakness of Félix Faure and had the opportunity of access to him. Empty capsules may be bought from any pharmacy. They may be filled with anything, from stimulants for an old man's lust to the most deadly and instant poison. Dr. Neill Cream, the Lambeth Poisoner seven years ago, was just such a killer."

"You think she poisoned him?"

He shook his head. "No, Watson. Not she. But what might not a man with evil in his mind do if he could fill one capsule with an instant poison and slip it among the others? Sooner or later his victim would take it. And when that victim was found dead with his mistress, as Félix Faure was found dead, would not his loyal servants act just as we have done? Who would demand an autopsy upon the body of a dead president in those circumstances? We believed that he had died from a foolish act of his own which would not bear the light of public scrutiny. Suppose it was worse—suppose it was poison. A murderer would scarcely need to cover his tracks, when we were eager to do it for him."

"Then it truly was his assassination that she feared!"

Holmes shrugged. "She had better fear for herself. If Félix Faure died by the hands of his enemies, the documents which those enemies feared are now in the hands of Marguerite Steinheil. I do not think, Watson, that I should care greatly to be in that young woman's shoes in the years to come."

VIII

I thought that it was one of our worst defeats, complete as it was rare. We had lost both battles with Alphonse Bertillon. We had failed to save Félix Faure from destruction or self-destruction, whichever it might be. We had not been the triumphant saviours of Alfred Dreyfus. Even Colonel Schwartzkoppen returned the card of Sherlock Holmes with his pencilled regrets that official duties in Pomerania made a personal meeting impossible. Sometimes, in the

months that followed, I wondered what had become of Félix Faure's "Secret History of France under the Third Republic." Did it ever exist? What did that matter now? The man to whom it would have been a shield was dead. His enemies might be uneasy at its existence but they would surely hesitate to commit murder as the price of its destruction. Though I read the daily news from Paris, I did not hear that Madame Steinheil had been murdered.

So we returned to London and I indulged Holmes so far as not to mention either Alphonse Bertillon or Marguerite Steinheil unless he did so first, which he did seldom and briefly. Yet the next twelve months saw a remarkable advance in the fortunes of Alfred Dreyfus. His persecutors had overreached themselves by arresting and imprisoning Colonel Picquart, Holmes's friend who was now head of counter-intelligence in the Deuxième Bureau. Picquart's crime had been to question the authorship of the treasonable letter to Colonel Schwartzkoppen.

Of the two men who had fabricated evidence against Captain Dreyfus, Colonel Hubert Henry cut his own throat with a razor on the day after his arrest. Lemercier-Picard anticipated his own arrest by hanging himself in his room. Among such events, the entire French civil judiciary demanded a retrial of Dreyfus, a call that the new President, Émile Loubet, dared not resist. At Rennes, to which he was brought haggard and white-haired from five years on Devil's Island, a military tribunal confirmed the guilt of Dreyfus but set him free. Frail but resolute, he promised to fight them until his innocence was recognised.

Time passed and Alfred Dreyfus won his last battle. His ally, Colonel Picquart, set free and vindicated, was about to become Minister of War in a new government led by Georges Clemenceau as Prime Minister, a man who had also demanded justice for Dreyfus.

"I fear," said Holmes, laying down his morning *Times*, in which he had just read the news, "that our friend Picquart will find nothing in the files to incriminate the persecutors of Alfred Dreyfus. The defeated party will have gone through the secret papers at the Élysée Palace and elsewhere with a fine comb to remove and destroy whatever might be used against them. More's the pity."

Had he really not seen it?

"You forget the secret history," I said gently. "That is not in the Élysée Palace but, if it exists, in the Impasse Ronsin."

He sighed, shook the paper out, and returned to it. The name of "that young woman" was not mentioned after all.

"Yes," he said quietly, "I daresay you are right. Perhaps the Impasse Ronsin is where that strange concoction of fact and imagination had best remain."

It was a matter of mere days before the wire came from Marguerite Steinheil, imploring the assistance of the great detective. She was in the prison of St. Lazare, awaiting trial for her life, on charges of having murdered both her mother and her husband on the night of 30 May. Had this been a fictional romance, I could not have believed such a thing. Next day, however, a brief report by the Paris correspondent of *The Times* assured us of its truth.

I quite expected that Holmes would decline to leave Baker Street. However, he withdrew to his room and I was presently serenaded by the sounds of cupboards and drawers being opened and closed, luggage being thrown about. I went to the door. Without question, he was packing all that he might need for Paris.

"You are going?" I said.

"We are going, Watson. By the night ferry."

"After the manner in which she made fools of us?"

"She?" He straightened up and looked at me. "She?"

"Marguerite Steinheil."

"Madame Steinheil!" Holmes raised his voice loud enough to bring Mrs. Hudson quite half-way up the stairs. "I care nothing for Madame Steinheil! They may guillotine her tomorrow at dawn, so far as that goes!"

"Then why?"

He opened a drawer and took out a shirt, each movement tense with exasperation.

"Why?" He looked at me grimly. "To seize an opportunity which will in all probability never present itself again. To settle a final account with Professor Alphonse Bertillon. That is why!"

With that he slammed shut the lid of the case and locked it.

IX

After all that, it was sweet as a nut, as the saying goes—one of the neatest of conclusions. Best of all, Holmes won the contest against Bertillon: game, set, and match.

The Impasse Ronsin behind the shabby Rue de Vaugirard had changed by scarcely a brick or a pane of glass since we last saw it. The double murder had occurred on the night of 30–31 May. On the following morning, Rémy Couillard, the Steinheils' valet, entered the upper floor, where Marguerite Steinheil, her husband, and her mother—Madame Japy—slept in three separate rooms. The valet found the rooms silent and ransacked. Adolphe Steinheil lay dead in the doorway of his bathroom, kneeling forward as if he had died without a struggle as the cord was tightened round his throat. Madame Japy, the mother, had died upon her bed. The old woman had been gagged with such violence that a broken false tooth was found in the back of her throat. It was certain that she must have suffocated before the noose was drawn round her neck.

Marguerite Steinheil was found tied to her bed, bound and gagged but still alive. She told a confused story of having woken in the night to be confronted by three men and a woman in black ecclesiastical habits of some kind, the woman and one of the men having red hair.

"Where is your family's money?" they demanded. "Where are your jewels? Tell us or we will kill you and them as well!"

Pleading with them not to harm her or the other members of her family, Madame Steinheil had told them. Until the valet came next morning, she lay on the bed with her wrists tethered above her head in such a way that at every attempt to move her hands the rope drew tighter about her throat. Her ankles were bound to the foot of the bed. Cotton wool had been forced into her mouth to silence her. Though she had heard Madame Japy's cries as the intruders gagged the old woman, she did not know until the morning that her mother and her husband were dead.

Madame Steinheil was not believed by the officers who investigated the crime. Her prosecutors insisted that she had first murdered her husband, then her mother, and had finally ransacked the house and tied herself up to support the story of a burglary. The motive was a wish to be rid of a weak-willed, improvident husband and to marry one of her numerous admirers.

Holmes glanced down the *résumé* of the evidence as we stood in the office of Gustave Hamard, Director of Criminal Investigations, opposite the monumental façade of the Palais de Justice, where Madame Steinheil appeared before her judges.

"The prosecution theory in that form may be disposed of at once," Holmes said quietly to the French detective. "I grant that Madame Steinheil might have strangled her husband, though the difference in their build and physical strength makes it unlikely. Why, though, would she first gag her mother, if her intention was to strangle the old lady?"

"Only the prisoner can tell us," Hamard said sceptically.

Holmes shook his head. "Consider this. The valet who released Madame Steinheil next morning did not undo the ropes. He cut them. The knots are still to be seen. She had been tied once or twice with a galley-knot. True, she might have tied herself to the bed but a galley-knot would be impossible in such places. It is, in any case, rarely used except among sailors or horse-dealers."

"It would require a single accomplice," Hamard said, "who, in return for a reward, tied up the young woman and disposed of the other two. What better than to tie up Madame Japy and gag her, so that she might later be a witness to seeing a stranger in the house? Her suffocation appears to have been an accident."

Again Holmes shook his head. "It will not do, monsieur. If Madame Japy's death was not intended, why was the cord tightened round her throat? The poor old woman could not be permitted to live. It argues that at least one intruder was someone whom she might recognise and identify."

For a week or two, the Steinheil murder case had threatened to cause almost as much disorder in Paris as the Dreyfus affair. One half of the city swore that Marguerite Steinheil was the victim of robbery, conspiracy, and worse. She had endured a night of terror, at the end of which the bodies of her husband and her mother were found lying in the other rooms. It was certainly true that four ecclesiastical costumes, identical to those in which she described her attackers, had been stolen from the property-room of the Théâtre Eden a few hours before the crime at the Impasse Ronsin. That in itself proved nothing.

The other half of Parisians thought her a notorious harlot who had paid villains as evil as herself to stage a make-believe robbery. The object was to murder her husband—of whom she was weary—so that she might make a better marriage. As for the pearls and other jewels, which Madame Steinheil claimed to have lost, they had never existed.

Holmes cared nothing for the jewels, whether they existed or not. There was another item which the valet and other servants testified to having seen in the house before the fatal night and never again after it. It was a package wrapped in brown paper and sealed. On its top was written the name of Marguerite Steinheil and the instruction, "Private Papers. To be burnt unopened after my death." Here and there the brown paper was torn and it was possible to see the corners of envelopes which the wrapping contained. This bundle of envelopes was, to all appearances, the secret history of the Third Republic and lay in a concealed wall-cupboard of Adolphe Steinheil's studio.

Madame Steinheil now swore that these were not the papers that might cause such embarrassment to the enemies of Félix Faure but a "dummy" package to deceive burglars. The papers from the Élysée Palace were hidden in a secret drawer of her writing-desk.

There was never so inconclusive an investigation for the police. Dr. Balthazard, forensic detective of the Sûreté, found nothing that would prove or disprove Madame Steinheil's story. Of the famous history of the Third Republic no more was said. As the judicial examination of Madame Steinheil began, it was widely doubted whether such a history existed—or had ever existed.

Professor Alphonse Bertillon used every means of scientific investigation at his disposal to identify those who had been at the Impasse Ronsin on the night of the crime. Despite his reservations over the technique, his assistants "fingerprinted" every room and every article of furniture in the house. It was all to no effect. To be sure, there were fingerprints by the dozen in every room, and they were photographed and catalogued. Unfortunately, the system had been so neglected by the Sûreté, that it was impossible to check the identity of such prints without great difficulty.

Holmes was on better terms with Gustave Hamard, whose authority allowed my friend to tread where the great Bertillon had gone before, to examine the interior of the house in the Impasse Ronsin on behalf of his client. He had no wish to consult Madame Steinheil in prison. If ever there was a case to be decided on cold and precise points of evidence—away from the hysteria of the mob and the suspect—it was this. Hamard had shrugged his broad shoulders at the futility of further examination but granted the request.

By the time that Holmes finished his examination, the trial of Marguerite Steinheil on charges of murder had begun at the Palais de Justice. The final leaves of autumn fell from the birch trees of the Île de la Cité, which we had last seen breaking into a green haze of spring across the Boulevard du Palais.

A few days later, Sherlock Holmes and Alphonse Bertillon faced each other across the desk of Gustave Hamard. The duel that Holmes had promised was about to begin, with Hamard and I as seconds. My companion took from his pocket a photographic card upon which the ridges and whorls of an index finger were plainly seen. He handed it to Bertillon, who shrugged and pulled a face.

"There were hundreds, Mr. Holmes," said the great anthropologist, taking off his glasses, brushing his eyes with the back of his hand, and replacing the spectacles. He took a page of fingerprints which was lying on the desk and ran his eye down it, looking aside from time to time at the image Holmes had given him.

"Try number eighty-four," Holmes suggested whimsically.

Bertillon picked up another card and glanced down it.

"Indeed, monsieur," he said affably, "you are quite correct. The print of this finger was found a number of times, among many many others, in the studio of Adolphe Steinheil. It was not found, I see, in the rooms of the upper floor where the crimes were committed. The studio was entered by so many visitors that it can count for little, I fear."

"Forgive me, monsieur," said Holmes quietly, "but the fingerprint upon the card I have handed you did not come from the studio of Adolphe Steinheil, nor from anywhere else in the Impasse Ronsin."

"Then where?" asked Bertillon sharply.

The voice of Sherlock Holmes was almost a purr of satisfaction.

"From the presidential apartments of the Élysée Palace on the sixteenth of February 1899, at a time when the late Félix Faure had just received the last rites. You will recall that you and I were at that time exchanging views on the use, or otherwise, of such prints. Having received as a present from Monsieur Faure's family a small pill-box of Sèvres ware—a charming thing—I was boorish enough to subject it to dusting with silver nitrate and exposure to a fixed-range Kodak, a contraption of my own."

Bertillon went pale. Hamard spoke first. "Who do you say this print comes from?"

"The Comte de Balincourt," said Holmes smoothly, "alias Viscount Montmorency, alias the Margrave of Hesse, sometime assistant chamberlain at the Élysée Palace—under what name I know not, as yet. Dismissed after the passing of President Faure for some trivial dishonesty. A dozen witnesses will tell you that, not a few weeks before his murder, Adolphe Steinheil began a commission to paint in his studio a portrait of the Comte de Balincourt in hunting costume."

Hamard's eyes narrowed. "Do you say, Mr. Holmes, that Steinheil knew such a man as Balincourt?"

"Not only knew him, Monsieur, but was heard in the studio discussing with him Félix Faure and the secret history of the Third Republic. There is a fingerprint, matching exactly the one I have shown you, on the door of a casually concealed wall-cupboard in the studio, where Balincourt was told that the papers of that secret history were kept. A package of papers remained there until the night of the two murders, inscribed with the name 'Marguerite Steinheil' and with instructions that it was to be burned unopened upon her death. On the morning following the crimes, that cupboard was empty. The scratches on the mirror of its lock indicate that it was opened by a little force and a good deal of fraud."

"Then the trial must be adjourned!" Hamard said. "My God! What if all this were to come to light and she had already been condemned?"

"And where," interrupted Bertillon, "is the Comte de Balincourt?"

Holmes shrugged. "At the bottom of the Seine, I imagine, or the bed of the River Spree, depending on whether his political masters are in Paris or Berlin. I do not think he will bother us again."

"The papers!" Hamard said furiously. "The manuscript! Where is that? Think of what it might do to the politics of France—to the peace of Europe!"

"The history of the Third Republic is quite safe," Holmes said coolly.

Hamard looked at him with narrowed eyes. "The cupboard was opened and the manuscript stolen, was it not?"

Holmes shook his head. "Madame Steinheil trusted no one, least of all the discretion of her weak-willed and garrulous husband. She let it be known in the household that the wall-cupboard contained the manuscript and the secret drawer of her writing-desk held a dummy package. Adolphe Steinheil did not know this when he boasted to the President's former chamberlain. In truth, it was the dummy package to which he unwittingly directed the man. After the blackest of crimes, the Comte de Balincourt handed his masters a bundle of old newspapers and blank pages. You may imagine how they will have rewarded him."

If an Anarchist bomb had gone off in the tree-lined Boulevard du Palais and blown the windows out, Hamard and Bertillon could scarcely have looked more aghast.

"You say Balincourt is a murderer?" Bertillon demanded. "Yet the same fingerprint was found nowhere upstairs."

"Not for one moment did I suppose he had committed murder. I think it likely that he entered the upper rooms and that he was accidentally seen by Madame Japy. The poor old woman would have recognised him from his portrait sittings, for which reason she was put to death. Balincourt or his masters had hired men who would not scruple to take that precaution for their own safety as well as his."

"A little convenient is it not?" said Hamard sceptically.

Holmes took from his pocket three more photographic prints.

"You will not know these fingerprints, for I believe they are unique to my own little collection. However, I shall be surprised if you do not find photographs of the three men in your Office of Judicial Identification. Baptistin is a young and violent criminal. Marius Longon, 'The Gypsy,' is a skilled and ruthless thief. Monstet de Fontpeyrine is a Cuban, a stage magician and a specialist in hotel robberies. He was seen last autumn, loitering in the Rue de Vaugirard, near the Impasse Ronsin. From there he was followed to the Métro station of Les Couronnes, where he met the other two men, a young woman with red hair, and a third man who is now identified as the Comte de Balincourt."

"You know where these other men are?"

"In the same deep water as Balincourt, I should imagine," said Holmes dismissively. "I scarcely think you will hear from them either."

"And the papers of the Third Republic?" Hamard persisted.

"Ah," said Holmes with an air of false regret. "They are where they will do no harm. I regret, however, that it is not in my power to produce them."

"You will be ordered to produce them!" Hamard shouted.

Holmes was moved invariably by poverty, misfortune, desperation in others, never by browbeating.

"Those papers, monsieur, are essential to my client's defence. You have my word that, as yet, they have been seen by no other eyes than my own. After she is acquitted, which on the evidence I have produced to you is what justice must demand, I can promise you that these documents will trouble the world no more. If, after all that has been said in this room, she is condemned to execution—worse, if she *goes* to the guillotine—I will stop at nothing to see every word of them published in the leading newspapers of every capital."

Gustave Hamard strode from the room and we heard his voice raised as he gave instructions to his subordinates. The trial of Madame Steinheil was adjourned early that day on the far side of the Boulevard du Palais. Two days later, its result was to be published across the world. After midnight, in the small hours of 14 November 1909, the jury that had retired to condemn Marguerite Steinheil was summoned into court again. De Valles, the president of the tribunal, imparted certain instructions to the jurors in the lamplit courtroom, his voice fraught with an anxiety that he had failed to show in the earlier stages of the proceedings. They retired and returned again to acquit Madame Steinheil of all the charges against her.

So much is history, as is the change in Professor Alphonse Bertillon's view on the usefulness of fingerprints. During the day or two left to us in Paris, he became almost a friend to Sherlock Holmes. The two men were now disposed to regard their past differences as something of a joke, each assuring the other that he had never really said the things that were reported—or that, if he had said them, he had never really meant them.

We came back to Baker Street by the night ferry to Charing Cross and arrived home in good time for lunch. That evening, as I watched Holmes arranging some experiment or other upon the familiar stained table, I brought up the subject that had lain between us for the last few days.

"If you are right about Balincourt, Holmes . . ."

"I am seldom wrong in such matters, Watson," he said gently, without looking up.

"If that man tampered with the box of capsules in the Élysée Palace . . ."

"Quite." He frowned and took a little brush to dust a surface with white powder.

"Then it was not an old man's lust that destroyed him, though it gave the opportunity."

"Quite possibly."

"Balincourt or one of their spies knew that Faure was about to change his policy—that he would turn to the *Dreyfusards*! That he would order a retrial! She had persuaded him."

"I daresay," he murmured, as if scarcely hearing me."

"It was not a love philtre but an instant poison, after all, disguised among the other capsules!"

He looked up, the aquiline features contracting in a frown of irritation.

"You will give me credit for something, I hope! My first analysis in Paris was confirmed by a more searching examination here. What was in the remaining capsules was a homeopathic quantity of canthar. They call such pills 'Diavolini.' The truth is that their contents would not even stimulate passion in a man, let alone kill him. Their effect, if any, is entirely upon the mind."

He returned to his studies.

"Then we witnessed it, after all!" I exclaimed.

"Witnessed what, my dear fellow?"

"The assassination of the President of France by those who had most to fear if Dreyfus were found innocent!"

"Oh, yes," said Holmes, as if it were the most ordinary thing in the world. "I had never supposed otherwise. However, it would not do for you to give that to the world as yet, Watson, in one of your little romances. Sleep on it a little, my old friend. Speaking of romances, there is one that requires our attention without delay."

He took a bundle of papers from a Gladstone bag and broke it open. A pile of well-filled foolscap envelopes slithered out randomly across the table.

"I have made my promise to Gustave Hamard," he said. "Madame Steinheil has paid me in kind. All debts are now discharged."

He took the first sheaf of papers, on which I just had time to catch sight of a few names and phrases in a neat plain hand. "General Georges Boulanger . . . Colonel Max von Schwartzkoppen, Königgrätzstrasse, Berlin . . . Pensées sur le suicide du Colonel Hubert Henry . . . Les crimes financières de Panama . . . L'affaire de Fashoda . . . Colonel Picquart et le tribunal . . ." An envelope lay addressed in black ink to Major Count Ferdinand Walsin-Esterhazy, Rue de la Bienfaisance, 27, Paris 8ᵉ.

The fire in the grate blazed whiter as the first pages burned. Holmes turned to take another envelope and emptied it. There fluttered down to the floor a note on the stationery of the Italian Embassy in the Rue de Varenne, inviting Colonel Schwartzkoppen to dine with Colonel Panizzardi. He scooped it up and dropped it into the flames. The fire blazed again and a shoal of sparks swept up the chimney. For half an hour, the secret ashes of the Third Republic dissolved in smoke against the frosty starlight above the chimney-pots of Baker Street.

The Abandoned Brigantine

SAM BENADY

ONE OF GIBRALTAR'S most distinguished citizens for many years, Dr. Samuel G. Benady (1937–) was born on the island into a family who has lived there since 1735 (an ancestor was kidnapped by pirates and had to be ransomed). After receiving his medical degree in London, he practiced pediatrics in Bristol and Jerusalem before returning to Gibraltar, where he has lived ever since.

Benady ran the Gibraltar Child Health service and single-handedly ran the Gibraltar Health Authority from 1980 until his retirement in 2002. He is a frequent lecturer at the Gibraltar Museum and regularly contributes articles to the newsletter of the Gibraltar Heritage Trust.

His lone book devoted to Sherlock Holmes was *Sherlock Holmes in Gibraltar* (1990), which featured two long short stories: the present one, in which Holmes solves one of the greatest mysteries of the sea, the abandonment of the *Mary Celeste*, and "The Gibraltar Letter," which narrates Holmes's involvement in the abduction of the Duke of Connaught while he was stationed in Gibraltar.

More recently, he has been cowriting (with Mary Chiappe) a series of mystery novels featuring Giovanni Bresciano, an amateur detective working in late eighteenth- and early nineteenth-century Gibraltar. The titles are *The Murder in Whirligig Lane* (2010), *Fall of a Sparrow* (2010), *The Pearls of Tangier* (2011), *The Prince's Lady* (2012), *The Devil's Tongue* (2013), and *Death in Paradise Ramp* (2014).

"The Abandoned Brigantine" was first published in *Sherlock Holmes in Gibraltar* (Gibraltar, Gibraltar Books, 1990).

THE ABANDONED BRIGANTINE

Sam Benady

I

"YES, WATSON," SAID Mr. Sherlock Holmes, raising his head briefly from his huge book of references, which he had been engaged in cross-indexing. "The sea is indeed mysterious and terrible."

"Most mysterious!" I replied absently, and then started with astonishment as I realised that, yet again, Holmes had penetrated my inmost thoughts.

"Holmes," I expostulated, "how could you possibly have known what was going through my mind? I have said not a word to you for over thirty minutes."

He looked up again with a chuckle. "True, you did not speak," he remarked. "But nevertheless you told me your thoughts as clearly as if you had shouted them from the roof-tops."

"This is too much, Holmes," I exclaimed. "Explain yourself!"

"Only if you promise not to say 'How absurdly simple' when you have heard my explanation."

"Done!"

"When you came into the room," said he, "you were carrying a copy of *The Strand Magazine*, which carries on its cover an illustration of a sailing ship in distress—a brigantine, if I am any judge. You then settled into the armchair and commenced to read. Within minutes, looks of perplexity and then of sadness appeared on your face. You put down the magazine and stared fixedly for a full minute at that picture of a tea clipper which hangs on our wall. You then rose, went to the bookshelf and withdrew one of the volumes which contain the somewhat sensational accounts which you have written of my cases, in particular, the one which includes the cases of the barque *Gloria Scott* and the one which you have chosen to entitle *Black Peter*. Having opened and perused this volume for a while, you returned to your chair, where you sat with an expression of gloom until I ventured to break into your thoughts with my not very profound observation, which merely followed the thoughts which were implicit in your face and actions."

"How absurdly simple—" I began, and then instantly joined him as he laughed heartily.

"Holmes," I said, passing him the magazine, "have you ever heard of a more mysterious and impenetrable problem than that detailed in these pages?"

He opened the magazine and glanced at the article in question.

"*An Unsolved Mystery*. I see that they have misspelled the name of the ship as usual and no doubt have repeated all the other errors and absurdities which were perpetrated some years ago by some scribbler named Boyle, or Doyle."

"You are acquainted with the case, then?"

"I have some slight recollection of it. Let us look it up in my book of references."

He opened the index volume and scanned it intently.

"Musgrave Ritual," he read. "That was a mysterious and tragic case. Moriarty; plenty of references to him, of course. Mazarin stone, Merton the pugilist—same case, those two. *Matilda Briggs*—another sea story there, Watson. Margolis the strangler. Ah, here it is, *Mary Celeste*." He selected the appropriate volume, turned over the pages, and handed the heavy volume to me.

I settled down to read the pages which he indicated. They were mainly abstracts of court proceedings and official reports, interspersed with cuttings from newspapers, mainly English and American, but including the *Gibraltar Chronicle* and a few which were presumably from Spanish and Portuguese papers.

"The real facts are certainly more prosaic," I remarked. "But the problem seems no easier to solve.

"Holmes," I continued, as a thought struck me, "surely you would find it easy to solve the case, which has baffled the whole world for years, by the application of those deductive methods of reasoning which you have so often employed in the past."

"You overestimate my powers, Watson," said Sherlock Holmes, with some amusement, although I could see that he was pleased by the compliment to his abilities. "I do not think that even I could reach the correct solution by pure reasoning from the facts available in these files."

Waving aside my protestations, he lapsed into a thoughtful silence for a few minutes. Then a gleam of amusement appeared in his deep-set eyes.

"Well, Watson," said he, languidly, "why do you yourself not make an attempt to formulate a hypothesis which will account for the facts? After all, you have been my colleague for many years, ample time to have absorbed the principles of deductive logic of which you speak so highly."

"I certainly shall!" I exclaimed hotly, for I thought I detected some slight irony in his voice. "We shall see whether by tomorrow I cannot present you with a logical explanation for the mysterious happenings on the *Mary Celeste*." With that, I went to my room, taking the book of references with me.

"We shall see," said Sherlock Holmes thoughtfully, as I left.

II

On the following morning I rose late, after a largely sleepless night. A wintry December sun shone through the windows of our rooms in Baker Street. Holmes was already at the breakfast table. He looked up as I entered.

"A fine day, Watson," said he, cheerfully. "Have you made any progress with the intellectual problem you have set yourself?"

"Indeed I have," I rejoined, somewhat coolly. "And I will give you a full account of my solution as soon as I have had some breakfast."

A little later, when we were seated in our armchairs, Holmes looked at me expectantly.

I arranged my papers in front of me. "The first thing to do," I said, I dare say somewhat self-importantly, "is to marshal the relevant facts. The *Mary Celeste* left New York on November the 7th '72 with a cargo of methylated spirits for Genoa. Her captain was Benjamin S. Briggs, who was accompanied by his wife and child. There was a crew of eight men. She was sighted by the brigantine *Dei Gratia* on December the 5th, derelict and abandoned, some 400 miles east of the Azores, and was boarded and taken into Gibraltar by a prize-crew from the latter vessel. At the subsequent hearing by the Vice-Admiralty Court in Gibraltar, it was established that the ship was sea-worthy, although she bore every sign of having been hastily abandoned. There was no sign of violence on board."

Holmes stirred in his seat. "Was there not a sword found in the captain's cabin?" he asked.

"There was, but it was in its scabbard, and stains found on it were analysed and found not to be blood. It was an Italian sword, with a cross of Savoy on the hilt, and was thought to be a souvenir acquired by Captain Briggs on his travels."

"Pray continue with your exposition."

"The last entry on the log slate was for 25th

November, giving the ship's position as six miles to the north of Santa Maria island in the Azores. The ship's boat was missing, and all the signs were that the ship had been abandoned hurriedly. There was no indication why this might have been done, and no trace of the boat or the crew has ever been found."

"I seem to recall that there were some strange marks on the hull."

"I cannot explain those," I admitted. "Each side of the bows had an almost symmetrical strip shaved off just above the water-line. I suppose that this could have been caused by rocks, during a near-shipwreck in the Azores, but all accounts state that the strips appeared very regular, as if they had been cut by a sharp instrument."

"What then is your solution to the mystery?"

I leaned backwards in my armchair. "I think that we can discard theories involving the slaughter of the crew by pirates, for the Atlantic has been free of these for almost a century. Mutiny by the ship's crew, or their murder by the crew of the *Dei Gratia* for the salvage money, which was the theory put forward by the Admiralty Advocate in Gibraltar, seems even more unlikely; in all these cases, signs of a struggle would surely have been found. I am prepared to discount theories of sea-monsters rising from the deep to swallow up the crew—"

"Are you?" said Sherlock Holmes, and smiled.

A little nettled, I continued, "The only remaining possibility, then, seems to be that the ship was abandoned voluntarily because of some danger to those on board her, and that the ship's boat was then swamped and all on board drowned. But the *Mary Celeste* was sea-worthy when found, although there had been a storm and the rigging and sails were damaged. I do not believe that an experienced captain, as all agree Captain Briggs was, would put those in his charge to the perils of an Atlantic storm in a small boat unless his ship were actually foundering, or if those on board were in deadly danger."

"You appear to have eliminated your last possibility," Holmes observed.

"Not quite," I replied triumphantly. "The sea is not the only possible source of peril to those on board a ship. A situation may have arisen on board which seemed so dangerous to the captain that he saw no alternative but to risk his wife and child, and his crew, to the fury of the Atlantic waves. Indeed, it has been suggested, on the strength of some minor damage to one of the casks in the cargo, that an explosion of spirit fumes may have been feared, and that the captain may have decided to launch the ship's boat and stand off from the ship until the fumes had dissipated, and that the *Mary Celeste* then drifted away, leaving them to their fate."

"But this, I take it, is not your preferred solution," Holmes observed.

"Indeed not," said I. "The evidence for a serious leak of methylated spirit is very poor, and in any case, I cannot imagine that seasoned seamen such as Captain Briggs and his crew would not have taken the precaution of fastening a tow-line to the ship. It is true that a tow-line might have snapped, but no trace of this was found aboard the ship.

"The true solution to the mystery was suggested to me by a remark which you once made during the case of the missing racehorse Silver Blaze, to the effect that sometimes it is not the presence but the absence of something which may be significant."

Holmes clapped his hands in approval.

"Excellent, Watson, excellent!" he cried. "I see that you have taken note of my methods, even while you were recounting them to the public in so sensational a manner. I believe there is hope for you yet."

Thus encouraged, I continued, "Those who boarded the abandoned vessel described in great detail what they found on her, but nowhere is there any mention of an animal on board. Now, there can be very few vessels which do not carry one or more cats on board, to keep down the rats, and frequently also a dog, to guard the ship against intruders when it is in port—"

"Might these animals not have been taken into the boat by the crew?"

"The *Mary Celeste* was abandoned in such haste that all personal belongings were left behind. There was then surely no time to hunt down the ship's pets. No, Holmes, the explanation for the absence of the animals is more sinister: I believe that these creatures had become infected with rabies, or hydrophobia, and this so terrorised the crew that in a mad panic they took to the boat, which was then swamped with the loss of all aboard. As the disease progressed, the rabid animals then jumped or fell overboard, leaving the ship deserted and a mystery which has remained unsolved—until today!" I added with some satisfaction.

"Capital, Watson, capital!" exclaimed Sherlock Holmes with a broad smile. "You have excelled yourself!"

"Do you then agree with me that I have divined the solution to this hitherto insoluble problem?" I inquired.

"Indeed not! But your solution is ingenious, and not entirely devoid of logical reasoning."

Somewhat crestfallen, I persisted.

"How can you maintain, then, that mine is not a possible solution?"

"For at least four reasons."

"Four!" I exclaimed, wounded. "Come, Holmes, I cannot believe that you have found so many flaws in my theory. Let us hear them!"

"Very well," said Holmes languidly. "*Primus.* I cannot believe that a crew of able-bodied men, used to facing all the dangers of the sea, would flee in panic from rabid animals into the greater danger of an Atlantic storm, rather than banding together with knives, boathooks, and belaying-pins to hunt the creatures down. *Secundus.* Should they indeed have decided to flee, which would presuppose not only cowardice but stupidity, as they would have been exposed to attack by the creatures while they laboured to launch the ship's boat, they would surely have seized every weapon available in order to defend themselves. Yet the sword remained in the cabin. *Tertius.* I think we must assume that there were several animals, even to attempt to justify this improbable panic. Yet the *Mary Celeste* was not found to be in total disorder, as it would have been had these creatures run wild through it in

their final frenzy, prior to casting themselves so conveniently overboard."

He paused for a second, and I returned to the attack.

"Your fourth reason, Holmes. Which is your fourth reason? Your first three only make my solution improbable, not impossible."

"My fourth reason you may well find more convincing. I *know* that matters did not proceed as you have conjectured, for I was on board the *Mary Celeste* on that fateful voyage."

I stared at Sherlock Holmes in disbelief.

"Holmes, that is impossible!" I ejaculated. "You were surely too young—"

"I was young," he agreed, "but not too young. I will recount to you what truly happened, but only on the condition that it remain a secret during the lifetime of all those involved."

"You may rely on me," said I earnestly.

III

The Lily of Aosta

Holmes rose, and filled his pipe from the Persian slipper on the mantelpiece. When he had returned to his seat, he lit the pipe, and spent some minutes smoking it thoughtfully. I was in a fever of impatience to hear his tale, but I knew better than to interrupt his reverie.

Finally he broke the silence.

"I have rarely spoken to you about my early life, Watson," said he. "And it is possible that you do not know that, after my schooling was completed, I spent a year abroad before going up to Cambridge. I had already determined to devote my life to the study of criminology, and considered that I might benefit from a period of apprenticeship in an organisation recognised as the foremost detective agency in the world."

"You mean—"

"Exactly, Watson, the Pinkerton Detective Agency. I must confess, though, that I was seriously disappointed; our American cousins show a sad deficiency of imagination both as criminals and as detectives. But I run ahead of my story."

. . .

My brother Mycroft, who even then had connections the world over, was instrumental in securing for me a junior position in the agency, and I sailed for New York early in '72.

A few months at the agency convinced me that I had nothing to learn from them about scientific detection, and I would have left and returned to England had I not been so fascinated by the energy and zest for life of the citizens of New York. Nevertheless, I was approaching a state of total *ennui* when one morning, a young man of swarthy complexion strode into the office.

He stopped at the doorway, and stared at me in amazement.

"Sherlock," he cried. "Can it possibly be you?"

For a second I had not recognised him, for since I had last seen him he had acquired a bristling black moustache. It was Luca D'Este, a young Italian of noble blood who had been a companion of my schooldays.

"Luca," I exclaimed, grasping him warmly by the hand. "What can have brought you here, so far from the Mediterranean sun which you always swore to return to and never leave again?"

"It is a matter of honour—my family's honour, and a lady's honour," he replied seriously. "May I speak with you privately; I remember your keen mind and your energy of old, and I feel sure that you are the only man who can help me in this strange quest."

I led him into an inner office, where, throwing himself into a chair, he launched himself impatiently into his tale.

"You may know, Sherlock, that I am a close relative of the King of Italy. Two years ago, his son, Amadeo of Savoy, Duke of Aosta, was chosen by the Spanish Parliament to be King of Spain. I travelled to that country with my cousin, as part of his entourage. Also in his party, as one of the ladies-in-waiting to his Queen, Maria Victoria, was a young girl of sixteen, who even at that early age, because of her surpassing beauty, was known as the Lily of Aosta; her name is Bianca Bernini.

"If you have followed the fortunes of Spain in the last year, you will know that the King's reign has not been easy; ignored and insulted by Madrid society, his rule threatened by Carlists and Republicans, he has become discouraged, and abandoning his high hopes of improving and modernising Spain through a popular constitutional monarchy, has retreated more and more into the company of those Italians who form his court. His eye lighted on Bianca; he became infatuated with her, until terrified by his advances the girl, virtuous and loyal to her queen, fled from the palace. Would that she had confided in me," Luca groaned. "She has not been seen since."

"How then do you know of all this?" I asked.

"As soon as her disappearance was known, the King summoned me and confided to me what had happened. We had high words—"

"You are then very fond of the lady," I observed.

His dark eyes flashed in astonishment.

"How did you know?" said he.

"One does not exchange angry words with a king, even if he is a cousin, for any lesser reason," I observed drily. "Proceed."

"He begged me, for the honour of the family, and because of a very natural concern about Bianca, for he feels the deepest remorse about his behaviour to her, to spare no effort to find her and bring her to safety."

"And how did this quest bring you to New York?"

"I soon found out, for Madrid is a hotbed of spies and gossip-mongers, that Bianca had been abducted by a group of Republicans. Their plan is either to hold her to ransom, or to force her to make public the conduct of the King, to further discredit him and the monarchy in the eyes of the Spaniards. Fearing that I was on their trail, they spirited her away to Vigo, and thence to New York, where a group of Republican *emigrés* have established themselves. I followed, hot on their heels, and have discovered that she is being held, under close guard, in an apartment not far from here."

"Why then, you have done all the detection yourself," said I. "All we need to do is to call on the excellent New York Police Department and they will release your beloved."

"That is impossible," said Luca. "Firstly, Bianca's life must not be put at risk; these men are desperate, and might well murder her if they feared capture—"

"And secondly, if the story of her capture and release were to reach the ears of the pertinacious American press, your cousin the King might be embarrassed, so you thought that it would be best to trust to the discretion of a private enquiry agency," I interposed. "Very well then, we must resort to subterfuge."

"You will then help me yourself? It would be more discreet if we were able to keep even this agency out of it."

"Of course."

Luca told me that he had observed the house in which Bianca was imprisoned. The apartment was on the second floor, and at all times there were at least three men guarding it. He had seen them going in and out, and it was only with difficulty, because of his concern for the lady's safety, that he had restrained himself from rushing in and confronting the ruffians on his own.

My plan was simple. On that very night we made our way to the building, and having introduced ourselves surreptitiously, with the aid of a jemmy, into the hall, crept up the stairs until we were outside the door of the apartment. A murmur of voices could be heard inside.

I knelt down, and placing an armful of rags and papers, which I had brought with me, by the door, set a light to them. Waiting only until I could see the smoke beginning to seep under the door, I put on my best Yankee accent, and on a hysterical note, shouted: "Fire! The building's alight! Fire!"

There was a confused babble of voices inside. Luca and I stationed ourselves on each side of the door, clutching heavy cudgels. The door burst open and three men rushed out. Luca's cudgel came down on the head of the first, and he collapsed to the floor without a sound. The other two were burdened with a form wrapped in a blanket, which could only be the drugged body of the girl; before they could put her down and defend themselves, we were on them, and they too fell senseless. Pausing only to verify that it was indeed Bianca, and that she breathed, we carried her out of the house and into a waiting cab, and drove away from the scene.

Our next problem was to get Bianca and Luca back to Europe without attracting the attention of her abductors, or the Press. Luca agreed that it would be best to return to Italy, and restore Bianca to her family; a return to Spain would only expose her to further danger. I therefore left my friend, with the aid of my Irish landlady, to look after the rapidly recovering Bianca in my room, and made my way to the waterfront early in the morning. There I ascertained that a cargo ship, the brigantine *Mary Celeste*, was leaving for Genoa two days later. The steam-packet to Lisbon, which was leaving on that very day, I rejected, as I did not wish for Bianca to return to the Iberian peninsula, and it seemed to me that the gang would assume that we would attempt to escape from New York by this means, and would be prepared to intercept us, but I boarded her and handed the captain a package, with instructions to forward it urgently on arrival in Lisbon.

I then sought out the captain of the *Mary Celeste*. I found Captain Briggs in a nearby lodging house with his wife and child. Captain Winchester, who was a part owner of the ship, was with them. Enjoining all to the utmost secrecy, I explained only that a lady and a gentleman, who were being pursued by criminals, desired immediate passage to Europe, for which they would pay a generous fee.

"Oh, Ben," cried Mrs. Briggs to her husband. "We must help this unfortunate young couple. I would never forgive myself if they came to any harm because of our failure to assist them."

Her husband and his partner, who had

seemed about to demur, were swayed by her appeal, and the transaction was agreed.

"Say," added Mrs. Briggs, "why don't your friends come and join us here? They'll be safer in company than alone."

I doubted this, as Bianca's pursuers would surely be haunting the area of the waterfront to foil any attempt at escape. We finally agreed that I would bring the passengers to the lodging house after dark on the following night, so that they might board the ship just before she sailed on the morning tide.

At Briggs's invitation, I accompanied him to the ship, where I met the crew, assuring myself that all were genuine seamen, and well-known to their captain. In particular the mate Richardson seemed a fine example of an honest, fearless Yankee mariner.

Returning to my apartment, I found Bianca fully recovered from her ordeal. As she attempted to thank me in pretty, broken English, I was able to observe her properly for the first time. She had the flawless, creamy skin and clear grey eyes which can often be observed in northern Italy, but combined with such perfect features as I have never seen before or since. Long, silky black hair, and a lissome figure, just above the medium height, completed the picture. As she became conscious of my gaze, she lowered her eyes, and the colour which flooded her cheeks seemed to add a further dimension to her beauty.

With Luca's assistance, she described to me how she had been waylaid as she rushed out of the palace, and confined in the cellar of a house in Madrid, from which she was taken to Vigo, where she and her captors embarked for New York. They had not used her ill, as they hoped to force her to make public a statement discrediting the King. This the brave girl had refused to do, but the constant brow-beating which she received because of this, together with her prolonged incarceration and the frequent soporifics administered in order to prevent her calling for help, had no doubt accentuated the natural pallor of her features.

After dark on the following evening a cab took us to Captain Briggs's lodging. As we approached, I noticed three sinister figures lurking on the other side of the road. It was clear that the house was being watched, and that my plan must be changed. As the cab halted, I quickly told the driver to drive to the rear of the building after we had alighted. We entered the lodging house, and I paused to warn Briggs of the watchers outside.

"I reckon I can take care of myself," said he with a laugh.

There was no time for argument; we ran swiftly to the back of the house, and jumped into the cab, which was waiting outside the back door, which fortunately did not appear to be watched. I ordered the cab-driver to take us to the *Mary Celeste*, and we boarded the ship. The mate, although surprised to see us, made us welcome, and installed Bianca in the captain's cabin, which it had been agreed she should share with Mrs. Briggs and the child.

I explained to Richardson what had happened, and that I feared that the captain and his family might be at grave risk from our pursuers.

"Let us go to his lodging and deal with the ruffians outside," said he. "I will give instructions to the men to guard the ship, and the lady. Then we will be off."

Luca remained, with drawn sword, outside the cabin door, and Richardson and I made our way swiftly to the lodging house. There was no sign of the watchers.

With grim foreboding we entered the house. The door of the room occupied by the captain and his family was ajar. As we entered the room a dreadful sight met our eyes. By the light of a fire which was even then spreading to the curtains we could see that Briggs and his wife had been savagely stabbed to death as they slept. As we recoiled in horror, the dry wood of the timber wall caught fire and the room became a sheet of flame. We turned to flee, and then the mate caught sight of the child, peacefully asleep in a cot by her murdered parents' bed.

"Sophia!" he cried, leaping forward through

the flames, and snatching the child from the cot, he followed me out of the burning house.

As we gained the roadway, the whole building became enveloped in flames. None of the other occupants can have had any chance of survival.

Soberly, we returned to the ship. Although we kept a keen lookout, we could detect no signs of pursuit, and it seemed likely to me that the murderers could have been deceived in the darkness, thinking that they had killed Bianca and Luca in the house, or that they had perished in the conflagration intended to hide the crime.

Once aboard, we held a council of war. Bianca took the bewildered and weeping child into her arms and attempted to console her. Richardson, once we had told him the whole story, suggested that we should proceed with the voyage as planned, and I was inclined to agree, as any attempt to report the murders and arson would inevitably cause us to be detained indefinitely in New York, and would undoubtedly expose Bianca and Luca to the publicity which they were so desperate to avoid.

"But what shall we do with the child?" asked Luca.

Bianca looked up with flashing eyes.

"Because of me her parents die," she said fervently. "I will take her and give her a new life!"

"We both will," said Luca, and took her hand.

She lifted her eyes to him with a brilliant smile which said more than words could.

IV

Sherlock Holmes paused at this point, and puffed reflectively at his pipe.

"If I might make a deduction of my own at this point, Holmes," I said, somewhat mischievously, "your description of the girl, Bianca, seems to indicate that you were considerably attracted to her."

"You must remember that I was very young," said Holmes tartly. "In any case the difference between us—"

"You mean because she was of the nobility—"

"No, Watson, because she was by far my intellectual inferior. But let me proceed with my story."

The *Mary Celeste* sailed with the morning tide. The next two weeks were uneventful, if any crossing of the Atlantic by sailing ship in winter can be said to be uneventful. Bianca and the child Sophia became great friends, and the ship frequently rang with their merry laughter. There was no sign of pursuit, yet I was not entirely at ease. It seemed likely that our pursuers would not long be deceived, and would find some way to follow us, and I spent many long hours on deck scanning the horizon through a telescope.

As it happened, however, it was not I who made the first sighting. As we approached the island of Santa Maria, which is the southernmost of the Azores, there was a cry from the other side of the deck. It was Bianca.

"A monster! A monster rises from the sea!"

I ran to her side. A great grey mass was emerging from the waves—your hypothetical monster, Watson. It was only a few yards away, and I could see that it was no sea-monster, but a man-made construction. Without doubt it was a submarine vessel, such as are now being constructed by all the great navies in the world, but at that time it was, as far as I knew, merely an inventor's pipe-dream. Was it friend or foe? We were not left long in doubt.

With a clanking sound, a hatch on the upper surface of the vessel opened, and a bearded face peered forth.

"Ees the brigantina *Mary Celeste*? Señor Holmes accompanied by two friends of the King of Espain?" it enquired cautiously.

"Who are you?" I called out.

"I am Don Narciso Monturiol, and this is my invento the submarino, the *Ictíneo III*. I have been charged by the King to escort you to where you wish to go."

"How did you know that we were on this ship?" I persisted, still a little suspicious.

"The King has received a message from you, from Lisboa."

I breathed a sigh of relief. My message had arrived safely.

"We welcome your escort, Don Narciso," I cried.

Monturiol and I agreed that my companions and I should remain on board the *Mary Celeste*, as the submarine would be rather uncomfortable, especially for a young lady and a child. He would patrol in our vicinity and report to us if he detected any vessel following us.

A few days after we had left the Azores behind, the submarine again surfaced near us. By this time, the weather had worsened considerably, with high seas and poor visibility, but Monturiol was able to make us understand that there was a brigantine following closely on our course, and that he proposed to take Bianca and Luca aboard.

"If the ship indeed carries our pursuers," said Luca, "then anyone left aboard the *Mary Celeste* is doomed, for in their fury that we have escaped them they will surely kill all those who have assisted us."

"You are right," said Richardson. "Can we not all be carried by the underwater vessel? We could then leave them to chase an empty ship, giving us more time to make our escape."

Monturiol confirmed that there was sufficient room in the submarine for us and the crew, and proceeded to attempt to bring his vessel alongside our ship. Because of the gale and the high seas, this proved extremely difficult. Twice the submarine came alongside, and on both occasions was flung violently against the bows, gouging deep strips out of the timber with its steel fins.

Finally, seeing that any further attempt was likely to endanger the submarine, Richardson shouted to the vessel to stand off: we would lower the ship's boat and row across to it.

This was done with great difficulty. More than once the boat was almost swamped by the waves, but eventually we reached the submarine. First the child and then Bianca were pulled through the hatch into safety; then Luca clambered in. As he turned to give me his hand in assistance, a tremendous wave hit the submarine, driving it into the boat, which was crushed, and all those in it were engulfed by the waves. I received a blow on the head, and was barely conscious of all this, and only afterwards was I told how Luca had kept his grip on my arm through it all and had dragged me to safety. We circled the area for some time, but no trace of the crew did we find. My good friend Richardson and his men had given their lives for us. Then the shape of the pursuing brigantine began to loom up through the mist, and Monturiol gave the order to dive.

"What was the name of the ship which you sighted?" I asked the inventor.

"The *Dei Gratia*," said he.

As our journey proceeded, I questioned Monturiol about his marvellous vessel, and found him most willing to expound on his invention.

"For more than one decade I have worked," he said, "and I started with a small wooden vessel driven by pedals; after, I build a big one, with steam engine, but that one also could only work in calm water, in harbour, and the Ministry of Marine are not interested. So I have worked for years on this third *submarino*, which will travel under the ocean."

"And very successful you have been!" I exclaimed.

"Alas no," said the inventor sadly. "*Ictíneo* is leaking badly after the heavy seas and the collision with your ship; she is taking in much water, and will be hard-pressed to bring us to the Espanish coast. Fear not," he added. "We shall be safe. But *Ictíneo* will never sail again, and the Navy will again pour scorn on my efforts. This will be my last *submarino*."

"Never fear," I rejoined. "If not you, someone else will take up your work, and perfect it."

.   .   .

"And I was right, Watson," added Sherlock Holmes.

A few years later, one Isaac Peral, a compatriot of Monturiol's, built an improved submarine, and since then many other countries have followed suit, and the submarine is now an important part of the world's navies.

Monturiol was true to his word, and landed us all safely and secretly at a small port near Cadiz, from where, with the help of letters which he carried from the King, Monturiol was able to arrange for a fast frigate of the Spanish Navy to take Bianca and Luca to Genoa, while I hastened to Madrid to report to King Amadeo.

"I am deeply grateful to you, Mr. Holmes," said Amadeo. "And I am happy that the wrong which I did has been righted. It is only just that I should have gained no benefit from all this. In a month or two I shall abdicate and return to Italy. From what you tell me, it seems that I may well be able to attend my cousin's wedding!"

While in Madrid I heard that the *Mary Celeste* had been taken into Gibraltar by the crew of the *Dei Gratia*, who had obviously decided to try to make a profit out of the affair. More disquieting news was that Captain Winchester had been called to Gibraltar to testify. I felt sure that he intended to keep his promise to say nothing of our transaction, but feared that the lawyers might wheedle out of him more than he intended to say. I travelled south again, to Gibraltar, and attended the court in disguise. Afterwards, I revealed myself to Winchester and learned from him that the deaths of Captain and Mrs. Briggs had passed unnoticed, as he alone knew that they had been staying in the ill-fated hotel, and it was assumed in New York that they had sailed on the *Mary Celeste*. Although he assured me that he would stand firm and say nothing, I thought it best to suggest to him that the court intended to arrest him for complicity in the murder of the crew of the *Mary Celeste*. He took fright and fled to America, taking no further part in the case.

The *Dei Gratia* sailed on to Genoa, even while the Admiralty Court was hearing the case, and much to the annoyance of the Judge Advocate. The Republican ruffians, knowing the proposed destination of the *Mary Celeste*, presumably suspected that Bianca and Luca, if they had survived, would make their way to that port, and were determined to have their revenge on them. Their deductions were correct as it happened, but the delay in Gibraltar meant that Luca and the Genoese *carabinieri* were waiting for them when they arrived, and the scoundrels paid the ultimate penalty for their crimes. The ship and its corrupt crew returned to Gibraltar, where the court obviously had serious doubts as to the *bona fides* of the salvagers, but nothing could be proved, and the Judge had to be satisfied with granting only a minuscule salvage award.

"Ah, yes, Watson, one other point. There *was* a ship's cat. It too found its way to safety—in the arms of Miss Sophia Briggs who, by the way, was adopted by Bianca and Luca D'Este after their marriage. She is now the Duchess of——."

The Adventure of the Curious Canary

BARRY DAY

NOTED FOR HIS career as an actor and the author of numerous books about the theater, literary figures, and entertainment celebrities, Barry Stuart Day also was one of the driving forces behind the reconstruction of Shakespeare's Globe Playhouse on London's Bankside, an experience about which he wrote *This Wooden "O": Shakespeare's Globe Reborn: Achieving an American's Dream* (1996), which featured an introduction by John Gielgud.

Among his other books are several in which his scholarship and perseverance produced such works as *The Letters of Noël Coward* (2007) and several charming collections of quotations: *Noël Coward: A Life in Quotes* (1999), *Oscar Wilde: A Life in Quotes* (2000), *P. G. Wodehouse in His Own Words* (2001), and *Sherlock Holmes: In His Own Words and in the Words of Those Who Knew Him* (2003).

He is the author of five novels about Sherlock Holmes: *Sherlock Holmes and the Shakespeare Globe Murders* (1997), *Sherlock Holmes and the Copycat Murders* (2000), *Sherlock Holmes and the Alice in Wonderland Murders* (2001), *Sherlock Holmes and the Apocalypse Murders* (2001), and *Sherlock Holmes and the Seven Deadly Sins Murders* (2002).

"The Adventure of the Curious Canary" was first published in *Murder, My Dear Watson*, edited by Martin H. Greenberg, Jon Lellenberg, and Daniel Stashower (New York, Carroll & Graf, 2002).

THE ADVENTURE OF
THE CURIOUS CANARY

Barry Day

"TELL ME, HOLMES, do you believe there is any such thing as the perfect crime?"

We were sitting in our rooms in 221B at a very loose end indeed. As an indication of the depth of his boredom, the world's most famous consulting detective was reduced to turning the detritus of the morning's newspapers into paper darts and launching them into the fire Mrs. Hudson had lit earlier in that morning to ward off autumn's first chill. More than once I had had reason to fear my friend's somewhat uncertain aim would end in a conflagration which would be recorded in the next day's equivalents—"HOLMES AND FRIEND PERISH IN MYSTERY BLAZE—ARSON SUSPECTED."

When I had almost forgotten the question—which had been asked more for something to fill the silence than anything else—Holmes finally answered.

"I am inclined to believe, Watson, that the only crimes that remain unsolved are the ones that have not been called to my attention."

As I glanced in his direction, I saw the small twitch of irony catch the corner of his mouth. It was an expression one had to be quick to spot and interpret. The next moment the face had regained its classically sculpted lines, something poised between Roman senator and an American Indian.

"I presume you are thinking of the icicle used as a dagger that subsequently melts?" he continued.

"Yes, or what about the case of the Barchester beekeeper who appeared to have been stung to death, until you proved that his wife had ad-ministered a fatal injection before dragging his body next to the hive and inciting the bees to attack. I should say that was a close run thing. If you hadn't been able to prove that the fellow was dead before the bees stung him, she'd have got away with it."

"A simple enough deduction for one versed in the kiss of the needle," Holmes replied, casting me a covert glance in expectation of a reaction. But I am too old a soldier to rise to such an obvious lure. Seeing that his ploy had failed, he continued. "And an insult to such a sophisticated species. One of these days I fully intend to . . ." But then another thought seemed to strike him.

"But, my dear chap, I confess I'm surprised you have failed to mention the infamous Anitnegra Affair—a story for which, like the Giant Rat of Sumatra, I suspect the world is not yet prepared."

"The Anitnegra Affair?" I exclaimed. "But I don't believe you have ever . . ."

"Oh, my dear fellow, how remiss of me. Do forgive me. It must have occurred during one of your many marital sabbaticals. I do declare, now that I think about it, that it comes very close to your definition of the perfect crime."

"Pray tell me the details," I said, reaching for the pad that was never far from my hand, ready for just such a recollection in tranquility.

"It was the rather sordid story of a purveyor of imported meats who became jealous of his partner. One evening in the warehouse there was a passionate altercation and the wretched fellow struck and killed his partner with a frozen steak, which he then proceeded to cook and eat—thus effectively destroying the evidence."

"But, Holmes, how was he brought to justice?"

"Oh, that was simple enough," my friend replied. "The man literally signed his crime. There was a livid mark on the corpse's head which read 'ANITNEGRA.'"

"ANITNEGRA? You mean that was the murderer's name?"

"Oh, no. ANITNEGRA is simply ARGENTINA spelt backwards. The meat had been stamped in its country of origin and had, so to speak, left its mark."

"And that was enough to convict him?"

"There was no need to convict him. The meat happened to be spoiled and the murderer died of food poisoning—along with twenty-three other innocent people. It was one of my least distinguished cases and caused me to give up red meat for at least a week. . . . Oh, my dear fellow, I do wish you could see your face!"

And the wretched man sank back into his chair and gave way to a paroxysm of that silent laughter that has often brought me close to throwing something at him.

It was at that very moment that the doorbell clanged that insistent call to arms that had heralded so many of our adventures. Only some time later did it occur to me that it was impossible for the imprint to have read ANITNEGRA anyway, since the letters E, G and R would have been reversed—but by that time it was too late to go over the whole wretched story again. Holmes was a leading actor with his timing, whereas I was merely a spear carrier.

Nonetheless, I was in the process of planning the form of my retribution when Mrs. Hudson knocked on the door and ushered in a slim, neatly dressed woman somewhere in her mid-thirties. Handsome rather than classically beautiful to my eye, and as Holmes often asserts, "The fair sex is your department, Watson," I consider myself a fair judge.

She was clearly nervous, as many of our first time visitors are, but Holmes is adept at putting women at their ease when he chooses to, solici-tous and soft of voice, and it was not long before he had her sitting comfortably in the visitors' chair opposite. I took up my accustomed place in a chair slightly to one side and behind Holmes, my pad ready on my knee.

"Pray do not concern yourself on at least one score, dear lady. You have plenty of time before your return to Lewes."

"But how . . . ?"

"A simple enough deduction, in all conscience. You are clutching tightly a rolled up newspaper of which the letters EWE are visible in the banner. The typography is that used by *The Lewes Examiner* and, while that publication enjoys a wide circulation in its part of Sussex, it is only available in the town itself at the time of day you must have caught the train that brought you here so early. Thus you have come here from Lewes.

"If one needed further corroboration, it is to be found in the numbers you have scribbled on the paper as an aide-memoire. To be sure 1415 could refer to the Battle of Agincourt but I suspect the terse prose of Mr. Bradshaw . . . Watson, would you be so kind?"

I reached to the shelf behind me and passed Holmes that well-thumbed red volume, which he proceeded to flick through with practised fingers.

"Ah, yes—here we are. Fourteen-fifteen London to Brighton, stopping at all stations, including Lewes. It was the first local train you felt you could be sure of catching after you had completed your business here. And by the way, Watson, I see those idle fellows are still engaged in their road works outside Victoria. The young lady has some of their sand on the instep of her shoe."

"Mr. Holmes, everything they say about you is true—you are a wizard." Then, as she reached down somewhat self-consciously to brush the offending sand away, she looked up at him with an expression both fascinated and a little frightened. It was one I was well used to.

"What else do you know about me?"

"Other than that you shop frugally at Gorringe's, are an excellent seamstress, are slightly astigmatic, have a Persian kitten of which you are very fond—and have been crying lately, I know practically nothing. Oh, except that you are a widow and expect to remarry in the near future. . . ."

The young lady's mouth literally dropped open. At which Holmes added—"Oh, and you appear to have no need for the service of a dental surgeon." This last made her laugh aloud and, as Holmes and I joined in, the social ice was effectively broken.

Holmes leaned forward in his chair and I have no doubt there was a distinct twinkle in those deep-set eyes. My department, indeed!

"My little parlour tricks are obvious enough, once explained, Miss—?"

"Lucas—Mary Lucas."

"As Watson knows, they are based on the observation of trifles where one may learn more from a lady's glove or the crease in a man's trouser than from a volume of an encyclopaedia. Take your own. They are obviously new, so much so that in your hurry to get here this morning you did not stay at the shop long enough for the sales assistant to take off the label properly. Only half has been removed, leaving the telltale GOR—. While clearly new, the gloves do not appear expensive and, in fact, were almost certainly a featured item in the shop's annual sale. Indeed, I seem to remember that rather distinctive design in an advertisement in today's *Chronicle*. The same can be said for your shoes."

Miss Lucas looked down at her feet, as though they had just betrayed her, while Holmes continued.

"I deduce that you are a seamstress of some accomplishment from the fact that, although your dress is of the latest style, the slight unevenness of the stitching in places tells me that it is not the work of the original designer. Therefore, you probably made it yourself—also from a Gorringe's pattern, I suspect. Your astigmatism is obvious enough from the two small indentations on either side of your nose, which indicate the use of reading glasses. Once again, they would not be deemed suitable for a visit where

you wished to impress on first acquaintance. The Persian kitten? When a lady embraces one of that particular breed—particularly on a regular basis—any item of her clothing will bear some evidence that even regular brushing will never quite eliminate. The colour of the hairs is quite distinctive and since the length is unusually short, it argues for either a very small specimen or—more probably—a kitten."

My friend's last remark produced a rather disconcerting reaction from our visitor. "Oh, Mr. Holmes, what I'd have done without Princess these last few days I cannot imagine . . ."

And Miss Mary Lucas burst into a flood of tears, which caused her to pull a rather crumpled lace handkerchief from the sleeve of her gown and press it to her eyes. As I moved over to give her what comfort I could, Holmes's eyes met mine in an expression that said "Q.E.D."

Then a sudden thought struck her.

"But how did you know about my being a widow and . . . ?"

"The ring finger of your left hand bears the unmistakable mark of a wedding band having been there for some considerable time. You now wear it on your right hand and involuntarily turn it around from time to time. It seems a reasonable assumption, then, that you are no longer married to your first husband but that the idea of marriage is by no means repugnant to you and is presently very much on your mind.

"Now, Miss Lucas, the sooner you tell us of the problem that has brought you here, the sooner we may be able to assist you. You may speak before my friend and associate, Dr. Watson, here with the utmost frankness. Few of my cases would be solved without his invaluable assistance"—and he made a grave nod in my direction, which pleased me greatly—"and none of them would be adequately recorded, were it not for his Boswellian qualities of rapportage.

"Tell us your story in your own words and, I pray you, omit no detail, no matter how insignificant it may appear. It is those details that invariably point the finger of truth." And he settled back in his chair, his lean fingers steepled before his face and his gaze fixed at some indeterminate point on the ceiling.

"Well, Mr. Holmes—Dr. Watson—there really was little to tell until a few weeks ago. I live—as you divined—not far from Lewes where I am housekeeper to Sir Giles Halliford at Halliford Hall. My dear husband died a few years ago quite unexpectedly, leaving me in very straitened financial circumstances. Some family friends were kind enough to recommend me to Sir Giles whose old housekeeper was about to retire after many years of service. I was offered the post and the arrangement has worked out to our mutual satisfaction. He is what one might call a confirmed old bachelor . . ."

"Sensible fellow," Holmes interrupted, then, not wishing to interrupt her flow, apologetically motioned her to continue.

". . . but underneath a gruff exterior which he puts up to keep the world at bay, he is the kindest and gentlest of men. Over the years we have discovered we have many interests in common and have grown comfortable in each other's company. To cut a long story short, Mr. Holmes, Sir Giles has asked me to become his wife . . . and I have accepted."

"But the problem does not lie there, I fancy?"

"Oh, indeed no. I should add, gentlemen, that this is of very recent occurrence and Sir Giles does not wish to announce our engagement until he has made certain family arrangements."

"But I thought you said Sir Giles was a bachelor?" I could not help interjecting.

"There is no immediate family as such," Miss Lucas continued. "He has a ward, a young lady called Emily Sommersby, not much younger than myself, who lives with him. She is the daughter of some old friends of his from his days in India. When they were killed in a climbing accident there some two years ago, he felt it was his duty to bring the girl back to England and give her a home."

"And how do the two of you get on?"

"To begin with everything was fine," Miss Lucas replied and her hand began to turn the ring around her finger, "but lately I seem to have sensed a change in her. Her manner has been more distant and if I may invoke a woman's intuition . . ."

"Indeed, I wish you would. How often have I not told Watson that a woman's impressions are frequently more valuable than the conclusion of an analytical reasoner."

"Well, then my sense of it is that she felt something in her guardian's behaviour that led her to suspect what he had in mind. . . ."

Looking at her I could not help but think that one woman might just as easily have detected that very same truth from the subtle but telltale conduct and tone of voice of another, but I kept that thought to myself.

Mary Lucas continued. "I am not even certain that she did not overhear the conversation between Sir Giles and myself the other evening, for she entered the room almost immediately afterwards. However, if that were all, I should not be here today taking your time. No, the real trouble began a few weeks ago when a young man arrived out of the blue claiming to be his nephew, Robert . . ."

"When you say 'claiming'?" Holmes interjected.

"Sir Giles had a younger brother who—he told me—had left home under something of a cloud. They had completely lost touch and he had no idea whether his brother had issue or not. It would take a long and costly legal search to ascertain the truth of his 'nephew's' claim—a search, incidentally, which he is about to put in hand."

"I take it that he did not warm to the young man?"

"Quite the opposite. His reaction was almost chemical. There was something about 'Robert Halliford'—for that is the only way I can think of him—that he distrusted on sight. Despite that, he felt obliged to give him board and lodging until the situation could be clarified. As for Robert, he acted as though he expected to have the fatted calf killed daily on his behalf, which only made matters worse, of course."

"Presumably the young 'Mr. Halliford' was able to provide some sort of credentials?"

"Not entirely. He claimed his effects had yet to arrive—they had been delayed at sea, he claimed—but he certainly knew a great deal about the family and Sir Giles in particular."

"And what had he to say about himself?"

"Not a great deal, now you come to mention it. He seemed to have worked in various parts of the Far East and most recently in India, which is where he learned of Sir Giles's whereabouts. I once asked him about his profession and he answered something about having knocked about doing a bit of this and a bit of that. I didn't like to press the point."

Holmes nodded thoughtfully. Then after a moment he said, "Did you notice his hands?"

Miss Lucas looked surprised, then furrowed her brow, as if conjuring up a vision of the man in question.

"Yes, they were strong hands. Not those of a gentleman. He had earned his living by them, now that I come to think of it. Strange, but I'd never thought of it before. But why . . . ?"

"It is of no immediate matter. Simply that I like to build up a mental picture of someone before I meet them and Mr. Halliford the Younger seems to be a leading character in whatever play you are about to lay out for us. Oh, by the way, how did he and Miss Sommersby get on?"

Miss Lucas thought for a moment.

"To begin with they were very formal with one another. 'Miss Sommersby, Mr. Halliford' sort of thing. Then they appeared to become very friendly, laughing and joking together." She paused, as if recollecting something. "There was one small incident, though, I remember . . ."

Holmes leaned forward.

"Which was . . . ?"

"One day she called him 'Tommy' by mistake and he took it very badly. He told her she must be confusing him with one of her rich friends from the old days. Then he changed the subject and pretended he was only teasing her but one could see another side of him."

"Tell us something of life at Halliford Hall."

Clearly relieved to be back on familiar territory, Mary Lucas continued.

"It is rather a solitary life we lead—but then, that is one of the things we like most about it, the peace and predictability. Sir Giles is what, I suppose, one might call a creature of habit. Even though it is—or has been until recently—only Emily and himself, he insists on dressing for dinner. Then, when the ladies—or, in this case, lady, retires"—she smiled involuntarily at the solecism, and I could perfectly well see the womanly quality that had charmed an old bachelor's heart—"why then Giles would retire himself to the library on the ground floor to smoke his cigars, pass himself the vintage port and—I am perfectly sure—relive the good old days. It is a habit I shall encourage him to continue when we are . . ."

She broke off in some confusion and a blush rose from the collar of her dress. Collecting herself, she continued. "More than once he has fallen asleep in his chair by the fire and I have found him there the following morning. It is something neither of us ever refers to and, frankly, Mr. Holmes, what harm does it do? My only concern is that, since Giles"—I could not help but notice that the "Sir" had been forgotten—"is a chronic asthmatic, the morning chill might prove upsetting."

"And now that there is another man in the house, Robert does not join him after dinner?" Holmes raised an interrogative eyebrow.

"For the first evening or two he did, now that you come to mention it." She spoke reflectively, as if she were trying to conjure up the events from memory. "He would talk about the importance of male tradition and ritual and how the ranking officer—that's how he put it, 'ranking officer'—by which he meant Giles, should be in a position to command the field of battle."

"Which meant?"

"Oh, he insisted that Giles's chair be moved next to the fireplace, so that he could survey the room and keep warm at the same time. He seemed most concerned that Giles should not sit in a draft."

"But I take it the smoking room battles did not last long?"

"Not for more than a day or two and then Giles made it perfectly clear that he preferred his own company. A Company of One, I think was how he put it. To make it even more obvious, when he went to the library, one could hear the key turn in the lock."

"So what was different about last night?"

"To begin with—nothing. Dinner was over and we had all said our good nights. I went to my room, played with Princess, and read for a while. Emily was in hers. Giles took himself off to the library as usual and Robert . . . I really don't know what Robert did in the evenings. He talked vaguely of some idea he was working on that would make him a fortune and I suppose he was working on that up in his room."

"Which was?"

"Next to mine in the west wing. I should explain that the house is far too big and many of the rooms, though partly furnished, have been unoccupied for years.

"By the very nature of my duties I am an early riser, Mr. Holmes, and since I had slept but fitfully, I was up and about before it was even light. Something—call it a protective instinct, if you will—drew me to the library and it was then that I heard it. . . ."

"Heard what?" I said.

"A laboured rhythmic sound like someone was breathing as if their life depended on it. I've never heard a sound quite like it—unless it was the old bellows at the local smithy. And then—gentlemen, you're going to think me quite mad. I wouldn't have credited it myself except that Princess, who goes with me everywhere, heard it, too. She was almost out of control . . ."

"Heard what?" I repeated.

"I heard a bird twittering."

"A bird?"

"Yes, Doctor, I know it sounds absurd but that is what it sounded like."

"And then what did you do?" This from Holmes, who was now leaning forward as if to snatch the words from her lips.

"I'm afraid my protective instincts overcame my professional discretion. I feared for Giles and, since I carry a set of keys to all the rooms, I ignored his instructions and invaded the sanctum sanctorum. It was as well I did, I can tell you, Mr. Holmes. He was slumped in his chair, fighting for breath, and scarcely seemed to know where he was. It was as much as I could do to get him out of there and into the hallway. Luckily, as soon as I did, I found Emily there. She had heard noises and come to see what was amiss."

"And Master Robert?"

"Oh, he appeared a moment later at the top of the stairs, saw what was happening and came down to help us get Giles to his room."

"Did you examine the library subsequently?"

"Certainly, but there was nothing misplaced. Giles's chair was where it always was—by the fire—and nothing else appeared to have been moved. Oh, there was one rather strange thing. There was an unusual smell in the room that I cannot recollect noticing there before. . . ."

"Can you describe it?"

"It was sweet, pungent—almost like incense, Mr. Holmes. But once I had opened the windows, it soon vanished.

"Mr. Holmes, I realise I may be bothering you unnecessarily. After all, nothing actually happened. All I can tell you is that there was something unbearably evil in that room this morning and I fear for Giles's life. What should I do?"

Holmes appeared to be examining his tented fingers and to address his remarks more to me than to Mary Lucas.

"The case most definitely has certain points of interest and I believe you are right in your sense of something being very wrong at Halliford Hall. My suggestion is that you return there forthwith. Try and act as though nothing untoward has occurred, particularly as far as Robert is concerned. Allow the evening to proceed as normal. Watson and I will arrive on the evening train and come to the house when everyone has gone to bed. Leave the front door on the latch, if you would be so kind. We will keep watch outside the room and see if we cannot determine the origin of these strange sounds and scents. Now, perhaps you will be good enough to draw a map of the ground floor for us . . . and you possess a spare key to the library? Excellent."

A few minutes later a still anxious but distinctly relieved Mary Lucas had dried her eyes, put on her gloves (having removed the offending label), and departed for the railway station.

"And what do you think of it all, Watson?" my friend asked, leaning back in his chair.

"For my money it's the nephew," I said. "Sees himself being cut out of the old man's inheritance; but how . . . ?"

"Yes, yes, Watson," Holmes interrupted impatiently. "Mr. Robert Halliford is clearly trying to secure what he thinks of as his—always supposing he is who he says he is—but, as you rightly ask, how? Not in this case, who—but how?

"This afternoon we shall make our pilgrimage to Lewes. Oh, and slip your service revolver into your pocket, would you, Watson? There's a good fellow. I always feel that Mr. Webley's No. 2 makes such a comfortable travelling companion. He can be so persuasive."

In the end we reached Lewes with ample time to spare and were able to enjoy an evening stroll around the Sussex county town before keeping our rendezvous. I have always been partial to country air, but to Holmes there is something almost sinister about the great outdoors. Where I see air and space, he perceives isolation and the privacy to perform all manner of secret wickedness. "In the lowest part of a big city, Watson, there is always someone to hear the cry for help and perhaps even to provide it but here . . . If Miss Lucas lived here in this bustling little town, I would have less to fear for her than in some brick mausoleum even a few miles distant."

As dusk began to fall we hired a pony and trap and drove to the small group of houses that passed for Halliford village. Since one of them was inevitably the village pub, we were able to make ourselves popular by buying drinks for the regulars and steering them—no great feat—into local gossip. They were able to confirm most of the facts of Miss Lucas's narrative. The squire, as they referred to Sir Giles, was irascible but well liked, as befitted one of the "old uns." For the "young un" they had no time at all. "A bit above 'isself" was the general verdict. "It'll be a sad day for Halliford if that one gets to be squire," said an old man in the chimney corner.

"Have you noticed, old fellow, that one often learns as much from the locals as from the protagonists in a case?" said Holmes, as we returned to our corner table. "They frequently do not know what they know."

We whiled away the evening pleasantly enough in this fashion until, consulting his watch, Holmes finished his drink. "What do you say to a visit to the library now, Watson?"

Our entry to Halliford Hall passed off without incident. The heavy front door opened to the touch and as we passed through the silent marbled hallway, a dark figure glided up to us.

"Thank heavens you're here, gentlemen," Mary Lucas whispered. "Everyone is in their rooms, except Giles"—and she indicated the door of what we now knew to be the famous library. "But there was a dreadful row over dinner between Giles and Robert and it was as though Robert was already the master of the house, the way he talked to Giles. Something is in the air, I know it."

"My best advice to you, Miss Lucas, is to take yourself off to bed now. Watson and I will stand guard from the room opposite." A moment later her ghostly presence could be seen flitting up the wide central staircase and Holmes and I were alone in our vigil.

We have been obliged to stay awake through the small hours on more than one occasion in the past but truth to tell, I have never found it easy. The mind is an easy prey to idle fancies and every noise carries too many disturbing possibilities. The creak of an old house settling can be a footstep approaching one with evil intent and, of course, Miss Lucas's premonitions did not exactly help matters. My only consolation was the reassuring presence of my two old friends—Mr. Holmes and Mr. Webley.

From time to time one or other of us would tiptoe across the hall and listen at the door. Each time the result was the same. There was the crackling of the fire—a sound which gradually diminished as the night wore on—and a regular, rather congested breathing, presumably the result of Sir Giles's asthma.

Then at around five, when I happened to be listening, there was a sudden staccato sound, as though one last ember was stubbornly giving up the ghost. It was over in a moment. Half an hour or so later the wheezing began. By this time we were both at the door.

It was rhythmic but erratic. The noise would build up and then suddenly stop. A minute or so later it would start up again. I looked at Holmes and mouthed, "What?" but he raised a finger to his lips in warning.

Now the noise had stopped altogether as suddenly as it had started. We looked at one another and I could see indecision written on Holmes's face. A moment later it had been replaced by determination as a new sound from inside the room came to our ears.

It was the sound of a small bird chirruping.

"Come along, Watson," Holmes shouted, "there isn't a moment to lose. Fool that I am, we may already be too late!" The key was ready in his hand.

Without ceremony we burst into the room. Before I could take in any of the detail, something bright yellow and in movement caught my eye. Flying around the room, briefly perching here and there and singing its heart out, was a small yellow canary.

Seeing that there was no immediate possibility of catching the little fellow, I turned my attention to Holmes. He was bending over the figure of a man slumped in a club armchair next to the open fireplace. His face as he rose told me the entire story.

"We are too late, Watson. I blame myself for this."

I went over and examined the corpse. As Holmes had indicated, there was no sign of a pulse. Sir Giles's face was flushed and the pupils dilated. At a guess, I would say that he had been dead no more than a few minutes.

"Heart attack, I would imagine," I offered, "probably brought on by his asthma."

"That, I am sure, is precisely what the murderer would like us to think, Watson. In fact, I venture to suggest that an autopsy would reveal nothing other than that. Technically, yes, he died because his heart stopped beating. The question is—what stopped it?"

By this time he was on his hands and knees by the grate in that trufflehound position I knew so well. He was busily sifting through the still warm ashes.

"Murder? How can this be murder? No one entered or left the room or we would have seen them. And as you can see, the room is sealed as tight as a drum."

"Exactly so, my dear fellow, and that is precisely what the murderer was counting on. Ah, Miss Lucas. I'm afraid we have failed you signally in your hour of need. You have my humblest apologies. . . ." Mary Lucas stood in the doorway. Behind her was a dark, rather plain young woman, presumably Emily Sommersby, whose eyes never left the housekeeper for an instant.

"I grossly underestimated the urgency of the situation. I confess I did not take your concerns seriously enough—or rather, I failed to appreciate the sense of urgency motivating the other party . . . or parties."

There was a pause before the significance of Holmes's words sank in and then Mary was clutching the frame of the door to prevent herself from falling. I went across and with Miss Sommersby's assistance helped her to a chair. I thought I saw the other woman flinch at Holmes's final words.

"Tell me it was a quick death, Mr. Holmes, and that he felt no pain. He was fond of joking that, as an old soldier, he didn't expect to die but only to fade away—preferably in his favourite chair with a glass of something by his side. At least he had that. But, oh!" And then she gave way to her grief.

As she spoke, Holmes continued to prowl around the periphery of the room. When he came to the large double French windows, he paused and ran his fingers around the frame.

"Come and take a look at this, old fellow."

As I joined him, I could see that attached to the original wooden frame was an additional construction of wood and metal which appeared to act as an extra seal.

"Oh, Mr. Holmes," a tearful Mary Lucas said, clearly relieved to have something to distract her, "that was Robert's idea. Giles had been complaining about the 'infernal draft,' as he put it, and Robert said 'Don't you worry about that. I'll take care of everything.' And he did the job himself only a day or two ago. I don't think a professional could have made a better job of it."

As she spoke, a glint of metal caught my eye. Some small object had fallen to the floor and been hidden by the heavy curtains Holmes had disarranged in his inspection. I bent down and retrieved it.

"Good heavens, Holmes," I heard myself exclaim, "I haven't seen one of these since my Army days."

In the palm of my hand lay a small multi-purpose spannerlike tool that had seen a good deal of wear. Partly worn away was an engraving which I tried to decipher.

"The property of Her Majesty's Royal Engineers, I think you'll find, Watson." Holmes spoke so that only I could hear. "I believe we have found the previous occupation of the would-be Young Master."

"Of course, that would account for the 'ranking officer' talk. Old habits die hard. Why, I know myself . . ."

"And does it not strike you as odd that at a moment like this the young man who is so very caring of his elders is noticeable by his absence?"

"You're right, Holmes. Why don't I go and . . . ?"

At that moment a sudden flash of yellow distracted us once more.

The canary, which had been perched on a high bookshelf and eyeing our doings beadily, now swooped down and landed on Miss Sommersby's shoulder. She reached up and patted it in an abstracted fashion.

Holmes continued as though nothing had occurred. "Yes, indeed, Miss Lucas—leaving a totally sealed environment. Would you be kind enough to come over here to the fireplace, please? Watson, perhaps you will assist her?" With obvious nervousness she did so. "Do you notice any unusual smell?"

She wrinkled her nose and frowned. "Well, now that you mention it, I do—just as I have for the last couple of days. A sort of sweet, sickly smell. I must have a word with our coal merchant."

"I don't think that will be necessary," Holmes said gently. "The source comes from somewhere a good deal south of Sussex. Now, since I presume you are the one to lay and clear the fire, what do you make of this?" And he opened a hand to reveal the results of his researches in the grate. On his palm was a small pile of what looked like grit.

She looked at it for a moment, then took a pinch of it between her finger and thumb.

"That's strange. I noticed the same stuff yesterday morning and that was the first time I'd seen it. If I didn't know any better, I'd say it looked like—bird seed. But how ever did a bird get in here?"

"Just what we are about to ascertain." Holmes carefully placed the pile of dust in an ashtray on a side table.

"You will, of course, have observed, Watson, that Sir Giles's chair is firmly bolted to the floor next to the fireplace. He would have been unable to change his position, had he wished to do so. Our indefatigable engineer at work again, I fancy. Miss Lucas, who occupies the room immediately above this one?"

"No one at present. As I told you, much of the house is unoccupied. But, Mr. Holmes, what do you think happened?"

"The foulest of foul play, dear lady. The locus invariably speaks for itself and this one shrieks its own story. Had I been here to listen to it twenty-four hours earlier, I could have prevented this tragic dénouement. As it is, the events of last night are emerging with great clarity and only a few pieces remain to be put into place. But, as Watson knows, I refuse to hypothesize until I have all those pieces in my possession. Ladies, shall we?"

Not surprisingly, the upstairs room was considerably smaller than the library, but the configuration was clearly similar. Dominating one side of it was the brick extension of the chimney. Immediately opposite were a set of mullioned windows. The room itself was entirely bare of furniture and it was apparent that it did not normally benefit from Miss Lucas's domestic attentions, for there was a distinct layer of dust everywhere except the floor area immediately next to the chimney embrasure and the central window. There were signs visible even to my eye of considerable activity.

"As I told you, gentlemen, this room is unused and normally kept locked," Miss Lucas said, looking around it in some surprise. Holmes and I followed her inside, though I noticed Miss Sommersby lingered in the doorway.

"And yet the key turned in the lock with surprising ease," Holmes remarked, moving purposefully over to the chimney, where he proceeded to tap with his fingernail at the brickwork.

"Ah, as I thought." His long fingers prised away a section of the brickwork exposing the chimney opening. Producing a lens from his inside pocket, Holmes examined the top edge of the exposed bricks with great care, before handing the lens to me to verify his findings.

"I think you will find clear indications that the brick has been scratched by a metal link chain, Watson. There are minute shavings of new metal embedded in the old brick and here and here are clear imprints of where the links have rested. And now . . ."

And with that—in the catlike manner that he invariably adopted when he was hot on the trail—he darted over to the window.

"And yes—although the rest of the windows are firmly shut and warped with age, this one"— and he demonstrated by opening and closing it—"has clearly been used very recently. And here again the metallic scratches . . . Now, let me see, somewhere near the chimney we should find . . ."

He dropped disconcertingly to his hands and knees and peered closely at the floorboards near the chimney aperture. Then, seeming to find what he was looking for, he gave a satisfied grunt, pulled two envelopes from the jacket pocket which was their invariable resting place, and carefully brushed the twin heaps of dust he had accumulated into them.

"What do you have there, Mr. Holmes?" It was Miss Lucas, riveted as anyone must be watching Holmes at work for the first time.

"The final pieces of our little puzzle, unless I am very much mistaken," Holmes replied. "Now, why don't we all repair to the morning room—I believe the local constabulary will require the library in due course—and I will attempt to explain the series of events."

"Don't you think I should ask Robert to join us?" Miss Lucas asked, looking around her as if she had suddenly mislaid him. "I don't know where he can be."

"I hardly think that would prove a very profitable request," Holmes replied, studying his watch. "I would estimate that Master Robert, realising that the game was up, and that a little bird would soon be telling us all we need to know, will have caught the—let me see—the 9:05 train to town. Watson, you might like to telephone our old friend Inspector Lestrade and ask him to have the gentleman in question met on his arrival. Main line stations can be so impersonal, especially to people who have been wandering the wild blue yonder and may even now be contemplating doing so again. Oh dear, Miss Sommersby appears to have fainted."

"It was obvious that Robert Halliford had to find some means of disposing of Sir Giles that appeared to be entirely natural." Holmes was sitting in an armchair covered in colourful chintz—a far cry from the battered Baker Street equivalent. Mary Lucas and I were opposite him on a sofa with Miss Sommersby propped among cushions on another. We had moved to the conservatory to allow the local constabulary I had called earlier to do their routine work in the library.

"Sir Giles's asthma gave him the idea. That, together with the fact that he invariably fell asleep in his usual chair conveniently placed by the log fire. At Robert's insistence, by the way. After that—like all good ideas—it was simple enough.

"First, he had to make sure the room was completely insulated. It wasn't, strictly speaking, a locked room. For his purposes it was better—it was a completely sealed room.

"I would be prepared to wager a small amount that we shall find 'Master Robert' or 'Tommy'—or whatever his real name turns out to be—was cashiered from the Royal Engineers for conduct unbecoming—though I somehow doubt he was either an officer or a gentleman—and thrown on his own dubious devices.

"So here we have a trained engineer who is also familiar with the strange and exotic ways of the Far East—even as my friend Watson is . . ." And he gave me an ambiguous little smile. "Many's the time he has regaled me with stories of how his more rakish friends were inclined to experiment with the inhalation of—shall we say—somewhat outré substances. This particular potion crossed my path during some rather extensive researches into perfumes and their origins. It is a particularly potent derivative of a species of the coriander, known to have an hallucinogenic effect on certain subjects. Its odour is particularly distinctive.

"I think we may assume that the young man brought a quantity of it back with him in powdered form for his personal use. But then it occurred to him that here at Halliford Hall he might find another and more deadly use for it.

"What a strong young constitution might tolerate in moderation might have a very different effect when administered in excess to a man in Sir Giles's condition, sitting captive in an alcohol-induced slumber. Literally a sitting target. It was certainly worth the experiment."

"But, Mr. Holmes, why wasn't I overcome with the same fumes when I went into the room the next morning?" Miss Lucas cried.

"You were witness to what turned out to be a failed test, my dear Miss Lucas. Halliford wasn't entirely sure that his mechanism would prove effective and did not use enough of the powder on that first occasion to have the desired effect. What it did prove was that the insulation worked. None of the fumes escaped and when you entered the room, all you detected was a faint residual odour, almost like a perfume."

"But how had he introduced the powder when, as you say, there was no one else in the room?" I asked.

"Simple. He had waited until Sir Giles was safely asleep and the fire down to its ashes, then poured it down the chimney from the room above—probably using a rubber tube. Traces of it remain in the room above and can easily be analysed. The heat from the embers created the fumes and Sir Giles, being in such close proximity, was the unknowing recipient. The first night he survived. The second, unfortunately, he did not.

"Robert Halliford's principal problem," Holmes continued, "was to remove the evidence—the poisonous smoke. And this is where his engineer's training came into play. For such a man it was child's play to obtain a simple bellows pump and convert it, so that instead of pumping air out—it would suck it in. With a simple hose attachment he could hope to drain the heavier, fume-laden air back up the chimney."

"And out of the open window," I cried.

"Precisely, Watson. So the evidence literally vanished into thin air. We find an ailing old man dead in his favourite chair in a room where he had palpably been alone. Who would think to analyse the ashes from the dead fire?"

"The perfect murder, Holmes?" I asked almost innocently, only to be rewarded by what I can only describe as an old-fashioned look.

"But what about the canary?" This from

Miss Lucas. Every eye turned to where the small yellow bird sat once again on Emily Sommersby's shoulder. She seemed to find its presence curiously comforting, for she was stroking it in an abstracted manner. Her eyes looked as though she, too, might be drugged. From the time we had first met her she had said not a word.

"Ah, yes, our little feathered friend. The unwitting accomplice who let him down badly. When the police drag the lake I noticed at the bottom of the garden—as I strongly suggest they do so without delay—they will undoubtedly find, in addition to the aforementioned and unpatented pumping device, a small bird cage. On the base, unless I am very much mistaken you will undoubtedly find the legend 'T. WILSON BERMONDSEY.' "

"Wilson the notorious canary trainer?"

"The very same, old fellow. Remind me one day to recount the full story of our earlier encounter. Yes, friend Halliford had clearly remembered the traditional coal miner's device of taking a caged canary down into the mine to ensure that the air below ground was pure enough to breathe. Why a canary rather than any other species, I have not the faintest idea but a canary it was.

"Having purchased a number of them, no doubt, from the disreputable Wilson, he adapted the practice for his own purposes. Once the fumes had been pumped out of the room, he would lower the bird in its gilded cage down the chimney, leave it there for several minutes and then retrieve it. The bird's continued good health would be an indication that the room was now clear. Unfortunately for him, on this occasion he had neglected to fasten the door of the cage securely. Seizing the opportunity, his bird literally flew the nest and there was nothing Halliford could do about it.

"Incidentally, there was one other factor he overlooked . . ."

"Which was . . . ?"

"The best laid plans of mice and men should not include the canary. Anyone who has ever owned one will tell you that they insist on spilling their food with unconfined abandon. In low-ering the cage Halliford was actually introducing alternative evidence."

"Ridiculous! The whole thing is ridiculous! You're making up a fairy tale!" Emily Sommersby was sitting up rigidly on the sofa, her face as white as parchment. These were the first words she had spoken. The bird fluttered around her head for a moment before settling again. It had never left her side from the moment she arrived at the scene of the crime.

"Ah, Miss Sommersby, I was wondering when we should hear from you." Holmes's voice had a flat and final tone that struck a chill even in that sunlit room.

As all eyes turned on her, he continued. "Fairy tales are designed to have happy endings. This one, I fear, will not. It seemed to me obvious that the soi-disant Robert Halliford must have an accomplice inside Halliford House, if he was to proceed with his plan without excessive risk of detection and you, I'm afraid, were the only candidate. I believe we shall find that you knew one another in India and perhaps had—shall we say?—some sort of 'understanding,' which was upset by your parents' death and his perpetual 'lack of funds.'

"Then circumstances—and Sir Giles's generosity—brought you back to England and landed you on your feet, as it seemed. Sir Giles was an old man and clearly ailing. Who else was there to inherit? But then you learned of his plan to remarry and instead of feeling happy that your benefactor had found a partner to brighten his last years, you felt cheated. Then, when you heard from your former lover of his own 'misfortune' in life, a sordid little plan began to take shape to destroy one of the people who had shown you kindness and defraud the other."

There was a gasp from Mary Lucas, who sat there ashen-faced.

"I suspect you were the one who actually poured the powder. Dust, my dear young lady, is a powerful medium and the shoe an equally fine expression of it. There were marks in the upstairs room of a man's footprint and also those of a woman of about your height. Since Miss Lucas has already told us that she is not in the habit of visiting the room in her professional capacity, it should prove a simple matter to make the necessary identification. Perhaps you have read my trifling monograph on *The Tracing of Footprints*—a seminal work? Ah, I see not."

Emily Sommersby was shrinking as far back in the sofa as she could and I felt fleetingly sorry for her, until I thought of the deed in which she had conspired. Holmes clearly shared the sentiment, for his voice was calmer when he resumed.

"I prefer to think that you had qualms when the theory turned to reality but your lover was determined. He could feel that the inheritance would come to him one way or another. For with Sir Giles dead, who would spend further time and money on a legal search? He became the driving force and you, perforce, went along with it. For, after all, Master Robert had promised to marry you, had he not? It would have been a union to rival the Borgias. Who would have been next—Miss Lucas? Or would you have been content to dismiss her without benefit of reference?

"You were the one who handled the canary. When you entered the room, the bird clearly recognised you and came to you, as it was trained to do. In a very real sense, it identified the murderer. Watson, I do believe Miss Sommersby has fainted again. Would you be so kind . . . ?"

An hour or so later we were on the train back to London. The local police had taken Emily Sommersby into custody and informed us that Robert Halliford had been apprehended as he stepped off the train at Victoria. Mary Lucas—her grief fighting with her gratitude—had thanked us with such simple dignity and grace that Holmes had exhibited signs of rare embarrassment.

"Mr. Holmes, I see now that some greater power must have intended that Sir Giles and I were not to be allowed a life together. Perhaps the differences between us were too great after all. All I know is that I am grateful for the few happy months we were given and more grateful to you than I can say for ensuring that his death will not go unavenged. He was a good man and so are you, Mr. Sherlock Holmes, and the world is a better place for your being in it."

As the train sped along, though, I could not forbear to ask my friend how she would manage.

"One thing the privileged classes understand, Watson, is the obligation of privilege. Having committed himself to the lady in question and being aware of his own fragile mortality, I think we shall find that Sir Giles had already taken care to make adequate provision for her, without ever saying a word to her. No, my dear fellow, money will not be Miss Lucas's chief concern."

"And what will be?"

"Persuading the cat and the canary to live together in reasonable accord."

And with that he slumped in his opposite corner of the carriage and proceeded to brood over what he considered his relative failure. I offered him a penny for his thoughts.

"About all they are worth, old fellow. I was thinking about that damned bird."

"What about it?"

"I should have asked her for a more explicit description of its song. Had I been able to identify it sooner as a canary, the game would have been ours. Watson, remind me to prepare a small monograph on *Bird Song and Its Application to the Solving of Crime*. It might prove quite invaluable."

Then a more pleasant thought struck him.

"We should be back in town just in time for lunch. What do you say to a decent steak at Simpson's–in–the–Strand?"

"It depends."

"On what, pray?"

"It depends on whether the steak has ANITNEGRA written on it. And by the way, Holmes, you do realise, don't you, that . . ."

The Adventure of the Murdered Art Editor

FREDERIC DORR STEELE

THE SUCCESSFUL CAREER of Frederic Dorr Steele (1873–1944) as an artist and illustrator reached its apex when he was asked by *Collier's Weekly* in 1903 to illustrate a new series of Sherlock Holmes stories that were later collected as *The Return of Sherlock Holmes* (1905).

Tall, thin, and hawk-nosed, Holmes was definitively illustrated in England by the artist Sidney Paget, whose illustrations in *The Strand Magazine* from 1891 to 1927 made Holmes immediately recognizable to millions of readers of Arthur Conan Doyle's stories.

In America, however, Steele modeled his portraits of Holmes on the American stage actor William Gillette, who played Holmes in more than thirteen hundred performances from 1899 to 1932. Although it has become iconic, the calabash pipe that Gillette invented for his dramatic appearances and that was featured in so many of Steele's illustrations of the great detective was not at all canonical.

Born in Michigan, Steele moved to New York to study at the National Academy of Design and took a job with *The Illustrated American* in 1896 and 1897 before becoming a freelance illustrator for the rest of his life, providing work for the top magazines of his day, including *The Century Magazine*, *Scribner's Magazine*, *McClure's*, *Woman's Home Companion*, and *The American Magazine*, among many others. He illustrated books and newspapers as well. His depiction of Holmes had become so beloved that he provided further illustrations of him for various publishers throughout the rest of his life.

In addition to the present story, Steele wrote two Sherlock Holmes parody/pastiches: "The Adventure of the Missing Hatrack" in the October 15, 1926, issue of *The Players Bulletin* and "The Attempted Murder of Malcolm Duncan" in the June 1, 1932, issue of *The Players Bulletin*.

"The Adventure of the Murdered Art Editor" was first published in *Spoofs*, edited by Richard Butler Glaenzer (New York, McBride, 1933).

THE ADVENTURE OF
THE MURDERED ART EDITOR

Frederic Dorr Steele

IT WAS ON a dark, misting day in March 1933, that Sherlock Holmes stamped into our lodgings in Baker Street, threw off his dripping raincoat, and sank into an armchair by the fire, his head bowed forward in deepest dejection.

At length he spoke. "Of all the cases we have had to deal with, Watson, none touches us more nearly than this." He tossed over a damp copy of the *Mail*, with an American despatch reading as follows:

ARTIST SUSPECTED OF MURDER

New York, March 27. (AP) The partially dismembered body of Elijah J. Grootenheimer was found today in a canvas-covered box which had been left on the curb in 10th Street near the East River. The face had been horribly mutilated by beating with some blunt instrument. Identification was made by means of a letter in the pocket of the dead man's coat, addressed to him and signed *Frederic Dorr Steele*. The police decline to give out the contents of this letter, but intimate that it was threatening in tone. Steele is an artist well known for his pictures illustrating Sherlock Holmes and other mystery tales, and it is thought that brooding over these stories may have affected his mind. The motive of the crime clearly was not robbery, since $4.80 in cash and a valuable ticket for the Dutch Treat Show were found undisturbed in his pockets. Steele's last known address was a garret in East 10th Street. Search has been made for him in his usual haunts, but thus far without success.

"Ah, but this is incredible—impossible!" I exclaimed. "Poor Steele wouldn't hurt a fly."

We sat in silence for a time, drawn together by our common anxiety. From time to time during some thirty years, beginning with "The Return of Sherlock Holmes," this Steele had been making illustrations for my little narratives. Though an American, he seemed a decent unobjectionable fellow who did his work conscientiously, and we had grown rather fond of him. His naïve simplicity and quaint American speech amused Holmes, who relished oddities among human beings in all walks of life.

"I can't make it out," I said. "What does it all mean?"

"It means, my dear Watson," said Holmes briskly, dragging out his old kit bag, "that you and I must catch the *Berengaria* at Southampton tomorrow morning."

We had fine weather as we sped westward. Holmes spent most of his waking hours pacing the deck, looking in now and again at the radio room for news—of which there was none. His nerves were as usual under iron control, but little indications of strain were plain to me who knew him so well; as for example when he abstractedly poured his glass of wine into the captain's soup plate, or when, on the boat deck, he suddenly picked up Lady Buxham's Pekinese and hurled it over the rail into the sea.

"Steady, Holmes," I said stanchly. "You must give yourself more rest."

"I cannot rest, Watson," he said, "until we have probed this hideous mystery to the bottom."

"Have you a theory?" I asked. "Surely you don't believe that that poor fellow has murdered an editor in cold blood!"

"Hot or cold, the thing is possible," said Holmes crisply. "It is well known that editors, especially art editors, are usually scoundrels, and sometimes able scoundrels, which makes them more dangerous to society. It is conceivable that our poor artist, after a lifetime of dealing with them, may have come to the end of his patience. Even a worm—" He broke off moodily and resumed his pacing of the deck.

When we reached New York, and Holmes had suffered with ill-disguised impatience the formal civilities of the Mayor's Committee for Distinguished Guests, we established ourselves in a hotel where English travelers had told us we might be assured of finding food properly prepared. But without waiting for even a kipper and a pot of tea, Holmes disappeared, and I did not see him again for three days.

When he reappeared he looked haggard and worn. "I have seen the garret studio," he said.

"Have you a clue to Steele's whereabouts?" I asked.

"A small one," he returned. "In fact, just sixteen millimeters long." He produced from his wallet a bit of cinema film. "I found it on the floor, Watson. What do you make of it?"

I held it to the light. "Well, I see a picture of a little girl and some queer-looking structures like giant mouse-traps behind her."

"Those mouse-traps, Watson, are lobster pots, and of a type peculiar to the coast of Maine. We are on the track of our man."

On a foggy day in May our motor boat crunched against the barnacle-covered timbers of the wharf at a small wooded island, on which stood perhaps twoscore bare gray buildings. Holmes wasted no time. To the leather-visaged lobsterman who had caught our bow line he said, "Sir, we are in quest of a certain artist, said to reside somewhere on your most picturesque coast. Do you know of any artist on this island?"

"Well, we used to know one, but he ain't any artist any longer. He itches all the time."

"Itches!" I said. "Perhaps, Holmes, that may be our man. He has a nervous temperament. He may have developed hives or some such ailment."

"Splendid, Watson. Your deduction is sound, but it is based on an incorrect pronunciation."

"But I don't see—" I began.

"You never see, my good Watson," said Holmes with a touch of asperity.

"He lives down in that shack by the Cove," said the lobsterman. "But if you cal'late to go down there you want to be careful. He bites."

"Bites!" I said in amazement.

"Yeah. Sid, here, was down there yesterday, with a mess o' tinkers, and got chased out. He said he was biting. I guess he's gone kind o' nutty-like, seems though."

"Is his name by any chance Steele?" asked Holmes.

"Seems like it was. But he calls himself Seymour Haden now."

"Seymour Haden!" I exclaimed. "That is the name of a great etcher."

"Precisely," said Holmes dryly. "He used to itch too."

Dreading a possible shock to our friend's mind, we approached him cautiously. He sat at a table in his little house, bent over a metal plate immersed in some villainous blue acid.

"Do you know us, Steele?" I asked timidly.

After a moment he turned his head toward us and we saw a wild gleam in his bloodshot eyes. His disheveled hair and beard and his grimy clothes made him uncouth, even repulsive in appearance. "I can't get up now. I'm biting a plate," he said.

"Another mystery solved," observed Holmes quietly.

"Don't you know us?" I repeated. "We have come all the way from London to find you."

"Sure I know you. You probably want me to illustrate another crime. I killed a man for less than that," said the artist vehemently.

"I daresay. I daresay," Holmes said soothingly. "But we're not hunting crimes now. We just want to help you."

"But you can't help me!" he shouted. "I have been a doomed man for thirty years. Ever since I began making pictures for your damned stories, those editors have called me a crime artist. No matter what else I do, they still try to feed me raw blood. But I got square with 'em. They made a criminal of me, and now, by Heaven, I've committed a perfect crime on one of them. And there are more to come, Mr. Holmes, more to come!"

After this outburst he turned his back on us again.

"Come, come," said Holmes gently, "we mustn't get excited. Think a minute. Is that why you have come off here and left all your friends—hidden from the world?"

"Yes, Mr. Holmes. And that is why I have had this old well cleaned out: I am going to fill it with editors' blood. It will take quite a lot of editors to fill it, but I have hopes."

We saw that it was useless to pursue the conversation further and rose to depart.

"Well, then, go take a walk," he said, "take the path straight over Light House Hill to White Head. After that you'd better come back here. I can give you a crust and perhaps a bit of short lobster if you're not too legally minded."

We crossed the island to the cliffs and stood for a time looking into the blue haze. "Strange, isn't it, Watson," Holmes reflected, "that crime and madness can lurk in so peaceful a spot. . . . I hate to do it, but I must question him further."

"But I say, Holmes, would it be quite sporting," I protested, "now that we are his guests?" But Holmes was resolute.

When we returned to the little house at sunset, we found its owner composed. We talked quietly together of his life on the island, where, he said, he meant to end his days. Only one subject seemed to bring on a return of abnormality,—the subject of editors.

"There is a big cavern up the shore," he said, "that I've got filled solid full of dynamite. There's a big boulder over it, and if an editor ever comes to this island, I'm going to pry it loose. . . ."

"But these editors," said Holmes gently. "Aren't they human beings?"

"Not after they become editors," was the reply. "They are machines. Machines that buy merchandise by the yard, put it in pigeon holes, label it . . ."

"Look here, my dear fellow," said Holmes, "you are happy here, aren't you? You are not bloodthirsty about other people—fishermen for example?"

"Oh, no."

"Well, then, I think Watson and I will go back to England and leave you in peace. You will be safe here. No one need ever know."

Two weeks later we were back in the old rooms in Baker Street. There had been no further developments in the Grootenheimer case. The police had given up the search for the missing artist, and now thought that the editor might have been killed by some Modernist or other deranged person.

But Holmes's watchful eye had caught this curious PERSONAL advertisement in the *New York Times*: "WANTED, an Art Editor, as companion for a summer vacation in Maine. All expenses paid. Must be full-blooded American."

"Poor soul," I said musingly, "no doubt his sorrows have driven him mad. But somehow I am not convinced that his crime is real. It may be entirely imaginary."

"Quite," said Holmes.

"No one could blame him, of course."

"Hardly."

The Darlington Substitution Scandal

DAVID STUART DAVIES

BEST KNOWN IN the Sherlockian community for his many fictional and nonfictional works about the great detective and Arthur Conan Doyle, David Stuart Davies (1946–) is also an internationally successful author of the popular Johnny One Eye private eye series.

Born in England, Davies worked as an English teacher before dedicating his life full-time to editing, writing, and theater. He is the editor of the Crime Writers' Association's monthly in-house publication, *Red Herrings*, editor of a crime fiction magazine titled *Sherlock*, one of three members of the literary performance group the Mystery Men, and, in his own words, an "all around good egg."

While Davies is generally best known for the detective series that records the adventures of Johnny Hawke, a private investigator in London who was medically discharged from the army after losing an eye to a rifle that exploded in his face, he has also written half a dozen Sherlock Holmes adventures throughout the 1990s and the early 2000s.

His love for Holmes and Conan Doyle started early on; in school he attempted to write his thesis on the famed author, but his university turned down his request because they deemed the subject "not of sufficient importance." Davies's passion was not deterred, and he went on to publish several nonfiction works on the author and his most famous creation, including *Holmes of the Movies: The Screen Career of Sherlock Holmes* (1976), *Bending the Willow: Jeremy Brett as Sherlock Holmes* (1996), *Starring Sherlock Holmes: A Century of the Master Detective on Screen* (2001, updated 2007), *Clued Up on Sherlock* (2004), and *Dancing in the Moonlight: Jeremy Brett—A Celebration* (2006). In 1999, his award-winning one-man play, *Sherlock Holmes*, premiered; it is still in production in the United Kingdom, France, Canada, the United States, Hong Kong, and Malta. Davies's Sherlockian pastiches include *Sherlock Holmes and the Hentzau Affair* (1991), *The Tangled Skein* (1992), *The Scroll of the Dead* (1998), and *The Veiled Detective* (2004).

"The Darlington Substitution Scandal" was originally published in *The Mammoth Book of New Sherlock Holmes Adventures*, edited by Mike Ashley (London, Robinson Publishing Company, 1997).

THE DARLINGTON
SUBSTITUTION SCANDAL

David Stuart Davies

SHERLOCK HOLMES AND I returned late one evening to our Baker Street rooms after spending some time in the realms of Wagner. My friend was still singing Siegfried's horn call even as we let ourselves in through the door of 221B. His recital was interrupted somewhat abruptly by the appearance of Mrs. Hudson at the foot of the stairs. She was wearing a long grey dressing gown and appeared to be quite perturbed.

"You have a visitor, Mr. Holmes," she whispered with a kind of desperate urgency. "He refuses to leave until he sees you. He is most insistent."

"Is he?" said Holmes. "Then we had better oblige the gentleman. Off to bed with you. Friend Watson and I will deal with the matter."

She gave an understanding nod, threw a brief smile in my direction, and disappeared behind her door.

The visitor was a short, burly figure of some sixty years. He possessed a high, bald forehead, a shiny face, and fierce blue eyes. He almost ran towards us as we entered our sitting room. "At last," he cried.

Holmes gave a gentle bow of the head in greeting as he flung off his coat and scarf. "Had his Lordship taken the courtesy to arrange an appointment he would not have had to wait over two hours to see me—the cigar butts in my ashtray indicate the length of time."

"You know me?"

"It is my business to know people. Even in this dim light it is not difficult to recognize the Queen's minister for foreign affairs, Lord Hec-tor Darlington. Now, pray take a seat and tell me about the theft."

Lord Darlington dropped open-mouthed into the wicker chair. "Who has told you?"

Holmes gave a brief chuckle. "A brandy night cap for us all, eh, Watson?" he said, before replying to his Lordship's question. "You would not be here alone at this time of night if your errand concerned government business. Therefore, it is a private affair which brings you to my door. A *very* private affair if the official police are not to be involved. It is well known that you are an avid collector of priceless paintings and possess a very rich collection. It does not need Sherlock Holmes to deduce that the matter on which you wish to consult me concerns your paintings or more likely one of your paintings. The matter is urgent and so therefore it relates to loss rather than damage. Ah, thank you Watson." He retrieved a brandy from the tray and took a sip.

Lord Darlington shook his large head in disbelief. "By Jove, you are right, sir. If only you can unravel the mystery as easily as you have guessed at its nature, I will be in your eternal debt."

Holmes raised an admonishing finger. "I never guess. It is an impractical pastime. Now, if you would be so kind as to familiarize me with the facts of the matter, I may be able to shed some light on your particular darkness." So saying he sat back in his chair, both hands cradling the brandy glass, and closed his eyes.

Lord Darlington cleared his throat and began his narrative. "As you rightly stated, my passion in life is art and over the years I have built up what I believe is an enviable collection, one of the finest private galleries in Europe. It is not for their financial value that I treasure my canvases, you understand: it is for their beauty and power, their vivid interpretation of life."

"Quite," remarked Holmes dryly.

"Recently I took possession of a seventeenth-century painting by Louis de Granville, his 'Adoration of the Magi.' It is the most magnificent painting."

"Louis de Granville—didn't he die very young?" I said.

His Lordship gave me a brief smile. "Indeed. He died of consumption at the age of twenty-seven. There are only thirty known canvases of his in existence and 'The Adoration' is regarded as his best. I was so fortunate to acquire this wonderful painting."

"Where did you obtain it?" asked Holmes.

"For years it was deemed a lost masterpiece and then it turned up in a Paris auction house last spring. The bidding was fierce but I was determined to have it. One American bidder chased me all the way, but I managed to shake him off in the end."

"And now it has disappeared."

Lord Darlington's face crumpled at this reminder of his loss. "I use my gallery as some men use tobacco or alcohol. Sitting alone with my pictures I am able to relax and allow the stresses and strains of the day flow out of me. Today I was due to make a visit to see my counterpart in the French government but at the last moment the trip was called off, so instead of catching the night train to Paris, I went home. Both my wife and my son were out on various social engagements, so I took myself to my gallery for a few hours' peace and relaxation. Imagine my horror when I pulled back the cord on my beloved de Granville to find that it was missing."

"The frame also?"

"Yes. There was no signs of forced entry and nothing else was disturbed. All my other pictures were there."

"How big is the painting?"

"It is about two foot by sixteen inches."

"Who has a key to the gallery besides yourself?"

"No one."

"No one?" I found myself repeating our visitor in surprise.

"My wife and son have no interest in my paintings and I welcome that. The gallery is my private domain."

"Who cleans and tidies the room?" asked Holmes languidly. It was clear that Lord Darlington's dilemma did not excite a great deal of interest within his breast.

"I do. It is a simple task. I perform it once a week."

"When did you last see the painting?"

"The previous evening. The charm of it is still so fresh for me that I rarely let a day go by when I don't spend some time with it. I know you may find it strange, gentlemen, but I was actually dreading my trip to France, knowing I would be deprived of my paintings for some days."

Sherlock Holmes drained his brandy glass and rose to his feet. "It is my experience that when the situation is so mysterious with no apparent clues, the solution must be quite simple. Do not lose sleep over it. I feel sure that we can recover your painting."

Our visitor beamed. "I do hope so."

"Watson and I will call around tomorrow morning to examine the scene of the crime and see if we can glean some suggestive facts."

"Won't you come now, gentlemen?"

Holmes yawned and stretched. "It is late, Lord Darlington. There is no danger in waiting for a new day before commencing our investigation. Shall we say at ten o'clock tomorrow morning? Watson will show you out."

When I returned, my friend was standing by the fireplace lighting up his pipe with a cinder from the grate clamped in the coal tongs. "You treated your new client in a rather cavalier fashion, Holmes," I said.

His head was momentarily enveloped in a cloud of grey smoke. When it cleared, I could see that he was smiling. "I object to being treated like a pet dog who will fetch and carry at the owner's whim. The privileged classes all too often forget the niceties of please and thank you. On this occasion it satisfied me to exercise my prerogative to act when *I* saw fit." He threw himself down in his chair. "Besides, it is a straightforward matter and I'm sure that we shall clear it up within the next twenty-four hours."

In this instance, Sherlock Holmes was wrong. The disappearance of Lord Darlington's painting turned out to be far from a straightforward matter.

The following morning we arrived as arranged at Lord Darlington's Mayfair town house a few minutes after ten. We were shown into the drawing room where his lordship greeted us in a most jovial manner. His demeanour was quite different from that of the night before. He introduced us to his wife, Sarah, a small, blonde-haired woman of about the same age as her husband. She seemed nervous in our company and soon made an excuse to leave us to our "business."

"I am sorry to have troubled you last night, Mr. Holmes," said his Lordship, "and it was remiss of me not to wire you this morning to save you a wasted journey. Nevertheless I am happy to pay whatever fees you deem appropriate for the services rendered."

"Indeed. Then the painting has reappeared."

"Yes. It is wonderful. I went into the gallery this morning and almost out of habit I pulled back the curtain and the de Granville was back in place as though it had never been missing."

"But it was missing yesterday," said my friend sternly, not sharing his client's glee.

"Yes, yes, it must have been, but that hardly matters now."

"I would beg to differ," snapped Holmes.

"You are sure that it is the genuine article?" I asked.

Lord Darlington looked puzzled for a moment. "Why, yes," he said slowly, with faltering conviction.

"What my friend is suggesting," said Holmes, "is that it is possible that the thief who stole the painting may well have replaced it with a very good copy, unaware that you knew of its disappearance. You were due to be in France when you discovered its loss, were you not?"

"Why, yes, but . . ."

"Come, come, Lord Darlington. There has been a theft. There must have been a reason for it. You cannot disregard the felony just because your painting has been returned to you."

Some of the sparkle left our client's eyes and he sat down on the sofa. "I suppose you are right. However, I am convinced that the picture resting in my gallery at this moment is the genuine article, but I will contact my friend Hillary Stallybrass, the art expert at the Royal Academy who verified the painting originally, to confirm my belief."

"You would be wise to—"

Holmes was cut short by the sudden entrance into the room of a tall young man with wavy blond hair and young, eager eyes. "Father, I must—" he cried and then on seeing us he faltered.

"Not now, Rupert. I am sure whatever it is you wish to see me about can wait."

The young man hesitated, uncertain whether to heed his father's injunction or proceed. His mouth tightened into a petulant grimace and he turned on his heel, leaving the room as swiftly as he had entered it.

"The impatience of youth," observed Lord Darlington mirthlessly.

"I should like to see your gallery," said Holmes as though the brusque interruption had not occurred.

With some reluctance Lord Darlington took us into his inner sanctum. It was a long chamber whose ceiling was studded with skylights, none of which, we were informed, could be opened. Down the two long walls were a number of red velvet curtains covering a series of paintings. In the centre of the room was a comfortable swivel chair and a table containing a tantalus and an ornate cigar box.

"May we see the de Granville?" asked Holmes.

Without replying, his Lordship pulled back

the cord on one of the curtains to reveal the masterpiece. I have only a layman's appreciation of art, but even I could see that this was a work of great beauty and skill.

"It is magnificent," said Lord Darlington, almost caressing the frame.

"Indeed," said Holmes, examining the canvas closely with his lens. "Tell me, Lord Darlington, do you keep a dog?"

"A dog?" Our client's mouth dropped open. "No. Why do you ask?"

Holmes shrugged. "It is no matter at the moment."

Lord Darlington seemed irritated at Holmes's vague response. He consulted his watch. "Gentlemen, I have an important appointment in the House at eleven-thirty . . ."

"Perhaps you could leave us in the capable hands of your wife. I should like to ascertain some details concerning the domestic arrangements."

"Very well, if you think it is important."

We were left in the hallway while our client arranged for his departure and informed his wife of our request. Holmes casually examined the calling cards in the tray. His face grew taut with excitement as he caught sight of one. He grinned. "Muddy waters grow clearer, my dear fellow," he said cheerily.

Once more we found ourselves in the drawing room. Lady Darlington had arranged coffee for us. She seemed to have lost her nervous edge and appeared composed and fully at ease, sitting on the edge of the sofa, hardly touching her drink.

"You do not share your husband's love of painting, Lady Darlington?"

"It is his passion. I could never match his devotion to art. He leads a difficult public life and his paintings afford him relief and a respite."

"You never visit the gallery?"

"Never."

"What about your son?"

"Rupert?" Her face softened at the mention of her son and a loving smile touched her lips. "He has a young man's interests, and old paintings form no part of those. Rupert and I are alike in that respect."

"He is a member of the Pandora Club."

Lady Darlington looked askance at Holmes. "He . . . he may be. I am not aware of all my son's leisure haunts."

"Or his acquaintances—like Lord Arthur Beacham, for example?"

"Lord Arthur, what of him?"

"He does not possess a very high reputation."

"Perhaps not in the circles in which you mix, Mr. Holmes. You must not listen to the gossip of maids and gardeners. Lord Arthur is a pleasant gentleman, but only one of many among Rupert's associates. Now if you have no further questions . . ."

"Just one more, Lady Darlington. Who has a key to the gallery?"

"There is only one and it never leaves my husband's possession. He carries it on his watch chain."

"Thank you. Thank you very much."

As we were being shown out of the house by a dour and decrepit butler we encountered a florid-faced, rotund man on the doorstep. He gave Holmes a polite smile of recognition and shook his hand. Holmes leaned forward and whispered some words in his ear before we set off down the street.

"Let us walk back to Baker Street," said my friend vigorously. "I am in need of fresh air and exercise."

"By all means," I agreed, falling in step with him. "I gather that rather red-faced gentleman was Hillary Stallybrass come to verify the de Granville."

"Indeed, it was, and I passed on a little advice that may be beneficial to him and certainly to us. Time will tell on that account."

"What is all this business of Lord Arthur Beacham and the Pandora Club? Your remarks were rather pointed in that direction."

Holmes beamed. "They were, weren't they? Someone was rather careless in leaving his calling card on show in the hall. Contrary to Lady Darlington's opinion, Lord Arthur has rather a doubtful reputation: he is a dissolute fellow whose activities sometimes stray into the realms of criminality. And Scotland Yard have had their eye on the Pandora Club, Beacham's office of operations, for some time. It is the centre for a number of somewhat nefarious dealings."

"How naïve of Lady Darlington to consider him a suitable companion for her son."

"How naïve of you, Watson, to think so."

I ignored my friend's riddle. "Do you think Beacham is mixed up with the missing picture?"

"I do. I am not sure yet what he is up to and quite who else is involved, but I have my theory, which I will put to the test later today."

After a simple lunch provided by Mrs. Hudson, Holmes busied himself with some malodorous chemical experiments, while I caught up with correspondence and prepared some case notes ready for publication. As dusk was falling, he retired to his room, emerging some forty-five minutes later in disguise. He was attired in evening dress, but he had padded out his lithe shape so that he appeared quite plump. His face was flushed and a large moustache adorned his upper lip, while a monocle twinkled in his left eye. The touches of disguise were light, but at the same time they transformed the familiar figure who was my friend and fellow lodger into a totally different character.

"I am ready for a night at the Pandora Club," he announced, his own voice seeming unnatural emanating from this stranger standing in our rooms. "After all my admonishments to you about the cavalier manner in which you throw your wound pension away on the guesses of the turf, I shall be very careful not to lose too much."

"You do not require my services, then?"

"Later, m'boy, but tonight I need to act, or rather observe, alone."

At this moment, Billy arrived with a telegram. Holmes ripped it open with gusto. "Aha," he cried, reading the contents and then throwing the missive over to me. It was from Hillary Stallybrass. It read: "de Granville is genuine. Some of the other works are not."

. . .

It was at breakfast the following morning when I next saw Holmes. He emerged, without disguise, clad in a purple dressing gown and beaming brightly.

"I gather from that grin," said I, tapping the shell of my boiled egg, "that your excursion to the Pandora Club was fruitful."

"The process of deduction is catching," he grinned, joining me at the table and pouring himself a cup of coffee. "One day I must pen a monograph on the importance in the art of detection of developing a knowledge of international crime and criminals."

"Riddles at breakfast? Come now, Holmes, speak your mind."

"Does the name Alfredo Fellini mean anything to you?"

I shook my head.

"You prove my point," my friend replied smugly. "Now I happen to know that he is the right-hand man of Antonio Carreras, one of the biggest gangland chiefs in the New York area. Blackmail and extortion are his methods and he has grown fat on them. So much so that he has been able to build up quite an impressive art collection. So my friend Barnes at Pinkerton's informs me in his regular reports."

"Art collection?" I dabbed my chin with the napkin and, pushing my half-eaten egg away, gave Holmes my full attention.

"Yes. Now I observed Fellini last night at the Pandora Club where he spent a great deal of his time deep in conversation with a certain member of the Darlington household."

"His Lordship's son, Rupert."

"Precisely. And the conversation was animated, not to say acrimonious at times. And all the while that sly cove Lord Arthur Beacham hovered in the background like a concerned mother hen."

"What does it all mean, Holmes?"

"To use a painting metaphor, which in this case is somewhat appropriate, I have sketched the outlines of the composition but I still need more time to fill in the detail and work on the light and shade. However, it is clear that Rupert Darlington is involved in some underhand deal which involves the unscrupulous Beacham *and* one of the most dangerous criminals in America—a deal that involves the theft of the de Granville canvas."

"But the painting was returned unharmed."

"It had to be. That is Rupert Darlington's problem."

Holmes loved to throw enigmatic statements at me to catch my reaction. I had long since learned that no matter how I responded he would not impart any information he held until he thought it the appropriate moment to do so. I had no conception of what Rupert Darlington's problem might be but I knew that should I press my friend to explain this conceit he would in some manner refuse. Therefore I tried to take our conversation in another, more positive direction, only to find it blocked by further enigma.

"What is our next move?" I asked.

"We visit 'the dog man,'" he replied with a grin.

Within the hour we were rattling in a hansom cab eastwards across the city. I had heard Holmes give the cabbie an address in Commercial Street near the Houndsditch Road, a rundown and unsavoury part of London. He sat back in the cab, his pale, gaunt features wrapped in thought.

"Who or what is 'the dog man' and what is the purpose of our visit? Since you requested my company on this journey it would seem sensible to let me know its purpose," I said tartly.

"Of course, my dear fellow," grinned my companion, patting my arm in an avuncular fashion, "what am I thinking of, keeping you in ignorance? Well now, 'the dog man' is my own soubriquet for Joshua Jones, whose house is overrun with the beasts. His fondness for canines has driven both his wife and children from his door. He lavishes love and attention on the various mutts he takes in, far more than he does upon his own kith and kin. However he has a great artistic talent." Holmes leaned nearer to me, dropping his voice to a dramatic whisper. "He is one of the greatest copy artists of all time. Only the keenest of experts could tell the real 'Mona Lisa' from a Jones copy. I have used the fellow on a couple of occasions myself when fake works of art were required to help clear up a case. You see where he might fit into our mystery?"

"Not precisely."

"I suspected Jones was involved in the matter yesterday morning. You may recall that when I examined the de Granville, I asked if Darlington kept a dog?"

"Yes. I do."

"That was because through my lens I observed several dog hairs adhering to the frame—hairs of at least three different breeds. It seemed quite clear to me that the painting had at some time recently been lodged in premises where several dogs had been able to brush past the canvas. Where else could this occur but in the home of Joshua Jones?"

"Because he was copying the canvas . . ."

Holmes nodded.

"I see that, but why then was the real painting returned and not the copy?"

"Ah, that is the crux of the matter and I wish to test my theory out on my friend Mr. Joshua Jones."

Commercial Street was indeed an unpleasant location. The houses were shabby and down-at-heel with many having boarded windows. The cab pulled up at the end of the street and Holmes ordered the cabbie to wait for us. With some reluctance he agreed. We then made our way down this depressing thoroughfare. A group of ragged, ill-nourished children were playing a ball game in the street and ran around us with shrill cries, taking no notice of our presence, their scrawny bodies brushing against us.

"If this Jones fellow is such a successful artist," I said, "why does he not live in a more salubrious neighbourhood?"

"I believe he has another house in town

where his wife and two children reside but she has forbidden him to bring a single dog over the threshold, so he seems quite content to stay here for most of the time with his horde of hounds. Ah, this is the one."

We had reached number 23: a house as decrepit as the rest with a dark blue door and a rusty knocker. The curtains at the window were closed, shunning the daylight and the outside world. Holmes knocked loudly. As the sound echoed through the house it was greeted by a cacophony of wailing, yapping, and barking cries as though a pack of hounds had been let loose.

"I trust these dogs are not dangerous," I said with some unease.

"I trust so too," replied Holmes, knocking loudly again and setting off a further fusillade of canine cries. Mingled with these came the sound of a human voice. Within moments the lock turned and the door creaked open a few inches; a beady eye and a beaky nose appeared at the crack.

"What do you want?" demanded the man.

"A little information, Joshua, if you please."

"Why it's Mr. Holmes," came the voice again, this time softer and warmer in tone. "Give me a moment to settle my little 'uns down. I don't want any of them to get out. Dog meat's at a premium around here." So saying he shut the door and he could be heard shepherding his pack of dogs back into the recesses of the house.

After a while the door opened again, this time wide enough to reveal the occupant, who was a scrawny individual of around seventy years of age, or so his wild white hair, rheumy eyes, and fine dry skin led me to believe. He was dressed in a pair of baggy trousers, a blue collarless shirt, and a shapeless green paint-spattered cardigan.

"Come in, gentlemen, come in."

Only two dogs appeared at their master's heels as he led us down a dingy corridor and into an equally dingy sitting room. The air was oppressive with the smell of hound. In a nearby room one could hear barking and yelping accompanied by the occasionally frantic scratching as some fretting dog attempted to burrow out.

Jones gave a throaty chuckle at the sound of the muted row. "The little 'uns don't like being separated from their daddy," he grinned, revealing a row of uneven brown teeth. With a casual wave of the hand he indicated we should take a seat on a dilapidated old sofa. "Well, Mr. Holmes, what can I do for you?"

"I need information."

A thin veil of unease covered Jones's face. "Ah, well," he said slowly, "I am reticent in that department, as you well know. I cannot be giving away the secrets of my clients or, soon enough, I'd have no clients."

"I have no wish to compromise you, Jones," said Sherlock Holmes evenly. "Indeed, it is not fresh information I require, merely confirmation of my deductions, confirmation which will allow me to proceed further in my case."

Jones frowned. "What you're asking is something I cannot give you. I treat all who cross over my threshold, be it man or dog, with the same regard and assurance of discretion."

Holmes appeared unperturbed by Jones's intransigence. "I am glad to hear it," he said. "I have no intention of asking you to betray anyone's trust, even that of such a lowly character as Lord Arthur Beacham."

Jones blanched somewhat at the mention of this name and his eyes flickered erratically. "Then what do you want from me?" he asked, his voice lacking the earlier assertiveness.

"I wish to present a series of suppositions to you regarding my current investigation which concerns the theft of Lord Darlington's painting the 'Adoration of the Magi' by de Granville—a work I understand you know intimately. All I require from you is a slight inclination of the head if you believe that I am in the possession of the correct interpretation of events and a shake of the head if you perceive my suppositions to be incorrect. There is no need for verbal confirmation. This would help me tremendously in the same way I believe I have helped you in the past."

Jones, who was by now sitting opposite us on a wicker chair with one of the dogs perched on his lap, bent over and kissed the creature on the nose and ruffled its fur. "As you know, I never ask questions of my clients. However I cannot prevent you from expressing your views in my company, Mr. Holmes," he said, as though he were addressing the dog.

"Indeed," agreed Holmes.

"And I may nod and shake my head as I feel fit. That is not to say that this will indicate definitely that I either agree or disagree with your statements."

"I understand perfectly. Now, sir, I happen to know that you have recently been asked to copy Louis de Granville's 'Adoration of the Magi' for a certain client."

Jones's head remained in close proximity to the dog but it moved downwards in a virtually imperceptible nod.

"I believe your client to be Lord Arthur Beacham . . ." Holmes paused but Jones did not move.

"And I believe you have copied many paintings for him over the last six months or so."

Another gentle nod.

"The work was carried out over a day and a night and both paintings, the original and the copy, were returned to your client. He then returned the fake to the premises of the owner and sold the original to one of several unscrupulous collectors."

"I have no notion of what happens to the paintings when they leave these premises, Mr. Holmes. I have no interest in the matter and would regard it as somewhat indiscreet to make enquiries."

"I can understand that. Such enquiries could lead you to learn information you would not wish to know."

For a moment a smile played on the old man's thin lips. He sat up, and looked Holmes in the eye and nodded.

Holmes continued: "I take it that you are able to carry out preparatory work on most copies as their images are easily accessible in lithographic form."

"That is correct. I prepare what I call my skeleton work in advance. It speeds up the process and lessens the time the original work needs to be with me in my gallery."

"But in the case of the de Granville this was not possible, was it? Being a 'lost painting' there were no lithographs available, so you required a longer time with the original."

Another imperceptible nod.

"You are an excellent listener," cried Holmes enthusiastically, rising to his feet and pulling me with him. "Your silences have been most eloquent. My case is all but complete. I thank you."

"In expressing your gratitude please remember that I conveyed no information to you, nor confirmed any of your statements."

"Of course. The players in this sordid drama will condemn themselves without involvement from outside sources. Come, Watson, let us see if the cabbie has waited for us."

And so in this hurried manner we took our leave of "the dog man."

I was surprised at the speed by which this case came to its conclusion; and a very dark conclusion it was too. I would never have guessed that what began as as a fairly inconsequential affair concerning a missing painting would end in murder and a family's disgrace.

The cabbie had been as good as his word and was still waiting for us at the corner of the street. However an expression of relief crossed his ruddy features as he saw us returning. "Back to Baker Street is it?" he asked as we climbed aboard.

"No," responded Holmes, "Mayfair."

"This is a sad affair, Watson," said my friend, lighting a cigarette as he lounged back in the recesses of the cab. "The person who will be hurt most by its outcome is the only innocent player in the drama."

"Lady Darlington?"

He shook his head. "Her husband. His career is likely to crumble to dust if the facts become public. Lady Darlington is far from innocent."

"You cannot mean she was involved in the theft?"

"Think, Watson, think. There was only one

key to the gallery. It was on Lord Darlington's watch chain. The only time he would not be wearing it would be at night when he was asleep. Then his wife, and only she, sleeping in the same room would have easy access to it. She is the only person who could have provided entry to the gallery. However improbable the circumstances, logic always provides certainties."

Lady Darlington was dismayed to see us and it was with a certain amount of ill grace that she bade us take a seat in the morning room. "I hope this will not take long, gentlemen. I have a series of pressing engagements today."

We had only just taken our seats when Holmes gave a sharp sigh of irritation and leapt to his feet. "I beg your pardon, Lady Darlington, my brain is addled today. I have just bethought me of a pressing matter that had slipped my mind. There is urgent need to send a telegram concerning another case of mine which is coming to fruition. If you will pardon me one moment, I will arrange for our cab-driver to deliver the message."

Before Lady Darlington had the opportunity to reply, Holmes had rushed from the room.

"What extraordinary behaviour," she observed, sitting stiffly upright, clutching her reticule.

"I am sure my friend will return shortly," I said, surprised as she was at at Holmes's sudden departure.

"I presume that you are not in a position to enlighten me as to the purpose of Mr. Holmes's visit."

"Not precisely," I replied lamely. "But I am sure he will not be many minutes."

Her ladyship sighed heavily and I sat in embarrassed silence, awaiting Holmes's return. Thankfully, he was as good as his word and in less than five minutes he was sitting opposite our client's wife once more.

"Now, Mr. Holmes, as you have already wasted some of my time, I beg you to be brief."

"My business here will take but a short time,

but I thought it would be best if I consulted you first before I told your husband the truth behind the disappearing and reappearing painting and the roles that you and your son played in the mystery."

Lady Darlington gave a startled gasp. "I don't know what you mean."

"Oh yes you do," asserted my friend coldly. "The time for pretence and dissembling is over. You cannot go on protecting your son any longer."

"Mr. Holmes, I will not tolerate any more of your nonsense. Would you please be kind enough to leave."

"I will leave, certainly, taking the key with me."

"The key?"

"I am afraid that I played a little trick on you just now. On leaving the room I did not go to instruct our waiting cabman as I intimated. Instead, I slipped upstairs to your son's room where it did not take me very long to discover the hiding place where he secreted the key." Holmes reached into his waistcoat pocket as though to retieve some small object. "The duplicate key that gains him access to your husband's gallery."

Lady Darlington's face turned white. "That is impossible," she cried in some agitation, snapping open her reticule.

"I agree," said Holmes, stepping forward and extracting a small golden key from her ladyship's bag. "I told you a tissue of lies in order for *you* to reveal the real hiding place of the duplicate key. It was a simple subterfuge engineered to reveal the truth."

At this, Lady Darlington broke down and sobbed uncontrollably. I was moved by her obvious distress and watched helplessly as her body shook with sorrow but Holmes remained stony-faced and waited until the lady had controlled herself enough to speak to him. "How much do you know?" she asked at last, dabbing her watery eyes with her handkerchief.

"I know all. I know your son has built up a series of very large gambling debts at the Pandora Club. In an endeavour to keep these from your husband you helped pay for them at first, but when the amounts became too great for you to contend with, you aided and abetted your son in his scheme of replacing the paintings in Lord Darlington's gallery with fakes while your son's crony Lord Arthur Beacham sold the originals."

"The situation as you portray it is more damning than the real circumstances," said Lady Darlington, regaining some of her composure. "Rupert is the son of my first marriage and has never been accepted by Hector. He even denied him the common courtesies. Certainly Rupert was never shown any love by his step-father. I suppose in a reaction to this I lavished love upon him. I gave him liberties and freedoms that were perhaps inappropriate for such a headstrong youth. He lacked a father's controlling guidance. When he formed a friendship with Lord Arthur Beacham I was pleased at first. I believed that the influence of this older man would be good for him. Alas, I did not know what a scoundrel the fellow was. The truth only emerged when it was too late and Rupert was completely under his evil spell. Beacham led my son into reckless habits. Yes, there were the gambling debts which, despite my pleas to Rupert to abandon the game, grew and grew. I knew that if Hector found out he would disinherit him and cast him out of the house. What would become of the boy then? How could I let that happen?"

Lady Darlington paused for a moment as though she was waiting for an answer to her questions, although she avoided our glances. Holmes remained silent.

"When the amounts became too great to deal with out of my allowance, Rupert presented me with the plan regarding the paintings. It had been suggested by Beacham of course. He knew of a skilled painter who could copy the pictures so that only an expert could tell the difference and he also had contacts who could provide eager customers for the original canvases. Beacham, of course, demanded a large fee for his 'services.' To my eternal shame, I agreed, believing it would be only the one painting. One night when my husband was asleep, I took the gallery

key from his chain and made a wax impression of it so that a copy could be made.

"The substitution of the first painting could not have been smoother. The exchange was carried out while my husband was away for two days on government business. Rupert took the picture early in the evening and returned the following morning with the forgery. My husband never suspected a thing. The apparent ease with which the plan had been carried out made Beacham bolder and greedier. He led my son into greater debt so that the substituition of another painting was needed. And so it became a regular process every two months or so."

"Until the de Granville fiasco when your husband's trip to France was postponed and he returned earlier than expected."

"It was Beacham's idea to take the de Granville. He said it would bring the greatest fee yet, but the copier required more time since it was an unknown painting. As you know, my husband discovered the masterpiece missing . . ." Lady Darlington's eyes watered afresh and she dabbed them with her handkerchief.

"Both your son and Beacham knew it would be foolish to place the forgery where the original had hung now that its absence had been discovered. They were aware that your husband would, as a matter of course, call in an expert to verify that it was the original."

Lady Darlington nodded mutely.

"You have been a foolish woman, Lady Darlington. Although you may have acted with the best of intentions towards your son, you have allowed a situation to develop that cannot fail but to bring pain and disgrace to those two men whom you hold dear."

"I beg you not to tell my husband."

"Your husband is my client. He must be told. Besides, we are not dealing with a family squabble here. This matter concerns the theft of a series of master paintings. Two of the culprits are the son and wife of the owner, who is a minister of the crown. A scandal now is inevitable."

"I appreciate that the truth has now to come out. But I want to be the one to tell Hector. It is the least I can do to atone for my sins. Give me a day—twenty-four hours—to do this and also to try and persuade my son to give himself up to the authorities."

Holmes hesitated. He was somewhat moved by the woman's plight.

"Please be merciful," she begged.

My companion consulted his watch. "It is now approaching four o'clock. I will send a telegram to reach Lord Darlington in the morning, indicating that I shall call on him at four in the afternoon to convey information of the greatest moment."

"Bless you, Mr. Holmes."

As events turned out, Holmes was never to make that visit. The following morning I was late down to breakfast and I found my friend slumped in his armchair perusing the paper. His face bore a grim expression.

"Violent delights have violent ends," he said, more to himself than me.

"Bad news?"

He shrugged. "Fate has entered the lists and we have effectively been relegated, old fellow." He waved the paper in my direction. "I refer to a report in here. Two bodies were washed up on the shingle below Tower Bridge late last night. They were bound and gagged and their brains had been blown out. They have been identified as Lord Arthur Beacham and Rupert Darlington, the son of the Minister for Foreign Affairs, Lord Hector Darlington."

"Great heavens what a tragedy. What happened?"

"It was no doubt the work of Alfredo Fellini and his cronies. Obviously Beacham, in his frustration regarding the de Granville painting, tried, foolishly, to pass the fake off as the original to the American. His treachery received the usual rough justice of the gangland courts. Rupert Darlington was seen as part of the conspiracy—which he may well have been. Ah, Watson, Scott had it aright: 'Oh what a tangled web we weave when we practise to deceive.'"

The Problem of the Purple Maculas

JAMES C. IRALDI

JAMES C. IRALDI (1907–1989) will always be remembered as the Sherlockian whose private library served as one of the foundations of the world's largest and most diverse collection of Sherlock Holmes material. In 1974, Iraldi sold to the University of Minnesota his collection of first-edition Sherlockiana, including about 160 early editions of the canon, as well as memorabilia, photographs, newspaper and magazine clippings, and more. Iraldi's cornerstone volumes would later be added to by many more collectors, paving the way for the University of Minnesota's holdings to grow from fewer than two hundred to over sixty thousand pieces of Holmes and Conan Doyle materials.

Though born in England, Iraldi resided in New Jersey for most of his life and was a prominent member of the Baker Street Irregulars, where his investiture, bestowed upon him in 1952, was "The Blanched Soldier."

Iraldi also was a collector of Jules Verne's work and collaborated with a number of other contributors on a reference work on the famous author, *The Jules Verne Encyclopedia*, published in 1996.

"The Problem of the Purple Maculas" is a previously untold case hinted at by Watson in "The Adventure of the Missing Three-Quarter," in which Holmes says, "and there was Henry Staunton, whom I helped to hang." It was originally published as a chapbook (Culver City, California, Luther Norris, 1968).

THE PROBLEM OF THE PURPLE MACULAS

James C. Iraldi

IT WAS TOWARDS the end of November, 1890, that I had a note from Sherlock Holmes, couched in his usual laconic style.

"Interesting problem at hand. Will expect you before noon. S. H."

Needless to say, I gave my patients a rest and eagerly went to keep the appointment. It was a pouring wet day when I set off, after making hurried arrangements at home, for the familiar address which had been the starting-point of so many of those adventures which were the normal condition of my friend's existence. Even an aching limb, protesting against the damp spell, failed to temper my enthusiasm as I hailed a cab, prepared to assist him in any way my slow methods and natural limitations permitted.

I found Sherlock Holmes seated near the hearth, his brier aglow and a pile of discarded newspapers crumpled on the floor beside him.

"Ah, come in, Watson, come in!" he cried cheerfully. "Draw up the basket-chair to the fire and take the seasonal chill out of your limbs!"

His keen, ever-active eyes scanned me meanwhile in that characteristic introspective fashion of his with which I was well familiar.

"I see Mrs. Watson is indisposed. Nothing serious I hope?"

"No. A slight chill. I've advised a few days in bed," I replied as I seated myself in the chair he had indicated with his pipe. I glanced over at him. "May I ask how you knew? You have not taken to pumping my maid, have you?"

"No, no, my dear Watson," he answered with a hearty chuckle which caused his grave, hawk-like features to relapse into more kindly lines. "Never that! It was a simple deduction, based upon the flour smeared on the underside of your left sleeve."

I raised my arm. It was as he said. A thin film of white still adhered to the fabric in spite of the chafing from my waterproof.

"Your explanation is equally obscure," I said, somewhat testily as I brushed it off. "I have no doubt that the connection between this and my wife's ailment is self-evident to a logical mind. Since I do not possess your gift, and am somewhat slow in my logical faculties . . ."

"Not slow, Watson," he broke in quickly, and quite seriously, "but merely undeveloped in so far as deducing from cause to effect. I have had occasion before to say that you possess faculties which though not sparkling nevertheless serve to illumine the qualities of keener minds. A by no means common gift, and one which I value highly, I assure you."

I shook my head dubiously. "I still fail to . . ."

"You still fail to grasp the connecting link between your sleeve and your wife? Yet the inference is clear. You no doubt had good reason for entering the kitchen this morning?"

I nodded. "Quite true. But how . . . ?"

"You could scarcely have gathered up flour in your dispensary," he cried, with an impatient wave of his arm. "Why does a solid British G.P.

enter the culinary domain? To speak to the cook; to arrange for this evening's supper—better still, to suggest a fitting meal for the ailing one. Why did not your wife undertake this typical household task? Because she herself is the bedridden one. I shall venture even further and add that in all probability you bid her good-bye simply by poking your head through the bedroom door."

It was quite so. Upon receiving Holmes's message I had hurried to the kitchen to leave instructions with our cook, hastened upstairs to tell my wife and had then flung myself out of the house without a further glance at my clothing.

"As usual," I said, "you have made it all seem absurdly simple. That final inference being based upon the fact that she would assuredly have noticed the sleeve had I presented myself to her before leaving."

"Quite so."

"Since you did not send me that note," I went on, "simply to tell me that I had got flour on my garments, you have, evidently, an enquiry afoot at this time?"

By way of reply, Holmes tossed over an envelope which contained the following message:

"Dear Mr. Holmes,

I have a splendid opportunity for you to utilize your methods in helping us identify the body of a man found yesterday morning in the river. No signs of violence. Thought you might be interested.

Patterson."

"We may have a clear field in which to start our inquiries. The papers have not yet got hold of it. What do you say, Watson? Care to join forces?"

My momentary hesitation, brief as it was, did not fail to catch his eye. He frowned. "Your wife?"

"No, no, Holmes, she will be perfectly all right without me."

"I may have need of a man of medicine."

"Oh, you need have no fears on that score. I shall come and with pleasure, you know that."

"Then why did you hesitate just now when I proposed having you along?"

"I have made no arrangements with my locum tenens . . . In the event that the case be of some duration."

The shadows fled from his brows. He smiled cheerfully. "Oh, in that case, it can easily be arranged. A telegram or two . . ."

And thus it came about that on that rainy November day we set off upon one of our most singular investigations, never dreaming that before it was over, it would become a "cause celebre" which would make all England ring.

We made a brief detour to the Wigmore Street Post Office where I sent off a telegram to my wife and another to Dr. Anstruther. Then we proceeded to Scotland Yard.

Inspector Patterson greeted us on our arrival in his customary dour fashion, and without wasting any time went along with us to the chill, dank mortuary wherein unknown derelicts are quartered until disposed of. On a sign from him, an attendant removed the shroud which covered one of the several stark figures lying on rough deal tables in various sections of the room. Revealed to our sober gaze lay the rigid form of a young man in his early twenties, with a clean-shaven face, thick black hair surmounting a high brow, dark eyes now bulging dimly from their sockets, a well-cut nose and full lips twisted in a dreadful grin which revealed even rows of sound teeth.

Here and there the white skin bore scratches and bruises and small irregular patches a deep purple in colour. The contusions and abrasions were most in evidence about the chest and shoulders; while the dark blemishes covered various portions of the trunk and face. That silent and pathetic figure with its blotched and contorted features gave even my professionally tempered nerves a jolt, but they failed to affect my friend's.

"These contusions," he remarked, pointing to the bruised form, "were most probably caused at the time of death, or very shortly afterwards.

But those purple marks are most peculiar. Any theory as to their cause, Inspector?"

Patterson stopped in the act of lighting a cigar. "Body was in the water most of the night," he said evasively. "May have got knocked about by the currents and eddies. There are a lot of piles and posts along Chelsea Reach, you know. Cadogan Pier isn't too far away from where the body was found."

"How long has he been dead?"

"The police surgeon says about ten hours before the grappling-irons brought him in. He was found by the river police at about nine yesterday morning, near the new Chelsea Bridge."

"Hum, that would place the time of death between eleven o'clock and midnight on Monday," mused Holmes. Then in a louder voice he asked, "Did the surgeon explain these discolourations?"

"Said they were simply scrapes most likely, caused perhaps by the fall into the river."

"Any indication as to the actual cause of death?"

"Well," said Patterson guardedly, with a slight shrug of his shoulders, "he didn't want to commit himself until after the inquest and autopsy. No water was found in the lungs; but neither have we uncovered any evidence of foul play. So far, the verdict seems to be 'Death by misadventure.'"

Holmes glanced towards me. "This is your territory, Doctor. What do you make of it?"

A gleam in his eye, a tensing of his attitude as he had spoken, served to put me on my guard. After another careful examination, I spoke cautiously.

"A sudden fall into cold water from a height," I said, "with the resultant shock and fear, might bring on a heart attack. Especially in in a person suffering from a cardiac condition." I pointed to the twisted features. "Such convulsions are sometimes indicative of painful, violent death, which might easily have been caused by heart failure."

"In other words, Watson, the man might have died in sheer panic before having even struck the water?"

"That's it exactly," I replied, pleased that he had accepted my theory without question. "It also explains," I concluded somewhat rashly, "the total absence of water in the lungs."

"But not the purple blemishes," observed Sherlock Holmes very quietly.

"The police surgeon," broke in the Inspector irrascibly at this moment, "didn't consider them to be serious at all, or in any way connected with the man's death. It's a clear case of accidental death caused by a fall into the river. The autopsy may clear up that aspect of it. What we would like to find out, before proceeding any further, is the man's identity. There's not a paper or personal identification of any description amongst his things. No one has yet come forward to claim the body. The lists of missing persons have been consulted, but no one answering his description has been reported."

Patterson snorted with exasperation, then turned to look at my friend who had listened with rapt attention to his words.

"Perhaps that's where you can help us, Mr. Holmes," he added. "Your scientific methods might give us a clue to his trade or profession, or some indication as to where he hails from. Any sort of lead which might put us on the track of his relations or his friends."

Holmes's eyes gleamed. A slight colour now tinged his cheek. The problem was a challenge: his analytical methods against the regular police investigation procedure. His present demeanor was that of a master-craftsman who sees his work ready at hand, called in after others less gifted had failed.

He was now standing over the lifeless form, examining it with swift appraising glances. After closely surveying the twisted, mottled features, he turned to the tightly clenched hands, then to the rest of the body. In silence, broken only by his rapid, nervous pacings, we watched his every move so intently that the sound of his voice, high-pitched and querulous, made us all start up in surprise when he asked:

"Where are his clothes, boots?"

Patterson was prepared for this, and a pile

of garments was quickly brought forward and spread out on a convenient work-bench. Again we relapsed into silence as my friend, completely oblivious of of our presence, quickly yet expertly examined the personal effects of the dead man. He turned out the pockets and scanned the water-matted dross and wool fragments which usually accumulate in the lining. Nothing escaped those keen bright eyes as he concentrated his attention on coat and shirt, then trousers and boots. This completed, he turned again to the Scotland Yard Inspector.

"Was a hat found?"

"No."

"Waterproof or outer coat?"

Patterson shook his head once more. "None."

Holmes pursed his lips, nodded thoughtfully. "I see," he murmured, before directing his attention to the articles found in the pockets.

These were more or less the customary things the average man carries about with him in his everyday life: a bunch of keys, some coins, a pencil and nail file, a comb, a water-soaked billfold which still retained some sodden paper currency, and a large, old-fashioned silver watch.

Holmes picked it up and eyed it intently. Glancing over his shoulder, I could see that it was one of those heavily engraved time-pieces of foreign manufacture, bearing the name of its maker on the enamelled dial. The ornate hands had stopped at exactly three minutes past 2:30. It carried no marks of blows or dents, and had evidently suffered no ill effects other than from immersion.

"This might be suggestive, Watson," he muttered, "most suggestive. Notice that it is quite undamaged. The crystal is still intact." He raised his head. There were traces of repressed excitement in his voice when he asked, "Has this watch been opened, Inspector? Or the hands moved or tampered with?"

"No, sir. That's exactly the way it was when we removed it from the man's waistcoat pocket. We don't consider it of any importance. It may have stopped days before, or the fellow just forgot to wind it."

"You may be right," said Holmes with a slight shrug. "Let us see what else there is. . . . Ah! What have we here?"

He was holding up a circular piece of glass-like substance, light brown in colour, of about an inch in thickness. After eyeing it speculatively for some seconds, he snapped off a small fragment and ground it to powder between his strong, lean fingers. These he carried first to his nose, then to his lips. The experiment appeared to satisfy him for I saw him nod to himself, a quick light coming to his eyes. Swiftly he walked back to the body, re-examined the dead man's hands, even to the extent of forcing open the rigid fingers of the left hand. Again he nodded as he gave vent to a grunt of satisfaction. Once more he returned to the work-bench, selected the trousers and submitted them to another rigorous inspection. When he had finished I could see that the light of triumph shone in his eyes as he said, "That is all. There is nothing else to be learned here."

To Patterson he asked, "Have you got a room where we can talk and smoke?"

The Inspector nodded. "This way, gentlemen."

Without another word we filed out of that sombre chamber and followed him up a flight of steps to a small room which, though bare of ornaments and sparsely furnished, nevertheless looked cozy and cheerful by comparison.

It was Inspector Patterson himself who first spoke after we had found chairs and charged our pipes.

"Well, Mr. Holmes," he remarked, "I don't suppose you learned very much from your probings?"

"The body's immersion has naturally robbed me of several suggestive facts, I concede," replied my friend quietly. "However, I can say with assurance that my researches have not been entirely barren."

"Then you did find out something about the man?" cried Patterson, making an effort to conceal his surprise.

"Only that he was a bachelor, inclined to be

vain of his personal appearance, did not smoke, and earned a precarious livelihood by playing the 'cello in some fashionable restaurant." Holmes paused, then added slowly, "And was without any doubt the victim of foul play."

Patterson started up, visibly shaken by this unexpected statement. "You mean the man was murdered?"

"I do."

The Scotland Yarder struggled to regain his composure. Naturally stolid and not easily moved, he resented any unexpected revelation which forced him to depart from his usual reserve. A note of irritation was quite noticeable in his voice when he added, "What makes you so certain of this, Mr. Holmes?"

"Those peculiar stains, to begin with," said my friend, "and the odd behavior of the watch, my dear Patterson."

"I don't attach much significance to those stains," said Patterson stubbornly. "If they are important, the medicos will tell us. But what has the watch to do with it?"

"According to the available data," replied Holmes, "the man died around midnight, presumably from a fall into the Thames. Is it likely that the watch should have continued to run, for two and a half hours, after its immersion?"

The Inspector removed the cigar from his lips, surveyed it thoughtfully for a moment, then slowly nodded his large gray head. "I'm beginning to see what you mean, Mr. Holmes. The man could have been dead at least two hours before his watch stopped running."

"Exactly."

"Does it not also give us the exact moment when the body fell into the water?" I put in.

"I should be more inclined to believe that it was hurled into the river!" observed Holmes ominously.

"And we blindly assumed that the difference between the time of death and the time registered by that watch was of no importance!" groaned Patterson, He faced my friend. "Mr. Holmes," he said, "if our investigations later confirm these deductions I shall swear you are a wizard!"

"And you would be wrong, Patterson. My inferences are based upon a series of facts, each one confirming the next. You are astonished by my conclusions because you are unfamiliar with the line of reasoning which I followed to reach them."

"I'll grant you that," said the Inspector. "Tell me. How did you conclude that he was a 'cellist? By his long hair? By the length of his fingers?"

"By no means," replied Holmes, a frosty smile appearing on his lips for a fleeting moment. "I deduced it from the calluses on the fingers of the left hand—the nails of which, by the way, were cut much shorter than those on the right. I also noticed the frayed shirt-cuff which brushes against the body of the instrument when the player is reaching for the higher positions. I was at first inclined towards a violinist, but subsequent examination of the trouser-legs gave me my most corroborative facts."

"In what way?" Patterson's steely gray eyes never left the detective's grave features as he put his question.

"The 'cellist," replied my friend, demonstrating with quick gestures of hands and knees, "holds his instrument between his knees, in this way. Now, at a point just below the knee of the trousers, on the inside of the leg, I noticed a distinct curve worn into the nap of the fabric. Only a violoncello, gentlemen, could make such a mark!"

"Wonderful!" exclaimed the usually imperturbable Patterson. "Incredible!"

"I assure you, Inspector," said Holmes deprecatingly, "that it is quite superficial." Yet I could see that Patterson's sincere praise had pleased him. "Furthermore," he resumed, "upon finding the rosin . . ."

"So that's what it was!" barked the Inspector, slapping his thigh indignantly. "And I thought it was glue!"

"You saw how easily it crumbled between my fingers. Glue—granting the possibility of its having resisted the action of water and retained its hardness—glue would never have done that. The rosin only confirmed my earlier suppositions. It gave me conclusive proof that the man was a string instrumentalist."

"Who was employed in a restaurant, you said," interposed the Inspector. "Why a restaurant? Why couldn't it have been a concert hall? Or a theatre?"

"Because of the floor-wax on the soles of the dead man's boots," replied the detective after a moment's reflection. "There are no waxed floors in music-halls or theatres."

"A dance-hall, then?"

"Have you ever seen a 'cellist playing in a dance-hall, Inspector? Reed and percussion instruments, yes; possibly violins, but violoncellos seldom if ever."

"I don't go to those places, so I wouldn't know," rumbled Patterson, "but I'll take your word for it, Mr. Holmes."

"Then start your enquiries for a missing musician among the better class cafes, where dancing is not only permitted but encouraged. These are not so numerous as you may think."

Patterson finished jotting down in his large notebook before asking my friend how he had deduced that the man was a bachelor.

Sherlock Holmes tapped his pipe against a convenient ash tray. "Did you take note of his stocking?" he asked. "A bachelor is prone to neglect them. But no self-respecting wife would ever permit her musician-husband to appear in public with holes in his footwear, or with buttons missing from shirt and coat. I counted no less than three lacking in both garments."

"Bachelor he was!" agreed the Inspector, duly noting the fact in his notebook. "And vain, too," he added, "if that comb, and the hair oil he used are any indication. No need to tell us how you found out he was not a smoking man, Mr. Holmes. There wasn't a trace of tobacco anywhere on him. No pipe, no loose shreds to indicate he was an habitual user of the weed." He closed his notebook before proceeding. "Now, as I see it—and this is only a tentative theory, mind you—the poor devil was waylaid in some dark street or alley, killed and then thrown into the river after the murderer had removed all identification from his pockets. In the darkness, he overlooked the watch. . . ."

"The victim, meanwhile," broke in Sherlock Holmes drily, "obligingly taking off his hat and coat to facilitate the murderer's work?"

"Well, I do admit there are some objections . . ."

"Several, in fact," interrupted the other, with a shake of the head. "It is far more likely that the man was indoors when he met his end. This would account for the missing outer garments as well as the missing personal papers. As for the watch, I do not think it was overlooked."

"You think it was left deliberately?"

"I do. The murderer might have thought to establish some sort of alibi in case the crime was laid at his door. However, it is still too early in the case to start theorizing."

"One more question, Mr. Holmes. What do you think he died of?"

Holmes stopped in the process of refilling his pipe. His shaggy brows corrugated deeply, his thin lips pressed together for a second before replying. "The man died from the effects of an alkaloid, as yet unknown, which was injected into the blood stream. I should like to draw your attention again to those purple blotches, Inspector. They are of the utmost significance." He rose to his feet as he finished his statement.

"Come, Watson," he added. "Back to Baker Street for a pipe or two over this matter. There are several fields of conjecture and speculation opened to us, worth at least half an ounce of shag."

Then turning to the Scotland Yarder he said, "Please keep me informed of further developments, will you, Inspector?"

As we jostled along in a cab through the rain-drenched streets, I refrained from asking my companion the many questions which lay on my tongue. As was his custom, he seldom discussed his cases until he held all his facts well in hand. Musing over the grim scene we had witnessed, I found myself formulating reasons and motives for such a crime. The untouched billfold, the silver watch, clearly indicated that it could not be robbery. Revenge was far more likely, but why so peculiar a means of causing death? Did not the murderer realize that its very strangeness might hold a clue to its solution? Did he actually think that he could cover up his tracks simply by using a strange and unknown poison? A glance around at my friend changed the trend of my thoughts.

Holmes, plunged deep in his waterproof, pipe clenched between his teeth, his long legs stretched out before him, seemed to be dozing all the way to 221B. But I, who knew him better than any other man, knew that he was at work on the problem. Knew that his keen, incisive mind was already balancing alternate theories, fitting the known facts into a clear, concise pattern. We pulled up at last before the door.

"There's a gentleman by the name of Mr. Edward Morrison waiting to see you, Mr. Holmes," cried the page as he admitted us. "Been waiting an 'alf hour, sir."

Holmes gave me a swift meaning look. He disliked overlapping cases, and the thought of another at this time nettled him, I could see. We ascended rapidly.

Our visitor rose as we entered. Holmes immediately apologized for having been delayed, and vanished into his room. I removed my waterproof, trying to appraise the thin young man as I attempted to put him at his ease with a polite phrase or two. Light-haired, he appeared to be in his late twenties. The dark suit he wore seemed to accentuate the paleness of his skin. It was not the pallor of ill health, however, but of those who spend a great deal of their time indoors. He had a pleasant smile, yet the creases of worry were apparent around his light blue eyes. I was about to make some trite reference to the weather when Holmes returned, whipping his old robe about his lank and spare frame, his keen eyes studying him as he introduced himself.

"Tell me, Mr. Morrison," he inquired, after we had taken our seats, "do you not find a wind instrument somewhat wearying to one who is evidently none too robust?"

Holmes seldom overlooked an opportunity to impress his clients with his powers of observation and deduction. He loved to astonish them by a display of his remarkable talents in making swift, analytical studies of their habits, traits or profession. In the present instance, though accustomed to my friend's extraordinary gifts, I confess to sharing Mr. Morrison's astonishment. Our new client could only stare in surprise before asking:

"How on earth did you guess that, Mr. Holmes? No one could have . . ."

Sherlock Holmes stopped him with a gesture. The quick smile of pleasure which had come to his lips vanished, and a frown creased his high forehead.

"Young man," he said sternly, "I never guess! It is destructive to the inferential faculties, and abhorrent to the trained analytical reasoner. I base my inferences upon a chain of reasoning drawn from the appearance of things." He stopped to apply a glowing coal to his pipe before resuming. "The links in my chain were forged, Mr. Morrison, by noticing your underlip and your right thumb. On your lip I observed the layer of protective skin left there by the reed; and when we shook hands I distinctly felt the horny ridge on the top knuckle of your thumb."

Turning to me he explained further.

"Such markings are indicative of the clarinet player. Pressure on the lip gives us our first clue; and the callus on the thumb is caused by the weight of the instrument which rests upon it."

His good humour returned as he watched with amused eyes our surprised faces and listened to our ejaculations of praise. He had now made himself quite comfortable in the depths of his favourite easy chair, and was puffing on his brier with contentment and abandon, his legs stretched out towards the blaze.

Musingly he added: "I have of late toyed with the idea of revising my monograph on 'The Influence of a Trade' to include a paragraph on the indelible marks left by musical instruments upon the hands and fingers of their performers. But of course," he put in quickly, "that need not be taken up at this time."

He faced the young man.

"Mr. Morrison, this is my friend and colleague, Dr. Watson. You may feel free to discuss your problem before him. In what way can I be of service to you?"

"By discreetly investigating the present whereabouts of a friend of mine," replied the other, after a slight hesitation, wetting his lips nervously, and exhibiting other signs of discomfort and disquietude.

"Discreetly?" repeated Holmes with a frown.

"There is a woman involved, sir. A married woman."

"But why come to me?" There was no mistaking the acerbity in my friend's tone, a bluntness which clearly spelled dislike for the kind of inquiry that Morrison's reply had evoked. "At present I am extremely occupied and cannot further burden myself with what may only be an illicit love affair. Why do you not go to the police? They are better equipped to undertake such cases."

"The police are not discreet, sir."

Sherlock Holmes stirred angrily in his chair.

"There are many detective agencies in the city who would be only too glad to delve into such unethical affairs. And with a discretion worthy of better things. I should suggest that you see one of them."

But Edward Morrison, with a display of determination which surprised me, refused to accept Holmes's dismissal. Evidently behind that sensitive exterior lay a core of firmness, a will to be heard.

"You must forgive me, Mr. Holmes," he said, "for insisting that you take this case. Perhaps I have not stated it very clearly. It is a delicate matter which, if improperly handled, might bring about the very disclosures I dread." He passed his white, long-fingered hand over his brow, then went on doggedly. "Yet, anxious as I am to avoid a scandal and fearful of committing what may well be an unpardonable breach of loyalty to a friend, I cannot sit idly by without making some effort to discover what has become of him."

"Your loyalty is most commendable, my dear Mr. Morrison," remarked Holmes ironically, "but why are you so anxious to protect the honour of a man who has shown such lack of principle, and disregard for the moral code by which we live?"

Our visitor did not reply. The picture of dejection, he kept his eyes on the worn rug, looking uncomfortable and ill at ease, his head held low.

Holmes turned round in his chair. "Come, come, sir!" he said, his voice strident with irritation. "Would you have me believe that your sole concern is your foolish friend's present circumstances?"

Morrison's voice was contrite when he spoke again. "Forgive me, Mr. Holmes, for trying to withhold a personal matter in the case. You see, I am engaged to marry Miss Geraldine Foote, sister of the missing man. As you have correctly surmised, my concern is less for him than for his family. They are fine people and I would not cause them unnecessary pain for all the world." He paused, then made a gesture of entreaty. "Cannot you see that I dare not go to the police? It would drag the whole disgraceful affair into the public prints!"

"Hum," murmured Holmes, relenting somewhat. "This changes the complexion of things." Then, more briskly, he added, "But I fail to see what can be done to avoid the resulting scandal, should it come out later that this person—what is his name? Foote?—should Foote have run off with another man's wife. Such deplorable behaviour can neither be condoned nor kept secret."

Morrison was about to speak at this point, but a gesture from the detective made him close his lips.

"However, on behalf of his people, I shall look into the matter and endeavour to trace him. But it must be clearly understood that my services will end there: that I shall not stand in the way of any justifiable redress which may be demanded by those whom he has injured." He reached for his notebook.

"Now, Mr. Morrison," he said, his voice still brisk and businesslike, but less harsh, "let me have a few pertinent facts. First, where does your friend live?"

"At 14 Dean Street, Soho."

"With his family?"

"No, sir. He lives alone, in a furnished suite

of rooms. His folks live in Dorsetshire. We visit them each year during the Summer holidays."

"Would you know his landlady's name?"

"Yes. I've had occasion to visit him at times. Her name is Mrs. Ferrucci, an Italian. . . ."

"Quite so. Could you describe Mr. Foote?"

"Easily. I've known him for many years. He is now twenty-six years of age, is five feet, nine inches in height, and weighs about twelve stone. Has very dark hair, thick and curly, and wears neither beard nor moustaches."

"No scars or other marks of identification?"

"Not to my knowledge, Mr. Holmes." A faint smile hovered around the troubled eyes as our client added: "He is considered quite handsome by most ladies."

"Such a description," commented Holmes drily, "would fit any number of men. How long has he been missing?"

"Since Monday evening, when he was called away . . ."

"Monday evening?" repeated Holmes quickly, a new note, a rising inflection of interest apparent now in his voice. His manner had changed suddenly. Until now listless and disinterested, his attitude assumed intense concentration at this point in the interrogation. He abruptly changed the trend of his questioning and asked:

"Is your friend a musician like yourself, Mr. Morrison?"

"Yes, sir, he is. But I can't understand how you could have known this, Mr. Holmes. I haven't . . ."

"What instrument does he play?" My friend's smooth voice broke in quickly. Although edged with excitement, it was well under control. Yet I could feel the suspense coiled beneath the surface.

"The violoncello. We play in the same orchestra."

Sherlock Holmes sprang to his feet, eyes gleaming, his face now flushed and darkened.

"And I thought it a coincidence, Watson," he exclaimed, his voice shrill, "a coincidence that both should be musicians! I was slow in connecting the two men, palpably slow, but no harm has been done by my lapse."

He turned brusquely towards our startled visitor who had witnessed the sudden metamorphosis of a languid form reclining in a shabby robe in an old armchair, to a veritable ferret in human guise, pacing swiftly back and forth, gesticulating, talking rapidly and asking questions.

"Mr. Morrison, you were saying that on Monday evening—that would be the day before yesterday—your friend was called away. Where did this take place? In the establishment in which you are both employed?"

"Yes, sir."

"And that is?"

"Henri Dumont's Cafe Continental, on Shaftsbury Avenue. We play concert and dance music there, from six until midnight."

"I see. Can you remember under what circumstances this call came for your friend? Please try to recall everything in connection with it. It may well be of the utmost importance."

"It was during the after supper lull. We were having our meal—which the Cafe supplies us, even though not paying us a very generous wage—when one of the dining room staff came to our table with a message for Arnold—for Mr. Foote."

"You have no idea of the contents of that note?"

"None whatever. But I do remember that Arnold seemed quite cut up after reading it."

"Did he leave at once?"

"No, sir. He first went to our orchestra leader, Mr. Orlando. Later, Mr. Orlando told us that Arnold had begged permission to leave, saying that some very urgent business had to be attended to immediately."

"And this permission was granted?"

"Yes, it was, but only after some heated discussion between them. You see, Mr. Holmes, there are only five of us, and each one is indispensable in such a small band. But Arnold swore he would return in time for the later dancing." Morrison stopped, shook his head sadly. "He never did. That was the last time I saw him."

"At what time did all this take place?"

"Around ten thirty, sir."

Holmes absorbed this in silence for a while. When he spoke again, his voice was casual. "Can you remember whether your friend wore his hat and coat when he left?"

Morrison did not answer at once. His brow creased in thought as he struggled with the question. Finally he said: "I did not see him leave. But when we went home that night, his things were no longer there in the usual place."

"It is then safe to assume that he had them on." Holmes rubbed his hands together, a faint grin of satisfaction appearing on his face. It was becoming quite evident to me now that he had as yet no intentions of telling our visitor the true facts behind Arnold Foote's disappearance. I confess to being unable, at this time, to fathom his reasons for this apparent insensitiveness. Holmes, although cold and unemotional, was neither callous nor cruel. However, I maintained a reserved silence, knowing that my friend's actions, no matter how incomprehensible to the outsider, would later prove to be justified.

Holmes reached over for his notes and a pencil.

"Now, Mr. Morrison," he said, "what can you tell us about the woman in the case?"

"Very little, I fear. Arnold spoke of her frequently to me. His experiences with women have been quite extensive, yet this particular person seems to have fascinated him far more than any of the others."

"This affair, then, is of some duration?"

"Well over a year at least, sir."

"Did you ever have occasion to meet her?"

"No. Although he would ask me to go along with him whenever he wanted to select a gift or token for her, my being an intimate of the family, as it were, made him naturally reticent and secretive where she was concerned."

"Then you cannot give us any information whatsoever with regard to her appearance, her age, height—anything which might help us identify or trace her?"

"All I can tell you, Mr. Holmes, is that she has honey-brown hair, is above medium in height, has very small hands and feet, is inordinately fond of costume jewelry, possesses very stylish clothes, and is two or three years older than Arnold himself. And according to his glowing description, she must be extremely attractive."

"Capital, my dear Mr. Morrison!" exclaimed my friend, sitting bolt upright in his chair, his bushy eyebrows raised in delighted surprise. "You are a model client, gifted with an exceptional memory for detail!"

My expression must have clearly mirrored the astonishment I felt on hearing this description from a man who had declared to have never set eyes upon the woman. But Holmes, chuckling as he caught sight of my face, easily explained it away.

"Mr. Morrison is merely repeating some of the phrases spoken by his friend. As for the other details did not our shrewd young friend here mention having accompanied Arnold Foote on various errands for the purpose of selecting presents for the charmer? He was thus enabled to obtain a fairly accurate picture of the woman's tastes, her height, size of gloves, and general appearance."

Edward Morrison nodded his agreement.

"It may prove to be of assistance to us," went on the detective, "you may be sure.

"Would you know where this person resides, Mr. Morrison?" he asked, becoming serious once more.

"From various chance remarks made by Arnold, at different times, I gathered that she lives somewhere in Chelsea."

"Chelsea?" Holmes's eyes sparkled. "Splendid! Did your friend ever mention her husband?"

"Rarely, sir, and only indirectly. It was a subject which was, of course, quite distasteful to him."

"Now, Mr. Morrison, I want you to think carefully before you answer my next question. It is this: Does Arnold Foote know whether the husband is aware of this illicit relationship?"

Morrison gave a visible start, then he nodded

slowly and pensively. "I have good reason for be-lieving that he does," he replied very quietly.

Holmes's shoulders stiffened almost imper-ceptibly.

"What makes you think so, Mr. Morrison?" he asked.

The young man stared gloomily at the rug as he made his reply. "Arnold has been depressed and worried for some time. No amount of ques-tioning ever elicited any replies, but I could see that there was something weighing on his mind. One night, about a week ago I think, as we walked home, he muttered something about 'skating on very thin ice' or some such phrase. Then—and I recall these words clearly—he said, 'Teddy, I think the old man smells a rat.'"

"He did not clarify the statement?" asked Holmes.

"No. At that moment we had reached the cor-ner of Dean Street, where he lives, and there we parted."

"And since then he has made no further ref-erence to the subject?"

"None whatsoever."

The detective relapsed into silence, and for several minutes not a word was exchanged. When he spoke again, it was to ask: "You have nothing further to add which may be of use?"

Morrison shook his head. "I'm afraid not, sir."

Something in my friend's manner as he re-moved the dottles from his pipe and started to refill it with slow deliberation, warned me that he was about to break the tragic news. I waited for the revelation with a troubled brow.

"Mr. Morrison," he said, "I deeply regret the necessity which has compelled me to withhold the news until now. My next words will shock you, I fear; yet they must be spoken. Your friend, Arnold Foote, is dead."

The thin face of our visitor turned deathly pale as he stared with dazed incomprehension at Holmes's grave features. His haggard eyes looked from one to the other with such pathos and grief that I all but sprang to my feet, ex-pecting him to pitch over in a dead faint. But he rallied instantly, for when he spoke his voice, al-though low, was firm and controlled.

"Are you certain of this, Mr. Holmes? Quite certain?"

Holmes nodded grimly. "As certain as I am that he met with foul play."

"Murdered?" Morrison's pale lips scarcely moved as he uttered the word.

"Yes, he was murdered," repeated my friend, "and it was to facilitate our investigations that I questioned you prior to revealing the fact that he was dead."

Morrison shuddered without raising his head which he had rested on his hands, and remained silent as the detective went on in a kindly tone: "So you see, my dear Mr. Morrison, your well-intentioned efforts to spare his people unneces-sary grief have proved to be of no avail."

The young man raised his drawn face.

"How did he die?" he asked.

"We have good reason for suspecting that he was poisoned," began the detective.

"Then it was she—she must have done it!" he exclaimed, his eyes wild and staring. "I tell you it was she!" Then he stopped, shook his head, muttering, "But why? In heaven's name, why?"

"That is what we are trying to discover," re-plied Holmes soberly. Then in a firmer tone he continued: "Now, sir, pull yourself together. The law claims forfeit for the life of your friend. You must do your utmost to help bring his murderer to justice."

"You are right, Mr. Holmes. I'm sorry I acted like an old woman. Tell me if there is anything I can do. . . ."

"Ah! That is much better," exclaimed Holmes. "You well understand, of course, that it is now a police matter and cannot be kept hidden or suppressed any longer. I advise you to go at once to Scotland Yard and to depose everything you have told us. You may also be asked to testify at the inquest and no doubt called upon to perform the unpleasant duty of identifying the body."

Edward Morrison rose shakily to his feet. "I

shall do as you say, Mr. Holmes." And with a faint nod of his head, he reached for his mackintosh and sadly took his leave.

After our unhappy visitor had departed upon his dismal errand, Holmes continued to smoke on in silence for several minutes. I had been quite shocked by his cold, deliberate lack of consideration, and was actually contemplating a few carefully chosen words of reproach on the subject when, as was often his habit, he broke into my thoughts without preamble.

"I quite agree with you, Watson. It was cruel, yet necessary, believe me. I am not so totally lacking in feeling as to ride roughshod over a sensitive person's susceptibilities without good cause. Yet," he went on, in that dogmatic tone he affected at certain times, "sentimentality has no place in the recesses of an analyst's brain. It interferes with the finely tempered tools which he uses. It nullifies his best efforts."

I nodded thoughtfully. I was recalling the words spoken by Stamford some years before: "Not out of malevolence, but simply in a spirit of inquiry."

"Whatever young Morrison's opinion of his friend's derelictions," he went on broodingly, "he could hardly be expected to return illuminating replies to my questions once his mind had been stunned by the news of Foote's tragic end. The dead influence the living at such moments."

And remembering the young man's reaction, I was forced to agree with his sober explanation. Mollified to some extent, and anxious to change the tone of the discussion, I asked: "Do you believe that the woman caused his death? That she poisoned him?"

Holmes had risen to his feet and was pacing restlessly about, puffing his brier, his hands clenched together behind his back. He shook his head in answer to my question. "No, I do not." He stopped and faced about. "I think I see your point, Watson. You are connecting my remark on the alkaloid used, with Morrison's somewhat hysterical outburst accusing the woman."

I nodded. "It seems fairly conclusive,

Holmes, that . . . oh, for any number of reasons, the woman decided to rid herself of her lover, and thereupon poisoned him."

Holmes did not reply at once to my observation, but resumed his nervous pacings, deep in thought, and evidently turning over in his mind the data he had gathered from our recent visitor. Finally he returned to his chair.

"It is often a mistake," he said, "to unload before one has taken on board a sufficient cargo. To theorize before our facts arrive can be misleading. I do not say that your theory is erroneous; poison is the legendary weapon of the female murderer, but that does not imply that the weaker sex retains a monopoly. Had we to contend with a common type—arsenic, antimony, strychnine—any one of a round half dozen in everyday medicinal or commercial use, I should tend to agree with you. But this was no ordinary alkaloid."

Knowing my friend's penchant for seeking the dramatic rather than the prosaic, I ventured a mild remonstrance, suggesting that perhaps something less fanciful might have been used.

His retort was brusque and sharp.

"The symptoms were unmistakable to the trained eye of a toxicologist. They clearly conveyed every indication of a toxic agent which, when injected into the blood stream, causes dark blemishes to appear on the skin. I do not possess all my data yet, Watson, but I shall have them! I must have them," he went on fiercely, "for then I may learn with whom we have to deal."

"Whom do you suspect? The husband?"

"It is still too early to reach conclusions which later discoveries may easily discount; but there is a strong balance of probability which favours such a suspicion."

"Perhaps," I suggested, "in a moment of blind, jealous rage, he might have . . ."

"No, Watson," he interrupted, "whoever killed Foote did so after thought and preparation. This was not a crime committed in an outburst of savage rage, but a carefully premeditated one."

"Nevertheless," I persisted, "a jealous man,

certain of his wife's unfaithfulness, might well commit such a crime. . . ." I stopped. A new thought struck a chill to my heart. "Holmes!" I exclaimed, "if your suspicions are well-founded, and the husband is the murderer, that woman may be in terrible danger. He may . . ."

"Perhaps he has already done so," broke in Holmes, the same thought no doubt crossing his mind at the same moment. There could be no mistaking the ominous tone in his voice.

"You think she is already dead, then?"

"What else is there to think, man? Foote's death took place most probably late Monday night. This is Wednesday. Why has she not come forward? Why does she choose to remain silent?"

"Perhaps she does not know that her lover is dead."

"It is quite possible," he replied, rising to his feet and starting to remove his robe, "but most unlikely."

"You are going out?"

"Yes, Watson, but I should like you to remain here. I am expecting developments, and with you holding the fort, I feel safe in going off for an hour or so."

"Where are you going, Holmes? To that Cafe-whatever-it-was?"

"The Cafe Continental? No. First I shall drop in at the British Museum. Then I intend to pay a visit to Arnold Foote's housekeeper—what was the name? Ah, yes, Ferrucci. I may uncover a salient fact or two before the hounds from Scotland Yard go baying towards Dean Street."

While speaking he had crossed over to his room, and I waited until he had emerged, buckling the belt of his waterproof, before asking: "What do you hope to find, Holmes?"

"In the Museum: data. In Dean Street: the woman—or at least some clue to her identity." He paused at the door and added reflectively: "Somewhere, in the course of my omnivorous readings, I have chanced upon the slenderest of allusions to a poison which stains the skin of its victims. I must try to find that reference, Watson. A purple blemish . . ." He was still

mechanically repeating that phrase as the door closed.

I watched from the window until my friend had vanished inside a a cab, then I turned to the early afternoon papers which Holmes's dealer had delivered in the meantime. The first reports of the identification of Arnold Foote's body ("thanks to the perspicacity and astuteness of Inspector Patterson and his able assistants") were appearing for the first time. Speculations were being made as to the cause of death, motives, possible culprits, but nothing new had been unearthed and fresh developments were being awaited with every passing hour. An article in the *Standard*, however, revealed that the earlier verdict of death by misadventure would have to be modified in the light of recent findings. Following upon the autopsy, which would no doubt bring in a charge of wilful murder by person or persons unknown. That the case was beginning to loom large in the press was proved by later editions which were brought up after four o'clock. I read them all eagerly, hoping to uncover some fresh details which might aid my friend in his investigations. But they contained merely rehashings of earlier reports and my search was in vain.

I spent another hour browsing through my friend's voluminous yearbooks and indexed cases, brushing up on earlier cases with an eye to future publication—subject to his approval, of course. I chatted over old times with Mrs. Hudson who, meanwhile, had very thoughtfully provided me with a pot of her excellent tea. It was not until well past five o'clock, when I was already beginning to fret and fume impatiently, that Billy came up with a telegram for me. It was from Holmes:

"View halloo. Meet me at Goldini's at six. S.H."

Holmes's use of hunting terms while on a case was not new to me. This could have but one interpretation; the game was breaking cover. His researches had not been fruitless.

My friend was already seated at the table when I reached the restaurant. My eager inquiries concerning his activities during the afternoon fell on deaf ears. Waving his hand towards a chair, he contented himself by saying briefly: "I've taken the liberty of ordering your dinner—and a bottle of Chianti. Fall to; we shall have time enough to discuss things later on."

I obeyed with alacrity for I was hungry and, I must confess, relieved that I could turn away even for only an hour, from the murky business on hand, to something warm and stimulating.

I have frequently had occasion to remark on one of Holmes's peculiar characteristics which permitted him to completely disconnect his mind from the problem under investigation and turn to that inexhaustible fund of fact and anecdote with which his remarkable memory was stocked. His spirited topics that evening, as I remember, touched upon the stains of old Cremona violins, the field of ancient musical instruments, and thence to the composition of intricate cryptograms over which he occasionally spent some of his leisure time in the British Museum.

The rain had stopped when we emerged, but a chilly damp fog enshrouded the streets as we strolled slowly and silently back to Baker Street. It was nearly eight o'clock when we reached our old quarters, and the light streaming brilliantly through the mist warned us that we had a visitor.

It proved to be Inspector Patterson, and the sight of his bulky, homely figure brought vividly back to mind the tragic affair which had haunted us throughout the day.

"I'm glad to see you have not been waiting long, Inspector," cried Sherlock Holmes cheerfully, as he tossed his damp mackintosh over a chair, and placed his cap on the mantle-piece.

"Your landlady told you?"

Holmes grinned and shook his head.

"I deduced that from the length of your cigar. However," he went on, his face becoming serious, "let us not waste time in banter. Only important business could have brought you out on such a dreary evening. What is it, Inspector? Have you traced the woman? Has another mysterious murder taken place?"

Patterson swayed his head in wonder and puzzlement. "There are times, Mr. Holmes," he said, "when I'm inclined to believe you're a mind reader."

"Then another murder *has* taken place?" he asked, half rising from the chair in which he was about to sit.

Patterson nodded grimly.

"A woman?"

"Aye, sir. A pretty but foolish young woman . . ."

"Whose body," broke in Sherlock Holmes, "is marked by a series of purple maculas, similar to those found on the body of Arnold Foote, late 'cellist?"

"My dear Holmes!" I gasped.

"Told you he was a mind reader," grumbled Patterson.

"Who is this woman?" snapped Holmes quickly, impervious to our remarks. "What is her name?"

"She was known at 134 Oakley Crescent as Mrs. Henry Staunton . . ." began the Inspector.

"And at 14 Dean Street?" My friend's eyes now gleamed with excitement.

"As Mrs. Arnold Foote," replied Patterson, cocking a shrewd eye at him. "I thought we had you there, Mr. Holmes!"

"A child could have followed such a trail, after Morrison's testimony. I suppose Foote's housekeeper identified her?"

"Positively!"

"Then the case is closed," said Holmes, sinking back into his chair with a sigh of disappointment. So far as he was concerned, his work was finished. I could tell by his tone and attitude that all interest in the case had evaporated.

"No, Mr. Holmes, the case is not closed," corrected the Scotland Yarder.

"You have only to arrest the woman's husband. Surely it is obvious that he is your man?" Holmes's voice, dry and brittle, showed annoyance at the other's stubbornness.

"There, I agree with you. In fact, he is being sought for questioning. But still . . ." He stopped, fumbled with his cigar, peering at the austere, grave face of the criminologist with anxious eyes.

"Come, Inspector, out with it!" urged my colleague in a sharp tone. "Is there any point in the case which needs clarifying?"

Patterson chewed and worried his cigar thoughtfully before speaking. Then he said, evasively: "Those were pretty neat deductions you made this morning, over at the mortuary. Hit the nail right on the head. Morrison corroborated every point you made."

Always susceptible to flattery where his work was concerned, Holmes thawed visibly. Encouraged, the Inspector continued: "You also implied that you know something about that purple stain poison which was used by the murderer. At least, you conveyed as much when you had me take note of the splotches on the skin. Now, frankly, I admit that we're up a tree there. The medicos don't know what it is. And we don't know either. As you well know, you can't convince a British jury . . ."

"Inspector," said Holmes at this moment, speaking as if he had ignored every word uttered by the good Patterson, "have you ever heard of matacalda?"

The Scotland Yarder shook his head without hesitation. "Never."

"Have you, Watson?"

"I can't say that I have," I replied guardedly.

"Well, until this afternoon, neither had I, so you need not be downcast about it." Assuming his best didactic manner, he continued: "Matacalda is a vegetable alkaloid extracted from an unknown plant by certain tribes in the Brazilian jungles. Very little is known about it. I myself only learned its name a few hours ago, although I had found obscure references to it in various books of travel. This much is known, however: it forms an important ingredient in the preparation of blow dart poison. It works swiftly once it enters the body, causing paralysis of the muscles which control the lungs, with death ensuing in a matter of minutes. Now mark this," he went on, emphasizing his next words with his pipe stem. "Victims of matacalda poisoning are invariably marked by deep purple splotches or maculas."

Patterson let out a cloud of smoke as Holmes ended his extraordinary statement. Then he observed:

"Sounds like a tall traveler's tale." But the intent expression on his face belied both his words and his scepticism.

"Nevertheless, that is the agent which destroyed both victims. Tell me, Patterson, have you any indication as to the manner in which it was administered?"

The Inspector glanced through his notebook, then looked up. "In Foote's case, the doctors believe it was injected by means of a thin sharp instrument which pierced the scalp just below the occ . . . occi-something bone." He looked over to me. "What's that, Doctor?"

"The occipital bone," I replied, "at the base of the skull where the spinal column . . ."

"Yes, yes," snapped Holmes testily, "cut the medical frills! The woman, man! What of the woman?"

Whatever feelings of justifiable pride he may have felt at this moment on having his findings confirmed by the medical evidence, his lean, drawn features did not reveal them.

Patterson consulted his notes again.

"Police surgeon cautious about committing himself, but suspects unknown toxic agent of virulent powers, similar to that discovered by post-mortem examination of the body of Arnold Foote." He stopped reading, then gloomily shook his head. "But we haven't found out yet how it was done," he concluded woefully.

Sherlock Holmes tensed in his chair.

"What do you mean?" he asked abruptly.

"I mean that, although we know, thanks to you, that some queer poison was used, there isn't a cut or puncture anywhere to show how that poison entered the woman's body!"

Almost at once I sensed an awakening of interest in my colleague's manner. His face had regained the old familiar alertness, his shoulders had stiffened, his eye held the gleam I knew so well. Here, at last, was something worthy of his steel. So far, the case had not called upon the full powers of his analytical genius. The deductions praised so highly by Inspector Patterson were, in his opinion, merely a demonstration of the more superficial aspects of crime detection and identification. They had whetted his appetite without satisfying it. Here, indeed, was a unique situation, and one calculated to appeal to his love of the complex and the seemingly inexplicable.

There was an odd light (I will not say of pleasure!) shining in his eyes as he asked quickly:

"Has the body been removed?"

"No. I thought you might care to look things over, so I gave orders to leave everything in status quo."

"Excellent!"

Holmes was already on his feet when he turned to me. "Well, Watson, one more sortie?" Then he chuckled heartily as he caught a glimpse of my expression.

As we clattered down the stairs I experienced anew that never-failing sense of exhilarating adventure which would sweep over me whenever we set off upon a new phase of one of my confrere's cases. It was the thrilling sensation of moments such as this which urged me to abandon my humdrum, everyday pursuits, and play a willing, secondary role in the dramas in which my friend and colleague invariably performed so brilliant a part.

During our drive through the foggy streets, with the gas lamps flickering eerily over the wet and glistening pavements, Inspector Patterson gave us a brief resume of the events which had transpired that afternoon.

Mrs. Emma Grant, part-time servant of the Stauntons, reporting to work at four p.m., her usual hour, had found the dead body of her mistress on the bedroom floor. The police, whom she had notified at once, impressed by the sight of the dark blemishes which disfigured the body, had promptly called in Scotland Yard. It was quickly ascertained by the investigators that the purple marks were identical to those found on the body of Arnold Foote, and had quite evidently been caused by the same agency. According to the police surgeon, the woman had been dead approximately fifteen hours, or since early morning of this day.

The husband, Henry Staunton, having presumably taken to his heels, a warrant had been issued for his arrest on suspicion of murder. It was further learned from the maid that the Staunton household was not a happy one. The couple were childless. Their frequent and bitter quarrels had alienated the few friends they had, and visitors were rare. The disparity of ages (she being some twenty years his junior) plus his moody nature and a jealous and vindictive character, had no doubt contributed much to the incompatibility which had wrecked their married life. An importer of medicinal herbs, Staunton was often away from home for weeks at a time. According to Mrs. Grant, he had only recently returned from a ten day stay on the Continent; Paris, she believed.

Sherlock Holmes stirred for the first time since we had entered the slow-moving vehicle. He had listened silently and intently to Patterson's succinct summary, with chin sunk low on chest, hands thrust deep in his raincoat pockets, his eyes closed. But at this moment he raised his head.

"Did the maid recall the exact day of his return?"

"Yes, as a matter of fact, she did. It was last Saturday, shortly before eight in the evening. She remembered it clearly because of the dreadful quarrel which broke out soon after his arrival. She also recalled hearing Staunton accusing his wife of infidelity, vilifying her brutally, and making ominous threats. To which Mrs. Staunton had retorted in furious rage, that all was over between them, and that she was leaving him. Thereupon, after having packed some of her more precious things, she had departed, swearing never to return."

"And yet, strangely enough," mused Holmes, "she was found dead in that house. What explanation did the maid offer, regarding her mistress's return?"

"She said Mrs. Staunton might have gone to get some of her clothes."

"She was not certain?"

"No. You see, Mrs. Grant had been told by Mr. Staunton that, since the place would be vacant for several days, she did not need to return until Wednesday—today. He was evidently going off on another of his trips."

"Or clearing the field for his next move, most likely," commented my friend. Then he asked: "Have you attempted to trace his movements since last Saturday?"

"I've put two good men to work on just that angle. The ports are being watched, and a descriptive circular has been issued by the Yard. He won't get far if he's still in England. We did uncover the fact that Mrs. Staunton visited Foote's quarters yesterday afternoon. We learned from the housekeeper that the lady looked terribly pale and ill, and when told that Arnold Foote had not spent the previous night (Monday, that is) in his rooms, she had exhibited great distress and had left immediately."

"A complex affair," muttered Holmes. "Mrs. Staunton was indubitably leading a double life, taking advantage of her husband's absences to live with her lover."

"That's how we view it," agreed Patterson.

For some minutes the only sounds to break the silence which followed were the crunch of wheels on wet asphalt and the steady clop-clop of the horse's hoofs. Occasionally the gaslight from a passing street lamp would fall on the grave, brooding faces of my companions. Holmes, pale and tense, his lips clamped tightly on the stem of his pipe. Patterson, stoical and calm, his heavy-set features showing no sign of strain or fatigue.

"We must be approaching the Thames!" cried Holmes suddenly. "I am sure I heard a boat whistle just now." He peered out into the foggy darkness for a moment. "Yes, yes, we ought to be there shortly," he exclaimed. "This is Flood Street, and those are the lights of the Embankment."

Holmes's accurate knowledge of London streets was never at fault, for a few minutes later we turned into Oakley Crescent.

No. 134 proved to be an old yet attractive Georgian dwelling, with wrought iron railings enclosing a narrow strip of garden. At the gate stood a stalwart police constable good-naturedly coping with a crowd of loafers staring up at the entrance. He saluted as he caught sight of the Inspector's large bulk, and waved the loiterers aside for us to pass.

I obtained only a shadowy glimpse of the narrow, dusty, panelled antechamber, lit by a gas chandelier, as we followed Patterson up a flight of carpeted steps, with its unpolished rods dully reflecting the light overhead. Then we were in the bedroom, the scene of the tragedy which, exploding in the press on the following morning, was to rock the entire country for weeks. A boyish-faced policeman rose hurriedly to his feet and saluted as we entered.

It was a largish room, tastefully decorated in blue and gold wall trimming, with heavy curtains at the wide windows, chairs in brocade and silks, soft rugs, and a vast gilt-framed mirror placed before a well carved dressing table. But I noticed all this later.

It was the slender, sheet-covered form, lying between the bed and the dressing table, which instantly caught my eye and held it with all the fascination that only swift and mysterious death can evoke. Mrs. Edna Staunton had been a beautiful creature, with clear blue eyes, light brown hair, and exquisitely modeled nose, lips, and throat. In spite of the hideous blemishes which now marred her features, she still radiated a faint, perfumed aura of feminine attractiveness which tugged at one's heartstrings.

While I had stood shaking my head sadly over the piteous ruin of one of Nature's perfect creations, Holmes, who never wasted a moment in maudlin sentiment, had been giving the room a searching examination. Lens in hand, he had carefully scrutinized the various toilet articles which littered the dressing table. Then, on his knees, he had meticulously gone over the carpet in the immediate vicinity of the body. Like some lank, weird bird of sombre plumage, he hopped about the room, muttering to himself, intent upon his work with all the powers of concentration at his command, completely unaware of those of us who were witnessing this strange spectacle. In silence we watched and waited, while he continued his investigations, impressed by the earnestness he exhibited, and his painstaking exactitude.

Finally he approached the sheeted figure, bent one knee and studied the lurid discolourations with frigid analytical detachment. An exclamation broke suddenly from his lips. A movement of his hand attracted my attention and in an instant I was at his side.

He had parted the soft brown hair and was pointing at the white scalp beneath. The keen, alert expression on his face, the tightening of thin lips and the quiver of nostrils were symptoms I diagnosed with ease.

"What do you think caused that, Watson?" he muttered, his voice hoarse with excitement. Craning my head, I could see to what he had alluded. Directly over the parietal bone, above the right ear, were a series of thin parallel scratches, less than an inch in length.

"What do you think it is, Holmes?" I countered, unable at the moment to account for so slight an abrasion.

"The solution to the mystery," he replied, rising to his feet and brushing the knees of his trousers as he went towards the dressing table.

"The mystery of her death?" I asked, following him.

"No, Watson, the mystery of how the poison was administered!"

I heard an ejaculation from Inspector Patterson and turned in time to see him retrieving the cigar which had toppled from his lax lips as my friend's ringing words fell on his ears.

As we eagerly approached the toilet table, watching Holmes with expectant eyes, he carefully lifted an object from its surface, then whirled round.

"And this," he cried dramatically, holding aloft a silver-mounted tortoise-shell comb, "this is the instrument of death!"

So long as memory serves, I shall never forget his face at that supreme moment of triumph. The colour had mounted to his usually sallow cheeks and his eyes glowed with sheer joy at the homage we paid him with our words of praise, our cries of astonishment. For the moment, the cold analytical reasoner became a human being, eager for admiration and applause. Then the hidden Holmes vanished as swiftly as he had appeared, the incisive reasoning machine returned.

After having scanned the spot on which the comb had lain, he was now intent upon examining the poisoned article itself, studying the long thin teeth through his pocket lens, turning it over with the utmost care.

"A conception worthy of the Borgias!" he cried at last, ill-repressed admiration in his voice. "This innocent-looking comb is deadlier than a cobra reared to strike! The merest scratch is sufficient to cause death."

Holding it out for us to see, but at a safe distance, he added: "Not only have the center teeth been filed to razor sharpness and smeared with poison, but the remaining teeth have been lowered a fraction of an inch. I could distinctly see the marks of the file through my lens!"

"What a devilish device!" I cried, horrified.

"Aye, Watson, devilish and cunning. Who would suspect so terrible a weapon masquerading under the guise of a common, everyday article such as this? With the possible exception of Culverton Smith's little ivory box, I cannot recall in all my experience of murder weapons another which filled me with such utter loathing."

"What made you suspect a comb in the first place?" asked Patterson, who had hardly uttered a word since entering the room.

"Where the others looked for the obvious, I sought for the unusual. Once having found the scratches, on the head, I could scarcely fail to recognize the object that had made them."

Patterson nodded. "Of course," he agreed, his shrewd eyes looking down at the covered body. "Must be a slow-acting poison," he observed as an afterthought. "She had time to replace the thing on the dressing table before collapsing."

"Perhaps the murderer himself did so," I interjected quickly, realizing with a sharp pang that Holmes had apparently failed to account for this most vital point.

But Sherlock Holmes merely shook his head. "No, no, gentlemen, I disagree with you. The poison acts too rapidly for the victim to do what you have implied, Patterson. The thought had already crossed my mind only to be discarded. I have a simpler explanation. You might ask the maidservant, Mrs. Grant, to step in here for a moment."

Inspector Patterson gave the necessary order, and the policeman who had remained on duty left the room at once. A minute or two later he returned with a sturdy, dour-faced woman, faded of feature and with gray-streaked hair.

Holmes greeted her with an encouraging smile. "No need for alarm, Mrs. Grant," he said, "I only wish to ask you a simple question."

The comb, which he had retained in his hand at his side, was suddenly level with the woman's pale, unblinking eyes, the silver mounting twinkling and shining under the gaslight.

"This comb was lying near Mrs. Staunton's body when you entered this room earlier this afternoon. What made you replace it on the table?"

She remained staring at him silently for several seconds, calm and unperturbed. In the hush which followed, I could hear the harsh sounds of a "growler" lumbering by, and the far-off hum of voices from the street. I held my breath, waiting for her to speak. Then the stolid features relaxed, the tightly pressed lips moved.

"You are a clever man, sir," she said, her voice still retaining traces of a Scottish burr worn thin from disuse. "A very clever man who makes a body remember things she had forgotten."

"What made you remove it?" insisted Holmes.

The heavy shoulders heaved in a helpless shrug.

"Who can say? I was that shocked to see the poor lass lying on the floor. I just had to do something. Ma'am was always so fussy about that comb, never a place she went to without taking it along with her. So . . ."

"So you automatically picked it up and put it back in its place, as a well-trained servant should," concluded Holmes for her, a glint of savage delight shining on his face. "Thank you, Mrs. Grant; your testimony has aided us materially."

"The comb will of course figure in the trial, Inspector," remarked my friend after the maid had left. "I entrust it to you. Remember, a careless movement resulting in the slightest scratch or abrasion will cause a frightful death. So handle it gingerly and advise your men accordingly."

Patterson nodded gravely. "I'll take proper care of it, never fear, Mr. Holmes, and so will my men." Then, shaking his grizzled head from side to side in wonderment, he added: "Wish I knew how you get your results."

"Yes, Holmes," I put in, "how did you discover it was the servant who had replaced the comb?"

"Simply by observing the dust on the dressing table," he replied. "As you can see," he went on, pointing with his finger, "a four day accumulation covers its surface, outlining every article. Upon lifting the comb, however, I could distinctly see that the dust beneath, although scuffed and disturbed, did not show the same clear imprint as the rest of the objects. Hence I deduced that it had only recently been placed there. The police would never have touched it. Who, then, had preceded them? The only person who met all the requirements was Mrs. Grant—the first person to enter the room and find the body."

"Holmes," I said, after a long silence, my voice quivering with emotion, "you have seldom risen to greater heights!"

"Best bit of detecting I've ever witnessed!" was Inspector Patterson's only comment, but it sufficed to bring a glow of pleasure to my friend's ascetic features.

"Well, Patterson," remarked Sherlock Holmes some time later as we were leaving the Staunton House, "there is your case. It is still incomplete, and some obscure details remain to be cleared up, but in the main, I believe you have got enough to hold Henry Staunton for questioning."

"Enough to hang him," said the Inspector grimly, tapping the leather case in which lay the tortoise-shell comb.

Retrospective

Three months had gone by. Henry Staunton, the Oakley Crescent murderer, had been tried and convicted of the poisoning of his wife and of her lover, Arnold Foote. The most dramatic trial of the decade had ended after four tempestuous weeks of controversy and debate. With the execution of the poisoner early in February, the whole sensational affair that had rocked the country was already in the process of being forgotten in the never-ending swirl and bustle of everyday life.

I had not seen Sherlock Holmes since that eventful evening in November. A hurried note from him which reached me on the 25th informed me that he had been called in by the French Government on a matter of grave importance. I could only conjecture as to what it was, for his terse messages which reached me from time to time conveyed only that his investigations might be of long duration.

I was, as a consequence, agreeably surprised on a late afternoon in mid-February to learn through Mycroft Holmes that my friend was back in town and wished to see me. My practice being quiet, I wasted no time but went to Baker Street the same evening.

As I knocked upon the well-remembered door, the sound of his strident voice made my heart leap with pleasure, and on entering, my eyes dimmed as I caught sight of the lean pale face, the faded bathrobe.

"Ah, Watson!" he exclaimed, "it is good to see you."

His face was thinner, more deeply lined than I ever remembered seeing it. His cheek bones were more prominent, and his thick, black eyebrows stood out against the pallor of his skin. Yet his keen, ever-alert eyes retained their old fire, his voice all of its commanding power and resonance.

He was seated at his desk, his long nervous fingers deftly inserting various papers and documents into a large blue envelope.

"But perhaps I am intruding upon you," I remarked, after having warmly responded to his greeting. "If you are busy . . ."

"No, Watson, only a preliminary weaving of my web. There is nothing more to be done at this stage." He held up the pale blue folder on the surface of which I noticed a large letter 'M.'"My case is almost complete, but I cannot spring into action for several weeks." He rose to his feet, placed the folder into one of the pigeonholes of his desk, then crossed over to his favourite chair by the fireplace.

"You must forgive me," he resumed, as I followed to take my accustomed place across from him, "for not notifying you earlier of my return. My present investigation necessitates the utmost secrecy. No one, save only those I trust implicitly, must know of my presence here in London at this time. I came back in disguise; the only persons with whom I have communicated are my brother and Police Inspector Patterson."

"This investigation, then, is of great importance?"

"So important," he replied very earnestly, "that if I bring it off successfully it will be the crowning achievement of my career."

"I need hardly have to say that I am at your disposal, Holmes. Should you need . . ."

"Rest assured, my dear Watson," he broke in, "that when the time comes I shall most certainly have need of a faithful ally. It is a waiting game that I play, against a formidable foe whose every move must be carefully weighed if I am to land him in the net I am preparing."

I experienced a pang of disappointment which I attempted to conceal. I ought to have known that it was not his nature to send for me just for the pleasure of seeing an old and trusted friend. His proud, self-contained personality and unemotional character made him shun any display of sentiment towards anyone, even his only friend.

"Come, come, Watson," he cried, a mischievous twinkle lurking in his eyes. "What I have to say will amply reward you for any time you may have to spend away from your patients."

"I am always happy to see you, Holmes," I said quietly, the bitterness thawed by the cordiality in his voice, "and to listen to whatever you might have to say. At present, having no serious cases to attend to, I am quite free to help you in any way I can."

"Splendid!" he exclaimed, crossing his thin knees and settling back more comfortably in his seat. "I suppose," he said, after a pause during which he sat thoughtfully puffing his pipe, "I suppose that you are wondering why I have asked you to drop in today?"

"You have a case to go over with me?"

"Right, Watson," he replied, glancing keenly in my direction, his heavy brows drawn low over his eyes, as if expecting a reaction from me. "The Staunton affair."

I started up in my chair in surprise.

"Is not that an unusual departure from your customary methods of work?" I asked, for none knew better than I that, in his clear and orderly mind, each case displaced the last, and present problems invariably blurred all recollections of past ones.

"It is," he agreed, "but there were unusual aspects about the case which prompted me to deviate from my rule."

"But what feature could have induced you to dwell upon the Oakley Crescent Murders at this time, three months after the conclusion of your investigations?"

"The significance of the tortoise-shell comb," he answered gravely, "in connection with the death of Mrs. Edna Staunton."

"I was not aware that there existed any significant aspect in connection with her death," I observed, my mind reverting to the grim scene in the Staunton bedroom. "The poisoned comb, I concede, was an extraordinary method of committing a crime, without precedent, perhaps, in modern criminal annals. But . . ."

"No, no, Watson," he said quickly, "say unusual if you like—even grotesque if you prefer

it, but not entirely unprecedented, for there *are* parallels in modern criminology."

"Indeed? I should like to hear some."

"Very well."

A reminiscent light came to his eyes as he resumed after a momentary reflection.

"I might mention, by way of illustration, the Wurlitzer Case at Salzburg, in 1877, in which a poisoned earring was used. The fact that the victim—a woman of means whose wealth was coveted by the murderer—had recently had her ears pierced at his insistence, was chiefly instrumental in bringing the poisoner to justice. Another, differing only in the method of application, is the Selmer Poisoning Case of Brittany, some two years ago. You may recall that a sharpened nail, driven through the sole of the boot, then smeared with a deadly acid, caused the death of its wearer, Francois Selmer, a rich cattle merchant. His nephew was later convicted of the crime when it was proved that the marks on the leather could only have been made by his own hammer. There are others, less striking perhaps, but these will suffice to bring out the various points of resemblance existing between them."

Holmes paused while he crammed his pipe with fresh shag, then tossed his pouch over to me as he continued.

"The singular circumstance which I alluded to just now concerns the presence of the sharpened comb at the side of Mrs. Staunton's body."

"Then the different theories," I put in, "evolved by the more sensational sheets to explain away that very aspect of the case were all inaccurate?"

"Do you mean those wild and absurd explanations advanced by unimaginative reporters?" he cried impatiently. "That Staunton suffered a mental lapse? That he lost his nerve? That he became careless and overconfident?" He gestured angrily. "Piffle, Watson, sheer piffle! Such implausible solutions outraged every logical faculty I possess! I read them all and found them to be wholly inconsistent with the facts, and with the character of the criminal himself."

He leaned forward in his chair, an intent look

on his face as he added: "Because it was the cunning and resourceful manner in which he murdered Arnold Foote and disposed of his body that gave me my first clear insight into the workings of his mind. This, in turn, enabled me to forge the links in my chain of reasoning which led me eventually to true solution."

"How did you bring this about?" I asked.

"By referring to my notes on the case, and the reading of a staggering pile of newspapers which carried a complete day-by-day account of the court proceedings. Having thus gathered in my harvest—and a goodly crop it proved to be!—I surrounded myself one evening with a motley assortment of shag, cushions, and hot coffee, and proceeded to thresh it out. It cost me a night's sleep, but at dawn I had my solution to the mystery."

"I should be very glad to hear what it was."

"And you shall, Watson, but all in good time. First, I should like to recapitulate briefly the sequence of events in the murder of Foote. It will serve to refresh your memory and thus enable you to obtain a firmer grip on the essentials."

He snuggled more deeply into his chair, and made certain that his brier was drawing properly before resuming.

"The true facts in the death of the 'cellist came out, as you know, in Henry Staunton's confession made soon after his arrest at Newhaven. This document is of particular interest, for not only did it tell us how the crime was done, but it also served to cast a revealing light upon what was to come.

"Staunton contrived, by a simple yet effective ruse, to entice this none-too-bright musician to his home on Oakley Crescent and there killed him by plunging a steel bodkin impregnated with an alkaloid into the base of his skull. Following a preconceived plan, the murderer then hid the body and calmly went to spend some hours with acquaintances in a near-by cafe."

"One moment, Holmes," I broke in, "there is one aspect of this which has never been clear to me. Where was his wife on this particular evening?"

"Have you forgotten that, following upon a last bitter quarrel, Mrs. Staunton had left him?"

"By Jove!" I exclaimed, "you are quite right! It had completely slipped my mind."

"Yet, it was of enormous importance," he observed. "But to return to Staunton. Having now established some sort of alibi, he returned some time around two a.m. leading a horse and cab which he had cooly appropriated without the owner's knowledge, and used it to carry the body to the river."

"Now that I come to think of it," I interjected, "that cabby never found out the grisly service his cab had rendered a murderer that night."

"Neither did he ever learn that a would-be murderer had been spying his movements, and knew of his habit of spending some time indoors on wet nights," added my friend. "And took full advantage of it later. Doubtless, the bad weather aided him, but his having donned the cabby's own hat and waterproof, which he had flung inside his vehicle—thus affecting a perfect disguise—was a master stroke of daring and of quick thinking, besides demonstrating a swift grasp of opportunity. Barely ten minutes after he had hurled Foote's body over the hand railing of the bridge, the cab was back at its place and no one the wiser."

I gave a reminiscent nod. "Staunton actually bragged about that exploit, I remember."

"And with some justification. The crime had been so cunningly planned, and had been carried out with such careful regard to detail and timing, that not a hitch occurred to mar it. I tell you, Watson, that the police might have been hard put to secure his conviction had he not made that wild, damning admission when he was arrested."

I had not forgotten the incident. Staunton, caught off guard when tendered the customary warning, had hotly denied all responsibility for the death of his wife, while conceding by his denial implications of guilt for the murder of Arnold Foote.

"Staunton possessed the three most dangerous qualities of the criminal," continued

Holmes; "cunning, resourcefulness, and daring. And, I might add, used them effectively."

"Then why did he not destroy that infernal comb?" I asked. "Surely self-preservation alone ought to have dictated so obvious a course."

"That, my dear fellow, was one of the very questions I asked myself when reviewing the case. How could a man of Staunton's calibre have overlooked so incriminating a piece of evidence? What had impelled this crafty schemer to make use of that strange and terrible matacalda twice in rapid succession—an obvious and fatal blunder?"

Holmes stopped to knock out the cold ashes from his pipe. Then he refilled it slowly, deep in thought, his brows drawn low, his eyes half closed.

"I could not reconcile these two facts," he resumed, "with Staunton's crafty and ingenious mind. Twist and turn them as I might, they refused to fit into an otherwise orderly pattern." He frowned. "Something was wrong, Watson. Instinctively I felt that somewhere in my chain of reasoning lay a defective link. By a process of elimination I succeeded in discovering my error. It lay in having until now gone along on the assumption that, having killed Arnold Foote, Staunton, of necessity, had also murdered his wife. But, I reasoned, if he had indeed committed both crimes, was it conceivable that he should bungle the second after having so cunningly covered up his tracks in the first? It was illogical, hence inadmissible.

"Confronted with this misconception, I began to cast about for an alternative theory, one which, while retaining the known facts, would enable me to reach a totally different conclusion. In view of the lapse of time, this could no longer be reached by the ordinary methods of observation and confirmation; only analytical deductions from these facts could give me the correct interpretation of them. Feverishly I began to go over my notes, sensing that somewhere among them was the answer I sought."

"You were successful?" I asked quickly.

"Beyond expectation," he replied, then re-lapsed once more into a deep thoughtful silence, his arms propped up on his knees, holding his pipe between his hands, contemplating the glowing sea-coals.

"Were I the ideal reasoner you so often have made me out to be," he began, after a long interval of silence, "I should have quickly perceived the significance underlying the Staunton maid's replies to my questions as to why she had replaced the comb."

"But what possible connection could there be between her replies and the solution to the death of Mrs. Staunton?"

"Do you recall her words?" he asked, countering my question with one of his own.

"Vaguely," I answered. "Was it not something about the 'poor lass lying dead on the floor'?"

"Good old Watson!" he said, with a dry chuckle.

"Well, she also referred to her mistress's fondness for that particular comb, and to the fact—and this is noteworthy—that she always took it with her wherever she went. We know that Mrs. Staunton, following the last quarrel with her husband, had packed a few things and had then fled from the house."

"Swearing never to return," I put in, as some of the details returned to me.

"Quite so. Now, at such moments of stress, a woman's instinct is to carry away her most cherished and useful possessions, is it not?"

"You mean . . . ," I began.

"I am prepared to stake my reputation on it," he put in, anticipating my question, "that when she left Oakley Crescent, the tortoise-shell comb was in her possession!"

I stared at him in blank surprise. "But if that is the case, how could Staunton have poisoned it?"

"Since he did not have access to the comb at any time during the three days which preceded her death, it was utterly impossible for him to have done so," he replied quietly.

"Really, Holmes," I cried, lifting my hands in a helpless gesture, "I am now more confused than ever. Would it not be better if you revealed the steps you took to unravel this intricate puzzle? How did you eventually solve it?"

"Simply by applying my oft-repeated formula. Having eliminated the impossible—that is, Staunton's complicity in the death of his wife—I had now to contend with whatever remained, however improbable, in order to arrive at the truth. No sooner had I reached this conclusion than the facts began to arrange themselves in their proper order. The old conceptions had perforce to give way to the new. Viewed thus from an entirely different angle, the true elements in the case now assumed their rightful perspective. The answer, of course, lay with the poisoned comb. Its very presence at the side of Mrs. Staunton's body finally suggested the true, the only possible solution.

"I make some claim to belated credit," he went on, "for remembering Mrs. Grant's words in connection with the poisoned instrument. But the truth is that I was woefully lacking in the mixture of imagination and exact knowledge which you are so fond of depicting. I also claim extenuating circumstances—for what man can cope with the warped mind of a vindictive woman, consumed by a hatred beyond description and a terrible sense of loss?"

I drew a deep breath. "Holmes," I begged, "who poisoned the comb? Who brought it back to the house?"

"Is it not obvious that it was—that it could only have been—Mrs. Staunton herself?"

"Good heavens!" I exclaimed aghast, staring wildly at his set features, my mind in a turmoil. "Do you mean to say that she . . . she actually committed suicide in that terrible fashion?"

"The facts speak for themselves, Watson. No other interpretation is possible."

"But why on earth could she not have gone to the police?" I asked, more calmly, now that the first shock had passed. "If she suspected, or knew, that her husband had murdered her lover, why could she not have brought the matter to their attention by less involved means? Why not a direct accusation?"

"And have the facts of her adulterous relationship aired in open court, to be later blazoned upon every newspaper in the kingdom?" he inquired sardonically. "Really, Watson," he went on, shaking his head in a puzzled manner, "I never quite get your limitations. Do you still fail to grasp the fact that her suicide, as you call it—that her self-murder, rather—was purely incidental to her scheme of revenge? That by purposely using the same poison—thereby attracting the attention of the police—she sent to the scaffold the man who had destroyed her lover?"

"Then Staunton's reiterated denials of all complicity in her death were justified?" I said, musingly.

"Entirely so," he replied. "Yet who believed him? Did not counsel for the prosecution stress the fact that Staunton, by insisting that his wife had committed suicide, hoped to escape the extreme penalty? It was futile effort, for without any doubt her violent death swayed the jury when they rendered their verdict."

"I wonder how she learned about the poison and its fearful properties?" I said, after a spell of silence. "Any theories, Holmes?"

He moved his head dubiously. "There, my dear Watson, we trespass into the field of surmise and conjecture. A wife has her own methods of finding out her husband's secrets. An unguarded word, a threat from him, perhaps even a boast as to the manner in which he had removed his young rival—any of these may have given her an inkling of the truth. The fact that she made use of it with such telling effect amply proves that she was fully aware of its potentialities. We shall have to be content with that."

"It was a fearful revenge, Holmes," I said, breaking into the long silence which followed his last words. "Yet, somehow, I cannot find it in my heart to condemn her too bitterly."

"And I," said my friend, reaching out for his pouch, "find that for the third time in my career, I have been beaten by a woman. Yet I cannot say that I shall ever begrudge Mrs. Staunton her triumph!"

YOU THINK THAT'S FUNNY?

The Adventure of the Second Swag

ROBERT BARR

(Writing as Luke Sharp)

BORN IN SCOTLAND, Robert Barr (1850–1912) moved to Canada with his family when he was four years old. While a teacher and later headmaster of the Central School of Windsor, Ontario, he wrote short stories that he placed with the *Detroit Free Press*. When he was twenty-six, he decided to devote himself full-time to writing and moved to Detroit to become a staff writer on that paper, eventually becoming its news editor.

His contributions to the newspaper were published under the pseudonym Luke Sharp, an amusing name but not one that Barr invented. As a schoolboy in Canada, he had regularly passed a storefront sign that proclaimed "Luke Sharpe, Undertaker," which he found too memorable to resist.

Barr's first Sherlock Holmes parody, "Detective Stories Gone Wrong: The Adventures of Sherlaw Kombs," published in May 1892, is often described as the first Holmes parody (it is early, yes, but not the first) and has been often anthologized, including in this collection. However, the present story, published more than a decade later and far more obscure, is an even funnier send-up of the great detective.

"The Adventure of the Second Swag" was first published in the December 1904 issue of *The Idler Magazine*; its first book appearance was as a chapbook limited to two hundred copies, *The Adventure of the Second Swag* (London, Ferret Fantasy, 1990).

THE ADVENTURE OF THE SECOND SWAG

Robert Barr

THE TIME WAS Christmas Eve, 1904. The place was an ancient, secluded manor house, built so far back in the last century as 1896. It stood at the head of a profound valley; a valley clothed in ferns waist deep, and sombrely guarded by ancient trees, the remnants of a primeval forest. From this mansion no other human habitation could be seen. The descending road which connected the king's highway with the stronghold was so sinuous and precipitate that more than once the grim baronet who owned it had upset his automobile in trying to negotiate the dangerous curves. The isolated situation and gloomy architecture of this venerable mansion must have impressed the most casual observer with the thought that here was the spot for the perpetration of dark deeds, were it not for the fact that the place was brilliantly illumined with electricity, while the silence was emphasised rather than disturbed by the monotonous, regular thud of an accumulator pumping the subtle fluid into a receptive dynamo situated in an outhouse to the east.

The night was gloomy and lowering after a day of rain, but the very sombreness of the scene made the brilliant stained glass windows stand out like the radiant covers of a Christmas number. Such was the appearance presented by "Undershaw," the home of Sir Arthur Conan Doyle, situated among the wilds of Hindhead, some forty or fifty miles from London. Is it any wonder that at a spot so remote from civilisation law should be set at defiance, and that the one lone policeman who perambulates the district should tremble as he passed the sinister gates of "Undershaw"?

In a large room of this manor house, furnished with a luxuriant elegance one would not have expected in a region so far from humanising influences, sat two men. One was a giant in stature, whose broad brow and smoothly shaven strong chin gave a look of determination to his countenance, which was further enhanced by the heavy black moustache which covered his upper lip. There was something of the dragoon in his upright and independent bearing. He had, in fact, taken part in more than one fiercely-fought battle, and was a member of several military clubs; but it was plain to be seen that his ancestors had used war clubs, and had transmitted to him the physique of a Hercules. One did not need to glance at the Christmas number of the *Strand*, which he held in his hand, nor read the name printed there in large letters, to know that he was face to face with Sir Arthur Conan Doyle.

His guest, an older man, yet still in the prime of life, whose beard was tinged with grey, was of less warlike bearing than the celebrated novelist, belonging, as he evidently did, to the civil and not the military section of life. He had about him the air of a prosperous man of affairs, shrewd, good-natured, conciliatory, and these two strongly contrasting personages are types of the men to whom England owes her greatness. The reader of the Christmas number will very probably feel disappointed when he finds, as he supposes, merely two old friends sitting amicably in a country house after dinner. There seems, to his jaded taste, no element of tragedy in such a situation. These two men appear comfortable enough, and respectable enough. It is true that there is whisky and soda at hand, and the box of cigars is open, yet there are latent possibilities of passion under the most placid natures, revealed only to writers of fiction in our halfpenny Press. Let the reader wait, therefore, till he sees these two men tried as by fire under a great temptation, and then let him say whether even the probity of Sir George Newnes comes scatheless from the ordeal.

"Have you brought the swag, Sir George?" asked the novelist, with some trace of anxiety in his voice.

"Yes," replied the great publisher; "but before proceeding to the count would it not be wise to give orders that will insure our being left undisturbed?"

"You are right," replied Doyle, pressing an electric button.

When the servant appeared he said: "I am not at home to anyone. No matter who calls, or what excuse is given, you must permit none to approach this room."

When the servant had withdrawn, Doyle took the further precaution of thrusting in place one of the huge bolts which ornamented the massive door studded with iron knobs. Sir George withdrew from the tail pocket of his dress coat two canvas bags, and, untying the strings, poured the rich red gold on the smooth table.

"I think you will find that right," he said; "six thousand pounds in all."

The writer dragged his heavy chair nearer the table, and began to count the coins two by two, withdrawing each pair from the pile with his extended forefingers in the manner of one accustomed to deal with great treasure. For a time the silence was unbroken, save by the chink of gold, when suddenly a high-keyed voice outside penetrated even the stout oak of the huge door. The shrill exclamation seemed to touch a chord of remembrance in the mind of Sir George Newnes. Nervously he grasped the arms of his chair, sitting very bolt upright, muttering:—

"Can it be he, of all persons, at this time, of all times?"

Doyle glanced up with an expression of annoyance on his face, murmuring, to keep his memory green:—

"A hundred and ten, a hundred and ten, a hundred and ten."

"Not at home?" cried the vibrant voice. "Nonsense! Everybody is at home on Christmas Eve!"

"You don't seem to be," he heard the servant reply.

"Me? Oh, I have no home, merely rooms in Baker Street. I must see your master, and at once."

"Master left in his motor car half an hour ago to attend the county ball, given tonight, at the Royal Huts Hotel, seven miles away," answered the servant, with that glib mastery of fiction which unconsciously comes to those who are members, even in a humble capacity, of a household devoted to the production of imaginative art.

"Nonsense, I say again," came the strident voice. "It is true that the tracks of an automobile are on the ground in front of your door, but if you will notice the markings of the puncture-proof belt, you will see that the automobile is returning and not departing. It went to the station before the last shower to bring back a visitor, and since its arrival there has been no rain. That suit of armour in the hall spattered with mud shows it to be the casing the visitor wore. The blazonry upon it of a pair of scissors above an open book resting upon a printing press, indicates that the wearer is first of all an editor; second, a publisher; and third, a printer. The only baronet in England whose occupation corresponds with his heraldic device is Sir George Newnes."

"You forget Sir Alfred Harmsworth," said the servant, whose hand held a copy of Answers.

If the insistent visitor was taken aback by this unlooked-for rejoinder, his manner showed no trace of embarrassment, and he went on unabashed.

"As the last shower began at ten minutes to

six, Sir George must have arrived at Haslemere station on the 6:19 from Waterloo. He has had dinner, and at this moment is sitting comfortably with Sir Arthur Conan Doyle, doubtless in the front room, which I see is so brilliantly lighted. Now, if you will kindly take in my card—"

"But I tell you," persisted the perplexed servant, "that the master left in his motor car for the county ball at the Royal—"

"Oh, I know, I know. There stands his suit of armour, too, newly black-leaded, whose coat of arms is a couchant typewriter on an automobile rampant."

"Great heavens!" cried Sir George, his eyes brightening with the light of unholy desire, "you have material enough there, Doyle, for a story in our January number. What do you say?"

A deep frown marred the smoothness of the novelist's brow.

"I say," he replied sternly, "that this man has been sending threatening letters to me. I have had enough of his menaces."

"Then triply bolt the door," advised Newnes, with a sigh of disappointment, leaning back in his chair.

"Do you take me for a man who bolts when his enemy appears?" asked Doyle fiercely, rising to his feet. "No, I will unbolt. He shall meet the Douglas in his hall!"

"Better have him in the drawing-room, where it's warm," suggested Sir George, with a smile, diplomatically desiring to pour oil on the troubled waters.

The novelist, without reply, spread a copy of that evening's *Westminster Gazette* over the pile of gold, strode to the door, threw it open, and said coldly:—

"Show the gentleman in, please."

There entered to them a tall, self-possessed, calm man, with clean-shaven face, eagle eye, and inquisitive nose.

Although the visit was most embarrassing at that particular juncture, the natural courtesy of the novelist restrained him from giving utterance to his resentment of the intrusion, and he proceeded to introduce the bidden to the unbidden guest as if each were equally welcome.

"Mr. Sherlock Holmes, permit me to present to you Sir George—"

"It is quite superfluous," said the newcomer, in an even voice of exasperating tenor, "for I perceive at once that one who wears a green waistcoat must be a Liberal of strong Home Rule opinions, or the editor of several publications wearing covers of emerald hue. The shamrock necktie, in addition to the waistcoat, indicates that the gentleman before me is both, and so I take it for granted that this is Sir George Newnes. How is your circulation, Sir George?"

"Rapidly rising," replied the editor.

"I am glad of that," asserted the intruder, suavely, "and can assure you that the temperature outside is as rapidly falling."

The great detective spread his hands before the glowing electric fire, and rubbed them vigorously together.

"I perceive through that evening paper the sum of six thousand pounds in gold."

Doyle interrupted him with some impatience.

"You didn't see it through the paper; you saw it in the paper. Goodness knows, it's been mentioned in enough of the sheets."

"As I was about to remark," went on Sherlock Holmes imperturbably, "I am amazed that a man whose time is so valuable should waste it in counting the money. You are surely aware that a golden sovereign weighs 123.44 grains, therefore, if I were you, I should have up the kitchen scales, dump in the metal, and figure out the amount with a lead pencil. You brought the gold in two canvas bags, did you not, Sir George?"

"In the name of all that's wonderful, how do you know that?" asked the astonished publisher.

Sherlock Holmes, with a superior smile, casually waved his hand toward the two bags which still lay on the polished table.

"Oh, I'm tired of this sort of thing," said Doyle wearily, sitting down in the first chair that presented itself. "Can't you be honest, even on Christmas Eve? You know the oracles of old did not try it on with each other."

"That is true," said Sherlock Holmes. "The fact is, I followed Sir George Newnes into the Capital and Counties Bank this afternoon, where he demanded six thousand pounds in gold; but when he learned this would weigh ninety-six pounds seven ounces avoirdupois weight, and that even troy weight would make the sum no lighter, he took two small bags of gold and the rest in Bank of England notes. I came from London on the same train with him, but he was off in the automobile before I could make myself known, and so I had to walk up. I was further delayed by taking the wrong turning on the top and finding myself at that charming spot in the neighbourhood where a sailor was murdered by two ruffians a century or so ago."

There was a note of warning in Doyle's voice when he said:—

"Did that incident teach you no lesson? Did you not realise that you are in a dangerous locality?"

"And likely to fall in with two ruffians?" asked Holmes, slightly elevating his eyebrows, while the same sweet smile hovered round his thin lips. "No; the remembrance of the incident encouraged me. It was the man who had the money that was murdered. I brought no coin with me, although I expect to bear many away."

"Would you mind telling us, without further circumlocution, what brings you here so late at night?"

Sherlock Holmes heaved a sigh, and mournfully shook his head very slowly.

"After all the teaching I have bestowed upon you, Doyle, is it possible that you cannot deduce even so simple a thing as that? Why am I here? Because Sir George made a mistake about those bags. He was quite right in taking one of them to "Undershaw," but he should have left the other at 221B, Baker Street. I call this little trip 'The Adventure of the Second Swag.' Here is the second swag on the table. The first swag you received long ago, and all I had for my share was some honeyed words of compliment in the stories you wrote. Now, it is truly said that soft words butter no parsnips, and, in this instance, they do not even turn away wrath. So far as the second swag is concerned, I have come to demand half of it."

"I am not so poor at deduction as you seem to imagine," said Doyle, apparently nettled at the other's slighting reference to his powers. "I was well aware, when you came in, what your errand was. I deduced further that if you saw Sir George withdraw gold from the bank, you also followed him to Waterloo station."

"Quite right."

"When he purchased his ticket for Haslemere, you did the same."

"I did."

"When you arrived at Haslemere, you sent a telegram to your friend, Dr. Watson, telling him of your whereabouts."

"You are wrong there; I ran after the motor car."

"You certainly sent a telegram from somewhere, to someone, or at least dropped a note in the post-box. There are signs, which I need not mention, that point irrevocably to such a conclusion."

The doomed man, ruined by his own self-complacency, merely smiled in his superior manner, not noticing the eager look with which Doyle awaited his answer.

"Wrong entirely. I neither wrote any telegram, nor spoke any message, since I left London."

"Ah, no," cried Doyle. "I see where I went astray. You merely inquired the way to my house."

"I needed to make no inquiries. I followed the rear light of the automobile part way up the hill, and, when that disappeared, I turned to the right instead of to the left, as there was no one out on such a night from whom I could make inquiry."

"My deductions, then, are beside the mark," said Doyle hoarsely, in an accent which sent cold chills up and down the spine of his invited guest, but conveyed no intimation of his fate to the self-satisfied later arrival.

"Of course they were," said Holmes, with exasperating self-assurance.

"Am I also wrong in deducing that you have had nothing to eat since you left London?"

"No, you are quite right there."

"Well, oblige me by pressing that electric button."

Holmes did so with much eagerness, but, although the trio waited some minutes in silence, there was no response.

"I deduce from that," said Doyle, "that the servants have gone to bed. After I have satisfied all your claims in the way of hunger for food and gold, I shall take you back in my motor car, unless you prefer to stay here the night."

"You are very kind," said Sherlock Holmes.

"Not at all," replied Doyle. "Just take that chair, draw it up to the table and we will divide the second swag."

The chair indicated differed from all others in the room. It was straight-backed, and its oaken arms were covered by two plates, apparently of German silver. When Holmes clutched it by the arms to drag it forward, he gave one half articulate gasp, and plunged headlong to the floor, quivering. Sir George Newnes sprang up standing with a cry of alarm. Sir Arthur Conan Doyle remained seated, a seraphic smile of infinite satisfaction playing about his lips.

"Has he fainted?" cried Sir George.

"No, merely electrocuted. A simple device the Sheriff of New York taught me when I was over there last."

"Merciful heavens! Cannot he be resuscitated?"

"My dear Newnes," said Doyle, with the air of one from whose shoulders a great weight is lifted, "a man may fall into the chasm at the foot of the Reichenbach Fall and escape to record his adventures later, but when two thousand volts pass through the human frame, the person who owns that frame is dead."

"You don't mean to say you've murdered him?" asked Sir George, in an awed whisper.

"Well, the term you use is harsh, still it rather accurately sums up the situation. To speak candidly, Sir George, I don't think they can indict us for anything more than manslaughter. You see, this is a little invention for the reception of burglars. Every night before the servants go to bed, they switch on the current to this chair.

That's why I asked Holmes to press the button. I place a small table beside the chair, and put on it a bottle of wine, whisky and soda, and cigars. Then, if any burglar comes in, he invariably sits down in the chair to enjoy himself, and so you see, that piece of furniture is an effective method of reducing crime. The number of burglars I have turned over to the parish to be buried will prove that this taking off of Holmes was not premeditated by me. This incident, strictly speaking, is not murder, but manslaughter. We shouldn't get more than fourteen years apiece, and probably that would be cut down to seven on the ground that we had performed an act for the public benefit."

"Apiece!" cried Sir George. "But what have I had to do with it?"

"Everything, my dear sir, everything. As that babbling fool talked, I saw in your eye the gleam which betokens avarice for copy. Indeed, I think you mentioned the January number. You were therefore accessory before the fact. I simply had to slaughter the poor wretch."

Sir George sank back in his chair well nigh breathless with horror. Publishers are humane men who rarely commit crimes; authors, however, are a hardened set who usually perpetrate a felony every time they issue a book. Doyle laughed easily.

"I'm used to this sort of thing," he said. "Remember how I killed off the people in 'The White Company.' Now, if you will help me to get rid of the body, all may yet be well. You see, I learned from the misguided simpleton himself that nobody knows where he is to-day. He often disappears for weeks at a time, so there really is slight danger of detection. Will you lend a hand?"

"I suppose I must," cried the conscience-stricken man.

Doyle at once threw off the lassitude which the coming of Sherlock Holmes had caused, and acted now with an energy which was characteristic of him. Going to an outhouse, he brought the motor car to the front door, then, picking up Holmes and followed by his trembling guest, he went outside and flung the body into the tonneau behind. He then threw a spade and a pick into the car, and covered everything up with a waterproof spread. Lighting the lamps, he bade his silent guest get up beside him, and so they started on their fateful journey, taking the road past the spot where the sailor had been murdered, and dashing down the long hill at fearful speed toward London.

"Why do you take this direction?" asked Sir George. "Wouldn't it be more advisable to go further into the country?"

Doyle laughed harshly.

"Haven't you a place on Wimbledon Common? Why not bury him in your garden?"

"Merciful motors!" cried the horrified man. "How can you propose such a thing? Talking of gardens, why not have him buried in your own, which was infinitely safer than going forward at this pace."

"Have no fear," said Doyle reassuringly, "we shall find him a suitable sepulchre without disturbing either of our gardens. I'll be in the centre of London within two hours."

Sir George stared in affright at the demon driver. The man had evidently gone mad. To London, of all places in the world. Surely that was the one spot on earth to avoid.

"Stop the motor and let me off," he cried. "I'm going to wake up the nearest magistrate and confess."

"You'll do nothing of the sort," said Doyle. "Don't you see that no person on earth would suspect two criminals of making for London when they have the whole country before them? Haven't you read my stories? The moment a man commits a crime he tries to get as far away from London as possible. Every policeman knows that, therefore, two men coming into London are innocent strangers, according to Scotland Yard."

"But then we may be taken up for fast driving, and think of the terrible burden we carry."

"We're safe on the country roads, and I'll slow down when we reach the suburbs."

It was approaching three o'clock in the morning when a huge motor car turned out of Trafalgar Square, and went eastward along the Strand. The northern side of the Strand was up, as it usually is, and the motor, skilfully driven, glided past the piles of wood-paving blocks, great sombre kettles holding tar, and the general debris of a repaving convulsion. Opposite Southampton Street, at the very spot so graphically illustrated by George C. Haite on the cover of the *Strand Magazine*, Sir Arthur Conan Doyle stopped his motor. The Strand was deserted. He threw pick and shovel into the excavation, and curtly ordered his companion to take his choice of weapons. Sir George selected the pick, and Doyle vigorously plied the spade. In almost less time than it takes to tell, a very respectable hole had been dug, and in it was placed the body of the popular private detective. Just as the last spadeful was shovelled in place the stern voice of a policeman awoke the silence, and caused Sir George to drop his pick from nerveless hands.

"What are you two doing down there?"

"That's all right, officer," said Doyle glibly, as one who had foreseen every emergency. "My friend here is controller of the Strand. When the Strand is up he is responsible, and it has the largest circulation in the—I mean it's up oftener than any other street in the world. We cannot inspect the work satisfactorily while traffic is on, and so we have been examining it in the night-time. I am his secretary; I do the writing, you know."

"Oh, I see," replied the constable. "Well, gentlemen, good morning to you, and merry Christmas."

"The same to you, constable. Just lend a hand, will you?"

The officer of the law helped each of the men up to the level of the road.

As Doyle drove away from the ill-omened spot he said:—

"Thus have we disposed of poor Holmes in the busiest spot on earth, where no one will ever think of looking for him, and we've put him away without even a Christmas box around him. We have buried him forever in the Strand."

Sheer Luck Again

STANLEY RUBINSTEIN

AS A PROMINENT lawyer specializing in literary and publishing matters, Stanley Jack Rubinstein (1890–1975) was the chairman of Burke Publishing and was instrumental in the formation of Andre Deutsch, a prominent British publishing house.

He was also a well-known historian, with his best-known work, *Historians of London* (1968), subtitled *An Account of the Many Surveys, Histories, Perambulations, Maps, and Engravings Made About the City and Its Environs, and of the Dedicated Londoners Who Made Them*, covering the era up to 1900. His other major contribution to the history of London is the colorful historical work *The Street Trader's Lot, London: 1851. Being an Account of the Lives, Miseries, Joys & Chequered Activities of the London Street Sellers as Recorded by Henry Mayhew* (1947), which is illustrated with twenty-five contemporary drawings representing various traders whose little stalls on crowded streets sold everything from oysters to Hindu tracts and birds' nests.

Evidence that the present parody was not Rubinstein's only foray into the mystery-writing world is his own crime novel *Merry Murder* (1949), which features Inspector Rogers and Thomas Willmott.

"Sheer Luck Again" was originally published in the April 1923 issue of *The Detective Magazine*.

SHEER LUCK AGAIN

Stanley Rubinstein

OWING TO MY wife's rooted objection to Sheerluck Combs, it was some little time since I had seen him, and I freely confess that it was with trepidation that I once more knocked upon the well-known door in Baker Street.

"Come in!" cried the voice of my revered master. And before I could turn the handle: "Welcome back, my prodigal Whatson!"

"How the dickens did you know it was me?" I gasped, forgetting my grammar in my admiration for my friend.

Combs watched a cloud of smoke up the chimney.

"Very simple," he said. "Your hair-oil, my dear chap, preceded you. Since I saw you last I have written a little monograph on the peculiar odour and flavour of over a hundred and fifty different varieties of hair-oils. I could distinguish your favourite brand a mile off."

I started to shower laudatory terms upon my illustrious friend, who, I was delighted to find, had lost none of his powers of perception, but Combs stopped me with an imperative gesture.

"Enough," he said. "Father, son—that is, Whatson, I cannot tell a lie even to you. As a matter of fact, I was standing at the window as you came up the street.

The simplicity with which he told the truth, even at the risk of losing a point, was wonderful. I gazed at my friend with an admiration which almost amounted to adoration.

"I have come on business," I said.

"I know," replied Combs.

"How?" I cried in amazement.

"You have just told me so," he replied. "It is important business," he added.

"Wonderful!" I could not help ejaculating. "How could you know that?"

Combs's answer was brilliantly characteristic of his marvellous reasoning.

"When an ordinary tidy man comes out without a tie on it denotes haste; haste in a man of your pronounced sloth denotes excitement; excitement in one of your temperament denotes importance. Simple deduction, my dear Whatson. You should really take up the study of elementary mathematics again; it refreshes the brain. I am inclined to the belief that you have lost something," he added.

I was too surprised to speak for a moment.

"And how in the name of good fortune have you guessed at the reason for my coming here?" I gasped.

Combs looked surprised for just the fraction of a second.

"When an educated gentleman sniffs instead of blowing his nose, it is a pretty good sign that he has lost his handkerchief."

The man's perception and knowledge of life was really remarkable.

"I could tell you more about yourself," he said.

"Do." I prompted him, ever eager for evidence of my friend's methods.

"You have taken to shaving with a safety razor," he replied.

It was true. My wife had presented me with

413

one as a wedding present, and some months back had persuaded me to use it.

"I am really at a loss to explain how you can detect that," I said.

"My dear Whatson, in the old days of your bachelorship you used to cut yourself with unfailing regularity every time you shaved; but now neither your chin nor your cheeks show any sign of those scars which I always used to think of as wounds honourably incurred in your daily wrestle with the razor. Your clean-shaven appearance is a sufficient sign that you have not ceased to shave, and your hand is, if anything, less steady than it used to be. In fact, if I did not fear to hurt your feelings, I should say that you had taken to drink."

I covered my burning face with my hands.

"I swear it was through no fault of mine," I cried.

"Your excuses must wait," said Combs coldly. "Let me hear what brought you here. State the facts as shortly as you can. I have not too much time. The case of the sugar king's lost pianola took me longer than I care to admit, and I am behindhand with two or three other important cases I am engaged on."

A dreary film spread over his eyes, and but for the irregular twitching of his interlocked finger-tips one could have thought him dead.

I cleared my throat and began.

"After dinner last night I went up to my study and locked the door."

"Ha!" cried Combs. "You were afraid of something. What was it? You blush, man. What's the matter?"

"Well, you see——" I stammered.

"I see nothing," said Combs impatiently. "I am a sleuthhound—*the* sleuthhound," he added, "not a mere spiritualist."

"Well, I must confess that my wife has turned vegetarian, and——"

"And that the dinner she provided proving unfilling, you repaired to your study to supply the deficiency by consuming the sandwiches which you had thoughtfully bought during the day. Am I right?" he asked.

"You are right—as you always are," I replied. "And for once I can almost follow your mental reasoning. Having consumed the sandwiches and—er—the contents of my flask, I unlocked my desk with the intention of doing that which I had many times contemplated, but had never up till now had the time to do."

"Go on," said Combs, "you interest me."

"My intention was to look through my notes of the cases in which I have been associated with you, and loose another selection upon an expectant and ever ready public."

Combs shrugged his eyebrows.

"Upon the same terms as before, I assume," he asked carelessly—"thirty per cent of the royalties to you, and—er—the balance to me?"

"Willingly," I said, trying to speak calmly, "but it can never be."

"Why not?" queried Combs curtly.

"Because the papers have been stolen," I said.

"Merciful powers!" cried Combs, springing from his seat, and with arms outstretched he flung himself towards me.

I verily believed that my last moments had come. But I had cruelly misjudged my friend, for he merely seized the 'cello which hung upon the wall over my head and began zigzagging, jazzing, and jigsawing all over the room. Up and down, in and out, the walls resounding to the wild music he extracted from the wonderful instrument, the gift of the Rajah of Shampoo, to whom Combs had once rendered some small service. At first it was a frenzied tune that he plucked from the strings, but as he became exhausted it gradually declined in violence, until, in the middle of a crooning lullaby, he flung the valuable instrument, the gift—er—yes, I mentioned that just now—into the wastepaper basket, and himself, a quivering mass, into his armchair.

He hardly had the strength to sob, but sob he did, such sobs as I have never heard but once before, an occasion when, disguised as Sultanas, we entered the harem of the Sultan of Badladd to rescue from his clutches a lady of high and royal lineage.

Presently he overcame his emotions.

"Whatson," he said, "I may in time learn to forget, but forgive—never. I relied upon you—you, my Boswell. However, tears avail me naught. I have been weak. I will be strong. Let me have the details. It may yet be time to save the papers." And Combs was once more the sleuthhound, prepared to listen with that passive attention which he gave to the most impersonal of cases.

"Having locked the door of my study," I said, "I took out all my notes, perused them, and arranged them in two piles upon the table. Upon the left-hand pile I placed those in which our efforts were—er—not so successful as they might have been. You remember, for instance, the mysterious disappearance of the seven-chinned lady?"

"I found the lady, but never recovered the chins," said Combs. "I remember! And the circus proprietor refused to take her back without them. Go on!" he added.

"And upon the right-hand pile," I continued, "I placed all the data of some dozen cases which I thought might now be safely placed before the public."

"And then?" queried Combs.

"I took two foolscap envelopes," I said, "and addressed one to you and one to the publishers. I placed these face downwards on the table——"

"I follow you with attention," said Combs.

"And shuffled them as if they had been dominoes. You see, I was undecided as to whether I should send the papers direct to the publishers or to you to peruse and, if necessary, revise. I knew, of course, that if you were not busy I should receive them back by return, but I feared lest in the rush of business you might overlook them."

"You were quite right," said Combs. "I probably should have."

"So I selected this method of determining which course to adopt. I was just about to turn over one of the envelopes which would have determined the destination of the papers, when I happened to glance at the clock on the mantelshelf."

"And the time?" said Combs. "This is important."

"It was 10:23," I replied. "I used to be, as you know, an abstemious man, but a prolonged vegetarian diet has lowered my stamina. In short, I seized my hat, coat, and umbrella, and ran round the corner to the Duke of Edinburgh to—er—refill my flask."

"Ah!" said Combs, and a long sigh escaped him. "Did you close the door behind you?"

"The front door, yes; the study door, no," I replied, "but I swear I was not away ten minutes, for, as you know, they turn you out—er—that is, close the doors at 10:30, and I came straight back. And as there are no roads to cross, there are no kerbs to trip over, either," I added rather irrelevantly.

"Did you find the front door open on your return?" asked Combs.

"No; all was apparently as I left it. I let myself in with my latchkey and went upstairs to my study. *The papers and the envelopes had vanished!*"

"Great Caesar!" cried Combs, and great beads of perspiration stood out on his forehead. "You have placed a mighty powerful weapon into the hands of my enemies," he added.

"Alas, I know!" I replied. "But do not rub it in."

"Come," said Combs, starting up, "there is no time to be lost. This is obviously the work of an opposition gang. I have had my eye upon them for a long time. They are an unscrupulous crowd, and will stick at nothing. Let us repair to the scene of the tragedy."

With Combs to think was to act, and in less time than it takes me to write it we were in the street and had hailed a passing taxi.

"Where to?" queried the driver.

I told him the address.

"I 'aven't enough petrol," he said, preparing to move on.

"You lie, George Blarnie, and you know it," said Combs quietly.

"'Ere, 'oo are you a-callin' nimes, anyway? Lor lumme, if it ain't Mister Sheerluck Combs! Jump in, yer worship! I'm sorry I didn't reckergnise yer before."

As the cab sped Hampstead Heath–ward, Combs lolled back in the corner, his brow knitted in deep thought.

"Have you formed any theories?" I asked.

"Not yet," replied Combs. "It is a capital offence to form theories before knowing all the facts. Besides, it is a waste of time. Have you communicated with Scotland Yard?" he queried.

"How can you ask such a question?" I cried. "Such an action on my part would have betokened a lack of faith in your powers."

"Oh, I wasn't thinking of the detective branch, but of the lost property office," he rejoined nonchalantly. "But here we are. Have you any change on you, my dear Whatson? I have left my purse at home."

I paid the cabman, who touched his hat, with a wink.

"You thort ter stop my little gimes," he said, "but I'm still hat it, yer see. Only this form of daylight 'igh robbery is licensed, so yer can't touch me. *Good-d'y* ter you, Mister Combs!" And he was off.

"A terrible villain that," said Combs. "He is one of the most expert bungalow-breakers in the kingdom. He was, you will recollect, the principal villain in the strange case of the commercial traveller's oil-stove."

"I remember it well," I replied.

My house is a basement one of the ordinary terrace type, three stories high, and with eleven steps leading down to the back door, which opens on to a narrow area, from which the coal-cellar, which is situated under the pavement, is also approached. There is no exit from the rear of the house, and the back windows overlook the Regents Canal, which is only separated from the wall of the house by a narrow towpath.

As I ascended the four stone steps up to the front door, and put my latchkey into the lock, fears assailed me for the first time; for Combs had not set foot in our house since my wife discovered the part he played in capturing those concerned in the bank robbery in Siam, as a result of which a second-cousin of hers by marriage had not yet returned to this country.

Evidently Combs had the same fears, for as I opened the door he whispered to me, "Remember, I'm the plumber."

As we stepped into the house my wife crossed the hall.

"The plumber, my dear," I said. "He has—er—come to see me about his windpipe." And I led the way straight up to my study, which is on the second floor and in the front of the house.

I must confess that I had expected Combs to praise me for this brilliant impromptuism. But as soon as I had closed the door he burst out, "Fool, idiot, dolt! I've come to repair something, not to be repaired. I may have to make a thorough examination both inside and out. Are your patients in the habit of crawling around the house on all fours?" And he crossed to the door and locked it.

"Now," he said, "let us start our investigations. I will commence by interviewing your staff."

"Alas!" I replied. "We have no staff; it left to make munitions, and is now making eyes from the back row of the chorus."

Combs frowned.

"I hate to have to suspect your wife so early in the proceedings, but your statement leaves me no alternative," he said.

"I can answer for my wife," I replied. "She was at the picture palace all the evening. She knows nothing of this, and, indeed, must never know. Remember, if she so much as suspected who you were she'd go home to her mother at once."

"And you do not propose to inform her who I am?" queried Combs.

"Not just yet, old friend," I replied. Combs shrugged his shoulders.

"*Comme vous voulez,*" he replied in an irreproachable accent. "You married men are much to be admired."

Then, dropping on his knees, he whipped out his tape measure and a large square magnifying glass.

"The *mise-en-scène* has not been touched since last night," I said. "There is the desk, and that is the table." And I pointed to the pieces of furniture in question.

"I wonder!" said Combs to himself, as he ceased for a moment crawling about the floor on all fours in order to draw a large note of interrogation in his note-book.

"Ha!" he suddenly exclaimed, with his eyes nearly on the carpet. "Fresh mud."

"I don't know how it can have come there," I said guiltily. "I took off my boots before dinner last night, and did not come into this room until after."

"You must have brought it back with you when you returned from the Duke of Edinburgh," said Combs, with a piercing glance.

I hung my head in silence.

His investigations concluded, Combs dropped into an armchair, and, lighting his pipe, was soon shrouded in thick smoke.

Suddenly he sprang up, walked across the room to the telephone, and made a noise like a telephone-bell.

"Go and tell your wife," he said, "that a friend whose name you were unable to catch has rung up and wants her to go round immediately on urgent private business."

I went and found my wife, and repeated Combs's message to her.

"Has she gone yet?" Combs asked eagerly on my return. "I want to examine the house."

"I'm afraid not," I replied. "She asked me how she was to know where to go if I hadn't caught the name of her would-be hostess."

"Bah!" hissed Combs. "You always bungle everything. I must proceed upon my usual plan of examination.

"If I run into your wife I shall repeat to her your absurd yarn about me being the plumber, and add that you have called me in to see the windpipes which you suspect of having developed a leak. Mind you support me in any questions you are asked." And before I had time to nod assent he had left the room.

I picked up a novel and tried to read, but I found my mind reverting to my tragic carelessness in having allowed my friend's precious documents to be stolen. I cursed the day I was born, the day I was introduced to Combs, the day my wife became a vegetarian, and, because it happened to be the same day, the day I first tasted alcoholic liquor.

I believe I must have dropped off to sleep, for I awoke to find Combs standing beside me. I could see at once that he had learnt nothing by his tour of the house.

"I should say from the dust that none of the windows or the back door have been opened for a twelvemonth," he said wearily.

"It would be about that time," I replied, "since the maids left."

Combs towered above me, lost in thought, his chin sunk upon his breast.

"I will not be baffled," he exclaimed suddenly. "It would be ill-fortune," he went on, "if, after years spent successfully solving the solutions of others, I were to fail upon the most important and intricate case I have ever had to deal with, particularly when it affects me personally."

At that moment my wife knocked at the door.

"The postman has just left a card for you," she said.

"Grocers and butchers I can understand," said Combs, "but I do not quite realise the value of being upon visiting terms with your postman."

"Put it under the door, please," I cried. And I leant down and picked up a postcard addressed to me, and which I read aloud to Combs. It ran as follows:

"Messrs. Emess and Script present their compliments to Mr. Whatson, and beg to inform him that an empty and unstamped foolscap envelope, addressed in his handwriting, was taken in by their office boy this morning, and the necessary surcharge postage paid thereon. They will be obliged if Mr. Whatson will kindly remit them threepence to cover this expenditure, or are prepared, if so desired, to debit it on Mr. Whatson's royalty account."

"Do you think it is genuine?" I asked, handing it across to Combs, who took it and studied it minutely through his glass.

"Undoubtedly," he replied.

"Then what do you make of it?" I queried.

Combs did not reply for a minute. Then he said, "I can imagine that the thief wished to rid himself of the valueless part of his booty at the earliest possible moment, and as he didn't know what to do with the envelope, he crossed the road and posted it."

"It sounds feasible," I said.

Combs flashed an angry glance at me.

"If you know of a better detective, you'd better go to him," he said. "You know that I know that you know that you cannot know of a better one, since none better exists."

I began to apologise. But Combs stopped me with another of his imperative gestures and rose.

"It's gone twelve o'clock," he said. "Do you turn to the right or the left for the Duke of Edinburgh? I want to measure the distance," he added.

I gave him the necessary directions, and ventured to add a warning as to certain drinks sold there which experience has taught me to avoid.

"Many thanks," said Combs. "Come and see me at seven o'clock this evening. I hope to have solved the problem." And he was gone.

I sat down and tried to think. I was in possession of all the facts, but could make nothing of them; while Combs, with the same facts, would, I felt happily sure, regain possession of the lost papers.

After some twenty minutes I gave up thinking in despair, and, slipping my revolver into my pocket, and telling my wife that I might not be home that night, I went off to the bedside of a patient who had been dying for the last three days, and who, I felt, might think he was being neglected.

I happily found him none the worse for my absence, but, owing to his insisting upon reading through his will to me before he would ask me to witness his signature thereto, it was nearer 7:15 than 7 o'clock when I knocked at Combs's door.

A young and fashionably-dressed lady, whose features seemed strangely familiar to me, was sitting in Combs's chair, smoking a pipe, and I was just about to withdraw an apology, when a sudden lifting of the eyebrow recalled her face to my recollection.

"Good evening, Miss Combs!" I said. "I assume your brother has not yet arrived home. May I come in and wait?"

"Mine name is Kammerad," said the lady. "I for Herr Combs on pizziness wait."

I judged from her accent that the lady was a German, a nation I had always disliked, and I decided that I would rather vait—I mean wait—for my friend in the street.

I was half-way down the stairs when a voice from upstairs called, "Herr Vatson! Herr Vatson!"

I returned to the room.

"Well?" I said testily.

"Don't you me know?" asked the lady, with a smile that was intended to be ingratiating.

"I haven't the pleasure," I said dryly.

"Then you ought to," said Combs in his ordinary voice, for it was he.

I expressed my admiration, and could not help reflecting, as I had many times reflected before, upon the genius of my friend. Not only was he a perfect past master in the art of making up, but he was able to throw himself into the character he impersonated with such success that even I, who knew him perhaps better than any other living soul, was unable to penetrate his disguise. The cinema-loving public lost a rare treat when Combs decided that he would not act for the films.

Combs chuckled.

"I am glad to find that I have not lost all my old powers," he said.

"Have you found the papers?" I asked anxiously.

"No," he replied, "but you will be glad to hear that your wife had not got them."

"How do you know that?" I cried in astonishment.

"I visited her in this disguise this afternoon," he replied, "and, telling her that I had been sent by a registry office, applied for the position of cook-parlour-maid. Fortunately, she shares your dislike for Germans, and my application was refused."

I suppose I showed all too clearly my disappointment at his failure to recover the papers.

"Cheer up," said Coombs, though the tone in which he said it was anything but cheering. "I am expecting the papers here at any moment."

I confess that at the time I thought that he only said it to buck me up.

"How, when, and where?" I cried excitedly.

"Ah-ha!" replied Combs mysteriously.

At that moment there was a knock at the front door.

"A visitor during the dinner-hour!" ejaculated Combs in surprise. "It must be something important."

"But you have just told me that you are expecting the papers," I said.

"How silly of me! Of course I did," replied Combs. "I had forgotten it for the moment."

The knock was repeated upon the door of the room.

"Come in!" said Combs.

A postman opened the door and inquired, "Mr. Combs in?"

"Yes," said Combs.

"Beggin' your pardon missie, but it's Mr. Combs as I want."

"It's all right, postman," said Combs, laughing, as he pulled off his wig.

"Oh, I beg your honour's pardon," said the man. "I didn't recognise you in them joy rags of yourn. One shilling to pay," he added, holding out a bulky-looking envelope.

"I never dispense charity at the door," said Combs, waving it aside.

"Do you formally refuse to take it?" queried the man.

"What is it?" parried Combs.

"'Ere you are, you can see for yourself. It's a handstamped letter. You was hout the hother two hoccasions I called tod'y, an' I couldn't leave it," replied the postman, his veneer of education wearing off in his excitement.

Combs took the proffered packet, and as he saw it a look of blank astonishment stole over his face.

"It's worth risking," he muttered, as he handed the postman a shilling.

He tore open the envelope, and glanced rapidly at its contents.

"Catch!" he cried, with a sigh of relief, tossing the envelope over to me. "There are your valuable papers. Mind you take more care of them in the future."

It was true. Not a paper was missing, and the envelope was the identical one I had myself addressed to Combs the previous evening.

I dropped on my knees at Combs's feet, and kissed his hands in gratitude.

"How did you manage it?" I gasped. But Combs waived the question aside.

"Leave me now," he said. "I'm very tired, and I think I'll go to bed. Come round tomorrow morning, and I'll have an explan—and I'll explain it to you." And he yawned.

I placed the precious packet securely in the inner lining of my waistcoat, and with reiterated thanks went home to bed and to sleep for the first time for two nights.

On the following morning I found Combs at breakfast, in a curiously shaped dressing gown of many colours. He had deep black lines under his eyes, which told me, as a medical man, quite clearly of the sleepless night he had spent pondering over the intricacies of some recent case, no doubt.

"You want to know how I found the papers," he said. "I will tell you. I have been thinking about it all night. It was really very simple when once I satisfied myself that no one could have entered the house while you were out. You will recollect that you confirmed my suspicions that none of the windows or the back door had been opened for several months. And, indeed, anyone jumping out of your study window must have inevitably broken his neck in falling into the area below. There was nobody there yesterday morning, because I looked, and I learnt from inquiry at the local police-station that none had been removed during the night.

"These facts established, I felt confident that no burglary had been committed, and as you have no maids, and I had myself ascertained that your wife was quite innocent, I was driven to the conclusion that *you took the papers out of the study yourself.*"

"Me!" I cried, forgetting my grammar again in my excitement.

"You," said Combs. "It is clear to me that before leaving the room for the Duke of Edinburgh you stuffed the papers into one of the envelopes, thought of putting them away for safety, but realised that you hardly had the time to put them away and lock up your desk again, and you dashed out with the envelopes in one of your hands—I am not sure which.

"On closing the front door you found yourself on the doorstep with the envelopes in your hand, and subconsciously assumed that you had come out to post the letters, so you crossed the road and slipped them into the pillar-box. Then when you found yourself on the doorstep again, and felt in your pocket for your latchkey you found your flask, and, forgetting in your excitement all about your little trip to the pillar-box, you dashed off to the Duke of Edinburgh.

"To be honest, and so prevent you from running away with the idea that I solved the problem by deduction alone, and without the aid of clues, I ought to mention that the mud on your study carpet set me wondering. There is no mud between here and the Duke of Edinburgh, and you remember *coming straight back*. You made no mention, however, of having *gone straight there*, and when I saw the muddy state of the road between your front door and the pillar-box, I felt that I was on the right track, and the publishers' postcard helped me farther.

"I think that's about all there is to it, except to say that to go round to the local post-office and inquire the time of the next delivery was but the work of five minutes, or, rather, would have been had I not been kept waiting fifty minutes for an answer to my query."

"Combs," I cried enthusiastically, seizing both his hands in mine, "you are really wonderful! How can I show my gratitude?"

"By leaving me, my dear chap," said Combs. "I am expecting a lady—er—an important client—at almost any moment, and her case is too private even for your ears."

And as I descended the stairs I heard him tuning his beloved 'cello, the gift—er—yes——

A Pragmatic Enigma

JOHN KENDRICK BANGS

(Writing as A. Conan Watson, M.D.)

OF THE MANY clever ideas of the great American humorist John Kendrick Bangs (1862–1922), none equaled his notion of "condensed novels." He published *Potted Fiction* (1908) with the subtitle *Being a series of extracts from the world's bestsellers put up in thin slices for hurried consumers.*

In his foreword, Bangs notes that "This library of Condensed Best Sellers is designed to meet the literary needs of those who have troubles of their own so numerous that they have not much spare time to devote to the trials and tribulations of the heroes and heroines of the hour. It is the purpose of the United States Literary Canning Company, of Pennsylvania, to put up in small packages, of which this is a sample, the most talked of literary products of our best, if not most famous, authors."

And thus was born *Reader's Digest*. Well, no, not really, but the spoof produced by Bangs is only slightly different from that enormously successful publishing enterprise. The concept was clearly a popular one, as the following testimonials illustrate.

From the mayor of Squantumville, S.D.: "Since using six cans of your *Potted Fiction* our Common Council has closed the Carnegie Library as superfluous." And from an insomniac of twenty years: "Your literary capsules have just arrived, and they are a revelation. I took two upon retiring last night, and have not waked up since. Many thanks."

"A Pragmatic Enigma" was first published in the magazine section of the April 19, 1908, issue of *The New York Herald*; it was first collected in book form in *Potted Fiction* (New York, Doubleday, Page & Co., 1908).

A PRAGMATIC ENIGMA

John Kendrick Bangs

IT WAS A drizzly morning in November. Holmes and I had just arrived at Boston, where he was to lecture that night on "The Relation of Cigar Stumps to Crime" before the Browning Club of the Back Bay, and he was playfully indulging in some deductive pranks at my expense.

"You are a doctor by profession, with a slight leaning toward literature," he observed, rolling up a small pill for his opium pipe and placing it in the bowl. "You have just come on a long journey over the ocean and have finished up with a five hour trip on the New York, New Haven, and Hartford Railroad. You were brushed off by a coloured porter and rewarded him with a sixpence taken from your right hand vest pocket before leaving the train. You came from the station in a cab, accompanied by a very handsome and famous Englishman; ate a lunch of baked beans and brown bread, opening with a Martini cocktail, and you are now wondering which one of the Boston newspapers pays the highest rates for press notices."

"Marvellous! Marvellous!" I cried. "How on earth do you know all this?"—for it was every bit of it true.

"It is the thing that we see the most clearly that we perceive the more quickly, my dear Watson," he replied, with a deprecatory gesture. "To begin with, I know you are a doctor because I have been a patient of yours for many years. That you have an inclination toward literature is shown by the fact that the nails on the fingers of your right hand are broken off short by persistent banging on the keys of a typewriting machine, which you carry with you wherever you go and with which you keep me awake at night, whether we are at a hotel or traveling on a sleeping car. If this were not enough to prove it I can clinch the fact by calling your attention to the other fact that I pay you a salary to write me up and can produce signed receipts on demand."

"Wonderful," said I, "but how did you know I had come on a long journey, partly by sea and partly by rail on a road which you specify?"

"It is simplicity itself," returned Holmes warily. "I crossed on the steamer with you. As for the railroad, the soot that still remains in your ears and mottles your nose is identical with that which decorates my own features. Having got mine on the New Haven and Hartford, I deduce that you got yours there also. As for the coloured porter, they have only coloured porters on those trains for the reason that they show the effects of dust and soot less than white porters would. That he brushed you off is shown by the streaks of gray on your white vest where his brush left its marks. Over your vest pocket is the mark of your thumb, showing that you reached into that pocket for the only bit of coin you possessed, a sixpence."

"You are a marvel," I murmured. "And the cab?"

"The top of your beaver hat is ruffled the wrong way where you rubbed it on the curtain roller as you entered the cab," said Holmes. "The handsome and famous Englishman who accompanied you is obvious. I am he, and am therefore sure of my deduction."

"But the lunch, Holmes, the lunch, with the beans and the cocktail," I cried.

"Can you deny them?" he demanded.

"No, I cannot," I replied, for to tell the truth his statement of the items was absolutely correct. "But how, how my dear fellow, can you have deduced a bean? That's what stumps me."

Holmes laughed.

"You are not observant, my dear Watson," he said. "How could I help knowing when I paid the bill?"

In proof he tossed me the luncheon cheque, and there it was, itemised in full.

"Aha!" I cried. "But how do you know that I am wondering which one of the Boston papers pays the best rates for press notices?"

"That," said he, "is merely a guess, my dear Watson. I don't know it, but I do know you."

And this was the man they had said was losing his powers!

At this moment there came a timid knock on our door.

"A would-be client," said Holmes. "The timidity of his knock shows that he is not a reporter. If it were the chambermaid, knowing that there were gentlemen in the room she would have entered without knocking. He is a distinguished man, also, who does not wish it known that he is calling, for if it were otherwise he would have been announced on the telephone from the office—a Harvard professor, I take it, for no other kind of living creature in Boston would admit that there was anything he did not know, and therefore no other kind of a Bostonian would seek my assistance. Come in."

The door opened and a rather distinguished looking old gentleman carrying a suit case and an umbrella entered.

"Good morning, professor," said Holmes, rising and holding out his right hand in genial fashion and taking his visitor's hat with his left. "How are things out at Cambridge this morning?"

"Marvellous! Marvellous!" ejaculated the visitor, infringing somewhat on my copyright, in fact taking the very words out of my mouth.

"How did you know I was a professor at Harvard?"

"By the matriculation mark on your right forefinger," said Holmes, "and also by the way in which you carry your umbrella, which you hold not as if it were a walking stick, but as if it were a pointer with which you were about to demonstrate something on a chart, for the benefit of a number of football players taking a four years' course in Life, at an institution of learning. Moreover, your address is pasted in your hat, which I have just taken from you and placed on the table. You have come to me for assistance, and your entanglement is purely intellectual, not spiritual. You have not committed a crime nor are you the victim of one—I can tell that by looking at your eyes, which are red, not with weeping, but from reading and writing. The tear ducts have not been used for years. Hence I judge that you have written a book, and after having published it, you suddenly discover that you don't know what it means yourself, and inasmuch as the critics over the country are beginning to ask you to explain it you are in a most embarrassing position. You must either keep silent, which is a great trial to a college professor, especially a Harvard professor, or you must acknowledge that you cannot explain—a dreadful alternative. In that bag you have the original manuscript of the book, which you desire to leave with me, in order that I may read it and if possible detect the thought, tell you what it is, and thus rid you of your dilemma."

"You are a wonderful man, Mr. Holmes," began our visitor, "but if you will let me—"

"One moment, please," said Holmes, eying the other closely. "Let us deduce next, if possible, just who you are. First let us admit that you are the author of a recently published book which nobody understands. Now, what is that book? It cannot be 'Six Months' by Helinor Quinn, for you are a gentleman, and no gentleman would have written a book of that character. Moreover, everybody knows just what that book means. The book we are after is one that cannot be understood without the assistance of a master like myself. Who writes such books? You may safely assert that the only books that nobody can understand these days are written by one James—Henry James. So far so good. But you are not Henry James, for Henry James is now in London translating his earlier works into Esperanto. Now, a man cannot be in London and in Boston at one and the same time. What is the inevitable conclusion? You must be some other James!"

The hand of our visitor trembled slightly as the marvellous deductive powers of Holmes unfolded themselves.

"Murmarvellulous!" he stammered.

"Now, what James can you be if you are not Henry?" said Holmes. "And what book have you written that defies the interpretation of the ordinary mind hitherto fed on the classic output of Hall Caine, Laura Jean Libbey, and Gertrude Atherton? A search of the Six Best Sellers fails to reveal the answer. Therefore the work is not fiction. I do not recall seeing it on the table of the reading room downstairs, and it is not likely, then, to be statistical. It was not handed me to read in the barber shop while having my hair cut and my chin manicured, from which I deduce that it is not humour. It is likely, then, that it is a volume either of history or philosophy. Now, in this country to-day people are too busy taking care of the large consignments of history in the making that come every day from Washington in the form of newspaper dispatches to devote any time to the history that was made in the past, and it is therefore not at all probable that you would go to the expense of publishing a book dealing with it. What, then, must we conclude? To me it is clear that you are therefore a man named James who has written a book on philosophy which nobody understands but yourself, and even you—"

"Say no more!" cried our visitor, rising and walking excitedly about the room. "You are the most amazingly astonishing bit of stupefying dumfounderment that I have ever stared at!"

"In short," continued Holmes, pointing his finger sternly at the other, "you are the man who wrote that airy trifle called 'Pragmatism!'"

There was silence for a moment, and then the Professor spoke up.

"I do not understand it at all," he said.

"What, pragmatism?" asked Holmes with a chuckle.

"No, you," returned the Professor coldly.

"Oh, it's all simple enough," said Holmes. "You were pointed out to me in the dining room at luncheon time by the head waiter, and, besides, your name is painted on the end of your suit case. How could your identity escape me?"

"Nevertheless," said the Professor, with a puzzled look on his face, "granted that you could deduce all these things as to my name, vocation, and so on, what could have given you the idea that I do not myself know what I meant when I wrote my book? Can you explain that?"

"That, my dear Professor, is the simplest of my deductions," said Holmes. "I have read the book."

Here the great man threw himself back in his chair and closed his eyes, and I, realising that I was about to be a witness of a memorable adventure, retired to an escritoire over by the window to take down in shorthand what Holmes said. The Professor, on the other hand, was walking nervously up and down the room.

"Well," said he, "even if you have read it, what does that prove?"

"I will tell you," said Holmes, going into one of his trances. "I read it first as a man should read a book, from first page to last, and when I got through I could not for the life of me detect your drift. A second reading in the same way left me more mystified than before, so I decided to read it backward. Inverted it was somewhat clarified but not convincing, so I tried to read it standing on my head, skipping alternate pages as I read forward, and taking in the omitted ones on the return trip. The only result of this was a nervous headache. But my blood was up. I vowed to detect your thought if it cost me my life. Removing the covers of the book, I cut the pages up into slips, each the size of a playing card, pasted these upon four packs of cards, shuffled them three times, cut them twice, dealt them to three imaginary friends seated about a circular table and played an equally imaginary game of muggins with them, at the end of which I placed the four packs one on top of the other, shuffled them twice again, and sat down to read the pages in the resulting sequence. Still the meaning of pragmatism eluded me."

There was a prolonged pause, interrupted only by the heavy breathing of the Professor.

"Go on," he said hoarsely.

"Well," said Holmes, "as a last resort I sent the book to a young friend of mine who runs a printing shop and had him set the whole thing in type, which I afterward pied, sweeping up the remains in a barrel and then drawing them out letter by letter, arranging them in the order in which they came. Of the result I drew galley proofs, and would you believe it, Professor, when I again proceeded to read your words the thing meant even less than it did before. From all of which I deduce that you did not know what pragmatism was, for if you had known the chances are you would have told us. Eh?"

I awaited the answer, looking out of the window, for the demolition of another man is not a pleasant thing to witness, even though it involves a triumph for one of our most respected and profitable heroes. Strange to say the answer did not come, and on turning to see the reason why I observed to my astonishment that Holmes and I were alone, and, what was worse, our visitor had vanished with both our suit cases and my overcoat as well.

Holmes, opening his eyes at the same moment, took in the situation as soon as I did and sprang immediately to the 'phone, but even as he took down the receiver the instrument rang of itself.

"Hello," said he, impatiently.

"Is this Mr. Holmes?" came a voice.

"Yes," replied the detective, irritably. "Hurry up and off the wire. I want to call the police. I've been robbed."

"Yes, I know," said the voice. "I'm the thief, Mr. Holmes. I wanted to tell you not to worry. Your stuff will be returned to you as soon as we have had it photographed for the illustration of an article in tonight's Boston Gazoozle. It will be on the newsstands in about an hour. Better read it; it's a corker; and much obliged to you for the material."

"Well, I'll be blanked!" cried Holmes, the 'phone receiver dropping from his nerveless fingers. "I fear, my dear Watson, that, in the language of this abominable country, I've been stung!"

Two hours later the streets of Boston were ringing with the cries of newsboys selling copies of the five o'clock extra of the Evening Gazoozle, containing a most offensive article, with the following headlines:

DO DETECTIVES DETECT?

A GAZOOZLE REPORTER DISGUISED AS A HARVARD PROFESSOR

CALLS ON SHERLOCK HOLMES, ESQ.
AND GETS AWAY WITH TWO SUIT CASES
FULL OF THE GREAT DETECTIVE'S
PERSONAL EFFECTS, WHILE
DR. WATSON'S HERO
TELLS WHAT HE DOES NOT KNOW ABOUT
PRAGMATISM

Herlock Shomes at It Again

ANONYMOUS

SOME PARODIES ARE better than others. One is usually able to recognize a good one from a bad one. However, in the six-part serial "Herlock Shomes at It Again," it is nearly impossible to be absolutely certain whether the inconsistencies are simply slovenly or are deliberate attempts at humor.

Clearly, the anonymous author intentionally ended one chapter with the notice "Next Week: An entirely new set of characters and another thrilling installment," then began the next chapter with the notice "Characters: Same as last week."

Similarly, one would like to think the author was clear-minded enough to have knowingly listed Dr. Hotsam in the cast of characters, only to have Shomes's assistant appear in the narrative as Dr. Plotsam, Dr. Flotsam, and Dr. Hotsam at various times. I am less convinced that one of the cast of characters, Harold Fitz Gibbons, who never appears in the story, was a deliberate omission.

As with many Sherlock Holmes parodies, this is an utterly silly story—and incomprehensible to boot. Why reprint it, you might ask. Not an unfair question. It is a rare story from an obscure publication, so it is possible that this is the first opportunity you have ever had to read it. Only you can decide if this is a good thing.

"Herlock Shomes at It Again" was first published in six issues of *The Wipers Times* (London, Herbert Jenkins, February 12–May 1, 1916); it was first published in book form in *The Wipers Times*, edited by F. J. Roberts and J. H. Pearson (London, Herbert Jenkins, 1918).

HERLOCK SHOMES AT IT AGAIN

Anonymous

CHARACTERS:

Bill Banks—A corpse.
Lizzie Jones—A Questionable Person Living at Hooge.
Harold Fitz Gibbons—Squire of White Chateau (in love with Honoria).
Intha Pink—A pioneer (in love with himself).
Honoria Clarenceaux—The Heroine (in love with Pink).
Herlock Shomes.
Dr. Hotsam, R.A.M.C.

Chapter 1
Shot in the Culvert

THE WIND WAS howling round the rugged spires of the Cloth Hall, and the moon shone down on the carriage bringing the elite of the old town to the festivities arranged to celebrate the 73rd term of office of Jacques Hallaert, the venerable mayor of Typers. Also the same moon shone down on the stalwart form of Intha Pink, the pioneer. He sighed as he passed the brilliantly lighted scene of festivity, thinking of days gone by and all that he had lost. As he plodded his way, clad in gum boots, thigh, pairs one, he soliloquised aloud thus: "What a blooming gime. They gives me a blooming nail, they gives me a blooming 'ammer, and then they tells me to go and build a blooming dug-out." At that moment Intha fell into a crump-hole, and then continued his soliloquies thus:
(To be Continued.)

Chapter 2
Shomes and His Methods

CHARACTERS:—SAME AS LAST WEEK.

SYNOPSIS:
Intha Pink, a pioneer, while passing the Cloth Hall, Typers, the scene of a dinner given to commemorate the 73rd year of office of the mayor of that town, falls into a crump-hole. Here we left him.

We now leave to the imagination of our gentle reader the nature of Intha's soliloquies in the crump-hole, and turn to a series of tragic events which were occurring in the Denin Road. It being feast night in Typers, the road was surging with a merry crowd pushing and jostling their way, eager to taste the delights the town had to offer, but there were, amongst that motley throng, two people who were destined to play principal parts in the most profound and murky mystery that had ever baffled the aged and doddering constabulary of Typers. One was Honoria, the fair but anemic daughter of the shell-fish merchant Hooge, and the other was—Shomes!

That night the shell-fish merchant, having run out of vinegar, had despatched his fair daughter to Typers to procure a fresh supply, and all had gone well with her until reaching the Culvert, she, catching sight of the lifeless form of Bill Banks, gazing placidly at the sky, had given three heart-rendering shrieks and fallen in the dark and silent waters of the Bellewarde Bec—the waters flowed on—but this was not to pass unnoticed. Shomes was in the district, and whipping out his vermoral sprayer with his right hand, he gave three rounds rapid into his forearm, while with his left he proceeded to tune up his violin. Dr. Plotsam, who had been walking in his shadow, hearing the haunting strains of the violin, rushed forward to his side, exclaiming "What is it, Shomes?" Shomes, with that grandiloquent gesture for which he is justly famed, said "You know my methods, Flotsam!" and fell in also. The waters of the Bec flowed on.

(To be Continued.)

N.B. Next week:—A fresh supply of characters, and another thrilling instalment.

Chapter 3
The Mystery of the Closed Gate

CHARACTERS:—SAME AS LAST WEEK.

SYNOPSIS:

Intha Pink, a pioneer, while passing the Cloth Hall, Typers, the scene of a dinner given to commemorate the 73rd year of office of the mayor of that town, falls into a crump-hole, where he is left soliloquizing. In the meantime, whilst a merry throng is making its way along the Denin Road towards Typers, Honoria, the fair but anemic daughter of the shell-fish merchant of Hooge, whilst passing by the Culvert, catches sight of the lifeless form of Bill Banks, and forthwith falls into the Bellewarde Bec, the waters of which flow on. This incident is noticed by Shomes and Dr. Flotsam, who were passing by the Culvert at the time. They both thereupon

fall into the Bec, the waters of which continue to flow on.

We now return to our friend Intha Pink, who, having soliloquized for exactly 13 minutes without once pausing to take breath or repeating himself, decides to extricate himself from the crump-hole into which he had so inadvertently fallen. While thus engaged, the silvery chimes of the clock on the Cathedral spire burst forth into song announcing the magic hour of zero p.m. "Bother!" ejaculated Pink in true Pioneer fashion. "At a quarter past zero I promised to meet Lizzie at Fell Hire Corner. I must indeed get a move on, otherwise she will be wroth."

With that he picked up his hammer and his nail from out of the crump-hole and proceeded at a rapid pace to the corner of the Square where, after having his boots polished and some of the mud brushed from his clothes by Bertie, the boss-eyed boot boy, he went off at the double along the road leading to the Denin Gate.

He had not proceeded very far when perforce his pace had to slacken on account of the density of the merry crowd advancing in the opposite direction in close column of humps, all bent on spending a merry evening at the Cloth Hall. But Pink's mission was not a gay one, neither was he in a merry mood; a deep plot was hatching in the Pioneer's fertile brain in which, let it be whispered, lovely Lizzie was to play a not unimportant part.

On reaching Trueside Corner he entered the little shop kept by Sandy Sam, the suspected spy and sandbag merchant. "Evening, Sam," said Pink. "What, you, Intha!" replied the old man. "What's in the air?" "Whizzbangs and air-crumps mostly, tonight" answered the other, "but I'm in a hurry. I want a good sandbag."

This article having been produced, and approved of, Intha paid the bill with a worthless check on Fox's, and placing his hammer and nail in the sandbag and, slinging the latter over his shoulder again, took to the road; such was his hurry that, generally observant as he was, he did not notice the shadowy figure of old Sam following in his wake. When within fifty yards of the Denin Gate the suspected spy took his S.O.S. signal from out of his pocket, unwrapped same, and hurled it into the air, this being almost immediately answered by three piteous howls from the direction of the gatekeeper's dug-out, where Tim Squealer, the sandbag merchant's foster son resided. Intha, still intent on his night's work, hurried on until he reached the Gate, where he fell over a cunningly concealed trip wire. At the same instant a soft, buzzing sound was heard, increasing in volume and ending in a loud crash! The Pioneer was trapped! The Denin Gate had closed!

(To be Continued).

Next Week: An entirely new set of characters, and another thrilling instalment.

Chapter 4

CHARACTERS:—SAME AS LAST WEEK.

Returning to our friend Shomes who has, for some time, been cooling his ardor in the Bec, during which period he has contrived to make the acquaintance of Honoria, his fair companion in distress. Breathing undying love and vowing to save her, he hoists her on one shoulder, his vermoral sprayer on the other, and commenced his itinerary towards Messrs. Crump, Hole and Co's circular scoop warehouse abutting on Hordon Goose Farm. Bending low with his precious burden, Shomes' mind begins to wander and so does his foot as he comes a terrific "purler" over a loose duck-board. Buzzing Bill, the Breezy Butcher of Bellewarde, witnessing the disaster, and being especially solicitous for the safety of his customers, shouts in stentorian terms "beat it for the tall timbers."

Meanwhile Intha Pink, having extricated himself from the disaster which overtook him at the Denin Gate, reappeared safely with his sandbag, hammer, and nail intent on reaching the trysting place where Lizzie is awaiting him.

"What of the night?" is his kindly remark to Vera, one of the "Cinema" girls, who has surreptitiously, tentatively, and furtively, dodged

the managerial eye, and had slipped out for a breath of fresh air.

"How you startled me, Intha!" she said. "Are you going to meet *that* woman again?"

"Ah! Vera, to what lengths will your jealously lead you?" said Intha chidingly.

At that moment Silent Percy arrived unheralded on the scene. "Poor Vera," said Intha, as he crawled out of the ditch and once more gathered up his hammer and nail, "she never would have been happy anyhow."

While this tender scene is being enacted, Chumley Marchbanks, the knut of Bond Street, having strolled down Grafton Street to pay a visit to the new night club "des Ramparts," which had sprung into fame very recently, inadvertently, and owing to the inadequate lighting, took the yellow bus at Fell Hire Corner and found himself in Bellewarde. All might yet have gone well with him had he not fallen over Crook, the Cambridge Cracksman, who after emptying his pockets pushed him into the Bec. The waters flowed on.

(To be Continued).

Next week: A new set of characters, and another thrilling instalment.

Chapter 5

CHARACTERS:—SAME AS BEFORE.

Snowflakes were falling heavily around Hordon Goose Farm, where we left Herlock with the fair Honoria. Breezy Bill, the Bouncing Butcher of Bellewarde, had just been hit in the neck by a whizzbang when the chug-chug of a motorcycle was heard. "Can it be Intha?" cried Honoria, while Shomes proceeded to tune his violin. "No!" roared he, as a motor despatch rider came round Fell Hire Corner. "News at last from my Baker Street Squad."

Hurriedly tearing open and reading the despatch, the true Shomes stood revealed in all his strength and method. Seizing his vermoral sprayer, he rapidly squirted an enormous dose into his forearm. Just then the voice of the faithful Hotsam was heard calling "Where are you,

Shomes?" "Here" replied the great detective, rapidly emptying his revolver at the approaching figure. "Thank goodness I've found you at last, but you nearly got me that time," said Hotsam admiringly. "Never mind, better luck next time," said Shomes, sotto voce, to Honoria. Aloud, "To work, there's mischief afoot. Thank heaven I attended that two day course at the Technical School. I shall now be up to all their dodges." Drawing a searchlight from his pocket, he read the fateful message:

Division moves tomorrow at dawn AAA. You will assemble all characters at zero fifteen outside Cloth Hall, Typers, P 13 D 1-1 in time to catch the underground for *—— —— at twenty AAA. On arrival there steal any rations you can find, and carry on with serial AAA —Editor. (*Censored —ED)

"At last!" shouted the great sleuth. "At last!" shouted the others, as they busily collected the usual paraphernalia of the great man. "Hotsam," cried Shomes, "send off the orderly sergeant at once to warn all Characters. Then meet me at the Denin Gate." With these words he disappeared into the gloom and a crump-hole. All these arrangements having been made, Hotsam and Honoria continued their journey down the Denin Road, arriving in Typers just in time to meet Intha Pink before he left for his nightly work. Having rapidly given him a summary of all that had happened, they went into a neighboring estaminet to await the fateful hour of zero.

(Another long and thrilling instalment next week).

Chapter 6
Shot in the Culvert

CHARACTERS:—SAME AS LAST WEEK.
Shomes and Co. having arrived at their new sphere of action speedily got going again. Intha Pink seized his hammer and nail and fell off the bus when near Hyde Park Corner. Meanwhile Hotsam had disappeared into the darkness, on a mysterious errand, taking the fair Honoria with him. Lizzie, as she saw his stalwart form disappearing from her sight, cried, "Do not leave me Herbert," but a curse was her only answer. In despair she threw herself in the way of a passing whizzbang and disappeared from our tale. Intha crept rapidly towards his objective, and had almost succeeded in attaining his end, when a machine gun spat in his direction. Completely perforated: yet he smiled happily, and murmured "It's a blightie."

Here we leave him and turn to a series of eventful happenings on the banks of the Douve. Hotsam, still dragging Honoria and perspiring freely, had managed to reach the lifeless form of Bill Banks, when a 17 in. shell detonated between them. Hissing out "We are discovered" he hurriedly grabbed Honoria and made off. But not far. Alas! His foot slipped, and with his burden he fell into the turbid waters below. The waters flowed on. Shomes, appearing on the scene some hours after, rapidly began looking for clues. Having found some, the great detective started off, but too late, the gas was on him, and he had left his vermoral sprayer in the bus.

And so ends this remarkable history of persistence and sagacity. The great enemy of the criminal is now only a name, but his methods must always remain one of the marvels of the criminal history of our nation.

THE END

[N.B. Should there be a few characters not dealt with in this Chapter the reader must understand that they all met their deaths in the liquid fire attack. —The Author.]

The Reigate Road Murder

ANTHONY ARMSTRONG

(Writing as A. Bonan Oil)

GEORGE ANTHONY ARMSTRONG WILLIS (1897–1976) was a pro-lific Canadian-born British author of historical and crime novels, humorous short stories and plays, and radio and film scripts in several literary genres. In 1924, he began to write humorous pieces for *Punch* and started to use the pseu-donym Anthony Armstrong. He wrote crime novels and humorous works and plays, some of which were adapted for radio from the 1930s through the 1960s. His published articles and short stories appeared in *The New Yorker*, *County Fair*, *The Strand Magazine*, *Gaiety*, the *Daily Mail*, and *The Evening News*.

Among his dozen mystery novels are *The Strange Case of Mr. Pelham* (1957), which served as the basis for the 1970 film *The Man Who Haunted Himself*, star-ring Roger Moore, and five novels about Jimmie Rezaire, a tough London thug who becomes a private eye with a somewhat underdeveloped sense of ethics.

Armstrong is perhaps best known for *Ten-Minute Alibi*, the hugely success-ful mystery play about a seemingly perfect murder, which he coauthored with Herbert Shaw; it made its debut on Broadway on October 17, 1933. Armstrong wrote a novelization that was published the following year, and an unloved low-budget film was released in 1935.

"The Reigate Road Murder" was first published in London in the December 1926 issue of *Gaiety*; its first book appearance was in *How to Do It* by Anthony Armstrong (London, Methuen, 1928).

THE REIGATE ROAD MURDER

Anthony Armstrong

I M A K E N O excuse for putting the following before the public, for the simple reason that the incidents narrated form the only occasion when my famous friend, Holmlock Shears, ever found himself at fault over a case.

I remember we were sitting in our room in Baker Street, one wet afternoon, occupied in our usual fashion—I with a pencil trying to write some further memoirs, and Shears playing the violin behind an impenetrable cloud of blue smoke—when a lady was shown into the room.

She was tall and of medium height, with dark light hair, a mouth and two eyes. She wore a ma-cintosh, face-powder, and a worried look, and advanced upon me from the doorway.

I dodged—not without difficulty, owing to my wound received at the battle of Maiwand—and speaking from cover, asked her what she wanted.

"Murder has been done," she gasped. "Where is Mr. Holmlock Shears? I do not see him."

I pointed silently to the smoke cloud from which issued the strains of Mendelssohn's *Lie-der*. Each strain was, of course, disguised so as to prevent Mendelssohn recognising his own property.

"He is inside there," I said proudly.

"Will he speak to me?"

I walked across and knocked on the edge of the smoke cloud.

"Lady to see you, Shears."

Mendelssohn's *Lieder*—what was left of it—changed abruptly to *I Don't Love Nobody*, played with the back of the bow and one cuff-link; three strings snapped; the smoke barrage drifted away; and Holmlock Shears was revealed to our sight.

It is totally unnecessary for me to describe in any way my well-known friend; his tallness, his leanness, his long fingeredness, and his pointed eyes. I need not weary the reader by mentioning his hawk-like nose which gave him such an air of alertness, and will pass over any reference to his chin, and to his hands, mottled with chemi-cals, spattled with nicotine, and measled with pricks from his hypodermic syringe. There is no need for me to describe—but by this time I have done it.

"You are married," suddenly flashed my companion, glancing at her left hand. "This af-ternoon you used face-powder."

"However did you know?" gasped the woman, recoiling in amazement at this sudden remark, and though I had had ample previous proof of Shears's superhuman powers of observation and deduction, even I was overcome with wonder.

"Now what is it you want with me?" he went on. "You'll have to be quick, because I'm only allowed two pages."

"There has been a murder at my house in South London. It's nothing serious—only my husband; but I should like, just as a matter of in-terest, you understand . . ."

"One minute. I suppose Scotland Yard are there and have no clue and are completely baf-fled?"

"Oh, yes, we got all the usual procedure over at the beginning and now they've gone away. But it is all most puzzling, for not only can we not find the murderer, but we can't even find the corpse. I am sorry to trouble you about such a little thing."

"To a great mind nothing is little. I will come at once." His eyes flashed swiftly over her. "It is raining," he said quietly, just as if it were the most commonplace remark in the world.

"Wonderful!" I ejaculated, while our visitor stood staring at him in amazement, which small incident I have only included to show the abnormal analytical power possessed by the great detective. In a flash he had deduced the above from her streaming macintosh and wet umbrella, whereas ordinary people would have looked out of the window.

Half an hour later we were in the very house where the dastardly crime had been committed. Shears was faced with the stupendous task of not only discovering the murderer, but also of discovering the corpse. But he was at once busy. He examined with a pocket lens the road outside, the path inside, the aspidistra in the front parlour, and everyone who happened to pass him—myself twice included—talking the whole time about Cremona fiddles and uttering little cries of self-encouragement.

Springing upon a small pile of grey dust in the hall, he scrutinised it closely.

"There are one hundred and fourteen different kinds of cigar and cigarette ash, my dear Watnot," he began. "I have written a monograph on the subject. This ash is the ash of a Trichinopoly cigar . . . No, I'm hanged," he broke off suddenly, "it isn't after all. I don't know what it is. Why can't they always smoke Trichinopoly cigars?" he went on petulantly. "They have always done so far, and between you and me it is the only one I really know."

But despite this serious setback, such was his amazing cleverness that within ten minutes he had formulated his theory about the murder. Summoning our hostess to the parlour, he began, "This is a very simple crime. The murder was committed by three men; one with a squint to the right, one with a squint to the left, and one without a squint at all. One of the three was

smoking a Trichin—no, was just smoking—and had a short while before purchased something for one shilling and elevenpence three farthings. They rode cycles and carried the corpse away in the direction of Reigate."

"By heavens, Shears, this is wonderful!" I ejaculated.

"Not at all, my dear Watnot; very elementary. Pass the hypodermic syringe."

"But you amaze me. What . . ."

"An intrinsically simple case of plain deduction with one or two instructive points. I reasoned thus. Our hostess here tells us that there has been a murder. Therefore a murder has been committed. There is no body. Therefore it has been taken away. So far, so good. But by whom, and how? By the murderers, who were three in number, and carried the corpse away on their bicycles; for there are three bicycle tracks on the Reigate road outside, and, moreover," he emphasises his words with his forefinger, "moreover, all exactly parallel, such as could only have been made by men carrying a rigid body laid across the handle-bars between them. I have already sent off my band of ragged urchins from Baker Street to follow up the tracks and tell the men they are wanted on the telephone. That little subterfuge will fetch them back, so that in half an hour we may expect to have them under lock and key."

"Marvellous!" I murmured feebly. "But the squint . . ."

"Elementary, Watnot, elementary. The two men on the outside carrying a body between them must each have had a squint inwards in order to be able to do it. Or if they hadn't they will have by now. As regards the article purchased for one and elevenpence three farthings, that follows simply on the finding of the cigar ash. That cigar the man was smoking could only have been given him instead of the farthing change . . ."

He broke off suddenly as a voice was heard outside, and our hostess rushed to the door.

Shears sprang to his feet.

"What is it?" he asked.

"Thank Heaven, the mystery is solved!" cried the lady triumphantly. "It is my husband alive and well. He was not murdered after all. He has just returned from a ride on his tricycle!"

Shears lit his pipe in baffled anger and disappeared in a cloud of blue smoke, drawing the violin, his last bow, and the hypodermic syringe after him.

The Succored Beauty

WILLIAM B. KAHN

WILLIAM B. KAHN appears to have made only a single contribution to the literature of Sherlock Holmes. It was published in 1905 in *The Smart Set Magazine*, a literary journal founded in 1900 and edited during its most successful years by H. L. Mencken and George Jean Nathan, who commissioned work by many of the best young writers of the time, including F. Scott Fitzgerald, Dashiell Hammett, Dorothy Parker, and James Joyce.

Parody was not unwelcome in its pages, and as the Sherlock Holmes character and stories were at the peak of their popularity, they were an obvious subject. Since this story was the first and only parody produced by Kahn, it should come as no surprise that its full published title was "More Adventures of Oilock Combs: The Succored Beauty," and that the parody is one of the first to recognize how many Holmes stories involved marital problems.

Nothing could be learned about the author, though there was a William Bonn Kahn (1882–1971) who wrote *The Avoidance of War, a Suggestion Offered by William B. Kahn, Written for the Society for Peace* in 1914. The possibility exists that it is the same person, though it seems unlikely that this would be of interest to anyone.

"The Succored Beauty" was first published in the October 1905 issue of *The Smart Set Magazine*; it was published separately in a chapbook limited to 222 copies titled *An Adventure of Oilock Combs* (San Francisco, Beaune Press, 1964).

THE SUCCORED BEAUTY

William B. Kahn

ONE NIGHT, AS I was returning from a case of acute indigestion—it was immediately after my divorce and I was obliged to return to the practice of my profession in order to support myself—it chanced that my way homeward lay through Fakir Street. As I reached the house where Combs and I had spent so many hours together, where I had composed so many of his adventures, an irresistible longing seized me to go once more upstairs and grasp my friend by the hand, for, if the truth must be told, Combs and I had had a tiff. I really did not like the way in which he had procured evidence for my wife when she sought the separation, and I took the liberty of telling Combs so, but he had said to me: "My dear fellow, it is my business, is it not?" and though I knew he was not acting properly I was forced to be placated. However, the incident left a little breach between us which I determined on this night to bridge.

As I entered the room I saw Combs nervously drinking a glass of soda water. Since I succeeded in breaking him of the morphine habit he had been slyly looking about for some other stimulant and at last he had found it. I sighed to see him thus employed.

"Good evening, Combs," said I, extending my hand.

"Hello, Spotson," cried he, ignoring my proffered digits. "You are well, I see. It is really too bad, though, that you have no servant again. You seem to have quite some trouble with your help." And he chuckled as he sipped the soda water.

Familiar as I was with my friend's powers, this extraordinary exhibition of them really startled me.

"Why, Oilock," said I, calling him in my excitement, by his praenomen, "how did you know it?"

"Perfectly obvious, Spotson, perfectly obvious. Merely observation," answered Combs as he took out his harmonica and began to play a tune thereon.

"But how?" persisted I.

"Well, if you really wish to know," he replied as he ceased playing, "I suppose I will be obliged to tell you. I see you have a small piece of court-plaster upon the index finger of your left hand. Naturally, a cut. But the plaster is so small that the cut must be very minute. 'What could have done it?' I ask myself. The obvious response is a tack, a pin, or a needle. On a chance I eliminate the tack proposition. I take another chance and eliminate the pin. Therefore, it must have been the needle. 'Why a needle?' query I of myself. And glancing at your coat I see the answer. There you have five buttons, four of which are hanging on rather loosely while the fifth is tightly sewn to the cloth. It had recently been sewn. The connection is now clear. You punctured your finger with the needle while sewing on the button. But," he continued musingly and speaking, it seemed, more to himself than to me, "I never heard of the man who would sew unless he was compelled to. Spotson always keeps a servant; why did she not sew the button on for him? The reply is childishly easy: his servant left him."

I followed his explanation with rapt attention. My friend's powers were, I was happy to see, as they were when I lived with him.

"Wonderful, Combs, wonderful," I cried.

"Merely observation," he replied. "Some day I think that I shall write a monograph on the subject of buttons. It is a very interesting subject and the book ought to sell well. But, hello, what is this?"

The sound of a cab halting before the door caused Combs's remark. Even as he spoke there was a pull at the bell, then the sound of hasty footsteps on the stairs. A sharp knock sounded upon the door. Combs dropped into his armchair, stuck out his legs in his familiar way and then said: "Come in."

The door opened and there entered, in great perturbation, a young lady, twenty-three years of age, having on a blue tailor-made suit, patent-leather shoes and a hat with a black pompon ornamenting it. She wore some other things, but these were all that I noticed. Not so Combs. I could see by the penetrating glance he threw at her that her secret was already known to that astute mind.

"Thank heaven," she cried, turning to me, "that I have found you in!"

"Are you ill, madam?" I began; but suddenly realizing that I was not in my office but in Combs's consultation-room, I drew myself up stiffly and said: "That is Mr. Combs."

The young lady turned to him. Then, lifting her handkerchief to her beautiful eyes she burst into tears as she said: "Help me, help me, Mr. Combs."

The great man did not reply. An answer to such a remark he would have regarded as too trivial. The lady took down her handkerchief and, after glancing dubiously at me, said to Mr. Combs, "Can I see you privately?"

Once, and once only did I ever before or, indeed, since, see such a look of rage on Combs's face. That was when Professor O'Flaherty and he had that altercation in Switzerland. (See "Memoirs of Oilock Combs." Arper & Co. $1.50.)

"Madam," said he in frigid tones, "whatever you desire to say to me you may say before Dr. Spotson. How under the sun, woman," he cried, losing control of himself for a moment, "would the public know of my adventures if he were not here to write them?"

I threw Combs a grateful look while he reached for the soda water. The visitor was momentarily crushed. At last, however, she recovered her equanimity.

"Well, then," she said, "I will tell you my story."

"Pray, begin," said Combs rather testily.

"My name is Ysabelle, Duchess of Swabia," the visitor commenced.

"One moment, please," interrupted Combs. "Spotson, kindly look up that name in my index."

I took down the book referred to, in which Combs had made thousands of notes of people and events of interest, and found between "Yponomeutidae" and "yttrium" the following item, which I read aloud:

"Ysabelle, Duchess of Swabia; Countess of Steinheimbach; Countess of Riesendorf, etc., etc. Born at Schloss Ochsenfuss, February 29, 1876. Her mother was the Duchess Olga, of Zwiefelfeld, and her father was Hugo, Duke of Kaffeekuchen. At three years of age she could say 'ha, ha!' in German, French, English, Italian, and Spanish. Between the ages of five and fifteen she was instructed by Professor Grosskopf, the eminent philosopher of the University of Kleinplatz. By sixteen her wisdom teeth had all appeared. A very remarkable woman!"

As I read this last sentence, the duchess again burst into tears.

"Pray, pray, compose yourself, duchess," said Combs, taking a pipe from the table and filling it with some tobacco which he absent-mindedly took from my coat-pocket.

The duchess succeeded in calming herself. Then, rising majestically and gazing at Combs with those wonderful eyes which had played havoc with so many royal hearts, she said, in solemn tones:

"I AM LOST!"

The manner in which she made this statement as well as the declaration itself seemed to make a deep impression upon Combs. Without uttering one word he sat there for fully four minutes. The way in which he puffed nervously at the pipe showed me that he was thinking. Suddenly, with an exclamation of delight, he dashed out of the room and down the stairs, leaving the amazed duchess and myself in his apartments. But not for long. In forty-three seconds he was again in the room and, dropping into his chair thoroughly exhausted, he triumphantly cried:

"I have it!"

Never had I seen my friend wear such a look of victory. The achievement which merited such an expression upon his countenance must have been remarkable. By and by he recovered from his fatigue. Then he spoke.

"Madam," he said, "I have the answer."

The duchess sobbed in ecstasy.

Combs continued:

"The moment that you said you were lost," he began, "an idea came to me. You must have noticed, Spotson, how preoccupied I seemed before. Well, that is the sign of an idea coming to me. Before it had time to vanish I dashed down the steps, into the vestibule, looked at the number of this house and jotted it down. Madam," he cried, drawing out a book and looking at one of the pages, "madam, you are saved! You are no longer lost! This is No. 62 Fakir Street. You are found!"

During this entire recital the duchess had not said a word. When Combs had finished she stood for a moment as if she did not understand and then, realizing the fact that she was rescued, she wept once more.

"My savior," she cried as she prepared to leave the room, "how can I ever thank you?" And she pressed into Combs's outstretched hand a large gold-mesh, diamond-studded purse.

The door closed, the carriage rolled away and the Duchess of Swabia was gone.

"Spotson," said Combs to me, "don't forget to write this one down. It has a duchess in it and will sell well to cooks and chambermaids. By the way, I wonder what she gave me."

He opened the purse and there, neatly folded, lay two hundred pounds in bills.

"Bah!" cried Combs contemptuously. "How ungrateful these royal personages always are."

The Marriage of Sherlock Holmes

GREGORY BREITMAN

(Translated from the Russian by Benjamin Block)

IT MAY BE true that Russians have a spectacular sense of humor, but it is equally true that this most precious of traits has not always been evident in the translated literature. It is an uncommon day indeed when even the best-natured individuals ache to share the laugh riot they encountered in a Dostoevsky novel or the hilarity of Tolstoy's dialogue.

Gregory Breitman has produced a story far funnier than one might have expected. That statement is true. When expectations are nil, *any* hint of humor is a welcome surprise. Actually, the premise of this story is extremely witty, and while its execution is unlikely to be confused with the best of Mark Twain or Dave Barry, it is more than tolerable.

Breitman was born in Russia on June 20, 1873, and emigrated to the United States in 1923; he died on June 11, 1943.

"The Marriage of Sherlock Holmes" was first published in the December 1926 issue of a man's magazine, *The Beau Book*; it was first published in book form in *The Beau Book*, a bound volume containing the issues of December 1926 through October 1927, edited by Samuel Roth and limited to five hundred copies, bound for subscribers (New York, Beau Publishing, 1927).

THE MARRIAGE OF SHERLOCK HOLMES

Gregory Breitman

"IS THAT YOU, Watson?"

Doctor Watson briskly entered Sherlock Holmes's cabinet and pressed warmly the extended hand of the host.

Sherlock shifted his pipe from one corner of his mouth to the other and pointed out the armchair to his friend.

Doctor Watson seated himself opposite the host and said:

"Sherlock, you have not changed a wee-bit! Think of it! We have not seen each other for three months, yet, as soon as I put my foot across the threshold of your apartment, you recognized me immediately!"

The famous detective did not smile, but an effort to do so was quite evident. Perhaps he only stirred his pipe, and the movement of his lips suggested a gentle smile.

"Who else, besides you, my dear friend," he began, "would have come into my apartment and freely groomed his hair before the big mirror, without even inquiring about me from the servant-maid? Every person possesses some subjective nuances of manner which accompany him wherever he goes and expose themselves unconsciously. Don't we recognize people by their gait?"

Watson, without doubt, was pleased silently with his friend's explanation. He leisurely lit his cigar and when his head, at last, became enveloped in clouds of gray smoke, he asked carelessly:

"My friend, you are married?"

Holmes raised his eyes at his friend, only to meet the latter's cynic glance; either was pretending to look less surprised than the other, as if some play was hidden in it. Holmes replied:

"You have reached your conclusions because of the new order in my house, the odor of perfume and a lady's apparel hanging on the clothes-rack in the ante-chamber?"

"Not at all, Sherlock, I haven't noticed that," calmly retorted Watson, "but I judge by the smooth, unmistakable marriage ring on the fourth finger of your left hand. To be sure, Sherlock, you never cared for trinkets!"

Holmes brought up the palm of his left hand to his face and for several minutes thoughtfully examined the gold ring on his finger.

"You are right, my friend," he murmured, "this is the proof, sure proof for any detective. Yes, I am married."

"What on earth has come over you, Sherlock?" inquired the doctor somewhat sympathetically, gazing reflectively at his friend.

Sherlock Holmes took out the pipe from his mouth and after having ascertained that the fire had burned out completely, he then remarked:

"One successful adventure, Watson!"

"Poor Sherlock!" sighed the doctor compassionately. A brief, but serious silence followed. Holmes was meditating and Watson was waiting.

"Watson," at last began the famous detective, "as you know, I was always wont to report to you all my adventures; at all times I feel the need to share with someone my observations and impressions; my thought works much faster then, and during a conversation I may arrive at a more practical decision much easier than during the process of thinking."

"If that be the case, my friend," fired back the doctor, "I very much regret that we have not seen each other for such a long time, still I presume that, had there been someone for you to have a heart-to-heart talk with, your situation would not have become so sadly complicated."

"Why do you suppose that I am unhappy in my marriage, Watson?" curiously rebutted Holmes, as sparks seemed to be playing in his eyes.

"Only because of my conviction that such a serious and self-existing person like yourself can never be satisfied with married life, however supernatural qualities your lively consort may possess. It is mainly up to you, not to her. Coupled life, especially with a woman, is a thing unnatural, as much as love without a woman is unnatural. Matrimony, in its present form, is a savagery, a survival of barbarism and ignorance, a violation of the nature of the modern human being, an impurity of some sort."

"And, most of all, it is a great inconvenience," concluded Sherlock Holmes. "Life begins to resemble a piano, into the strings of which a cane with a gold head has been stuck. Absolutely incompatibility."

"What a misfortune it is for mankind that the woman is denied the ideal franchise with the man!" remarked the doctor bitterly.

Sherlock spoke up slowly: "I would gladly bear her name, carry out all household duties, make her the head of the family, just to be given the means to reckon with a definite quantity, only to know with whom I am dealing!"

"You are right, Sherlock; the psychic life of the woman is utterly inconceivable to the man, while the woman proper is always a puzzle to him. In that alone lies the nature of her relationship to him. Since Creation there was not, nor will there be such a man who could understand a woman. Not because there were not and there will not be any erudite and perspicacious men, but simply because it would be almost as supernatural if there were a man who could understand the languages of dogs, birds, and jackasses."

"Why, then, does a woman understand a man so well?" asked Sherlock sighingly.

"Because this is one of the peculiarities of her nature. She was thus created by God," quickly and assuredly asserted Watson. "It is one of her inborn qualities, without which she is—a weakling, a defective, like a cat without whiskers and special pupils, a dog without his scent, a hedgehog without his prickles. This is the weapon she employs in her struggle for her existence and against the man."

Watson began to reek with perspiration; he took out his handkerchief and wiped his high forehead. Sherlock lit up his pipe and puffed away at it till a thick, gray smoke enveloped him fully. Then, as if speaking to himself, he said:

"Most remarkable! During my life I had fought with all possible criminals, such criminals that police the world over refused to mingle with; I caught the most ingenious swindlers, cleverest thieves, brave robbers and beastly murderers; I traced the most amazing crimes, conceived the secrets of the most complicated adventures and unfolded them; I had dealt with prisoners, bullies, half-wits, and maniacs."

Watson's face bubbled with astonishment, and stretching himself out to a comfortable position, he interrupted his friend:

"Only your wife you cannot catch!" he shouted.

The pipe in Sherlock's mouth began to tremble, as if someone had struck it. A minute later the famous detective made the following reply:

"My good friend, Watson, I love you so, that I know not what to answer you!"

A stifled reproach was heard in the detective's voice. Watson grasped his hand and flared up in ardent exaltation:

"My dear teacher, whatever has come over you? You seem to have forgotten your first and main principle; to regard everything subjectively and seriously! I fail to recognize you, Sherlock!"

"I am not at all sure whether she has committed any crime at all."

"Then, you are jealous, Sherlock!"

"No, not jealous, but suspicious. I have sufficient proof to sustain my contention. I alone am aware of it. To another man she would seem an ideal wife, true and loving. It does not seem as if she had many male acquaintances. She does not spruce or receive letters from anyone, nor does she mention any names in her sleep; in a word, she conducts herself superbly."

"What do you want from her, then?"

"To know to whom she is betraying me!"

"Are you sure about it?"

"You, Watson, if anyone else, should know me at least a little bit!"

"Forgive me, Sherlock! But what is it, namely, that makes you suffer?"

"I am not suffering at all, Watson, I am merely interested. Two hearts have met in collision; hers and mine. My nature, however, does not tolerate a concrete secret."

"Of course! But, on what do you base your assumption, Sherlock?"

"I am certain, for instance, that she is taking someone home before she returns to the house. The individual she is riding with is a man, and lives not far from here. Judging by your raised eyebrows, you are deeply interested in the affair. Very well, then. I have observed her through the window several times when she was returning from an appointment. She never sat in the center of the seat, but always on the right-hand side. I conclude, therefrom, that at her left-hand side sat her escort who, undoubtedly, left the cab before. That her escort is a man is evinced by two outstanding incidents: First, that he sat at her left-hand side; second, that my wife never paid the driver. Consequently, he must have been paid off before, by a man, of course."

"The observation, in all probability, is correct!"

"Then, after the appointment, my wife usually brings home with her the odor of his perfume and cigars. One thing, Watson, you must admit, that I am endowed with a very keen, almost dog-like scent, and I can very easily discern the difference between a cigar and a pipe. Besides, you know well yourself that tobacco smoke assails the nostrils of the non-smoking neighbor more readily than the smoker himself."

The detective filled up his pipe with fresh tobacco; lighting it, he puffed away at it for a brief moment. Then, he stretched and straightened up his back awhile and continued:

"As you can see now, I possess a sufficient supply of watchfulness and observation; both of us are engaged in a definite, silent, but stubborn struggle. My wife, for instance, knows well that not until I bear witness of her actions will I utter a single syllable of rebuke to her; I am too serious a man for that. Her general behavior toward me is beyond reproach; neither do I suspect nor feel that she has grown cold toward me; she pretends not to be bored in my company; on the contrary, she is very kind, sweet, and amiable. Yet, I have on hand some well-founded material which proves to me that it is nothing but make-believe on her part, that she is playing a very subtle game—which must end some day."

"Still, I believe she will come out of this unmarred," remarked the visitor somewhat sadly, "unless you get her in the very act, when it will be impossible for her to prove or to deceive you any longer; when all roads leading to it will become locked. Otherwise, it is very difficult to test a woman; you cannot subject her love to an examination. She can make-believe and simulate as much as she desires. It is not like us men; we are mere mechanisms in the process of love."

"You are perfectly right, my friend; but my profession and art have forced me to discount all the time the views on love and women you have just propounded, and which so opportunely coincide with my own convictions. May I not, therefore, take the liberty of asking you, who is deceiving you, my friend?"

Watson doubtless became confused, but succeeded in retaining the composure of his mind. He met Sherlock's keen look with real fortitude, and discharging heavy clouds of smoke, he charged back, slowly, but very emphatically:

"This is a groundless accusation, Sherlock. I merely expressed my views and convictions. They bound me to nothing whatever."

"Perhaps! Yet, I firmly believe that they come to one only through personal experience, and their origin, I may say, is without doubt, the same as mine. But, whereas you are an admirer of concrete facts, I shall permit you to avail yourself of my material with regards to your case."

Watson's face became flooded with color. He was silent, holding the cigar tight in his mouth.

"The fact of the matter is, my friend, that it is more than three months since you have hidden yourself away, and although you have not left London, you have severed all connections with me. That happened for the first time during our uninterrupted friendship. I presume you were not sick, nor have we had any discord."

"This, if you like, is a thought, but not a reason. I might have been very much occupied."

"Just as I thought it was; you were very much occupied with your party. Tell me, Watson, since when is it that you began to spruce, wear such cravats, frizzle your hair, and in general employ methods of rejuvenation? The odor of your perfume is such as I have met in café-chantants only. Besides, where have your streaks of gray hair disappeared to? And why this white flower in your coat-lapel? I remember you never gave a snap for all that. And that gold tooth in your mouth, you didn't have it before! All this, my friend, forces me to fully presuppose that a woman is at the bottom of it all."

"I admit that your presumption is not without substantial logic, but it is no proof by any means, Sherlock."

Watson overcame his confusion, but refused to yield.

"I shall now unleash my last reserves, Watson," continued the detective unperturbed. "About a month ago, when I was tracing my wife, I found myself, much to my surprise, near your house. Thinking of you, I decided to step in and share with you my affairs. Alas, my friend, you could not receive me because there was a woman in your apartment. I confess, however, never be-fore have I met a female in your house, with the sole exception of your servant-maid who, on that occasion revealed the secret; she was fetching up to your room freshly bought candies, fruits, and flowers. Oh, Watson, how I wished I could share with you then my frame of mind. I, perhaps, would not have been married now!"

"But that happened only about three weeks ago, Sherlock!" surprisingly remarked Watson.

"Yes, and I was married only a week ago. Till then I was busily engaged in an unsuccessful search for my competitor. A strong depression of mind suddenly possessed me and I became doubtful of my suspicion and art and . . . put on this ring."

A concentrated silence ensued. Finally, hard pressed and silenced, the doctor meekly brushed away the ashes from his cigar and confessed naively.

"You are right, Sherlock, I am in love!"

"What happened then; you have parted with your sweetheart?"

Watson's face turned dead white suddenly.

"What makes you think so, Sherlock?"

"I judge by the sadness and disappointment you have expressed about women, and most of all, by the fact that you have come to me. I presume you were overwhelmed with the desire to have a heart-to-heart talk with someone; you felt lonesome, and your first thought, undoubtedly, was about me, your old, reliable friend. Why, you look awfully bad, Watson! I see you have not shaved for several days. I heartily congratulate you, my dear friend, upon the loss of your woman!"

"You are terrible, Sherlock," declared Watson, and continued sullenly, "Why, I am experiencing now a silent heart-tragedy. I have been searching her for the last ten days, but, alas; as if the earth itself had swallowed her down! I have availed all the methods of sleuthing you have taught me, but without success. Her traces lose themselves somewhere in this neighborhood. Having strayed down here, I ran in to have a chat with you and forget myself a bit."

Sherlock puffed away at his pipe with great

effort, as if vexed by it, and after a short pause, he began with a grimace of anxiety on his face:

"The more searches I conduct, the more convinced I become of how dangerous and deceitful the art of a detective sometimes is. What horrid, strange and incomprehensible concurrences of circumstances there are in our life—concurrences that create a full picture, an illusion of truth, which at the end turn out to be nothing but falsehoods and myths. How many people have been sent to the jails, hard-labor prisons, to the gallows, because of such mistakes of the courts of justice!"

"Why do you say that, Sherlock?" exclaimed Watson, being amazed at the sudden change of subject on the part of the detective. He took the cigar from his mouth and remained agape for awhile; he continued in complete stupor for some time, unable to determine whether his friend was merely joking or spoke in earnest.

"Don't be surprised, Watson," calmly continued Sherlock Holmes, without even looking at his guest; instead, he concentrated his eyes upon the edge of his fuming pipe, "even though it may sound unpleasant to you. Haven't we agreed and concluded long since, that everything in this world is possible, is natural and has its organic reasons? Well, then—only an hour ago you tried to convince me that I should regard the affair with my wife objectively and abstractedly. And so, my friend, I am following your kind advice. But, have you considered, at least for a brief moment, this very strange coincidence, that, when I have been looking for my wife, traces have brought me down to your house, and when you have been searching for your sweetheart, her traces led you straight to me? Of course, this is a mere coincidence, one of those coincidences which usually cause the mistakes of the courts. On the other hand, the very circumstance which brought us together today is misleading us. Now, supposing I were not acquainted with you, I would, even then, beyond all doubts, have entered your house, not in a friendly way, of course, but by means of direct detective indication. Presently, you have come

to me also by means of detective indication, although if I were not your friend, you would have been here just the same. And during our conversation I caught the odor of your handkerchief, when you were wiping your forehead, and recalled immediately the redolence of that unknown man's perfume my wife always brings with her after she returns from her rendezvous. Besides, I have already told you that she also brought with her the smell of cigars; indeed, you are smoking cigars . . ."

Watson availed himself of the chance when Holmes stopped to fix the ashes in his pipe and turned to the detective:

"You are right, Sherlock, and presently you will convince yourself how curious and amusing the pranks of sleuthing sometimes are. In order to prove to you that my case has nothing to do with yours, I shall relate to you briefly the history of my romance, the beginning of which you know, without any doubt."

The latter made a move, seated himself more comfortably in his armchair, and with an imperturbed expression on his face, prepared himself to listen to his friend's love affair.

"Surely, you remember, Sherlock," began Watson, after he lit up a new cigar, "our last adventure about three months ago, after which we first met today. Perhaps you have by now forgotten that charming young lady with the golden tresses and celestial eyes—the girl that kissed our hands and begged us to save her father, whom the agents of the king's police were about to seize and arrest. Your genius then manifested itself in its full glory; in half an hour you put the police to shame and made them confess of the rude mistake they had committed. They suspected the poor gentleman, a cashier of the Trade Bank of England, of embezzlement of two thousand pounds sterling, while, as you directly pointed out, it was stolen by his assistant, who lost the money on the stock exchange."

"I do remember, Watson," confirmed Sherlock through his pipe, "the investigation was brief, but beautiful. Yes, I remember that well."

"But I doubt whether you remember the

statement the charming young lady had made—about her going to business every morning at 10 a.m. I confess, Sherlock, the young lady has made a powerful impression on me. I fully agree now with those individuals who claim that love is an infectious disease, sometimes more obstinate than malaria. Promptly at 10 a.m. the next morning, I was at her house and walked her over to her place of business. Thank God, it was a long way off and I had plenty of time to enamor myself, more and more, with her exquisite charms. I have thus been escorting her to her place of business every day.

"Sherlock, I was infinitely happy. All this time she filled my life with love, caresses, and sweetness; she respected my principle never to marry, never to bind my fate with another, nor to surrender my liberty and comfort. Suddenly, about ten days ago, she disappeared. I have not found her yet, and while searching for her, false traces have brought me to you, my dear Sherlock. I believe, however, that it was the instinct, rather than the track, that led me here; I must have just felt the need of some counsel from a man like you."

Sherlock Holmes for several minutes sat with eyes shut. Then he took out the pipe from his mouth, placed it on his knees and then only did he look up to his guest.

"I remember," said he, "that I could not forget that girl with the golden tresses and celestial eyes. Nor have I forgotten when she had remarked about her going to business at 10 a.m. in the morning, the exact hour when I am eating my breakfast. But you apparently have forgotten that the very same charming girl added also that she is returning from business at 4 p.m., at the time you are accustomed to have your dinner. And, if you, my friend, were wont to escort her every day to the office, then I was escorting her every day from the office to her house. I also have succumbed to the fever of love. In my case, my friend, it ended in a catastrophe: I married her, sparing you from such fate."

Watson was all white and deeply shaken by the phlegmatic confession of his friend, whose malaise was evinced by the quivering pipe he now held in his hand and with which he beat against his knee, in order to mask his emotions. Nothing interested him more now than his competitor, upon whom he riveted an obstinate look of his dark gray eyes. Both were silent. It is not an easy venture to guess what the outcome would have been of their unusual, stiffened silence, but presently they heard a sound that set both of them to tremble and an unforeseen shadow of uneasiness spread over their faces. That brief moment was nothing short of horror. Both host and guest were aghast. They were ready to run. But fate had decreed that each look into the other's eyes and that assimilated look brought light into their hearts, and the lacking roads of retreat and exits out of the created situation, led them into a silent agreement. And when the door flung open and into the room briskly entered Mrs. Holmes, the two chums sat like statues, true to themselves, and returned to their school of life.

Mrs. Holmes indeed was very charming. Beside the golden tresses and celestial eyes, her round face, with its soft and delicate colors and shades, seemed almost enameled; it gleamed with moral chastity and cheerful indolence; a sort of elegant naivete, which combined both that which is childish and feminine into one beautiful smile and look.

Smartly dressed and childishly cheerful she stopped suddenly, as if rooted down to the very spot, and after a second of thoughtful gazing at the two friends, she smilingly extended her hand to Watson, exclaiming in her sweet elastic voice:

"Ah, Mr. Watson! I know you! My husband has spoken to me a great deal about you. Besides, I actually could not forget you since the first moment I met you. I had dreamed ever since I married my Sherlock to become acquainted with you more closely. Sherlock had told me a great many fine and interesting things about you, Mr. Watson."

"Poor Watson is in a quandary," explained Sherlock calmly, "he was left flat by a woman whom he was madly in love with and, on whose account, he forgot everyone in this world, even me, his bosom friend. He should be appeased, don't you think so, Mary? I wish you would take upon yourself this task."

"Poor Mr. Watson," sincerely exclaimed Mrs. Holmes, as she shot a cunning glance at the sad and silent doctor, who sat in his armchair with downcast eyes.

Sherlock Holmes by now completely regained his composure and watched, not without pleasure, the transpiring scene. He intended, apparently, to carry on his intrigue against his wife, but presently the latter noticed the strange turns of mind on the part of the men and a flash of suspicion flit through her eyes and face.

The spark of animation the young lady brought in with her into the room was suddenly extinguished and all at once a weird silence, which none seemed willing to interrupt, filled up the whole room. Mrs. Holmes began to feel the grip of danger, but could not yet compute its proportion. Finally, Watson could hold out no longer. Determination glowed in his look; the instinct of self-preservation was abetting his desire to put an end to this tormenting situation from which, it seemed, there was no way out. His voice sounded dull, he was staring into the distance:

"Stop that, Mary, Sherlock knows it all . . ."

Mrs. Holmes turned white at once, and tears appeared in her eyes.

"You did not act fairly, Mr. Watson, not in the least gentleman-like!" was all she was able to utter.

Watson instantly jumped to his feet, as if someone had struck him. His voice quivered now, he was unspeakably agitated.

"Ah, my dear Mrs. Holmes," he exclaimed plaintively, "please do not condemn me; is it my fault that your husband is a great detective?"

During Watson's brief complimentary praise to the detective, the latter attentively puffed away at his pipe, and having inhaled a goodly portion of smoke, he spoke up in his usual tone:

"Most important of all is that this mystery has at last been brought to a satisfactory conclusion; the whole affair has been cleared up in all its details. I can make you rejoice but at a single fact, my darling Mary, that during my long career as a detective, I have not yet tackled such an enigma."

Mrs. Holmes somewhat regained her self-possession. Hearing, at last, her husband's words, she dropped slowly on the edge of the sofa and began:

"Act as you like, Sherlock, but I have not deceived you. When you and Mr. Watson displayed so much interest in me, by saving my father, my whole being became filled with affection for you; the two of you became so dear to me that I began to feel a strong penchant for your society—the society of both of you. That was at the beginning. I was at a loss then, not knowing for whom to show my preference. Were the two of you to come to me together, it would have been much easier for me to decide on either one of you. But right then you two parted, and each one separately made a different impression upon me. In the beginning, when we first met, I did not even suppose that you, Sherlock, had any intentions of marrying me. You proposed marriage to me only three days before our wedding. And because of that, am I to blame that Mr. Watson proved himself to be more ardent and willing than you were, Sherlock? Both of you were aiming at one and the same object, but through different roads. Still, Sherlock, I have not deceived you, just as I have not deceived Mr. Watson, yet you two have made me suffer. You are men, and, therefore, you cannot conceive the heart of a woman when it is filled with gratitude; it begets all sorts of feelings and sufferings. When you proposed to me, I left Mr. Watson immediately because to you, my dear, I had already given away myself, my freedom, and the right over my feelings. You may do as you please, Sherlock, but it would have been far more proper on your part had you informed me of your intentions beforehand, rather than occupy yourself with investigations that permeate our relationship with a spirit of strife and enmity. Sometime in the future I shall relate to you how I strove against your art and I hope that you will extol my contriving spirit, my dexterity and ingenuity."

The young woman grew silent, encouraged by the address she had delivered, and darting a glance at the men, a shade of crimson unwillingly passed through her cheeks; a current of delight and appeasement filled up her heart.

The two friends exchanged furtive glances, and it seemed that, in another second, they would begin to smile.

"It is quite a different task to fathom a woman's heart and soul," at last spoke up Watson, with a nonchalant shrug of his shoulders.

"And a hopeless one!" concluded Sherlock Holmes, as he pressed heartily the hand of the doctor.

The Return of Sherlock Holmes

E. F. BENSON AND
EUSTACE H. MILES

LIKE HIS TWO brothers, Edward Frederic Benson (1867–1940) was a master of ghost and horror stories, but his first great success was a society novel, *Dodo* (1893), which remained in print for more than eighty years. Its continued sales enabled him to devote himself full-time to writing and he produced a prodigious amount of social satire, notably his series about Emmeline "Lucia" Lucas and Elizabeth Mapp, which was adapted for TV by London Weekend Television as *Mapp and Lucia* in 1985–1986.

Benson also wrote highly regarded biographies, including the standard one at the time for Charlotte Brontë—more than seventy books in all. While most of his novels of manners and society are now predictably dated, his frequent forays into the realm of supernatural and horror fiction remain high points in the literature. All four volumes of his ghost stories—*The Room in the Tower* (1912), *Visible and Invisible* (1923), *Spook Stories* (1928), and *More Spook Stories* (1934)—are in print today and still avidly read, with a more recent volume, *The Flint Knife* (1988), collecting previously uncollected work.

Benson's collaborator on this excellent parody, Eustace H. Miles (1868–1948), was a British amateur tennis champion who also wrote, among other works, a book on improving memory, *How to Remember* (1901), and a physical exercise book, *Daily Training* (1902), with some emphasis on being vegetarian, cowritten with Benson.

"The Return of Sherlock Holmes" was first published in *The Mad Annual* (London, Grant Richards, 1903).

THE RETURN OF SHERLOCK HOLMES

E. F. Benson and Eustace H. Miles

MY FRIEND, Mr. Sherlock Holmes, was apparently killed, as the many millions of my readers will remember, somewhere in Switzerland, by Mr. Moriarty. Since then, however, he appears to have been exercising his deductive faculties somewhere down in Devonshire in connection with a large dog painted with phosphorus. So, as the many millions of my readers will already have come to the conclusion that he was not really killed in Switzerland, I may as well tell them, in my usual manner, what really took place between his supposed death and his rather feeble reincarnation at the damp house of the Baskervilles.

I was sitting in the front room at Baker Street, the flat we shared together, some two years after his disappearance, neatly dressed, as is my custom, in a bowler-hat and morning tail-coat. In the interval, I had read over again and again the notes of the strange cases he had so considerately forgotten to take with him to Switzerland, and I had come to the conclusion that his disappearance—as I gave it to the world—was a mistake on my part. I had a very fair working knowledge of his methods, and had learned to distinguish fifty-seven sorts of blotting paper, forty-three cigar-ashes, and with the aid of his pocket-glass, which he had also left behind, could from the marks on the carpet ascertain with fair correctness whether anyone with extremely muddy boots had lately been in the room. Consequently, if only I had not given to the world the story of his disappearance, I might have gone on to write almost any number of these reminiscences which have so taken the world by storm. Then,

to my inexpressible relief, came the story of his marvellous power of intuition in the matter of the phosphorescent dog, and since the public swallowed that, they might be pleased to swallow more, or indeed anything. The story, as every reader will remember, was supposed to be told by me, but somebody else really made it up. As soon as I saw it, I thought of applying for a breach of patent, but Mrs. (now Lady) Watson restrained me. But from that moment I began to plan a whole new series of tales, and if these should ever see the light, I do not think that anyone will fail to be thrilled over "King Cophetua's Beggar-maid," "The Mystery of Hampstead Heath," "The Moth-eaten Boa Constrictor," "The King of Spain's Purple Inkstand," and the short monograph on the tails of cab-horses.

As I said, I was sitting in the front room at Baker Street—what had happened to my wife I can't remember. As every reader will have noticed, she disappears at intervals from these stories. Some day I shall watch her, after the methods of my revered master, Sherlock Holmes. Anyhow, I was sitting in the front room at Baker Street when the door-bell rang. I had already learned to distinguish many sorts of ringing—the routine ringing, for instance, of the baker; the Wagnerian ringing of Mr. Sherlock Holmes's relations, who think they have a claim on me; the hopeless ringing of the dun; the expectant ringing of the boon-companion; and the merely *enragé* ringing of the incurable maniac. But I had hardly time to turn up my classification of ringing when my visitor was announced, and a middle-aged woman of below the middle height was ushered into the room. She had a splash of yolk of egg on her jacket, from which I concluded that she was not penniless, or she would have had no breakfast, and that she was of an untidy habit, while, from the muddy bootlace that trailed on the carpet, I inferred with lightning rapidity that she was in a hurry and had also probably walked here. At her throat she wore a diamond, which I saw at once to be worth a king's ransom, and from the fact that she was smoking a short clay pipe I gathered she was not English, or, at any rate, not belonging to the so-called fashionable world of London. So, adopting my usual confidential professional manner—"Well, my good woman," I said, "what can I do for you?"

The crone replied in a slightly cracked voice. "Is it Mr. Sherlock Holmes?" she said.

The temptation—if indeed it was a temptation—prevailed. It would have been tedious to explain to her that I was his greater chronicler, adducing the obvious parallel of Johnson and Boswell; and, indeed, I doubted whether she had ever heard of either.

"You may speak to me quite frankly," I said. "I only wish my friend Lord—I mean Mr. Watson was here, whom I often consult in cases where superior penetration is required."

As I spoke I dropped my eyes to adjust the stethoscope that was sticking out of my pocket. It is my custom—rightly or wrongly, I do not know—to carry my stethoscope somewhere where it can be easily seen, as it leads to patients. As I did this, I heard a faint chuckle, and remembered whom I impersonated.

So I lit an ounce or two of shag tobacco, and, closing my eyes slightly, extemporised on my late friend's violin.

"Mitral regurgitation," I said, referring to the chuckle. "I perceive, also, that you have walked some distance, and are of an untidy temperament. This is apt to grow on elderly females. From your height, I should infer you had rickets when young, but that your father was a man of wealth."

"You mean my diamond," said she; "it was given me by my husband."

This was weary work.

"Then where is your wedding-ring?" I asked, looking at the thin tapering hands, and striking a series of consecutive fifths.

My visitor made a movement of impatience.

"The *E* string is slightly out of tune," she observed.

I handed her the violin. The *E* string was altogether missing.

"You forget whom you are talking to," said I. "But pray name your business! Two kings and three marchionesses are already on the telephone, and I cannot give you long. Also the purple Emperor of Paraguay has been consulting me on a matter of the most urgent importance."

I had learned this trick, I must confess, from Sherlock. Whenever, in the old days, I challenged his deductions, he always used to refer me to the case of the Green Sparrow of Pesth, or the Aurora of Candahar. Even as I spoke, I got up and rang up a false telephone, with which it was my custom to impress patients. Once Mrs., I mean Lady——

But even as I turned, I heard a well-known voice——

"You have gone up a little in weight, Watson," it said; "I should say you were seven-stone-six."

In an instant I knew who it was.

"Holmes, this is unworthy of you!" I cried. "Besides, I am thirteen stone," and I stood on the weighing-machine. It only registered fourteen stone and instantly burst with a loud report.

"That convinces us both of its fallibility," he remarked. "I should be obliged, Watson, if you would sit down, and not pretend to ring up imaginary people. It was I who invented the purple Emperor of Paraguay. But it was you who broke my *E* string."

Even in this short space of time he had entirely divested himself of the habiliments of the slovenly spinster, and in the chair there lay back the figure of Sherlock Holmes, clad in his usual dressing-gown, his thin, hawk-like, athletic face irradiated by a painful kind of smile.

"You have attempted to impersonate me," he said.

"You have been fooling around in Devonshire long after I had killed you," I retorted.

His face became filled by that egotism which I have often deplored in these and similar pages.

"I do not deny," he said, "that you have been on occasions of some slight use to me. But the times when your infernal tail-coat and bowler-hat have irritated me beyond endurance are without number."

This roused me.

"If it hadn't been for me," I said, "you would never have been heard of."

"We are quits," he replied; "if it hadn't been for me you would never have found anything to write about. Oblige me by the tobacco."

I handed him his purple shag, and watched him with extreme interest, for I saw he was in his most intuitive mood. I should get copy out of this.

"I observe," he said, "that in my absence you have not been idle. A lady of title has called here today; you were very busy before dinner; you planted a polyanthus at Uxbridge a few days ago, and have an idle servant; you have lately read a volume by Mr. Alfred Austin; you have a young dog which it has been necessary to chastise because he dug up the polyanthus; you smoked a cigarette just before I came into the room; and replied, this afternoon, to a letter from your mother-in-law, who proposed herself to come and stay with you; you have a brother who used to drink, but who was buried on Thursday; Sir Richard Calmady's mother has married again; you went to the wedding."

I paced up and down the room in incontrollable agitation.

"Holmes, this is not fair!" I cried. "You have been spying on me!"

A look of pained surprise covered his face.

"Do you not know my methods yet?" he said. "All this is, or should be to one who has access to my note-book, perfectly simple. To begin with—there is a countess's coronet lying on the floor: I inferred a countess had been to see you. A large ink-stain on your forefinger, my dear Watson, indicates that you have been writing, and in a man of your scrupulous cleanliness, it is fair to infer that if you had written before lunch you would have washed before dinner. On your instep there is a withered polyanthus leaf, imbedded in a small crust of pleiocene clay, which occurs only at Uxbridge, where I know you have a cottage. The clay is rather dry, and from that I inferred a lazy servant, who did not clean your boots properly. The volume of Mr. Alfred Austin which you have lately read is surely indicated by the fragments in the grate, on which, even from here, I detect *Veron . . . Gar . . .* , surely *Veronica's Garden*. Out of your pocket is sticking a small dog-whip with a leaf of polyanthus on it; I infer you have beaten the dog that dug up the polyanthus at Uxbridge. The fact of a cigarette before dinner was purely guesswork, but I see no cigar-butt in the ash-tray, from which I assume you smoked a cigarette before dinner, just before I came into the room. The letter from your mother-in-law proposing to come and stay with you I inferred from the fact that in the hall there was lying a reply from you, addressed to Mrs. Smith, and in the top corner the word *"Damn,"* instead of "To be forwarded." Your drunken brother I have often heard you mention; the fact that he was buried on Thursday is an easy deduction from the funeral card on the mantelshelf. Sir Richard Calmady's mother is a rather longer shot; but I see footprints of a heavy man on your carpet only a few inches apart. No one but Sir Richard with his deplorable absence of shin could have made them. The orange-blossom on your table, in conjunction with the piece of wedding-cake, indicates the rest. Besides," he added, "I saw it in the evening paper."

His fascination and extraordinary brilliance instantly asserted their old spell over me. There sat Holmes the sleuth-hound; Holmes the violin virtuoso; Holmes the hero of the Speckled Band; Holmes the authority on cigar-ashes; Holmes my friend. The room, too, was a monument to him. On the walls was the elaborate design of revolver bullets instead of a paper, which he used to idly plant there while thinking out some crime which had baffled all Scotland Yard; the bookshelves were filled with his monographs, and behind the door hung up several of his more remarkable disguises. Even the tail-coat and bowler-hat that I wore were indirectly the fruits of his incomparable brain.

"Holmes!" I cried with unparalleled devotion, forgetting all his egotism, forgetting even the vast store of thrilling adventures I could have made from his note-books, "Holmes, welcome home!"

I could see from his half-closed eye that he was much gratified.

"And tell me," I went on, "what really happened to you."

He shifted in his chair.

"You will not altogether like it, Watson," he said, "but it is fair you should know. My disappearance was carefully planned to deceive you into thinking I was dead. I led you to believe that Moriarty was on my track, intent to kill me. That was not the case. The supposed Moriarty was none other than my brother, who joined me in Switzerland. Since then we have been investigating crime in Turkestan."

"But why this elaborate ruse?" said I.

He paused a moment.

"Well, my dear Watson, the reason is not very complimentary to you; but the fact is, that I simply could not stand any more of you. You got on to my nerves quite indescribably, and it was necessary for my peace of mind that you should not be with me. I knew your almost too faithful nature. I knew how you would leave your practice to take care of itself if I evinced the slightest desire for your companionship; and the only thing to do was to make you think I was dead. In fact, my dear fellow, I rather thought you would commit suicide as soon as you were convinced I was no longer living—but you did not. I must confess my deductions were a little at fault there. Well, you may blame me if you wish, but neither my brother nor I could stand you. So we made this extremely simple little plot to throw you off the track. And now I have come back because I find I can't do without you any more."

I was indescribably touched at his frankness; at the same time, I was a little hurt.

"What was it in me that got on your nerves?" I asked.

Holmes shook his head impatiently.

"Your hat, your coat, your obtuseness, your whole personality," he said.

"Then why have you come back?" I asked. "My hat, my coat (or others exactly like them), my—my obtuseness and personality are all here."

"I know my dear fellow," he said; "but you have something which I now know outweighs them all. It is your matchless mediocrity of mind and literary style which is the one and proper medium for the telling of my adventures, since it leaves the mind of the reader entirely free to follow what I do. You are my pen, my right hand. I am your brain. We are both perfectly useless alone. Together we dominate the English-reading public. So, Watson, I came back."

Even as he spoke a prodigious peal came from the door-bell, followed by a succession of piercing screams. "And adventure meets me on the threshold," said Holmes. "That is a good omen for our future work."

He hastily refilled his pipe, his eyelids half closed, and the room grew dense with tobacco smoke.

"My landlady is out," I shouted to make myself heard above the screaming, "and no one will answer the bell. In the meantime somebody is being murdered on the doorstep."

Holmes sighed wearily.

"You will never distinguish the essential from the incidental, Watson," he said. "Those screams—I think I recognise the *timbre* of the Queen of Bohemia—are not those of pain but of passion. We will wait till they are quieted. Then you shall bring her Majesty in."

"Have you seen much of them lately?" I asked.

"Yes; I have been able to be of some small service to the King," said Holmes, "whereby I saved a European war. It was a very simple little problem. He rewarded my services in a manner quite beyond their deserts by presenting me with the remarkably fine diamond that perhaps you noticed I was wearing."

The door-bell had long since had its wire broken, but our fair visitor continued to hammer on the door. The screams had died down, and at a sign from Holmes I took off my bowler-hat, and went to let her Majesty in.

A woman of transcendent loveliness was standing on the threshold. She was tall and commanding in figure, but her face was distorted with passion.

"Take me to Mr. Sherlock Holmes," she said.

I preceded her upstairs and threw open the door. The room was quite empty, but a sound of furniture being pushed as a barricade against the bedroom door from the inside told me that my friend was exercising his usual caution in dealing with this problem.

"He is in there!" she cried. "Come out, Mr. Holmes! I will not hurt you! I only want my diamond! Otherwise, I shall shoot this man, whom I recognise as Watson, barricade the bedroom door from this side, and set fire to the house. You know my hasty temper."

Some unusually strong emotion must have been excited in Sherlock Holmes at this speech, for he trembled so much in the adjoining room that the whole house shook.

"Does your Majesty swear not to make an attack on my person?" he asked.

"I would not touch you with a barge-pole," she replied. "Come out!"

We heard the barricade slowly moved away, and in another moment Sherlock Holmes emerged, and with an impressive sweep of his right arm deposited the diamond in the Queen's hand.

"I restore the stone to your Majesty with pleasure," he said. "it is false, and worth about £10."

She looked at it a moment curiously.

"Very stupid of the King," she said; "he telegraphed to me in London that you had stolen the Blue Gem and left for England. But I see you only got hold of the imitation one, which I wear on second-rate occasions. One does not leave valuable gems about, Mr. Holmes, when people of shady character are at the Palace. Goodbye! Next time you leave Bohemia you will leave it sitting on a donkey's back, face to the tail."

She swept from the room, and for a few moments there was silence. Then the dreamy look that I know so well came into my friend's face.

"There are a few little *lacunae* to be supplied," he said, "in what, after all, is a very commonplace affair. You see, the theft could not have been found out till I had left Bohemia, which, as you know, has no extradition treaty with any other country. Therefore I was safe in that respect. But a superficial examination of the stone by a jeweller in Paris convinced me it was false. Therefore I had not stolen the real gem. I did not tell you it was false, my dear Watson, because the announcements made by you that I have been engaged in investigations for crowned heads help my prestige very much, and to let you know that my reward has been only a £10 paste diamond would not lead you to believe I have been of any great service to them. And now that you do know all, I am sure my secret is safe with you, for otherwise you would spoil the market for both of us. The Queen is a woman of great force."

He reached out for his violin.

"Let me play you a little thing of my own which I have not published," he said. "Tomorrow we will begin writing some more adventures."

The Unmasking of Sherlock Holmes

ARTHUR CHAPMAN

ARTHUR CHAPMAN (1873–1935) is most widely known as a writer of cowboy poetry—verse that depicts the people and the land of the Midwest frontier in early twentieth-century America, most famously "Out Where the West Begins," which, a decade after its creation in 1910, was hailed as the "best-known bit of verse in America."

Frequently reprinted, quoted, and parodied, it was published in book form in 1916. *Out Where the West Begins, and Other Small Songs of a Big Country* was a modest fifteen-page volume issued by Carson-Harper in Denver but was such a huge success that Houghton Mifflin quickly published a larger collection with fifty-eight poems, *Out Where the West Begins, and Other Western Verses*, in 1917. In addition, the poem was put to music composed by Estelle Philleo in the same year.

Chapman also had a long career in the newspaper business, working for the *Chicago Daily News* as a reporter, *The Denver Republican* as a literary editor and columnist, and *The Denver Times* as managing editor. In 1919 he left the frontier for New York City, where he became a staff writer for the Sunday edition of the *New York Tribune* (later the *New York Herald Tribune*). He was a writer of fiction and nonfiction throughout his life, and published four books over the span of a dozen years: *Mystery Ranch* (1921), a western adventure and murder mystery; *The Story of Colorado, Out Where the West Begins* (1924), a history of the state; *John Crews* (1926), a western combining adventure and romance; and *The Pony Express: The Record of a Romantic Adventure in Business* (1932), a nonfiction account.

"The Unmasking of Sherlock Holmes" was originally published in the February 1905 issue of *The Critic and Literary World*.

THE UNMASKING OF
SHERLOCK HOLMES

Arthur Chapman

IN ALL MY career as Boswell to the Johnson of Sherlock Holmes, I have seen the great detective agitated only once. We had been quietly smoking and talking over the theory of thumbprints, when the landlady brought in a little square of pasteboard at which Holmes glanced casually and then let drop on the floor. I picked up the card, and as I did so I saw that Holmes was trembling, evidently too agitated either to tell the landlady to show the visitor in or to send him away. On the card I read the name:

Monsieur C. Auguste Dupin,
Paris.

While I was wondering what there could be in that name to strike terror to the heart of Sherlock Holmes, M. Dupin himself entered the room. He was a young man, slight of build and unmistakably French of feature. He bowed as he stood in the doorway, but I observed that Sherlock Holmes was too amazed or too frightened to return the bow. My idol stood in the middle of the room, looking at the little Frenchman on the threshold as if M. Dupin had been a ghost. Finally, pulling himself together with an effort, Sherlock Holmes motioned the visitor to a seat, and, as M. Dupin sunk into the chair, my friend tumbled into another and wiped his brow feverishly.

"Pardon my unceremonious entrance, Mr. Holmes," said the visitor, drawing out a meerschaum pipe, filling it, and then smoking in long, deliberate puffs. "I was afraid, however, that you would not care to see me, so I came in before you had an opportunity of telling your landlady to send me away."

To my surprise Sherlock Holmes did not annihilate the man with one of those keen, searching glances for which he has become famous in literature and the drama. Instead he continued to mop his brow and finally mumbled, weakly:

"But—but—I thought y-y-you were dead, M. Dupin."

"And people thought you were dead, too, Mr. Sherlock Holmes," said the visitor, in his high, deliberate voice. "But if you can be brought to life after being hurled from a cliff in the Alps, why can't I come out of a respectable grave just to have a chat with you? You know my originator, Mr. Edgar Allan Poe, was very fond of bringing people out of their graves."

"Yes, yes, I'll admit that I have read that fellow, Poe," said Sherlock Holmes testily. "Clever writer in some things. Some of his detective stories about you are not half bad, either."

"No, not half bad," said M. Dupin, rather sarcastically, I thought. "Do you remember that little story of 'The Purloined Letter,' for instance? What a little gem of a story that is! When I get to reading it over I forget all about you and your feeble imitations. There is nothing forced there. Everything is as sure as fate itself—not a false note—not a thing dragged in by the heels. And the solution of it all is so simple that it makes most of your artifices seem clumsy in comparison."

"But if Poe had such a good thing in you, M. Dupin, why didn't he make more of you?" snapped Sherlock Holmes.

"Ah, that's where Mr. Poe proved himself a real literary artist," said M. Dupin, puffing away at his eternal meerschaum. "When he had a good thing he knew enough not to ruin his reputation by running it into the ground. Suppose, after writing 'The Murders of the Rue Morgue' around me as the central character, he had written two or three books of short stories in which I figured. Then suppose he had let them dramatize me and further parade me before the public. Likewise suppose, after he had decently killed me off and had announced that he would write no more detective stories, he had yielded to the blandishments of his publishers and had brought out another interminable lot of tales about me? Why, naturally, most of the stuff would have been worse than mediocre, and people would have forgotten all about that masterpiece, 'The Murders of the Rue Morgue,' and also about 'The Purloined Letter,' so covered would those gems be in a mass of trash."

"Oh, I'll admit that my string has been overplayed," sighed Sherlock Holmes moodily, reaching for the hypodermic syringe, which I slid out of his reach. "But maybe Poe would have overplayed you if he could have drawn down a dollar a word for all he could write about you."

"Poor Edgar—poor misunderstood Edgar!— maybe he would," said Dupin, thoughtfully. "Few enough dollars he had in his stormy life. But at the same time, no matter what his rewards, I think he was versatile genius enough to have found something new at the right time. At any rate he would not have filched the product of another's brain and palmed it off as his own."

"But great Scott, man!" cried Sherlock Holmes. "You don't mean to say that no one else but Poe has a right to utilize the theory of analysis in a detective story, do you?"

"No, but see how closely you follow me in all other particulars. I am out of sorts with fortune and so are you. I am always smoking when thinking out my plans of attack, and so are you. I have

an admiring friend to set down everything I say and do, and so have you. I am always dazzling the chief of police with much better theories than he can ever work out, and so are you."

"I know, I know," said Sherlock Holmes, beginning to mop his forehead again. "It looks like a bad case against me. I've drawn pretty freely upon you, M. Dupin, and the quotation marks haven't always been used as they should have been where credit was due. But after all I am not the most slavish imitation my author has produced. Have you ever read his book, 'The White Company' and compared it with 'The Cloister and the Hearth'? No? Well do so, if you want to get what might be termed 'transplanted atmosphere.'"

"Well, it seems to be a great age for the piratical appropriating of other men's ideas," said M. Dupin, resignedly. "As for myself, I don't care a rap about your stealing of my thunder, Sherlock Holmes. In fact, you're a pretty decent sort of a chap, even though you are trying my patience with your continual refusal to retire; and besides you only make me shine the brighter in comparison. I don't even hold that 'Dancing Men' story against you, in which you made use of a cryptogram that instantly brought up thoughts of 'The Gold-Bug.'"

"But you did not figure in 'The Gold-Bug,'" said Sherlock Holmes with the air of one who had won a point.

"No, and that merely emphasizes what I have been telling you—that people admire Poe as a literary artist owing to the fact that he did not overwork any of his creations. Bear that in mind, my boy, and remember, when you make your next farewell, to see that it is not one of the Patti kind, with a string to it. The patience of even the American reading public is not exhaustless, and you cannot always be among the 'six best-selling books of the day.'"

And with these words, M. Dupin, pipe and all, vanished in the tobacco-laden atmosphere of the room, leaving the great detective, Sherlock Holmes, looking at me as shamefacedly as a schoolboy who had been caught with stolen apples in his possession.

The Adventure of the Diamond Necklace

GEORGE F. FORREST

AS A PUBLISHING venture, a slim volume of parodies by a virtually unknown author seems a risky business, but that did not prevent Frank Harvey of 21 & 22 Broad Street, a small house in Oxford, from committing to the publication of *Misfits: A Book of Parodies* by George Forrest (as his name appears on the front cover, or G. F. Forrest, as he is identified on the title page); it was released in 1905.

As with all story collections, some are inevitably better than others; in the case of parodies, some are funnier than others, and this volume is no exception. It contains burlesques of such disparate authors as Rudyard Kipling, Francis Bacon, William Shakespeare, and the very popular adventure writer H. Rider Haggard, as well as several poets. "The Deathless Queen," narrated by a cowardly Allan Quarterslain, is set in the heart of Africa and features an idolized queen known as "She-Who-Must-Be-Decayed." For his spoof of Arthur Conan Doyle, Forrest subtitled the story "Dedicated as a study in grotesque criminology."

In addition to a regular trade edition in paper covers, *Misfits* was also issued in a handsome large paper hardcover edition, limited to one hundred fifty copies. Limited editions, then as now, are generally reserved for the great names in literature, so it appears that the publisher had oddly high hopes for a book by the little-known Forrest or, as seems more likely, that the author himself may have had a hand in the publication. Subsidy publishing, also known as vanity publishing, was not unknown in Edwardian times.

THE ADVENTURE OF
THE DIAMOND NECKLACE

George F. Forrest

AS I PUSHED open the door, I was greeted by the strains of a ravishing melody. Warlock Bones was playing dreamily on the accordion, and his keen, clear-cut face was almost hidden from view by the dense smoke-wreaths, which curled upwards from an exceedingly filthy briar-wood pipe. As soon as he saw me, he drew a final choking sob from the instrument, and rose to his feet with a smile of welcome.

"Ah, good morning, Goswell," he said cheerily. "But why do you press your trousers under the bed?"

It was true—quite true. This extraordinary observer, the terror of every cowering criminal, the greatest thinker that the world has ever known, had ruthlessly laid bare the secret of my life. Ah, it was true.

"But how did you know?" I asked in a stupor of amazement.

He smiled at my discomfiture.

"I have made a special study of trousers," he answered, "and of beds. I am rarely deceived. But, setting that knowledge, for the moment, on one side, have you forgotten the few days I spent with you three months ago? I saw you do it then."

He could never cease to astound me, this lynx-eyed sleuth of crime. I could never master the marvelous simplicity of his methods. I could only wonder and admire—a privilege, for which I can never be sufficiently grateful. I seated myself on the floor, and, embracing his left knee with both my arms in an ecstasy of passionate adoration, gazed up inquiringly into his intellectual countenance.

He rolled up his sleeve, and, exposing his thin nervous arm, injected half a pint of prussic acid with incredible rapidity. This operation finished, he glanced at the clock.

"In twenty-three or twenty-four minutes," he observed, "a man will probably call to see me. He has a wife, two children, and three false teeth, one of which will very shortly have to be renewed. He is a successful stockbroker of about forty-seven, wears Jaegers, and is an enthusiastic patron of Missing Word Competitions."

"How do you know all this?" I interrupted breathlessly, tapping his tibia with fond impatience.

Bones smiled his inscrutable smile.

"He will come," he continued, "to ask my advice about some jewels which were stolen from his house at Richmond last Thursday week. Among them was a diamond necklace of quite exceptional value."

"Explain," I cried in rapturous admiration. "Please explain."

"My dear Goswell," he laughed, "you are really very dense. Will you never learn my methods? The man is a personal friend of mine. I met him yesterday in the City, and he asked to come and talk over his loss with me this morning. *Voilà tout.* Deduction, my good Goswell, mere deduction."

"But the jewels? Are the police on the track?"

"Very much off it. Really our police are the veriest bunglers. They have already arrested twenty-seven perfectly harmless and unoffending persons, including a dowager duchess, who is still prostrate with the shock; and, unless I am very much mistaken, they will arrest my friend's wife this afternoon. She was in Moscow at the time of the robbery, but that, of course, is of little consequence to these amiable dolts."

"And have you any clue as to the whereabouts of the jewels?"

"A fairly good one," he answered. "So good, in fact, that I can at this present moment lay my hands upon them. It is a very simple case, one of the simplest I have ever had to deal with, and yet in its way a strange one, presenting several difficulties to the average observer. The motive of the robbery is a little puzzling. The thief appears to have been actuated not by the ordinary greed of gain so much as by an intense love of self-advertisement."

"I can hardly imagine," I said with some surprise, "a burglar, *qua* burglar, wishing to advertise his exploits to the world."

"True, Goswell. You show your usual common sense. But you have not the imagination, without which a detective can do nothing. Your position is that of those energetic, if somewhat beef-witted enthusiasts, the police. They are frankly puzzled by the whole affair. To me, personally, the case is as clear as daylight."

"That I can understand," I murmured with a reverent pat of his shin.

"The actual thief," he continued, "for various reasons I am unwilling to produce. But upon the jewels, as I said just now, I can lay my hand at any moment. Look here!"

He disentangled himself from my embrace, and walked to a patent safe in a corner of the room. From this he extracted a large jewel case, and, opening it, disclosed a set of the most superb diamonds. In the midst a magnificent necklace winked and flashed in the wintry sunlight. The sight took my breath away, and for a time I groveled in speechless admiration before him.

"But—but how"—I stammered at last, and stopped, for he was regarding my confusion with evident amusement.

"*I* stole them," said Warlock Bones.

The Adventure of the Ascot Tie

ROBERT L. FISH

ROBERT LLOYD FISH (1912–1981) was a successful civil engineer working in Brazil when he faced a dull day with no immediate obligations. An aficionado of Sherlock Holmes, he decided to fill the empty hours by writing a parody of the great detective for his own amusement, never before having written anything of a creative nature.

He had one scene in mind when he began to write, of the frequently recorded moment when Holmes makes a series of deductions about a client that invariably stupefies Watson, as well as the client, for its inspired brilliance. In Fish's parody, Schlock Homes is entirely wrong and, when corrected on his absurd statements, retorts, "Ah, yes. Well, it was certain to have been one or the other."

"The Adventure of the Ascot Tie" immediately sold to *Ellery Queen's Mystery Magazine*, marking the beginning of a career that led to more than thirty novels, two Edgar Awards (for *The Fugitive*, the best first novel of 1961, and for "The Moonlight Gardener," the best short story of 1970), a position as president of the Mystery Writers of America, and the legacy of the Robert L. Fish Memorial Award, sponsored by the author's estate, which has been awarded annually since 1984 by MWA for the best first short story by an American author.

In addition to Schlock Homes, Fish's best-known characters are José da Silva, a police detective in Rio de Janeiro, and Kek Huuygens, a brilliant smuggler. *Kek Huuygens, Smuggler* (1976) was the first book ever published by the Mysterious Press. Fish also wrote under the pseudonym Robert L. Pike, under which name he produced *Mute Witness* (1963), the novel that was the basis for the popular motion picture *Bullitt* (1968). It starred Steve McQueen, Robert Vaughn, and Jacqueline Bisset, and remains memorable for the thrilling car chase scene through the streets of San Francisco; the film won an Edgar Award.

"The Adventure of the Ascot Tie" was first published in the February 1960 issue of *Ellery Queen's Mystery Magazine*; it was first collected in *The Incredible Schlock Homes* (New York, Simon & Schuster, 1966).

THE ADVENTURE OF THE ASCOT TIE

Robert L. Fish

IN GOING OVER my notes for the year '59, I find many cases in which the particular talents of my friend Mr. Schlock Homes either sharply reduced the labours of Scotland Yard or eliminated the necessity of their efforts altogether. There was, for example, the case of the Dissembling Musician who, before Homes brought him to justice, managed to take apart half of the instruments of the London Symphony Orchestra and cleverly hide them in various postal boxes throughout the city where they remained undiscovered until the dénouement of the case. Another example that comes readily to mind is the famous Mayfair Trunk Murder, which Homes laid at the door of Mr. Claude Mayfair, the zookeeper who had goaded one of his elephants into strangling a rival for Mrs. Mayfair's affection. And, of course, there was the well-publicized matter involving Miss Millicent Only, to whom Homes refers, even to this day, as the "Only Woman." But of all the cases which I find noted for this particular year, none demonstrates the devious nature of my friend's analytical reasoning powers so much as the case I find I have listed under the heading of *The Adventure of the Ascot Tie.*

It was a rather warm morning in the month of June in '59 when I appeared for breakfast in the dining room of our quarters at 221B Bagel Street. Mr. Schlock Homes had finished his meal and was fingering a telegram which he handed me as I seated myself at the table.

"Our ennui is about to end, Watney," said he, his excitement at the thought of a new case breaking through the normal calm of his voice.

"I am very happy to hear that, Homes," I replied in all sincerity, for the truth was I had begun to dread the long stretches of inactivity that often led my friend to needle both himself and me. Taking the proffered telegram from his outstretched hand, I read it carefully. "The lady seems terribly upset," I remarked, watching Homes all the while for his reaction.

"You noticed that also, Watney?" said Homes, smiling faintly.

"But, of course," I replied. "Her message reads, 'Dear Mr. Homes, I urgently request an audience with you this morning at 9 o'clock. I am terribly upset.' And it is signed Miss E. Wimpole."

He took the telegram from me and studied it with great care. "Typed on a standard post-office form," he said thoughtfully, "by a standard post-office typewriter. In all probability by a post-office employee. Extremely interesting. However, I fear there is little more to be learned until our client presents herself."

At that moment a loud noise in the street below our open window claimed my attention, and as I glanced out I cried in great alarm, "Homes! It's a trap!"

"Rather a four-wheeler I should have judged," replied Homes languidly. "These various vehicles are readily identified by the tonal pitch of the hub-squeal. A trap, for example, is normally pitched in the key of F; a four-wheeler usually in B-flat. A hansom, of course, is always in G. However, I fear we must rest this discussion, for here, if I am not mistaken, is our client."

At that moment the page ushered into our rooms a young lady of normal beauty and of about twenty-five years of age. She was carefully dressed in the fashion of the day, and appeared quite distraught.

"Well, Miss Wimpole," said Homes, after she had been comfortably seated and had politely refused a kipper, "I am anxious to hear your story. Other than the fact that you are an addict of sidesaddle riding; have recently written a love letter; and stopped on your way here to visit a coal mine, I am afraid that I know little of your problem."

Miss Wimpole took this information with mouth agape. Even I, who am more or less familiar with his methods, was astonished.

"Really, Homes," I exclaimed. "This is too much! Pray explain."

"Quite simple, Watney," he replied, smiling. "There is a shiny spot on the outside of Miss Wimpole's skirt a bit over the exterior central part of the thigh, which is in the shape of a cut of pie with curved sides. This is the exact shape of the new type African saddle horn which is now so popular among enthusiasts of equestrianism. The third finger of her right hand has a stain of strawberry-coloured ink which is certainly not the type one would use for business or formal correspondence. And lastly, there is a smudge beneath her left eye which could only be coal dust. Since this is the month of June, we can eliminate the handling of coal for such seasonal purposes as storage or heating, and must therefore deduce her visit to a place where coal would reasonably be in evidence the year around—namely, a coal mine."

Miss Wimpole appeared quite confused by this exchange. "I was forced to leave the house in quite a hurry," she explained apologetically, "and I am afraid that I was not properly careful in applying my mascara. As for the jam on my finger, it is indeed strawberry," and she quickly licked it clean before we could remonstrate with her manners. She then contemplated her skirt ruefully. "These new maids," she said sadly, with a shake of her head. "They are so absentminded! The one we now have continues to leave the flatiron connected when she goes to answer the door!"

"Ah, yes," said Homes, after a moment of introspection. "Well; it was certain to have been one or the other. And now, young lady, if you should care to reveal to us the nature of your problem?" He noticed her glance in my direction and added reassuringly, "You may speak quite freely in Dr. Watney's presence. He is quite hard of hearing."

"Well, then, Mr. Homes," said she, leaning forward anxiously, "as you undoubtedly deduced from my telegram, my name is Elizabeth Wimpole, and I live with my uncle Jno. Wimpole in a small flat in Barrett Street. My uncle is an itinerant Egyptologist by trade, and for some time we have managed a fairly comfortable living through the itineraries he has supplied to people contemplating visits to Egypt. However, since the recent troubles there, his business has been very slow, and as a result he has become extremely moody, keeping to his own company during the day, and consorting with a very rough-looking group at the local in the evening.

"In order to understand the complete change in the man, it is necessary to understand the type of life we enjoyed when itinerant Egyptologists were in greater demand. Our home, while always modest, nonetheless was the meeting place for the intelligentsia. No less than three curators, an odd politician or two, and several writers on serious subjects counted themselves as friends of my uncle; and the head mummy-unwrapper at the British Museum often dropped by for tea and a friendly chat on common subjects.

"Today this has all changed. The type of person with whom my uncle is now consorting is extremely crude both in appearance and language, and while I hesitate to make accusations which may be solely based upon my imagination, I fear that several of these ruffians have even been considering making advances against my person, which I am certain my uncle would never have countenanced at an earlier day.

"While this situation has naturally worried

me a bit, I should have passed it off without too much thought, except that yesterday a rather odd thing occurred. In the course of casually arranging my uncle's room, I chanced upon a telegram in a sealed envelope sewn to the inner surface of one of his shirts in a locked drawer. The nature of the message was so puzzling that I felt I needed outside assistance, and therefore made bold to call upon you." With this, she handed Homes a telegram form which she had drawn from her purse during her discourse.

Homes laid it upon the table and I stood over his shoulder as we both studied it. It read as follows: "WIMPY—WE HEIST THE ORIENTAL ICE SATURDAY. AMECHE OTHERS. HARDWARE NEEDLESS—THE FIX IS IN. WE RIG THE SPLIT FOR TUESDAY. JOE."

A curious change had come over Homes's face as he read this cryptic message. Without a word he turned to a shelf at his side and selected a heavy book bound in calfskin. Opening it, he silently studied several headings in the index and then, closing it, spoke quietly to our visitor.

"I wish to thank you for having brought me what promises to be a most interesting problem," he said, tilting his head forward politely. "I shall devote my entire time to the solution. However, I fear there is little I can tell you without further cogitation. If you will be so kind as to leave your address with Dr. Watney here, I am sure that we shall soon be in touch with you with good news."

When the young woman had been shown out, Homes turned to me in great excitement. "An extremely ingenious code, Watney," he chuckled, rubbing his hands together in glee. "As you know, I have written some sixteen monographs on cryptography, covering all phases of hidden and secret writings, from the Rosetta stone to my latest on the interpretation of instructions for assembling Yule toys. I believe I can honestly state, without false modesty, that there are few in the world who could hope to baffle me with a cipher or code. I shall be very much surprised, therefore, if I do not quickly arrive at the solution to this one. The difficulty, of course, lies in

the fact that there are very few words employed, but as you know the only problems which interest me are the difficult ones. I fear this is going to be a five-pipe problem, so if you do not mind, Watney, handing down my smoking equipment before you leave, I shall get right to it!"

I reached behind me and furnished to him the set of five saffron pipes which had been the gift of a famous tobacconist to whom Homes had been of service: a case which I have already related in *The Adventure of the Five Orange Pipes*. By the time I left the room to get my medical bag he had already filled one and was sending clouds of smoke ceilingward, as he hunched over the telegram in fierce concentration.

I had a very busy day, and did not return to our rooms until late afternoon. Homes was pacing up and down the room in satisfaction. The five pipes were still smoking in various ashtrays about the room, but the frown of concentration had been replaced by the peaceful look Homes invariably employed when he saw daylight in a particularly complex problem.

"You have solved the code," I remarked, setting my bag upon the sideboard.

"You are getting to be quite a detective yourself, Watney," replied Schlock Homes with a smile. "Yes. It was devilishly clever, but in the end I solved it as I felt sure I would."

"I was never in doubt, Homes," I said warmly.

"Watney, you are good for me," answered my friend, clasping my hand gratefully. "Well, the solution is here. You will note the message carefully. It says: 'WIMPY—WE HEIST THE ORIENTAL ICE SATURDAY. AMECHE OTHERS. HARDWARE NEEDLESS—THE FIX IS IN. WE RIG THE SPLIT FOR TUESDAY. JOE.' Now, disregarding the punctuation that separates this gibberish, I applied the various mathematical formulae which are standard in codifying, as well as several which have not been known to be in use for many years, but all to no avail.

"For some hours I confess to having been completely baffled. I even tested the telegram form for hidden writing, applying benzedrine hypochloric colloid solution to both surfaces, but other than an old shopping list which some post-office clerk had apparently written and then erased, there was nothing to be discovered.

"It was then that I recalled that Mr. Jno. Wimpole was acquainted with a mummy-unwrapper, and the possibility occurred to me that in the course of their many conversations, it was possible that the secret of ancient Egyptian secret writing had entered their discussions. Beginning again on this basis, I applied the system originally developed by Tutankhamen for the marking of palace laundry, and at once the thing began to make sense. Here, Watney; look at this!"

Bending over triumphantly he underlined the letter *W* in the word *Wimpy*, and then proceeded to underline the first letter of each alternate word, glancing at my startled face in satisfaction as he did so. The message now read: WHOS ON FIRST.

"Remarkable, Homes," I said dubiously; "but if you will forgive me, I find I am as much in the dark as before."

"Ah, Watney," said my friend, now laughing aloud. "When I first read this message, I also found myself baffled. But that was some hours ago, and I have not spent this time idly. I am now in possession of the major outline of the plot, and while it does not involve any serious crime, still it has been quite ingenious and clever. But there is nothing more to be done tonight. Pray send a telegram to our client advising her that we shall stop by and pick her up in a cab tomorrow morning at ten, and that we shall then proceed to the locale where the entire mystery shall be resolved."

"But, Homes!" I protested. "I do not understand this thing at all!"

"You shall, Watney; the first thing tomorrow," said Homes, still smiling broadly. "But no more for tonight. The Wreckers are at Albert Hall, I believe, and we just have time to change and get there if we are to enjoy the performance."

. . .

The following morning at ten o'clock sharp our hansom pulled up before a small building of flats in Barrett Street, and Miss Wimpole joined us. Both the young lady and myself looked askance at Homes, but he leaned forward imperturbably and said to the driver, "Ascot Park, if you please, cabby," and then leaned back smiling.

"Ascot Park?" I asked in astonishment. "The solution to our problem lies at a racing meet?"

"It does indeed, Watney," said Homes, obviously enjoying my mystification. Then he clapped me on the shoulder and said, "Pray forgive my very poor sense of humour, Watney; and you also, Miss Wimpole. I have practically solved the problem, and the solution does indeed lie at Ascot Park. Watney here knows how I love to mystify, but I shall satisfy your curiosity at once."

He leaned forward in thought, selecting his words. "When I first decoded the message and found myself with another message almost as curious as the first, namely, WHOS ON FIRST, I considered it quite carefully for some time. It could have been, of course, some reference to a person or commercial establishment named 'Whos' which was located on a First Avenue or Street. While I did not believe this to be true, it is in my nature to be thorough, and since New York is the only city to my knowledge with a First Avenue, I cabled my old friend Inspector LeStride, asking him to take steps. His reply in the negative eliminated this possibility, and I returned to my original thesis.

"Note carefully the last word, which is 'First.' This might, of course, have been an obscure reference to the Bible, in which it is promised that the last shall be first, but in perusing the original message I sensed no religious aura, and I am particularly sensitive to such emanations. No; instead I allowed myself to consider those cases in which it might be important to be first. I do not, of course, refer to queues or obstacles of that nature. The logical answer, naturally, is in wagering. The various means available to the

Englishman of today to place a wager are extremely proscribed, and after checking the team standings and finding Nottingham still firmly in the lead, I turned to the racing news.

"And there I found, as I had honestly expected to find, that in the second race at Ascot today, the entry of the Abbott-Castle stables is a three-year-old filly named *Who's On First*."

He turned to the young woman at his side. "My dear," said he, "I fear that your uncle is involved in a touting scheme and that the group with whom he has been meeting lately have been using the telegraph system to send advices regarding probable winners. This is, of course, frowned upon in most racing circles; but as I have so often stated, I am not of the official police, and therefore feel no responsibility for bringing people to their so-called justice over minor vices. I shall look forward, however, to the proof of my ratiocination at the track in a few moments."

"Oh, Mr. Schlock Homes," cried Miss Wimpole, clasping his hand in gratitude, "you have relieved my mind greatly. I have been so worried, especially since I have accidentally come across large sums of money hidden in obscure places in the house and feared that my uncle had become involved with some desperate characters engaged in nefarious practices. Now that I am cognizant of the nature of the enterprise, I can relax and may even replace at least a part of these sums with my conscience at rest, knowing that they were not gained through fearful means. But you must let me pay you for your efforts in this matter, Mr. Homes. Pray tell me what your fee is."

"No, Miss Wimpole," replied Homes with simple dignity. "If my theory is as good as I believe it to be, there shall be no question of payment. I shall take as payment the benefits of the information which you yourself were so kind as to bring to my attention."

Within a few minutes our hansom drew up at the ornate gate of the famous racing meet, and while Homes went to study the posted odds and speak with some of the bookmakers with whom he enjoyed acquaintance, I purchased the latest journal and retired to the stands to await his return. He was with me in a few moments, smiling broadly.

"It is even better than I had imagined, Watney!" said he. "The true genius of these people arouses my profoundest admiration. I note that in addition to *Who's On First* in the second race, this same Abbott-Castle stable has entered a horse named *What On Second* in the first race. And when I spoke to one of the track stewards just a moment ago, he informed me that because of rumours which have been flooding the steward's office—rumours apparently started by one of the hansom drivers at the gate—they propose to combine the two races. Now, at long last, the true nature of this ingenious plot finally emerges!"

"But what might that be, Homes?" I asked in bewilderment. "Can it be that the stewards are cognizant of the touting scheme and are using this means to combat it?"

"Your faith in track stewards is touching, Watney," said Homes dryly. "I am quite convinced that without the aid of one of their members, named Joseph, the entire scheme could not have been contemplated. No, no, Watney! The plan is far more intricate. These people know that if they go to a bookmaker with a bet on any one horse to win, the maximum odds which they can expect will be in the nature of five, or at most ten, to one. But think, Watney, think! Consider! What would the odds be against a *tie*?"

At once the devilish cleverness of the entire business burst upon my brain. "What do you propose to do, Homes?" I asked, searching his strong face for a clue.

"I have already done it, Watney," he replied calmly, and withdrew from his weskit five separate betting slips, each for the sum of £20, and each to be redeemed at the rate of 200 to 1 should the combined race end in a tie.

"Well, Watney," said Homes, when we were once again seated comfortably in our rooms in Bagel Street, "I can honestly state that to my mind this was one of my most successful cases—certainly from the financial standpoint. I feel that the ingenuity involved in codifying the betting information, while leaving out certain obvious factors, places our Mr. Wimpole and his associates in a special category of brilliance. We must be thankful that they have selected this relatively harmless means of breaching the law, and not something more nefarious. I certainly do not begrudge him his gains, although I must say that in seeing through their clever scheme, I feel quite justified in keeping mine."

Homes lit his pipe, and when it was pulling to his satisfaction, spoke again. "And now, Watney, we must search for another case to ward off boredom. Is there any crime news in that journal you are perusing which might prove to be of interest to us?"

"Only this," I said, folding the sheet in half and handing it to Homes with the indicated article on top. "Some three million pounds' worth of diamonds were stolen last night from the home of the Japanese ambassador. They were known as the Ogima Diamonds, and were considered the most valuable collection of their type in the world. The article states that the police believe it to be the work of a gang, but that otherwise they find themselves without a clue."

"Ah, really?" murmured Homes, his nostrils distended in a manner I had long since come to recognize as indicating intense interest. "May I see the article, Watney? Ah, yes! Ogima . . . Ogima . . . There is something faintly familiar . . ." He reached behind himself to the shelf where the reference books were kept and, drawing one out, opened it to the letter *O*.

"Ogima in basic Swahili means pencil-sharpener," he said, half to himself, "while the same word in ancient Mandarin referred to the type of pick used with the one-string guitar. No; I doubt if this is of much help. It would be far too subtle."

He returned the reference book to the shelf, and studied the article once again. Suddenly his faced cleared, and he leaned forward excitedly.

"Of course! You will note, Watney, that *Ogima* spelled backwards becomes *Amigo*. I shall be very much surprised if the answer to this problem does not lie somewhere south of the border. Your timetable, Watney, if you please."

CONTEMPORARY

VICTORIANS

A Case of Mis-Identity

COLIN DEXTER

THE CREATOR OF the irascible but beloved Inspector Morse, Norman Colin Dexter (1930–) shares many qualities with his detective (though not the irascibility). They both love English literature, cask ale, the music of Richard Wagner, and extremely difficult crossword puzzles. In November 2008, Dexter was featured on a BBC broadcast, *How to Solve a Cryptic Crossword*, where he spoke about Morse's dexterity with crossword clues.

The first novel featuring Morse was *Last Bus to Woodstock* (1975), and he was the central character in all of Dexter's thirteen novels and six of the stories in *Morse's Greatest Mystery* (1993). Already widely read, the series about the Oxford police detective achieved even greater success when it was televised over thirty-three episodes of the TV series *Inspector Morse*, produced between 1987 and 2000. Much like Alfred Hitchcock, with his brief moments in front of the camera in the films he directed, Dexter enjoyed making a cameo appearance in almost all episodes. A lesser character from the Morse series, Sergeant (now Inspector) Lewis, became the star of a television series, *Lewis*; Dexter has cameos on this series as well.

The (British) Crime Writers' Association has honored two of his novels—*The Wench Is Dead* (1989) and *The Way Through the Woods* (1992)—with Gold Daggers, and awarded him the Cartier Diamond Dagger for lifetime achievement in 1997. In the tradition of other distinguished British mystery writers like Dorothy L. Sayers, Nicholas Blake, Edmund Crispin, and Michael Innes, Dexter's mysteries combine scholarly erudition, well-constructed plots, and humor.

"A Case of Mis-Identity" was originally published in *Winter's Crimes*, edited by Hilary Hale (London, Macmillan, 1989); it was collected in *Morse's Greatest Mystery* (London, Macmillan, 1993).

A CASE OF MIS-IDENTITY

Colin Dexter

LONG AS HAD been my acquaintance with Sherlock Holmes, I had seldom heard him refer to his early life; and the only knowledge I ever gleaned of his family history sprang from the rare visits of his famous brother, Mycroft. On such occasions, our visitor invariably addressed me with courtesy, but also (let me be honest!) with some little condescension. He was—this much I knew—by some seven years the senior in age to my great friend, and was a founder member of the Diogenes Club, that peculiar institution whose members are ever forbidden to converse with one another. Physically, Mycroft was stouter than his brother (I put the matter in as kindly a manner as possible); but the single most striking feature about him was the piercing intelligence of his eyes—greyish eyes which appeared to see beyond the range of normal mortals. Holmes himself had commented upon this last point: "My dear Watson, you have recorded—and I am flattered by it—something of my own powers of observation and deduction. Know, however, that Mycroft has a degree of observation somewhat the equal of my own; and as for deduction, he has a brain that is unrivalled—*virtually* unrivalled—in the northern hemisphere. You may be relieved, however, to learn that he is a trifle lazy, and quite decidedly somnolent—and that his executant ability on the violin is immeasurably inferior to my own."

(Was there, I occasionally wondered, just the hint of competitive envy between those two unprecedented intellects?)

I had just called at 221B Baker Street on a fog-laden November afternoon in 188–, after taking part in some research at St. Thomas's Hospital into suppurative tonsilitis (I had earlier acquainted Holmes with the particulars). Mycroft was staying with Holmes for a few days, and as I entered that well-known sitting room I caught the tail-end of the brothers' conversation.

"Possibly, Sherlock—possibly. But it is the *detail*, is it not? Give me all the evidence and it is just possible that I could match your own analyses from my corner armchair. But to be required to rush hither and thither, to find and examine witnesses, to lie along the carpet with a lens held firmly to my failing sight . . . No! It is not my *métier*!"

During this time Holmes himself had been standing before the window, gazing down into the neutral-tinted London street. And looking over his shoulder, I could see that on the pavement opposite there stood an attractive young woman draped in a heavy fur coat. She had clearly just arrived, and every few seconds was looking up to Holmes's window in hesitant fashion, her fingers fidgeting with the buttons of her gloves. On a sudden she crossed the street, and Mrs. Hudson was soon ushering in our latest client.

After handing her coat to Holmes, the young lady sat nervously on the edge of the nearest armchair, and announced herself as Miss Charlotte van Allen. Mycroft nodded briefly at the newcomer, before reverting to a monograph on polyphonic plainchant; whilst Holmes himself made observation of the lady in that abstracted yet intense manner which was wholly peculiar to him.

"Do you not find," began Holmes, "that with your short sight it is a little difficult to engage in so much type-writing?"

Surprise, apprehension, appreciation, showed by turns upon her face, succeeded in all by a winsome smile as she appeared to acknowledge Holmes's quite extraordinary powers.

"Perhaps you will also tell me," continued he, "why it is that you came from home in such a great hurry?"

For a few seconds, Miss van Allen sat shaking her head with incredulity; then, as Holmes sat staring towards the ceiling, she began her remarkable narrative.

"Yes, I did bang out of the house, because it made me very angry to see the way my father, Mr. Wyndham, took the whole business—refusing even to countenance the idea of going to the police, and quite certainly ruling out any recourse to yourself, Mr. Holmes! He just kept repeating—and I *do* see his point—that no real harm has been done . . . although he can have no idea of the misery I have had to endure."

"Your father?" queried Holmes quietly. "Perhaps you refer to your step-father, since the names are different?"

"Yes," she confessed, "my step-father. I don't know why I keep referring to him as 'father'—especially since he is but five years older than myself."

"Your mother—she is still living?"

"Oh, yes! Though I will not pretend I was over-pleased when she remarried so soon after my father's death—and then to a man almost seventeen years younger than herself. Father—my real father, that is—had a plumbing business in the Tottenham Court Road, and Mother carried on the company after he died, until she married Mr. Wyndham. I think he considered such things a little beneath his new wife, especially with his being in a rather superior position as a traveller in French wines. Whatever the case, though, he made Mother sell out."

"Did you yourself derive any income from the sale of your father's business?"

"No. But I do have £100 annual income in my own right; as well as the extra I make from my typing. If I may say so, Mr. Holmes, you might be surprised how many of the local businesses—including *Cook and Marchant*—ask me to work for them a few hours each week. You see" (she looked at us with a shy, endearing diffidence) "I'm quite good at *that* in life, if nothing else."

"You must then have some profitable government stock—?" began Holmes.

She smiled again: "New Zealand, at four and a half per cent."

"Please forgive me, Miss van Allen, but could not a single lady get by very nicely these days on—let us say, fifty pounds per annum?"

"Oh, certainly! And I myself live comfortably on but ten shillings per week, which is only half of that amount. You see, I never touch a single penny of my inheritance. Since I live at home, I cannot bear the thought of being a burden to my parents, and we have reached an arrangement whereby Mr. Wyndham himself is empowered to draw my interest each quarter for as long as I remain in that household."

Holmes nodded. "Why have you come to see me?" he asked bluntly.

A flush stole over Miss van Allen's face and she plucked nervously at a small handkerchief drawn from her bag as she stated her errand with earnest simplicity. "I would give everything I have to know what has become of Mr. Horatio Darvill. There! Now you have it."

"Please, could you perhaps begin at the beginning?" encouraged Holmes gently.

"Whilst my father was alive, sir, we always received tickets for the gas-fitters' ball. And after he died, the tickets were sent to my mother. But neither Mother nor I ever thought of going, because it was made plain to us that Mr. Wyndham did not approve. He believed that the class of folk invited to such gatherings was inferior; and furthermore he asserted that neither of us—without considerable extra expenditure—

had anything fit to wear. But believe me, Mr. Holmes, I myself had the purple plush that I had never so much as taken from the drawer!"

It was after a decent interval that Holmes observed quietly: "But you *did* go to the ball?"

"Yes. In the finish, we both went—Mother and I—when my step-father had been called away to France."

"And it was there that you met Mr. Horatio Darvill?"

"Yes! And—do you know?—he called the very next morning. And several times after that, whilst my step-father was in France, we walked out together."

"Mr. Wyndham must have been annoyed once he learned what had occurred?"

Miss van Allen hung her pretty head. "Most annoyed, I'm afraid, for it became immediately clear that he did not approve of Mr. Darvill."

"Why do you think that was so?"

"I am fairly sure he thought Mr. Darvill was interested only in my inheritance."

"Did Mr. Darvill not attempt to keep seeing you—in spite of these difficulties?"

"Oh yes! I thought, though, it would be wiser for us to stop seeing each other for a while. But he did write—every single day. And always, in the mornings, I used to receive the letters myself so that no one else should know."

"Were you engaged to this gentleman?"

"Yes! For there was no problem about his supporting me. He was a cashier in a firm in Leadenhall Street——"

"Ah! Which office was that?" I interposed, for that particular area is known to me well, and I hoped that I might perhaps be of some assistance in the current investigation. Yet the look on Holmes's face was one of some annoyance, and I sank further into my chair as the interview progressed.

"I never did know exactly which firm it was," admitted Miss van Allen.

"But where did he live?" persisted Holmes.

"He told me that he usually slept in a flat on the firm's premises."

"You must yourself have written to this man, to whom you had agreed to become engaged?"

She nodded. "To the Leadenhall Street Post Office, where I left my letters *poste restante*. Horatio—Mr. Darvill—said that if I wrote to him at his work address, he'd never get to see my envelopes first, and the young clerks there would be sure to tease him about things."

It was at this point that I was suddenly conscious of certain stertorous noises from Mycroft's corner—a wholly reprehensible lapse into poor manners, as it appeared to me.

"What else can you tell me about Mr. Darvill?" asked Holmes quickly.

"He was very shy. He always preferred to walk out with me in the evening than in the daylight. 'Retiring,' perhaps, is the best word to describe him—even his voice. He'd had the quinsy as a young man, and was still having treatment for it. But the disability had left him with a weak larynx, and a sort of whispering fashion of speaking. His eyesight, too, was rather feeble—just as mine is—and he always wore tinted spectacles to protect his eyes against the glare of any bright light."

Holmes nodded his understanding; and I began to sense a note of suppressed excitement in his voice.

"What next?"

"He called at the house the very evening on which Mr. Wyndham next departed for France, and he proposed that we should marry before my step-father returned. He was convinced that this would be our only chance; and he was so dreadfully in earnest that he made me swear, with my hand upon both Testaments, that whatever happened I would always be true and faithful to him."

"Your mother was aware of what was taking place?"

"Oh, *yes*! And she approved so much. In a strange way, she was even fonder of my fiancé than I was myself, and she agreed that our only chance was to arrange a secret marriage."

"The wedding was to be in church?"

"Last Friday, at St. Saviour's, near King's Cross; and we were to go on to a wedding breakfast afterwards at the St. Pancras Hotel. Horatio called a hansom for us, and put Mother and me into it before stepping himself into a four-wheeler which happened to be in the street. Mother and I got to St. Saviour's first—it was only a few minutes' distance away. But when the four-wheeler drove up and we waited for him to step out—he never did, Mr. Holmes! And when the cabman got down from the box and looked inside the carriage—*it was empty*."

"You have neither seen nor heard of Mr. Darvill since?"

"Nothing," she whispered.

"You had planned a honeymoon, I suppose?"

"We had planned," said Miss van Allen, biting her lip and scarce managing her reply, "a fortnight's stay at The Royal Gleneagles in Inverness, and we were to have caught the lunch-time express from King's Cross."

"It seems to me," said Holmes, with some feeling, "that you have been most shamefully treated, dear lady."

But Miss van Allen would hear nothing against her loved one, and protested spiritedly: "Oh, no, sir! He was far too good and kind to treat me so."

"Your own opinion, then," said Holmes, "is that some unforeseen accident or catastrophe has occurred?"

She nodded her agreement. "And I think he must have had some premonition that very morning of possible danger, because he begged me then, once again, to remain true to him—whatever happened."

"You have no idea what that danger may have been?"

"None."

"How did your mother take this sudden disappearance?"

"She was naturally awfully worried at first. But then she became more and more angry; and she made me promise never to speak to her of the matter again."

"And your step-father?"

"He seemed—it was strange, really—rather more sympathetic than Mother. At least he was willing to discuss it."

"And what was his opinion?"

"He agreed that some accident must have happened. As he said, Mr. Darvill could have no possible interest in bringing me to the very doors of St. Saviour's—and then in deserting me there. If he had borrowed money—or if some of my money had already been settled on him—then there might have been some reason behind such a cruel action. But he was absolutely independent about money, and he would never even look at a sixpence of mine if we went on a visit. Oh, Mr. Holmes! It is driving me half-mad to think of—" But the rest of the sentence was lost as the young lady sobbed quietly into her handkerchief.

When she had recovered her composure, Holmes rose from his chair, promising that he would consider the baffling facts she had put before him. "But if I could offer you one piece of advice," he added, as he held the lady's coat for her, "it is that you allow Mr. Horatio Darvill to vanish as completely from your memory as he vanished from his wedding-carriage."

"Then you think that I shall not see him again?"

"I fear not. But please leave things in my hands. Now! I wish you to send me a most accurate physical description of Mr. Darvill, as well as any of his letters which you feel you can spare."

"We can at least expedite things a little in those two respects," replied she in business-like fashion, "for I advertised for him in last Monday's *Chronicle*." And promptly reaching into her handbag, she produced a newspaper cutting which she gave to Holmes, together with some other sheets. "And here, too, are four of his letters which I happen to have with me. Will they be sufficient?"

Holmes looked quickly at the letters, and nodded. "You say you never had Mr. Darvill's address?"

"Never."

"Your step-father's place of business, please?"

"He travels for *Cook and Marchant*, the great Burgundy importers, of Fenchurch Street."

"Thank you."

. . .

After she had left Holmes sat brooding for several minutes, his fingertips still pressed together. "An interesting case," he observed finally. "Did you not find it so, Watson?"

"You appeared to read a good deal which was quite invisible to me," I confessed.

"Not invisible, Watson. Rather, let us say—unnoticed. And that in spite of my repeated attempts to impress upon you the importance of sleeves, of thumb-nails, of boot-laces, and the rest. Now, tell me, what did you immediately gather from the young woman's appearance? Describe it to me."

Conscious of Mycroft's presence, I sought to recall my closest impressions of our recent visitor.

"Well, she had, beneath her fur, a dress of rich brown, somewhat darker than the coffee colour, with a little black plush at the neck and at the sleeves—you mentioned sleeves, Holmes? Her gloves were dove-grey in colour, and were worn through at the right forefinger. Her black boots, I was not able, from where I sat, to observe in any detail, yet I would suggest that she takes either the size four and a half or five. She wore small pendant earrings, almost certainly of imitation gold, and the small handkerchief into which the poor lady sobbed so charmingly had a neat darn in the monogrammed corner. In general, she had the air of a reasonably well-to-do young woman who has not quite escaped from the slightly vulgar inheritance of a father who was—let us be honest about it, Holmes!—a plumber."

A snort from the chair beside which Holmes had so casually thrown Miss van Allen's fur coat served to remind us that the recumbent Mycroft had now reawakened, and that perhaps my own description had, in some respect, occasioned his disapproval. But he made no spoken comment, and soon resumed his former posture.

"'Pon my word, Watson," said Holmes, "you are coming along splendidly—is he not, Mycroft? It is true, of course, that your description misses almost everything of real importance. But the method! You have hit upon the *method*,

Watson. Let us take, for example, the plush you mention on the sleeves. Now, plush is a most wonderfully helpful material for showing traces; and the double line above the wrist, where the type-writist presses against the table, was beautifully defined. As for the short-sightedness, that was mere child's play. The dent-marks of a *pince-nez* at either side of the lady's nostrils—you did not observe it? Elementary, my dear Watson! And then the boots. You really *must* practise the art of being positioned where all the evidence is clearly visible. If you wish to observe nothing at all, like brother Mycroft, then you will seek out the furthest corner of a room where even the vaguest examination of the client will be obscured by the furniture, by a fur coat, by whatever. But reverting to the lady's boots, I observed that although they were very like each other in colour and style, they were in fact *odd* boots; the one on the right foot having a slightly decorated toe-cap, and the one on the left being of a comparatively plain design. Furthermore, the right one was fastened only at the three lower buttons out of the five; the left one only at the first, third, and fifth. Now the deduction we may reasonably draw from such evidence is that the young lady left home in an unconscionable hurry. You agree?"

"Amazing, Holmes!"

"As for the glove worn at the forefinger—"

"You would be better advised," suddenly interposed the deeper voice of Mycroft, "to concentrate upon the missing person!"

May it have been a flash of annoyance that showed itself in Holmes's eyes? If so, it was gone immediately. "You are quite right, Mycroft! Come now, Watson, read to us the paragraph from *The Chronicle*."

I held the printed slip to the light and began: "Missing on the 14th November 188–. A gentleman named Mr. Horatio Darvill: about 5' 8" in height; fairly firmly built; sallow complexion; black hair, just a little bald in the centre; bushy black side-whiskers and moustache; tinted spectacles; slight infirmity of speech. When last seen, was dressed in——"

"But I think," interrupted Holmes, "he may by now have changed his wedding vestments, Watson?"

"Oh, certainly, Holmes."

There being nothing, it seemed, of further value in the newspaper description, Holmes turned his attention to the letters, passing them to me after studying them himself with minute concentration.

"Well?" he asked.

Apart from the fact that the letters had been typed, I could find in them nothing of interest, and I laid them down on the coffee-table in front of the somnolent Mycroft.

"Well?" persisted Holmes.

"I assume you refer to the fact that the letters are type-written."

"Already you are neglecting your newly acquired knowledge of the *method*, Watson. Quite apart from the point you mention, there are three further points of immediate interest and importance. First, the letters are very short; second, apart from the vague 'Leadenhall Street' superscription, there is no precise address stated at any point; third, it is not only the body of the letter which has been typed, but the signature, too. Observe here, Watson—and here!—that neat little 'Horatio Darvill' typed at the bottom of each of our four exhibits. And it will not have escaped you, I think, how conclusive that last point might be?"

"Conclusive, Holmes? In what way?"

"My dear fellow, is it possible for you not to see how strongly it bears upon our present investigations?"

"*Homo circumbendibus*—that's what you are, Sherlock!" (It was Mycroft once more.) "Do you not appreciate that your client would prefer some positive action to any further proofs of your cerebral superiority?"

It is pleasing to report here that this attempt of Mycroft to provoke the most distinguished criminologist of the century proved largely ineffectual, and Holmes permitted himself a fraternal smile as his brother slowly bestirred his frame.

"You are right, Mycroft," he rejoined lightly. "And I shall immediately compose two letters: one to Messrs. *Cook and Marchant;* the other to Mr. Wyndham, asking that gentleman to meet us here at six o'clock tomorrow evening."

Already I was aware of the easy and confident demeanour with which Holmes was tackling the singular mystery which confronted us all. But for the moment my attention was diverted by a small but most curious incident.

"It is just as well, Sherlock," said Mycroft (who appeared now to be almost fully awakened), "that you do not propose to write three letters."

Seldom (let me admit it) have I seen my friend so perplexed: "A *third* letter?"

"Indeed. But such a letter could have no certain destination, since it apparently slipped your memory to ask the young lady her present address, and the letters she entrusted to you appear, as I survey them, to be lacking their outer envelopes."

Momentarily Holmes looked less than amused by this light-hearted intervention. "You are more observant today than I thought, Mycroft, for the evidence of eye and ear had led me to entertain the suspicion that you were sleeping soundly during my recent conversation with Miss van Allen. But as regards her address, you are right." And even as he spoke I noted the twinkle of mischievous intelligence in his eyes. "Yet it would not be too difficult perhaps to *deduce* the young lady's address, Mycroft? On such a foul day as this it is dangerous and ill-advised for a lady to travel the streets if she has a perfectly acceptable and comfortable alternative such as the Underground; and since it was precisely 3:14 p.m. when Miss van Allen first appeared beneath my window, I would hazard the guess that she had caught the Metropolitan-line train which passes through Baker Street at 3:12 p.m. on its journey to Hammersmith. We may consider two further clues, also. The lady's boots, ill-assorted as they were, bore little evidence of the mud and mire of our London streets; and we may infer from this that her own home is perhaps as adjacent to an Underground station as is our own. More significant, however, is the fact, as we all observed, that Miss van Allen wore a dress of linen—a fabric which, though it is long-lasting and pleasing to wear, is one which has the disadvantage of creasing most easily. Now the skirt of the dress had been most recently ironed, and the slight creases in it must have resulted from her journey—to see me. And—I put this forward as conjecture, Mycroft—probably no more than three or four stops on the Underground had been involved. If we remember, too, the 'few minutes' her wedding-carriage took from her home to St. Saviour's, I think, per-haps . . . perhaps . . ." Holmes drew a street-map towards him, and surveyed his chosen area with his magnification-glass.

"I shall plump," he said directly, "for Cow-cross Street myself—that shabbily genteel little thoroughfare which links Farringdon Road with St. John Street."

"Very impressive!" said Mycroft, anticipat-ing my own admiration. "And would you place her on the north, or the south side, of that thor-oughfare, Sherlock?"

But before Holmes could reply to this small pleasantry, Mrs. Hudson entered with a slip of paper which she handed to Holmes. "The young lady says she forgot to give you her address, sir, and she's written it down for you."

Holmes glanced quickly at the address and a glint of pride gleamed in his eyes. "The answer to your question, Mycroft, is the south side—for it is an even-numbered house, and if I remember correctly the numbering of houses in that part of London invariably begins at the east end of the street with the odd numbers on the right-hand side walking westwards."

"And the number is perhaps in the middle or late thirties?" suggested Mycroft. "Thirty-six, perhaps? Or more likely thirty-eight?"

Holmes himself handed over the paper to us and we read:

Miss Charlotte van Allen
38, Cowcross Street

I was daily accustomed to exhibitions of the most extraordinary deductive logic employed by Sherlock Holmes, but I had begun at this point to suspect, in his brother Mycroft, the existence of some quite paranormal mental processes. It was only some half an hour later, when Holmes himself had strolled out for tobacco, that My-croft, observing my continued astonishment, spoke quietly in my ear.

"If you keep your lips sealed, Dr. Watson, I will tell you a small secret—albeit a very simple one. The good lady's coat was thrown rather carelessly, as you noticed, over the back of a chair; and on the inside of the lining was sewn a tape with her name and address clearly printed on it. Alas, however, my eyes are now not so keen as they were in my youth, and sixes and eights, as you know, are readily susceptible of confu-sion."

I have never been accused, I trust, of undue levity, but I could not help laughing heartily at this coup on Mycroft's part, and I assured him that his brother should never hear the truth of it from me.

"Sherlock?" said Mycroft, raising his mighty eyebrows. "He saw through my little joke imme-diately."

It was not until past six o'clock the following evening that I returned to Baker Street after (it is not an irrelevant matter) a day of deep interest at St. Thomas's Hospital.

"Well, have you solved the mystery yet?" I asked, as I entered the sitting room.

Holmes I found curled up in his armchair, smoking his oily clay pipe, and discussing medi-eval madrigals with Mycroft.

"Yes, Watson, I believe——"

But hardly were the words from his mouth when we heard a heavy footfall in the passage and a sharp rap on the door.

"This will be the girl's step-father," said Holmes. "He has written to say he would be here at a quarter after six. Come in!"

The man who entered was a sturdy, middle-sized fellow, about thirty years of age, clean-shaven, sallow-skinned, with a pair of most penetrating eyes. He placed his shiny top-hat on the sideboard, and with an insinuating bow sidled down into the nearest chair.

"I am assuming," said Holmes, "that you are Mr. James Wyndham and" (holding up a type-written sheet) "that this is the letter you wrote to me?"

"I am that person, sir, and the letter is mine. It was against my expressed wish, as you may know, that Miss van Allen contacted you in this matter. But she is an excitable young lady, and my wife and I will be happy to forgive her for such an impulsive action. Yet I must ask you to have nothing more to do with what is, unfortunately, a not uncommon misfortune. It is clear what took place, and I think it highly unlikely, sir, that even you will find so much as a single trace of Mr. Darvill."

"On the contrary," replied Holmes quietly, "I have reason to believe that I have already discovered the whereabouts of that gentleman."

Mr. Wyndham gave a violent start, and dropped his gloves. "I am delighted to hear it," he said in a strained voice.

"It is a most curious fact," continued Holmes, "that a type-writer has just as much individuality as does handwriting. Even when completely new, no two machines are exactly alike; and as they get older, some characters wear on this side and some on that. Now in this letter of yours, Mr. Wyndham, you will note that in every instance there is some slight slurring in the eye of the 'e'; and a most easily detectable defect in the tail of the 't.' "

"All our office correspondence," interrupted our visitor, "is typed on the same machine, and I can fully understand why it has become a little worn."

"But I have four other letters here," resumed Holmes, in a slow and menacing tone, "which purport to come from Mr. Horatio Darvill. And in each of these, also, the 'e's are slurred, and the 't's un-tailed."

Mr. Wyndham was out of his chair instantly and had snatched up his hat: "I can waste no more of my valuable time with such trivialities, Mr. Holmes. If you can catch the man who so shamefully treated Miss van Allen, then catch him! I wish you well—and ask you to let me know the outcome. But I have no interest whatsoever in your fantastical notions."

Already, however, Holmes had stepped across the room and turned the key in the door. "Certainly I will tell you how I caught Mr. Darvill, if you will but resume your chair."

"What?" shouted Wyndham, his face white, his small eyes darting about him like those of a rat in a trap. Yet finally he sat down and glared aggressively around, as Holmes continued his analysis.

"It was as selfish and as heartless a trick as ever I encountered. The man married a woman much older than himself, largely for her money. In addition, he enjoyed the interest on the not inconsiderable sum of the step-daughter's money, for as long as that daughter lived with them. The loss of such extra monies would have made a significant difference to the life-style adopted by the newly married pair. Now the daughter herself was an amiable, warm-hearted girl, and was possessed of considerable physical attractions; and with the added advantage of a personal income, it became clear that under normal circumstances she would not remain single for very long. So he—the man of whom I speak—decided to deny her the company and friendship of her contemporaries by keeping her at home. But she—and who shall blame her?—grew restive under such an unnatural regimen, and firmly announced her intention to attend a local ball. So what did her step-father do? With the connivance of his wife, he conceived a cowardly plan. He disguised himself cleverly: he covered those sharp eyes with dully tinted spectacles; he masked that clean-shaven face with bushy side-whiskers; he sank that clear voice of his into the strained whisper of one suffering from the quinsy. And then, feeling himself doubly secure because of the young lady's short sight, he appeared *himself* at the ball, in the guise of one Horatio Darvill, and there he wooed the fair Miss van Allen for his own—thereafter taking further precaution of always arranging his assignations by candlelight."

(I heard a deep groan which at the time I assumed to have come from our visitor, but which, upon reflection, I am inclined to think originated from Mycroft's corner.)

"Miss van Allen had fallen for her new beau; and no suspicion of deception ever entered her pretty head. She was flattered by the attention she was receiving, and the effect was heightened by the admiration of her mother for the man. An 'engagement' was agreed, and the deception perpetuated. But the pretended journeys abroad were becoming more difficult to sustain, and things had to be brought to a head quickly, although in such a *dramatic* way as to leave a permanent impression upon the young girl's mind. Hence the vows of fidelity sworn on the Testaments; hence the dark hints repeated on the very morning of the proposed marriage that something sinister might be afoot. James Wyndham, you see, wished his step-daughter to be so morally bound to her fictitious suitor that for a decade, at least, she would sit and wilt in Cowcross Street, and continue paying her regular interest directly into the account of her guardian: the same blackguard of a guardian who had brought her to the doors of St. Saviour's and then, himself, conveniently disappeared by the age-old ruse of stepping in at one side of a four-wheeler—and out at the other."

Rising to his feet, Wyndham fought hard to control his outrage. "I wish you to know that it is you, sir, who is violating the law of this land—and not me! As long as you keep that door locked, and thereby hold me in this room against my will, you lay yourself open——"

"The law," interrupted Holmes, suddenly unlocking and throwing open the door, "may not for the moment be empowered to touch you. Yet never, surely, was there a man who deserved punishment more. In fact . . . since my hunting-crop is close at hand——" Holmes took two swift strides across the room; but it was too late. We heard a wild clatter of steps down the stairs as Wyndham departed, and then had the satisfaction of watching him flee pell-mell down Baker Street.

"That cold-blooded scoundrel will end on the gallows, mark my words!" growled Holmes.

"Even now, though, I cannot follow all the steps in your reasoning, Holmes," I remarked.

"It is this way," replied Holmes. "The only person who profited financially from the vanishing-trick was the step-father. Then, the fact that the two men, Wyndham and Darvill, were never actually seen *together*, was most suggestive. As were the tinted spectacles, the husky voice, the bushy whiskers—all of these latter, Watson, hinting strongly at disguise. Again, the type-written signature betokened one thing only—that the man's handwriting was so familiar to Miss van Allen that she might easily recognise even a small sample of it. Isolated facts? Yes! But all of them leading to the same inevitable conclusion—as even my slumbering sibling might agree?"

But there was no sound from the Mycroft corner.

"You were able to verify your conclusion?" I asked.

Holmes nodded briskly. "We know the firm for which Wyndham worked, and we had a full description of Darvill. I therefore eliminated from that description everything which could be the result of deliberate disguise——"

"Which means that you have *not* verified your conclusion!" Mycroft's sudden interjection caused us both to turn sharply towards him.

"There will always," rejoined Holmes, "be a need and a place for informed conjecture——"

"*Inspired* conjecture, Holmes," I interposed.

"Phooey!" snorted Mycroft. "You are talking of nothing but wild *guesswork*, Sherlock. And it is my opinion that in this case your guesswork is grotesquely askew."

I can only report that never have I seen Holmes so taken aback; and he sat in silence as Mycroft raised his bulk from the chair and now stood beside the fireplace.

"Your deductive logic needs no plaudits from me, Sherlock, and like Dr. Watson I admire your desperate hypothesis. But unless there is some firm evidence which you have thus far concealed from us . . . ?"

Holmes did not break his silence.

"Well," stated Mycroft, "I will indulge in a little guesswork of my own, and tell you that the gentleman who just stormed out of this room is as innocent as Watson here!"

"He certainly did not *act* like an innocent man," I protested, looking in vain to Holmes for some support, as Mycroft continued.

"The reasons you adduce for your suspicions are perfectly sound in most respects, and yet—I must speak with honesty, Sherlock!—I found myself sorely disappointed with your reading—or rather complete misreading—of the case. You are, I believe, wholly correct in your central thesis that there is no such person as Horatio Darvill." (How the blood was tingling in my veins as Mycroft spoke these words!) "But when the unfortunate Mr. Wyndham who has just rushed one way up Baker Street rushes back down it the other with a writ for defamation of character—as I fear he will!—then you will be compelled to think, to analyse, and to act, with a little more care and circumspection."

Holmes leaned forward, the sensitive nostrils of that aquiline nose a little distended. But still he made no comment.

"For example, Sherlock, two specific pieces of information vouchsafed to us by the attractive Miss van Allen herself have been strongly discounted, if not wholly ignored, in your analysis." (I noticed Holmes's eyebrows rising quizzically.) "First, the fact that Mr. Wyndham was older than Miss van Allen *only by some five years*. Second, the fact that Miss van Allen is so competent and speedy a performer on the type-writer that she works, on a free-lance basis, for several firms in the vicinity of her home, including Messrs. *Cook and Marchant*. Furthermore, you make the astonishing claim that Miss van Allen was totally deceived by the disguise of Mr. Darvill. Indeed, you would have her not only blind, but

semi-senile into the bargain! Now it is perfectly true that the lady's eyesight is far from perfect— *glaucopia Athenica*, would you not diagnose, Dr. Watson?—but it is quite ludicrous to believe that she would fail to recognise the person with whom she was living. And it is wholly dishonest of you to assert that the assignations were always held by candlelight, since on at least two occasions, the morning after the first meeting—the *morning*, Sherlock!—and the morning of the planned wedding ceremony, Miss van Allen had ample opportunity of studying the physical features of Darvill in the broadest of daylight."

"You seem to me to be taking an unconscionably long time in putting forward your own hypothesis," snapped Holmes, somewhat testily.

"You are right," admitted the other. "Let me beat about the bush no longer! You have never felt emotion akin to love for any woman, Sherlock—not even for the Adler woman—and you are therefore deprived of the advantages of those who like myself are able to understand both the workings of the male and also the female mind. Five years her superior in age—her step-father; *only five years*. Now one of the sadnesses of womankind is their tendency to age more quickly and less gracefully than men; and one of the truths about mankind in general is that if you put one of each sex, of roughly similar age, in reasonable proximity . . . And if one of them is the fair Miss van Allen—then you are inviting a packet of trouble. Yet such is what took place in the Wyndham ménage. Mrs. Wyndham was seventeen years older than her young husband; and perhaps as time went by some signs and tokens of this disproportionate difference in their ages began to manifest themselves. At the same time, it may be assumed that Wyndham himself could not help being attracted—however much at first he sought to resist the temptation—by the very winsome and vivacious young girl who was his step-daughter. It would almost certainly have been Wyndham himself who introduced Miss van Allen to the part-time duties she undertook for *Cook and Marchant*—where the two of them were frequently thrown together, away from the restraints of wife and home, and with a result which it is not at all difficult to guess. Certain it is, in my own view, that Wyndham sought to transfer his affections from the mother to the daughter; and in due course it was the daughter who decided that whatever her own affections might be in the matter she must in all honour leave her mother and step-father. Hence the great anxiety to get out to dances and parties and the like—activities which Wyndham objected to for the obvious reason that he wished to have Miss van Allen as close by himself for as long as he possibly could. Now you, Sherlock, assume that this objection arose as a result of the interest accruing from the New Zealand securities—and you are *guessing*, are you not? Is it not just possible that Wyndham has money of his own—find out, Brother!—and that what he craves for is not some petty addition to his wealth, but the love of a young woman with whom he has fallen rather hopelessly in love? You see, she took *him* in, just as she took *you* in, Sherlock—for you swallowed everything that calculating little soul reported."

"Really, this is outrageous!" I objected—but Holmes held up his hand, and bid me hear his brother out.

"What is clear, is that at some point when Wyndham was in France—and why did you not verify those dates spent abroad? I am sure *Cook and Marchant* would have provided them just as quickly as it furnished the wretched man's description—as I was saying, with Wyndham in France, mother and daughter found themselves in a little *tête-à-tête* one evening, during the course of which a whole basketful of dirty linen was laid bare, with the daughter bitterly disillusioned about the behaviour of her step-father, and the mother hurt and angry about her husband's infidelity. So, together, the pair of them devised a plan. Now, we both agree on one thing at least, Sherlock! There appears to be no evidence whatsoever for the independent existence of Horatio Darvill except for what we have heard from Miss van Allen's lips. Rightly, you drew our attention to the fact that the two men were never seen together. But, alas, having appreciated the

importance of that clue, you completely misconceived its *significance*. *You* decided that there is no Darvill—because he is Wyndham. *I* have to tell you that there is no Darvill—*because he is the pure fabrication of the minds of Mrs. Wyndham and her daughter.*"

Holmes was staring with some consternation at a pattern in the carpet, as Mycroft rounded off his extravagant and completely baseless conjectures.

"Letters were written—and incidentally I myself would have been far more cautious about those 'e's and 't's: twin faults, as it happens, of my very own machine! But, as I say, letters were written—*but by Miss van Allen herself;* a wedding was arranged; a story concocted of a non-existent carriage into which there climbed a non-existent groom—and that was the end of the charade. Now, it was you, Sherlock, who rightly asked the key question: *cui bono?* And you concluded that the real beneficiary was Wyndham. But exactly the contrary is the case! It was the mother and daughter who intended to be the beneficiaries, for they hoped to rid themselves of the rather wearisome Mr. Wyndham—but not before he had been compelled, by moral and social pressures, to make some handsome money-settlement upon the pair of them—especially perhaps upon the young girl who, as Dr. Watson here points out, could well have done with some decent earrings and a new handkerchief. And the *social* pressure I mention, Sherlock, was designed—carefully and cleverly designed—to come from *you.* A cock-and-bull story is told to you by some wide-eyed young thing, a story so bestrewn with clues at almost every point that even Lestrade—given a week or two!—would probably have come up with a diagnosis identical with your own. And why do you think she came to you, and not to Lestrade, say? Because 'Mr. Sherlock Holmes is the greatest investigator the world has ever known'—and his judgements are second only to the Almighty's in their infallibility. For if you, Sherlock, believed Wyndham to be guilty—then Wyndham *was* guilty in the eyes of the whole world—the whole world except for one, that is."

"Except for two," I added quietly.

Mycroft Holmes turned his full attention towards me for the first time, as though I had virtually been excluded from his previous audience. But I allowed him no opportunity of seeking the meaning of my words, as I addressed him forthwith.

"I asked Holmes a question when he presented his own analysis, sir. I will ask you the same: have you in any way verified your hypothesis? And if so, how?"

"The answer, Dr. Watson, to the first part of your question is, in large measure, 'yes.' Mr. Wyndham, in fact, has quite enough money to be in no way embarrassed by the withdrawal of Miss van Allen's comparatively minor contribution. As for the second part . . ." Mycroft hesitated awhile. "I am not sure what my brother has told you, of the various offices I hold under the British Crown——"

It was Holmes who intervened—and impatiently so. "Yes, yes, Mycroft! Let us all concede immediately that the, shall we say, 'unofficial' sources to which you are privy have completely invalidated my own reconstruction of the case. So be it! Yet I would wish, if you allow, to make one or two observations upon your own rather faithful interpretation of events? It is, of course, with full justice that you accuse me of having no first-hand knowledge of what are called 'the matters of the heart.' Furthermore, you rightly draw attention to the difficulties Mr. Wyndham would have experienced in deceiving his stepdaughter. Yet how you under-rate the power of disguise! And how, incidentally, you *over*-rate the intelligence of Lestrade! Even Dr. Watson, I would suggest, has a brain considerably superior——"

For not a second longer could I restrain myself. "Gentlemen!" I cried, "you are both—*both* of you!—most tragically wrong."

The two brothers stared at me as though I had taken leave of my senses.

"I think you should seek to explain yourself, Watson," said Holmes sharply.

"A man," I began, "was proposing to go to Scotland for a fortnight with his newly married wife, and he had drawn out one hundred pounds in cash—no less!—from the Oxford Street branch of the Royal National Bank on the eve of his wedding. The man, however, was abducted after entering a four-wheeler on the very morning of his wedding-day, was brutally assaulted, and then robbed of all his money and personal effects—thereafter being dumped, virtually for dead, in a deserted alley in Stepney. Quite by chance he was discovered later that same evening, and taken to the Whitechapel Hospital. But it was only after several days that the man slowly began to recover his senses, and some patches of his memory—and also, gentlemen, his *voice*. For, you see, it was partly because the man was suffering so badly from what we medical men term suppurative tonsilitis—the quinsy, as it is commonly known—that he was transferred to St. Thomas's where, as you know, Holmes, I am at present engaged in some research on that very subject, and where my own professional opinion was sought only this morning. Whilst reading through the man's hospital notes, I could see that the only clue to his identity was a tag on an item of his underclothing carrying the initials 'H.D.' You can imagine my excitement——"

"Humphry Davy, perhaps," muttered Mycroft flippantly.

"Oh no!" I replied, with a smile. "I persisted patiently with the poor man, and finally he was able to communicate to me the name of his bank. After that, if I may say so, Holmes, it was almost child's play to verify *my* hypothesis. I visited the bank, where I learned about the withdrawal of money for the honeymoon, and the manager himself accompanied me back to St. Thomas's where he was able to view the patient and to provide quite unequivocal proof as to his identity. I have to inform you, therefore, that not only does Mr. Horatio Darvill exist, gentlemen; he is at this precise moment lying in a private ward on the second floor of St. Thomas's Hospital!"

For some little while a silence fell upon the room. Then I saw Holmes, who these last few minutes had been standing by the window, give a little start: "Oh, no!" he groaned. And looking over his shoulder I saw, dimly beneath the fogbeshrouded lamplight, an animated Mr. Wyndham talking to a legal-looking gentleman who stood beside him.

Snatching up his cape, Holmes made hurriedly for the door. "Please tell Mr. Wyndham, if you will, Watson, that I have already written a letter to him containing a complete recantation of my earlier charges, and offering him my profound apologies. For the present, I am leaving—by the back door."

He was gone. And when, a minute later, Mrs. Hudson announced that two angry-looking gentlemen had called asking to see Mr. Holmes, I noticed Mycroft seemingly asleep once more in his corner armchair, a monograph on polyphonic plainchant open on his knee, and a smile of vague amusement on his large, intelligent face.

"Show the gentlemen in, please, Mrs. Hudson!" I said—in such peremptory fashion that for a moment or two that good lady stared at me, almost as if she had mistaken my voice for that of Sherlock Holmes himself.

The Startling Events in the Electrified City

THOMAS PERRY

THOMAS PERRY (1947–), noted for his sophisticated and humorous suspense novels, has written more than twenty books, including eight that feature Jane Whitefield and three that star the Butcher's Boy, who made his debut in *The Butcher's Boy* (1982), which won an Edgar Award for best first novel.

Jane Whitefield, Perry's most beloved character—the books in which she is featured were often bestsellers—is a powerful Seneca Indian whose great skill is helping people to disappear and create new identities as they escape violent situations. The first novel in the Whitefield saga, *Vanishing Act* (1995), was named one of the one hundred Favorite Mysteries of the Century by the Independent Mystery Booksellers Association.

The three novels about the Butcher's Boy feature a nameless (or, more accurately, pseudonymous) hit man who nonetheless garners the sympathy of readers for his own code of honor, which tends to pit him and his exceptional skills against villains and gangsters.

Perry has been praised by scores of top professional writers, including Stephen King, who wrote, "The fact is, there are probably only half a dozen suspense writers now alive who can be depended upon to deliver high-voltage shocks, vivid, sympathetic characters, and compelling narratives each time they publish. Thomas Perry is one of them."

Prior to becoming a full-time novelist, Perry was the writer and producer of numerous episodes of such TV series as *Simon & Simon*, *21 Jump Street*, and *Star Trek: The Next Generation*.

"The Startling Events in the Electrified City" was originally published in *A Study in Sherlock*, edited by Laurie R. King and Leslie S. Klinger (New York, Bantam Books, 2011).

THE STARTLING EVENTS IN THE ELECTRIFIED CITY

Thomas Perry

(A Manuscript Signed "John Watson," in the Collection of Thomas Perry)

DURING THE MANY years while I was privileged to know the consulting detective Sherlock Holmes and, I fancy, serve as his closest confidant, he often permitted me to make a record of the events in which we played some part, and have it printed in the periodicals of the day. It would be false modesty to deny that the publication of these cases, beginning in 1887, added something to his already wide reputation.

There were a number of cases presented to him by people responding to the new, larger reputation my amateurish scribbles brought upon him. There were others on which I accompanied him that I have never intended to submit for publication during my lifetime or his. The event in Buffalo is a bit of both. It is a case that came to him from across the Atlantic because his reputation had been carried past the borders of this kingdom between the covers of *The Strand Magazine*. And yet it is a case deserving of such discretion and secrecy that when I finish this narrative, I will place the manuscript in a locked box with several others that I do not intend to be seen by the public until time and mortality have cured them of their power to harm.

It was the twenty-fifth of August in 1901, the year of Queen Victoria's death. I was with Holmes that afternoon in the rooms that he and I had shared at 221B Baker Street since Holmes returned to London in 1894. I was glad I had closed my medical office early that day, because he seemed to be at a loss, in a bout of melancholy,

which I silently diagnosed as a result of inactivity. It was a day of unusually fine late summer weather after a week of dismal rainstorms, and at last I managed to get him to extinguish the tobacco in his pipe and agree to stroll with me and take the air. We had already picked up our hats and canes from the rack and begun to descend the stairs, when there came a loud ringing of the bell.

Holmes called out, "Hold, Mrs. Hudson. I'm on sentry duty. I'll see who goes there." He rapidly descended the seventeen steps to the door and opened it. I heard a man say, "My name is Frederick Allen. Am I speaking to Mr. Holmes?"

"Come in, sir," said Holmes. "You have come a long way."

"Thank you," the man said, and followed Holmes up the stairs to Holmes's sitting room. He looked around and I could see his eyes taking in the studied disorder of Holmes's life. His eyes lingered particularly on the papers spread crazily on the desk, and the very important few papers that were pinned to the mantel by a dagger.

"This is my good friend, Dr. John Watson."

The stranger shook my hand heartily. "I've heard of you, Doctor, and read some of your writings."

"Pardon, Mr. Allen," Holmes said at this juncture. "But I wish to use this moment for an experiment. Watson, what would you say is our guest's profession?"

"I'd guess he was a military man," I said. "He has the physique and the bearing, the neatly trimmed hair and mustache. And I saw the way he looked at the manner in which you've arranged your rooms. He's a commissioned officer who has inspected quarters before."

"Excellent, my friend. Any further conjecture?"

"He's American, of course. Probably late of the conflict with Spain. American army, then, judging from his age and excellent manners, with a rank of captain or above."

Mr. Allen said, "Remarkable, Dr. Watson. You have missed in only one particular."

"Yes," said Holmes. "The branch of service. Mr. Allen is a naval officer. When I heard his accent, I too knew he was American, and said he'd come a long way, implying he'd just come off a transatlantic voyage. He didn't deny it. And we all know that the weather the past week has been positively vile. Yet he didn't think it worth a mention, because he's spent half his life at sea." He nodded to Allen. "I'm sorry to waste your time, sir. Watson and I play these games. What brings you to us, Captain Allen?"

"I'm afraid it's a matter of the utmost urgency and secrecy, gentlemen."

Holmes strolled to the window and looked down at the street. "I assure you that I have been engaged in matters of trust many times before. And Dr. Watson has been with me every step in most of these affairs. He is not only an accomplished Royal Medical Officer who has been through the Afghan campaigns, he is also a man of the utmost discretion."

"I believe you, Mr. Holmes. I have permission from the highest levels to include Dr. Watson in what I'm about to impart."

"Excellent."

"No doubt you know that in my country, in the city of Buffalo, New York, the Pan-American Exposition opened on the first of May. It's been a highly publicized affair."

"Yes, of course," Holmes said. "A celebration of the future, really, wouldn't you say? Calling the world together to witness the wonders of electricity."

"That's certainly one of the aspects that have made us most proud. It was hoped that President McKinley would visit in June, but he had to postpone because of Mrs. McKinley's ill health. At least that was the public story."

"If there's a public story, then there must be a private story," said Holmes.

"Yes. There were indications that there might be a plot on the president's life."

"Good heavens," I said.

"I know how shocking it must be to you. Your country is renowned for its stability. Not since Charles the First in 1649 has there been the violent death of a head of state, and when your late, beloved Queen Victoria's reign ended a few months ago, it had lasted nearly sixty-four years. In my country, during just the past forty years, as you know, there have been a civil war that killed six hundred thousand men, and two presidents assassinated."

"It's not a record that would instill complacency," I admitted, but Holmes seemed to be lost in thought.

He said, "Who is suspected of plotting to kill President McKinley?"

"I'm afraid that I've reached the limit of what I'm authorized to say on that topic at present," Captain Allen said.

I felt the same frustration I often have at official obfuscation in my own military experience, where a doctor is outside the chain of command. "If your business is a secret from Holmes, then how can you expect him to help you?"

"I spoke as freely as my orders allowed. My mission is to deliver a request that you two gentlemen come for a personal and private meeting with the President of the United States, who will tell you the rest." He reached into his coat and produced a thin folder. "I have purchased a pair of tickets on the SS *Deutschland* of the Hamburg Amerika line. The ship is less than a year old, a four-stack steamship capable of twenty-two knots that has already set a record crossing the Atlantic in just over five days."

"Very fast indeed," I conceded.

Holmes lit his pipe and puffed out a couple of times to produce curlicues of bluish smoke. "How did the President of the United States come to think of me, when he can have many capable men at his command within minutes?"

"President McKinley is an avid reader. I gather he's read of your accomplishments in *The Strand Magazine*."

I confess that when I heard those words, I found that my ears were hot and my collar suddenly seemed to have tightened around my neck. Vanity is a powerful drug, able to strengthen the heartbeat and circulation extraordinarily.

Holmes said, "I can answer *for* myself, because I only have to answer *to* myself. I shall be happy to meet with the president. When does the *Deutschland* weigh anchor?"

"High tide is tomorrow at nineteen hundred."

Holmes turned to me. "And you, Watson?" It was not the first time when I thought I detected in Holmes a slight resentment of my relationship with the lovely creature who was, within the year, to become my second wife. It seemed to me a tease, almost a challenge, an implication that I was no longer my own man and able to have adventures.

I did not take the bait and say something foolish in an attempt to save face. "I must speak with a dear friend of mine before I give you my word. But I'm almost certain I will join you."

Allen smiled and nodded. "I thank you both, gentlemen. I'll leave the tickets with you. Once again, I must bring up the uncomfortable issue of secrecy. I must adjure you both to absolute silence about the nature of your voyage."

"Of course," I said, since the request was clearly addressed to me. Holmes could never have been prevailed upon to reveal anything he didn't wish to. I, on the other hand, was about to go to Queen Anne Street to speak to a beautiful and loving woman, and get her to agree I should go to another continent without being able to tell her which one or why.

What was said during that night's discussions, and what inducements were offered to break my oath of silence I leave to the reader's own experience. I did present myself on the London docks at nineteen hundred the next evening with my steamer trunk packed. Holmes, upon seeing me arrive in a carriage, merely looked up and said, "Ah, Watson. Prompt as always."

We sailed on the tide. The steamship *Deutschland* was a marvel of modern design, but also of modern impatience. The powerful engines in the stern below decks could be heard and felt without difficulty anywhere on board at any hour of the twenty-four, despite the fact that the bow was more than six hundred feet from them. I had been accustomed after several tours in India to long voyages under sail. The old, graceful, and soothing push of wind, where the only sound is the creaking of boards and ropes as they stand up to the sea is disappearing rapidly. Even HMT *Orontes*, which brought me back to Portsmouth after my last tour of duty, had its three masts of sails supplemented by steam power below deck. Some day, no doubt, travel by sail will be a pleasure reserved for the leisured rich, the only ones who will be able to afford the time for it.

Our enormous steamship pushed on at full tilt, regardless of the weather. Holmes and I walked the deck and speculated on the true nature of our enigmatic invitation. Rather, I speculated, but Holmes maintained the irritating silence into which he often retreated when a case began. It was something between a boxer's silent meditation before a match—among Holmes's several skills was a mastery of the pugilist's art—and a scientist's cogitation on a natural phenomenon. Long before the ship steamed its way into New York harbor, I was grateful that its soulless speed would deliver me of the need to be with a man who neither spoke nor listened.

It was late afternoon when the crew tied the bow and stern to cleats, and stevedores hauled our steamer trunks from our cabin. We were on the main deck prepared to step down the gangplank to the new world. Captain Allen joined us, and he engaged a closed carriage to take us to a different dock. "Have either of you been to the United States before?" Allen asked.

"I have," Holmes said. "In 1879 I traveled here with a Shakespeare company as Hamlet. I hope to play a less tragic part on this visit."

When we arrived at the new jetty, we found that all the sailors there were in military uniform. They rapidly loaded our trunks aboard a much smaller craft, a Coast Guard vessel of some fifty feet in length, with a steam engine. Once we were aboard, the vessel was pushed from the dock, oriented itself due north, and began to move across the harbor. The air was hot and humid that afternoon, and I was grateful when the vessel began to lay on some speed. I came to understand from one of the crew that the purpose of the vessel was to outrun the craft of smugglers and other miscreants and bring them to a halt, so its speed was considerable. Before long we were out of the congested waters of the harbor and heading up the majestic Hudson River.

Much of the land along the river was wooded, but here and there on the shore we could see charming villages, most of them apparently supported by a combination of agriculture and light manufacturing. I could see growing fields of maize and other vegetables on the distant hillsides, but nearer the water were smokestacks and railroad tracks.

As I explored the Coast Guard cutter, I happened upon Allen and Holmes at the bow. "Excellent means of travel," Holmes said, and Allen replied, "It's not the usual way, but it was determined that a government vessel would not be suspected to be smuggling two Englishmen to Buffalo."

"Is the secrecy warranted?" Holmes asked.

Allen said, "If all goes well, we may never know."

"Indeed."

We disembarked at a city called Albany. I found all of the names of British places in America—York, Albany, Rochester—disturbing in some fundamental way. It was like emerging from a wilderness trail and hearing that I had arrived at Charing Cross. But I said nothing. At Albany we were transferred to a railroad train, and moved on at still greater speed. We followed roughly the course of a narrow, straight waterway called the Erie Canal, which had for the past seventy years or so brought the natural resources and products of the western parts—lumber, produce, and so on—back to the ports like New York. I found the vastness of the place a bit unnerving. By the time we reached Buffalo we had gone more than the distance between London and Edinburgh, and not left the state of New York, one of forty-five states, and by no means the largest.

The next day at four in the afternoon, we arrived at the train station in Buffalo. It was an imposing piece of architecture for such a distant and provincial place, with patterned marble floors and high stone galleries like a church. There I received my introduction to the peculiarity of the American mind. In the center of the large marble floor was a statue of an American bison covered in a layer of what I believe to be polished brass. Although this beast is commonly called a "buffalo," it is nothing of the sort, not at all like either the Asian buffalo or the African. The Americans simply like to call it a buffalo, as they like to grant the name "robin" to a native migratory thrush that is not a near relative of a British robin. Further, although the bison posing as a buffalo is the informal mascot of the city, the city's name has nothing to do with animals. It seems that Buffalo is a corruption of the seventeenth-century French name for the place, "Beau fleuve," beautiful river, an accurate description of the Niagara, on whose banks the city is situated. The logic was all virtually incomprehensible, but even the dimmest visitor could see that the inhabitants of the place had built themselves what looked like a golden calf and placed it in the station. As I was soon to learn, this was a city that worshipped industry, technological progress, and prosperity as fervently as the biblical sinners worshipped their own false deities. Holmes and I were about to happen upon one of their greatest pagan celebrations: the Pan-American Exposition was a festival of electrical power.

We were rushed from the station to a carriage and taken to the Genesee Hotel at Main and Genesee Streets. The Genesee was one of several large and thriving hotels in the central part of the city, with more under construction. The hotel served to seal my impression of the city, which was full of people from elsewhere, there to sell or buy or negotiate or merely gawk, as a place that grew and changed so rapidly that one had better write down his address because the next time he saw the location it might look different.

Captain Allen waited while we checked in and let the bellmen take our trunks to our suite. Then he took his leave. "I shall call upon you gentlemen at ten this evening on the matter of which we spoke," he said, turned on his heel, and went out the door. The carriage took him away.

Holmes and I went upstairs to our quarters. "We shall be here for at least a week," he said. "We may as well do some unpacking."

I took his advice, and watched out of the corner of my eye as he did the same. He had an array of unexpected items with him that I had not noticed during the six days at sea or the two days of travel into the interior. In addition to the clothing and accessories that he wore in London, there were some clothes and shoes that looked like those of a workman, some firearms and ammunition, an actor's makeup kit, and wooden boxes that were plain and unlabeled, which he left unopened in the trunk.

We took the opportunity to bathe and dress appropriately for our evening appointment. Holmes was a tall, trim man who looked positively elegant when he chose to, and a visit to the President of the United States was one occasion he considered worthy of some effort. In all modesty I must assert that my somewhat broader body was also suitably dressed. The elegant and tasteful lady I had been courting had, long before the voyage, insisted on going with me to a fine tailor on Savile Row where I was outfitted with several suits I could barely afford.

At exactly ten there was a knock on the door of our suite. Captain Frederick Allen was there to escort us. He conducted us to a waiting cabriolet, and we went down a broad and nicely paved street called Delaware Avenue. On both sides there were stately, well-kept homes of three stories, made of wood or brick or both, and surrounded by impressive lawns and gardens. We stopped at number 1168. When the cabriolet

pulled out of earshot to wait, Captain Allen said, "This is the home of a local attorney, Mr. John Milburn, who is serving as president of the Exposition."

We mounted the steps and a pair of American soldiers in dress blues opened the doors for us, then stood outside for a few moments to be sure that we had not been followed. Then they stepped back inside and resumed their posts. Mr. Allen led us across a broad foyer to a large set of oak doors. He knocked, and the man who opened the door surprised me.

I had seen photographs of William McKinley during the election of 1900, and there was no mistaking him. He was tall, about sixty years old, with hair that had not yet gone gray. His brow was knitted in an expression of alertness that made him look more stern than he proved to be. His face broadened into a smile instantly, and he said, "Ah, gentlemen. Please come in. I must thank you for coming halfway around the world to speak with me."

"It's a pleasure, sir," Holmes said, and shook his hand.

I said, "I'm honored to meet you."

We were inside the library in a moment, and then someone, presumably Allen, closed the door behind us. Holmes said, "I don't mind if our friend Captain Allen hears what we say."

The president shook his head. "He knows what I'm about to tell you, and some day in the future having been here might make him subject to unwanted inquiry."

The president went to the far end of the library and sat in a leather armchair. I noticed he had a glass on the table beside him that appeared to be some local whiskey-like spirit mixed with water. "Would you care to join me in a drink?"

I saw that there were a decanter of the amber liquid and a pitcher of water on a sideboard, and a supply of glasses. In the interest of politeness, I poured myself three fingers of the distillate. Holmes said, "Water for me, Watson, at least until I'm sure I won't need a clear head."

I brought him the water and we each sat in armchairs facing the president. Holmes leaned back, crossed his legs at the knee, and said confidently, "You're a president who has learned of recent plots against his life. You are about to appear in public at an international exposition. I assume that what you want is for me to take charge of your personal security to ensure that you are not assassinated."

"Why no, sir," President McKinley said. "I called you all this way because I want you to ensure that I *am* assassinated."

"What?" I said. "Perhaps I—"

"Your surprise proves you heard the president correctly," Holmes said. Then he looked at President McKinley judiciously. "Dr. Watson will agree you appear to be in perfect health, so you're not avoiding the pain of a fatal illness. I can see from the lack of broken vessels in your facial skin that the alcohol you're drinking now is not your habitual beverage, but an amenity for guests. You were only recently reelected by a nation grateful for your service. Unless there's some curious delay in the delivery of bad news in this country, I don't think there's a scandal. And if you wanted to kill yourself, you're fully capable of obtaining and operating a firearm, since you fought in your Civil War. Why would a leader at the apex of his career wish to be murdered?"

"I don't wish to be murdered. I wish to appear to have been murdered."

"But why? Your life seems to be a series of victories."

"I've become a captive of those victories," he said.

"How so?"

"Five years ago, with the help of my friend the party boss Mark Hanna, I assembled a coalition of businessmen and merchants, and ran for president on a platform of building prosperity by giving every benefit to business. Using protective tariffs and supporting a currency based on the gold standard, I helped lift the country out of the depression that had started in 1893, and made her an industrial power."

"Then what can be the matter?"

"I'm a man who got everything he wanted,

and has only now discovered that his wishes weren't the best things for his country."

"Why not?"

"Unintended consequences. Mark Hanna got me elected, but in doing so he spent three and a half million dollars. I'm afraid we have irrevocably tied political success to money, and that the connection, once made, will be disastrous for this country. The men with the most money will buy the government they want. I got us out of a depression by favoring business. I believed men of wealth and power would be fair to their workers because it was the right thing to do. Instead, the giant companies I helped act like rapacious criminals. They employ children in inhuman conditions in factories and mines, murder union spokesmen, keep wages so low that their workers live like slaves. Their own workmen can't buy the products they make, and the farmers live in debt and poverty. Since my reelection, I have been trying to bring sane and moderate regulation to business, but I have had no success. My allies, led by my friend Senator Hanna, won't hear of such a thing. My opponents don't trust me because I was champion of their oppressors. I wanted a second term to fix all the mistakes of the first term, but I find I can't fix any of them. I am clearly not the man for this job."

"Your people reelected you."

"I should not have run. I am a man of the nineteenth century. I understood the challenges of the time—bringing an end to slavery, building the railroads, settling the western portions of the country. But my time is now over. We have moved into the twentieth century, and I have overstayed history's welcome."

I said, "Mr. President, if you were to be assassinated, what would become of your nation?"

He smiled. "That is one of the few things that don't worry me. I selected a special man to be my vice presidential running mate. His name is Theodore Roosevelt. He's what I can never be—a man of the twentieth century."

"I'm afraid I know little about him," said Holmes. "I remember reading that he led a cavalry charge up San Juan Hill."

McKinley nodded. "He was running the U.S. Navy when war was declared. He resigned his Washington job and then organized his own troop of cavalry, fought alongside his men, and was recognized for his bravery. He is a genuine hero. And that should help when the country has to accept him as president. He is as well educated as a man in this country can be, is a respected historian, but also spent years running cattle in the Dakota Territory. He is only forty-two years old. He is fearless, intelligent, and utterly incorruptible. He is a man who sees these times so clearly that to a nineteenth-century man like myself, he seems clairvoyant. He is the man for the challenging times that are coming."

"What challenges do you mean?" I asked.

"The ethnic and linguistic groups of Europe have been forging themselves into nations and joining alliances for decades now—Germany and Italy have risen, and Germany defeated France in 1870. The pan-Slav movement has united Russia with the Balkans. The strength of Russia places it at odds with the Turks and the Japanese. Now all of these nations, and dozens more, are in the process of arming themselves. They're galloping toward a conflagration."

"And what can Mr. Roosevelt do?"

"In a few days, he can begin by showing the world that once again, there will be an orderly succession here. When one American leader dies, another stronger and better leader will immediately step up into his place. And then Mr. Roosevelt will show the world that the United States has might. Knowing him, I believe he will begin with the navy, which he knows best. He has already suggested sending a Great White Fleet around the world to show the flag. Germany has been working to build a fleet stronger than the British navy. Maybe if the kaiser becomes aware that he would need to defeat two strong navies, he will hesitate to attack anyone for a time."

"So you see Roosevelt as buying time?"

"Yes. I believe that if he does the job right, he can delay a general war by ten years. If he's better than that, he can delay it by fifteen years. America is on the rise. Each day that our leaders can keep the peace makes the country richer, stronger, and less vulnerable. Keeping the peace will also give him the time to begin conserving the country's wild places for posterity, and to begin curtailing and breaking up the trusts that have sprung up in industry to strangle competition and impoverish farmers and workers. I don't know what else he'll do. He is the man of the future, and I'm only a man of the past. I just know the time has come to get out of his way."

"And what would become of you?"

"That, sir, will be up to you. I would like to have you arrange my assassination within the next few days. Then I want you to help me with my afterlife. My wife, Ida, and I want to go off somewhere to live the years allotted to us in anonymity and privacy. I love my country and I've done my best for it all my life. But now I would be content to watch it from a distance." As he looked at Holmes, the president's brows knitted in that stern way he had.

Holmes sat in silence for a moment. "Sir, I accept your charge. Tonight, I believe, is the third of September. We must move quickly and keep the number of conspirators very small. I believe we'll be ready to move on the sixth." He stood.

McKinley smiled and stood with him, so I had little choice but to do the same, although I felt a bit confused by their haste. I too took my leave, and Holmes and I went outside to find Captain Allen waiting by our cabriolet. We got in, and Allen said to the driver, "The Genesee Hotel," and then stepped aside and let the cab go by.

On the way up Delaware, Holmes told the driver to stop at the telegraph office. There was one on Main Street, which was not far from our quarters. He went inside and wrote out a message he covered with his hand so I couldn't accidentally glance at it, handed it to the telegraph operator, and paid him a sum of three dollars.

When we were back in the cabriolet, he said, "Take us to the Exposition grounds, please."

"The buildings will be closed, sir," said the driver. "It's nearly midnight."

"Exactly," said Holmes.

The cab took us north along the deserted Delaware Avenue. The clopping of the horse's hooves on the cobblestone pavement was the only sound. All of the great houses were closed and darkened.

After no more than ten minutes, we reached a section of the avenue that curved, and as we came around, the Pan-American Exposition rose before us. From this distance it was a strange and ghostly sight. It was 350 acres of buildings constructed on the site of the city's principal park. Because the Exposition was, above all, a celebration of progress exemplified by electrical power, all of the principal buildings were decorated and outlined with lightbulbs, and all of them were lit, so the place looked like the capital of fairyland.

The countless bulbs glowed with a warm pink hue which never glared or fatigued the eyes, so a spectator's attention was drawn to every detail, every color. I was dumbstruck at the sights. The Exposition grounds were bisected by a grand promenade running from the Triumphal Bridge at the south end to the Electric Tower at the north end. There were canals, lakes, and fountains surrounding all the buildings, so these large, complicated, and beautiful constructions with heavily ornamented walls were not only illuminated and outlined by the magical lighting, but the glow was repeated in lakes and canals that served as reflecting pools. As we approached, the impression was of a city, with domes and towers and spires everywhere.

The architecture was indescribable—a fanciful mixture of neoclassical, Spanish Renaissance baroque, and pure whimsy all placed side by side along the midway in every direction. There were some constructions that reminded me of the more ornate Hindu temples I'd seen, with their red and yellow paint and green panels.

Whenever I thought I had perceived the organizing principle of the Exposition, I saw my guess was inadequate and partial. The colors of the buildings at the south end were bright and vivid. The Temple of Music was a garish red, with green panels in its dome and a liberal use of gold and blue-green. Nearer the north end, by the Electric Tower, the colors had grown to be subtler, gentler, and more subdued, as though they represented a change from barbaric splendor to modern sophistication. I also saw monumental sculptures, like frozen plays, that purported to represent the Rise of Man, the Subjugation of Nature, the Achievements of Man. Another series was labeled the Age of Savagery, the Age of Despotism, the Age of Enlightenment. Perhaps if there was an organizing principle, it was that these were people who worshipped progress and pointed it out wherever they could detect it.

From time to time Holmes would jump down from our carriage and look closely at some building or press his face against the windows to see inside. Or he would stand on the raised edge of a fountain and stare along a prospect as though aiming a rifle at a distant target. He craned his neck to look along the tops of parapets, as though he were looking for imaginary snipers.

At length I got out and walked with him. "What are we doing?" I asked.

"The Exposition has been open all summer, and it's now enjoying advertising by word of mouth. Current estimates are that it will have been visited by eight million people by its closing next month. If we came to do our examination tomorrow morning, not only would we draw attention to ourselves, but we would be trampled by the crowds."

"But what are we examining it for?"

"Vulnerabilities and opportunities, my friend. Not only must we find the best means, time, and place to conduct our feigned murder of the president, we must also make sure that we retain a monopoly on presidential murders for the day."

"What?"

"You recall that President McKinley managed to give Spain a crushing defeat in 1898. That must make him seem to many European powers a dangerous upstart. He also has let the unscrupulous owners and operators of large U.S. companies and their political minions know that he intends to rescind many of their privileges and powers. I can hardly imagine a person with worse enemies than he has."

"Is what you're saying that we must keep Mr. McKinley alive in order to assassinate him?"

"Precisely. Our little charade can only flourish in the absence of genuine tragedy." He walked along a bit farther. "That is why I told him we would move on the sixth. Giving ourselves until the tenth or twelfth might expose him to unacceptable risk."

I remained silent, for I had finally realized what he was looking for. He showed special interest in the Acetylene Building, examining it from all sides and shaking his head. "The danger of explosion is too obvious," he said. "We can avoid the hazard by keeping him away."

We got out again at the Stadium in the northeast corner of the Exposition. It was a formidable place, considering it was built only for this summer, and like the other buildings, would be torn down at the end of it. The place could hold twelve thousand spectators. "This spot is tempting," he said. "The marvel of large open spaces like this is that we could have him stand at a podium in the center, and assemble twelve thousand witnesses in the seats. They would all later swear that they saw the president killed, but none of them would have been close enough to really see anything but a man fall over."

"It's something to keep in mind," I said. "We could contrive a rifle shot from up high—maybe on the Electric Tower—and pretend he'd been hit."

"Let's see what else is available." We returned to our cab and Holmes directed the driver farther down the main thoroughfare.

We moved south to the ornate Temple of Music. It was about 150 feet on a side, with truncated corners so its square shape looked rounded. It had a domed roof, and every exposed surface was plastered with ornate decorations and painted garish colors, primarily red, and surrounded by statuary representing some sort of allegory that no living man could decipher—kinds of music, I supposed.

Holmes showed particular interest in this building. He walked around it from every side, looked in the windows, and, finally, picked the lock on the door and went inside. It was a large auditorium with a stage at the far end and removable seats in the center. "I believe we may have found what we were looking for," he said.

When we went out, he took a moment to relock the door.

We took our cab back to the Genesee Hotel and paid our tired driver handsomely for the long evening he'd had.

The next morning, as Holmes and I were having breakfast in our room, there was a quiet knock on the door. I got up to open it, expecting it to be Captain Allen. But there, standing in front of me, was an elderly man. Judging from his snow-white hair, his clothing, worn and a bit discolored from many washings, and the positively ancient shoes he was wearing, I thought him to be a tradesman who had gotten too old to pursue his trade. As kindly as I could, I said, "May I help you, sir?"

"Yes, my friend," said the old man in a cracked voice. "Is this the suite of Mr. Holmes?"

"Why, yes it is. Would you like to come in?"

As he stepped into the sitting room, Holmes emerged from his bedroom and grinned. "Ah, Mr. Booth. I'm very glad to see you could come so quickly." He added, "And thank you for hiding your identity so effectively."

The elderly gentleman immediately straightened, stepped athletically to Holmes, and shook his hand with a smile. "The journey was by night, and very quick," he said. "I came as soon as my final show was over. We're due to begin rehearsals for the next one in New York in a month, and if I'm not back, my understudy will stand in for me." He looked at each of us in turn. "Do you mind if I make myself at ease?" he said, as he pulled off the white hair, then carefully removed the mustache and put them in the pocket of his oversized coat. He had become a young man, perhaps twenty-one to twenty-five, as tall and healthy-looking as before he had been bent and weak.

"This is my friend Watson," said Holmes. "He has my utmost confidence and trust. Watson, this is Mr. Sydney Barton Booth, a member of the premier family of actors in this country."

I pulled him aside and whispered. "Booth?" I said. "But Holmes—"

"Yes." He spoke loudly and happily. "The same."

The young man said, "I'm twenty-three years old. My uncle John Wilkes Booth's terrible deed took place twelve years before I was born. He was the only one of my father, grandfather, and nine aunts and uncles who sympathized with the Confederacy. The others were staunch Union people and supporters of President Lincoln."

"The Booth family have long ago outlived any suspicion," Holmes said. "In the interim, they have continued their tradition of fine acting, and particularly in the realistic portrayal of human emotion. Mr. Sydney Booth is considered the finest of his generation. I had deduced from our invitation that we would need the services of an excellent American actor. A friend of mine from the British stage whom I contacted before we left informed me that the Booths have always searched for a way to make up for the mad actions of Mr. Booth's uncle. He also gave me his professional opinion that the present Mr. Booth was likely to be our man. We need him more than I had predicted, although in a performance with a very different ending."

"But have you warned Mr. Booth of the delicacy and danger of the role he would be playing?"

Holmes turned to Booth. "Mr. Booth, our scheme is dangerous in the extreme, and will earn you little thanks if you are successful. The only reward is that it is a patriotic task that I am persuaded will strengthen your country—and with it, ours, at least for a time."

Booth said, "I can think of nothing that would make me happier."

Holmes said, "There will be only a handful who are invited to join in our conspiracy. In addition to us there will be the president, of course; his trusted secretary, Mr. Cortelyou; the chief of police of Buffalo, Mr. William Bull; the head of the military contingent, whom I hope will be our friend Captain Allen; and Dr. Roswell Park, the most respected physician in the city. Each of them may have a trusted ally or two who will need to be told some part of the plan, but not all."

"That reminds me," I said. "I must be on my way. I'm meeting with Dr. Park this morning." I took my hat and cane and left the suite.

I found that my American medical counterpart, Dr. Roswell Park, was a man of great learning and a citizen of some standing in the medical community. He and I toured the University of Buffalo medical school facilities, the county morgue, and three of the local hospitals, as well as the field hospital that had been established at the edge of the grounds of the Pan-American Exposition. Everywhere we went, all doors opened and he was welcomed, something between a visiting potentate and a fatherly benefactor.

He and I examined the X-ray machine that was on display at the Exposition, which made it possible to see inside the body to detect a break in a bone or identify dangerous lesions. There was also an infant incubator on the midway, which I found particularly promising.

In many of our moments we were in places where the only possible eavesdroppers were the dead—the cadavers used for dissection by medical students, or the fresh bodies of transients found near the docks off Canal Street. During these times we discussed the difficulties of the assignment that the president and Holmes had given us, but we found a number of solutions in accepted medical protocols and in the simple matter of being prepared in advance to make sure events unfolded in certain ways and not others. Dr. Park was a man of such thoroughness that he thought of some things I had not—making sure that certain interns and nurses would be the ones on duty the afternoon and evening of September 6, because they would unhesitatingly follow his every order, and arranging to have horse-drawn ambulances prepared to make certain clandestine deliveries during the nights that followed. By the end of that day I was ready to entrust my life to Dr. Park. It was a sentiment that went unexpressed, because that was precisely what I was doing, as he was entrusting his life to me.

I returned to the Genesee Hotel in the evening, and found Holmes and Booth still in earnest conference. Holmes had brought out the makeup kit that I'd sometimes seen him use in London. It was a mixed collection of substances he had borrowed from the art of the theater, but even more liberally borrowed from the more subtle paints and powders employed by fashionable ladies in the interest of beauty. He had often gained information in the past by posing as a longshoreman or a gypsy or an old bookseller, and this kit had helped transform his face. It seemed from the change in his appearance that the young actor Mr. Booth was as expert as Holmes. He had changed once more. He now appeared to be a rough sort of fellow of thirty years who worked outdoors with his hands. His skin and hair had darkened a bit so he seemed to be from somewhere in continental Europe.

They had also laid out a series of maps of the Pan-American Exposition grounds that Holmes appeared to have drawn from memory. Booth was studying one of them.

"You'll have to wait long enough so the first hundred or so get through the doors and meet the president," Holmes said. "By then the line will be moving in an orderly way, and the guards will be getting overconfident and bored. Remember that the first move is mine. You will act only after I do."

"I understand," said Mr. Booth. "And then I'll make some hasty attempt at departure."

"Certainly, but be careful not to succeed. You must remain embroiled with the guards and police officers. If you make it into the open, one of them will surely get a shot off."

"I'll be sure to be overwhelmed promptly," said Booth.

And on they went. Since my presence was not required I retired to my bedchamber and settled my mind with a nap, which helped me to digest the many details I would need to remember two days hence. It was a few hours later before Mr. Booth stood and shook Holmes's hand. By then, I noticed, he had once again become the old white-haired man.

"I won't see you again until the afternoon of the sixth, Mr. Holmes. I'm sure we agree on all of the essentials of the performance. If you learn of any changes, please let me know. I'm staying at the boardinghouse at Main and Chippewa Streets."

"I will, Mr. Booth. In the meantime, know that we have great confidence in you, and we salute you for your patriotism."

"Good-bye. And good-bye to you, Dr. Watson. I'll see you in a couple of days."

"Good-bye, Mr. Booth."

And he was gone. Holmes quickly put away his disguise kit and some other items he and Booth had studied, and said, "I'm hungry, Watson. It's time for a late supper."

We left the hotel and walked around the block to a small establishment that had many of the qualities of a London public house. Sitting at a table in the rear of the house was a large man in a blue police uniform. His hat was on the table next to an empty beer glass, and as we came in the door, I saw him move it to the seat beside him.

"Mr. Bull," said Holmes.

"Sit down," said the policeman.

Holmes and I took a pair of seats across the table from him, and he raised his hand and beckoned, and the bartender arrived. Mr. Bull said, "Have you had dinner?"

"Well, no," I said.

"These two gentlemen will have dinner, please. And a pitcher of beer. Put it on my tab."

"Thank you," said Holmes. "Do you happen to know what dinner consists of this evening?"

"Roast beef on kummelweck, pickled hard-boiled eggs, beer, sauerkraut, and pickles," said the barman. "All you want."

"Excellent," Holmes said, with what appeared to be sincerity.

I was surprised at the eagerness with which Holmes and the police chief attacked the strange food, but I joined in with little hesitation, and found that the bar fare was exactly what I needed after a long day with my medical colleague. I particularly liked incidentals that had been judged not worth mentioning—short lengths of sausage and small pieces of chicken, primarily thighs and wings. I have often found that in exotic countries the native diet is exactly what is required for the maintenance of health and vigor.

Holmes stood and looked up the hallway behind the barroom to be sure there were no eavesdroppers, then opened the conversation almost immediately. "Chief Bull, do you know why I asked for a chance to meet with you?"

"I do," he said. "When Captain Allen came to me on your behalf, I made inquiries with the president's secretary, Mr. Cortelyou. I'll confess I was feeling insulted that they would hire a private citizen from another country to do my job of protecting important guests in my home city."

"And did Mr. Cortelyou settle your mind on that score?"

"He did," said Bull, then leaned closer to us and kept his voice low. "Now I'm not insulted. I'm afraid for everyone involved. If this goes wrong, it will be difficult for anyone to believe that we weren't joined in a murderous conspiracy. Once the name 'Booth' is mentioned . . ." He shuddered.

"We must be certain that there are no mistakes," said Holmes. "The fact that you are with us has helped to settle my mind considerably."

"And what will you need from me?"

"First," said Holmes, "we must request that you maintain the utmost secrecy. This is not a hoax that can later be revealed. We mean to establish a historical event that will remain enshrined in public knowledge for centuries. The men who know of it are the three of us, the president, Mr. Cortelyou, Dr. Roswell Park, Mr. Booth, and Captain Allen. I believe we can keep it within a small circle of honorable men, only those who must know."

Chief Bull sipped his beer thoughtfully. "Agreed. Any of my men will do as I say because I say it. They don't need to know why I say it."

"Exactly," said Holmes. "The portions for which we most need your help are the arrangement and disposition of the audience, the immediate aftermath of the performance, and then, just as important, the events of the following two weeks."

"You have my cooperation," he said. "We'll need to go over exactly what you want to happen, and what you don't want to happen."

"I propose to do that as soon as we have finished this sumptuous repast," said Holmes.

And he did. It took only about an hour spent pleasantly in the American pub for Holmes to choreograph exactly what he wanted—where each officer was to stand, how the citizens would be lined up to meet the president, what would happen as soon as Mr. Booth discharged his part, and so on. Chief Bull, I must say, proved to be a canny and intelligent strategist, picking up every detail and foreseeing more than a few that came from his professional knowledge of the behavior of crowds. By the end of the hour, when he stood and retrieved his policeman's hat, he and Holmes had a clear understanding.

Holmes was extremely thorough by habit and temperament, and in the time that followed he made sure that each member of the group knew something of the role of each of the others, so that none would mistakenly impede the execution of another's part. At his urging, each went to the Exposition alone and studied the areas he would need to know during the fateful day, like an actor blocking his part in a play.

And then, before I was even prepared for the day to come, it was the sixth of September. The moment I awoke I knew that the day was going to be hot. The sun had barely risen on the slightly overcast morning when it began to exert a power over the city. The humidity reminded me of those days in Delhi just before the government would decamp each year to the higher, cooler climate of Simla.

At 7:15 a.m. the president awoke at 1168 Delaware Avenue, the home of Mr. Milburn. He took a walk along the avenue, where he met another solitary figure, a tall, trim gentleman equipped as a peddler on the way to the Exposition with a tray of souvenirs to sell. I'm told they walked together for only a couple of blocks, but in that time, a great deal of information was conveyed in both directions. Then the mysterious salesman parted with the president, and they went their separate ways.

Later in the morning Holmes and I were at the railway station to board a train which was to take us to Niagara Falls. I noticed that there seemed to be a large number of prosperous-looking and well-dressed gentlemen waiting on the platform, even after Holmes and I had climbed aboard. The train was held up at the last moment, to take on a particular passenger. The president and his party arrived by coach and were ushered to a special car. The local dignitaries were far too numerous to be admitted to the car, but they filled in on the nearest alternative cars as well as they could, with little jostling.

I whispered to Holmes, "Where is Mrs. McKinley?"

He whispered back, "She's still at the Milburn house. Her husband fears this heat would be too much for her." He paused, significantly. "And she has a great many preparations to make. She will have a large role to play in the next few weeks."

The train took us along the Niagara River, which I judged to be a half-mile wide with a current of three to five knots for most of its length. It was pleasant to ride along at a brisk pace in the heat. But Holmes insisted on standing and walking the length of the train. I said, "What are we doing?"

"Looking," he said. "Look for faces that are familiar, faces that don't belong here, faces that don't want to meet our gaze, faces that look at us with too much interest."

We walked from one car to another, with a leisurely gait, looking at the many passengers. At times Holmes would stop and speak to someone in a seat. "A wonderful day to visit the falls, isn't it?" he would say. Or "Do you have any idea when this train reaches the falls?" Or even, "Is this seat taken?" The person would reply, he would nod and touch the brim of his hat, and then go on. I can be sure that nobody who was in the public sections of the train escaped his scrutiny. At the end, when we were standing at the back railing of the front car, staring ahead at the coal car and the engine, I said, "Well, we've looked. What have we seen?"

"Not enough," he said. "But we'll see more on the way back."

"What do you expect to see?"

"You and I have a plan. But what if someone else has a plan of his own? This is a fine day for

it. The Exposition is a fine place for it. But an even better place might be the falls."

"You mean—"

"I mean nothing more than that. Search the faces, Watson." He opened the door and went up the aisle. This time we were facing the passengers, and had a better opportunity to stare at each one.

At the end of the last carriage before the president's, he whispered, "We shall have to be vigilant today. There are three on this train who are not what they seem."

"Which ones?"

"There is a man in a coal black suit in the third car up. He is thin, with long elegant fingers that play idly along the length of his walking stick. He has on the floor between his feet a hard-sided case. I wondered at it because he didn't put it in the luggage rack."

"Do you suspect it holds a weapon?" I asked. "Perhaps something silent like the air gun that the blind craftsman Von Herder made and Colonel Moran used in his crime some years ago?"

"The same idea crossed my mind when I saw it, but then I noticed that the clasp on the case bears the emblem of Bergmann-Bayer, a maker of military firearms for the Spanish army," he said. "The weapon needn't be silent if he intends to fire it after we reach the falls. I'm told that the roar of the water is so loud that you could fire a field piece and the report would seem no more than a pop. No, I think with him, we have time."

"An angry Spaniard, trying to get revenge for the war. Who are the other two?"

"One is the middle-aged lady, quite small, wearing the brown dress with green trim in the front car."

"A lady? Surely you can't be serious."

"She's an unusual lady. She has a very slight but fresh cut, half an inch and nearly vertical, along her jaw line on the left side. I noticed from her movements that she is right-handed. And that is why she cut herself on the left side while shaving. It's harder to reach with her razor."

"So it's a man."

"And one who shaved extra closely this morning. The makeup powder she must have applied after it happened has run in this heat."

"Incredible," I said. "She . . . he could be carrying anything under those skirts. A brace of pistols. A cavalry sword. Even a rifle." I thought for a moment. "If we'd only had time, we could have devised a way of ensuring safety."

"Oh?" said Holmes.

"A device of some kind—perhaps an archway that each passenger had to walk through that had powerful magnets hanging from strings. They would detect the iron and steel of a weapon, swing right to it, and stick."

"We may consider the idea another time, perhaps," he said. "I believe we must get close to the third man before the train arrives. He is the one who seems to offer us the most imminent competition."

"Who is he?"

"Think about this. We bought a ticket. We got on the train. We walked from back to front, then from front to back. We've stopped to talk. I just saw a sign that said we were entering La Salle, which is the last place before Niagara Falls. Has the conductor punched your ticket?"

"Why, no."

"He hasn't checked anyone else's either. When I looked at him he avoided my eyes and stared ahead as though he were driving the train. The conductors I've observed can practically feel where they are on a line without looking. They have an almost miraculous sense of the exact duration of the journey. I would guess that in a moment he will be making his way to the back of the train looking very conductorly, if you'll permit me to coin a term. But what he'll be doing is using his uniform to be admitted to the car where the president sits."

And within minutes, there he was. As we were reaching the outskirts of a larger city that could only be Niagara Falls, the false conductor suddenly came down the aisle, taking tickets and punching them. He punched them without looking closely at them, which made him seem very experienced, but he was actually too en-grossed in judging the distance to his destination, the door of the last car.

Holmes sat in the aisle seat on the right of the car, and I sat in the seat across the aisle from him as we watched the man's progress. I waited for Holmes to make a move, but he allowed the conductor to continue his advance. I looked at Holmes repeatedly, but saw no sign in his expression that he had even noticed. He actually was gazing out the window at passing glimpses of the river between the quaint buildings of the City of Niagara Falls. The conductor continued his approach. He was ten feet from the door, then five, but Holmes never moved. Finally I could stand it no more. I had my cane across my lap, and as he stepped to the door of the presidential car, I jabbed it between his ankles, tripped him up so he sprawled on the floor, swung the stout ivory handle across the back of his skull, and then threw myself on top of him. I could tell he was dazed, half-conscious, and somewhat deprived of wind. Holmes rather casually reached into his waistcoat pocket and handed me a pair of handcuffs without even standing up. The sight irritated me, but I could see I had only a single choice to make—accept them or reject them, and either must be without comment. I chose to accept them because the conductor was a man of some size and probable strength, and I pulled his arms behind his back and clasped the irons on his wrists quickly before his senses fully returned.

Holmes helped me roll him to his side, and patted his blue uniform tunic. He pulled from the man's uniform a loaded .45 caliber Colt revolver, a quite sizable weapon for concealment. Holmes slipped it under his coat, and looked up at the nearby passengers, who were all members of the group of local dignitaries not important enough to sit with the president. He fanned the fallen culprit with his conductor's hat and said to the others, "This heat can make a man faint with just light exercise."

The man had planned his crime rather well. The train was already pulling up to the platform at Niagara Falls. He had clearly intended to go in, shoot the president, then jump from the last car as the train slowed while approaching the platform. He could have thrown away the conductor's hat and coat in a second and looked like anyone else in the crowd gathering at the station to see the president's arrival.

The train stopped, and we waited for the other passengers to make their exit. Then Holmes knocked on the president's car, and a young soldier opened the door. We could see four other soldiers behind him. "This man was attempting to get in and shoot the president," Holmes said. "Be sure he is locked up in the Niagara Falls police station right away. Take no chances. You are dealing with a murderer." He handed the soldier the gun, helped the failed assassin to his feet, and walked down the aisle toward the exit at the front of the car.

Seeing that we were alone, I said, "Why did you do nothing while I fought an armed assassin?"

"Untrue, Watson. I cheered you on—silently, for reasons of security."

I straightened my clothing as we walked out onto the platform and soon caught up with the American president and his party. They made their way down a broad street lined with trees to a series of staircases that led down to the very brink of Niagara Falls. The blue, wide river narrows at this point into the brink of a semicircular cliff, then drops 170 feet to a churning white cauldron below. The sheer volume of water pouring over the falls was astonishing. It threw a white cloud of mist hundreds of feet into the firmament that was visible for miles. The roar of the water was constant, unchanging, hypnotic. It didn't matter that the falls were so loud, because their immensity and beauty rendered all sensible men mute, and made all commentary inadequate. Whatever we might have said would have seemed irrelevant.

I noticed as we approached the giant falls and the sight and sound overwhelmed all else, Holmes's visage seemed to cloud and then freeze in a stoic expression. He walked along, and for a moment, his eyes lost their focus.

"Steady, Holmes," I said. "I know what you're remembering, but right now, I need you here and on duty."

Holmes patted my arm. "Good point, my friend. Reichenbach Falls is a good ten years behind us. It is uncanny how sounds and smells can bring back moments from the past. But we linger in them at our peril."

We walked along about three hundred feet behind the presidential party, and I could see that Holmes was not watching them, but studying the faces of the people in the crowd. Seeing so many well-dressed men and women in a single group on a promenade along the railing that separated them from the chasm made an impression on all the strangers who were there on holiday. It was difficult for me to tell whether the average American citizen recognized William McKinley, but it was also often difficult for me to tell whether any individual was an American or not. I heard speech that was French, German, Spanish, and several kinds of central European Slavic. There were several Asian voices also, including some speaking Hindi or Punjab. We were, after all, at one of the seven wonders of the modern world, and people had come from all the continents to see it. Very few took their eyes off the water except to watch their steps to keep from falling into it. Presidents, kings, or emperors were tiny, paltry sights compared with nature's titanic spectacle.

But suddenly Holmes picked up the pace. He walked straight away from the group along the railing, then ran up the stairs toward the street level. I followed him at a distance, not wanting to draw attention to myself, and consequently, to him.

As soon as I was up at the level of the street, I could see that he was watching a man in a dark suit. He followed him to the south, along the river above the falls. He went two blocks, and I could not quite imagine what harm the man could cause going away from the president's party at the brink of the falls. But then I saw what Holmes must have perceived instantly: the man was making his way along the path to the footbridge to the largest of the islands above the falls, which I later learned was called Goat Island. His approach was rendered nearly invisible by the many trees growing on the island, shading the paths. From there, he moved along the shore of Goat Island to a second footbridge that led to a much smaller island called Luna Island, a tiny wedge of land right at the edge of the falls.

Holmes was moving at a terrific pace now, running along, hat and cane in hand, jumping over low bushes, always staying out of the man's sight by taking a longer way around. I felt that because he was circling the man, I should walk along in a more leisurely and direct way on the well-marked footpath, so we could capture him in a pincer maneuver, if necessary.

As I came to a straight stretch of pathway, I feared the man would turn around and see me, so I too moved onto a more verdant route, walking along beyond a row of rather large trees. As it happened, I had the man in clear sight when Holmes came into view again. The man was the tall, thin man with the black suit from the train, and I saw he was still carrying his hard-sided case. He stood at the edge of the falls, looking over. Then he looked to his right along the jagged rim of the falls toward the observation point. From his vantage he could see President McKinley and his party clearly.

The dark-suited man went to a spot in the nearby bushes within a yard of the brink, where water amounting to millions of gallons was propelling itself at some thirty miles an hour off a cliff. He knelt, opened his box, pulled out what looked like the tripod of a surveyor's transom, opened it, and extended the legs. He placed a small brass scope on the top and sighted along it, making a few adjustments. He was clearly looking in the direction of the president and his hosts. Then he knelt again and worked to assemble several pieces of gleaming metal. As he rose to his feet, I could see that what he had was a metal tube a bit thicker than the barrel of a rifle, and at the butt end of it, a mechanism that looked like the receiver of a pistol. From a

distance it looked like a telescope. He attached the device to the top of the tripod, adjusting a set of thumbscrews, and Holmes began to run.

I ran too, and as I did, I realized that what the assassin had was a specially designed rifle with a smaller telescopic sight mounted independently to the tripod. He had spotted his prey and aimed the gunsight before attaching the rifle. Holmes and I came close, then stopped and began to approach him silently from two directions. We walked toward him, watching him peer into the scope at the president. Then he knelt and reached into his carrying case, pulled out a box magazine, and inserted it into the now-assembled rifle.

As the assassin's eye reached the eyepiece of the telescopic sight, Holmes and I surged forward like two rugby players lunging into a scrum. I crashed into the man's shoulder, throwing him against the railing, while Holmes hit the tripod and pushed it over the railing, where it fell, turning over and over, toward the churning water below.

"Oh, excuse me, please, gentlemen," said Holmes to both of us. "I tripped on that protruding rock along the path. I hope neither of you is injured." He helped me up first, and then took the arm of the man in the black suit and began to brush the dust off him, roughly.

"I'm terribly sorry about your telescope," he said to the man. "Or was it a camera? Either way, I insist on paying you its full value."

"You—" The man suddenly contained his rage, like a man turning off a faucet. "You haven't hurt me at all," he said. Now I could hear the Spanish accent that I was expecting. "And the telescope, it was just a trifle, a toy that I bought in New York."

"I insist," Holmes said. He took out his billfold and produced a sheaf of American money. It looked to be a great deal, but since American money consisted of identically colored, sized, and shaped currency, I couldn't tell how much at a glance. When the man wouldn't reach out for it, Holmes stuffed it in the breast pocket of the black suit. "Please, sir. I've already ruined your day. It's all I can do."

And then Holmes turned and walked off quickly, leaving me with the frustrated murderer. It occurred to me that with his weapon being churned about underwater far below, the man was relatively harmless. Nonetheless I tipped my hat as a pretext for backing away, then turned and went after Holmes. Just before the pathway took a turn to the pedestrian bridge off Luna Island I looked back to see him throw the hard-sided gun case over the railing into the chasm.

As I reached the main walkway above the falls I saw that the president's party, having observed the cataract from nearly every prospect, and seen the electrical power plant invented by Mr. Tesla on the shore below, was now walking toward the nearest city street. Holmes left the group and joined me. "They're going to lunch, Watson."

I was ravenous, not having eaten since my hasty breakfast of tea and toast in the hotel. "Shall we join them?"

"In a manner of speaking, yes. But I believe we must feed our eyes and noses today, and not our bellies." He broke into a brisk walk, and I noted that instead of the front door to one of the row of restaurants, Holmes headed up a narrow alley and stopped at an open door.

Hearing the noises coming from inside, I said, "The kitchen?"

He nodded. "Your medical education and experience make you the ideal man to ensure that no poison made of a medical derivative is introduced to the food—opiates, for instance—or any of the biological toxins like botulism. And I have some familiarity with most of the common substances like arsenic and strychnine, as well as a few that have seldom been heard of outside a shaman's hut. Come, my friend. Anything that doesn't look or smell right must be discarded."

We entered the kitchen. Outside it was a hot, humid day, but inside it was like the engine room of a ship steaming through hell. The *sous-chefs* were working stripped to the waist, their bodies glistening with sweat as they labored over their bubbling soups and sauces, braised their meats, and baked their fish. Holmes and I threw off our coats and waistcoats and joined the staff, examining every dish that went out through the swinging doors to the dining room, sniffing each uncooked carcass, tasting a pinch of every spice, and inquiring into the freshness and provenance of every comestible. We found no poisons and only one dish of elderly oysters, but the work lasted nearly two hours, and when we went outside to join the president's party on its walk to the train, I felt as though I had been catapulted out of Hades into paradise.

At one the train loaded and left for Buffalo, and I stood outside the car on the small area above the rear coupling where there was a railing, enjoyed the wind moving over me, and watched the passengers through the glass from there. Holmes joined me after a time. He said, "When we reach Buffalo the president will rest for an hour in his room at Mr. Milburn's home on Delaware Avenue. At four o'clock they'll bring him to the Exposition, and he will greet his constituents at the Temple of Music. That's our hour and I must prepare for it. After this, you and I will not see each other for a day or two. I trust that you and Dr. Park have made all the preparations you'll need?"

"I'm certain of it," I said. "He's a brilliant doctor with a scientist's mind, and he took to conspiracy quickly."

"Good," said Holmes. "Then I wish all of us the favor of fortune." He turned, walked off into the next car toward the rear of the train, and disappeared from my sight.

The train arrived in the station in Buffalo at one thirty, and the president and his party left in carriages, but I didn't spot Holmes among the throng. Nor did I see him anywhere else. It was as though he had crumbled into dust and blown away in the breeze.

I took a carriage directly to the Exposition grounds. I walked to the hospital that had been set up on the site, introduced myself as Dr. Mann, and indicated that I was to be the physician in charge for the shift that began at five p.m. As we had anticipated, the administrative nurse, a formidable woman of about fifty years, sent a messenger to Dr. Park to verify my credentials, even though she had seen him give me a tour of the facilities only two days earlier. The delay gave me an opportunity to leave, so I went off on the pretense of inspecting the ambulances stationed on the midway in case of emergency. Actually I made my way to the Temple of Music and introduced myself to the policeman at the door as Dr. Mann. He called for Chief Bull to come to the door, and Chief Bull greeted me warmly and admitted me. Through the windows I could see that there were already large crowds of people who had been arranged into an orderly queue waiting outside for the president. I pitied them, and fancied that before long I would be catering to cases of heat exhaustion.

During the next minutes I stood in the building inspecting the arrangements for the president's visit. Many chairs had been removed, to make way for the president's receiving line. He was to be standing approximately in the center of the auditorium with some of his entourage and the soldiers. People would be permitted inside, and each would shake hands with him, and then be turned and sent out.

I heard a murmur outside. It grew into a commotion. The doors opened, and President McKinley entered. He took his place flanked by Mr. John Milburn and Mr. Cortelyou. There were eleven soldiers and four police officers in the building, including Chief Bull. The president gave the order at four o'clock, and the soldiers opened the doors.

The orderly line of citizens advanced into the building. There were men, women, and a fair number of children. When I saw the children I shuddered, but then I saw that their parents were keeping them in close order, so I worried less. The president met each person with a smile and a greeting, and then the policemen moved each person out of the way so others would get their turns. I conjectured that the soldiers and police officers had agreed to move the crowd along smartly so more of them could get inside into the shade.

And then there was trouble. I could see it developing as the crowd inched forward. There came a tall, thin, swarthy man with a handlebar mustache and black curly hair. He was muttering angrily to himself as he stood in the queue, in a language which after a moment I realized was Italian.

He began to draw glances from the onlookers, and then from the guardsmen. Three of the policemen sidled along up the row of people, apparently straightening the line and narrowing it strictly to single file as it got close to the president. When they reached the Italian, one of them spoke to him in a low voice and took his arm like an usher to move him a pace to the left. He reacted like a madman. He punched the policeman, and turned to charge the other two. They were taken by surprise, so he bowled them over into a pair of ladies, who were thrown roughly backward onto the carpet.

That part of the line became a battle royal, with eight or nine soldiers and all the policemen diving onto the pile and delivering blows with less judiciousness than fervor. When the sudden motion froze into a contest of tugging and resisting, I recognized that the swarthy Italian had a profile very familiar to me. I also noticed that he had one of the women in an apparently unbreakable embrace. After a second I realized the offended woman was the disguised man Holmes had recognized on the train.

Just then, as the crowd ahead of the Italian swept forward, partly to meet the president and partly to get out of the way of the fighting, one of their number, a man who looked Central European—perhaps a Serb or a Croatian, with dark skin, hair, and mustache—stepped into the vanguard. He had a white handkerchief in his hand, as several others did, to wipe away the perspiration before shaking the president's hand. I saw that nearly all of the policemen and soldiers were occupied with the disorderly Italian and the ones still near the president were watching the fray, mesmerized. So when the man aimed a revolver he'd hidden under the handkerchief at the president, there was no one there in time to prevent it.

He fired once, and a brass button on the president's coat threw sparks. His second shot was not deflected. The president gripped his belly and fell. As the president fell, the soldiers and policemen let go of the unruly Italian. Some went to the president's side, and the others surrounded the assassin. Fortunately, a tall man of African descent had been behind the shooter in the line. He batted the gun from the man's hand and kept him from escaping. If he had not done that, the soldiers almost certainly would have shot the culprit. Instead, they dragged him to the floor and delivered a series of kicks and punches.

The president, lying on the carpet in the arms of his secretary and Mr. Milburn, called out, "Don't hurt him, boys!" The calm, wise words seemed to bring the men to their senses. They subdued the culprit and took him out to a police van that was parked near the building.

Meanwhile, I pushed my way to the president's side. "I'm a doctor," I called out, and the guards made room. I opened his coat as I leaned close to listen to his breathing. As I did, I surreptitiously produced a small vial of fresh chicken blood from my waistcoat and spilled it on the white shirt just above the belt. "He's wounded, but alive," I said. "Lift the president to his carriage," I ordered. "We'll take him to the field hospital on the Exposition grounds."

The strong young soldiers nearby lifted the president and placed him in the carriage. I joined him and Captain Allen jumped into the driver's seat and whipped the horses to such a gallop that I feared the president would die in a carriage accident and take me with him. I managed to speak with him a bit in a low voice. "How are you, sir?" I asked.

"Excellent, Dr. Watson," he said. "Seldom better."

"Good. We'll try to keep you that way. Now put on this coat and hat." It was a rather dull brown coat that looked very different from his tailored black one, and a bowler hat like the ones many men wore that day. When we were near the Indian Congress, Captain Allen drove the coach into a horse barn. Allen and I got into a second

coach that was waiting there. Our horses had easily outrun word of the attack on the president, and as we pulled away, I could see that none of the visitors touring the Exposition noticed Mr. McKinley in his new garb entering the Indian Congress.

Captain Allen whipped the new set of horses, and I went to work on the substitute patient already waiting on the seat, a cadaver that Dr. Park and I had selected at the medical school the previous day. I covered his torso with Mr. McKinley's black coat, and his face with my handkerchief, as though keeping the sun out of his eyes. When we reached the field hospital, I jumped out, and Captain Allen and I put the corpse on a stretcher. Two orderlies loitering outside rushed to carry it in. "To the operating room immediately," I shouted. We took the stretcher inside and locked the door.

After a few minutes, Dr. Roswell Park arrived at the door with several of his assistants and nurses, and made the little hospital look as though it were being run with great professional skill. With him to assist, I began the operation. I had removed bullets from a number of soldiers while on duty in India, so I was extremely familiar with the procedure and the many ways in which it can succeed or fail. As I worked on the cadaver to make it look as though it had been opened to search for the bullet, he complimented my technique several times.

We had only the open part of the abdomen uncovered by sheets, and the deceased man who was supposed to be the president lay on his back with a face mask over his mouth and nose and a surgical cap on his head. Nonetheless, it occurred to me that we were fortunate that while millions of lightbulbs were displayed everywhere throughout the Exposition, nobody had thought to install a single bulb in the hospital.

Through Dr. Park's nurses and assistants, we slowly fed our fiction to the outside world. We said the president was a healthy specimen, and he had been lucky. The first bullet had hit a brass button and ricocheted, leaving a shallow gash along his side. The second shot entered the abdomen at close range, but the pistol had been a small caliber, and most likely Dr. Mann would find and remove the bullet in the present surgery. Once that happened, McKinley could be expected to recover fully. But after more than four hours of surgery, we changed the news slightly. Dr. Mann had not found the bullet, which must have fragmented in the body.

This was the story all that evening. It was still the story when we moved the cadaver to Mr. Milburn's house to recover. At various times during the next few days we issued reports that the president was recovering nicely, that his spirits were high, and that we expected an early return to health.

Meanwhile, as Holmes told me later, the rest of the deception went tolerably well. The assassin captured at the Temple of Music was taken to the police station. He, of course, was Mr. Booth. He identified himself as Leon Czolgosz, the son of Polish immigrants, who had been struck by the inequality in the way the president was treated compared with an ordinary man. Because of Chief Bull's fears of public emotion aroused by his crime, Czolgosz was kept apart from other prisoners.

The president had made his way into the Indian village, where he met Holmes, no longer an Italian madman. Holmes was waiting for the president with three Iroquois Indians he had met while they were studying at the University of London years before—two Senecas and a Mohawk. Holmes applied some of the makeup he had brought, and within a few minutes he and the president were the fourth and fifth Iroquois Indians. After nightfall, the five men left the Exposition in the midst of a growing crowd, and rowed across the Niagara River into Canada.

With the help of his Iroquois friends, Holmes conveyed Mr. McKinley to Montreal, where he put him on the steamship *Arcturus*, which sailed on September 9 for London. I'm told he was an impressive figure, registered in the ship's manifest as Selim Bey, first cousin to the third wife of the Sultan of Turkey. He wore some makeup, a large turban, and a sash with a curved dagger

in it. After he reached London he took another ship for Tangiers as the Reverend Dr. Oliver McEachern, a Methodist missionary.

Five days after the *Arcturus* sailed, on September 14, I was forced to declare President William McKinley dead. He had been said to be recovering, but a few days later he succumbed to blood poisoning. There was some speculation, especially in the papers in New York City and Washington, that Dr. Mann had botched the surgery. There was even some lamentation that on the grounds of the Exposition had been an experimental X-ray machine, which could easily have found even fragments of a bullet. That was precisely why I, or Dr. Mann, had forbidden its use.

Nine days later, on the testimony of eyewitnesses, Leon Czolgosz, the young man who had shot the president, was convicted of murder. He was taken from the court to Auburn Penitentiary, where he was executed in an electric chair, another application of the marvels of electricity celebrated by the Pan-American Exposition in Buffalo. The one flaw of the modern method in comparison to hanging was that when a single wire was loosened, an electric chair became simply a chair. A fine actor can perform a set of death throes that would make a gravedigger faint.

Holmes and Dr. Mann were among the dignitaries who attended the very small funeral held at the penitentiary for the murderer. The casket had been nailed shut because the face of the killer Czolgosz had been disfigured by sulfuric acid poured on the corpse by persons unknown. Presiding over the funeral was a young clergyman who gave an extremely impressive elegy, inspiring all listeners with the notion that even the worst sinner can be forgiven and admitted to the kingdom of heaven. Afterward we took him to the nearest railway station and bought him a ticket, not to heaven, but only to New York, where he was in time to begin rehearsals for a Broadway play called *Life*, which opened the following March to appreciative notices.

After the state funeral of the president in

Washington, it was popularly supposed that Mrs. Ida McKinley returned to Ohio where she was to live with her sister. I often thought of her during the next seven years, knowing that she was living happily by turns as the wife of Selim Bey or of the Reverend Dr. McEachern—a veiled Moslem to the Christians, and a Christian to the Moslems, a person who pretended never to speak the language of those around her, and never had to explain herself. When she died after seven years, her body was secretly shipped back to Ohio and then buried by her sister, as though she had lived as a reclusive widow all along.

On the fourteenth of September, 1901, when it was first announced that President McKinley was dying, a number of notables rushed to Buffalo. One of them was his old friend Senator Mark Hanna, and another was the young vice president, Theodore Roosevelt. He stayed at the Ansley Wilcox mansion at 641 Delaware Avenue, where he was sworn in late that night as the twenty-sixth president of the United States. Whether in later years Roosevelt lived up to his predecessor's hopes, I cannot say. As Selim Bey or Dr. McEachern, the former president declared himself to be happy in retirement and never gave another political opinion. But the Great War he had feared did not begin until 1914, did not involve America until 1917, and ended a year later as he had hoped it would, with his country victorious and growing stronger.

. . .

Curator's Note: Although Dr. Watson's claims cannot be verified, the circumstances of the manuscript's discovery in a locked metal box hidden in his great-grandson's home in London with several other, equally startling manuscripts might add credibility for some readers. Many personalities in Dr. Watson's story were real people, e.g. Mark Hanna, Ida and William McKinley, Dr. Roswell Park, Mr. John Milburn, George Cortelyou, Chief William Bull, "Dr. Mann," Leon Czolgosz, Theodore Roosevelt, Ansley Wilcox, and Sherlock Holmes. Watson's description of the assassination appears to agree with descriptions by eyewitnesses, even in the particular of the distraction of the guards by the unidentified Italian. Czolgosz's body actually was rendered unrecognizable because of sulfuric acid poured on it by persons unknown after his execution. The actor Sydney Barton Booth really was a descendant of Edwin Booth, a pro-Lincoln member of the acting family, and he had a fine career that lasted long enough for him to appear in several successful motion pictures. As for timing, we do know that the whereabouts of Holmes and Watson are unknown between Thursday, May 16, 1901, when the "Priory School" events took place, and Tuesday, November 19, 1901, when they were seen during the "Sussex Vampire" case.

The Case of Colonel Warburton's Madness

LYNDSAY FAYE

AFTER TEN YEARS as a professional actress on the West Coast, Lyndsay Faye (1980–) moved to New York in 2005 to further her career but quickly found the competition and lifestyle daunting so turned to writing.

A lifelong aficionado of Sherlock Holmes, Faye pitted Holmes against Jack the Ripper in her first book, *Dust and Shadow: An Account of the Ripper Killings by Dr. John H. Watson* (2000). It was given blessings by the Arthur Conan Doyle Estate and received praise from many sources, including Caleb Carr, who wrote his own pastiche, *The Italian Secretary*, in 2005.

Faye followed *Dust and Shadow* with *The Gods of Gotham* (2012), an ambitious first novel in a series about Timothy Wilde, a bartender who becomes a policeman at the time that New York was creating its police department in 1846, coincidentally the year of the great Irish potato famine; it was nominated for an Edgar Award. Her massive historical research was put to use again for the second Wilde novel, *Seven for a Secret* (2013), which deals with "blackbirders," underworld thugs who kidnap northern Negroes and sell them into slavery in the South.

"The Case of Colonel Warburton's Madness" was selected for the prestigious *The Best American Mystery Stories 2010*, edited by Lee Child; it is one of ten stories Faye has written about Holmes, the most recent and longest being "The Gospel of Sheba" (2014). "The Case of Colonel Warburton's Madness" was first published in *Sherlock Holmes in America*, edited by Martin H. Greenberg, Jon L. Lellenberg, and Daniel Stashower (New York, Skyhorse, 2009).

THE CASE OF COLONEL
WARBURTON'S MADNESS

Lyndsay Faye

MY FRIEND Mr. Sherlock Holmes, while possessed of one of the most vigorous minds of our generation, and while capable of displaying tremendous feats of physical activity when the situation required it, could nevertheless remain in his armchair perfectly motionless longer than any human being I have ever encountered. This skill passed wholly unrecognized by its owner. I do not believe he held any intentions to impress me so, nor do I think the exercise was, for him, a strenuous one. Still I maintain the belief that when a man has held the same pose for a period exceeding three hours, and when that man is undoubtedly awake, that same man has accomplished an unnatural feat.

I turned away from my task of organizing a set of old journals that lead-gray afternoon to observe Holmes perched with one leg curled beneath him, firelight burnishing the edges of his dressing gown as he sat with his head in his hand, a long-abandoned book upon the carpet. The familiar sight had grown increasingly unnerving as the hours progressed. It was with a view to ascertain that my friend was still alive that I went so far against my habits as to interrupt his reverie.

"My dear chap, would you care to take a turn with me? I've an errand with the bootmaker down the road, and the weather has cleared somewhat."

I do not know if it was the still-ominous dark canopy that deterred him or his own pensive mood, but Holmes merely replied, "I require better distraction just now than an errand which is not my own and the capricious designs of a March rainstorm."

"What precise variety of distraction would be more to your liking?" I inquired, a trifle nettled at his dismissal.

He waved a slender hand, at last lifting his dark head from the upholstery where it had reclined for so long. "Nothing you can provide me. It is the old story—for these two days I have received not a shred of worthwhile correspondence, nor has any poor soul abused our front doorbell with an eye to engage my services. The world is weary, I am weary, and I grow weary with being weary of it. Thus, Watson, as you see I am entirely useless myself at the moment, my state cannot be bettered through frivolous occupations."

"I suppose I would be pleased no one is so disturbed in mind as to seek your aid, if I did not know what your work meant to you," I said with greater sympathy.

"Well, well, there is no use lamenting over it."

"No, but I should certainly help if I could."

"What could you possibly do?" he sniffed. "I hope you are not about to tell me your pocket watch has been stolen, or your great-aunt disappeared without trace."

"I am safe on those counts, thank you. But perhaps I can yet offer you a problem to vex your brain for half an hour."

"A problem? Oh, I'm terribly sorry—I had forgotten. If you want to know where the other key to the desk has wandered off to, I was given cause recently to test the pliancy of such objects. I'll have a new one made—"

"I had not noticed the key," I interrupted him with a smile, "but I could, if you like, relate a series of events which once befell me when I was in practice in San Francisco, the curious details of which have perplexed me for years. My work on these old diaries reminded me of them yet again, and the circumstances were quite in your line."

"I suppose I should be grateful you are at least not staring daggers at my undocked case files," he remarked.

"You see? There are myriad advantages. It would be preferable to venturing out, for it is already raining again. And should you refuse, I will be every bit as unoccupied as you, which I would also prefer to avoid." I did not mention that if he remained a statue an instant longer, the sheer eeriness of the room would force me out of doors.

"You are to tell me a tale of your frontier days, and I am to solve it?" he asked blandly, but the subtle angle of one eyebrow told me he was intrigued.

"Yes, if you can."

"What if you haven't the data?"

"Then we shall proceed directly to the brandy and cigars."

"It's a formidable challenge." To my great relief, he lifted himself in the air by his hands and crossed his legs underneath him, reaching when he had done so for the pipe lying cold on the side table. "I cannot say I've any confidence it can be done, but as an experiment, it has a certain flair."

"In that case, I shall tell you the story, and you may pose any questions that occur to you."

"From the beginning, mind, Watson," he admonished, settling himself into a comfortable air of resigned attention. "And with as many details as you can summon up."

"It is quite fresh in my mind again, for I'd set it down in the volumes I was just mulling over. As you know, my residence in America was relatively brief, but San Francisco lives in my memory quite as vividly as Sydney or Bombay—an impetuous, thriving little city nestled among the great hills, where the fogs are spun from ocean air and the sunlight refracts from Montgomery Street's countless glass windows. It is as if all the men and women of enterprise across the globe determined they should have a city of their own, for the Gold Rush built it and the Silver Lode built it again, and now that they have been linked by railroad with the eastern states, the populace believes nothing is impossible under the sun. You would love it there, Holmes. One sees quite as many nations and trades represented as in London, all jostling one another into a thousand bizarre coincidences, and you would not be surprised to find a Chinese apothecary wedged between a French milliner and an Italian wine merchant.

"My practice was based on Front Street in a small brick building, near a number of druggist establishments, and I readily received any patients who happened my way. Poor or well-off, genteel or ruffianly, it made no difference to a boy in the first flush of his career. I'd no long-established references, and for that reason no great clientele, but it was impossible to feel small in that city, for they so prized hard work and optimism that I felt sudden successes lay every moment round the next corner.

"One hazy afternoon, as I'd no appointments and I could see the sun lighting up the masts of the ships in the Bay, I decided I'd sat idle long enough, and set out for a bit of exercise. It is one of San Francisco's peculiar characteristics that no matter what direction one wanders, one must encounter a steep hill, for there are seven of them, and within half an hour of walking aimlessly away from the water, I found myself striding up Nob Hill, staring in awe at the array of houses.

"Houses, in fact, are rather a misnomer; they call it Nob Hill because it is populated by mining and railroad nabobs, and the residences are like something from the reign of Ludwig the Second or Marie Antoinette. Many are larger than our landed estates, but all built within ten years of the time I arrived. I ambled past a gothic near-castle and a neo-classicist mansion only to spy an Italianate villa across the street, each making an effort to best all others in stained glass, columns, and turrets. The neighborhood—"

"Was a wealthy one," Holmes sighed, hopping out of his chair to pour two glasses of claret.

"And you would doubtless have found that section of town appalling." I smiled at the thought of my Bohemian friend eyeing those pleasure domes with cool distaste as he handed me a wineglass. "There would have been others more to your liking, I think. Nevertheless, it was a marvel of architecture, and as I neared the crest of the hill, I stopped to take in the view of the Pacific.

"Standing there watching the sun glow orange over the waves, I heard a door fly open and turned to see an old man hobbling frantically down a manicured path leading to the street. The mansion he'd exited was built more discreetly than most, vaguely Grecian and painted white. He was very tall—quite as tall as you, my dear fellow—but with shoulders like an ox. He dressed in a decades-old military uniform, with a tattered blue coat over his gray trousers, and a broad red tie and cloth belt, his silvery hair standing out from his head as if he'd just stepped from the thick of battle.

"Although he cut an extraordinary figure, I would not have paid him much mind in that mad metropolis had not a young lady rushed after him in pursuit, crying out, 'Uncle! Stop, please! You mustn't go, I beg of you!'

"The man she'd addressed as her uncle gained the curb not ten feet from where I stood, and then all at once collapsed onto the pavement, his chest no longer heaving and the leg which had limped crumpled underneath him.

"I rushed to his side. He breathed, but shallowly. From my closer vantage point, I could see one of his limbs was false, and that it had come loose from its leather straps, causing his fall. The girl reached us not ten seconds later, gasping for breath even as she made a valiant effort to prevent her eyes from tearing.

"'Is he all right?' she asked me.

"'I think so,' I replied, 'but I prefer to be certain. I am a doctor, and I would be happy to examine him more carefully indoors.'

"'I cannot tell you how grateful we would be. Jefferson!' she called to a tall black servant hurrying down the path. 'Please help us get the Colonel inside.'

"Between the three of us, we quickly established my patient on the sofa in a cheerful, glass-walled morning room, and I was able to make a more thorough diagnosis. Apart from the carefully crafted wooden leg, which I reattached more securely, he seemed in perfect health, and if he were not such a large and apparently hale man I should have imagined that he had merely fainted.

"'Has he hurt himself, Doctor?' the young woman asked breathlessly.

"Despite her evident distress, I saw at once she was a beautiful woman, with a small-framed, feminine figure, and yet a large measure of that grace which goes with greater stature. Her hair was light auburn, swept away from her creamy complexion in loose waves and wound in an elegant knot, and her eyes shone golden brown through her remaining tears. She wore a pale blue dress trimmed with silver, and her ungloved hand clutched at the folds in her apprehension. She—my dear fellow, are you all right?"

"Perfectly," Holmes replied with another cough which, had I been in an uncharitable humor, would have resembled a chuckle. "Do go on."

"'This man will be quite all right once he has rested,' I told her. 'My name is John Watson.'

"'Forgive me—I am Molly Warburton, and the man you've been tending is my uncle, Colonel Patrick Warburton. Oh, what a fright I have had! I cannot thank you enough.'

"'Miss Warburton, I wonder if I might speak with you in another room, so as not to disturb your uncle while he recovers.'

"She led me across the hall into another tastefully appointed parlor and fell exhaustedly into a chair. I hesitated to disturb her further, and yet I felt compelled to make my anxieties known.

"'Miss Warburton, I do not think your uncle would have collapsed in such a dramatic manner had he not been under serious mental strain. Has anything occurred recently which might have upset him?'

"'Dr. Watson, you have stumbled upon a

family embarrassment,' she said softly. 'My uncle's mental state has been precarious for some time now, and I fear recently he—he has taken a great turn for the worse.'

"'I am sorry to hear it.'

"'The story takes some little time in telling,' she sighed, 'but I will ring for tea, and you will know all about it. First of all, Dr. Watson, I live here with my brother, Charles, and my uncle, the Colonel. Apart from Uncle Patrick, Charles and I have no living relatives, and we are very grateful to him for his generosity, for Uncle made a great fortune in shipping during the early days of California statehood. My brother is making his start in the photography business, and I am unmarried, so living with the Colonel is for the moment a very comfortable situation.'

"'You must know that my uncle was a firebrand in his youth, and saw a great deal of war as a settler in Texas, before that region was counted among the United States. The pitched fighting between the Texians—that is, the Anglo settlers—and the Tejanos so moved him that he joined the Texas Army under Sam Houston, and was decorated several times for his valor on the field, notably at the Battle of San Jacinto. Later, when the War Between the States began, he was a commander for the Union, and lost his leg during the Siege of Petersburg. Forgive me if I bore you. From your voice, I do not think you are a natural-born American,' she added with a smile.

"'Your story greatly interests me. Is that his old Texas uniform he is wearing today?' I asked.

"'Yes, it is,' she replied as a flicker of pain distorted her pretty face. 'He has been costuming himself like that with greater and greater frequency. The affliction, for I do not know what to call it, began several weeks ago. Indeed, I believe the first symptom took place when he changed his will.'

"'How so? Was it a material alteration?'

"'Charlie and I had been the sole benefactors,' she replied, gripping a handkerchief tightly. 'His entire fortune will now be distributed amongst various war charities. Texas War for Independence charities, Civil War charities. He is obsessed with war,' she choked, and then hid her face in her hands.

"I was already moved by her story, Holmes, but the oddity of the Colonel's condition intrigued me still further.

"'What are his other symptoms?' I queried when she had recovered herself.

"'After he changed his will, he began seeing the most terrible visions in the dark. Dr. Watson, he claims in the most passionate language that he is haunted. He swears he saw a fearsome Tejano threatening a white woman with a pistol and a whip, and on another occasion he witnessed the same apparition slaughtering one of Houston's men with a bayonet. That is what so upset him, for only this morning he insisted he saw a murderous band of them brandishing swords and torches, with the identical Tejano at their head. My brother believes that we have a duty as his family to remain and care for him, but I confess Uncle frightens me at times. If we abandoned him, he would have no one, save his old manservant; Sam Jefferson served the colonel for many years, as far back as Texas, I believe, and when my uncle built this house, Jefferson became the head butler.'

"She was interrupted in her narrative as the door opened and the man I knew at once to be her brother stepped in. He had the same light brown eyes as she, and fine features, which twisted into a question at the sight of me.

"'Hello, Molly. Who is this gentleman?'

"'Charlie, it was horrible,' she cried, running to him. 'Uncle Patrick ran out of the house and collapsed. This is Dr. John Watson. He has been so helpful and sympathetic that I was telling him all about Uncle's condition.'

"Charles Warburton shook my hand readily. 'Very sorry to have troubled you, Doctor, but as you can see, we are in something of a mess. If Uncle Patrick grows any worse, I hate to think what—'

"Just then a great roar echoed from the morning room, followed by a shattering crash. The three of us rushed into the hallway and found Colonel Warburton staring wildly about him, a vase broken into shards at his feet.

"'I left this house once,' he swore, 'and by the devil I will do it again. It's full of vengeful spirits, and I will see you all in hell for keeping me here!'

"The niece and nephew did their utmost to calm the Colonel, but he grew even more enraged at the sight of them. In fact, he was so violently agitated that only Sam Jefferson could coax him, with my help, toward his bedroom, and once we had reached it, the Colonel slammed the door shut in the faces of his kinfolk.

"By sheer good fortune, I convinced him to take a sedative, and when he fell back in a daze on his bed, I stood up and looked about me. His room was quite Spartan, with hardly anything on the white walls, in the simple style I supposed was a relic of his days in Texas. I have told you that the rest of the house also reflected his disdain for frippery. The bed rested under a pleasant open window, and as it was on the ground floor, one could look directly out at the gardens.

"I turned to rejoin my hosts when Sam Jefferson cleared his throat behind me.

"'You believe he'll be all right, sir?'

"He spoke with the slow, deep tones of a man born on the other side of the Mississippi. I had not noticed it before, but a thick knot of scarring ran across his dark temple, which led me to believe he had done quite as much fighting in his youth as his employer.

"'I hope so, but his family would do well to consult a specialist. He is on the brink of a nervous collapse. Was the Colonel so fanciful in his younger days?'

"'I don't rightly know about fanciful, sir. He's as superstitious a man as ever I knew, and more afeared of spirits than most. Always has been. But sir, I've a mind to tell you something else about these spells the Colonel been having.'

"'Yes?'

"'Only this, Doctor,' and his low voice sunk to a whisper. 'That first time as he had a vision, I set it down for a dream. Mister Patrick's always

been more keen on the bogeymen than I have, sir, and I paid it no mind. But after the second bad spell—the one where he saw the Tejano stabbing the soldier—he went and showed me something that he didn't show the others.'

"'What was it?'

"He walked over to where the Colonel now slept and pointed at a gash in the old uniform's breast, where the garment had been carefully mended.

"'The day Mister Patrick told me about that dream was the same day I mended this here hole in his shirt. Thought himself crazy, he did, and I can't say as I blame him. Because this hole is in exactly the spot where he dreamed the Tejano stabbed the Texian the night before. What do you think of that, sir?'

"'I've no idea what to think of it,' I replied. 'It is most peculiar.'

"'Then there's this third vision,' he went on patiently. 'The one he had last night. Says he saw a band of 'em with torches, marching toward him like a pack of demons. I don't know about that. But I sure know that yesterday morning, when I went to light a fire in the library, half our kindling was missing. Clean gone, sir. Didn't make much of it at the time, but this puts it in another light."

Sherlock Holmes, who had changed postures a gratifying number of times during my account, rubbed his long hands together avidly before clapping them once.

"It's splendid, my dear fellow. Positively first-class. The room was very bare indeed, you say?"

"Yes. Even in the midst of wealth, he lived like a soldier."

"I don't suppose you can tell me what you saw outside the window?"

I hesitated, reflecting as best I could.

"There was nothing outside the window, for I made certain to look. Jefferson assured me that he examined the grounds near the house after he discovered the missing firewood, and found no sign of unusual traffic. When I asked after an odd hole, he mentioned a tall lilac had been torn out from under the window weeks previous because it blocked the light, but that cannot have had any bearing. As I said, the bed faced the wall, not the window."

Holmes tilted his head back with a light laugh. "Yes, you did say that, and I assure you I am coming to a greater appreciation of your skills as an investigator. What happened next?"

"I quit the house soon afterward. The younger Warburtons were anxious to know what had transpired in the sick room, and I comforted them that their uncle was asleep, and unlikely to suffer another such outburst that day. But I assured them all, including Jefferson, that I would return the following afternoon to check on my patient.

"As I departed, I could not help but notice another man walking up the side path leading to the back door. He was very bronzed, with a long handlebar mustache, unkempt black hair, and he dressed in simple trousers and a rough linen shirt of the kind the Mexican laborers wore. This swarthy fellow paid me no mind, but walked straight ahead, and I seized the opportunity to memorize his looks in case he should come to have any bearing on the matter. I did not know what to make of the Colonel's ghostly affliction or Jefferson's bizarre account of its physical manifestation, but I thought it an odd enough coincidence to note.

"The next day, I saw a patient or two in the afternoon and then locked my practice, hailing a hack to take me up Nob Hill. Jefferson greeted me at the door and led me into a study of sorts, shelves stacked with gold-lettered military volumes and historical works. Colonel Warburton stood there dressed quite normally, in a gray summer suit, and he seemed bewildered by his own behavior the day before.

"'It's a bona fide curse, I can't help but think, and I'm suffering to end it,' he said to me. 'There are times I know I'm not in my right senses, and other times when I can see those wretched visions before me as clear as your face is now.'

"'Is there anything else you can tell me which might help in my diagnosis?'

"'Not that won't make me out to be cracked

in the head, Dr. Watson. After every one of these living nightmares, I've awakened with the same pain in my head, and I can't for the life of me decide whether I've imagined the whole thing, or I really am haunted by one of the men I killed during the war in Texas. Affairs were that muddled—I've no doubt I came out on one or more of the wrong Tejanos. So much bloodshed in those days, no man has the luxury of knowing he was always in the right.'

"'I am no expert in disorders of the mind,' I warned him, 'although I will do all I can for you. You ought to consult a specialist if your symptoms persist or worsen. May I have your permission, however, to ask a seemingly unrelated question?'

"'By all means.'

"'Have you in your employ, or do any of your servants or gardeners occasionally hire, Mexican workers?'

"He seemed quite puzzled by the question. 'I don't happen to have any Hispanos on my payroll. And when the staff need day labor, they almost always engage Chinese. They're quick and honest, and they come cheap. Why do you ask?'

"I convinced him that my question had been purely clinical, congratulated him on his recovery, and made my way to the foyer, mulling several new ideas over in my brain. Jefferson appeared to see me out, handing me my hat and stick.

"'Where are the other members of the household today?' I inquired.

"'Miss Molly is out paying calls, and Mister Charles is working in his darkroom.'

"'Jefferson, I saw a rather mysterious fellow yesterday as I was leaving. To your knowledge, are any men of Mexican or Chileno descent ever hired by the groundskeeper?'

"I would swear to you, Holmes, that a strange glow lit his eyes when I posed that question, but he merely shook his head. 'Anyone does any hiring, Dr. Watson, I know all about it. And no one of that type been asking after work here for six months and more.'

"'I was merely curious whether the sight of

such a man had upset the Colonel,' I explained, 'but as you know, he is much better today. I am no closer to tracing the source of his affliction, but I hope that if anything new occurs, or if you are ever in doubt, you will contact me.'

"'These spells, they come and they go, Dr. Watson,' Jefferson replied, 'but if I discover anything, I'll surely let you know of it.'

"When I quit the house, I set myself a brisk pace, for I thought to walk down the hill as evening fell. But just as I began my descent, and the wind picked up from the west, I saw not twenty yards ahead of me the same sun-burnished laborer I'd spied the day before, attired in the same fashion, and clearly having emerged from some part of the Warburton residence moments previous. The very sight of him roused my blood; I had not yet met you, of course, and thus knew nothing whatever of detective work, but some instinct told me to follow him to determine whether the Colonel was the victim of a malignant design."

"You followed him?" Holmes interjected, with a startled expression. "Whatever for?"

"I felt I had no choice—the parallels between his presence and Colonel Warburton's nightmares had to be explained."

"Ever the man of action." My friend shook his head. "Where did he lead you?"

"When he reached Broadway, where the land flattened and the mansions gave way to grocers, butcheries, and cigar shops, he stopped to mount a streetcar. By a lucky chance, I hailed a passing hack and ordered the driver to follow the streetcar until I called for him to stop.

"My quarry went nearly as far as the waterfront before he descended, and in a trice I paid my driver and set off in pursuit toward the base of Telegraph Hill. During the Gold Rush days, the ocean-facing slope had been a tent colony of Chilenos and Peruanos. That colony intermixed with the lowest hell of them all on its eastern flank: Sydney-Town, where the escaped Australian convicts and ticket-of-leave men ran the vilest public houses imaginable. It is a matter of historical record that the Fierce Grizzly employed a live bear chained outside its door."

"I have heard of that district," Holmes declared keenly. "The whole of it is known as the Barbary Coast, is it not? I confess I should have liked to see it in its prime, although there are any number of streets in London I can visit should I wish to take my life in my hands. You did not yourself encounter any wild beasts?"

"Not in the strictest sense; but inside of ten minutes, I found myself passing gin palaces that could have rivaled St. Giles for depravity. The gaslights appeared sickly and meager, and riotous men stumbled from one red-curtained den of thieves to the next, either losing their money willingly by gambling it away, or drinking from the wrong glass only to find themselves propped insensate in an alley the next morning without a cent to their name.

"At one point I thought I had lost sight of him, for a drayman's cart came between us, and at the same moment he ducked into one of the deadfalls. I soon ascertained where he had gone, however, and after a moment's hesitation entered the place myself.

"The light shone from cheap tallow candles and ancient kerosene lamps with dark purple shades. Losing no time, I approached the man and asked if I could speak with him.

"He stared at me silently, his dark eyes narrowed into slits. At last, he signaled the barman for a second drink, and handed me a small glass of clear liquor.

"I thanked him, but he remained dumb. 'Do you speak English?' I inquired finally.

"He grinned, and with an easy motion of his wrist flicked back his drink and set the empty glass on the bar. 'I speak it as well as you, *señor*. My name is Juan Portillo. What do you want?'

"'I want to know why you visited the Warburton residence yesterday, and again this afternoon.'

"His smile broadened even further. 'Ah, now I understand. You follow me?'

"'There have been suspicious events at that house, ones which I have reason to believe may concern you.'

"'I know nothing of suspicious events. They

hire me to do a job, and to be quiet. So I am quiet.'

"'I must warn you that if you attempt to harm the Colonel in any way, you will answer for it to me.'

"He nodded at me coldly, still smiling. 'Finish your drink, *señor*. And then I will show you something.'

"I had seen the saloon keeper pour my liquor from the same bottle as his, and thus could not object to drinking it. The stuff was strong as gin, but warmer, and left a fiery burn in the throat. I had barely finished it when Portillo drew out of some hidden pocket a very long, mother-of-pearl-handled knife.

"'I never harm the Colonel. I never even see this Colonel. But I tell you something anyway. Men who follow me, they answer to this,' he said, lifting the knife.

"He snarled something in Spanish. Three men, who had been sitting at a round table several yards away, stood up and strode toward us. Two carried pistols in their belts, and one tapped a short, stout cudgel in his hand. I was evaluating whether to make do with the bowie knife I kept on my person, or cut my losses and attempt an escape, when one of the men stopped short.

"'*Es el doctor!* Dr. Watson, yes?' he said eagerly.

"'After a moment's astonishment, I recognized a patient I had treated not two weeks before even though he could not pay me, a man who had gashed his leg so badly in a fight on the wharf, his friends had carried him to the nearest physician. He was profoundly happy to see me, a torrent of Spanish flowing from his lips, and before two minutes had passed of him gesturing proudly at his wound and pointing at me, Portillo's dispute had been forgotten. I did not press my luck, but joined them for another glass of that wretched substance and bade them farewell, Portillo's unblinking black eyes upon me until I was out of the bar and making for Front Street with all speed.

"The next day, I determined to report Portillo's presence to the Colonel, for as little as I understood, I now believed him an even more sinister character. To my dismay, however, I found the house in a terrible uproar."

"I am not surprised," Holmes nodded. "What had happened?"

"Sam Jefferson stood accused of breaking into Charles Warburton's darkroom with the intent to steal his photographic apparatus. The servant who opened the door to me was hardly lucid for her tears, and I heard cruel vituperations even from outside the house. Apparently, or so the downstairs maid said in her state of near-hysterics, Charles had already sacked Jefferson, but the Colonel was livid his nephew had acted without his approval, theft or no theft, and at the very moment I knocked, they were locked in a violent quarrel. From where I stood, I could hear Colonel Warburton screaming that Jefferson be recalled, and Charles shouting back that he had already suffered enough indignities in that house to last him a lifetime. Come now, Holmes, admit to me that the tale is entirely unique," I could not help but add, for the flush of color in my friend's face told me precisely how deeply he was interested.

"It is not the ideal word," he demurred. "I have not yet heard all, but there were cases in Lisbon and Salzburg within the last fifty years which may possibly have some bearing. Please, finish your story. You left, of course, for what gentleman could remain in such circumstances, and you called the next day upon the Colonel."

"I did not, as a matter of fact, call upon the Colonel."

"No? Your natural curiosity did not get the better of you?"

"When I arrived the following morning, Colonel Warburton as well as Sam Jefferson had vanished into thin air."

I had expected this revelation to strike like a bolt from the firmament, but was destined for disappointment.

"Ha," Holmes said with the trace of a smile. "Had they indeed?"

"Molly and Charles Warburton were beside themselves with worry. The safe had been opened and many deeds and securities, not to mention paper currency, were missing. There was no sign of force, so they theorized that their uncle had been compelled or convinced to provide the combination.

"A search party set out at once, of course, and descriptions of Warburton and Jefferson circulated, but to no avail. The mad Colonel and his servant, either together or separately, voluntarily or against their wills, quit the city without leaving a single clue behind them. Upon my evidence, the police brought Portillo in for questioning, but he provided a conclusive alibi and could not be charged. And so Colonel Warburton's obsession with war, as well as the inscrutable designs of his manservant, remain to this day unexplained.

"What do you think of it?" I finished triumphantly, for Holmes by this time leaned forward in his chair, entirely engrossed.

"I think that Sam Jefferson—apart from you and your noble intentions, my dear fellow—was quite the hero of this tale."

"How can you mean?" I asked, puzzled. "Surely the darkroom incident casts him in an extremely suspicious light. All we know is that he disappeared, probably with the Colonel, and the rumor in San Francisco told that they were both stolen away by the Tejano ghost who possessed the house. That is rubbish, of course, but even now I cannot think where they went, or why."

"It is impossible to know where they vanished," Holmes replied, his gray eyes sparkling, "but I can certainly tell you why."

"Dear God, you have solved it?" I exclaimed in delight. "You cannot be in earnest—I've wracked my brain over it all these years to no avail. What the devil happened?"

"First of all, Watson, I fear I must relieve you of a misapprehension. I believe Molly and Charles Warburton were the authors of a nefarious and subtle plot which, if not for your intervention and Sam Jefferson's, might well have succeeded."

"How could you know that?"

"Because you have told me, my dear fellow, and a very workman-like job you did in posting me up. Ask yourself when the Colonel's mental illness first began. What was his initial symptom?"

"He changed his will."

"It is, you will own, a very telling starting point. So telling, in fact, that we must pay it the most stringent attention." Holmes jumped to his feet and commenced pacing the carpet like a mathematician expounding over a theorem. "Now, there are very few steps—criminal or otherwise—one can take when one is disinherited. Forgery is a viable option, and the most common. Murder is out, unless your victim has yet to sign his intentions into effect. The Warburtons hit upon a scheme as cunning as it is rare: they undertook to prove a sane man mad."

"But, Holmes, that can scarcely be possible."

"I admit that fortune was undoubtedly in their favor. The Colonel already suffered from an irrational preoccupation with the supernatural. Additionally, his bedroom lacked any sort of ornament, and young Charles Warburton specialized in photographic technique."

"My dear chap, you know I've the utmost respect for your remarkable faculty, but I cannot fathom a word of what you just said," I confessed.

"I shall do better, then," he laughed. "Have we any reason to think Jefferson lied when he told you of the ghost's earthly manifestations?"

"He could have meant anything by it. He could have slit that hole and stolen that firewood himself."

"Granted. But it was after you told him of Portillo's presence that he broke into the photography studio."

"You see a connection between Portillo and Charles Warburton's photographs?"

"Decidedly so, as well as a connection between the photographs, the blank wall, and the torn-out lilac bush."

"Holmes, that doesn't even—"

I stopped myself as an idea dawned on me. Finally, after the passage of many years, I was beginning to understand.

"You are talking about a magic lantern," I said slowly. "By God, I have been so blind."

"You were remarkably astute, my boy, for you took note of every essential detail. As a matter of fact, I believe you can take it from here," he added with more than his usual grace.

"The Colonel disinherited his niece and nephew, possibly because he abhorred their mercenary natures, in favor of war charities," I stated hesitantly. "In a stroke of brilliance, they decided to make it seem war was his mania and he could not be allowed to so slight his kin. Charles hired Juan Portillo to appear in a series of photographs as a Tejano soldier, and promised that he would be paid handsomely if he kept the sessions dead secret. The nephew developed the images onto glass slides and projected them through a magic lantern device outside the window in the dead of night. His victim was so terrified by the apparition on his wall, he never thought to look for its source behind him. The first picture, threatening the white woman, likely featured Molly Warburton. But for the second plate . . ."

"That of the knife plunging into the Texian's chest, they borrowed the Colonel's old garb and probably placed it on a dummy. The firewood disappeared when a number of men assembled, further off on the grounds, to portray rebels with torches. The lilac, as is obvious—"

"Stood in the way of the magic lantern apparatus," I cried. "What could be simpler?"

"And the headaches the Colonel experienced afterward?" my friend prodded me.

"Likely an aftereffect of an opiate or narcotic his family added to his meal in order to heighten the experience of the vision in his bedchamber."

"And Sam Jefferson?"

"A deeply underestimated opponent who saw the Warburtons for what they were and kept a constant watch. The only thing he stole was a look at the plates in Charles's studio as his final piece of evidence. When they sent him packing, he told the Colonel all he knew and they—"

"Were never heard from again," Holmes finished with a poetic flourish.

"In fact, it was the perfect revenge," I laughed. "Colonel Warburton had no interest in his own wealth, and he took more than enough to live from the safe. And after all, when he was finally declared dead, his estate was distributed just as he wished it."

"Yes, a number of lucky events occurred. I am grateful, as I confess I have been at other times, that you are an utterly decent fellow, my dear doctor."

"I don't understand," I said in some confusion.

"I see the world in terms of cause and effect. If you had not been the sort of man willing to treat a rogue wounded in a knife fight who had no means of paying you, it is possible you would not have had the opportunity to tell me this story."

"It wasn't so simple as all that," I muttered, rather abashed, "but thank—"

"And an admirable story it was too. You know, Watson," Holmes continued, extinguishing his pipe, "from all I have heard of America, it must be an exceedingly fertile ground for men of mettle. The place lives almost mythically in the estimations of most Englishmen. I myself have scarcely met an American, ethically inclined or otherwise, who did not possess a certain audacity of mind."

"It's the pioneer in them, I suppose. Still, I cannot help but think that you are more than a match for anyone, American or otherwise," I assured him.

"I would not presume to contradict you, but that vast expanse boasts more than its share of crime as well as of imagination, and for that reason commands some respect. I am not a complete stranger to the American criminal," he said with a smile.

"I should be delighted to hear you expound on that subject," I exclaimed, glancing longingly at my notebook and pen.

"Another time, perhaps." My friend paused, his long fingers drumming along with the drops as he stared out our front window, eyes glittering brighter than the rain-soaked street below.

"Perhaps one day we may both find occasion to test ourselves further on their soil." He glanced back at me abruptly. "I should have liked to have met this Sam Jefferson, for instance. He had a decided talent."

"Talent or no, he was there to witness the events; you solved them based on a secondhand account by a man who'd never so much as heard of the Science of Deduction at the time."

"There are precious few crimes in this world, merely a hundred million variations," he shrugged. "It was a fetching little problem, however, no matter it was not matchless. The use of the magic lantern, although I will never prove it, I believe to have been absolutely inspired. Now," he proclaimed, striding to his violin and picking it up, "if you would be so kind as to locate the brandy and cigars you mentioned earlier, I will show my appreciation by entertaining you in turn. You've come round to my liking for Kreutzer, I think? Capital. I must thank you for bringing your very interesting case to my attention; I shall lose no time informing my brother I solved it without moving a muscle. And now, friend Watson, we shall continue our efforts to enliven a dreary afternoon."

The Infernal Machine

JOHN LUTZ

WITH MORE THAN forty novels and two hundred short stories to his credit, John Thomas Lutz (1939–) has demonstrated both the ingenuity and work ethic of historically prolific writers who turned out entertaining prose year after year. Born in Dallas, Lutz moved to St. Louis when young and has lived there ever since. Before becoming a full-time writer in 1975, he had jobs as a construction worker, theater usher, warehouse worker, truck driver, and switchboard operator for the St. Louis Metropolitan Police Department.

His writing career has been as varied as his background, producing private-eye stories and many other types of fiction, including political suspense, humor, occult, psychological suspense, espionage, historical, futuristic, police procedural, and urban suspense. When asked why he writes serial-killer novels, he replied, "Serial paychecks." His first series character, Alo Nudger, who debuted in *Buyer Beware* (1976), is an unlikely private eye, so compassionate that he appears meek, a borderline coward paralyzed by overdue bills, clients who refuse to pay him, and a blood-sucking former wife.

A more traditional character is the Florida-based P.I. Fred Carver, a former cop forced off the job when a street punk kneecapped him; his first appearance is in *Tropical Heat* (1986). Lutz's most commercially successful book is probably *SWF Seeks Same* (1990), a suspense thriller that served as the basis for the 1992 movie *Single White Female* starring Bridget Fonda and Jennifer Jason Leigh. His novel *The Ex* (1996) was adapted for an HBO movie of the same title in 1997; Lutz coauthored the screenplay.

Lutz has served as the president of the Mystery Writers of America and has been nominated for three Edgar Awards, winning in 1986 for best short story for "Ride the Lightning."

"The Infernal Machine" was first published in *The New Adventures of Sherlock Holmes*, edited by Martin Harry Greenberg and Carol-Lynn Rössel Waugh (New York, Carroll & Graf, 1987).

THE INFERNAL MACHINE

John Lutz

NOT THAT, AT times, my dear friend and associate Sherlock Holmes can't play the violin quite beautifully, but at the moment the melancholy, wavering tunelessness produced by the shrill instrument was getting on my nerves.

I put down my copy of the *Times*. "Holmes, must you be so repetitious in your choice of notes?"

"It's in the very repetition that I hope to find some semblance of order and meaning," he said. He held his hawkish profile high, tucked the violin tighter beneath his narrow chin, and the screeching continued—certainly more piercing than before.

"Holmes!"

"Very well, Watson." He smiled and placed the violin back in its case. Then he slumped into the wing chair opposite me, tamped tobacco into his clay pipe, and assumed the attitude of a spoiled child whose mince pie has been withheld for disciplinary purposes. I knew where he'd turn next, after finding no solace in the violin, and I must confess I felt guilty at having been harsh with him.

When he's acting the hunter in his capacity as consulting detective, no man is more vibrant with interest than Holmes. But when he's had no case for some weeks, and there's no prospect of one on the horizon, he becomes zombielike in his withdrawal into boredom. It had been nearly a month since the successful conclusion of the case of the twice-licked stamp.

Holmes suddenly cocked his head to the side, almost in the manner of a bird stalking a worm, at the clatter of footsteps on the stairs outside our door. From below, the cheerful voice of Mrs. Hudson wafted up, along with her light, measured footfalls. A man's voice answered her pleasantries. Neither voice was loud enough to be understood by us.

"Visitor, Watson." Even as Holmes spoke there was a firm knock on the door.

I rose, crossed the cluttered room, and opened it.

"A Mr. Edgewick to see Mr. Holmes," Mrs. Hudson said, and withdrew.

I ushered Edgewick in and bade him sit in the chair where I'd been perusing the *Times*. He was a large, handsome man in his mid-thirties, wearing a well-cut checked suit and polished boots that had reddish mud on their soles. He had straight blond hair and an even blonder brush-trimmed mustache. He looked up at me with a troubled expression and said, "Mr. Holmes?"

I smiled. "You've recently come from Northwood," I said. "You're unmarried and are concerned about the well-being of a woman."

Holmes, too, was smiling. "Amazing, Watson. Pray tell us how you did it."

"Certainly. The red clay on Mr. Edgewick's boots is found mainly in Northwood. He's not wearing a wedding ring, so he isn't married. And since he's a handsome chap and obviously in some personal distress, the odds are good there's a young woman involved."

Holmes's amused eyes darted to Edgewick, who seemed flustered by my incisiveness.

"Actually," he said, "I am married—my ring is

at the jewelers being resized. The matter I came here about only indirectly concerns a woman. And I haven't been to Northwood in years."

"The hansom cab you arrived in apparently carried a recent passenger from Northwood," Holmes said. "The mud should dry on this warm day as the hansom sits downstairs awaiting your return."

I must admit my mouth fell open, as did Edgewick's. "How on earth did you know he'd instructed a hansom to wait, Holmes? You were nowhere near the window."

Holmes gave a backhand wave, trailing his long fingers. "If Mr. Edgewick hasn't been to Northwood, Watson, the most logical place for him to have picked up the red mud is from the floor of the hansom cab."

Edgewick was sitting forward, intrigued. "But how did you know I'd arrived in a hansom to begin with, and instructed the driver to wait downstairs?"

"Your walking stick."

I felt my eyebrows raise as I looked again where Edgewick sat. "What walking stick, Holmes?"

"The one whose tip left the circular indentation on the toe of Mr. Edgewick's right boot as he sat absently leaning on it in the cab, as is the habit of many men who carry a stick. The soft leather still maintains the impression. And since he hasn't the walking stick with him, and his footfalls on the stairs preclude him from having brought it up with him to leave outside in the hall, we can deduce that he left it in the hansom. Since he hardly seems a careless man, or the possessor of a limitless number of walking sticks, this would suggest that he ordered the cab to wait for him."

Edgewick looked delighted. "Why, that's superb! So much from a mere pair of boots!"

"A parlor game," Holmes snapped, "when not constructively applied." Again his slow smile as he made a tent with his lean fingers and peered over it. His eyes were unwavering and sharply focused now. "And I suspect you bring some serious matter that will allow proper application of my skills."

"Oh, I do indeed. Uh, my name is Wilson Edgewick, Mr. Holmes."

Holmes made a sweeping gesture with his arm in my direction. "My associate, Dr. Watson."

Edgewick nodded to me. "Yes, I've read his accounts of some of your adventures. Which is why I think you might be able to help me—rather help my brother Landen, actually."

Holmes settled back in his chair, his eyes half closed. I knew he wasn't drowsy when he took on such an appearance, but was in fact a receptacle for every bit of information that might flow his way, accepting this as pertinent, rejecting that as irrelevant—acutely alert.

"Do tell us about it, Mr. Edgewick," he said.

Edgewick glanced at me. I nodded encouragement.

"My brother Landen is engaged to Millicent Oldsbolt."

"Oldsbolt Munitions?" Holmes asked.

Edgewick nodded, not surprised that Holmes would recognize the Oldsbolt name. Oldsbolt Limited was a major supplier of small arms for the military. I had, in fact, fired Oldsbolt rounds through my army revolver while in the service of the Queen.

"The wedding was to be next spring," Edgewick went on. "When Landen, and myself, would be financially well-off."

"Well-off as a result of what?" Holmes asked.

"We're the English representatives of one Richard Gatling, the inventor of the Gatling gun."

I couldn't help but ask, "What on earth is that?"

"It's an infernal machine that employs many barrels and one firing chamber," Holmes said. "The cartridges are fed to the chamber by means of a long belt, while the barrels revolve and fire one after the other in rapid succession. The shooter need only aim generally and turn a crank with one hand while the other depresses the trigger. It's said the Gatling gun can fire almost a hundred rounds per minute. It was used in the Indian Wars in America, on the plains, with great effectiveness."

"Very good, Mr. Holmes!" Edgewick said. "I see you're well versed in military ordnance."

"It sounds a fiendish device," I said, imagining those revolving barrels spewing death to man and beast.

"As war itself is fiendish," Holmes said. "Not at all a game. But do continue, Mr. Edgewick."

"Landen and I were staying at the King's Knave Inn in the town of Alverston, north of London. To be near the Oldsbolt estate. You see, we were trying to sell the idea of the Gatling gun to Sir Clive Oldsbolt for manufacture for the British forces. The gun had passed all tests, and Sir Clive had offered a price I'm sure the American manufacturer would have accepted."

Holmes pursed his thin lips thoughtfully, then said, "You speak often in the past tense, Mr. Edgewick. As if your brother's wedding has been canceled. As if now Oldsbolt Limited is no longer interested in your deadly gun."

"Both those plans have been dealt the severest blow, Mr. Holmes. You see, last night Sir Clive was murdered."

I drew in my breath with shock. Holmes, however, leaned forward in his chair, keenly interested, almost pleased. "Ah! Murdered how?"

"He was returning home late from the King's Knave Inn, alone in his carriage, when he was shot. A villager found him this morning, after hearing the noise last night."

Holmes's nostrils actually quivered. "Noise?"

"Rapid gunfire, Mr. Holmes. Shots fired in quick, rhythmic succession."

"The Gatling gun."

"No, no. That's what the chief constable at Alverston says. But the gun we used for demonstration purposes had been cleaned and not fired again. I swear it! Of course, the local constabulary and villagers all say that Landen cleaned it after killing Sir Clive."

"Your brother has been arrested for his future father-in-law's murder?" I asked in astonishment.

"Indeed!" Edgewick said in great agitation. "That's why I rushed here after he was taken into custody. I thought only Mr. Holmes could make right of such a mistake."

"Does your brother Landen have any motive for murdering his fiancée's father?"

"No! Quite the opposite! Sir Clive's death means the purchase of the Gatling gun manufacturing rights has been canceled. As well, of course, as Landen and Millicent's wedding. And yet . . ."

Holmes waited, his body perfectly still.

"Yet, Mr. Holmes, the sound the villagers in the inn described could be none other than the rattling, measured firing of the Gatling gun."

"But you said you examined it and it hadn't been recently fired."

"Oh, I'll swear to that, Mr. Holmes—for all the good it will do poor Landen."

"Perhaps a different Gatling gun."

"There is no other in England, Mr. Holmes. Of that you can be sure. We crossed the Atlantic just last week with this one, and Mr. Gatling knows the whereabouts of all his machines. Understand, sir, this is a formidable weapon that threatens the very existence of nations if in the wrong hands. It will change the nature of warfare and isn't to be taken lightly."

"How many times was Sir Clive shot?" Holmes asked.

"Seven. All through the chest with large-caliber bullets, like those fired by the Gatling gun. The village doctor removed the two bullets that didn't pass through Sir Clive, but they became misshapen when striking bone, so their precise caliber can't be determined."

"I see. It's all very interesting."

"Will you come at once to Alverston, Mr. Holmes, and determine what can be done for my brother?"

"You *did* say Sir Clive had been shot seven times, Mr. Edgewick?"

"I did."

Holmes stood up from the wing chair as abruptly as if he'd been stuck by a cushion spring. "Then Watson and I shall take the afternoon train to Alverston and meet you at the King's Knave Inn. Now, I suggest you return to your brother and his fiancée, where you're no doubt sorely needed."

Edgewick smiled broadly with relief and

stood. "I intend to pay you well, Mr. Holmes. Landen and I are not without means."

"We'll discuss all that later," Holmes said, placing a hand on Edgewick's shoulder and guiding him to the door. "In the meantime, tell your brother that if he's innocent he need have no concern and might well outlive the hangman."

"I'll tell him that, Mr. Holmes. It will comfort him, I'm sure. Good day to both of you." He went out the door, burst back in momentarily, and added, "Thank you, Mr. Holmes! For me and for Landen!"

Holmes and I stood listening to his descending tread on the stairs.

Holmes parted the curtain and looked after our visitor as he emerged onto Baker Street. The shouts of vendors and the clattering of horses' hooves drifted into the room, along with the pungent smells of London. "An extremely distressed young man, Watson."

"Indeed, Holmes."

He rubbed his hands together with a glee and animation that would have been impossible to him fifteen minutes ago. "We must pack, Watson, if we're to catch the afternoon train to Alverston." His gaunt face grew momentarily grave. "And I suggest you bring along your service revolver."

I had fully intended to do that. Where a member of nobility is shot seven times on his way from inn to home, any act of the direst nature might be possible.

The King's Knave Inn was but a short distance from the Alverston train depot, just outside the town proper. It was a large tudor structure, bracketed by huge stone chimneys, one at each end of its steeply pitched slate roof.

Wilson Edgewick wasn't among the half-dozen local patrons seated at small wooden tables. A beefy, red-faced man, with a thinning crop of ginger hair slicked back on his wide head, was dispensing drinks, while a fragile blond woman with a limp was carrying them to the tables.

I made arrangements for satisfactory rooms while Holmes surveyed the place. There was a young man seated at a nearby table, looking disconsolate, as if he were too far into his cups. Two old-timers—one with a bulbous red nose, the other with a sharp gray hatchetlike face—sat at another table engrossed in a game of draughts. Three middle-aged men of the sort who work the land sat slumped about a third table, their conversation suspended as they mildly observed us.

"Now, you'd be Mr. Holmes, the famous detective," the red-faced pub owner, whose name was Beech, said to Holmes with a tinge of respect as he studied the guest register I'd signed; "or my guess'd be far wrong." Alcohol fumes wafted on his breath.

Holmes nodded. "I've enjoyed my share of successes."

"Look just like your pictures drawed in the *Daily Telegraph*, you do."

"I find them distinctly unflattering."

One of Beech's rheumy eyes was running, and he swiped at it with the back of his hand as he said, "Don't take a detective to know why you're here, though."

"Quite so," Holmes said. "A tragic affair."

"Weren't it so!" Beech's complexion got even ruddier, and a blue vein in his temple began a wild pulsation. A conspiratorial light entered his eyes. He sniffed and wiped again at the watery one. "We heard it all here, Mr. Holmes. Witnesses to murder, we was, here at the inn."

"How is that?" asked Holmes, much interested.

"We was standing here as we are now, sir, late last night, when we heard the infernal machine spitting its death."

"The Gatling gun?"

"That's what it was." He leaned forward, wiping his strong, square hands on his stained apron. "A sort of 'rat-a-tat-tat-tat,' it was." Spittle flew as he described the sound of the repeating-fire gun. "Well, we'd heard the gun fired before and knew the noise right off, sir. But not from that direction." He waved a hand toward the north. "In the morning, Ingraham Codder was on the north road to go and see

Lord Clive at the house. Instead he sees one of the lord's gray geldings and the fine two-hitch carriage the lord comes to town in. The other gelding somehow got unhitched and was standing nearby. Lord Clive himself was slumped down in the carriage dead. Shot full of holes, Mr. Holmes. Seven of 'em, there was."

"So I've heard. Did anyone else hear this 'rat-a-tat-tat' sound?" Holmes managed to describe the gunfire without expectorating.

"All three of us did," spoke up one of the farmers at the table. "It was just as Mr. Beech described."

"And what time was it?" Holmes asked.

"Half past eleven on the mark," Beech said. "Just about ten minutes after poor Sir Clive left here after downing his customary bit of stout." The patrons all agreed.

The young man alone at his table gazed up at us, and I was surprised to see that he wasn't as affected by drink as I'd assumed by his attitude. His gray eyes were quite clear in a well-set-up face; he had a firm jawline and a strong nose and cheekbones. "They've got Sir Clive's murderer under lock," he said. "Or so they say."

"And you are, sir?" Holmes asked.

"He's Robby Smythe," Beech cut in. "It's horseless carriages what's his folly. If you can imagine that."

"Really?" Holmes said.

"Yes, sir. I have two of them that I'm improving on and will soon manufacture and sell in great numbers, Mr. Holmes. In ten years everyone in England shall drive one."

I couldn't contain myself. "Everyone? Come now!"

Holmes laughed. "Not you, Watson, not you, I'd wager."

"Young Robby here's got a special interest in seeing justice done," Beech said. "He's engaged to Sir Clive's youngest daughter, Phoebe."

"Is he now?" Holmes said. "Then you know the Edgewick brothers, no doubt."

Smythe nodded. "I've met them both, sir."

"And would you say Landen Edgewick is capable of this act?"

Smythe seemed to look deep into himself for the answer. "I suppose, truth be told, under certain circumstances we're all capable of killing a man we hate. But no one had reason to hate Sir Clive. He was a kind and amiable man, even if stern."

"Point is," Beech said, "only the Edgewick brothers had knowledge and access to the Gatling gun. I say with the law that Landen Edgewick is the killer."

"It would seem so," Holmes acknowledged. "But why Landen Edgewick? Where was Wilson?"

Beech grinned and swiped again at the watery eye. "Up in his room at the top of them stairs, Mr. Holmes. He couldn't have had a fig to do with Sir Clive's murder. Had neither the time nor the opportunity. I came out from behind the serving counter and seen him step out of his room just after the shots was fired. He came down then and had himself a glass of stout. We told him we'd heard the gun, but he laughed and said that was impossible, it was locked away in the carriage house him and his brother had borrowed out near Sir Clive's estate." He snorted and propped his ruddy fists on his hips. "Locked away, my eye, Mr. Holmes!"

"Very good, Mr. Beech," Holmes said. "You remind me of my friend Inspector Lestrade of Scotland Yard."

Looking quite pleased, Beech instructed the waitress and maid, Annie, to show us to his best rooms.

Wilson Edgewick arrived shortly thereafter, seeming overjoyed to see us. He was, if anything, even more distraught over the plight of his brother. He had been to see Landen's fiancée Millicent Oldsbolt, the daughter of the man his brother had allegedly murdered, and the meeting had obviously upset him. A wedding was hardly in order under the circumstances.

Wilson explained to us that Landen had arrived here from London two days before he and had taken up lodgings at the inn. The brothers had declined an invitation to stay at the Oldsbolts' home, as they had final adjustments and technical decisions to make preparatory to demonstrating the Gatling gun to Sir Clive.

The night of the murder, from Wilson's point of view, was much as had been described by Beech and the inn's patrons, though Wilson himself had been in his room at the precise time of the shooting and hadn't heard the gun.

"The next morning, after Sir Clive's body was found," he said, "I hurried directly to the carriage house. The Gatling gun was there, mounted on its wagon, and it hadn't been fired since the last test and cleaning."

"And did you point this out to the local constable?" Holmes asked.

"I did, after Landen was taken in for the crime. Chief Constable Roberts told me there'd been plenty of time for him to have cleaned the Gatling gun after Sir Clive had been shot, then return on the sly to his room. No one saw Landen until the morning after the murder, during which he claimed to have been asleep."

Holmes paced slowly back and forth, cupping his chin in his hand.

"What, pray God, are we going to do?" Wilson blurted out, unable to stand the silence.

Holmes stood still and faced him. "Watson and I will unpack," he said, "then you can take us to examine the scene of Sir Clive's murder, and to talk to the victim's family."

The rest of that afternoon was spent gathering large as well as minute pieces of information that might mean little to anyone other than Sherlock Holmes, but which I'd seen him time and again use to draw the noose snug around those who'd done evil. It was a laborious but unerringly effective process.

We were driven out the road toward Sir Clive's estate, but our first stop was where he'd been killed.

"See this, Watson," Holmes said, hopping down out of the carriage. "The road dips and bends here, so the horses would have to slow. And there is cover in that thick copse of trees. A perfect spot for an ambush."

He was right, of course, in general. The rest of the land around the murder scene was almost flat, however, and any hidden gunman would have had to run the risk that someone in the vicinity might see him fleeing after the deed was done.

I got down and stood in the road while Holmes wandered over and examined the trees. He returned walking slowly, his eyes fixed to the ground, pausing once to stoop and drag his fingers along the earth.

"What's he looking for?" Wilson Edgewick whispered.

"If we knew," I told him, "it wouldn't mean much to us."

"Were any spent cartridges found?" Holmes asked Edgewick, when he'd reached us. He was wiping a dark smudge from his fingers with his handkerchief.

"No, Mr. Holmes."

"And the spent shells stay in the ammunition belt of the Gatling gun rather than being ejected onto the ground after firing?"

"Exactly. The belts are later refitted with fresh ammunition."

"I see." Holmes bent down suddenly. "Hello. What have we here, Watson?" He'd withdrawn something small and white almost from beneath my boot.

I leaned close for a better look. "A feather, Holmes. Only a white feather."

He nodded, absently folding the feather in his handkerchief and slipping it into his waistcoat pocket. "And here is where the body was found?" He pointed to the sharp bend in the road.

"Actually down there about a hundred feet," Edgewick said. "The theory is that the horses trotted on a ways after Sir Clive was shot and the reins were dropped."

"And what of the horse that was found standing off to the side?"

Edgewick shrugged. "It had been improperly hitched, I suppose, and worked its way loose. It happens sometimes."

"Yes, I know," Holmes said. He walked around a while longer, peering at the ground. Edgewick glanced at me, eager to get on to the house. I raised a cautioning hand so he wouldn't interrupt Holmes's musings. In the distance a flock of wrens rose from the treetops, twisting as one dark form with the wind.

After examining the murder scene we drove to the carriage house and saw the Gatling gun itself. It was manufactured of blued steel and smelled of oil and was beautiful in a horrible way.

"This shouldn't be allowed in warfare," I heard myself say in an awed voice.

"It is so terrible," Edgewick said, "that perhaps eventually it will eliminate warfare as an alternative and become the great instrument of peace. That's our fervent hope."

"An interesting concept," Holmes said. He sniffed at the clustered barrels and firing chambers of the infernal machine. Then he wiped from his fingers some gun oil he'd gotten on his hand, smiled, and said, "I think we've seen quite enough here. Shall we go on to the house?"

"Let's," Edgewick said. He seemed upset as well as impatient. "It appears that progress will be slow and not so certain."

"Not at all," Holmes said, following him out the door and waiting while he set the lock. "Already I've established that your brother is innocent."

I heard my own intake of breath. "But Holmes—"

"No revelations yet," Holmes said, waving a languid hand. "I merely wanted to lessen our young friend's anguish for his brother. The explanation is still unfolding."

When we reached the house we were greeted by Eames the butler, a towering but cadaverously thin man, who ushered us into the drawing room. The room took up most of the east wing of the rambling, ivy-covered house, and was oak-paneled and well furnished with comfortable chairs, a game table, a Persian carpet, and a blazing fire in a ponderous stone fireplace. French doors opened out onto a wide lawn.

Wilson Edgewick introduced us around. The delicately beautiful but sad-eyed woman in the leather chair was Millicent, Landen's fi-

ancée. Standing by the window was a small, dark-haired girl of pleasant demeanor: Phoebe Oldsbolt, Millicent's younger sister and Robby Smythe's romantic interest. Robby Smythe himself lounged near the stone fireplace. Standing erectly near a sideboard and sipping a glass of red wine was a sturdily built man in tweeds who was introduced as Major Ardmont of the Queen's Cavalry.

"Sir Clive was a retired officer of cavalry, was he not?" Holmes asked, after offering his condolences to the grieving daughters of the deceased.

"Indeed he was," Ardmont said. "I met Sir Clive in the service at Aldershot some years ago, and we served together in Afghanistan. Of course, that was when we were both much younger men. But when I cashiered out and returned from India, I heard the news that Sir Clive had been killed; I saw it as my duty to come and offer what support I could."

"Decent of you," I said.

"I understand you were a military man, Dr. Watson," Ardmont said. He had a tan skin and pure blue, marksman's eyes that were zeroed in on me. That look gave me a cold feeling, as if I were quarry.

"Yes," I said. "Saw some rough and tumble. Did my bit as a surgeon."

"Well," Ardmont said, turning away, "we all do what we can."

"You and Doctor Watson must move from the inn and stay here until this awful thing is settled!" Millicent said to Holmes.

"Please do!" her sister Phoebe chimed in. Their voices were similar, high and melodious.

"I'd feel better if you were here," Robby Smythe said. "You'd afford the girls some protection. I'd stay here myself, but it would hardly be proper."

"You live at the inn, do you not?" Holmes asked.

"Yes, but I don't know what it is those fools heard. I was in my shop working on my autocar when the shooting occurred."

Holmes stared at Major Ardmont, who

looked back at him with those unrattled blue eyes. "Major, you hardly seem old enough to have just retired from service."

"It isn't age, Mr. Holmes. I've been undone by an old wound, I'm afraid, and can no longer sit a horse."

"Pity," I said.

"I understand," Holmes said, looking at Millicent, "that Eames overheard your father and Landen Edgewick arguing the evening of the murder."

"That's what Eames said, Mr. Holmes, and I'm sure he's telling the truth. At the same time, I know that no matter what their differences, Landen wouldn't kill my father—nor anyone else!" Her eyes danced with anger as she spoke. A spirited girl.

"You haven't answered us, Mr. Holmes," Phoebe Oldsbolt said. "Will you and Dr. Watson accept our hospitality?"

"Kind of you to offer," Holmes said, "but I assure you it won't be necessary." He smiled thinly and seemed lost for a moment in thought. Then he nodded, as if he'd made up his mind about something. "I'd like to talk with Eames the butler, and then spend a few hours in town."

Millicent appeared puzzled. "Certainly, Mr. Holmes. But you and Dr. Watson shall at least dine here tonight, I insist."

Holmes nodded with a slight bow. "It's a meal I anticipate with pleasure, Miss Oldsbolt."

"As do I," I added, and followed Holmes toward the door.

Outside, while waiting for the buggy to be brought around, Holmes drew me aside.

"I suggest you stay here, Watson. And see that no one leaves."

"But no one seems to have any intention of leaving, Holmes."

He gazed skyward for a moment. "Have you noticed any wild geese since we've been here, Watson?"

"Uh, of course not, Holmes. There are no wild geese in this part of England in October. I know; I've hunted in this region."

"Precisely, Watson."

"Holmes—"

But the coachman had brought round the buggy, and Holmes had cracked the whip and was gone. I watched the black, receding image of the buggy and the thin, erect figure on the seat. As they faded into the haze on the flat landscape I thought I saw Holmes lean forward, urging the mare to go faster.

When Holmes returned later that evening, and we were upstairs dressing for dinner, I asked him why he'd gone into town.

"To talk to Annie," he told me, craning his lean neck and fastening his collar button.

"Annie?"

"The maid at the King's Knave Inn, Watson."

"But what on earth for, Holmes?"

"It concerned her duties, Watson."

There was a knock on the door, and Eames summoned us for dinner. I knew any further explanation would have to wait for the moment when Holmes chose to divulge the facts of the case.

Everyone who had been in the drawing room when we'd first arrived was at the table in the long dining hall. The room was high-ceilinged and somewhat gloomy, with wide windows that looked out on a well-tended garden. Paintings of various past Oldsbolts hung on one wall. None of them looked particularly happy, perhaps because of the grim commerce the family had long engaged in.

The roast mutton and boiled vegetables were superb, though the polite dinner conversation was commonplace and understandably strained.

It was afterward, in the oak-paneled drawing room where we were enjoying our port, that Millicent Oldsbolt said, "Did you make any progress in your trip to town, Mr. Holmes?"

"Ah, yes," Major Aldmont said, "did you discover any clues as to the killer's identity? That's what you were looking for, was it not?"

"Not exactly," Holmes said. "I've known for a while who really killed Sir Clive; my trip into town was in the nature of a search for confirmation."

"Good Lord!" Ardmont said. "You've actually known?"

"And did you find such confirmation?" Robby Smythe asked, tilting forward in his chair.

"Indeed," Holmes said. "One might say I reconstructed the crime. The murderer lay in wait for Sir Clive in a nearby copse of trees, saw the carriage approach, and moved into sight so Sir Clive would stop. With very little warning, he shot Sir Clive, emptying his gun to be sure his prey was dead."

"Gatling gun, you mean," Major Ardmont said.

"Not at all. A German Army sidearm, actually, of the type that holds seven rounds in its cylinder."

"But the rapid-fire shots heard at the inn!" Robby Smythe exclaimed.

"I'll soon get to that," Holmes said. "The murderer then made his escape, but found he couldn't get far. He had to return almost a mile on foot, take one of Sir Clive's horses from the carriage hitch, and use it to pull him away from the scene of the crime."

Robby Smythe tilted his head curiously. "But why would Landen—"

"Not Landen," Holmes cut him off. "Someone else. The man Eames only assumed it was Landen when he heard a man arguing with Sir Clive earlier that evening. Landen was where he claimed to be during the time of the murder, asleep in his room at the inn. He did *not* later return unseen through his window as the chief constable so obstinately states."

"The constable's theory fits the facts," Major Ardmont said.

"But I'm telling you the facts," Holmes replied archly.

"Then what shooting did the folks at the inn hear?" Millicent asked.

"They heard no shooting," Holmes said. "They heard the rapid-fire explosions of an internal combustion engine whose muffling device had blown off. The driver of the horseless carriage had to stop it immediately lest he awaken everyone in the area. He then returned to the

scene of the murder and got the horse to pull the vehicle to where it could be hidden. Then he turned the animal loose, knowing it would go back to the carriage on the road, or all the way here to the house."

"But who—"

Phoebe Oldsbolt didn't get to finish her query. Robby Smythe was out of his chair like a tiger. He flung his half-filled glass of port at Holmes, who nimbly stepped aside. Smythe burst through the French doors and ran toward where he'd left his horseless carriage alongside the west wing of the house.

"Quick, Holmes!" I shouted, drawing my revolver. "He'll get away!"

"No need for haste, Watson. It seems that Mr. Smythe's tires are of the advanced pneumatic kind. I took the precaution of letting the air out of them before dinner."

"Pneumatic?" Major Ardmont said.

"Filled with atmosphere under pressure so they support the vehicle on a cushion of air," Holmes said, "as you well know, Major."

I hefted the revolver and ran for the French windows. I could hear footsteps behind me, but not in front. I prayed that Smythe hadn't made his escape.

But he was frantically wrestling with a crank on the front of a strange-looking vehicle. Its motor was coughing and wheezing but wouldn't supply power. When he saw me, he gave up on the horseless carriage and ran. I gave chase, realized I'd never be able to overtake a younger man in good condition, and fired a shot into the air. "Halt, Smythe!"

He turned and glared at me.

"I'll show you the mercy you gave Sir Clive!" I shouted.

He hesitated, shrugged, and trudged back toward the house.

"Luckily, the contraption wouldn't start," I said, as we waited in the drawing room for Wilson Edgewick to return with the Chief Constable.

"I was given to understand the horseless carriage can be driven slowly on deflated tires," Holmes said, "but not at all with this missing." He held up what looked like a length of stiff black cord. "It's called a spark wire, I believe. I call removing it an added precaution."

Everyone seemed in better spirits except for Robby Smythe and Phoebe. Smythe appealed with his eyes to the daughter of the man he'd killed and received not so much as a glance of charity.

"How could you possibly have known?" Millicent asked. She was staring in wonder at Holmes, her fine features aglow, now that her world had been put back partly right.

Holmes crossed his long arms and rocked back on his heels while I held my revolver on Smythe.

"This afternoon, when Watson and I examined the scene of the murder, I found a feather on the ground near where the body was discovered. I also found a black sticky substance on the road."

"Oil!" I said.

"And thicker than that used to lubricate the Gatling gun, as I later ascertained. I was reasonably sure then that a horseless carriage had been used for the murder, as the oil was quite fresh and little had been absorbed into the ground. The machine had to have been there recently. When Smythe here tried to make his escape after shooting Sir Clive, the muffling device that quiets the machine's motor came off or was blown from the pressure, and the hammering exhaust of the internal combustion made a noise much like the rapid-fire clatter of the Gatling gun. Which led inn patrons to suppose the gun was what they'd heard near the time of the murder. Smythe couldn't drive his machine back to its stall in such a state, and couldn't silence it, so he had one of Sir Clive's horses pull him back. If only the earth hadn't been so hard, this would all have been quite obvious, perhaps even to Chief Constable Roberts."

"Not at all likely," Millicent said.

"It was Smythe whom Eames overheard arguing with Sir Clive," Holmes continued. "And

Major Ardmont, who is a member of the German military, knows why."

Ardmont nodded curtly. "When did you realize I wasn't one of your Cavalry?" he asked.

"I knew you were telling the truth about being in the cavalry, and serving in a sunny clime," Holmes said, "but the faint line of your helmet and chinstrap on your sunburned forehead and face doesn't conform to that of the Queen's Cavalry helmet. They do suggest shading of the helmet worn by the German horse soldier. I take it you received your sun-darkening not in India but in Africa, in the service of your country."

"Excellent, Mr. Holmes!" Ardmont said, with genuine admiration. "Mr. Smythe," he said, "had been trying to convince Sir Clive to get the British military interested in his horseless machine as a means to transport troops or artillery. A hopeless task, as it turned out, with an old horseman like Sir Clive. Smythe contacted us, and introduced me to Sir Clive. He told Sir Clive that if the British didn't show interest in his machines, he'd negotiate with us. And we were quite willing to negotiate, Mr. Holmes. We Germans do feel there's a future for the internal combustion engine in warfare."

I snorted. Much like a horse. I didn't care. The image of a thousand sabre-waving troops advancing on hordes of sputtering little machines seemed absurd.

"Sir Clive," Ardmont went on, "showed his temper, I'm afraid. He not only gave his final refusal to look into the idea of Smythe's machine, he absolutely refused to have as his son-in-law anyone who would negotiate terms with us. Possibly that's what the butler overheard in part, thinking Sir Clive was referring to Landen Edgewick and Millicent rather than to Mr. Smythe and Phoebe."

"Then you were with Sir Clive and Smythe when they clashed," I said, "yet you continued to let the police believe it was Landen Edgewick who'd had the argument."

"Exactly," Major Ardmont said. "To see Mr. Smythe off to the hangman wouldn't have given Germany first crack at a war machine, would it?"

"Contemptible!" I spat.

"But wouldn't you do the same for your country?" Ardmont asked, grinning a death's head grin.

I chose not to answer. "The feather?" I said. "Of what significance was the feather, Holmes?"

"It was a goose feather," Holmes said, "of the sort used to stuff pillows. I suspected when I found it that a pillow had been used to muffle the sound of the shots when Sir Clive was killed. Which explains why the actual shots weren't heard at the inn."

"Ah! And you went into town to talk to Annie, then."

"To find out if she'd missed a pillow from the inn lately. And indeed one had turned up missing—from Robby Smythe's room."

"An impressive bit of work, Mr. Holmes," Ardmont said. "I'll be leaving now." He tossed down the rest of his port and moved toward the door.

"He shouldn't be allowed to leave, Holmes!"

"The good major has committed no crime, Watson. English law doesn't compel him to reveal such facts unless questioned directly, and what he knew about the argument had no exact bearing on the crime, I'm afraid."

"Very good, Mr. Holmes," Ardmont said. "You should have been a barrister."

"Lucky for you I'm not," Holmes said, "or be sure I'd find some way to see you swing alongside Mr. Smythe. Good evening, Major."

. . .

Two days later, Wilson and Landen Edgewick appeared at our lodgings on Baker Street and expressed appreciation with a sizable check, a wedding invitation, and bone-breaking handshakes all around. They were off to Reading, they said, to demonstrate the Gatling gun to the staff of British Army Ordnance Procurement. We wished them luck, I with a chill of foreboding, and sent them on their way.

"I hope, somehow, that no one buys the rights to their weapon," I said.

"You hope in vain," Holmes told me, slouching deep in the wing chair and thoughtfully tamping his pipe. "I'm afraid, Watson, that we're poised on the edge of an era of science and mechanization that will profoundly change wartime as well as peacetime. It mightn't be long before we're experimenting with the very basis of matter itself and turning it to our own selfish means. We mustn't sit back and let it happen in the rest of the world, Watson. England must remain in the forefront of weaponry, to discourage attack and retain peace through strength. Enough weapons like the Gatling gun, and perhaps war will become untenable and a subject of history only. Believe me, old friend, this can be a force for tranquillity among nations."

Perhaps Holmes is right, as he almost invariably is. Yet as I lay in bed that night about to sleep, never had the soft glow of gaslight, and the clatter of horses' hooves on the cobblestones below in Baker Street, been so comforting.

The Specter of Tullyfane Abbey

PETER TREMAYNE

FINDING PLEASURE IN combining his favorite writing subjects—mystery, horror, and history—Peter Berresford Ellis (1943–) has enjoyed enormous worldwide success following this formula. Ellis was born in Coventry, Warwickshire, and his family can be traced back in the area to 1288. Ellis, most of whose fiction has been published under the Peter Tremayne pseudonym, followed his father's footsteps to become a journalist. His first book was *Wales—A Nation Again: The Nationalist Struggle for Freedom* (1968), a history of the Welsh fight for independence, followed by popular titles in Celtic studies; as a leading authority on Celtic history, he has thirty-four nonfiction titles to his credit. He has served as International Chairman of the Celtic League (1988–1990) and is the honorary Life President of the Scottish 1820 Society and honorary Life Member of the Irish Literary Society.

He has produced nearly one hundred books, a similar number of short stories, and numerous scholarly pamphlets. As Tremayne, he has written twenty-three internationally bestselling novels about the seventh-century Irish nun-detective Sister Fidelma, with more than three million copies in print. As Peter MacAlan, he produced eight thrillers (1983–1993). In the horror field, he has written more than two dozen novels, mostly inspired by Celtic myths and legends, including *Dracula Unborn* (1977), *The Revenge of Dracula* (1978), and *Dracula, My Love* (1980).

"The Specter of Tullyfane Abbey" was first published in *Villains Victorious*, edited by Martin H. Greenberg and John Helfers (New York, DAW, 2001).

THE SPECTER OF TULLYFANE ABBEY

Peter Tremayne

Somewhere in the vaults of the bank of Cox and Co., at Charing Cross, there is a travel-worn and battered tin dispatch box with my name, John H. Watson MD, Late Indian Army, painted on the lid. It is filled with papers, nearly all of which are records of cases to illustrate the curious problems which Mr. Sherlock Holmes had at various times to examine.

—"The Problem of Thor Bridge"

THIS IS ONE of those papers. I must confess that there are few occasions on which I have seen my estimable friend, Sherlock Holmes, the famous consulting detective, in a state of some agitation. He is usually so detached that the word *calm* seems unfit to describe his general demeanor. Yet I had called upon him one evening to learn his opinion of a manuscript draft account I had made of one of his cases which I had titled "The Problem of Thor Bridge."

To my surprise, I found him seated in an attitude of tension in his armchair, his pipe unlit, his long pale fingers clutching my handwritten pages, and his brows drawn together in disapproval. "Confound it, Watson," he greeted me sharply as I came through the door. "Must you show me up to public ridicule in this fashion?"

I was, admittedly, somewhat taken aback at his uncharacteristic greeting. "I rather thought you came well out of the story," I replied defensively. "After all, you helped a remarkable woman, as you yourself observed, while, as for Mr. Gibson, I believe that he did learn an object lesson—"

He cut me short. "Tush! I do not mean the case of Grace Dunbar, which, since you refer to it, was not as glamorous as your imaginative pen elaborates on. No, Watson, no! It is here"—he waved the papers at me—"here in your cumbersome preamble. You speak of some of my unsolved cases as if they were failures. I only mentioned them to you in passing, and now you tell me, and the readers of the *Strand Magazine*, that you have noted them down and deposited the record in that odious little tin dispatch box placed in Cox's Bank."

"I did not think that you would have reason to object, Holmes," I replied with some vexation.

He waved a hand as if dismissing my feelings. "I object to the manner in which you reveal these cases! I read here, and I quote . . ." He peered shortsightedly at my manuscript. "'Some, and not the least interesting, were complete failures, and as such will hardly bear narrating, since no final explanation is forthcoming. A problem without a solution may interest the student, but can hardly fail to annoy the casual reader. Among these unfinished tales is that of Mr. James Phillimore, who, stepping back into his own house to get his umbrella, was never more seen in this world.' There!" He glanced up angrily.

"But, Holmes, dear fellow, that is precisely the matter as you told it to me. Where am I in error?"

"The error is making the statement itself. It

is incomplete. It is not set into context. The case of James Phillimore, whose title was Colonel, incidentally, occurred when I was a young man. I had just completed my second term at Oxford. It was the first time I crossed foils, so to speak, with the man who was to cause me such grief later in my career . . . Professor Moriarty."

I started at this intelligence, for Holmes was always unduly reticent about his clashes with James Moriarty, that sinister figure whom Holmes seemed to hold in both contempt as a criminal and regard as an intellect.

"I did not know that, Holmes."

"Neither would you have learned further of the matter, but I find that you have squirreled away a reference to this singular event in which Moriarty achieved the better of me."

"You were bested by Moriarty?" I was now really intrigued.

"Don't sound so surprised, Watson," he admonished. "Even villains can be victorious once in a while." Then Holmes paused and added quietly, "Especially when such a villain as Moriarty enlisted the power of darkness in his nefarious design."

I began to laugh, knowing that Holmes abhorred the supernatural. I remember his outburst when we received the letter from Morrison, Morrison, and Dodd which led us into "The Adventure of the Sussex Vampire." Yet my laughter died on my lips as I caught sight of the ghastly look that crossed Holmes's features. He stared into the dancing flames of the fire as if remembering the occasion.

"I am not in jest, Watson. In this instance, Moriarty employed the forces of darkness to accomplish his evil end. Of that there can be no shadow of doubt. It is the only time that I have failed, utterly and miserably failed, to prevent a terrible tragedy whose memory will curse me to the grave."

Holmes sighed deeply and then appeared to have observed for the first time that his pipe was unlit and reached for the matches.

"Pour two glasses from that decanter of fine Hennessy on the table and sit yourself down.

Having come thus far in my confession, I might as well finish the story in case that imagination of yours decides to embellish the little you do know."

"I say, Holmes—" I began to protest, but he went on, ignoring my words.

"I pray you, promise never to reveal this story until my clay has mingled with the earth from which I am sprung."

If there is a preamble to this story, it is one that I was already knowledgeable of and which I have already given some account of in the memoir I entitled "The Affray at the Kildare Street Club." Holmes was one of the Galway Holmes. Like his brother, Mycroft, he had attended Trinity College, Dublin, where he had, in the same year as his friend Oscar Wilde, won a demyship to continue his studies at Oxford. I believe the name Sherlock came from his maternal side, his mother being of another well-established Anglo-Irish family. Holmes was always reticent about this background, although the clues to his Irish origins were obvious to most discerning people. One of his frequent disguises was to assume the name of Altamont as he pretended to be an Irish-American. Altamont was his family seat near Ballysherlock.

Armed with this background knowledge, I settled back with a glass of Holmes's cognac and listened as he recounted a most singular and terrifying tale. I append it exactly as he narrated it to me.

"Having completed my first term at Oxford, I returned to Dublin to stay with my brother Mycroft at his house in Merrion Square. Yet I found myself somewhat at a loose end. There was some panic in the fiscal office of the chief secretary where Mycroft worked. This caused him to be unable to spare the time we had set aside for a fishing expedition. I was therefore persuaded to accompany Abraham Stoker, who had been at Trinity the same year as Mycroft, to the Royal to see some theatrical entertainment. Abraham, or Bram as he preferred to be called, was also a close friend of Sir William and Lady Wilde, who lived just across the square, and with whose younger son, Oscar, I was then at Oxford with.

"Bram was an ambitious man who not only worked with Mycroft at Dublin Castle but wrote theatrical criticism in his spare time and by night edited the *Dublin Halfpenny Press*, a journal which he had only just launched. He was trying to persuade me to write on famous Dublin murders for it, but as he offered no remuneration at all, I gracefully declined.

"We were in the foyer of the Royal when Bram, an amiable, booming giant with red hair, hailed someone over the heads of the throng. A thin, white-faced young man emerged to be clasped warmly by the hand. It was a youth of my own age and well known to me; Jack Phillimore was his name. He had been a fellow student at Trinity College. My heart leaped in expectation, and I searched the throng for a familiar female face which was, I will confess it, most dear to me. But Phillimore was alone. His sister Agnes was not with him at the theater.

"In the presence of Bram, we fell to exchanging pleasantries about our alma mater. I noticed that Phillimore's heart was not in exchanging such bonhomie nor, to be honest, was mine. I was impatient for the opportunity to inquire after Phillimore's sister. Ah, let the truth be known, Watson, but only after I am not in this world.

"Love, my dear Watson. Love! I believe that you have observed that all emotions, and that one in particular, are abhorrent to my mind. This is true, and since I have become mature enough to understand, I have come to regard it as opposite to that true cold reason which I place above all things. I have never married lest I bias my judgment. Yet it was not always my intention, and this very fact is what led to my downfall, causing the tragedy which I am about to relate. Alas, Watson, if . . . but with an *if* we might place Paris in a bottle.

"As a youth I was deeply in love with Agnes Phillimore who was but a year older than I. When Jack Phillimore and I were in our first year at Trinity, I used to spend time at their town house by Stephen's Green. I confess, it was not the company of Phillimore that I sought then but that of Agnes.

"In my maturity I could come to admire *the* woman, as you insist I call Irene Adler, but admiration is not akin to the deep, destructive emotional power that we call love.

"It was when Bram spotted someone across the foyer that he needed to speak to that Phillimore seized the opportunity to ask abruptly what I was doing for recreation. Hearing that I was at a loose end, he suggested that I accompany him to his father's estate in Kerry for a few days. Colonel James Phillimore owned a large house and estate in that remote county. Phillimore said he was going down because it was his father's fiftieth birthday. I thought at the time that he placed a singular emphasis on that fact.

"It was then that I managed to casually ask if his sister Agnes was in Dublin or in Kerry. Phillimore, of course, like most brothers, was ignorant that his sister held any attraction for the male sex, least of all one of his friends. He was nonchalant. 'To be sure she is at Tullyfane, Holmes. Preparing for her marriage next month.'

"His glance was distracted by a man jostling through the foyer, and so he missed the effect that this intelligence had on me.

"'Married?' I gasped. 'To whom?'

"'Some professor, no less. A cove by the name of Moriarty.'

"'Moriarty?' I asked, for the name meant little to me in that context. I knew it only as a common County Kerry name. It was an Anglicizing of the Irish name Ó Muircheartaigh, meaning 'expert navigator.'

"'He is our neighbor, he is quite besotted with my sister, and it seems that it is arranged that they will marry next month. A rum cove, is the professor. Good education and holds a chair of mathematics at Queen's University in Belfast.'

"'Professor James Moriarty,' I muttered savagely. Phillimore's news of Agnes's intentions had shattered all my illusions.

"'Do you know him?' Phillimore asked, observing my displeasure. 'He's all right, isn't he? I mean . . . he's not a bounder, eh?'

"'I have seen him once only and that from a distance in the Kildare Street Club,' I confessed. I had nothing against Moriarty at that time. 'My brother Mycroft pointed him out to me. I did not meet him. Yet I have heard of his reputation. His *Dynamics of an Asteroid* ascended to such rarefied heights of pure mathematics that no man in the scientific press was capable of criticizing it.'

"Phillimore chuckled.

"'That is beyond me. Thank God I am merely a student of theology. But it sounds as though you are an admirer.'

"'I admire intellect, Phillimore,' I replied simply. Moriarty, as I recalled, must have been all of ten years older than Agnes. What is ten years at our age? But to me, a callow youth, I felt the age difference that existed between Agnes and James Moriarty was obscene. I explain this simply because my attitude has a bearing on my future disposition.

"'So come down with me to Tullyfane Abbey,' pressed Phillimore, oblivious to the emotional turmoil that he had created in me.

"I was about to coldly decline the invitation when Phillimore, observing my negative expression, was suddenly very serious. He leaned close to me and said softly: 'You see, Holmes, old fellow, we are having increasing problems with the family ghost, and as I recall, you have a canny way of solving bizarre problems.'

"I knew enough of his character to realize that jesting was beyond his capacity.

"'The family ghost?'

"'A damned infernal specter that is driving my father quite out of his wits. Not to mention Agnes.'

"'Your father and sister are afraid of a specter?'

"'Agnes is scared at the deterioration in my father's demeanor. Seriously, Holmes, I really don't know what to do. My sister's letters speak of such a bizarre set of circumstances that I am inclined to think that she is hallucinating or that my father has been driven mad already.'

"My inclination was to avoid opening old wounds now by meeting Agnes again. I could spend the rest of my vacation in Marsh's Library, where they have an excellent collection of medieval cryptogram manuscripts. I hesitated— hesitated and was lost. I had to admit that I was intrigued to hear more of the matter in spite of my emotional distress, for any mystery sends the adrenaline coursing in my body.

"The very next morning I accompanied Jack Phillimore to Kingsbridge Railway Station and boarded the train to Killarney. En route he explained some of the problems.

"Tullyfane Abbey was supposed to be cursed. It was situated on the extremity of the Iveragh Peninsula in a wild and deserted spot. Tullyfane Abbey was, of course, never an abbey. It was a dignified Georgian country house. The Anglo-Irish gentry in the eighteenth century had a taste for the grandiose and called their houses *abbeys* or *castles* even when they were unassuming dwellings inhabited only by families of modest fortune.

"Phillimore told me that the firstborn of every generation of the lords of Tullyfane were to meet with terrible deaths on the attainment of their fiftieth birthdays even down to the seventh generation. It seems that first lord of Tullyfane had hanged a young boy for sheep stealing. The boy turned out to be innocent, and his mother, a widow who had doted on the lad as insurance for comfort in her old age, had duly uttered the curse. Whereupon each lord of Tullyfane, for the last six generations, had met an untimely end.

"Phillimore assured me that the first lord of Tullyfane had not even been a direct ancestor of his, but that his great-grandfather had purchased Tullyfane Abbey when the owner, concerned at the imminent prospect of departing this life on his fiftieth birthday, decided to sell and depart for healthier climes in England. This sleight of hand of ownership had not prevented Jack's great-grandfather, General Phillimore, from falling off his horse and breaking his neck on his fiftieth birthday. Jack's grandfather, a redoubtable judge, was shot on his fiftieth birthday. The local inspector of the Royal Irish Constabulary had assumed that his untimely demise could be ascribed more to his profession than to the paranormal. Judges and policemen often experienced sudden terminations to their careers in a country where they were considered part of the colonial occupation by ordinary folk.

"'I presume your father, Colonel James Phillimore, is now approaching his fiftieth birthday and hence his alarm?' I asked Phillimore as the train rolled through the Tipperary countryside toward the Kerry border.

"Phillimore nodded slowly.

"'My sister has, in her letters, written that she has heard the specter crying at night. She reports that my father has even witnessed the apparition, the form of a young boy, crying on the turret of the abbey.'

"I raised my eyebrows unintentionally.

"'Seen as well as heard?' I demanded. 'And by two witnesses? Well, I can assure you that there is nothing in this world that exists unless it is due to some scientifically explainable reason.'

"'Nothing in this world,' muttered Phillimore. 'But what of the next?'

"'If your family believes in this curse, why remain at Tullyfane?' I demanded. 'Would it not be better to quit the house and estate if you are so sure that the curse is potent?'

"'My father is stubborn, Holmes. He will not quit the place, for he has sunk every penny he has into it apart from our town house in Dublin. If it were me, I would sell it to Moriarty and leave the accursed spot.'

"'Sell it to Moriarty? Why him, particularly?'

"'He offered to buy Father out in order to help resolve the situation.'

"'Rather magnanimous of him,' I observed. 'Presumably he has no fear of the curse?'

"'He reckons that the curse would only be directed at Anglo–Irish families like us, while he, being a pure Milesian, a Gael of the Gaels, so to speak, would be immune to the curse.'

"Colonel Phillimore had sent a calèche to Killarney Station to bring Phillimore and me to Tullyfane Abbey. The old colonel was clearly not in the best of spirits when he greeted us in the library. I noticed his hand shook a little as he raised it to greet me.

"'Friend of Jack's, eh? Yes, I remember you. One of the Galway Holmeses. Mycroft Holmes is your brother? Works for Lord Hartington, eh? Chief Secretary, eh?'

"He had an irritating manner of putting *eh* after each telegraphic phrase as a punctuation.

"It was then that Agnes Phillimore came in to welcome us. God, Watson, I was young and ardent in those days. Even now, as I look back with a more critical eye and colder blood, I acknowledge that she was rare and wonderful in her beauty. She held out her hand to me with a smile, but I saw at once that it lacked the warmth and friendship that I thought it had once held for me alone. Her speech was reserved, and she greeted me as a distant friend. Perhaps she had grown into a woman while I held to her image with boyish passion? It was impossible for me to acknowledge this at that time, but the passion was all on my side. Ah, immature youth, what else is there to say?

"We dined in somber mode that evening. Somber for me because I was wrestling with life's cruel realities; somber for the Phillimores because of the curse that hung over the house. We were just finishing the dessert when Agnes suddenly froze, her fork halfway to her mouth. Then Colonel Phillimore dropped his spoon with a crash on his plate and gave a piteous moan.

"In the silence that followed I heard it plainly. It was the sound of a sobbing child. It seemed to echo all around the room. Even Jack Phillimore looked distracted.

"I pushed back my chair and stood up, trying to pinpoint the direction from which the sounds came.

"'What lies directly beneath this dining room?' I demanded of the colonel. He was white in the face, too far gone with shock to answer me.

"I turned to Jack Phillimore. He replied with some nervousness.

"'The cellars, Holmes.'

"'Come, then,' I cried, grabbing a candelabra from the table and striding swiftly to the door.

"As I reached the door, Agnes stamped her foot twice on the floor as if agitated.

"'Really, Mr. Holmes,' she cried, 'you cannot do battle with an ethereal being!'

"I paused in the doorway to smile briefly at her.

"'I doubt that I shall find an ethereal being, Miss Phillimore.'

"Jack Phillimore led the way to the cellar, and we searched it thoroughly, finding nothing.

"'What did you expect to find?' demanded Phillimore, seeing my disappointment as we returned to the dining room.

"'A small boy, corporeal in form and not a spirit,' I replied firmly.

"'Would that it were so.' Agnes greeted our return without disguising her look of satisfaction that I could produce no physical entity in explanation. 'Do you not think that I have caused this house to be searched time and time again? My father is on the verge of madness. I do believe that he has come to the end of his composure. I fear for what he might do to himself.'

"'And the day after tomorrow is his fiftieth birthday,' added Phillimore soberly.

"We were standing in the entrance to the dining room when Malone, the aging butler, answered a summons to the front door by the jangle of the bell.

"'It's a Professor Moriarty,' he intoned.

"Moriarty was tall and thin, with a forehead domed in a white curve and deeply set eyes. His face protruded forward and had a curious habit of slowly oscillating from side to side in what, in the harsh judgment of my youth, I felt to be a curiously reptilian fashion. I suppose, looking back, he was handsome in a way and somewhat distinguished. He had been young for his professorship, and there was no doubting the sharpness of his mind and intellect.

"Agnes greeted him with warmth while Phillimore was indifferent. As for myself, I felt I had to suppress my ill humor. He had come to join us for coffee and brandy and made sympathetic overtures to the colonel over his apparent state of ill health.

"'My offer still stands, dear sir,' he said. 'Best be rid of the abbey and the curse in one fell swoop. Not, of course, that you would lose it entirely, for when Agnes and I are married, you will always be a welcome guest here.'

"Colonel Phillimore actually growled. A soft rumbling sound in the back of his throat, like an animal at bay and goaded into response.

"'I intend to see this through. I refuse to be chased out of my home by a specter when Akbar Khan and his screaming Afghans could not budge me from the fort at Peiwar Pass. No, sir. Here I intend to stay and see my fiftieth birthday through.'

"'I think you should at least consider James's offer, Father,' Agnes rebuked him. 'This whole business is affecting your nerves. Better get rid of the place and move to Dublin.'

"'Nonsense!' snapped her father. 'I shall see it through. I will hear no more.'

"We went to bed early that night, and I confess, I spent some time analyzing my feelings for Agnes before dropping into a dozing slumber.

"The crying woke me. I hauled on a dressing gown and hastened to the window through which a full white moon sent its soft light. The cry was like a banshee's wail. It seemed to be coming from above me. I hastened from the room and in the corridor outside I came across Jack Phillimore, similarly attired in a dressing gown. His face looked ghastly.

"'Tell me that I am not dreaming, Holmes,' he cried.

"'Not unless we share a dream,' I replied tersely. 'Do you have a revolver?'

"He looked startled.

"'What do you hope to achieve with a revolver?' he demanded.

"'I think it might be efficacious in dealing with ghosts, ghouls, and apparitions.' I smiled thinly.

"Phillimore shook his head.

"'The guns are locked below in the gun room. My father has the key.'

"'Ah well,' I replied in resignation, 'we can probably proceed without them. This crying is emanating from above. What's up there?'

"'The turret room. That's where Father said he saw the apparition before.'

"'Lead me to the turret room, then.'

"Spurred on by the urgency of my tone, Phillimore turned to lead the way. We flew up the stairs of a circular tower and emerged onto a flat roof. At the far end of the building rose a similar, though larger, tower or, more accurately, a round turret. Encircling it, ten feet above the roof level, there ran a small balcony.

"'My God!' cried Phillimore, halting so abruptly that I cannoned in to him.

"It took me a moment to recover before I saw what had caused his distress. On this balcony there stood the figure of a small boy. He was clearly lit in the bright moonlight and yet, yet I will tell you no lie, Watson, his entire body and clothes glowed with a strange luminescence. The boy it was who was letting out the eerie, wailing sounds.

"'Do you see it, Holmes?' cried Phillimore.

"'I see the young rascal, whoever he is!' I yelled, running toward the tower over the flat roof.

"Then the apparition was gone. How or where, I did not observe.

"I reached the base of the tower and looked for a way to scramble up to the balcony. There was only one way of egress from the roof—a small door in the tower which seemed clearly barred on the inside.

"'Come, Phillimore, the child is escaping!' I cried in frustration.

"'Escaping, eh?' It was the colonel who emerged out of the darkness behind us. His face was ashen. He was clad only in his pajamas.

"'Specters don't need to escape, eh! No, sir! Now that you have seen it, too, I can say I am not mad. At least, not mad, eh?'

"'How do I get into the turret?' I demanded, ignoring the colonel's ranting.

"'Boarded up for years, Holmes,' Phillimore explained, moving to support his frail father for fear the old man might topple over. 'There's no way anyone could have entered or left it.'

"'Someone did,' I affirmed. 'That was no specter. I think this has been arranged. I think you should call in the police.'

"The colonel refused to speak further of the matter and retired to bed. I spent most of the night checking the approaches to the turret room and was forced to admit that all means of entrance and exit seemed perfectly secured. But I was sure that when I started to run across the roof toward the tower, the boy had bobbed away with such a startled expression that no self-respecting ghost in the middle of haunting would have assumed.

"The next morning, over breakfast, I was forceful in my exhortations to the colonel that he should put the matter forthwith in the hands of the local police. I told him that I had no doubts that some bizarre game was afoot. The colonel had recovered some of his equilibrium and listened attentively to my arguments.

"Surprisingly, the opposition came from Agnes. She was still in favor of her father departing the house and putting an end to the curse.

"We were just finishing breakfast when Malone announced the arrival of Professor Moriarty.

"Agnes went to join him in the library while we three finished our meal, by the end of which, Colonel Phillimore had made up his mind to follow my advice. It was decided that we accompany Colonel Phillimore directly after breakfast to discuss the matter with the local Inspector of the Royal Irish Constabulary. Agnes and Moriarty joined us, and having heard the story from Agnes, Moriarty actually said that it was the best course of action, although Agnes still had her doubts. In fact, Moriarty offered to accompany us. Agnes excused herself a little ungraciously, I thought, because she had arranged to make an inventory of the wines in the cellar.

"So the colonel, Phillimore, Moriarty, and I agreed to walk the two miles into the town. It must be observed that a few miles' walk was nothing for those who lived in the country in those days. Now, in London, everyone is forever hailing hansom carriages even if they merely desire to journey to the end of the street.

"We left the house and began to stroll down the path. We had barely gone twenty yards when the colonel, casting an eye at the sky, excused himself and said he needed his umbrella and would be but a moment. He turned, hurried back to his front door, and entered. That was when he disappeared from this world forever.

"The three of us waited patiently for a few moments. Moriarty then said that if we continued to stroll at an easy pace, the colonel would catch us up. Yet when we reached the gates of the estate, I began to grow concerned that there was still no sign of the colonel. I caused our party to wait at the gates. Ten minutes passed, and then I felt I should return to find out what had delayed the colonel.

"The umbrella was still in the hall stand. There was no sign of the colonel. I rang the bell for old Malone and he swore that as far as he was aware the colonel had left with us and had not returned. There was no budging him on that point. Grumbling more than a little, he set off to the colonel's room; I went to the study. Soon the entire house was being searched as Jack Phillimore and Moriarty arrived back to discover the cause of the delay.

"It was then that Agnes emerged from the cellars, looking a little disheveled, an inventory in her hand. When she heard that her father had simply vanished, she grew distraught and Malone had to fetch the brandy.

"In the wine cellar, she told me, she had heard and seen nothing. Moriarty volunteered to search the cellar just to make the examination of the house complete. I told Phillimore to look after his sister and accompanied Moriarty. While I disliked the man, there was no doubt that Moriarty could hardly have engineered the colonel's disappearance as he had left the house with us and remained with us outside the house. Naturally, our search of the cellars proved futile. They were large, and one could probably have hidden a whole army in them if one so desired.

But the entrance from the hall led to the area used for wine storage, and no one could have descended into the cellar without passing this area and thus being seen by Agnes. No answer to Colonel James Phillimore's disappearance presented itself to me.

"I spent a week at Tullyfane attempting to form some conclusion. The local RIC eventually gave up the search. I had to return to Oxford, and it became obvious to me that neither Agnes nor Moriarty required my company further. After that, I had but one letter from Jack Phillimore, and this several months later and postmarked at Marseille.

"Apparently, at the end of two weeks, a suicide note was found in the colonel's desk stating that he could not stand the strange hauntings in Tullyfane Abbey. Rather than await the terrible death on his fiftieth birthday, he proposed to put an end to it himself. There was attached a new will, giving the estate to Agnes in acknowledgment of her forthcoming marriage and the house in Stephen's Green to Jack. Phillimore wrote that although the will was bizarre, and there was no proof of his father's death, he nevertheless had refused to contest it. I heard later that this was against the advice of Phillimore's solicitor. But it seemed that Jack Phillimore wanted no part of the curse or the estate. He wished his sister joy of it and then took himself to Africa as a missionary where, two years later, I heard that he had been killed in some native uprising in British East Africa. It was not even on his fiftieth birthday. So much for curses.

"And Agnes Phillimore? She married James Moriarty and the property passed to him. She was dead within six months. She drowned in a boating accident when Moriarty was taking her to Beginish, just off the Kerry coast, to show her the columnar basaltic formations similar to those of the Giant's Causeway. Moriarty was the only survivor of the tragedy.

"He sold Tullyfane Abbey and its estate to an American and moved to London to become a gentleman of leisure, although his money was soon squandered due to his dissipated lifestyle.

He resorted to more overt illegal activities to replenish his wealth. I have not called him the 'Napoleon of crime' without cause.

"As for Tullyfane, the American tried to run the estate, but fell foul of the Land Wars of a few years ago when the Land Leaguers forced radical changes in the way the great estates in Ireland were run. That was when a new word was added to the language—boycott—when the Land Leaguers ostracized Charles Boycott, the estate agent of Lord Erne at Lough Mask. The American pulled out of Tullyfane Abbey, which fell into ruin and became derelict.

"Without being able to find out what happened when James Phillimore stepped back beyond his front door to retrieve his umbrella, I was unable to bring the blame to where, I believed with every fiber in my body, it lay; namely, to James Moriarty. I believe that it was Moriarty who planned the whole dastardly scheme of obtaining the estate which he presumed would set him up for life. He was not in love with poor Agnes. He saw her as the quick means of becoming rich and, not content to wait for her marriage portion, I believe he forged the suicide note and will and then found an ingenious way to dispatch the colonel, having failed to drive him insane by playing on the curse. Once he had secured the estate, poor Agnes became dispensable.

"How he worked the curse, I was not sure until a singular event was reported to me some years later.

"It was in London, only a few years ago, that I happened to encounter Bram Stoker's younger brother, George. Like most of the Stoker brothers, with the exception of Bram, George had gone into medicine and was a Licentiate of the Royal College of Surgeons in Dublin. George had just married a lady from County Kerry, actually the sister of the McGillycuddy of the Reeks, one of the old Gaelic nobility.

"It was George who supplied me with an important piece of the jigsaw. He was actually informed of the occurrence by none other than his brother-in-law, Dennis McGillycuddy, who had been a witness to the event.

"About a year after the occurrences at Tullyfane Abbey, the body of a young boy was found in an old mine working in the Reeks. I should explain that the Reeks are the mountains on the Iveragh Peninsula which are the highest peaks in Ireland and, of course, Tullyfane stands in their shadows. The boy's body had not badly decomposed, because it had lain in the ice-cold temperatures of the small lochs one gets in the area. It so happened that a well-known Dublin medical man, Dr. John MacDonnell, the first person to perform an operation under anesthetic in Ireland, was staying in Killarney. He agreed to perform the autopsy because the local coroner had noticed a peculiar aspect to the body; he observed that in the dark the corpse of the boy was glowing.

"MacDonnell found that the entire body of the boy had been coated in a waxy yellow substance; indeed, it was the cause of death, for it had so clogged the pores of his skin that the unfortunate child had simply been asphyxiated. Upon analysis, it was discerned that the substance was a form of natural phosphorus, found in the caves in the area. I immediately realized the significance of this.

"The child, so I presumed, was one of the hapless and miserable wretches doomed to wander the byways of Ireland, perhaps orphaned during the failure of the potato crops in 1871, which had spread starvation and typhus among the peasants. Moriarty had forced or persuaded him to act the part of the wailing child whom we had observed. This child was our specter, appearing now and then at Moriarty's command to scream and cry in certain places. The phosphorus would have emitted the ethereal glow.

"Having served his purpose, Moriarty, knowing well the properties of the waxy substance with which he had coated the child's body, left the child to suffocate and dumped the body in the mountains."

I waited for some time after Holmes had finished the story, and then I ventured to ask the question to which he had, so far, provided no answer. As I did so, I made the following preamble.

"Accepting that Moriarty had accomplished a fiendish scheme to enrich himself and that it was only in retrospect you realized how he managed to use the child to impersonate a specter—"

Holmes breathed out sharply as he interrupted. "It is a failure of my deductive capabilities that I have no wish to advertise, Watson."

"Yet there is one thing—just how did Moriarty manage to spirit away the body of James Phillimore after he stepped back inside the door of the house to retrieve his umbrella? By your own statement, Moriarty, Jack Phillimore, and yourself were all together, waiting for the colonel, outside his house. The family retainer, old Malone, swore the colonel did not reenter the house. How was it done? Was Malone in the pay of Moriarty?"

"It was a thought that crossed my mind. The RIC likewise questioned old Malone very closely and came to the conclusion that he was part of no plot. In fact, Malone could not say one way or another if the colonel had returned, as he was in the kitchen with two housemaids as witnesses at the time."

"And Agnes? . . ."

"Agnes was in the cellar. She saw nothing. When all is said and done, there is no logical answer. James Phillimore vanished the moment he stepped back over the threshold. I have thought about every conceivable explanation for the last twenty years and have come to no suitable explanation except one. . . ."

"Which is?"

"The powers of darkness were exalted that day, and Moriarty had made a pact with the devil, selling his soul for his ambition."

I stared at Holmes for a moment. I had never seen him admit to any explanation of events that was not in keeping with scientific logic. Was he correct that the answer lay with the supernatural, or was he merely covering up for the fact of his own lack of knowledge or, even more horrific to my susceptibilities, did the truth lie in some part of my old friend's mind which he refused to admit even to himself?

Pinned to John H. Watson's manuscript was a small yellowing cutting from the *Kerry Evening News;* alas the date had not been noted.

"During the recent building of an RIC Barracks on the ruins of Tullyfane Abbey, a well-preserved male skeleton was discovered. Sub-Inspector Dalton told our reporter that it could not be estimated how long the skeleton had lain there. The precise location was in a bricked-up area of the former cellars of the abbey.

"Doctor Simms-Taafe said that he adduced, from the condition of the skeleton, that it had belonged to a man in midlife who had met his demise within the last twenty or thirty years. The back of the skull had been smashed in due to a severe blow, which might account for the death.

"Sub-Inspector Dalton opined that the death might well be linked with the disappearance of Colonel Phillimore, then the owner of Tullyfane Abbey, some thirty years ago. As the next owner, Professor James Moriarty was reported to have met his death in Switzerland, the last owner having been an American who returned to his homeland, and the Phillimores being no longer domiciled in the country, the RIC are placing the matter in their file of unsolved suspicious deaths."

A few lines were scrawled on the cutting in Dr. Watson's hand, which ran, "I think it was obvious that Colonel Phillimore was murdered as soon as he reentered the house. I have come to believe that the truth did lie in a dark recess of my old friend's mind which he refused to admit was the grotesque and terrible truth of the affair. Patricide, even at the instigation of a lover with whom one is besotted, is the most hideous crime of all. Could it be that Holmes had come to regard the young woman herself as representing the powers of darkness?" The last sentence was heavily underscored.

The Adventure of the Agitated Actress

DANIEL STASHOWER

ALREADY ESTABLISHED AS a writer of excellent mystery fiction, Daniel Meyer Stashower (1960–) has enjoyed even greater success in recent years with his nonfiction works.

After winning a Raymond Chandler Fulbright Fellowship in Detective Fiction to work at Oxford University for a year, Stashower produced his first novel, *The Adventure of the Ectoplasmic Man* (1985), which featured Sherlock Holmes and Harry Houdini, the fictional mystery novel blending with the author's real-life fascination with magic and conjuring; it was nominated for an Edgar Award for best first novel.

Houdini became a favorite protagonist and appeared in several of Stashower's subsequent novels: *The Dime Museum Murders* (1999), *The Floating Lady Murder* (2000), and *The Houdini Specter* (2001).

Having turned to nonfiction, but continuing to focus on the late nineteenth and early twentieth centuries, he wrote *Teller of Tales: The Life of Arthur Conan Doyle* (1999), for which he won his first Edgar. He followed this with additional critically acclaimed works on a variety of subjects, including such highly readable tomes as *The Beautiful Cigar Girl: Mary Rogers, Edgar Allan Poe, and the Invention of Murder* (2006), which narrates the true story of the brutal murder on which Poe based his second C. Auguste Dupin story, "The Mystery of Marie Roget"; and the Edgar-winning *The Hour of Peril: The Secret Plot to Murder Lincoln Before the Civil War* (2013), which recounts the Pinkertons' tireless efforts to thwart an assassination plot during Lincoln's journey to Washington, a plan that could have forever divided the nation.

"The Adventure of the Agitated Actress" was first published in *Murder, My Dear Watson*, edited by Martin H. Greenberg, Jon Lellenberg, and Daniel Stashower (New York, Carroll & Graf, 2002).

THE ADVENTURE OF
THE AGITATED ACTRESS

Daniel Stashower

"WE'VE ALL HEARD stories of your wonderful methods, Mr. Holmes," said James Larrabee, drawing a cigarette from a silver box on the table. "There have been countless tales of your marvelous insight, your ingenuity in picking up and following clues, and the astonishing manner in which you gain information from the most trifling details. You and I have never met before today, but I dare say that in this brief moment or two you've discovered any number of things about me."

Sherlock Holmes set down the newspaper he had been reading and gazed languidly at the ceiling. "Nothing of consequence, Mr. Larrabee," he said. "I have scarcely more than asked myself why you rushed off and sent a telegram in such a frightened hurry, what possible excuse you could have had for gulping down a tumbler of raw brandy at the Lion's Head on the way back, why your friend with the auburn hair left so suddenly by the terrace window, and what there can possibly be about the safe in the lower part of that desk to cause you such painful anxiety." The detective took up the newspaper and idly turned the pages. "Beyond that," he said, "I know nothing."

"Holmes!" I cried. "This is uncanny! How could you have possibly deduced all of that? We arrived in this room not more than five minutes ago!"

My companion glanced at me with an air of strained abstraction, as though he had never seen me before. For a moment he seemed to hesitate, apparently wavering between competing impulses. Then he rose from his chair and crossed down to a row of blazing footlights. "I'm sorry, Frohman," he called. "This isn't working out as I'd hoped. We really don't need Watson in this scene after all."

"Gillette!" came a shout from the darkened space across the bright line of lights. "I do wish you'd make up your mind! Need I remind you that we open tomorrow night?" We heard a brief clatter of footsteps as Charles Frohman—a short, solidly built gentleman in the casual attire of a country squire—came scrambling up the side access stairs. As he crossed the forward lip of the stage, Frohman brandished a printed handbill. It read: "William Gillette in his Smash Play! Sherlock Holmes! Fresh from a Triumphant New York Run!"

"He throws off the balance of the scene," Gillette was saying. "The situation doesn't call for an admiring Watson." He turned to me. "No offense, my dear Lyndal. You have clearly immersed yourself in the role. That gesture of yours—with your arm at the side—it suggests a man favoring an old wound. Splendid!"

I pressed my lips together and let my hand fall to my side. "Actually, Gillette," I said, "I am endeavoring to keep my trousers from falling down."

"Pardon?"

I opened my jacket and gathered up a fold of loose fabric around my waist. "There hasn't been time for my final costume fitting," I explained.

"I'm afraid I'm having the same difficulty,"

said Arthur Creeson, who had been engaged to play the villainous James Larrabee. "If I'm not careful, I'll find my trousers down at my ankles."

Gillette gave a heavy sigh. "Quinn!" he called.

Young Henry Quinn, the boy playing the role of Billy, the Baker Street page, appeared from the wings. "Yes, Mr. Gillette?"

"Would you be so good as to fetch the wardrobe mistress? Or at least bring us some extra straight pins?" The boy nodded and darted backstage.

Charles Frohman, whose harried expression and lined forehead told of the rigors of his role as Gillette's producer, folded the handbill and replaced it in his pocket. "I don't see why you feel the need to tinker with the script at this late stage," he insisted. "The play was an enormous success in New York. As far as America is concerned, you *are* Sherlock Holmes. Surely the London audiences will look on the play with equal favor?"

Gillette threw himself down in a chair and reached for his prompt book. "The London audience bears little relation to its American counterpart," he said, flipping rapidly through the pages. "British tastes have been refined over centuries of Shakespeare and Marlowe. America has only lately weaned itself off of *Uncle Tom's Cabin.*"

"Gillette," said Frohman heavily, "you are being ridiculous."

The actor reached for a pen and began scrawling over a page of script. "I am an American actor essaying an English part. I must take every precaution and make every possible refinement before submitting myself to the fine raking fire of the London critics. They will seize on a single false note as an excuse to send us packing." He turned back to Arthur Creeson. "Now, then. Let us continue from the point at which Larrabee is endeavoring to cover his deception. Instead of Watson's expression of incredulity, we shall restore Larrabee's evasions. Do you recall the speech, Creeson?"

The actor nodded.

"Excellent. Let us resume."

I withdrew to the wings as Gillette and Creeson took their places. A mask of impassive self-possession slipped over Gillette's features as he stepped back into the character of Sherlock Holmes. "Why your friend with the auburn hair left so suddenly by the terrace window," he said, picking up the dialogue in midsentence, "and what there can possibly be about the safe in the lower part of that desk to cause you such painful anxiety."

"Ha! Very good!" cried Creeson, taking up his role as the devious James Larrabee. "Very good indeed! If those things were only true, I'd be wonderfully impressed. It would be absolutely marvelous!"

Gillette regarded him with an expression of weary impatience. "It won't do, sir," said he. "I have come to see Miss Alice Faulkner and will not leave until I have done so. I have reason to believe that the young lady is being held against her will. You shall have to give way, sir, or face the consequences."

Creeson's hands flew to his chest. "Against her will? This is outrageous! I will not tolerate—"

A high, trilling scream from backstage interrupted the line. Creeson held his expression and attempted to continue. "I will not tolerate such an accusation in my own—"

A second scream issued from backstage. Gillette gave a heavy sigh and rose from his chair as he reached for the prompt book. "Will that woman never learn her cue?" Shielding his eyes against the glare of the footlights, he stepped again to the lip of the stage and sought out Frohman. "This is what comes of engaging the company locally," he said in an exasperated tone. "We have a mob of players in ill-fitting costumes who don't know their scripts. We should have brought the New York company across, hang the expense." He turned to the wings. "Quinn!"

The young actor stepped forward. "Yes, sir?"

"Will you kindly inform—"

Gillette's instructions were cut short by the sudden appearance of Miss Maude Fenton, the actress playing the role of Alice Faulkner, who rushed from the wings in a state of obvious agitation. Her chestnut hair fell loosely about her shoulders and her velvet shirtwaist was imperfectly buttoned. "Gone!" she cried. "Missing! Taken from me!"

Gillette drummed his fingers across the prompt book. "My dear Miss Fenton," he said, "you have dropped approximately seventeen pages from the script."

"Hang the script!" she wailed. "I'm not playing a role! My brooch is missing! My beautiful, beautiful brooch! Oh, for heaven's sake, Mr. Gillette, someone must have stolen it!"

Selma Kendall, the kindly, auburn-haired actress who had been engaged to play Madge Larrabee, hurried to Miss Fenton's side. "It can't be!" she cried. "He only just gave it—that is to say, you've only just acquired it! Are you certain you haven't simply mislaid it?"

Miss Fenton accepted the linen pocket square I offered and dabbed at her streaming eyes. "I couldn't possibly have mislaid it," she said between sobs. "One doesn't mislay something of that sort! How could such a thing have happened?"

Gillette, who had cast an impatient glance at his pocket watch during this exchange, now stepped forward to take command of the situation. "There, there, Miss Fenton," he said, in the cautious, faltering tone of a man not used to dealing with female emotions. "I'm sure this is all very distressing. As soon as we have completed our run-through, we will conduct a most thorough search of the dressing areas. I'm sure your missing bauble will be discovered presently."

"Gillette!" I cried. "You don't mean to continue with the rehearsal? Can't you see that Miss Fenton is too distraught to carry on?"

"But she must," the actor declared. "As Mr. Frohman has been at pains to remind us, our little play has its London opening tomorrow evening. We shall complete the rehearsal, and then—after I have given a few notes—we shall locate the missing brooch. Miss Fenton is a fine

actress, and I have every confidence in her ability to conceal her distress in the interim." He patted the weeping actress on the back of her hand. "Will that do, my dear?"

At this, Miss Fenton's distress appeared to gather momentum by steady degrees. First her lips began to tremble, then her shoulders commenced heaving, and lastly a strange caterwauling sound emerged from behind the handkerchief. After a moment or two of this, she threw herself into Gillette's arms and began sobbing lustily upon his shoulder.

"Gillette," called Frohman, straining to make himself heard above the lamentations, "perhaps it would be best to take a short pause."

Gillette, seemingly unnerved by the wailing figure in his arms, gave a strained assent. "Very well. We shall repair to the dressing area. No doubt the missing object has simply slipped between the cushions of a settee."

With Mr. Frohman in the lead, our small party made its way through the wings and along the backstage corridors to the ladies' dressing area. As we wound past the scenery flats and crated property trunks, I found myself reflecting on how little I knew of the other members of our troupe. Although Gillette's play had been a great success in America, only a handful of actors and crewmen had transferred to the London production. A great many members of the cast and technical staff, myself included, had been engaged locally after a brief open call. Up to this point, the rehearsals and staging had been a rushed affair, allowing for little of the easy camaraderie that usually develops among actors during the rehearsal period.

As a result, I knew little about my fellow players apart from the usual backstage gossip. Miss Fenton, in the role of the young heroine Alice Faulkner, was considered to be a promising ingenue. Reviewers frequently commented on her striking beauty, if not her talent. Selma Kendall, in the role of the conniving Madge Larrabee, had established herself in the provinces as a dependable support player, and was regarded as something of a mother hen by the younger actresses. Arthur Creeson, as the wicked James Larrabee, had been a promising romantic lead in his day, but excessive drink and gambling had marred his looks and scotched his reputation. William Allerford, whose high, domed forehead and startling white hair helped to make him so effective as the nefarious Professor Moriarty, was in fact the most gentle of men, with a great passion for tending the rosebushes at his cottage in Hove. As for myself, I had set out to become an opera singer in my younger days, but my talent had not matched my ambition, and over time I had evolved into a reliable, if unremarkable, second lead.

"Here we are," Frohman was saying as we arrived at the end of a long corridor. "We shall make a thorough search." After knocking on the unmarked door, he led us inside.

As was the custom of the day, the female members of the cast shared a communal dressing area in a narrow, sparsely appointed chamber illuminated by a long row of electrical lights. Along one wall was a long mirror with a row of wooden makeup tables before it. A random cluster of coat racks, reclining sofas, and well-worn armchairs were arrayed along the wall opposite. Needless to say, I had never been in a ladies' dressing room before, and I admit that I felt my cheeks redden at the sight of so many underthings and delicates thrown carelessly over the furniture. I turned to avert my eyes from a cambric corset cover thrown across a ladderback chair, only to find myself gazing upon a startling assortment of hosiery and lace-trimmed drawers laid out upon a nearby ottoman.

"Gracious, Mr. Lyndal," said Miss Kendall, taking a certain delight in my discomfiture. "One would almost think you'd never seen linens before."

"Well, I—perhaps not so many at once," I admitted, gathering my composure. "Dr. Watson is said to have an experience of women which extends over many nations and three separate continents. My own experience, I regret to say, extends no further than Hatton Cross."

Gillette, it appeared, did not share my sense of consternation. No sooner had we entered the dressing area than he began making an energetic and somewhat indiscriminate examination of the premises, darting from one side of the room to the other, opening drawers and tossing aside cushions and pillows with careless abandon.

"Well," he announced, after five minutes' effort, "I cannot find your brooch. However, in the interests of returning to our rehearsals as quickly as possible, I am prepared to buy you a new one."

Miss Fenton stared at the actor with an expression of disbelief. "I'm afraid you don't understand, Mr. Gillette. This was not a common piece of rolled plate and crystalline. It was a large, flawless sapphire in a rose gold setting, with a circle of diamond accents."

Gillette's eyes widened. "Was it, indeed? May I know how you came by such an item?"

A flush spread across Miss Fenton's cheek. "It was—it was a gift from an admirer," she said, glancing away. "I would prefer to say no more."

"Be that as it may," I said, "this is no small matter. We must notify the police at once!"

Gillette pressed his fingers together. "I'm afraid I must agree. This is most inconvenient."

A look of panic flashed across Miss Fenton's eyes. "Please, Mr. Gillette! You must not involve the police! That wouldn't do at all!"

"But your sapphire—?"

She tugged at the lace trimming of her sleeve. "The gentleman in question—the man who presented me with the brooch—he is of a certain social standing, Mr. Gillette. He—that is to say, I—would prefer to keep the matter private. It would be most embarrassing for him if his—if his attentions to me should become generally known."

Frohman gave a sudden cough. "It is not unknown for young actresses to form attachments with certain of their gentlemen admirers," he said carefully. "Occasionally, however, when these matters become public knowledge, they are attended by a certain whiff of scandal. Especially if the gentleman concerned happens to be married." He glanced at Miss Fenton, who held his gaze for a moment and then looked away. "Indeed," said Frohman. "Well, we can't have those whispers about the production, Gillette. Not before we've even opened."

"Quite so," I ventured, "and there is Miss Fenton's reputation to consider. We must discover what happened to the brooch without involving the authorities. We shall have to mount a private investigation."

All eyes turned to Gillette as a mood of keen expectation fell across the room. The actor did not appear to notice. Having caught sight of himself in the long mirror behind the dressing tables, he was making a meticulous adjustment to his waistcoat. At length, he became aware that the rest of us were staring intently at him.

"What?" he said, turning away from the mirror. "Why is everyone looking at me?"

"I am *not* Sherlock Holmes," Gillette said several moments later, as we settled ourselves in a pair of armchairs. "I am an actor *playing* Sherlock Holmes. There is a very considerable difference. If I did a turn as a pantomime horse, Lyndal, I trust you would not expect me to pull a dray wagon and dine on straw?"

"But you've studied Sherlock Holmes," I insisted. "You've examined his methods and turned them to your own purposes. Surely you might be able to do the same in this instance? Surely the author of such a fine detective play is not totally lacking in the powers of perception?"

Gillette gave me an appraising look. "Appealing to my vanity, Lyndal? Very shrewd."

We had been arguing back and forth in this vein for some moments, though by this time—detective or no—Gillette had reluctantly agreed to give his attention to the matter of the missing brooch. Frohman had made him see that an extended disruption would place their financial interests in the hazard, and that Gillette, as head of the company, was the logical choice to take command of the situation. Toward that end, it was arranged that Gillette would question each member of the company individually, beginning with myself.

Gillette's stage manager, catching wind of the situation, thought it would be a jolly lark to re-place the standing set of James Larrabee's drawing room with the lodgings of Sherlock Holmes at Baker Street, so that Gillette might have an appropriate setting in which to carry out his investigation. If Gillette noticed, he gave no sign. Stretching his arm toward a side table, he took up an outsize calabash pipe and began filling the meerschaum bowl.

"Why do you insist on smoking that ungainly thing?" I asked. "There's no record whatsoever of Sherlock Holmes having ever touched a calabash. Dr. Watson tells us that he favors an oily black clay pipe as the companion of his deepest meditations, but is wont to replace it with his cherrywood when in a disputatious frame of mind."

Gillette shook his head sadly. "I am *not* Sherlock Holmes," he said again. "I am an actor *playing* Sherlock Holmes."

"Still," I insisted, "it does no harm to be as faithful to the original as possible."

Gillette touched a flame to the tobacco and took several long draws to be certain the bowl was properly ignited. For a moment, his eyes were unfocused and dreamy, and I could not be certain that he had heard me. His eyes were fixed upon the fly curtains when he spoke again. "Lyndal," he said, "turn and face downstage."

"What?"

"Humor me. Face downstage."

I rose and looked out across the forward edge of the stage.

"What do you see?" Gillette asked.

"Empty seats," I said.

"Precisely. It is my ambition to fill those seats. Now, cast your eyes to the rear of the house. I want you to look at the left-hand aisle seat in the very last row."

I stepped forward and narrowed my eyes. "Yes," I said. "What of it?"

"Can you read the number plate upon that seat?"

"No," I said. "Of course not."

"Nor can I. By the same token, the man or woman seated there will not be able to appreciate the difference between a cherrywood pipe and an oily black clay. This is theater, Lyndal. A real detective does not do his work before an audience. I do. Therefore I am obliged to make my movements, speech, and stage properties readily discernible." He held the calabash aloft. "This pipe will be visible from the back row, my friend. An actor must consider even the smallest object from every possible angle. That is the essence of theater."

I considered the point. "I merely thought, inasmuch as you are attempting to inhabit the role of Sherlock Holmes, that you should wish to strive for authenticity."

Gillette seemed to consider the point. "Well," he said, "let us see how far that takes us. Tell me, Lyndal. Where were you when the robbery occurred?"

"Me? But surely you don't think that I—"

"You are not the estimable Dr. Watson, my friend. You are merely an actor, like myself. Since Miss Fenton had her brooch with her when she arrived at the theater this morning, we must assume that the theft occurred shortly after first call. Can you account for your movements in that time?"

"Of course I can. You know perfectly well where I was. I was standing stage right, beside you, running through the first act."

"So you were. Strange, my revision of the play has given you a perfect alibi. Had the theft occurred this afternoon, after I had restored the original text of the play, you should have been high on the list of suspects. A narrow escape, my friend." He smiled and sent up a cloud of pipe smoke. "Since we have established your innocence, however, I wonder if I might trouble you to remain through the rest of the interviews?"

"Whatever for?"

"Perhaps I am striving for authenticity." He turned and spotted young Henry Quinn hovering in his accustomed spot in the wings near the scenery cleats. "Quinn!" he called.

The boy stepped forward. "Yes, sir?"

"Would you ask Miss Fenton if she would be so good as to join us?"

"Right away, sir."

I watched as the boy disappeared down the long corridor. "Gillette," I said, lowering my voice, "this Baker Street set is quite comfortable in its way, but do you not think a bit of privacy might be indicated? Holmes is accustomed to conducting his interviews in confidence. Anyone might hear what passes between us here at the center of the stage."

Gillette smiled. "I am *not* Sherlock Holmes," he repeated.

After a moment or two Quinn stepped from the wings with Miss Fenton trailing behind him. Miss Fenton's eyes and nose were red with weeping, and she was attended by Miss Kendall, who hovered protectively by her side. "May I remain, Mr. Gillette?" asked the older actress. "Miss Fenton is terribly upset by all of this."

"Of course," said Gillette in a soothing manner. "I shall try to dispense with the questioning as quickly as possible. Please be seated." He folded his hands and leaned forward in his chair. "Tell me, Miss Fenton, are you quite certain that the brooch was in your possession when you arrived at the theater this morning?"

"Of course," the actress replied. "I had no intention of letting it out of my sight. I placed the pin in my jewelry case as I changed into costume."

"And the jewelry case was on top of your dressing table?"

"Yes."

"In plain sight?"

"Yes, but I saw no harm in that. I was alone at the time. Besides, Miss Kendall is the only other woman in the company, and I trust her as I would my own sister." She reached across and took the older woman's hand.

"No doubt," said Gillette, "but do you mean to say that you intended to leave the gem in the dressing room during the rehearsal? Forgive me, but that seems a bit careless."

"That was not my intention at all, Mr. Gillette. Once in costume, I planned to pin the brooch to my stockings. I should like to have worn it in plain view, but James—that is to say, the gentleman who gave it to me—would not have approved. He does not want anyone—he does not approve of ostentation."

"In any case," I said, "Alice Faulkner would hardly be likely to own such a splendid jewel."

"Yes," said Miss Fenton. "Just so."

Gillette steepled his fingers. "How exactly did the jewel come to be stolen? It appears that it never left your sight."

"It was unforgivable of me," said Miss Fenton. "I arrived late to the theater this morning. In my haste, I overturned an entire pot of facial powder. I favor a particular type, Gervaise Graham's Satinette, and I wished to see if I could persuade someone to step out and purchase a fresh supply for me. I can only have been gone for a moment. I stepped into the hallway looking for one of the stagehands, but of course they were all in their places in anticipation of the scene three set change. When I found no one close by, I realized that I had better finish getting ready as best I could without the powder."

"So you returned to the dressing area?"

"Yes."

"How long would you say that you were out of the room?"

"Two or three minutes. No more."

"And when you returned the brooch was gone?"

She nodded. "That was when I screamed."

"Indeed." Gillette stood and clasped his hands behind his back. "Extraordinary," he said, pacing a short line before a scenery flat decorated to resemble a bookcase. "Miss Kendall?"

"Yes?"

"Has anything been stolen from you?" he asked.

"No," she answered. "Well, not this time."

Gillette raised an eyebrow. "Not this time?"

The actress hesitated. "I'm sure it's nothing," she said. "From time to time I have noticed that one or two small things have gone astray. Nothing of any value. A small mirror, perhaps, or a copper or two."

Miss Fenton nodded. "I've noticed that as well. I assumed that I'd simply misplaced the items. It was never anything to trouble over."

Gillette frowned. "Miss Fenton, a moment ago, when the theft became known, it was clear that Miss Kendall was already aware that you had the brooch in your possession. May I ask who else among the company knew of the sapphire?"

"No one," the actress said. "I only received the gift yesterday, but I would have been unlikely to flash it about, in any case. I couldn't resist showing it to Selma, however."

"No one else knew of it?"

"No one."

Gillette turned to Miss Kendall. "Did you mention it to anyone?"

"Certainly not, Mr. Gillette."

The actor resumed his pacing. "You're quite certain? It may have been a perfectly innocent remark."

"Maude asked me not to say anything to anyone," said Miss Kendall. "We women are rather good with secrets."

Gillette's mouth pulled up slightly at the corners. "So I gather, Miss Kendall. So I gather." He turned and studied the false book spines on the painted scenery flat. "Thank you for your time, ladies."

I watched as the two actresses departed. "Gillette," I said after a moment, "if Miss Kendall did not mention the sapphire to anyone, who else could have known that it existed?"

"No one," he answered.

"Are you suggesting—" I leaned forward and lowered my voice. "Are you suggesting that Miss Kendall is the thief? After all, if she was the only one who knew—"

"No, Lyndal. I do not believe Miss Kendall is the thief."

"Still," I said, "there is little reason to suppose that she kept her own counsel. A theatrical company is a hotbed of gossip and petty jealousies." I paused as a new thought struck me. "Miss Fenton seems most concerned with protecting the identity of her gentleman admirer, although this will not be possible if the police have to be summoned. Perhaps the theft was orchestrated to expose him." I considered the possibility for a moment. "Yes, perhaps the intended victim is really this unknown patron, whomever he might be. He is undoubtedly a man of great wealth and position. Who knows? Perhaps this sinister plot extends all the way to the—"

"I think not," said Gillette.

"No?"

"If the intention was nothing more than to expose a dalliance between a young actress and a man of position, one need not have resorted to theft. A word in the ear of certain society matrons would have the same effect, and far more swiftly." He threw himself back down in his chair. "No, I believe that this was a crime of opportunity, rather than design. Miss Kendall and Miss Fenton both reported having noticed one or two small things missing from their dressing area on previous occasions. It seems that we have a petty thief in our midst, and that this person happened across the sapphire during those few moments when it was left unattended in the dressing room."

"But who could it be? Most of us were either onstage or working behind the scenes, in plain view of at least one other person at all times."

"So it would seem, but I'm not entirely convinced that someone couldn't have slipped away for a moment or two without being noticed. The crew members are forever darting in and out. It would not have drawn any particular notice if one of them had slipped away for a moment or two."

"Then we shall have to question the suspects," I said. "We must expose this nefarious blackguard at once."

Gillette regarded me over the bowl of his pipe. "Boucicault?" he asked.

"Pardon?"

"That line you just quoted. I thought I recognized it from one of Mr. Boucicault's melodramas."

I flushed. "No," I said. "It was my own."

"Was it? How remarkably vivid." He turned to young Henry Quinn, who was awaiting his instructions in the wings. "Quinn," he called,

"might I trouble you to run and fetch Mr. Allerford? I have a question or two I would like to put to him."

"Allerford," I said, as the boy disappeared into the wings. "So your suspicions have fallen upon the infamous Professor Moriarty, have they? There's a bit of Holmes in you, after all."

"Scarcely," said Gillette with a weary sigh. "I am proceeding in alphabetical order."

"Ah."

Young Quinn returned a moment later to conduct Allerford into our presence. The actor wore a long black frock coat for his impersonation of the evil professor, and his white hair was pomaded into a billowing cloud, exaggerating the size of his head and suggesting the heat of the character's mental processes.

"Do sit down, Allerford," Gillette said, as the actor stepped onto the stage, "and allow me to apologize for subjecting you to this interview. It pains me to suggest that you may in any way have—"

The actor held up his hands to break off the apologies. "No need, Gillette. I would do the same in your position. I presume you will wish to know where I was while the rest of you were running through the first act?"

Gillette nodded. "If you would be so kind."

"I'm afraid the answer is far from satisfactory. I was in the gentlemen's dressing area."

"Alone?"

"I'm afraid so. All the others were onstage or in the costume shop for their fittings." He gathered up a handful of loose fabric from his waistcoat. "My fitting was delayed until this afternoon. So I imagine I would have to be counted as the principal suspect, Gillette." He allowed his features to shift and harden as he assumed the character of Professor Moriarty. "You'll never hang this on me, Mr. Sherlock Holmes," he hissed, as his head oscillated in a reptilian fashion. "I have an ironclad alibi! I was alone in my dressing room reading a magazine!" The actor broke character and held up his palms in a gesture of futility. "I'm afraid I can't offer you anything better, Gillette."

"I'm sure nothing more will be required, Allerford. Again, let me apologize for this intrusion."

"Not at all."

"One more thing," Gillette said, as Allerford rose to take his leave.

"Yes?"

"The magazine you were reading. It wasn't *The Strand*, by any chance?"

"Why, yes. There was a copy lying about on the table."

"A Sherlock Holmes adventure, was it?"

Allerford's expression turned sheepish. "My tastes don't run in that direction, I'm afraid. There was an article on the sugar planters of the Yucatán. Quite intriguing, if I may say."

"I see." Gillette began refilling the bowl of his pipe. "Much obliged, Allerford."

"Gillette!" I said in an urgent whisper, as Allerford retreated into the wings. "What was that all about? Were you trying to catch him out?"

"What? No, I was just curious." The actor's expression grew unfocused as he touched a match to the tobacco. "Very curious." He sat quietly for some moments, sending clouds of smoke up into the fly curtains.

"Gillette," I said after a few moments, "shouldn't we continue? I believe Mr. Creeson is next."

"Creeson?"

"Yes. If we are to proceed alphabetically."

"Very good. Creeson. By all means. Quinn! Ask Mr. Creeson to join us, if you would."

With that, Gillette sank into his chair and remained there, scarcely moving, for the better part of two hours as a parade of actors, actresses, and stagehands passed before him. His questions and attitude were much the same as they had been with Allerford, but clearly his attention had wandered to some distant and inaccessible plateau. At times he appeared so preoccupied that I had to prod him to continue with the interviews. At one stage he drew his legs up to his chest and encircled them with his arms, looking for all the world like Sidney Paget's illustration of Sherlock Holmes in the grip of one of his three-pipe problems. Unlike the great detective, however, Gillette soon gave way to meditations of a different sort. By the time the last of our interviews was completed, a contented snoring could be heard from the actor's armchair.

"Gillette," I said, shaking him by the shoulder. "I believe we've spoken to everyone now."

"Have we? Very good." He rose from the chair and stretched his long limbs. "Is Mr. Frohman anywhere about?"

"Right here, Gillette," the producer called from the first row of seats. "I must say this appears to have been a colossal waste of time. I don't see how we can avoid going to the police now."

"I'm afraid I have to agree," I said. "We are no closer to resolving the matter than we were this morning." I glanced at Gillette, who was staring blankly into the footlights. "Gillette? Are you listening?"

"I think we may be able to keep the authorities out of the matter," he answered. "Frohman? Might I trouble you to assemble the company?"

"Whatever for?" I asked. "You've already spoken to—Say! You don't mean to say that you know who stole Miss Fenton's brooch?"

"I didn't say that."

"But then why should you—?"

He turned and held a finger to his lips. "I'm afraid you'll have to wait for the final act."

The actor would say nothing more as the members of the cast and crew appeared from their various places and arrayed themselves in the first two rows of seats. Gillette, standing at the lip of the stage, looked over them with an expression of keen interest. "My friends," he said after a moment, "you have all been very patient during this unpleasantness. I appreciate your indulgence. I'm sure that Sherlock Holmes would have gotten to the bottom of the matter in just a few moments, but as I am not Sherlock Holmes, it has taken me rather longer."

"Mr. Gillette!" cried Miss Fenton. "Do you mean to say you've found my brooch?"

"No, dear lady," he said, "I haven't. But I trust that it will be back in your possession shortly."

"Gillette," said Frohman, "this is all very irregular. Where is the stone? Who is the thief?"

"The identity of the thief has been apparent from the beginning," Gillette said placidly. "What I did not understand was the motivation."

"But that's nonsense!" cried Arthur Creeson. "The sapphire is extraordinarily valuable! What other motivation could there be?"

"I can think of several," Gillette answered, "and our 'nefarious blackguard,' to borrow a colorful phrase, might have succumbed to any one of them."

"You're talking in circles, Gillette," said Frohman. "If you've known the identity of the thief from the first, why didn't you just say so?"

"I was anxious to resolve the matter quietly," the actor answered. "Now, sadly, that is no longer possible." Gillette stretched his long arms. Moving upstage, he took up his pipe and slowly filled the bowl with tobacco from a ragged Persian slipper. "It was my hope," he said, "that the villain would come to regret these actions—the rash decision of an instant—and make amends. If the sapphire had simply been replaced on Miss Fenton's dressing table, I should have put the incident behind and carried on as though I had never discerned the guilty party's identity. Now, distasteful as it may be, the villain must be unmasked, and I must lose a member of my company on the eve of our London opening. Regrettable, but it can't be helped."

The members of the company shifted uneasily in their seats. "It's one of us, then?" asked Mr. Allerford.

"Of course. That much should have been obvious to all of you." He struck a match and ran it over the bowl of his pipe, lingering rather longer than necessary over the process. "The tragedy of the matter is that none of this would have happened if Miss Fenton had not stepped from her dressing room and left the stone unattended."

The actress's hands flew to her throat. "But I told you, I had spilled a pot of facial powder."

"Precisely so. Gervaise Graham's Satinette. A very distinctive shade. And so the catalyst of the crime now becomes the instrument of its solution."

"How do you mean, Gillette?" I asked.

Gillette moved off to stand before the fireplace—or rather the canvas and wood strutting that had been arranged to resemble a fireplace. The actor spent a moment contemplating the plaster coals that rested upon a balsa grating. "Detective work," he intoned, "is founded upon the observation of trifles. When Miss Fenton overturned that facial powder, she set in motion a chain of events that yielded a clue—a clue as transparent as that of a weaver's tooth or a compositor's thumb—and one that made it patently obvious who took the missing stone."

"Gillette!" cried Mr. Frohman. "No more theatrics! Who took Miss Fenton's sapphire?"

"The thief is here among us," he declared, his voice rising to a vibrant timbre. "And the traces of Satinette facial powder are clearly visible upon—Wait! Stop him!"

All at once, the theater erupted into pandemonium as young Henry Quinn, who had been watching from his accustomed place in the wings, suddenly darted forward and raced toward the rear exit.

"Stop him!" Gillette called to a pair of burly stagehands. "Hendricks! O'Donnell! Don't let him pass!"

The fleeing boy veered away from the stagehands, upsetting a flimsy side table in his flight, and made headlong for the forward edge of the stage. Gathering speed, he attempted to vault over the orchestra pit, and would very likely have cleared the chasm but for the fact that his ill-fitting trousers suddenly slipped to his ankles, entangling his legs and causing him to land in an awkward heap at the base of the pit.

"He's out cold, Mr. Gillette," came a voice from the pit. "Nasty bruise on his head."

"Very good, Hendricks. If you would be so good as to carry him into the lobby, we shall decide what to do with him later."

Miss Fenton pressed a linen handkerchief to her face as the unconscious figure was carried past. "I don't understand, Mr. Gillette. Henry took my sapphire? He's just a boy! I can't believe he would do such a thing!"

"Strange to say, I believe Quinn's intentions were relatively benign," said Gillette. "He presumed, when he came across the stone on your dressing table, that it was nothing more than a piece of costume jewelry. It was only later, after the alarm had been raised, that he realized its value. At that point, he became frightened and could not think of a means to return it without confessing his guilt."

"But what would a boy do with such a valuable stone?" Frohman asked.

"I have no idea," said Gillette. "Indeed, I do not believe that he had any interest whatsoever in the sapphire."

"No interest?" I said. "What other reason could he have had for taking it?"

"For the pin."

"What?"

Gillette gave a rueful smile. "You are all wearing costumes that are several sizes too large. Our rehearsals have been slowed for want of sewing pins to hold up the men's trousers and pin back the ladies' frocks. I myself dispatched Quinn to find a fastener for Mr. Lyndal."

"The essence of theater," I said, shaking my head with wonder.

"Pardon me, Lyndal?"

"As you were saying earlier. An actor must consider even the smallest object from every possible angle. We all assumed that the brooch had been taken for its valuable stone. Only you would have thought to consider it from the back as well as the front." I paused. "Well done, Gillette."

The actor gave a slight bow as the company burst into spontaneous applause. "That is most kind," he said, "but now, ladies and gentlemen, if there are no further distractions, I should like to continue with our rehearsal. Act one, scene four, I believe . . ."

It was several hours later when I knocked at the door to Gillette's dressing room. He bade me enter and made me welcome with a glass of ex-

cellent port. We settled ourselves on a pair of makeup stools and sat for a few moments in a companionable silence.

"I understand that Miss Fenton has elected not to pursue the matter of Quinn's theft with the authorities," I said after a time.

"I thought not," Gillette said. "I doubt if her gentleman friend would appreciate seeing the matter aired in the press. However, we will not be able to keep young Quinn with the company. He has been dismissed. Frohman has been in touch with another young man I once considered for the role. Charles Chapman."

"Chaplin, I believe."

"That's it. I'm sure he'll pick it up soon enough."

"No doubt."

I took a sip of port. "Gillette," I said, "there is something about the affair that troubles me."

He smiled and reached for a pipe. "I thought there might be," he said.

"You claimed to have spotted Quinn's guilt by the traces of face powder on his costume."

"Indeed."

I lifted my arm. "There are traces of Miss Fenton's powder here on my sleeve as well. No doubt I acquired them when I was searching for the missing stone in the dressing area—after the theft had been discovered."

"No doubt," said Gillette.

"The others undoubtedly picked up traces of powder as well."

"That is likely."

"So Quinn himself might well have acquired his telltale dusting of powder *after* the theft had occurred, in which case it would not have been incriminating at all."

Gillette regarded me with keen amusement. "Perhaps I noticed the powder on Quinn's sleeve before we searched the dressing area," he offered.

"Did you?"

He sighed. "No."

"Then you were bluffing? That fine speech about the observation of trifles was nothing more than vain posturing?"

"It lured a confession out of Quinn, my friend, so it was not entirely in vain."

"But you had no idea who the guilty party was! Not until the moment he lost his nerve and ran!"

Gillette leaned back and sent a series of billowy smoke rings toward the ceiling. "That is so," he admitted, "but then, as I have been at some pains to remind you, I am *not* Sherlock Holmes."

The Adventure of the Dorset Street Lodger

MICHAEL MOORCOCK

ONE OF THE most prolific writers in the world of science fiction and fantasy, Michael John Moorcock (1939–) is also one of the most honored. He has received lifetime achievement awards from every significant organization in those genres. He was inducted into the Science Fiction and Fantasy Hall of Fame in 2002 and the ultimate awards for his body of work have been presented at the World Fantasy Convention in 2000 (World Fantasy Award), at the Utopiales International Festival in 2004 (Prix Utopia), from the Horror Writers Association in 2004 (Bram Stoker Award), and from the Science Fiction and Fantasy Writers of America in 2008, when he was chosen as its twenty-fifth Grand Master. He was the Co–Guest of Honor at the 1976 World Fantasy Convention in New York City and also a Guest of Honor at the 1997 World Science Fiction Convention in San Antonio, Texas.

He has produced work in other forms, notably literary fiction, and *The Times* of London named him to its list of "The 50 Greatest British Writers Since 1945."

His most popular works have featured the antihero Elric of Melniboné in a series of fantasy novels in which Moorcock deliberately reverses the clichés of such "sword and sorcery" authors as Robert E. Howard and Fritz Leiber (whom he nonetheless admires).

"The Adventure of the Dorset Street Lodger" was originally privately printed as a chapbook for David Shapiro and Joe Piggott (1993); it was first collected in book form in *The Improbable Adventures of Sherlock Holmes*, edited by John Adams (San Francisco, Night Shade Books, 2009).

THE ADVENTURE OF THE DORSET STREET LODGER

Michael Moorcock

IT WAS ONE of those singularly hot Septembers, when the whole of London seemed to wilt from over-exposure to the sun, like some vast Arctic sea-beast foundering upon a tropical beach and doomed to die of unnatural exposure. Where Rome or even Paris might have shimmered and lazed, London merely gasped.

Our windows wide open to the noisy staleness of the air and our blinds drawn against the glaring light, we lay in a kind of torpor, Holmes stretched upon the sofa while I dozed in my easy chair and recalled my years in India, when such heat had been normal and our accommodation rather better equipped to cope with it. I had been looking forward to some fly fishing in the Yorkshire Dales but meanwhile, a patient of mine began to experience a difficult and potentially dangerous confinement so I could not in conscience go far from London. However, we had both planned to be elsewhere at this time and had confused the estimable Mrs. Hudson, who had expected Holmes himself to be gone.

Languidly, Holmes dropped to the floor the note he had been reading. There was a hint of irritation in his voice when he spoke.

"It seems, Watson, that we are about to be evicted from our quarters. I had hoped this would not happen while you were staying."

My friend's fondness for the dramatic statement was familiar to me, so I hardly blinked when I asked: "Evicted, Holmes?" I understood that his rent was, as usual, paid in advance for the year.

"Temporarily only, Watson. You will recall that we had both intended to be absent from London at about this time, until circumstances dictated otherwise. On that initial understanding, Mrs. Hudson commissioned Messrs. Peach, Peach, Peach, and Praisegod to refurbish and decorate 221B. This is our notice. They begin work next week and would be obliged if we would vacate the premises since minor structural work is involved. We are to be homeless for a fortnight, old friend. We must find new accommodations, Watson, but they must not be too far from here. You have your delicate patient and I have my work. I must have access to my files and my microscope."

I am not a man to take readily to change. I had already suffered several setbacks to my plans and the news, combined with the heat, shortened my temper a little. "Every criminal in London will be trying to take advantage of the situation," I said. "What if a Peach or Praisegod were in the pay of some new Moriarty?"

"Faithful Watson! That Reichenbach affair made a deep impression. It is the one deception for which I feel thorough remorse. Rest assured, dear friend. Moriarty is no more and there is never likely to be another criminal mind like his. I agree, however, that we should be able to keep an eye on things here. There are no hotels in the area fit for human habitation. And no friends or relatives nearby to put us up." It was almost touching to see that master of deduction fall into deep thought and begin to cogitate our domestic problem with the same attention he would give to one of his most difficult cases. It was this power of concentration, devoted to any matter in hand, which had first impressed me with his unique talents. At last he snapped his fingers, grinning like a Barbary ape, his deep-set eyes blazing with intelligence and self-mockery . . . "I have it, Watson. We shall, of course, ask Mrs. Hudson if she has a neighbour who rents rooms!"

"An excellent idea, Holmes!" I was amused by my friend's almost innocent pleasure in discovering, if not a solution to our dilemma, the best person to provide a solution for us!

Recovered from my poor temper, I rose to my feet and pulled the bellrope.

Within moments our housekeeper, Mrs. Hudson, was at the door and standing before us.

"I must say I am very sorry for the misunderstanding, sir," she said to me. "But patients is patients, I suppose, and your Scottish trout will have to wait a bit until you have a chance to catch them. But as for you, Mr. Holmes, it seems to me that hassassination or no hassassination, you could still do with a nice seaside holiday. My sister in Hove would look after you as thoroughly as if you were here in London."

"I do not doubt it, Mrs. Hudson. However, the assassination of one's host is inclined to cast a pall over the notion of vacations and while Prince Ulrich was no more than an acquaintance and the circumstances of his death all too clear, I feel obliged to give the matter a certain amount of consideration. It is useful to me to have my various analytical instruments to hand. Which brings us to a problem I am incapable of solving—if not Hove, Mrs. Hudson, where? Watson and I need bed and board and it must be close by."

Clearly the good woman disapproved of Holmes's unhealthy habits but despaired of converting him to her cause.

She frowned to express her lack of satisfaction with his reply and then spoke a little reluctantly. "There's my sister-in-law's over in Dorset Street, sir. Number Two, sir. I will admit that her cookery is a little too Frenchified for my taste, but it's a nice, clean, comfortable house

with a pretty garden at the back and she has already made the offer."

"And she is a discreet woman, is she Mrs. Hudson, like yourself?"

"As a church, sir. My late husband used to say of his sister that she could hold a secret better than the Pope's confessor."

"Very well, Mrs. Hudson. It is settled! We shall decant for Dorset Street next Friday, enabling your workman to come in on Monday. I will arrange for certain papers and effects to be moved over and the rest shall be secure, I am sure, beneath a good covering. Well, Watson, what do you say? You shall have your vacation, but it will be a little closer to home than you planned and with rather poorer fishing!"

My friend was in such positive spirits that it was impossible for me to retain my mood and indeed events began to move so rapidly from that point on, that any minor inconvenience was soon forgotten.

Our removal to number 2, Dorset Street, went as smoothly as could be expected and we were soon in residence. Holmes's untidiness, such a natural part of the man, soon gave the impression that our new chambers had been occupied by him for at least a century. Our private rooms had views of a garden which might have been transported from Sussex and our front parlour looked out onto the street, where, at the corner, it was possible to observe customers coming and going from the opulent pawn-brokers, often on their way to the Wheatsheaf Tavern, whose "well-aired beds" we had rejected in favour of Mrs. Ackroyd's somewhat luxurious appointments. A further pleasing aspect of the house was the blooming wisteria vine, of some age, which crept up the front of the building and further added to the countrified aspect. I suspect some of our comforts were not standard to all her lodgers. The good lady, of solid Lancashire stock, was clearly delighted at what she called "the honour" of looking after us and we both agreed we had never experienced better attention. She had pleasant, broad features and a practical, no nonsense manner to her which suited us both. While I would never have said so to either woman, her cooking was rather a pleasant change from Mrs. Hudson's good, plain fare.

And so we settled in. Because my patient was experiencing a difficult progress towards motherhood, it was important that I could be easily reached, but I chose to spend the rest of my time as if I really were enjoying a vacation. Indeed, Holmes himself shared something of my determination, and we had several pleasant evenings together, visiting the theatres and music halls for which London is justly famed. While I had developed an interest in the modern problem plays of Ibsen and Pinero, Holmes still favoured the atmosphere of the Empire and the Hippodrome, while Gilbert and Sullivan at the Savoy was his idea of perfection. Many a night I have sat beside him, often in the box which he preferred, glancing at his rapt features and wondering how an intellect so high could take such pleasure in low comedy and Cockney character-songs.

The sunny atmosphere of 2 Dorset Street actually seemed to lift my friend's spirits and give him a slightly boyish air which made me remark one day that he must have discovered the "waters of life," he was so rejuvenated. He looked at me a little oddly when I said this and told me to remind him to mention the discoveries he had made in Tibet, where he had spent much time after "dying" during his struggle with Professor Moriarty. He agreed, however, that this change was doing him good. He was able to continue his researches when he felt like it, but did not feel obliged to remain at home. He even insisted that we visit the kinema together, but the heat of the building in which it was housed, coupled with the natural odours emanating from our fellow customers, drove us into the fresh air before the show was over. Holmes showed little real interest in the invention. He was inclined to recognize progress only where it touched directly upon his own profession. He told me that he believed the kinema had no relevance to criminology, unless it could be used in the reconstruction of an offence and thus help lead to the capture of a perpetrator.

We were returning in the early evening to our temporary lodgings, having watched the kinema show at Madame Tussaud's in Marylebone Road, when Holmes became suddenly alert, pointing his stick ahead of him and saying in that urgent murmur I knew so well, "What do you make of this fellow, Watson? The one with the brand new top hat, the red whiskers, and a borrowed morning coat who recently arrived from the United States but has just returned from the north-western suburbs where he made an assignation he might now be regretting?"

I chuckled at this. "Come off it, Holmes!" I declared. "I can see a chap in a topper lugging a heavy bag, but how you could say he was from the United States and so on, I have no idea. I believe you're making it up, old man."

"Certainly not, my dear Watson! Surely you have noticed that the morning coat is actually beginning to part on the back seam and is therefore too small for the wearer. The most likely explanation is that he borrowed a coat for the purpose of making a particular visit. The hat is obviously purchased recently for the same reason while the man's boots have the 'gaucho' heel characteristic of the South Western United States, a style found only in that region and adapted, of course, from a Spanish riding boot. I have made a study of human heels, Watson, as well as of human souls!"

We kept an even distance behind the subject of our discussion. The traffic along Baker Street was at its heaviest, full of noisy carriages, snorting horses, yelling drivers, and all of London's varied humanity pressing its way homeward, desperate to find some means of cooling its collective body. Our "quarry" had periodically to stop and put down his bag, occasionally changing hands before continuing.

"But why do you say he arrived recently? And has been visiting north-west London?" I asked.

"That, Watson, is elementary. If you think for a moment, it will come clear to you that our friend is wealthy enough to afford the best in hats and Gladstone bags, yet wears a morning coat too small for him. It suggests he came with little luggage, or perhaps his luggage was stolen, and had no time to visit a tailor. Or he went to one of the ready-made places and took the nearest fit. Thus, the new bag, also, which he no doubt bought to carry the object he has just acquired. That he did not realize how heavy it was is clear and I am sure if he were not staying nearby, he would have hired a cab for himself. He could well be regretting his acquisition. Perhaps it was something very costly, but not exactly what he was expecting to get . . . He certainly did not realize how awkward it would be to carry, especially in this weather. That suggests to me that he believed he could walk from Baker Street Underground Railway station, which in turn suggests he has been visiting north west London, which is chiefly served from Baker Street."

It was rarely that I questioned my friend's judgements, but privately I found this one too fanciful. I was a little surprised, therefore, when I saw the top-hatted gentleman turn left into Dorset Street and disappear. Holmes immediately increased his pace. "Quickly, Watson! I believe I know where he's going."

Rounding the corner, we were just in time to see the American arrive at the door of Number 2 Dorset Street, and put a latch-key to the lock!

"Well, Watson," said Holmes in some triumph. "Shall we attempt to verify my analysis?" Whereupon he strode up to our fellow lodger, raised his hat and offered to help him with the bag.

The man reacted rather dramatically, falling backwards against the railings and almost knocking his own hat over his eyes. He glared at Holmes, panting, and then with a wordless growl, pushed on into the front hall, lugging the heavy Gladstone behind him and slamming the door in my friend's face. Holmes lifted his eyebrows in an expression of baffled amusement.

"No doubt the efforts with the bag have put the gentleman in poor temper, Watson!"

Once within, we were in time to see the man, hat still precariously on his head, heaving his bag up the stairs. The thing had come undone and I caught a glimpse of silver, the gleam of gold, the representation, I thought, of a tiny human hand. When he recognized us he stopped in some confusion, then murmured in a dramatic tone:

"Be warned, gentleman. I possess a revolver and I know how to use it."

Holmes accepted this news gravely and informed the man that while he understood an exchange of pistol fire to be something in the nature of an introductory courtesy in Texas, in England it was still considered unnecessary to support one's cause by letting off guns in the house. This I found a little like hypocrisy from one given to target practice in the parlour!

However, our fellow lodger looked suitably embarrassed and began to recover himself. "Forgive me, gentlemen," he said. "I am a stranger here and I must admit I'm rather confused as to who my friends and enemies are. I have been warned to be careful. How did you get in?"

"With a key, as you did, my dear sir. Doctor Watson and myself are guests here for a few weeks."

"Doctor Watson!" The man's voice established him immediately as an American. The drawling brogue identified him as a South Westerner and I trusted Holmes's ear enough to believe that he must be Texan.

"I am he." I was mystified by his evident enthusiasm but illuminated when he turned his attention to my companion.

"Then you must be Mr. Sherlock Holmes! Oh, my good sir, forgive me my bad manners! I am a great admirer, gentlemen. I have followed all your cases. You are, in part, the reason I took rooms near Baker Street. Unfortunately, when I called at your house yesterday, I found it occupied by contractors who could not tell me where you were. Time being short, I was forced to act on my own account. And I fear I have not been too successful! I had no idea that you were lodging in this very building!"

"Our landlady," said Holmes dryly, "is renowned for her discretion. I doubt if her pet cat has heard our names in this house."

The American was about thirty-five years old, his skin turned dark by the sun, with a shock of red hair, a full red moustache and a heavy jaw. If it were not for his intelligent green eyes and delicate hands, I might have mistaken him for an Irish prize fighter. "I'm James Macklesworth, sir, of Galveston, Texas. I'm in the import/export business over there. We ship upriver all the way to Austin, our State Capital, and have a good reputation for honest trading. My grandfather fought to establish our Republic and was the first to take a steam-boat up the Colorado to trade with Port Sabatini and the river-towns." In the manner of Americans, he offered us a resume of his background, life and times, even as we shook hands. It is a custom necessary in those wild and still largely unsettled regions of the United States.

Holmes was cordial, as if scenting a mystery to his taste, and invited the Texan to join us in an hour, when, over a whiskey and soda, we could discuss his business in comfort.

Mr. Macklesworth accepted with alacrity and promised that he would bring with him the contents of his bag and a full explanation of his recent behaviour.

Before James Macklesworth arrived, I asked Holmes if he had any impression of the man. I saw him as an honest enough fellow, perhaps a business man who had got in too deep and wanted Sherlock Holmes to help him out. If that were all he required of my friend, I was certain Holmes would refuse the case. On the other hand, there was every chance that this was an unusual affair.

Holmes said that he found the man interesting and, he believed, honest. But he could not be sure, as yet, if he were the dupe of some clever villain or acting out of character. "For my guess

is there is definitely a crime involved here, Watson, and I would guess a pretty devilish one. You have no doubt heard of the Fellini Perseus."

"Who has not? It is said to be Fellini's finest work—cast of solid silver and chased with gold. It represents Perseus with the head of Medusa, which itself is made of sapphires, emeralds, rubies, and pearls."

"Your memory as always is excellent, Watson. For many years it was the prize in the collection of Sir Geoffrey Macklesworth, son of the famous Iron Master said to be the richest man in England. Sir Geoffrey, I gather, died one of the poorest. He was fond of art but did not understand money. This made him, I understand, prey to many kinds of social vampires! In his younger years he was involved with the aesthetic movement, a friend of Whistler's and Wilde's. In fact Wilde was, for a while, a good friend to him, attempting to dissuade him from some of his more spectacular blue and white excesses!"

"Macklesworth!" I exclaimed.

"Exactly, Watson." Holmes paused to light his pipe, staring down into the street where the daily business of London continued its familiar and unspectacular round. "The thing was stolen about ten years ago. A daring robbery which I, at the time, ascribed to Moriarty. There was every indication it had been spirited from the country and sold abroad. Yet I recognized it—or else a very fine copy—in that bag James Macklesworth was carrying up the stairs. He would have read of the affair, I'm sure, especially considering his name. Therefore he must have known the Fellini statue was stolen. Yet clearly he went somewhere today and returned here with it. Why? He's no thief, Watson, I'd stake my life on it."

"Let us hope he intends to illuminate us," I said as a knock came at our door.

Mr. James Macklesworth was a changed man. Bathed and dressed in his own clothes, he appeared far more confident and at ease. His suit was of a kind favoured in his part of the world, with a distinctly Spanish cut to it, and he wore a flowing tie beneath the wings of a wide-collared soft shirt, a dark red waistcoat and pointed ox-blood boots. He looked every inch the romantic frontiersman.

He began by apologizing for his costume. He had not realized, he said, until he arrived in London yesterday, that his dress was unusual and remarkable in England. We both assured him that his sartorial appearance was in no way offensive to us. Indeed, we found it attractive.

"But it marks me pretty well for who I am, is that not so, gentlemen?"

We agreed that in Oxford Street there would not be a great many people dressed in his fashion.

"That's why I bought the English clothes," he said. "I wanted to fit in and not be noticed. The top hat was too big and the morning coat was too small. The trousers were the only thing the right size. The bag was the largest of its shape I could find."

"So, suitably attired, as you thought, you took the Metropolitan Railway this morning to—?"

"To Willesden, Mr. Holmes. Hey! How did you know that? Have you been following me all day?"

"Certainly not, Mr. Macklesworth. And in Willesden you took possession of the Fellini Perseus, did you not?"

"You know everything ahead of me telling it, Mr. Holmes! I need speak no more. Your reputation is thoroughly deserved, sir. If I were not a rational man, I would believe you possessed of psychic powers!"

"Simple deductions, Mr. Macklesworth. One develops a skill, you know. But it might take a longer acquaintance for me to deduce how you came to cross some six thousand miles of land and sea to arrive in London, go straight to Willesden, and come away with one of the finest pieces of Renaissance silver the world has ever seen. All in a day, too."

"I can assure you, Mr. Holmes, that such adventuring is not familiar to me. Until a few months ago I was the owner of a successful shipping and wholesaling business. My wife died several years ago and I never remarried. My children are all grown now and married, living far from Texas. I was a little lonely, I suppose, but reasonably content. That all changed, as you have guessed, when the Fellini Perseus came into my life."

"You received word of it in Texas, Mr. Macklesworth?"

"Well, sir, it's an odd thing. Embarrassing, too. But I guess I'm going to have to be square with you and come out with it. The gentleman from whom the Perseus was stolen was a cousin of mine. We'd corresponded a little. In the course of that correspondence he revealed a secret which has now become a burden to me. I was his only living male relative, you see, and he had family business to do. There was another cousin, he thought in New Orleans, but he had yet to be found. Well, gentlemen, the long and the short of it was that I swore on my honour to carry out Sir Geoffrey's instructions in the event of something happening to him or to the Fellini Perseus. His instructions led me to take a train for New York and from New York the *Arcadia* for London. I arrived yesterday afternoon."

"So you came all this way, Mr. Macklesworth, on a matter of honour?" I was somewhat impressed.

"You could say so, sir. We set high store by family loyalty in my part of the world. Sir Geoffrey's estate, as you know, went to pay his debts. But that part of my trip has to do with a private matter. My reason for seeking you out was connected with it. I believe Sir Geoffrey was murdered, Mr. Holmes. Someone was blackmailing him and he spoke of 'financial commitments.' His letters increasingly showed his anxiety and were often rather rambling accounts of his fears that there should be nothing left for his heirs. I told him he had no direct heirs and he might as well reconcile himself to that. He did not seem to take in what I said. He begged me to help him. And he begged me to be discreet. I promised. One of the last letters I had from him told me that if I ever heard news of his death, I must immediately sail for England and upon arriving take a good sized bag to 18 Dahlia Gardens, Willesden Green, North West London, and supply proof of my identity, whereupon I would take responsibility for the object most precious to the Macklesworths. Whereupon I must return to Galveston with all possible speed. Moreover I must swear to keep the object identified with the family name forever.

"This I swore and only a couple of months later I read in the Galveston paper the news of the robbery. Not long after, there followed an account of poor Sir Geoffrey's suicide. There was nothing else I could do, Mr. Holmes, but follow his instructions, as I had sworn I would. However I became convinced that Sir Geoffrey had scarcely been in his right mind at the end. I suspected he feared nothing less than murder. He spoke of people who would go to any lengths to possess the Fellini Silver. He did not care that the rest of his estate was mortgaged to the hilt or that he would die, effectively, a pauper. The Silver was of overweaning importance. That is why I suspect the robbery and his murder are connected."

"But the verdict was suicide," I said. "A note was found. The coroner was satisfied."

"The note was covered in blood, was it not?" Holmes murmured from where he sat lounging back in his chair, his finger tips together upon his chin.

"I gather that was the case, Mr. Holmes. But since no foul play was suspected, no investigation was made."

"I see. Pray continue, Mr. Macklesworth."

"Well, gentlemen, I've little to add. All I have is a nagging suspicion that something is wrong. I do not wish to be party to a crime, nor to hold back information of use to the police, but I am honour-bound to fulfil my pledge to my cousin. I came to you not necessarily to ask you to solve a crime, but to put my mind at rest if no crime were committed."

"A crime has already been committed, if Sir Geoffrey announced a burglary that did not happen. But it is not much of one, I'd agree. What did you want of us in particular, Mr. Macklesworth?"

"I was hoping you or Dr. Watson might accompany me to the address—for a variety of obvious reasons. I am a law-abiding man, Mr. Holmes, and wish to remain so. There again, considerations of honour . . ."

"Quite so," interrupted Holmes. "Now, Mr. Macklesworth, tell us what you found at 18 Dahlia Gardens, Willesden!"

"Well, it was a rather dingy house of a kind I'm completely unfamiliar with. All crowded along a little road about a quarter of a mile from the station. Not at all what I'd expected. Number 18 was dingier than the rest—a poor sort of a place altogether, with peeling paint, an overgrown yard, bulging garbage cans and all the kind of thing you expect to see in East Side New York, not in a suburb of London.

"All this notwithstanding, I found the dirty knocker and hammered upon the door until it was opened by a surprisingly attractive woman of what I should describe as the octoroon persuasion. A large woman, too, with long but surprisingly well-manicured hands. Indeed, she was impeccable in her appearance, in distinct contrast to her surroundings. She was expecting me. Her name was Mrs. Gallibasta. I knew the name at once. Sir Geoffrey had often spoken of her, in terms of considerable affection and trust. She had been, she told me, Sir Geoffrey's housekeeper. He had enjoined her, before he died, to perform this last loyal deed for him. She handed me a note he had written to that effect. Here it is, Mr. Holmes."

He reached across and gave it to my friend, who studied it carefully. "You recognize the writing, of course?"

The American was in no doubt. "It is in the flowing, slightly erratic, masculine hand I recognize. As you can see, the note says that I must accept the family heirloom from Mrs. Gallibasta and, in all secrecy, transport it to America, where it must remain in my charge until such time as the other 'missing' Macklesworth cousin was found. If he had male heirs, it must be passed on to one of them at my discretion. If no male heir can be found, it should be passed on to one of my daughters—I have no living sons—on condition that they add the Macklesworth name to their own. I understand, Mr. Holmes, that to some extent I am betraying my trust. But I know so little of English society and customs. I have a strong sense of family and did not know I was related to such an illustrious line until Sir Geoffrey wrote and told me. Although we only corresponded, I feel obliged to carry out his last wishes. However, I am not so foolish as to believe I know exactly what I am doing and require guidance. I want to assure myself that no foul play has been involved and I know that, of all the men in England, you will not betray my secret."

"I am flattered by your presumption, Mr. Macklesworth. Pray, could you tell me the date of the last letter you received from Sir Geoffrey?"

"It was undated, but I remember the post mark. It was the fifteenth day of June of this year."

"I see. And the date of Sir Geoffrey's death?"

"The thirteenth. I supposed him to have posted the letter before his death but it was not collected until afterward."

"A reasonable assumption. And you are very familiar, you say, with Sir Geoffrey's handwriting."

"We corresponded for several years, Mr. Holmes. The hand is identical. No forger, no matter how clever, could manage those idiosyncracies, those unpredictable lapses into barely readable words. But usually his hand was a fine, bold, idiosyncratic one. It was not a forgery, Mr. Holmes. And neither was the note he left with his housekeeper."

"But you never met Sir Geoffrey?"

"Sadly, no. He spoke sometimes of coming out to ranch in Texas, but I believe other concerns took up his attention."

"Indeed, I knew him slightly some years ago, when we belonged to the same club. An artistic type, fond of Japanese prints and Scottish furniture. An affable, absent-minded fellow, rather retiring. Of a markedly gentle disposition. Too good for this world, as we used to say."

"When would that have been, Mr. Holmes?" Our visitor leaned forward, showing considerable curiosity.

"Oh, about twenty years ago, when I was just starting in practice. I was able to provide some evidence in a case concerning a young friend of his who had got himself into trouble. He was gracious enough to believe I had been able to turn a good man back to a better path. I recall that he frequently showed genuine concern for the fate of his fellow creatures. He remained a confirmed bachelor, I understand. I was sorry to hear of the robbery. And then the poor man killed himself. I was a little surprised, but no foul play was suspected and I was involved in some rather difficult problems at the time. A kindly sort of old-fashioned gentleman. The patron of many a destitute young artist. It was art, I gather, which largely reduced his fortune."

"He did not speak much of art to me, Mr. Holmes. I fear he had changed considerably over the intervening years. The man I knew became increasingly nervous and given to what seemed somewhat irrational anxieties. It was to quell these anxieties that I agreed to carry out his request. I was, after all, the last of the Macklesworths and obliged to accept certain responsibilities. I was honoured, Mr. Holmes, by the responsibility, but disturbed by what was asked of me."

"You are clearly a man of profound common sense, Mr. Macklesworth, as well as a man of honour. I sympathize entirely with your predicament. You were right to come to us and we shall do all we can to help!"

The relief on the American's face was considerable. "Thank you, Mr. Holmes. Thank you, Doctor Watson. I feel I can now act with some coherence."

"Sir Geoffrey had already mentioned his housekeeper, I take it?"

"He had, sir, in nothing less than glowing terms. She had come to him about five years ago and had worked hard to try to put his affairs in order. If it were not for her, he said, he would have faced the bankruptcy court earlier. Indeed, he spoke so warmly of her that I will admit to the passing thought that—well, sir, that they were . . ."

"I take your meaning, Mr. Macklesworth. It

might also explain why your cousin never married. No doubt the class differences were insurmountable, if what we suspect were the case."

"I have no wish to impugn the name of my relative, Mr. Holmes."

"But we must look realistically at the problem, I think." Holmes gestured with his long hand. "I wonder if we might be permitted to see the statue you picked up today?"

"Certainly, sir. I fear the newspaper in which it was wrapped has come loose here and there—"

"Which is how I recognized the Fellini workmanship," said Holmes, his face becoming almost rapturous as the extraordinary figure was revealed. He reached to run his fingers over musculature which might have been living flesh in miniature, it was so perfect. The silver itself was vibrant with some inner energy and the gold chasing, the precious stones, all served to give the most wonderful impression of Perseus, a bloody sword in one hand, his shield on his arm, holding up the snake-crowned head which glared at us through sapphire eyes and threatened to turn us to stone!

"It is obvious why Sir Geoffrey, whose taste was so refined, would have wished this to remain in the family," I said. "Now I understand why he became so obsessed towards the end. Yet I would have thought he might have willed it to a museum—or made a bequest—rather than go to such elaborate lengths to preserve it. It's something which the public deserves to see."

"I agree with you completely, sir. That is why I intend to have a special display room built for it in Galveston. But until that time, I was warned by both Sir Geoffrey and by Mrs. Gallibasta, that news of its existence would bring immense problems—not so much from the police as from the other thieves who covet what is, perhaps, the world's finest single example of Florentine Renaissance silver. It must be worth thousands!

"I intend to insure it for a million dollars, when I get home," volunteered the Texan.

"Perhaps you would entrust the sculpture with us for the night and until tomorrow evening?" Holmes asked our visitor.

"Well, sir, as you know I am supposed to take the *Arcadia* back to New York. She sails tomorrow evening from Tilbury. She's one of the few steamers of her class leaving from London. If I delay, I shall have to go back via Liverpool."

"But you are prepared to do so, if necessary?"

"I cannot leave without the Silver, Mr. Holmes. Therefore, while it remains in your possession, I shall have to stay." John Macklesworth offered us a brief smile and the suggestion of a wink. "Besides, I have to say that the mystery of my cousin's death is of rather more concern than the mystery of his last wishes."

"Excellent, Mr. Macklesworth. I see we are of like mind. It will be a pleasure to put whatever talents I possess at your disposal. Sir Geoffrey resided, as I recall, in Oxfordshire."

"About ten miles from Oxford itself, he said. Near a pleasant little market town called Witney. The house is known as Cogges Old Manor and it was once the centre of a good-sized estate, including a working farm. But the land was sold and now only the house and grounds remain. They, too, of course, are up for sale by my cousin's creditors. Mrs. Gallibasta said that she did not believe it would be long before someone bought the place. The nearest hamlet is High Cogges. The nearest railway station is at South Leigh, about a mile distant. I know the place as if it were my own, Mr. Holmes, Sir Geoffrey's descriptions were so vivid."

"Indeed! Did you, by the by, contact him originally?"

"No, sir! Sir Geoffrey had an interest in heraldry and lineage. In attempting to trace the descendants of Sir Robert Macklesworth, our mutual great-grandfather, he came across my name and wrote to me. Until that time I had no idea I was so closely related to the English aristocracy! For a while Sir Geoffrey spoke of my inheriting the title—but I am a convinced republican. We don't go much for titles and such in Texas—not unless they are earned!"

"You told him you were not interested in inheriting the title?"

"I had no wish to inherit anything, sir." John

Macklesworth rose to leave. "I merely enjoyed the correspondence. I became concerned when his letters grew increasingly more anxious and rambling and he began to speak of suicide."

"Yet still you suspect murder?"

"I do, sir. Put it down to an instinct for the truth—or an overwrought imagination. It is up to you!"

"I suspect it is the former, Mr. Macklesworth. I shall see you here again tomorrow evening. Until then, goodnight."

We shook hands.

"Goodnight, gentlemen. I shall sleep easy tonight, for the first time in months." And with that our Texan visitor departed.

"What do you make of it, Watson?" Holmes asked, as he reached for his long-stemmed clay pipe and filled it with tobacco from the slipper he had brought with him. "Do you think our Mr. Macklesworth is 'the real article' as his compatriots would say?"

"I was very favourably impressed, Holmes. But I do believe he has been duped into involving himself in an adventure which, if he obeyed his own honest instincts, he would never have considered. I do not believe that Sir Geoffrey was everything he claimed to be. Perhaps he was when you knew him, Holmes, but since then he has clearly degenerated. He keeps an octoroon mistress, gets heavily into debt, and then plans to steal his own treasure in order to preserve it from creditors. He involves our decent Texan friend, conjuring up family ties and knowing how important such things are to Southerners. Then, I surmise, he conspires with his housekeeper to fake his own death."

"And gives his treasure up to his cousin? Why would he do that, Watson?"

"He's using Macklesworth to transport it to America, where he plans to sell it."

"Because he doesn't want to be identified with it, or caught with it. Whereas Mr. Macklesworth is so manifestly innocent he is the perfect one to carry the Silver to Galveston. Well, Wat-

son, it's not a bad theory and I suspect much of it is relevant."

"But you know something else?"

"Just a feeling, really. I believe that Sir Geoffrey is dead. I read the coroner's report. He blew his brains out, Watson. That was why there was so much blood on the suicide note. If he planned a crime, he did not live to complete it."

"So the housekeeper decided to continue with the plan?"

"There's only one flaw there, Watson. Sir Geoffrey appears to have anticipated his own suicide and left instructions with her. Mr. Macklesworth identified the handwriting. I read the note myself. Mr. Macklesworth has corresponded with Sir Geoffrey for years. He confirmed that the note was clearly Sir Geoffrey's."

"So the housekeeper is also innocent. We must look for a third party."

"We must take an expedition into the countryside, Watson." Holmes was already consulting his Bradshaw's. "There's a train from Paddington in the morning which will involve a change at Oxford and will get us to South Leigh before lunch. Can your patient resist the lure of motherhood for another day or so, Watson?"

"Happily there's every indication that she is determined to enjoy an elephantine confinement."

"Good, then tomorrow we shall please Mrs. Hudson by sampling the fresh air and simple fare of the English countryside."

And with that my friend, who was in high spirits at the prospect of setting that fine mind to something worthy of it, sat back in his chair, took a deep draft of his pipe, and closed his eyes.

We could not have picked a better day for our expedition. While still warm, the air had a balmy quality to it and even before we had reached Oxford we could smell the delicious richness of an early English autumn. Everywhere the corn had been harvested and the hedgerows were full of colour. Thatch and slate slid past our window which looked out to what was best in an England whose people had built to the natural roll of the land and planted with an instinctive eye for beauty as well as practicality. This was what I had missed in Afghanistan and what Holmes had missed in Tibet, when he had learned so many things at the feet of the High Lama himself. Nothing ever compensated, in my opinion, for the wealth and variety of the typical English country landscape.

In no time we were at South Leigh station and able to hire a pony-cart with which to drive ourselves up the road to High Cogges. We made our way through winding lanes, between tall hedges, enjoying the sultry tranquillity of a day whose silence was broken only by the sound of bird-song and the occasional lowing of a cow.

We drove through the hamlet, which was served by a Norman church and a grocer's shop which also acted as the local post office. High Cogges itself was reached by a rough lane, little more than a farm track leading past some picturesque farm cottages with thatched roofs, which seemed to have been there since the beginning of time and were thickly covered with roses and honeysuckle, a rather vulgar modern house whose owner had made a number of hideous additions in the popular taste of the day, a farmhouse and outbuildings of the warm, local stone which seemed to have grown from out of the landscape as naturally as the spinney and orchard behind it, and then we had arrived at the locked gates of Cogges Old Manor which bore an air of neglect. It seemed to me that it had been many years since the place had been properly cared for.

True to form, my friend began exploring and had soon discovered a gap in a wall through which we could squeeze in order to explore the grounds. These were little more than a good-sized lawn, some shrubberies and dilapidated greenhouses, an abandoned stables, various other sheds, and a workshop which was in surprisingly neat order. This, Holmes told me, was where Sir Geoffrey had died. It had been thoroughly cleaned. He had placed his gun in a vice and shot himself through the mouth. At the inquest, his housekeeper, who had clearly been

devoted to him, had spoken of his money worries, his fears that he had dishonoured the family name. The scrawled note had been soaked in blood and only partially legible, but it was clearly his.

"There was no hint of foul play, you see, Watson. Everyone knew that Sir Geoffrey led the Bohemian life until he settled here. He had squandered the family fortune, largely on artists and their work. No doubt some of his many modern canvasses would become valuable, at least to someone, but at present the artists he had patronized had yet to realize any material value. I have the impression that half the denizens of the Café Royal depended on the Macklesworth millions until they finally dried up. I also believe that Sir Geoffrey was either distracted in his last years, or depressed. Possibly both. I think we must make an effort to interview Mrs. Gallibasta. First, however, let's visit the post office—the source of all wisdom in these little communities."

The post office–general store was a converted thatched cottage, with a white picket fence and a display of early September flowers which would not have been out of place in a painting. Within the cool shade of the shop, full of every possible item a local person might require, from books to boiled sweets, we were greeted by the proprietress whose name over her doorway we had already noted.

Mrs. Beck was a plump, pink woman in plain prints and a starched pinafore, with humorous eyes and a slight pursing of the mouth which suggested a conflict between a natural warmth and a slightly censorious temperament. Indeed, this is exactly what we discovered. She had known both Sir Geoffrey and Mrs. Gallibasta. She had been on good terms with a number of the servants, she said, although one by one they had left and had not been replaced.

"There was talk, gentlemen, that the poor gentleman was next to destitute and couldn't afford new servants. But he was never behind with the wages and those who worked for him were loyal enough. Especially his housekeeper. She had an odd, distant sort of air, but there's no question she looked after him well and since his prospects were already known, she didn't seem to be hanging around waiting for his money."

"Yet you were not fond of the woman?" murmured Holmes, his eyes studying an advertisement for toffee.

"I will admit that I found her a little strange, sir. She was a foreign woman, Spanish I think. It wasn't her gypsy looks that bothered me, but I never could get on with her. She was always very polite and pleasant in her conversation. I saw her almost every day, too—though never in church. She'd come in here to pick up whatever small necessities they needed. She always paid cash and never asked for credit. Though I had no love for her, it seemed that she was supporting Sir Geoffrey, not the other way around. Some said she had a temper to her and that once she had taken a rake to an under-footman, but I saw no evidence of it. She'd spend a few minutes chatting with me, sometimes purchase a newspaper, collect whatever mail there was and walk back up the lane to the manor. Rain or shine, sir, she'd be here. A big, healthy woman she was. She'd joke about what a handful it all was, him and the estate, but she didn't seem to mind. I only knew one odd thing about her. When she was sick, no matter how sick she became, she always refused a doctor. She had a blind terror of the medical profession, sir. The very suggestion of calling Doctor Shapiro would send her into screaming insistence that she needed no 'sawbones.' Otherwise, she was what Sir Geoffrey needed, him being so gentle and strange and with his head in the clouds. He was like that since a boy."

"But given to irrational fears and notions, I gather?"

"Not so far as I ever observed, sir. He never seemed to change. She was the funny one. Though he stayed at the house for the past several years and I only saw him occasionally. But when I did he was his usual sunny self."

"That's most interesting, Mrs. Beck. I am grateful to you. I think I will have a quarter-pound of your best bullseyes, if you please. Oh, I forgot to ask. Do you remember Sir Geoffrey receiving any letters from America?"

"Oh, yes, sir. Frequently. He looked forward to them," she said. "I remember the envelope and the stamps. It was almost his only regular correspondent."

"And Sir Geoffrey sent his replies from here?"

"I wouldn't know that, sir. The mail's collected from a pillar-box near the station. You'll see it, if you're going back that way."

"Mrs. Gallibasta, I believe, has left the neighbourhood."

"Not two weeks since, sir. My son carried her boxes to the station for her. She took all her things. He mentioned how heavy her luggage was. He said if he hadn't attended Sir Geoffrey's service at St. James's himself he'd have thought she had him in her trunk. If you'll pardon the levity, sir."

"I am greatly obliged to you, Mrs. Beck." The detective lifted his hat and bowed. I recognized Holmes's brisk, excited mood. He was on a trail now and had scented some form of quarry. As we left, he murmured: "I must go round to 221B as soon as we get back and look in my early files."

As I drove the dog-cart back to the station, Holmes scarcely spoke a further word. He was lost in thought all the way back to London. I was used to my friend's moods and habits and was content to let that brilliant mind exercise itself while I gave myself up to the world's concerns in the morning's *Telegraph*.

Mr. Macklesworth joined us for tea that afternoon. Mrs. Ackroyd had outdone herself with smoked salmon and cucumber sandwiches, small savouries, scones, and cakes. The tea was my favourite Darjeeling, whose delicate flavour is best appreciated at that time in the afternoon, and even Holmes remarked that we might be guests at Sinclair's or the Grosvenor.

Our ritual was overseen by the splendid Fellini Silver which, perhaps to catch the best of the light, Holmes had placed in our sitting-room window, looking out to the street. It was as if we ate our tea in the presence of an angel. Mr. Macklesworth balanced his plate on his knee wearing an expression of delight. "I have heard of this ceremony, gentlemen, but never expected to be taking part in a High Tea with Mr. Sherlock Holmes and Doctor Watson!"

"Indeed, you are doing no such thing, sir," Holmes said gently. "It is a common misconception, I gather, among our American cousins that High- and Afternoon-tea are the same thing. They are very different meals, taken at quite different times. High Tea was in my day only eaten at certain seats of learning, and was a hot, early supper. The same kind of supper, served in a nursery, has of late been known as High Tea. Afternoon-tea, which consists of a conventional cold sandwich selection, sometimes with scones, clotted cream, and strawberry jam, is eaten by adults, generally at four o'clock. High Tea, by and large, is eaten by children at six o'clock. The sausage was always very evident at such meals when I was young." Holmes appeared to shudder subtly.

"I stand corrected and instructed, sir," said the Texan jovially, and waved a delicate sandwich by way of emphasis. Whereupon all three of us broke into laughter—Holmes at his own pedantry and Mr. Macklesworth almost by way of relief from the weighty matters on his mind.

"Did you discover any clues to the mystery in High Cogges?" our guest wished to know.

"Oh, indeed, Mr. Macklesworth," said Holmes, "I have one or two things to verify, but think the case is solved." He chuckled again, this time at the expression of delighted astonishment on the American's face.

"Solved, Mr. Holmes?"

"Solved, Mr. Macklesworth, but not proven. Doctor Watson, as usual, contributed greatly to my deductions. It was you, Watson, who suggested the motive for involving this gentleman in what, I believe, was a frightful and utterly cold-blooded crime."

"So I was right, Mr. Holmes! Sir Geoffrey was murdered!"

"Murdered or driven to self-murder, Mr. Macklesworth, it is scarcely material."

"You know the culprit, sir?

"I believe I do. Pray, Mr. Macklesworth," now Holmes pulled a piece of yellowed paper from an inner pocket, "would you look at this? I took it from my files on the way here and apologize for its somewhat dusty condition."

Frowning slightly, the Texan accepted the folded paper and then scratched his head in some puzzlement, reading aloud. "My dear Holmes, Thank you so much for your generous assistance in the recent business concerning my young painter friend . . . Needless to say, I remain permanently in your debt. Yours very sincerely . . ." He looked up in some confusion. "The notepaper is unfamiliar to me, Mr. Holmes. Doubtless the Athenaeum is one of your clubs. But the signature is false."

"I had an idea you might determine that, sir," said Holmes, taking the paper from our guest. Far from being discommoded by the information, he seemed satisfied by it. I wondered how far back the roots of this crime were to be found. "Now, before I explain further, I feel a need to demonstrate something. I wonder if you would be good enough to write a note to Mrs. Gallibasta in Willesden. I would like you to tell her that you have changed your mind about returning to the United States and have decided to live in England for a time. Meanwhile, you intend to place the Fellini Silver in a bank vault until you go back to the United States, whereupon you are considering taking legal advice as to what to do with the statue."

"If I did that, Mr. Holmes, I would not be honouring my vow to my cousin. And I would be telling a lie to a lady."

"Believe me, Mr. Macklesworth, if I assure you, with all emphasis, that you will not be breaking a promise to your cousin and you will not be telling a lie to a lady. Indeed, you will be doing Sir Geoffrey Macklesworth and, I hope, both our great nations, an important service if you follow my instructions."

"Very well, Mr. Holmes," said Macklesworth, firming his jaw and adopting a serious expression, "if that's your word, I'm ready to go along with whatever you ask."

"Good man, Macklesworth!" Sherlock Holmes's lips were drawn back a little from his teeth, rather like a wolf which sees its prey finally become vulnerable. "By the by, have you ever heard in your country of a creature known as 'Little Peter' or sometimes 'French Pete'?"

"Certainly I have. He was a popular subject in the sensational press and remains so to this day. He operated out of New Orleans about a decade ago. Jean 'Petit Pierre' Fromental. An entertainer of some sort. He was part Arcadian and, some said, part Cree. A powerful, handsome man. He was famous for a series of particularly vicious murders of well-known dignitaries in the private rooms of those establishments for which Picayune is famous. A woman accomplice was also involved. She was said to have lured the men to their deaths. Fromental was captured eventually but the woman was never arrested. Some believe it was she who helped him escape when he did. As I remember, Mr. Holmes, Fromental was never caught. Was there not some evidence that he, in turn, had been murdered by a woman? Do you think Fromental and Sir Geoffrey were both victims of the same murderess?"

"In a sense, Mr. Macklesworth. As I said, I am reluctant to give you my whole theory until I have put some of it to the test. But none of this is the work of a woman, that I can assure you. Will you do as I say?"

"Count on me, Mr. Holmes. I will compose the telegram now."

When Mr. Macklesworth had left our rooms, I turned to Holmes, hoping for a little further illumination, but he was nursing his solution to him as if it were a favourite child. The expression on his face was extremely irritating to me. "Come, Holmes, this won't do! You say I helped solve the problem, yet you'll give me no hint as to the solution. Mrs. Gallibasta is not the murderess, yet you say a murder is most likely involved. My theory—that Sir Geoffrey had the Silver spirited away and then killed himself so

that he would not be committing a crime, as he would if he had been bankrupted—seems to confirm this. His handwriting has identified him as the author of letters claiming Mr. Macklesworth as a relative—Macklesworth had nothing to do with that—and then suddenly you speak of some Louisiana desperado known as 'Little Pierre,' who seems to be your main suspect until Mr. Macklesworth revealed that he was dead."

"I agree with you, Watson, that it seems very confusing. I hope for illumination tonight. Do you have your revolver with you, old friend?"

"I am not in the habit of carrying a gun about, Holmes."

At this, Sherlock Holmes crossed the room and produced a large shoe-box which he had also brought from 221B that afternoon. From it he produced two modern Webley revolvers and a box of ammunition. "We may need these to defend our lives, Watson. We are dealing with a master criminal intelligence. An intelligence both patient and calculating, who has planned this crime over many years and now believes there is some chance of being thwarted."

"You think Mrs. Gallibasta is in league with him and will warn him when the telegram arrives?"

"Let us just say, Watson, that we must expect a visitor tonight. That is why the Fellini Silver stands in our window, to be recognized by anyone who is familiar with it."

I told my friend that at my age and station I was losing patience for this kind of charade, but reluctantly I agreed to position myself where he instructed and, taking a firm grip on my revolver, settled down for the night.

The night was almost as sultry as the day and I was beginning to wish that I had availed myself of lighter clothing and a glass of water when I heard a strange, scraping noise from somewhere in the street and risked a glance down from where I stood behind the curtain. I was astonished to see a figure, careless of any observer, yet fully visible in the yellow light of the lamps, climbing rapidly up the wisteria vine!

Within seconds the man—for man it was, and a gigantic individual, at that—had slipped a knife from his belt and was opening the catch on the window in which the Fellini Silver still sat. It was all I could do to hold my position. I feared the fellow would grasp the statue and take it out with him. But then common sense told me that, unless he planned to lower it from the window, he must come in and attempt to leave by the stairs.

The audacious burglar remained careless of onlookers, as if his goal so filled his mind that he was oblivious to all other considerations. I caught a glimpse of his features in the lamplight. He had thick, wavy hair tied back in a bandanna, a couple of day's stubble on his chin and dark, almost negroid skin. I guessed at once that he was a relative of Mrs. Gallibasta.

Then he had snapped back the catch of the window and I heard his breath hissing from his lips as he raised the sash and slipped inside.

The next moment Holmes emerged from his hiding place and levelled the revolver at the man who turned with the blazing eyes of a trapped beast, knife in hand, seeking escape.

"There is a loaded revolver levelled at your head, man," said Holmes evenly, "and you would be wise to drop that knife and give yourself up!"

With a wordless snarl, the intruder flung himself towards the Silver, placing it between himself and our guns. "Shoot if you dare!" he cried. "You will be destroying more than my unworthy life! You will be destroying everything you have conspired to preserve! I underestimated you, Macklesworth. I thought you were an easy dupe—dazzled by the notion of being related to a knight of the realm, with whom you had an intimate correspondence! I worked for years to discover everything I could about you. You seemed perfect. You were willing to do anything, so long as it was described as a matter of family honour. Oh, how I planned! How I held myself in check! How patient I was. How noble in all my deeds! All that I would one day own

not merely that fool Geoffrey's money, but also his most prized treasure! I had his love—but I wanted everything else besides!"

It was then I realized suddenly what Holmes had been telling me. I almost gasped aloud as I understood the truth of the situation!

At that moment I saw a flash of silver and heard the sickening sound of steel entering flesh. Holmes fell back, his pistol dropping from his hand and with a cry of rage I discharged my own revolver, careless of Fellini or his art, in my belief that my friend was once again to be taken from me—this time before my eyes.

I saw Jean-Pierre Fromental, alias Linda Gallibasta, fall backwards, arms raised, and crash through the window by which he had entered. With a terrible cry he staggered, flailed at the air, then fell into an appalling silence.

At that moment, the door burst open and in came John Macklesworth, closely followed by our old friend Inspector Lestrade, Mrs. Beck, and one or two other tenants of 2 Dorset Street.

"It's all right, Watson," I heard Holmes say, a little faintly. "Only a flesh wound. It was foolish of me not to think he could throw a Bowie-knife! Get down there, Lestrade, and see what you can do. I'd hoped to take him alive. It could be the only way we'll be able to locate the money he has been stealing from his benefactor over all these years. Good night to you, Mr. Macklesworth. I had hoped to convince you of my solution, but I had not expected to suffer quite so much injury in the performance." His smile was faint and his eyes were flooded with pain.

Luckily, I was able to reach my friend before he collapsed upon my arm and allowed me to lead him to a chair, where I took a look at the wound. The knife had stuck in his shoulder and, as Holmes knew, had done no permanent damage, but I did not envy him the discomfort he was suffering.

Poor Macklesworth was completely stunned. His entire notion of things had been turned topsy-turvy and he was having difficulty taking everything in. After dressing Holmes's wound, I told Macklesworth to sit down while I fetched everyone a brandy. Both the American and myself were bursting to learn everything Holmes had deduced, but contained ourselves until my friend would be in better health. Now that the initial shock was over, however, he was in high spirits and greatly amused by our expressions.

"Your explanation was ingenious, Watson, and touched on the truth, but I fear it was not the answer. If you will kindly look in my inside jacket pocket, you will find two pieces of paper there. Would you be good enough to draw them out so that we might all see them?"

I did as my friend instructed. One piece contained the last letter Sir Geoffrey had written to John Macklesworth and, ostensibly, left with Mrs. Gallibasta. The other, far older, contained the letter John Macklesworth had read out earlier that day. Although there was a slight similarity to the handwriting, they were clearly by different authors.

"You said this was the forgery," said Holmes, holding up the letter in his left hand, "but unfortunately it was not. It is probably the only example of Sir Geoffrey's handwriting you have ever seen, Mr. Macklesworth."

"You mean he dictated everything to his—to that devil?"

"I doubt, Mr. Macklesworth, that your namesake had ever heard of your existence."

"He could not write to a man he had never heard of, Mr. Holmes!"

"Your correspondence, my dear sir, was not with Sir Geoffrey at all, but with the man who lies on the pavement down there. His name, as Doctor Watson has already deduced, is Jean-Pierre Fromental. No doubt he fled to England after the Picayune murders and got in with the Bohemian crowd surrounding Lord Alfred Douglas and others, eventually finding exactly the kind of dupe he was looking for. It is possible he kept his persona of Linda Gallibasta all along. Certainly that would explain why he became so terrified at the thought of being examined by a

doctor—you'll recall the postmistress's words. It is hard to know if he was permanently dressing as a woman—that, after all, is how he had lured his Louisiana victims to their deaths—and whether Sir Geoffrey knew much about him, but clearly he made himself invaluable to his employer and was able, bit by bit, to salt away the remains of the Macklesworth fortune. But what he really craved was the Fellini Silver, and that was when he determined the course of action which led to his calculating deception of you, Mr. Macklesworth. He needed a namesake living not far from New Orleans. As an added insurance he invented another cousin. By the simple device of writing to you on Sir Geoffrey's stationery he built up an entire series of lies, each of which had the appearance of verifying the other. Because, as Linda Gallibasta, he always collected the mail, Sir Geoffrey was never once aware of the deception."

It was John Macklesworth's turn to sit down suddenly as realization dawned. "Good heavens, Mr. Holmes. Now I understand!"

"Fromental wanted the Fellini Silver. He became obsessed with the notion of owning it. But he knew that if he stole it there was little chance of his ever getting it out of the country. He needed a dupe. That dupe was you, Mr. Macklesworth. I regret that you are probably not a cousin of the murdered man. Neither did Sir Geoffrey fear for his Silver. He appears quite reconciled to his poverty and had long since assured that the Fellini Silver would remain in trust for his family or the public forever. In respect of the Silver he was sheltered from all debt by a special covenant with Parliament. There was never a danger of the piece going to his creditors. There was, of course, no way, in those circumstances, that Fromental could get the Silver for himself. He had to engineer first a burglary—and then a murder, which looked like a consequence of that burglary. The suicide note was a forgery, but hard to decipher. His plan was to use your honesty and decency, Mr. Macklesworth, to carry the Silver through to America. Then he planned to obtain it from you by any means he found necessary."

Macklesworth shuddered. "I am very glad I found you, Mr. Holmes. If I had not, by coincidence, chosen rooms in Dorset Street, I would even now be conspiring to further that villain's ends!"

"As, it seems, did Sir Geoffrey. For years he trusted Fromental. He appears to have doted on him, indeed. He was blind to the fact that his estate was being stripped of its remaining assets. He put everything down to his own bad judgement and thanked Fromental for helping him! Fromental had no difficulty, of course, in murdering Sir Geoffrey when the time came. It must have been hideously simple. That suicide note was the only forgery, as such, in the case, gentlemen. Unless, of course, you count the murderer himself."

Once again, the world had been made a safer and saner place by the astonishing deductive powers of my friend Sherlock Holmes.

Postscript

And that was the end of the Dorset Street affair. The Fellini Silver was taken by the Victoria and Albert Museum who, for some years, kept it in the special "Macklesworth" Wing before it was transferred, by agreement, to the Sir John Soane Museum. There the Macklesworth name lives on. John Macklesworth returned to America a poorer and wiser man. Fromental died in hospital, without revealing the whereabouts of his stolen fortune, but happily a bank book was found at Willesden and the money was distributed amongst Sir Geoffrey's creditors, so that the house did not have to be sold. It is now in the possession of a genuine Macklesworth cousin. Life soon settled back to normal and it was with some regret that we eventually left Dorset Street to take up residence again at 221B. I have occasion, even today, to pass that pleasant house and recall with a certain nostalgia the few days when it had been the focus of an extraordinary adventure.

The Adventure of the Venomous Lizard

BILL CRIDER

BORN AND RAISED in Texas, Bill Crider (1941–) has been a highly prolific author of mystery novels (as well as numerous westerns, horror novels, and
books for young readers) for thirty years. Apart from *Blood Marks* (1991), a violent serial-killer book, his work tends to be traditional and soft-boiled.

The Sheriff Dan Rhodes series features the adventures of a sheriff in a small
Texas county where, as Crider has written, "there are no serial killers, where a
naked man hiding in a Dumpster is big news, and where the sheriff still has time
to investigate the theft of a set of false teeth." The first book in the series, *Too
Late to Die* (1986), won an Anthony Award.

Crider's past as an English professor may have served as background for his
series about Carl Burns, a teacher at a small denominational college who is a
reluctant amateur sleuth, as well as the books about Sally Good, the chair of the
English Department at a community college near the Texas Gulf Coast who is
also a reluctant amateur sleuth. The first Burns novel is *One Dead Dean* (1988);
the first Good book (so to speak) is *Murder Is an Art* (1999). Crider also writes a
series about a Galveston private detective, Truman Smith, whose first adventure
was *Dead on the Island* (1991), which was nominated for a Shamus Award by the
Private Eye Writers of America.

"The Adventure of the Venomous Lizard" was first published in *The New
Adventures of Sherlock Holmes*, edited by Martin H. Greenberg, Jon L. Lellenberg, and Carol-Lynn Rössel Waugh (New York, Carroll & Graf, 1999).

THE ADVENTURE OF THE VENOMOUS LIZARD

Bill Crider

I AM AN old man now, but on days like today, at the dank late end of spring, when the chill rain has been falling steadily for days, I can still feel the ache of the Jezail bullet that wounded me at the Battle of Maiwand, so long ago that I am no longer sure where I was struck. Sometimes the ache is in my leg, and at other times in my shoulder, so that more than once I have wondered whether I was actually shot at all or whether my memory of the event is nothing more than a dream.

But no, it was not a dream. I was there at Maiwand, and other places, too, places that I helped make known to those who were so kind as to read my tales about my great friend Sherlock Holmes. And so it is, on days like this, when going outside is a prospect with no appeal, yet staying inside has become increasingly hard to bear, that I find myself sitting quietly in a chair and going back over those recorded cases of Sherlock Holmes in which I myself played no small part. I do so both to assure myself that what I once did was indeed no dream, and in some minor way to relive those days and to experience again something of the thrill that I felt in times gone by.

And sometimes, as I go through those yellowing manuscripts, I recall other adventures, as yet unrecorded, and I find myself smoothing a sheet of paper and reaching for pen and ink to set down the facts before they flee my mind forever. How I wish, at those times, that I had in my possession Holmes's carefully indexed volume of cases, through which he would occasionally pore! Then I would have at my fingertips a veritable trove of information. But I find that I

do not need it. As I write, those days come back to me with the clarity of a vision, and give me, if not a chance to relive my life in actual fact, a chance at least to remember what it was, in the days that Holmes and I embarked on the singular adventure of the venomous lizard.

It was on a day very much like the present one. The winter seemed reluctant to release its hold on the land and hovered over the city for weeks past its allotted time filling the air with the chill of fog and rain. The Jezail bullet discomfited me. The cobbles were slick and glistened in the evening lamplight. Raindrops slid down the windows of 221B Baker Street as Sherlock Holmes stared gloomily out at them and smoked his pipe, the smoke curling up from the bowl and wreathing his head. There had been no one by our quarters, of late, who needed the services of the world's only consulting detective, and Holmes was growing restive. I knew the signs.

But he was momentarily startled out of his nonchalance. Pointing the stem of his pipe at the window, he said, "Come, Watson, and observe a desperate man."

I rose from the chair where I had been sitting and walked to the window. Outside in the thin rain, a man walked rapidly down the street in the direction of our dwelling.

"How do you know that he is desperate, Holmes?" I asked.

"Try your own powers, my dear Watson," he replied. "It is a simple matter of observation.

Note that I do not say *seeing*, for the difference between *seeing* and *observing* is as vast as the earth."

He had often harped on the same string, so I was prepared, though my feeble efforts at observation never came near to equaling his own.

"For one thing," said I, "he hunches forward and walks quickly. He is quite determined, and—look there!—he has slipped because of the careless placement of a foot. Clearly he is a man with something other than his own safety in mind."

"Very good, Watson," said Holmes. "Everything you say is true. But you have missed the most telling detail. Sometimes it is the most obvious things that elude us."

"And what might that be?"

"He has no umbrella," said Holmes. "Who would venture out in weather such as this with no umbrella, Watson? An Englishman without one on an evening like this is practically unimaginable, yet here he is. He is a man who left home in great haste, without thought for anything except whatever mission dominates his mind. I suspect that he will be knocking on our door at any moment now, for he is clearly a man in dire need of our services."

Soon enough, he was proven correct, as there was a tapping on the door and Mrs. Hudson announced herself outside our room. I opened the door to admit our landlady and the dripping visitor, one of a long line of unusual and sometimes disreputable personages who had sought out the aid of Sherlock Holmes.

"I most humbly apologise for any damages," the man said, as water from his outer garments bedewed our floor. "In my hurry, I may say, my desperation to reach you I seem to have neglected to pick up an umbrella. I hope that you will forgive me."

"Of course," said Holmes, only too happy to forgive what was really a very minor annoyance in the anticipation of the tale that our visitor would soon be telling, for it was clear that the young man, for such he was, was not merely desperate but distraught.

His eyes were wide and staring, and they failed to focus on any one person or object in the room, roving, as it were, from here to there, from our cluttered sideboard to the patriotic V. R. that Holmes had fashioned on our wall by firing bullets into it, from Holmes's face to mine, from the windows to the rug.

At last he drew a deep breath and said, "Which one of you is Sherlock Holmes?"

"I am," said Holmes. "Watson, fetch our visitor a blanket. Mrs. Hudson, a dry towel if you please."

In no time at all, that much-used woman had returned with a towel, which our visitor used to soak some of the water from both his clothing and the floor, after which she took the towel from him and let herself out. Our visitor wrapped himself in the blanket I had brought and was shivering on our sofa, where he began to tell us as strange a tale as it was ever my pleasure to hear inside that room on Baker Street.

"My name," said he, "is William Randolph, and I believe I have murdered my sister."

One may easily imagine the thrill of horror I felt to think that a confessed murderer was sitting on our sofa, wrapped in a blanket from my own room. But Holmes remained impassive. He had often told me that the capacity to retain one's objectivity was of the utmost importance in the reasoning process. He did not form his theories in advance. He listened instead, and approached each case with a mind that resembled as much as possible a tabula rasa.

"When did this happen?" Holmes asked.

"I have made the discovery only just now," the miserable young man said. "And I immediately came to you because you were nearby and because I have read of your accomplishments."

Holmes nodded at the implied compliment, though he sometimes complained that my modest attempts to convey his adventures to the public exaggerated in one way or the other. "You say that you 'made the discovery.' That does not seem to indicate any action on your part that could be construed as murder."

Randolph waved a hand. "I am afraid that my

mind is not working in an orderly manner. Let me gather my thoughts and begin again."

He sat quietly for a moment. Holmes smoked his pipe. I watched both of them in suspense and awe.

After several moments, Randolph began his tale again.

"Up until a year ago," said he, "I had been living in America, in California and in that part of the country inhabited by the Mormons."

Holmes gave me a significant look, as if to say that he knew full well what I was thinking of, a case of his that had the scarlet thread of murder running all through it.

"I was there for business reasons, not religion," Randolph continued, oblivious to what had passed between me and Holmes. "The business is not material, but while I was there, I was attracted to the peculiar fauna of the region to the south of where I was living, in particular a type of lizard known as the Gila."

"Ah," Holmes said. "The venomous lizard, *Heloderma suspectum*."

Randolph looked at Holmes in amazement. He was not so familiar as I with the breadth of Holmes's knowledge when it came to things relating to poison, or, for that matter, anything deadly or dangerous, about which Holmes knew as much, or more, than any man alive.

"You are correct," Randolph said. "So you know about the Gila."

Holmes gave the slightest of nods. "I know that it can grow quite large, that it is mostly black with irregular orange and pink areas on its body, and that it can store food in its body for long periods of time. I also know, among other things, that its bite is thought to be fatal. I have never seen such a lizard myself, however."

"I hope that you soon shall," Randolph said, though he did not explain himself at that time. "As for me, I saw several in a collection in the house of a man who befriended me, and I was quite fascinated. I even wrote to my sister and her husband of the unique creatures, which led to the horrible scene I discovered only a short while ago."

"You have not yet described that scene for us," said Holmes, "nor have you told us why you are here."

"I will come to that. I promise that I will. But first I must tell you what my fascination with the creatures led me to do: I brought one back as a gift for my sister and her husband."

"And that, I take it, led to the situation that brings you here," said Holmes.

"Indeed," Randolph replied, and he put his head in his hands.

Holmes smoked and waited, as I continued to await the revelation that was coming.

At last Randolph looked up. "Earlier this evening," he said, "only moments before coming to your door, I went to visit my sister at her home. It was there that I found her lying dead, poisoned by the very lizard that I had given her."

"Good Lord," said I. "Does this mean that even now she lies dead upon the floor of her house?"

"Indeed," Randolph said. "And I have come to Sherlock Holmes to find the thing that killed her, for I cannot."

"It is loose in the house?" I asked, my blood freezing at the thought.

"So it must be, for the glass cage where it lived is broken, and it was not in the room where she lay."

As he said those words, all the colour that had remained in his face drained away, and his shoulders shook with his silent sobs.

Holmes's face was impassive. "Watson," said he, "I believe that you should fetch your revolver—and your medical bag. It is possible that we shall find ourselves in need of them. There are dark doings here, Watson."

The rain had resolved itself into a heavy mist that put a frosty halo around the lamps by the time we left our apartments, and an umbrella was no longer necessary. We eagerly followed Randolph to his sister's home, a Georgian structure that was located on Blandford Street, not far from our own lodgings.

We entered through an unlocked door, and went down a hallway in which there was an elephant-foot umbrella stand. Holmes paused momentarily as we passed the stand and looked at the umbrellas there. One of them, I noticed, was still wet. Then we walked through a dark parlor in which the embers of a fire smouldered dimly on the grate and thence into a sort of solarium, with one wall being taken up mostly by windows, though all light was now provided by two flickering lamps. There were potted green plants of several kinds, but I paid them no attention, for my eyes were arrested by what lay on the floor.

It was the body of a young woman, her resemblance to her brother plain to see even in the dim light of the room. Her dark hair was spread upon the floor, and her skin appeared to have a slight bluish tinge, obviously caused by the venom of the Gila, aptly referred to in this instance as a monster.

I immediately went to kneel beside the body to see if there was any possibility that the young woman was merely unconscious, perhaps paralyzed by the Gila's poison. Setting my medical bag beside me, I felt for any trace of a pulse, but it was far too late for such false hopes. She was quite dead.

Holmes knelt beside me to examine the skin of the young woman's arm, which was deeply punctured in several places where the lizard had bitten her.

As for the Gila, it was gone. There was a large glass case, its bottom lined with sand, that was lighted and warmed by one of the lamps. However, one side of the case was shattered, as if it had been broken in a struggle of some kind. Sand was scattered on the floor.

Holmes and I stood up. Randolph remained where he had stopped at the threshold of the room, as if unable to will himself to enter. His face was a study in sorrowful apprehension.

"Where could the thing be?" he asked. "To think that I brought it into this house, that I am the cause of her death! Murderer! Murderer!"

"An accident is not murder," said Holmes. "Have you any idea whether your sister frequently handled the Gila?"

"Her name was Sofia," said Randolph dolefully. "Sofia Randolph Bingham. I would have to say that she seldom, if ever, touched the thing. It did not require frequent feeding, and it was certainly not of an affectionate nature. You must find it!"

Holmes nodded grimly. "I do not believe that will prove difficult. I am surprised that you did not find it yourself."

Randolph hung his head. "I confess that I was frightened of the creature. And I hardly knew where to begin."

"It would seek warmth," said Holmes. "An English home in winter is hardly the kind of place that the Gila would find an agreeable dwelling place. I am surprised that it has survived for this long."

"I brought it only a month ago," Randolph said. "However, the journey here was a long one."

"The Gila can survive for quite a long time without food," said Holmes, "but it needs water occasionally and warmth rather more often."

"My room aboard ship was quite warm," Randolph said. "Do you suppose that the lack of a temperate environment could have caused the thing to kill my sister?"

"That seems doubtful," said Holmes. "Tell me, what of your sister's husband?"

"He is the one who encouraged me to bring the Gila to them," Randolph said. "He seemed as interested in the beast as I. But as soon as he saw it, he was repelled by its appearance. My sister, being of a gentler nature, pitied it, and so it remained here."

Holmes looked around the room where we stood. "Your brother-in-law must be a man of substance to own a home such as this," said he.

Randolph smiled feebly. "He is a physician, like your friend, Dr. Watson. While he does much good for others, I fear that he does not do well for himself."

"The house, then, is your sister's."

"Yes. Our family was quite successful in the business I mentioned earlier."

"I do not believe you mentioned what that business was," said I.

"It is one that was begun by my father, who

was something of an adventurer. It involves the mining of borax, and I was sent to America after his death to learn how to conduct the business." His eyes turned to the body on the floor. "Now, as a result of that, Sofia is gone like my father, and the fault lies with me."

"Perhaps not," said Holmes.

"Of course not," I added. "You cannot blame yourself for the actions of an animal that you believe to be quite harmless."

"Oh, I knew of its venom," Randolph protested. "While I was in the American West, I heard several tales of its potent bite. They formed a part of my fascination with the lizard, and I even related several of them in letters to my sister. They were often quite vivid, and one claimed that when the Gila attached itself to a victim, it refused to let go and had to be cut away." He shuddered. "At least my sister was spared that horror."

"Yes," said Holmes, "but not others."

Randolph straightened his shoulders. "No," he said. "But we must not allow it to happen to anyone else. Can you help me find the Gila?"

Holmes nodded. "As I said, it should not be difficult to locate him. Come."

"Wait, Holmes," said I. "Should we not do something with the . . . with Miss Sofia?"

"It is unfortunate," he said, "but I think it would be best to leave her for now. You may cover her face, if you wish."

I did as he suggested, using my clean linen handkerchief to conceal the sad dead face from the eyes of the world.

Holmes then led us to the shadowy parlour and said, "Is there a lamp?"

"Of course," said Randolph, and just as the light reddened his face, there was the sound of the door opening and of someone coming into the hallway.

"Sofia?" someone called. "Is that you in the parlour?"

"God help me," Randolph said. "It is Bertie, Dr. Bingham, I mean. Sofia's husband. What shall I say?"

"Say that we are here, in the parlour," Holmes suggested.

Randolph did as he was bid, and Dr. Bingham bustled in after doffing his coat and settling his bag in the hallway. He was a youngish man, not much older than Randolph himself, and he had a round, smiling visage that must have offered a great deal of comfort to those who needed his aid.

"Ah, William," said the doctor. "So good to see you. And who are these gentlemen you have with you?"

Randolph indicated me with a turn of his hand. "This is Dr. John Watson. And this," he turned to Holmes, "is Mr. Sherlock Holmes."

Bingham's pleasant face brightened at the mention of our names. "I have heard of both of you," he said. "Living so near, I had hoped that I would one day have the pleasure of meeting you, and now that day has arrived. Where is Sofia? Has she offered you sherry?"

Randolph seemed to have no idea how to answer the query, and he turned helplessly to Holmes.

"I'm sorry to tell you," said Holmes, "that your wife is dead."

I thought it a rather harsh way to broach the information, but I suppose that there was really no other way. Bingham's smile faltered.

"Surely you must be making some sort of joke," he said. "You cannot mean—"

Holmes's face was grim. "I am sorry to say that I do mean exactly what you have heard. Your wife lies dead in the other room."

With a strangled cry, Bingham broke away from us and ran into the solarium. Randolph, after a glance in our direction, followed him.

"What now, Holmes?" I asked, completely at a loss.

"Now let us find the Gila monster," said Holmes. "I think it must be nearby."

He picked up the lamp that Randolph had lighted, and walked in the direction of the fireplace. The embers that had earlier blushed on the grate had now turned nearly to ash. Holmes raised the lamp in his left hand.

"There," he said, pointing with his right forefinger to a spot on the low hearth.

And there, indeed, it was.

It looked almost like a creature from another time, thick, torpid, and black with splotches of color that showed but dimly in the lamplight. Its clawed feet clutched at the bricks of the hearth where it had come, drawn, no doubt, by the warmth of the dying fire. Its hooded eyes stared blankly.

"It does not appear to be quite as aggressive as I had thought," said I, clutching the handle of my revolver in the event that the creature should attempt to spring upon us. I slowly drew my revolver from my coat. "Shall I kill it?" I asked.

Holmes, ever observant, smiled at my nervousness. "I do not believe we have anything to fear from the Gila. It appears hardly to notice our existence."

And indeed it did not. It was as motionless as the graven image of some pagan god. It hardly seemed even to breathe.

"But how can we return it to its cage? The glass is broken."

"We shall see," said Holmes. "For now, let us join Dr. Bingham and attempt to alleviate his grief."

I did not think that would be possible. To have lost a beautiful young wife in the prime of her existence—it was a marrow-deep melancholy that I knew all too well. But I put away my revolver and followed Holmes into the solarium, where Bingham sat on a wicker couch, sobbing into his hands as Randolph stood impotently by.

Bingham looked up at our entrance, his eyes red and hollow. "I do not blame my brother-in-law for this," he said. "Although he has tried to take the fault upon himself, it is mine alone, for I am the one who allowed my wife to keep such a monster in our home."

"I believe that you are correct," said Holmes. "The fault is indeed yours alone, for you are the one who killed your wife."

Randolph's face mirrored the astonishment on mine, though neither of us appeared quite as surprised as Bingham.

"What are you saying?" he asked. "Could you possibly accuse me of murder in such circumstances?"

His pain seemed so genuine that I was moved to speak in his defense. "I say, Holmes, it hardly seems right to intrude on a man's grief with such an accusation."

"It is more than an accusation, my dear Watson," said Holmes. "It is an incontrovertible fact."

Bingham came to his feet. "I have heard that you seldom err, Mr. Holmes, but this is one time that you have made a grave mistake."

"No," said Holmes, "I have not. The mistakes, and there were many, were all yours. I think it would be best if you went for the police now, Mr. Randolph. We will want them here when I confirm all that I have said."

Randolph turned with a wordless appeal to Bingham, who snarled, shoved him aside, and ran past us toward the parlour.

"Stop!" I shouted, removing my revolver from my coat and firing a shot into the lintel beam.

The sound of the shot echoed around the room, and Bingham froze in mid-step.

Holmes smiled grimly. "That was quick action, Watson. I am glad that you were ready."

"I have known you longer than Dr. Bingham," said I. "And I have not known you to err."

"And yet you doubted for a moment."

"A moment," I admitted, keeping a close watch on Bingham, who, however, seemed to have lost his desire to flee. "But for a moment only."

"It is just as well," said Holmes.

Randolph's eyes went from one of us to the other, and then to Bingham, who was standing listlessly, his hands at his side.

"I do not understand," said Randolph. "If the venomous lizard killed my sister, how could her husband be to blame? It seems impossible that you could know."

"I knew while we were still at Baker Street that something was very wrong with your story," said Holmes. "We had only to arrive here to confirm my suspicions."

His remarks puzzled me. "But I thought you did not theorize until you had the facts."

"I had the facts, and they pointed to the

crime of murder," said Holmes. "For one thing, the Gila has never been known to attack a human being except in cases of extreme provocation. It did not seem likely to me that a woman at home alone would be so obtuse as to provoke the creature into attacking her. In addition, although the bite of the Gila is indeed poisonous, there has been, as far as I know, not a single recorded instance of its bite having killed anyone."

"But the stories I heard!" Randolph protested.

"Are merely that—stories. Miners are prone to exaggerate, though it may well be true that one of them might have provoked a Gila to bite him. And it may even be true that the creature's bite was so tenacious that it would have to be cut away from its victim. But it does not kill."

"But what of the bite on my sister?"

"That is one reason we could not afford to kill the monster and risk the destruction of its unique dental structure. There was some attempt to make the marks on your sister's arm look like the bite of some reptile, a snake perhaps, but the Gila's teeth are not like fangs at all, as a simple examination will show. It chews on the victim's skin and mangles it to introduce the poison rather than injecting it."

Randolph's puzzlement had not ended. "But Sofia is dead, and apparently of poison."

"Yes, but the color of her skin would indicate that the poison is more likely curare than that of the Gila. And curare is a poison that a physician can obtain with ease. I observed a spot on your sister's arm that was undoubtedly caused by an injection, an injection that Dr. Bingham gave

to her after rendering her unconscious by other means. He then broke the cage and freed the monster to make it appear that his wife's death was an accident."

Randolph, now almost convinced, stared at Bingham. "But why?" he asked.

"Money," said Holmes, "is almost always the answer. Your sister had the fortune, not he. Perhaps he was going to leave her for another but could not do it without her money. Or perhaps it was merely that he was tired of her. He can tell us that."

Bingham stood silently.

"If the police examine your bag and find curare in it, will you be able to show that you are currently using it in some medical case?" asked Holmes.

Once again, Bingham ran for the other room. But I had worked my way closer to him, and I was able to grasp his arm firmly in one hand and show him the revolver. That was quite enough to stop him. At another word from Holmes, Randolph went to fetch the police and bring an end to our adventure.

And yet such adventures never really end. As I sit here and write about the events of that day so long ago, and the streetlights outside my window flicker to life in the rain, I can see the Gila monster crouching on the warm hearth almost as clearly as if it were in the room where I now sit. The dull ache of the Jezail bullet fades. And I feel alive and young again, in a way that I have not since last I saw the face of Sherlock Holmes.

The Case of the Friesland Outrage

JUNE THOMSON

ALTHOUGH THE MAJORITY of the novels by June Valerie Thomson (1930–) feature Inspector Jack Finch (named Inspector Rudd in American editions after the first book in order to avoid confusion with the Septimus Finch series written by Margaret Erskine) and Sergeant Tom Boyce, she has become a staple in the world of Sherlock Holmes, having written seven books about Dr. Watson and the great detective. In addition to *Holmes and Watson: A Study in Friendship* (1995), an examination of numerous elements of the canon, including the reasons for the close relationship between the two roommates, Thomson has written six collections of pastiches of nearly uniformly high quality, noted both for their original plotting and the adherence to the background, tone, and atmosphere of the originals.

The Rudd/Finch series of twenty novels about the wily policeman in the quiet Essex village of Abbots Stacey began with *Not One of Us* in 1971 and appears to have ended with *Going Home*, as there have been no new books since 2006.

Thomson's Holmes story collections began with *The Secret Files of Sherlock Holmes* (1990), followed by *The Secret Chronicles of Sherlock Holmes* (1992), *The Secret Journals of Sherlock Holmes* (1993), *The Secret Documents of Sherlock Holmes* (1999), *The Secret Notebooks of Sherlock Holmes* (2004), and *The Secret Archives of Sherlock Holmes* (2012).

"The Case of the *Friesland* Outrage" was originally published in *The Secret Journals of Sherlock Holmes* (London, Constable, 1993).

THE CASE OF THE *FRIESLAND* OUTRAGE

June Thomson

I

IT WAS, I recall, late one stormy evening in November 1894, some months after Sherlock Holmes's miraculous return from death at the hands of his arch-enemy, Professor Moriarty, at the Reichenbach Falls,* that the following remarkable events occurred which were so nearly to cost us both our lives.

Having dined, we had retired to our armchairs on either side of the blazing fire, Holmes deep in a volume on Early Elizabethan ciphers, I absorbed in nothing more abstruse than the *Evening Standard*, content that my old friend had no case on hand to force us out of doors in such tempestuous weather.

Hardly had the thought crossed my mind than Holmes lifted his head and, laying aside his book, remarked, "A cab has just drawn up outside, Watson. I believe we have a visitor. Rather than allow the maid to be disturbed at such an hour, I shall let him in myself."

"Him?" I inquired.

---

* The fateful encounter between Mr. Sherlock Holmes and Professor Moriarty took place on 4 May 1891 on a ledge overlooking the Reichenbach Falls, near the village of Meiringen in Switzerland, after Dr. John H. Watson had been lured away by a false message. On his return, he found Mr. Sherlock Holmes had disappeared, leaving a farewell message. Assuming both men had plunged to their death, Dr. Watson, much saddened, returned to London. However, Mr. Sherlock Holmes had survived and three years later, in the spring of 1894, reappeared in London to Dr. Watson's great joy and relief. *Vide* "The Adventure of the Final Problem" and "The Adventure of the Empty House." Dr. John F. Watson.

"Oh, it is undoubtedly a man. Did you not hear the slam of the cab door? No woman would act in quite so positive a manner."

I had heard nothing above the sound of the wind roaring in the chimney and rattling the windows in their frames although I was not surprised that Holmes had discerned these distant noises. His hearing is keener than that of any other man I know.

He left the room, returning soon afterwards with a short, powerfully built, bearded man, so broad across the shoulders and so stocky of frame that he appeared quite square in shape. From his pea jacket and peaked cap, I took him to be a seafarer, a supposition which proved correct when Holmes introduced him.

"This is Captain Hans Van Wyk, Watson." Turning to our visitor, he continued, "Pray be seated, sir."

Van Wyk removed his cap, revealing a head of grey hair, as thick and as grizzled as his beard. His weather-beaten face was deeply creased about the eyes with humorous lines, suggesting a jovial nature, although the gravity of his general demeanour revealed that whatever business had brought him to consult Holmes was of a serious nature.

"Master of the Dutch vessel, the SS *Friesland*," said he, sinking down into the chair which Holmes had indicated. Although his English was on the whole excellent, he spoke with a guttural accent. "I apologize for intruding on you so late in the evening, gentlemen. But the lady insisted I come to you, not the official police."

"I think," said Holmes, resuming his own seat, "that you had better begin by telling us who the lady is and why she is in such urgent need of my help."

"Of course, Mr. Holmes. However, I ought first to explain a little of the background to the affair. The SS *Friesland* is a small cargo vessel, plying between the coasts of Germany and Holland and the south-east of England. We also carry passengers; not many as there is cabin accommodation for only a dozen. Yesterday, we docked at the Free Trade Wharf* in the Port of London where we unloaded and took on a fresh cargo, ready for the return voyage to Rotterdam. We are due to sail at half-past one tomorrow morning on the high tide.

"A few passengers embarked earlier this evening, among them an elderly gentleman, a Mr. Barnaby Pennington, and his daughter. I did not see them come on board although I understand from the steward that they went straight to their cabins.

"Some time later, Miss Pennington went on deck and approached the mate in some distress. It seems that, after she had settled herself into her own cabin, she went to her father's which was opposite hers to make sure that he, too, was comfortable for the night. Having knocked and received no reply, she let herself in, only to find the cabin empty and signs that a struggle had taken place. Her father's luggage had been rifled and a large sum of money, together with some important documents, was missing.

"The mate alerted me and I ordered an immediate search of the whole ship but no trace of Mr. Pennington was found. I also questioned the crew. But no one had noticed anything suspicious although that is understandable. It is a dark, wet night and the men were busy about their own tasks."

"Miss Pennington had heard nothing?"

---

* The Free Trade Wharf is situated on the north bank of the Thames, a mile and a half downstream from the Tower of London. Known originally as the East India Wharf, it was renamed the Free Trade Wharf in 1858 after tariff reform had lifted former trading restrictions. Dr. John F. Watson.

"Evidently not, Mr. Holmes, apart from some muffled thuds which she took to be coming from the deck. The storm was then at its height."

"And what of the other passengers. Have you spoken to them?"

"Not personally. I was too occupied with supervising the search and examining the crew. However, the steward questioned them on my instructions. He reported that none of them had heard or seen anything out of the ordinary. There are only four of them on this voyage and the cabins between theirs and Mr. Pennington's are unoccupied. I have since taken the precaution of posting a man at the head of the gangplank in case anyone should try to take Mr. Pennington ashore. Of course, it may be a case, as you English say, of bolting the door after the horse has vanished."

"You mean that someone could have come on board and abducted Mr. Pennington without your knowledge?"

Captain Van Wyk spread out his large, gnarled hands.

"On such a night, anything is possible," he replied.

"You said you spoke to Miss Pennington," Holmes continued. "Had she any idea who might be responsible for her father's disappearance?"

"No, none at all, sir; except she seemed to think robbery might be a motive."

There was a hesitation in the captain's voice which Holmes was quick to perceive.

"You yourself do not believe it?"

"I think there may be more to the case than simple theft, Mr. Holmes. When I spoke to the lady, she was strangely reluctant to discuss her father's business affairs. She was also most insistent that I was to come directly to you and no one else. She has written a letter which she asked me to deliver to you personally."

Feeling in his jacket pocket, Captain Van Wyk produced an envelope which he handed to Holmes who, having opened it and glanced quickly over the sheet of paper it contained, read the message aloud for our visitor's benefit as well as my own.

"'Dear Mr. Holmes, Captain Van Wyk will

have explained to you the circumstances surrounding my father's disappearance. As I have great fear for his safety, I beg you to make inquiries on my behalf. My father has often spoken of your detective skills in relation to one specific investigation.'"

At this point, Holmes broke off to ask Captain Van Wyk, "Did Miss Pennington happen to mention any particulars of this inquiry?"

"Yes, she did, Mr. Holmes!" the captain replied eagerly. "It was the Blackmore case."

"Indeed!" my old friend murmured. "As I remember, it was a most delicate business." Seeing my look of inquiry, he explained, "It was an investigation I carried out in '89 when you were in practice in Paddington. I did not call on your services, Watson, as you were laid up at the time with an attack of bronchitis. To continue with the letter. Miss Pennington goes on to add, and the sentence is underlined twice, 'On no account must Scotland Yard be informed of this affair.' The letter is signed Maud Pennington. Well, Captain Van Wyk," Holmes concluded, folding up the sheet of paper and placing it in his pocket, "I shall certainly accept the young lady's request. The case presents some unusual features. You came in a four-wheeler, I believe, which you have retained?"

"It is outside, Mr. Holmes," the captain replied, looking surprised. "But how did you know I had asked the driver to wait?"

"It is quite simple. I have not heard the cab drive away," Holmes said nonchalantly. "Watson, if you care to accompany Captain Van Wyk downstairs, I shall follow you shortly. I must leave a note for Mrs. Hudson in case we are delayed by our inquiries. I should not wish to cause our inestimable landlady any undue concern. You go ahead, my dear fellow, and make sure you wear something suitable against this appalling weather."

Taking my old friend's advice, I put on a long waterproof and, followed by Captain Van Wyk, led the way out into the street where a four-wheeler was drawn up beside the kerb. While we waited for Holmes, we took shelter inside it from the driving rain.

He joined us several minutes later, limping so heavily that it was with some difficulty he climbed into the cab.

On my inquiring what had happened, he said impatiently, "In my haste, I sprained my ankle coming down the stairs and had to return in order to strap it up. But it is a mere trifle. Shall we proceed? We have already wasted valuable time through my carelessness."

Captain Van Wyk gave instructions to the driver and we set off for the docks along deserted streets running with water like so many minor tributaries of the Thames itself, as if that great river had burst its banks and inundated the entire city.

Holmes said nothing during the journey. He sat huddled in his ulster, the flaps of his travelling cap pulled well down about his ears, staring out through the rain-drenched window at the passing scene. From time to time in the light of the street lamps, I caught a glimpse of his profile, looking very austere, his lips compressed and his brows heavily contracted.

I put his silence down to the pain of his ankle but said nothing, not wishing to exasperate him further by referring to his mishap.

Captain Van Wyk and I exchanged a few desultory remarks but we, too, soon fell silent, oppressed by Holmes's taciturn mood and the melancholy drumming of the rain on the roof of the cab.

Eventually, it drew up at the end of a narrow, ill-lit street where we alighted and followed Captain Van Wyk as he led the way on to the Free Trade Wharf.

Here, the full strength of the gale, blowing straight off the river, caught us in its blast. Heads bowed against its onslaught, we struggled forward in the darkness, the captain striding ahead of us, quite at home, it seemed, in this elemental world of wind and water.

I had nothing more than a fleeting impression of my surroundings. Battered by the storm and half blinded by the rain, I was aware only of the tall edifices of warehouses, like the sides of a grimy brick canyon, towering above us on our left and, to the right, the huge hulks of ships at anchor, their masts and rigging pitching to and fro against the night sky and groaning audibly with every squall.

There were no moon or stars to illuminate the scene, only the fitful light of a few lamps, guttering in the wind and casting a tremulous yellow glow over those looming hulks and the river which ran between them as black as oil.

We arrived eventually at the foot of a gang-plank which Captain Van Wyk nimbly mounted, while we followed more slowly behind him, gripping fast to the rail, especially Holmes who had to haul himself up the steep incline.

At the top, a member of the crew in oilskins was standing guard, lantern in hand. Captain Van Wyk conferred with him briefly before, turning to us, he roared out above the storm, "He says no one has left the ship in my absence, gentlemen! Follow me! I will show you Mr. Pennington's cabin."

Taking the lantern from the man, Van Wyk set off at a brisk pace towards the stern of the vessel, Holmes and I groping our way as best we could after that bobbing light over the deck which shifted uneasily under our feet on the swelling tide.

At last we saw glimmering out of the darkness aft of the wheel-house a white-painted, flat-roofed structure housing the passengers' accommodation, with a row of port-holes along its side and lifeboats slung above it on davits. Ducking through a low doorway, we found ourselves in a small vestibule which gave access to a passage, lit by hanging lamps, with several doors leading off it on either side.

Captain Van Wyk threw one of these open.

"Mr. Pennington's cabin," he announced.

The interior was small, most of it taken up by a pair of bunks, one of which was strewn with articles of clothing, carelessly flung about. A leather valise, emptied of its contents, lay on its side on the floor.

There were signs, too, that a struggle had taken place inside that confined space. One of the curtains at the port-hole was wrenched from its rings while the basin, which was set below it in a locker, was heavily blood-stained.

Holmes stood just inside the doorway, looking about him, his head lifted like a gun dog scenting game. Then, limping forward, he examined first the basin and the valise, before turning his attention to the port-hole, lifting aside the torn curtain to examine the large brass screw which secured it. But it was tightly fastened down and showed no signs of having been loosened. Even if it had been, the opening was too small to admit even a child, let alone a grown man.

Meanwhile Van Wyk watched these activities with the keenest interest, murmuring to me in an aside, "It warms up the cockle of my heart to see such an expert at work!" Then, raising his voice, he continued, "If you have seen enough, Mr. Holmes, I suggest we speak to Miss Pennington. I know she is most anxious to meet you."

Holmes agreed and we followed the captain across the passage to a door opposite on which Van Wyk tapped several times. Receiving no answer, he finally turned the handle and, opening the door, thrust his head inside.

In the light of the lamp, we saw at once that the cabin was empty although there were indications that it had recently been occupied. A lady's mantle hung behind the door and a nightgown, neatly folded, lay upon the pillow.

There were no signs, however, of a violent physical struggle, such as we had seen in the other cabin, and yet there was clear evidence that Miss Pennington had not left of her own volition. Hanging in the air was the unmistakable sweet, sickly reek of chloroform.

It was apparent that the odour was familiar also to the captain for no sooner had he smelt it than he turned and made for the deck, shouting to us to follow him.

By the time we had joined him, he was already deep in animated conversation in a foreign language which I took to be Dutch with a broad, heavily bearded man who, as I was later to learn, was the mate, Bakker.

From the latter's expression and gestures, I deduced that he was as bewildered as we were by the disappearance of Miss Pennington, following so closely upon her father's.

Captain Van Wyk flung out an arm in an

abrupt movement of command and barked out an order to the mate. Then, motioning with his head to us, he led the way up an open companion-way, its iron treads made treacherous by the rain, to his own quarters which were situated below the bridge.

His cabin was more spacious than the passengers' accommodation although it was similarly equipped with a bunk and a range of lockers including, in this instance, a shelf for logs and a broad table to serve as a desk. Charts were pinned upon the walls and a brass spittoon was screwed to the floor beside the table.

"Well, gentlemen, this is indeed a strange business," Van Wyk said, when we had divested ourselves of our wet outer garments. "Two passengers disappeared! Such a thing has never happened before in all the years I have been at sea! I have ordered the mate to make another search of the vessel. He will report to me as soon as it is completed."

"And if Miss Pennington is not found?" Holmes inquired.

"Then I shall be forced to send for the official police, despite her instructions to the contrary. I cannot see that I have any other choice. The young lady's disappearance has indeed put the cat among the birds. She has not been taken ashore. The man posted at the head of the gang-plank was quite sure no one has left the ship. Have you any explanation to offer for this mysterious affair, Mr. Holmes?"

"I confess I am utterly at a loss," my old friend admitted with a rueful expression. "Mr. Pennington's disappearance might be accounted for. He could have been abducted. But his daughter's! That is a different matter altogether. The only logical conclusion is that she must still be on board."

"That is my thought exactly. But the search will take at least two hours. There are many places on a vessel where someone could be hidden. If I have to delay the ship's departure, then so be it!" Van Wyk said, shrugging his broad shoulders philosophically. "In the meantime, you will take a glass of schnapps with me? It will help to keep out the cold."

I was about to refuse, not having much taste for strong liquor and preferring to keep a clear head for whatever inquiries still lay ahead of us. But when Holmes agreed, I felt it might appear churlish if I declined, so I, too, accepted.

"Then we shall drink to the successful outcome of the case!" our host exclaimed.

Turning away, he opened a locker and took out a squat bottle and three glasses which he filled in turn, handing one each to Holmes and myself and raising his own in salutation.

"Down the hatchway!" cried he, his blue eyes sparkling as, throwing back his head, he swallowed down the brandy in one single draught.

I followed his example, feeling the schnapps burn its way down my throat like liquid fire. As a protection against the cold of that stormy night it was indeed effective. Within seconds, its warmth had begun to circulate through my blood, spreading out to tingle down to the very fingertips.

Meanwhile, Holmes, glass in hand, had wandered across the cabin to examine one of the charts pinned up on the wall above the desk. He seemed abstracted, his mind no doubt still on the mysterious disappearance of Mr. Pennington and his daughter. I had seen him in this mood many times before when the problems presented by a case so occupied his mind that he was oblivious of everything else about him.

"You have not yet drunk our toast, Mr. Holmes," Captain Van Wyk reminded him.

"I beg your pardon," Holmes replied. "My thoughts were elsewhere. To our success, Captain!"

He was about to raise his glass when he gave a sudden lurch sideways, only saving himself from falling by clutching at the table with his free hand. However, he quickly recovered and, standing upright once more, he threw back his head and swallowed the brandy.

Whether the ship had been struck by a particularly heavy swell or his sprained ankle had caused Holmes that momentary loss of balance, I could not tell for at that moment I myself was overcome by a violent bout of dizziness. The cabin seemed to be rising and falling in a most extraordinary manner, as if the *Friesland* had already set sail and was tossing about on the high seas.

My last recollection was of Holmes, setting down his empty glass and saying, with a smile of apology, "I am afraid I am a poor sailor, Captain Van Wyk. I appear not yet to have acquired my sea-legs. But your excellent brandy should soon set that to rights."

The next instant, the cabin spun about me and I felt myself pitching forward into a black abyss of oblivion.

II

I do not know how long I remained unconscious but, some time later, I was aware of Holmes shaking me urgently by the shoulder. For a moment, I fancied I was in my own bed in our lodgings in Baker Street and that some crisis had occurred for which Holmes required my immediate presence.

However, as I struggled to sit up, I found that I could not move. It was only then I realized that I was lying, facing the wall, on the bunk in Captain Van Wyk's cabin, my hands secured behind my back by a rope which was drawn tightly across my chest, my legs and feet similarly bound. A pad of cotton wadding, placed across my mouth and held in position by a strip of cloth, made breathing difficult and I felt half suffocated for lack of air.

"Lie still and do not make a sound," Holmes whispered close to my ear as he removed the gag.

I next heard the rasp of something metal cutting into the cords and, as my bonds fell away, I was able to sit upright at last to see Holmes standing beside me, one finger against his lips, his deep-set eyes glittering in the lamp-light.

Leaving me seated on the bunk to recover my full senses, he moved with a cat-like speed and silence across the cabin, showing no sign of the limp which had earlier impeded his movements. Kneeling down in front of the door, he inserted into the keyhole a thin metal rod which he began to manipulate to and fro with great care, his head pressed against the panel as he listened for the wards to yield.

While he was thus engaged, I looked about me, still dazed, trying to piece together what had happened in the time I had been unconscious.

From the lengths of rope lying on the far side of the cabin, together with a pad and piece of cloth, I deduced that Holmes, like me, had been trussed up and gagged although I had no idea how he had managed to release himself.

Nor could I see why Captain Van Wyk had wished to lure us aboard the *Friesland* and to offer us schnapps laced with some strong narcotic drug, for that was what must have happened. There was no other explanation for my sudden loss of consciousness.

I assumed that Holmes, too, had been drugged although looking at him as he knelt by the door, every sense alert, his fingers probing delicately at the keyhole, it was difficult to imagine. He appeared to have suffered no ill effects, a recovery I put down to his iron constitution and that seemingly bottomless well of nervous energy on which he was able to draw in times of crisis.

At last, there came a faint click as the lock gave way but instead of opening the door and beckoning to me to follow him on deck as I had expected, he secured the top and bottom bolts before crossing silently back to the bunk on which I was sitting, his finger again pressed to his lips. Seeing my look of interrogation, he mouthed the word, "Wait."

But for what? I wondered. For Van Wyk to return and break down the door when he discovered it barred against him? Although the bolts were strong, it would take no more than two men to burst them open.

And then what would happen to us?

I was under no illusions that we were not in mortal danger. The captain had not made us his prisoners only to let us walk free. Indeed, I was surprised that he had not dispatched us when he had us drugged and at his mercy.

Such thoughts clamoured in my mind and yet I dared not voice them out loud to Holmes. He had taken the captain's chair at the desk and was leaning back, his eyes closed, as he strained to pick up the faintest sounds beyond the four walls of the cabin.

The storm had abated a little and it was possible to distinguish other noises aboard the *Friesland* besides the relentless roar of the wind and the beating of the rain. I heard footsteps occasionally passing below on deck and the sound of distant voices. Once there came a faint metallic crash, as if a heavy iron door had been slammed shut. As a background to these signs of human activity, there was the constant creak and groan of the vessel itself as it swung restlessly at its moorings.

My tension was exacerbated by Holmes's inactivity. Although we were unarmed, all my instincts told me it would be better to make a dash for it on to the deck where, in the darkness and ensuing confusion, we might have a chance of escape. And even if we failed in our attempt, we would have the satisfaction of going down fighting like men which was infinitely preferable to sitting there, like trapped animals, tamely awaiting our fate.

For the first time in my long association with Sherlock Holmes, I felt that he had failed me and I was bitterly disappointed. I could not believe that this was the same man who had met his arch-enemy, Moriarty, face to face without flinching and, by grappling with him on that narrow ledge above the Reichenbach Falls, had sent him plunging to his death.

With each succeeding minute, my exasperation mounted until I could contain it no longer and prepared myself to make a dash for the door, my intention being to force Holmes into action by taking the initiative. If I moved first, surely he would follow?

As events were to prove, it was fortunate that Holmes forestalled me. Before I could rise from the bunk, he had sprung to his own feet, an expression of intense relief lighting up his keen features.

"There is our signal!" he exclaimed aloud.

"What signal?" I inquired, greatly astonished not only at the sound of his voice after so long a silence but at the remark itself. I had heard nothing apart from the usual sounds on board the *Friesland* and a double blast on a steam whistle from some passing vessel.

"Of Inspector Patterson's arrival. Hurry, Watson! There is no time to lose!"

Suddenly he was in a positive whirl of activity, snatching our coats from the hooks and throwing my waterproof at me before flinging his own ulster about his shoulders. With two rapid movements, he had slid back the bolts and, opening the door, disappeared outside. By the time I had caught up with him, he was already scrambling down the companion-way which led on to the deck.

The sight which met me when I finally descended, close on Holmes's heels, was one of utter confusion. Lanterns were darting to and fro like fireflies in the darkness, their yellow beams illuminating briefly portions of the stern deck, shining black in the rain, and flashing on to a struggling group of men whose mingled shouts and curses, raised to a dreadful pitch, added to the impression that I had stumbled into a scene from a mediaeval inferno.

In the centre of all this wild activity, as if forming its nucleus, I could dimly discern the huge figure of Bakker and the stocky form of Captain Van Wyk, both fighting like mad men.

The next moment, Van Wyk had broken free from the mêlée and, turning rapidly about, came charging forward to where Holmes and I were standing in the lee of the wheel-house.

I doubt if he saw us in the shadows. His goal seemed to be the gang-plank which lay over to our left. Two constables, recognizable by their helmets and their black waterproof capes, were guarding it but their attention was on the main struggle which was taking place further along the deck. Within seconds, all could be lost. Van Wyk would reach the gang-plank and, taking the constables by surprise, might force his way down on to the wharf from where he would easily make his escape among the surrounding labyrinth of alleyways and side-streets.

I must confess that I, who only a short time

before had been so eager for action and silently upbraiding Holmes for his lack of it, found it impossible to move. As the powerful figure of the captain came hurtling towards us, his face contorted by rage, I was suddenly overcome by nausea, caused no doubt by the effects of the drug still present in my system.

It was Holmes who responded. As I stood helplessly by, he took a step forward, the muscles of his left arm bunched at the shoulder, his whole body as tense as a coiled spring. Then his fist went flashing past me, the knuckles gleaming white in the lamp-light, and there came a heavy thud as the blow struck the side of Van Wyk's jaw. Like a tree felled by a single stroke of an axe, he went crashing down on to the deck.

Holmes turned to me, his lean features transfigured by an expression of fierce jubilation.

"I think, Watson," said he, "that our account with Captain Van Wyk is finally settled."

Before I had time to reply, a bulky figure, dressed in unofficial tweeds, detached itself from the group of struggling men in the centre of the deck and came striding in our direction: Inspector Patterson of Scotland Yard, I perceived as he drew nearer. I had already made his acquaintance through my association with Holmes and had found him an excellent officer, efficient, co-operative, and possessing a wide knowledge of London's criminal fraternity.

"Well, Mr. Holmes," cried he, coming to a halt beside Van Wyk's recumbent body and regarding it with a look of satisfaction, "I have not seen a better straight left than yours outside the professional ring.* And with the captain down and out for the count, thanks to you, we now have all the crew safely rounded up."

He gestured to where the knot of men was already breaking up and was making its way in a more orderly fashion towards the gang-plank, each member of the crew escorted by a police officer, some in uniform, some in plain clothes. Among them, I recognized the mate, Bakker, his hands secured behind his back and his dark, bearded features made even more ill-favoured by a large swelling above his left eye.

On Inspector Patterson's orders, the two constables guarding the gang-plank came forward and, heaving Van Wyk upright, snapped a pair of handcuffs over his wrists. He had recovered a little from the blow Holmes had dealt him although he was still unsteady on his feet. As he was dragged away, he directed towards us a scowl of such intense hatred that my blood ran cold at the thought that only a short time ago, Holmes and I had lain drugged and bound at the mercy of this unspeakable villain.

With the departure of the crew of the *Friesland*, all of whom with the exception of Captain Van Wyk and the mate were later released as having played no part in our abduction and imprisonment, the night's activities were almost completed. Inspector Patterson left a guard on board the vessel and the four passengers who were found cowering in their cabins, too terrified by the sounds of the violent struggle taking place on deck to emerge, were reassured and escorted ashore.

Holmes and I then left in the company of Inspector Patterson to drive to Scotland Yard where, after we had formally identified Van Wyk and Bakker, they were later charged and taken away into custody.

---

* Mr. Sherlock Holmes, who had practised boxing while at university, used his skill at the sport on several occasions, notably against Woodley whom he defeated with a straight left. *Vide* "The Adventure of the Solitary Cyclist." In "The Adventure of the Yellow Face," Dr. John H. Watson refers to him as "one of the finest boxers of his weight" that he had ever seen. Mr. Sherlock Holmes had also fought three rounds with a professional prize-fighter, McMurdo, at the latter's benefit night and was considered by him expert enough to have turned professional. *Vide The Sign of Four.* Dr. John F. Watson.

III

"And now, my good Inspector, you will no doubt wish to hear a more detailed and personal account of last night's extraordinary events than the official statement I have already made," Holmes said.

It was the following evening when, on my old friend's insistence, Patterson had called at our Baker Street lodgings.

"First, the identity of the villain behind last night's attempted abduction."

"We already know that!" Patterson interjected. "It was Van Wyk, the master of the SS *Friesland*, with the assistance of Bakker, the mate."

"Oh, no, Inspector. He was merely the agent of someone much more powerful and dangerous whose name is familiar to both of you. Can you not guess? Then I shall have to tell you. It is Professor Moriarty."

"Moriarty!" Patterson and I exclaimed in unison.

"But Holmes," I protested, as the inspector fell silent in utter astonishment, "Professor Moriarty met his death at the Reichenbach Falls at your hands. You are surely not suggesting that by some miracle he survived."

"No, my dear fellow. There is not the smallest likelihood of that. No one, not even he, could have emerged alive from that dreadful abyss. But it is perfectly possible for a man with Moriarty's genius for evil to continue exerting his influence from beyond the grave. He warned me once, here in this very room, that if I brought about his destruction, he would see to it that I, in turn, would be destroyed.[*] On that same occasion, he also informed me that he was the head of a syndicate, the full extent of which even I could not appreciate. In that, he was mistaken. From my inquiries, I had already deduced that Moriarty controlled an international criminal fraternity, responsible for at least forty major crimes, including murder, robbery, and forgery.

"I believe I once described him to you, Watson, as a malignant spider. It was an apt simile. His organization was composed of many threads and extended over a vast area. When, with Inspector Patterson's help,[†] we set about smashing that web by rounding up members of Moriarty's gang, a few managed to elude us, including Van Wyk and his associate Bakker, whose task it was, should Moriarty fail in his attempt on my life at the Reichenbach Falls, to take revenge on his master's behalf.

"The scheme was a simple one and was planned to take place several years after the Reichenbach encounter,[‡] by which time Moriarty estimated that I should feel secure and my guard would consequently be lowered. But he omitted to take into account two vital considerations. Firstly, unlike him, I have never underestimated my opponent's capabilities. That man possessed the most phenomenal intellect which I could only admire, much as I detested the criminal ends to which he devoted those remarkable powers. For that reason, I was able to study him objectively as one might a specimen under a microscope. By so doing, I concluded that our minds worked on a very similar plane. In short, I could deduce his reasoning and anticipate his every action as if I had entered his mind and shared with him his very thoughts.

"I therefore asked myself the following question. Were I Professor Moriarty, what would I do if, when brought face to face with a protagonist such as myself, I ran the risk of losing my life at his hands?

"The answer was obvious. I should so ar-

[†] In his farewell letter left at the Reichenbach Falls, Mr. Sherlock Holmes instructs Dr. John H. Watson to inform Inspector Patterson that all the papers he needed to convict Professor Moriarty and his criminal associates were in a blue envelope, marked Moriarty, in the M pigeon-hole of his desk. The Moriarty gang was later brought to trial but two of them, including Colonel Moran, escaped justice. The other presumably was Captain Van Wyk. *Vide* "The Adventure of the Final Problem" and "The Adventure of the Empty House." Dr. John F. Watson.

[‡] Over three years had elapsed between Mr. Sherlock Holmes's encounter with Professor Moriarty at the Reichenbach Falls in May 1891 and the attempt made on Mr. Sherlock Holmes's life on board the SS *Friesland* in November 1894. Dr. John F. Watson.

[*] For a full account of Mr. Sherlock Holmes's interview with Professor Moriarty, readers are referred to "The Adventure of the Final Problem." Dr. John F. Watson.

range matters that, at some future date, his life, too, would become forfeit.

"Moriarty's second mistake was in choosing Captain Van Wyk to carry out his plot. Van Wyk is essentially a man of violence, prepared to commit murder and therefore necessary to the scheme but lacking that subtlety of imagination which a swindler or a confidence trickster might have possessed. When he presented himself yesterday evening here at Baker Street with his story of the disappearance of his elderly passenger, Mr. Pennington, I was suspicious of it almost at once."

"Were you, Holmes?" I interjected. "It sounded perfectly plausible to me. What made you doubt it?"

"The behaviour of Miss Pennington, the alleged passenger's daughter. Once more, it was a question of putting myself in someone else's place. Here was a young lady whose father had apparently disappeared on board ship on a dark and stormy night. Were I in her shoes, my first action would have been to rouse one of my fellow passengers in the nearby cabins. Instead, we were told that she rushed out on deck to seek help from the mate.

"I might, however, have passed over this discrepancy had I not read the letter which Miss Pennington had supposedly written to me. It was undoubtedly in a young lady's handwriting but showed no sign of the agitation that one would have expected from someone in her situation.

"In this letter, she mentioned an unspecified case which I had undertaken and which she claimed to have heard about from her father. I decided to test out my suspicions by asking Van Wyk if he knew to what precise investigation she referred. It was then that Van Wyk demonstrated that lack of imaginative finesse which was to confirm my doubts and bring about his arrest. So eager was he to lure me aboard the *Friesland* that, instead of pleading ignorance, he made the mistake of mentioning the Blackmore affair. I am afraid that I am not at liberty to divulge all the details nor are they relevant to the present case. Suffice it to say that it was a highly delicate inquiry involving the attempted blackmail of a well-known member of the aristocracy, carried out on Professor Moriarty's orders by one of his agents, a man called Blackmore. By means of a ruse, I was able to arrange for Blackmore's arrest by Inspector Lestrade of Scotland Yard on a quite separate charge of handling stolen property on the understanding that he would receive all the credit, providing I was allowed to remove certain private papers from Blackmore's safe.

"Consequently, although Blackmore's trial was widely publicized in the press, nowhere in those reports was there any mention of my name.

"How, then, had Van Wyk learned of my connection with the case unless he were a member of Moriarty's syndicate and had heard it discussed among his associates? I therefore concluded that the Penningtons did not exist and that the story of the father's disappearance was part of a plot against my life, almost certainly arranged by the late professor before his demise."

"Yet, knowing this, you were prepared to accompany Captain Van Wyk aboard the *Friesland*?" Inspector Patterson inquired in great astonishment. "Surely you were aware in what grave danger you were placing not only yourself but also Dr. Watson?"

"Indeed I was and I can assure you it was not a decision I took lightly." Turning to me, Holmes continued, "My only excuse, my dear fellow, is that, throughout our long friendship, I have never known you refuse to assist me in a case, however dangerous it might prove. I acknowledge it was wrong of me to assume you would do so on this occasion and for that I offer you my sincere apologies. I would have suggested that you remained behind on some pretext or other had I not known that you would have objected and, by so doing, might have aroused Van Wyk's suspicions. It was essential to my plan that he believed I had accepted his story unequivocally."

"Oh, please, Holmes!" I exclaimed, deeply touched. "There is no need to apologize. Even if I had known the full circumstances, I should have agreed to accompany you."

"Thank you, Watson. That is what I had expected you would say. Nevertheless, I am deeply grateful. As Cicero so aptly states: '*Adminiculum in amicissimo quoque dulcissimum est.*'"*

There was a short silence and then Holmes resumed his account.

"As you will recall, Watson, I sent you and Van Wyk ahead of me to wait in the cab with the excuse that I had to leave a note for Mrs. Hudson. Instead, having roused our landlady, I wrote to you, Inspector Patterson, briefly describing the situation and asking for your immediate assistance but not mentioning Professor Moriarty by name for reasons which I shall shortly explain. In the letter, as you know, I suggested that you bring at least a dozen colleagues with you and that you signal your arrival by two blasts on the steam whistle of a police launch. I then handed the letter to Mrs. Hudson, with strict instructions that, as soon as our cab had departed, she was to take a hansom to Scotland Yard and deliver the letter into your hands.

"At the same time, I took the precaution of arming myself as best I could. I knew it would be quite useless to take my revolver with me. If my deductions regarding Van Wyk's plans were correct, he would not make an attempt on our lives until the *Friesland* had sailed on the high tide at 1:30 a.m. and was safely out to sea. He would then murder us and fling our bodies overboard. To do so while the vessel was still in port was too dangerous. Had we put up a struggle, our outcries might have roused the passengers and those members of the crew who were not involved in the plot. Besides, our bodies, even if weighted down, might later have been dredged up by the anchor of another ship. Once out in the Channel, he ran no such risk.

"In the meantime, he would have to keep us secure and silent. The best method of achieving this was, I deduced, first to drug us and then make sure we were safely locked away until

* The quotation is from Cicero's *De Amicitia* and translates as: Man's best support is a very dear friend. Dr. John F. Watson.

after the vessel had set sail. One of the precautions I expected Van Wyk to take was to search our pockets. Had I carried a revolver, it would have been immediately discovered and removed. Those, at least, were my suppositions.

"What occurred after we had boarded the *Friesland* is, of course, known to you, my dear Watson, as you participated in the events. But I am sure you will bear with me while I elaborate on them a little for Inspector Patterson's benefit.

"With the intention of persuading Van Wyk that I accepted his account, I made a pretence of examining Mr. Pennington's cabin, incidentally discovering one further mistake which Van Wyk had made in setting up his trap for us. I assume you failed to notice it yourself, Watson, for you made no reference to it, not even by so much as a raised eyebrow."

"I confess I noticed nothing apart from the obvious signs that a struggle had taken place and that Mr. Pennington's luggage had been searched. To what do you refer?"

"To the basin which was liberally splashed with blood and yet there were no other stains elsewhere. Had someone bled so copiously, I should have expected to find evidence of it on the floor or upon the curtains, one of which had been wrenched from its rings during that apparent struggle.

"With the discovery of the alleged disappearance of Miss Pennington, Van Wyk suggested that we retire to his cabin while a second search of the vessel was supposedly made and that, while we waited, we join him in drinking a glass of schnapps. The glasses as well as the bottle were kept in a locker and I noticed that, when he took them out, he was most careful to keep the two glasses intended for our use separate from the one he subsequently drank from himself, causing me to suspect that they already contained a few drops of some powerful opiate, its taste and odour effectively disguised by the brandy.

"I am afraid there was nothing I could do, Watson, to prevent you from responding to Van Wyk's toast. However, you may recall that I carried my own glass to the far side of the cabin where I appeared to lose my balance. Under cover of this, I emptied the contents of my glass into the spittoon which stood beside the captain's desk."

"But Holmes!" I expostulated. "I distinctly recall you drank your brandy only a short time later!"

"No, my dear fellow," said Holmes, laughing heartily. "What you saw was the pretence of drinking. It is one of the oldest and simplest tricks in the repertoire of any stage magician. An object, a coin say, is placed inside a receptacle such as a box from which it apparently vanishes. The truth is, of course, that the coin has remained concealed in the man's palm and he has merely faked the action of putting it into the container. In much the same way, I kept the empty glass shielded in my cupped hand but went through all the motions of drinking from it, evidently successfully as neither you nor Van Wyk suspected me of legerdemain.

"After you had succumbed to the effects of the drug, I waited for a few moments and then, having observed your symptoms, I proceeded to imitate them, collapsing on the floor beside you. Once we were both apparently unconscious, Van Wyk summoned the mate, Bakker, and the two of them then set to work to search us and truss us up. It was at this point that my knowledge of baritsu* proved its usefulness."

"Baritsu?" Inspector Patterson inquired. "I have not heard of it."

"It is a Japanese form of wrestling which I have studied and which I had used before to great effect in my struggle with Professor Moriarty on the path above the Reichenbach Falls. One of its benefits lies in the development of the muscles in the upper arms and torso. When Van Wyk and his accomplice, Bakker, bound the ropes about

---

* Baritsu, or Bartitsu, was a form of self-defence, the name of which was derived from *bujitsu*, the Japanese word for martial arts. Mr. Sherlock Holmes used his skill at the sport to escape from Professor Moriarty's grasp and send him plunging to his death at the Reichenbach Falls. *Vide* "The Adventure of the Empty House." Dr. John F. Watson.

my chest and secured my arms behind my back, I flexed those muscles and, by releasing the tension after they had left, I was able to loosen the ropes sufficiently to allow me to reach the blade of a scalpel I had concealed in the cuff of my coat. After ten minutes' laborious work, I succeeded in cutting through the cord round my wrists and, once my hands were free, the other bonds were soon released. The rest you know. Having roused you, my dear Watson, and untied you, it was simply a matter of waiting for the signal from the steam whistle announcing the arrival of the excellent inspector here and his colleagues."

"You have forgotten one thing, Holmes," I pointed out.

"Have I? And what is that, pray?"

"The picklock with which you opened the cabin door."

"Did I omit to mention it? How remiss of me!" Holmes said carelessly. "The explanation is quite simple. At the same time as I concealed the scalpel blade, I took the precaution of strapping a small selection of picklocks round my left ankle. It made walking somewhat painful, hence my excuse of having sprained my foot. But it was worth the discomfort. The implements proved indispensable.

"And now, Inspector Patterson—and you, too, Watson, for the consequences will affect you as well—I must offer you an explanation of why I failed to refer to Professor Moriarty by name in the letter I sent by Mrs. Hudson. The omission was deliberate.

"You will not have heard, my dear fellow, of the murder in Rotterdam in January '90 of a Hendrik Van den Vondel, although Inspector Patterson was informed of it at the time. Van den Vondel was fatally stabbed one night, apparently in the course of an attempted robbery, near the docks by two men who were seen running away by a passer-by. Unfortunately, the witness was not able to describe them and the two malefactors were never brought to justice. However, there were rumours of a darker and more sinister motive behind Van den Vondel's death.

"Those suspicions were later confirmed by the Dutch authorities who, in the strictest confidence, consulted my brother Mycroft who, as you know, has connections with our own government.[*] They had reason to believe that an international organization was behind the murder and that it was carried out by two of its Dutch agents whose identities were then unknown.

"It was revealed that Van den Vondel was a plain-clothes inspector of police who was investigating this organization which, with the aid of forged documents, was engaged in smuggling known criminals from the Continent to this country. They included such notorious villains as Larsson, the Swedish forger, and the Nihilist, Boris Orlov, wanted by the Russian authorities for the bombing of a post office in St. Petersburg. Most of these criminals were later rounded up by Inspector Patterson and his colleagues at the Yard.

"This traffic in human cargo was centred on the port of Rotterdam and was apparently carried out with the assistance of certain dock officials who had been bribed to cover up the truth although the Dutch authorities had no proof either of this or of the identities of those who had organized the illicit trade.

"However, in the light of last night's events aboard the SS *Friesland*, I think we may safely assume that Van Wyk and Bakker were part of the conspiracy and it was they who had murdered the unfortunate Van den Vondel on Professor Moriarty's orders. I suggest therefore, Inspector Patterson, that you make a thorough search of the captain's cabin for you may well find sufficient evidence among his papers to prove his and Bakker's guilt as well as the names of those port officials who were bribed to keep silent.

"It was because of these international connections that I thought it wiser to make no mention of Professor Moriarty until I had discussed the whole affair with Mycroft which I did earlier this afternoon. Rather than bring Van Wyk and Bakker to trial in this country, Her Majesty's Government has decided to hand them over to the Dutch authorities who will no doubt wish to question them closely about the murder as well as the allegations of conspiracy.

"In addition, Inspector Patterson and his men are still hunting for Luigi Bertorelli, an important member of the Sicilian Mafia, and, until he is arrested, not a word of this must be made public.

"For these reasons, Watson, you will not be permitted to publish an account of our adventure on board the SS *Friesland*. I very much regret this, my dear fellow, but Mycroft's decision is final."

However, I could not allow the case to pass totally into oblivion for it illustrates not only the ingenuity and deductive skills of my old friend Sherlock Holmes but also his great personal courage in the face of mortal danger. In addition, it allowed me my sole contact, albeit posthumously, with that arch-villain, Professor Moriarty, whom Holmes once referred to as the Napoleon of crime[†] and whose genius for evil has never to my knowledge been surpassed in this century.

But it is not only for this reason that I have decided to write this confidential account of the outrageous events that took place on board the SS *Friesland*, which I shall deposit among my private papers.[‡]

It is also intended as a tribute to the courage of my old friend, Sherlock Holmes, and as a form of apology to him for my doubting, however briefly, his lion-hearted valour.

---

[*] Mr. Mycroft Holmes, Mr. Sherlock Holmes's elder brother, acted as a confidential adviser to various government departments while ostensibly employed by them as an auditor. *Vide* "The Adventure of the Bruce-Partington Plans." Dr. John F. Watson.

[†] *Vide* "The Adventure of the Final Problem." Dr. John F. Watson.

[‡] The only reference which Dr. John H. Watson makes to the case is in "The Adventure of the Norwood Builder," in which he states that "the shocking affair of the Dutch steamship, *Friesland*, which so nearly cost" both him and Mr. Sherlock Holmes their lives, occurred in the months following Mr. Holmes's return to London in 1894. Dr. John F. Watson.

The Strange Case of the Tongue-Tied Tenor

CAROLE BUGGÉ

C. E. LAWRENCE (1953–), pseudonym Carole Buggé, is the author of two Sherlock Holmes novels, *The Star of India* (1998) and *The Haunting of Torre Abbey* (2000), and a series featuring Claire Rawlings in the detective adventures *Who Killed Blanche DuBois?* (1999), *Who Killed Dorian Gray?* (2000), and *Who Killed Mona Lisa?* (2001).

Under her real name, Lawrence has written four thrillers starring Lee Campbell: *Silent Screams* (2009), *Silent Victim* (2010), *Silent Kills* (2011), and *Silent Slaughter* (2012). Her short fiction has appeared in numerous anthologies and magazines and has been nominated for a Pushcart Prize. She has won numerous prizes for her poetry. Her plays and musicals have been presented regionally and in New York City. Her advanced physics play, *Strings*, which dramatized string theory and cosmology, was described by John Simon as "the most absorbing play in New York today." Lawrence is also a professional singer, actress, and improvisational comedian.

"The Strange Case of the Tongue-Tied Tenor" was first published in *The Game Is Afoot*, edited by Marvin Kaye (New York, St. Martin's Press, 1994).

THE STRANGE CASE OF THE
TONGUE-TIED TENOR

Carole Buggé

THE SPRING OF 1890 brought a week of grainy London afternoons which depressed my medical practice as well as my spirits, and so it was on one of those dull grey days that I escaped my dreary surgery and headed for my old digs at 221B Baker Street to pay a visit on my friend Mr. Sherlock Holmes.

Mrs. Hudson greeted me with more than her usual effusiveness, for she had not seen me for some weeks, and the company of her only tenant, while undoubtedly invigorating, was also a trial which she bore with the fierce stoicism of her Scottish ancestors. As we ascended the familiar staircase, she threw her hands up in dismay.

"Oh, Dr. Watson, thank heaven you've come—maybe now he'll eat and sleep like a normal human being for a change!"

If Holmes was neither eating nor sleeping—bodily necessities which he did not always regard as such—it meant either that he was on a case or subject to the influence of the evil drug he turned to in his constant battle against ennui.

As I entered Holmes's sitting room, I saw that he was not alone. Seated on the sofa opposite the door was a stocky, red-faced gentleman with a full head of curly ginger hair and a face which was the likely result of a cross between a cherub and a bulldog. Holmes was sprawled out in his usual chair.

"Ah, Watson—come in; you are just in time to hear a most amusing little problem."

The red-faced man appeared to bristle at Holmes's words.

"My dear Mr. Holmes, forgive me for saying so, but to me there is nothing amusing about it," he said, or rather whispered, for his voice was nothing more than a faint throaty croak.

"Yes, yes, I'm sure—please forgive me," Holmes replied, with more impatience than contrition. "And allow me to introduce my colleague and very good friend, Dr. Watson. Watson, may I present Mr. Gerald Huntley."

"Not *the* Gerald Huntley—"

"The one and same—operatic tenor extraordinaire. Mr. Huntley has come to me on a matter of some distress to a singer of his caliber. Simply put, Watson, he has lost his voice."

Mr. Huntley's face grew redder as Holmes spoke.

"Well, that's terrible, of course, but surely that is a matter for a medical doctor—"

"Ah, but there's more, isn't there, Mr. Huntley?" Holmes said smoothly, with a smile which in the dim light looked almost predatory. The tenor blinked rapidly and shook his red curls, which offset the deepening flush on his face.

"I don't know what you mean, exactly—"

Holmes rose and stood over Huntley, his tall, spare frame looming like a bird of prey over the man.

"Mr. Huntley," he said in a sharp voice, "I am a busy man, and an impatient one, as you have perhaps gathered. I therefore suggest to you that you withhold nothing from me, either now or later, if you have any hope of my taking your case. You will therefore start by telling me why you feel you are in mortal danger and what connection that might have to your current clandestine love affair."

The singer swallowed hard and fell back against the couch. He drew a lace handkerchief from his breast pocket and passed it over his damp brow.

"You are truly everything they said you were, Mr. Holmes, and more," he croaked, making another pass with the handkerchief.

"That's better," said Holmes, settling into his chair again with a satisfied smile, though whether he was referring to the implied cooperation or the compliment I could not say.

"You are correct, sir, in everything that you say, though before I tell you my story I must say I cannot see how you could possibly know—"

"Tut, tut, man, there is nothing so mysterious about it," answered Holmes, though evidently pleased to have scored an impression. Holmes was, in his own way, no less a performer than our tenor, and his most faithful audience— apart from myself—was his steady stream of clients. No magician ever flourished his hat and cape with more relish or flair than Holmes unveiled his deductions to the breathless gasps of his admirers.

"That you are frightened is not hard to deduce. I happened to be looking out the window when you alighted from your cab, and only a criminal or a man who believes his life is threatened looks about furtively the way you did. I do you the honour to suppose you are not the former; I may therefore logically take you to be the latter."

Our illustrious guest hung his head.

"Quite right, I'm afraid, Mr. Holmes."

"As to the woman, there are so many signs I hardly know where to begin. If your fresh manicure and haircut had not alerted me, I could not have helped but notice that your boots, though unaccustomed to frequent polishings, have recently been shined to a glimmer. Your hat"— and here he brandished our guest's bowler—"is scented with one cologne, and yet this morning you put on quite a different, muskier scent. Add this to the baggy appearance of your vest and the fact that you have cinched your pants in an extra loop. When a man changes his perfume, takes extraordinary care over his person, and on top of that loses weight so rapidly that he cannot change his wardrobe quickly enough to keep his clothes from hanging loosely upon him—surely even to the inexperienced eye that bespeaks a recent and consuming infatuation of the most virulent kind."

With that Holmes went to the mantel, where he kept the Persian slipper which contained his shag tobacco. From the pipe rack he selected a long carved cherrywood pipe and stood waiting for our guest to recover his breath. Mr. Huntley looked very sheepish and defeated; at last he spoke.

"I must admit everything you say is true, and that furthermore, everything I have done has been in spite of my better instincts."

Holmes smiled disdainfully. "Affairs of the heart usually manage to override one's better instincts. Pray continue, Mr. Huntley," he said, folding his long frame into his favourite chair.

"There is not much to tell, really," the tenor whispered, and I felt a pang at witnessing the ruin of so great a voice. "I have been engaged to sing Don José in a production of *Carmen;* it is a role I have done many times, of course, but this was the first time I had performed with—her."

"You refer of course to Madame Olga Rayenskavya, the Russian mezzo-soprano."

"Well, yes, but how—?"

"Oh, come, come, Mr. Huntley; a casual perusal of the entertainment section of any number of London dailies would reveal that you are both appearing in *Carmen* in repertory for the next two weeks at the Royal Albert Hall."

"Yes, of course."

"So how did you come to be involved with this—temptress?"

"Enchantress would be more like it," said our guest, rubbing his eyes wearily. "I have neither eaten nor slept more than a few hours since she wrapped her spell around me. It is a sickness, a fever; I am like one of Ulysses's men Circe turned into pigs: it seems all I can do is grunt and grovel at her feet. I am powerless to extricate myself, even though I feel this affair has brought danger upon my head."

"What form has this danger taken?"

"Well, there have been several signs, but last night I stayed somewhat late after the performance; it is my custom to take tea in my dressing room after I sing. When I had finished my tea I remembered I had left my scarf in the wings somewhere; the Royal Albert is very drafty, as you may know, and so I had worn my scarf about my neck right up until my first entrance. It was very dark and quiet, as most everyone had gone home. Nonetheless, I thought I heard footsteps on the catwalk above the stage as I crossed to get my scarf. As I reached the stage left wings I heard a sound directly above me, and if I had not had my wits about me and leapt out of the way, I doubt that I would be sitting here now."

"Out of the way of what?" I asked, caught up in his story.

"A sandbag fell directly upon the spot where I had been standing. I had thought up until that moment that I was imagining everything, but sandbags do not simply fall from the sky for no reason at all. After last night I am convinced that someone is trying to get me out of the way."

"Out of the way of what, I wonder," said Holmes, pulling pensively at his pipe.

"I don't know, but I am convinced there is a connection with this wretched affair."

"The lady in question is married, is she not, to a conductor?" I said, recalling having read something about her engagement in the paper.

Mr. Huntley smiled bitterly. "Oh, yes, and that is not the least of the irony in my situation. Her husband is none other than Sir Terrance Farthingale, the maestro for this production of *Carmen*."

"Hmm, I see," said Holmes, tapping his pipe out into a potted plant on the tea table, a habit Mrs. Hudson hated. "You have pitched your tent rather close to the lion's den."

"I have made a rotten mess of things, if that's what you mean," said our downcast friend with a sigh.

"From what you know of Sir Terrance, do you think he would be capable of—?" I started to say, but Mr. Huntley interrupted me with a gesture.

"Dr. Watson, if I have learned one thing from all of this it is that when it comes to love, a man might be capable of anything at all."

"But what makes you think that losing your voice is somehow connected to all of this?" I inquired.

"Oh, I don't think there's a connection, except maybe that it was brought on by fatigue and worry—"

"Oh, but there I disagree with you, Mr. Huntley," Holmes interrupted. "Quite the contrary: I believe it to be a key to solving the case."

Both of us stared at him. He proceeded to fill and light his pipe before continuing, increasing our anticipation by making us wait for his response. He took a deep draught and exhaled slowly.

"Consider the facts. A man has a liaison with another man's wife. Soon he comes to feel his life is in peril. Shortly after a narrow escape he finds himself unable to perform his chosen profession—in short, he finds himself out of commission, temporarily or otherwise. He is still alive, but harm has undoubtedly been done to him; more importantly, as you yourself stated, Mr. Huntley, he is *out of the way*. So it seems it was not necessary to kill him after all, merely get him out of the way."

"Out of the way of what?" I interjected.

"That is precisely what we must find out, Watson." Holmes laid down his pipe and rose from his chair. "Good day, Mr. Huntley—if I have need of further information I shall be in contact with you."

Mr. Huntley scrambled to his feet rather confusedly, not used to Holmes's characteristically unceremonious treatment.

"We did not discuss the subject of fee—"

"There will be plenty of time for that, Mr. Huntley; I think you will find my fees by no means extravagant," said Holmes, bustling him to the door.

"Well, then, I will take my leave of you—"

"What about Mr. Huntley's safety?" I asked, seeing the anxious expression on his face.

"Oh, I should think Mr. Huntley's safety is for the time being assured; so long as he has no voice, he is certain to remain alive and well. Good day, Mr. Huntley. I shall let you know if there are any developments."

"Thank you, Mr. Holmes. Good day, Dr. Watson."

"Good day."

"Oh, one more question, Mr. Huntley. Who serves you your tea?"

"My dresser, McPearson. He has been with me for years."

"Very well. Thank you—I will be in touch."

After our guest was gone Holmes sprawled out on the couch and intertwined his long fingers behind his head.

"There, you see, Watson: you upbraid me with my refusal to have anything to do with the fairer sex, and yet this is the likely outcome of such an encounter. A man loses his means of livelihood and nearly his life, all for the sake of a woman."

"Oh, Holmes, you're incorrigible. Mr. Huntley has acted indiscreetly, to say the least. To use this as a moral for the entire—" but I stopped when I saw Holmes laughing that peculiar silent laugh of his.

"Ah, Watson, forgive me for taking advantage of your earnestness. Sometimes I cannot help tweaking you to see how you will react."

"I should think you would find the consistency of my responses rather boring by now," I said, feeling somewhat put out.

"Oh, come along, Watson, don't be cross! Let me make it up to you by standing you to the Wellington at Simpson's: I do believe theirs is the best Yorkshire pudding in town."

I am used to accompanying my friend in the testing of his many various hypotheses, but I must say this was one theory I was by no means averse to examining. And so it was that less than half an hour later I found myself seated across from Holmes, confronted by an undeniably agreeable specimen of Wellington's lesser known victory.

"Well, Watson," said my companion after we had finished our cigars and coffee, "what do you say to a little trip 'round to the Royal Albert, to the scene of the crime, as it were?"

"No crime has as yet been committed, Holmes."

"As yet, Watson; but it is only a matter of time."

"What do you expect to find at the Royal Albert?"

"I expect nothing, but I shall know when and if I find it."

The backstage area at the Royal Albert Hall is not usually accessible to the public, but the man guarding the stage door was more impressed by the mention of the name Sherlock Holmes than by the considerable tip offered to him by that august person. In any event, we soon found ourselves in the winding corridors leading to the various dressing rooms. Holmes headed straight for Gerald Huntley's, and upon knocking was greeted by an ancient gentleman of impressive sidewhiskers and rheumatic eyes of a remarkably pale blue hue.

"Ah, Mr. McPearson, isn't it?" said Holmes brightly.

"At your service, Sir. I'm afraid Mr. Huntley isn't in at the moment, Sir," he wheezed in a burr as Scottish as a field of mountain heather.

"Yes, yes, I know," answered Holmes, "we've come on his behalf. I am Mr. Sherlock Holmes, and this is my companion, Dr. Watson."

"Well, I'm glad he finally had the sense to see a doctor," the old man snorted. "I told him something like this would happen if he didn't take better care of himself."

I opened my mouth to explain but a look from Holmes silenced me.

"Yes, well, my colleague here has reason to believe Mr. Huntley may have ingested something—hazardous."

"Hmmp! Not very likely—he hasn't 'ingested' much of anything in the last few weeks!"

"You serve him his tea, do you not?"

"Indeed I do, as I have for the last eight years. That's one thing, at least; I've never known Mr. Gerald to refuse a good cup of tea, if it's made the way he likes it, and I know just the way he likes it."

"Yes, yes, I'm sure you do," said Holmes, trying unsuccessfully to bury the edge of impatience in his tone. "I wonder if you would grant me a very great favor—"

"If it'll help Mr. Huntley get better, I'd be glad to."

"Would you show me how you make him his tea? I—uh, that is, Dr. Watson here wants to assure that Mr. Huntley's routine remains undisturbed during his—convalescence."

McPearson seemed pleased by Holmes's interest in his tea-making skills. He bent closer and spoke in a conspiratorial whisper.

"Do you know you're the second man who's asked me about my methods in the last week?"

"Oh, really?" Holmes said casually.

"Aye; Mr. Huntley has always said no one could brew a cup quite like myself, and if I do say so—"

"You said another gentleman inquired earlier in the week—?" Holmes interrupted, his tone one of absent-minded disinterest.

"Aye, and a strange one he was at that. I fancy I have a fair eye for a man, and he was a right odd laddie. Said he was a stagehand here, but I can't say as I ever noticed him around. A fellow like that would be hard to miss, too—"

"What was he like?"

"Well, first off he had this yellow hair—it was really more like straw than hair, and so pale that it was almost white—as though he had been scared by something. It weren't the white hair of an old man—he was just a young laddie. And he spoke with a stutter, which was so bad that sometimes I was wantin' to finish the word for him just so's we could get on with it."

As our garrulous Scotsman described his visitor, Holmes's eyes narrowed and his lean face tightened.

"What did you show him?"

"I just showed him how I make the tea—my little 'secret,' if you can call it that, is that I put just a wee bit of water in at first and let it steep in that and then add the rest of the water straight from the kettle right at the end. That way it's strong and hot and warms you up, and

Mr. Huntley swears the flavor is better, too. I learned the trick off a Norwegian sea captain by the name of Olaf Niels."

Holmes glanced around the dressing room.

"Is that your teapot?" he said, pointing to a stout blue willow pot which looked as though it had seen years of service.

"Aye—they keep the kettle down the hall, so I have to go down there twice to fill the pot."

"And you generally leave the pot unattended while you wait for it to steep?"

"Aye, I've other things to do than hover around waiting for tea leaves. I usually lay out Mr. Huntley's dressing gown and then go back for the tea."

"I see. Do you mind if we have a look at the kettle?"

"No—in fact, if you like, I'll make you gentlemen a cup of tea right now."

Holmes was already out the door, so I answered.

"Thank you, Mr. McPearson; that would be very nice."

We followed Mr. McPearson down narrow hallways to the communal tea area. A few stagehands lingered around a much-used kettle, smoking and playing cards. Ignoring them, Holmes pulled out his magnifying glass and began poking around. McPearson did not comment on this but set about to making the tea. Suddenly Holmes stiffened and a muffled cry escaped his throat.

"Ha! Watson—it is a sloppy workman who leaves behind traces such as this!" With a flourish, he pulled out the small leather pouch he always carried and swept something into it. "Thank you, Mr. McPearson; you've been enormously helpful," he said, pulling me after him toward the exit.

"What about your tea?" McPearson called after us in a hurt voice.

"Another time, perhaps—" I called back as Holmes swept me out the door and into a hansom cab.

"What is it, Holmes?" I said as the cab rattled through the streets. "What did you find there?"

"I'm not certain, Watson, but I may have

found what I was looking for. First, however, some experimentation is required."

I had some business to attend to at my neglected surgery, and so agreed to meet Holmes later in the evening.

When I entered the front hallway Mrs. Hudson was there to greet me.

"Oh, Dr. Watson—he'll drive me batty with those experiments of his! See if you can't take his mind off of his work for a while."

"I'll do my best, Mrs. Hudson," I said dubiously, as a bitter odor drifted down the stairs toward us. Rolling her eyes, Mrs. Hudson bustled me into my old sitting room, closing the door behind her with a click.

The lamp by the window lit the room with its yellow glow, and I saw the lean frame of my friend bent over his improvised lab table, sheathed in the green smoke which swirled about his head. His thick black hair, usually impeccably neat, fell in unruly locks over his forehead. At first I thought Holmes had not heard me enter, and was startled to hear him address me without turning to look at me.

"Ah, Watson, your timing is, as usual, impeccable. Come have a look."

I stopped by the door to remove my coat.

"Come, Watson, come—it won't last forever, you know!" His face, in the lingering azure smoke, was pale and taut.

"What is it, Holmes?"

"Poison, Watson—a rare South African curare derivative I had the notion to write a small monograph about once."

I bent over the beaker from which the green smoke emanated. Immediately I began to feel weak and dizzy. Holmes evidently noticed this, because I felt his strong grip on my shoulder.

"Not so close, Watson—not so close! It is a very concentrated tincture. Come, let us get some fresh air."

With that he guided me over to the window, where he opened the shutters wide to let in a breeze. Even the thick air of London was a welcome relief to me after inhaling the stultifying fumes of Holmes's experiment.

"What is the connection, Holmes?"

"Curare, as you may know, acts in part as an agent of paralysis—you may perhaps have heard of its use in certain voodoo rituals to paralyze the victim."

"Yes, I have heard of it, but—"

"This particular derivative, Watson, owes its effectiveness to its ability to localize its effect, thus paralyzing only a single muscle or group of muscles. Administered as a drink—"

"Huntley's vocal cords—paralyzed!"

"Precisely, Watson. Fortunately for Mr. Huntley, the effect will eventually wear off, but someone evidently took great pains to remove him from the picture temporarily."

"But why, Holmes? And who would—?"

"The why is not yet entirely clear to me, Watson. But the who . . ." A shadow passed over my friend's stern face, and I fancied I saw him shudder. He rose and walked to the window, looking out into the night, where a soft rain had started to fall.

"The gentleman described to us by Mr. McPearson is well known to me. His name is Freddie Stockton, and he is an agent of"— here Holmes paused and drew his hand across his brow—"Professor Moriarty."

"Good God, Holmes."

"Yes. These are deeper waters than I at first suspected, Watson, and we must watch our step if we do not wish to find ourselves at the bottom of the river."

"But Holmes, how is Moriarty involved—?"

"That is exactly what I intend to discover. I suggest you disassociate yourself from me for a while, Watson. It will be better if I proceed on my own from now on."

"Don't be ridiculous, Holmes. I wouldn't think of abandoning the chase now."

Holmes suddenly looked very tired and worn. His shoulders drooped and he looked as if he could hardly stand.

"You don't understand, Watson," he said in a weary voice. "Moriarty is no ordinary villain; he has half the criminals of London at his beck and call. And I would never forgive myself if something should happen to you through my carelessness. No, it really would be better if I go on alone from here. I can't put you at risk."

"Holmes, since when have you ever known me to abandon you in times of danger? I beg you not to speak of this again unless you wish to risk seriously insulting me."

Holmes looked at me and then laughed softly.

"Good old Watson, stalwart to the last," he said with an unaccustomed softness in voice. "All right; I admit I did not expect you to budge for a moment, but I had to try—surely you can understand that."

"Yes, I suppose so. Now, what is our next step?"

"To penetrate the web, Watson, that surrounds the spider."

"And how do we do that?"

"We might start by interviewing some of the flies."

And so I soon found myself seated next to my friend in a hansom, revolver in my coat pocket, the thrill of the chase tight in my throat. Holmes sat back in the shadows of the cab, his long fingertips pressed tightly together, hat low over his eyes. If I did not know better I would have said he did not draw a breath during the entire ride, so still he sat.

Finally we arrived at our destination: the heart of London's East End, teeming with vermin of both the animal and human variety. We wound our way through stalls of vegetable sellers and past women selling another kind of ware, until finally we reached a squalid alley. The sign said PLUMMER'S COURT, and although I instinctively shrank back from entering the narrow, dark corridor framed by a brick wall on one side and a shuttered building on the other, Holmes strode forth with such confidence that I was ashamed not to follow him. As we walked along the flagstone pavement I thought I heard scurrying noises at our feet. We stopped at a doorway which to my untrained eye looked boarded up and deserted, but when Holmes rapped three times with his stick there were answering sounds from within. Presently a latch was drawn and the door opened slightly. An unshaven face appeared, and a gruff voice asked, "What is it you want?"

"I want to speak with Mr. Freddie Stockton."

"And who might you be?"

"I am Sherlock Holmes."

The name evidently had an effect, because I could hear muffled voices from within. In response to something said to him, the man at the door opened it wide enough to admit us, closing it quickly after we entered.

The room was dark and smelled of horses—it had evidently until recently been used as a stable. Four men sat around a thick oaken table, smoking cigarettes and drinking. They were a rough-looking lot, none more so than the one with the stiff white-blond hair. He had thick shoulders and a snarling mouth, which curled in disgust when Holmes addressed him.

"So, Mr. Stockton, we meet again. I trust all has gone well for you since you were a guest of Scotland Yard after that unfortunate incident involving the jewelry theft. Pity they did not see it your way, really it is. Still, you seem none the worse for wear."

The surly fellow rose from his chair and put his face close to Holmes's. My hand closed round my revolver as he spoke.

"You got a lotta nerve c-c-comin' here. You—"

"Come, come, Mr. Stockton; there's no need to be uncivil. I just would like you to deliver a message to the Professor from me. If you like I can come back at a more convenient time—"

Stockton's bloodshot eyes narrowed.

"What kinda m-m-message?"

"Simply that I'm on to his game, and that he should be more judicious in his use of poisons. I have a bit of expertise in the various forms of curare, I'm afraid, and I saw through his little charade."

Stockton's already florid face reddened, and it was then I saw the long curved dagger hanging from his belt. Holmes certainly had seen it, and yet he was as cool as always. He turned to leave.

"Oh, and one more thing. He really should send someone a little less—memorable—than yourself on such public errands. Good day, gentlemen."

And before any of the men could intervene, Holmes pulled me along with him and we were out the door. As we hurried back down the narrow street I glanced over my shoulder nervously, but evidently no one had followed us.

"That was awfully risky, Holmes. Why did you do it?"

"To put the fear of God into Moriarty, Watson. The more closely he believes he is being watched, the more likely he is to make a mistake. Besides, I knew we were in no great danger. Moriarty's men do nothing without instructions from him, and if he wanted to abduct us he could do that anytime he wished."

In spite of Holmes's brave words, I could not help feeling we were in danger, and it was with regret that I turned off in the direction of my surgery once we were back in familiar territory. I pleaded with Holmes to take a cab to Baker Street, but he refused, saying the night air would clear his brain. As I watched his tall, spare form recede, I felt a shiver go down my spine, and I almost ran after him.

The next morning my fears were realized when I was awakened before dawn by a telegram from Mrs. Hudson summoning me urgently to Baker Street. I arrived unshaven and barely dressed, so great was my dread. Mrs. Hudson greeted me at the door.

"They brought him in last night, Dr. Watson. I begged him to go to hospital, but he would have none of it."

"What's happened? Where is he?"

"He's upstairs, Dr. Watson. I'd like to get my hands round the villain that did this to him."

I took the stairs two at a time and in an instant was in the sitting room. Holmes was lying on the couch, and standing over him was Dr. Leslie Oakshott, the surgeon who would soon make a name for himself all over London, receiving a knighthood in the process.

"I'm afraid Mr. Holmes has refused a hospital bed, though I still feel it would be better in his condition," said Dr. Oakshott.

I looked down at Holmes. His left shoulder was heavily bandaged, and he was unconscious.

"What happened?"

"A gunshot wound to the chest. Missed the heart by only inches. He lost a lot of blood, Dr. Watson; we nearly lost him."

"Is he—?"

"He has been unconscious for several hours, and needs careful watching. The bullet went clean through but there is always the possibility of infection." Dr. Oakshott glanced at his watch. "I've several appointments awaiting me; I've done what I can, and would be grateful if you—"

"Of course; I'll stay with him as long as necessary. Thank you, Dr. Oakshott."

"Certainly, Dr. Watson. If he awakens you may need some morphine for the pain. Call me at once if he shows any sign of fever."

When Dr. Oakshott had gone, I sat down next to the couch and looked at my friend. His face was pale and drawn, and a dark patch of blood had soaked through the dressing on his shoulder. He who prided himself in his mastery and control lay now before me utterly helpless, and I felt a wave of rage at the fiend Moriarty, who was doubtless behind this assault.

Outside the first cries of the pickle-sellers and fishmongers were breaking through the early morning haze, and I settled back in my chair in a sort of reverie, remembering all the times Holmes and I had dashed out of these very rooms at all hours of the day and night, on the track of some crime or another. I bitterly reproached myself for letting Holmes walk home alone on the previous night, knowing all the while that if I had been with him I would have likely been shot too; still, I could not help feeling angry with myself for abandoning him against my better judgement. My daydreaming was interrupted only by Mrs. Hudson coming and going with tea, and I watched the grey light of morning dissolve into the greenish glow of a misty London afternoon. Sometime in the early evening Holmes stirred and moaned. I knelt beside him.

"Watson," he whispered, his voice very faint. "What time is it? How long have I been out?"

I glanced at the mantel clock.

"It's six o'clock."

"In the evening?" He tried to sit up, but sank back with a groan.

"Yes, Holmes."

He paused, and I could see he was breathing hard from the effort of speaking.

"Holmes, don't try to talk."

"I must, Watson; it is imperative that we move quickly."

"Holmes, you're not moving anywhere."

"Then you must help me, Watson. A life may depend on it."

"Very well. Tell me what to do."

"There is a performance of *Carmen* tonight. When Moriarty had me attacked, he tipped his hand: whatever is going to happen will happen soon, most probably tonight."

"What is going to happen?"

"I have several theories. I will follow the mostly likely first. Kindly get down my volume of *Who's Who*."

I moved to Holmes's bookcase, extracting the weighty volume, taking care not to drop the many slips of paper Holmes had inserted between the pages over the years.

"Hand it to me, please."

I did so reluctantly, for I could see from his white face and compressed lips that the effort of holding the book was causing him considerable pain.

"Holmes, let me—"

"No, Watson—you must send a telegram by runner to the Royal Albert Hall. Immediate reply requested."

"What am I to say?"

"Inquire as to who is singing the role of Don José tonight."

"Is that all?"

"Quite all. Thank you."

I did as was requested of me, and then sat down next to Holmes. The room was quite cool,

and yet beads of sweat gathered upon his forehead, and he breathed with difficulty.

"Holmes, I must take your temperature."

"No, Watson! Time is of the essence. Read to me," he said, handing me *Who's Who*, "under the entry Farthingale."

"There are two. Sir Terrance, the conductor, and his brother, Sir Anthony, Member of Parliament—"

"Yes, curious, isn't it?"

"I don't see why—"

"No, no, of course not. Now, Watson, you are somewhat more up on operatic plots than I. Refresh my memory as to the story of *Carmen*, if you would." He settled back on the couch, but the movement caused him to grimace with pain.

"Holmes, at least let me get you some morphine—"

"No, Watson; I need my mind clear. Now, *Carmen*, if you please."

"Well, it's a love triangle of sorts, about a vixen who attracts the attentions of a jealous lover—"

"Don José?"

"Yes. In the end he stabs her outside the bullring—"

"Yes, just as I thought. Now we only await the arrival of our telegram," he said, leaning his head back and closing his eyes. I was grateful that he was resting and tiptoed about, making myself busy by clearing the tea things. Eight o'clock came and went, with still no answer to our telegram. Finally I heard Mrs. Hudson's knock on the door, and she entered with the telegram. No sooner had I taken it from her than I heard Holmes's voice calling me from the couch asking to see it. I handed it to him and he looked at it intently, then before I could speak, suddenly rose from the couch. He staggered, but waved off my offer of assistance and went straight to his crime files, where he kept notes on criminals from around the world. He emerged with the file labelled "Q" and, after rifling through it, evidently found what he was looking for. After studying it intently for some moments, he scribbled something on a piece of paper and thrust it at Mrs. Hudson.

"Have that sent to Inspector Lestrade at Scotland Yard immediately."

"Yes, Mr. Holmes."

Holmes glanced up at the clock.

"Good God, Watson—we must hurry!"

"You're not going anywhere in your condition, Holmes."

Holmes gripped me by the shoulders.

"Watson, there is no time to explain, but believe me when I say that I am all that stands between a murderer and his victim!" He relaxed his grip, and I saw that he was about to faint. I helped him over to the couch.

"I believe I will take you up on the offer of some morphine—not too much, just enough to dull the pain, if you don't mind."

"Very well, Holmes. I'll get my syringe, but I cannot condone this—"

"Watson, I swear to you if there were any other way I would take it, but there isn't. Please believe me."

I injected the morphine and helped him get into his coat, then into a cab, with the assistance of Mrs. Hudson. Holmes told the driver to hurry to the Royal Albert Hall. I wanted to ask Holmes what was up, but the sight of his grim, pale face next to me silenced my questions.

When we arrived at the Royal Albert he led me not to the main entrance but around to the backstage door, where, fortunately for us, the same man stood guard and recognized us. It did not take Holmes long to convince the man to let us in, and soon we were at the heavy red fire door marked Stage Right. Singers in exotic Spanish costumes came and went around us, and Holmes hovered momentarily just outside the door. Then he pushed it open slowly, and I could see the vast stage of the Royal Albert Hall. I followed him into the darkened wings, where a few stagehands stood with their hands in their pockets. It was quite dark, so no one took particular notice of the two cloaked forms who picked their way over coiled ropes and sandbags toward the stage.

Two lone figures stood on a gaudily painted set of a bullring. I recognized the lady as the regal Olga Rayenskavya, but did not recognize the man, who was short and swarthy and had his back to me. They were singing the duet I thought I recognized as the Act Four finale, near the end of the opera. Just then I felt Holmes's grip on my arm. My eyes followed his hand as he pointed toward the stage, and in an instant I saw what he saw: a flash of steel under the bright rainbow lights. Before I could cry out, Holmes had sprung onto the stage and grasped the hand that held the gleaming weapon, holding it aloft and away from its intended target. Immediately cries went up from the house, and then pandemonium broke loose. The orchestra stopped playing, and several members rose from their chairs to better see what was happening on stage. Two stagehands sprang from the wings at Holmes, while the tenor surprised everyone by bolting offstage as fast as he could.

"Stop him!" Holmes cried to his captors. "Stop that man! He is a murderer!"

No one had the presence of mind to follow Holmes's instructions, so when I saw the man approaching me at top speed, I set myself for a good old-fashioned rugby tackle and brought him down heavily upon the floorboards, knocking the wind out of him. It was only when I got up that I realized he still clutched the knife, with its blade of real steel. Fortunately, neither of us had fallen on it, but I picked it up to examine it; it was curved and reminded me of the blade which hung from Freddie Stockton's belt. It was at that moment I saw Inspector Lestrade walking purposefully toward me, flanked by several of London's finest, and I was never so glad to see the good Inspector as at that moment. I handed over my charge, surprised that Lestrade seemed to recognize him, and then hurried onto the stage, where Holmes lay propped up against the set, flushed and panting. Madame Olga knelt beside him, wiping his brow. Removing his overcoat, I saw that his wound had begun to bleed again, and summoned two stagehands to help me carry him outside. Madame Olga followed us, and when we laid Holmes in a cab she stood at the door while I got in.

"Your friend, he has saved my life," she said in a thick Russian accent. "I will never forget this." She lowered her beautiful black eyes. "There are some who would say I am a bad woman, but—I will never forget what he has done."

As the cab drove off I looked back and saw her standing in the light rain which had begun to fall, looking after us. A tall figure which I took to be Sir Terrance came and put his arm around her. I thought to myself that I too would forgive many things for such a woman, just as Sir Terrance undoubtedly had.

By the time we got to Baker Street Holmes had lost consciousness and remained in a delirium for the better part of the night. By the next day he had regained consciousness, but I was master now and would not let him speak, so that in spite of my curiosity it was several days before I heard the whole story.

"You see, Watson," he said as he lay propped up with pillows in front of the fire, "I felt all along that the good professor had no business with our friend Mr. Huntley except to get him out of the way. That is why he sent Mr. Stockton to put curare in his tea, so he could put his understudy Mr. Quintaros in his stead."

"But how did you know Quintaros would try to murder Madame Rayenskavya?"

"I didn't know, Watson; I deduced. The question to answer was why Moriarty needed Huntley out of the way. When I thought to look up Sir Terrance, and saw that he had a brother who is a Member of Parliament, my suspicions were close to being confirmed, and when I saw Mr. Huntley's understudy was to be the notorious South American singer Juan Quintaros, who fled his own country under suspicion of murder—well, if you want to commit a murder, get a murderer, and that is precisely what Moriarty did."

"But I still don't see that connection with Sir Terrance—"

"Consider, Watson. A man's wife is having an affair, and is then murdered during a performance by the substitution of a real knife for a fake one. The understudy who actually commits the crime might be excused for several reasons: he has no reason to kill a woman he does not even know, he is undoubtedly preoccupied with his performance and therefore less likely to notice the substitution of the real knife when he has never seen the fake one. No, Watson, the suspicion falls not on the actual murderer but on the person who substituted the real knife, and that could be anyone. The most likely suspect is of course the jealous husband. Moriarty thought all of this out, of course, and then when all signs point to Sir Terrance, Moriarty pulls the rug out from under his unsuspecting accomplice, sacrifices Quintaros to the jury, and Sir Terrance is left bewildered but very much in Moriarty's debt. And who better to have in your debt than the brother of a Member of Parliament?"

"I see. It was a complicated hand he played, Holmes, and I doubt if anyone else but you could have figured it out."

"Well, Watson, perhaps you are right. But Moriarty played his cards a little too freely, and he forgot that sometimes the joker is wild. And now, Watson, if you will permit me to smoke, I would appreciate it if you would hand me my pipe."

The Human Mystery

TANITH LEE

ALTHOUGH TANITH LEE (1947–) has been best known over the past four decades as a prodigiously productive author of fantasy, horror, gothic romance, and historical and science fiction, both for children and adults, with more than ninety novels and nearly three hundred short stories to her credit, she has occasionally wandered into the mystery genre with excellent results.

It is not only quantity, however, that has elevated her to the top of the writing world, but also quality, as attested to by her numerous awards, including the following:

Nebula: *The Birthgrave* (1975), nominated for Best Novel; "Red as Blood" (1979), nominated for Best Short Story.

World Fantasy Award: *Night's Master* (1978), nominated for Best Novel; "The Gorgon" (1982), winner for Best Short Story; "Elle Est Trois (La Mort)" (1983), winner for Best Short Story; "Nunc Dimitis" (1983), nominated for Best Novella; *Red as Blood, or, Tales from the Sisters Grimmer* (1983), nominated for Best Anthology/Collection; *Night Visions 1* (1984), nominated for Best Anthology/Collection; *Dreams of Dark and Light* (1986), nominated for Best Anthology/Collection; *Night's Sorceries* (1986), nominated for Best Anthology/Collection; "Scarlet and Gold" (1999), nominated for Best Novella; "Uous" (2005), nominated for Best Novella.

British Fantasy Award: Six nominations, including *Death's Master* (1979), which won for Best Novel.

"The Human Mystery" was originally published in *More Holmes for the Holidays*, edited by Martin H. Greenberg, Jon L. Lellenberg, and Carol-Lynn Waugh (New York, Berkley, 1999).

THE HUMAN MYSTERY

Tanith Lee

1

ALTHOUGH I HAVE written so often of the genius of Mr. Sherlock Holmes, a reader may have noticed, it was not always to Holmes's satisfaction. With that in mind, I suspect the reader may also have wondered if, on occasion, certain exploits were never committed to paper. This I confess to be true.

The causes are various. In some instances the investigation had been of so delicate a nature that, sworn to secrecy myself, as was Holmes, I could not break my vow. Elsewhere Holmes had perhaps acted alone, and never fully enlightened me, due mostly, I believe, to a certain boredom he often exhibited, when a case was just then complete. Other adventures proved ultimately dull, and dullness I have never readily associated with Sherlock Holmes.

Otherwise a small body of events remain, rogues of their kind. They would not please the more devoted reader, as indeed at the time they had not pleased Holmes, or myself. I do not mean to imply here any failure, anything dishonourable or paltry on the part of Holmes. Although he has his faults, that glowing brain of his, when once electrically charged, transcends them. In this, or in any age, I daresay, he would be a great man. Nevertheless, certain rare happenings have bruised his spirit, and in such a way that I, his chronicler, have let them lie.

A year has gone by, however. An insignificant item in the newspaper brings me to my pen. No other may ever read what it writes. It seems to me, even so, that what was a distasteful, sad curiosity has become a tragedy.

Holmes, although he will, almost undoubtedly, have seen the item, has not alluded to it. I well remember his sometime comment that more recent work pushes from his memory the ventures of the past. It is therefore possible he has forgotten the case of the Caston Gall.

One winter afternoon, a few days before Christmas, Holmes and I returned to our rooms from some business near Trafalgar Square. The water in the fountain had been frozen, and I had great sympathy with it. The Baker Street fire was blazing, and the lamps soon lit, for the afternoon was already spent and very dark, with a light snow now falling.

Holmes regarded the snow from the window a moment, then turning, held out to me a letter. "I wonder if the weather will deter our visitor?"

"Which visitor is that?"

"This arrived earlier. I saved it to show you on our return."

Dear Mr. Holmes,

I should like to call upon you this afternoon at three o'clock. Hopefully, this will be of no inconvenience to you. Should it prove otherwise, I will return at some more favourable hour.

I looked up. "How unusual, Holmes. A client who fails to assume you are always in residence, awaiting them!"

"Indeed. I also was struck by that."

The letter continued:

I am divided in my mind whether or not to ask your opinion. The matter at hand seems strange and foreboding to me, but I am acutely conscious your time is often filled, and perhaps I am fanciful. Finally I have decided to set the facts before you, that you may be the judge. Please believe me, Mr. Holmes, if you can assure me I have no cause for fear, I shall depart at once with a light heart.

"Good heavens!" I exclaimed.

Holmes stood by the window. "She sets great store by my opinion, it seems. She will allow me to decide her fate merely on hearsay."

"She? Ah yes, a lady." The signature read "Eleanor Caston." It was a strong, educated hand, and the paper of good quality.

"What do you make of it, Watson?" Holmes asked, as was his wont.

I told him my views on the paper, and added, "I think she is quite young, although not a girl."

"Ah, do you say so. And why?"

"The writing is formed, but there is none of the stiffness in it which tends to come with age. Nor does she seem querulous. She has all the courteous thought of someone used to getting her own way. Conversely, she knows of and trusts you. Wisdom, but with a bold spirit. A young woman."

"Watson, I stand in awe."

"I suppose," I added, not quite liking his tone, "an elderly lady will now enter the room."

"Probably not. Mrs. Hudson caught sight of her earlier. But do go on."

"I can think of nothing else. Except I have used this writing paper myself. It is good but hardly extravagant."

"Two other things are apparent," said Holmes, leaning to the letter. "She wears a ring slightly too large for her, on her right hand. It has slipped and caught in the ink, here and here, do you see? And she does not, as most of her sex do, favour scent."

I sniffed the paper. "No, it seems not."

"For that reason, I think, Watson, you at first deduced the letter had been penned by a man. A faint floweriness is often present in these cases. Besides, her writing is well-formed but a trifle masculine."

Below, I heard the bell ring. "And here she is."

Presently Eleanor Caston was admitted to the room.

She was slim, and quite tall, her movements extremely graceful. She wore a tawny costume, trimmed with marten fur, and a hat of the same material. Her complexion was white and clear, and she had fine eyes of a dark grey. Her hair was decidedly the crowning glory, luxuriant, elegantly dressed, and of a colour not unlike polished mahogany. I was surprised to note, when she had taken off her gloves, that contrary to Holmes's statement, she wore no rings.

Although her appearance was quite captivating, she was not, I thought, a woman one would especially notice. But I had not been in her company more than five minutes, before I realized hers was a face that seemed constantly changeable. She would, in a few moments, pass from a certain prettiness to an ordinariness to vivid flashes of beauty. It was quite bewitching.

"Thank you, Mr. Holmes, Doctor Watson, for allowing me this interview today. Your time is a precious commodity."

Holmes had sat down facing her. "Time is precious to all of us, Miss Caston. You seem to have some fear for yours."

Until that moment she had not looked directly at him. Now she did so, and she paled. Lowering her eyes, she said, rather haltingly, "You must forgive me. This is, as you suspect, perhaps a matter of life or death to me."

Without taking his eyes from her, Holmes signalled to me. I rose at once and poured for her a glass of water. She thanked me, sipped it, and set it aside.

She said, "I have followed many of your cases, Mr. Holmes, in the literature of Doctor Watson."

"Literature—ah, yes," Holmes remarked.

"The curiosity of it is, therefore, that I seem almost to be acquainted with you. Which enables me to speak freely."

"Then by all means, Miss Caston, speak."

"Until this summer, I have lived an uneventful life. My work has been in the libraries of others, interesting enough, if not highly remunerative. Then I was suddenly informed I had come into a house and an amount of money which, to me, represents a fortune. The idea I need no longer labour for others, but might indulge in study, books and music on my own account, was a boon beyond price. You see, a very distant relative, a sort of aunt I had never known I had, died last Christmas, and left all her property to me, as her only relation. You will note, I am not in mourning. As I say, I did not know her, and I dislike hyprocrisy. I soon removed to the large house near Chislehurst, with its grounds and view of fields and woodland. Perhaps you can envisage my happiness."

She paused. Holmes said, "And then?"

"Autumn came, and with it a change. The servants, who until then had been efficient and cheerful, altered. My maid, Lucy, left my service. She was in tears and said she had liked her position very well, but then gave some pretext of a sick mother."

"And how could you be sure it was a pretext, Miss Caston?"

"I could not, Mr. Holmes, and so I had to let her go. But it had been my understanding that she, as I, was without family or any close friends."

At this instant she raised her head fiercely, and her eyes burned, and I saw she was indeed a very beautiful woman, and conceivably a courageous one. Despite her self-possession, it was obvious to me that Holmes made her shy and uneasy. She turned more often to me in speech. This phenomenon was not quite uncommon, I must admit. She had admitted after all to reading my histories, and so might have some awareness of Holmes's opinion of women.

"Presently," she went on, "I had recourse to my aunt's papers. I should have explained, a box of them had been left for me, with instructions from my aunt to read them. That is, the instruction was not directed solely at me, but at any woman bearing the Caston name, and living alone in the house. Until then I had put the task off. I thought I should be bored."

"But you were not," said Holmes.

"At first I found only legal documents. But then I came to these. I have them here." She produced and held out to him two sheets of paper. He read the first. Then, having got up and handed both papers to me, Holmes walked about the room. Reaching the window, he stayed to look out into the soft flurry of the falling snow and the darkness of impending night. "And she had died at Christmas?"

"Yes, Mr. Holmes, she had. So had they all."

The first paper was a letter from Miss Caston's aunt. It bore out my earlier amateur theory, for the writing was crochety and crabbed. The aunt was a woman in her late sixties, it seemed, her hand tired by much writing.

To any female of the Caston family, living in this house a single life, unwed, or lacking the presence of a father or a brother: Be aware now that there is a curse put on the solitary spinsters of our line.

You may live well in this house at any time of year save the five days which forerun and culminate in Christmas Eve. If you would know more, you must read the following page, which I have copied from Derwent's Legends of Ancient Houses. *You will find the very book in the library here. Take heed of it, and all will be well. It is a dogged curse, and easy to outwit, if inconvenient. Should you disregard my warning, at Christmas, you will die here.*

I turned to the second paper. Holmes all this while stood silent, his back to us both. The young woman kept silent too, her eyes fixed on him now as if she had pinned them there, with her hopes.

"Watson," said Holmes, "kindly read Derwent's commentary aloud to me."

I did so.

In the year 1407, the knight Hugh de Castone is said to have left his bane on the old manor-farm at Crowby, near Chislehurst. A notorious woman-hater, Sir Hugh decreed that if any Castone woman lived on the property without husband, father or brother to command her obedience, she would die there a sudden death at Yuletide. It must be noted that this was the season at which de Castone's own wife and sister had conspired to poison him, failed, and been mercilessly hanged by his own hands. However, the curse is heard of no more until the late seventeenth century, when Mistress Hannah Castone, her husband three months dead, held a modest festival in the house. She accordingly died from choking on the bone of a fowl, on Christmas Eve. One curiosity which was noted at the time, and which caused perplexity, was that a white fox had been spotted in the neighbourhood, which after Mistress Castone's burial, vanished. A white fox, it seems, had been the blazon of Sir Hugh de Castone, as depicted on his coat of arms.

I stopped here and glanced at Miss Caston. She had turned from us both and was gazing in the fire. She appeared calm as marble, but it occurred to me that might be a brave woman's mask for agitation.

"Watson, why have you stopped?" came from the window.

I went on.

Again the curse fell dormant. It may be that only married ladies thereafter dwelled at the farm, sisters with brothers or daughters with their fathers. However, in 1794, during the great and awful Revolution in France, a French descendant of the Castons took refuge in the house, a woman whose husband had been lost to the guillotine. Three nights before the eve of Christmas, charmed, as she said, by glimpsing a white fox running along the terrace, the lady stepped out, missed her footing on the icy stair, and falling, broke her neck. There has in this century been only one violent death of a Caston woman at the house in Crowby. Maria Caston, following the death of her father the previous year, set up her home there. But on the evening preceeding Christmas Eve, she was shot and killed, supposedly by an unwanted lover, although the man was never apprehended. It is generally said that this curse, which is popularly called the Caston Gall, is abridged by midnight on Christmas Eve, since the holiness of Christmas Day itself defeats it.

I put down the paper, and Holmes sprang round from the window.

"Tell me, Miss Caston," he said, "are you very superstitious?"

"No, Mr. Holmes. Not at all. I have never credited anything which could not be proved. Left to myself, I would say all this was nonsense."

"However?"

"The lady I call my aunt died on Christmas Eve, about eleven o'clock at night. She had had to break her own custom. Normally she would leave the house ten days before Christmas, staying with friends in London, and returning three days after St. Stevens. But this year she fell ill on the very day she was to leave. She was too unwell to travel, and remained so. I heard all this, you understand, from the servants, when once I had read the papers in the box, and questioned my staff firmly."

"How did she die?"

"She was asleep in her bed, and rallying, the doctor believed. The maid slipped out for a moment, and coming back found my aunt had risen as if much frightened, and was now lying by the fireplace. Her face was congested and full of horror. She was rigid, they told me, as a stone."

"The cause?"

"It was determined as a seizure of the heart."

"Could it not have been?"

"Of course her heart may have been the culprit."

Holmes glanced at me. His face was haughty and remote but his eyes had in them that dry mercurial glitter I connect with his interest.

"Mr. Holmes," said Eleanor Caston, standing up as if to confront him, "when I had questioned my servants, I put the story away with the papers. I engaged a new maid to replace Lucy. I went on with my improved life. But the months passed, and late in November, Lucy wrote to me. It was she who found my aunt lying dead, and now the girl told me she herself had also that day seen a white fox in the fields. It would be, of course, an albino, and our local hunt, I know, would think it unsporting to destroy such a creature. No, no. You must not think for a moment any of this daunted me."

"What has?"

"Three days ago, another letter came."

"From your maid?"

"Possibly. I can hardly say."

On the table near the fire she now let fall a thin, pinkish paper. Holmes bent over it. He read aloud, slowly, "'Go you out and live, or stay to die.'" He added, "Watson, come and look at this."

The paper was cheap, of a type that might be found in a thousand stationers who catered to the poor. Upon it every word had been pasted. These words were not cut from a book or newspaper, however. Each seemed to have been taken from a specimen of handwriting, and no two were alike. I remarked on this.

"Yes, Watson. Even the paper on which each word is written is of a different sort. The inks are different. Even the implement used to cut them out, unless I am much mistaken, is different." He raised the letter, and held it close to his face, and next against the light of a lamp. "A scissors here, for example, and there a small knife. And see, this edge—a larger, blunter blade. And

there, the trace of a water-mark. And this one is very old. Observe the grain, and how the ink has faded, a wonder it withstood the paste—Hallo, this word is oddly spelled."

I peered more closely and saw that what had been read as "out" was in fact "our." Some error," said Holmes, "or else they could not find the proper word and substituted this. Miss Caston, I trust you have kept the envelope."

"Here it is."

"What a pity! The postmark is smudged and unreadable—from light snow or rain, perhaps."

"There had been sleet."

"But a cheap envelope, to coincide with the note-paper. The writing on the envelope is unfamiliar to you, or you would have drawn some conclusion from it. No doubt it is disguised. It looks malformed." He tossed the envelope down and rounded on her like an uncoiling snake.

"Mr. Holmes—I assure you, I was no more than mildly upset by this. People can be meddlesome and malicious."

"Do you think that you have enemies, Miss Caston?"

"None I could name. But then, I have been struck by fortune. It is sometimes possible to form a strong passion concerning another, only by reading of them say, in a newspaper. I gained my good luck suddenly, and without any merit on my part. Someone may be envious of me, without ever having met me."

"I see your studies include the human mystery, Miss Caston."

Her colour rose. One was not always certain with Holmes, if he complimented or scorned. She said, rather low, "Other things have occurred since this letter."

"Please list them."

She had gained all his attention, and now she did not falter.

"After the sleet, there was snow in our part of the country, for some days. In this snow, letters were written, under the terrace yesterday. An E, an N and an R and a V. No footsteps showed near them. This morning, I found, on coming into my study, the number five written large, and in red, on the wall. I sleep in an adjoining room and had heard nothing. Conversely, the servants say the house is full of rustlings and scratchings."

"And the white fox? Shall I assume it has been seen?"

"Oh, not by me, Mr. Holmes. But by my cook, yes, and my footman, a sensible lad. He has seen it twice, I gather, in the last week. I do not say any of this must be uncanny. But it comes very near to me."

"Indeed it seems to."

"I might leave, but why should I? I have gone long years with little or nothing, without a decent home, and now I have things I value. It would appal me to live as did my aunt, in flight each Christmas, and at length dying in such distress. Meanwhile, the day after tomorrow will be Christmas Eve."

2

After Miss Caston had departed, Holmes sat a while in meditation. It seemed our visitor wished to collect some rare books, as now and then she did, from Lightlaws in Great Orme Street. We were to meet her at Charing Cross station and board the Kentish train together at six o'clock.

"Well, Watson," said Holmes at length, "let me have your thoughts."

"It appears but too simple. Someone has taken against her luck, as she guesses. They have discovered the Caston legend and are attempting to frighten her away."

"Someone. But who is that someone?"

"As she speculated, it might be anyone."

"Come, Watson. It might, but probably things are not so vague. This would seem a most definite grudge."

"Some person then who reckons the inheritance should be theirs?"

"Perhaps."

"It has an eerie cast, nonetheless. The letters in the snow: ENRV. That has a mediaeval sound which fits Sir Hugh. The number five on the study wall. The fox."

"Pray do not omit the rustlings and scratchings."

I left him to cogitate.

Below, Mrs. Hudson was in some disarray. "Is Mr. Holmes not to be here for the festive meal?"

"I fear he may not be. Nor I. We are bound for Kent."

"And I had bought a goose!"

Outside the night was raw, and smoky with the London air. The snow had settled only somewhat, but more was promised by the look of the sky.

On the platform, Miss Caston awaited us, her parcel of books in her arm.

Holmes did not converse with us during the journey. He brooded, and might have been alone in the carriage. I was glad enough to talk to Miss Caston, who now seemed, despite the circumstances, serene and not unhappy. She spoke intelligently and amusingly, and I thought her occasional informed references to the classics might have interested Holmes, had he listened. Not once did she try to break in upon his thoughts, and yet I sensed she derived much of her resolution from his presence. I found her altogether quite charming.

Her carriage was in readiness at Chislehurst station. The drive to Crowby was a slow one, for here the snow had long settled and begun to freeze, making the lanes treacherous. How unlike the nights of London, the country night through which we moved. The atmosphere was sharp and glassy clear, and the stars blazed cold and white.

Presently we passed through an open gateway, decorated with an ancient crest. Beyond, a short drive ran between bare lime trees, to the house. It was evident the manor-farm had lost, over the years, the greater part of its grounds, although ample gardens remained, and a small area of grazing. Old, powerful oaks, their bareness outlined in white, skirted the building. This too had lost much of its original character to a later restoration, and festoons of ivy. Lights burned in tall windows at the front.

Miss Caston's small staff had done well. Fires

and lamps were lit. Upstairs, Holmes and I were conducted to adjacent rooms, supplied with every comfort. The modern wallpaper and gas lighting in the corridors did not dispell the feeling of antiquity, for hilly floors and low ceilings inclined one to remember the fifteenth century.

We descended to the dining room. Here seemed to be the heart of the house. It was a broad, high chamber with beams of carved oak, russet walls, and curtains of heavy plush. Here and there hung something from another age, a Saxon double-axe, swords, and several dim paintings in gilded frames. A fire roared on the great hearth.

"Watson, leave your worship of the fire, and come out on to the terrace."

Somewhat reluctantly I followed Holmes, who now flung open the terrace doors and stalked forth into the winter night.

We were at the back of the house. Defined by snow, the gardens spread away to fields and pasture, darkly blotted by woods.

"Not there, Watson. Look down. Do you see?"

Under the steps leading from the terrace— those very steps on which the French Madame Caston had met her death—the snow lay thick and scarcely disturbed. The light of the room fell full there, upon four deeply incised letters: ENRV.

As I gazed, Holmes was off down the stair, kneeling by the letters and examining them closely.

"The snow has frozen hard and locked them in," I said. But other marks caught my eye. "Look, there are footsteps!"

"A woman's shoe. They will be Miss Caston's," said Holmes. "She too, it seems, did as I do now."

"Of course. But that was brave of her."

"She is a forthright woman, Watson. And highly acute, I believe."

Other than the scatter of woman's steps, the letters themselves, nothing was to be seen.

"They might have dropped from the sky."

Holmes stood up. "Despite her valour, it was a pity she walked about here. Some clue may

have been defaced." He looked out over the gardens, with their shrubs and small trees, towards the wider landscape. "Watson, your silent shivering disturbs me. Go back indoors."

Affronted, I returned to the dining room, and found Miss Caston there, in a wine-red gown.

"They will serve dinner directly," she said. "Does Mr. Holmes join us, or shall something be kept hot for him?"

"You must excuse Holmes, Miss Caston. The problem always comes first. He is a creature of the mind."

"I know it, Doctor. Your excellent stories have described him exactly. He is the High Priest of logic and all pure, rational things. But also," she added, smiling, "dangerous, partly unhuman, a leopard, with the brain almost of a god."

I was taken aback. Yet, in the extreme colourfulness of what she had said, I did seem to make out Sherlock Holmes, both as I had portrayed him, and as I had seen him to be. A being unique.

However, at that moment Holmes returned into the room and Miss Caston moved away, casting at him only one sidelong glance.

The dinner was excellent, ably served by one of Miss Caston's two maids, and less well by the footman, Vine, a surly boy of eighteen or so. Miss Caston had told us she had dispensed with all the servants but these, a gardener and the cook.

I noticed Holmes observed the maid and the boy carefully. When they had left the room, he expressed the wish to interview each of the servants in turn. Miss Caston assured him all, save the gardener, who it seemed had gone elsewhere for Christmas, should make themselves available. The lady then left us, graciously, to our cigars.

"She is a fine and a most attractive woman," I said.

"Ah, Watson," said Holmes. He shook his head, half smiling.

"At least grant her this, she has, from what she has said, known a life less than perfect, yet she has a breeding far beyond her former station. Her talk betrays intellect and many accomplishments. But she is also womanly. She deserves her good fortune. It suits her."

"Perhaps. But our mysterious grudge-bearer does not agree with you." Then he held up his hand for silence.

From a nearby room, the crystal notes of a piano had begun to issue. It seemed very much in keeping with the lady that she should play so modestly apart, yet so beautifully, and with such delicate expression. The piece seemed transcribed from the works of Purcell, or Handel, perhaps, at his most melancholy.

"Yes," I said, "indeed, she plays delightfully."

"Watson," Holmes hissed at me. "Not the piano. Listen!"

Then I heard another sound, a dry sharp scratching, like claws. It came, I thought, from the far side of the large room, but then, startling me, it seemed to rise up into the air itself. After that there was a sort of soft quick rushing, like a fall of snow, but inside the house. We waited. All was quiet. Even the piano had fallen still.

"What can it have been, Holmes?"

He got up, and crossed to the fireplace. He began to walk about there, now and then tapping absently on the marble mantle, and the wall.

"The chimney?" I asked. "A bird, perhaps."

"Well, it has stopped."

I too went to the fireplace. On the hearth's marble lintel, upheld by two pillars, was the escutcheon I had glimpsed at the gate.

"There it is, Holmes, on the shield. De Castone's fox!"

3

To my mind, Holmes had seemed almost leisurely so far in his examination. He had not, for example, gone upstairs at once to view the study wall. Now however, he took his seat by the fire of the side parlour, and one by one, the remaining servants entered.

First came the cook, a Mrs. Castle. She was a large woman, neat and tidy, with a sad face which, I hazarded, had once been merry.

"Now, Mrs. Castle. We must thank you for your splendid dinner."

"Oh, Mr. Holmes," she said, "I am so glad that it was enjoyed. I seldom have a chance to cook for more than Miss Caston, who has only a little appetite."

"Perhaps the former Miss Caston ate more heartily."

"Indeed, sir, she did. She was a stout lady who took an interest in her food."

"But I think you have other reasons to be uneasy."

"I have seen it!"

"You refer—?"

"The white fox. Last week, before the snow fell, I saw it, shining like a ghost under the moon. I know the story of wicked old Sir Hugh. It was often told in these parts. I grew up in Chislehurst Village. The fox was said to be a legend, but my brother saw just such a white fox, when he was a boy."

"Did he indeed."

"Then there are those letters cut in the snow. And the number upstairs, and all of us asleep—a five, done in red, high upon the wall. The five days before Christmas, when the lady is in peril. A horrible thing, Mr. Holmes, if a woman may not live at her own property alone, but she must go in fear of her life."

"After the death of your former employer, you take these signs seriously."

"The first Miss Caston had never had a day's indisposition until last Christmas. She always went away just before that time. But last year her carriage stood ready on the drive every day, and every day the poor old lady would want to go down, but she was much too ill. Her poor hands and feet were swollen, and she was so dizzy she could scarce stand. Then, she was struck down, just as she had always dreaded."

"And the fox?" Holmes asked her.

The cook blinked. She said, "Yes, that was strange."

"So you did not yourself see it, on that former tragic occasion?"

"No, sir. No one did."

"But surely, Mrs. Castle, the present Miss

Caston's former maid, Lucy, saw the white fox in the fields at the time of the elder lady's death?"

"Perhaps she did, sir. For it would have been about," Mrs. Castle replied ominously.

"Well, I must not keep you any longer, Mrs. Castle."

"No, sir. I need to see to my kitchen. Some cold cuts of meat have been stolen from the larder, just as happened before."

"Cold meat, you say?"

"I think someone has been in. Someone other than should have been, sir. Twice I found the door to the yard unlocked."

When she had left us, Holmes did not pause. He called in the footman, Vine. The boy appeared nervous and awkward as he had during dinner. From his mumblings, we learned that he had seen the white fox, yesterday, but no other alien thing.

"However, food has been stolen from the kitchen, has it not?"

"So cook says," the boy answered sullenly.

"A gypsy, perhaps, or a vagrant."

"I saw no one. And in the snow, they would leave their footprints."

"Well done. Yes, one would think so."

"I saw the letters dug out there," blurted the boy, "and Miss Caston standing over them, with her hand to her mouth. Look here, she says to me, who has written this?"

"And who had?"

The boy stared hard at Holmes. "You are a famous gentleman, sir. And I am nothing. Do you suspect me?"

"Should I?"

Vine cried out, "I never did anything I should not have! Not I. I wish I never had stayed here. I should have left when Lucy did. Miss Caston was a hard mistress."

I frowned, but Holmes said, amiably, "Lucy. She was obliged to care for her ailing mother, I believe."

Vine looked flustered, but he said, "The mistress never mourned her aunt, the old woman. Mistress likes only her books and piano, and her

thoughts. I asked her leave to go home for the Christmas afternoon. We live only a mile or so distant, at Crowby. I should have been back by nightfall. And she says to me, Oh no, Vine. I will have you here."

"It was your place to be here," I said, "at such a time. You were then the only man in the house."

Holmes dismissed the boy.

I would have said more, but Holmes forestalled me. Instead we saw the maid, Reynolds, who had waited at dinner. She had nothing to tell us except that she had heard recent noises in the house, but took them for mice. She had been here in old Miss Caston's time, and believed the old woman died of a bad heart, aggravated by superstitious fear. Reynolds undertook to inform Holmes of this without hesitation. She also presented me with a full, if untrained, medical diagnosis, adding, "As a doctor, you will follow me, I am sure, sir."

Lastly Nettie Prince came in, the successor to Lucy, and now Miss Caston's personal maid. She had been at the house only a few months.

Nettie was decorous and at ease, treating Holmes, I thought, to his surprise, as some kind of elevated policeman.

"Is your mistress fair to you?" Holmes asked her at once.

"Yes, sir. Perfectly fair."

"You have no cause for complaint."

"None, sir. In my last employment the mistress had a temper. But Miss Caston stays cool."

"You are not fond of her, then?"

Nettie Prince raised her eyes. "I do not ask to love her, sir. Only to please her as best I can. She is appreciative of what I do, in her own way."

"Do you believe the tales of a curse on the Caston women?"

"I have heard stranger things."

"Have you."

"Miss Caston is not afraid of it, sir. I think besides she would be the match for any man, thief, or murderer—even a ghost. Old Sir Hugh de Castone himself would have had to be wary of her."

"Why do you say that?"

"She talks very little of her past, but she made her way in the world with only her wits. She will not suffer a fool. And she knows a great deal."

"Yet she has sent for me."

"Yes, sir." Nettie Prince looked down. "She spoke of you, sir, and I understand you are a very important and clever gentleman."

"And yet."

Nettie said, "I am amazed, sir, at her, wanting you in. From all I know of Miss Caston, I would say she would sit up with a pistol or a dagger in her lap, and face anything out—alone!"

"Well, Watson," said Holmes, when we were once more by ourselves in the parlour.

"That last girl, Nettie Prince, seems to have the right of it. An admirable woman, Miss Caston, brave as a lioness."

"But also cold and selfish. Unsympathetic to and intolerant of her inferiors. Does anything else strike you?"

"An oddity in names, Holmes."

Holmes glanced my way. "Pray enlighten me."

"The letters in the snow, ENRV. And here we have a Nettie, a Reynolds and a Vine."

"The E?"

"Perhaps for Eleanor Caston herself."

"I see. And perhaps it strikes you too, Watson, the similarity between the names Castle and Caston? Or between Caston and Watson, each of which is almost an anagram of the other, with only the C and the W being different. Just as, for example, both your name and that of our own paragon, Mrs. Hudson, end in S.O.N."

"Holmes!"

"No, Watson, my dear fellow, you are being too complex. Think."

I thought, and shook my head.

"ENR," said Holmes, "I believe to be an abbreviation of the one name, Eleanor, where the E begins, the N centres, and the R finishes."

"But the V, Holmes."

"Not a V, Watson, a Roman five. A warning of the five dangerous days, or that Miss Caston will be the fifth victim of the Gall. Just as the number five is written in her study, where I should now like to inspect it."

Miss Caston had not gone to bed. This was not to be wondered at, yet she asked us nothing when she appeared in the upper corridor, where now the gas burned low.

"The room is here," she said, and opened a door. "A moment, while I light a lamp."

When she moved forward and struck the match, her elegant figure was outlined on the light. As she raised the lamp, a bright blue flash on the forefinger of her right hand showed a ring. It was a square cut gem, which I took at first for a pale sapphire.

"There, Mr. Holmes, Doctor. Do you see?"

The number was written in red, and quite large, above the height of a man, on the old plaster of the wall which, in most other areas, was hidden by shelves of books.

"Quite so." Holmes went forward, looked about, and took hold of a librarian's steps, kept no doubt so that Miss Caston could reach the higher book shelves. Standing up on the steps, Holmes craned close, and inspected the number. "Would you bring the lamp nearer. Thank you. Why, Miss Caston, what an exquisite ring."

"Yes, it is. It was my aunt's and too big for me, but in London today it was made to fit. A blue topaz. I am often fascinated, Mr. Holmes, by those things which are reckoned to be one thing, but are, in reality, another."

"Where are you, Watson?" asked Holmes. I duly approached. "Look at this number." I obeyed. The five was very carefully drawn, I thought, despite its size, yet in some places the edges had run, giving it a thorny, bloody look. Holmes said no more, however, and descended from the steps.

"Is it paint, Holmes?"

"Ink, I believe."

Miss Caston assented. She pointed to a bottle standing on her desk, among the books and papers there. "My own ink. And the instrument too—this paper knife."

"Yes. The stain is still on it. And here is another stain, on the blotting paper, where it was laid down."

Holmes crossed the room, and pulled aside

one of the velvet curtains. Outside the night had again given way to snow. Opening the window, he leaned forth into the fluttering darkness. "The ivy is torn somewhat on the wall." He leaned out yet further. Snow fell past him, and dappled the floor. "But, curiously, not further down." He now craned upwards and the lamplight caught his face, hard as ivory, the eyes gleaming. "It is possible the intruder came down from the roof rather than up from the garden below. The bough of a tree almost touches the leads just there. But it is very thin."

"The man must be an acrobat," I exclaimed.

Holmes drew back into the room. He said, "Or admirably bold."

Miss Caston seemed pale. She stared at the window until the curtain was closed again. The room was very silent, so that the ticking of a clock on the mantle seemed loud.

Holmes spoke abruptly. "And now to bed. Tomorrow, Miss Caston, there will be much to do."

Her face to me seemed suddenly desolate. As Holmes walked from the room, I said to her, "Rest as well as you can, Miss Caston. You are in the best of hands."

"I know it, Doctor. Tomorrow, then."

4

The next morning, directly after breakfast, Holmes dispatched me to investigate the hamlet of Crowby. I had not seen Miss Caston; it seemed she was a late riser. Holmes, abroad unusually early, meanwhile wished to look at the bedchamber of the deceased elder Miss Caston. He later reported this was ornate but ordinary, equipped with swagged curtains and a bell-rope by the fire.

As I set out, not, I admit, in the best of humours, I noted that the sinister letters and the Roman number five had been obliterated from the ground below the terrace by a night's snow.

Elsewhere the heavy fall had settled, but not frozen, and in fact I had a pleasing and bracing walk. Among the beech coppices I spied pheasant, and on the holly, red berries gleamed.

Crowby was a sleepy spot, comprising two or three scattered clusters of houses, some quite fine, a lane or two, and an old ruin of a tower, where birds were nesting. There was neither a church nor an inn, the only public facility being a stone trough for the convenience of horses.

Vine's people lived in a small place nearby, but since Holmes had not suggested I look for it, or accost them, I went round the lanes and returned.

My spirits were quite high from the refreshing air, by the time I came back among the fields. Keeping to the footpath, I looked all about. It was a peaceful winter scene, with nothing abnormal or alarming in it.

When I came in sight of the house, I had the same impression. The building looked gracious, set in the white of the snow, the chimneys smoking splendidly.

Indoors, I found Vine, Reynolds and Nettie engaged in decorating the dining room with fresh-cut holly, while a tree stood ready to be dressed.

Holmes and Miss Caston were in the side parlour and I hesitated a moment before entering. A fire blazed on the parlour hearth, and a coffee pot steamed on the table. Holmes was speaking of a former case, affably and at some length. The lady sat wrapt, now and then asking a sensible question.

Seeing me, however, Holmes got up and led me in.

"I have been regaling Miss Caston with an old history of ours, Watson. It turns out she has never read your account of it, though nothing else seems to have escaped her."

We passed an enjoyable couple of hours before luncheon. I thought I had seldom seen Holmes so unlike himself in company, so relaxed and amenable. Miss Caston cast a powerful spell, if even he was subject to it. But presently, when he and I were alone, he changed his face at once, like a mask.

"Watson, I believe this interesting house is no less than a rat-trap, and we are all the rats in it."

"For God's sake, Holmes, what do you mean?"

"A plot is afoot," he said, "we must on no account show full knowledge of."

"Then she is in great danger?" I asked.

He glanced at me and said, coldly, "Oh, yes, my dear Watson. I do believe she is. We are dealing with high villainy here. Be on guard. Be ready. For now, I can tell you nothing else. Except that I have looked at the elder Miss Caston's papers myself, and made an obvious discovery."

"Which is?"

"The warning or threatening letter which was sent my client had all its words cut from various correspondence kept here. I have traced every word, save one. No doubt I would find that if I persisted. They were part of bills and letters, one of which was written in the early seventeenth century. Our enemy effaced them without a care. One other incidental. The footman, Vine, resents the dismissal of his sweetheart, Lucy, who was Miss Caston's former maid."

"His sweetheart?"

"Yes, Watson. You will remember how Vine spoke of his employer, saying that she was a hard mistress."

"But surely that was because she would not let him go off for Christmas."

"That too, no doubt. But when he mentioned her hardness, it was in the past tense, and in the same breath as Lucy's dismissal. He declared he 'should have left when Lucy did.'"

"She was not dismissed, Holmes. She went of her own accord."

"No. During our morning's friendly conversation, I put it to Miss Caston that she had perhaps sent Lucy away due to some misconduct with Vine. Our client did not attempt to deceive me on this. She said at once there had been trouble of that sort."

"That then furnishes Vine and Lucy with a strong reason for malice."

"Perhaps it does."

"Did she say why she had not told you this before?"

"Miss Caston said she herself did not think either Lucy or Vine had the wit for a game of this sort. Besides, she had not wanted to blacken the girl's character. Indeed, I understand she gave Lucy an excellent reference. Miss Caston expressed to me the opinion that Lucy had only been foolish and too ardent in love. She would be perfectly useful in another household."

"This is all very like her. She is a generous and intelligent woman."

Reynolds alone attended to us at lunch. The hall was by now nicely decked with boughs of holly. Miss Caston announced she would dress the tree herself in the afternoon. This she did, assisted by myself. Holmes moodily went off about his investigations.

My conversation with her was light. I felt I should do my part and try to cheer her, and she seemed glad to put dark thoughts aside. By the time tea was served, the tree had been hung with small gold and silver baubles, and the candles were in place. Miss Caston lit them just before dinner. It was a pretty sight.

That night too, Mrs. Castle had excelled. We dined royally on pheasant, with two or three ancient and dusty bottles to add zest.

Later, when Miss Caston made to leave us, Holmes asked her to remain.

"Then, I will, Mr. Holmes, but please do smoke. I have no objection to cigars. I like their smell. I think many women are of my mind, and sorry to be excluded."

The servants had withdrawn, Vine too, having noisily seen to the fire. The candles on the tree glittered. Nothing seemed further from this old, comfortable, festive room than our task.

"Miss Caston," said Holmes, regarding her keenly through the blue smoke, "the time has come when we must talk most gravely."

She took up her glass, and sipped the wine, through which the firelight shone in a crimson dart. "You find me attentive, Mr. Holmes."

"Then I will say at once what I think you know. The author of these quaint events is probably in this house."

She looked at him. "You say that I know this?"

"Were you not suspicious of it?"

"You are not intending to say that after all I believe Sir Hugh de Castone haunts me?"

"Hardly, Miss Caston."

"Then whom must I suspect? My poor servants? The affair with Lucy was nothing. She was too passionate and not clever enough. Vine was a dunce. They were better parted."

"Aside from your servants, some other may be at work here."

Just at that moment the most astonishing and unearthly screech burst through the chamber. It was loud and close and seemed to rock the very table. Holmes started violently and I sprang to my feet. Miss Caston gave a cry and the glass almost dropped from her hand. The shriek then came again, yet louder and more terribly. The hair rose on my head. I looked wildly about, and even as I did so, a scratching and scrabbling, incorporeal yet insistent, rushed as it seemed through thin air itself, ascending until high above our heads in the beamed ceiling, where it ended.

I stood transfixed, until I heard Holmes's rare dry laughter.

"Well, Watson, and have you never heard such a noise?"

Miss Caston in her turn also suddenly began laughing, although she seemed quite shaken.

"A fox, Watson. It was a fox."

"But in God's name, Holmes—it seemed to go up through the air—"

"Through the wall, no doubt, and up into the roof."

I sat and poured myself another glass of brandy. Holmes, as almost always, was quite right. A fox has an uncanny, ghastly cry, well known to country dwellers. "But then the creature exists?"

"Why not?" said Holmes. "White foxes sometimes occur hereabouts, so we have learnt from Mrs. Castle, and from Derwent's book. Besides, in this case, someone has made sure a white fox is present. Before we left London, I made an inquiry of Messrs. Samps and Brown, the eccentric furriers in Kempton Street, who deal in such rarities. They advised me that a live albino fox had been purchased through them, a few months ago."

"By whom?" I asked.

"By a man who was clearly the agent of an-

other, a curious gentleman, very much muffled up and, alas, so far untraceable." Holmes looked directly at Miss Caston. "I think you can never have read all the papers which your aunt left you. Or you would be aware of three secret passages which run through this house. None is very wide or high, but they were intended to conceal men at times of religious or political unrest, and are not impassable."

"Mr. Holmes, I have said, I never bothered much with the papers. Do you mean that someone is hiding—in my very walls?"

"Certainly the white fox has made its earth there. No doubt encouraged to do so by a trail of meat stolen from the larder."

"What is this persecutor's aim?" she demanded fiercely. "To frighten me away?"

"Rather more than that, I think," said Holmes, laconically.

"And there is a man involved?"

"It would seem so, Miss Caston, would you not say?"

She rose and moved slowly to the hearth. There she stood in graceful profile, gazing at the shield above the fireplace.

"Am I," she said at last, "surrounded by enemies?"

"No, Miss Caston," I replied. "We are here."

"What should I do?"

Holmes said, "Perhaps you should think very clearly, Miss Caston, delve into the library of your mind, and see what can be found there."

"Then I will." She faced him. She was not beseeching, more proud. "But you mean to save me, Mr. Holmes?"

He showed no expression. His eyes had turned black as two jets in the lamplight. "I will save whomever I can, Miss Caston, that deserves it. But never rate me too highly. I am not infallible."

She averted her head suddenly, as if at a light blow. "But you are one of the greatest men living."

So saying, and without bidding us good night, she gathered her skirts and left the room. Holmes got up, and walked to the fire, into which he cast the butt of his cigar.

"Watson, did you bring your revolver?"

"Of course I did."

"That is just as well."

"Tomorrow is Christmas Eve," I said, "according to the story, the last day of the Gall."

"Hmm." He knocked lightly on the wall, producing a hollow note. "One of the passages runs behind this wall, Watson, and up into the attics, I am sure. The other two I have not yet been able to locate, since the plans are old and hardly to be deciphered. Just like the postmark on the letter sent to Miss Caston. Did you notice, by the by, Watson, that although the envelope had been wetted and so conveniently smudged, no moisture penetrated to the letter itself?"

I too tossed my cigar butt into the flames.

"Fires have the look of Hell, do you think, Watson? Is Hell cheerful after all, for the malign ones cast down there?"

"You seem depressed. And you spoke to her as if the case might be beyond you."

"Did I, old man? Well, there must be one or two matches I lose. I am not, as I said, infallible."

Leaving me amazed, he vacated the room, and soon after I followed him. In my well-appointed bedchamber, I fell into a restless sleep, and woke with first light, uneasy and perplexed.

5

I now acknowledged that Holmes was keeping back from me several elements of the puzzle he was grappling with. This was not the first occasion when he had done so, nor would it be the last. Though I felt the exclusion sharply, I knew he would have reasons for it, which seemed wise to him, at least.

However, I checked my revolver before breakfast. Going downstairs, I found I would eat my toast and drink my coffee alone. Miss Caston, as yesterday, was above, and Holmes had gone off, Vine grudgingly told me, on his own errands.

I amused myself as I could, examining the old swords, and finding a distinct lack of newspapers, tried the books in the library. They proved too heavy for my present scope of concentration.

About noon, Holmes returned, shaking the snow off his coat and hat. A blizzard was blowing up, the white flakes whirling, hiding the lawns, trees and fields beyond the windows. We went into the dining room.

"Read this," said Holmes, thrusting a telegram into my hands. I read it. It came from the firm of Samps and Brown, Furriers to the Discerning. A white fox had been purchased through their auspices on 15th October, and delivered to the care of a Mr. Smith.

"But Holmes, this was the very information you relayed last night."

"Just so. It was the information I expected to get today. But the telegram was kept for me at Chislehurst Village."

"Then why—"

"I gambled for once on its being a fact. I dearly wanted to see how Miss Caston would take it."

"It frightened her, Holmes, I have no doubt. What else?"

"Oh, did it frighten her? She kept a cool head."

"She is brave and self-possessed."

"She is a schemer."

He shocked me. I took a moment to find words. "Why on earth do you say so?"

"Watson, I despair of you. A lady's charms can disarm you utterly. And she well knows that, I think."

"She speaks more highly of you," I angrily asserted.

"I am sure that she does, which is also a way of disarming you, my dear fellow. Sit down, and listen to me. No, not there, this chair, I suggest, away from the fire."

I obeyed him. "You believe someone listens in the secret passage behind the wall there?"

"I think it possible. But this is a peculiar business and certainly its heroine has got me into a mode of distrust."

We sat down, and Holmes began to talk: "Miss Caston came to us, Watson, well-versed in all your tales of my work, inaccurate and embellished as they are. She brought with her the legend of the Caston Gall, which legend seems to be real enough, in as much as it exists in Derwent and elsewhere. Four Caston women, widows or spinsters, have apparently died here on one of the five days before Christmas. But the causes of Miss Caston's recent alarm—the writing in the snow, the number on the wall, the warning letter, the white fox—all these things have been achieved, I now suppose, by the lady herself."

"You will tell me how."

"I will. She had easy access to the letters and documents of her aunt, and herself cut out the words, using different implements, and pasting them on a sheet of cheap paper which may be come on almost anywhere. She was impatient, it is true, and used the word 'our' where 'out' eluded her. In her impatience, too, she hired some low person of no imagination to procure the fox and bring it here—Mr. Smith, indeed. Then she herself took cold meat from the larder to lure the animal to a tenancy inside the passageway, where it has since been heard scratching and running about. The door of the kitchen was found—not forced, nor tampered with, I have checked—but unlocked, twice. And if unlocked from the outside, why not from the inside? Again, her impatience, perhaps, led her to this casualness. She would have done better to have left some sign of more criminal work, but then again, she may have hoped it would be put down to the carelessness of her staff. The letters in the snow she scratched there herself, then stood over them exclaiming. Hence her footsteps mark the snow, but no others. The abbreviation of her name and the use of the Roman five are not uningenious, I will admit—she has been somewhat heavy-handed elsewhere. In the study, she herself wrote the number five upon the wall. Standing on the librarian's steps, I had to lean down some way, the exact distance needed for a woman of her height, on those same steps, to form the number. You noticed the five, though drawn carefully, was also three times abruptly smeared, particularly on the lower curve. This was where her blue topaz ring, which at that time did not properly fit her, slipped down and pulled the ink, just as it had on her note to me. The ivy she herself disarranged from the window, with an almost insolent lack of conviction."

"Holmes, it seems to me that this once you assume a great deal too much—"

"At Baker Street I watched her in the window as she looked at me. My back was turned to her, and in her obvious unease, she forgot I might see her lamplit reflection on the night outside. Her face, Watson, was as predatory as that of any hawk. I fancied then she was not to be trusted. And there is too much that fits my notion."

"When the fox screamed, I thought she would faint."

"It is a frightful cry, and she had not anticipated it. That one moment was quite genuine."

"Vine," I said, "and Lucy."

"I have not decided on their rôle in this, save that the boy is obviously disgruntled and the girl maybe was not sensible. As for the letter Lucy is said to have written to Miss Caston, that first warning which so unfortunately was thrown away, being thought at the time of no importance—it never existed. Why should Lucy, dismissed from her employment and her lover, desire to warn the inventor of her loss?"

"Perhaps Lucy meant to frighten her."

"An interesting deduction, Watson, on which I congratulate you. However, you must look at the other side of the coin. If the inventor of Lucy's loss received a sinister warning from her, would she too not conclude it was an attempt to frighten?"

"Very well. But the deaths, Holmes. I too have read Derwent. The elder Miss Caston undeniably died here. The other three women certainly seem to have done."

"There is such a thing as coincidence, Watson. Mistress Hannah Castone choked on a chicken bone. The French lady slipped on the icy stair. Maria Caston was shot by a spurned and vengeful suitor. The aunt was apoplectic and terrified out of her wits by having to remain in the house at Christmas. You as a doctor will easily see the possibility of death in such a situation."

"She had left her bed and lay by the fireplace."

"In her agony, and finding herself alone, she struggled to reach the bell-rope and so summon help."

"And the bell-rope is by the fire."

"Phenomenal, Watson."

"By God, Holmes, for once I wish you might be in error."

"I seldom am in error. Think of our subject, Watson. She has come from a miserable life, which has toughened her almost into steel, to a great fortune. Now she thinks she may have anything she wants, and do as she wishes. She flies in the face of convention, as exemplified in her refusal to wear mourning for the old lady. She prefers, now she can afford better, an inferior writing-paper she likes—a little thing, but how stubborn, how wilful. And she has got us here by dint of her wiles and her lies."

"Then in God's name why?"

"Of that I have no definite idea. But she is in the grip of someone, we may be sure of it. Some powerful man who bears me a grudge. He has a honed and evil cast of mind, and works her strings like a master of marionettes. Certain women, and often the more strong among their sex, are made slaves by the man who can subdue them. And now, old chap, I shall be delighted to see you later."

I was so downcast and irascible after our talk, I went up to my room, where I wrote out the facts of the case up to that point. These notes have assisted me now, in putting the story together at last.

When I went down to lunch, I found Holmes once more absent, and Miss Caston also. She sent me her compliments by Nettie, who said her mistress was suffering from a cruel headache to which she was prone. Naturally I asked if I could be of any help. I was rather relieved, things standing as now they did, when Nettie thanked me and declined.

Vine waited on me at lunch, in a slapdash

manner. Afterwards I played Patience in the side parlour, and was soundly beaten, as it were, nothing coming out. Beyond the long windows which ran to the floor, as they did in the dining room, the snow swirled on with a leaden feverishness.

Finally I went upstairs again to dress for dinner. I had on me, I remember, that sensation I experienced in my army days when an action was delayed. Some great battle was imminent, but the facts of it obscured. I could only curb my fretfulness and wait, trusting to my commander, Sherlock Holmes.

Outside, night had thickened, and the snow still fell. Dressed, I kept my revolver by me. Tonight was the fifth night of the Caston curse, and despite Holmes's words, perhaps because of them, I still feared not only for my friend, but for Eleanor Caston.

As I went down the corridor, for some reason I paused to look out again, through a window there. Before me on the pale ground I saw something run glimmering, like a phantom. Despite what we had learned, I drew back, startled. It was the Caston fox, pure white, its eyes flashing green in the light of the windows.

"Yes, sir. The beast exists."

I turned, and there stood the footman, Vine. He was clad, not in his uniform, but in a decent farmer's best, and looked in it both older and more sober.

"The fox is not a myth," I said.

"No, sir."

"Why are you dressed in that way?"

"I am going home. I have given her my notice. I have no mind to stay longer. I will take up my life on the land, as I was meant to. There is a living to be made there, without bowing and scraping. And when I have enough put by, I shall bring Lucy home, and marry her."

From a bad-tempered boy he had become a man, I saw. My instinct was to respect him, but I said, "And what of your mistress, Miss Caston?"

"She may do as she pleases. There was love, but nothing improper between Lucy and me.

That was her excuse. Miss Caston threw Lucy out on account of her reading—and I will say it now, on account of you, sir, and Mr. Holmes."

Dumbfounded, I asked what he meant.

"Why, sir, when Miss Caston came here, she would rather have read the coal-scuttle than anything of yours."

"Indeed."

"Any popular story was beneath her. She likes the Greek philosophers and all such. But when she had her headaches, Lucy read to her, and one day it was a tale of yours, sir, concerning Mr. Holmes. And after that, Lucy read others, since Miss Caston asked for them."

My vanity was touched, I confess. But there was more to this than my vanity.

"She made a regular study of Mr. Holmes, through your tales, Doctor. And then, this last September, she said Lucy must go, as her conduct with me was unseemly, which it never was. Even so, she gave my girl a fine reference, and Lucy has work now in a house better than this one."

I was searching in my mind for what to say, when the lad gave me a nod, and walked away. There was a travelling bag in his hand.

"But the weather, the snow," I said.

"This is a cold house," said he. "Snow is nothing to that." And he was gone.

Downstairs, I found Holmes, as I had hoped to. He stood by the dining room hearth, drinking a whisky and soda.

"Well, Watson, some insight has come your way."

"How do you know?"

"Merely look in a mirror. Something has fired you up."

We drew back from the hearth, mindful of a listener in the secret place behind it, and I told him what Vine had said.

"Ah, yes," said Holmes. "She has studied me. This confirms what I suspected. I think you see it too, do you not?"

"It is very strange."

"But the man who is her master, despite all my efforts, with which I will not tax you, he eludes me. What is his purpose? His name? It is a long way round to come at me."

Just then, Eleanor Caston entered the room. She wore a gown the dark colour of the green holly, which displayed her milk-white shoulders. Her burnished hair was worn partly loose. Seldom have I seen so fetching a woman.

Our dinner was an oddity. Only Reynolds waited on us, but efficiently. No one spoke of the affair at hand, as if it did not exist and we were simply there to celebrate the season.

Then Miss Caston said, "At midnight, all this will be over. I shall be safe, then, surely. I do believe your presence, Mr. Holmes, has driven the danger off. I will be forever in your debt."

Holmes had talked during the meal with wit and energy. When he set himself to charm, which was not often, there was none better. Now he lit a cigarette, and said, "The danger is not at all far off, Miss Caston. Notice the clock. It lacks only half an hour to midnight. Now we approach the summit, and the peril is more close than it has ever been."

She stared at him, very pale, her bright eyes wide.

"What then?" she asked.

"Watson," said Holmes, "be so kind, old man, as to excuse us. Miss Caston and I will retire into the parlour there. It is necessary I speak to her alone. Will you remain here, in the outer room, and stay alert?"

I was at once full of apprehension. Nevertheless I rose without argument, as they left the table. Eleanor Caston seemed to me in those moments almost like a woman gliding in a trance. She and Holmes moved into the parlour, and the door was shut. I took my stance by the fireplace of the dining room.

How slowly those minutes ticked by. Never before, or since, I think, have I observed both hands of a clock moving. Through a gap in the curtains, snow and black night blew violently about together. A log settled, and I started. There was no other sound. Yet then I heard Miss Caston laugh. She had a pretty laugh, musical as her piano. There after, the silence came again.

I began to pace about. Holmes had given me no indication whether I should listen at the door, or what I should do. Now and then I touched the revolver in my pocket.

At last, the hands of the clock closed upon midnight. At this hour, the curse of the Gall, real or imagined, was said to end.

Taking up my glass, I drained it. The next second I heard Miss Caston give a wild shrill cry, followed by a bang, and a crash like that of a breaking vase.

I ran to the parlour door and flung it open. I met a scene that checked me.

The long doors stood wide on the terrace and the night and in at them blew the wild snow, flurrying down upon the carpet. Only Eleanor Caston was in the room. She lay across the sofa, her hair streaming, her face as white as porcelain, still as a waxwork.

I crossed to her, my feet crunching on glass that had scattered from a broken pane of the windows. I thought to find her dead, but as I reached her, she stirred and opened her eyes.

"Miss Caston—what has happened? Are you hurt?"

"Yes," she said, "wounded mortally."

There was no mark on her, however, and now she gave me an awful smile. "He is out there."

"Who is? Where is Holmes?"

She sank back again and shut her eyes. "On the terrace. Or in the garden. Gone."

I went at once to the windows, taking out the revolver as I did so. Even through the movement of the snow, I saw Holmes at once, at the far end of the terrace, lit up by the lighted windows of the house. He was quite alone. I called to him, and at my voice he turned, glancing at me, shaking his head, and holding up one hand to bar me from the night. He too appeared unharmed and his order to remain where I was seemed very clear.

Going back into the dining room I fetched a glass of brandy. Miss Caston had sat up, and took it from me on my return.

"How chivalrous you always are, Doctor."

Her pulse was strong, although not steady. I hesitated to increase her distress but the circumstances brooked no delay. "Miss Caston, what has gone on here?"

"Oh, I have gambled and lost. Shall I tell you? Pray sit down. Close the window if you wish. He will not return this way."

Unwillingly I did as she said, and noted Holmes had now vanished, presumably into the icy garden below.

"Well then, Miss Caston."

She smiled again that sorry smile, and began to speak.

"All my life I have had nothing, but then my luck changed. It was as if Fate took me by the hand, and anything I had ever wanted might at last be mine. I have always been alone. I had no parents, no friends. I do not care for people much, they are generally so stupid. And then, Lucy, my maid, read me your stories, Doctor, of the wonderful Mr. Holmes. Oh, I was not struck by your great literary ability. My intimates have been Dante and Sophocles, Milton, Aristotle and Erasmus. I am sure you do not aspire to compete with them. But Holmes, of course—ah, there. His genius shines through your pages like a great white light from an obscure lantern. At first I thought you had invented this marvellous being, this man of so many parts: chemist, athlete, actor, detective, deceiver—the most effulgent mind this century has known. So ignorant I was. But little Lucy told me that Sherlock Holmes was quite real. She even knew of his address, 221B Baker Street, London."

Miss Caston gazed into her thoughts and I watched her, prepared at any moment for a relapse, for she was so blanched, and she trembled visibly.

"From your stories, I have learned that Holmes is attracted by anything which engages his full interest. That he honours a mind which can duel with his own. And here you have it all, Doctor. I had before me in the legend of this house the precise means to offer him just such a plot as many of your tales describe—the Caston Gall, which of course is a farrago of anecdote, coincidence, and superstition. I had had nothing, but now I had been given so much, why should I not try for everything?"

"You are saying you thought that Holmes—"

"I am saying I wanted the esteem and friendship of Mr. Sherlock Holmes, that especial friendship and esteem which any woman hopes for, from the man she has come to reverence above all others."

"In God's name, Miss Caston! Holmes!"

"Oh, you have written often enough of his coldness, his arrogance, and his dislike of my sex. But then, what are women as a rule but silly witless creatures, geese done up in ribbons. I have a mind. I sought to show him. I knew he would solve my riddle in the end, and so he did. I thought he would laugh and shake my hand."

"He believed you in the toils of some villain, a man ruthless and powerful."

"As if no woman could ever connive for herself. He told me what he thought. I convinced him of the truth, and that I worked only for myself, but never to harm him. I wanted simply to render him some sport."

"Miss Caston," I said, aghast, "you will have angered him beyond reason."

Her form drooped. She shut her eyes once more. "Yes, you are quite right. I have enraged him. Never have I seen such pitiless fury in a face. It was as if he struck me with a lash of steel. I was mistaken, and have lost everything."

Agitated as I was, I tried to make her sip the brandy but she only held it listlessly in one hand, and stood up, leaning by the fireplace.

"I sent Lucy away because she began, I thought, to suspect my passion. There has been nothing but ill-will round me since then. You see, I am becoming as superstitious as the rest. I should like to beg you to intercede for me—but I know it to be useless."

"I will attempt to explain to him, when he is calmer, that you meant no annoyance. That you mistakenly thought to amuse him."

As I faltered, she rounded on me, her eyes flaming. "You think you are worthy of him, Watson? The only friend he will tolerate. What I

would have offered him! My knowledge, such as it is, my ability to work, which is marvellous. All my funds. My love, which I have never given any other. In return I would have asked little. Not marriage, not one touch of his hand. I would have lain down and let him walk upon me if it would have given him ease."

She raised her glass suddenly and threw it on the hearth. It broke in sparkling pieces.

"There is my heart," said she. "Good night, Doctor." And with no more than that, she went from the room.

I never saw her again. In the morning when we left that benighted house, she sent down no word. Her carriage took us to Chislehurst, from where we made a difficult Christmas journey back to London.

Holmes's mood was beyond me, and I kept silent as we travelled. He was like one frozen, but to my relief his health seemed sound. On our return, I left him alone as much as I could. Nor did I quiz him on what he did, or what means he used to allay his bitterness and inevitable rage. It was plain to me the episode had been infinitely horrible to him. He was so finely attuned. Another would not have felt it so. She had outraged his very spirit. Worse, she had trespassed.

Not until the coming of a new year did he refer to the matter, and then only once. "The Caston woman, Watson. I am grateful to you for your tact."

"It was unfortunate."

"You suppose her deranged and vulgar, and that I am affronted at having been duped."

"No, Holmes. I should never put it in that way. And she was but too plausible."

"There are serpents among the apples, Watson," was all he said. And turning from me, he struck out two or three discordant notes on his violin, then put it from him and strode into the other room.

We have not discussed it since, the case of the Caston Gall.

A year later, this morning, which is once more

the day of Christmas Eve, I noted a small item in the paper. A Miss Eleanor Rose Caston died yesterday, at her house near Chislehurst. It is so far understood she had accidentally taken too much of an opiate prescribed to her for debilitating headaches. She passed in her sleep, and left no family nor any heirs. She was twenty-six years of age.

Whether Holmes, who takes an interest in all notices of death, has seen this sad little obituary, I do not know. He has said nothing. For myself, I feel a deep regret for her. If we were all to be punished for our foolishness, as I believe Hamlet says, who should 'scape whipping? Although crime is often solvable, there can be no greater mystery than that of the human heart.

Hostage to Fortune

ANNE PERRY

AN INTERNATIONALLY BESTSELLING author of historical mystery fiction with more than twenty-six million copies sold, Juliet Marion Hulme (1938–), using the pseudonym Anne Perry, has produced more than seventy books, most of them about Thomas and Charlotte Pitt or about William Monk. In addition to these classic Victorian-era detective novels, she has written a highly successful Christmas-themed novella annually since 2003, five novels set during World War I, two fantasy novels, four young adult books, and several stand-alone novels, and has edited five anthologies.

Hulme's first book as Perry was *The Cater Street Hangman* (1979), featuring Thomas Pitt, a Victorian policeman, and his high-born wife, Charlotte, who helps her husband solve mysteries out of boredom. She is of enormous help to him, as she is able to gain access to people of high social rank, which would be extremely difficult for a common police officer to do. There are thirty books in the series, set in the 1880s and 1890s.

The Monk series, with twenty novels, is set in the 1850s and 1860s. Monk, a private detective, is assisted on his cases by the excitable nurse Hester Latterly. The events in the first Monk book, *The Face of a Stranger* (1990), precede Sherlock Holmes's investigations by a quarter of a century, though Holmes is frequently described as the world's first consulting detective.

After winning an Edgar in 2000 for her short story "Heroes," which was set during World War I, Perry began a series of five novels featuring its protagonist, British Army chaplain Joseph Reavely, whose exploits and character were suggested by the author's grandfather; the first book was *No Graves as Yet* (2003).

"Hostage to Fortune" was first published in *The New Adventures of Sherlock Holmes*, edited by Martin H. Greenberg, Jon L. Lellenberg, and Carol-Lynn Rössel Waugh (New York, Carroll & Graf, 1999).

HOSTAGE TO FORTUNE

Anne Perry

HOLMES AND I had just returned to 221B Baker Street after a brisk walk in the most agreeable spring weather. I had picked up the newspaper to read, and he was wandering around the familiar room touching one thing after another in a most dissatisfied manner, when Mrs. Hudson knocked on the door.

"What is it?" he asked, hope lighting his keen face that the interruption would offer some interest at a time when he was growing increasingly bored.

"A gentleman to see you, sir," she replied with a frown, indicating that there was at least one thing about our visitor of which she disapproved. "Says it is a matter of life or death." Her tone made it clear she did not believe it, as she deplored exaggeration, unless she was the one doing it. Also she did not like people who made much of their misfortunes, and I confess we had had a few of those lately. As Holmes said to me, somewhat testily, they had proven to be domestic matters, trivia, things the ordinary police could have dealt with perfectly adequately, nothing whatever worth the skill of Sherlock Holmes.

"Well, ask him in!" he commanded. "Show him up!"

Mrs. Hudson withdrew with a swish of skirts.

"I am full of optimism, Watson," Holmes said briskly. "Our visitor may at last bring a challenge for the mind, a quest worth pursuing. Everything else in the last month has been fit only for Lestrade! Burglaries, forgeries so obvious a child should not have been deceived. Ah!"

He gave this last exclamation as a large, burly man came into the room, his eyes going immediately to Holmes. He wore a full beard and had a fine head of dark hair, but even so his expression of acute anxiety was clear, and everything in the movement and attitude of his body betrayed that he laboured under great emotion.

"Mr. Holmes!" He thrust out his hand, then instantly withdrew it as if he had not time for such courtesies. "I am at my wit's end, sir, or I would not have burst in upon you like this, without so much as a by-your-leave."

I was examining him more closely, as Holmes had so long taught me to do. His clothes were of very good quality both in fabric and in cut, but I fancied not in high fashion. He had large feet, yet his boots appeared comfortable. I dare say they were custom-made for him. Altogether, I doubted his trouble was financial.

"Mrs. Hudson said your problem was a matter of life or death," Holmes reminded him. Already, impatience was there in his face and the edge of his voice. "Be seated, sir, and tell me what I may do for you."

Our visitor sat, but on the edge of the chair, as if such restriction to his movement was a hardship to him.

"My name is Robert Harris," he introduced himself. "I do not know whether to begin my story at the beginning, or at the end."

"Is the beginning necessary for me to know?" Holmes asked, a slight frown between his brows. He loathed indulgence in the irrelevant.

"I believe it is."

"Then tell me. Leave out no detail that has to do with the catastrophe that threatens you."

"Catastrophe is indeed the right word, Mr.

Holmes," Harris answered him. "It is the kidnapping of my only child, my daughter, Naomi, as good and lovely a young woman as walks the earth." His voice was tight with the strain of containing his terror.

Holmes leaned forward a little. I could see in the sharp lines of his face that Mr. Harris had every whit of his attention. Mrs. Hudson could have fallen down the stairs with every piece of crockery in the house, and he would barely have noticed.

"Tell me," he urged. "Omit nothing at all. We do not yet know what may turn out to be crucial." He glanced at me. "You may trust Dr. Watson with anything at all. He is a man of the utmost discretion and loyalty."

For the first time Harris turned to me. His smile was charming. "I apologise, sir. My manners are appalling. The only mitigation I can offer is my distress. I have heard of you, of course, and I already know you to be all that Mr. Holmes has said of you. It never crossed my mind not to consider you part of any assistance he may give me." With that he looked back again, and began his story.

"Naomi is twenty-three, and is married to a most excellent young man of whom I heartily approve. He has made her very happy. Nevertheless I am a widower of many years, and she and I are very close. She comes to visit me, with her husband's good wishes, several times a year. She had just arrived yesterday . . ." His voice cracked with his distress. He required a moment to regain his composure.

It cost Holmes an effort I could read in his face not to betray his impatience.

"We went to a concert together—she is very fond of music, most particularly a good chamber quartet—at the Prince's Hall on Trafalgar Road. It was wonderful. I have never seen her look in better spirits." Harris breathed in and out slowly before continuing. "The concert finished a little after ten o'clock. We left the hall together, but a few yards from the steps I was waylaid by friends whom Naomi did not know. I spoke with them as briefly as I could, trying to excuse myself, but when I turned to find her, she was not there. I

assumed she had also seen old friends, and I waited five minutes or so for her to rejoin me. When she did not, I asked those few people still about, but they had not seen her. Then I thought perhaps she had gone on ahead of me."

"Was that likely?" Holmes interrupted.

"No, but I could not think what else," Harris answered, his voice sharpening in the remembered panic. "We live on Groom's Hill, not far from the hall, a comfortable distance to walk. I had looked forward to it. The streets are pleasant and quiet. We could have talked."

"But she had not gone ahead of you," Holmes assumed. "Did you see her again, Mr. Harris?"

"No! No, I did not, Mr. Holmes. I walked more and more rapidly, expecting with each corner to see her ahead of me. But she was not there. I had been home not more than twenty minutes or so when there was a knock on the door. I answered it myself, certain it would be her, ready to scold her for the fright she had given me, but above all, relieved to see her face." Again he required a moment to steady himself, but he did it admirably. I admit my heart ached for the man.

"Who was it?" Holmes demanded, leaning forward, his eyes intent upon Harris's.

"It was a boy, Mr. Holmes, an urchin, with a note for me." He reached in his inside pocket and produced it, handing it across.

Holmes read it aloud, for my benefit.

"We have your daughter. For the moment she is unharmed. You can have her back for ten thousand pounds. If you do not pay, we keep her for our entertainment, until we are bored. Then the sewer rats can have her. They'll eat anything.

"Bring the money on Wednesday, to the yard behind the Duck and Dragon on Brick Lane, off Tench Street, by the Wapping Basin. Midnight exact. Any trouble and she's gone. Understand? I'd rather have the money, but the choice is yours."

"Extremely ugly," Holmes said softly, turning the paper over in his long fingers, examining the texture and quality of it. From where I was sitting I could see that the words were not written, but cut out from newspaper and pasted on.

Harris watched him with growing desperation.

"How curious," Holmes said thoughtfully. "He has taken the trouble to make this note as anonymous as possible, as if he thought you would recognise his hand, or even that you might take it to the police . . ."

"No!" Harris cried vehemently. "Any trouble and he will harm her! For God's sake, he has made that plain enough! I must pay! Only that is the thing, I cannot! I do not have the means to raise such a sum."

"Do you have any idea who sent this note?" Holmes asked him. "Think carefully, sir. You are a prosperous man, who knows his business well. You have succeeded in a competitive trade. There must be many who envy you, perhaps even believe your gain has been at their expense."

Harris looked startled. "You know me by repute?"

The ghost of a smile curved Holmes's thin lips. "No, sir. But I observe your clothing and your manner. The sum for which you are asked is what others perceive you to have. You have told me the area in which you live. You are used to command and to being obeyed. You live in London, and yet you have seen much exposure to sun and wind. There are old scars upon your hands and what appears to be the shadow where a tattoo has been removed from your wrist. I would guess that in your earlier years you followed the sea. Now you are an importer of some standing."

"I knew I had come to the right man!" Harris said, that remarkable smile lighting his face again. "Indeed it is true, all true!" Then the joy vanished and darkness took its place. "But I cannot raise ten thousand pounds, Mr. Holmes! I have spent all day since the banks opened, doing everything I can, everything humanly possible! I can raise no more than six thousand four hundred and a few shillings. They demand it tomorrow night. That is where I need your help, sir." His voice became firmer, his resolve absolute.

"I need someone of undisputed honour, someone who cannot and will not be duped or used, to persuade these men, whoever they are, that this is all the money I have. I will give it to them, if they return Naomi to me, unharmed. If they refuse, I cannot give what I do not have, and if they injure her in the slightest, I will spend the rest of my life hunting them down. Nothing else will matter to me until I have exacted the last ounce of revenge . . . as terrible as that with which they have threatened her. And believe me, Mr. Holmes, from my days at sea, and in the east, I know how to do that!"

Looking at his massive shoulders, and the burning intensity in his black eyes, I believed him utterly. I could see that Holmes also held no doubt.

"Look into my affairs, Mr. Holmes!" Harris urged. "My business is an open book to you. Convince yourself that I am speaking the truth when I say I can raise no more, then I implore you . . . go in my place at midnight, and persuade these men to return Naomi to me for the money I can give, less the fee for your time and services . . . I apologise, but that is truly every penny I own . . . and I will pursue them no further."

"You will let them get away with this?" I was aghast. The wickedness of it was an affront to all decency. "They will do it again, to some other poor young woman!"

Harris turned to me. "Perhaps, Dr. Watson, but if I give them my word that this is all the money I have, which it is, and I use Mr. Sherlock Holmes's honour as pledge to the truth of that, then I must abide by my word not to pursue them. I am bound. Can you not see that?"

I could see. And I regarded it as a peculiar honour that Harris should take my friend's reputation so seriously as to believe it would save his daughter's life. I confess I felt a thrill of pride that his esteem included me equally.

"Of course," I conceded. "But the wickedness of it still galls me."

"And me," he said bitterly. "But Naomi is all my concern. When we care for someone, Dr. Watson, we are uniquely hostages to fortune, and sometimes that ransom has to be paid." Then he looked again at Holmes. "Will you help me?"

Holmes did not hesitate. I believe it was as much from compassion for Harris as for the challenge it offered him, although he would never have said so. Certainly the financial reward was the least of importance to him. There were times when I worried that his disregard for such necessities would see him in difficulty. The general public had no idea how frequently he undertook cases without accepting any reward other than the satisfaction of helping a creature in distress, and always, of course, the exercise of his intellect and his daring.

I was very sure he would understand only too clearly the plight of a man like Harris who was perceived by others to have far greater wealth than indeed he did have.

"Of course I will," he answered. "We shall begin this afternoon. I shall accept your offer to make myself familiar with your business and your circumstances, so I may argue your case with detail and prove beyond a doubt to them that you are offering all you have. You may rest assured, Mr. Harris, that nothing whatever will be left undone in the effort to restore your daughter to you, in no way harmed beyond the fear she must inevitably feel."

"Thank you!" Harris's relief and gratitude positively shone around him. "Sir, I shall be forever in your debt!"

I could not see then how prophetic those words would be.

Harris gave us every assistance, and Holmes and I spent that afternoon and all of the following day examining the business that Harris had built up since retiring from the sea, and it was indeed most successful. He had achieved it honestly, and was held in considerable respect. But he had undeniably made enemies, and as the hours passed, it became increasingly easy to see that envy could well be the source of his present trouble. He was a clever and imaginative man, frequently beating his rivals to a fortunate deal.

However he had given his daughter the best of everything he could afford, the finest education, including travel and tuition in arts and foreign languages. Much of the money he earned he had also spent, but I could not begrudge the man such a manner of doing it. He had not lavished jewels upon her, or worldly things of no worth. I began to picture her in my mind, and wonder what manner of young woman she was, that everyone spoke so well of her honour and her kindness and I wished more fervently that we should succeed in our task of rescuing her.

We also retraced Harris's steps to the concert hall, and verified as far as possible what he had told us. Of course we could find no one who had been there on the evening of Naomi's disappearance, but when Holmes taxed Harris with this, he willingly gave us the names and addresses of two of the friends who had waylaid him. We called upon them, and they confirmed his tale. Of course we gave a quite inoffensive excuse for our enquiry. As I recall I said something to the effect of having known Harris myself when I was in the east, and had attended the concert, and thought I had caught sight of him. Could they verify it was indeed he.

I am afraid in the pursuit of the truth when assisting Holmes in one of his cases, I appear to have become rather good at telling lies myself. It is a habit I shall have to watch very carefully.

So it was that a little after eleven o'clock Holmes and I set out to keep our rendezvous at the yard behind the Duck and Dragon. Holmes had with him the six thousand and four hundred pounds of Harris's money—he had declined to take anything for himself, although he had not told Harris this. I admired him for it, although I was not in the least surprised. I had expected he would do so. His only concern was to get Naomi back. After that he would wish next to pursue in some way the evil man who had abducted her. His own purpose would be well served by that alone. He never thought greatly of money; it could not buy the intellectual challenge he loved, the music, the learning or the thrill of the chase. Nor did it ever buy friendship.

It was a most insalubrious area. In spite of the pleasant spring evening, the mild air was filled with a cloying mist, and the odours of inadequate drains, uncleared rubbish, and cramped living were all about us like a suffocating hand.

The darkness away from the lighted thoroughfares was relieved only by glimpses of candles through filthy windows, and the occasional reflection of distant gas lamps on wet walls. I fear I heard the slither and rattle of rats' feet, and now and again a pile of refuse collapsed as some creature within it moved.

"What a godforsaken place!" I said under my breath. "The sooner our business is completed, the better."

"That would be equally true, were we in flowered walks by the river," Holmes retorted. "It is an evil matter to kidnap, Watson, to try and sell human life and trade on one person's love for another. It outweighs the theft of any material object, be it the crown jewels."

I agreed with him heartily, but knew I did not need to say so.

We felt our way forward carefully. The stones were slimy under our feet, and although we had both brought bull's-eye lanterns, we were loath to draw attention to ourselves by using them. And I freely admit, I did not greatly wish to see what might lie around us.

The Duck and Dragon was thirty yards ahead, its sign faintly lit by a lamp hanging above it, but so grimy as to serve its purpose ill. So far I could see no one in the shadows beneath.

"Are we early?" I asked, fingering the revolver I had insisted upon bringing. After all, Holmes was carrying a great deal of money, and I had no intention of our being robbed of it before we could effect the rescue of Naomi.

"They will no doubt ascertain who it is before they show themselves," Holmes replied. "They will be expecting Harris himself. It is my task to convince them I am acting on his behalf."

I had considerable misgivings as to his ability to do that, now that we were come to the point. I looked around me. The shadows seemed to move. I had a hideous vision that they were all alive, the isolated and rejected of society crouched in doorways, cold and hungry, perhaps riddled with fever or tuberculosis, waiting for death to take them.

I heard a hacking cough and started in momentary terror.

Somewhere a glass or bottle dropped and smashed on the stone. How could this hell on earth exist so close to the warmth of homes with fires and food and laughter?

Holmes was several yards ahead of me. I hurried to keep up with him. This was not the time to indulge in morbid thoughts, and leave him unguarded as he met the kind of men who would kidnap a young woman.

Please heaven they had not held her anywhere like this! She would be half-mad with fear by now.

I strained my eyes to see through the gloom and discern a human figure ahead of us, all the while keeping my hand steady on my revolver.

Holmes walked silently until he was directly under the feeble light above the sign of the Duck and Dragon, then he stopped, signaling me to remain a few yards away, almost concealed.

The dampness condensed and dripped from the eaves. I could hear its steady sound amid the creaking of rotting wood and the slither and scamper of rodent feet. Nothing on earth would have induced me to remain here, but the knowledge that the life of a young woman depended upon us.

Still nothing moved but the wavering shadows as the wind swung the lantern.

Then I saw him, a huge bulk in the gloom, appearing as if from nowhere, his hat drawn down to conceal his features, his coat ragged at the skirts but high-collared. He beckoned to Holmes as if he recognised him. Holmes walked across the slick cobbles toward him, and I moved also, now drawing my revolver out so I could fire it at any moment, should this highly unsavoury man offer any violence.

Holmes reached him and they spoke together

so quietly I did not hear the words. Then the man nodded, as if he had agreed to something, and the two of them moved toward an alleyway.

I was apprehensive. Anyone might lurk in the darkness under those dripping eaves, but I had no alternative but to follow, all the while doing my best to mark the way we had come, so I might be able to return.

We emerged from the alley onto a cross street. Ahead of me, Holmes was still talking softly to the huge man, inclining slightly toward him as if listening.

We plunged into more darkness. I felt my way, one hand before me. I wished profoundly that Holmes would charge the man to remain still until they had reached an agreement, but I did not interrupt in case I should destroy some moment of trust.

Once again I came out into relative light. But no one was visible ahead of me. I looked left and right, but there was no sign of either Holmes, or anyone else.

I swiveled around to look the way I had come, but saw only the gaping entrance of the alley. Surely I could not have passed them. I looked again to see if there were any openings that I had missed, but there was nothing! What had happened to Holmes?

Panic swelled up in me. My revolver was useless against someone I could not see! Should I cry out? There was no one to ask. In the short space that I could see, there seemed to be no living soul but myself.

Then dimly I made out the slumped, motionless shapes of men asleep huddled in doorways, trying to gain some few minutes' rest, starved and homeless men who lived on the refuse even this desperate neighbourhood did not want. There was little purpose in disturbing them. I already knew had I been sufficiently close behind Holmes I would have seen him when I first emerged had he been on this street. He and his guide must have gone through some doorway hidden in the darkness of the alley.

I turned back, lighting my lantern, now not caring if I were seen, and began to make my way back.

But I did not find him, or his companion. There were doorways surely enough, and wide broken and boarded-up windows, but no indication which of them they had gone through. There were no footprints on the glistening cobbles, no obvious way cleared through the scattering of rubbish, and no one to ask.

Had he lost me on purpose? Was he even now inside one of these damp, creaking buildings negotiating the release and safety of Harris's daughter?

I had no way of knowing.

What should I do? Wait until he reappeared? Go and look for him? But where?

Time dragged by, five minutes, ten, fifteen. There was silence except for the incessant dripping, and now and then the creak of rotting wood, as if the houses shifted their weight. I found myself shivering violently. The cold ate into my bones, and I confess it, a mounting fear that something terrible had happened to Holmes.

I had let him down. What should I do? It was pointless waiting here any longer, and I had no idea in this foetid warren where I should begin to search for him. At least I knew the way I had come, and could return to Baker Street.

I moved more and more rapidly, in the hope that I should find him there, and we should laugh together over the adventure, and I should regard in hindsight my present fears as ridiculous. By the time I was within a hundred yards, I was at a run.

But the rooms were in darkness, and there was no familiar figure to welcome me. I lit the gas brackets and poured myself a stiff whiskey. It warmed my throat, but it could do nothing to assuage my fears.

I paced the floor uselessly, turning over every possibility for action, both sensible and absurd, until I realised that they were all ineffective unless I knew what had happened. There was no purpose in contacting Harris. I would only drive the poor man to despair, and maybe needlessly. There was nothing I could tell Lestrade, and I would only further endanger Naomi's life if the kidnapper were to learn of it.

It was a quarter past three in the morning. I

was no longer cold, but in every other respect I had never felt worse. I tried to remind myself of every adventure I had shared with my friend, how many had had moments when it had seemed all was lost, and yet he had always managed to pull victory from defeat. He was brilliant, endlessly perceptive, full of imagination, and had the greatest intelligence allied with courage of any man I know. Even his brother, Mycroft, could not match him for vigour of mind.

With morning light he would return with Naomi, and chide me for my lack of faith in him.

But with morning came a messenger carrying a handwritten note addressed to me. I tore it open.

"Dear Dr. Watson,

I am afraid I deceived you. There was no kidnap on Monday. Naomi is safe and well.

However, today there is! If you wish to see Sherlock Holmes again, you will pay ten thousand pounds for that privilege. You have seen the distasteful neighbourhood of the Duck and Dragon. You will not disbelieve a man could disappear there and not ever be seen again.

I will allow you two days to raise the money, and bring it to me. I think the front of the Duck and Dragon will do this time. Again, do not contact the police. Surely it is not necessary to spell out for you the consequences of such an action?

I enclose an authorisation in Holmes's own hand, so you may raise the necessary funds."

It was unsigned.

Folded inside it was a torn piece of paper, on one side of which was written in Holmes's hand:

"This is to entitle Dr. John Watson to redeem on my behalf all such stocks and securities as I hold, to the value of ten thousand pounds, to be paid to him in cash upon his demand.

Sherlock Holmes"

It was dated that day.

I found myself shaking almost uncontrollably. I wanted to rush out and find that unspeakable villain Harris, and beat him with my fists until he regretted the day he was born. But I realised that that would only place Holmes in greater danger, perhaps even bring about his injury or death.

Calm was required, a cool and intelligent mind, logical thought, deduction.

What a blackguard Harris was! He had played upon Holmes's good nature and abused it to extort money! His words about affection for anyone providing a hostage to fortune came back to me with bitter irony. He had placed me in exactly the position he claimed to be in himself.

I had never felt more bereft, or helpless. And Holmes's very life rested upon my skill!

I paced the floor trying to compose my thoughts. It was far too early to attempt to contact banks and houses of finance in order to raise the amount demanded. I thought for a moment of going to see Mycroft to ask his assistance. He was the only man clever enough to find a solution to this without jeopardising Holmes's life. I was as far as the front door when I recalled that Holmes had told me Mycroft was on a trip to Italy, he did not specify where, and would not return for at least three weeks.

I realised with horror that it depended entirely on me.

I climbed back up the stairs with a feeling of such desolation I hardly knew what to do with myself. The price of my failure was far higher than shame, inadequacy, even the world's blame and contempt, it was the life of the best friend and the finest man I ever knew.

I sat down in my favourite chair and willed myself to think . . . clearly and rationally. What would Holmes do were our positions reversed?

I was well enough acquainted with his affairs to know he did not possess ten thousand pounds, even were he willing to have it paid in ransom to a villain like Harris. The note he had sent must have been at gunpoint.

He also knew that Mycroft was in Italy, and there would be no one to whom I could turn. I could not imagine that even the fear for his life would make him lose control of his intellect so as to forget such things.

Then why had he written the note?

I stood up and went over to where I had left it, and read it again. Then I turned it over and looked at the other side. It was quite obviously torn from a letter, only portions of which were visible. There was no date, and no address of the sender. It was the top left-hand quarter of the paper. It must surely be from the very woman we had believed we were rescuing, and about whom we had ascertained so much, independently of anything Harris had told us.

> *"Dearest Papa,*
>
> *Thank you very much for your*
> *I am so glad that you are*
> *Naturally spring here is not so*
> *as far south as you are. Nevertheless*
> *tulips are beautiful. Yesterday Rose*
> *Donald said that the whole Black*
> *they are going to widen the road, but*
> *Did I tell you that we*
> *saw most wonderful dolphins! What*
> *greatest happiness! I wish you were"*

I stared at it, reading it over and over. It was all I had! Had he sent me this intending me to learn from it some fact that could help him?

The phrase "hostage to fortune" kept beating in my mind. Harris had used it speaking of his love for his daughter. I had thought then that I heard anguish in his voice, and an honesty.

I was caught in exactly the trap he had claimed to be in. Except that I had no Sherlock Holmes to turn to!

But that was not true! Surely I, of all men, could turn to the years of friendship and the shared experiences of the past? What would Holmes say were he here? Use what I have. Look at the clues and read them!

I turned over the piece of paper again. It had to be a letter from Naomi! I did not know when it had been written, but it was safe to as-

sume it was recent, or he would not have been still carrying it. Had it been an old one, but of sentimental value, then he would not have been willing to tear it for Holmes to use.

Did Harris love Naomi as he had told us? Perhaps she was truly his one vulnerability? If so then I had to use it. I had no compunction. Did he care what she thought of him? Assuredly. All his actions toward her were witness of that.

Where was she? If I put my mind to it, surely there was information I could use. She had indicated that she was to the north, but that must include most of England, and all of Scotland. The tulips were out and she had spoken of roses, but with a capital letter. Possibly Rose was a person.

The tulips were long since out in London. Perhaps her climate was noticeably cooler, and the season later.

And it must be country, or a village, she had spoken of widening a road, something impossible in a city where houses would prevent it.

That still left half the nation. I began to see the futility of what I was proposing.

But Holmes had sent this pointless message. He must mean me to read the back, and deduce something! It could only be where Naomi was. Perhaps in his arrogance Harris had allowed him to see even more clearly his regard for his daughter, imagining Holmes could do nothing to turn it to his advantage.

Dolphins. Beautiful, joyous creatures. I had admired their grace and seeming humour in foreign waters many times. We did not see them around our own coasts.

But she had written of seeing them. I strode to the bookshelf and took down a natural-history encyclopedia. My fingers fumbled as I turned the pages and found the reference to dolphins. I skimmed their history and attributes and read eagerly where they might be found. There were two places in Britain: Cardigan Bay in Wales, and the Moray Firth, lying between Inverness-shire and the Black Isle.

Black! Could that be the "Black" in Naomi's letter?

This time it was a detailed atlas that I sought. I examined the Black Isle minutely, not sure what I hoped to find, except somewhere where one might view dolphins. That was absurd! An island had nothing but sea coasts!

But it was not a true island, instead it was a long isthmus with water to the north, south, and east. The north coast faced onto the almost enclosed Cromarty Firth, an unlikely place for such seagoing creatures. The south coast was far more open, and following it round I saw the small town of Rosemarkie. There was my "Rose."

I was in a fever of hope. Now at last I had something to do! A plan was already beginning to form in my mind. It was desperate, but I had nothing else. Harris himself had indicated the weapon—if he had spoken the truth about Naomi, and I now believed he had, because he had invited Holmes to verify it, and every evidence showed that he was indeed devoted to her.

I seized pen and paper and wrote to Harris.

"I have your letter, and the authorisation from Holmes to raise the necessary funds, however, I require to add some of my own in order to reach the amount in the form you wish. Therefore you must allow me greater time. I shall need at least another day, possibly two.

I shall contact you when I have succeeded. Should any harm whatever have befallen Holmes while in your care, you will receive no money whatever, and my eternal enmity. I fancy you will understand this very well.

John Watson"

I felt a certain satisfaction with this. It held an irony that pleased me. I addressed it and posted it immediately, then I packed a small bag sufficient to last me for three days, which was all I had, and set out for Euston Railway Station to take the very next train to Inverness.

It is a long journey, some eleven and a half hours, and I sat impatiently while the countryside streamed past me. We stopped at York, Durham, and Edinburgh. I was desperately impatient to continue, but all the while I attempted to define more clearly in my mind exactly what I should do when I reached Rosemarkie.

We proceeded north, and beyond Stirling moved into the Highlands, and some of the most beautiful country I have ever seen. But even the mountain grandeur and the light on rivers and lochs could not lift my heart or hold my attention this time.

As soon as we reached Inverness I leaped off the train. It was now half past nine in the evening, and quite dark, even this far north where the sun in midwinter barely shines for more than the middle of the day, but in summer sets in a glory across the sky, leaving a rim of fire above the mountains that remains the brief hour or two until dawn.

I contained myself with difficulty, finding lodgings for the night where I was able to enquire about a ferry at sunrise, and some means of transport once I had arrived at North Kessock on the Black Isle. I had already settled upon my story, that I was seeking the daughter of a friend who was in most serious difficulty and my need to find her was urgent. Should any harm come to Holmes, I intended to make that the truth.

I was given every assistance by those most hospitable people. I could not say I slept well, but that was no lack of comfort or warmth, simply my own rising fears for Holmes's safety, and my own ability to affect his release.

I rose early, ate an excellent breakfast of fresh herrings rolled in oatmeal, a delicacy of the area, and toast and Dundee marmalade, then thanking my host, I set out as he directed.

It was mid-morning when I drove my hired pony and trap into the picturesque village of Rosemarkie. It was a beautiful day, sharp and sweet with the peculiarly clear light of the north making all the outlines of crowstep gables and budding trees sharp against the blue sky. I had no time to spare for subtlety. I had to find Naomi straight away. I was considerably hampered by not knowing her married name, but there was no help for that. I stayed with my story. I was seeking a young Englishwoman named Naomi, whose father was in serious trouble of which she was unaware.

I asked first at the local grocery store, and met with a courteous reticence. I met with nothing better at the apothecary or the hardware store. I then decided in a flash of desperation to trade upon my profession. I enquired for the nearest general practitioner, and there, after repeating my tale, I was successful. I blushed to use a colleague in such fashion, but Holmes's life hung in the balance, and nothing would have shamed me into silence.

She lived with her husband a little way inland, at Upper Eathie, and I was given her address willingly. I thanked them and followed their directions.

It was late morning when I finally met Naomi MacAllister. She was a charming, sensitive woman with most beautiful hair, and only a fleeting resemblance to her father in colouring and pattern of speech.

I had already decided to remain with the story, which had served me so well.

"Good morning, Mrs. MacAllister. My name is John Watson, Dr. Watson," I introduced myself. "I have come as speedily as I could from London." I saw her instant look of concern, and I admit I felt a stab of guilt. But there was no alternative, no kinder way to use her, as I intended to.

"Is my father ill?" she asked in a voice already sharp with anxiety.

"He is not ill," I answered. "But he is in most serious trouble . . . which may yet be averted from its worst outcome, if you will give me your assistance."

"Anything!" she almost cut my words off in her eagerness. There was a warmth in her face and a softness about the lips, which can only have come from her mother. I wondered fleetingly what that lady could have been like, and if Robert Harris would have sunk to this appalling depth were she still alive. But the instant passed. There was no time for speculation.

"I am afraid we must return to London," I answered, prepared to offer all manner of safeguards to her reputation, even to her husband accompanying us as a last resort, although his presence must hamper my plan to end this matter without harm to her. Then another idea came to me. "Mr. Sherlock Holmes is involved in the affair, and it is his effort, and mine, to prevent your father from suffering in a dreadful crime that would devastate the whole of his life, if not indeed end it." This was the truth, although hardly in the way I implied. If Holmes were to die at Harris's hand, I would see to it myself that Harris ended his days at the end of a rope.

She was very pale, and put her hand to the door post to steady herself. But she certainly did not lack courage.

"Of course I will come, Dr. Watson. Mr. Holmes's reputation is beyond doubt or question. Even as far north as this, we have heard of him. And of course I visit London to see my father frequently. We must catch the train from Inverness. Please come in. I must make arrangements. Tell me what you need me to do."

"Simply to be there, Mrs. MacAllister. If our plan succeeds, your presence will in itself be sufficient," I answered.

She did not question me further, but set about filling a small valise with the needed toiletries and clean linen in order to accompany me. She informed her neighbour of the necessity for her departure, and wrote a letter for her husband, who was not expected home until the following day, having taken a trip in the course of his business, over the mountains to Ullapool on the West Coast.

We left late in the afternoon, hoping to find seats on the night train to Euston, and were fortunate to do so.

Several times she expressed her concern, and asked me to tell her more of the nature of her father's predicament, and the danger that threatened him, and I was obliged to think very rapidly. I confess I hated lying to her. The longer I was in her company the greater became my regard for her. She was intelligent, generous of spirit, and I believe, in other circumstances, would have had a marked sense of humour. At moments, forgetting our cause, it flashed through in wry observation of others at the railway station as we boarded the train. At one awkward moment she stopped to assist an elderly woman with too much luggage, and a crying child, a very simple act of kindness, and done with such grace it seemed most natural to her.

But it was my growing conclusion of her integrity that most moved me. It was the quality upon which my plan depended, but it wounded me that I was making such use of her.

Fortunately for my feelings, and perhaps my nerve, it was a night train, and therefore most people made some attempt to sleep. I find it difficult, but I kept my eyes closed as if I were deep in slumber, to avoid the necessity of speaking with her again. I fear it was a cowardly thing to do. My excuse is that I also needed time to think.

We arrived at Euston station about eight o'clock in the morning, and immediately disembarked and set about finding a hansom cab to Baker Street. The rooms were strangely empty. I felt the silence, the fresh air without the odour of Holmes's tobacco, like a desolation.

I could no longer put off action. I faced her frankly.

"Mrs. MacAllister, your father is about to embark upon a course of action that will lead him very possibly to physical harm, most certainly to moral destruction. His motives may be good" . . . that was a lie I was prepared to tell for her sake . . . "but the act is not. I believe his love for you is great enough that if you write to him, begging him not to go ahead, then he will desist. I shall write a covering letter, and deliver it where I must. It is dangerous and unpleasant, I cannot require that you accompany me." Though I relied upon her spirit and her devotion to her father that she would.

I was not mistaken.

"I most certainly will come with you, Dr. Watson." Honest to the last, she made no claim to be unafraid.

"Thank you," I said with total sincerity.

I sent a message to Harris at his home that I had the full value he had requested, and would meet him in front of the Duck and Dragon, but would pass it to him only if he had Holmes with him, alive and well. Then I awaited his answer.

It came by return, with the same messenger. He was willing. I could almost feel his eagerness in the scrawl upon the paper.

Accordingly, Naomi and I set out before midnight in the damp and blustery weather and rode in tense silence. There was no sound but the rattle of the wheels over the cobbles and the clatter of the horses' hooves as we moved from the dim circle of one gas lamp to the next through ever narrower and grimier streets.

Naomi was worried, I saw the fear in her face as we passed through each patch of light, her eyes straining forward, lips pressed together. How could she have felt anything else? She was in the dreariest of places with a man she knew only by repute, and her father was in the utmost danger. How I admired her courage, and my rage was almost beyond control that all her love was for someone as unworthy as Harris. I found myself caring profoundly, not merely that I should rescue Holmes sound and well, but that I should be able to force Harris to a more honourable path.

At last we reached the Duck and Dragon, and I confess, my heart was in my mouth as I assisted her out, and paid the driver. I asked him to wait, but I had little confidence that he would do so.

It was a most gloomy and sinister place, even though it had stopped raining and the wind was not cold. Everything about us seemed to drip and creak as if the entire street were subsiding upon itself. The smell of rotting timber and stale beer filled the air and the occasional shout or cry seemed less than human.

I took her by the arm. "Come," I said with a cheer I did not feel. "It is only a few steps, and we are in excellent time." I held her firmly in case she should see her father and run to him. I would use her as bargain if I had to.

The seconds ticked by. I searched the shadows for a sign of Harris, or of Holmes. Suddenly I was desperately afraid Harris would think me a man of too much honour or kindness to use his daughter in this way. What if he were certain I would never harm her, and he did not come?

Then I steadied myself. Harming her had never been my intent. My weapon against him was to allow her to know exactly what manner of man he was. And I still had his ransom note, written in his hand. I would show it to her, and explain it all, if I must.

I led her farther toward the faint light of the one lamp above the door to the public house, so if Harris were somewhere in the shadows, he would see her.

It worked. A huge, dim figure detached itself and moved forward. I felt Naomi stiffen in terror, then relax as she recognised something in the outline of him.

Still I held her so hard she winced.

"Where is Holmes?" I asked grimly.

Harris stopped. He seemed to be taking the measure of me, perhaps judging how much I was capable of, and willing to do, or even if I had already damaged his daughter's opinion of him beyond redeeming.

Then I knew what I should say.

"Have you managed to save Holmes?" I asked, my voice as clear and steady as I could make it.

He hesitated only a moment before he surrendered.

"Yes," the single word grated with all the anger and frustration he dared not reveal.

"Show me," I demanded.

He made a sharp gesture with one arm.

Holmes stepped forward. I was horrified by the appearance of him: His clothes were torn and stained with mud and there were bruises and dried blood on his face. He had certainly given his captor a fight, but he was doubtlessly taken by surprise, and far outweighed.

My heart soared at the sight of him. I felt like laughing with sheer relief. But we were not yet entirely free.

"Good!" I said breathlessly. "Then we may take our leave, and our mission is complete. As you had said, Mr. Harris, your daughter is a woman of both courage and honour, and you are rightly proud of her. It has been my pleasure to make her acquaintance." I wished him to know I had told her nothing ill of him, he still had everything to gain by allowing us to leave in peace.

He understood me. I saw in that ill light the anger in his face, and a kind of relief as well, as if defeat were not all bitter.

Then Holmes walked toward me, and I let go of Naomi's arm and she went to her father.

"Well done, Watson," Holmes said softly as he reached me. "I have never wished more to go home."

"It was nothing," I said airily. "Just a little exercise in logical deduction, and an understanding of values. When one cares, one has a hostage to fortune, whoever one is."

"Indeed," he murmured. "But you did it well."

The Adventure of the Missing Countess

JON KOONS

BEST KNOWN AS a performer, Jon Koons (1962–) has also written in various genres, including nonfiction, arts criticism, and short stories. He is the author of the highly successful children's books *A Confused Hanukkah: An Original Story of Chelm* (2004), illustrated by S. D. Schindler, and *Arthur and Guen: An Original Tale of Young Camelot* (2008), illustrated by Igor Oleynikov.

Koons is an exceptionally versatile entertainer, having first been on stage at the age of nine, subsequently becoming a singer and actor on Broadway and Off-Broadway, and in summer and regional theater productions, feature films, television programs, and commercials. He has become accomplished in magic, ventriloquism, stilt-walking, fire-eating, juggling, mime, and just about anything that can be performed on stage or screen or at private events. He has performed everywhere from New York to Hollywood to Kenya.

In addition to his career as an entertainer, he has worked as a producer, director, and stage manager for opera, theater, and film companies, and is a leading teacher of theatrical, circus, and performing arts. It is his background with circuses and circus performers that inspired his story about Holmes and the fascinating world that lies beneath the Big Top.

"The Adventure of the Missing Countess" was originally published in *The Game Is Afoot*, edited by Marvin Kaye (New York, St. Martin's Press, 1994).

THE ADVENTURE OF
THE MISSING COUNTESS

Jon Koons

IT WAS A glorious spring day in the year 1889. The air was still brisk, but surprisingly fresh for the city, and the walks and lanes down which I trod were lined with fragrant and colorful rosebay willow and London Pride.

I awoke this morning fully with the intent of escorting my lovely wife, Mary, at her request, to the travelling circus that had made nearby Tunbridge Wells its temporary home, but those plans were laid aside, much to my wife's dismay, by an urgent communication from my friend and associate, Sherlock Holmes. As I walked the accustomed route to 221B Baker Street, I reflected on some of Holmes's past adventures which started out in this exact same manner. Upon arriving at my destination, Holmes greeted me warmly.

"Ah, Watson, so good of you to come."

"Come, Holmes," I replied, "I have rarely declined an opportunity to accompany you on one of your cases."

"Quite so, but since Mary Morstan made an honest man of you, your availability has been somewhat more limited."

"One of the small disadvantages of married life, I'm afraid."

"A small disadvantage to be sure. Married life agrees with you, old boy."

"Not that I disagree, mind you, but what leads you to that conclusion, Holmes?"

"Elementary, my friend. You have, of late, been more ebullient than ever. Your apparel has been more carefully coordinated, the obvious influence of a woman's keen eye for fashion, and is

better tended to, save for the small stain there on your vest . . . kippers, I would say . . . which indicates that you are being well fed. The fact that your ample stature has become even more so by eight or ten pounds would tend to support this conclusion. You are more precisely groomed, your shoes are finely polished and you appear more rested and less tense, an obvious benefit of the sort of companionship that you formerly lacked. Your occasional discourse regarding your wife is always favorable, and the very fact that you have been less available to join me lately clearly indicates that you are enjoying your current situation and reaping the benefits."

"Holmes, you never cease to amaze me."

"Nor I myself, old boy."

"So, what are we on to today?"

"Come, Watson. I'll tell you all I know in the cab."

In the carriage, Holmes explained what he knew of the case.

"Do you know the name Countess Virginia Thorgood Willoughby?"

"As a matter of fact I do. I read an account of the Countess Willoughby recently in the society pages of the *Strand Magazine*. If memory serves, she's a widow who lives alone with her seventeen-year-old daughter. She lost her husband during a visit to America last year, although the particulars of the event elude me."

"Very good, Watson. What else do you recall?"

"She returned with her daughter to London six months ago to leave the incident behind and raise her daughter with a sense of proper British morality, something which, according to the article, the Countess found lacking in America."

"Precisely. She did not wish her young, impressionable daughter, Alexandra, to succumb to the improper influences that she said the Americans seemed to thrive on. Apparently she was a bit too late, as her daughter was already enamored of American ways and was, by all accounts, unhappy with the sudden move back to England. She caused her mother a good deal of embarrassment by making her feelings known at every opportunity, not least of all in public."

"But what does this have to do with us?"

"It seems, Watson old man, that upon arriving home from the opera late last night, Countess Willoughby found her home a shambles and her daughter missing. She has not been seen since approximately five hours before the discovery of the transgression, which is why our destination is their Kensington residence. The Countess immediately sent word to Scotland Yard, which investigated with its usual fervor but aside from finding a concise ransom note, is unable to fathom the meaning of any of the available clues. As has happened more than once, as well you know, Inspector Lestrade sent for my aid, which he will gladly employ and thereafter forget to acknowledge. But no matter, my dear Watson. I have been hungry for a new mystery to occupy my time. I was, of course, dismayed to be called so long after the crime had been discovered, but Lestrade assures me that the scene, and any evidence which might be present, will be left undisturbed until our arrival. So now you know as much as I about this case, save that we are presently going to meet the Countess in the company of her legal advisor and recent social companion, Kent Osgood, whose role in these proceedings has yet to be determined."

"Surely, Holmes, this is a simple case of kidnapping, not worthy of your extraordinary talents."

"Perhaps, Watson," Holmes replied. "Perhaps."

Holmes then fell silent and gazed out the window, his fingers pressed together in a steepled attitude, as was his custom during moments of deep thought. As I looked upon my friend, bedecked in his customary deerstalker cap, cape-backed overcoat and pipe, all of which had become, I daresay largely due to my accounts of his adventures, his trademarks, I pondered my own good fortune not only to be in the presence of greatness, but to be his personal friend and longtime companion as well.

We arrived at the address in Kensington shortly afterwards and were ushered into the house with all due haste by a maid who appeared utterly distraught. She took us directly to the sitting room where Inspector Lestrade, the Countess, and Mr. Osgood were waiting. At once we could see the disarray caused by the perpetrators. Furniture had been knocked askew or overturned. Drawers were opened and rummaged through, and all manner of things were strewn about the room.

"Mr. Holmes," cried the Countess, "I am at my wits' end. You are the only man in all of London who can save my little girl. Please say that you will help me."

"I shall do what I can, madame. Please try to calm yourself so that you may answer some questions for me."

"I will do my best," said the Countess as she grasped the hand of her companion. After some brief introductions, Holmes began his questioning.

"Countess Willoughby, I am told you discovered your daughter missing when you returned from the opera last night . . ."

"Yes, Mr. Holmes, that is so. I blame myself. Had I not been out of the house last night for so frivolous a reason perhaps my little girl would still be here with me now . . ." She began to weep, and Mr. Osgood embraced her.

"Now we've been all through that, Virginia. You are not to blame," said Osgood in a comforting tone.

"Mr. Osgood is quite right. You cannot be

held accountable for actions about which you had no prior knowledge. If I may continue? Is it your custom to frequent the opera, or was last evening a special event?"

"If I may, Mr. Holmes," Osgood interjected. "Since Virginia and I have been keeping company these last several months we have made it a weekly ritual to visit the opera, or perhaps a concert. We generally do so on a Friday evening, but this past Friday Virginia was feeling a bit under the weather, so we postponed our weekly entertainment until last night, Tuesday."

"Was anyone else aware of this change of plans?"

"Not to my knowledge. It was the maid's day off. We had invited Alexandra, as we usually do, but she unfortunately declined, as she usually does."

"And at exactly what time did you leave the premises?"

"The opera we saw was *The Magic Flute*, at Royal Albert Hall. It was to begin at eight o'clock. As you are no doubt aware, Albert Hall is not far, so we left here at a quarter past seven, I would say."

"And you returned . . . ?"

"They returned," piped Lestrade, obviously feeling left out, "at exactly seventeen past midnight, according to my report."

"Thank you, Inspector. Your assistance, as always, has been invaluable. Now if you will permit me to inspect the premises, I shall see what clues I can unearth. If you please, Watson."

As we began to scrutinize the room, Inspector Lestrade commented on the lack of available clues, save a knife thrust through a photograph of Alexandra hanging over the mantel. Holmes nodded. I followed my friend to and fro, carefully noting every item that he examined.

I spotted something unusual on the floor near the entrance.

"What do you make of this, Holmes?" I called out. He joined me at the door, stooped down on his knees and pulled his glass from his pocket.

"Good show, Watson. Sawdust!"

"Sawdust? Then perhaps we are looking for someone in the construction trade. Or perhaps woodworking."

"Perhaps, Watson. Come look at this photograph. Young Miss Willoughby is quite an attractive lass, is she not?" She was indeed, I agreed. The hand-tinted photograph showed her long golden hair and lovely, delicate features.

Holmes pulled the knife from the photograph and handed it to me. "What can you tell me about this knife?"

"Well . . ." I studied the knife carefully but could not see what he was getting at. "The handle is worn more on the left side than the right, so . . . our suspect is left-handed?"

"Excellent. Please continue."

"The blade is very dull, which means that it is used by someone who is either neglectful of its poor condition or else who does not require a sharp edge."

"Bravo, Watson. Very astute. There is more, but time is fleeting. Inspector," Holmes said, turning to Lestrade, "I would like to see the ransom note, then I want to inspect the girl's bed chamber."

"Here's the note. No point looking into the bedroom."

"Quite," was all Holmes said. He glanced briefly at the note and then handed it to me. "Please read this aloud, Watson."

"If you ever want to see Alexandra alive again, deliver a sum of one thousand British pounds to the Charing Cross train station on April 29th at noon. Put it in a small bag and leave it at the signal flag at track 9. Go to ticket window five afterwards and Alexandra will be waiting. Come alone. If we see police, I will kill her." As I finished reading, the Countess once again burst into tears.

Holmes asked the maid to direct him to the girl's bedroom, and went off directly, only to return a few moments later.

"I told you it was pointless, Holmes." Inspector Lestrade looked at me with a smug look.

"I have seen all I need to," Holmes replied simply. "I shall contact Watson three days hence and he shall relay my instructions. In the meantime, feel free to tidy up the damage and go about your business. Countess, your daughter is safe, so you needn't fear. Three days, then!" And with that he nodded to the group and was out the door. Both Lestrade and the Countess were obviously bewildered, and looked to me for clarification, which I could not provide.

I quickly followed. "No time to explain, Watson," Holmes stated, as he hailed a cab. "Be at Baker Street in three days." As he climbed into the cab, he turned and said, "And bring your lovely wife Mary with you."

"Holmes . . . ?"

"Time is short, Watson. I've clues and motives to juggle." The cab started off.

Puzzled by Holmes's behavior, I took advantage of my proximity to Kensington Gardens, and strolled through the park pondering the events of the day. Could Holmes have pieced together the clues and unravelled the mystery so quickly? I had, of course, witnessed his uncanny abilities on numerous occasions before, but it seemed he reached some conclusion in an impossibly brief amount of time. Why did he leave so abruptly? What purpose would his three day absence serve? And to what end was my wife's presence requested? Think as I might, I could not decipher his reasoning. Winded from my exertions, I sat upon the steps of the Albert Memorial and watched two badgers frolic through some oxeye daisies, Mary's favorite flower. I knew only one thing for certain. Holmes had been right. I was putting on weight.

Three days later my wife and I arrived at Baker Street. It had been some little time since Mary had been there, but she remembered it well and felt quite comfortable, although no less curious than I about the circumstances. Shortly after our arrival, Mrs. Hudson, the landlady, handed me a wire from Holmes. It instructed me, and Mary, to meet him, at, of all places, R. J. Toby Colossal Travelling Circus in Tunbridge Wells. He entreated us to enjoy the three o'clock show, and then wait afterwards at the Torture King tent on

the midway where he would meet us. Mary was delighted to be included in Holmes's adventure, but even more now that it appeared she would get to see the circus after all. We departed immediately for Tunbridge Wells.

The festival was a splendid sight to behold. A great tent, striped in bright red and blue, was the centerpiece to a dizzying display of color and movement. Wonderful carriages, arranged in a half circle, resplendent in their brilliant reds and whites, were trimmed out with yellows and greens and gaudy rococo gold leaf. Some of the carriages bore cages which held magnificent beasts of all types, while others displayed performers' names and promises of wonders to come. While looking closely at a caged lion I discovered, curiously enough, that my inclination to sneeze while in the presence of common house cats was also very much a reality in the presence of these larger rather less amiable cats, a fact which did not please me but apparently amused my wife no end. A carousel hosting painted horses and carriages turned round and round for the amusement of the children, and the sound of calliope music filled the air. Aromas of all types, some pleasant and some not so, assaulted the nose. The midway was quite a sight, sporting tall impressively illustrated banners describing the likes of such oddities as the Incredible Bearded Woman, the Tantalizing Egyptian Snake Charmer, the Amazing Dog-Faced Boy, and the Death-Defying Torture King. I noted the location of the latter's tent for future reference.

In our wanderings I saw no sign of Holmes. Having strolled the grounds of the circus, and after having partaken, at Mary's behest, of some sort of gooey confection made from nuts, bits of dried fruit, chocolate and caramel, much of which I was still trying unobtrusively to pry from my teeth, we headed for the main tent, as it was nearly three. While purchasing our tickets we were met by Countess Willoughby, Mr. Osgood, and Inspector Lestrade. I introduced my wife to the gathering, and we took seats near the large wooden ring which served as the stage area. The ring was floored with a generous amount of sawdust, and much to my dismay, I began to sneeze once again.

"Mr. Watson . . ." began the Countess.

"Doctor, Countess," I corrected her.

"Forgive me. Dr. Watson, I do not understand what we are doing here. Perhaps you can shed some light?"

"I should be delighted to, but I am as much in the dark as you. Sherlock Holmes is the most knowledgeable person I know, but I must confess that I still do not entirely understand all of his methodology. If it is any comfort to you, from what I know of my friend, you shall have your answers, and most likely your daughter, before the day is up."

Lestrade complained, "No good will come of building this lady's hopes up. Scotland Yard has been investigating this case for three days as well, and we have drawn no conclusions. Holmes is good, I'll grant you, but I dare say he's not so good as to deliver this lady's daughter on a silver platter!"

Mr. Osgood agreed. "Yes, Dr. Watson. Suppose you are wrong. I should think that instilling false hope is something you would wish to avoid."

"Mr. Osgood, Inspector Lestrade," said my wife, "I was once a client of Sherlock Holmes. I am confident that he will solve this mystery and return your daughter to you. If anyone can, he can."

"Thank you, my dear," replied the Countess. "You are very kind."

At that moment, the crowd fell silent. The circus was about to begin. Mary took my hand and we settled down to enjoy the show. Neither of us had been to the circus since we were children.

The ringmaster, in his jodhpurs, red frock coat, and top hat, introduced the acts each and all, and the band played merrily as the performers took their places in the large circular stage area. A lovely young lady led six stallions of varied colors around the ring, and demonstrated her mastery of horsemanship. The tent fairly vibrated with applause. Next, a colorful clown on stilts juggled three lit torches. He tried to blow them out, one by one, but every time he transferred them from hand to hand they relit, one by one, much to Mary's delight. Finally dousing the flames, he walked across the ring, but seemingly unaware of the tightrope which blocked his passage, became entangled in it. His stilts shot out from under him, leaving him dangling from the rope. After many precarious antics he gained the top of the rope and proceeded to walk its length to a small platform. He bowed to the thunderous applause of the crowd, and in doing so fell to the net below, and then ran off. Next came the elephants, followed by some acrobats and then it was again time for the clowns, this time several of them dressed in the costume of a fire brigade. The "fire clowns" ran circles around one another in an attempt to "save" a burning building, bumping into each other, falling down, dusting off, and falling down again. One clown jumped into the crowd, tweaked Mary's nose, pulled my moustache and bolted back into the ring. Mary told me that the clown was very familiar somehow, but I explained that he had been the same stilt-walking clown from earlier in the show. After the clowns had failed to "save" the building, they rapidly retreated from the tent, as the crowd roared with laughter. Several foreign chaps and scantily clad young ladies flew through the air on trapeze, after which a young man, about twentyish, I would say, led a teenaged boy to a door-sized wooden wall and fastened him to it by the arms and legs. The man then stepped back and displayed a set of dangerous looking knives, which he proceeded to throw directly at the boy. Mary held my hand as I caught my breath, and the crowd was silent with fear. He hurled the knives one by one, impaling them in the wooden wall, each time narrowly missing the boy. Only when the boy was completely surrounded by knives was he released and able to take his bows with the young man. Several additional acts followed, including trained dogs, more clown antics, a dancing Russian bear, and an additional display of acrobatics. At the end of the show, Mary and I, along with Countess Willoughby, Mr. Osgood, and Inspector Lestrade, headed for the Torture King tent, which I took note of previously.

"How did you enjoy the show?" Mary asked the group as a whole.

"Very amusing," the Countess answered, although it was obvious she was distracted by other concerns. Osgood agreed.

"Well, since you asked," Lestrade said unpleasantly, "I think it was rubbish. All just stuff and nonsense."

We stood silently as a group in front of the designated meeting area, awaiting Holmes's arrival. Numerous patrons, and even many of the performers on their way to the changing tent, passed by, but there was as yet no sign of Holmes. One clown, the featured performer throughout the show, stopped before us to further display his antics. He pulled three colored balls from a pocket and juggled them in a number of different patterns before tossing them high into the air and allowing them to fall directly on his head. His body crunched lower to the ground as each ball hit until he was flat on his back. Mary, Osgood and I applauded. The Countess then turned to me and said, "Dr. Watson. While this is all quite amusing, I am finding it hard to keep my spirits light in the face of our purpose here."

"Quite right," added Osgood, "where is this Sherlock Holmes of yours?"

Just then the clown jumped up and onto his hands, where he stood momentarily. "I seem to have turned myself around. You all look so tall. But if I keep this up I'll lose my head." He righted himself, then placed a pipe between his teeth, from where he retrieved it I could not say,

and then blew into the stem, causing a great cloud of ash to erupt into the air. "I say, would you have some tobacco that I can borrow? My pipe has gone empty."

"Well, no actually, I do not," I said.

"Just as well," said the clown, "it would probably smell like an old Persian slipper, anyway."

"As a matter of fact . . . wait a moment. How could you know that?"

"Elementary, my dear Watson."

"Holmes!?"

"Holmes? Sherlock Holmes?" The startled Countess asked.

"What's all this then, Holmes?" Lestrade said.

"Excuse me, but I seem to be a bit confused . . ." Osgood said.

"All your questions will be answered. Please follow me." Holmes started off in the direction of the dressing tent and our party obligingly followed. "Sorry to have taken you all by surprise like this, but it was necessary," he explained. "My theatrical inclinations have been a long time without expression. It was good to utilize my talents once again." He stopped outside the tent, and proceeded with his explanation. "While at your home, Countess, I found several clues which led me here. The sawdust on your floor was fouled with soil and animal refuse. Had it been tracked in from a carpentry shoppe or similar establishment it would have been purer." He removed his red rubber nose and yarn fringed bald pate wig. "The knife that impaled your daughter's photograph was not thrust in, but thrown from across the room, as indicated by the angle at which it hit. Furthermore, the knife is a specially balanced one, edged for use in a knife throwing act. The shattered glass from the frame was spread in a pattern that suggested an impact of great force. Had the knife been thrust into the photograph manually, the pattern would have been less remarkable. Finally I detected a faint odor of greasepaint in the room. Someone connected with this circus, the only one within reasonable distance, seemed the logical choice."

"Astounding," I said.

"Simple deductive reasoning, Watson. The culprit, obviously an amateur, overturned and disturbed both furniture and belongings in an effort to simulate a robbery, or perhaps a struggle, but the ruse was unconvincing. Had he sought to rob the house, valuables would have been missing, and furniture left undisturbed. If the purpose of the break-in was a kidnapping, belongings would not have been touched, and had there been an actual struggle, I find it unlikely that large, heavy pieces of furniture would have been overturned while trying to apprehend a small, seventeen year old girl."

"Mr. Holmes," the Countess interposed, "you said at my house that my daughter is safe. How can you be so sure? And where is she?"

"She is here, madame. You have seen her. You all have."

"Here," objected Lestrade. "What do you mean?"

"You'll see soon enough. Please accompany me into the tent."

Once inside, we found ourselves in the company of several performers in varying stages of undress, many in the process of removing make-up. Holmes walked to the center of the room and spoke aloud. "Pardon me, but my friends have joined me so that we may solve a crime." He looked around the room, and his gaze fell upon the young man who had performed the knife throwing act, who suddenly appeared nervous, and began edging his way towards the exit. Holmes nodded to a burly toff, the Man of Steel, from the show, who blocked the young man's passage and said, "Aye wouldn' go nowheres if aye was you," and so he gave up the attempt.

"Now, young Master Errol Smithy, or should I use your real name, Chuck Hanson? I shall make a series of statements, and you will answer yes or no depending on the accuracy. You are personally acquainted with Countess Willoughby's daughter, Alexandra, are you not?"

"Well, I . . . We kind of . . ." Hanson stam-mered and looked around the room for help, but none was forthcoming.

"Yes or no, Mr. Hanson?"

"Yes."

"You are in love with Alexandra, and have been since you met her in America last year."

"Hey, how could you know that?"

"That qualifies as a yes, wouldn't you say, Watson?"

"Indubitably, Holmes."

"You have, in fact, been lovers, and plotted this kidnapping ruse so that you could be married." Countess Willoughby gasped. Osgood helped her to a seat.

"Look, we knew her mother would never approve of us. I'm just a circus brat from the poor side of the tracks. We planned to get hitched back home, in New Jersey, but when they moved back to England, I had to find a way to be with her. I sold all of my belongings, except my knives, and used all of my savings to book cheap passage to England and then got the job with the circus here. I contacted her as soon as I could and we planned the whole thing."

"Logically, your lack of money would present a problem, and hence the reason for the kidnapping ruse."

"At first we were just going to run off and elope, but I thought of the kidnapping scheme to get some money to make our start in life a little easier. Don't blame Alex. It's all my fault. I just love her so." He flopped down into the nearest chair and laid his head in his hands.

Holmes asked Lestrade for the ransom note. The inspector handed it to him. "This was the most incriminating piece of evidence in unravelling the puzzle. Attend. 'If you ever want to see Alexandra alive again, deliver a sum of one thousand British pounds to the Charing Cross train station on April 29th at noon.' The note refers to 'Alexandra,' a familiar use of the name, indicating personal acquaintance. Secondly, the reference to 'British pounds' suggested to me that the 'kidnapper' was someone who thinks in terms of a different monetary system. American dollars are unique and standard across that country, whereas the European designation of 'pound notes' as currency are issued by any of several countries. Local residents would not specify the country of origin. Only an American in a foreign country would make such a distinction. Next point," Holmes continued, "the use of 'train station' rather than 'railway station' is American, as is the note's poor grammatical style in general. There are numerous other clues, but they are of no great moment." He handed the note back to Lestrade. "I left the home of the Countess and came immediately to this circus, where I was hired temporarily as a new performer. Over the past three days I have had the opportunity to discover, at leisure, all of the additional information that I required from the company of performers and from young Chuck himself. He is twenty-one years old, from Hackensack, New Jersey, in America, and as you may have observed during his act, is left-handed.

"When the circus arrived in Tunbridge Wells, the closest stop to London on the touring schedule, he and Alexandra waited for an opportunity to carry out their plan. The only time the Countess left the house with any regularity was on Friday, but the circus had late performances those nights. When the Countess rescheduled her outing, it was exactly the turn of luck that they had hoped for. Tuesday is the only day on which the circus has no performances. It was a very fortunate happenstance indeed that the supposed abduction could be carried out without his absence from the circus being noticed."

"All right, Holmes." Lestrade interrupted, a little too loudly. "You've told us how you found him out, and that he had means and motive, but aside from what he says, what evidence do you have that the girl was involved of her own free will?"

"Inspector, your investigation of the Willoughby premises was incomplete. When I investigated Miss Alexandra's bed chamber, I took particular note of the items on, or rather the items missing from, her vanity and wardrobe.

Nothing was disturbed to suggest a theft, but small gaps with empty hangers in the wardrobe indicated the removal of a few select pieces of necessary apparel. And no young lady of proper breeding would feel complete without her brush and hand mirror, which were conspicuously missing from the vanity. In addition, only Alexandra knew the exact time that her mother and the maid would be away from the house, and for precisely how long."

"Mr. Holmes, please. My daughter would never do such a thing!"

"I quite agree, Holmes," Osgood added. "Your conjectures are bordering on slanderous. I suggest you prove your theory immediately, if you can, otherwise I shall be forced to advise Countess Willoughby to file suit against you on behalf of her daughter."

"Kent, please!" the Countess chided. "I have no interest in proof or legal suits. I only want my daughter back. Mr. Holmes, you have brought us all the way here to listen to your brilliant deductions, but where is my daughter?"

"Walking through that very tent flap at any moment," Holmes stated calmly. As if on cue, the tent flap pulled back and a lone figure entered the tent.

"Ha!" Lestrade scoffed. "It's just the boy from the knife act." The boy had entered, seeing a crowd of curious faces intently staring at him, and stopped frozen in his tracks. His face went ashen. Tears started to well up in his eyes.

"ALEXANDRA!" The Countess was beside herself.

"Hi, Mummy," the girl said sheepishly through her tears.

"Alexandra, indeed!" Holmes said triumphantly. "Hair dyed black and cut in the style of a young lad, dressed as a young lad, but Alexandra, nonetheless. Her boyish figure made it a convincing disguise. I learned her habit to change costume out of sight of the others, but she always returns to the tent so as not to draw attention to her absence."

The Countess embraced her daughter.

"But why, Alexandra? Why?"

"Because I love him, Mother."

"Well now," Lestrade coughed, embarrassed, "seems like Mr. Holmes has done a right good piece of reasoning, after all. But it's all in the hands of the law now. I assume, Countess, that you would like to press charges against this young scalawag?"

"No, Inspector, I would not."

"Virginia, really! As your legal advisor I must advise you to . . ."

"Do be quiet, Kent."

"Mother . . . ?"

"I think we must all sit down and have a long chat," said the Countess. "If you love this boy so much that you staged this elaborate deception, and if he left behind his life in America to follow you here, well . . . we shall all discuss it at length when we get home."

"Oh, Mother," said the girl as she heartily embraced her dam. They walked out of the tent, followed by Hanson and Osgood, who, still cowed, nodded to us with a shrug before departing. Lestrade looked as if about to say something, but simply turned and left.

After the others departed, Sherlock Holmes took a seat and immediately began rubbing some sort of white cream on his face to remove the remains of his clown make-up. He spoke as he cleansed.

"Mrs. Watson, so good of you to come."

"Likewise, Mr. Holmes. But why did you ask me to accompany my husband?"

"Watson mentioned your desire to see the circus, which I so rudely interrupted. Besides, I wanted to see what it was that has been making my old friend appear so happy lately."

"Why, thank you, Mr. Holmes."

"Think nothing of it, madame. Now then, you two must stay on with me for the next show."

"What on earth for?"

"I would like to see it rather than be a part of it just once . . ."

"By the way, Holmes," I asked, "how did you learn the juggling and stilt-walking and such?"

"Simply a matter of balance, coordination, and concentration, if one is physically fit. As a young lad I was always fascinated with clowns, so I learned the basics of the craft, thinking I might one day become a circus performer. It seems I've managed to do just that. I was able to learn the intricacies of the skills once I arrived. The routines themselves haven't changed much since I saw the circus as a boy, so I was familiar with them already. So, what do you say? Will you see the next show with me?"

"Mary and I would be delighted to spend an entertaining evening with my closest friend and companion. Can you, by any chance, deduce who that might be, Mr. Sherlock Holmes?"

"I haven't a clue, Watson. I haven't a clue."

The Adventure of Zolnay, the Aerialist

RICK BOYER

THE FIRST NOVEL by Richard Lewis Boyer (1943–) was *The Giant Rat of Sumatra* (1976), a Sherlock Holmes pastiche, because, the author claimed, he wanted to learn from the best. He then went on to write a series about Charlie "Doc" Adams, an oral surgeon with a practice in New England.

Boyer is a native of Evanston, Illinois. He majored in English at Denison University and earned an MFA in Creative Writing at the University of Iowa, studying under renowned science fiction writer Kurt Vonnegut. Boyer worked as a sales representative for the publisher Little, Brown, has been a high school teacher, and taught English at Western Carolina University.

The first "Doc" Adams mystery was *Billingsgate Shoal* (1982), for which he won an Edgar for the best novel of the year. Adams is an unexciting figure, an ordinary man to whom people bring their problems, with which he tries to help. In an interview, Boyer stated that "Adams is me in more extraordinary circumstances. . . . I was pretending to be somebody else. . . . I tried to combine the unexceptional guy, basically a suburbanite, who runs into extraordinary circumstances."

In addition to nine "Doc" Adams novels, Boyer has written the bizarre *Mzungu Mjina: Swahili for "Crazy White Man"* (2004) and *Buck Gentry* (2005). *The Giant Rat of Sumatra* was reissued in *A Sherlockian Quartet* (1998), to which he added three new short stories.

"The Adventure of Zolnay, the Aerialist" was originally published in *A Sherlockian Quartet* (Alexander, North Carolina, Alexander Books, 1998).

THE ADVENTURE OF ZOLNAY, THE AERIALIST

Rick Boyer

"WHOEVER OUR MYSTERIOUS visitor is, he is certainly an impressive physical specimen," observed Sherlock Holmes as he doffed his overcoat.

"Whatever do you mean?" I asked. It was a blustery spring afternoon in mid May. Holmes and I had just returned from a brisk walk in Regent's Park; our cheeks were flushed from the fresh air. His comment had taken me entirely off guard.

"Come now, Watson, don't you see that new pair of gloves he left behind on the sofa cushion? Here they are, now let me show you something . . ."

So saying, he took the right one and plunged his hand into it in a twinkling. Then he clenched and unclenched his fist inside the garment, twirling his thin fingers about.

"Loose fit, eh? *Quite*, I'd say. But my hands are extraordinarily thin. So let's try one of yours. There, try it on for size."

I did as instructed, and was amazed to discover how easily my hand slid in. Once inside, there was still half an inch of finger room left.

"Hmmmm! Amazing, Watson. You are a perfect mesomorph in the prime of life, yet you now resemble a child trying on his father's glove, correct?"

"Yes, it certainly is large. The man must be a giant."

"Let's see what else he is. Grab the mate, will you, and bring them over to the window—let us see what these mis-laid items will reveal about the man who came calling while we were away."

He examined them for some time, checking the label sewn inside, and finally turned them both inside out. Upon seeing faint red blotches along the upper extremity of the palm of the right glove, a cry of satisfaction broke from his lips.

"Hah! You see that, Watson? Surely these stains tell us quite a bit about our absent friend."

"Is it blood? I don't see how—"

"Let us start at the beginning. First, as you can see, the gloves are new—probably not more than a few days old. I can tell by the odour and texture of the flannel that they have not been cleaned, for the sizing is still present. But they show no signs of dirt: therefore they are quite new. There is, however, a trace of wax along the index finger of the left glove, so we can assume our man wears a moustache. Observe also the label: E.J. Stanhope, Ltd. It's one of Bond Street's most exclusive shops—far too posh for the likes of us, eh? Therefore the man is rich, or well off anyway. It is here that a curious anomaly emerges . . ."

"What anomaly? So far all your observations make sense, Holmes; it appears you're putting together quite a portrait of the fellow."

"The quirk is this: he is well-off financially and well-dressed, yet he is *not* a gentleman. In fact, it appears he makes his living by performing physical feats of the most prodigious sort . . ."

"A labourer?"

"No. Remember he is wealthy, or relatively so. I draw your attention once more to the faint bloodstains on the inside of the right glove. Obviously they are the result of extreme trauma to the palm of the hand just below the fingers. You know that this is the spot on the hand most subject to abrasion or callouses—"

"Which again would suggest the man is a labourer who swings a hammer or plies a shovel."

"Let's not be too hasty. Would a workingman earn the money to buy gloves like these? Certainly not. Furthermore, as I showed in the case of the apprentice Smythe, a workingman's hand soon becomes coated with callouses that are thick and shiny, and very hard. Yet these bloodstains show us that the skin has been ripped off by extreme trauma, a force so great as to destroy even hardened callouses. What sort of activity would cause this kind of terrific strain to the hand? And while you're pondering that question, let us consider another possibility: that the man does not ordinarily wear gloves—at least not dress gloves of fine grey flannel like these."

"How do you know this?"

"I do not know it, I *infer* it as a probability. First, he left the gloves behind. Now he could be extremely agitated, yet a gentleman who is in the habit of wearing dress gloves regularly would not forget them, and this fellow has. Also, the fact that they are new is suggestive. Perhaps he has bought these fine gloves for a special occasion, or as a result . . ."

He pondered the facts and possibilities before him for a few minutes, then fetched the morning's newspapers and retired to the sofa with a pipe. I had settled myself comfortably with a cigar and the most recent issue of *Lancet*, when there came a series of heavy bounds upon the staircase, followed by a robust knocking upon our door. Holmes, putting aside the paper with a gleam in his eye, rose and went to the door. But before he opened it, he turned to me and proclaimed in a loud voice: "Ah, Watson, I see *Mr. Gregor Zolnay* has returned. Come in, Mr. Zolnay, and welcome!"

With this he threw open the door, and revealed a personage with the most awesome physique I have ever seen. He was a full head taller than either of us, with broad shoulders, a piercing face set off by green eyes and a giant brown moustache. All in all, his appearance was striking in the extreme; he seemed to exude strength and vitality. And when he spoke, it was with a booming baritone voice, modulated somewhat by halting speech and a thick accent.

"Mr. Holmes, yes?" he enquired, stepping into the parlour and extending a huge hand wrapped in bandages.

"Yes, Mr. Zolnay, and this is my friend Dr. John Watson. Tell me, what brings you back from the circus grounds so soon?"

Our visitor was so stunned he nearly reeled into my armchair with amazement. I must confess that, accustomed as I was to Holmes's feats of observation and deduction, my wonder almost equalled that of our caller.

"Mr. Holmes, you are *mizand*, eh . . . eh . . ."

"A sorcerer?"

"Yes! You are magic, Mr. Holmes! You have been to the Chipperfield's? No? Then how do you know me? I leave no card; I speak with no one! Gregor Zolnay comes and goes, and *pfffffi*! Sherlock Holmes knows who I am even before he sees me—*mizand*!"

"Come now, my dear sir, it wasn't really all that difficult, eh, Watson?" said my companion, filling his pipe.

I mumbled an assent, but for the life of me was at a loss as to Holmes's thinking processes.

"You see, Mr. Zolnay, you forgot your gloves earlier this afternoon, and they served very well as your calling card."

"Yes, I leave them. I forget. Zolnay does not wear gloves except in wintertime . . ."

"Or except to hide his injured hand," continued Holmes, winking in my direction.

The giant bounded back, drawing the hand under his coat.

"Zolnay is not injured!" he cried, and then added thoughtfully, "It is only to *myself* I am injured, not to others."

"I think we understand, don't we, Watson? You have a reputation to uphold. But guessing your identity was not hard. Watson and I were discussing the possible occupations of the man who owned these gloves. We concluded the man was well-paid, yet evidently possessed great strength, and *used* it too, as we saw by these bloodstains. Now what sort of job would it be that pays a nice salary for physical exertion? There is only one: a performer of some sort. Focusing my efforts along this line, I seemed to recall a notice for the circus in this morning's *Telegram*. Finding it, I scanned the advertisement for a lead. Certainly the performer was either a strongman or an acrobat, but odds favored the acrobats, especially a trapeze artist who would undoubtedly subject his hands to incredible abrasion. You see, Mr. Zolnay, I do a bit of boxing in my spare time at Sullivan's gymnasium, and so am familiar with the torn hands of the gymnasts who train there—"

The huge man stared dumbstruck at Holmes, glowing with admiration and wonder.

"Prominently featured in the advertisement was a reference to 'Gregor the Great—Aerialist Supreme,' alias Gregor Zolnay."

"But how did you know it was Zolnay behind the closed door?" I asked.

"Ah yes, Herr Doctor," joined Zolnay, wagging a huge finger in Holmes's direction, "you have magic eyes too, eh?"

"There are seventeen steps leading to our flat," returned Holmes. "You bounded up in four leaps plus a step. Would an ordinary man be able to ascend a staircase four at a time? No. Could an acrobat? With ease, as you have proven. Now, sir, what is it I can do for you?"

Recollecting his reason for seeking assistance, Gregor Zolnay's strong face assumed a forlorn expression. He sank wearily into my armchair and sighed deeply.

"Mr. Holmes, Herr Doctor . . . I have much sadness in my heart. My dear Anna is crippled, she—"

Here the man, so outwardly strong, buried his head in his hands and rocked to and fro in grief. Holmes, after waiting some time for the man to continue, began to ask him questions.

"Is her condition the result of illness or injury?"

"She fell. It was two nights ago, during the time we rehearse. We were doing the triple pirouette. It is very difficult, and dangerous, and demands much attention. Also, Mr. Holmes, the net was down, as it must be during the performance."

"I take it the stunt miscarried, and as a result she fell to the ground—"

"Yes, forty feet down into the ring. When I saw her fall I grabbed a cable and slid down after her. So *this*," and he held up his bandaged hand.

"I see, that would be the natural thing to do. Anna is your wife then?"

"No, we are to be married—that is we had planned to be married. She may never walk again. She can barely talk. It is very sad."

"You mean she is unconscious?" I asked.

"Sometimes she wakes, sometimes she sleeps—mostly she sleeps—"

"Is she hospitalized?"

"Yes, Herr Doctor, at the London Hospital. When she wakes she talks nonsense. Always it is the same thing she says. She grabs my head and whispers in my ear: 'Gregor, the elephant man, *it is the elephant man!*'"

Holmes and I exchanged bewildered glances. I assumed Zolnay's rather cryptic phrase was due to his heavy accent and marginal command of English.

"Surely," said Holmes, "Anna was referring to the man who cares for the elephants: their keeper. Is this not the case?"

The giant shook his head dumbfoundedly.

"No, Mr. Holmes. I ask her this. *Is it Panelli who feeds the animals?* No, she says. I don't know what she is trying to say, gentlemen. Until this morning I think she is mad with fever and talking nonsense. But then this morning I remember something odd, and come to see you."

Holmes leaned forward eagerly.

"I am remembering that just before she fell, she said too: the *elephant man*. I think too she screamed a little just before—"

"—just before the accident?"

"Yes, Herr Doctor. Let me explain please. I am catcher who hangs on centre bar—"

"On the trapeze?"

"Yes, I hang head downwards by my legs, swinging. Anna leaps from platform holding onto her bar. She releases, pirouettes three times—quick like this—then extends her wrists for me."

"Then you grab them."

"Yes, and after one, maybe two swings, she releases to grab again the bar held by Vayenko. Then she swings to other platform."

"Who is Vayenko?"

"Vayenko is third man in team. A Russian, from Kiev. He is long time with Chipperfield's. He is now too old for much performing—he holds bar for Anna. When we are in correct place on the swing, he releases it from far platform so it will be there for Anna to catch. We are not friends. He loved Anna before I joined Chipperfield's in Buda-Pesth three years ago."

Holmes shot a keen glance in my direction.

"Naturally, he was disappointed, and angered, that Anna should abandon him for you," I pursued.

Zolnay remained silent for a short while before replying. He looked down at his hands, assuming almost a guilty look.

"He does not talk of his feelings, Herr Doctor. But I think they are as you say. He proposed to Anna after we met, and she refused him."

"Can you relate the details of the accident?" asked Holmes, changing the subject.

"It is as I say: Anna on the platform, I am in the middle, hanging upside down on the bar, Vayenko is on the far platform holding the other bar . . ."

"Yes," I said, recounting, "and Anna leaps from her platform, releasing the bar at the height of her swing—"

"Yes, then turning like this you see—"

At this point the huge man jumped from the chair and turned around three times with amazing quickness and grace.

"—then she was to extend to me her arms so—then I to grab her wrists, but she did not do this gentlemen. She went into a ball and fell."

"And you remember her crying out?"

"Yes, she cried out something about the el-ephant man . . . I think she said the word *horrible*, or *horrid* . . . but I am not sure now because then I am watching her fall—going fast down away from me and I cannot think—"

Here the aerialist winced with the memory of the tragedy.

"And Vayenko never left his place on the far platform?"

"No, Mr. Holmes. He never moved, from the time we start the rehearsal until Anna is falling . . . and afterwards he is at my side as I am leaning over her."

Holmes pondered what had been said for some time before responding.

"And you have come to me solely because of Anna's strange talk about the elephant man?"

"It is not much perhaps, Mr. Holmes. But Anna is a great flyer. She would not miss the triple like that—bent over, like a baby who sleeps in a little ball. It was something . . . something horrible that frightened her so that she could not think of the triple."

"And there was nothing unusual in the ring, or tent? Nothing strange about the grounds?"

Zolnay shook his head.

"No. In fact, Vayenko fastened the tent so that no one could enter during the rehearsal—so there would be no interference."

"And I take it that was the usual procedure."

"No. Only then was the tent fastened."

"That is interesting . . . decidedly so. Feel like taking in the circus, Watson? Shall we shed our middle-age stuffiness and become boys again?"

He fetched his coat and flung mine across the armchair.

"Come on, man! Can't you hear the steam whistle blowing? You're encamped on the fairgrounds at Wimbledon I suppose, eh, Mr. Zolnay? Good, then let's have a look around the grounds before going to visit poor Anna at London Hospital."

Inside of an hour's time, we were standing at the edge of the *tober* (as Zolnay called it) or field at Wimbledon. In its centre rose the immense tent, an elliptical mountain of cloth over a hundred yards in length. Pennants fluttered gaily from its summit while, as predicted by Holmes, the robust tones of the steam piano could be heard from afar. Long queues of anxious people streamed to the centre tent, while throngs of curious onlookers packed into the "sideshows" that ringed the circus grounds. Encircling the show, so as to form a crude fence round it, were scores of wagons and caravans, all painted red with "CHIPPERFIELD'S" painted in huge silver letters on their sides. Drawing closer, the heavy odour of animals and the smell of hay reached us, and a wave of nostalgia passed over me.

Soon we were inside the ring of wagons, and our famous companion was besieged by countless admirers. Zolnay informed us that this area was the "back yard" where the performers congregated between acts, and where the properties and wardrobes were kept. Many people came to offer their condolences and best wishes for Anna's recovery. Among the interesting people we met were Bruno Baldi, the strongman who could lift a horse. "Black Jack" Houlihan could swallow a scimitar, bending the trunk of his body to accommodate the curved blade. Several clowns approached and offered their best wishes too, and it seemed strange to hear normal, sober voices emerge from the grotesque faces. Zolnay hailed one fellow, a slight little man with a twisted body who limped along the sawdust like an urchin.

"Sidney, Sidney Larkin!" he called, and the stunted figure stopped, turned and bounded over to us. Zolnay, who had to prepare for the afternoon show, instructed him to take us to Panelli's caravan. The man complied instantly, obviously an indication of his affection for the aerialist. He led us, with his hobbling gait, to a caravan that resembled the ones owned by Gypsies and Tinkers. It was immediately apparent that someone was home; we saw the plume of grey smoke rising from the tin stack that projected through the wagon's roof. Drawing closer, the delicious aroma of onions and garlic frying in olive oil issued from the open window.

Larkin lurched up the rear ladder and rapped on the door.

"'Ey, Panelli," he said under his breath, "couple of flatties out here to see you . . ."

"What the devil is a '*flattie*'?" I asked Holmes.

"I believe it's circus parlance for 'outsider.' "

"You in a kip? Eh? Allright, mate, we'll wait a bit."

Shortly afterwards the caravan's owner appeared in the minute rear doorway, and motioned us all inside. Panelli was a short, stout man with an enormous drooping moustache and swarthy features. He wore a tattered hat, and most strange and engaging of all—had a small black monkey riding on his shoulder. The monkey too wore a tiny hat, and a bright jacket, which gave him an almost humanoid appearance. Already I was glad to have accompanied Holmes on this errand, since I had always been most curious to see the inside of a traveling caravan. We ducked in and were surprised to find not only Panelli, but his wife and five children too! How they could survive in those cramped quarters I couldn't say, yet the place, crowded as it was, certainly had a cozy air about it. Mrs. Panelli stirred the iron pot on the stove, and offered us tea.

Panelli, who was sprawled on a cot feeding his monkey (whose name was Jocko), was most cooperative in answering our questions. It was a curious experience sitting on a steamer trunk in the tiny traveling home, listening to the babble of the throng outside as the noise entered through the windows that were cheerfully decorated with curtains of blue gingham.

"You will come with me please, gentlemen," said Panelli, who bade his family goodbye and led us back down the ladder and towards a large tent.

Lifting the flap for us to pass through, Panelli led us around a haystack. I was met with a sight that fairly took my breath away, and made me take several steps backwards.

"Not to be afraid, gentlemen, they will not hurt you," said the Italian, and walked calmly into the midst of a small herd of elephants that stood eating not ten feet away from us. One huge tusker caught my attention as he flicked the heavy chain which fettered him to and fro with his trunk as if it were a piece of twine. The beasts flapped their ears and swayed rhythmically as they ate. I could hear the grinding of their molars.

"Now, Mr. Panelli, am I given to understand that when the accident occurred you were in this very tent with the elephants?"

"Yes, it was late when they were rehearsing. I remember it was dark outside. The elephants were all as you see them now. Sidney sees me here then, also Rocco the clown. Panelli here the whole time."

"And all of the elephants too? None amiss?"

"No, all here, all twelve, as you can count now—"

At that instant the big bull, head swaying, backed up three steps and would have stepped on Holmes had he not backed off.

"Hannibal!" shouted Panelli, and the bull resumed his original place.

"They are easy, you see. Now, gentlemen, I go eat my lunch?"

"Certainly. Thanks you for your help," replied Holmes.

We stared at the great animals for perhaps ten more minutes, but then the big bull showed signs of restlessness again so we departed the tent and resumed walking around the grounds.

Holmes, as was his custom, walked slightly hunched over peering downwards in thought, his hands clasped behind his back.

"Well, did you observe anything remarkable either about Mr. Panelli or his elephants?"

"I'm afraid not, Holmes. Everything seemed to be entirely above board. Besides, Panelli has several witnesses to attest to his presence in the tent."

"I concur. I think we can rule him out . . . and the beasts too."

"But why then Anna's constant referral to the elephant man?"

"Humf! That is why we must see her personally. It is good you are a physician, Watson, for it will make our visit to London Hospital much easier. Of course this means that we must miss the show. Let's look up Zolnay and—good heavens, what's that?"

A piercing cry reached us over the din of the crowd. It came again, and I recognized it as the scream of an elephant. We made our way back to Panelli's tent in time to see him scurry out of the caravan, a driving hook in his hand. Jocko the monkey rode chattering on his shoulder.

"It is Hannibal again," he said to us as he hurried towards the canvas flap. "He is near musth, and restless lately, as you saw. I must chain him apart from the others."

Having dispersed the crowd that was beginning to gather, we followed the trainer back into the tent. The animals were restless. Their rocking, swaying motion had increased, and they swung their trunks about with hollow blowing noises. The great bull Hannibal raised his head and trunk upwards and walked deliberately into the young bull tethered next to him. That animal in turn trumpeted and prepared to charge back. It was then I realized how frail indeed was the canvas tent that enclosed the animals. Panelli rushed between the huge beasts, goad upraised. I couldn't help but admire his courage. The monkey shrieked with rage and delight. The animals backed away from each other and the massive chains straightened, then sprung into the air, thrumming like guitar strings. Holmes and I watched fascinated at the incredible strength and energy being displayed. Talking softly to the animals—whose behavior had much improved since his arrival—Panelli then crept round behind Hannibal and in a twinkling had affixed another chain to his right rear leg. This he then fastened to an enormous iron stake (its head flared like a mushroom from countless hammer blows) at the rear of the tent. After several minutes of tricky maneuvering, he had succeeded in isolating the bull between two stakes—far away from the others.

All seemed in order, yet there occurred the next instant one of the most violent and ghastly spectacles I've ever witnessed. And though it involved no human life, the incident remains grimly marked in my memory for life.

Panelli had finished drawing tight the rear chain and was walking past the animal towards us when Jocko, seeing the elephant's tail swinging a few feet away, was overcome by temptation. Whether the huge tail resembled a rope or vine I cannot say, but the monkey sprang from the trainer's shoulders and grasped the tail, then scrambled up along the huge back. There it pranced delightedly, turning backward somersaults and flinging about the straw that lay upon the elephant's back. But in an instant the excited chattering was replaced by a muffled groan as the enraged beast's trunk found the interloper and wrapped tightly round him. I heard Panelli cry out an admonition to Hannibal, but it was too late. The trunk snapped downward like a gigantic buggy-whip, and the monkey was slammed to earth. It tried to flee, and rose spastically for an instant, but was then blotted out by the descending grey foot. Before the trainer could call off the elephant, it had drawn up the small limp form again in its trunk and flung it through the tent flap.

We all stared dumbstruck for a few seconds, so great was the shock and violence of the occurence. Then, recovering our wits, the three of us raced outside the tent to meet the gathering crowd that had formed a circle around the tiny furred carcass that lay sprawled upon the sawdust. The dead monkey lay on its back, its mouth, full of gore, opened in a horrid mocking grin which exposed the large teeth.

"*Hoodoo!*" cried Rocco the clown.

"*Hoodoo!*" echoed Black Jack Houlihan.

"Oh lord! It's the *hoodoo* sure enough!" responded Sidney Larkin, looking with horror on the dead monkey.

"Holmes! The '*hoodoo?*' What's the *hoodoo?*"

"I take it to be an ill omen, a Jonah," he replied.

"Aye, sir, that it is—a Jonah! And the worst sort," said Larkin, backing off in fear. "The worst sort of sign there can be, for if a monkey is killed, it means that *three people shall die!*"

"Humph!" I exclaimed in disbelief, as we watched the elephant trainer sadly gather up his departed friend and wend his way back to the wagon. But despite my incredulity, I noticed the look of fear and wonder on the faces of the circus people, and the comment I heard more than once: "I hope it ain't me!"

We paused in the tent yard long enough for a pipe. At the end of that time, Holmes frankly admitted to me that the case appeared confusing. Since we'd struck a dead-end at the circus grounds for the time being, he thought it best to go to Anna's bedside directly and have Zolnay join us there at the performance's close.

"Perhaps we'll learn more at the hospital, Watson, though I must say this is not an auspicious beginning."

The ride to London Hospital was not a long one, and before half an hour had elapsed we were at its entrance. Sir Frederick Treves, the brilliant doctor and surgeon who was one of the hospital's directors, was an acquaintance of mine. I therefore approached the head nurse and informed her of my relationship with Treves, and said we wished to see a patient in the hospital.

"I'm sorry, Doctor, he's not to be seen unless so directed personally by Dr. Treves, we've had enough of the curious—"

"I beg pardon, Miss," I pursued, "but the patient we wish to see is a woman: Miss Anna Tontriva . . ."

"Oh I'm sorry. I thought it was . . . another matter entirely. This way please."

I was shown into the chamber alone whilst Holmes waited outside. We had agreed that if she were in sufficient condition, he would join me in asking her questions. But upon examining the lady for only a few seconds, I uttered a sigh of despair, for I knew she would not live. I again checked her vital signs to make certain, but I had not been mistaken: the woman was in a deep coma, and running a high fever. Moreover, from examining her chart and palpitating her abdomen, I could tell that peritonitis had set in. There was nothing to be done . . .

"What is it then, old fellow?" enquired my companion as I emerged, dejected. "Come on, man, raise up your head—"

I shook my head sadly.

"Fetch Zolnay. I'm afraid there's much unpleasantness ahead for us. I'll get the physician in charge, or his assistant. But believe me, Holmes, she hasn't a chance."

Holmes said nothing, but his expression told me that he too was thinking of the monkey.

"The '*hoodoo*,' eh, Holmes?"

"Bah! Rubbish!" he cried, and spun off to bring the acrobat.

I needn't relate to you, dear reader, the painful events that followed. We saw the gigantic Hungarian, Gregor the Great, reduced to a weeping hulk as the body of his beloved Anna was borne away on a litter. We summoned various people from Chipperfield's to comfort the man, and to arrange for the funeral. Leaving the hospital to continue our investigation, we passed Treves in the hallway. He was speaking to an orderly as we approached, and I heard a snatch of the conversation.

". . . so fortunate that he has quarters *here* now, don't you see, for he won't have people gaping at him all the time. Yes, women have been known to faint—oh hullo, Watson, what brings you here?"

I briefly explained our grim mission to Treves, who extended his sincere sympathy, and we made our way back to the circus grounds. We had no trouble finding Sidney Larkin and Rocco, for they were in Rocco's caravan, heads bowed in grief. All claimed it was the hoodoo working, and shuddered at the thought of the two additional deaths to follow. Panelli, feeling he was somehow to blame, would see no one. The show had been over for several hours and we were at liberty to examine the main tent. We entered and were immediately overwhelmed by the enormity of it. With the assistance of Larkin and Rocco, Holmes lighted several of the big carbon-arc lamps that served as spotlights. These he aimed upwards at the flying bars and platforms. Then, much to the amazement of all present, he approached the rope ladder that hung down into the centre ring and began to climb.

"Halt!" came a voice. "What are you doing here?"

We turned to see a powerful-looking man approach the centre ring and glare up at Holmes, who was almost to the top.

"Vayenko, this man is Sherlock Holmes, a detective who is helping Gregor discover the cause of Anna's fall—" began Rocco, but he was cut short.

"Get down!" cried the Russian, shaking his fist.

"Mr. Vayenko, I am here at the request of Mr. Gregor Zolnay. I would be most anxious for your assistance in this matter," said Holmes coolly. "However, if you do not wish to cooperate, I would request you not interfere."

Holmes continued climbing toward the aerialist's platform. He had almost reached the platform when Vayenko, with a curse, started up the ladder in pursuit with a speed that was unbelievable. In short order he had overtaken my comrade and seized him by the ankle.

"See here!" I shouted and ran to the ladder, Larkin and the clown at my heels.

Holmes assayed the situation calmly, and asked the acrobat to release his grip. I was appalled at the aerialist who, of all of us, should have been the most keenly aware of the danger to which he was subjecting Holmes. Yet I watched terrified as the Russian began pulling at his leg, and drew Holmes's other foot from the rung on which it rested. My friend dangled there, forty feet up, carrying not only his own weight, but much of the other man's as well. However, just as I thought his grip would fail, I saw his free foot snap back and the boot drive into the Russian's hand. The man let out a howl of pain, and allowed Holmes to reach the platform.

"What is going on here?" cried a deep voice. We saw an elegantly dressed man approach the ring and look up.

"Vladimir, is that you? Who the devil is that up there with you?"

The man made himself known as Lamar Chipperfield, the owner and manager of the show. Upon hearing the nature of our business, Mr. Chipperfield gladly consented, and instructed Vayenko to dismount the ladder immediately. Upon receiving this order, the man's demeanor changed markedly; he assumed a meek and dutiful manner, and went to great pains to assure Mr. Chipperfield that he was acting only out of concern for the circus—preventing a stranger and trespasser from damaging the apparatus.

"You know, Mr. Chipperfield, that our lives depend on the wires. To have them damaged in any way . . ."

"I fully understand, Vladimir. You made an honest mistake. Kindly wait in your wagon until these gentlemen are through, for they may have questions to ask you. Goodnight."

The Russian moved off most humbly, even bowing slightly in my direction. But my loathing for him remained, and I felt that his servile attitude was a sham, for I saw him glare again in Holmes's direction just before he departed the tent.

I returned directly beneath the platform and spent the next several minutes helping to direct the spotlights in the directions Holmes indicated.

"A little to the left and up," he would say, peering about the tent from his lofty perch, "no, not so far—there, hold it steady for a moment . . ."

Apparently tiring of this, he amazed us by drawing the middle bar over to the platform by means of a light rope. In a few seconds we saw him swinging in a wide arc over our heads. We were all afright for his situation, but he displayed that remarkable coolness which was his hallmark; he sat on the bar as if enjoying himself tremendously, gazing about and shouting directions to us.

"Don't be a moron, Holmes!" I cautioned. "You'll break your neck! I say, come down at once!"

But he stayed up another ten minutes before returning, bright-eyed, to the sawdust ring.

"I say, Larkin, what's that?" he enquired, pointing to a canvas canopy that emerged between tiers of wooden benches.

"That, sir, is the *run in*."

"The *run in?*"

"Yes, sir. The animals make their entrance through it. It's a canvas tunnel that runs out to the backyard and wagons. It's kept sealed until showtime, for the children would sneak in through it to avoid paying."

The three of us examined the cloth-covered entranceway. It was about four feet in diameter. We entered the tunnel, stooping low as we walked, until we came to a wall of canvas tightly laced. Larkin undid the laces for us and we passed out into the night air. Sure enough, we were in the midst of the menagerie of wagons. The faint growling and acrid stench indicated the presence of lions.

"And this is always kept laced?"

"Yessir. Until the middle of showtime. As you can see, there's nobody hereabouts most times—since the performers gather over near the front line tent for tea and a chat . . ."

"I see. And not only is this area deserted, but remarkably near the outer fence too," observed Holmes as he walked slowly about, eyes glued to the ground. "It may interest you to know, Watson, that the entranceway of the run in is visible from the platform, but not from the centre bar . . ."

"You don't say," I replied, unable to follow his train of thought.

"Larkin, are the flaps to the run in kept closed also?"

"The inside ones? Yes, sir. It allows the trainers to lead their animals into the run without them being seen."

"And how are the flaps raised?"

"By means of stout cords, which are held by the ringmaster—Mr. Chipperfield, the gentleman you met. After announcing the act, he gives a sharp pull to the cords, see, which raises the flaps, signaling the animals to prance into the ring. It's a pretty sight sir, ain't it, Rocco?"

"I see," mused my companion, and returned through the tunnel of canvas to the grounds. There he requested a lantern, which Rocco promptly brought. He spent the next half hour, lantern in hand, tracing wide half-circles over the "pitch," or grounds. I seated myself on an enormous coil of rope and smoked three cigarettes during this procedure. Finally I heard the yelp of satisfaction that announced a discovery.

"Like a hound, eh?" I said to my companions. "His cries tell us he's found the scent."

Holmes, thirty yards distant, was kneeling upon the earth, eyes and face aglow with excitement.

"You see here, Watson . . . you *see*?" he cried tensely, pointing at the ground.

I saw nothing save a rough scrabbling on the earth that seemed to repeat itself at regular intervals. It certainly did not resemble footprints of any sort I had ever seen. Yet the regular repetition of the strange pattern indicated a locomotive motion, albeit a strange one.

"Ah, look here," said Holmes, pointing to a small round depression in the earth that was likewise repeated with the pattern.

"A cane?"

"Yes, or a crutch. So it is a human—or is it? Certainly it leaves no ordinary footprints. Let us follow them . . ."

The track led to the outer fence, and there, fastened upon a slat of wood that formed the fence, was a cloth object that Holmes removed from its perch and examined with much interest.

"What is it, Holmes?"

"I'm not yet sure, but it appears to be some kind of garment . . ."

He held the weird object under the lantern's beam, mumbling to himself. He then made additional efforts to pick up the strange track on the other side of the fence but, owing to the darkness, was forced to relinquish the chase.

"The track was clear enough in the earth and sawdust of the pitch, but will be extremely difficult to follow in the meadow that surrounds it. It's a wonder we ever found it at all considering the enormous traffic flowing over the grounds. However, as you saw, I discovered it only by circling far out towards the fence. Whoever, or *whatever* it was clearly headed straight for the fence, and over it. No, Watson, we'd be wasting

our time to search further tonight. Better to return tomorrow in full daylight. For the present, I think we've learned all we can from our inspections. Tell me, Larkin, is it true the flyers were alone in the main tent the night of the accident?"

The stunted man hobbled alongside us in the darkness for several minutes before replying.

"Yes, sir, to the best of my knowledge. I think we was all in the side tent, or tending to our own affairs in our caravans. As you know, I was with Panelli and Rocco."

Holmes spent another half-hour questioning the remaining circus people: had any of them been in the main tent during the ill-fated rehearsal? Was it true that the flaps were fastened shut so no one could enter? Had they seen a strange animal amongst the wagons, or loitering near the big tent? The answer to these questions was no. Therefore we boarded a hansom and within the hour found ourselves once again at our quarters. Saddened over Anna's death, we sat for some time before the fireplace in silence. Then Holmes retrieved the strange article of clothing he had found on the circus fence. It resembled a huge sleeve, yet one end was sewn up in heavy canvas, which was blackened with dirt and macadam. He drew it over his arm; his hand was then encircled by the canvas end, which he inspected carefully with the aid of his lens and the glare of the student lamp. After twenty minutes of scrutiny, broken only by occasional sighs and grunts, he flung it nonchalantly into my lap.

"What do you make of it?"

"It looks like some kind of slipper," I replied at last, "since we can see by the condition of the canvas end that it has had repeated, even constant, contact with the ground."

He nodded his head in agreement as he drew on his pipe, expelling clouds of smoke into the lamp's glare.

"The strange part is, it is not shaped like something that would fit over a leg and foot," I continued. "In fact, from its dimensions, I would say it was made more for a fin, or flipper, than for a human limb—"

"If it were made for a normal human foot,

even disregarding its intense size and grotesque shape, we could assume that the *footprint* on the canvas—the dark stain that has been produced by the limb within pushing the cloth onto the ground—would bear a roughly elongated shape comparable to a foot. It would show a series of smudges at one end corresponding to the balls of the feet and perhaps the toes—"

"Yes!" he interrupted. "And a slightly smaller smudge at the other end which would be made by the heel . . ."

"Of course. But in this case, we see that the stain is an irregular blob. Instead of delineating a foot, even roughly, it delineates nothing."

"Or nothing that is a foot," he corrected.

"Then *what is it?*" I enquired, the horror growing in me.

"I don't know, Watson, except to say that it is perhaps human, or half-human, as the case may be. I can tell by the remnants of sawdust stuck to the tar that this was on the limb—one of the limbs rather, that made the strange track near the tent."

". . . the elephant man . . ." I mused.

"My thoughts exactly. Is it possible? What sort of man—if such he could be called—would require a boot like this one, eh? He would have to be terribly—"

"Deformed?"

"*Yes!* Only—I say, wait a minute! I seem to remember a column in the *personals* of about a month ago . . . let's see here . . ."

He flung himself down upon his knees and began rummaging like a pack rat through the stacks of newspapers that littered our floor.

"Drat, Watson! I see you've been housecleaning again—shame on you! How am I to solve these puzzles if you persist in raiding my stores of information, eh? Neatness is a loathsome trait, Watson; never forget it!"

I spent the better part of an hour convincing him that, were it not for my 'housecleaning,' our flat would soon become a jackdaw's nest. As a further balm for his distress, I offered to buy our dinner, and soon we were off to Morley's Chop House. Throughout the meal he plied me with questions. As a medical man, was I aware of any disease or condition that would result in horrendous deformities? I replied that there were a few, like *elephantiasis*, that could result in unbelievable swelling of the flesh and lymph glands, and a corresponding ulceration and scaling of the skin.

"By Jove! And the correct name as well! Surely then that is the answer, and yet . . ."

He fell silent again, and we finished the meal talking of other subjects.

"Tell me, Watson," he pursued as we left Morley's, "does elephantiasis, damaging though it is to the flesh and glands, affect the bones?"

When I replied in the negative, Holmes observed that we had best rule out the disease.

"As you yourself stated after examining the strange slipper we found, the *limbs* are misshapen, not just the tissue on them, correct?"

I nodded. "I must say I'm entirely at a loss, Holmes. If indeed it is a human afflicted with a malady, the malady's identity escapes me. I don't see how you expect to find the answer to this puzzle either, unless you plan to continue following the strange track in tomorrow's daylight . . ."

"There may be an easier way, Watson. Tomorrow morning shall find me at the *Times* office. I'm quite sure it was in that paper—in the agony columns—that I saw the notice a month ago. Well, shall we return directly to Baker Street or would you rather stop by Drury Lane on the way?"

I had scarcely dressed next morning when Holmes burst into my room full of excitement.

"Your surgeon friend at London Hospital, Watson, his name is *Treves* is it not?"

"Yes. Sir Frederick Treves. You saw him yesterday in the hospital corridor, if you recollect—"

"Of *course* I recollect," he snapped, "but, though the name was faintly familiar to my ear, I failed to assemble all the pieces . . ."

"Eh? All the pieces?"

"I take it that until yesterday you had not spoken to Treves in some time? That would seem plausible, since you work at different hospitals. It is unlikely, then, that you have heard about his recent charge."

"No, I confess I haven't."

"A unique charge, to say the least. Come along, there's a cab waiting at our kerb. No! You must skip your tea, old fellow—one of the penalties for being a slugabed!"

He half-dragged me down the staircase and flung me into the waiting hansom. We dashed off in the direction of London Hospital.

"Now, Watson," said he, drumming his fingers on his knee impatiently, "don't you recall that yesterday when you introduced yourself as a friend of Treves the head nurse assumed you were visiting another patient . . ."

"I think I do remember . . . she said they had seen enough of the curious . . ."

"Yes!" he beamed. "And also, you may recollect that Treves himself, whilst speaking to a colleague in the hallway, mentioned that *women have been known to faint*! . . .'"

". . . since time immemorial, I'm afraid! . . ."

"Dash it, Watson, you really are slow sometimes!"

"I beg pardon—"

"At first I thought it coincidence that Anna Tontriva should be confined in the same building that contains the solution to our problem. But upon reflection it makes sense, since London is the closest hospital to the circus grounds . . ."

"Whatever are you talking about, Holmes?" I said with a yawn, for I was not entirely at my best without my morning cup.

"Never mind, Watson, you'll see the answer for yourself soon enough. Here we are. I'll meet you inside directly I pay the cabbie."

Shortly afterwards Holmes joined me at the head nurse's station, where he enquired for Treves.

"Mr. Holmes? He is expecting you. Yes, Doctor Treves received your wire. This way please."

She led us to the rear wing of the hospital, where, set off by two sets of doors from the remainder of the building, was a suite of rooms which looked out onto an enclosed grassy courtyard. Being vaguely familiar with the hospital, I had heard this referred to as Bedstead Square. It was an isolation ward, and usually used to house lunatics temporarily before they were transferred to asylums. The nurse bade us sit down in the first of the rooms, and after several minutes' wait, Treves entered the room and drew up a chair opposite us. "Hullo again, Watson. Mr. Holmes, I received your urgent wire this morning. Surely your keen powers are much as Watson has proclaimed, for we've done our level best to keep Merrick's confinement here a secret."

"I'm sure you have, sir. And may I express my sincere admiration to you and Mr. Carr Gomm. Your advertisement in the *Times*, I take it, was successful."

"Oh quite. Merrick now has the means to sustain himself in comfort here for the remainder of his life, thanks to the generosity of the British public. He was unaware of his newfound fortune until yesterday, for we didn't want to disappoint him were it not to materialise. But now he knows he can stay here for good, and is most joyous. Now you, Watson, have not heard of John Merrick?"

"Not until this very minute."

Treves paused for a moment before continuing.

"Are you familiar with *neurofibromatosis*?"

"Recklinghausen's disease?"

"Right you are! It's known by both names. As you no doubt know, it causes a proliferation of cells around the delicate connective tissue surrounding nerve endings. It usually affects only the nerves and skin."

I nodded. It was indeed a rare disorder; in my dozen or so years of practice, I'd seen half as many instances of it, if that.

"But in the strange—and tragic—case of John Merrick, the disease has run rampant over his entire body with alarming consequences. Not only that, but it has affected his *bones* as well, with the most monstrously deforming results . . ."

"Doctor Treves, is Merrick free to come and go as he pleases?" asked Holmes.

"In what sense do you mean? Certainly in the legal or medical sense he is free to go wherever he pleases at any time. He is not bound here. Yet, considering his frightful appearance, he remains a voluntary recluse in these chambers since even a brief glance at his form has caused people to go into shock."

"Was Merrick here three nights ago?" pursued Holmes.

"Now that you mention it, Mr. Holmes, that night he made one of his rare nocturnal excursions. He goes about after dark, and clothed in the most amazing rig of garments you have ever laid eyes on."

"Is this part of the wardrobe?" enquired my companion, holding up the strange slipper he had found the previous night.

"Dear me, so it is! Where did you find it? Merrick will be most grateful, I'm sure. But come along, you may see him now, if your nerves and stomach can take it."

He led us to a closed door and turned the knob. He was about to open it when he hesitated, turned to us, and spoke.

"I know you two gentlemen, considering your many dangerous adventures together, have stronger nerves than most people. Still in all, I must caution even you, Watson, who have seen so many medical oddities and loathsome sights, that you surely have never seen a human so horribly disfigured as the man who lies beyond this door. Likewise, Mr. Holmes, even considering the myriad smashed corpses you have examined closely—the countless maimed and injured on either side of the law—the person you are about to meet is all the more horrid and pathetic because he is *alive*, trapped inside his own monstrous form."

He then opened the door and led us in. In the centre of the large room was a bed with a hospital screen round it. We approached this, and Treves drew back the screen partially, revealing a foot that was so hideous that, despite my inner steeling and Treves's words of warning, I could not suppress a short gasp.

The foot didn't in the least resemble a human one, as Holmes and I had surmised from inspecting the slipper that had covered it. It was a flat slab of lumpy flesh. The skin was of a warty texture, resembling a head of cauliflower.

"You can see, gentlemen, the extent of poor Merrick's plight. When he was first confined here, the attending nurse, who was not forewarned of his appearance, fainted dead away at the sight of him."

With this, Treves then slowly slid the screen back to reveal the pitiable wretch who lay stretched upon the bed. His skin throughout was of the same lumpy, fibrous appearance as we had observed on his foot. But in addition, the limbs themselves were grotesquely twisted and gnarled.

The back was bowed as a hunchback's, and from his chest, neck and back there hung great masses of lumpy flesh. The head was most gruesome of all, for it was nearly twice normal size, and had protruding from it—where the face should have been—a number of bony masses, loaflike in shape and covered with the same loathsome, fungeous-looking skin. The projection near the mouth was huge, and stuck out like a pink stump, turning the upper lip inside out, leaving the mouth a cavernous fissure. This singular deformity gave the appearance of a rudimentary trunk. It, coupled with the cauliflower-like skin, was obviously responsible for the epithet of "elephant man."

"Dear God . . ." I murmured, against my will, and found myself involuntarily looking away. But the next moment, I observed Sherlock Holmes, and felt ashamed at myself. For my companion, although obviously revolted by this disgusting specimen of humanity, bore not the look of loathing upon his face, but pity. Obviously, whatever personal reaction he had to viewing Merrick was eclipsed by his pity for the poor wretch. Once again I was struck by the compassion and sympathy that so clearly marked his character, and which lay so close under the surface of his cold exterior.

Treves asked us to shake hands with Merrick who, he assured us, despite his strange appearance, enjoyed meeting people from the outside world, particularly when they showed no fright at meeting him. Holmes, typically composed, strode forward and extended his hand in greeting. To my amazement, I saw that one part, at least, of Merrick's body was completely free from the scourge that had transfigured him. It was his left arm, which he eagerly thrust in my companion's direction.

It was not only normal; it was beautiful. Finely shaped and covered with skin of a delicate, glowing texture, it was a limb any woman might have envied. The other arm, by contrast, resembled the rest of Merrick's body. In fact, there was no distinguishing between the palm and the back of the hand. The thumb looked like a stunted radish, whilst the fingers resembled twisted carrots.

Holmes grasped the normal arm and shook Merrick heartily by the hand. The wretch babbled something unintelligible, but it was obvious from general tone of the reply, and the excited twitching of his prostrate form, that he was delighted to meet my companion. I followed suit, and found that, once having become accustomed to the hideous appearance of the man, being in his company was not at all unbearable.

"As you can no doubt surmise," said Treves in an offhand way, "Merrick's facial deformities render normal speech impossible. You can see that his speech has a slurred quality, and seems to issue from a deep cavern rather than from a mouth. I, therefore, will translate his responses to you, Mr. Holmes, as I have grown accustomed to his utterances and can discern their meaning."

So for the next hour Holmes plied the man with questions. The man answered willingly enough, with a boyish enthusiasm and desire to please (he was, in fact, a very young man, though telling it from looking at him was, of course, impossible).

"Now, John, I want you to remember all you can about the last several days," began Holmes. "First of all, where did you go Monday night, and why did you go there?"

The wretch babbled and snorted an unintelligible reply which Treves quickly translated.

"He went to the circus grounds to seek a job. Ah, Mr. Holmes, that would make some sense. You see, up until recently John was forced to make his 'living,' if such it could be called, by exhibiting himself as an oddity at local fairgrounds and circuses, right, John?"

The man nodded his huge head slowly in sadness.

"But now, thanks to the public's concern and generosity, he need no longer worry about being gaped and jeered at. Obviously, he went to the circus unaware of his endowment, and reluctantly, yet he reasoned it was that or starve. Well you needn't worry any longer, my friend . . ."

Here Holmes and I stared dumbstruck as the man threw his head down upon his deformed chest and wept with joy and relief, the tears covering his monstrous face. I could almost have wept myself, so pathetic was the sight of this poor creature who had endured so much, without a friend or comforter in the world. And yet, were tears to come to my eyes, they would also have been tears of joy and renewed faith in the human heart: for now clearly John Merrick *had* friends and comforters, and his life as a public horror had drawn to a close.

"He went to the grounds that night," Treves continued, "alone and in secret, as strictly instructed by the circus representative—"

Holmes and I glared at each other. We had little doubt as to the identity of the "representative."

"And did you meet this man at the edge of the grounds?" pursued Holmes.

"Yes, he did," continued Treves. "He was helped over the fence and led into a narrow tunnel in the tent. There he was told to remain, squatting in his great cloak, which conceals him in public, until the signal was given."

"And what was the signal?"

"When the flaps were raised, Merrick was to fling off his cloak, rise up and wave his limbs about. Thereupon, he was told, the flaps would immediately close again, and he was to refasten his cloak and scurry outside again the same instant—returning to the hospital secretly, and telling no one of this 'audition.'"

"Was he paid, or offered employment?" I asked.

"He was paid two pounds for his appearance which is, as we know, remarkably good pay. If the owners decided to hire him, he was to be notified in a week. Otherwise, he was strictly instructed to keep the matter quiet, accepting the generous payment for his efforts."

Merrick answered all the questions in a forthright manner, obviously blissfully unaware of the nefarious purpose to which his "appearance" had been put.

"Finally, John, can you please describe this representative who approached you?"

When we heard the description, which fit Vladimir Vayenko in every detail, we knew the last piece of the puzzle had fallen into place. However, so as not to upset Merrick, Holmes and I departed without further questions.

"Well, we've truly met a *monster* on this case, Watson," remarked Holmes as he hailed a cab, "although it's not the poor follow who lies yonder . . ."

"The coward! Rather than face his rival directly, he chose to seek revenge by killing his loved one!"

"Yes. But I'm sure the revenge was *direct* as well. Love can turn quickly to hate, as you know. He never forgave Anna for throwing him away for Zolnay."

"And to use poor Merrick as the means— after all the wretched soul has been through . . ."

"It is ugly in every respect, Watson. Also, considering his recent actions towards me, I'm convinced that, like most cowards, Vayenko is a bully."

"Lucky for him he didn't choose to confront you on the ground!"

"I was thinking the same thing. Like most heavily muscled men, he would be slow to the punch and block. But we digress. The question is: what to do now?"

"Why, summon the police, of course! It's clear now that Vayenko caused Anna's death: he somehow rigged the flaps so they could be opened from the far platform. Then, just as Anna began her difficult stunt, he opened them quickly, revealing a sight so horrid that she lost control—"

"Yes, of course. *We* know that's what happened. But who else would believe us? Zolnay, due to his position high up on the centre bar saw nothing. Anna is dead. We have poor Merrick, who can scarcely speak. Can you imagine his appearing in a public courtroom against Vayenko? On whose side would the jury's sympathy lie? Also, who would believe such an outlandish tale? The only evidence that Vayenko was directly related to a *planned* act was his closing of the tent before the rehearsal. No, Watson, it won't do. Vayenko is a coward and a blackguard, but a deucedly clever one. Somehow, probably in connection with his career, he became acquainted with the whereabouts of Merrick, the *elephant man*, and has used the unfortunate man in a diabolically clever murder."

"Is there nothing we can do, then?" I asked with a curse.

"Yes," he answered after several minutes of deep thought. "That is why we're headed for Chipperfield's."

Once again we found the circus people, usually so gay and sociable, downcast in clouds of fear and gloom. To add to their woes the weather had turned cold and rainy with heavy winds. This is the worst possible weather for the circus, and attendance had fallen to a mere trickle. Accordingly nobody seemed surprised, in fact most seemed relieved, when Lamar Chipperfield announced the afternoon show postponed. Holmes and I ambled along the back yard, splashing through puddles and watching the performers idle about. Most were snug in their caravans, and from the noise issuing from many of them, we could tell that the ale and calvados were flowing freely. Passing close by some of them, we heard more talk of the *hoodoo*, and how the ugly weather was but one manifestation of the dead monkey's curse.

We found Zolnay in his wagon, brooding over

a bottle of *schnapps*. He welcomed us warmly, and managed to keep a composed exterior for several minutes before breaking down into a fit of weeping. We comforted him as best we could. Then my companion, fixing his steely gaze upon the Hungarian giant, said in a low whisper: "Mr. Zolnay, Dr. Watson and myself are close to finding the solution to your beloved Anna's death. But there remains one matter that must be attended to. Will you help us?"

As expected, he complied fully and eagerly.

"Good," continued Holmes. "Now tonight, the doctor and I shall return here to your caravan. We will arrive late, when everyone should be asleep. Do not tell anyone of our intended visit, not even Larkin. Is that clear?"

"Yes, Mr. Holmes. But is there nothing more you can tell me about my poor Anna?"

"Not at this time, I'm afraid. Just be here at one o'clock fully dressed. *Adieu.*"

To my surprise, we retraced our route back to London Hospital. There, Holmes dashed from the cab, telling me to wait. In less than ten minutes he came bounding back, a hospital laundry bag slung over his shoulder.

"Marvelous fellow Treves, and most cooperative as well," said he after directing the cabbie to Baker Street.

"Eh, what's in the bag, Holmes?"

"Tut! You shall find out soon enough, dear fellow. I think I have devised a rather clever way for Vayenko to confess his guilt, as you shall see tonight. Now where shall we dine? It's my turn to treat, is it not?"

Shortly after mid-night Holmes roused me from my fitful dozing in front of the fireplace.

"I must say I sometimes envy your lethargic nature, Watson," he remarked, drawing on his coat. "You seem to be able to sleep anywhere at any time, regardless of impending action. Well, up you go and let's be off. But first, will you lend me your leather coin purse?"

We arrived at the circus grounds shortly before the appointed hour. I was dumbstruck to see that Holmes had brought the laundry bag with him, as well as a walking stick. It certainly had my curiosity up. We were about to scale the fence when the sound of measured footfalls reached our ears.

"Watchman!" cried Holmes in a hoarse whisper. "Drat! I'd forgotten him."

But we scurried behind a wagon until the man passed, then scaled the fence without difficulty. Slinking from shadow to shadow, we worked our way to Zolnay's caravan. We were careful to avoid the menagerie wagons, for if aroused, the lions would certainly betray our presence.

We entered the wagon and Holmes instructed Zolnay to light a single taper, keeping the curtains drawn tight over all the windows. He then stood before Zolnay's bunk and proceeded to empty the contents of the laundry bag upon it. Out tumbled a ragged pile of clothes, including the strangest, and largest, cap I have ever seen.

"Good Lord, Holmes, what on earth—?"

"John Merrick's walking apparel, Watson. Treves is correct, a most amazing—not to say *outlandish*—bit of haberdashery, eh? You see how clever it is? Not a bit of the person can be seen. Notice especially the hat. See the canvas visor that hangs down on all sides? The eye slit is the only opening. Now the cloak, as you can see, actually is more of a tent. The long sleeves conceal the arms. These mittens somewhat resemble the coarse 'slipper' we examined at our quarters . . ."

Zolnay stared silently in amazement as Holmes held up each strange article.

"Finally," he continued, "we have these baggy trousers, which I shall now draw on over my own . . ."

I was beginning to follow Holmes's scheme, and had an inkling of the purpose to which he would put my leather coin purse.

"Now the two of you must help me. Master of disguise that I am, impersonating the 'elephant man' will surely be my most ambitious enterprise to date. Now, Watson, fetch those two rolls of sticking plaster will you. Zolnay, if you'd be good enough to wad up that newspaper yonder and stuff it into this great hat—hardly a task worthy of your strength—that's a good fellow."

Next he brought out an empty snuff tin from his coat. I noticed that its bottom had been removed so that, with the lid off, it became a metal tube about four inches in length. To my utter amazement, Holmes placed the tube against his mouth and, with my help, fastened it there securely with the sticking plaster. When next he spoke, it was in a hollow, distorted voice remarkably similar to Merrick's!

"This miniature megaphone does the trick, eh? And the cap's visor will keep it well-concealed."

He then drew on the grotesque slippers and gloves, finally topping off the disguise with the giant peaked cap, from which hung down, from all sides, the curtain of cloth. And when he hobbled about the caravan with his cane, bent over in the strange costume and babbling incoherently behind the visor, the transformation into Merrick, the "elephant man," was complete. Zolnay continued to gape in confusion until Holmes, unable to keep him in the dark any longer, explained our night-time mission: Holmes, impersonating Merrick, was to go to Vayenko's wagon—in the dead of night as Merrick would have been forced to do—and ask for more money for performing his "feat." Hopefully Vayenko's reaction would implicate him. As expected, the Hungarian trembled with wrath, and almost burst from his wagon in fury to seek the Russian. Holmes and I restrained him with difficulty.

"There, there, old fellow! I've gone to much trouble to arrange this nocturnal visit. If properly carried off, Vayenko will hang. Seek revenge now, and *you* could hang, and Anna's killer will go free."

The man saw our logic and restrained himself, yet I could hear that his breathing was heavy and fast, and he swore an oath under his breath as we departed the wagon.

We ambled about in the dark with Holmes in the lead. I was surprised that he headed towards the fence instead of Vayenko's wagon. But his intentions were made clear by the silent approach of a figure who had been waiting near the fence. In a moment, Lestrade was standing beside us.

We made our way to Vayenko's wagon. There Holmes bade us crawl underneath it and sit behind the rear axle. From there, we had a clear view of Holmes as he stood at the foot of the ladder. I felt the excitement growing in me, and noticed that Zolnay's agitation had increased still; he clenched and unclenched his huge fists and ground his teeth in rage. We hadn't long to wait. The "elephant man" hobbled up the steps and rapped upon the wagon's door with his walking stick. A long silence followed, and Holmes rapped a second time. We then heard a thumping and stumbling above us, and the door opened with a curse.

"Who's there?" cried a voice still heavy with drink. "What do you want?"

Holmes backed down the ladder and held up my coin purse. We could hear the unintelligible, hollow groaning that issued from his mask.

"Oh it's *you*, is it?" said Vayenko in a threatening tone. "What have you come back for? I told you not to return!"

Yet Holmes remained, holding up the purse and groaning.

"You monster! You have your nerve, you hideous beast! What are you trying to tell me, eh? What?"

Holmes was busy gesticulating with his arms and mumbling. We could see he was trying to indicate a fall from a high place.

"Ah, so you know of *that*, do you?" said Vayenko in a low voice. "So you saw her fall. You have discovered my little scheme, eh? And you now want more money to keep quiet . . ."

There was a period of silence. Holmes stood still, as if to indicate that that was indeed what he wanted. When Vayenko spoke next, his voice was full of treachery.

"See here, man. People will hear us talking out here, won't you come inside my wagon? There we can share a bottle and discuss the payment . . ."

Holmes backed off, still holding the purse upraised towards Vayenko, who began to descend the ladder towards my companion.

"No need to be afraid, Merrick. I'll pay you five pounds not to tell anyone about Anna's death . . ."

At that instant, the Russian lunged at Holmes, who would have raised his stick in defence were it not for the cloth that covered his face and so affected his vision. For the night was dark to begin with, and the small eye slit rendered him almost blind. Likewise the loosely draped clothes hindered his normally quick limbs, and Holmes fell beneath the rush of the heavy man.

Vayenko was no doubt surprised that the man he supposed to be stunted and clumsy was in fact a sinewy boxer of tremendous strength. After recovering from his momentary disadvantage, Holmes dealt his attacker two quick punches to the face. His blows staggered the acrobat, who seized the cane Holmes had dropped. Although we three had already sprung from our hiding place and were racing towards the two combatants, we were too late to prevent Vayenko from striking Holmes on the side of the head and knocking him to the ground. The man turned in time to see us, and went pale with terror at the sight of Zolnay bearing down on him.

I knelt down over Holmes, who was not seriously hurt, though he had a nasty welt on the side of his face. We heard the din of running feet and shouted oaths as he removed the awkward disguise and joined me in pursuit. Before we had gone ten steps, however, there came a scream that froze the blood in my veins. It was filled with terror and agony, and ended abruptly in a hoarse choke.

Owing to the darkness, it was several minutes before we discovered the body. By this time scores of people had joined us at the site, as we gazed at the twisted figure that lay bent backwards over a wagon tongue. Vayenko's eyes were open, and showed the ghostly white of death. His head was flung backwards at a grotesque angle, the back of the neck resting on the wooden beam. A quick inspection with my hands revealed what I had thought from the first: his neck was snapped entirely through. We called for a lantern, and in the light Holmes pointed out four great bruises upon the dead man's forehead. Each was the size of a shilling. Holmes attempted to place his fingers upon them but they were far too wide apart. In my mind's eye I swiftly recalled the great gloves that had enveloped my hand, and had no doubts as to how Vladimir Vayenko had met his death. Holmes shot a knowing glance in my direction.

"You see, Watson," he whispered softly, "using this projecting wagon tongue as a fulcrum, and placing his hand along Vayenko's forehead, he bent the head back—"

"Yes, I know," I said shortly. Certainly only a man with superhuman strength could have broken the massive neck of Vayenko. Yet I felt no remorse for the scoundrel who lay at our feet. Moreover, my concern was for the Hungarian giant, who was no doubt at that very instant in flight for his life across the fields of Wimbledon.

I felt a jostling at my side and saw Lestrade, recently arrived, peering down at the corpse.

"How did this fellow meet his end?" he enquired. "Did he fall in the dark and break his neck?"

Holmes and I glanced at each other momentarily.

"That would certainly seem possible," admitted Holmes noncommittally.

"And the other fellow, where is he?"

"We've no idea," I replied. "I say, Lestrade, shouldn't I call a hospital van? Eh? Yes, I'll do so directly whilst you and Holmes see to matters here." By the time the van arrived, Lestrade, still assuming Vayenko's death was accidental, had lost all interest in Zolnay. Holmes and I suspected that he was hiding in one of the many caravans belonging to his friends, or else was flying from London, and the horrendous events he was part of, aboard an express train.

"Wherever he may be," mused Holmes as we made our way back to the flat as dawn was breaking, "I wish him Godspeed."

Epilogue

But in the end, the *hoodoo* claimed its final victim.

Scarcely two months after our adventure with Zolnay the aerialist, Holmes interrupted our morning tea with the announcement that Merrick was dead. The piece in the *Telegraph* was brief, and obviously devoid of the pain and pathos that had marked the tragic life of young John Merrick:

"ELEPHANT MAN" DIES IN SLEEP

London, August 24—John Merrick, the human monstrosity known also as the "Elephant Man," died in his sleep last night in his private room at London Hospital. According to Dr. Frederick Treves, the physician in attendance, death occurred around 3:00 a.m., and was caused by a dislocation of the neck. Dr. Treves explained that Merrick was accustomed to sleeping in an upright position, yet, perhaps to fulfill his lifelong dream to "be like other people," he had this night attempted to sleep recumbent, with the result that his massive head—over three times normal size and weight, must have fallen back upon the soft pillow in such a fashion as to dislocate the vertebrae and sever major nerves. All evidence seems to point to a peaceful, if untimely death, since the coverlets weren't in the slightest disturbed. In accordance with a voluntary arrangement with the hospital, the body shall be donated to the Medical School of the University of London. Merrick was 27 years old.

"Poor chap," I said. "At least his death was quick and painless."

"I suppose that adds to the irony. The poor fellow seems to have been fortunate only in death. The more I ponder upon it, Watson, the real hero of this adventure was Merrick. He bore his pain and suffering stoically, with tremendous fortitude and bravery. Think of it! Think of his childhood, Watson! Abandoned as a horror by his mother—sold to a local fair at the age of four. Treated as a living monster by the human race, mocked and scorned by children his own age—shut up for days on end in dreary closets

and cold compartments! And after this living hell, he emerges not only unscathed, but *grateful* for his last few months in Bedstead Square! Was there ever in human history a tale of greater courage?"

I glanced out the window and sighed.

"Thank the Lord for people like Treves, and the British public," I said at last.

"Amen, Watson. And now, on a cheerier note, I have a surprise for you which I know you'll like. I received this package yesterday. You notice the postmark?"

". . . Salzberg . . ."

"Open it, Watson," said Holmes, gleefully rubbing his hands.

I tore off the brown wrappings and found within a cardboard box containing two leathern cases, each the size of a butter loaf.

"One is for you, the other for me," he said. "Would you prefer the fullbent or the bulldog?"

His question reached my ears as I was opening one of the leathern cases, revealing the handsomest meerschaum pipe I'd ever laid eyes on. Its bowl glowed with a creamy lustre, and the amber mouthpiece was a radiant golden hue.

"Holmes, a pipe like this is worth a fortune! Who wishes to bestow gifts like these upon us?"

"I've no idea, Watson," he answered with a twinkle in his eye, "yet he enclosed his calling card—here it is—"

He flung a grey flannel glove in my direction.

"Now let's see if we can discern his identity: he is rich, yet not a gentleman, and seems to make his living by performing physical feats of the most prodigious sort . . ."

Author's Notes for the Story "The Adventure of Zolnay, the Aerialist"

John Merrick, "The Elephant Man," actually lived. His disease, and consequent deformities, were as described in the story. Furthermore, the history of his life was, for the most part, as it was told. Frederick Treves was the greatest London physician of his time—with the exception of course, of John H. Watson. It was Treves who befriended Merrick and, with the assistance of Carr Gomm (the director of London Hospital) obtained private quarters in the hospital and an endowment to sustain Merrick for the rest of his days which were few in number. Aside from this gallant show of philanthropy, Treves is perhaps best known for removing the inflamed appendix of Edward VII on the eve of his coronation.

For a detailed account of Merrick's life, see Treves's book *The Elephant Man and Other Reminiscences,* or the excellent review of the book (and a capsule summary of Merrick's unfortunate life) by Ashley Montagu that appeared in the March 1971 issue of *Natural History* magazine.

This story was written with my friend Tom Zolnay especially in mind. He knows "Vayenko" only too well, having escaped from Hungary in 1956.

RLB

The Adventure of the Giant Rat of Sumatra

JOHN T. LESCROART

AS THE AUTHOR of numerous national bestsellers, John T. Lescroart (1948–) created a much-loved character in Dismas Hardy, a San Francisco ex-cop and lawyer (yes, lawyers *can* be loved) who made his first appearance in *Dead Irish* (1989); later books in the series have often featured previously adjunct characters as the main protagonist, notably Hardy's best friend, Abe Glitsky, a policeman, and Wyatt Hunt, a private investigator. Lescroart has also written several stand-alone urban thrillers.

After publishing *Sunburn* (1981), a paperback original, Lescroart turned to writing Sherlockian novels featuring Auguste Lupa, the son of Sherlock Holmes and Irene Adler, who may well have been a young Nero Wolfe (though Wolfe is never mentioned by name). The Lupa novels are *Son of Holmes* (1986) and *Rasputin's Revenge* (1987). The next time Lescroart turned to Holmes was with "The Adventure of the Giant Rat of Sumatra."

"I'd already enjoyed a couple of the humorous takes . . . on this most famous of the apocryphal Holmesian titles," Lescroart wrote, "[and] suddenly one day it came to me. I simply *knew* the story. It was amazing to me that it hadn't already been written, for what else could a Holmes rat story be about except for the plague? It has to be the plague, a missing (or found) serum, and, of course, Prof. Moriarty. . . . [It] really felt as if someone were dictating the words to me (Watson?) (Doyle?) and I were a mere conduit."

"The Adventure of the Giant Rat of Sumatra" was first published in the Summer/Fall 1997 issue of the *Mary Higgins Clark Mystery Magazine*; it was first published in book form in *The Best American Mystery Stories 1998*, edited by Sue Grafton (Boston, Houghton Mifflin, 1998).

THE ADVENTURE OF
THE GIANT RAT OF SUMATRA

John T. Lescroart

WE WERE SEATED over breakfast, my friend Mr. Sherlock Holmes deeply engrossed in his morning paper, when I heard him mutter something. "I beg your pardon, Holmes?" I asked.

"Sumatra," he repeated, all but to himself. "My God, even for Moriarty this is appalling!"

"Holmes," I exclaimed, "what is it?"

He put down the paper and looked in my direction, but he appeared not to see me. That in itself was so singular that I was immediately on my guard. When Sherlock Holmes looked, he saw—it was one of his dicta. But on that cold December morning in 1888, he stared as if through me out to the drizzly fog that enshrouded London.

I tried again to speak to him, but he waved me off impatiently. "Watson, please, don't interrupt me. It may already be too late."

Accustomed as I was to his outbursts, his tone still smarted. I started to remonstrate, but he had already risen and gone to the corner by the coal scuttle in our rooms at 221B Baker Street. There he kept his stack of past editions of London's newspapers. As I watched in growing concern, he attacked the pile, throwing whole sections out behind him when they didn't contain that for which he was searching.

Then, with an armload of papers, he half fell into his chair, grabbing his pipe on the way down. For the next quarter hour he sat engulfed in tobacco smoke, muttering or cursing one moment, and the next falling into a quiet and desperate depression. After watching him for a time, I ventured another syllable.

"Holmes?"

He flung some of the papers at me. "Read it for yourself, Watson. It may be the end of us all."

I picked the papers from the floor and began perusing them. Some were up to two years old, and I must confess I saw nothing in them but yesterday's news. Nevertheless, I slogged through the sections, pausing from time to time at a familiar name or at the mention of a case in which Holmes and I had been involved. While I read, Holmes evidently finished his work and rang for Mrs. Hudson. When our landlady appeared, he sent her to fetch Billy the page, saying it was a matter of the utmost urgency.

Quickly, he scratched a note on a pad and then, filling another pipe, turned to me as he lit it. "Well, Watson, I must say that as a doctor you are calm enough about it."

I must have looked at him blankly.

"The plague, Watson! The plague! Can it be you don't see it?"

Before I could respond, he had rushed to the table and snatched several of the papers away from me. "Look here!" he exclaimed. "And here! And here! You see nothing? Nothing?" He was grabbing and pulling the sections every which way. I had never seen him so agitated.

"Holmes! There's no need to be rude."

That brought him up short. He visibly summoned that control upon which he prides himself, straightening himself to his full height, taking a deep breath. "My dear man, please forgive me."

"It's nothing, Holmes, it's forgotten. But what is it? Please tell me."

Looking at the door, he came to some decision. "Well, I guess there is time before Billy comes." And he sat down, pulling that day's *Times* in front of him.

"Here, Watson, on page five—the article on our old friend Colonel Sebastian Moran."

I had read it, of course. The travels of the famous hunter were always of interest to me, both because they were often fascinating in themselves, but also and not least because of his position as Professor Moriarty's chief lieutenant. The article was an account of a Boer pirate attack on Moran's ship as it had been rounding the Horn on its return from Sumatra, loaded with hunting trophies. Moran and his crew had fought off the belligerents, hauled the injured ship back to Johannesburg and delivered it and its dead crew to the British authorities. A particular point of interest was that they had neither docked nor resupplied at port and had allowed no one to board their vessel.

"It seems like a typical Moran adventure," I said upon rereading it.

"By itself, you may be right, Watson. But what of this?"

He placed before me the oldest of the newspapers and pointed to a piece on the outbreak of bubonic plague that had occurred two years before on Siberut, a tiny island off the west coast of Sumatra.

"And these . . ."

The other articles related to a Dr. Culverton-Smith, who had announced and then retracted the news that he had developed and hoped shortly to perfect a serum that would prevent and cure bubonic plague.

I had just finished the last of these when there was a sharp rap at out door, followed immediately by the entrance into our quarters of Billy. One of the street urchins who frequented the alleys hereabouts, Billy had more than once proved a useful ally to my friend and me.

Holmes wasted no time on greeting him but handed him the note he'd scribbled earlier. "Ah, Billy, here. Deliver this at once to the address listed, and wait there for a reply."

Without a word, the boy was off, and I was again left alone with Holmes, pondering the obscure links in this bizarre chain. "What is this about, Holmes? What was that note?"

Now that he had taken some action, he reverted to that languid pose I knew so well. His eyes had become so black they appeared nearly hooded. But this time there was none of the sparkle in them that always appeared after the "view halloo" had been sounded, when the game was afoot. This time it was no game.

"The note was to Dr. Culverton-Smith, Watson—one of the most evil and brilliant men to ever grace your profession." He took a long pull at his pipe. "I wondered how long it would be before Professor Moriarty and he made each other's acquaintance." Then he sighed with an ineffable sadness. "I only wish I had acted to prevent it. I only hope now I'm not too late." He sighed again, wearily.

"What did the note say?"

He waved his pipe. "Oh, it was prosaic enough. It said, 'England will pay you more than Moriarty.'"

"For what?"

"For the serum, of course. The cure for bubonic plague."

"My God, Holmes, could it be . . . ?"

"I don't know yet. I won't know for sure until Billy comes back. Halloa? That would be him now."

He jumped up and ran to the door, opening it before the panting boy could even knock. Breathlessly, Billy handed a missive to Holmes, who ripped open the engraved envelope. As he read, his shoulders sagged.

Absently, he forced some coins on Billy and rather unceremoniously shooed him out. I thought he was a little too brusque with the boy and told him so.

"Watson, it's as I suspected. Moriarty, Moran, and Culverton-Smith are in it together, and no one must know. There would be panic."

"What does the reply say?"

Holmes smiled but with no humor. "'My dear Mr. Holmes,'" he read, "'Your offer is interesting. Unfortunately, what England can pay me is rather off the point, since within a year, my associates and I will *be* England.'"

"Holmes!" I exclaimed.

"Exactly. Moriarty plans to inoculate himself and his henchmen against the plague, then introduce the disease into England."

"How would he do that?"

"Probably through an animal that Moran has captured and smuggled onto his ship."

The pieces were beginning to fit, though my own enlightenment had none of the epiphanic quality of Holmes's. "But if they merely patented the serum," I argued, "they would be millionaires many times over."

Again that frigid grin. "Power, Watson. Power is more seductive than money, and for Moriarty it is everything. His mind envisions an England desolate and depopulated but one where he is absolute ruler, a medieval king. The population not under his power—including you and me, my friend—would die in swollen, boil-infested agony."

"You shock me!"

"Depend on it, Watson. I know my man."

"What can we do?"

The grin softened to a smile. "Good old Watson," he said. "Where there is danger, you have no fear. Where courage is needed, you have no peer. It would be a good epitaph."

The warmth I felt at the compliment quickly chilled at the vision of my own tomb. "Still," I said, "what can be done?"

Within moments, I had my answer. I had been reading again, trying to piece together the disparate elements of this diabolical plot, when Holmes tapped my shoulder. I must have been deeply engrossed in my researches not to have noticed Holmes leave the room. But now he was back, dressed and bundled for an excursion.

"Get your coat, Watson. I think we should pay a visit to the Diogenes Club."

The Diogenes was perhaps the strangest club in a city of strange clubs. Its members were the most private men in the City, and the charter and by-laws of the club colluded to keep them that way, since no one was allowed to speak within the club's walls, the sole exception being in the Visitor's Room. But even there, only whispering was permitted.

After a bitterly cold ride in a hansom, we found ourselves before the forbidding double doors of the building. Inside, Holmes passed his card to the doorman and we were ushered into the Visitor's Room to await the arrival of Holmes's brother, Mycroft.

Mycroft's dour face and huge bulk surprised me anew, though I had met him once before during our adventure with the Greek interpreter. That episode had not ended happily, and I found myself praying that his intercession here would produce more positive results. He took me in at a glance, somehow included a welcoming nod and turned to his brother, twelve years younger than himself. According to Holmes, Mycroft was the smartest and most powerful man in England. I reflected that his position, however it was defined, might be one that Moriarty would covet. But there was no more time for reflection.

"Sherlock," he whispered with affection, "what brings you to these hermit's haunts?"

In a few words Holmes outlined the situation. Hearing him retell it in his logical and orderly fashion, I was horrified again by the boldness and grandeur of Moriarty's twisted vision.

Could he actually pull it off? As I watched and listened to Mycroft and his brother formulate their own plan, I had no doubts at all that if Moriarty could be stopped, only one man living could do it, and that man was my friend Sherlock Holmes.

Eight days later, Holmes and I paced the deck of the HMS *Birmingham*, the twenty-eight-gun flagship of the Atlantic fleet. Earlier in the day we had passed the Canaries and now were beating farther south in African waters. Holmes had estimated that we would meet up with Colonel Moran's ship somewhere near the latitude of Dakar, off the coast of French West Africa, and that would be another day or two's hard sail.

The air was balmy, a far cry from the London winter. Some of the sailors had thought to bring a Christmas tree along—had tied it to the forward mast, decked it in red and green trimming and even placed a few wrapped boxes under it for the effect. I couldn't help but admire the spirit of these men, facing Her Majesty's sometimes terrible tasks with dignity, honor and even humor. This was an England worth fighting, even dying, for!

Of course, we were not alone. Twenty-six ships of the line were arrayed in a crescent pattern out to the sides and behind us. Mycroft had persuaded an outraged prime minister to assign the convoy to try to blockade the oncoming vessel. It was the largest armada to be assembled since the Franco-Prussian War, and I hope it will be a long, long time before such a force is needed again.

To get the kind of commitment needed for an expedition of this magnitude, Holmes had had to go to the limits of his imagination and persuasiveness, convincing Scotland Yard that Dr. Culverton-Smith must be arrested and questioned. Though none of the serum had been found in his possession—what a boon to mankind that would have been!—his personal notes and laboratories provided enough evidence, and the potential danger was serious enough, that the reluctant PM had finally assigned the fleet. But he had made it clear that if Holmes were wrong, both his career and that of his brother would be finished. Even criminal charges against them would not be out of the question!

But these concerns were the last things on Holmes's mind as we restlessly paced the deck, checking and rechecking the horizon for any sign of the hostile ship.

"It is too easy," he said. "Even now, as we stalk the prey, I am filled with misgivings."

"Whatever for, Holmes? Surely Colonel Moran is no match for Her Majesty's Navy?"

"Moran, though formidable, is not the opponent I fear. No, Watson, I speak of Moriarty, the Napoleon of Crime. His net is worldwide, his contacts rival those of any government. Just when you think you have set your trap is when you must be on your closest guard."

"But . . ."

"Mark my words! It has happened before. His brain is like a spider's web—spirals within spirals. Moriarty lives to spin that web, and he feels the slightest tremor at its periphery. You may rest assured he knows we are on the seas, and that he is somehow . . ." Holmes paused, taking in a lungful of tobacco smoke and letting it out slowly. "Somehow, he is stalking us."

"Come now, Holmes—stalking the Royal Navy?"

"You may laugh, Watson, but it is difficult to overestimate Moriarty's determination."

One of the crewmen appeared with a couple of cups of tea spiked with a tot of rum, saying that the bridge thought we might appreciate a little refreshment. We thanked him and continued pacing. The tin cups were hot to the touch, so we rested them against a coil of rope.

I looked out again at the calm sea, thinking that the tension of our voyage had affected Holmes's judgment. His respect for his arch rival seemed exaggerated, bordering on the ludicrous. It occurred to me that, expecting a long ocean voyage with little outside stimulation, he might have brought along some of his cocaine, which he occasionally injects when his overactive mind needs surcease from boredom. The drug could have produced such paranoia. Lost in these thoughts, I absently took the cup of tea into my hand, blew on it and sipped.

"Spit it out, Watson! Spit it out!" Holmes was slapping me on the back, having dashed the cup to the deck. "Poison!" he said. "The tea has been poisoned! Are you all right?"

Shaking, my mouth already feeling a kind of dry numbness though I had obeyed Holmes's command instantly, I turned to my friend. "Where is that mate?" I mumbled.

But the deck was filled with uniformed men, all indistinguishable from a distance. My legs seemed to be getting weaker, and it was becoming harder to focus, to recognize any of the men. Even Holmes appeared wavy and indistinct, as though I were looking at him from under water. Then all went dark.

I could feel strong fingers digging into my shoulder, pressing against the Jezail bullet that had lodged there when I had been wounded in Afghanistan. I opened my eyes, and an unfamiliar room swam before me.

There was a hoarse whisper. "Watson?" The fingers gripped harder. "Watson? Can you hear me?"

I tried to bring the towering figure into focus in the darkened room. "Holmes? Where am I?"

"You're alive. That's what's important. You very nearly weren't."

It began to come back to me—the mate, the tea, my last memories before losing consciousness. What a fool I had been to doubt Holmes! Once again he'd been right. Moriarty's agents, it appeared, were with us even aboard this ship.

"Where are we now?" I asked. "What day is it?" The questions kept coming. "Why us, Holmes? Why poison us? Does he think we can make a difference, when the entire Navy is out to get him?"

Holmes chuckled. "I rather fancy he thinks just that. Flattering, eh?"

Groggily I sat up. "I wish I could take some pleasure in it. Just now I'm too confused."

"Come, can you get up?"

Holmes took me by the arm and walked me about the small cabin. Outside, it appeared to be closing on dusk. After a few turns from wall to wall, I regained my sea legs and my mind cleared. "What did I take? What was it?"

"One of the cyanamids, I presume. You were extremely lucky, Watson. Even trace amounts can kill. You mustn't have swallowed any at all."

The reason for that did not for a moment escape me. Once again Sherlock Holmes had saved my life.

"As to how long you've been under, thirty hours is a reasonable estimate. And as you can see, night descends." He reached into his pock-

ets and pulled forth most of a loaf of bread, some dried meat and an orange. "You must be hungry, and you'll need all your strength. I packed this food myself as a precaution against just this sort of thing."

Twenty minutes later we were again on the deck. I had naturally brought my revolver along, and now I gratefully felt its cold weight in my pocket. Shadow figures scattered here and there, swabbing, stowing, making the vessel shipshape for the night. Even armed, I was not without trepidation, knowing that one of these men had tried to kill us only the day before. It could easily happen again.

Captain John Wagner approached. Ginger-haired and bearded, he was a sturdy sailor of the old school—hale, hearty, and profane. In spite of my accident, I felt I was safe within his domain. He ran the tightest of ships.

"Good evening, Mr. Holmes. Ah, Dr. Watson," he blustered, "that such a thing should happen on my ship! I swear to you we'll find the blackguard, and I'll personally keelhaul him. My best men are on it." His voice then softened. "You had us all right worried there, sir. Good to see you back up and about."

I thanked him for his good wishes and struck up a conversation about our quarry. "Tomorrow looks to be the day, doesn't it, captain?"

He laughed. "That's your friend's estimate, doctor. But it's a big ocean. Hard to pinpoint a meeting date. Could happen any time."

"Could we miss him entirely?"

His face hardened. "We won't miss him. And once we encounter the blighter, we'll bring him to. I'll stake my reputation on that."

"Who's at the wheel now, captain?" Holmes asked blandly, walking up to us. Throughout our discussion, he had stood at the ship's rail, peering into the darkness.

"That'd be my first mate, Jeffers."

"And the lookout?"

Justifiably, I thought, the captain's eyes narrowed. "What's all this about, Mr. Holmes?"

Holmes turned and pointed out over the bow. "Unless I'm very much mistaken, captain, there's a ship running dark just off to starboard."

Wagner and I ran to the railing, squinting to make out a shape where Holmes had indicated. Before I had seen anything, the captain had turned, uttering a foul oath. As he rushed back to the bridge, his voice bellowing "Battle stations!" shook the very timbers of the ship.

We were the wedge of the armada, and within minutes flares had alerted the rest of the fleet that something had been spotted. We had no way to be sure it was Colonel Moran, but the fact that the ship had its running lights covered was more than enough to convince me.

Holmes stood beside me at the bow rail, his face a study in determination. "Now remember, Watson," he said. "No one from that ship must be allowed aboard. All its crew will have been inoculated against the plague, but there's no telling if any of them are infested with the fleas or lice that carry the disease."

"Are we to kill them all, then?" The men were fiends, but it was not like Holmes to be so cold-blooded.

"No, no, we'll shepherd them and their cargo of death to Gorée, a small island in Dakar's harbor which used to hold slaves waiting for transport. Captain Wagner knows the drill."

"And then . . . ?"

"And then Moran and his men can swim for it while we blow their ship out of the water. The salt water will leach away any vermin, and the men are all sailors—they'll have no trouble finding work. . . ."

He was about to continue when we heard a shot from somewhere behind us. I reached for my revolver and raced toward the sound, Holmes at my heels.

"Here! Up here!"

It was Jeffers, the first mate, staggering to his feet on the bridge, his hands to his bleeding head. At his feet lay a prostrate Captain Wagner.

"The captain . . ." Jeffers began.

I was there beside him, but there was nothing I could do. Captain Wagner had a bullet hole in the back of his head. The gallant sailor had completed his last command.

"What happened?" I demanded.

The mate appeared to be in shock. "I don't know. I was hit from behind, and then . . ."

At that moment, the lookout shouted from above. "Enemy ship preparing to engage!"

We looked over our shoulders and there, its running lights suddenly lit, a ship was bearing down on us on a collision course. Our crew, at battle stations, waited for the orders, but Jeffers seemed incapable of movement, watching horrified as the vessel approached.

"We can't let them engage." Holmes spoke calmly to Jeffers, but his voice cut like a knife. "Think of your orders, man."

On the deck of the enemy ship, we could see the crew manning their battle stations, with small arms and grappling hooks at the ready. These were the same men who had captured the deadly Boer pirates only two weeks before. Jeffers looked about in panic, like a caged rat, and then suddenly screamed to his own waiting crew: "Fire! Fire! Fire all guns!"

"*No!*" Holmes yelled, but his voice was drowned out by the simultaneous roar of fourteen cannons. Moran must have kept a magazine below decks, for no sooner had we recovered from the shock of the first sally than the night turned into day as the enemy ship, less than fifty yards from us now, exploded in a huge fireball.

The force of the explosion knocked us off our feet, and we lay dazed for a moment in a shocking, deathly silence. And then, as though the brutality of what we'd just witnessed were not enough, a ghastly rain of burning timber and flesh began to fall and litter our deck.

The falling debris started several small fires, and Jeffers forced himself up to direct the crew. Holmes and I sat by Wagner's body and watched the floating remains of Moran's ship flare, then smoke, as they slowly sank into the ocean.

Holmes's eyes were glazed over. His elbows rested on his knees, his hands limp between them. Glancing first at me, then at the fallen captain, he sighed aloud. "Wrong," he muttered half to himself in a tone of pure anguish. "Where could it have gone so wrong?"

There was no chance of sleeping. Eight bells in the third watch came and went, and still the crew kept at its cleanup duties. Jeffers had convened an officer's tribunal and ordered that every man account for his whereabouts at the time the captain had been murdered. One by one, the men filed wearily into the captain's stateroom, resentful and edgy. Holmes stood silent at the railing, smoking. His hunched shoulders left no doubt that he carried the burden of the deaths of Moran's crewmen as though they were his own.

I went to him. "It could not be helped," I said.

He looked coldly at me.

"Holmes," I insisted. "It was not your fault."

He shook his head. "It was not supposed to be that way. No one had to die. And we never got the proof."

"But surely the fact that they intended to engage . . . ?"

"It doesn't prove . . . Halloa," he exclaimed. "What's that?"

I looked out at the black ocean. A glint of phosphorous showed above something moving in the dark water. "What could that be?" I asked.

Holmes's dark eyes glinted in the light from his pipe. A kind of smile began to play at the corners of his mouth, and I recognized that look: He was on a scent, when he thought it had eluded him. Then, at once, the half smile faded, replaced by a grimness I had never before witnessed in him. "The monster," he said under his breath. "The unspeakable monster."

"Holmes," I began, "what—"

"Follow me," he said, "and keep your gun handy." He headed toward the bridge.

"Mate Jeffers," he yelled up from the deck, "there is a boat in the water."

The first mate, more haggard than ever, was struggling with the onus of command. He glared at Holmes as another interruption in an already impossible night. "What's that you say, sir?" he yelled down.

"There's a boat in the water." Holmes pointed. "There, at forty-five degrees off port."

The small boat could just barely be seen coming into the circle of light thrown by our ship. "My God," said Jeffers. He seemed instantly rejuvenated, taking the steps down from the bridge in bounding leaps. "Could it be that someone survived?"

"It would appear so," my friend answered. I glanced then at Sherlock Holmes, and he had in his eye a look so dangerous that even I, who knew him so well, shuddered. Yet I could not for the life of me see what had so aroused him. Questions formed in my mind, but the fierceness of his countenance forced me to hold my tongue.

Jeffers called for some men and had them begin preparing for the rescue. Out in the night, I could just make out the lifeboat. On board was a single man, standing and waving. His "Ahoy," small yet haunting, carried across the water. In the boat with him appeared to be a large box of some sort—probably, I thought, some possessions he'd managed to escape with before the ship exploded.

As the boat approached, Jeffers leaned farther over the water to direct the crewmen's operations. Just at that moment, Holmes lurched forward, grabbed the mate from behind and lifted him up and over the railing. With flailing arms and an anguished cry, Jeffers hit the water with a tremendous splash.

"Holmes!" I cried.

"There's no time to explain! Quick, Watson, your weapon!"

In a flash I had drawn my revolver and leveled it at the crew members gathered around us. Holmes remained calm. "I apologize for this inconvenience, gentlemen," he said to them, "and after a moment it won't be necessary, but for now I think it better that no one try to save Mr. Jeffers."

The mate rose to the surface, spluttering. "Holmes!" he called. "What's the meaning of this? It's mutiny! Watson, I'll have you both hanged!"

"I think the pleasure will be the other way round!" Holmes countered. "If you don't drown first."

"Why should I hang?"

"First for murdering Captain Wagner, then for blowing up Moran's ship, and not least for trying to poison Watson and me."

"You're mad. They were going to ram us!"

"No," Holmes replied. "But for a moment it certainly did look that way, so that your disobedience of orders seemed logical."

"What are you saying?"

"The convoy was to herd the ship to Gorée, not destroy it. And no one—no one at all, even a survivor—was to come aboard."

Jeffers treaded water awkwardly. Fully dressed as he was, the weight of his clothes would pull him down within minutes. The lifeboat, all but forgotten by us, was drifting steadily away from him.

Jeffers went under briefly and came up gagging. Looking at the lifeboat, he tried a few half-hearted breaststrokes in its direction, but the effort was too great for him. He turned back to us, breathing heavily. "Help me, Watson, and I'll see that you're pardoned!"

"If my friend hangs," I called down, "I will gladly hang beside him." Then, to Holmes, I said softly, "You're not going to let him drown, are you?"

"I rather think he'll be saved."

But as we watched, Jeffers went under again. I thought the mate was gone, but once again he broke the surface. This time the panic in his voice was not feigned. He looked up at Holmes, then across to the lifeboat and came to his fateful decision. "Moran!" he yelled. "Help me! I'm drowning!"

"You fool, Jeffers! Shut up!"

Sherlock Holmes addressed me, finally allowing himself a smile. "As I suspected, they know each other by name. It is all the proof we need." He called overboard. "You'd better see to Jeffers, Moran! The game is up."

"Who is that I'm speaking to?"

Holmes chuckled mirthlessly. "You don't recognize the voice, colonel? We've met occa-sionally." He leaned over the railing. "Mr. Sherlock Holmes at your service."

"Holmes? What is this?"

"You thought I'd be dead by now, eh? Poisoned?"

"What are you talking about?"

"We had better discuss it after you've saved your accomplice."

And, indeed, Moran had set to with his oars. Before long, the exhausted mate had been pulled into the lifeboat.

"Now in the name of decency, Holmes, let us aboard!" Moran cried.

"You have a great deal of gall using that word, colonel. What is that box behind you, sir?"

Moran uncovered a huge cage in which skulked something large and black, looking from our deck like a small bear. "It is nothing more than a giant Sumatran tree rat, Holmes. I was taking it to the London Zoo. It was the only thing I could save from the ship."

"Before you blew it up?"

"What are you saying?"

"I'm saying you sacrificed your entire crew so that we would naturally pluck you and your giant rat of Sumatra from the lifeboat. You thought by now that Watson, Captain Wagner, and I would all be dead and that no one would think to question your rescue."

"No!"

"That rat is infested with bubonic plague, and you yourself are host to its deadly carrier fleas. Both you and Jeffers are inoculated, but once you or the rat comes aboard this ship, the England we all love is gone."

At the word *plague*, a general murmuring arose from the men behind us. Holmes turned and addressed them. "You heard me correctly. All your officers, including Jeffers, had been briefed—no one from Moran's ship was to board a British ship of the line. Would any of you let Moran and Jeffers aboard?"

"What should we do, sir?" one of the men asked.

"Run to the stateroom and ask the ranking officer to take control here. Be off now!" Holmes turned back to the lifeboat. "Drop the cage over-board, Moran. Now!"

We could hear the vicious growls and squeals of the caged beast. It stalked back and forth, beady eyes fixed on the lights of our ship. Moran hesitated a moment, then reached behind him.

"Holmes, have pity . . ." he began.

"Fire a shot into the boat, Watson."

I did so.

Holmes continued: "Colonel, you're going to have a hard time staying afloat with a hull full of bullet holes."

"Please . . ."

"Another, Watson, if you would."

After the second shot, Moran quickly lifted the cage and dropped it into the black water. It sank like a stone, leaving no trace.

One of the officers came running up. "What's going on here, Mr. Holmes? Where's Mr. Jeffers?"

In a few dozen words the situation had been explained.

"What should we do with these two men?"

Holmes smiled. "I should think that that life-boat, if towed at a goodly distance behind us, would make for an interesting journey back to England. Both men should be deloused by the time we arrive."

Back in our digs in Baker Street, Holmes put his feet up before the fire. We'd been back for nearly three weeks, and the trials of Moran and Jeffers were coming up, yet there were still elements unclear to me. "When did you know, exactly?" I asked.

Holmes exhaled a heady Cavendish smoke. "I believe I have mentioned before, Watson, that when all other possibilities have been exhausted, whatever remains, however implausible, must be the truth. As soon as I saw the lifeboat in the water, a conjecture occurred to me. No lifeboat could have survived that explosion. Therefore, it had been lowered before the explosion. It follows, then, that the explosion was planned. When Jeffers did not hesitate to try to bring the survivor aboard, I surmised that he was in on the plot. Of course, I had to risk mutiny to prove it, but Jeffers's involvement was the only thing that fit all the facts."

"But he was bleeding when we came upon him and Captain Wagner."

"Nothing is more convincing and easier to self-inflict than a superficial head wound."

"And our—ahem—my poisoning?"

"The crewman said that the tea was from the bridge. We both assumed he meant from the captain. But a man of Captain Wagner's person-ality would imprint it on his men, and if he had personally sent the drinks, the crewman would have said, 'Captain Wagner sends his compli-ments,' or some such thing."

"Now that you explain it, it seems so clear."

"Don't punish yourself, my friend. Neither of us saw it at the time. It was not until I saw Moran in the lifeboat that I was forced to recon-sider the smallest events in the chain."

The fire burned low. "And what, finally, of Professor Moriarty?" I asked.

Holmes sighed. "Not Moran, nor Jeffers, nor Culverton-Smith will implicate him. For the present we've foiled him, but I fear Moriarty and I must await another confrontation."

"And what then?" I asked, looking into my friend's troubled face.

Sherlock Holmes gazed glassy-eyed into the fire. "And then, Watson," he said, "then one of us must surely die."

THE FOOTSTEPS OF
A GIGANTIC AUTHOR

Did Sherlock Holmes Meet Hercule . . . ?

JULIAN SYMONS

IN ADDITION TO writing nearly thirty mystery novels and a half-dozen short story collections, Julian Gustave Symons (1912–1994) was an outstanding scholar of mystery fiction as well as one of its foremost practitioners. In addition to biographies of Edgar Allan Poe, Arthur Conan Doyle, and a critical study of Dashiell Hammett, he wrote an excellent history of the genre, *Bloody Murder* (1972; titled *Mortal Consequences* in the United States), in which he also defined the genre as he thought it ought to be, insisting that it move away from pure puzzle-solving to a greater reliance on psychological elements of crime; it won an Edgar. He has been honored with lifetime achievement awards from the Mystery Writers of America, the (British) Crime Writers' Association, and the Swedish Crime Writers' Academy.

Symons, a great admirer of Sherlock Holmes and an even greater one of Arthur Conan Doyle, chided Sherlockians for their game of treating Conan Doyle as merely the literary agent for Dr. Watson. In addition to the present story, Symons wrote two short story pastiches, "How a Hermit was Disturbed in His Retirement," published in *The Great Detectives* (1981), and "The Affair of the Vanishing Diamonds" (1987). He also wrote two modern-day Sherlockian novels: *A Three Pipe Problem* (1975), in which a television actor, Sheridan Hayes, wears the mask of Sherlock Holmes and assumes his character; and, more than a decade later, the less successful *The Kentish Manor Murders* (1988), featuring the same character.

"Did Sherlock Holmes Meet Hercule . . . ?" was originally published in the April 1987 issue of *The Illustrated London News*. It was collected in *The Man Who Hated Television and Other Stories* (London, Macmillan, 1995).

DID SHERLOCK HOLMES MEET HERCULE . . . ?

Julian Symons

Did Sherlock Holmes ever meet Hercule Poirot? This is not so unlikely a supposition as it might seem. The last recorded Sherlock Holmes case takes place in 1914 on the eve of World War I, after which he retired to bee-keeping on the Sussex Downs. At that time Poirot, according to the best information we have, was fifty and still active, the account of his retirement in 1904 (in *The Mysterious Affair at Styles*) being no doubt a printing error.

It is this possibility that gives peculiar interest to the following story, particularly as it does not come from Dr. Watson's battered tin despatch-box containing details of many important cases which he placed "somewhere in the vaults of the bank of Cox & Company at Charing Cross," where it presumably remains. It was found, rather, among the papers of Poirot's friend Captain Arthur Hastings, who recorded a number of the great Belgian detective's cases. Why should a case involving Sherlock Holmes and narrated by Dr. Watson be among the Hastings papers? Perhaps the narrative itself answers the question. It is unfortunately not quite complete, but there can be no more than a few lines missing at the end. Of course, no absolute guarantee of its authenticity, or of its relevance to the two great detectives, can be given.

SHERLOCK HOLMES WOULD shake his head when I mentioned the name of Mulready and say the world was not yet prepared to hear about an affair that involved a chief Minister of the Crown, secret papers, and the threat of war. Yet it can do no harm to set down the extraordinary series of events involving the inhabitants of Mulready House while they remain fresh in my mind.

It was an autumn morning a couple of years before Holmes's retirement, and I had spent the night with my old friend in Baker Street. Breakfast was finished, he had done with the papers, and was roaming about the room, talking discursively as was his wont, when he stopped at the window.

"Halloa, Watson. Our humble lodgings are about to be unusually honoured."

"Holmes, if you are going to give me some of those far-fetched deductions about——"

Holmes laughed. "No, no, my dear fellow. It is true that when I see a man being driven up in the latest model of Rolls-Royce motorcar, and when that vehicle has a crest on the door panel, I know a person of some distinction is likely to step out of it. But in fact I recognized the man himself. It is Lord Rivington."

A moment later, our Secretary for War was in the room. His features were familiar to me through many photographs and cartoons, but none had done full justice to the force in those craggy features, the intensity of the deep-set eyes behind the bushy brows. He looked from one of us to the other.

"Mr. Holmes, I have come to ask your help in a matter of great importance, and one that is absolutely confidential."

I rose, but Holmes stopped me. "You may speak in Dr. Watson's presence as freely as you would if I were alone."

"Nevertheless . . ." Sherlock Holmes was

filling his pipe. He said nothing. Lord Riving-ton looked at him fiercely, then shrugged. "Very well, there is no time for argument. You are aware that negotiations are going on between this country and France that involve a plan for joint action if the Kaiser's sabre-rattling should turn to the drawing of swords?"

"I know what is said in the newspapers, nothing more."

"The negotiations have reached a most delicate stage. You can imagine my feelings when I discovered through our Intelligence Service that everything we have discussed was known in Berlin, down to the last detail. And it was shown to me quite inescapably that the information must have reached Germany through the office of the man in charge of negotiations, Sir Charles Mulready. He is one of my oldest friends, we were at school and the Varsity together. I could swear that he is a man of honour. Yet these papers have passed through no hands but his. You may ask how I can be so sure of this, Mr. Holmes. The answer is simple. I heard it yesterday from Sir Charles's own lips."

"Nobody in his office had access to them?"

"Nobody. They were kept in a safe, and were under lock and key when he took them home. And there has been no betrayal from the French side." Lord Rivington coughed. "Allies may have their own secrets. Certain matters mentioned in memoranda accompanying the documents have not been discussed with the French, yet these, too, are known in Berlin. They have not been stolen, hence they must have been either copied or photographed."

Holmes had been following with the keenest attention. "Does Sir Charles have any family links with Germany?"

"There you've hit it, Mr. Holmes. He married a German lady who had been left a widow with a young son when her husband, Count von Brankel, was killed in a hunting accident. The boy, Hans, has been brought up as if he were Charles's own son. He is intelligent, but I fear not manly. He was expelled from his public school—I am sure I need not enter into details. Then he studied medicine for a year, but gave it

up and expressed a wish to become a stage actor, something which of course could not be countenanced. Accordingly, he follows no profession, lives at home, and sponges on his family. They have a daughter of their own, Lilian, who has some ridiculous idea that women should be allowed to vote, and that what she calls weapons of murder should be abolished. My friends have not been fortunate in their children."

"One more question. Am I right in thinking that our French allies would be interested in the memoranda they have not seen?"

For a moment the Secretary for War looked surprised. "Possibly, but the relations between our countries are entirely friendly. Monsieur Calamy, who is handling the negotiations, is in London and staying at Mulready House."

Holmes nodded.

"And now I come to the tragic climax. A draft known as Plan X has been prepared, setting out in detail our military and naval commitments to France in the event of war. Together with it was a memorandum about the defence of Britain which was for our eyes only, not those of M. Calamy. Both of these were in Sir Charles's possession. Yesterday, when what had been suspicions became certainties, I asked him to come and see me. He had been away from Whitehall corridors for a couple of days with an attack of gout, but he limped along to see me, and I told him what I had learned.

"He behaved as I would have expected, was first incredulous and then horrified. He protested his innocence, and I believed him." The great head bent down for a moment, then he looked from one of us to the other in despair. "Yet last night he made a confession of guilt, not in words but in his actions. He took an overdose of a medicine he used to ease his sufferings from gout. And there is worse to say. Both Plan X and the memorandum were with him, taken home for study. Both are missing."

A few minutes later, we were sitting in the Rolls-Royce, on the way to the Mulready home in Mayfair.

The blinds were drawn over the long windows, and within the house we felt the sombre atmosphere of sudden death. Lord Rivington led the way up to Sir Charles's suite, separated from his wife's by a dressing-room.

"Lady Mulready found him in pain at some time in the night and immediately called his doctor, whose name is Cardew. He said Sir Charles must have suffered an acute attack of gout and taken an overdose of his medicine, but I fear it was taken deliberately."

"I know Dr. Cardew," I said. "A most reliable practitioner." I approached the bed where the body lay, decently covered by a sheet, and looked at the distorted features. An empty glass stood on a bedside table, with a bottle beside it, perhaps one-third full, labelled *Colantium*. "This is a medicine often used for gout. It contains colchicum, which relieves the pain. I see no unusual circumstances here."

"Do you not, Watson?" Holmes had been prowling the room and the dressing-room beyond, examining pictures, ornaments, a pipe rack, using his magnifying glass to look closely at a bureau in the dressing-room. Now he, too, lifted the sheet, then looked carefully at the glass and bottle, tipping the latter and holding it to the light.

"Colchicum is a poison, like many plants and flowers that play a part in relieving pain. Yellow jasmine, spotted hemlock, the foxglove, the Calabar bean, and the paternoster pea—these can be as deadly as the poppy or laburnum seeds. I have in preparation a little pamphlet called 'The Poison Garden,' which should be useful to every medical practitioner. And colchicum may ease pain in small quantities, but in larger ones it can kill. Did you remark the amount of precipitation in that bottle, Watson? It should not be there, and there are marks of sediment in the glass. Somebody added more colchicum to the bottle, and made this gout remedy a poisonous drink."

I looked again at the bottle. "Holmes, you are right. But how——"

"That is what we must discover. And colchicum is bitter, the first taste should have warned

Sir Charles." He turned to Lord Rivington. "I take it that Plan X and the memorandum were kept in the dressing-room bureau. The lock has been picked skilfully, but scratches show under the magnifying glass. Perhaps we may now talk to Lady Mulready."

The widow was a tall, stately grey-haired lady. Lord Rivington called her Ilse, and she spoke to him as Gerald. She greeted Holmes warmly.

"Mr. Holmes, I know what Lord Rivington believes, but I can assure you he is wrong. I am a German and proud of my ancestry, and I know my husband's equal pride in being British. Some terrible mistake has been made."

"I believe we shall find an explanation that will be entirely honourable to his name. If you could tell me what happened yesterday after his return from Whitehall, I should be grateful."

"My husband told me little or nothing of political affairs. When he returned home, I could see that he was upset, but he said nothing of the cause and I had learned that it was useless to ask. He remained in his private rooms until dinner. We were five at table, our children, Hans and Lilian, and M. Calamy making up the rest of the party. It was not a cheerful meal. My husband's gout was troubling him and he hardly spoke, except when Lilian provoked him by speaking of some suffragette meeting she had attended. Hans seemed preoccupied and M. Calamy was concerned, as always, with his food."

A fleeting smile crossed her face. "We live simply here. My husband did not care what he ate, and the years have reconciled me to English cooking, but M. Calamy cannot endure it. He has brought his chef as well as his valet, but although his meals are specially prepared he still grumbles. So he did last night. After dinner, my husband called me aside and said, "I have painful decisions to make, Ilse, and I fear the results will cause you grief." Those were his last words to me."

"When was the tragedy discovered?"

"At three o'clock this morning. I heard cries coming from my husband's room. I went in and found him in terrible pain. Dr. Cardew was summoned immediately, but by the time he arrived Charles was in a coma and he could do nothing. The end came just after seven."

"Were your son and daughter present?"

"Lilian, yes. Hans . . ." She hesitated. "It proved almost impossible to rouse him and, when at last the housemaid did so, he staggered, as though under the influence of drink. Coming from his room to his father's, he slipped, fell down several stairs, and, as it proved, broke his ankle. He had to be carried back to bed, and Dr. Cardew says he must stay in his room."

"A last question, and I have done. You said your husband didn't care what he ate. Was there a special reason for that?"

"Yes. A nasal operation a few years ago almost deprived him of taste and smell, so that he could barely distinguish chicken from beef or claret from brandy. Surely that cannot be important?"

"It is one piece in the jigsaw, no more."

Outside the drawing room, we were met by a young girl. It was easy to see this was Ilse Mulready's daughter, although there was a light in her eye and a spring in her step that her mother lacked. She held out an envelope. "Which of you gentlemen is Mr. Sherlock Holmes? Here is a letter for you."

Holmes looked at the envelope, tore it open, read it, and passed it to me. Some words were printed in capitals on a single sheet of paper:

MISTER HOLMES GO AWAY
YOUR PRESENTS HERE IS UNNECESSARY

"Written with a Waverley nib on a standard Ranelagh-weave paper," Holmes said. "Was this delivered by hand, Miss Mulready?"

"No, one of the footmen found it on the hall table. What does it say?" Holmes showed it to her, and she flushed. "I think he's right. Of course, I am sorry my father is dead, but he should be allowed to rest in peace. I know he died because he was a man of war, as you are, Lord Rivington. He hated poor Hans, because

Hans had no interest in fighting and killing people. I heard them arguing last night in Father's room."

"And what was the subject?"

"I don't know. And if I did, I shouldn't tell you." She turned away from us and ran upstairs. Lord Rivington coughed, hummed under his breath, said nothing.

"Surely this note is important, Holmes," I said. "It was obviously written by somebody almost illiterate."

"Or somebody who wants us to think so. Or——"

He was interrupted by the appearance of a gentleman dressed with rather too obvious elegance, his hair glossy, his beard wonderfully neat. My feeling that there is something unmanly about the French is reinforced by their use of pomades and perfumes. This, of course, was M. Calamy, who now expressed his regrets to Lord Rivington, smiling as he did so.

"Perhaps after this tragedy our negotiations should be given up—postponed, as you say."

"Not at all." Lord Rivington spoke sharply. "They are more than ever urgent, and I shall take charge of them in person."

"That will make me happy. We shall, of course, conduct them on both sides with entire frankness." The Frenchman's smile perhaps broadened a little. "Later today I move from this house of sorrow to our Embassy."

"With your staff?" Lord Rivington said with heavy irony.

"My valet, my chef, what should I do without them?" He bowed slightly and was gone. The Secretary for War muttered something among which I thought I heard the words "primping popinjay."

Holmes looked after him with a puzzled air, then stood deep in thought. Lord Rivington said impatiently, "Mr. Holmes, this is no time for brooding."

"I beg your pardon. I agree, Plan X must be returned to you at once."

"You know where it is?" the Secretary for War said in astonishment.

"It was an elementary problem."

. . .

Holmes asked a maid to take us to Mr. Hans's room. As we walked up the great stairs and down a long passage, Holmes murmured to me, "Nevertheless, Watson, there is something I do not understand."

We found the son of the house on a sofa, one foot heavily bandaged. He was a good-looking young fellow with delicate, almost pretty features, but at this moment they were taut with anguish. A bowl of flowers stood on a window ledge beside him and Holmes picked it up.

"The autumn crocus," he said musingly. "A charming but dangerous flower."

The young man started, then said, "Before God, Mr. Holmes, I never intended——"

"I am prepared to believe you, but I am not your judge. Let me tell you what I think happened and you can say how nearly it approaches the truth."

He turned to us. "Hans here is one of those unfortunate people with a strong feminine streak that leads them into dubious, even criminal associations. Such deviations have touched our own Royal family—you will recall the need to hush up the scandal of the noble visitors to the male brothel in Cleveland Street. The German Intelligence department became aware of Hans's propensities and they have been blackmailing him. He has abstracted documents from his stepfather's bureau, copied, and then returned them. When you, Lord Rivington, told Sir Charles what had happened, he knew who the culprit must be."

The young man wrung his hands. "They threatened to expose me. I would have gone to prison. What else could I do?"

"You should have told your stepfather," Holmes said sternly. "I come to the events of last night. Sir Charles called you to his room. I don't know what he said, perhaps that you must leave the country, but it made you desperate. You had sufficient medical knowledge to know that colchicum was in your stepfather's medicine, and that it is easily distilled from the autumn crocus. Perhaps you prepared it then, perhaps you had

some already prepared for just such an emergency. You added it to the medicine."

"It was to make sure he slept soundly. I swear I never meant him to die."

"I don't suppose you did. A little medical knowledge may be not merely dangerous but fatal. Otherwise, your scheme worked well enough. You took the papers, I suppose meaning to copy and return them. Why did you not do so?"

"Because I was drugged. All you say is true, Mr. Holmes, but can you explain what happened to me? When I knew my stepfather would be asleep, I went to his dressing-room and took the plan and the memorandum—the bureau drawer was easy to open. I had done it before. I brought them in here to copy and return them, and then I was going to post the copy at once. But I was too sleepy, my fingers wouldn't move over the paper. I put the papers away and fell asleep, and when I was woken I felt so dizzy I could hardly stand. It was because of the dizziness that I fell and broke my ankle." He gestured at the bandages. "Then Dr. Cardew gave me an opiate and I slept until ten o'clock this morning. Now I am told not to move."

"The papers are still here?" Lord Rivington cried. "Then if you want a chance of saving your villainous skin, tell me where they are."

"In that bookcase," the young man said sullenly. "Behind the top row of books, on the right."

Lord Rivington went to the bookcase, took out some books in the top row, put his hand in, took out more books, and turned with a furious face. "There is nothing here! What trick are you trying to play?"

"Nothing?" I have never seen a ghastlier look of fear and apprehension on a man's face. "Impossible." He shrank back as Lord Rivington approached him threateningly.

"Wait," Sherlock Holmes said in an imperative tone. "Something is wrong here, there is something I have not understood." He paced up and down the room while the rest of us watched. "Did you write a card saying my presence here was unnecessary? I thought not, yet it came from within the house. Last night you all ate the same food at dinner?"

"Except M. Calamy. His food is specially prepared by his chef."

"And afterwards?"

"My stepfather left us. Coffee was served, but my digestion is poor. I always have a cup of chocolate."

"A cup of chocolate, yes. And M. Calamy was very pleased with himself. I have been stupid, Watson."

"Holmes, I don't know what you're talking about." I could see from Lord Rivington's expression that he was similarly bewildered.

"The card, Watson, the card. It was a Frenchman's English misspelling. But quick, there is not a moment to lose, he is leaving."

"M. Calamy?"

"The man who drugged the cup of chocolate—his so-called chef."

We found him in a servants' bedroom, under the eaves, packing his bag for departure. He did not seem surprised to see us.

"Ah, Monsieur Holmes. Here is what you look for." A large envelope lay on the bed. "The excellent Plan X, and the other paper."

"Which you have copied."

"Precisely, *mon cher*. Now Britain and France have no secrets from each other, we can be entirely frank in discussion."

"It was you who sent me the postcard."

"My spelling, she is not of the best, but that is so."

"You drugged the chocolate, and then took the documents."

"On behalf of *la belle France*. I am called the good M. Calamy's chef, but he gets the indigestion from my cooking." He chuckled. "I make my investigation, and soon understand that the young Hans is—like your Oscar Wilde, shall we say?—and is responsible for what has happened. And I see things are, as you say, coming to the head, so I arrange for the young Hans to have a little harmless sleep while I take possession of Plan X and the memorandum. No harm is done—except to our friend Sir Charles. That is a great tragedy."

He was an odd-looking little fellow, very short, his head a perfect egg shape. His hair was very black and parted in the middle, his moustaches long and pointed. He wore patent-leather shoes. He looked like a perfect musical-comedy Frenchman.

"You are an agent of the French government," Holmes said rather stiffly.

"At the moment that is so, but I am like yourself a private detective. It is truly an honour to meet the greatest detective in Britain."

Holmes rarely smiled but he did so then, although his smile vanished at the little man's next words.

"I am myself the greatest detective in Europe. My name is——"

The narrative ends here, so that the pseudo-chef's identity remains uncertain. The scandal of Sir Charles's death was evidently hushed up. Hans Mulready had in later life a successful stage career as a female impersonator.

A Trifling Affair

H. R. F. KEATING

A PROLIFIC NOVELIST with more than fifty books to his credit, as well as the author of scores of short stories, Henry Reymond Fitzwalter Keating (1926–2011) also worked as a journalist until 1960, when he became a full-time fiction writer and literary critic, achieving success with *The Perfect Murder* (1964). Introducing his most famous character, Inspector Ganesh Ghote (pronounced GO-tay), of the Bombay CID, it won the (British) Crime Writers' Association (CWA) Gold Dagger for the best novel of the year; it also was nominated for an Edgar Award by the Mystery Writers of America. Regarded as one of the great writers of fair-play detective fiction, Keating served as president of the prestigious Detection Club (1985–2000) and was awarded a Cartier Diamond Dagger for lifetime achievement by the CWA in 1996.

In addition to reviewing crime fiction for the London *Times* for fifteen years, he wrote many nonfiction books devoted to mysteries, including *Murder Must Appetize* (1975), *Great Crimes* (1982), *Writing Crime Fiction* (1986; revised 2nd ed. 1994), *Crime and Mystery: The 100 Best Books* (1987), and *The Bedside Companion to Crime* (1989). As a dedicated aficionado of Sherlock Holmes, he produced *Sherlock Holmes, the Man and His World* (1979) and several pastiches of the great detective.

"A Trifling Affair" was first published in *John Creasey's Crime Collection*, edited by Herbert Harris (London, Gollancz, 1980).

A TRIFLING AFFAIR

H. R. F. Keating

TRIFLES, SHERLOCK HOLMES was wont to remark, may bear an importance altogether contrary to their apparent worth, and I venture to think that there cannot have been a case more trifling in all Holmes's adventures than that of the affair of the poet of childhood and the ink-blotted verse volume. Yet, unimportant though it was, it nevertheless had in it for me a lesson which I hope I shall not forget.

It was a day in the spring of 1898 when from among the early post Holmes selected a particular letter, still in its envelope, and tossed it to me across the breakfast table.

"Well, Watson," he said, "tell me what you make of that. A somewhat unusual missive for a consulting detective to receive, I think."

I took the envelope and turned it over once or twice in my hands. It appeared to be of no particular distinction. The paper was neither cheap nor very expensive. The postmark, I saw, was that of Brighton and Hove for the previous afternoon. The writing of the address, "Sherlock Holmes Esq., 221B Baker Street, London W.," was plainly that of a gentleman, though the letters were not perhaps as confidently formed as they might have been. The sole peculiarity that I could observe was that the writer's name had been put upon the reverse of the envelope, "Phillip Hughes Esq."

"Possibly an American who writes," I ventured at last, when from the tapping of Holmes's lean fingers on the tablecloth I became aware of his impatience. "I believe that the custom of putting the writer's name on the outside of a letter is more practised on the far side of the Atlan-

tic than here. And certainly the handwriting is not that of any contintental."

"Good, Watson. Excellent. Clearly my correspondent does not come from the Continent of Europe. But is there no more you can tell from the plentiful signs that any person addressing an envelope is bound to leave behind?"

I looked at the letter once more, a little mortified that Holmes had added his disparaging rider to the praise for my first deduction.

"Perhaps the writer was in a state of some perturbation," I suggested. "The formation of some of the letters is certainly rather ragged, although the hand in itself is by no means uneducated. It is just the sort I learnt painfully at school myself."

Holmes clapped his hands in delight.

"Yes, indeed, Watson. You have gone to the heart of it with all your usual perspicacity."

I busied myself in taking some marmalade. The truth of the matter was that I could not for the life of me see in what I had been so perspicacious, though I was not sorry to have earned Holmes's unstinted praise.

A silence fell. Darting a glance at my companion from my perhaps over-busy buttering of my hot toast, I found that he was leaning back in his chair, half-empty coffee cup neglected, regarding me with unremitting steadiness.

I was constrained to look back at him.

"You have no further comment to make?" he asked me at last.

I picked up the envelope once again.

"No, no, my dear fellow, not the envelope. I must suppose that you have long ago extracted all the information you are likely to get from that. I meant have you no comment to make upon my remarking on your perspicacity in pointing to the style of my correspondent's hand."

"Why, no, Holmes. No, I think not. No, there is nothing more to be said about that. I think."

"Not even that undoubtedly the writer of the letter is a schoolboy?"

"A schoolboy? But how . . ."

"That educated hand, yet with many of the letters curiously unformed. Why, you have only to compare the capital H of Holmes with that of Hughes to observe the significant differences. No, undoubtedly my correspondent is still at school, and indeed not yet at any of our great public schools but a mere boy of no more than twelve. And, as you must know, the South Coast is greatly favoured by private scholastic establishments. Open the letter, Watson, and let us hear why a schoolboy wishes to consult Sherlock Holmes."

Obediently I took up a paperknife and slit open the envelope, hoping the while, I must confess, that just once Holmes's confident deductions might prove false. But a single glance at the address on the letter within confirmed him exactly in his surmise. "St. George's School, Hove," it was headed.

"Read it, Watson. Read it."

"Dear Mr. Holmes," I read. "All of us boys at St. George's are jolly interested in your cases, except that Dr. Smyllie, our headmaster, forbids us to read about you. But, Mr. Holmes, a fearful injustice has been done. He has said that our holiday for St. George's Day, which has been our right ever since the beginning of the world, will be cancelled unless someone owns up. But, Mr. Holmes, nobody did it. Every chap in the school is certain of that. No one did it at all, and still he says our holiday will be cancelled. Your obedient servant, Phillip Hughes. P.S. It was spilling ink on his precious book, and why should any fellow do that?"

I laid down Master Hughes's letter with tears of laughter in my eyes.

"Upon my soul, Holmes," I said. "Here's a case that will try your methods to the utmost."

"Yes, indeed, Watson. There are features in it, are there not, of considerable interest. I think a trip to the Sussex coast might prove distinctly stimulating."

My laughter was quenched.

"Surely," I said, "you cannot be serious?"

Yet already I knew from the look of deep preoccupation on my friend's countenance that he did indeed fully intend to go down to Hove and investigate our young correspondent's indignant complaint.

"My dear Watson," he answered with some asperity. "If a council of schoolboys declares upon oath in a purely private communication that a certain event did not occur among them, you can take it as pretty much of a fact that that event did not happen. They know altogether too much about each other. There is only one circumstance I can think of that might prove an exception."

"And that is?"

He gave me a quick frown.

"Why, if the deed in question should have been perpetrated by the writer of the letter himself, of course. And we can make certain of that only by speaking to the young man face to face."

"Yes, I suppose so," I answered. "But all the same, a visit to Hove will take us most of a day if not more, and you have the business of the Bank of England oyster dinner still in hand."

"My dear Watson, an injustice has been done. Or almost certainly so. I hope I am not the man to allow any mere pecuniary considerations to stand in my way under such circumstances. St. George's Day is but two days hence. Have the goodness to look up a train to Brighton. We will go down this morning."

I went at once to Bradshaw in its familiar place upon our shelves.

But I was not yet to tell Holmes how soon we could be off on this extraordinary errand. Before I had had time to run my finger down the Brighton departures column there entered our page, Billy, with upon the salver that he carried a single large visiting card.

Holmes picked it up and read it aloud.

"Dr. A. Smyllie, MA, PhD, St. George's School for the Preliminary Education of Young

Gentlemen, Hove, near Brighton, Sussex. Why, Watson, here is the very dominie under whose stern edict our young friend is suffering. Bring him up, Billy. Bring him up."

In a few moments Master Hughes's headmaster stood before us. He was not the sort of man I would have imagined a headmaster to be, even the headmaster of an establishment for twelve-year-olds. Far from being an imposing figure able to exert authority with a glance, he was reedy and undulating to a degree. Correctly enough dressed in frock-coat and striped trousers, he yet wore a loosely knotted cravat at his throat. His face was very pale, and he seemed more than a little agitated.

"Mr. Sherlock Holmes?" he asked in a high-pitched, almost squeaky, voice, turning not to Holmes but to myself.

I corrected his mistake, which seemed unduly to disconcert him, and introduced my friend.

Dr. Smyllie extended a somewhat limp hand at the end of an extraordinarily long arm, and winced a little when Holmes took it in his firm grasp.

"And what can I have the honour of doing for the poet of childhood?" Holmes asked.

Upon Dr. Smyllie's pallid countenance there appeared a faint flush of pleasure.

"You know my work, Mr. Holmes? I had hardly dared to hope that a person of your—of your—of your direction in life would be aware of my few, humble efforts."

"You do yourself an injustice, Dr. Smyllie," Holmes replied. "Who does not know those lines of yours that conclude so touchingly 'Take up the spangled web of words—'"

"'Then lay it gently on my grave,'" I completed the poem, surprised only that Holmes, so contemptuous of the softer things of life, should be able to quote those verses from "For My Infant Son," often though they have been reprinted.

Now I understood why Holmes had addressed Dr. Smyllie as "the poet of childhood." For such Algernon Smyllie had been dubbed some thirty years earlier when his very successful volume of verse had first appeared, poems

concerned with every tender aspect of a child's life, of which the verses "For My Infant Son" were the crown.

But now, it seemed, the young poet had become the mature schoolmaster. Algernon Smyllie had become Dr. A. Smyllie, MA, PhD. Yet he still looked, I thought to myself, more the sensitive poet than the awe-inspiring headmaster.

Indeed, faced with telling Holmes the reason for his visit, he positively hung his head and scraped at our Turkey carpet with the inside of his right foot, upon which, I saw, the boot buttons were mismatched at the top.

"Now, sir," Holmes said encouragingly.

Dr. Smyllie blushed again.

"It is a trifling matter, Mr. Holmes," he said.

Holmes's lips flickered in the merest hint of a smile.

"But trifling matters, as I have more than once explained to my friend, Dr. Watson, can on occasion be of the utmost significance," he said.

Dr. Smyllie stepped back a pace, and even glanced at the door as if he were contemplating immediate flight. But he succeeded in standing his ground at last.

"No, no, Mr. Holmes," he said, the words tumbling out of him. "No, indeed. I assure you, my dear sir, quite the contrary. Altogether the other way about. I would not have disturbed you at all, my dear sir, only that I happened to be passing this way and I thought—I thought . . ."

Holmes stayed silent, sucking at an empty pipe which he had picked up from the mantelpiece.

Dr. Smyllie gave an immense swallow, the Adam's apple in his long throat above that loosely tied cravat rising and falling.

"No, my dear sir," he resumed, "I would have dismissed the matter by writing a mere note, perhaps not even by that, only it so happened that my business takes me past—er—your door and it—er—occurred to me to call and settle it with a few words."

"And the matter is?" Holmes asked, with a certain sharpness.

"Oh, nothing, sir. A mere trif— Nothing, sir, of any importance."

"But, nevertheless, since you have called upon us, it would be as well to unburden yourself of its substance."

The willowy poet-headmaster blushed again at Holmes's rebuke. But he did now contrive to bring out what it was that had brought him to call.

"Mr. Holmes," he said, "I have reason to believe that one of my pupils—I assure you, sir, that they are not generally so disgracefully behaved—that one of my pupils may have had the temerity to address a letter to your good self. A letter concerning a trifling—that is, the merest matter of necessary discipline. And happening, as I say, to be passing, I—er—thought I would merely call in to—to assure you, sir, that you need do nothing in the matter. Nothing at all, sir. I merely wished to offer you an apology, as it were. An apology on behalf of—er—St. George's School."

Holmes replaced his pipe upon the mantelpiece and gave our visitor a cool nod.

"If you will excuse me one moment, Dr. Smyllie," he said. "I have a small domestic matter to attend to. A word with our landlady about my arrangements for the day. She needs to know in good time in order to do her marketing."

He left the room, quietly closing the door behind him, and Dr. Smyllie and I stood facing each other in a somewhat awkward silence. I felt myself a little annoyed with my friend. He did not usually leave me with a client in this manner, nor was it often his custom to consult so much Mrs. Hudson's convenience. However, he returned before I had had time to do more than offer our visitor some few comments on the prevailing weather, and he at once resumed the consultation.

"I take it then, sir," he said to Dr. Smyllie, "that this extempore visit was with the intention simply of reassuring me that I need take no particular notice of any communication I might receive from any of your pupils?"

"Exactly so, sir. Exactly so."

Holmes regarded the schoolmaster-poet with an expression of the utmost seriousness.

"Then, sir, you may take it that the object of your visit has been thoroughly achieved," he said.

Dr. Smyllie bowed and thanked Holmes with, I thought, perhaps more effusiveness than was necessary, and in a few minutes he had left us.

"Well, Watson," Holmes said, as our visitor's tread could be heard descending the stairs, "have you any observations to make?"

I pondered.

"I hardly think so," I replied. "Except perhaps that Dr. Smyllie need hardly have put himself out even to the extent of halting his cab outside our door to tell us that young Hughes's letter is, after all, a very trifling—that is, not a matter of great importance."

"You think so? But, tell me, did you notice anything more about our poet of childhood?"

"Why, no. No. Unless perhaps that his right boot was mis-buttoned."

"Good, Watson. I knew I could rely upon you to seize on the significant detail."

"Significant, Holmes?"

"Why, surely so. When a person comes to our rooms here all the way from the Sussex coast while we are at breakfast, and, though correctly dressed, appears with a mis-buttoned boot and with a small shaving cut upon his right cheek, something which I fear you failed to notice, then there is only one conclusion to be drawn."

"And that is?"

"That he left home in a very great hurry precisely in order to see myself as soon as he possibly could."

"But, no, Holmes," I could not help expostulating. "He told us that he had an appointment in town elsewhere. No doubt it was for an early hour and he is already on his way there again."

"You think so? Well, perhaps we shall soon see."

At that moment Billy came back into the room, a look of sharp triumph on his always eager face.

"Victoria Station, Mr. Holmes, sir," he announced without preliminary.

"There you are, Watson."

"But I don't quite understand. What about Victoria Station?"

"That it was to there that Dr. Smyllie directed his cab," Holmes replied. "I made an opportunity to leave the room and instruct Billy to wait out on the steps and overhear any directions our visitor might give. You surely did not think I was so concerned about our dinner tonight that I went out for that purpose?"

"No, no. Of course not. So Dr. Smyllie is returning directly to Hove. What do you see as the significance of that?"

"Simply that he is unduly concerned that I should take no action as the result of that letter. Now, if what might seem to be a mere trifle caused him to go to so much trouble, I think we should make all haste to follow in his footsteps. You were consulting Bradshaw, I believe."

Although Sherlock Holmes is a master of disguise, and I have frequently seen him so transformed that it has taken me no little time to recognize him even at close quarters, it has been seldom in the course of our adventures that he has called upon me to assume an appearance other than my own. At Hove, however, once we had found St. George's School and examined the neighbourhood round about, he did require me to adopt a disguise. So it was that I found myself on the afternoon of that day waiting in the road where the school stood, clad in a not altogether sweet-smelling coat belonging to the owner of a four-wheeler whom Holmes had persuaded for a consideration to lend us both vehicle and garment. From where I sat high up on the driving seat I could see in the garden of the house next to St. George's, a residence that had luckily chanced to be unoccupied, the stooping figure of a gardener methodically digging in a flower-bed close to the fence dividing the two premises. Had I not known for a fact that this man was Holmes himself I would not, even at the comparatively short distance that separated us, have recognized him.

I had not been in position long before I heard the clangour of a bell from within the school and saw a few moments later some score of youngsters come pouring out into the grounds to play. None of them, I think, paid any heed to the old gardener at work on the other side of the fence. But when, after a little, one of the boys happened to go near, Holmes called out something in a quiet voice, and before long I was able to see another of the happy youngsters running and playing there, a handsome red-headed lad, go over and lean against the fence just where the gardener was at work. But no one who was not within a yard or two of the boy could have seen that he was engaged in conversation with the man on the far side. It was a conversation that lasted a full quarter of an hour, and at its end the gardener carefully scraped clean his spade and made his way off, trudging along as if well tired after a good day's labour.

I jerked the reins in my lap and the four-wheeler's old horse set off at a sedate walk. Round the next corner I saw waiting for me a tall, upright, and sprightly figure resembling not at all the ancient gardener in the empty garden, for all that his clothes were not unalike.

In a moment Holmes was seated in the cab behind me and telling me the result of his unconventional consultation with master Phillip Hughes.

"It is much as I thought, Watson. It seems that in the entrance hall of the school there is kept in a place of honour, in a locked glass case, a copy of Algernon Smyllie's book *Poems of Childhood*, together with a letter to the poet from Her Majesty herself. It is the custom for the chief boy of the school, the Dux as they call him, to turn one page of the book each day. Now, just a week ago our friend, young Hughes, who had omitted to learn the evening before a prescribed passage from Horace, came downstairs very early to, as he said, 'mug up the beastly stuff.' Glancing at the display case to see which in particular of (again I use his own words) 'the vicious verses' was on show, since if he failed to present his passage of Horace correctly it would be his punishment by tradition to learn that poem, he saw, not entirely to his dismay, that someone had poured ink with conspicuous liberality all over the page, which happened indeed to be that on which appear the quatrains you yourself so much admire, the ones entitled 'For My Infant Son.'"

"Ah, yes. 'Take up the spangled web of words, Then lay it gently on my grave.'"

"Exactly. Though I fear young Hughes does not share your enthusiasm. However, that is not the end of his account. Scarcely had he, he told me, absorbed the fact of the desecration than he heard behind him the voice of his headmaster which a moment later, when he too had perceived what had happened, was raised in the most terrible ire. An anger that persisted, when no culprit would come forward, and soon resulted in the cancellation of the long-honoured St. George's Day holiday."

"And are you satisfied, Holmes, that young Hughes did not himself commit the very act he summoned you to investigate?"

"Yes, I flatter myself that no young man of twelve years of age could long deceive me. And, besides, there is no possible advantage to him in committing the crime."

"I suppose not. Yet, pray, consider. Youngsters are notoriously mettlesome. They revel in all sorts of pranks. Why, I remember from my own schooldays—"

"I dare say, Watson. And I am very aware of the nature of schoolboys. It would not have been inconceivable that one of these youngsters had crept down in the middle of the night and played this trick were it not for two circumstances."

"Yes?"

"First, as I explained to you at the outset of the affair, the act would be certain to have become known to at least one of his fellow pupils, aware of each other's habits and inclinations as schoolboys invariably are. And, secondly, the case in which the book is kept is always locked, and there are only two keys to it, one held by Dr. Smyllie himself and the other by his son, Arthur, a young man of twenty-two or twenty-

three who assists in the running of the establishment."

"Then it seems to me that we must find some way of speaking to young Arthur Smyllie, if you are indeed satisfied that the cabinet can be opened in no other way than by its keys."

"Watson, I could not yet be satisfied of that myself. But Phillip Hughes and his fellow pupils most certainly are so, and I am well disposed to take their word for it, as interested parties."

Holmes had ascertained from young Hughes that Mr. Arthur Smyllie was in the habit of taking an evening stroll. "The young shaver intimated, Watson, that the Lion Hotel might be his destination, a suggestion that I felt bound to scout." But it was outside the Lion Hotel that we waited that evening in the expectation of accosting the son of the headmaster of St. George's School. I was myself a little apprehensive over what reception we might be given when we disclosed the reason for our seeking his company. But I need not have worried. The moment Holmes greeted the young fellow, a fine upstanding ruddy-faced specimen of British manhood, and pronounced his own name, his face lit up in an expression of profound delight.

"Mr. Sherlock Holmes," he exclaimed. "Why, I could not have wished more dearly to meet any other soul upon earth. And is this Dr. Watson? Sir, I have read your accounts of Mr. Holmes's cases with the keenest interest. I must tell you, Mr. Holmes, that I am of a scientific turn myself. Indeed, I hope to be leaving for London at the start of the next university year to read for a degree in the physical sciences."

"A most commendable ambition," Holmes said. "But won't you miss the rewards of schoolmastering?"

The young man grinned.

"Keeping all those cheeky young devils in order for my father? Well, I shan't altogether miss that, I promise you. And yet you're right, Mr. Holmes, of course. There are rewards for a schoolmaster, and I dare say I shall miss the little blighters in the end after all."

Holmes offered the young man some hospitality and we all three repaired to the hotel to discuss a bottle of wine. It was some time before Holmes was able to bring the conversation round to the affair of St. George's School so keen was Arthur Smyllie to learn all he could of scientific methods of detection. But at last Holmes contrived an adroitly phrased question about our guest's present life among his father's "little blighters."

"Well, yes, Mr. Holmes, they can be nothing but pests at times, I admit, for all that at other times they are delightfully willing to learn every blessed thing I can teach them."

"Up to all sorts of tricks, however, I make no doubt," Holmes said.

Arthur Smyllie laughed.

"Oh, yes, indeed. Can you guess what their latest escapade has been?"

"I am sure I cannot."

"Well, one of the little beasts has poured ink all over a precious copy of my father's book *Poems of Childhood*. You know that I am the only heir of the man who wote 'For My Infant Son'?"

"Are you, indeed, Mr. Smyllie? And you say that one of your father's pupils poured ink on a copy of that book?"

"A copy, sir? More than just a copy, I assure you. A very precious one, signed by Her Majesty, no less, and enclosed in a glass case together with a letter from the Queen to my father. It really was too bad of the little beast who spoiled it. And yet . . . Well, to tell you the truth, that poem has hung round my neck like a millstone all my life, and I'm not altogether sorry that it was that particular page that received the inky deluge."

"I'm surprised that the display case was left open when there are schoolboys about, always apt to carelessness and pranks."

"Oh, no, Mr. Holmes, the case was never left open. Once a day, true, it is unlocked by the Dux of the school and a page is turned. But he always had to obtain a key from either my father or myself and to return it immediately."

"But perhaps the case can be opened without benefit of key?"

"No, again, Mr. Holmes. It's stoutly locked, I can assure you."

Holmes smiled.

"Why then," he said, "it seems you have produced for me a mystery worthy of my best powers. Who committed the crime within the locked cabinet? And how was the deed done?"

Arthur Smyllie laughed aloud in delight.

"Yet, you know," Holmes interjected with some acerbity, "if there were a problem of more importance but with the identical set of circumstances, it would not take me long to put my finger on the crux of it. If it were possible for a room or a cabinet to be opened except with its keys, then I should look pretty sharply to the holders of the keys, whoever they were, for my criminal."

Young Smyllie lost his cheerful look in an instant.

"Mr. Holmes," he said, "you are not suggesting that I defaced that book of my father's?"

"My dear sir, I am asking only if it has to be the holders of the keys and no one else who could gain access to the volume."

Arthur Smyllie's face, formerly so ruddily cheerful, was white now as a sheet.

"Mr. Holmes," he said, rising abruptly from the table, "I will bid you good night."

He had left before either of us had had time to remonstrate.

"Holmes," I asked, "is there some way to get into that display case without using either of its keys?"

"My dear Watson, you heard yourself Arthur Smyllie tell us that there was not."

"Is there no other key then? A key that one of the boys could have obtained by some means?"

"If there were such a thing," Holmes answered me, "we should have heard about it from Hughes. Nothing could keep its existence a secret within a school, believe me."

"But then Arthur Smyllie must have defaced the book himself, as indeed his conduct just now can only lead us to believe. But why should he do such a thing? It escapes me."

"Oh, come," Holmes replied. "Did you not hear Arthur tell us that he is going to London University to read for a degree in science? Did you not hear how that poem of his father's, with its public plea to him to 'take up the spangled web of words,' to become a poet in his turn, weighs like a millstone on him?"

I sighed. Holmes's words were only too convincing.

"Then I suppose that tomorrow we must go to Dr. Smyllie and tell him that no boy in his school committed the outrage," I said.

"Yes, that certainly we must do."

Our adventures in Hove were not, however, yet ended. We took the only room which the Lion had vacant for the night, and I know that I lay long restless thinking of the message that we had to deliver the next day, although it seemed to me that Holmes in the other bed slept soundly enough. So it was I who heard at an hour well after midnight an insistent creaking sound just outside our window. At first I took it for the action of the wind on the branches of the tree that grew close to the building at just that point. But before long I realized that the night was, in fact, singularly calm, and yet the creaking persisted.

Without waking Holmes, I slipped from my bed, put on slippers and a dressing-gown and looked about the darkened room for some weapon. At last I recalled that there was a good set of fire-irons in the chimney place. I crept across and secured the poker.

Armed with this, I advanced to the window, paused for a moment, heard the creaking continue and flung wide the casement. There was a swift movement among the branches of the tree just outside. I leapt forward, snatching with my free hand at a pale form I could vaguely discern. There came a loud yelp. The form wriggled, abominably in my grasp. I raised the poker to deliver a sound blow.

"Oh, come, Watson, spare the rod," said the voice of Sherlock Holmes from behind me.

"Spare the rod?" I said refraining from bring-ing the poker down but keeping a firm grip on my opponent's clothing. "Holmes, we have a burglar here. Pray assist me."

"A burglar, yes," Holmes answered. "But only a small one, I venture to think."

I heard the sound of him striking a match behind me. The rays from the candle he lit shone out into the night. By then I saw that I was detaining none other than the young red-haired Phillip Hughes.

I hauled him out of the tree and inside.

"Now, young sir," I said, "what is the meaning of this new jape of yours?"

But Sherlock Holmes answered for him.

"No new jape, Watson, I think, since I believe I told you that in my opinion the lad committed no old jape."

"But, Holmes, he has this instant proved himself a night prowler, and a determined one at that. There can no longer be any doubt about who blotted that book."

"No, Watson, there never has been any doubt about that. But let us hear what brought our determined little ally prowling all the way over to us here."

The boy looked up at Holmes, his eyes alight with admiration.

"You knew then that I had come to tell you, sir?" he asked.

Holmes's lips curved in a faint smile.

"I hardly think you would have risked so perilous a journey for any other purpose," he said. "I take it that you found out from Mr. Arthur Smyllie where we lodged?"

"Yes, sir."

"Then tell us what you have to tell us."

"Sir, I think I know how that book got to be covered in ink, sir."

Holmes's eyes gleamed momentarily.

"I wonder if you do," he said. "Let us hear."

"Well, sir, it's not easy to believe."

"The truth very often isn't. Your human being is a very tricky piece of machinery, my lad."

"Yes, sir. Well, sir, I was lying awake tonight, thinking about you coming all the way down from London and everything, and wondering whether you would solve the mystery, sir. Well, not really that. I knew you would solve it, sir, but I wondered what the answer could possibly be. And then, sir, I remembered Thompson Minor. He left last year, sir."

"Thompson Minor," I exclaimed. "Did a boy come back to the school and—"

"Watson, let young Hughes tell us in his own way."

"Of course, of course. Speak up, young fellow me lad."

"Yes, sir. Well, I thought about Thompson Minor and the way he used to get into great bates. And then, Mr. Holmes, well, he would do things that only hurt him himself. Once when he was in a specially bad temper he threw his champion pocket-knife into the fire, sir. He did really."

Holmes's eyes were glowing sombrely now.

"So, young Hughes," he said, "draw your conclusions. Bring your account to a proper end, and my friend Watson here shall record it for you."

The boy looked back at him, white-faced and intent in the candlelight.

"Sir, Dr. Smyllie did it himself, didn't he, sir? It must have been him. Mr. Arthur's too decent ever to do a thing like that, and the only other key was Dr. Smyllie's. Sir, he did it to spite himself because Mr. Arthur won't be a poet but a scientist, sir. Isn't that it? Isn't it?"

"Yes," said Sherlock Holmes. "That is it, my boy."

He turned to me.

"And, as you suggested, Watson," he said, "in the morning we shall have to go to Dr. Smyllie and tell him what his son guessed this evening, that no boy committed our crime. And it's 'Hurrah for St. George' and a whole day of holiday."

Raffles: The Enigma of the Admiral's Hat
and
Raffles on the Trail of the Hound

BARRY PEROWNE

WITH THE POSSIBLE exception of Professor Moriarty, who appears too seldom in the canon, the greatest criminal character in literature is, of course, A. J. Raffles, the gentleman jewel thief created by E. W. Hornung at the end of the Victorian era, his first book appearance being in *The Amateur Cracksman* (1899). A few years after the author's death in 1921, the popularity of the character remained at such a high level that the British magazine *The Thriller* asked Philip Atkey (1908–1985), already a regular contributor to its pages, to continue the rogue's adventures. After making arrangements with the estate of Hornung, Atkey, using the pseudonym Barry Perowne, produced many more stories and novels about Raffles than his creator had.

Atkey wrote hundreds of stories and more than twenty novels, many featuring the suave safecracker and his sidekick, Bunny Manders, including *Raffles After Dark* (1933; American title: *The Return of Raffles*), *Raffles in Pursuit* (1934), *Raffles Under Sentence* (1936), *Raffles and the Key Man* (1940), and the short story collections *Raffles Revisited* (1974), *Raffles of the Albany* (1976), and *Raffles of the M. C. C.* (1979).

It was inevitable, of course, that the great criminal and the great detective would be matched against each other, and the finest examples of their confrontations are in Perowne's "Raffles: The Enigma of the Admiral's Hat," first published in the March 1975 issue of *Ellery Queen's Mystery Magazine*, and its sequel, "Raffles on the Trail of the Hound," first published in the July 1975 issue of *Ellery Queen's Mystery Magazine*. They were first collected in *Raffles of the Albany: Footprints of a Famous Gentleman Crook in the Times of a Great Detective* (London, Hamish Hamilton, 1976).

RAFFLES: THE ENIGMA OF THE ADMIRAL'S HAT

Barry Perowne

"MORAL OR OTHERWISE, Bunny," said Raffles, "it's a fact of life that possession is nine points of the law."

Immaculate in a grey suit, a pearl in his cravat, his dark hair crisp, his keen face tanned, he tossed aside the London *Times*, in which a correspondence had been going on for months about some ancient bas-reliefs, the Thracian Marbles, unearthed by an archaeologist on a field expedition and presented by him to the British Museum.

"This savant," Raffles added, offering me a Sullivan from his cigarette-case, "probably hopes to be rewarded with a knighthood by the Queen—talking of whom, Bunny, this royal occasion we're on our way to should be a pretty good week, with luck."

The train in which we were speeding through the sun-basking countryside was bound for the naval town of Portsmouth, which Her Majesty, making one of her now rare public appearances, was visiting for the purposes of declaring Navy Week open.

Among the official functions and sporting events arranged for the week was a three-day cricket match between the Royal Navy and a Gentlemen-of-England team captained by A. J. Raffles.

At Portsmouth Town station we found our host, the skipper of the Navy team, Lieutenant-Commander Braithwaite, in dazzling white naval uniform, waiting to greet us off the train.

"You're the first of the Gentlemen blokes to arrive, Raffles," he said, as we followed a porter carrying our valises and Raffles's cricket-bag to the open four-wheeler Braithwaite had waiting. "The Navy Week opening ceremony went off very well this morning. I've just come from it. The Queen seemed quite her regal self, though still in widow's weeds. You'll get a chance to see her after lunch. She's due to board the royal yacht at two o'clock, at Portsmouth Hard, and proceed to her summer residence, Osborne House, in the Isle-of-Wight, just across the water. To see her pass by, I'd hoped to get you on board H.M.S. *Victory*—"

"Horatio Nelson's old flagship," I said, "at the Battle of Trafalgar?"

"Yes, indeed," said Braithwaite, as our cab jingled through streets ablaze with flags and pictures of the Queen. "*Victory* lies, perfectly preserved, at a permanent anchorage in our harbour here, but only invited bigwigs are allowed on board her to-day—including a bunch of millionaires."

"Millionaires?" said Raffles.

"The international social crowd," explained Braithwaite. "Commodore Vanderbilt, the Duke of Westminster, one of the Rothschilds, the Prince of Monaco, Mr. Leonard Jerome of New York with his beautiful daughter Jennie and her husband Lord Randolph Churchill. Real swells! They've come over in parties for the day from their glittering private steam-yachts gathered at Cowes, in the Isle-of-Wight, for the Regatta."

I met Raffles's grey eyes. Cowes Regatta! He gave me a rueful look. We had clean forgotten the most brilliant event of the summer social season. At Cowes we might have found some financial way to improve the shining hour. Instead, he had tied himself up in a three-day cricket match on just the wrong side of the water.

"So near, Bunny," he murmured to me, "and yet so far!"

"By courtesy," our host Braithwaite was saying, "of the Royal Navy Museum at Greenwich, Portsmouth's been loaned, in honour of the Queen's visit, a national treasure—the uniform, the hat and bloodstained knee-breeches, waistcoat, and swallowtail blue coat with epaulettes, which Nelson was wearing when he fell mortally wounded on *Victory*'s quarter-deck in the very hour of his decisive triumph at Trafalgar. From to-morrow *Victory* will be open for the public to view Nelson's uniform, but only invited bigwigs are on board her to-day. Still, I can get you on board a Navy tug, *Gosport Jezebel*, to see the Queen pass by presently in the royal yacht."

After lunch at the fine old waterfront inn, The Lord Nelson, where our Navy hosts had billeted the Gentlemen cricket team with myself as supernumerary, we boarded a tug flying the white ensign. As *Jezebel* steamed out from her berth, the great harbour, backed by the Portsdown Hill forts built to repel the Grand Army of Napoleon, was crowded with craft of every description, all laden with sightseers.

Besides Raffles and myself, there were a few other favoured civilians on board *Jezebel* and, as I leaned with Raffles and Braithwaite against the tug's throbbing rail, taking in the spectacular scene in the blazing sunshine, there drifted my way a cloud of strong shag-tobacco smoke from the pipe of some man who had come up behind us.

"There she is, Watson," I heard a voice say, "the old *Victory*, as sound and trim as on the day Nelson sailed her, at the head of the fleet, into the blood and thunder of Trafalgar."

"A study in scarlet, that day," a second voice said. "Is Mr. Sherlock Holmes a patriotic man?"

"Unquestionably so. Look, Watson, there's a vacant space at the rail along there. Let's claim it."

Braithwaite, seeing me glance round at the two frock-coated, silk-hatted men as they strolled away along the deck, the taller man tossing pipe-smoke over his shoulder, told me who they were.

"The shorter chap," he said, "is a Mr. James Watson, Secretary of the Portsmouth and Southsea Literary and Scientific Society. The big, burly man is Dr. A. Conan Doyle, in medical practice in Southsea, the residential part of Portsmouth. As to Mr. Sherlock Holmes"—Braithwaite chuckled—"I'll lend you something to-night that'll introduce you to him, if you haven't yet met. I say, though! By Jove, look at those nobs on the old *Victory*!"

Our tug had hove-to as near as was permitted to Nelson's flagship, around which circling whaleboats manned by Navy oarsmen with capbands marked H.M.S. *Victory* preserved a space of water clear of the clustering sightseeing craft.

The bowsprit chains of the old seventy-four-gun ship-of-the-lines shone like silver. Her masts and yards towered above us to the blue sky. Her oaken hull was freshly tarred. Through her open gunports, framed in fresh white paint, the guns of her broadsides looked ready to rumble out with a lion's roar at the drop of a hat.

On her decks, her distinguished visitors stood about in groups, conversing. Others were gathered in the old ship's carven stern-gallery. Beautiful women twirled their parasols languidly. Jewels sparkled. Tophats and gold watch-chains glistened.

"Millionaires all," Raffles murmured to me. "So near—and yet so far!"

Braithwaite explained to us that some of the unfamiliar naval uniforms visible on board *Victory* were those of Captains from American, Greek, German, Italian, and other foreign warships which, on courtesy visits for Navy Week at Portsmouth, were lying at anchor off the Isle-of-Wight.

The report of a cannon clapped across the harbour.

"First minute-gun of the royal salute," said

Braithwaite. "The *Victoria-and-Albert* is putting out from Portsmouth Hard."

The guns of the saluting battery at Haslar Point continued to fire at one-minute intervals through the storm of cheering as the Queen's yacht, flying the scarlet-and-gold of the Royal Standard, steamed through the multitude of small craft that made way for her stately progress.

Up the rigging of *Victory*, as the royal yacht approached, raced barefoot sailors in the uniforms of Nelson's time, the two topmost men running out to either tip of the mainmast-yard, to stand rigid, away up there, as the whole team formed a gigantic V—alike for *Victory* and for the royal widow whose tiny figure, in black shawl and jet-beaded bonnet, stood in regal solitude, well apart from her clustered attendants, on the deck of her yacht steaming slowly by.

As the Queen passed and, to the continued firing of the minute-guns, the royal yacht began to recede toward the harbour-mouth, I heard a wild cry, and I was just in time to see the sailor standing at the larboard tip of *Victory*'s mainmast-yard sway on his dizzy perch—and fall, turning helplessly in the air, to strike the water with a glittering splash.

I hardly heard the continued cheering, further off, or the measured reports of the saluting battery's guns, as our *Jezebel* tug's bridge-telegraph bell clanged, the tug throbbed to life, and, with a dozen other assorted craft, sightseers, and Navy whaleboats, surged to the rescue.

One of the Navy whaleboats beat us to it. As our tug's screws reversed, slowing us alongside, I saw sailors in the whaleboat heaving in the drenched man, unconscious or dead, over their gunwale. They stretched him on the floorboards and, at a barked order from their midshipman coxswain, bent to their oars, pulled around under the chains of *Victory*'s great bowsprit, and, leaving a dozen flung lifebelts and a confusion of would-be rescue craft bobbing on the water, passed from my view.

It was smartly done. Even before the last report of the saluting cannons marked the passing of the Queen's yacht out of the harbour-mouth, the incident was over.

Yet, if rumour was to be believed, something else had happened on board H.M.S. *Victory*. From what source the rumour emanated I had no idea, but by the time we disembarked from the tug *Jezebel* at Portsmouth Hard the excited crowd there was abuzz with a story that a Marine sentry on solitary duty in *Victory*'s wardroom, where Nelson's uniform was displayed, had been found chloroformed shortly after the Queen had passed, and that, with the exception of the hat, Horatio Nelson's uniform, stained at Trafalgar with his lifeblood, had disappeared.

"Impossible!" said Braithwaite, as he, Raffles, and I jostled our way through the crowd besieging some waiting cabs. "Nelson's uniform stolen? It just *can't* be true!"

A whiff of shag-tobacco smoke from the pipe of Dr. Conan Doyle, who, with Mr. Watson, was just ahead of us, making for the cabs, floated back to me.

"*Can* it be true?" I heard Mr. Watson ask.

"The mention of the hat, Watson, has a circumstantial ring. Yes, I fear this rumour *could* have some factual basis."

"In which case, Doctor, does any point occur to you to which our friend Holmes would be likely to devote particular attention?"

"The hat, Watson—the enigma of the Admiral's hat."

"But people are saying the hat was *not* taken!"

"That is the enigma, Watson."

People jostled between us at that moment, and I lost sight of the two men.

Raffles and I dined, that night, at the Royal Naval Barracks. The rest of the Gentlemen-of-England cricket team had arrived during the day and all of us were dinner guests of the Navy team in a vast room with walls from which gilt-framed portraits of bygone admirals, of Mr. Samuel Pepys, sometime Secretary of the Navy, and of Horatio Nelson himself, wearing what was in all probability the very uniform which now had been stolen from his old flagship, gazed down on us.

At dinner, the talk was of nothing but the crime committed on the *Victory*, which was indeed a fact. The sailor who had fallen from the yardarm was a naval rating called John S. Hayter. His fall was said to have been due to sunstroke; he was now in Haslar Naval Hospital with a dislocated shoulder. The Marine sentry had, apparently, been chloroformed from behind and could say only that his assailant had been a man of great strength.

"What about the distinguished guests, Braithwaite?" Raffles asked.

"They had to be regarded, of course, as above suspicion. They've all dispersed now."

"The millionaires gone back to their steamyachts at Cowes, have they?" said Raffles "H'm! Has the Navy called in the County Constabulary?"

"Of course. Police reinforcements are pouring in from all over."

"Including the Isle-of-Wight?"

"Naturally. Except for the Queen's bobbies, guarding her at Osborne House, there'll be damned few police left, over in the island."

"Steward," said Raffles, "I'll have a drop more of that wine."

As we were leaving the Barracks, Braithwaite handed Raffles an obviously much read copy of *Beeton's Christmas Annual*.

"The thing I told you I'd lend you," said Braithwaite. "It's a shilling shocker, published quite recently. Dr. Conan Doyle wrote the main story. It's called *A Study in Scarlet*. I don't think he gets many patients."

"Or he wouldn't have time to write shockers," said Raffles, putting the magazine under his red-lined evening cape. "I'll skim through this to-night, and see you in the morning, Braithwaite, ten-thirty on the cricket ground."

Out of curiosity, I borrowed *A Study in Scarlet* from Raffles next morning. He told me he had skimmed through it in bed. At the cricket ground I found myself a chair on the pavilion terrace in the sunshine and sat reading the story while the cricket went on.

The Mr. Sherlock Holmes I had heard mentioned turned out to be the leading character in the book. A private investigator of crime, who claimed to have methods of his own, he held my interest. Even when Raffles went in to bat, I read on with increasing absorption, until a sudden collective groan from the spectators, mostly in Navy white, made me look up.

Out at the wicket, on the green expanse of flawless turf, Raffles had thrown down his bat and was pulling off his right-hand batting-glove. Blood dripped from his fingers.

"Bad luck, Raffles," I heard Braithwaite call, as Raffles wrapped his handkerchief round his hand. "Will it put you out of the match?"

"I'm afraid so, Braithwaite," Raffles said. He came to the pavilion. "Kicking ball, Bunny," he told me. "Split my forefinger open. It'll need a stitch or two, by the look of it. I'll get changed and join you."

I had an uneasy suspicion about the mishap and, when he rejoined me, I accused him of contriving the damage.

"Not entirely, Bunny," he said, as we left the ground. "I intended to get out of the match, but that ball came at me very fast and I mistimed it more than I'd planned. No matter, I'm out of the game. It's only a friendly one, and you and I have fish to fry at Cowes Regatta—goldfish!"

He hailed a passing hansom and, as the horse jingled to a standstill, asked the cabbie, "D'you know the address of a Dr. Doyle?"

"Yes, sir, Number One, Bush Villas, Elm Grove, Southsea."

"No, Raffles," I said. "Not *that* doctor!"

"Why not?" said Raffles, surprised.

"I can't say exactly. This story of his—I just feel, somehow—"

"Nonsense! Nothing wrong with the story. It's an interesting little tale. Besides, Braithwaite said this Dr. Doyle doesn't get too many patients, so he'll probably be glad of a fee. Come—hop in, Bunny!"

Bush Villas, in residential tree-shaded Elm

Grove, proved to be four attached houses, tall and dignified, with lace-curtained windows and bathbricked front steps. Raffles gave the bell-pull of Number One a tug with his undamaged hand. The polished brass nameplate on the door had a newish look, as though the doctor had not been long in practice; and in fact, when he himself opened the door to us, he looked to be—though tall and dignified, with a bushy brown moustache—no more than thirty, half-a-dozen or so years Raffles's senior.

Powerfully built, frockcoated, a silver watch-chain looped across his white waistcoat, the doctor seemed to take us in at a single glance of his keen, direct blue eyes.

"Ah," he said, "one of the Gentlemen crick-eters had a knock on the hand, eh? Come in."

"That was a quick diagnosis," said Raffles, as we entered.

"Navy versus Gentlemen is the Match of the Week," said Dr. Doyle, leading us into a small surgery. "You're not in uniform, so you're not Navy. You're wearing a Zingari Club cravat, so you *are* a cricketer."

"Hence," said Raffles, with a laugh, "one of the Gents? I see. Doctor, my name's Raffles. This is my friend Manders."

"Well, let's have a look at that hand, Mr. Raffles."

"A study in scarlet," said Raffles, unwinding the gory handkerchief.

"From that remark," said Dr. Doyle, "I deduce you're one of the dozens who've read my little shocker. H'm! Who did this to your finger—the Navy's fast bowler? That fellow always leaves a trail of walking wounded. Incidentally"—he went to work on Raffles's finger—"didn't I see you two on the tug *Jezebel* yesterday?"

"We were there," said Raffles. "What would your Mr. Sherlock Holmes make of this theft from H.M.S. *Victory*?"

"He'd be interested, I fancy, in the minute-guns."

"The guns?" said Raffles.

"Everything indicates that the crime was the carefully planned, co-ordinated work of a num-ber of men. They can have arranged to time their respective actions by noting the cannon reports of the royal salute."

"What a novel use of the royal salute!" Raffles exclaimed.

"The crime presents several features which would have interested Holmes." The doctor bandaged Raffles's finger, then slid a kid-leather black finger-stall over it. "There you are, Mr. Raffles."

"Thank you, Dr. Doyle. What fee do I owe you?"

"You won't be able to play," said the doctor, "but I take it you'll be at the cricket ground? Very well, we'll see about a fee when I take the stitches out of that finger. Drop in here towards the end of the week."

The door of No. 1 Bush Villas, with the name *Dr. A. Conan Doyle* on its polished brassplate, closed on us.

Late that afternoon found us, not at the cricket ground, but over in the nearby Isle-of-Wight, observing the millionaires' steam-yachts anchored off Cowes—among them, Commodore Vanderbilt's; the Duke of Westminster's, with Mr. Leonard Jerome and Lord and Lady Randolph Churchill in his party; the S/Y *Achilleion*, property of the Greek merchant-shipping magnate, Mr. Aristotle Andiakis; and the luxurious yacht flying the candy-striped burgee of the wealthy ocean-racer and ichthyologist, Prince Albert of Monaco.

"Fine, Bunny," said Raffles, as the puffing-billy train rattled us back through the buttercup meadows to Ryde, to board the paddle-steamer ferry across to Clarence Pier, Southsea. "To-morrow, as captain of the Gentleman team, I must put in an appearance at the cricket match for a few hours. While I'm there, you can pick up a few things we shall need, and in the evening we'll return, suitably attired, to Cowes, then make our move as opportunity offers. There's a small fortune in sparklers to be picked up in the ladies' cabins of any one of those yachts."

Next morning, while Raffles was at the cricket ground, I hunted Old Portsmouth for a sailors' second-hand slopshop, and found one in Landport Terrace, childhood home of Charles Dickens when his Mr. Micawberish father had been a civilian clerk employed by the Navy. I bought a couple of blue jerseys and well-worn peaked caps of the longshoreman type.

Just as I was about to leave the shop, I saw Dr. Doyle and Mr. Watson. They were on the other side of the street, looking in at the window of a foreign-looking little restaurant—The Corfu Restaurant, according to the name on the window—where lobsters waved languid antennae among kegs of oysters and pickled vine-leaves on a bed of seaweed. The two men went in.

"You can get good shellfish across the street," said the slopshop man, seeing the direction of my gaze. "Belongs to a Mrs. Miranda Hayter, widder of a Royal Navy gunner-rating."

"It's far too early for lunch," I said, which was in fact so true that, as I slunk out of the slopshop with my parcel, I wondered what Dr. Doyle and Mr. Watson were doing in the restaurant across the way.

Suddenly I remembered something. I hailed a cab, went to The Lord Nelson Inn, locked the parcel into the valise in my room there, then continued to the cricket ground. I found Raffles watching the cricket from a deckchair on the pavilion terrace. I told him I had just seen Dr. Doyle and Mr. Watson.

"The name of the woman who owns the restaurant they went into is Hayter," I said. "Raffles, the name of the sailor who fell from *Victory*'s yardarm is Able-Seaman John S. Hayter!"

"Splendid, Bunny!" said Raffles. "Dr. Doyle's obviously stumbled on to something to do with the *Victory* crime. He's following it up. The game's afoot for him. And the major part of the Hampshire Constabulary's fully preoccupied with the same crime. Nothing could suit us better! As opportunists, you and I've never had such a chance as this. Over in the Isle-of-Wight to-night, we'll be on an easy wicket, and you'll see—something will turn up for us."

"That," I said, thinking uneasily of the Dickens house in Landport Terrace, "is what Mr. Micawber used to say."

I still felt uneasy when, dressed as jerseyed longshoremen, we stepped off the little puffing-billy island train at Cowes Station that evening. The small town, all yacht-building yards, sail lofts, rope-walks, and ship's chandler stores, was *en fête* for the Regatta.

We sauntered around the harbour. The beautiful racing-yachts, their masts a forest of bare poles, lay moored against the harbour-wall. The millionaires' steam-yachts, lying out at anchor, were ablaze with lights. In evening dress, jewelled women and elegant men were dining under the deck-awnings. Music drifted to us from the instruments of the millionaires' private trios and quintets. Much farther out, in the Channel, twinkled the lights of warships, British and visiting foreign ironclads lying at anchor.

Throngs of sailors, many of them on liberty from the foreign warships, were roistering in and out of the waterfront taverns.

"We haven't a chance, Raffles," I said. "There are too many people on those millionaires' steam-yachts."

He put a hand on my arm. "Bunny, there's a boat putting ashore from the *Achilleion*, and there's a carriage pulling up on the wharf along there and a crowd of sailors gathering round it. Let's see what's going on."

We walked along the cobbled wharf, added ourselves to the throng around the carriage, and saw at once why it had attracted interest. The tophatted driver and groom on the box wore the royal livery; on the doors of the carriage were the initials V.R. surmounted by a crown.

"The Queen sending a carriage to take somebody to Osborne House?" Raffles murmured. "Bunny, it's extremely unusual for Her Majesty to receive a visitor at her summer residence."

Alongside the seaweedy, water-lapped steps of the harbour wall, the S/Y *Achilleion*'s boat drew in. Oars were shipped and the boat held steady for a tall man of striking appearance to step out. His face leather-dark, aquiline, with a square-cut iron-grey beard and a monocle, he wore full evening-dress, the ribbon of some foreign Order of Chivalry slanting across his shirtfront, on his scarlet-lined cape a glittering jewelled star.

He was the Greek merchant-shipping millionaire, Mr. Aristotle Andiakis.

With the demeanour of a king, he came up the steps and, the groom holding the door open for him, mounted into the carriage. The groom climbed back up to the box, to sit stiffly there with folded arms, as the driver touched up the two magnificent black horses with his whip and the royal carriage clattered off along the wharf.

The boat's crew from S/Y *Achilleion* tied up their boat and, like the sailors who had gathered around, repaired to the nearest tavern.

"Bunny," Raffles said, "I told you something would turn up. Look at *Achilleion* out there. Very few lights on board. Mr. Andiakis evidently has no party of guests. The owner and half the crew are now ashore. The yacht will only be keeping an anchor watch. Now's our chance! Let's borrow a dinghy. There are dozens moored around the harbour-wall."

From a lampless section of the harbour we commandeered a dinghy. I took the oars and, with Raffles instructing me so as to avoid the lights reflected on the water from the other millionaires' steam-yachts, pulled out towards S/Y *Achilleion*. From the Greek yacht, as we neared it, I heard laughter—and a sudden sharp report.

"Champagne-cork," Raffles whispered to me. "There are a couple of men on the yacht's bridge. They're excited about something—seem to be drinking toasts. Pull on your right oar a bit. Now, both together—gently—to bring us under the yacht's counter."

As the jut of the counter loomed shadowy over us, Raffles was gone, rocking the dinghy as he leaped up, gripped the yacht's scupper-edge, and pulled himself soundlessly on board. Letting my oars trail in the rowlocks, I checked the

dinghy against the yacht's stern. And here, in the deep shadow cast by the S/Y *Achilleion*'s counter, the sultry thumping of my heart measured out my vigil.

It seemed interminable. Reflected ribbons of light trembled on the harbour water. Music, laughter, voices reached me faintly from the other millionaires' steam-yachts. Sweat stung my eyes, salted my lips. My throat grew parched. What in God's name was Raffles doing? I strained my ears. No sound from *Achilleion*. I cursed Raffles. He had been gone too long. I cursed him again. I wished I never had met him. I consigned him to nethermost hell.

And there, suddenly, he was—not in hell, but a dark-jerseyed figure in a peaked cap, dangling by his hands in front of my eyes. I brought the dinghy under him. He dropped into it almost without sound.

"Shove off, Bunny," he whispered. "The quicker we're off this island, the better!"

I asked no questions. All seemed quiet on S/Y *Achilleion*, but I knew from Raffles's tone that something had gone wrong.

We tied up the dinghy where we had found it. In the distance, a train whistled officiously.

"Puffing Billy coming in from Ryde," said Raffles. "It'll start back in a few minutes, and we'll be on it!"

We were on the wooden platform of the station as the diminutive train approached, steaming and clattering, and I ventured to ask, "What happened?"

"Most of the cabins seemed unused, Bunny. But I found Mr. Andiakis's day cabin—furnished as a study, luxurious. There was a small safe in it—combination-lock—fairly simple. I got it open—" He broke off, gripped my arm, jerked me into the tiny Waiting Room. "Look there!"

The train had pulled up. Getting off it were Dr. Doyle, pipe in mouth, and Mr. Watson. They strode with an intent, purposeful air out of the station.

"What on earth brings *them* to Cowes?" I whispered.

"It can only be one thing, Bunny—the contents of Mr. Aristotle Andiakis's safe. That Southsea doctor's got on the trail somehow."

"The trail of what?"

"Horatio Nelson's blood-stained uniform, Bunny—in the safe on the S/Y *Achilleion*."

I felt stunned as we boarded the train. We had a compartment to ourselves. Raffles lighted a Sullivan as the train clattered along towards Ryde and the ferry-steamers. Never had I seen him so tense.

"What did you do?" I said.

"I shut the safe," said Raffles, "re-set the combination, wiped off everything I'd touched, and got off that yacht. I don't know what's going on, Bunny, but you and I want nothing to do with the *Victory* crime. As captain of the visiting cricket team, I must be at the ground when the match ends, then we'll get out of Portsmouth—and follow the *Victory* crime developments in the newspapers."

Next morning, in the newspapers, there was not one word about the *Victory* crime. The sudden, total silence on the subject seemed unnatural and sinister.

The cricket match ended just after five o'clock that afternoon, the Navy winning by six wickets. Raffles excused us from the usual post-match carouse. We went straight to The Lord Nelson Inn and packed our valises.

I carried mine into Raffles's room, added it to his valise and cricket-bag on the fourposter bed where many a bygone seacaptain had slept. His grey suit immaculate, a pearl in his cravat, Raffles was standing in the window-bay with its wide-open leaded-paned casements. He was smoking a cigarette and gazing out over Portsmouth Harbour.

"Look at the old *Victory*, Bunny," he said, as I joined him at the window, "lying peacefully at anchor out there—and keeping her secret."

Horse's hooves clacked on cobbles, harness jingled, wheels ground. A hansom pulled up below. Two frockcoated, silk-hatted men stepped out—Dr. Conan Doyle and Mr. James Watson. They entered the Inn. We looked at each other.

"Can't be anything to do with us," Raffles said.

But we waited tensely. A firm knock sounded on the door. I had a sense of doom. Raffles called, "Come in," and the door opened. His silk hat, which he did not remove, almost touching the beams of the low ceiling, the Elm Grove doctor came in, followed by Mr. Watson.

"Just leaving?" Dr. Doyle said, noting instantly our luggage on the bed. "Mr. Raffles, there's a bill outstanding."

"Doctor," said Raffles, and I sensed and shared his relief as he glanced at his fingerstalled hand, "I'd clean forgotten this. How much do I owe you?"

"That depends. Watson, make sure that door is quite closed." The big doctor, his blue, direct eyes fixed on Raffles, took pipe and pouch from his pocket. "Mr. Raffles, let's discuss the *Victory* crime. First, the enigma of the Admiral's hat. Why was it not taken? Reflection suggested to me that the large, stiff hat was not amenable, like the blood-stained garments, to being tightly rolled-up for concealment in some receptacle—a receptacle that would have to be very quickly spirited off of *Victory*, since a minute search of the ship would have been in progress even before the distinguished guests left her. Perforce, those guests had to be regarded as above suspicion. They were neither questioned nor searched. Yet, even had one of them been guilty, in what receptacle could the uniform have been concealed?"

"One of the distinguished ladies' reticules?" Raffles suggested.

"Not big enough. However, Mr. Raffles, recall the scene of the fallen sailor's rescue. When we saw him pulled into the whaleboat, a number of objects bobbed around on the water—objects flung from *Victory* and from several sightseeing craft, including the tug *Jezebel*. I refer to life-belts."

The doctor lighted his pipe, exhaling smoke

under his bushy moustache, his steady eyes always on Raffles.

"I came to the conclusion that Nelson's bloodstained uniform left his old flagship inside one of her own lifebelts—prepared beforehand by cutting out part of the cork, thus hollowing the lifebelt, then plugging the orifice with part of the cut-out cork and roughly stitching back the canvas cover. The prepared lifebelt was then concealed in *Victory's* wardroom. All the man who chloroformed the Marine sentry had then to do was slash the stitches of the canvas, pull out the cork plug, thrust the tightly-rolled uniform into the orifice, and replace the cork plug. Meantime, every eye on board *Victory*—except his own—was watching the Queen pass. But for that lifebelt to be thrown overboard by the man, almost certainly a member of *Victory's* crew, somebody had to fall into the water."

"Able-Seaman John S. Hayter," said Dr. Doyle's companion.

"Just so, Watson. The intrepid foretopman and his crewmate confederate coordinated their respective actions to the minute-guns of the royal salute, while other confederates, in one of the sightseeing small craft, watched for their fellow-conspirator, the chloroformer, to throw the relevant lifebelt, so that they could retrieve and make off with it in the confusion of the rescue."

"Quite simple, really," said Dr. Doyle's companion.

"When analysed, Watson, and explained."

"I trust I did not, by my inadvertent remark—"

"By no means, Watson." But the Elm Grove doctor's keen eyes remained fixed on Raffles. "Inquiry at the Navy Records Office provided me with the home address of Seaman Hayter, who proved to be a Portsmouth-born man, like many sailors. Mr. Watson and I visited that address, a small restaurant owned by his mother—a woman from the Greek island of Corfu. From 1815 until 1863 in this century, Corfu was under British jurisdiction, and Hayter's mother, a Corfu girl, married a British sailor, Hayter's

late father. Their Portsmouth-born son, Able-Seaman Hayter, was brought up—due to the mother—with loyalties divided between Britain, land of his father, and Greece, the land of his mother. But these are simple people."

The doctor puffed thoughtfully at his pipe.

"Seaman Hayter is still in Haslar Naval Hospital with a dislocated shoulder. Could a foretopman, certainly a physical type, have conceived and co-ordinated the *Victory* crime? Improbable. Could his crewmate confederate—no doubt a man of the same type and, on the evidence of the chloroformed Marine, remarkably strong—have conceived the crime? Improbable. No, Mr. Raffles, those men were *paid* by somebody. Whose was the *mind* behind the *Victory* crime?"

Raffles and I both knew. But we neither moved nor spoke.

"Our local newspaper, the *Portsmouth and Southsea Chronicle*," said Dr. Doyle, "published a list of the distinguished persons invited to be present on board *Victory* on Navy Day. The newspaper published a second list—those invited guests who actually were on board *Victory* on that day. On comparing the lists, I noted that, of the yacht-owning visitors at Cowes, who had all received invitations to *Victory*, only one had not availed himself of the invitation."

"Mr. Aristotle Andiakis," said Mr. Watson, "of the S/Y *Achilleion*."

"Precisely, Watson. Mr. Andiakis. A powerful mind—a Greek mind. A man, moreover, with seamen at his disposal—the crew of the *Achilleion*—to pose as sightseers and, in some hired boat, manoeuvre into a convenient position to pick up the lifebelt flung for them from *Victory*."

Dr. Doyle tamped down the tobacco in his pipe.

"Why was Mr. Andiakis not on board *Victory*? Was it from fear of personal involvement in the crime he possibly had planned? I wondered. I noted an absence of violence in the crime. Seaman Hayter's dislocated shoulder was unforeseeable. The Marine sentry was not brutally blackjacked, as would have been quicker and easier. He was harmlessly chloroformed. Was Mr. Andiakis, then, if his was in fact the mind behind the crime, a man of some nicety of scruple—sufficient nicety, perhaps, to decline to be a guest on board a ship he planned to rob? To you personally, Mr. Raffles, would such a scruple be comprehensible?"

I did not like the question. I could sense trouble coming. But Raffles said quietly, "Yes, Dr. Doyle, it would."

"But if Mr. Aristotle Andiakis," said the Elm Grove doctor, "were a man of scruple, what possible motive could he have for so drastic a deed as the illicit acquisition of a national treasure of the British nation?"

"I cannot imagine," said Raffles. "Unless—" He stopped.

"Something has occurred to you?" said Dr. Doyle.

"The Thracian Marbles," said Raffles.

"Ah!" said Dr. Doyle. "You read the London *Times*. So do I. And when I recalled a long-standing wrangle in its correspondence columns about the moral right of the British Museum to possess those ancient bas-reliefs commemorating a battle as important in Greek history as is the battle of Traflagar in British history, I felt sure of my ground."

"Dr. Doyle," said Mr. Watson, "immediately invited me to accompany him to the Isle-of-Wight."

"To Cowes, Watson, to be precise. Millionaires! Millionaires were all around us there. But some things," said Dr. Conan Doyle, "cannot be bought with minted money. We found Mr. Andiakis absent from his yacht. He was being granted the extremely unusual privilege of being received in audience by our Queen at her summer residence, Osborne House. Mr. Watson and I were invited on board the yacht to await his return. On his arrival, I immediately accused him of being in possession of the uniform in which Horatio Nelson died at Trafalgar."

In this room, in this ancient waterfront inn, there was for a moment no sound.

"Realising," Dr. Conan Doyle said, then, "that I had found him out, Mr. Andiakis immediately—under seal of secrecy—confided to me the outcome of his audience with Her Majesty. Mr. Raffles, the Nelson uniform is in due course to be returned to the Royal Navy Museum at Greenwich. In due course, in return, the Thracian Marbles will be restored to Greece, the ancient land of their origin. By command of Her Majesty, no explanation will ever be given. But, as to this—well, a danger exists."

My heart thumped slow, stifling. I could not breathe.

"Mr. Raffles," said the Southsea doctor, "Mr. Andiakis's possession of the Nelson uniform became known—last night—to an intruder. The safe on the S/Y *Achilleion* was opened."

I stared at the floor. Raffles was as still as a statue.

"I asked Mr. Andiakis," Dr. Doyle said, "if Mr. Watson and I might see the uniform. You've read, you told me, my story, *A Study in Scarlet*. Nelson's blood is not scarlet. Time has blackened those honoured stains. But I noticed a faint red blemish on Nelson's swallowtail blue epauletted coat. Blood, Mr. Raffles. Mr. Andiakis assured me that, when he set the combination of the safe just before leaving for his audience with the Queen, that blemish of fresh red blood was not on the coat."

"Dr. Doyle," said the big doctor's companion, "thereupon made a close examination of the safe's exterior—"

"And found on the carpet before it something that led me to the conclusion that the intruder had been wearing a fingerstall." Coldly blue as an arctic iceberg, Dr. Doyle's eyes were fixed on Raffles. "For greater tactile sensitivity in the manipulation of that relatively simple combination-lock, the intruder took off his fingerstall. For greater sensitivity still, he removed from the finger, probably with his teeth, two surgical stitches and, with his tongue, flicked them from his mouth. I have them—together with my bill, Mr. Raffles—in this envelope."

So it had come. Raffles was exposed. We were

finished. I could not swallow the great lump in my throat.

"Seaman Hayter," Dr. Doyle said, "and his bosun confederate in *Victory*'s crew will not be charged before a Court of Admiralty. They are no longer in the Royal Navy. They have been bought out by Mr. Andiakis and will be employed in his merchant-shipping fleet. Further, because a ban of silence has been imposed on every facet of the *Victory* crime, the intruder last night on S/Y *Achilleion* cannot be charged at Winchester Assizes. I don't know why you left the Nelson uniform where you found it, Mr. Raffles. Perhaps the devil looks after his own. You remain free to catch your train. But I, personally, have a bill to present. I shall hold it pending. If ever, traceable to you or your friend Manders, there comes to my ears any mention of what you know about Mr. Andiakis, I shall seek you out, Mr. A. J. Raffles, and infallibly present my bill—at a price a great deal higher than you will care to pay."

The doctor of Bush Villas, Elm Grove, knocked out his pipe-bowl into an ashtray on the dressing-table.

"To each," his strong voice said, "his own. To every nation, the mystery of its own soul, which is born of its past. Our Queen grows old. Her heart has known sorrow, but in that heart is the pride of kings. And the man who stood before her in Osborne House last night is a king among men—a self-made aristocrat, an Odysseus of our own century. He was confident of the lady to whom he spoke, and he knew how to present his case to her. He quoted to her four lines from one of her favourite poets, Lord Macaulay:

For how can man die better
Than facing fearful odds
For the ashes of his fathers
And the temples of his gods?

And that great Greek gentleman, Mr. Aristotle Andiakis, told me that the little, aging, indomitable Widow looked long at him. Then she turned to her Private Secretary and said, 'In this matter of the Thracian Marbles, convey to Ten Downing Street this, Our Royal Command: *Let right be done.*'"

Staring blindly at the floor, I heard the door open.

"Come, Watson."

The door-latch clicked shut.

Neither Raffles nor I moved.

Through the open window-casements, the breeze from the sea blew cool and salty upon us. Thinly over Portsmouth Harbour floated the bugle notes of the day's end call, "Retreat." The report of the sunset gun clapped across the water. From the masthead of H.M.S. *Victory*, as on all the Queen's ships at their anchors, the flag of her Realm fluttered down.

I heard Raffles draw in his breath, deeply.

"From now on, Bunny," he said, "an unsettled bill hangs over us."

"In account," I muttered, "with Dr. A. Conan Doyle."

"Or in account," Raffles said, in a strange tone, "with the other name he uses for himself—in the pages of that story."

On the fourposter bed, with our valises and Raffles's cricket-bag, lay the copy of *A Study in Scarlet*.

Historical Note

Not only does Mr. Manders's foregoing narrative, now at last become available, seem to explain the official silence which for so long has enshrouded the circumstances of the *Victory* crime, but it appears also to corroborate a perceptive remark made by Mr. John Dickson Carr on page 194 of his *Life of Sir Arthur Conan Doyle* (Harper & Row, 1949).

"When we consider," remarks Mr. Carr, "Conan Doyle's detective work in the case of George Edalji, we may ask ourselves a question to which the answer will be self-evident: Who *was* Sherlock Holmes?"

In Mr. Carr's book appears a photograph of Dr. Conan Doyle taken at approximately the period of the *Victory* crime, together with a photograph of the handwriting and signature of Mr. James Watson, Secretary of the Portsmouth & Southsea Literary & Scientific Society.

H.M.S. *Victory*, now preserved in drydock, may still be visited in Portsmouth Harbor, and the uniform stained with the lifeblood of Admiral Lord Horatio Nelson may be viewed today in the Royal Navy Museum at Greenwich.

Due, presumably, to the official sequestration of documents touching upon the *Victory* crime, no mention of it appears in Mr. Carr's book, but it may be of interest to note that the Thracian Marbles were quietly returned to Greece not long after the events described by Mr. Manders in his private writings about the career of his friend, A. J. Raffles.

RAFFLES ON THE TRAIL OF THE HOUND

Barry Perowne

"I WONDER IF by any chance, Mr. Raffles, you're one of those discriminating people who may be described, perhaps, as Sherlockians?"

The question was tossed suddenly at A. J. Raffles by Mr. Greenhough Smith, distinguished editor of England's leading monthly periodical, *The Strand Magazine*.

It was a morning in dubious springtime, and a fitful sun shone in through the windows of Mr. Smith's editorial sanctum in Southampton Street, just off London's busy Strand.

Mr. Smith had invited Raffles, England's best-known cricketer, to contribute an article on the game, and dropping in on Mr. Smith to discuss the matter, Raffles had brought me along with him.

Knowing what I knew about the least suspected side of Raffles's life, the criminal side, I felt uncomfortable when Mr. Smith, agreement having been reached with Raffles for the cricket article, asked his unexpected question.

"Why, yes, Mr. Smith," Raffles replied, at ease in a saddlebag chair, his suit immaculate, a pearl in his cravat, his dark hair crisp, his keen face tanned. "I think Bunny Manders and I can claim to be—shall we say—amateur Sherlockians. Eh, Bunny?"

"Certainly, Raffles," I murmured uneasily, taking my cue from him and accepting a Sullivan from his proffered cigarette-case.

"You may be interested, then," said Mr. Greenhough Smith, "to note this big basketful of letters on my desk. They're just a small part of the mail that's been flooding in from readers of Dr. Conan Doyle's latest tale, *The*

Hound of the Baskervilles. It's the twenty-sixth published adventure of Sherlock Holmes. Its first instalment appeared last year, in *The Strand Magazine* for August 1901. Its eighth and final instalment is in the current issue—practically vanished already from the bookstalls. You may have been reading the tale?"

"Bunny Manders and I consider it," said Raffles, "the most enthralling Holmes adventure that's so far appeared."

"An opinion, to judge from these letters," said Mr. Smith, "concurred in by most readers—with one curious exception."

The jingle of passing hansoms was faintly audible from Southampton Street as Mr. Smith, polishing his scholarly glasses, frowned at a letter that lay open before him on his blotting-pad.

"You know, Mr. Raffles," he went on, "Dr. Doyle was asked recently if he'd based the character of Sherlock Holmes on any real-life original. He replied that he had had in mind a preceptor of his undergraduate days at Edinburgh University, a certain Dr. Joseph Bell. On being told of this, Dr. Bell smiled. He said that Dr. Doyle's kind remembrance of his old teacher had made much of very little and that the real-life Sherlock Holmes is, in fact, Dr. Conan Doyle himself."

My palms moistened with embarrassment, for Raffles and I knew from personal experience that Dr. Joseph Bell's remark was only too true. Back at a time when Dr. Conan Doyle had been an obscure medical practitioner in the naval town of Portsmouth and had published, to no great acclaim, only the first of his Sherlock Holmes tales, *A Study in Scarlet*, Raffles and I had had an encounter with Dr. Doyle and had nearly gone to prison as a result.

Now here in Mr. Greenhough Smith's editorial sanctum twenty-five Sherlock Holmes tales later, with the great detective and his creator known the world over, the conversation had taken a turn I found distinctly disquieting.

But Raffles merely tapped ash casually from his cigarette and said, "To amateur Sherlockians, Dr. Joseph Bell's remark provides food for thought, Mr. Smith."

"Of late," Mr. Smith said, "Dr. Doyle's own great investigative ability has been concentrated on a challenge of the times we live in. As you may know, on the success of the Holmes tales, he abandoned medicine for literature. However, when the recent regrettable war with the Boers broke out, he abandoned literature for medicine—in order to serve in South Africa with the Langman Field Hospital. That photograph of him was taken at the time."

Among the framed drawings and signed photographs on the walls of Mr. Smith's Sanctum was the original, I saw now, of an illustration for *The Hound of the Baskervilles*, depicting Sherlock Holmes, in deerstalker cap and Inverness cape, firing his revolver at the apparition of a gigantic hound charging with lambent eyes and slavering jaws out of the fog of a Dartmoor night.

Beside this illustration of the fictional Holmes hung a photograph of his creator, the real-life Sherlock Holmes. Big, burly, bushy-moustached, wearing khaki fatigues and a sun-helmet and smoking a Boer curved pipe, he was shown standing, a stalwart, uncompromising figure, against a background of Red Cross bell-tents on the parched South African *veld*.

"You may have met Dr. Doyle out there?" Mr. Smith asked.

"As Yeomanry subalterns for the duration, Bunny Manders and I served in a different sector," said Raffles, naturally making no mention of our Portsmouth encounter with Dr. Doyle, which had occurred years before the Boer War.

"Now that peace has been restored," said Mr. Smith, "Dr. Doyle has felt it his duty to investigate foreign allegations, not made by the Boers themselves, that the British used dum-dum bullets and committed other transgressions. As a doctor who had a good many Boer prisoners, wounded and sick, pass through his hands, he saw no evidence to support the allegations. He considers them to emanate from tainted sources with a vested interest in maintaining discord among nations."

"The traffickers in armaments," said Raffles.

"Exactly! And our government," said Mr. Smith, "apparently considering it beneath its dignity to heed such allegations, Dr. Doyle has undertaken the task of investigation himself, at great personal expense of time and money. He has, nowadays, a world-wide audience. He feels a duty to it and to the cause of Peace, for he knows that when he speaks it's with a voice known to the world—the voice of Sherlock Holmes."

"Quite so," said Raffles.

"Dr. Doyle has gathered his documented evidence in rebuttal," said Mr. Smith, "in a book he calls *The South African War: Its Cause and Conduct*, written without fee and printed far below cost by a sympathetic publisher. With the object of financing the translation of the book into many languages and its printing and world-wide distribution, gratis, a Fund has been opened for the receipt of contributions—"

"A Fund?" said Raffles, his grey eyes alert.

"A 'War Book Fund,'" said Mr. Smith, "administered by Dr. Doyle's own bank—and also, you may recall, as Sherlockians, Holmes's bank—the Capital and Counties, Oxford Street branch. Of course, this great task which Dr. Doyle has taken upon his broad shoulders leaves him no time for fiction. In fact, he tells me he intends *The Hound of the Baskervilles* to be his last Holmes tale—which is bad news, of course, for the writers of all these letters. Strange as it may seem, I dare not bother him with them in his present mood—which is a pity, because there's one here in particular that—"

He broke off and called, "Come in!"

The door opened to admit a tall young man,

meticulously frock-coated, with a high collar and clean-cut, intellectual features.

"My Assistant Editor," said Mr. Smith, introducing us and handing the newcomer a sheaf of page proofs. "You want these for Mr. W. W. Jacobs? Very well, they can go off to him now. We mustn't keep humorists waiting. By the way, I was thinking of getting Mr. Raffles's impression of that letter from Dartmoor."

"It's a hoax, Mr. Smith," said the Assistant Editor firmly. "It's another humorist at work—an unlicenced one. It's be a mistake to bother Dr. Doyle with it, especially at this time. An impudent hoax would not only annoy Dr. Doyle, it'd just about put the lid on his determination to write no more Holmes tales. Gentlemen, if you'll excuse me—"

With a brisk nod to Raffles and myself, the Assistant Editor, obviously busy, left us.

"He's probably right about this letter," said Mr. Smith, as the door closed. "It came in this morning, in an envelope postmarked Bovey Tracey. That's a small town—the 'Coombe Tracey' of *The Hound of the Baskervilles*—on the edge of Dartmoor. No harm in getting a fresh eye cast on this letter. As a man of the world, Mr. Raffles, what d'you make of this?"

I read the letter, amateurishly typewritten on a machine with a faded blue ribbon, over Raffles's shoulder:

> Dartmoor,
> Devonshire.
> 27th March 1902

The Editor,
The Strand Magazine,
London.

Sir,

As a resident in the Dartmoor area, scene of The Hound of the Baskervilles, *now concluded in the current issue of your magazine, I have read the narrative with particular interest.*

Your author, A. Conan Doyle, has based his tale on the case, well known in this area since 1677, of Sir Richard Cabell, Lord of the Manor of Brooke in the parish of Buckfastleigh. This evil-living baronet, in the act of raping a virgin, had his throat torn out by an avenging hound, which then, according to legend, took on phantom form, to range evermore upon Dartmoor.

Your author has adapted the legend to his own purpose, making the Phantom Hound "the curse of the Baskervilles" and skilfully using the topography and certain phenomena of Dartmoor to lend his tale verisimilitude. Among such phenomena mentioned by him are strange nocturnal howlings sometimes heard, as indeed of some huge hound baying the moon. Sceptics attribute these sounds to natural causes—the wind in the rocks of the moorland tors, or the slow upwelling and escape of vegetable gas from the depths of the treacherous Dartmoor mires, such as the Fox Tor morass which your author chooses to call "the great Grimpen Mire."

These sounds, and other phenomena mentioned in his tale, have never in fact been satisfactorily explained. I had hoped that your author might advance some theory to account for them. I now find, however, that he is content to end his tale with Mr. Sherlock Holmes destroying the "phantom hound" with five shots from a revolver, proving the beast to be mortal and doctored with phosphorescent paste in order for an evildoer to secure an inheritance by chicanery.

Sir, I must confess to a slight sense of disappointment, and I feel constrained to describe to you a recent experience of my own.

As something of a folklorist, I have cultivated the acquaintance, for the sake of his unique knowledge of the moor, of a certain local deer-poacher, sheep-stealer, all-around ne'er-do-well. I am, frankly, ashamed of my furtive association with the man. However, he came stealing one night to my back door not long ago. His poacher's sawed-off shotgun had been confiscated.

He begged the loan of my twelve-bore and a handful of cartridges. For some time, I gathered, a lurcher-like bitch he owned, a rangy, grizzly-grey beast he called Skaur, had been wild on the moor. Trouble was now brewing over sheep wantonly hamstrung and other depredations. The police were on the look-out for the culprit—Skaur, my acquaintance was certain, though he had long ago given it out that the bitch was dead and buried. If the police now got her and proved his ownership, it would mean gaol for him, as he could not pay the fines and damages.

He was in such a panic to down Skaur before the police did so that I lent him my gun. About a week later, he appeared again one night at my door, a deeply shaken man. He had sighted Skaur, shot her, and crippled her. Following her blood trail, he found her laired among the rocks. She lay panting, bloodstained, with three grizzly-grey whelps so savagely at her dugs that she was like to be eaten while yet alive.

As he crouched, peering into the lair in the failing daylight and howling wind, some instinct made him look round. He swears that, stealing towards him, was a creature, big as a pony, shadowy—some species of enormous hound. He shot at it, wildly—and the apparition was gone.

The fellow was in such a state when he came to me that it was all I could do to get him, the following day, to take me on the long, rough trudge across some of the worst parts of Dartmoor to the alleged lair.

It exists. Skaur lay there dead, ripped and torn by her own whelps. Sir, I have never seen on canine pelts such curious markings as those on these savage creatures. I have penned them into the lair and, at considerable inconvenience, kept them alive. Curious as to their sire, I have maintained long vigils at the lair by day and night, but have caught no glimpse of the creature described by my ne'er-do-well

acquaintance, though I have heard, on two occasions, a distant, grievous, hound-like howling—but no conclusion, of course, can be drawn from that nocturnal phenomenon.

I can devote no further time to this matter. I intend to shoot the whelps. I have no desire, as you will appreciate, for my association with my unsavoury acquaintance to become known. I must guard my local good repute—and hence maintain my anonymity in this matter. However, I will make this much concession: If your author should wish to view the strange whelps, he should insert forthwith, in the Personal column of the daily Devon & Cornwall Gazette, an announcement to this effect: 'Sirius— instructions awaited.'

There will then be mailed to your office a map of Dartmoor with, clearly marked upon it, the precise location of the lair of the strange whelps. What your author may then choose to do about them, should he look into the matter, will be his responsibility, not mine.

In the event of no announcement appearing, as specified above, by 7th April, I shall carry out the intention I have expressed in this notification.

Meantime, I have the honour to be, Sir, yours truly,

Sirius

"Well, Mr. Raffles?" said Mr. Greenhough Smith, as Raffles returned the letter to him.

"A hoax, obviously," Raffles said. "Eh, Bunny?"

"Undoubtedly, Raffles," I said.

"How well, Mr. Smith," Raffles asked, glancing at the illustration of the fictional Sherlock Holmes and the photograph of the real-life Sherlock Holmes, on the wall, "is Dr. Doyle actually acquainted with Dartmoor?"

"He spent a few days there, researching for *The Hound of the Baskervilles*," said Mr. Smith, "at just about this time last year. He was with his friend, Mr. Fletcher Robinson, of Ipplepen,

Devonshire, who knows Dartmoor well and told Dr. Doyle of the legend of the Phantom Hound which inspired his *Baskerville* tale. You know, I'm sorry—in a way—that you consider this letter a hoax. I had just a faint hope that, if I let Dr. Doyle see it, it might kindle a spark in his creative mind—and result perhaps in a sequel to *The Hound of the Baskervilles*."

"I'm afraid," Raffles said, with a smile, "it would be more likely to annoy him, as your Assistant Editor remarked."

"Common sense tells me you're right, of course. Ah, well!" Mr. Smith put the letter, rather reluctantly, into a drawer of his desk and became business-like. "Now, Mr. Raffles, about a delivery date for your cricket article—"

A date readily agreed upon by Raffles, we took our leave.

"I suppose that, as usual when you get an invitation to write about cricket, Raffles," I said, as we sauntered down Southampton Street, "you expect me, as a one-time journalist, to ghost-write this article for you?"

"Why else, except for you to hear Mr. Smith's briefing for it, would I have brought you with me this morning, Bunny? Innocent appearances in print are useful cover for—shall we say—less innocent activities. But literary toil's more your cup of tea than mine, though it would have been impolitic to mention your spectral function to Mr. Smith."

"I appreciate that," I said. "I'm not complaining. I just feel, seeing that the throes of composition fall upon me, that you might have held out for a later delivery date."

"You'll manage, Bunny," said Raffles absently. "Dartmoor air will stimulate your muse."

"Dartmoor air?" I stopped dead. "Why should we go to Dartmoor?"

Raffles gave me a strange look.

"To see a man about a dog, Bunny—if we can find him!"

In the first-class smoking compartment we had to ourselves in the train going down to Devon-shire next day, Raffles explained his reasoning to me.

"Dr. Doyle's probably long ago forgotten our Portsmouth encounter with him, Bunny, but I never have. I made a humiliating mistake on that occasion. He detected it. I respect that man. The figure I cut in his eyes on that Portsmouth occasion is something I can't forget till I've levelled the score with him. If I could do him a service, even though he may never know of it, I'd feel—in my own mind—that I'd settled an account long outstanding to my own self-respect. And I could turn the page and forget."

A heavy shower lashed the train windows.

"Raffles," I said uneasily, "we'd be well advised to let sleeping dogs lie."

"Every instinct tells me, Bunny, that the dog in that 'Sirius' letter is very wide-awake. I think that letter's an attempt to set a trap. I think 'Sirius' is a man with a mission. I think he's a running dog of those 'tainted sources' who'd like to stop the translation and free world-wide distribution of Dr. Doyle's book disproving their mischief-making allegations. He carries that whole project on his own shoulders. Remove Dr. Doyle, in some way that would appear mere accident, and the world-wide project would die on the vine, and, incidentally, the career of the fictional Sherlock Holmes would end with the career of the real-life one."

"Who," I argued, "being what we know him to be, would be as quick as you are to suspect a trap in that letter!"

"Of course he would, Bunny. And, being the man he is, he might decide—if he saw that letter—to track down 'Sirius' himself. That's why I told Mr. Greenhough Smith I thought the letter a hoax. 'Sirius' thought, of course, that the letter would be passed on immediately to Dr. Doyle. 'Sirius' couldn't know what we know, which is that Mr. Smith was in two minds about it—an editorial predicament. *We* don't want Dr. Doyle to see that letter, Bunny, because *we* want to be the ones to kennel 'Sirius'!"

"How?"

"He has a weak spot, Bunny. His whole letter proclaims it. He's a Sherlockian!"

I stared. The train rat-tatted along, vibrating, through the wind-blown rain. Raffles offered me a Sullivan from his case.

"Consider what's probably happened, Bunny. Assume 'Sirius' to be a man briefed to queer Dr. Doyle's pitch. Seeking ways and means to get at him, 'Sirius' reads *The Hound of the Baskervilles*—with its vivid descriptions of the natural hazards of Dartmoor. Where most likely, thinks 'Sirius,' for Dr. Doyle to meet with a fatal accident than among the scenes of his own tale—if somehow he could be lured there?"

My heart began to thump.

"If I'm right," said Raffles, "the idea of a trap probably began to shape in the mind of 'Sirius' as he finished his reading of *The Hound of the Baskervilles*—the end of which, he says, 'disappointed' him. It's highly unlikely that the man is, in fact, a Dartmoor resident. So what would he do?"

"Reconnoitre the area himself," I said, "to decide just where and how he could best contrive a trap."

"Furthermore, Bunny, he'd want to find out just how familiar Dr. Doyle really is with the area. 'Sirius' would probably ask a question here and there, to find out if Dr. Doyle had personally explored Dartmoor and, if so, how extensively. So—what are you and I to look for?"

"An inquisitive stranger!"

"Asking questions, Bunny, within—probably—the past couple of weeks, because the current issue of *The Strand Magazine*, containing the end of the *Baskerville* tale, only became available about then. No, Bunny, 'Sirius' shouldn't be hard to find. He's like you and me—a deviant Sherlockian."

"Deviant?"

"Avowed Sherlockians, Bunny, are interested in the *fictional* Sherlock Holmes. You and I are interested in tracing the footsteps of the real-life Sherlock Holmes, Dr. Doyle. So, I suspect, is 'Sirius.' Now, as Mr. Greenhough Smith told us, Dr. Doyle *did* visit Dartmoor almost exactly

a year ago. If we can find out who's been sniffing, just recently, to pick up a scent of Doyle on Dartmoor, we'll have discovered the prowling hound, the deviant Sherlockian—'Sirius.' And here, by the look of it," Raffles added, "is our first glimpse of the moor coming up."

The daylight was fading. Bleak hills swept by wind and rain loomed in the distance—the outlying bastions of Dartmoor with its sombre tors and quaking morasses, its neolithic hut circles and notorious prison. As I peered through the train window at those brooding sentinel hills, my own reading of *The Hound of the Baskervilles* gave me a haunting sense of having been here before—in the company of Sherlock Holmes, Dr. Watson, and the menaced Sir Henry Baskerville.

After changing to a local train, Raffles and I arrived that night at Lydford Station and put up at an inn under Black Down on the moor's edge.

"Dr. Conan Doyle?" said the landlady, in reply to Raffles's inquiry. "In these parts this time last year? No, sir, I don't recolleck any Dr. Doyle."

"Have you had any visitors during the last couple of weeks?" Raffles asked.

"No, sir, you're the first for many a month. Dartmoor gets visitors in the summer, more. Mostly they like to see the Sepulchre—which is the tomb of Sir Richard Cabell, 'im as was Lord o' the Manor, wenching and carrying on in 'is prime, over Buckfastleigh way. Ended up with 'is throat tore out by the 'Ound that turned phantom, as is well known in these parts."

Raffles and I exchanged a glance.

"There's a key'ole in the door of Sir Richard's tomb," said the landlady, "an' to this day, if you pokes yer finger through, 'is skeleton'll up an' gnaw at it."

"There are mysteries on Dartmoor, Missus," agreed Raffles, "and you'll join us in a nightcap to steady us. What'll you take?"

"Just a small port-and-peppermint," said Missus graciously.

All next day Raffles was out on the moor on a hired hunter, seeking word of Dr. Doyle's visit to these parts a year ago. The weather was vile, and I was not sorry that my duty as Raffles's "ghost" kept me indoors by the snuggery fire, working on his cricket article while the wind wuthered in the thatched and dripping eaves.

As the wan daylight faded and Missus brought the lamp in, lighted, and drew closed the snuggery curtains against the howling dark, there still was no sign of Raffles. It was a night when one could believe in the Phantom Hound, a night for it to be abroad on the desolate moor. I began to grow anxious. But, at last, Raffles returned, soaked to the skin. And when he had changed, and Missus set before us on the snuggery table a great round of beef and a foaming jug of nut-brown ale drawn from the wood, I was left alone with him, and I asked how he had got on.

"Not badly, Bunny," he said. "I made a start at Bovey Tracey, on the far side of the moor. That's the 'Coombe Tracey' of *The Hound of the Baskervilles*, and I struck what we're seeking—the trail behind the tale." He began, obviously famished, to carve the juicy sirloin, perfectly roast. "Dr. Conan Doyle's remembered at Bovey Tracey, both he and his friend Mr. Fletcher Robinson. Two big, genial, moustached gentlemen, Bunny, making a holiday of their explorations on Dartmoor for Dr. Doyle's tale of the Hound."

"What about 'Sirius'?"

"Not a sniff, as yet, of that inquisitive Sherlockian. I'll get his scent to-morrow, with luck. After you with the horseradish, Bunny."

But it was not until our fourth night at the Black Down inn that Raffles returned from his own explorations with a glint in his eyes that I knew well.

"Got him, Bunny! I picked up his scent at Widecombe-in-the-Moor. I had the luck to fall into conversation with the Vicar there—elderly man, a devoted Sherlockian himself. He told me about a man who'd called at the Vicarage about ten days ago—a tall, lean, mean-eyed individual, a stranger to the Vicar, who said there was something about the look of the chap that made him

think of some lines the poet Shelley once wrote. The old Vicar quoted them to me:

"I met Murder on the way.
He had a mask like Castlereagh.
Very grey he looked and grim.
Seven bloodhounds followed him."

"My God, Raffles!" I breathed.

"Apparently," Raffles said, "he told the Vicar he was a bookdealer visiting country houses and would give a good price for any first editions they might care to part with—such as first editions of Dr. Conan Doyle's books. A good gambit, Bunny, to start asking if Dr. Doyle was known to have visited the area."

"It's 'Sirius,' for a certainty!"

"You can lay to that. But there are only *two* bloodhounds following him—you and me, Bunny. And the scent's now hot and rank, because the old Vicar told me he recognised the horse the fellow was riding—a hack hired from an inn called Rowe's Duchy Hotel at Princetown."

"That's where that damnable prison is, Raffles."

"The highest point on Dartmoor, Bunny—Princetown. And we'll shift our base to there in the morning."

In the night, the wind dropped. The weather changed. We hired a dogcart from Missus. Raffles took the reins. Under a leaden sky, we clattered along the potholed road to Princetown. A strange stillness brooded over the moor, its desolation relieved here and there by great, smooth patches of green among the rocks and heather—the deceptive, inviting green of the deadly quagmires. The distant tors loomed up, strange and jagged in the distance, out of a growing hint of mist.

Suddenly, on that lonely road, we came upon a grisly procession—a shuffling file of convicts in knickerbockers and tunics stamped with broad arrows. Under a strong escort of blue-uniformed Civil Guards armed with carbines and fixed bayonets, Britain's born losers trudged along with picks and shovels over their shoulders, their sullen, shaved heads sunk on their chests.

"There, Bunny," Raffles muttered, "but for the grace of God—"

I knocked on wood as our dogcart clattered on past. And, about lunchtime, there loomed up ahead of us the house of a thousand hatreds, the most notorious of penitentiaries, its great, gaunt complex of buildings towering starkly over the squat little cluster of dwellings, Princetown, isolated under the gunmetal sky.

"Caution's our watchword, Bunny," Raffles said, as he reined in our horse before the long, low, stone-built inn that faced the prison across a deep dip in the moor. "We'll feel out the ground."

We found the landlord behind his counter in the Bar Parlour. A stout man in his shirtsleeves, with an oiled cowlick of hair, he was polishing the shove-ha'p'ny board. He gave us good-day and Raffles ordered a Scotch-and-soda for each of us.

"See any lags on the road?" a voice asked.

We turned from the bar. There was one other customer present, sitting on a settle by the window. Lean, tall, powerfully built, gaunt of face, with a mean, tight mouth under a small, wax-pointed, sergeant-major type moustache, he wore a buttoned-up frockcoat and a bowler.

"Yes," Raffles said, "we saw a group."

"Being marched in from the stone quarries, huh? At this hour? That means there's fog coming up."

The man drained his tankard, mopped his moustache with a red bandanna handkerchief, stood up and, with a curt nod to the landlord, went out.

"Have a drink yourself, landlord," said Raffles.

"Thank 'ee, sir—just a small nip o' gin, then, to give me an appetite. You gents on holiday?"

"Snatching a few days from the treadmill," said Raffles. "Like that gentleman, perhaps, who just went out?"

"Well, no, sir, that's—but I better not mention his name, he likes to keep it quiet." The landlord glanced around, lowered his voice. "Between ourselves, gents, he's the Man with the Cat."

I stared. We had come to Dartmoor to see a man about a dog.

"The Man with the Cat?" said Raffles.

The landlord nodded. "It's not like the bad old days, sir, when it was done 'ap'azard. We're in a new century now. When a lag's ordered strokes nowadays, it has to be done civilized. So the Man with the Cat comes down from the Prison Commissioners in London to do it. He brings the Cat-o'-Nine-Tails in proper hygienic wrappings. He has to do the job within a prescribed time of the lag bein' sentenced, to avoid mental anguish, and lay the Cat on for the best effect—scientific.

"He lodges with me for a night or two when he comes down on 'is business. If 'e lodges in the prison, the lags seem to smell 'e's arrived. They catcalls all night, yowling *miaouw miaouw* like a thousand randy toms on the roof, to keep him from sleepin'. They kick up a hell of a shindy, to sap 'is strength. The man's a bit too much in love with 'is work, for my taste. I gets a lodgin' allowance for him from the Commission, but I can't say I like the man."

"I'm sure," said Raffles. "Landlord, I think we'll have another drink. Is that gentleman your only guest just now?"

"No, sir, we've one other in the house. Book-dealer gent. Rides round to country 'ouses, tryin' to buy up old books, not that he seems to have much luck. Asked me, he did, when he arrived a week or so ago, if I'd 'appened to read the tale about our Phantom 'Ound in a magazine. Well, I don't get the time for reading, but we had the writer of it lodgin' here about a year ago, a Dr. Doyle, 'oo 'ad a Mr. Robinson an' Mr. Baskerville with him."

"Mr. *Baskerville?*" Raffles exlaimed.

The landlord chuckled. "I showed the book-dealer gent our Guest Book to prove it." He produced a leather-covered volume from under his counter, consulted the pages, then turned the book to Raffles and me. "See for yourselves, sir."

Under the date 2nd April 1901 were two signatures, one firm and clear, the other boldly scrawled:

A. Conan Doyle, M.D., Norwood, London.

Fletcher Robinson, Ipplepen, Devon (and coachman, Harry M. Baskerville)

"Mr. Robinson brought 'is own dogcart and coachman, see," said the landlord. "Mr. Baskerville'd drive the two gents 'ere an' there on the moor, then wait with the dogcart when the gents trudged off to points they could only get to afoot. Mr. Baskerville took 'is meals in the kitchen with me an' my family an' staff. 'E was tickled pink because Dr. Doyle'd asked him if he'd mind bein' knighted and put in a tale as Sir 'Enry Baskerville. Talk about laugh."

"Well, well!" said Raffles. "There's more behind some of these magazine stories than meets the eye. Is your book-dealer guest still staying here?"

"Yes, sir. He's out just now. He's out all day, most days, on a horse I hires him. If he ain't back well before dark, by the look of it, he'll get fogged in an' have to put up in some shepherd's bothy. Dartmoor's dangerous in fog."

"Then perhaps we'd be wise to spend the night here ourselves," said Raffles. "Got a couple of vacant rooms?"

"Certainly, sir."

As soon as we had been shown to our rooms, I joined Raffles in his.

"The so-called book-dealer's our man, Bunny. He's 'Sirius,' all right. I want to find his room and take a look at his things while he's out." Raffles opened a door, listened at the crack, then turned. "Mealtime sounds from downstairs, Bunny. The inn folk are in the kitchen, eating. Now's my chance. Watch from that window. If a grey-faced man on a horse arrives, open this door and start whistling *Drink, Puppy, Drink*."

He was gone. I watched from the window. I thought of the "Sirius" letter that implied the existence of "Baskerville whelps," and Whyte-Melville's old hunting ditty ran eerily through my mind:

Drink, puppy, drink, and let every puppy drink
That's old enough to lap and swallow,
For he'll grow into a hound,
so let's pass the bottle round,
And merrily we'll whoop and hollo!

Outside, a stealing mist was beginning faintly to obscure the gaunt buildings of the prison across the plunging dip in the moorland. In front of the inn our dogcart still stood, the horse munching in its nosebag. No man came riding enigmatic out of the mist. And suddenly, silently, Raffles was back in the room.

"Got him, Bunny—knew his room because it's the only one with a few books in it. There was a locked portmanteau. I opened it with the little gadget I carry. There's a small Blick typewriter with a faded ribbon in the portmanteau."

"That settles it," I said.

"Not quite, Bunny. There's also an envelope containing five sheaves of currency notes, each sheaf £100. I dared not take it, of course. There's an Ordinance Survey map of Dartmoor in the portmanteau. I took a look at the map. I could faintly make out the pressure marks left by a pencil when a tracing had been made over the map, and a small *x* marked on it."

"The alleged 'lair of the whelps,' Raffles!"

"Not only that, Bunny. There's also in the portmanteau a copy of the daily *Devon & Cornwall Gazette*, with a small announcement in the Personal column ringed round in pencil: 'Sirius—instructions awaited.'"

My heart stopped.

"The one thing we didn't want, Bunny," Raffles said, his grey eyes hard, "must have happened. Mr. Greenhough Smith *has* shown the 'Sirius' letter to Dr. Doyle, and that real-life Sherlock Holmes has smelled the trap in it—damn it, he'd be bound to, knowing what *we* know of him! If he inserted that announcement, it's because he's decided to catch 'Sirius' himself, knowing the 'tainted sources' he's probably working for. But, Bunny, that copy of the *Devon & Cornwall Gazette* is four days old! I checked the date on it."

Raffles was searching, as he spoke, through the things in his own valise.

"You see what it means, Bunny? If the map tracing showing the alleged lair of the whelps was posted to *The Strand Magazine* the day the announcement appeared in the *Gazette*, the tracing could have reached Dr. Doyle the day before yesterday, assuming normal mail. He may be on the moor now—the real-life Holmes! He may already have caught 'Sirius' in a counter-trap."

"Or"—I hardly dared say it—"'Sirius' caught him?"

"My money—remembering Portsmouth—is on the real-life Holmes," Raffles said grimly. He was studying his own Ordinance Map, dug out from his valise. He made a small *x* on the map with a pencil. "There we are, Bunny. There it is—out on the moor—the alleged 'lair of the whelps,' at the neolithic Stone Rows near Higher White Tor. There's where 'Sirius' has set his trap and where he's been keeping vigil over it every day for Doyle to walk blindly into it, 'Sirius' *hopes*!"

"For all we know," I said, "he may be out there at this moment!"

"Bunny," Raffles said grimly, "they may *both* be out there at this moment, stalking each other in this fog that's closing in. There may be *just* a chance that we can take a hand and square a long-outstanding account. The dogcart's outside. The map shows Higher White Tor and the Stone Rows to lie almost due north from Princetown here. Come on!"

Raffles at the reins, the horse jingled along, now at a trot, now at a canter, along a rough track through the heather, the wheels of the dogcart jolting and grinding. Mist, slowly deepening over the moor, was beginning to take on the grey tinge that presaged the menace of a Dartmoor peasouper.

Presently, the track became impossible for the dogcart. We left it and trudged on afoot. Heather, sparse and tough, grew among scattered, loose flints, which became more plentiful as we went on.

"Prehistoric flint-chippings, Bunny," Raffles said, "workings of our skin-clad ancestors, the beetle-browed Dawn Men. We must be getting near their settlement, the Stone Rows."

Suddenly a cry came, thin and inhuman, from somewhere ahead. We checked, listening. Again came the cry, soaring to a neighing, despairing screech, and abruptly ceased.

"There's a Dartmoor pony gone," said Raffles, "mired in some morass, and not far off."

I felt the insidious vapour, dankly chill like grave sweat on my face, as we trudged on—blindly, for my part—up a slope that now was virtually a glacis of flint-chippings, debris of the Dawn Men.

"Down!" breathed Raffles. "Listen!"

Flat on my belly beside him, I discerned a thickening in the mist ahead. A little above our level, the thickening was probably one of the Stone Age hut circles, up there on a small plateau. I heard a slight crunching sound. Somebody was walking around among the ruins.

Raffles inched higher, keeping flat. I followed. The rock-edge of the plateau loomed now just above us. I made out the shadowy form of a man up there. From our low-angle viewpoint, he looked like a very thin, tall funeral mute in a high hat and cemetery black.

"The 'book-dealer,'" Raffles breathed in my ear. "'Sirius.'"

The man's elongated legs moved like scissors as he paced slowly to and fro between the plateau-edge and a ruined hut-wall dimly perceptible in the mist. A strange figure, this gaunt assassin who had been riding about Dartmoor on a hired horse, sniffing at the year-old trail of the author of *The Hound of the Baskervilles*.

The man passed from view around the angle of the hut wall. We seized our chance to clamber higher, then froze as he reappeared. He resumed his pacing. We kept low. I could feel the thumping of my heart against the ground. Hours seemed to pass. A man of deadly patience, this "Sirius," who must thus for two, perhaps three days now have been keeping vigil here over his trap, baited with whelps that never were.

Even as the thought crossed my mind, as I crouched there beside Raffles on the steep slope in this mist-muffled, silent solitude, the man checked his pacing and stood as though intently listening. Then he did a thing that raised the hair on my head.

He howled like a mournful hound.

The wailing cry died away in the mist. All was still, the man a long shadow, listening. I heard faintly, as from the further slope of this tumulus or plateau, the clink of a shod horse's hooves, then walking. The sounds stopped.

A yelp sounded, a sudden ky-yi-ing as of pain, a sharp bark, snarls and growling. Had the human source of these canine sounds not been dimly visible there above on the ledge, I would have sworn they emanated from a litter of whelps contending in a lair among the ruins.

"Bait," Raffles breathed. "He's got a revolver in his hand now. He's holding it clubbed. He's drawing his man on to look for the lair. As he comes around the hut wall, he'll be clubbed senseless and dragged down for disposal in the mire where we heard that pony scream as it was sucked under."

"Who comes?" I whispered. "Dr. Doyle?"

I had no answer from Raffles, for just then, out of the mist-dim ruins of the Dawn Age dwellings, a voice rang, calling: "Is there anybody here?"

Silence. Then sudden, sharp barks, on a note of challenge and interrogation, as from the hidden lair of the "Baskerville Whelps." And, before I sensed his intention, Raffles lunged upwards to the ledge, seized the barking man by the ankles, and jerked his feet out from under him.

He toppled backwards against the hut wall, tore his ankles free, aimed a kick at Raffles's head, then with flying coat-tails made a huge bound clean over the both of us. He landed on

the glacis, went slithering down it in a cascade of loose flints, and vanished into the mist.

"Who's there?"—again the voice, peremptory above us.

We looked up. From our angle, the man who stood now on the ledge above us loomed tall in the mist—not a burly figure like Dr. Conan Doyle, but a lean man, a man in a deerstalker cap and an Inverness cape, a figure known the world over, a figure out of *The Hound of the Baskervilles.*

I seemed to hear the cracking of the thin ice of human reason.

Neither Raffles nor I moved, staring up.

"Who are you?" the man on the ledge demanded, firmly authoritative, conspicuous on his eminence. "I require an answer. You recognise with whom you have to deal!"

I heard Raffles, beside me, draw in his breath, slowly, deeply, as though released from a thrall. Clambering up to the ledge, he stood erect there.

"Yes, we have met," he told the newcomer courteously. "You're the Assistant Editor of *The Strand Magazine.* How d'you do?"

My own bespelled trance dissolved. My reason restored to me, with reservations regarding the newcomer's garments, I clambered up on to the ledge.

Glibly, Raffles explained that, as amateur Sherlockians, he and I had been prompted by our reading of *The Hound of the Baskervilles* to spend a few days on Dartmoor while he worked on his cricket article. Visiting this prehistoric site, the Stone Rows, we had noticed a man here who was behaving oddly. As we watched the man, he suddenly had begun to foam at the mouth and emit canine sounds. Believing him to be seized of a fit of some kind, we had tried to succour him, but he had eluded our helpful attentions and bolted.

"I thought I heard a horse galloping away," said Raffles. "He must have had one tethered down there in the mist somewhere."

"But good God!" exclaimed the Assistant

Editor. "Don't you realize, Mr. Raffles? That must've been the man himself—'Sirius'—the *Baskerville* hoaxer!"

"Indeed?" said Raffles, astonished. "Bunny, what a pity we lost him!"

The Assistant Editor, seeming rather nettled by our ineptitude, explained that he had been convinced from the first that the "Sirius" letter was a hoax. To prove it to Mr. Greenhough Smith, who still had been half inclined to let Dr. Doyle see the letter, the Assistant Editor had persuaded Mr. Smith to let him insert the reply—"Instructions awaited"—in *The Devon & Cornwall Gazette*.

On receipt by mail of a map tracing marked with the lair of the alleged whelps, he had come down from London by train, spent the night at Coryton, then hired a horse and set out across the moor to find the marked spot, the Stone Rows.

"Lucky to find the spot, with this mist coming on," he said, not knowing how lucky he was not to have had his skull fractured, in mistake for Dr. Doyle's, and to have ended up in the mire that had swallowed the pony. "I borrowed this deerstalker and cape," he said, "from the studio of our artist, Sidney Paget, who illustrates the Holmes stories. My idea was, if the hoaxer should show himself, to give the fellow the shock of his life by suddenly appearing before him as—Sherlock Holmes!"

"You gave *us* a shock," said Raffles ruefully. "Eh, Bunny?"

"Absolutely, Raffles," I said.

"Listen!" exclaimed the Assistant Editor. "What's that sound?"

From somewhere distant in the mist came, faintly, a prolonged, eerie howling. The Assistant Editor blenched, listening, a wild surmise in his eyes.

"It's all right," said Raffles. "That, I think, comes from Dartmoor Prison. The convicts must have learned they have a certain visitor in the vicinity."

. . .

From time to time, that night, we heard yowling and catcalling from the nearby prison.

Raffles mentioned it when we set off, very early next morning, in the dogcart, to return it to Missus and catch our train at Lydford. The Assistant Editor, who had also put up at Rowe's Duchy Hotel and who was to go up to London in the same train with us, was astride his hired horse, trotting a hundred yards ahead of us in the grey, foggy morning.

"The yowling from the prison didn't keep the Man with the Cat awake, Bunny," Raffles said. "He was snoring when I paid his room a visit in the night. Have a look in my valise."

Mystified, I unstrapped his valise and took out, in its hygienic wrappings bearing the seal of the Prison Commissioners, the Cat-o'-Nine-Tails.

"If sentence must be carried out within a prescribed time of its order," Raffles said, "there's a chance we may have saved some poor devil a flayed back to-day. There's a nice little quagmire just ahead on the left."

He reined in the horse, looked each way along the road, took the Cat from me and, standing up in the cart, hurled the Cat from him, overarm. It arched high through the air, fell in the green scum, remained for a moment upright like some sordid Excalibur, then was dragged under by its heavy stock.

"The other visit I paid in the night, Bunny," said Raffles, as the horse jingled us on again, "was to the room of 'Sirius.' We gave him a shock at the Stone Rows. He hadn't returned to the inn. He wasn't in his room. I think he must have left Dartmoor. So I now have in my pocket the £500 from his portmanteau."

Raffles was mistaken, however. "Sirius" had not left Dartmoor, as I learned two days later, when I completed the cricket article to be signed "by A. J. Raffles" and took it round to his rooms in The Albany, just off Piccadilly.

He showed me a brief newspaper item. It stated that the finding of a riderless horse had led to the discovery on Dartmoor of a man, a guest at Rowe's Duchy Hotel, whose identity had not been satisfactorily established. The horse evidently had had a fall. The man's neck was broken.

"That's what comes," said Raffles, "of galloping a horse in a Dartmoor fog. Not really a clever man, Bunny—certainly not clever enough to catch the real-life Sherlock Holmes in a trap, even if Dr. Doyle had been shown the 'Sirius' letter. Now, about this money. Tainted as its source is, we'll retain £100 to cover our expenses. For the rest, we have an account to settle. It's been outstanding since twenty-five Sherlock Holmes stories ago, so it's high time we squared the account, for the sake of our self-esteem."

We jingled round in a hansom, in the springtime sunshine, to the bank mentioned to us by Mr. Greenhough Smith—Dr. Conan Doyle's own bank, the Oxford Street branch of the Capital & Counties, which he had named in his tales as the bank also of his fictional alter ego, Mr. Sherlock Holmes.

"There is here," Raffles said to the cashier at the counter, "the sum of £400—a contribution to the Fund for the translation into many languages and free world-wide distribution of Dr. Conan Doyle's book exposing the evil of slander between nations."

"Very good, sir," said the cashier, counting the currency notes with deft fingers. "To whom do you wish this handsome contribution to be attributed?"

"As amateur Sherlockians, keenly looking forward to the appearance, some day, of a sequel to *The Hound of the Baskervilles*, my friend here and I would like to honour the gentleman who inspired Dr. Doyle's tale of the Phantom Hound. So attribute this contribution, please, to Sir Richard Cabell, and post the formal acknowledgment," said A. J. Raffles, "to his country seat—The Sepulchre, Parish of Buckfastleigh, Dartmoor, Devon."

The Adventure of the Cipher in the Sand

EDWARD D. HOCH

ALTHOUGH MOST AUTHORS of mystery fiction have produced short stories, it has been virtually impossible for them to earn a living writing exclusively in this form. Edward D. Hoch (1930–2008) was a rare exception. He produced more than nine hundred stories in his career, approximately half of them published in *Ellery Queen's Mystery Magazine*, beginning in 1962. In May 1973, Hoch started a remarkable run of publishing at least one story in every issue of *EQMM* until his death—and beyond, as he had already delivered additional stories.

Readers have never been able to decide which of Hoch's series characters is their favorite, as he created numerous protagonists, from the bizarre Simon Ark, who claims to be two thousand years old and is the central character of his first published story, "Village of the Dead" (1955), to Nick Velvet, the thief who steals only innately worthless objects (the first story in which he appears is "The Theft of the Clouded Tiger," 1966), to Dr. Sam Hawthorne, who specializes in solving locked-room and other impossible crimes and makes his first appearance in 1974 in "The Problem of the Covered Bridge."

Hoch also wrote numerous stories featuring Sherlock Holmes and was able to capture the sound of the nineteenth-century and English (as opposed to American) speech patterns, even though he was born and lived almost his entire life in the very American city of Rochester, New York. The Holmes tales were collected in *The Sherlock Holmes Stories of Edward D. Hoch* (2013).

"The Adventure of the Cipher in the Sand" was first published as a chapbook limited to 221 copies (New York, Mysterious Bookshop, 1999).

THE ADVENTURE OF
THE CIPHER IN THE SAND

Edward D. Hoch

IT WAS A fine autumn morning in late September of '99 when Sherlock Holmes and I received an unexpected visitor at our Baker Street lodgings. Accustomed as Holmes was to welcoming paying clients, it was rare indeed for Inspector Lestrade to visit us.

"Is this official business?" Holmes asked, pausing in the act of filling his pipe to study the lean, ferret-like countenance of the Scotland Yard inspector.

"It is indeed, Mr. Holmes."

"I trust it has to do with a body discovered along the shore of the Thames River, near Wapping, within the last three hours."

Lestrade seemed taken aback by his words. "My God, Holmes! Has one of your Baker Street urchins brought you news of it already?"

"I hardly need that," he replied with the superior gaze I'd seen so many times. "You know my methods, Watson. Explain to the inspector how I knew the location of the killing."

I studied him up and down for a moment. "Well, I can see moist sand dried to the knees of his trousers," I suggested with some uncertainty.

Holmes finished lighting his pipe. "Of course! Moist sand in the city on a sunny September morning most likely comes from the banks of the Thames at low tide. That particular grade of sand is mainly found near Wapping. A man of your rank, Inspector, would only have been called out for the most serious of crimes. The fact that you knelt in the moist sand tells me you were examining a body."

"You never fail to amaze me, Holmes," the inspector said, brushing the sand from his knees. "The body of a man was indeed found near Wapping this morning. Some sort of message was left in the sand near his body. It appears to be a cipher, and I heard of your success last year with the problem of the dancing men. I hope you can come with me to view this message before it is washed away by the rising tide."

Holmes glanced in my direction. "What say you, Watson? Is your calendar clear for the next few hours?"

"Certainly, Holmes."

The area of Wapping near the Liverpool docks was made up mainly of four-story buildings with shops on the ground floors and lodgings above. Facing west, one could see the Tower of London looming in the distance. Holmes and I followed Lestrade down to the stretch of damp sand by the water's edge where a pair of bobbies stood guard. I could see that the tide had already turned.

"The body has been removed," Lestrade told us. "It was sighted just after dawn by the Metropolitan Special Constabulary—the river police—and officers were dispatched to the scene."

"What was the cause of death?" Holmes asked.

"Stabbed once in the back. The knife was still in the wound. The victim was dressed like a seaman, with black hair and a short beard. Perhaps he was off one of the merchant ships at the Liverpool docks. He had no money or identification in his pockets, suggesting robbery as the motive. However the killer missed this." He held out a white disk, apparently made of ivory, with the number 5 imprinted on it in gold ink.

Sherlock Holmes grunted, his attention taken by three rows of block letters in the damp sandy soil at our feet:

YVI YAH
TOMIT
WAHT YH

"It's a cipher of some sort," I agreed, "but hardly anything like the dancing men. Perhaps Roman numerals, mixed with other letters."

"The letters are much too regular to have been made by a person's finger," Holmes said thoughtfully, "certainly not by a dying man's finger. It looks more as if they were imprinted. Where was the body found, Inspector?"

"Right here by the message. There were some footprints, but by the time the body was discovered and the police arrived, I'm afraid the original tracks could not be determined with any degree of accuracy."

Holmes shook his head hopelessly but still went through the motions of squatting down and examining the nearest footprints with his magnifying glass. He asked the two bobbies to lift their feet and examined the bottoms of their shoes as well. "I can find very little," he admitted. "The area is too cluttered."

Holmes jotted down the apparent cipher in his notebook and we left the scene as the rising tide began to fill some of the letters with water. "Did you see anything I missed?" Lestrade asked.

"Many things, Inspector, but nothing that points directly to the killer. Please let me examine that disk you showed us earlier."

Lestrade handed over the ivory marker with the number 5 on it. "Could it be a coat check?" I suggested.

Holmes shook his head. "Coat checks usu-ally have a hole in them. And they're not made of ivory. I would guess this is a roulette chip from a fashionable casino, in the amount of five pounds."

"That was my thinking exactly," the inspector said.

"The casinos for the affluent are to be found in the West End. Are there any places near here, in the East End, which might use such chips?"

Lestrade considered the question. "Certainly not in this area, with its wretchedly poor people."

"Still, there is a fine row of eighteenth-century houses to be seen in Wapping High Street. I could easily imagine one of those as an illegal gambling establishment."

"We have heard rumors," he admitted.

Holmes nodded. "I will look into the matter."

"But what of the cipher?"

"All in good time, Inspector."

Holmes said very little about the case when we returned to our lodgings in Baker Street, but I noticed him more than once puzzling over the message in the sand that he'd copied into his notebook. After dinner, when I was giving some thought to retiring early, he suddenly roused himself from his favorite armchair and announced, "Come, Watson, it is time we visited Wapping High Street."

"Now, Holmes? It's after nine o'clock!"

"This is just the time when London's night life begins to awaken."

Holmes directed our hansom cab to the block he sought on Wapping High Street, and when we arrived he pretended he'd forgotten the number we sought. "What is it you're looking for, gents?" the driver asked from above.

"The casino."

"Parkleigh's?"

"That's the one."

The cab moved down a few houses and stopped before a three-story brick home of eighteenth-century design, where two gentlemen were just entering ahead of us. Holmes paid the man and said as we alighted, "Lestrade should check with the hansom drivers for his information."

Once inside the door of the establishment Holmes and I passed through a red velvet drape into a passage where a porter awaited us. "Welcome to Parkleigh's," he said, and showed us into a large ballroom which must have occupied a large portion of the ground floor. An attractive blond woman played a piano at one end and there was a bar at the other end, with small tables and chairs along the walls. About a dozen couples were dancing to waltz music, and I expressed my surprise at the presence of women. "They are hostesses provided by the establishment," Holmes explained.

We proceeded upstairs to the gambling room, which was much more crowded. Perhaps fifty young and middle-aged men were grouped around the gaming tables playing roulette and dice and *chemin-de-fer*. All were well dressed, some in formal evening attire. I saw at once that Holmes had been correct. The ivory disk in the dead man's pocket was indeed a roulette chip. In fact, the five-pound chip seemed to be the highest denomination in play. At the far side of the room was a glass-domed tape machine that supplied race results by means of a telegraph ticker. Apparently the establishment was open in the afternoons for wagering on horse races.

The murmur of conversation was low, broken only by an occasional shout or curse from an emotional player. Tobacco smoke hung heavy in the air, though there were no drinks served upstairs. We'd been observing the scene for some minutes when a short, thick-set man who might have been a former prize fighter came over to introduce himself. "I'm Jerry Helmsphere, the manager here. Can I help you gentlemen with anything?"

Sherlock Holmes smiled. "I had thought that I might help you. I understand that you have had some criminal activity here of late."

The man seemed taken aback by his words. "Could you step into my office, please?" We followed him into a small office where Holmes introduced us. It was obvious at once that the man recognized the name. "Sherlock Holmes, the consulting detective?"

"The very same."

"How did you learn of the theft of our tape machine?"

"I may have a clue to its whereabouts," Holmes said, pointedly ignoring the question. "Would you care to hire me in an official capacity?"

The short man was hesitant. "How much are you asking?" Holmes mentioned a figure and the man sighed. "I am only the manager here. I don't possess that sort of money."

"But you cannot request help from the police, since your entire operation is illegal," Holmes remarked. "And you dare not report it to your owner."

"The owner resides in Paris. He is better left undisturbed." Helmsphere made a counteroffer. "That is as high as I can go."

"Very well," Holmes agreed. "Now tell me exactly what happened to your missing tape machine."

"You may have noticed one machine against the opposite wall as you entered. Its ticker reports the results from Epsom, Ascot, and the other tracks. We had two such machines to accommodate more of our patrons who wished to read the results before they are posted. One was stolen overnight. I need not tell you that the tape machines are expensive, and illegal possession of one could lead to all manner of chicanery."

I observed that beads of perspiration had collected on Jerry Helmsphere's upper lip as he spoke. Clearly the disappearance of the machine was a matter of grave importance to him. Holmes sensed it too, and asked, "What sort of chicanery?"

He wiped a hand across his lips. "Many of the smaller bookmaking establishments do not have tape machines like these. Whoever stole it could use it to place bets on winning horses before the official results reached those places. The other bookmakers might hold me responsible for their losses."

His meaning was all too clear. The man feared for his life unless he could recover the stolen machine. "How heavy is it?" Holmes inquired. "Could one man have carried it out alone?"

"Not easily. Two would be much safer."

"At about what time would the theft have taken place?"

"We close here at two a.m. I'm usually around until three checking the books and making certain the place is cleaned up. We open at one in the afternoon on race days, so it makes for long hours." He paused, then added, "The theft would have taken place between three a.m. and noon, when I discovered it."

"A man's body was found this morning down by the river. He was dressed as a seaman and had one of your roulette chips in his pocket. Do you remember anyone like that being in here last night?"

Helmsphere shook his head. "We generally attract a better clientele. A man in seaman's dress would not have been allowed upstairs. However he might have remained downstairs to mingle with the girls. Let me ask Frances."

He sent someone downstairs to get her, and after a moment the blond piano player joined us. Her name was Frances Poole and she seemed to be in her late twenties. She eyed Holmes and me with some apprehension. My friend smiled, trying to put her at ease. "There is nothing to fear, Miss Poole. We are only inquiring about one of last evening's customers. This would be a man with black hair and a beard, dressed as a seaman."

She nodded at once. "He danced with some of the girls and then he wanted to go upstairs, but Tim told him he wasn't dressed for it."

"Tim?"

"That would be Tim Thaw, one of our croupiers. They often go downstairs on their breaks," the manager told us.

"Could I speak to him?"

"Frances, have someone relieve Tim and tell him to come in here."

She nodded and went off on her mission. Through the open door I saw her approach a sandy-haired young man at the roulette table. Presently he came in to join us, with someone else taking his place at the table. "How can I help you, Mr. Helmsphere?" he asked.

"I have invited this gentleman here to investigate the overnight theft of our tape machine."

Holmes shook Thaw's hand and said, "Miss Poole tells me a bearded seaman was downstairs last evening and spoke with you about coming up here for gambling."

"I informed him that proper attire was needed for the gaming room and he remained downstairs with the ladies."

"Did he mention his name, or his ship?"

"His name was Drexel, I believe, off one of the Liverpool ships. I didn't see him again after my break ended."

"He left a bit later," Frances Poole confirmed.

"Alone?"

"I believe so."

We seemed to have learned all there was to learn, and as we left the office we walked out with young Thaw. "Have you worked here long?" I asked.

He shrugged. "A few months. I owned a country pub near Henley but couldn't make a go of it. I think I was always meant to live in London. This is a nice place to start out."

Holmes and I watched him for a time at the roulette table, then went back downstairs. Frances Poole was at her piano. Some of the ladies had disappeared from the dance floor and I wondered aloud to Holmes where they might be. "Good old Watson," he said. "That needn't concern us. We have quite enough, with the murder by the river and the stolen tape machine."

"Do you think the two are linked, Holmes?"

"Almost certainly. The thief needed help to carry the stolen machine out of here and hired this seaman. They had a falling-out, no doubt over money, and the thief stabbed him."

"But if that's true, Holmes, what happened to the killer and the stolen machine? And what was the meaning of that cipher message?"

"I believe I know, but we must wait until morning."

. . .

It was quite unusual for Mrs. Hudson to interrupt our breakfast with news of an early morning visitor, but she did so the following day, announcing that Inspector Lestrade had come calling once more.

"Send him up, by all means!" Holmes exclaimed. "He may have news for us, Watson."

The inspector apologized for his early arrival. "I thought you'd want to know, Mr. Holmes, that the dead man has been identified. He was missing off the Irish freighter *Antrim*, and the captain identified him as a third mate named Sean Drexel."

"I suspected as much," Holmes said. "Watson and I visited Parkleigh's last evening and his name was mentioned. He was there shortly before his death."

"Parkleigh's!" Lestrade repeated. "How did you ever find such a place?"

"It matters not. Could the Metropolitan Special Constabulary supply us with a police boat this morning?"

"It might be arranged, but to what purpose?"

"Give me a boat and I will deliver the murderer before noon."

Within the hour we finished breakfast and Holmes donned the pea jacket and red scarf he'd worn before when we ventured onto the Thames. "Do you have your revolver, Watson?"

"You believe I'll need it?"

"Perhaps."

Lestrade insisted on coming with us in the launch, and we met it at Westminster Wharf. Its green running lights had been removed from the sides so it was not readily identifiable as a police boat, and we set off down river toward Wapping. A morning mist still hung over the water, but the sun was gradually burning it off. We passed tugboats pulling lines of loaded barges, but Holmes paid no attention to the river traffic. He seemed alone with his thoughts until we had gone under Tower Bridge. Then he sprang instantly to life.

"Steer us toward the south shore," he instructed the officer at the wheel. There was another man tending the coal-fired steam engines below deck. As the launch moved closer to shore, Holmes scanned the damp soil with his binoculars. The tide was still low, though it was beginning to rise as it had on the previous morning.

"What are we looking for?" Lestrade asked. "And why here? The murder occurred on the opposite bank."

Without lowering the glasses from his eyes, Holmes began to speak. "The facts of the case seem clear enough. The casino chip in the victim's pocket led Watson and me to Parkleigh's in nearby Wapping. There we learned that a valuable ticker tape machine, used for receiving race results, had been stolen during the early morning hours, after three o'clock. This is a relatively heavy machine, and since some sort of carrying case was necessary to protect the glass dome, the thief would have wanted someone to help transport it out of the casino. The seaman Sean Drexel was recruited and given a five-pound casino chip as a down payment."

"How can you possibly know that, Holmes?"

"Drexel was barred from the casino floor because of his seaman's attire. He could only have acquired that chip if someone on the ground floor gave it to him."

"Come now," Lestrade argued. "I can think of another explanation. A fellow seaman, having visited the casino, might have brought it back to their ship and given it to him."

But Holmes shook his head. "No, Inspector. If that were the case the fellow seaman would surely have remarked upon the proper attire for admittance to Parkleigh's."

The police launch was moving closer to shore, and we were directly opposite the place on the north shore where the body was found. "Soon, now," Holmes said, almost to himself.

"You believe the killer came across the river to this area?" Lestrade asked. "Why not the other direction? Why not the north side?"

"You are full of questions today," my friend answered, a slight smile on his lips. "He obviously left the scene of the crime by boat. Working alone, he would have had to drag his heavy box back up to the street if a vehicle awaited him, and there were no drag marks. The use of a boat implies a destination across the river in an easterly direction. If he were going west it would have made more sense to hire a vehicle and go back over Tower Bridge. But there is no other bridge to the east of Tower. Rather than risk a long carriage ride and the driver's suspicions as to his cargo, he acquired a small boat, no doubt a rowboat, to carry himself and his loot across the river. His destination was a location in this area where the tape machine could be installed to deliver early race results."

Suddenly he gripped my shoulder. "Quick, Watson, look through these binoculars and tell me what you see!"

I did as he asked. "It seems to be a small warehouse of some sort, probably abandoned."

"No, no—on the sand leading up to it!"

"Drag marks above the tidal line," I confirmed. "They might be from a boat."

"No doubt. And something else besides."

As we drew nearer I could see that one of the doors stood open a few inches for ventilation. It seemed likely that our quarry was inside. Lestrade directed the officer at the wheel to dock the launch at a pier about a hundred feet down river. As Holmes and I left the vessel, the inspector and the two-man crew were right behind us.

When we neared our destination I drew my revolver. "You won't need that," Lestrade told me.

"The man is a murderer."

"It has yet to be proven."

Holmes flung open the warehouse door, revealing a figure bent over a tape machine identical to the one we had seen at Parkleigh's. "I must interrupt your work," Holmes said, like the voice of judgment. "The police are here to arrest you for murder, Mr. Tim Thaw."

When he saw the revolver in my hand, and the officers behind us, Thaw offered no resistance. Instead, he tried to argue his way out. "I know nothing about a murder."

As the officers took him into custody, Holmes went over to inspect a rowboat and a wooden packing case. The latter had obviously been nailed together by Thaw from scrap boards. "This was an investigation where I suspected I knew the killer's name even before I met him. Thaw told us he'd owned a pub near Henley, and that was the final clue I needed."

He showed us again the apparent cipher we'd found in the wet sand, only he'd rewritten it to move the second line to the top:

TOMIT
WAHT YH
YVI YAH

"Do you see it now?" Holmes asked. "The letters were raised on the bottom of this home-made box made out of scrap lumber. In the damp sand their impression was printed backward, like a metal die. These pieces came from Thaw's old pub sign." He turned over the box so we could see the embossed bottom:

TIMOT
HY THAW
HAY IVY

"*Timothy Thaw, Hay & Ivy.* You'll note the spacing device between his first and last names, and the ampersand between *Hay* and *Ivy.* Both are painted rather than embossed, so they did not leave their marks in the soil. He cut the sign apart, using the wood for the bottom of the box where it wouldn't be seen. By some curious coincidence all of these letters are symmetrical, appearing the same forward and backward."

"Why didn't he notice the imprint on the sand?" Lestrade wanted to know.

"Because it was dark when Drexel was killed. Remember the river police spotted the body just after dawn."

"And Thaw rowed across here alone?"

"No great feat for a young man, especially one from Henley where rowing is a popular sport, at least at Regatta time. But he had to drag the box up here, and I was counting on its having left marks above the tidal line."

Lestrade turned to confront their captive. "Do you have anything to say for yourself?"

The man curled back his lips. "He wanted more money. He made threats. I stabbed him. There's nothing more to say."

"You should have stayed in the pub business," Holmes said.

The South Sea Soup Co.

KENNETH MILLAR

FAR BETTER KNOWN under his Ross Macdonald pseudonym, Kenneth Millar (1915–1983) has long been recognized as a major American novelist, not purely a writer of mystery fiction. His series of detective novels about Lew Archer are ranked alongside the works of Raymond Chandler and Dashiell Hammett as the apotheosis of the quintessential American private eye novels of the twentieth century.

Millar had issues with his byline for some time. He had married Margaret Sturm, who took his name and published distinguished crime fiction as Margaret Millar, beginning with *The Invisible Worm* (1941); she was eventually given the Grand Master Award for lifetime achievement by the Mystery Writers of America, as was her husband. Her success in the genre revived his own interest (he had been a devoted reader of mysteries when he was younger), so he published his first four novels under his own name, beginning with *The Dark Tunnel* (1944), but when some readers confused their names, he adopted the pseudonym John Macdonald, only to be confused again, this time with John D. MacDonald. His only book under this nom de plume is *The Moving Target* (1949), which introduced Archer, a lonely, introspective private investigator in the California town of Santa Teresa (a fictionalized Santa Barbara, where the Millars lived). The novel served as the basis for *Harper* (1966), starring Paul Newman as the renamed detective; Newman reprised the Archer/Harper character in 1975 in *The Drowning Pool*. Millar quickly switched his byline to John Ross Macdonald, publishing five novels and a short story collection. He permanently took the Ross Macdonald name in 1956 with the publication of *The Barbarous Coast*.

"The South Sea Soup Co." is Millar's first fictional writing, produced for *The Grumbler*, his Kitchener, Ontario, high school magazine, in 1931. (Curiously, his high school sweetheart, Margaret Sturm, also had her first story published in the same issue.) It was first published commercially in a chapbook, *Early Millar: The First Stories of Ross Macdonald & Margaret Millar* (Santa Barbara, California, Cordelia Editions, 1982), which was limited to one hundred fifty paper-bound copies and fifteen hardcover copies.

THE SOUTH SEA SOUP CO.

Kenneth Millar

THE AMBITIOUS YOUNG investigator, Herlock Sholmes, yawned behind his false moustache and poured for himself a cocaine-and-soda. He then lightly tapped with his knuckles a Burmese wacky-wara, which he had secured from an Odd-Fellows' Temple in French Indo-China. For it was thus he summoned his obtuse assistant, Sotwun. Sotwun crawled into the room, an idiotic expression on his face.

"I say, Sotwun, I'm sorry to disturb your reading of the 'Ju-Ju Journal' for March 1, 1927."

Sotwun stood awed by Herlock's amazing perspicuity and perspicacity. "How did you know that I was reading that, huh?"

Sholmes smiled and explained:

"Well, there's a minute speck of fresh plaster-of-paris on your nose. The only place there is fresh plaster-of-paris in these rooms is the nose on the bust of Julius Caesar in the next room, which I repaired this morning. Therefore your nose must have touched the nose of the bust. As I have often noticed your resemblance to a monkey, physically and mentally, Sotwun, I thought you must have imitated some picture you saw. The only picture in this house of people touching noses is in the Ju-Ju Journal for March 1, 1927, which I scanned several years ago."

When Sotwun had overcome his astonishment, Sholmes explained the reason for his summons.

"Sotwun, has the South Sea Soup Company yet accepted my application for the position as head of their detective force, whose business is to discover oysters in their oyster soup? No? How strange!

Just then Herlock sneezed.

"Aha!" said he. "The phone!"

Instead of ringing, his telephone had been made to loose a quantity of gas whenever there was a call. This gas had the peculiar property of causing one to sneeze. Thus Sholmes could be informed of the call without any undesirable noise.

He lifted the receiver. Immediately he recognized the voice of a man sixty-three years of age, wearing a brown suit and other clothes, who had been married eighteen times.

The strained voice said, "Mr. Sholmes? Oh! Come quickly to the office of the South Sea Soup Company. Mr. Ox-Tailby has been murdered!"

Nonchalantly flicking an imaginary speck of dust from his eyebrow, Sholmes quickly undressed himself and donned his clothes again, thus changing his appearance from that of a handsome, thoughtful, young man to that of a good-looking, pensive youth. He then bounded out of the room and down the stairs, eight at a time, tying his shoelace and lighting his opium-pipe on the way.

He then hailed a passing cab and rode his bicycle, with Sotwun running behind, to the office of the South Sea Soup Company.

With a burst of speed he burst into the room, bursting his vest-buttons.

There on the floor lay the corpse of Oswald Ox-Tailby, the gravel commissioner in the company's barley department, a bullet-wound in its chest. The body, to the experienced eye of Herlock Sholmes, was evidently quite dead.

Sholmes thought steadily for a full second. Then,—"Aha! Sotwun, go and ask Raring Riley, my Limehouse man, to look up Jamaica Jo."

For seventeen minutes and forty-five seconds the occupants of the room, friends and colleagues of the murdered man, stared at Herlock's thoughtful brow. Then Sotwun came into the room with somebody behind him.

Nonchalantly flicking an imaginary speck of dust from his necklace, Sholmes said, "Allow me, gentlemen, to introduce to you Miss Josephine Bartley, commonly appellated Jamaica Jo!"

It was a woman!

"Miss Bartley," said Sholmes, "has anyone ever said you were beautiful?"

The woman blushed. "Why, yes, sir. My sweetheart has often said so."

With a cry of triumph, our hero grasped her by the arm. "Tell me where he lives," he thundered.

The woman gave him the street and number and he drove his bicycle madly to the designated dwelling. He ran to the door, struck it violently, and deftly handcuffed the man that answered.

Before giving him time to speak, Sholmes flung him across the handle bars of his bicycle and, drawing on his vast resources of Herculean strength, pedalled back to the office.

"Here is your man!" he said, nonchalantly flicking a speck of dust from his moccasins, which he had secured while hunting colleoptera in the Antarctic.

Everyone shouted, "Huh?"

"I suppose you wish me to explain," said the detective, as he took out his grammar-book to continue his study of the Lithuanian tongue.

Assent was evidenced.

Sholmes began: "The first thing that struck me when I entered this room (besides that dictionary yonder) was that the corpse had a bullet-wound in it. This reminded me of the famous Ugga-Wulla case which you all must remember.

In that case the murdered man also had a bullet-wound in him. The similarity of the two crimes is astonishing, as I have just shown you, and consequently I deducted that the same criminal committed them both. I had already solved this Ugga-Wulla mystery, though I forgot to denounce the murderer to the police. The murderer was Black Bleerstone.

"My Limehouse man, Raring Riley, had told me a month before that Black Bleerstone was the lover of this woman, Jamaica Jo. Black Bleerstone, having once used a pair of spectacles from Woolworth's, has very poor eyesight. To confirm the message that Bleerstone was her lover, I asked Jo if anyone had ever called her beautiful. She said that her lover had, and, as only a man with poor eyesight would call her beautiful, her lover is a man with poor eyesight. That man there is her lover, and he has, as you perceive by his powerful spectacles, poor eyesight. And Bleerstone has poor eyesight! The coincidence is too great, and the man that killed Oswald Ox-Tailby stands before you in the person of Black Bleerstone, Jamaica Jo's lover."

Then forth from the circle of onlookers strode Peter P. Soup, the superintendent of horse-flesh cutting in the chicken-soup department, and said, "Herlock Sholmes, I cannot let an innocent man go to the scaffold. I am the man who killed Oswald Ox-Tailby, for he made the vile insinuation that I did not put any veal in our last week's output of chicken-soup. But I did! Lots of it! Didn't I, my friends?" and he turned a pleading face to his former co-workers.

"No, you didn't. Only horse-flesh," said they. On these fateful words Sholmes, nonchalantly flicking an imaginary speck of dust from his boxing gloves, which he secured in Hindustan during the Boxer Rebellion, threw himself at Peter P. Soup, self-confessed murderer.

But Soup, with one blow of his mighty fist, strengthened by years of pounding horse meat to make it as tough as ordinary spring chicken, knocked Herlock through the open window.

Sholmes alighted unhurt on the grass below.

Nonchalantly flicking several thousand real specks of dust from his face, Sholmes ran back into the office just in time to see Peter P. Soup place a little white pellet in his mouth. Sholmes tried to take it from him, but he was too late, for the mint from a slot-machine had been swallowed. In a few seconds it began to do its deadly work. Soup fell to the floor, his limbs slowly stiffening. With his last breath he sang that fine old song so reminiscent of slot-machine mints in general, "Rock of Ages."

After these evidences of his detective abilities, Sholmes was accepted as the head detective of the South Sea Soup Company's detective force.

But he never succeeded in finding an oyster in the oyster-soup, although he found several oyster-shell buttons.

The Adventure of the Clothes-Line

CAROLYN WELLS

H O W   I S   I T possible that someone so enormously popular and prominent in her lifetime could be so largely forgotten and unread today? The bibliophilic Carolyn Wells (1862–1942) wrote and edited one hundred seventy books, of which eighty-two are mysteries, many of which had exceptionally ingenious plot ideas, and most of which are achingly dull—reason enough to ignore them. As famous as she was for her mystery novels, sixty-one of which featured the scholarly, book-loving Fleming Stone, she was equally noted in her time for such anthologies as *Nonsense Anthology* (1902), considered a classic of its kind, and her *Parody Anthology* (1904), which remained in print for more than a half-century. Wells also wrote the first instructional manual in the detective fiction genre, *The Technique of the Mystery Story* (1913). Her first mystery novel, *The Clue* (1909), was selected for the Haycraft-Queen Definitive Library of Detective-Crime-Mystery Fiction.

Her affection for satires and parodies led her to write many of them herself, including *Ptomaine Street* (1921), a full-length parody of Sinclair Lewis, and several stories involving Sherlock Holmes, including "The Adventure of the 'Mona Lisa'" (1912) and "Sure Way to Catch Every Criminal. Ha! Ha!" (1912).

"The Adventure of the Clothes-Line" was first published in the May 1915 issue of *The Century Magazine*; its first appearance in book form was in *The Misadventures of Sherlock Holmes*, edited by Ellery Queen (Boston, Little, Brown, 1944).

THE ADVENTURE OF
THE CLOTHES-LINE

Carolyn Wells

THE MEMBERS OF the Society of Infallible Detectives were just sitting around and being socially infallible, in their rooms in Fakir Street, when President Holmes strode in. He was much saturniner than usual, and the others at once deduced there was something toward.

"And it's this," said Holmes, perceiving that they had perceived it. "A reward is offered for the solution of a great mystery—so great, my colleagues, that I fear none of you will be able to solve it, or even to help me in the marvelous work I shall do when ferreting it out."

"Humph!" grunted the Thinking Machine, riveting his steel-blue eyes upon the speaker.

"He voices all our sentiments," said Raffles, with his winning smile. "Fire away, Holmes. What's the prob?"

"To explain a most mysterious proceeding down on the East Side."

Though a tall man, Holmes spoke shortly, for he was peeved at the inattentive attitude of his collection of colleagues. But of course he still had his Watson, so he put up with the indifference of the rest of the cold world.

"Aren't all proceedings down on the East Side mysterious?" asked Arsène Lupin, with an aristocratic look.

Holmes passed his brow wearily under his hand.

"Inspector Spyer," he said, "was riding on the Elevated Road—one of the small numbered Avenues—when, as he passed a tenement-house district, he saw a clothes-line strung from one high window to another across a courtyard."

"Was it Monday?" asked the Thinking Machine, who for the moment was thinking he was a washing machine.

"That doesn't matter. About the middle of the line was suspended—"

"By clothes-pins?" asked two or three of the Infallibles at once.

"Was suspended a beautiful woman."

"Hanged?"

"No. *Do listen!* She hung by her hands, and was evidently trying to cross from one house to the other. By her exhausted and agonized face, the inspector feared she could not hold on much longer. He sprang from his seat to rush to her assistance, but the train had already started, and he was too late to get off."

"What was she doing there?" "Did she fall?" "What did she look like?" and various similar nonsensical queries fell from the lips of the great detectives.

"Be silent, and I will tell you all the known facts. She was a society woman, it is clear, for she was robed in a chiffon evening gown, one of those roll-top things. She wore rich jewelry and dainty slippers with jeweled buckles. Her hair, unloosed from its moorings, hung in heavy masses far down her back."

"How extraordinary! What does it all mean?" asked M. Dupin, ever straightforward of speech.

"I don't know yet," answered Holmes, honestly. "I've studied the matter only a few months. But I will find out, if I have to raze the whole tenement block. There *must* be a clue somewhere."

"Marvelous! Holmes, marvelous!" said a phonograph in the corner, which Watson had fixed up, as he had to go out.

"The police have asked us to take up the case and have offered a reward for its solution. Find out who was the lady, what she was doing, and why she did it."

"Are there any clues?" asked M. Vidocq, while M. Lecoq said simultaneously, "Any footprints?"

"There is one footprint; no other clue."

"Where is the footprint?"

"On the ground, right under where the lady was hanging."

"But you said the rope was high from the ground."

"More than a hundred feet."

"And she stepped down and made a single footprint. Strange! Quite strange!" and the Thinking Machine shook his yellow old head.

"She did nothing of the sort," said Holmes, petulantly. "If you fellows would listen, you might hear something. The occupants of the tenement houses have been questioned. But, as it turns out, none of them chanced to be at home at the time of the occurrence. There was a parade in the next street, and they had all gone to see it."

"Had a light snow fallen the night before?" asked Lecoq, eagerly.

"Yes, of course," answered Holmes. "How could we know anything, else? Well, the lady had dropped her slipper, and although the slipper was not found, it having been annexed by the tenement people who came home first, I had a chance to study the footprint. The slipper was a two and a half D. It was too small for her."

"How do you know?"

"Women always wear slippers too small for them."

"Then how did she come to drop it off?" This from Raffles, triumphantly.

Holmes looked at him pityingly.

"She kicked it off because it was too tight. Women always kick off their slippers when playing bridge or in an opera box or at a dinner."

"And always when they're crossing a clothes-line?" This in Lupin's most sarcastic vein.

"Naturally," said Holmes, with a taciturnine frown. "The footprint clearly denotes a lady of wealth and fashion, somewhat short of stature, and weighing about one hundred and sixty. She was of an animated nature—"

"Suspended animation," put in Luther Trant, wittily, and Scientific Sprague added, "Like the Coffin of Damocles, or whoever it was."

But Holmes frowned on their light-headedness.

"We must find out what it all means," he said in his gloomiest way. "I have a tracing of the footprint."

"I wonder if my seismospygmograph would work on it," mused Trant.

"I am the Prince of Footprints," declared Lecoq, pompously. "*I* will solve the mystery."

"Do your best, all of you," said their illustrious president. "I fear you can do little; these things are unintelligible to the unintelligent. But study on it, and meet here again one week from tonight, with your answers neatly typewritten on one side of the paper."

The Infallible Detectives started off, each affecting a jaunty sanguineness of demeanor, which did not in the least impress their president, who was used to sanguinary impressions.

They spent their allotted seven days in the study of the problem; and a lot of the seven nights, too, for they wanted to delve into the baffling secret by sun or candlelight, as dear Mrs. Browning so poetically puts it.

And when the week had fled, the Infallibles again gathered in the Fakir Street sanctum, each face wearing the smug smirk and smile of one who had quested a successful quest and was about to accept his just reward.

"And now," said President Holmes, "as nothing can be hid from the Infallible Detectives, I assume we have all discovered *why* the lady hung from the clothes-line above that deep and dangerous chasm of a tenement courtyard."

"We have," replied his colleagues, in varying tones of pride, conceit, and mock modesty.

"I cannot think," went on the hawk-like voice, "that you have, any of you, stumbled upon the real solution of the mystery; but I will listen to your amateur attempts."

"As the oldest member of our organization, I will tell my solution first," said Vidocq, calmly. "I have not been able to find the lady, but I am convinced that she was merely an expert trapezist or tight-rope walker, practising a new trick to amaze her Coney Island audiences."

"Nonsense!" cried Holmes. "In that case the lady would have worn tights or fleshings. We are told she was in full evening dress of the smartest set."

Arsène Lupin spoke next.

"It's too easy," he said boredly; "she was a typist or stenographer who had been annoyed by attentions from her employer, and was trying to escape from the brute."

"Again I call your attention to her costume," said Holmes, with a look of intolerance on his finely cold-chiseled face.

"That's all right," returned Lupin, easily. "Those girls dress every old way! I've seen 'em. They don't think anything of evening clothes at their work."

"Humph!" said the Thinking Machine, and the others all agreed with him.

"Next," said Holmes, sternly.

"I'm next," said Lecoq. "I submit that the lady escaped from a near-by lunatic asylum. She had the illusion that she was an old overcoat and the moths had got at her. So of course she hung herself on the clothes-line. This theory of lunacy also accounts for the fact that the lady's hair was down—like *Ophelia's*, you know."

"It would have been easier for her to swallow a few good moth balls," said Holmes, looking at Lecoq in stormy silence. "Mr. Gryce, you are an experienced deducer; what did *you* conclude?"

Mr. Gryce glued his eyes to his right boot toe, after his celebrated habit. "I make out she was a-slumming. You know, all the best ladies are keen about it. And I feel that she belonged to the Cult

for the Betterment of Clothes-lines. She was by way of being a tester. She had to go across them hand over hand, and if they bore her weight, they were passed by the censor."

"And if they didn't?"

"Apparently that predicament had not occurred at the time of our problem, and so cannot be considered."

"I think Gryce is right about the slumming," remarked Luther Trant, "but the reason for the lady hanging from the clothes-line is the imperative necessity she felt for a thorough airing, after her tenemental visitations; there is a certain tenement scent, if I may express it, that requires ozone in quantities."

"You're too material," said the Thinking Machine, with a faraway look in his weak, blue eyes. "This lady was a disciple of New Thought. She had to go into the silence, or concentrate, or whatever they call it. And they always choose strange places for these thinking spells. They have to have solitude, and, as I understand it, the clothes-line was not crowded?"

Rouletabille laughed right out.

"You're way off, Thinky," he said. "What ailed that dame was just that she wanted to reduce. I've read about it in the women's journals. They all want to reduce. They take all sorts of crazy exercises, and this crossing clothes-lines hand over hand is the latest. I'll bet it took off twenty of those avoirdupois with which old Sherly credited her."

"Pish and a few tushes!" remarked Raffles, in his smart society jargon. "You don't fool me. That clever little bear was making up a new dance to thrill society next winter. You'll see. Sunday-paper headlines: STUNNING NEW DANCE! THE CLOTHES-LINE CLING! CAUGHT ON LIKE WILDFIRE! *That's* what it's all about. What do you know, eh?"

"Go take a walk, Raffles," said Holmes, not unkindly; "you're sleepy yet. Scientific Sprague, you sometimes put over an abstruse theory, what do you say?"

"I didn't need science," said Sprague, carelessly. "As soon as I heard she had her hair down,

I jumped to the correct conclusion. She had been washing her hair, and was drying it. My sister always sticks her head out of the skylight; but this lady's plan is, I should judge, a more all-round success."

As they had now all voiced their theories, President Holmes rose to give them the inestimable benefit of his own views.

"Your ideas are not without some merit," he conceded, "but you have overlooked the eternal-feminine element in the problem. As soon as I tell you the real solution, you will each wonder why it escaped your notice. The lady thought she heard a mouse, so she scrambled out of the window, preferring to risk her life on the perilous clothes-line rather than stay in the dwelling where the mouse was also. It is all very simple. She was doing her hair, threw her head over forward to twist it, as they always do, and so espied the mouse sitting in the corner."

"Marvelous! Holmes, marvelous!" exclaimed Watson, who had just come back from his errand.

Even as they were all pondering on Holmes's superior wisdom, the telephone bell rang.

"Are you there?" said President Holmes, for he was ever English of speech.

"Yes, yes," returned the impatient voice of the chief of police. "Call off your detective workers. We have discovered who the lady was who crossed the clothes-line, and why she did it."

"I can't imagine you really know," said Holmes into the transmitter; "but tell me what you think."

"A-r-r-rh! Of course I know! It was just one of those confounded moving-picture stunts!"

"Indeed! And why did the lady kick off her slipper?"

"A-r-r-r-h! It was part of the fool plot. She's Miss Flossy Flicker of the Flim-Flam Film Company, doin' the six-reel thriller, 'At the End of Her Rope.'"

"Ah," said Holmes, suavely, "my compliments to Miss Flicker on her good work."

"Marvelous, Holmes, marvelous!" said Watson.

Sherlock Holmes and the Muffin

DOROTHY B. HUGHES

THE UNDERAPPRECIATED DOROTHY BELLE HUGHES (1904–1993) is historically important as being the first female writer to fall squarely into the hard-boiled school. She wrote eleven novels in the 1940s, beginning with *The So Blue Marble* (1940) and including *The Cross-Eyed Bear* (1940), *The Bamboo Blonde* (1941), *The Fallen Sparrow* (1942), *Ride the Pink Horse* (1946), and *In a Lonely Place* (1947), the latter three all made into successful films noir. *The Fallen Sparrow* was released by RKO in 1943 and stars John Garfield and Maureen O'Hara; *Ride the Pink Horse* (1947) stars Robert Montgomery and Thomas Gomez; *In a Lonely Place* (1950) was a vehicle for Humphrey Bogart, Gloria Grahame, and Martha Stewart, and was directed by Nicholas Ray. This classic film noir portrays an alcoholic screenwriter who is prone to violent outbursts and is accused of murdering a hatcheck girl. He is given an alibi by his attractive blond neighbor, who soon becomes fearful that he really did commit the crime and that she might be next. In the book, the writer is, in fact, a psychopathic killer, but the director found it too dark and softened the plot.

At the height of her powers and success, Hughes largely quit writing due to domestic responsibilities. She reviewed mysteries for many years, winning an Edgar for her critical acumen in 1951; in 1978, the Mystery Writers of America named her a Grand Master for lifetime achievement.

"Sherlock Holmes and the Muffin" was first published in *The New Adventures of Sherlock Holmes*, edited by Martin Harry Greenberg and Carol-Lynn Rössel Waugh (New York, Caroll & Graf, 1987).

SHERLOCK HOLMES AND THE MUFFIN

Dorothy B. Hughes

I

THE ICICLES DID indeed hang by the wall on that early December morning; quite as Sherlock Holmes was caroling as he came from his bedroom into our sitting room:

> *"When icicles hang by the wall,*
> *"And Dick the shepherd blows his nail,*
> *"And Tom bears logs . . ."*

A bump on the corridor door interrupted. It was half after six and our early morning tea had arrived. As he was nearby, Holmes opened the door. Lustily, he resumed his song:

> *"And greasy Joan doth keel the pot . . ."*

The tweeny entered, balancing the heavy silver tray, with its two brown china pots of Jackson's best English Breakfast blend, a large container of steaming water, two cups and saucers of Wedgewood china, a sugar bowl and milk pitcher also of Wedgewood, and two silver spoons. She managed with care to put down the tray without spilling anything. She then faced up to Holmes. "My name is not Joan," she stated, "and I am not greasy. I wash myself every morning and every night, and on Saturday I take a full bath in m'Mum's washtub." She emphasized, "Every Saturday."

She was a little thing, of no more than ten or eleven years by the looks of her. Over her dress she wore an overall, evidently one of Mrs. Hudson's in the way it hung almost to her ankles. Her mousy brown hair was cut as a small boy's, a straight fringe to the eyebrows and square below the ears. Her eyes were as gray as this wintry morning.

Tweenies came and went at Mrs. Hudson's. Our exemplary landlady was not so goodhearted to underservants as to her tenants. I had frequently heard her berating one or another tearful child. Tweenies being on the lowest rung of domestics, and hence lowest paid, none remained long in Mrs. Hudson's employ.

But this one had spunk. And Sherlock himself was in fine fettle, by which I assumed a new case had come his way. As he so often said, "Give me problems, give me work. I abhor stagnation." Without a problem, he took to his mournful Stradivari violin and his pipe of 7½ percent solution.

Although his eyes were laughing now, his face remained grave as did his voice. "If you are not Greasy Joan," he said, "what name are you called?"

"My name is Muffin."

"Muffin?"

"Muffin," she repeated firmly, daring him to disdain it.

"Well, Mistress Muffin," he bowed slightly, "you may pour me a cup of your excellent tea. First a spill of milk, then the tea, and lastly two lumps of sugar."

She hesitated, as if it were not her job, as indeed it wasn't, to pour the tea. I had already serviced my cup, with a generous pour of the milk, and with one lump of sugar, and stir and stir, as we were taught in boarding school. But she followed his instructions, quite as if she were accustomed to this extra duty. She knew how, I must say. She probably played Mother for her Mum of an evening.

"And where did you get that fine name, Mistress Muffin?" Sherlock inquired politely as he ventured a sip of his scalding tea.

"M'Mum named me that," she replied. "Ever before I was born, she once saved a ha'penny from her wages, and she bought for herself a muffin from the Muffin Man. She says it was the best thing she had ever in her life. And when I came to her, she named me Muffin." As she was concluding, she had edged her way to the door. "Excuse me, sirs, but she'll be accusing me of twattling if I don't get backstairs. I will return for the tray later on."

With that she was gone like a streak.

When she was well away, Sherlock burst into laughter. "Muffin. Because it was the best thing she ever had." Then his face became serious. "Poor woman. Waiting—how long?—until she could spare a ha'penny for her special treat. I daresay the child has not ever tasted one."

"Not on a tweeny's wages," I agreed. I poured myself more tea. "You are up early. A new case?"

"It would seem so. A chest of jewels shipped from India on *The Prince of Poona* is missing. This morning I meet with the ship's captain and representatives of the viceroy. After I learn more of the details, I shall decide whether or not I wish to undertake this case."

"Not the Gaekwar of Baroda's gems!" I had read of their worth this past week in the dallies.

"Indeed, yes. From your service in India, Watson, I daresay you know that the Gaekwar receives each year from his subjects his weight in gold and jewels. Doubtless this is why he emulates a Strasbourg goose at table." We could exchange a smile, having seen news photographs of the present Gaekwar. Holmes continued, "It seems he has decided to have some of his treasure set in pieces—breastplates, coronets, rings and things, possibly as gifts to his ladies and to favored courtiers."

"But why London?" The East Indians were noted for their skills as lapidaries.

"Why indeed? Because the best stone-cutters are now in London, it seems. At least the Gaekwar considers this to be so. And he will have no one else cut these gems."

Beneath his dressing gown, Holmes was dressed save for his coat jacket. Briefly, he returned to his room, only to emerge in his stout boots, his Inverness topcoat, several woolen mufflers wrapped about his neck, and carrying his fur-lined winter gloves. On his head was a fur hat he had bought in Russia. He had lowered the ear flaps.

Because of the weather, I suggested he take a hansom cab to his meeting place. He scoffed at that. "Cold fresh air is what my lungs have needed." And he was off. I envied him. I was still more or less housebound, nursing the wounds of my services in Afghanistan. I gathered by the fire, settling in an easy chair with my briar and the morning *London Times*. Sherlock claimed that the *Times* was read only by intellectuals, of which ilk I make no claim. But for me, the *Times* was the only paper which gave proper news.

I'd forgotten about Muffin until she thumped the door later and reappeared. In one breath she said, "Miz Hudson says your breakfast will be ready in one hour is that too late and will you be down?"

Holmes and I usually took our breakfast in the downstairs dining room, it being difficult, if not impossible, to keep toast and eggs and bacon properly warm when a tray has to be loaded and carried two flights from the kitchen to the first floor front, where we had our quarters.

"Yes, I will be down." I told her. "And eight o'clock will suit me properly. And please to inform Mrs. Hudson that Mr. Holmes will not be coming to breakfast as he has already gone out." This was not unusual when he was on a case. There were times when he actually left before early morning tea!

"Yessir," said Muffin. She had been stacking the tray with the remains of this early morning's. She made as if to take it up now, but I halted her.

"I want you to know," I said, "that Mr. Holmes was not speaking of you when he spoke of greasy Joan. He was just singing one of Mr. Will Shakespeare's songs."

Her face lighted. "Oh. I have heard some of them before. When I was little, m'Mum took me to see some of his plays at the Lyceum. There was one where a father's ghost appears to a prince named Hamlet. Ever so scary. And another one called *Twelfth Night* where a girl pretends to be a boy and where there are two old gentlemen who sing and dance. Very comical they are."

I wondered, "Your mother is in theatre?"

"Oh, no, Dr. Watson, sir. It was when she was charing at the Lyceum. It is not far from the docks, just off the Strand. The usher let her bring me in if I would sit quiet on the steps." She tossed her head. "I can tell you, young as I was, I was much more quiet than the folks in the stalls or the balcony." She hoisted the tray, it was not so heavy with the teapots empty. "I'd best hurry before Miz Hudson gets crotchety again." And off she went.

That evening by the fireplace I regaled Holmes with the further revelations of Muffin. He was as impressed as I at her knowing of Shakespeare. "I wonder can she read and write," he reflected.

Education for females was still scarce to nonexistent, although the National Education Act was initiated by Parliament some years before. To a goodly extent, Parliament had acted because of John Stuart Mill's movement for the improvement of schools for females, to which Miss Florence Nightingale had added her influence. Both Holmes and I were staunch supporters of education for all.

That night Holmes did not talk of his new case, save to say he had accepted it and would be leaving early in the morning for the docks. Possibly the docks were somewhat improved now, in the late 19th century, but they were still unsavoury at best and dangerous below that. Not that Holmes was ever fearful walking even the meanest alleys. His lean frame gave no hint of the muscular power beneath. Holmes was as fine a boxer as any professional, and with exercise and proper diet, he kept himself fit. Nevertheless, he did not rely on brute strength alone. The stick he carried was weighted, as more than one malefactor could testify.

He did remark, "It is to be hoped that the cache is not in the hands of a dredger. It might be somewhat difficult to retrieve."

For the most part dredgermen were steady, hardworking men of the lowest class, searching among the flotsam for objects of possible value. They also had the duty of recovering drowned bodies from the river. For this latter they were paid "inquest money." Unfortunately, smugglers larded themselves among the decent dredgers. These were most active when East Indian ships rode at anchor in the river.

Holmes puffed placidly on his after-dinner shag. "Certainly, with diamonds the stakes, time is of the essence."

"Diamonds!" I could not help but exclaim.

"The cache contains diamonds, in weight near 500 stone."

"And you are to recover it?"

"I intend to try." His lips were unsmiling. "I do not intend to fail."

II

The following morning Muffin did not linger after bringing our early morning tea. I daresay Mrs. Hudson had dressed her down for yesterday's lapses. Holmes had his tea with his customary before-breakfast pipe, filled, as always, with the day-before dottle, which he dried on his bureau overnight. With it he had his usual two cups with two sugars, but he did not linger over them. He was off to his room in no time to dress, eager to get himself down to the docks.

I lighted my briar and poured myself a third cup. Without warning, without even her customary thump, Muffin burst into the room. In each hand she held a man's walking boot. "Is not Mr. Holmes here?" she demanded.

"He is here. In his room, dressing," I replied.

She gasped, "Someone put his boots in the dustbin. I went to empty the kitchen baskets into the bin and saw them atop the leavings. The dust cart comes this afternoon, and they would have been taken to the dust yard." She tossed her head. "If the dustman did not keep them to sell."

From his doorway, Holmes called out, "What is this you say?"

Muffin spun around, and the boots fell from her fingers. In a moment, she gulped, "Gor, Mr. Holmes. You gave me such a start." She let out a deep breath. "I took you for a lascar."

Holmes was now concealed in the guise of one of those fierce East Indian sailors. An angry scar slanted down his entire left cheek. His face was colored as brown as coffee. Even to me, a medical man, and in these close quarters, it appeared to be an actual scar.

"You are familiar with the lascars?" Holmes asked her.

"Oh yes, m'Mum and I live near the docks. My Da was a seafaring man until his ship was lost in the Indian Ocean, all hands aboard. I never knew him; I was just a babe." She shook off memories and returned to the present. "Lascars are mean. They'd as leave knife you as give you the time of day."

Holmes now turned to me. "And do I pass inspection with you, Doctor Watson?"

"You've passed a stiffer test," I informed him. "It is more difficult to deceive children than it is their elders." I then explained to him, "Muffin rescued your boots from the dustbin."

Having recovered them from the floor, she held them out to him.

"How good of you to look out for me, Mistress Muffin. However, these are boots I have discarded."

"But Mr. Holmes," she protested. "The leather is not broken. Look. And the soles! Yet strong—"

"I no longer need them," he told her. "My Jermyn Street bootmaker delivered my new ones this week. These you may consign again to the dustheap."

"If you say." Reluctantly she turned to depart, still rubbing her thumb on the smooth leather. And then she turned back to him again, asking in a small voice, "Would you mind if instead of the dustbin, I kept them myself?"

He was taken aback for a moment. "Not at all. But I fear they would be rather too big for you, Mistress Muffin."

"Oh, not for me, sir. For m'Mum. Her feet are that cold when she comes home late at night from her charing, like sticks of ice they are. When it's damp out her shoes are wet clean through to her skin. Her soles are paper cardboard."

"Won't they be too big for her?" I put in dubiously. "A woman's foot is different from a man's."

"Not with new-old stockings. Maybe two pair to fill the chinks."

"New-old stockings?" It was an expression I had not heard.

She told me, "All the Mums make them. They cut off the worn foot and sew together what's left. And then they cut a top piece off another old stocking and sew that to the top to make them long enough. And you have a new-old stocking."

A peremptory knock on the door silenced her. It was Mrs. Hudson's knock. I noted only then that Sherlock had made an unobtrusive exit while Muffin and I were engaged.

I opened the door to our landlady. She bade me goodmorning, then directed her gaze to Muffin. "You are needed below."

"Yes'm," the child said meekly and scuttled away.

"I am sorry I kept her this long helping me," I assumed the blame, hoping it would be of some help to Muffin. I noted that she had managed to conceal the boots under her overall before her quick exit.

"Any time you need help, Dr. Watson," Mrs. Hudson said graciously, "just inform me. I will spare one of the maids."

With that, she rustled away. From the fullness of her skirts she must always wear several petticoats and at least one of taffety. I had no doubt that, by now, Muffin would have the boots well secreted below until she departed that evening.

It was after dark before Holmes returned. From his morose visage, his day had not gone well, and I asked no questions. Not until he had scrubbed away all vestiges of the lascar, and was comfortably by the fire, wrapped in his purple dressing gown, did he discuss the venture.

"The docks were teeming with lascars, Watson. Although I speak several of their dialects, none were willing to talk with me. Otherwise the area was near deserted of its denizens. Whether for fear of them or on orders from one Jick Tar, I was unable to ascertain."

"Jick Tar?" I repeated. The name had no meaning to me.

"Or Jicky Tar. He has a chandler's shop down there and seems to rule the neighborhood as absolutely as an Oriental potentate."

I continued to puzzle. "Not Jack Tar? Jick Tar."

"Possibly once he was a Jack Tar and changed the name when he left the Royal Navy. For good and sufficient reasons, I have no doubt. I did discover him to have been a dredger, or to have used that cover for his operations. I understand he lost a leg in one such and could no longer work in the water, and therefore opened the shop. I made to enter it but was thrust away roughly by one of the bullies at his door."

"You will not need to return?" I hoped.

"I must if I am to discover the jewels. But I shall vary my guise."

Our dinner arrived at that point. I had ordered it sent up when I realized he would not return in time to dress for the dining room. I was pleased to see that far from retreating into the doldrums, he had good appetite. After the sweet, he opened a bottle of claret, and I brought out the Havana cigars. The day's setback obviously only added to the challenge of solving the case.

He was by the fire in our sitting room before I was up, next day. For all of my knowledge he may have sat there through the night. But he

was far from disheartened, which I took as an indication he had thought of one or more other plans of procedure.

At promptly six thirty, Muffin arrived with the morning tea tray. She looked worried. After setting it down, she approached Holmes. "I have done you a wrong," she quavered. "It was the boots. When I was carrying them home last evening, I met up with Jacky and Little Jemmy and they said I had stole them and I said indeed I had not and that Mr. Sherlock Holmes had given me them."

Holmes was endeavoring not to laugh at her childish agitation. "Not so fast," he pleaded.

She gulped a breath. "They said they were going to tell Jicky Tar, but when I spoke your name they took off like rabbits. Only—" she took breath again, "they followed me this morning. I fear they mean harm to you. And m'Mum was so grateful for the boots, she even cried tears."

Holmes asked, "Where are these boys?"

"Across the roadway." She led us to the broad front windows and pointed down and across. "There, by the second dun house." In the morning darkness we could just make out the shapes of two small figures huddled together on the cold kerb.

"They are Jicky Tar's boys?" Holmes inquired.

"Oh no, they are Mud Larks." This was the name given to those miserable children who scavenged the muddy verges on the banks of the river for bottles or lumps of coal or whatever lost articles they might sell for a few pence. In spite of modern reforms, there were still too many street children in London, those whose parents, unable to care for them, had turned them out to beg or otherwise do for themselves. "But Jicky Tar buys some of their findings," she said. "And they fear his displeasure."

"I will see them," Holmes stated. "Go tell Mrs. Hudson to send up the fireboy to do an errand for me."

The fireboy turned out to be a dour old man whom I had never seen before, as he came to build our fire before I was awake. He stumped up the stairs and Holmes met him at our door. "There are two boys across the road. I want you to bring them along to me. I would speak with them."

With neither aye nor nay, the man stumped off again, down the stairs.

Holmes left the door ajar and came to the table. "Today greasy Joan has indeed keeled the pot."

"I'll ring for more hot water," I said.

"This will do. There isn't time to be particular." Even as he spoke we could hear voices below, and shortly thereafter the door opened wider and an urchin, bundled in all manner of mufflers and mittens, peered in. He was about the size of Muffin, but better fed, with a round nose and round blue eyes in a round face. His cheeks were red from the cold.

Holmes said, "Come in, boy. You are—"

"Jacky, sir." His voice was hoarse with cold.

"And where is Jemmy?"

"M'brother's over there," he gestured. "Minding the box."

Holmes contained his excitement. "The box—"

"It's too heavy to carry far."

"What is in the box?" Holmes queried.

"Rocks," the boy said. "Nuffin but rocks."

"Then why did you bring it here?"

The boy looked about the room suspiciously, particularly at me.

"Why?" Holmes repeated.

"I want you should see it. I want you to see it's nuffin but rocks. I don't want Jicky Tar to be saying I stole from it."

"Fetch it," Holmes directed. "Can you carry it up the staircase?"

"Me and Little Jemmy together can. Like we carried it all the way to Baker Street."

Holmes waited at the head of the stairs, just in case Mrs. Hudson should not allow Jacky to return with Jemmy. Not that she was unused to the queer company which Holmes often kept. I moved to the doorway and watched as the two boys appeared, hoisting a wooden box step by step until Holmes took it from them up top. Little Jemmy scarcely reached to Jacky's shoul-

der. He could not have been more than seven or eight years. Like Jacky, he was bundled, but his thin face seemed parched white from the bitter weather. All of us entered the sitting room and Holmes directed the boys to the hearth by the fire. He set the box before them on the floor. "Will you open it?" he asked.

The box or chest seemed to be made of fine heavy teak, although much abused from having been immersed in river water. It was perhaps half the size of a child's traveling trunk. Jacky lifted the latch and raised the lid.

It contained rocks. Nothing but dirty rocks. Some were small as a cherry but most were large as plums.

"What do you want me to do with these?" Holmes inquired of the boys.

"Do what you like," Jacky told him. "But don't tell Jicky Tar we brought them to you."

Little Jemmy cautioned fearfully, "He give you a clout with that stick of his to knock you down, and he stomp you like a bug."

Holmes assured them, "I shall have none of him."

After the boys had departed, each clutching a new sixpence within his mitten, Holmes turned to me. "Come, Watson. We must dress and be off at once. If these rocks are what I surmise them to be, I need you for a witness."

"And our breakfast?" I reminded him.

"We will breakfast later."

I did not dispute him. In record time both of us were ready to depart. I went ahead, carrying his stick, while he carried the chest down. I was fortunate in procuring a hansom cab for us almost immediately. Holmes directed the driver, "To Ironmonger's Lane."

When we were underway, Holmes explained, "I am taking the chest to a certain Signor Antonelli, who is, I have been informed, the finest lapidary in London. For centuries the East Indians were the only lapidaries in the civilized world. As you doubtless learned in your years in India, that country was the only known source of diamonds until the early 18th century and the discovery of them in Brazil."

"Indeed yes," I recalled. "The best and most famous stones have come from the Golconda area near Hyderabad. The Kuh-a-Nur, which was a gift from India to our royal crown, is the longest diamond known. The Darya-i-Nur, another of the great stones, is in Persia. It was taken there along with all those now known as the Persian Crown Jewels, by the Nadir Shah when he sacked Delhi in 1739. They say the Persian jewels surpass all others in vastness of number, size, and quality, although our own crown jewels contain some of the most precious gems, particularly in diamonds." The toe of my boot nudged the chest. "You believe these rocks are diamonds?"

"I do," replied Holmes. "Both in India and Brazil, diamonds were found only in gravel deposits. As sedimentary rocks come from some deeper deposit, obviously this was not the original source. But only with the discovery of diamonds in South Africa, less than twenty years ago, have we learned that they come from within deep pipes of igneous rocks. In its uncut form, the diamond cannot be distinguished from any sizable rock."

When Holmes investigated a subject, he did it with thoroughness. "Diamonds are pure carbon. True, some poorer stones have small crystals of other minerals embedded, but these are not used as gem stones, only for diamond dust and other mean purposes." He mused. "The history of diamonds is fascinating, Watson. They are known to have been worn as precious stones as far back as 300 B.C. In ancient documents it is recorded that Alexander, the Macedonian Greek who conquered Persia, and added 'The Great' to his title as he proceeded to take over all the mid-east, decked himself in diamonds. The very name is from the Greek, *adamas* or 'invincible.'"

Holmes had evidently found time, along with all else he was engaged in, to visit the reading room of the British Museum. He continued, "The diamond is the hardest of gemstones, therefore the most difficult to cut. It alone ranks ten, the highest point, on Mohs's recently tabulated scale. Of special interest to me are the differences in judging the beauty of a diamond. In the East the beauty is primarily in its weight, whereas in the West it is in color and form. The Indian lapidaries devised the rose cut, which best preserved the weight. But they found it next to impossible to polish this cut to bring out its fire.

"It was the Venetian lapidary, Vincenti Peruzzi, who in the late seventeenth century began experimenting with adding facets to the table cut. The result was the first brilliant cut. Cutting is a science. Peruzzi had studied with East Indian lapidaries. As has Signor Antonelli. And that is why we are here," he concluded as the cab drew up before a very old shop on Ironmonger's Lane.

Holmes alighted. While he was paying off the driver, I pushed the chest over to where he could lift it out more easily. I then stepped down to the walk and started across to the shop door. At that instant I saw a man who was approaching at a rapid pace, despite the hindrance of a peg leg.

"Holmes!" I warned quickly.

At the alarm in my voice, he turned, and he too recognized who this person must be. None other than Jicky Tar. He was large although not tall, and his seaman's knit jumper could not conceal his bulging muscles. His visage was a malevolent mask. He brandished a cudgel, knobby as are those heavy clubs which come from the village of Shillelagh.

One glance, and Holmes thrust the box at me. He extricated his stick from under my arm, then advanced a few paces and stood waiting. Only then did I see the two bully boys who had come round the corner in Jicky Tar's wake. One had Jacky immobilized in an arm lock, the other had a viselike fist around Jemmy's small arm.

Holmes saw them as I did, and he thundered, "Release those boys! At once!"

"Not until you return my property," Jicky snarled. He had advanced to a distance of several yards from Holmes before taking his stance. It was obvious that he was accustomed to street fighting, where striking distance was needed in order to swing a cudgel for the fullest impact.

"What property of yours do you claim I have?" Holmes asked.

"The box." Jicky gave a quick glance to where I was standing. "The box those picaroons stole from me and gave to you."

The boy Jacky shouted atop his words. "He's lying, Mr. Holmes! He's lying! It wasn't his, it was ours. We found it. Not him."

Jacky was twisting and straining to release himself from his captor, aiming his kicks to where they would do the most good. One found its mark. The bully howled, and for a moment his grip on the boy was loosed. Jacky wrenched away and darted at high speed up the lane.

The bully shouted, "Jicky, he's got away! The bloody little wretch got away! I'll go after him."

"No," Jicky ordered. "Stay! We'll get him later. He won't go far. Not without his sniveling little brother." He then turned his full attention to Holmes. "Will you give me the box or do I take it?"

Holmes stated with authority, "The property belongs to the Gaekwar of Baroda and I shall return it to him."

Without warning "on guard," Jicky Tar swung his cudgel, while the unencumbered bully came under it toward Holmes. Holmes's well-aimed feint at Jicky became a blow to the bully's head, felling him. It was then just the two men, both experts, in this tit for tat, manoeuvering as swordsmen, one to disarm the other. The bully came to his feet too soon and moved in to join the fray. I feared for Holmes with two against one, but I need not have. With enviable deftness, Holmes's stick struck and dropped the bully again. Holmes's stick was then raised to disarm Jicky Tar when a police whistle sounded.

"It's Jacky," Jemmy cried out. "He's brought the Peelers."

It was indeed Jacky, running ahead of one bobby while another followed, blasting his whistle. The police quickly took charge of Tar and his henchman. The one who had mishandled Jemmy had faded away during the rumpus, releasing the boy, who ran to his brother's side.

Holmes told the policemen, "Take these men

to Inspector Lestrade. I will be there shortly to inform him as to their misdeeds. And take the boys with you."

"Gor blimey," Jacky cried, while Jemmy clung to him. "He's shopped us!"

"Not at all," Holmes told them. "It isn't safe for you to return to your old haunts. Just stay with the police until I come, and I will then find a better place for you to live."

While he was speaking, the police wagon, summoned by the whistle-blasts, came down the alley. The villains were quickly locked inside. With great reluctance the boys were boosted beside the driver and the wagon clip-clopped back up the road. Holmes brushed off his coat and straightened his cap. He then took the box from me and we proceeded to enter Signor Antonelli's shop.

It was dim and dingy inside. There was just the one room, a counter separating the front from the larger rear. There, shelves were laden with all manner of rocks, and on a long table were more, in various stages of grinding. The diamond dust recovered from grinding is the only substance hard enough to produce the necessary high polish for fine stones.

At this table, bent to his work, was a wizened old man, his face scarred doubtless from rogue bits of gemstone. His scant yellow-white hair fell below his ears and he wore spectacles with lenses of heavy magnification. If he was aware of the recent commotion outside his shop, he gave no indication. He ignored our entrance.

After a moment, Holmes spoke. "You are Signor Antonelli?" The question was ignored. Holmes continued, "I am Sherlock Holmes, and this is my friend, Dr. Watson."

The old man did not respond.

As the awkward silence continued, Holmes hoisted the chest to the counter and unhasped it. He took one of the rocks and held it out to Signor Antonelli. "Will you tell me what this is?"

Antonelli ceased work and shuffled over to us. He took the rock from Holmes. "I will see," he muttered.

We watched as he carried the rock back to his worktable. With instruments which had no meaning to either Holmes or myself, he began grinding a bit at the edge. Shortly he brought it back to the counter. "It is a diamond," he stated.

"From the *Prince of Poona* cargo," Holmes told him.

The Signor muttered, "I have been waiting for these. I was told you might bring them here."

"Then I may leave the chest with you?" Again there was no response. But Holmes continued as if there had been. "I shall so advise the viceroy. He will inform you about what is wanted by the Gaekwar."

The ancient nodded once. Without a word of farewell to us, he lifted the chest as if it were no heavier than a dog's bone, carrying it back to his working area. Holmes and I, exchanging amused glances, took our own departure.

It was necessary to walk to a more traveled thoroughfare before finding a hansom cab. "I will drop you off," Holmes told me. "It may be that Mrs. Hudson will serve you a late breakfast. At least she will fetch something to tide you to the lunch hour."

"And you will eat . . . ?"

"Later," he said. "First I must go to Scotland Yard to confer with Lestrade. From now on I am certain that he will keep a wary eye on Jicky Tar. I must also arrange a place where the boys can be safe. Thanks to Muffin they came to me with their find. If they had gone to that villain, I daresay by now the 'rocks' would all have been flung into the river."

III

It was nearing the dinner hour before Holmes returned.

"And will ye be wanting your breakfast now?" I jested him in the cook's broad Scots. "Or will ye be waiting for the dinner?"

"Lestrade and I had lunch after we reported to the viceroy," Holmes replied. "I may just pass our dinner tonight. After the cuisine prepared by the chef of the Savoy, Mrs. Hudson's cook does not tempt my appetite."

"Although she does prepare a bountiful Scotch breakfast."

"True," he agreed as he laid off his coat and cap.

"What of the boys?" I inquired.

He answered with enthusiasm. "I have turned them over to a pair of my Irregulars. Stalwart young chaps who will not only arrange a place for Jacky and Jemmy to live but will initiate them into the ways of the Irregulars. We will be seeing them again, I have no doubt."

"Nor I," I nodded.

"In case you puzzled, as I, how Jicky Tar knew of Signor Antonelli's shop; he had an informer from the *Poona* who advised him that the chest would find its way there. Once he learned that I was on the case, Jicky had me watched. Hence our being followed. All's well that ends well," he quoted, and suggested, "Perhaps a small glass of amontillado would not go amiss?" He walked to our sideboard, fetched two wine glasses and the bottle. After he poured, I lifted my glass. "To yet another success."

He dismissed the tribute. "Pure happenstance this time."

"But based upon accumulated knowledge," I amended.

"And a tweeny." He now raised his glass. "To our Mistress Muffin," he toasted. "You know, John," he said as he seated himself, "I am not accustomed to accepting remuneration for help I give to those in need of solutions to their problems. But now and again, I do make a settlement. This was a time when I did. The Gaekwar can well afford it."

He sipped his sherry. "I have in mind to send Muffin to a school—a good school for females. But how to arrange it? It is quite obvious that both she and her Mum are independent personages who would not accept charity, or anything that hinted of it." He shook his head. "Yet for their living they find it necessary for both to go out to work."

"With the cost of living these days, it seems to be essential," I commented.

"I have been pondering this problem." He

refilled our glasses. "I have thought of some kind of scholarship. Not to cover fees alone, but with enough over to at least pay for their lodgings. This way her mother could afford to have Muffin take advantage of schooling. The child has such a bright mind and unusual spirit, it would be wasteful not to allow her to better herself. Perhaps become a teacher."

"Or perhaps a scientist," I suggested.

"Or a doctor of medicine," he countered.

"That day will come for women," I agreed. "And before too long."

"But how to devise a scholarship? And how to make sure that Muffin will make use of it? This is as knotty a problem as yet I have encountered."

"You will solve it," I spoke with certainty.

"I must," he responded. "It is, if I may invent a phrase, a 'finder's fee.'"

The first bell sounded from below. We began to gather ourselves together, to be ready to descend the stairs before the second. Holmes smiled as he put down his wineglass. "I have a notion to play Father Christmas to our young friends. A warm coat and winter cap for Muffin, and the same for the boys. Perhaps even a new pair of stout boots for each of them."

The second bell sounded.

"Do you not think I could pass muster, even to wise children, in a long white beard and a long red coat and a red bonnet on my head?"

I made no reply. To the boys, yes, I believed he could. But not to our Muffin.

The Man from Capetown

STUART M. KAMINSKY

THE PROLIFIC AND varied career of Stuart Melvin Kaminsky (1934–2009) produced several long-running mystery series, screenplays, books on writing, and works about the film industry.

As a professor of film at Northwestern for sixteen years and at Florida State for six, Kaminsky was well-qualified to write about film genres, as well as produce biographies of such significant figures as Don Siegel, Clint Eastwood, Gary Cooper, and John Huston. He also cowrote the screenplay for *Once Upon a Time in America* (1984).

Kaminsky enjoyed great success with his twenty-four-volume series about Toby Peters, a slightly seedy private detective during Hollywood's golden age who became involved with the greatest stars of the era, including Humphrey Bogart *(Bullet for a Star*, 1977), the Marx Brothers (*You Bet Your Life*, 1978), Bela Lugosi (*Never Cross a Vampire*, 1980), and Mae West (*He Done Her Wrong*, 1983).

Equally well-received was the series about Porfiry Rostnikov, an honorable Russian police detective in Moscow, which began with *Death of a Dissident* (1981) and ran for sixteen books; *A Cold Red Sunrise* (1988) won the Edgar Award for best novel.

Kaminsky produced more than sixty books in his career, had eight Edgar nominations, and was named a Grand Master for lifetime achievement by the Mystery Writers of America in 2006.

"The Man from Capetown" was originally published in *Murder in Baker Street*, edited by Martin H. Greenberg, Jon L. Lellenberg, and Daniel Stashower (New York, Carroll & Graf, 2001).

THE MAN FROM CAPETOWN

Stuart M. Kaminsky

IT WAS RAINING. It was not the usual slow, cold gray London rain that spattered on umbrellas and broad brimmed hats but the heavy relentless downpour that came several times a year jungle drumming on the rooftops of cabs reminding me of the more mild monsoons I had witnessed in my years in India.

Time in India always moved slowly. Time in the apartment I shared with Sherlock Holmes had moved at the pace of a torpid Bombay cat during the past two weeks.

I kept myself busy trying to write an article for *The Lancet* based on Holmes's findings about the differences he had discovered between blood from people native to varying climates. At first Holmes had entered into the endeavor with vigor and interest, pacing, smoking his pipe, pausing to remind me of subtle differences and the implications of his discovery both for criminology and medicine.

Several days into the enterprise, however, Holmes had taken to standing at the window for hours at a time, staring into the rain-swept street, thinking thoughts he chose not to share with me.

Twice he picked up the violin. The first time he woke me at five in the morning with something that may have been Liszt. The second time was at one in the afternoon when he repeatedly played a particularly mournful tune I did not recognize.

On this particular morning, Holmes was sitting in his armchair, pipe in hand, looking at the coal scuttle.

"Rather interesting item in this morning's *Times*," I ventured as I sat at the table in our sitting room with the last of my morning tea and toast before me.

Holmes made a sound somewhere between a grunt and a sigh.

"A Mr. Morgan Fitchmore of Leeds," he said. "Found in a cemetery on his back with a railroad spike plunged into his heart. He was gripping the spike, apparently in an attempt to remove it. The night had been damp and the police found no footprints in the mud other than those of the deceased. About twenty feet from the body a hammer was found. The police are baffled."

Holmes grunted again and looked toward the window where the rain beat heavily on the glass.

"Yes," I said. "That is the story. I thought it might interest you."

"Minimally," said Holmes. "Read the rest of the story, Watson, as I have. Fitchmore was a petty thief. He was found lying on his back. The dead man appears to have left no signs that he attempted to defend himself."

"Yes, I see," I said reading further.

"What was a petty thief doing in a graveyard on a rainy night?" Holmes said drawing on his pipe. "Why would someone attack him with a railroad spike? Why were there no other footprints? Why did he not struggle?"

"I couldn't say," I said.

"Railroad spikes make passable chisels, Watson. A thief might well go into a graveyard at night with a spike and hammer to chisel away some cameo or small crucifix or other item he might sell for a slight sum. Such assaults on the resting place of the dead are not uncommon. A rainy night would ensure a lack of intrusion."

"I fail to see . . ."

"It is not a matter of seeing, Watson. It is a matter of putting together what has been seen with simple logic. Fitchmore went to the grave-yard to rob the dead. He slipped in the mud flinging his hammer away as he fell forward on the spike he held in his hand. He rolled over on his back, probably in great agony, and attempted to pull the spike from his chest, but he was al-ready dying. There is no mystery, Watson. It was an accidental if, perhaps, ironically apropos end for a man who would steal from the dead."

"Perhaps we should inform the police in Leeds," I said.

"If you wish," said Holmes indifferently.

"May I pour you a cup of tea? You haven't touched your breakfast."

"I am not hungry," he said, his eyes now turned to the fireplace where flames crackled and formed kaleidoscope patterns which seemed to mesmerize Holmes who had not bothered to fully dress. He wore his gray trousers, a shirt with no tie and a purple silk smoking jacket that had been given to him by a grateful client several years earlier.

In the past month, Holmes had been offered three cases. One involved a purloined pearl necklace. The second focused on an apparent at-tempt to defraud a dealer in Russian furs and the third a leopard missing from the London zoo. Holmes had abruptly refused all three entreaties for his help and had directed the potential cli-ents to the police.

"If the imagination is not engaged," he said when the zoo director had left, "and there is no worthy adversary, I see no point in expending energy and spending time on work that could be done by a reasonably trained Scotland Yard ju-nior inspector."

Holmes suddenly looked up at me.

"Do you have that letter readily at hand?"

I knew the letter of which he spoke and in the hope of engaging his interest I retrieved it from the portmanteaus near the fireplace which crack-led with flames which cast unsettling morning shadows across the sitting room.

The letter had arrived several weeks ago and aside from the fact that it bore a Capetown post-mark, it struck me as in no way singular or more interesting than any of a dozen missives that Holmes had done no more than glance at in the past several weeks.

"Would you read it aloud once more, Watson, if you please?"

"Mr. Sherlock Holmes," it read:

I have a matter of the greatest importance to set before you. I have some business to attend to here in Capetown. It should take no more than a few days. I will then set forth for En-gland in the hope of seeing you immediately upon my arrival. I must hurry now to get this letter on the next ship bound for Portsmouth. This is a matter of money, love, and a pal-pable threat to my life. I beg you to give me a consultation. Cost is no object.

The letter was signed, *Alfred Donaberry*.

I folded the letter and looked at Holmes wondering why this particular correspondence, among the many so much like it he had received over the years, should draw his interest and why he had chosen this moment to return to it.

As he had done so many times before, Holmes answered my unspoken questions.

"Note the order in which our Mr. Donaberry lists his concerns," said Holmes, looking in my direction and pointing his pipe at the missive in my hand. "Money, love, and life. Mr. Donaberry lists the threat to his life last. Curious. As to why I am now interested in the letter, I ask a ques-tion. Did you hear a carriage stop in the street a moment ago?"

I had and I said so.

"If you check the arrival of ships in the paper from which you have just read you will note that the *Principia*, a cargo ship, arrived in Ports-mouth from Capetown yesterday. If our Mr. Donaberry is as concerned as his letter indicates, he may well have been on that ship and braved the foul weather to make his way to us."

"It could be anyone," I said.

"The rig, judging from the sound of its wheels on the cobblestone, is a large one, not a common street cab and it is drawn by not one but two horses. I hear no other activity on the street save for this vehicle. The timing is right and, I must confess to a certain curiosity about a man who would venture from as far as Capetown to pay us a visit. No, Watson, if this man is as anxious to meet me as his letter indicates, he will have been off the boat and on his way catching the seven o'clock morning train."

A knock at the door and a small smile from Holmes accompanied by a raised eyebrow in satisfaction were aimed my way.

"Enter, Mrs. Hudson," Holmes called.

Our landlady entered, looked at the plate of untouched food in front of Holmes, and shook her head.

"A lady to see you," she said.

"A lady?" Holmes asked.

"Most definitely," Mrs. Hudson said.

"Please tell the lady that I am expecting a visitor and that she will have to make an appointment and return at a future time."

Mrs. Hudson was at the door with tray in hand. Over her shoulder she said, "The lady said to tell you that she knows you are expecting a visitor from South Africa. That is why she must see you immediately."

Holmes looked at me with arched eyebrows. I shrugged.

"Please show her in, Mrs. Hudson, and, if you would be so kind, please brew us a fresh pot of tea," Holmes said.

"You've eaten nothing, Mr. Holmes," she said. "Perhaps I can bring you some fresh biscuits and jam?"

"Tea and biscuits will be perfect," Holmes said as she closed the door behind her, the tray balanced carefully in one hand.

"So our Mr. Donaberry is not the only one who would willingly venture out in a storm like this," I said, pretending to return to the newspaper.

"So it would seem, Watson."

The knock at the door was gentle. A single knock. Holmes called out, "Come in," and Mrs. Hudson ushered in an exquisite dark creature with clear white skin and raven hair brushed back in a tight bun. She wore a prim black dress buttoned to the neck. The woman stepped in, looked from me to Holmes and stood silently for a moment till Mrs. Hudson had closed the door.

"Mr. Holmes," she said in a soft voice suggesting just the touch of an accent.

"I am he," said Holmes.

"My name is Elspeth Belknapp, Mrs. Elspeth Belknapp," she said. "May I sit?"

"By all means, Mrs. Belknapp," Holmes said, pointing to a chair near the one in which I was sitting.

"I have come . . . this is most delicate and embarrassing," she said as she sat. "I have come to . . ."

"First a few questions," said Holmes, folding his hands in his lap. "How did you know Donaberry was coming to see me?"

"I . . . a friend in Capetown sent me a letter, the wife of a clerk in Alfred's office," she said. "May I have some water?"

I rose quickly and moved to the decanter Mrs. Hudson had left on the table. I poured a glass of water and handed it to her. She drank as I sat down and looked over at Holmes who seemed to be studying her carefully.

"Mr. Holmes," she said. "I was, until five months ago, Mrs. Alfred Donaberry. Alfred is a decent man. He took me in when my own parents died in a fire in Johannesburg. Alfred is considerably older than I. I was most grateful to him and he was most generous to me. And then, less than a year ago John Belknapp came to South Africa to conduct business with my then husband."

"And what business is that?" Holmes asked.

"The diamond trade," she said. "Alfred has amassed a fortune dealing in diamonds. Though I tried not to do so, I fell in love with John

Belknapp and he with me. I behaved like a coward, Mr. Holmes. John wanted to confront Alfred but I wanted no scene. I persuaded John that we should simply run away and that I would seek a divorce citing Alfred's abuse and infidelity."

"And was he abusive and unfaithful?" asked Holmes.

She shook her head.

"I am not proud of what I did. Alfred was neither abusive nor unfaithful. He loved me but I thought of him less as a husband than as a beloved uncle."

"And so," said Holmes, "you obtained a divorce."

"Yes, I came to London with John and obtained a divorce. John and I married the day after the divorce was approved by the Court. I thought that Alfred would read the note I had left for him when I fled with John and that Alfred would resign himself to the reality. But now I find . . ."

"I see," said Holmes. "And what would you have me do?"

"Persuade Alfred not to cause trouble, to leave England, to return to South Africa, to go on with his life. Should he confront John . . . John is a fine man, but he is somewhat on occasion and when provoked given to unconsidered reaction."

The woman removed a kerchief from her sleeve and dabbed at her eyes.

"He can be violent?" asked Holmes.

"Only when provoked, Mr. Holmes. Alfred Donaberry is a decent man, but were he to confront John . . ."

At this point Mrs. Hudson knocked and entered before she was bidden to do so. She placed biscuits and jam upon the table with three plates, knives, and a fresh pot of tea. She looked at the tearful Elspeth Belknapp with sympathy and departed.

"Next question," Holmes said, taking up a knife and using it to generously coat a biscuit with what appeared to be gooseberry jam. "You say your former husband is a man of considerable wealth?"

"Considerable," she said, accepting a cup of tea from me.

"Describe him."

"Alfred? He is fifty-five years of age, pleasant enough looking though I have heard people describe him as homely. He is large, a bit, how shall I say this . . . Alfred is an uneducated, a self-made man, perhaps a bit rough around the edges, but a good, gentle man."

"I see," said Holmes, a large piece of biscuit and jam in his mouth. "And he has relatives, a mother, sister, brother, children?"

"None," she said.

"So, if he were to die, who would receive his inheritance?"

"Inheritance?"

"In his letter to me, he mentions that his visit is in part a matter of money."

"I suppose I might unless he has removed me from his will."

"And your new husband? He is a man of substance?"

"John is a dealer in fine gems. He has a secure and financially comfortable position with London Pembroke Gems Limited. If you are implying that John married me in the hope of getting Alfred's estate, I assure you you are quite wrong, Mr. Holmes."

"I am merely trying to anticipate what direction Mr. Donaberry's concerns will take him when we meet. May I ask what you are willing to pay for my services in dissuading Mr. Donaberry from further pursuit of the issue?"

"I thought . . . Pay you? John and I are not wealthy," she said, "but I'll pay what you wish should you be successful in persuading Alfred to return to South Africa. I do not want to see him humiliated or hurt."

"Hurt?" asked Holmes.

"Emotionally," she said quickly.

"I see," said Holmes. "I'll take your case under advisement. Should I decide to take it, how shall I reach you?"

Elspeth Belknapp rose and removed a card from her small purse. She handed the card to Holmes.

"Your husband's business card," Holmes said.

"My home address is on the back."

She held out her hand to me. I took it. She was trembling.

"Holmes failed to introduce me," I said, glancing reproachfully at my friend.

"You are Dr. Watson," she said. "I've read your accounts of Mr. Holmes's exploits and have remarked on your own humility and loyalty."

It was my turn to smile. She turned to Holmes, who had risen from his chair. He took her hand and held it, his eyes on her wedding ring.

"A lovely diamond and setting," he said.

"Yes," she said, looking at the ring. "It is far too valuable to be worn constantly. A simple band would please me as much but John insists and when John makes up his mind . . . Please, Mr. Holmes, help us, John, me, and Alfred."

The rain was still beating and the wind blowing even harder as she departed, closing the door softly as she left.

"Charming woman," I said.

"Yes," said Holmes.

"Love is not always kind or reasonable," I observed.

"You are a hopeless romantic, Watson," he said, moving to the window and parting the curtains.

"Not much of a challenge in this one," I observed.

"We shall see, Watson. We shall see. Ah, she wears a cape and carries an umbrella. Sensible."

I could hear the carriage door close and listened as it pulled away, horses clomping slowly into the distance.

Holmes remained at the window without speaking. He checked his watch from time to time but did not waver from his vigil till the sound of another carriage echoed down Baker Street.

"And this shall be our forlorn former husband," said Holmes, looking back at me. "Ah yes, the carriage has stopped. He has gotten out. No umbrella. A big man. Let us move a chair near the fire. He will be drenched."

And indeed, when Mrs. Hudson announced and ushered Alfred Donaberry into the room, he was wet, thin hair matted against his scalp. His former wife had been kind in describing him as homely. He had sun darkened skin and a brooding countenance and bore a close resemblance to a bull terrier. In his left hand he carried a large and rather battered piece of luggage. His clothing, trousers, shirt, and jacket were of good quality though decidedly rumpled and the man himself was quite disheveled and in need of a shave. His wrinkled suit was dark, a bit loose.

"Please forgive my appearance. I came here straightaway from the railway station," he said, setting down his suitcase and holding out his hand. "Donaberry. Alfred Donaberry."

Holmes shook it. I did the same. Firm grip. Troubled face.

"I am Sherlock Holmes and this is my friend and colleague Dr. Watson. Won't you sit by the fire."

"I thank you, sir," Donaberry said, moving to the chair I had moved next to the warmth of the hearth.

"I may as well get right to it," the man said, holding his hands toward the fire.

"Your wife has left you," Holmes said. "Some three months ago. You recently discovered that she is in London and you've come in pursuit of her."

"How did you . . . ?"

"You missed her by but a few minutes," Holmes said.

"How did she know I . . . ?" Donaberry said perplexed.

"Let us lay that aside for the moment," said Holmes "and, if you will, get to the heart of your problem."

"Heart of the problem. Ironical choice of words, Mr. Holmes," he said. "No, I am not pursuing Elspeth. If she wants no more of an old man, I can understand though I am broken of heart. The minute I read the note she had left me those months ago I accepted reality and removed my wedding ring."

He held up his left hand to show a distinct white band of skin where a ring had been.

"You do not want to find her or her new husband?" Holmes asked.

"No sir," he said. "I want nothing to do with him, the jackanapes who stole her from me and polluted her mind. I want you to find them and stop them before they succeed in murdering me within the next month."

I looked at Holmes with a sense of shock but Holmes simply popped yet another piece of biscuit and jam into his mouth.

"Why should they want to murder you, Mr. Donaberry?" I asked.

He looked at me.

"I have entered my will for change in the courts," he said. "In one month's time, Elspeth will be my heir no longer."

"Why a month?" I asked.

Donaberry shifted uncomfortably in his chair and looked down before speaking.

"When we married, because of my age and sometimes fragile health, I feared for Elspeth's future should I die. Though by law she would inherit, I have distant relatives in Cornwall who might well make claim on my estate or some part of it. Therefore, I entered specifically into my will that Elspeth should inherit everything and that there should be no revocation or challenge to my will and my desire. My solicitor now informs me, and Elspeth well knows and has certainly informed her new husband, that it will take a month longer to execute the changing of the will, so carefully has it been worded. For you see, the word 'wife' never appears in the will, only the name Elspeth Donaberry."

"But what," I asked, "makes you think they plan to kill you?"

"The two attempts which have already been made upon my life in South Africa," he answered with a deep sigh. "Once when I was in field a fortnight past. I spend much of my time when weather permits and the beating sun is tolerable, in the flats and mountains searching for gem deposits. It was a particularly blistering day when I was fired upon. Three shots from the cover of trees. One shot struck a rock only inches from my head. I was fortunate enough to escape with my life. In the second instance, an attempt was made to push me off a pier onto a trio of sharpened pilings. Only by the grace of God did I fall between the pilings."

"You have other enemies besides Belknapp and your wife?"

"None, and Mr. Holmes, I don't blame Elspeth necessarily, but that John Belknapp is a piece of work with friends of an unsavory bent and though he might have persuaded her otherwise, I know from my most reliable sources that John Belknapp is in serious financial trouble. He is a profligate, a speculator, and a gambler. I think he wants not just my wife but my fortune."

"And you want me to protect you?" asked Holmes.

"I want you to do whatever it takes to keep Belknapp from killing me or having me killed. He's more than half a devil."

It sounded to me like the kind of case Holmes would have sent straightaway to Lestrade and the Yard.

"The price will be two hundred pounds, payment in advance," said Holmes.

Donaberry did not hesitate. He stood up, took out his wallet, and began placing bills on the table, counting aloud as he did so.

"Thank you," said Holmes. "Dr. Watson and I will do our utmost to see to it that murder does not take place. Where will you be staying in London?"

"I have a room reserved at The Cadogan Hotel on Sloane Street," he said.

The Cadogan was a small hotel known to be the London residence of Lilly Langtree and rumored to be an occasional hideaway for the notorious playwright Oscar Wilde.

"You've told no one," said Holmes.

"Only you and Dr. Watson," he said.

"Very good," said Holmes. "Remain in your room. Eat in the hotel. We will contact you when we have news. And Mr. Donaberry, do not go out the front door and do not take the cab that is waiting for you. You may be watched. Dr. Watson will show you how to get out the back entrance. There is a low fence. I suggest you climb it and work your way out to the street beyond. Mrs. Hudson will provide you with an umbrella."

"My suitcase," he said.

"Dr. Watson or I will return it to you the moment it is safe to do so. I cannot see a man of your size and age climbing fences with the burden of this luggage."

Donaberry looked as if he were thinking deeply before deciding to nod his head in reluctant agreement.

"Then be off," Holmes said. "Remember, stay in the hotel. In your room as much as possible with the door locked. Take all your meals in the hotel dining room. The food is not the best but it is tolerable."

Donaberry nodded and I led him out the door and down to the back entrance after he had retrieved his coat and Mrs. Hudson had provided an umbrella.

Holmes was pacing the floor, hands behind his back when I returned to our rooms and said, "Holmes, while I sympathize with Mr. Donaberry's situation, I see nothing in it to capture your attention or make use of your skills."

"I'm sorry, Watson, what did you say? I was lost in a thought about this curious situation. There are so many questions."

"I see nothing curious about it," I said.

"We are dealing with potential murder here and a criminal mind that is worth confronting," he responded. "And we have no time to lose. Let us take Mr. Donaberry's waiting cab and pay a visit."

"To whom?" I asked.

In response, Holmes held up the card Elspeth Belknapp had handed him.

"To John Belknapp," he said. "Of course."

In the carriage, to the beating of the rain on the carriage roof and the jostling of the wheels along the cobblestones, Holmes said that he had examined the contents of Alfred Donaberry's luggage when I had ushered Donaberry to the rear entrance to Mrs. Hudson's.

"The suitcase was neatly packed, shirts and trousers, toiletries, underclothing and stockings, plus a pair of serviceable shoes."

"And what did you discover from that?" I asked as lightning cracked in the west.

"That Alfred Donaberry packs neatly and keeps his clothing and shoes clean," said Holmes.

"Most significant," I said, trying to show no hint of sarcasm at this discovery.

"Perhaps," said Holmes, looking out the window.

We arrived on a side street off Portobello Road within twenty minutes. The rain had let up considerably and I negotiated with the cabby to await our return. Considering that we were now going to pay for Donaberry's trip plus our own, the slicker-shrouded driver readily agreed. Holmes and I moved quickly toward the entrance to the four-story office building which bore a bronze plate inscribed Pembroke Gems, Ltd., by Appointment of His Majesty, 1721.

Despite its history, the building was less than nondescript. It was decidedly shabby. We knocked at the heavy wooden door which dearly needed painting and were ushered inside by a very old man in a suit that seemed much too tight even for his frail frame.

"We are here to see Mr. John Belknapp," said Holmes.

"Mr. Belknapp is in," the frail old man said, "but . . . do you have an appointment?"

"Tell him it is Mr. Sherlock Holmes and that I have come about a matter concerning Alfred Donaberry."

"Sherlock Holmes, about Alfred Donaberry," the old man repeated. "Please wait here."

The man moved slowly up the dark wooden stairway in the small damp hallway.

"Why the urgency, Holmes?"

"Perhaps there is none, Watson, but I prefer to err on the side of caution in a situation such as this."

The frail old man reappeared in but a few minutes and turned to lead us up the stairs after saying, "Mr. Belknapp can see you now."

On the narrow second floor landing with creaking floorboards, we were ushered to a door with *John Belknapp* written in peeling black paint.

The frail old man knocked and a voice called, "Come in."

We entered and the old man closed the door behind us as he left.

Our first look at Belknapp immediately provoked in me a sense of caution. He was, as we had been told, a handsome man of no more than forty, reasonably well dressed in a dark suit and vest. His hair, just beginning to show signs of distinguished gray at the temples, was brushed back. He was standing behind his desk in an office that showed no great distinction or style. Plain dark wooded furniture, several chairs, cabinets, and a picture of the queen upon the wall. The view through his windows was really no view at all, simply a brick wall no more than half a dozen feet away. Prosperity did not leap from the surroundings.

Sensing my reaction perhaps, Belknapp in an impatient response said, "My office is modest. It is designed for work and not for entertaining clients. For that there is a conference space on the ground floor."

I nodded.

"I hope this will be brief," he said.

"Dr. Watson and I will take but a few minutes of your time," Holmes said. "We have no need to sit."

"Good," said Belknapp, "I have a client to meet if I can find a cab in this confounded rain. You said this is about Alfred Donaberry."

"Yes," said Holmes. "Perhaps you know why we have come."

"Alfred Donaberry is a fool so I assume you are on a fool's errand. He could not hold on to a beautiful wife, did not appreciate her. I rescued her from a life of potential waste in a barely civilized country torn by potential war. If he is in England or has commissioned you in some way to persuade or threaten me and my wife, I . . ."

"Mr. Donaberry is, indeed, in England."

"Money," said Belknapp as if coming to a sudden understanding. "It's about the money."

"In part," said Holmes. "If you answer but one question, we shall leave you to attend to your client."

"Ask," said Belknapp with distinct irritation.

"What would you say your business is worth?"

"That is of no concern to you," Belknapp responded angrily.

"Incorrect," said Holmes. "It is precisely my concern. You wish us to depart so that you can get on with your client, simply answer the question."

"My business is worth far less than I would like. The inevitable war with the Boers has already affected mining and my sources are threatened. My personal savings and holdings have dwindled. What has this to do with . . . ?"

"We shall leave now," said Holmes. "I have one suggestion before we do so."

"And what might that be?" asked Belknapp with a sneer that made it clear he was unlikely to take any suggestion made by a representative of Alfred Donaberry.

"Stay away from Mr. Donaberry," said Holmes. "Stay far away."

"A threat? You issue me a threat?" asked Belknapp, beginning to come around his desk, fists clenched.

"Let us say it is a warning," said Holmes, standing his ground.

Belknapp was now in front of Holmes, his face pink with anger. I took a step forward to my friend's side. Holmes held up a hand to keep me back.

"You should learn to control your temper," said Holmes. "In fact I would say it is imperative that you do so."

I thought Belknapp was certainly about to strike Holmes but before he could do so, Holmes held his right hand up in front of the gem dealer's face.

"Were you to lose control," Holmes said, "it is likely that you would be the one injured. Would you like to explain a swollen eye or lip and a disheveled countenance to your expected client?"

Belknapp's fists were still tight but he hesitated.

"Good morning to you," said Holmes, turning toward the door, "and remember my warning. Stay away from Alfred Donaberry."

I followed Holmes out the door and down the stairs. The rain had stopped and the streets were wet under a cloudy sky that showed no promise of sun.

When we were on the move again, I looked at Holmes who sat frowning.

"I don't see how your warning will stop Belknapp from his plan to do away with Donaberry. While your reputation precedes you, he did not seem the kind who would be concerned about the consequences of any violence that might come to Donaberry."

"I'm afraid you are right, Watson," Holmes said with a sigh. "I'm afraid you are right."

We were no more than five minutes from Baker Street when Holmes suddenly said, "We must stop the carriage."

"Why?" I asked.

"No time to explain," he said, rapping at the hatchway in the roof. "We must get to Alfred Donaberry at once. It is a matter of life or death."

The driver opened the flap. Though the rain had now stopped, a spray from the roof hit me through the open portal. Holmes rose and spoke to the driver. I did not clearly hear what he said beyond Holmes's order and statement that there was a full pound extra in it if he rode like the wind.

He did. Holmes and I were jostled back and forth holding tightly to the carriage straps. The noise of the panting horse and the wheels against the uneven cobblestones made it difficult to understand Holmes who seemed angry with himself. I thought I heard him say, "The audacity, Watson. Not even to wait a day. To use me for a fool."

"You think Belknapp is on his way to The Cadogan Hotel?" I asked.

"I'm convinced of it," Holmes said. "Pray we are not too late."

We arrived in, I am certain, record time. Holmes leaped out of the carriage before the horse had come to a complete halt.

"Wait," I called to the driver, following Holmes past the doorman and into the hotel lobby.

As it turned out, we were too late.

The lobby was alive with people and two uniformed constables trying to keep them calm. Holmes moved through the crowd not worrying about who he might be elbowing out of the way.

"What has happened here?" Holmes demanded of a bushy mustached constable.

"Nothing you need concern yourself with, sir," the constable said, paying no attention to us.

"This," I said, "is Sherlock Holmes."

The constable turned toward us and said, "Yes, so it is. How did you get here so fast? I know you have a reputation for . . . but this happened no more than five minutes ago."

"This?" asked Holmes. "What is 'this'?"

"Man been shot dead in room upstairs, Room 116 I think. We have a man up there with the shooter and we're waiting for someone to show up from the Yard. So . . ."

Holmes waited for no more. He moved past the constable who was guarding the steps with me in close pursuit. Holmes moved more rapidly up the stairs than did I. My old war wound allowed for limited speed, but I was right behind him when he made a turn at the first landing and headed for a young constable standing in front of a door, a pistol in his hand. The sight of a London constable holding a gun was something quite new to me.

"Where is he?" Holmes demanded.

The constable looked bewildered.

"Are you from the Yard?" the young man asked hopefully.

"We are well known at the Yard," I said. "I'm a doctor. I expect an Inspector will be right behind us."

"Is that the murder weapon?" Holmes asked.

"It is, sir," the young man said, handing it to

me. "He gave it up without a word. He's just sitting in there now as you can see."

I looked through the door. There was a man on his back in the middle of the floor, eyes open, a splay of blood on his white shirt. Another man sat at the edge of a sturdy armchair, head in hands.

The dead man was John Belknapp. The man in the chair was Alfred Donaberry.

"We are," said Holmes, "too late."

At the sound of Holmes's voice, Donaberry looked up. His eyes were red and teary. His mouth was open. A look of pale confusion covered his face.

"Mr. Holmes," he said. "He came here just minutes ago. He had a gun. I don't . . . He gave no warning. He fired."

Donaberry pointed toward the window. I could see that it was shattered.

"I grabbed at him and managed to partially wrest the gun away," Donaberry went on. "We struggled. I thought he had shot me, but he backed away and . . . and fell as you see him now. My God, Mr. Holmes, I have killed a man."

Holmes said nothing as I moved to Donaberry and called for the constable at the door to bring a glass of water. Had I my medical bag there were several sedatives I could have administered but barring that, I could only minister to his grief, horror, and confusion, which I did to the best of my limited ability.

Holmes had now moved to and sat on a wooden chair near a small table on which rested a washing bowl and pitcher. He had made a bridge of his fingers and placed the edge of their roof against his pursed lips.

I know not how many minutes passed with me trying to calm Donaberry but it could not have been many before Elspeth Belknapp came rushing into the room. Her eyes took in the horror of the scene and she collapsed weeping at the side of her dead husband.

"I . . . Elspeth, believe me it was an accident," Donaberry said. "He came to . . ."

"We know why he came," Inspector Lestrade's voice came from the open door.

Lestrade looked around the room. I retrieved the gun from my pocket and handed it to him.

"Mrs. Belknapp came to Scotland Yard," said Lestrade, looking at Holmes, who showed no interest in his arrival or the distraught widow. "It seems Mr. Belknapp left a note which Mrs. Belknapp found no more than an hour ago. He told her he was going to see Alfred Donaberry and end his intrusion forever. Constable Owens has filled me in on what took place. We'll need a statement from Mr. Donaberry."

"May I see the note, Inspector?" Holmes said.

Lestrade retrieved the missive from his pocket and handed it to Holmes who read it slowly and handed it back to the Inspector.

"Lady says her husband had quite a temper," Lestrade said. "He owned several weapons, protection from gem thieves."

"Yes," said the kneeling widow. "I asked him repeatedly to keep the weapons out of our house, but he insisted that they were essential."

"Temper, weapon, note, struggle," said Lestrade. "I'd say Mr. Donaberry is fortunate to be alive."

"Indeed," said Holmes. "But that danger has not yet passed."

Elspeth Belknapp turned to Holmes.

"I harbor no wishes of death for Alfred," she said. "I have had enough loss, Mr. Holmes."

"Well," said Lestrade with a sigh. "That pretty much takes care of this unfortunate situation. We'll need a detailed statement from you, Mr. Donaberry, when you're able."

Donaberry nodded.

"A very detailed statement," said Holmes. "Mr. Donaberry, would you agree that my part of our agreement has been fulfilled albeit not as we discussed it?"

"What?" asked the bewildered man.

"You paid me two hundred pounds to keep John Belknapp from killing you. You are not dead. He is."

"The money is yours," said Donaberry with a wave of his hand.

"Thank you," said Holmes. "Now, with that settled, we shall deal with the murder of John

Belknapp, a murder which I foresaw but failed to act upon with sufficient haste to save his life. The audacity of the murderer took me, I admit, by surprise. I'll not let such a thing to again transpire."

"What the devil are you talking about, Holmes?" Lestrade said.

Holmes rose from his chair and looking from Elspeth Belknapp to Alfred Donaberry said, "These two have conspired to commit murder, which is bad enough, but what I find singularly outrageous is that they sought to use me to succeed in their enterprise."

"Use you?" asked Donaberry. "Mr. Holmes, have you gone mad? I went to you for help. Belknapp tried to kill me."

Holmes was shaking his head "no" even before Alfred Donaberry had finished.

"Can you prove this, Holmes?" Lestrade asked.

"Have I ever failed to do so in the past to your satisfaction?"

"Not that I recall," said Lestrade.

"Good, then hear me," said Holmes, pacing the floor. "First, I thought it oddly coincidental that Mrs. Belknapp should visit me only minutes before her former husband. Ships are notoriously late and occasionally early. Yet the two visits were proximate."

"Which proves?" asked Lestrade.

"Nothing," said Holmes. "I accepted it as mere coincidence. As I accepted Mrs. Belknapp's statements about the basic goodness of her former spouse. She said she wanted to protect her husband. I now believe she came for the sole purpose of describing her former husband as a kind and decent man who would hurt no one and her now dead husband as a man of potentially uncontrollable passion."

"But that . . ." Lestrade began.

Holmes held up his hand and continued.

"And then Mr. Donaberry here arrived, rumpled, suitcase in hand showing us the finger from which he had supposedly removed his wedding ring three months earlier."

"Supposedly?" asked Lestrade.

"Mr. Donaberry told Watson and me that he worked almost daily with his hands in subtropical heat and sun. His skin is, indeed, deeply tanned. In three months, one would expect that the mark of the removed ring, though it might linger somewhat, would be covered by the effects of the sun. The band of skin where the ring had been is completely white. The band has been removed for no more than a few days."

"That's true," I said, looking down at Donaberry's left hand.

"So, why lie? I asked myself," Holmes went on, "and so allowed my prospective client to continue as I observed that his clothes were badly rumpled and that he was in a disheveled state."

"I had hurried from the train, hadn't changed clothes since arriving in port yesterday," Donaberry said.

"Yet," said Holmes, "when I examined the contents of your suitcase when Dr. Watson led you out the rear of Mrs. Hudson's, I found everything neatly pressed and quite clean. You could have at least changed shirts and put on clean trousers in your travel to an appointment that meant life and death to you."

"I was distraught," said Donaberry.

"No doubt," said Holmes. "But I think you wanted to give the impression that you had not yet had time to check into this hotel."

"I had not," Donaberry said, looking at me for support.

"I know," said Holmes, "but neither had you rushed to see me from the train station. I asked the cabby where he had picked you up. You had hailed him from the front of the Strathmore Hotel which is at least three miles from the railway station."

"I took a cab there and quarreled with the cabby who was taking advantage of my lack of familiarity with London," said Donaberry. "I got out at the Strathmore and hailed another cab."

"Possible," said Holmes, "not plausible. My guess is that you were staying at the Strathmore, probably under an assumed name."

"But why on earth would I want to kill Belknapp?" said Donaberry. "I was not jealous."

"On that I agree," said Holmes. "You were not. It was not jealousy that led you to murder. It was simple greed."

"Greed?" asked Elspeth Belknapp, rising.

"Yes," said Holmes. "While John Belknapp's offices may seem shabby, the firm is an old and respected one and he supplied to my satisfaction that he was not only solvent but had an estate of some value. It will not be difficult to determine how valuable that estate might be."

"Not difficult at all," said Lestrade.

"And Mr. Donaberry, it should not be difficult to determine your financial status," Holmes went on. "You tell us you have a small fortune which Belknapp coveted. I doubt if that is the case."

"We can check that too," said Lestrade.

"Then, you counted on something that on the surface seemed to remove suspicion from you and your former wife. Mrs. Belknapp, even with tearful eyes, is a lovely young woman while you are, let us say, a man of less than handsome countenance. Belknapp, on the other hand, was decidedly younger than you and even as he lies there in death, he makes a handsome corpse."

"This is absurd," said Elspeth Belknapp.

"Indeed it is," said Holmes, "but easy for Inspector Lestrade to check. A final point, how did John Belknapp know that you were staying at The Cadogan?"

"He must have followed me from your apartment," said Donaberry.

"But you went out the rear," said Holmes. "However, even if we give you the benefit of the doubt, Watson and I went immediately to Belknapp's office after you departed. We were probably on our way before you found a cab in the rain. And he was in his office when we arrived."

"He could have had someone . . ." Elspeth Belknapp said, and then stopped, realizing that she was now actively trying to protect the man who had shot her husband.

"No," said Holmes. "Mr. Donaberry made an appointment with your deceased husband, probably not giving his real name. John Belknapp went on the assumption that he was going to see a potential client. When he entered this room, he was murdered. We have only Mrs. Belknapp's word that her husband had many weapons and even if he did, we have no evidence that he brought a weapon with him. And then there is the note."

Holmes held up the note.

"I had a moment or two to glance at Belknapp's papers on his desk. There is definitely a similarity. However, I think careful scrutiny will show that it is at best a decent forgery. I suspect that Mrs. Belknapp wrote the note herself. Is that sufficient, Inspector?"

"I think so, Mr. Holmes. Easy enough to check it all through."

"But, Holmes," I interjected, looking at the mismatched accused, "are you telling us that Donaberry and Mrs. Belknapp are lovers still, that he allowed his wife to not only marry but to enter into marital relations with another man?"

"I would suggest, Watson, that the white band on Mr. Donaberry's ring finger resulted from removing the wedding band from his marriage to Elspeth Belknapp's mother. I would suggest that she was not his wife but was and continues to be his daughter."

With that the woman ran into the arms of her father who took her in clear admission of their defeat.

"They made too many mistakes," Lestrade said, motioning for the constable to take the pair into custody.

"Yes," said Holmes. "But the biggest of them was thinking they could make a dupe of Sherlock Holmes. I can sometimes forgive murder. It is their hubris which I find intolerable."

But Our Hero Was Not Dead

MANLY WADE WELLMAN

BORN IN KAMUNDONGO, Portuguese West Africa (now Angola), Manly Wade Wellman (1903–1986) and his family moved to Washington, DC, when he was still a child. Wellman worked as a reporter for two Wichita newspapers, the *Beacon* and the *Eagle*, then moved east in 1934 to become the Assistant Director of the WPA's Folklore Project. He moved to North Carolina in 1955 and remained there for the rest of his life, becoming an expert in mountain music, the Civil War, and the historic regions and peoples of the Old South.

Writing mainly in the horror field in the 1920s, by the 1930s Wellman was selling stories to the leading pulps in the genre: *Weird Tales, Wonder Stories,* and *Astounding Stories.* He had three series running simultaneously in *Weird Tales*: Silver John, also known as John the Balladeer, the backwoods minstrel with a silver-stringed guitar; John Thunstone, the New York playboy and adventurer who was also a psychic detective; and Judge Keith Hilary Persuivant, an elderly occult detective, whose stories were written under the pseudonym Gans T. Fields.

Wellman also wrote numerous nonfiction books, including *Dead and Gone: Classic Crimes of North Carolina* (1954), which won the Edgar Award for Best Fact Crime Book. He also wrote fourteen children's books and wrote for the comic books, producing the first Captain Marvel issue for Fawcett Publishers.

Wellman's short story "A Star for a Warrior" won the Best Story of the Year award from *Ellery Queen's Mystery Magazine* in 1946, beating out William Faulkner, who wrote an angry letter of protest. Other major honors include Lifetime Achievement Awards from the World Fantasy Writers (1980) and the British Fantasy Writers (1985), and the World Fantasy Award for Best Collection for *Worse Things Waiting* (1975).

"But Our Hero Was Not Dead" was first published in the August 9, 1941, issue of *Argosy.* It was first published in book form in *The Misadventures of Sherlock Holmes,* edited by Ellery Queen (Boston, Little, Brown, 1944) under the title "The Man Who Was Not Dead."

BUT OUR HERO WAS NOT DEAD

Manly Wade Wellman

OUT OF THE black sky plummeted Boling, toward the black earth. He knew nothing of the ground toward which he fell, save that it was five miles inland from the Sussex coast and, according to Dr. Goebbels's best information, sparsely settled.

The night air hummed in his parachute rigging, and he seemed to drop faster than ten feet a second, but to think of that was unworthy of a trusted agent of the German Intelligence. Though the pilot above had not dared drop him a light, Boling could land without much mishap . . . Even as he told himself that, land he did. He struck heavily on hands and knees, and around him settled the limp folds of the parachute.

At once he threw off the harness, wadded the fabric and thrust it out of sight between a boulder and a bush. Standing up, he took stock of himself. The left leg of his trousers was torn, and the knee skinned—that was all. He remembered that William the Conquerer had also gone sprawling when he landed at Hastings, not so far from here. The omen was good. Boling stooped, like Duke William, and clutched a handful of pebbles.

"Thus do I seize the land!" he quoted aloud, for he was at heart theatrical.

His name was not really Boling, though he had prospered under that and other aliases. Nor, though he wore the uniform of a British private, was he British. Born in Chicago late in 1917, of unsavory parents, he had matured to a notable career of imposture and theft. He had entered the employment of the Third Reich, not for love of its cause or thirst for adventure, but for the very high rate of pay. Boling was practical as well as gifted. He had gladly accepted the present difficult and dangerous mission, which might well be the making of his fortune.

Now the early gray dawn came and peered over his shoulder. Boling saw that he was on a grassy slope, with an ill-used gravel road below it. Just across that road showed lighted windows—a house with early risers. He walked toward those lights.

Which way was Eastbourne, was his first problem. He had never seen the town; he had only the name and telephone number there of one Philip Davis who, if addressed by him as "Uncle," would know that the time had arrived to muster fifteen others.

They, in turn, would gather waiting comrades from the surrounding community, picked, hard men who whole years ago had taken lodging and stored arms thereabouts. These would organize and operate as a crack infantry battalion. After that, the well-tested routine that had helped to conquer Norway, Holland, Belgium, France— seizure of communications, blowing up of rails and roads, capture of airdromes.

Reinforcements would drop in parachutes from overhead, as he, Boling, had done. At dusk this would be done. In the night, Eastbourne would be firmly held, with a picked invasion corps landing from barges.

Crossing the road toward the house, Boling considered the matter as good as accomplished.

He needed only a word from the house-dwellers to set him on his way.

He found the opening in the chin-high hedge of brambles and flowering bushes, and in the strengthening light he trod warily up the flagged path. The house, now visible, was only a one-story cottage of white plaster, with a roof of dark tiling. Gaining the doorstep, Boling swung the tarnished knocker against the stout oak panel.

Silence. Then heavy steps and a mumbling voice. The door creaked open. A woman in shawl and cap, plump and very old—past ninety, it seemed to Boling—put out a face like a cheerful walnut.

"Good morning," she said. "Yes, who is that?" Her ancient eyes blinked behind small, thick lenses like bottle bottoms. "Soldier, ain't you?"

"Right you are," he responded in his most English manner, smiling to charm her. This crone had a London accent, and looked simple and good-humored. "I'm tramping down to Eastbourne to visit my uncle," he went on plausibly, "and lost my way on the downs in the dark. Can you direct me on?"

Before the old woman could reply, a dry voice had spoken from behind her: "Ask the young man to step inside, Mrs. Hudson."

The old woman drew the door more widely open. Boling entered one of those living rooms that have survived their era. In the light of a hanging oil lamp he could see walls papered in blue with yellow flowers, above gray-painted wainscoting. On a center table lay some old books, guarded by a pudgy china dog. At the rear, next a dark inner doorway, blazed a small but cheerful fire, and from a chair beside it rose the man who had spoken.

"If you have walked all night, you will be tired," he said to Boling. "Stop and rest. We're about to have some tea. Won't you join us?"

"Thank you, sir," accepted Boling heartily. This was another Londoner, very tall and as gaunt as a musket. He could not be many years younger than the woman called Mrs. Hudson, but he still had vigor and presence.

He stood quite straight in his shabbiest of blue dressing gowns. The lamplight revealed a long hooked nose and a long lean chin, with bright eyes of blue under a thatch of thistledown hair. Boling thought of Dr. Punch grown old, dignified and courteous. The right hand seemed loosely clenched inside a pocket of the dressing gown. The left, lean and fine, held a blackened old briar with a curved stem.

"I see," said this old gentleman, his eyes studying Boling's insignia, "that you're a Fusilier—Northumberland."

"Yes, sir, Fifth Northumberland Fusiliers," rejoined Boling, who had naturally chosen for his disguise the badges of a regiment lying far from Sussex. "As I told your good housekeeper, I'm going to Eastbourne. If you can direct me, or let me use your telephone—"

"I am sorry, we have no telephone," the other informed him.

Mrs. Hudson gulped and goggled at that, but the old blue eyes barely flickered a message at her. Again the gaunt old man spoke: "There is a telephone, however, in the house just behind us—the house of Constable Timmons."

Boling had no taste for visiting a policeman, especially an officious country one, and so he avoided comment on the last suggestion. Instead he thanked his host for the invitation to refreshment. The old woman brought in a tray with dishes and a steaming kettle, and a moment later they were joined by another ancient man.

This one was plump and tweedy, with a drooping gray mustache and wide eyes full of childish innocence. Boling set him down as a doctor, and felt a glow of pride in his own acumen when the newcomer was so introduced. So pleased was Boling with himself, indeed, that he did not bother to catch the doctor's surname.

"This young man is of your old regiment, I think," the lean man informed the fat one. "Fifth Northumberland Fusiliers."

"Oh, really? Quite so, quite so," chirruped

the doctor, in a katydid fashion that impelled Boling to classify him as a simpleton. "Quite. I was with the old Fifth—but that would be well before your time, young man. I served in the Afghan War." This last with a proud protruding of the big eyes. For a moment Boling dreaded a torrent of reminiscence; but the Punch-faced man had just finished relighting his curved briar, and now called attention to the tea which Mrs. Hudson was pouring.

The three men sipped gratefully. Boling permitted himself a moment of ironic meditation on how snug it was, so shortly before bombs and bayonets would engulf this and all other houses in the neighborhood of Eastbourne.

Mrs. Hudson waddled to his elbow with toasted muffins. "Poor lad," she said maternally, "you've torn them lovely trousers."

From the other side of the fire bright blue eyes gazed through the smoke of strong shag. "Oh, yes," said the dry voice, "you walked over the downs at night, I think I heard you say when you came. And you fell?"

"Yes, sir," replied Boling, and thrust his skinned knee into view through the rip. "No great injury, however, except to my uniform. The King will give me a new one, what?"

"I daresay," agreed the doctor, lifting his mustache from his teacup. "Nothing too good for the old regiment."

That led to discussion of the glorious past of the Fifth Northumberland Fusiliers, and the probable triumphant future. Boling made the most guarded of statements, lest the pudgy old veteran find something of which to be suspicious; but, to bolster his pose, he fished forth a wad of painstakingly forged papers—pay-book, billet assignment, pass through lines, and so on. The gaunt man in blue studied them with polite interest.

"And now," said the doctor, "how is my old friend Major Amidon?"

"Major Amidon?" repeated Boling to gain time, and glanced as sharply as he dared at his interrogator. Such a question might well be a trap, simple and dangerous, the more so because his research concerning the Fifth Northumber-

land Fusiliers had not supplied him with any such name among the officers.

But then he took stock once more of the plump, mild, guileless face. Boling, cunning and criminal, knew a man incapable of lying or deception when he saw one. The doctor was setting no trap whatever; in fact, his next words provided a valuable cue to take up.

"Yes, of course—he must be acting chief of brigade by now. Tall, red-faced, monocle—"

"Oh, Major Amidon!" cried Boling, as if remembering. "I know him only by sight, naturally. As you say, he's acting chief of battalion; probably he'll get a promotion soon. He's quite well, and very much liked by the men."

The thin old man passed back Boling's papers and inquired courteously after the uncle in Eastbourne. Boling readily named Philip Davis, who would have been at pains to make for himself a good reputation. It developed that both of Boling's entertainers knew Mr. Davis slightly—proprietor of the Royal Oak, a fine old public house. Public houses, amplified the doctor, weren't what they had been in the eighties, but the Royal Oak was a happy survival from that golden age. And so on.

With relish Boling drained his last drop of tea, ate his last crumb of muffin. His eyes roamed about the room, which he already regarded as an ideal headquarters. Even his momentary nervousness about the constable in the house behind had left him. He reflected that the very closeness of an official would eliminate any prying or searching by the enemy. He'd get on to Eastbourne, have Davis set the machinery going, and then pop back here to wait in comfort for the ripe moment when, the chief dangers of conquest gone by, he could step forth . . .

He rose with actual regret that he must get about his business. "I thank you all so much," he said. "And now it's quite light—I really must be on my way."

"Private Boling," said the old man with the blue gown, "before you go, I have a confession to make."

"Confession?" spluttered the doctor, and Mrs. Hudson stared in amazement.

"Exactly." Two fine, gaunt old hands rose and placed their finger tips together. "When you came here I couldn't be sure about you, things being as they are these days."

"Quite so, quite so," interjected the doctor. "Alien enemies and all that. You understand, young man."

"Of course," Boling smiled winningly.

"And so," continued his host, "I was guilty of a lie. But now that I've had a look at you, I am sure of what you are. And let me say that I do have a telephone, after all. You are quite free to use it. Through the door there."

Boling felt his heart warm with self-satisfaction. He had always considered himself a prince of deceivers; this admission on the part of the scrawny dotard was altogether pleasant. Thankfully he entered a dark little hallway from the wall of which sprouted the telephone. He lifted the receiver and called the number he had memorized.

"Hello," he greeted the man who made guarded answer. "Is that Mr. Philip Davis? . . . Your nephew, Amos Boling, here. I'm coming to town at once. I'll meet you and the others wherever you say . . . What's the name of your pub again? . . . The Royal Oak? Very good, we'll meet there at nine o'clock."

"That will do," said the dry voice of his host behind his very shoulder. "Hang up, Mr. Boling. At once."

Boling spun around, his heart somersaulting with sudden terror. The gaunt figure stepped back very smoothly and rapidly for so aged a man. The right hand dropped again into the pocket of the old blue dressing gown. It brought out a small, broad-muzzled pistol, which the man held leveled at Boling's belly.

"I asked you to telephone, Mr. Boling, in hopes that you would somehow reveal your fellow agents. We know that they'll be at the Royal Oak at nine. A party of police will appear to take them in charge. As for you—Mrs. Hudson, please step across the back yard and ask Constable Timmons to come at once."

Boling glared. His right hand moved, as stealthily as a snake, toward his hip.

"None of that," barked the doctor from the other side of the sitting room. He, too, was on his feet, jerking open a drawer in the center table. From it he took a big service revolver, of antiquated make but uncommonly well kept. The plump old hand hefted the weapon knowingly. "Lift your arms, sir, and at once."

Fuming, Boling obeyed. The blue dressing gown glided toward him, the left hand snatched away the flat automatic in his hip pocket.

"I observed that bulge in your otherwise neat uniform," commented the lean old man, "and pondered that pocket pistols are not regulation for infantry privates. It was one of several inconsistencies that branded you as an enemy agent. Will you take the armchair, Mr. Boling? I will explain."

There was nothing to do, under the muzzles of those guns, but to sit and listen.

"The apparition of a British soldier trying hard to disguise an American accent intrigued me, but did not condemn you at first. However, the knee of your trousers—I always look first at the trouser knee of a stranger—was so violently torn as to suggest a heavy fall somewhere. The rest of your kit was disarranged as well. But your boots—I always look at boots second—were innocent of scuff or even much wear. I knew at once that your story of a long night's tramp, with trippings and tumblings, was a lie."

Boling summoned all his assurance. "See here," he cried harshly, "I don't mind a little joke or whatever, but this has gone far enough. I'm a soldier and as such a defender of the realm. If you offer me violence—"

"There will be no violence unless you bring it on yourself. Suffer me to continue: You caused me even more suspicion when, calling yourself a private of the Fifth Northumberland Fusiliers, you yet patently failed to recognize the name of my old friend here. He, too, was of the Fifth, and in civilian life has won such fame as few Fusiliers can boast. The whole world reads his writings—"

"Please, please," murmured the doctor gently.

"I do not seek to embarrass you, my dear fellow," assured the lean host, "only to taunt this sorry deceiver with his own clumsiness. After that, Mr. Boling, your anxiety to show your credentials to me, who had not asked for them and had no authority to examine them; your talk about the service, plainly committed to memory from a book; and, finally, your glib talk about one Major Amidon who does not exist—these were sufficient proof."

"Does not exist?" almost barked the doctor. "What do you mean? Of course Major Amidon exists. He and I served together . . ."

Then he broke off abruptly, and his eyes bulged foolishly. He coughed and snickered in embarrassed apology.

"Dear me, now I know that I'm doddering," he said more gently. "You're right, my dear fellow—Major Amidon exists no longer. He retired in 1910, and you yourself pointed out his death notice to me five years ago. Odd how old memories cling on and deceive us—good psychological point there somewhere . . ."

His voice trailed off, and his comrade triumphantly resumed the indictment of Boling:

"My mind returned to the problem of your disordered kit and well-kept shoes. By deductive reasoning I considered and eliminated one possibility after another. It was increasingly plain that you had fallen from a height, but had not walked far to get here. Had you traveled in a motor? But this is the only road hereabouts, and a bad one, running to a dead end two miles up the downs. We have been awake for hours, and would have heard a machine. A horse, then? Possible, even in these mechanized times, but your trousers bear no trace of sitting astride a saddle. Bicycle? But you would have worn a clip on the ankle next to

the sprocket, and that clip would have creased your trouser cuff. What does this leave?"

"What?" asked the fat doctor, as eagerly as a child hearing a story.

"What, indeed, but an airplane and a parachute? And what does a parachute signify in these days but German invasion—which has come to our humble door in the presence of Mr. Boling?" The white head bowed, like an actor's taking a curtain call, then turned toward the front door. "Ah, here returns Mrs. Hudson, with Constable Timmons. Constable, we have a German spy for you to take in charge."

Boling came to his feet, almost ready to brave the two pistols that covered him. "You're a devil!" he raged at his discoverer.

The blue eyes twinkled. "Not at all. I am an old man who has retained the use of his brains, even after long and restful idleness."

The sturdy constable approached Boling, a pair of gleaming manacles in his hands. "Will you come along quietly?" he asked formally, and Boling held out his wrists. He was beaten.

The old doctor dropped his revolver back into its drawer, and tramped across to his friend.

"Amazing!" he almost bellowed. "I thought I was past wondering at you, but—amazing, that's all I can say!"

A blue-sleeved arm lifted, the fine lean hand patted the doctor's tweed shoulder affectionately. And even before the words were spoken, as they must have been spoken so often in past years, Boling suddenly knew what they would be:

"Elementary, my dear Watson," said old Mr. Sherlock Holmes.

The Adventure of The Marked Man

STUART PALMER

AFTER A SUCCESSFUL career as a novelist, Stuart Hunter Palmer (1905–1968) became a prolific screenwriter, writing thirty-seven scripts, mostly mysteries about the adventures of such famous characters of detective fiction as the Lone Wolf, Bulldog Drummond, and the Falcon. While working at a wide variety of jobs, Palmer began writing for pulp magazines under his own name and as Theodore Orchards. When he was only twenty-six, his first novel, *The Penguin Pool Murder* (1931), was published. It introduced his famous series character, Hildegarde Withers, a spinster sleuth often referred to as the American Miss Marple, though she is far funnier than the Agatha Christie heroine.

A film version of *The Penguin Pool Murder* was released the following year, starring Edna May Oliver, with James Gleason as a crusty New York City policeman. The success of the book induced Palmer to write thirteen additional adventures of the acerbic amateur sleuth, including *Murder on the Blackboard* (1932), which was adapted for a film of the same title in 1934 with the same casting of the chief protagonists; *The Puzzle of the Pepper Tree* (1933), filmed as *Murder on a Honeymoon* (1935), again with Oliver and Gleason; *The Puzzle of the Silver Persian* (1934); *The Puzzle of the Red Stallion* (1936, published in England as *The Puzzle of the Briar Pipe*), filmed as *Murder on a Bridle Path* (1936), with Helen Broderick replacing Oliver but with Gleason still present; and *The Puzzle of the Blue Banderilla* (1937), among others.

Palmer wrote two Sherlock Holmes pastiches while working as a training-film instructor and liaison officer between the army and Hollywood's war effort at a military outpost in Oklahoma during World War II. In addition to the present story, he produced "The Adventure of the Remarkable Worm" (1944).

"The Adventure of the Marked Man" was first published in the July 1944 issue of *Ellery Queen's Mystery Magazine*; it was first collected in a chapbook titled *The Adventure of the Marked Man and One Other* (Boulder, Colorado, Aspen Press, 1973).

THE ADVENTURE OF THE MARKED MAN

Stuart Palmer

IT WAS ON a blustery afternoon late in April of the year '95, and I had just returned to our Baker Street lodgings to find Sherlock Holmes as I had left him at noon, stretched out on the sofa with his eyes half-closed, the fumes of black shag tobacco rising to the ceiling.

Busy with my own thoughts, I removed the litter of chemical apparatus which had overflowed into the easy chair, and settled back with a perturbed sigh. Without realizing it, I must have fallen into a brown study. Suddenly Holmes's voice brought me back to myself with a start.

"So you have decided, Watson," said he, "that not even this difference should be a real barrier to your future happiness?"

"Exactly," I retorted. "After all, we cannot—" I stopped short. "My dear fellow!" I cried. "This is not at all like you!"

"Come, come, Watson. You know my methods."

"I had not known," I said stiffly, "that they embraced having your spies and eavesdroppers dog the footsteps of an old friend, simply because he chose a brisk spring afternoon for a walk with a certain lady."

"A thousand apologies! I had not realized that my little demonstration of a mental exercise might cause you pain," murmured Holmes in a deprecating voice. He sat up, smiling. "Of course, my dear fellow, I should have allowed for the temporary mental aberration known as falling in love."

"Really, Holmes!" I retorted sharply. "You should be the last person to speak of psycho-pathology—a man who is practically a walking case history of manic-depressive tendencies—"

He bowed. "A touch, a distinct touch! But Watson, in one respect you do me an injustice. I was aware of your plans to meet a lady only because of the excessive pains you took with your toilet before going out. The lovely Emilia, was it not? I shall always remember her courage in the affair of the Gorgiano murder in Mrs. Warren's otherwise respectable rooming house. And indeed, why not romance? There has been a very decent interval since the passing of your late wife, and the widow Lucca is a most captivating person."

"That is still beside the point. I do not see—"

"None so blind, Watson, none so blind," retorted Holmes, stuffing navy-cut into his cherrywood pipe, a sure sign that he was in one of his most argumentative moods. "It is really most simple, my dear fellow. It was not difficult for me to deduce that your appointment, on an afternoon as pleasantly gusty as this, was in the park. The remnants of peanut shell upon your best waistcoat speak all too plainly of the fact that you have been amusing yourself by feeding the monkeys. And your return at such an early hour, obviously having failed to ask the lady to dine with you, indicates most clearly that you have had some sort of disagreement while observing the antics of the hairy primates."

"Granted, Holmes, for the moment. But pray continue."

"With pleasure. As a good medical man, you cannot fail to have certain deep convictions as to the truth contained in the recent controversial publications of Mr. Charles Darwin. What is more likely than that in the warmth of Indian Summer romance you were unwise enough to start a discussion of Darwin's theories with the Signora Lucca, who like most of her countrywomen is no doubt deeply religious? Of course she prefers the Garden of Eden account of humanity's beginning. Hence your first quarrel and your hasty return home, where you threw yourself into a chair and permitted your pipe to go out while you threshed through the entire situation in your mind."

"That is simple enough, now that you explain it," I admitted grudgingly. "But how could you possibly know the conclusion which I had just reached?"

"Elementary, Watson, most elementary. You returned with your normally placid face contorted into a pout, the lower lip protruding most angrily. Your glance turned to the mantelpiece, where lies a copy of *The Origin of Species*, and you looked even more belligerent than before. But then after a moment the flickering flames of the fireplace caught your eye, and I could not fail to see how that domestic symbol reminded you of the connubial felicity which you once enjoyed. You pictured yourself and the lovely Italian seated before such a fire, and your expression softened. A distinctly fatuous smile crossed your face, and I knew that you had decided that no theory should be permitted to come between you and the lady you plan to make the second Mrs. Watson." He tapped out the cherrywood pipe into the grate. "Can you deny that my deductions are substantially correct?"

"Of course not," I retorted, somewhat abashed. "But Holmes, in a less enlightened reign than this our Victoria's, you would be in grave danger of being burned as a witch."

"A wizard, pray," he corrected. "But enough of mental exercises. Unless I am mistaken, the persistent ringing of the doorbell presages a client. If so, it is a serious case and one which may absorb all my faculties. Nothing trivial would

bring out an Englishman during the hour sacred to afternoon tea."

There was barely time for Holmes to turn the reading lamp so that it fell upon the empty chair, and then there were quick steps on the stair and an impatient knocking at the door. "Come in!" cried Holmes.

The man who entered was still young, some eight and thirty at the outside, well-groomed and neatly if not fashionably attired, with something of professorial dignity in his bearing. He put his bowler and his sturdy malacca stick on the table, and then turned toward us, looking questioningly from one to the other. I could see that his normally ruddy complexion was of an unhealthy pallor. Obviously our caller was close to the breaking point.

"My name is Allen Pendarvis," he blurted forth, accepting the chair to which Holmes was pointing. "I must apologize for bursting in upon you like this."

"Not in the least," said Holmes. "Pray help yourself to tobacco, which is there in the Persian slipper. You have just come up from Cornwall, I see."

"Yes, from Mousehole, near Penzance. But how—?"

"Apart from your name—'By the prefix Tre-, Pol-, Pen- ye shall know the Cornishmen'—you are wearing a raincoat, and angry storm clouds have filled the southwest sky most of the day. I see also that you are in great haste, as the Royal Cornishman pulled into Paddington but a few moments ago, and you have lost no time in coming here."

"*You*, then, are Mr. Holmes!" decided Pendarvis. "I appeal to you, sir. No other man can give me the help I require."

"Help is not easy to refuse, and not always easy to give," Holmes replied. "But pray continue. This is Dr. Watson. You may speak freely in his presence, as he has been my collaborator on some of my most difficult cases."

"No one of your cases," cried Pendarvis, "can be more difficult than mine! I am about to be murdered, Mr. Holmes. And yet—and yet I have not an enemy in the world! Not one person, living or dead, could have a reason to wish me in my coffin. All the same, my life has been thrice threatened, and once attempted, in the last fortnight!"

"Most interesting," said Holmes calmly. "And have you any idea of the identity of your enemy?"

"None whatever. I shall begin at the beginning, and hold nothing back. You see, gentlemen, my home is in a little fishing village which has not changed materially in hundreds of years. As a matter of fact, the harbor quay of Mousehole, which lies just beyond my windows, was laid down by the Phoenicians in the time of Uther Pendragon, the father of King Arthur, when they came trading for Cornish tin . . ."

"I think in this matter we must look closer home than the Phoenicians," said Holmes dryly.

"Of course. You see, Mr. Holmes, I live a very quiet life. A small income left to me by a deceased aunt makes it possible for me to devote my time to the avocation of bird photography." Pendarvis smiled with modest pride. "A few of my photographs of terns on the nest have been printed in ornithology magazines. Only the other day—"

"Nor do I suspect the terns," Holmes interrupted. "And yet someone seeks your life, or your death. By the way, Mr. Pendarvis, does your wife inherit your estate in the unhappy event of your demise?"

Pendarvis looked blank. "Sir? But I have never married. I live alone with my brother Donal. Bit of a gay dog, Donal. Romantic enough for us both. All of the scented missives in the morning mail are addressed to him."

"Ah," said Holmes. "We need not apply the old rule of *cherchez la femme*, then? That eliminates a great deal. You say that your brother is your heir?"

"I suppose so. There is not much to inherit, really. The income stops at my death, and who would want my ornithological specimens?"

"That puts a different light on it, most certainly. But let us set aside the problem of *cui bono*, at least for the moment. What was the first intimation that someone had designs upon your life?"

"The first threat was in the form of a note, roughly printed upon brown butcher's-paper and shoved beneath the door last Thursday week. It read: 'Mr. Allen Pendarvis, you have but a short while to live.' "

"You have that note?"

"Unfortunately, no. I destroyed it, thinking it to be but the work of a stupid practical joker." Pendarvis sighed. "Three days later came the second."

"Which you kept, and brought with you?"

Pendarvis smiled wryly. "That would be impossible. It was chalked upon the garden wall, repeating the first warning. And the third was marked in the mud of the harbor outside my bedroom window, visible on last Sunday morning at low tide, but speedily erased. It said 'Ready to die yet, Mr. Allen Pendarvis?' "

"These warnings were of course reported to the police?"

"Of course. But they did not take them seriously."

Holmes gave me a look, and nodded. "We understand that official attitude, do we not, Watson?"

"Then you can also understand, Mr. Sherlock Holmes, why I have come to you. I am not used to being pooh-poohed by a local sub-inspector! And so, when it finally happened last night—" Pendarvis shuddered.

"Now," interrupted Holmes, as he applied the flame of a wax vesta to his clay pipe, "we progress. Just what did happen?"

"It was late," the ornithologist began. "Almost midnight, as a matter of fact, when I was awakened by the persistent ringing of the doorbell. My housekeeper, poor soul, is hard of hearing, and so I arose and answered the door myself. Imagine my surprise to find no one there. Without all was Stygian blackness, the intense gloomy stillness of a Cornish village at that late hour. I stood there for a moment, shivering, holding my candle and peering into the darkness. And then a bullet screamed past me, missing my heart by a narrow margin and extinguishing the candle in my hand!"

Holmes clasped his lean hands together, smiling. "Really! A pretty problem, eh, Watson? What do you make of it?"

"Mr. Pendarvis is lucky in that his assailant is such a poor shot," I replied. "He must have presented a very clear target, holding a light in the doorway."

"A clear target indeed," Holmes agreed. "And why, Mr. Pendarvis, did not your brother answer the door?"

"Donal was in Penzance," Pendarvis answered. "For years it has been his invariable custom to attend the Friday night boxing matches there. Afterwards he usually joins some of his cronies at the Capstan and Anchor."

"Returning in the wee sma' hours? Of course, of course. And now, Mr. Pendarvis, I believe I have all that I need. Return to your home. You shall hear from us shortly." Holmes waved a languid hand at the door. "A very good evening to you, sir."

Pendarvis caught up his hat and stick, and stood dubiously in the doorway. "I must confess, Mr. Holmes, that I had been led to expect more of you."

"More?" said Holmes. "Oh, yes. My little bill. It shall be mailed to you on the first of the month. Goodnight, sir."

The door closed upon our dissatisfied client, and Holmes, who had been leaning back on the sofa in what appeared to be the depths of dejection, abruptly rose and turned toward me. "Well, Watson, the solution seems disappointingly easy, does it not?"

"Perhaps so," I said stiffly. "But you are skating upon rather thin ice, are you not? You may have sent that poor man to his death."

"To his death? No, my dear Watson. I give you my word on that. Excuse me, I must write a note to our friend Gregson of the Yard. It is most important that an arrest be made at once."

"An arrest? But of whom?"

"Who else but Mr. Donal Pendarvis? A telegram to the authorities of Penzance should suffice."

"The brother?" I cried. "Then you believe that he was not actually attending the boxing matches at the time of the attempted murder of our client?"

"I am positive," said Sherlock Holmes, "that he was engaged in quite other activities." I waited, but evidently he preferred not to take me further into his confidence. Holmes took quill and paper, and did not look up again until he had finished his note and dispatched it by messenger. "That," he said, "should take care of the situation for the time being." Whereupon he rang for Mrs. Hudson, requesting a copious dinner.

My friend maintained his uncommunicative silence during the meal, and devoted the rest of the evening to his violin. It was not until we were at the breakfast table next morning that there was any reference whatever to the case of the Cornish ornithologist.

The doorbell rang sharply, and Holmes brightened. "Ah, at last!" he cried. "An answer from Gregson. No, it is the man himself, and in a hurry, too." The steps on the stairs came to our door, and in a moment Tobias Gregson, tall, pale, flaxen-haired as ever, entered.

Smartest and sharpest of the Scotland Yard Inspectors, Holmes had always called him. But Gregson was in a bad frame of mind at the moment.

"You have had us for fair, Mr. Holmes," he began. "I felt in my bones that I should not have obeyed your unusual request, but remembering the assistance you have given us in the past, I followed out your suggestion. Bad business, Mr. Holmes, bad business!"

"Really?" said Holmes.

"Quite. It's this man Pendarvis, Donal Pendarvis, that you wanted arrested."

"No confession?"

"Certainly not. And moreover, the fellow is no doubt instituting a suit at law this very minute, for false arrest."

Holmes almost dropped his cup. "You mean that he is no longer in custody?"

"I mean exactly that. He was arrested last night and held in Penzance gaol, but he made such a fuss about it that Owens, the sub-inspector, was forced to let him go free."

Sherlock Holmes drew himself up to his full height, throwing aside his napkin. "I agree, sir. Bad business it is." He stood in deep thought for a moment. "And the other request I made? Have they located a man of that description?"

"No, Mr. Holmes. Sub-inspector Owens has lived in Penzance all his life, and he swears that no such person exists."

"Impossible, quite impossible," said Holmes. "He must be mistaken!"

Gregson rose. "We all have our successes and our failures," he said comfortingly. "Good morning, Mr. Holmes. Good morning, doctor."

As the door closed behind him, Holmes turned suddenly to me. "And why, Watson, are you not already packing? Do you not choose to accompany me to Cornwall?"

"To Cornwall? But I understood . . ."

"You have heard everything, and understood nothing. I shall have to demonstrate to you, and to the sub-inspector, on the scene. But enough of this. The game is afoot. You had best bring your service revolver and a stout ash, for there may be rough work before this little problem is solved." He consulted his watch. "Ah, we have just half an hour to catch the ten o'clock train from Paddington."

We boarded it with but a moment or two to spare, and when we were rolling southwest through the outskirts of London my friend began a dissertation upon hereditary tendencies in fingerprint groupings, a subject upon which he was planning a monograph. I kept my impatience to myself as long as I could, and finally interrupted him. "I have but one question, Holmes. Why are we going to Cornwall?"

"The spring flowers, Watson, are at the height of their season. The perfume will be pleasant after the fogs of London. Meanwhile, I intend to have a nap. You might occupy your-

self with considering the unusual nature of the warning notes received by Mr. Allen Pendarvis."

"Unusual? But they seemed clear enough to me. They were definitely intended to let Mr. Pendarvis know that he was a marked man."

"Brilliantly put, Watson!" said Sherlock Holmes, and placidly settled down to sleep.

He did not awaken until we were past Plymouth, and the expanse of Mount's Bay was outside our window. There were whitecaps rolling in from the sea, and a gusty wind. "I fancy there will be more rain by dusk," said Holmes pleasantly. "An excellent night for the type of hunting we expect to engage in."

We had hardly alighted at Penzance when a broad man in a heavy tweed ulster approached us. He must have stood fifteen stone of solid brawn and muscle, and his face was grave. An apple-cheeked young police constable followed him.

"Mr. Holmes?" said the elder man. "I am Sub-inspector Owens. We were advised that you might be coming down. And high time it is. A sorry muddle you have got us into."

"Indeed?" said Holmes coolly. "It has happened, then?"

"It has," replied Sub-inspector Owens seriously. "At two o'clock this afternoon." The constable nodded in affirmation, very grave.

"I trust," Holmes said, "that you have not moved the body?"

"The body?" The two local policemen looked at each other, and the constable guffawed. "I was referring," Owens went on, "to the suit for false arrest. A writ was served upon me in my office."

My companion hesitated only a moment. "I should not, if I were you, lose any sleep over the forthcoming trial of the case. And now before going any farther, Dr. Watson and I have just had a long train journey and are in need of sustenance. Can you direct us to the Capstan and Anchor, inspector?"

Owens scowled, then turned to his assistant. "Tredennis, will you be good enough to show these gentlemen to the place?" He turned back to Holmes. "I shall expect you at the police station in an hour, sir. This affair is not yet settled to my satisfaction."

"Nor to mine, sir," said Holmes, and we set off after the constable. That strapping young man led us at a fast pace to the sign of the Capstan and Anchor. "Into the saloon bar with you, Watson," my companion said to me in a low voice. He lingered a moment at the door, and then turned and joined me. "Just as I thought. Constable Tredennis has taken up his post in a doorway across the street. We are not trusted by the local authorities."

He ordered a plate of kidneys and bacon, but left them to cool while he chatted with the barmaid, a singularly ordinary young woman from all that was apparent to me. But Holmes returned to the table smiling. "She confesses to knowing Mr. Donal Pendarvis, at least to the point of giggling when his name is mentioned. But she says that he has not been frequenting the public house in recent weeks. By the way, Watson, suppose I asked you for a description of our antagonist? What sort of game are we hunting, should you say?"

"Mr. Donal Pendarvis?"

Holmes frowned. "That gentleman resembles his extraordinarily dull brother, from best accounts. No, Watson, dig deeper than that. Look back upon the history of the case, the warning messages—"

"Very well," said I. "The intended murderer is a poor shot with a rifle. He is a person who holds a grudge a long time—even a fancied grudge, for Mr. Allen Pendarvis does not even have an idea of the identity of his assailant. He is a man of primitive mentality, or else he would not have stooped to the savagery of torturing his intended victim with warning messages. He is a newcomer to the town, a stranger . . ."

"Hold, Watson!" interrupted Holmes, with an odd smile. "You have reasoned amazingly. Yet I hear the patter of rain against the panes, and we must not keep our constable waiting in the doorway."

A brisk walk uphill, with the rain in our faces, brought us at last to the steps of the po-

lice station, but there I found that the way was barred, at least to me. Sub-inspector Owens, it appeared, wished to speak to Mr. Holmes alone.

"And so it shall be," replied Holmes pleasantly, to the burly constable in the door. He turned to me. "Watson, I stand in need of your help. Would you be good enough to occupy the next hour or so in a call on one or two of your local colleagues? You might represent yourself as in search of a casual patient whose name has escaped you. But you have, of course, some important reason for locating him. A wrong prescription, I fancy . . ."

"Really, Holmes!"

"Be as vague as you can about age and appearance, Watson, but specify that the man you seek is a crack shot, he is very conversant with the locality, of unimpeachable respectability and—most important of all—he has a young and beautiful wife."

"But Holmes! You imply that is the description of our murderer? It is the exact opposite of what I had imagined."

"The reverse of the coin, Watson. But you must excuse me. Be good enough to meet me here in—shall we say—two hours? Off with you now, I must not keep the sub-inspector cooling his heels."

He passed on inside and I turned away into the rain-swept street, shaking my head dubiously. How I wished, at the moment, for the warmth and comfort of my fireside, any fireside! But well I knew that Holmes had some method in his madness. With difficulty I managed to secure a hansom cab, and for a long time rattled about the steep streets of the ancient town of Penzance, in search of the ruby lamp outside the door which would signify the residence of a medical man.

My heart was not in the task, and it was no surprise to me that, in spite of the professional courtesy with which I was greeted by my medical colleagues, they were unable to help me by so much as one iota. Owens, for all his pomposity, had been correct when he reported that of all the citizenry of Penzance, no such person as

Holmes sought had ever existed. Or if he had, he was not among their patients.

I returned to the police station to find Holmes waiting for me. "Aha, Watson!" he cried genially. "What luck? Very little, I suppose, else you should not wear the hangdog look of a retriever who has failed to locate the fallen bird. No matter. If we cannot go to our man, he shall come to us. I have to some extent regained the confidence of the sub-inspector, Watson. You see, I have given my word that before noon tomorrow Mr. Donal Pendarvis shall have withdrawn his suit for false arrest. In return we are to have the support of a stalwart P.C. for this night's work."

In a few moments there appeared down the street the figure of a uniformed man astride a bicycle. It turned out to be our friend Tredennis, who apologized for his delay. This was to have been his evening off duty, and it had been necessary to hurry home and explain matters to his better half.

"Maudie she worries if I'm not reporting in by nine o'clock," he said, his pink cheeks pinker than ever with the exertion of his ride. "But I told her that any man would be glad to volunteer for a tour of duty with Mister Holmes, the celebrated detective from England."

"From *England*?" I put in wonderingly. "And where are we now?"

"In Cornwall," said Holmes, nudging me gently with his elbow. "Ah, Watson, I see that your hansom has been kept waiting. Any moment now and we shall be setting our trap, somewhere near the home of Mr. Pendarvis."

"It's a good three miles, sir," said Constable Tredennis. "By the road, that is. Along the shore it's a good bit less, but it's coming high tide and no easy going at any season."

"We shall take the road," Holmes decided. Soon we were rattling along a cobbled street that wound up and down dale, past looming ranks of fisherman's houses, with the wind blowing ever wet and fresh against our cheeks. "A land to make a man cherish his hearth, eh, Watson?"

We rode on in silence for some time, and then the constable stopped the cab at the head of a steep sloping street that wound down toward the shore. There was a strong odor of herring about the place, mingled with that of tar and salt seaweed. I observed that as we went down the sloping street Holmes gave a most searching glance right and left, and that at every subsequent street corner he took the utmost pains to see that we were not followed.

Frankly, I knew not what near-human game we were hoping to entrap in this rain-swept, forgotten corner of a forgotten seaside town, but I was well assured, from the manner in which Holmes held himself, that the adventure was a grave one, and nearing its climax. I felt the reassuring weight of the revolver in my coat pocket, and then suddenly the constable caught my arm.

"In here," he whispered. We turned into a narrow passage near the foot of the street, passed through what appeared to be in the dimness a network of mews and stables, and came at last to a narrow door in the wall, which Holmes unlocked with a key affixed to a block of wood. We entered it together, and closed it behind us.

The place was black as ink, but I felt that it was an empty house. The planking beneath my feet was old and bare, and my outstretched hand touched a stone wall wet with slime. Then we came to an empty window with a broken shutter, through which the dank night air came chilly.

"We are in what was the Grey Mouse Inn," whispered the young constable. "Yonder, Mr. Holmes, is the house."

We peered across a narrow street and through the open, unshaded window panes of a library, brilliantly lighted by two oil lamps. I could see a line of bookcases, a table, and a mantelpiece in the background. For a long while there was nothing more to see except the dark street, the darker doorway of the house, and that one lighted window.

"There is no other entrance?" demanded Holmes in a whisper.

"None," said the constable. "The other windows give out onto the harbor, and at this hour the tide is passing high."

"Good," said Holmes. "If our man comes, he

must come this way. And we shall be ready for him."

"More than ready," said young Tredennis stoutly. He hesitated. "Mr. Holmes, I wonder if you would be willing to give a younger man a word of advice. What, do you think, are the opportunities for an ambitious policeman up London way? I have often thought of trying to better myself . . ."

"Listen!" cried Holmes sharply. There had come a sharp screaming sound, like the shriek of a rusty gate. It came again, and I recognized it as the cry of a gull.

The silence crept back again. From far away came the barking of a dog, suddenly silenced. Then suddenly appeared in the room across the way, a man in a wine-colored dressing gown who entered the library, turned down the lamps, and blew them out. It could be none other than our client, Mr. Allen Pendarvis.

"As usual he keeps early hours," said Holmes dryly. We waited until one might have counted a hundred, and then another light showed in the room. The man returned, bearing a lamp—but mysteriously, in the few minutes that had passed, he had changed his apparel. Mr. Pendarvis now wore a dinner coat with the collar and tie askew. He crossed to the bookcase, removed a volume, and from the recess took out a small flask, which he placed in his pocket. Then he put back the book and left the room.

"A lightning-change artist!" I cried.

Holmes, gripping my arm, said, "Not quite, Watson. That is the brother. They are very alike, from this distance."

We waited in silence, for what seemed an interminable length of time. But no light reappeared. Finally Holmes turned to me. "Watson," he said, "we have drawn another blank. I should have sworn that the murderer would have struck tonight. I dislike to turn back . . ."

"My orders, sir, are to remain here until sunrise," put in the constable. "If you wish to return to the town, rest assured that I shall keep my eyes open."

"I am sure of it," said Holmes. "Come, Wat-son. The game is too wary. We have no more to do here."

He led me back across the sagging floor, through the door into the mews, and finally brought me out into the street again. But once there, instead of heading up the slope toward where our hansom was waiting, he suddenly drew me into the shadows of an alleyway. I would have spoken, but I felt his bony fingers across my lips. "Shh, Watson. Wait here—and never take your eyes off that doorway."

We waited, for what seemed an eternity. I stared with all my might at the doorway of the Pendarvis house. But I saw nothing, not even when Holmes gripped my arm.

"Now! Watson," he whispered, and started out in that direction, I tardily at his heels.

As we came closer I saw that a man was standing with his finger pressed against the Pendarvis doorbell. Holmes and I flung ourselves upon him, but he was a wiry customer, and we for all our superior strength and numbers were flung back and forth like hounds attacking a bear. And then the door was opened suddenly from within, and we all tumbled into a hallway lighted only by a candle held aloft in the hand of the surprised householder.

Our captive suddenly ceased his struggles, and Holmes and I drew back to see that we had succeeded in overcoming none other than Constable Tredennis himself. He held in his right hand an extremely businesslike revolver, which fell to the carpet with a dull thump.

"Mr. Pendarvis," said Holmes, "Mr. Donal Pendarvis, permit me to introduce you to your intended murderer."

No one spoke. But the apple-cheeked constable now had a face the color of the under side of a flounder. All thought of resistance was gone. "You are uncanny, Mr. Holmes," the young man muttered. "How could you know?"

"How could I fail to know?" said Holmes, arranging his disheveled clothing. "It was fairly evident that since there was no citizen in Penzance who possessed both an ability as a marksman, a knowledge of the tides, and an attractive young wife, our man must be a member of the profession where marksmanship is encouraged." He turned toward the man who still held the candle, though with trembling fingers. "It was also evident that your brother, who still sleeps soundly upstairs, was never intended as a victim at all. Else the murderer would hardly have bothered with warning messages. It was you, Mr. Donal Pendarvis, who was the bull's-eye of the target."

"I—I do not understand," said the man with the candle, backing away. I kept a close grip upon the unresisting form of the prisoner, and watched Holmes as he quietly produced his cherrywood pipe and lighted it.

"There was an excellent motive for Constable Tredennis to murder you, sir," said Holmes to our unwilling host. "No man cares to have his garden plucked by a stranger. Your death would have begun an inquiry which would have led straight to the husband of the lady you see on Friday nights . . ."

"That is a black lie!" shouted Tredennis, and then subsided.

"Unless," Holmes continued quietly, "it was obvious to all the world that Donal Pendarvis was killed by accident, that he met his death at the hands of a madman with an unexplained grudge against his brother Allen. That is why the warning notes so unnecessarily stressed the name of *Allen* Pendarvis. That is why the murderer-to-be carefully missed his supposed victim and shot out the candle. I did my best, Mr. Pendarvis, to assure your safety by having you taken into custody. That subterfuge failed, and so I was forced to this extreme means."

Tredennis twisted out of my grasp. "Very well, make an end of it!" he cried. "I admit it all, Mr. Holmes, and shall gladly leave it to a jury of my peers—"

"You had best leave it to me, at the moment," advised Holmes. "Mr. Pendarvis, you do not know me, but I have saved your life. May I ask a favor in return?"

Donal Pendarvis hesitated. "I am listening," he said. "You understand, I admit nothing . . ."

"Of course. I venture to suggest that, in-stead of remaining here in the household of your brother and amusing yourself with dangerous dalliance, you betake yourself to fields which offer a greater opportunity for the use of your time and energy. The wheat fields of Canada, perhaps, or the veldt of South Africa . . ."

"And if I refuse?"

"The alternative," said Holmes, "is an exceedingly unpleasant scandal, involving a lady's name. Your lawsuit for false arrest will present the yellow press with unusual opportunities, will it not, when they learn that it all arose from an honest attempt upon my part to save your neck from a just punishment?"

Mr. Donal Pendarvis lowered the candle, and a slow smile spread across his handsome face. "I give you my word, Mr. Holmes. I shall leave by the first packet."

He extended his hand, and Holmes grasped it. And then we turned back into the night, our prisoner between us. We went up the cobbled street in silence, the young constable striding forward as to the gallows.

We found the hansom still waiting, and set off at once for Penzance. But it was Holmes who called on the driver to stop as we pulled into the outskirts of the town.

"Can we drop you off at your dwelling, constable?" he asked.

The young man looked up, his eyes haunted. "Do not make sport of me, Mr. Holmes. You copped me for fair and I am ready to—"

Holmes half-shoved him out of the hansom. "Be off with you, my young friend. You must leave it to me to satisfy your sub-inspector with a story which Doctor Watson and I shall contrive out of moonbeams. For your part, you must make up your own mind as to your tactics in dealing with your Maudie. After all, the immediate problem is removed, and if you wish to transfer to some other duty with less night work, here is my card. I shall be glad to say a word in your behalf to the powers at Scotland Yard."

The hansom, at Holmes's signal, rolled onward again, cutting short the incoherent thanks of the chastened young constable.

"I am quite aware of what is in your mind," said Holmes to me as we approached our destination. "But you are wrong. The ends of justice will be better served by sending our young culprit back to his Maudie instead of by publicly disgracing him . . ."

"It is of no use, Holmes," said I firmly. "Nothing that you can say will change my decision. Upon our return to London I shall ask Emilia to become my wife."

Sherlock Holmes let his hand fall on my shoulder, in a comradely gesture. "So be it. Marry her and keep her. One of these days I shall return to the country and the keeping of bees. We shall see who suffers the sharpest stings."

PERMISSIONS ACKNOWLEDGMENTS

Kingsley Amis: "The Darkwater Hall Mystery" by Kingsley Amis, copyright © 1978 by Kingsley Amis, copyright © 2014 by the Kingsley Amis Estate. Originally published in *Playboy* (May 1978). Reprinted by permission of The Wylie Agency LLC, on behalf of the Estate of Sir Kingsley Amis.

Poul Anderson: "The Martian Crown Jewels" by Poul Anderson, copyright © 1958 by the Trigonier Trust. Originally published in *Ellery Queen's Mystery Magazine* (February 1958). Reprinted by permission of Karen K. Anderson.

Bliss Austin: "The Final Problem" by Bliss Austin, copyright © 1946 by Bliss Austin. Originally published in *The Queen's Awards*, edited by Ellery Queen (Little, Brown and Company, 1946). Reprinted by permission of Winifred Morton and Peter Austin.

Sam Benady: "The Abandoned Brigantine" by Sam Benady, copyright © 1990 by Sam Benady. Originally published in *Sherlock Holmes in Gibraltar* (Gibraltar Books, 1990). Reprinted by permission of the author.

Anthony Boucher: "The Adventure of the Bogle-Wolf" by Anthony Boucher, copyright © 1949 by Anthony Boucher. Originally published in *Illustrious Client's Second Case-Book*, edited by J. N. Williamson (Indianapolis, Ind.: The Illustrious Clients, 1949). Reprinted by permission of Curtis Brown, Ltd.

Carole Buggé: "The Strange Case of the Tongue-Tied Tenor" by Carole Buggé, copyright © 1994 by Carole Buggé. Originally published in *The Game Is Afoot*, edited by Marvin Kaye (St. Martin's Press, 1994). Reprinted by permission of the author.

Anthony Burgess: "Murder to Music" by Anthony Burgess, copyright © 1989 by Anthony Burgess. Originally published in *The Devil's Mode*, by Anthony Burgess (Random House, 1989). Reprinted by permission of David Higham Associates Limited, London.

Peter Cannon: "The Adventure of the Noble Husband" by Peter Cannon, copyright © 1998 by Peter Cannon. Originally published in *The Confidential Casebook of Sherlock Holmes*, edited by Marvin Kaye (St. Martin's Press, 1998). Reprinted by permission of the author.

A. B. Cox: "Holmes and the Dasher" by A. B. Cox, copyright © 1925 by A. B. Cox. Originally published in *Jugged Journalism* (Herbert Jenkins Ltd., 1925). Reprinted by permission of The Society of Authors, London.

Dorothy B. Hughes: "Sherlock Holmes and the Muffin" by Dorothy B. Hughes, copyright © 1987 by Dorothy B. Hughes. Originally published in *The New Adventures of Sherlock Holmes*, edited by Martin Harry Greenberg and Carol-Lynn Rössel Waugh (Carroll & Graf, 1987). Permission granted by Blanche C. Gregory Inc., on behalf of the Dorothy B. Hughes Trust.

Stuart M. Kaminsky: "The Man from Capetown" by Stuart M. Kaminsky, copyright © 2001 by Double Tiger Productions, Inc. Originally published in *Murder in Baker Street: New Tales of Sherlock Holmes*, edited by Martin H. Greenberg, Jon L. Lellenberg, and Daniel Stashower (Carroll & Graf, 2001). Reprinted by permission of Double Tiger Productions, Inc.

H. R. F. Keating: "A Trifling Affair" by H. R. F. Keating, copyright © 1980 by H. R. F. Keating. Originally published in *John Creasey's Crime Collection*, edited by Herbert Harris (Gollancz, 1980). Reprinted by permission of Sheila Keating.

Laurie R. King: "Mrs. Hudson's Case" by Laurie R. King, copyright © 1997 by Laurie R. King. Originally published in *Crime Through Time*, edited by Miriam Grace Monfredo and Sharan Newman (Berkley, 1997). Reprinted by permission of the author.

Stephen King: "The Doctor's Case" by Stephen King, copyright © 1987 by Stephen King. Originally published in *The New Adventures of Sherlock Holmes*, edited by Martin Harry Greenberg and Carol-Lynn Rössel Waugh (Carroll & Graf, 1987) and collected in *Nightmares & Dreamscapes*, by Stephen King (Pocket Books, 2009). Print and electronic rights outside of North America are administered by Hodder and Stoughton Limited. Reprinted by permission of Darhansoff & Verrill Literary Agents and Hodder and Stoughton Limited. All rights reserved.

Hugh Kingsmill: "The Ruby of Khitmandu" by Arth_r C_n_n D_yle and E. W. H_rn_ng, copyright © 1932 by Hugh Kingsmill. Originally published in *The Bookman* (April 1932). Reprinted by permission of the Executor of the Estate of Hugh Kingsmill.

Leslie S. Klinger: "The Adventure of the Wooden Box" by Leslie S. Klinger, copyright © 1999 by Leslie S. Klinger (The Mysterious Bookshop, 1999). Reprinted by permission of the author.

Jon Koons: "The Adventure of the Missing Countess" by Jon Koons, copyright © 1994 by Jon Koons. Originally published in *The Game Is Afoot*, edited by Marvin Kaye (St. Martin's Press, 1994). Reprinted by permission of the author.

Tanith Lee: "The Human Mystery" by Tanith Lee, copyright © 1999 by Tanith Lee. Originally printed in *More Holmes for the Holidays*, edited by Martin H. Greenberg, Jon L. Lellenberg, and Carol-Lynn Waugh (Berkley, 1999). Reprinted by permission of the author.

John T. Lescroart: "The Adventure of the Giant Rat of Sumatra" by John T. Lescroart, copyright © 1997 by Lescroart Corporation. Originally published in *Mary Higgins Clark Mystery Magazine* (Summer/Fall 1997). Reprinted by permission of the author.

John Lutz: "The Infernal Machine" by John Lutz, copyright © 1987 by John Lutz. Originally published in *The New Adventures of Sherlock Holmes*, edited by Martin Harry Greenberg and Carol-Lynn Rössel Waugh (Carroll & Graf, 1987). Reprinted by permission of the author.

PERMISSIONS ACKNOWLEDGMENTS

June Thomson: "The Case of the *Friesland* Outrage" by June Thomson, copyright © 1993 by June Thomson. Originally published in *The Secret Journals of Sherlock Holmes* (Constable, 1993). Reprinted with permission of the Curtis Brown Group, Ltd., London.

Peter Tremayne: "The Specter of Tullyfane Abbey" by Peter Tremayne, copyright © 2001 by Peter Tremayne. Originally published in *Villains Victorious*, edited by Martin H. Greenberg and John Helfers (DAW Books, 2001). Used by permission of Brandt & Hochman Literary Agents, Inc. All rights reserved.

Manly Wade Wellman: "But Our Hero Was Not Dead" by Manly Wade Wellman, copyright © 1941 by Manly Wade Wellman. Originally published in *Argosy* (August 9, 1941). Reprinted by permission of David Drake.

P. G. Wodehouse: "From a Detective's Notebook" by P. G. Wodehouse, copyright © 1959 by P. G. Wodehouse. Originally published in *Punch* (May 1959). Reprinted with permission of the Estate of P. G. Wodehouse.